Introduction to Fiction

Introduction to Fiction

Jack David/Robert Lecker

Holt, Rinehart and Winston of Canada, Limited,
Toronto.

Canadian Cataloguing in Publication Data
Main entry under title:
Introduction to fiction

ISBN 0-03-920202-X

1. Short stories. I. David, Jack, 1946-
II. Lecker, Robert, 1951-

PN6120.2.I57 808.83′1 C81-095143-6

Acquisitions Editor: Anthony Luengo
Production Editor: Marilyn S. Brooks
Design: Jim McLachlan
Typesetting and Assembly: Compeer Typographic Services Limited

Printed in Canada

1 2 3 4 5 86 85 84 83 82

Preface

Introduction to Fiction is unique in three ways.

First, our wide-ranging selection, which comprises one hundred stories from the mainstream of international writing, can be used to illustrate the historical development of fictional modes or to exemplify the traditional, modern, or contemporary narrative form.

Second, *Introduction to Fiction* is organized by story length. It contains short short stories (under 2000 words), which can be read in a few minutes and discussed in class while ideas are still fresh; short stories (2000–10 000 words), which can be studied at more leisure; and five classic novellas (10 000–50 000 words), which invite extended consideration of the elements of fiction.

Third, the anthology has no apparatus: no questions, no glossaries, no biographical notes, no sample analyses. Teachers don't have to buy the editors' prose in order to buy the prose they have selected. And most teachers find the critical information they want outside the anthology they have adopted. The reason for this is clear: anthologies of fiction are not anthologies of criticism. In editing this book we have concentrated on selecting readable, teachable, and in many cases famous stories. We hope teachers will use these stories as their own critical assumptions, and the needs of their courses, dictate.

Jack David
Robert Lecker

Contents

PART 1: SHORT SHORT STORIES

Richard Brautigan Sea, Sea Rider 3
Roch Carrier The Hockey Sweater 5
Kate Chopin Ripe Figs 7
Matt Cohen Keeping Fit 8
Julio Cortázar Continuity of Parks 9
Jacques Ferron The Bridge 10
L. P. Hartley A High Dive 11
Edna O'Brien Mary 13
Frederic Raphael Bridal Suite 14
Alain Robbe-Grillet The Secret Room 16
William Saroyan Love, Here Is My Hat 19
Steven Schrader Whole 21
Sam Selvon When Greek Meets Greek 22
William Carlos Williams The Use of Force 24

PART 2: SHORT STORIES

Chinua Achebe The Voter 29
Sherwood Anderson I Want to Know Why 32
Margaret Atwood The Resplendent Quetzel 36
James Baldwin Sonny's Blues 42
Honoré de Balzac La Grande Bretèche 56
John Barth Lost in the Funhouse 64
Donald Barthelme The Balloon 74
Saul Bellow Looking for Mr. Green 77
Ambrose Bierce An Occurrence at Owl Creek Bridge 86
Clark Blaise Grids and Doglegs 90
Heinrich Böll The Adventure 96
Jorge Luis Borges The Garden of Forking Paths 99
George Bowering The Elevator 104
Erskine Caldwell Where the Girls Were Different 108
Morley Callaghan Last Spring They Came Over 111
Italo Calvino The Count of Monte Cristo 115
Albert Camus The Guest 120
John Cheever The Country Husband 126

Anton Chekhov The Darling 137
Arthur C. Clarke The Star 143
Samuel Clemens (Mark Twain) The Notorious Jumping Frog of Calaveras County 146
Robert Coover A Pedestrian Accident 149
Stephen Crane The Open Boat 158
Réjean Ducharme The Wedding Gown 168
Stanley Elkin A Poetics for Bullies 172
Ralph Ellison King of the Bingo Game 179
William Faulkner A Rose for Emily 183
F. Scott Fitzgerald Babylon Revisited 187
Gustave Flaubert A Simple Heart 196
E. M. Forster The Celestial Omnibus 210
Mavis Gallant The Accident 217
Hugh Garner The Yellow Sweater 223
William H. Gass In the Heart of the Heart of the Country 228
Dave Godfrey The Hard-Headed Collector 239
Nicolai Gogol The Nose 245
Nathaniel Hawthorne My Kinsman, Major Molineux 256
Anne Hébert The Coral Frock 264
Ernest Hemingway The Snows of Kilimanjaro 267
Jack Hodgins The Trench Dwellers 277
Hugh Hood New Country 283
Shirley Jackson The Lottery 288
Henry James The Tree of Knowledge 292
James Joyce Araby 299
W. P. Kinsella Dance Me Outside 302
Ring Lardner Haircut 305
Margaret Laurence A Bird in the House 310
D. H. Lawrence The Rocking-Horse Winner 318
Doris Lessing A Room 325
Alistair MacLeod The Boat 327
Bernard Malamud The Magic Barrel 335
Katherine Mansfield The Fly 342
Gabriel Garcia Márquez A Very Old Man with Enormous Wings 345
Guy de Maupassant The Necklace 348
Carson McCullers A Tree, A Rock, A Cloud 352
Yukio Mishima Patriotism 356
Alice Munro The Found Boat 366
Vladimir Nabokov Signs and Symbols 371
V. S. Naipaul A Christmas Story 374
Alden Nowlan Miracle at Indian River 383
Joyce Carol Oates How I Contemplated the World from the Detroit House of Correction and Began My Life Over Again 386
Flannery O'Connor A Good Man Is Hard to Find 393
Tillie Olsen I Stand Here Ironing 400
Edgar Allan Poe The Fall of the House of Usher 404
Katherine Anne Porter The Grave 412
Leon Rooke Standing in for Nita 415
Sinclair Ross The Painted Door 422
Philip Roth Defender of the Faith 431
Gabrielle Roy My Aunt Thérésina Veilleux 443
Irwin Shaw The Girls in Their Summer Dresses 449
Isaac Bashevis Singer Gimpel the Fool 453

John Steinbeck The Chrysanthemums 459
Audrey Thomas Xanadu 464
James Thurber The Catbird Seat 470
Ivan Turgenev A Country Doctor 474
John Updike A & P 479
W. D. Valgardson Red Dust 482
Kurt Vonnegut, Jr. Report on the Barnhouse Effect 490
Eudora Welty Powerhouse 496
Rudy Wiebe Where is the Voice Coming From? 501
Virginia Woolf The New Dress 505
Richard Wright The Man Who Was Almost a Man 509

PART 3: NOVELLAS

Joseph Conrad Heart of Darkness 517
Franz Kafka The Metamorphosis 554
Herman Melville Billy Budd, Foretopman 574
John Metcalf Girl in Gingham 607
Leo Tolstoy The Death of Ivan Ilych 630

Short Short Stories

RICHARD BRAUTIGAN

Sea, Sea Rider

The man who owned the bookstore was not magic. He was not a three-legged crow on the dandelion side of the mountain.

He was, of course, a Jew, a retired merchant seaman who had been torpedoed in the North Atlantic and floated there day after day until death did not want him. He had a young wife, a heart attack, a Volkswagen and a home in Marin County. He liked the works of George Orwell, Richard Aldington and Edmund Wilson.

He learned about life at sixteen, first from Dostoevsky and then from the whores of New Orleans.

The bookstore was a parking lot for used graveyards. Thousands of graveyards were parked in rows like cars. Most of the books were out of print, and no one wanted to read them any more and the people who had read the books had died or forgotten about them, but through the organic process of music the books had become virgins again. They wore their ancient copyrights like new maidenheads.

I went to the bookstore in the afternoons after I got off work, during that terrible year of 1959.

He had a kitchen in the back of the store and he brewed cups of thick Turkish coffee in a copper pan. I drank coffee and read old books and waited for the year to end. He had a small room above the kitchen.

It looked down on the bookstore and had Chinese screens in front of it. The room contained a couch, a glass cabinet with Chinese things in it and a table and three chairs. There was a tiny bathroom fastened like a watch fob to the room.

I was sitting on a stool in the bookstore one afternoon reading a book that was in the shape of a chalice. The book had clear pages like gin, and the first page in the book read:

BILLY

THE KID

BORN

NOVEMBER 23,

1859

IN

NEW YORK

CITY

The owner of the bookstore came up to me, and put his arm on my shoulder and said: "Would you like to get laid?" His voice was very kind.

"No," I said.

"You're wrong," he said, and then without saying anything else, he went out in front of the bookstore, and stopped a pair of total strangers, a man and a woman. He talked to them for a few moments. I couldn't hear what he was saying. He pointed at me in the bookstore. The woman nodded her head and then the man nodded his head.

They came into the bookstore.

I was embarrassed. I could not leave the bookstore because they were entering by the only door, so I decided to go upstairs and go to the toilet. I got up abruptly and walked to the back of the bookstore and went upstairs to the bathroom, and they followed after me.

I could hear them on the stairs.

I waited for a long time in the bathroom and they waited an equally long time in the other room. They never spoke. When I came out of the bathroom, the woman was lying naked on the couch, and the man was sitting in a chair with his hat on his lap.

"Don't worry about him," the girl said. "These things make no difference to him. He's rich. He has 3,859 Rolls Royces." The girl was very pretty and her body was like a clear mountain river of skin and muscle flowing over rocks of bone and hidden nerves.

"Come to me," she said. "And come inside me for we are Aquarius and I love you."

I looked at the man sitting in the chair. He was not smiling and he did not look sad.

I took off my shoes and all my clothes. The man did not say a word.

The girl's body moved ever so slightly from side to side.

There was nothing else I could do for my body was like birds sitting on a telephone wire strung out down the world, clouds tossing the wires carefully.

I laid the girl.

It was like the eternal 59th second when it becomes a minute and then looks kind of sheepish.

"Good," the girl said, and kissed me on the face.

The man sat there without speaking or moving or sending out any emotion into the room. I guess he *was* rich and owned 3,859 Rolls Royces.

Afterwards the girl got dressed and she and

the man left. They walked down the stairs and on their way out, I heard him say his first words.

"Would you like to go to Ernie's for dinner?"

"I don't know," the girl said. "It's a little early to think about dinner."

Then I heard the door close and they were gone. I got dressed and went downstairs. The flesh about my body felt soft and relaxed like an experiment in functional background music.

The owner of the bookstore was sitting at his desk behind the counter. "I'll tell you what happened up there," he said, in a beautiful anti-three-legged-crow voice, in an anti-dandelion side of the mountain voice.

"What?" I said.

"You fought in the Spanish Civil War. You were a young Communist from Cleveland, Ohio. She was a painter. A New York Jew who was sightseeing in the Spanish Civil War as if it were the Mardi Gras in New Orleans being acted out by Greek statues.

"She was drawing a picture of a dead anarchist when you met her. She asked you to stand beside the anarchist and act as if you had killed him. You slapped her across the face and said something that would be embarrassing for me to repeat.

"You both fell very much in love.

"Once while you were at the front she read *Anatomy of Melancholy* and did 349 drawings of a lemon.

"Your love for each other was mostly spiritual. Neither one of you performed like millionaires in bed.

"When Barcelona fell, you and she flew to England, and then took a ship back to New York. Your love for each other remained in Spain. It was only a war love. You loved only yourselves, loving each other in Spain during the war. On the Atlantic you were different toward each other and became every day more and more like people lost from each other.

"Every wave on the Atlantic was like a dead seagull dragging its driftwood artillery from horizon to horizon.

"When the ship bumped up against America, you departed without saying anything and never saw each other again. The last I heard of you, you were still living in Philadelphia."

"That's what you think happened up there?" I said.

"Partly," he said. "Yes, that's part of it."

He took out his pipe and filled it with tobacco and lit it.

"Do you want me to tell you what else happened up there?" he said.

"Go ahead."

"You crossed the border into Mexico," he said. "You rode your horse into a small town. The people know who you were and they were afraid of you. They knew you had killed many men with that gun you wore at your side. The town itself was so small that it didn't have a priest.

"When the rurales saw you, they left the town. Tough as they were, they did not want to have anything to do with you. The rurales left.

"You became the most powerful man in town.

"You were seduced by a thirteen-year-old girl, and you and she lived together in an adobe hut, and practically all you did was make love.

"She was slender and had long dark hair. You made love standing, sitting, lying on the dirt floor with pigs and chickens around you. The walls, the floor and even the roof of the hut were coated with your sperm and her come.

"You slept on the floor at night and used your sperm for a pillow and her come for a blanket.

"The people in the town were so afraid of you that they could do nothing.

"After a while she started going around town without any clothes on and the people of the town said that it was not a good thing, and when you started going around without any clothes, and when both of you began making love on the back of your horse in the middle of the zocalo, the people of the town became so afraid that they abandoned the town. It's been abandoned ever since.

"People won't live there.

"Neither of you lived to be twenty-one. It was not necessary.

"See, I do know what happened upstairs," he said. He smiled at me kindly. His eyes were like the shoelaces of a harpsichord.

I thought about what happened upstairs.

"You know what I say is the truth," he said. "For you saw it with your own eyes and traveled it with your own body. Finish the book you were reading before you were interrupted. I'm glad you got laid."

Once resumed, the pages of the book began to speed up and turn faster and faster until they were spinning like wheels in the sea.

ROCH CARRIER

The Hockey Sweater

Translated by Sheila Fischman

The winters of my childhood were long, long seasons. We lived in three places — the school, the church and the skating-rink — but our real life was on the skating-rink. Real battles were won on the skating-rink. Real strength appeared on the skating-rink. The real leaders showed themselves on the skating-rink. School was a sort of punishment. Parents always want to punish children and school is their most natural way of punishing us. However, school was also a quiet place where we could prepare for the next hockey game, lay out our next strategies. As for church, we found there the tranquillity of God: there we forgot school and dreamed about the next hockey game. Through our daydreams it might happen that we would recite a prayer: we would ask God to help us play as well as Maurice Richard.

We all wore the same uniform as he, the red, white and blue uniform of the Montreal Canadiens, the best hockey team in the world; we all combed our hair in the same style as Maurice Richard, and to keep it in place we used a sort of glue — a great deal of glue. We laced our skates like Maurice Richard, we taped our sticks like Maurice Richard. We cut all his pictures out of the papers. Truly, we knew everything about him.

On the ice, when the referee blew his whistle the two teams would rush at the puck; we were five Maurice Richards taking it away from five other Maurice Richards; we were ten players, all of us wearing with the same blazing enthusiasm the uniform of the Montreal Canadiens. On our backs, we all wore the famous number 9.

One day, my Montreal Canadiens sweater had become too small; then it got torn and had holes in it. My mother said: 'If you wear that old sweater people are going to think we're poor!' Then she did what she did whenever we needed new clothes. She started to leaf through the catalogue the Eaton company sent us in the mail every year. My mother was proud. She didn't want to buy our clothes at the general store; the only things that were good enough for us were the latest styles from Eaton's catalogue. My mother didn't like the order forms included with the catalogue; they were written in English and she didn't understand a word of it. To order my hockey sweater, she did as she usually did; she took out her writing paper and wrote in her gentle schoolteacher's hand: 'Cher Monsieur Eaton, Would you be kind enough to send me a Canadiens' sweater for my son who is ten years old and a little too tall for his age and Docteur Robitaille thinks he's a little too thin? I'm sending you three dollars and please send me what's left if there's anything left. I hope your wrapping will be better than last time.'

Monsieur Eaton was quick to answer my mother's letter. Two weeks later we received the sweater. That day I had one of the greatest disappointments of my life! I would even say that on that day I experienced a very great sorrow. Instead of the red, white and blue Montreal Canadiens sweater, Monsieur Eaton had sent us a blue and white sweater with a maple leaf on the front — the sweater of the Toronto Maple Leafs. I'd always worn the red, white and blue Montreal Canadiens sweater, all my friends wore the red, white and blue sweater; never had anyone in my village ever worn the Toronto sweater; never had we even seen a Toronto Maple Leafs sweater. Besides, the Toronto team was regularly trounced by the triumphant Canadiens. With tears in my eyes, I found the strength to say:

'I'll never wear that uniform.'

'My boy, first you're going to try it on! If you make up your mind about things before you try, my boy, you won't go very far in this life.'

My mother had pulled the blue and white Toronto Maple Leafs sweater over my shoulders and already my arms were inside the sleeves. She pulled the sweater down and carefully smoothed all the creases in the abominable maple leaf on which, right in the middle of my chest, were written the words 'Toronto Maple Leafs.' I wept.

'I'll never wear it.'

'Why not? This sweater fits you . . . like a glove.'

'Maurice Richard would never put it on his back.'

'You aren't Maurice Richard. Anyway, it isn't what's on your back that counts, it's what you've got inside your head.'

'You'll never put it in my head to wear a Toronto Maple Leafs sweater.'

My mother sighed in despair and explained to me:

'If you don't keep this sweater which fits you perfectly I'll have to write to Monsieur Eaton and explain that you don't want to wear the Toronto sweater. Monsieur Eaton's an *Anglais*; he'll be insulted because he likes the Maple Leafs. And if he's insulted do you think he'll be in a hurry to answer us? Spring will be here and you won't have played a single game, just because you didn't want that perfectly nice blue sweater.'

So I was obliged to wear the Maple Leafs sweater. When I arrived on the rink, all the Maurice Richards in red, white and blue came up, one by one, to take a look. When the referee blew his whistle I went to take my usual position. The captain came and warned me I'd be better to stay on the forward line. A few minutes later the second line was called; I jumped onto the ice. The Maple Leafs sweater weighed on my shoulders like a mountain. The captain came and told me to wait; he'd need me later, on defense. By the third period I still hadn't played; one of the defensemen was hit in the nose with a stick and it was bleeding. I jumped on the ice: my moment had come! The referee blew his whistle; he gave me a penalty. He claimed I'd jumped on the ice when there were already five players. That was too much! It was unfair! It was persecution! It was because of my blue sweater! I struck my stick against the ice so hard it broke. Relieved, I bent down to pick up the debris. As I straightened up I saw the young vicar, on skates, before me.

'My child,' he said, 'just because you're wearing a new Toronto Maple Leafs sweater unlike the others, it doesn't mean you're going to make the laws around here. A proper young man doesn't lose his temper. Now take off your skates and go to the church and ask God to forgive you.'

Wearing my Maple Leafs sweater I went to the church, where I prayed to God; I asked him to send, as quickly as possible, moths that would eat up my Toronto Maple Leafs sweater.

KATE CHOPIN

Ripe Figs

Maman-Nainaine said that when the figs were ripe Babette might go to visit her cousins down on the Bayou-Lafourche where the sugar cane grows. Not that the ripening of figs had the least thing to do with it, but that is the way Maman-Nainaine was.

It seemed to Babette a very long time to wait, for the leaves upon the trees were tender yet, and the figs were like little hard, green marbles.

But warm rains came along and plenty of strong sunshine, and though Maman-Nainaine was as patient as the statue of la Madone, and Babette as restless as a humming-bird, the first thing they both knew it was hot summer-time. Every day Babette danced out to where the fig-trees were in a long line against the fence. She walked slowly beneath them, carefully peering between the gnarled, spreading branches. But each time she came disconsolate away again. What she saw there finally was something that made her sing and dance the whole long day.

When Maman-Nainaine sat down in her stately way to breakfast, the following morning, her muslin cap standing like an aureole about her white, placid face, Babette approached. She bore a dainty porcelain platter, which she set down before her godmother. It contained a dozen purple figs, fringed around with their rich, green leaves.

"Ah," said Maman-Nainaine, arching her eyebrows, "how early the figs have ripened this year!"

"Oh," said Babette, "I think they have ripened very late."

"Babette," continued Maman-Nainaine, as she peeled the very plumpest figs with her pointed silver fruit-knife, "you will carry my love to them all down on Bayou-Lafourche. And tell your Tante Frosine I shall look for her at Toussaint — when the chrysanthemums are in bloom."

MATT COHEN

Keeping Fit

When he had started training it was always the breath that went first. That didn't surprise him; he knew that at thirty-two and with ten years of inactivity behind him it would take a long time. But after a couple of weeks, when he had worked up to doing a slow mile and had quit smoking, it became his legs and ankles. It wasn't for several months, when he was running six and seven miles at a stretch, that his feet began to bother him. It was funny; he had never thought of himself as having particularly good feet but somehow he had never encountered the problem of blisters and sores. But by the time he was up to ten miles the pain was always and exclusively in his feet. No matter what he did — he had tried all sorts of salves — even an antibiotic a couple of times — there didn't seem to be any way he could prevent the blistering. He remembered the difficulty of getting into condition too well to stop running for a couple of weeks to let his feet heal so he just bandaged them up and did his best to ignore them. If he was running smoothly, and lately he was always running smoothly, it took at least six miles for the bandages to work themselves off. After the first irritation of squashing them to a more comfortable place in his shoes it was two or three miles until they really started to hurt. He would run another fifteen minutes thinking of almost nothing but his feet and feeling the separateness of each sharp pain. Finally the hurt would melt together and he would run until he had to stop. The bandages were coming off now, he had felt the first twitch at the bottom of the hill; once they started they worked loose pretty fast. He ran easily along the shoulder of the level stretch of highway. The cars didn't bother him and he had long ago quit caring about people staring at him. Actually, he liked running along level ground even better than downhill and had, for a while, considered moving west. There was a feeling of continuous motion that, after the first few minutes, he would slowly sink into. When he had first been able to do ten miles he had thought about giving up his project and becoming a long-distance runner. He went out one night to a track club; it was summer and they practised in the evening. But, not really to his surprise, he found running with other people distracting. So he never went back and instead kept running on the streets and by the highway. He was half way at least through the painful part now. It didn't seem as bad today though he wasn't sure whether he liked that or not. As usual he couldn't think very clearly when he ran. In fact he could hardly think at all. That was one of the things that had attracted him to it. He thought a lot afterwards, about what he was doing and about other things. But when he ran he thought of nothing and was only barely conscious of his own movements and, of course, the cycle of his foot blisters. Going around a bend of the highway there was a last brief moment of sharp pain and then it all diffused. He loped along for another couple of hundred yards and turned onto a dirt road. It extended at least ten miles, according to the map, and he knew that would be far enough. He kept running. The motion had taken him over. After a while, he didn't know how long, he noticed he was slowing down and speeded up a little before settling into his customary rhythm. He had wanted it to be like that, smooth and easy, an imperceptible transition, and when they found him the next day they thought he had collapsed in mid-stride.

JULIO CORTAZÁR

Continuity of Parks

Translated by Paul Blackburn

He had begun to read the novel a few days before. He had put it down because of some urgent business conferences, opened it again on his way back to the estate by train; he permitted himself a slowly growing interest in the plot, in the characterizations. That afternoon, after writing a letter giving his power of attorney and discussing a matter of joint ownership with the manager of his estate, he returned to the book in the tranquillity of his study which looked out upon the park with its oaks. Sprawled in his favorite armchair, its back toward the door — even the possibility of an intrusion would have irritated him, had he thought of it — he let his left hand caress repeatedly the green velvet upholstery and set to reading the final chapters. He remembered effortlessly the names and his mental image of the characters; the novel spread its glamour over him almost at once. He tasted the almost perverse pleasure of disengaging himself line by line from the things around him, and at the same time feeling his head rest comfortably on the green velvet of the chair with its high back, sensing that the cigarettes rested within reach of his hand, that beyond the great windows the air of afternoon danced under the oak trees in the park. Word by word, licked up by the sordid dilemma of the hero and heroine, letting himself be absorbed to the point where the images settled down and took on color and movement, he was witness to the final encounter in the mountain cabin. The woman arrived first, apprehensive; now the lover came in, his face cut by the backlash of a branch. Admirably, she stanched the blood with her kisses, but he rebuffed her caresses, he had not come to perform again the ceremonies of a secret passion, protected by a world of dry leaves and furtive paths through the forest. The dagger warmed itself against his chest, and underneath liberty pounded, hidden close. A lustful panting dialogue raced down the pages like a rivulet of snakes, and one felt it had been decided from eternity. Even to the caresses which writhed about the lover's body, as though wishing to keep him there, to dissuade him from it; they sketched abominably the frame of that other body it was necessary to destroy. Nothing had been forgotten: alibis, unforeseen hazards, possible mistakes. From this hour on, each instant had its use minutely assigned. The cold-blooded, twice-gone-over re-examination of the details was barely broken off so that a hand could caress a cheek. It was beginning to get dark.

Not looking at one another now, rigidly fixed upon the task which awaited them, they separated at the cabin door. She was to follow the trail that led north. On the path leading in the opposite direction, he turned for a moment to watch her running, her hair loosened and flying. He ran in turn, crouching among the trees and hedges until, in the yellowish fog of dusk, he could distinguish the avenue of trees which led up to the house. The dogs were not supposed to bark, they did not bark. The estate manager would not be there at this hour, and he was not there. He went up the three porch steps and entered. The woman's words reached him over the thudding of blood in his ears: first a blue chamber, then a hall, then a carpeted stairway. At the top, two doors. No one in the first room, no one in the second. The door of the salon, and then, the knife in hand, the light from the great windows, the high back of an armchair covered in green velvet, the head of the man in the chair reading a novel.

JACQUES FERRON

The Bridge

Translated by Betty Bednarski

This was some time ago. The Seaway Canal had not yet been dug. In the evenings I was in the habit of forgetting my practice and seeking out another world on the other side of the river. The bridge marked the half-way point, and was itself divided, both architecturally and according to the direction in which I was going. When I approached it from the south, crossing over to the north, no structure was visible overhead, and I hardly noticed I had left the road. I would walk under an open sky as far as the Ile Sainte-Hélène. There it seemed I was already in Montreal. I was no longer aware of the bridge, so eager was I for promising encounters. But as I returned, tired, disappointed, my eyes could not escape the compelling power of its superstructure and the magnificent tracery of its steel girders. Night enclosed it like a cathedral. I would enter it with remorse, regretting the time I had wasted and my neglected duties. The high black arch came to an end and opened out onto the lights of the lowest stars, and those along the plain which stretches from Longueuil to Chambly, from Saint Lambert to Saint-Amable, these lights variously grouped in constellations, small villages, and large suburbs. In the midst of this glimmering rose the dark shapes of the mountains — Saint-Bruno, Beloeil, and Rougemont. This sight would reconcile me to my side of the river. Each time I would vow never to leave it again.

Sometimes I would pass a horse and cart. The driver was a woman. In the cart she carried scrap-metal to Montreal, then headed back to Coteau Rouge, where she was a fellow-citizen of mine. I knew her. She was one of those English women still marked by Europe who for some strange reason flee their race and feel happy only among French Canadians. The latter in return assimilate them. This is where we get a good many of our red-heads. One does one's best to gallicize, usually from the bottom up, while Englishness asserts itself from the top down. Nothing could have been more wretched nor at the same time more proud than this woman. The shack she lived in was divided in two by a semi-partition: on one side the horse, on the other side her family. This family: her husband, pin boy in a bowling alley, a good-for-nothing, and two rather snotty children.

There and back, her expedition took her about four hours. She left around ten o'clock in the evening. That was roughly the hour I left the south shore. And my return often coincided with hers. Now, at the time, because of a photographer friend who wanted to go into film-making, I was thinking in terms of cinema. I had thought of using this strange group. The action of the film, its climax and its dénouement, would take place within four hours. By showing from time to time the horse, the cart, the English woman, I felt I could indicate in an interesting way the precious moments allotted to the characters for their happiness or unhappiness. However the idea was not new, and I was all the less original for having seen "The Phantom Carriage". Besides the photographer did not go into films, and I stopped thinking about my scenario. Yet I was left with the pretext for the film — this little group, which measured the passing of time and was a reminder of destiny. Today I cannot think of the bridge without remembering them. I have always had a weakness for fine words and beautiful images — even secondhand. That is probably why I write.

During the day the English woman would go along the streets of the suburb before the arrival of the garbage trucks. Old springs, the remains of washing machines and stoves, any old metal interested her. She went to a great deal of trouble and earned very little money. Perhaps it was to make use of her horse, quite a fine animal. But what do I know? What did I ever know about her? Everything was an enigma, even her age. Was she twenty-five, thirty, thirty-five? Thin, bony, red haired, and not in the least feminine, she did not arouse desire or even pity. She seemed to expect nothing from anyone and to remain, in everything she did, an outsider. Perhaps she was mad. She had fine features and her skin was extremely white. She never struck me as vulgar; on the contrary, by a strange air of authority, she commanded respect. But this authority was due perhaps to her origins and to our own feeling of inferiority. I had noticed that she was growing rather stout. One night I was called to her shack. She had given birth alone. I cut the cord and completed the delivery. She did not utter a word or make a sound. She seemed to be thinking of something else. This third child did not prevent her from going back to her work. But a few months later she disappeared. I still meet her good-for-nothing husband reeling along. No one has seen her since, neither her nor her horse, the last one to cross the river regularly. The cart has become, like that carriage, a phantom one. If I see it again some night on the deserted bridge I shall know I have had an accident.

L. P. HARTLEY

A High Dive

The circus-manager was worried. Attendances had been falling off and such people as did come — children they were, mostly — sat about listlessly, munching sweets or sucking ices, sometimes talking to each other without so much as glancing at the show. Only the young or little girls, who came to see the ponies, betrayed any real interest. The clowns' jokes fell flat, for they were the kind of jokes that used to raise a laugh before 1939, after which critical date people's sense of humour seemed to have changed, along with many other things about them. The circus-manager had heard the word 'corny' flung about and didn't like it. What did they want? Something that was, in his opinion, sillier and more pointless than the old jokes; not a bull's-eye on the target of humour, but an outer or even a near-miss — something that brought in the element of futility and that could be laughed at as well as with: an unintentional joke against the joker. The clowns were quick enough with their patter but it just didn't go down: there was too much sense in their nonsense for an up-to-date audience, too much articulateness. They would do better to talk gibberish, perhaps. Now they must change their style, and find out what really did make people laugh, if people could be made to; but he, the manager, was over fifty and never good himself at making jokes, even the old-fashioned kind. What was this word that everyone was using — 'sophisticated'? The audiences were too sophisticated, even the children were: they seemed to have seen and heard all this before, even when they were too young to have seen and heard it.

'What shall we do?' he asked his wife. They were standing under the Big Top, which had just been put up, and wondering how many of the empty seats would still be empty when they gave their first performance. 'We shall have to do something, or it's a bad look-out.'

'I don't see what we can do about the comic side,' she said. 'It may come right by itself. Fashions change, all sorts of old things have returned to favour, like old-time dances. But there's something we could do.'

'What's that?'

'Put on an act that's dangerous, really dangerous. Audiences are never bored by that. I know you don't like it, and no more do I, but when we had the Wall of Death — '

Her husband's big chest-muscles twitched under his thin shirt.

'You know what happened then.'

'Yes, but it wasn't our fault, we were in the clear.'

He shook his head.

'Those things upset everyone. I know the public came after it happened — they came in shoals, they came to see the place where someone had been killed. But our people got the needle and didn't give a good performance for I don't know how long. If you're proposing another Wall of Death I wouldn't stand for it — besides, where will you find a man to do it? — especially with a lion on his bike, which is the great attraction.

'But other turns are dangerous too, as well as dangerous-looking. It's *being* dangerous that is the draw.'

'Then what do you suggest?'

Before she had time to answer a man came up to them.

'I hope I don't butt in,' he said, 'but there's a man outside who wants to speak to you.'

'What about?'

'I think he's looking for a job.'

'Bring him in,' said the manager.

The man appeared, led by his escort, who then went away. He was a tall, sandy-haired fellow with tawny leonine eyes and a straggling moustache. It wasn't easy to tell his age — he might have been about thirty-five. He pulled off his old brown corduroy cap and waited.

'I hear you want to take a job with us,' the manager said, while his wife tried to size up the newcomer. 'We're pretty full up, you know. We don't take on strangers as a rule. Have you any references?'

'No, sir.'

'Then I'm afraid we can't help you. But just for form's sake, what can you do?'

As if measuring its height the man cast up his eyes to the point where one of the two poles of the Big Top was embedded in the canvas.

'I can dive sixty feet into a tank eight foot long by four foot wide by four foot deep.'

The manager stared at him.

'Can you now?' he said. 'If so, you're the very man we want. Are you prepared to let us see you do it?'

'Yes,' the man said.

'And would you do it with petrol burning on the water?'

'Yes.'

'But have we got a tank?' the manager's wife asked.

'There's the old Mermaid's tank. It's just the thing. Get somebody to fetch it.'

While the tank was being brought the stranger looked about him.

'Thinking better of it?' said the manager.

'No, sir,' the man replied. 'I was thinking I should want some bathing-trunks.'

'We can soon fix you up with those,' the manager said. 'I'll show you where to change.'

Leaving the stranger somewhere out of sight, he came back to his wife.

'Do you think we ought to let him do it?' she asked.

'Well, it's his funeral. You wanted us to have a dangerous act, and now we've got it.'

'Yes, I know, but — ' The rest was drowned by the rattle of the trolley bringing in the tank — a hollow, double cube like a sarcophagus. Mermaids in low relief sported on its leaden flanks. Grunting and muttering to each other the men slid it into position, a few feet from the pole. Then a length of hosepipe was fastened to a faucet, and soon they heard the sound of water swishing and gurgling in the tank.

'He's a long time changing,' said the manager's wife.

'Perhaps he's looking for a place to hide his money,' laughed her husband, and added, 'I think we'll give the petrol a miss.'

At length the man emerged from behind a screen, and slowly walked towards them. How tall he was, lanky and muscular. The hair on his body stuck out as if it had been combed. Hands on hips he stood beside them, his skin pimpled by gooseflesh. A fit of yawning overtook him.

'How do I get up?' he asked.

The manager was surprised, and pointed to the ladder. 'Unless you'd rather climb up, or be hauled up! You'll find a platform just below the top, to give you a foot-hold.'

He had started to go up the chromium-plated ladder when the manager's wife called after him: 'Are you still sure you want to do it?'

'Quite sure, madam.'

He was too tall to stand upright on the platform, the awning brushed his head. Crouching and swaying forty feet above them he swung his arms as though to test the air's resistance. Then he pitched forward into space, unseen by the manager's wife who looked the other way until she heard a splash and saw a thin sheet of bright water shooting up.

The man was standing breast-high in the tank. He swung himself over the edge and crossed the ring towards them, his body dripping, his wet feet caked with sawdust, his tawny eyes a little bloodshot.

'Bravo!' said the manager, taking his shiny hand. 'It's a first-rate act, that, and will put money in our pockets. What do you want for it, fifteen quid a week?'

The man shook his head. The water trickled from his matted hair on to his shoulders, oozed from his borrowed bathing-suit and made runnels down his sinewy thighs. A fine figure of a man: the women would like him.

'Well, twenty then.'

Still the man shook his head.

'Let's make it twenty-five. That's the most we give anyone.'

Except for the slow shaking of his head the man might not have heard. The circus-manager and his wife exchanged a rapid glance.

'Look here,' he said. 'Taking into account the draw your act is likely to be, we're going to make you a special offer — thirty pounds a week. All right?'

Had the man understood? He put his finger in his mouth and went on shaking his head slowly, more to himself than at them, and seemingly unconscious of the bargain that was being held out to him. When he still didn't answer, the knot of tension broke, and the manager said, in his ordinary, brisk voice,

'Then I'm afraid we can't do business. But just as a matter of interest, tell us why you turned down our excellent offer.'

The man drew a long breath and breaking his long silence said, 'It's the first time I done it and I didn't like it.'

With that he turned on his heel and straddling his long legs walked off unsteadily in the direction of the dressing-room.

The circus-manager and his wife stared at each other.

'It was the first time he'd done it,' she muttered. 'The first time.' Not knowing what to say to him, whether to praise, blame, scold or sympathize, they waited for him to come back, but he didn't come.

'I'll go and see if he's all right,' the circus-manager said. But in two minutes he was back again. 'He's not there,' he said. 'He must have slipped out the other way, the crack-brained fellow!'

EDNA O'BRIEN

Mary

Dear Sadie

I am in the toilet as it's the only place I get a bit of peace. She is calling me down to do the dinner as I am a good cook and she is not. He raised ructions yesterday about cabbage water and I got red and you won't believe it but he smiled straight into my face. He never smiles at her. If I tell you a secret don't tell anyone. She sees another man. Didn't I walk straight into them the night I was to meet Tom Dooley and he never came. Next day she gave me a frock of hers, I suppose so's I'd keep my mouth shut. And now I am in a fix because she expects me to wear it when I go dancing and I want to wear a frock of my own. It is brushed wool, mine is, and I know it is brushed wool but I am not telling her.

Tom Dooley came the next night. He got the nights mixed up, a good job I was there. We went for a walk in the park opposite this house — there's a park, I told you that, didn't I? It's nice in the summer because there's a pavilion where they sell icecream and stuff but dead boring in the winter. Anyhow we had a walking race through the woods and he beat me blind and I got so winded I had to sit down and he sat next to me and put his arm around me. Then he kissed me and all of a sudden he raised the subject of SEX and I nearly died. I got such a fright that I took one leap off the seat and tore across the field and he tore after me and put his arms around me and then I burst out crying, I don't know why. And I had to come in home and when I did he was here by himself. She's always out. Goes to pubs on her own or wandering around the road gathering bits of branches saying how sad and how beautiful they are. Did you ever hear such nonsense in all your life. She wouldn't darn a sock. Anyhow he was here listening to music. He always is. And he called me in to warm my feet and sat me down and we hardly said one word except that he asked me was I all right and I had to say something, so I said I got a smut in my eye. Didn't he get an eye-glass and was poking away at it with a little paint brush and didn't she come in real quiet in her crêpe-soled shoes.

'Oh, togetherness,' she said in her waspy voice and you wouldn't see me flying up the stairs to bed. Next morning — and you mustn't breathe this to a soul — she was up at cock-crow. Said she had heartburn and went out to do some weeding. It's winter and there's nothing in those flower beds only clay. Guess what, wasn't she waiting for the postman and no sooner had he come than she was all smiles and making coffee and asking me what kind of dancing did I like, and didn't the phone ring and when she tripped off to answer it I had a gawk at the letter she got. I could only scan it. Real slop. It was from a man. It said darling be brave. See you a.m. Now I haven't told you this but I love their child. He has eyelashes as long as daisies and lovely and black. Like silk. I admired them one day and he wanted to pull one out for me. I'd do anything for that kid.

Anyhow I discovered where she keeps the letters — under the hall carpet. She presses flowers there too. Of course if I wanted to, I could show them to hubby, find them, pretend I didn't know what they were. I'm not sure whether I will or not. I heard him telling her once that he'd take the kid and go to Australia. I'd love to go. The kid has a pet name — he's called Buck — and he loves bread and jam and I think he prefers me to her. I have to go now as she's calling me. Not a word to my mother about this. I'll let you know developments.

Your fond friend
Mary

PS I am thinking of changing my name. How do you like the sound of Myrtle?

FREDERIC RAPHAEL

Bridal Suite

'Strange things honeymoons,' he said to her in the limousine on the way to the airport.

'Stranger still,' she said, 'when you've been together as long as we have.'

'I sure hope we did the right thing,' he said, when Central American Airways called the flight.

'Getting married?' she said. 'Not much we can do about it now. We already ate the cake.'

'Maybe we did,' he said, 'but do we have to fly to the dysentery belt to blow out the candles?'

'You seem different,' she said, with a smile to prove she wasn't.

'Maybe I am,' he said, 'I was never married before.'

'I was,' she said. 'And please don't be. Different. I like you the way you were.'

'That was yesterday,' he said, and seemed to resent the way she helped him fasten his safety belt.

He had known her three, going on four years. He had always thought her face unique for its wide blue eyes and its white, incisive teeth above that neat, narrow jaw. It was rather a shock to observe, at the wedding breakfast, that she had three sisters and, almost more disconcerting, two brothers (Alvin and MacMichael, for God's sakes), all of whom had the eyes and the teeth and the neat, narrow jaw.

They were going only two and a bit hours from Dallas, but the faces in the jet were mainly swarthy; the Spanish announcements were more clearly understood than the English. He just hoped that the hotel was going to be all right. It was American-owned, but he still thought maybe the whole thing was a mistake. 'The honeymoon,' he meant, 'not the wedding.'

They drove at last into the modern section of the city, concretely rebuilt since the recent earthquake, along a fancy avenue named after the American president whose vice-president had had to dodge the stones of the mob on his way to the *casa del presidente* where the prevailing general had taken receipt of the funds for the construction of the highway. The general now lived in some luxury in Lucerne; the highway was not as long as the purse allotted to it.

There was nothing obviously wrong with the hotel. It had a coffee shop and a gourmet restaurant and a heated pool and two hire car desks and there were tours available to the unspoiled hinterland. The bridal suite was on the seventh floor and it was already embarrassingly effusive with flowers and good wishes from the folks they hoped they had left behind. The management had been thoughtful with fruit. She watched, dismayed at his dismay, as he winced at the florists' cellophane. She wished that they were back at the twelve bucks a night motel where their affair began, in a place called Alexandria, Louisiana. It had been a hundred and fifteen in the shade when they checked in and the shower wasn't working and who cared? Now she took a shower, but he didn't seem to want to come in and get anything. She came out and he was standing at the window looking down, without enthusiasm, on the crowded evening buses taking workers back to their shanties. The sides of the buses were badged with the portraits of the new generation of contending generals who hoped one day, if elected, to live in Lucerne.

The hotel promised American service, but it was staffed mainly by local Indians. There was trouble getting a drink; there was more trouble obtaining a sandwich. As darkness fell, the sky was luminous with flashes. They heard distant explosions. 'Sounds like they have a fiesta going on,' she said. 'I hate fiestas,' he said, and made it sound as though he also hated her. She wriggled silken toes and smoothed her stockings up her gleaming thighs. He stared out of the window. 'We're going to have folksongs next,' he said, 'you wait and see.' He sighed as a crackle of festive fire made him flinch. He opened the terrace window and stepped into the flashing night. She followed him, accepting an invitation which had not been offered. The sky was splenetic with low and temporary constellations. The evening air pricked in her nostrils like a summer cold. She stood by her husband and willed him to admire the gaudy dazzle of the city.

Suddenly a mass of people, shouting and waving things, came running out of a side street opposite the hotel and spilled into the avenue. They were followed by a squad of masked and shielded police who seemed rather comically slow on cue as they began, with no evident order or purpose, to fire into the crowd. People screamed and ran in various directions. From the high terrace they could look directly down to where two men were being thumped with rifle butts as they slid down the railings of the hotel compound, access to which was blocked by a limousine carrying a diplomatic quartet.

She looked down then with appalled condescension at the bloody scene below them. In the distance, as she glanced away, she could see the trickling raw redness of a volcano, like a picked scab against the far sky. Her throat was sour with the tear-gas which, even at the height of the seventh floor, rasped her lungs. 'You're right,' she said, 'we have to get out of here; it's horrible.' Fear and revulsion made uneasy stilts of the high heels she had decided to put on. She leaned her head on his shoulder, for help. His arms promptly bracketed her, his hands hard where she was soft. She wanted to go in, out of the vicious dark, but he held her there on the terrace, while the violence from the street rose like a savage drug. She shook her head — no, not now — but he was smiling. 'It *is* our honeymoon,' he said.

ALAIN ROBBE-GRILLET

The Secret Room

Translated by Barbara Wright

To Gustave Moreau

At first it is a red patch — a vivid, brilliant, but dark red, with shadows which are almost black. It is in the form of an irregular rosette, with well-defined contours, which are extended on several sides into broad rivulets of unequal length, afterwards dividing and narrowing until they are reduced to sinuous trickles. The whole stands out against the pallor of a surface which is smooth, rounded, and at the same time both matt and somehow nacreous, a semi-sphere, joined by gentle curves to an expanse of the same pale hue — a whiteness attenuated by the darkness of the setting: dungeon, underground room or cathedral — glowing with diffused brightness in the half-light.

Beyond, the space is taken up by the cylindrical shafts of pillars which grow progressively more prolific and more indistinct the nearer they get to the background, where the beginning of a vast stone staircase can be made out; it curves a little as it ascends, and gets gradually narrower as it rises up to the high vaults, where it disappears.

The whole of this decor, staircase and colonade, is empty. In the foreground, alone, and faintly shining, is the outstretched body with its red patch — a white body whose substance one imagines to be full and supple, fragile, no doubt; vulnerable. Beside the blood-stained semi-sphere, another, identical, round form, this one unblemished, may be observed from exactly the same angle; but the areolated point that crowns it, of darker hue, is here completely recognisable, while the first has been almost entirely destroyed, or at least masked by the wound.

In the background, towards the top of the staircase, a black silhouette is moving further away, a man enveloped in a long, flowing cloak, who is climbing the last steps without looking back, his task fulfilled. A tenuous column of smoke rises in spirals from a sort of incense-burner placed on a high, wrought-iron stand with silvery highlights. The milky body is lying quite near, with the broad trickles of blood running from the left breast down the side and on the hip.

It is the body of a woman, full-figured but not heavy, quite naked, lying on her back, her bust slightly raised by thick cushions thrown on to the ground, which is covered with rugs of oriental design. Her waist is very narrow, her neck long and slim, bent over to one side, her head thrown back into a darker area in which the features can nevertheless be divined; the half-open mouth, the big, open eyes, fixed and shining, and the mass of long, black hair, spread out in waves of well-regulated disorder on a material, perhaps velvet, with heavy folds, on which the arm and shoulder are also lying.

It is an even, dark violet velvet, or that is how it appears in this light. But violet, brown and blue also seem to predominate in the colours of the cushions — of which only a very small part is covered by the velvet material and which are very visible lower down, under the bust and waist — as also in the oriental design of the rugs on the floor. Further away, the same colours also appear in the actual stone of the floor, the arches of the vaults, the staircase, and the less clearly defined surfaces at the far ends of the room.

It is difficult to specify the dimensions of the room; the young woman who has been sacrificed seems at first sight to occupy a place of importance in it, but the vast proportions of the staircase leading down to her would rather indicate that, on the contrary, this is not the whole of the room, whose considerable expanse must in reality continue on all sides, to the right and to the left, and also past the rows of pillars in all directions, towards those distant browns and blues, perhaps towards other sofas, thick rugs, piles of cushions and materials, other tortured bodies, other incense-burners.

It is also difficult to say where the light is coming from. There is no indication on the pillars or on the ground to show the direction of its rays. Furthermore, there is no window visible, no torch. It is the milky body itself that seems to illuminate the scene, the bust with its swelling breasts, the curve of the hips, the stomach, the full thighs, the wide-open, outstretched legs, and the black hair of the exposed sex, provocative, offered, henceforth useless.

The man has already moved several paces away. He is now already on the first steps of the staircase, which he is preparing to climb. The lower stairs are long and wide, like the steps leading to some building, temple or theatre; they get progressively smaller as they rise, and at the same time start a broad, spiral movement, which is so slight that the staircase has not even completed half a revolution when, reduced to a steep narrow passage without a hand-rail, and even more precarious in the deepening darkness, it disappears near the top of the vaults.

But the man isn't looking in that direction, even though that is where his feet are taking him; with his left foot on the second step and his right already touching the third, his knee bent, he has turned round to contemplate the sight for the last time. The long, flowing cloak which he has hurriedly thrown over his shoulders and is holding with one hand, at waist level, has followed the rapid, rotary movement which has just brought the head and bust round to face the opposite direction from that in which he is going, and a piece of the material is floating in the air as if affected by a sudden gust of wind; the corner, which is curling over in a rather loose S shape, reveals the red silk lining with gold embroidery.

The man's features are impassive, but tense, as if he were expecting — or perhaps fearing — some sudden occurrence, or rather as if he were surveying, with one last glance, the total immobility of the scene. Though he is looking behind him in this way, his whole body is still leaning slightly forward, as if he were still continuing his ascent. His right arm — the one which is not holding his cloak in place — is half stretched out towards the left, towards a point in space where the handrail would be, if this staircase had one; an interrupted gesture, almost incomprehensible, at least unless it is seen as an instinctive attempt to cling to the absent support.

As to the object of his gaze, there is no doubt that it is the body of the victim lying exposed on the cushions, the limbs stretched out in the shape of a cross, the bust slightly raised, the head thrown back. But the face may perhaps be hidden from the man's eyes by one of the pillars at the bottom of the stairs. The young woman's right hand is touching the ground just by the foot of this pillar. A thick iron bracelet encircles her fragile wrist. Her arm is almost in the shadows; only her hand is sufficiently visible against the circular swelling which serves as a base to the stone shaft. A black metal chain surrounds it and passes through a ring with which the bracelet is equipped, thus fastening the wrist tightly to the pillar.

At the other end of the arm, a round shoulder, raised by the cushions, is also well-lit, as are the neck, the throat and the other shoulder, the armpit with its down, the left arm, also stretched out behind the head, and the wrist, which is secured in the same way to the base of another pillar, quite near the foreground; here the iron bracelet and the chain are very prominent, every detail depicted with perfect clarity.

The same applies, still in the foreground but on the other side, to a similar chain, though it is a little less thick, which directly imprisons the ankle, is twisted round it twice, and immobilises it against a powerful ring embedded in the ground. About a yard behind it, or perhaps a little more, the right foot is chained in the identical manner. But the left ankle and its chain are depicted with greater precision.

The foot is small, fragile, delicately modelled. The chain has crushed the flesh in places, making appreciable depressions in it, although only over a small area. The links are oval in shape, thick, as big as an eye. The ring is similar to those used for tying up horses; it is almost flat on the paving stone to which it is attached by a massive eyebolt. The border of a rug can be seen an inch or so away; it is slightly folded back here, the result, no doubt, of the convulsive, though perforce limited, movements of the victim in her struggle to defend herself.

The man is still half-leaning over her, standing, some three feet away. He is contemplating her back-tilted head, her dark eyes, enlarged by make-up, her wide-open mouth that looks as if it were in the middle of a scream. The position of the man allows nothing to be seen of his face but a vague profile, but one divines it to be a prey to a violent exultation, in spite of his rigid attitude, his silence, his immobility. His back is slightly rounded. His left hand, the only one that is visible, is holding, some distance away from his body, a piece of material, some dark-coloured article of clothing, the end of which reaches down to the rug, and which must be the long cloak with the gold-embroidered lining.

This bulky silhouette largely conceals the naked flesh down which the red patch, which has spread over the curve of the breast, is running in long trickles, which narrow as they divide, against the pale background of the torso and the whole side. One trickle has reached the armpit and is tracing a fine, almost straight, line down the arm; others have reached the waist and formed, on one side of the stomach, the hip, and the upper part of the thigh, a more perilous network which is already congealing. Three or four veinlets have reached the hollow of the groin and met in a sinuous line which joins the apex of the V formed by the open legs, and disappears into the black tuft of hair.

But now — the flesh is still intact; the black tuft of hair and the white stomach, the soft curve of the hips, the narrow waist and, higher up, the nacreous breasts which rise and fall to the rhythm of the rapid breathing, which is now becoming more agitated. The man, close against her, kneeling on one knee, leans over further. The head alone, with its long, curly hair, has kept some freedom of movement, and writhes and struggles;

finally the girl's mouth opens convulsively, while the flesh succumbs, the blood spurts over the tender, tense flesh, the carefully blackened eyes grow out of all proportion, the mouth opens even wider, the head moves from right to left; violently, for the last time, and then more gently, and at last falls back into immobility, in the mass of black hair spread out over the velvet.

At the very top of the stone staircase the little door is open, letting in a yellow but continuous light, against which the dark silhouette of the man wrapped in his long cloak stands out. He has only a few more stairs to climb to reach the threshold.

Then the whole decor is empty; the immense, violet-shadowed room with its stone pillars proliferating on all sides, the monumental staircase without a handrail, curving round as it ascends, and becoming narrower and more uncertain as it rises into obscurity, up to the high vaults, where it disappears.

Near the body, whose wound has congealed, whose brilliance is already diminishing, the tenuous column of smoke from the incense-burner describes complicated spirals in the calm air; at first it is a coil lying horizontally over to the left, which then straightens and gains a little height, after which it moves back towards the axis of its departure point and even extends beyond it to the right, starts again in the other direction, and comes back once more, describing in this way an irregular, gradually diminishing sinusoid, which rises vertically to the top of the painting.

WILLIAM SAROYAN

Love, Here Is My Hat

When I woke up I didn't know what time it was, what day, or what city. I knew I was in a hotel room. It seemed to be either pretty late or a small town. I didn't know whether to get up or go on lying on the bed in my clothes. It was dark.

I knew I was feeling the same.

Love is absurd, always has been, always will be. It's the only thing, but it's absurd. It's too good for anything but birds. It's too spendid for any form of life that's cluttered up with all the crazy things the human form of life is cluttered up with. It's too fine for creatures which wear clothes, which inhabit the world, who must work, who must earn money, who cannot live on air and water.

It's too good for animals that can talk.

I woke up and remembered where I was and why. I was in a room in the Riverside Hotel in Reno and I wasn't in Reno for divorce because I wasn't married. I was in Reno because she was in San Francisco.

I'm not a canary, oriole, dove, quail, robin, hummingbird or any other kind of feathered creature that lives in or near trees, and exists only to love another canary, oriole, dove, quail, robin, or hummingbird, and sing about it. I'm an American. Fun is fun, but I know the difference between good wholesome fun and love, and love is too good for me or anybody like me. It's too wonderful. I can't fly and I can't sing and I need honest-to-God nourishment. I've got to have rare roast beef at least once a day and when I'm in love I can't eat.

I can't be that nice, either, and not feel ridiculous. It isn't my nature to be that nice. That may be all right for an oriole, but it's just a little absurd for me. I can be that nice when I don't mean it, but when I mean it, it's just too wonderful for words. Being that nice is all right for some good-looking dope in a movie, but it's just too wonderful in San Francisco.

I was in Reno because I wanted her to start eating regularly again and let me eat regularly too. I wanted her to get well, so I could get well too.

Look, I told her in San Francisco. I'm getting awfully hungry. Will you excuse me while I leave town?

Leave town? she said. If you go, I go.

Nothing would please me more, I said, but if you go with me, we won't be able to eat and what we need is food. We're both undernourished. Look at me. I'm scarcely a shadow of what I was three weeks ago.

You look wonderful, she said.

No, I don't, I said. I look hungry. I *am* hungry. You look hungry too.

I don't care if I do, she said. If you go away, I'm going with you. I can't live without you.

Yes, you can, I said. What you can't live without is roast beef.

I don't care if I never eat again, she said.

Look, I said. You've got to get some food and sleep, and so do I.

I won't let you go, she said.

All right, I said, then we'll die of starvation together. It's all right with me if it's all right with you.

It's all right with me, she said.

All right, I said. I won't go. What shall we do? I mean, first?

It was a little after eleven and we had just gotten home after a movie and an attempt to eat sandwiches that wouldn't go down, except dry. We ate the pickles and drank the coffee.

Let's stay here and listen to the phonograph, she said.

Or shall we go out and have a few drinks? I said.

Wouldn't you rather stay here and listen to the phonograph? she said.

I guess I would, I said.

So we went to bed.

It might have been a couple of orioles.

Three days later, though, we decided to let me go away. We laughed and she said she wouldn't try to find out where I had gone to and wouldn't follow me and I said I wouldn't write, wire or telephone her.

I feel sick, she said.

Don't be silly, I said. Get in bed and go to sleep and when you wake up, have them bring you a big tray of food. Keep that up for a week.

All right, she said.

I rode to the airport in a cab and two hours later I was in Reno. Fifteen minutes later I was asleep in this room in the Riverside Hotel. I slept like a baby and when I woke up I didn't know what time it was, what day, or what city. Little by little I began to remember.

I got up and yawned. Then I went downstairs and ate a hearty but sad supper of rare roast beef. I don't think it did me much good. After supper I took a walk around town. It was bright and pleasant, but I didn't feel right. I wished I was back in San Francisco, so I got into a cab and rode out of town to The Tavern where I had eight or nine drinks. When I got back to the hotel it was a quarter after two. The desk clerk handed me the key to my room and eleven slips of paper asking me to telephone 783-J. That was a local number. I went to my room and telephoned 783-J.

Where are you? I said.

I'm in Reno, she said.

I know, I said. But where?

I'm at Leon & Eddy's, she said. That number's the number of the phone in the booth here. I'm drunk.

I'll come and get you, I said.

Are you all right? she said.

I'm fine, I said. Are you all right?

I want to cry, she said.

I'll come and get you, I said.

Did you eat? she said.

Yes, I said. Did you?

No, she said. I couldn't.

I'll be right down, I said. How did you know I was in Reno?

The desk clerk told me, she said. I asked him if he knew where you had gone and he told me you had gone to Reno. He told me the name of the hotel too. Did you tell him?

Yes, I said.

I didn't think you would, she said. Why did you do it?

I don't know, I said. I guess I thought maybe you might ask him. Why did you ask him?

I thought maybe you might tell him, she said.

I'll be right down, I said.

Leon & Eddy's was two blocks from the hotel, but I took a cab anyway.

When I saw her sitting at the small table, holding the tall glass and looking alone and lonely, I felt sick and happy again, only worse. It was goofy. It was the only thing but it was crazy.

Come on, I said.

It was too good for me or anybody like me, but it seemed to be the will of the good Lord.

We walked to the hotel.

What we'll have to do, I said, is quarrel and hate one another. It's no use getting married.

I won't quarrel, she said.

We're bound to find something to quarrel about, I said. It may take another day or two, but we're bound to find something. If we don't, it'll be just too bad. This is terrible. I love you.

I love you too, she said.

We stayed in Reno eleven days. Then I told her what I knew she knew I was going to tell her.

Everything's fine, I said. I want it to stay that way.

All right, she said. But we didn't quarrel, did we?

No, I said. Would you prefer a small quarrel?

No, she said.

I'm glad we met, I said.

I took a train back to Frisco and was sick all the way. I knew I would get well, though, and I did.

It took me a long time, but after I got well, nothing was spoiled, and the next time I saw her, three months later, she was well too, so we had supper together.

It was the biggest and finest supper we ever had together, and we enjoyed everything.

Isn't it wonderful? she said.

It certainly is, I said.

STEVEN SCHRADER

Whole

The first morning I slipped off the ladder of my loft bed and landed on my ass. I cried. I cursed my ex-wife. Then I laughed. I flexed my ankles and stood up. My ass didn't fall off. I was whole.

I joined the block association to meet girls. They were all afraid of getting raped and mugged. A police captain came to the meeting and handed out whistles so the victim could blow it and summon neighbors. The girls collected money for brighter lights.

My wife missed me and we started sleeping together. It was just like a new girl friend. I left early before my son got up, so as not to confuse him.

It was a mild winter with many sunny, springlike days. Time didn't seem to pass. I was separated but I was still sleeping with my wife so I stopped. I needed change. I started sleeping with a girl in Riverdale. She was heavy and couldn't assume some of the athletic positions I was used to. On the other hand, I didn't have the warmth of Bernie, her previous boyfriend. We had awkward breakfasts on Sunday mornings. I wanted to rush away to visit my son, but I chewed toast and grinned. She smoked.

There was always snow on the ground in Riverdale. It never seemed to melt or get cleared away. People could ski. It was a resort area. I left and never returned. We spoke on the phone and became friends. You call me. I'll call you. Lose some weight. Develop some warmth.

I went to a party and fell in love. She was quiet and serene, the way my wife had been before she got angry. This girl had a boyfriend, though. Forget him, I told her. I'll show you a good time. Call me in a few weeks, she said. I'm tied up. I waited celibately. Almost. Just my wife a couple of times. She was there. It was convenient. My son saw me leave one morning and I said hello guiltily.

I cleaned my new place, bought some lamps and dishes and a rug. Never again with my wife.

I called the girl I loved but she was still tied up. You're not in love with him, I told her. You're too quiet. I could turn you on, perk you up. Theater, movies, and dance, songs and jokes. I'm terrific. She told me to call in a few months.

I bought colored sneakers and went to parties and danced for hours. I tried to connect. But the beautiful girls were all taken. And I hated the imperfect ones. One breast smaller than the other. Or else braces. I wanted a beautiful white smile. Now. I didn't want to wait two years for someone's bite to be corrected.

I went back to sleeping with my wife. In the morning my son came in and played on the bed and asked if I was moving back.

Spring came and I had to have extensive dental work. My teeth were okay but the gums had to go. I felt older. My body sagged. I was eating french fries too much, so I started cooking home. Lettuce and tomatoes. I learned macrobiotic cooking. I went to exercise class and took up yoga. My muscle tone changed. I was lean and wiry.

I fell in love with a young, beautiful girl from England. She told me I had lovely muscles in my arms, a thick chest, flared nostrils, and distinguished features. We ran our bodies gently over our hands. I don't sleep with a man right away, she told me. Fine, take your time. A couple of years, decades, even. I can wait.

She broke the next date. I'm in love with someone else, she said.

I slept with my wife again.

What are you doing here, my son asked.

I fell in love with a girl who taught history in college. I want a relationship, I told her. Not just fucking. Communication. I'll try, she said. But I'm busy. I went to protests with her. Marched in the rain. Read the News of the Week in Review with her till three in the morning and fell asleep with a hard-on.

I answered a personal ad in a magazine, a mineralogist who wanted to meet people outside her field. She had nice breasts and a horrible twitch which distorted one side of her face. I started twitching, too.

Are you making fun of me?

No, I'm sorry. I can't help it.

We climbed up to my bed and made love on top of the sheets, in time to our twitches. At the end her twitch had stopped. She thanked me profusely.

I began answering lots of ads. None of those sensitive, nubile, whimsical, esthetic, artistic, and warm ladies mentioned their twitches or problems in the ads. But I discovered them right away. I laid my hand on their foreheads and took away birth marks. I cured stammers and club feet.

By summer I was tired. My apartment was steamy. My wife called and begged me to come over. I refused. I had my last personal to respond to. I was with a girl who wanted to kill her baby and I helped her throw it in the river.

That night I dreamed my wife had bought a gun and shot me. I woke with a pain in my stomach, the sheets red, and realized I was dying.

SAM SELVON

When Greek Meets Greek

One morning Ramkilawansingh (after this, we calling this man Ram) was making a study of the notice-boards along Westbourne Grove what does advertise rooms to let. Every now and then he writing down an address or a telephone number, though most of the time his eyes colliding up with *No Colours, Please, or Sorry, No Kolors*.

"Red, white and blue, all out but you," Ram was humming a little ditty what children say when they playing whoop. Just as he get down by Bradley's Corner he met Fraser.

"You look like a man who looking for a place to live," Fraser say.

"You look like a man who could tell me the right place to go," Ram say.

"You try down by Ladbroke Grove?" Fraser ask.

"I don't want to go down in that criminal area," Ram say, "at least, not until they find the man who kill Kelso."

"Then you will never live in the Grove," Fraser say.

"You are a contact man," Ram say, "which part you think I could get a room, boy?"

Fraser scratch his head. "I know of a landlord up the road who vow that he ain't ever taking anybody who come from the West Indies. But he don't mind taking Indians. He wouldn't know the difference when he see you is a Indian ... them English people so foolish they believe every Indian come from India."

"You think I stand a chance?" Ram ask.

"Sure, you stand a chance. All you have to do is put on a turban."

"I never wear a turban in my life; I am a born Trinidadian, a real Creole. All the same, you best hads give me the address, I will pass around there later."

So Fraser give him the address, and Ram went on reading a few more boards, but he got discourage after a while and went to see the landlord.

The first thing the landlord ask him was: "What part of the world do you come from?"

"I am an Untouchable from the heart of India," Ram say. "I am looking for a single room. I dwelt on the banks of the Ganges. Not too expensive."

"But you are not in your national garments," the landlord say.

"When you are in Rome," Ram say, making it sound like an original statement, "do as the Romans do."

While the landlord sizing up Ram, an Indian tenant come up the steps to go inside. This fellar was Chandrilabodoo (after this, we calling this man Chan) and he had a big beard with a hair-net over it, and he was wearing a turban. When he see Ram, he clasp his hands with the palms touching across his chest by way of greeting.

The old Ram catch on quick and do the same thing.

"*Acha, Hindustani,*" Chan say.

"*Acha, pilau, papadom, chickenvindaloo,*" Ram say desperately, hoping for the best.

Chan nod his head, say good morning to the landlord and went inside.

"That was a narrow shave," Ram thought, "I have to watch out for that man."

"That was Mr. Chan," the landlord say, "he is the only other Indian tenant I have at the moment. I have a single room for two pounds. Are you a student?"

"Who is not a student?" Ram say, getting into the mood of the thing. "Man is forever studying ways and means until he passes into the hands of Allah."

Well, to cut a long story short, Ram get a room on the first floor, right next door to Chan, and he move in that same evening.

But as the days going by, Ram had to live like cat-and-mouse with Chan. Every time he sees Chan, he have to hide in case this man start up this Hindustani talk again, or start to ask him questions about Mother India. In fact, it begin to get on Ram nerves, and he decide that he had to do something.

"This house too small for the two of we," Ram say to himself, "one will have to go."

So Ram went down in the basement to see the landlord.

"I have the powers of the Occult," Ram say, "and I have come to warn you of this man Chan. He is not a good tenant. He keeps the bathroom dirty, he does not tidy up his room at all, and he is always chanting and saying his prayers loudly and disturbing the other tenants."

"I have had no complaints," the landlord say.

"But I am living next door to him," Ram say, "and if I concentrate my powers I can see through the wall. That man is a menace, and the best thing you can do is to give him notice. You have a good house here and it would be a pity to let one man spoil it for the other tenants."

"I will have a word with him about it," the landlord say.

Well, the next evening Ram was in his room when he hear a knock at the door. He run in the corner quick and stand upon his head and say, "Come in."

The landlord come in.

"I am just practising my yoghourt," Ram say.

"I have had a word with Mr. Chan," the landlord say, "and I have reason to suspect that you have deceived me. You are not from India, you are from the West Indies."

Ram turn right-side up. "I am a citizen of the world," he say.

"You are flying false colours," the landlord say. "You do not burn incense like Mr. Chan, you do not dress like Mr. Chan, and you do not talk like Mr. Chan."

"Give me a break, old man," Ram say, falling back on the good old West Indian dialect.

"It is too late. You have already started to make trouble. You must go."

Well, the very next week find Ram out scouting again, giving the boards a perusal, and who he should chance to meet but Fraser.

He start to tell Fraser how life hard, how he had to keep dodging from this Chan fellar all the time, and it was pure torture.

"Listen," Fraser say, "you don't mean a big fellar with a beard, and he always wearing a turban?"

"That sound like him," Ram say. "You know him?"

"Know him!" Fraser say. "Man, that is a fellar from Jamaica who I send to that house to get a room!"

WILLIAM CARLOS WILLIAMS

The Use of Force

They were new patients to me, all I had was the name, Olson. Please come down as soon as you can, my daughter is very sick.

When I arrived I was met by the mother, a big startled looking woman, very clean and apologetic who merely said, Is this the doctor? and let me in. In the back, she added. You must excuse us, doctor, we have her in the kitchen where it is warm. It is very damp here sometimes.

The child was fully dressed and sitting on her father's lap near the kitchen table. He tried to get up, but I motioned for him not to bother, took off my overcoat and started to look things over. I could see that they were all very nervous, eyeing me up and down distrustfully. As often, in such cases, they weren't telling me more than they had to, it was up to me to tell them; that's why they were spending three dollars on me.

The child was fairly eating me up with her cold, steady eyes, and no expression to her face whatever. She did not move and seemed, inwardly, quiet; an unusually attractive little thing, and as strong as a heifer in appearance. But her face was flushed, she was breathing rapidly, and I realized that she had a high fever. She had magnificent blonde hair, in profusion. One of those picture children often reproduced in advertising leaflets and the photogravure sections of the Sunday papers.

She's had a fever for three days, began the father, and we don't know what it comes from. My wife has given her things, you know, like people do, but it don't do no good. And there's been a lot of sickness around. So we tho't you better look her over and tell us what is the matter.

As doctors often do I took a trial shot at it as a point of departure. Has she had a sore throat?

Both parents answered me together, No ... No, she says her throat don't hurt her.

Does your throat hurt you? added the mother to the child. But the little girl's expression didn't change nor did she move her eyes from my face.

Have you looked?

I tried to, said the mother, but I couldn't see.

As it happens we had been having a number of cases of diphtheria in the school to which this child went during that month and we were all, quite apparently, thinking of that, though no one had as yet spoken of the thing.

Well, I said, suppose we take a look at the throat first. I smiled in my best professional manner and asking for the child's first name I said, come on, Mathilda, open your mouth and let's take a look at your throat.

Nothing doing.

Aw, come on, I coaxed, just open your mouth wide and let me take a look. Look, I said opening both hands wide. I haven't anything in my hands. Just open up and let me see.

Such a nice man, put in the mother. Look how kind he is to you. Come on, do what he tells you to. He won't hurt you.

At that I ground my teeth in disgust. If only they wouldn't use the word "hurt" I might be able to get somewhere. But I did not allow myself to be hurried or disturbed but speaking quietly and slowly I approached the child again.

As I moved my chair a little nearer suddenly with one cat-like movement both her hands clawed instinctively for my eyes and she almost reached them too. In fact she knocked my glasses flying and they fell, though unbroken, several feet away from me on the kitchen floor.

Both the mother and father almost turned themselves inside out in embarrassment and apology. You bad girl, said the mother, taking her and shaking her by one arm. Look what you've done. The nice man ...

For heaven's sake, I broke in. Don't call me a nice man to her. I'm here to look at her throat on the chance that she might have diphtheria and possibly die of it. But that's nothing to her. Look here, I said to the child, we're going to look at your throat. You're old enough to understand what I'm saying. Will you open it now by yourself or shall we have to open it for you?

Not a move. Even her expression hadn't changed. Her breaths however were coming faster and faster. Then the battle began. I had to do it. I had to have a throat culture for her own protection. But first I told the parents that it was entirely up to them. I explained the danger but said that I would not insist on a throat examination so long as they would take the responsibility.

If you don't do what the doctor says you'll have to go to the hospital, the mother admonished her severely.

Oh yeah? I had to smile to myself. After all, I had already fallen in love with the savage brat, the parents were contemptible to me. In the ensuing struggle they grew more and more abject, crushed, exhausted while she surely rose to magnificent heights of insane fury of effort bred of her terror of me.

The father tried his best, and he was a big man but the fact that she was his daughter, his shame at her behavior and his dread of hurting her made him release her just at the critical moment several times when I had almost achieved success, till I wanted to kill him. But his dread also that she might have diphtheria made him tell me to go on, go on though he himself was almost fainting, while the mother moved back and forth behind us raising and lowering her hands in an agony of apprehension.

Put her in front of you on your lap, I ordered, and hold her wrists.

But as soon as he did the child let out a scream. Don't, you're hurting me. Let go of my hands. Let them go I tell you. Then she shrieked terrifyingly, hysterically. Stop it! Stop it! You're killing me!

Do you think she can stand it, doctor! said the mother.

You get out, said the husband to his wife. Do you want her to die of diphtheria?

Come on now, hold her, I said.

Then I grasped the child's head with my left hand and tried to get the wooden tongue depressor between her teeth. She fought, with clenched teeth, desperately! But now I also had grown furious — at a child. I tried to hold myself down but I couldn't. I know how to expose a throat for inspection. And I did my best. When finally I got the wooden spatula behind the last teeth and just the point of it into the mouth cavity, she opened up for an instant but before I could see anything she came down again and gripping the wooden blade between her molars she reduced it to splinters before I could get it out again.

Aren't you ashamed, the mother yelled at her. Aren't you ashamed to act like that in front of the doctor?

Get me a smooth-handled spoon of some sort, I told the mother. We're going through with this. The child's mouth was already bleeding. Her tongue was cut and she was screaming in wild hysterical shrieks. Perhaps I should have desisted and come back in an hour or more. No doubt it would have been better. But I have seen at least two children lying dead in bed of neglect in such cases, and feeling that I must get a diagnosis now or never I went at it again. But the worst of it was that I too had got beyond reason. I could have torn the child apart in my own fury and enjoyed it. It was a pleasure to attack her. My face was burning with it.

The damned little brat must be protected against her own idiocy, one says to one's self at such times. Others must be protected against her. It is social necessity. And all these things are true. But a blind fury, a feeling of adult shame, bred of a longing for muscular release are the operatives. One goes on to the end.

In a final unreasoning assault I overpowered the child's neck and jaws. I forced the heavy silver spoon back of her teeth and down her throat till she gagged. And there it was — both tonsils covered with membrane. She had fought valiantly to keep me from knowing her secret. She had been hiding that sore throat for three days at least and lying to her parents in order to escape just such an outcome as this.

Now truly she *was* furious. She had been on the defensive before but now she attacked. Tried to get off her father's lap and fly at me while tears of defeat blinded her eyes.

Short Stories

CHINUA ACHEBE

The Voter

Rufus Okeke — Roof for short — was a very popular man in his village. Although the villagers did not explain it in so many words Roof's popularity was a measure of their gratitude to an energetic young man who, unlike most of his fellows nowadays had not abandoned the village in order to seek work, any work, in the towns. And Roof was not a village lout either. Everyone knew how he had spent two years as a bicycle repairer's apprentice in Port Harcourt, and had given up of his own free will a bright future to return to his people and guide them in these difficult times. Not that Umuofia needed a lot of guidance. The village already belonged *en masse* to the People's Alliance Party, and its most illustrious son, Chief the Honourable Marcus Ibe, was Minister of Culture in the outgoing government (which was pretty certain to be the in-coming one as well). Nobody doubted that the Honourable Minister would be elected in his constituency. Opposition to him was the proverbial fly trying to move a dunghill. It would have been ridiculous enough without coming as it did now, from a complete nonentity.

As was to be expected Roof was in the service of the Honourable Minister for the coming elections. He had become a real expert in election campaigning at all levels — village, local government or national. He could tell the mood and temper of the electorate at any given time. For instance he had warned the Minister months ago about the radical change that had come into the thinking of Umuofia since the last national election.

The villagers had had five years in which to see how quickly and plentifully politics brought wealth, chieftaincy titles, doctorate degrees and other honours some of which, like the last, had still to be explained satisfactorily to them; for in their naïvety they still expected a doctor to be able to heal the sick. Anyhow these honours and benefits had come so readily to the man to whom they had given their votes free of charge five years ago that they were now ready to try it a different way.

Their point was that only the other day Marcus Ibe was a not too successful mission school teacher. Then politics had come up to their village and he had wisely joined up, some said just in time to avoid imminent dismissal arising from a female teacher's pregnancy. Today he was Chief the Honourable; he had two long cars and had just built himself the biggest house anyone had seen in these parts. But let it be said that none of these successes had gone to Marcus's head as well they might. He remained devoted to his people. Whenever he could he left the good things of the capital and returned to his village which had neither running water nor electricity, although he had lately installed a private plant to supply electricity to his new house. He knew the source of his good fortune, unlike the little bird who ate and drank and went out to challenge his personal spirit. Marcus had christened his new house "Umuofia Mansions" in honour of his village, and he had slaughtered five bulls and countless goats to entertain the people on the day it was opened by the Archbishop.

Every one was full of praise for him. One old man said: "Our son is a good man; he is not like the mortar which as soon as food comes its way turns its back on the ground." But when the feasting was over, the villagers told themselves that they had underrated the power of the ballot paper before and should not do so again. Chief the Honourable Marcus Ibe was not unprepared. He had drawn five months' salary in advance, changed a few hundred pounds into shining shillings and armed his campaign boys with eloquent little jute bags. In the day he made his speeches; at night his stalwarts conducted their whispering campaign. Roof was the most trusted of these campaigners.

"We have a Minister from our village, one of our own sons," he said to a group of elders in the house of Ogbuefi Ezenwa, a man of high traditional title. "What greater honour can a village have? Do you ever stop to ask yourselves why we should be singled out for this honour? I will tell you; it is because we are favoured by the leaders of PAP. Whether or not we cast our paper for Marcus, PAP will continue to rule. Think of the pipe-borne water they have promised us ..."

Besides Roof and his assistant there were five elders in the room. An old hurricane lamp with a cracked, sooty, glass chimney gave out yellowish light in their midst. The elders sat on very low stools. On the floor, directly in front of each of them, lay two shilling pieces. Outside beyond the fastened door, the moon kept a straight face.

"We believe every word you say to be true," said Ezenwa. "We shall, every one of us, drop his paper for Marcus. Who would leave an ozo feast and go to a poor ritual meal? Tell Marcus he has our papers, and our wives' papers too. But what we do say is that two shillings is shameful." He brought the lamp close and tilted it at the money before him as if to make sure he had not mistaken its value. "Yes, two shillings is too shameful. If Marcus were a poor man — which our ancestors forbid — I should be the first to give him my paper free, as I did before. But today Marcus is a great man and does his things like a great man. We did not ask him for money yesterday; we shall not ask him tomorrow. But today is our day, we have climbed the iroko tree today and would be foolish not to take down all the firewood we need."

Roof had to agree. He had lately been taking down a lot of firewood himself. Only yesterday he had asked Marcus for one of his many rich robes — and had got it. Last Sunday Marcus's wife (the teacher that nearly got him in trouble) had objected (like the woman she was) when Roof pulled out his fifth bottle of beer from the refrigerator; she was roundly and publicly rebuked by her husband. To cap it all Roof had won a land case recently because, among other things, he had been chauffeur-driven to the disputed site. So he understood the elders about the firewood.

"All right," he said in English and then reverted to Ibo. "Let us not quarrel about small things." He stood up, adjusted his robes and plunged his hand once more into the bag. Then he bent down like a priest distributing the host and gave one shilling more to every man; only he did not put it into their palms but on the floor in front of them. The men, who had so far not deigned to touch the things, looked at the floor and shook their heads. Roof got up again and gave each man another shilling.

"I am through," he said with a defiance that was no less effective for being transparently faked. The elders too knew how far to go without losing decorum. So when Roof added: "Go cast your paper for the enemy if you like!" they quickly calmed him down with a suitable speech from each of them. By the time the last man had spoken it was possible, without great loss of dignity, to pick up the things from the floor ...

The enemy Roof had referred to was the Progressive Organization Party (POP) which had been formed by the tribes down the coast to save themselves, as the founders of the party proclaimed, from "total political, cultural, social and religious annihilation." Although it was clear the party had no chance here it had plunged, with typical foolishness, into a straight fight with PAP, providing cars and loud-speakers to a few local rascals and thugs to go around and make a lot of noise. No one knew for certain how much money POP had let loose in Umuofia but it was said to be very considerable. Their local campaigners would end up very rich no doubt.

Up to last night everything had been "moving according to plan," as Roof would have put it. Then he had received a strange visit from the leader of the POP campaign team. Although he and Roof were well known to each other, and might even be called friends, his visit was cold and business-like. No words were wasted. He placed five pounds on the floor before Roof and said, "We want your vote." Roof got up from his chair, went to the outside door, closed it carefully and returned to his chair. The brief exercise gave him enough time to weigh the proposition. As he spoke his eyes never left the red notes on the floor. He seemed to be mesmerized by the picture of the cocoa farmer harvesting his crops.

"You know I work for Marcus," he said feebly. "It will be very bad ... "

"Marcus will not be there when you put in your paper. We have plenty of work to do tonight; are you taking this or not?"

"It will not be heard outside this room?" asked Roof.

"We are after votes not gossip."

"All right," said Roof in English.

The man nudged his companion and he brought forward an object covered with a red cloth and proceeded to remove the cover. It was a fearsome little affair contained in a clay pot with feathers stuck into it.

"The *iyi* comes from Mbanta. You know what that means. Swear that you will vote for Maduka. If you fail to do so, this *iyi* take note."

Roof's heart nearly flew out when he saw the *iyi*; indeed he knew the fame of Mbanta in these things. But he was a man of quick decision. What could a single vote cast in secret for Maduka take away from Marcus's certain victory? Nothing.

"I will cast my paper for Maduka; if not this *iyi* take note."

"Das all," said the man as he rose with his companion who had covered up the object again and was taking it back to their car.

"You know he has no chance against Marcus," said Roof at the door.

"It is enough that he gets a few votes now; next time he will get more. People will hear that he gives out pounds, not shillings, and they will listen."

Election morning. The great day every five years when the people exercise power. Weather-beaten posters on walls of houses, tree trunks and telegraph poles. The few that were still whole called out their message to those who could read. Vote for the People's Alliance Party! Vote for the Progressive Organization Party! Vote for PAP! Vote for POP! The posters that were torn called out as much of the message as they could.

As usual Chief the Honourable Marcus Ibe was doing things in grand style. He had hired a highlife band from Umuru and stationed it at such a distance from the voting booths as just managed to be lawful. Many villagers danced to the music, their ballot papers held aloft, before proceeding to the booths. Chief the Honourable Marcus Ibe sat in the "owner's corner" of the enormous green car and smiled and nodded. One enlightened villager came up to the car, shook hands with the great man and said in advance, "Congrats!" This immediately set the pattern. Hundreds of admirers shook Marcus's hand and said "Corngrass!"

Roof and the other organizers were prancing up and down, giving last minute advice to the voters and pouring with sweat.

"Do not forget," he said again to a group of illiterate women who seemed ready to burst with enthusiasm and good humour, "our sign is the motor-car ..."

"Like the one Marcus is sitting inside."

"Thank you, mother," said Roof. "It is the same car. The box with the car shown on its body is the box for you. Don't look at the other with the man's head: it is for those whose heads are not correct."

This was greeted with loud laughter. Roof cast a quick and busy-like glance towards the Minister and received a smile of appreciation.

"Vote for the car," he shouted, all the veins in his neck standing out. "Vote for the car and you will ride in it!"

"Or if we don't, our children will," piped the same sharp, old girl.

The band struck up a new number: "Why walk when you can ride ... "

In spite of his apparent calm and confidence Chief the Honourable Marcus was a relentless stickler for detail. He knew he would win what the newspapers called "a landslide victory" but he did not wish, even so, to throw away a single vote. So as soon as the first rush of voters was over he promptly asked his campaign boys to go one at a time and put in their ballot papers.

"Roof, you had better go first," he said.

Roof's spirits fell; but he let no one see it. All morning he had masked his deep worry with a surface exertion which was unusual even for him. Now he dashed off in his springy fashion towards the booths. A policeman at the entrance searched him for illegal ballot papers and passed him. Then the electoral officer explained to him about the two boxes. By this time the spring had gone clean out of his walk. He sidled in and was confronted by the car and the head. He brought out his ballot paper from his pocket and looked at it. How could he betray Marcus even in secret? He resolved to go back to the other man and return his five pounds ... Five pounds! He knew at once it was impossible. He had sworn on that *iyi*. The notes were red; the cocoa farmer busy at work.

At this point he heard the muffled voice of the policeman asking the electoral officer what the man was doing inside. "Abi na pickin im de born?"

Quick as lightning a thought leapt into Roof's mind. He folded the paper, tore it in two along the crease and put one half in each box. He took the precaution of putting the first half into Maduka's box and confirming the action verbally: "I vote for Maduka."

They marked his thumb with indelible purple ink to prevent his return, and he went out of the booth as jauntily as he had gone in.

SHERWOOD ANDERSON

I Want to Know Why

We got up at four in the morning that first day in the East. On the evening before, we had climbed off a freight train at the edge of town and with the true instinct of Kentucky boys had found our way across town and to the race track and the stables at once. Then we knew we were all right. Hanley Turner right away found a nigger we knew. It was Bildad Johnson, who in the winter works at Ed Becker's livery barn in our home town, Beckersville. Bildad is a good cook as almost all our niggers are and of course he, like everyone in our part of Kentucky who is anyone at all, likes the horses. In the spring Bildad begins to scratch around. A nigger from our country can flatter and wheedle anyone into letting him do most anything he wants. Bildad wheedles the stable men and the trainers from the horse farms in our country around Lexington. The trainers come into town in the evening to stand around and talk and maybe get into a poker game. Bildad gets in with them. He is always doing little favors and telling about things to eat, chicken browned in a pan, and how is the best way to cook sweet potatoes and corn bread. It makes your mouth water to hear him.

When the racing season comes on and the horses go to the races and there is all the talk on the streets in the evenings about the new colts, and everyone says when they are going over to Lexington or to the spring meeting at Churchill Downs or to Latonia, and the horsemen that have been down to New Orleans or maybe at the winter meeting at Havana in Cuba come home to spend a week before they start out again, at such a time when everything talked about in Beckersville is just horses and nothing else and the outfits start out and horse racing is in every breath of air you breathe, Bildad shows up with a job as cook for some outfit. Often when I think about it, his always going all season to the races and working in the livery barn in the winter where horses are and where men like to come and talk about horses, I wish I was a nigger. It's a foolish thing to say, but that's the way I am about being around horses, just crazy. I can't help it.

Well, I must tell you about what we did and let you in on what I'm talking about. Four of us boys from Beckersville, all whites and sons of men who live in Beckersville regular, made up our minds we were going to the races, not just to Lexington or Louisville, I don't mean, but to the big Eastern track we were always hearing our Beckersville men talk about, to Saratoga. We were all pretty young then. I was just turned fifteen and I was the oldest of the four. It was my scheme. I admit that, and I talked the others into trying it. There was Hanley Turner and Henry Rieback and Tom Tumberton and myself. I had thirty-seven dollars I had earned during the winter working nights and Saturdays in Enoch Myer's grocery. Henry Rieback had eleven dollars and the others, Hanley and Tom, had only a dollar or two each. We fixed it all up and laid low until the Kentucky spring meetings were over and some of our men, the sportiest ones, the ones we envied the most, had cut out. Then we cut out too.

I won't tell you the trouble we had beating our way on freights and all. We went through Cleveland and Buffalo and other cities and saw Niagara Falls. We bought things there, souvenirs and spoons and cards and shells with pictures of the falls on them for our sisters and mothers, but thought we had better not send any of the things home. We didn't want to put the folks on our trail and maybe be nabbed.

We got into Saratoga as I said at night and went to the track. Bildad fed us up. He showed us a place to sleep in hay over a shed and promised to keep still. Niggers are all right about things like that. They won't squeal on you. Often a white man you might meet, when you had run away from home like that, might appear to be all right and give you a quarter or a half dollar or something, and then go right and give you away. White men will do that, but not a nigger. You can trust them. They are squarer with kids. I don't know why.

At the Saratoga meeting that year there were a lot of men from home. Dave Williams and Arthur Mulford and Jerry Myers and others. Then there was a lot from Louisville and Lexington Henry Rieback knew but I didn't. They were professional gamblers and Henry Rieback's father is one too. He is what is called a sheet writer and goes away most of the year to tracks. In the winter when he is home in Beckersville he don't stay there much but goes away to cities and deals faro. He is a nice man and generous, is always sending Henry presents, a bicycle and a gold watch and a boy scout suit of clothes and things like that.

My own father is a lawyer. He's all right, but don't make much money and can't buy me things, and anyway I'm getting so old now I don't expect it. He never said nothing to me against Henry, but Hanley Turner and Tom Tumberton's fathers did. They said to their boys that money so come by is no good and they didn't want their boys brought up to hear gamblers' talk and be thinking about such things and maybe embrace them.

That's all right and I guess the men know what they are talking about, but I don't see what it's got to do with Henry or with horses either. That's what I'm writing this story about. I'm puzzled. I'm getting to be a man and want to think straight and be O.K., and there's something I saw at the race meeting at the Eastern track I can't figure out.

I can't help it, I'm crazy about thoroughbred horses. I've always been that way. When I was ten years old and saw I was growing to be big and couldn't be a rider I was so sorry I nearly died. Harry Hellinfinger in Beckersville, whose father is Postmaster, is grown up and too lazy to work, but likes to stand around in the street and get up jokes on boys like sending them to a hardware store for a gimlet to bore square holes and other jokes like that. He played one on me. He told me that if I would eat a half a cigar I would be stunted and not grow any more and maybe could be a rider. I did it. When father wasn't looking I took a cigar out of his pocket and gagged it down some way. It made me awful sick and the doctor had to be sent for, and then it did no good. I kept right on growing. It was a joke. When I told what I had done and why, most fathers would have whipped me, but mine didn't.

Well, I didn't get stunted and didn't die. It serves Harry Hellinfinger right. Then I made up my mind I would like to be a stableboy, but had to give that up too. Mostly niggers do that work and I knew father wouldn't let me go into it. No use to ask him.

If you've never been crazy about thoroughbreds, it's because you've never been around where they are much and don't know any better. They're beautiful. There isn't anything so lovely and clean and full of spunk and honest and everything as some race horses. On the big horse farms that are all around our town Beckersville there are tracks, and the horses run in the early morning. More than a thousand times I've got out of bed before daylight and walked two or three miles to the tracks. Mother wouldn't of let me go, but father always says, "Let him alone." So I got some bread out of the breadbox and some butter and jam, gobbled it and lit out.

At the tracks you sit on the fence with men, whites and niggers, and they chew tobacco and talk, and then the colts are brought out. It's early and the grass is covered with shiny dew and in another field a man is plowing and they are frying things in a shed where the track niggers sleep, and you know how a nigger can giggle and laugh and say things that make you laugh. A white man can't do it and some niggers can't, but a track nigger can every time.

And so the colts are brought out and some are just galloped by stableboys, but almost every morning on a big track owned by a rich man who lives maybe in New York, there are always, nearly every morning, a few colts and some of the old race horses and geldings and mares that are cut loose.

It brings a lump up into my throat when a horse runs. I don't mean all horses, but some. I can pick them nearly every time. It's in my blood like in the blood of race track niggers and trainers. Even when they just go slop-jogging along with a little nigger on their backs, I can tell a winner. If my throat hurts and it's hard for me to swallow, that's him. He'll run like Sam Hill when you let him out. If he don't win every time it'll be a wonder and because they've got him in a pocket behind another or he was pulled or got off bad at the post or something. If I wanted to be a gambler like Henry Rieback's father I could get rich. I know I could and Henry says so too. All I would have to do is to wait till that hurt comes when I see a horse and then bet every cent. That's what I would do if I wanted to be a gambler, but I don't.

When you're at the tracks in the morning — not the race tracks but the training tracks around Beckersville — you don't see a horse, the kind I've been talking about, very often, but it's nice anyway. Any thoroughbred, that is sired right and out of a good mare and trained by a man that knows how, can run. If he couldn't, what would he be there for and not pulling a plow?

Well, out of the stables they come and the boys are on their backs and it's lovely to be there. You hunch down on top of the fence and itch inside you. Over in the sheds the niggers giggle and sing. Bacon is being fried and coffee made. Everything smells lovely. Nothing smells better than coffee and manure and horses and niggers and bacon frying and pipes being smoked out of doors on a morning like that. It just gets you, that's what it does.

But about Saratoga. We was there six days and not a soul from home seen us and everything came off just as we wanted it to, fine weather and horses and races and all. We beat our way home and Bildad gave us a basket with fried chicken and bread and other eatables in, and I had eighteen dollars when we got back to Beckersville. Mother jawed and cried, but Pop didn't say much. I told everything we done, except one thing. I did and saw that alone. That's what I'm writing about. It got me upset. I think about it at night. Here it is.

At Saratoga we laid up nights in the hay in the shed Bildad had showed us and ate with the niggers early and at night when the race people had all gone away. The men from home stayed mostly in the grandstand and betting field and didn't come out around the places where the horses are kept except to the paddocks just before a race when the horses are saddled. At Saratoga they don't have paddocks under an open shed as at Lexington and Churchill Downs and other tracks down in our country, but saddle the horses right out in an open place under trees on a lawn as smooth and nice as Banker Bohon's front yard here in Beckersville. It's lovely. The horses are sweaty and nervous and shine and the men come out and smoke cigars and look at them and the trainers are there and the owners, and your heart thumps so you can hardly breathe.

Then the bugle blows for post and the boys that ride come running out with their silk clothes on and you run to get a place by the fence with the niggers.

I always am wanting to be a trainer or owner, and at the risk of being seen and caught and sent home I went to the paddocks before every race. The other boys didn't, but I did.

We got to Saratoga on a Friday, and on Wednesday the next week the big Mullford Handicap was to be run. Middlestride was in it and Sunstreak. The weather was fine and the track fast. I couldn't sleep the night before.

What had happened was that both these horses are the kind it makes my throat hurt to see. Middlestride is long and looks awkward and is a gelding. He belongs to Joe Thompson, a little owner from home who only has a half dozen horses. The Mullford Handicap is for a mile and Middlestride can't untrack fast. He goes away slow and is always 'way back at the half, then he begins to run and if the race is a mile and a quarter he'll just eat up everything and get there.

Sunstreak is different. He is a stallion and nervous and belongs on the biggest farm we've got in our country, the Van Riddle place that belongs to Mr. Van Riddle of New York. Sunstreak is like a girl you think about sometimes but never see. He is hard all over and lovely too. When you look at his head you want to kiss him. He is trained by Jerry Tillford who knows me and has been good to me lots of times, lets me walk into a horse's stall to look at him close and other things. There isn't anything as sweet as that horse. He stands at the post quiet and not letting on, but he is just burning up inside. Then when the barrier goes up he is off like his name, Sunstreak. It makes you ache to see him. It hurts you. He just lays down and runs like a bird dog. There can't anything I ever see run like him except Middlestride when he gets untracked and stretches himself.

Gee! I ached to see that race and those two horses run, ached and dreaded it too. I didn't want to see either of our horses beaten. We had never sent a pair like that to the races before. Old men in Beckersville said so and the niggers said so. It was a fact.

Before the race, I went over to the paddocks to see. I looked a last look at Middlestride, who isn't such a much standing in a paddock that way, then I went to see Sunstreak.

It was his day. I knew when I see him. I forgot all about being seen myself and walked right up. All the men from Beckersville were there and no one noticed me except Jerry Tillford. He saw me and something happened. I'll tell you about that.

I was standing looking at that horse and aching. In some way, I can't tell how, I knew just how Sunstreak felt inside. He was quiet and letting the niggers rub his legs and Mr. Van Riddle himself put the saddle on, but he was just a raging torrent inside. He was like the water in the river at Niagara Falls just before it goes plunk down. That horse wasn't thinking about running. He don't have to think about that. He was just thinking about holding himself back till the time for the running came. I knew that. I could just in a way see right inside him. He was going to do some awful running and I knew it. He wasn't bragging or letting on much or prancing or making a fuss, but just waiting. I knew it and Jerry Tillford his trainer knew. I looked up, and then that man and I looked into each other's eyes. Something happened to me. I guess I loved the man as much as I did the horse because he knew what I knew. Seemed to me there wasn't anything in the world but that man and the horse and me. I cried and Jerry Tillford had a shine in his eyes. Then I came away to the fence to wait for the race. The horse was better than me, more steadier and, now I know, better than Jerry. He was the quietest and he had to do the running.

Sunstreak ran first of course and he busted the world's record for a mile. I've seen that if I never see anything more. Everything came out just as I expected. Middlestride got left at the post and was 'way back and closed up to be second, just as I knew he would. He'll get a world's record too some day. They can't skin the Beckersville country on horses.

I watched the race calm because I knew what would happen. I was sure. Hanley Turner and Henry Rieback and Tom Tumberton were all more excited than me.

A funny thing had happened to me. I was thinking about Jerry Tillford the trainer and how happy he was all through the race. I liked him that afternoon even more than I ever liked my own father. I almost forgot the horses thinking that way about him. It was because of what I had seen in his eyes as he stood in the paddocks beside Sunstreak before the race started. I knew he had been watching and working with Sunstreak since the horse was a baby colt, had taught him to run and be patient and when to let himself out and not to quit, never. I knew that for him it was like a mother seeing her child do something brave or wonderful. It was the first time I ever felt for a man like that.

After the race that night I cut out from Tom and Hanley and Henry. I wanted to be by myself and I wanted to be near Jerry Tillford if I could work it. Here is what happened.

The track in Saratoga is near the edge of town. It is all polished up and trees around, the evergreen kind, and grass and everything painted and nice. If you go past the track you get to a hard road made of asphalt for automobiles, and if you go along this for a few miles there is a road turns off to a little rummy-looking farmhouse set in a yard.

That night after the race I went along that road because I had seen Jerry and some other men go that way in an automobile. I didn't expect to find them. I walked for a ways and then sat down by a fence to think. It was the direction they went in. I wanted to be as near Jerry as I could. I felt close to him. Pretty soon I went up this side road — I don't know why — and came to the rummy farmhouse. I was just lonesome to see Jerry, like wanting to see your father at night when you are a young kid. Just then an automobile came along and turned in. Jerry was in it and Henry Rieback's father, and Arthur Bedford from home, and Dave Williams and two other men I didn't know. They got out of the car and went into the house, all but Henry Rieback's father who quarreled with them and said he wouldn't go. It was only about nine o'clock, but they were all drunk and the rummy-looking farmhouse was a place for bad women to stay in. That's what it was. I crept up along a fence and looked through a window and saw.

It's what give me the fantods. I can't make it out. The women in the house were all ugly mean-looking women, not nice to look at or be near. They were homely too, except one who was tall and looked a little like the gelding Middlestride, but not clean like him, but with a hard ugly mouth. She had red hair. I saw everything plain. I got up by an old rosebush by an open window and looked. The women had on loose dresses and sat around in chairs. The men came in and some sat on the women's laps. The place smelled rotten and there was rotten talk, the kind a kid hears around a livery stable in a town like Beckersville in the winter but don't ever expect to hear talked when there are women around. It was rotten. A nigger wouldn't go into such a place.

I looked at Jerry Tillford. I've told you how I had been feeling about him on account of his knowing what was going on inside Sunstreak in the minute before he went to the post for the race in which he made a world's record.

Jerry bragged in that bad woman house as I knew Sunstreak wouldn't never have bragged. He said that he made that horse, that it was him that won the race and made the record. He lied and bragged like a fool. I never heard such silly talk.

And then, what do you suppose he did! He looked at the woman in there, the one that was lean and hard-mouthed and looked a little like the gelding Middlestride but not clean like him, and his eyes began to shine just as they did when he looked at me and at Sunstreak in the paddocks at the track in the afternoon. I stood there by the window — gee! — but I wished I hadn't gone away from the tracks, but had stayed with the boys and the niggers and the horses. The tall rotten-looking woman was between us just as Sunstreak was in the paddocks in the afternoon.

Then, all of a sudden, I began to hate that man. I wanted to scream and rush in the room and kill him. I never had such a feeling before. I was so mad clean through that I cried and my fists were doubled up so my fingernails cut my hands.

And Jerry's eyes kept shining and he waved back and forth, and then he went and kissed that woman and I crept away and went back to the tracks and to bed and didn't sleep hardly any, and then next day I got the other kids to start home with me and never told them anything I seen.

I been thinking about it ever since. I can't make it out. Spring has come again and I'm nearly sixteen and go to the tracks mornings same as always, and I see Sunstreak and Middlestride and a new colt named Strident I'll bet will lay them all out, but no one thinks so but me and two or three niggers.

But things are different. At the tracks the air don't taste as good or smell as good. It's because a man like Jerry Tillford, who knows what he does, could see a horse like Sunstreak run, and kiss a woman like that the same day. I can't make it out. Darn him, what did he want to do like that for? I keep thinking about it and it spoils looking at horses and smelling things and hearing niggers laugh and everything. Sometimes I'm so mad about it I want to fight someone. It gives me the fantods. What did he do it for? I want to know why.

MARGARET ATWOOD

The Resplendent Quetzal

Sarah was sitting near the edge of the sacrificial well. She had imagined something smaller, more like a wishing well, but this was huge, and the water at the bottom wasn't clear at all. It was mud-brown; a few clumps of reeds were growing over to one side, and the trees at the top dangled their roots, or were they vines, down the limestone walls into the water. Sarah thought there might be some point to being a sacrificial victim if the well were nicer, but you would never get her to jump into a muddy hole like that. They were probably pushed, or knocked on the head and thrown in. According to the guidebook the water was deep but it looked more like a swamp to her.

Beside her a group of tourists was being rounded up by the guide, who obviously wanted to get the whole thing over with so he could cram them back onto their pink and purple striped *turismo* bus and relax. These were Mexican tourists, and Sarah found it reassuring that other people besides Canadians and Americans wore big hats and sunglasses and took pictures of everything. She wished she and Edward could make these excursions at a less crowded time of year, if they had to make them at all, but because of Edward's teaching job they were limited to school holidays. Christmas was the worst. It would be the same even if he had a different job and they had children, though; but they didn't have any.

The guide shooed his charges back along the gravel path as if they were chickens, which was what they sounded like. He himself lingered beside Sarah, finishing his cigarette, one foot on a stone block, like a conquistador. He was a small dark man with several gold teeth, which glinted when he smiled. He was smiling at Sarah now, sideways, and she smiled back serenely. She liked it when these men smiled at her or even when they made those juicy sucking noises with their mouths as they walked behind her on the street; so long as they didn't touch. Edward pretended not to hear them. Perhaps they did it so much because she was blonde: blondes were rare here. She didn't think of herself as beautiful, exactly; the word she had chosen for herself some time ago was "comely." Comely to look upon. You would never use that word for a thin woman.

The guide tossed his cigarette butt into the sacrificial well and turned to follow his flock. Sarah forgot about him immediately. She'd felt something crawling up her leg, but when she looked nothing was there. She tucked the full skirt of her cotton dress in under her thighs and clamped it between her knees. This was the kind of place you could get flea bites, places with dirt on the ground, where people sat. Parks and bus terminals. But she didn't care, her feet were tired and the sun was hot. She would rather sit in the shade and get bitten than rush around trying to see everything, which was what Edward wanted to do. Luckily the bites didn't swell up on her the way they did on Edward.

Edward was back along the path, out of sight among the bushes, peering around with his new Leitz binoculars. He didn't like sitting down, it made him restless. On these trips it was difficult for Sarah to sit by herself and just think. Her own binoculars, which were Edward's old ones, dangled around her neck; they weighed a ton. She took them off and put them into her purse.

His passion for birds had been one of the first things Edward had confided to her. Shyly, as if it had been some precious gift, he'd shown her the lined notebook he'd started keeping when he was nine, with its awkward, boyish printing — *Robin, Bluejay, Kingfisher* — and the day and the year recorded beside each name. She'd pretended to be touched and interested, and in fact she had been. She herself didn't have compulsions of this kind; whereas Edward plunged totally into things, as if they were oceans. For a while it was stamps; then he took up playing the flute and nearly drove her crazy with the practising. Now it was pre-Columbian ruins, and he was determined to climb up every heap of old stones he could get his hands on. A capacity for dedication, she guessed you would call it. At first Edward's obsessions had fascinated her, since she didn't understand them, but now they merely made her tired. Sooner or later he'd dropped them all anyway, just as he began to get really good or really knowledgeable; all but the birds. That had remained constant. She herself, she thought, had once been one of his obsessions.

It wouldn't be so bad if he didn't insist on dragging her into everything. Or rather, he had once insisted; he no longer did. And she had encouraged him, she'd let him think she shared or at least indulged his interests. She was becoming less indulgent as she grew older. The waste of energy bothered her, because it was a waste, he never stuck with anything, and what use was his encyclopaedic knowledge of birds? It would be different if they had enough money, but they were always running short. If only he would take all that energy and do something productive with it, in his job for instance. He could be a principal if he wanted to, she kept telling him that. But he wasn't interested, he was content to poke along doing the same thing year after year. His Grade Six children adored him, the boys especially. Perhaps it was because they sensed he was a lot like them.

He'd started asking her to go birding, as he called it, shortly after they'd met, and of course she had gone. It would have been an error to refuse. She hadn't complained, then, about her sore feet or standing in the rain under the dripping bushes trying to keep track of some nondescript sparrow, while Edward thumbed through his *Peterson's Field Guide* as if it were the Bible or the bird was the Holy Grail. She'd even become quite good at it. Edward was nearsighted, and she was quicker at spotting movement than he was. With his usual generosity he acknowledged this, and she'd fallen into the habit of using it when she wanted to get rid of him for a while. Just now, for instance.

"There's something over there." She'd pointed across the well to the tangle of greenery on the other side.

"Where?" Edward had squinted eagerly and raised his binoculars. He looked a little like a bird himself, she thought, with his long nose and stilt legs.

"That thing there, sitting in that thing, the one with the tufts. The sort of bean tree. It's got orange on it."

Edward focused. "An oriole?"

"I can't tell from here.... Oh, it just flew." She pointed over their heads while Edward swept the sky in vain.

"I think it lit back there, behind us."

That was enough to send him off. She had to do this with enough real birds to keep him believing, however.

Edward sat down on the root of a tree and lit a cigarette. He had gone down the first side-path he'd come to; it smelled of piss, and he could see by the decomposing Kleenexes further along that this was one of the places people went when they couldn't make it back to the washroom behind the ticket counter.

He took off his glasses, then his hat, and wiped the sweat off his forehead. His face was red, he could feel it. Blushing, Sarah called it. She persisted in attributing it to shyness and boyish embarrassment, she hadn't yet deduced that it was simple rage. For someone so devious she was often incredibly stupid.

She didn't know, for instance, that he'd found out about her little trick with the birds at least three years ago. She'd pointed to a dead tree and said she saw a bird in it, but he himself had inspected that same tree only seconds earlier and there was nothing in it at all. And she was very careless: she described oriole-coloured birds behaving like kingbirds, woodpeckers where there would never be any woodpeckers, mute jays, neckless herons. She must have decided he was a total idiot and any slipshod invention would do.

But why not, since he appeared to fall for it every time. And why did he do it, why did he chase off after her imaginary birds, pretending he believed her? It was partly that although he knew what she was doing to him, he had no idea why. It couldn't be simple malice, she had enough outlets for that. He didn't want to know the real reason, which loomed in his mind as something formless, threatening and final. Her lie about the birds was one of the many lies that propped things up. He was afraid to confront her, that would be the end, all the pretences would come crashing down and they would be left standing in the rubble, staring at each other. There would be nothing left to say and Edward wasn't ready for that.

She would deny everything anyway. "What do you mean? Of course I saw it. It flew right over there. Why would I make up such a thing?" With her level gaze, blonde and stolid and immovable as a rock.

Edward had a sudden image of himself, crashing out of the undergrowth like King Kong, picking Sarah up and hurling her over the edge, down into the sacrificial well. Anything to shatter that imperturbable expression, bland and pale and plump and smug, like a Flemish Madonna's. Self-righteous, that's what it was. Nothing was ever her fault. She hadn't been like that when he'd met her. But it wouldn't work: as she fell she would glance at him, not with fear but with maternal irritation, as if he'd spilled chocolate milk on a white tablecloth. And she'd pull her skirt down. She was concerned for appearances, always.

Though there would be something inappropriate about throwing Sarah into the sacrificial well, just as she was, with all her clothes on. He remembered snatches from the several books he'd read before they came down. (And that was another thing: Sarah didn't believe in reading up on places beforehand. "Don't you want to understand what you're looking at?" he'd asked her. "I'll see the same thing in any case, won't I?" she said. "I mean, knowing all those facts doesn't change the actual statue or whatever.") Edward found this attitude infuriating and now that they were here, she resisted his attempts to explain things to her by her usual passive method of pretending not to hear.

"That's a Chac-Mool, see that? That round thing on the stomach held the bowl where they put the hearts, and the butterfly on the head means the soul flying up to the sun."

"Could you get out the suntan lotion, Edward. I

think it's in the tote bag, in the left-hand pocket."

And he would hand her the suntan lotion, defeated once again.

No, she wouldn't be a fit sacrifice, with or without lotion. They only threw people in — or perhaps they jumped in, of their own free will — for the water god, to make it rain and ensure fertility. The drowned were messengers, sent to carry requests to the god. Sarah would have to be purified first, in the stone sweat-house beside the well. Then, naked, she would kneel before him, one arm across her breast in the attitutde of submission. He added some ornaments: a gold necklace with a jade medallion, a gold circlet adorned with feathers. Her hair, which she usually wore in a braid coiled at the back of her head, would be hanging down. He thought of her body, which he made slimmer and more taut, with an abstract desire which was as unrelated as he could make it to Sarah herself. This was the only kind of desire he could feel for her any more: he had to dress her up before he could make love to her at all. He thought about their earlier days, before they'd married. It was almost as if he'd had an affair with another woman, she had been so different. He'd treated her body then as something holy, a white and gold chalice, to be touched with care and tenderness. And she had liked this; even though she was two years older than he was and much more experienced she hadn't minded his awkwardness and reverence, she hadn't laughed at him. Why had she changed?

Sometimes he thought it was the baby, which had died at birth. At the time he'd urged her to have another right away, and she'd said yes, but nothing had happened. It wasn't something they talked about. "Well, that's that," she said in the hospital afterwards. A perfect child, the doctor said; a freak accident, one of those things that happen. She'd never gone back to university either and she wouldn't get a job. She sat at home, tidying the apartment, looking over his shoulder, towards the door, out the window, as if she was waiting for something.

Sarah bowed her head before him. He, in the feathered costume and long-nosed, toothed mask of the high priest, sprinkled her with blood drawn with thorns from his own tongue and penis. Now he was supposed to give her the message to take up to the god. But he couldn't think of anything he wanted to ask for.

And at the same time he thought: what a terrific idea for a Grade Six special project! He'd have them build scale models of the temples, he'd show the slides he'd taken, he'd bring in canned tortillas and tamales for a Mexican lunch, he'd have them make little Chac-Mools out of papier-mâché ... and the ball game where the captain of the losing team had his head cut off, that would appeal to them, they were blood-thirsty at that age. He could see himself up there in front of them, pouring out his own enthusiasm, gesturing, posturing, acting it out for them, and their response.... Yet afterwards he knew he would be depressed. What were his special projects anyway but a substitute for television, something to keep them entertained? They liked him because he danced for them, a funny puppet, inexhaustible and a little absurd. No wonder Sarah despised him.

Edward stepped on the remains of his cigarette. He put his hat back on, a wide-brimmed white hat Sarah had bought for him at the market. He had wanted one with a narrower brim, so he could look up through his binoculars without the hat getting in his way; but she'd told him he would look like an American golfer. It was always there, that gentle, patronizing mockery.

He would wait long enough to be plausible; then he would go back.

Sarah was speculating about how she would be doing this whole trip if Edward had conveniently died. It wasn't that she wished him dead, but she couldn't imagine any other way for him to disappear. He was omnipresent, he pervaded her life like a kind of smell; it was hard for her to think or act except in reference to him. So she found it harmless and pleasant to walk herself through the same itinerary they were following now, but with Edward removed, cut neatly out of the picture. Not that she would be here at all if it wasn't for him. She would prefer to lie in a deck chair in, say, Acapulco, and drink cooling drinks. She threw in a few dark young men in bathing suits, but took them out: that would be too complicated and not relaxing. She had often thought about cheating on Edward — somehow it would serve him right, though she wasn't sure what for — but she had never actually done it. She didn't know anyone suitable, any more.

Suppose she was here, then, with no Edward. She would stay at a better hotel, for one thing. One that had a plug in the sink; they had not yet stayed in a hotel with a plug. Of course that would cost more money, but she thought of herself as having more money if Edward were dead: she would have all of his salary instead of just part of it. She knew there wouldn't be any salary if he really were dead, but it spoiled the fantasy to remember this. And she would travel on planes, if possible, or first-class buses, instead of the noisy, crowded second-class ones he insisted on taking. He said you saw more of the local colour that way and there was no point going to another country if you spent all your time with other tourists. In theory she agreed with this, but the buses gave her headaches and she could do without the close-up tour of squalor, the miserable thatched or tin-roofed huts, the turkeys and tethered pigs.

He applied the same logic to restaurants. There was a perfectly nice one in the village where they were staying, she'd seen it from the bus and it didn't look that expensive; but no, they had to eat in a seedy linoleum-tiled hutch, with plastic-covered tablecloths. They were the only customers in the place. Behind them four adolescent boys were playing dominoes and drinking beer, with a lot of annoying laughter, and some smaller children watched television, a program that Sarah realized was a rerun of *The Cisco Kid,* with dubbed voices.

On the bar beside the television set there was a crêche, with three painted plaster Wise Men, one on an elephant, the others on camels. The first Wise Man was missing his head. Inside the stable a stunted Joseph and Mary adored an enormous Christ Child which was more than half as big as the elephant. Sarah wondered how the Mary could possibly have squeezed out this colossus; it made her uncomfortable to think about it. Beside the crêche was a Santa Claus haloed with flashing lights, and beside that a radio in the shape of Fred Flintstone, which was playing American popular songs, all of them ancient.

"*Oh someone help me, help me, plee-ee-ee-eeze ...*"

"Isn't that Paul Anka?" Sarah asked.

But this wasn't the sort of thing Edward could be expected to know. He launched into a defence of the food, the best he'd had in Mexico, he said. Sarah refused to give him the consolation of her agreement. She found the restaurant even more depressing than it should have been, especially the crêche. It was painful, like a cripple trying to walk, one of the last spastic gestures of a religion no one, surely, could believe in much longer.

Another group of tourists was coming up the path behind her, Americans by the sound of them. The guide was Mexican, though. He scrambled up onto the altar, preparing to give his spiel.

"Don't go too near the edge, now."

"Who me, I'm afraid of heights. What d'you see down there?"

"Water, what am I supposed to see?"

The guide clapped his hands for attention. Sarah only half-listened: she didn't really want to know anything more about it.

"Before, people said they threw nothing but virgins in here," the guide began. "How they could tell that, I do not know. It is always hard to tell." He waited for the expected laughter, which came. "But this is not true. Soon, I will tell you how we have found this out. Here we have the altar to the rain god Tlaloc ... "

Two women sat down near Sarah. They were both wearing cotton slacks, high-heeled sandals and wide-brimmed straw hats.

"You go up the big one?"

"Not on your life. I made Alf go up, I took a picture of him at the top."

"What beats me is why they built all those things in the first place."

"It was their religion, that's what he said."

"Well, at least it would keep people busy."

"Solve the unemployment problem." They both laughed.

"How many more of these ruins is he gonna make us walk around?"

"Beats me. I'm about ruined out. I'd rather go back and sit on the bus."

"I'd rather go shopping. Not that there's much to buy."

Sarah, listening, suddenly felt indignant. Did they have no respect? The sentiments weren't that far from her own of a moment ago, but to hear them from these women, one of whom had a handbag decorated with tasteless straw flowers, made her want to defend the well.

"Nature is very definitely calling," said the woman with the handbag. "I couldn't get in before, there was such a lineup."

"Take a Kleenex," the other woman said. "There's no paper. Not only that, you just about have to wade in. There's water all over the floor."

"Maybe I'll just duck into the bushes," the first woman said.

Edward stood up and massaged his left leg, which had gone to sleep. It was time to go back. If he stayed away too long, Sarah would be querulous, despite the fact that it was she herself who had sent him off on this fool's expedition.

He started to walk back along the path. But then there was a flash of orange, at the corner of his eye. Edward swivelled and raised his binoculars. They were there when you least expected it. It was an oriole, partly hidden behind the leaves; he could see the breast, bright orange, and the dark barred wing. He wanted it to be a Hooded Oriole, he had not yet seen one. He talked to it silently, begging it to come out into the open. It was strange the way birds were completely magic for him the first time only, when he had never seen them before. But there were hundreds of kinds he would never see; no matter how many he saw there would always be one more. Perhaps this was why he kept looking. The bird was hopping further away from him, into the foliage. Come back, he called to it wordlessly, but it was gone.

Edward was suddenly happy. Maybe Sarah hadn't been lying to him after all, maybe she had really seen this bird. Even if she hadn't, it had come anyway, in answer to his need for it. Edward felt he was allowed to see birds only when they wanted him to, as if they had something to tell him, a secret, a message. The Aztecs thought hummingbirds were the souls of dead warriors, but why not all birds, why just warriors? Or perhaps they were the souls of the unborn, as some believed. "A jewel, a precious feather," they called an unborn baby, according to *The Daily Life of the Aztecs. Quetzal,* that was *feather.*

"This is the bird I want to see," Sarah said when they were looking through *The Birds of Mexico* before coming down.

"The Resplendent Quetzal," Edward said. It was a green and red bird with spectacular iridescent blue tail plumes. He explained to her that Quetzal Bird meant Feather Bird. "I don't think we're likely to see it," he said. He looked up the habitat. "*'Cloud forests.'* I don't think we'll be in any cloud forests."

"Well, that's the one I want," Sarah said. "That's the only one I want."

Sarah was always very determined about what she wanted and what she didn't want. If there wasn't anything on a restaurant menu that appealed to her, she would refuse to order anything; or she would permit him to order for her and then pick around the edges, as she had last night. It was no use telling her that this was the best meal they'd had since coming. She never lost her temper or her self-possession, but she was stubborn. Who but Sarah for instance would have insisted on bringing a collapsible umbrella to Mexico in the dry season? He'd argued and argued, pointing out its uselessness and the extra weight, but she'd brought it anyway. And then yesterday afternoon it had rained, a real cloudburst. Everyone else had run for shelter, huddling against walls and inside the temple doorways, but Sarah had put up her umbrella and stood under it, smugly. This had infuriated him. Even when she was wrong, she always managed, somehow, to be right. If only just once she would admit... what? That she could make mistakes. This was what really disturbed him: her assumption of infallibility.

And he knew that when the baby had died she had blamed it on him. He still didn't know why. Perhaps it was because he'd gone out for cigarettes, not expecting it to be born so soon. He wasn't there when she was told; she'd had to take the news alone.

"It was nobody's fault," he told her repeatedly. "Not the doctor's, not yours. The cord was twisted."

"I know," she said, and she had never accused him; nevertheless he could feel the reproach, hanging around her like a fog. As if there was anything he could have done.

"I wanted it as much as you did," he told her. And this was true. He hadn't thought of marrying Sarah at all, he'd never mentioned it because it had never occurred to him she would agree, until she told him she was pregnant. Up until that time, she had been the one in control; he was sure he was just an amusement for her. But the marriage hadn't been her suggestion, it had been his. He'd dropped out of Theology, he'd taken his public-school teaching certificate that summer in order to support them. Every evening he had massaged her belly, feeling the child move, touching it through her skin. To him it was a sacred thing, and he included her in his worship. In the sixth month, when she had taken to lying on her back, she had begun to snore, and he would lie awake at night listening to these gentle snores, white and silver they seemed to him, almost songs, mysterious talismans.... Unfortunately Sarah had retained this habit, but he no longer felt the same way about it.

When the child had died, he was the one who had cried, not Sarah. She had never cried. She got up and walked around almost immediately, she wanted to get out of the hospital as quickly as possible. The baby clothes she'd been buying disappeared from the apartment; he never found out what she'd done with them, he'd been afraid to ask.

Since that time he'd come to wonder why they were still married. It was illogical. If they'd married because of the child and there was no child, and there continued to be no child, why didn't they separate? But he wasn't sure he wanted this. Maybe he was still hoping something would happen, there would be another child. But there was no use demanding it. They came when they wanted to, not when you wanted them to. They came when you least expected it. A jewel, a precious feather.

"Now I will tell you" said the guide. "The archaeologists have dived down into the well. They have dredged up more than fifty skeletons, and they have found that some of them were not virgins at all but men. Also, most of them were children. So as you can see, that is the end of the popular legend." He made an odd little movement from the top of the altar, almost like a bow, but there was no applause. "They do not do these things to be cruel," he continued. "They believe these people will take a message to the rain god, and live forever in his paradise at the bottom of the well."

The woman with the handbag got up. "Some paradise," she said to her friend. "I'm starting back. You coming?"

In fact the whole group was moving off now, in the scattered way they had. Sarah waited until they had gone. Then she opened her purse and took out the plaster Christ Child she had stolen from the crêche the night before. It was inconceivable to her that she had done such a thing, but there it was, she really had.

She hadn't planned it beforehand. She'd been standing beside the crêche while Edward was paying the bill, he'd had to go into the kitchen to do it as they were very slow about bringing it to the table. No one was watching her: the domino-playing boys were absorbed in their game and the children were riveted to the television. She'd just suddenly reached out her hand, past the Wise Men and through the door of the stable, picked the child up and put it into her purse.

She turned it over in her hands. Separated from the dwarfish Virgin and Joseph, it didn't look quite so absurd. Its diaper was cast as part of it, more like a tunic, it had glass eyes and a sort of page-boy haircut, quite long for a newborn. A perfect child, except for the chip out of the back, luckily where it would not be noticed. Someone must have dropped it on the floor.

You could never be too careful. All the time she was pregnant, she'd taken meticulous care of herself, counting out the vitamin pills prescribed by the doctor and eating only what the books recommended. She had drunk four glasses of milk a day, even though she hated milk. She had done the exercises and gone to the classes. No one would be able to say she had not done the right things. Yet she had been disturbed by the thought that the child would be born with something wrong, it would be a mongoloid or a cripple, or a hydrocephalic with a huge liquid head like the ones she'd seen taking the sun in their wheelchairs on the lawn of the hospital one day. But the child had been perfect.

She would never take that risk, go through all that work again. Let Edward strain his pelvis till he was blue in the face; "trying again," he called it. She took the pill every day, without telling him. She wasn't going to try again. It was too much for anyone to expect of her.

What had she done wrong? She hadn't done anything wrong, that was the trouble. There was nothing and no one to blame, except, obscurely, Edward; and he couldn't be blamed for the child's death, just for not being there. Increasingly since that time he had simply absented himself. When she no longer had the child inside her he had lost interest, he had deserted her. This, she realized, was what she resented most about him. He had left her alone with the corpse, a corpse for which there was no explanation.

"*Lost,*" people called it. They spoke of her as having lost the child, as though it was wandering around looking for her, crying plaintively, as though she had neglected it or misplaced it somewhere. But where? What limbo had it gone to, what watery paradise? Sometimes she felt as if there had been some mistake, the child had not been born yet. She could still feel it moving, ever so slightly, holding on to her from the inside.

Sarah placed the baby on the rock beside her. She stood up, smoothing out the wrinkles in her skirt. She was sure there would be more flea bites when she got to the hotel. She picked up the child and walked slowly towards the well, until she was standing at the very brink.

Edward, coming back up the path, saw Sarah at the well's edge, her arms raised above her head. *My God,* he thought, *she's going to jump.* He wanted to shout to her, tell her to stop, but he was afraid to startle her. He could run up behind her, grab her . . . but she would hear him. So he waited, paralyzed, while Sarah stood immobile. He expected her to hurtle downwards, and then what would he do? But she merely drew back her right arm and threw something into the well. Then she turned, half stumbling, towards the rock where he had left her and crouched down.

"Sarah," he said. She had her hands over her face; she didn't lift them. He kneeled so he was level with her. "What is it? Are you sick?"

She shook her head. She seemed to be crying, behind her hands, soundlessly and without moving. Edward was dismayed. The ordinary Sarah, with all her perversity, was something he could cope with, he'd invented ways of coping. But he was unprepared for this. She had always been the one in control.

"Come on," he said, trying to disguise his desperation, "you need some lunch, you'll feel better." He realized as he said this how fatuous it must sound, but for once there was no patronizing smile, no indulgent answer.

"This isn't like you," Edward said, pleading, as if that was a final argument which would snap her out of it, bring back the old calm Sarah.

Sarah took her hands away from her face, and as she did so Edward felt cold fear. Surely what he would see would be the face of someone else, someone entirely different, a woman he had never seen before in his life. Or there would be no face at all. But (and this was almost worse) it was only Sarah, looking much as she always did.

She took a Kleenex out of her purse and wiped her nose. *It is like me,* she thought. She stood up and smoothed her skirt once more, then collected her purse and her collapsible umbrella.

"I'd like an orange," she said. "They have them, across from the ticket office. I saw them when we came in. Did you find your bird?"

JAMES BALDWIN

Sonny's Blues

I read about it in the paper, in the subway, on my way to work. I read it, and I couldn't believe it, and I read it again. Then perhaps I just stared at it, at the newsprint spelling out his name, spelling out the story. I stared at it in the swinging lights of the subway car, and in the faces and bodies of the people, and in my own face, trapped in the darkness which roared outside.

It was not to be believed and I kept telling myself that, as I walked from the subway station to the high school. And at the same time I couldn't doubt it. I was scared, scared for Sonny. He became real to me again. A great block of ice got settled in my belly and kept melting there slowly all day long, while I taught my classes algebra. It was a special kind of ice. It kept melting, sending trickles of ice water all up and down my veins, but it never got less. Sometimes it hardened and seemed to expand until I felt my guts were going to come spilling out or that I was going to choke or scream. This would always be at a moment when I was remembering some specific thing Sonny had once said or done.

When he was about as old as the boys in my classes his face had been bright and open, there was a lot of copper in it; and he'd had wonderfully direct brown eyes, and great gentleness and privacy. I wondered what he looked like now. He had been picked up, the evening before, in a raid on an apartment downtown, for peddling and using heroin.

I couldn't believe it: but what I mean by that is that I couldn't find any room for it anywhere inside me. I had kept it outside me for a long time. I hadn't wanted to know. I had had suspicions, but I didn't name them, I kept putting them away. I told myself that Sonny was wild, but he wasn't crazy. And he'd always been a good boy, he hadn't ever turned hard or evil or disrespectful, the way kids can, so quick, so quick, so especially in Harlem. I didn't want to believe that I'd ever see my brother going down, coming to nothing, all that light in his face gone out, in the condition I'd already seen so many others. Yet it had happened and here I was, talking about algebra to a lot of boys who might, every one of them for all I knew, be popping off needles every time they went to the head. Maybe it did more for them than algebra could.

I was sure that the first time Sonny had ever had horse, he couldn't have been much older than these boys were now. These boys, now, were living as we'd been living then, they were growing up with a rush and their heads bumped abruptly against the low ceiling of their actual possibilities. They were filled with rage. All they really knew were two darknesses, the darkness of their lives, which was closing in on them, and the darkness of the movies, which had blinded them to that other darkness, and in which they now, vindictively, dreamed, at once more together than they were at any other time, and more alone.

When the last bell rang, the last class ended, I let out my breath. It seemed I'd been holding it for all that time. My clothes were wet — I may have looked as though I'd been sitting in a steam bath, all dressed up, all afternoon. I sat alone in the classroom a long time. I listened to the boys outside, downstairs, shouting and cursing and laughing. Their laughter struck me for perhaps the first time. It was not the joyous laughter which — God knows why — one associates with children. It was mocking and insular, its intent was to denigrate. It was disenchanted, and in this, also, lay the authority of their curses. Perhaps I was listening to them because I was thinking about my brother and in them I heard my brother. And myself.

One boy was whistling a tune, at once very complicated and very simple, it seemed to be pouring out of him as though he were a bird, and it sounded very cool and moving through all that harsh, bright air, only just holding its own through all those other sounds.

I stood up and walked over to the window and looked down into the courtyard. It was the beginning of the spring and the sap was rising in the boys. A teacher passed through them every now and again, quickly, as though he or she couldn't wait to get out of that courtyard, to get those boys out of their sight and off their minds. I started collecting my stuff. I thought I'd better get home and talk to Isabel.

The courtyard was almost deserted by the time I got downstairs. I saw this boy standing in the shadow of a doorway, looking just like Sonny. I almost called his name. Then I saw that it wasn't Sonny, but somebody we used to know, a boy from around our block. He'd been Sonny's friend. He'd never been mine, having been too young for me, and, anyway, I'd never liked him. And now, even though he was a grown-up man, he still hung around that block, still spent hours on the street corners, was always high and raggy. I used to run into him from time to time and he'd often work around to asking me for a quarter or fifty cents. He always had some real good excuse, too, and I always gave it to him. I don't know why.

But now, abruptly, I hated him. I couldn't stand the way he looked at me, partly like a dog, partly like a cunning child. I wanted to ask him what the hell he was doing in the school courtyard.

He sort of shuffled over to me, and he said, "I see you got the papers. So you already know about it."

"You mean about Sonny? Yes, I already know about it How come they didn't get you?"

He grinned. It made him repulsive and it also brought to mind what he'd looked like as a kid. "I wasn't there. I stay away from them people."

"Good for you." I offered him a cigarette and I watched him through the smoke. "You come all the way down here just to tell me about Sonny?"

"That's right." He was sort of shaking his head and his eyes looked strange, as though they were about to cross. The bright sun deadened his damp dark brown skin and it made his eyes look yellow and showed up the dirt in his kinked hair. He smelled funky. I moved a little away from him and I said. "Well, thanks. But I already know about it and I got to get home."

"I'll walk you a little ways," he said. We started walking. There were a couple of kids still loitering in the courtyard and one of them said goodnight to me and looked strangely at the boy beside me.

"What're you going to do?" he asked me. "I mean, about Sonny?"

"Look. I haven't seen Sonny for over a year, I'm not sure I'm going to do anything. Anyway, what the hell *can* I do?"

"That's right," he said quickly, "ain't nothing you can do. Can't much help old Sonny no more, I guess."

It was what I was thinking and so it seemed to me he had no right to say it.

"I'm surprised at Sonny, though," he went on — he had a funny way of talking, he looked straight ahead as though he were talking to himself — "I thought Sonny was a smart boy, I thought he was too smart to get hung."

"I guess he thought so too," I said sharply, "and that's how he got hung. And how about you? You're pretty goddamn smart, I bet."

Then he looked directly at me, just for a minute. "I ain't smart," he said. "If I was smart, I'd have reached for a pistol a long time ago."

"Look. Don't tell *me* your sad story, if it was up to me, I'd give you one." Then I felt guilty — guilty, probably, for never having supposed that the poor bastard *had* a story of his own, much less a sad one, and I asked, quickly, "What's going to happen to him now?"

He didn't answer this. He was off by himself some place.

"Funny thing," he said, and from his tone we might have been discussing the quickest way to get to Brooklyn, "when I saw the papers this morning, the first thing I asked myself was if I had anything to do with it. I felt sort of responsible."

I began to listen more carefully. The subway station was on the corner, just before us, and I stopped. He stopped too. We were in front of a bar and he ducked slightly, peering in, but whoever he was looking for didn't seem to be there. The juke box was blasting away with something black and bouncy and I half watched the barmaid as she danced her way from the juke box to her place behind the bar. And I watched her face as she laughingly responded to something someone said to her, still keeping time to the music. When she smiled one saw the little girl, one sensed the doomed, still-struggling woman beneath the battered face of the semi-whore.

"I never *give* Sonny nothing," the boy said finally, "but a long time ago I come to school high and Sonny asked me how it felt." He paused, I couldn't bear to watch him, I watched the barmaid, and I listened to the music which seemed to be causing the pavement to shake. "I told him it felt great." The music stopped, the barmaid paused and watched the juke box until the music began again. "It did."

All this was carrying me some place I didn't want to go. I certainly didn't want to know how it felt. It filled everything, the people, the houses, the music, the dark, quicksilver barmaid, with menace; and this menace was their reality.

"What's going to happen to him now?" I asked again.

"They'll send him away some place and they'll try to cure him." He shook his head. "Maybe he'll even think he's kicked the habit. Then they'll let him loose" — he gestured, throwing his cigarette into the gutter. "That's all."

"What do you mean, that's *all*?"

But I knew what he meant.

"I *mean,* that's *all.*" He turned his head and looked at me, pulling down the corners of his mouth. "Don't you know what I mean?" he asked, softly.

"How the hell *would* I know what you mean?" I almost whispered it, I don't know why.

"That's right," he said to the air, "how would *he* know what I mean?" He turned toward me again, patient and calm, and yet I somehow felt him shaking, shaking as though he were going to fall apart. I felt that ice in my guts again, the dread I'd felt all afternoon; and again I watched the barmaid, moving about the bar, washing glasses, and singing. "Listen. They'll let him out and then it'll just start all over again. That's what I mean."

"You mean — they'll let him out. And then he'll

just start working his way back in again. You mean he'll never kick the habit. Is that what you mean?"

"That's right," he said, cheerfully. "*You* see what I mean."

"Tell me," I said at last, "why does he want to die? He must want to die, he's killing himself, why does he want to die?"

He looked at me in surprise. He licked his lips. "He don't want to die. He wants to live. Don't nobody want to die, ever."

Then I wanted to ask him — too many things. He could not have answered, or if he had, I could not have borne the answers. I started walking. "Well, I guess it's none of my business."

"It's going to be rough on old Sonny," he said. We reached the subway station. "This is your station?" he asked. I nodded. I took one step down. "Damn!" he said, suddenly. I looked up at him. He grinned again. "Damn it if I didn't leave all my money home. You ain't got a dollar on you, have you? Just for a couple of days, is all."

All at once something inside gave and threatened to come pouring out of me. I didn't hate him any more. I felt that in another moment I'd start crying like a child.

"Sure," I said. "Don't sweat." I looked in my wallet and didn't have a dollar, I only had a five. "Here," I said. "That hold you?"

He didn't look at it — he didn't want to look at it. A terrible, closed look came over his face, as though he were keeping the number on the bill a secret from him and me. "Thanks," he said, and now he was dying to see me go. "Don't worry about Sonny. Maybe I'll write him or something."

"Sure," I said. "You do that. So long."

"Be seeing you," he said. I went on down the steps.

And I didn't write Sonny or send him anything for a long time. When I finally did, it was just after my little girl died, and he wrote me back a letter which made me feel like a bastard.

Here's what he said:

Dear brother,

You don't know how much I needed to hear from you. I wanted to write you many a time but I dug how much I must have hurt you and so I didn't write. But now I feel like a man who's been trying to climb up out of some deep, real deep and funky hole and just saw the sun up there, outside. I got to get outside.

I can't tell you much about how I got here. I mean I don't know how to tell you. I guess I was afraid of something or I was trying to escape from something and you know I have never been very strong in the head (smile). I'm glad Mama and Daddy are dead and can't see what's happened to their son and I swear if I'd known what I was doing I would never have hurt you so, you and a lot of other fine people who were nice to me and who believed in me.

I don't want you to think it had anything to do with me being a musician. It's more than that. Or maybe less than that. I can't get anything straight in my head down here and I try not to think about what's going to happen to me when I get outside again. Sometime I think I'm going to flip and *never* get outside and sometime I think I'll come straight back. I tell you one thing, though, I'd rather blow my brains out than go through this again. But that's what they all say, so they tell me. If I tell you when I'm coming to New York and if you could meet me, I sure would appreciate it. Give my love to Isabel and the kids and I was sure sorry to hear about little Gracie. I wish I could be like Mama and say the Lord's will be done, but I don't know it seems to me that trouble is the one thing that never does get stopped and I don't know what good it does to blame it on the Lord. But maybe it does some good if you believe it.

Your brother,
Sonny

Then I kept in constant touch with him and I sent him whatever I could and I went to meet him when he came back to New York. When I saw him many things I thought I had forgotten came flooding back to me. This was because I had begun, finally, to wonder about Sonny, about the life that Sonny lived inside. This life, whatever it was, had made him older and thinner and it had deepened the distant stillness in which he had always moved. He looked very unlike my baby brother. Yet, when he smiled, when we shook hands, the baby brother I'd never known looked out from the depths of his private life, like an animal waiting to be coaxed into the light.

"How you been keeping?" he asked me.

"All right. And you?"

"Just fine." He was smiling all over his face. "It's good to see you again."

"It's good to see you."

The seven years' difference in our ages lay between us like a chasm: I wondered if these years would ever operate between us as a bridge. I was remembering, and it made it hard to catch my breath, that I had been there when he was born; and I had heard the first words he had ever spoken. When he started to walk, he walked from our mother straight to me. I caught him just before he fell when he took the first steps he ever took in his world.

"How's Isabel?"

"Just fine. She's dying to see you."

"And the boys?"

"They're fine, too. They're anxious to see their uncle."

"Oh, come on. You know they don't remember me."

"Are you kidding? Of course they remember you."

He grinned again. We got into a taxi. We had a lot to say to each other, far too much to know how to begin.

As the taxi began to move, I asked, "You still want to go to India?"

He laughed. "You still remember that. Hell, no. This place is Indian enough for me."

"It used to belong to them," I said.

And he laughed again. "They damn sure knew what they were doing when they got rid of it."

Years ago, when he was around fourteen, he'd been all hipped on the idea of going to India. He read books about people sitting on rocks, naked, in all kinds of weather, but mostly bad, naturally, and walking barefoot through hot coals and arriving at wisdom. I used to say that it sounded to me as though they were getting away from wisdom as fast as they could. I think he sort of looked down on me for that.

"Do you mind," he asked, "if we have the driver drive alongside the park? On the west side — I haven't seen the city in so long."

"Of course not," I said. I was afraid that I might sound as though I were humoring him, but I hoped he wouldn't take it that way.

So we drove along, between the green of the park and the stony, lifeless elegance of hotels and apartment buildings, toward the vivid, killing streets of our childhood. These streets hadn't changed, though housing projects jutted up out of them now like rocks in the middle of a boiling sea. Most of the houses in which we had grown up had vanished, as had the stores from which we had stolen, the basements in which we had first tried sex, the rooftops from which we had hurled tin cans and bricks. But houses exactly like the houses of our past yet dominated the landscape, boys exactly like the boys we once had been found themselves smothering in these houses, came down into the streets for light and air and found themselves encircled by disaster. Some escaped the trap, most didn't. Those who got out always left something of themselves behind, as some animals amputate a leg and leave it in the trap. It might be said, perhaps, that I had escaped, after all, I was a school teacher; or that Sonny had, he hadn't lived in Harlem for years. Yet, as the cab moved uptown through streets which seemed, with a rush, to darken with dark people, and as I covertly studied Sonny's face, it came to me that what we both were seeking through our separate cab windows was that part of ourselves which had been left behind. It's always at the hour of trouble and confrontation that the missing member aches.

We hit 110th Street and started rolling up Lenox Avenue. And I'd known this avenue all my life, but it seemed to me again, as it had seemed on the day I'd first heard about Sonny's trouble, filled with a hidden menace which was its very breath of life.

"We almost there," said Sonny.

"Almost." We were both too nervous to say anything more.

We live in a housing project. It hasn't been up long. A few days after it was up it seemed uninhabitably new, now, of course, it's already rundown. It looks like a parody of the good, clean faceless life — God knows the people who live in it do their best to make it a parody. The beat-looking grass lying around isn't enough to make their lives green, the hedges will never hold out the streets, and they know it. The big windows fool no one, they aren't big enough to make space out of no space. They don't bother with the windows, they watch the TV screen instead. The playground is most popular with the children who don't play at jacks, or skip rope, or roller skate, or swing, and they can be found in it after dark. We moved in partly because it's not too far from where I teach, and partly for the kids; but it's really just like the houses in which Sonny and I grew up. The same things happen, they'll have the same things to remember. The moment Sonny and I started into the house I had the feeling that I was simply bringing him back into the danger he had almost died trying to escape.

Sonny has never been talkative. So I don't know why I was sure he'd be dying to talk to me when supper was over the first night. Everything went fine, the oldest boy remembered him, and the youngest boy liked him, and Sonny had remembered to bring something for each of them; and Isabel, who is really much nicer than I am, more open and giving, had gone to a lot of trouble about dinner and was genuinely glad to see him. And she's always been able to tease Sonny in a way that I haven't. It was nice to see her face so vivid again and to hear her laugh and watch her make Sonny laugh. She wasn't, or, anyway, she didn't seem to be at all uneasy or embarrassed. She chatted as though there were no subject which had to be avoided and she got Sonny past his first, faint stiffness. And thank God she was there, for I was filled with that icy dread again. Everything I did seemed awkward to me, and everything I said sounded freighted with hidden meaning. I was trying to remember everything I'd heard about dope addiction and I couldn't help watching Sonny for signs. I wasn't doing it out of malice. I was trying to find out something about my brother. I was dying to hear him tell me he was safe.

"Safe!" my father grunted, whenever Mama suggested trying to move to a neighborhood which might be safer for children. "Safe, hell! Ain't no place safe for kids, nor nobody."

He always went on like this, but he wasn't, ever, really as bad as he sounded, not even on weekends, when he got drunk. As a matter of fact, he was always on the lookout for "something a little better," but he died before he found it. He died suddenly, during a drunken weekend in the middle of the war, when Sonny was fifteen. He and Sonny hadn't ever got on too well. And this was partly because Sonny was the apple of his father's eye. It was because he loved Sonny so much and was frightened for him, that he was always fighting with him. It doesn't do any good to fight with Sonny. Sonny just moves back, inside himself, where he can't be reached. But the principal reason that they never hit it off is that they were so much alike. Daddy was big and rough and loud-talking, just the opposite of Sonny, but they both had — that same privacy.

Mama tried to tell me something about this, just after Daddy died. I was home on leave from the army.

This was the last time I ever saw my mother alive. Just the same, this picture gets all mixed up in my mind with pictures I had of her when she was younger. The way I always see her is the way she used to be on a Sunday afternoon, say, when the old folks were talking after the big Sunday dinner. I always see her wearing pale blue. She'd be sitting on the sofa. And my father would be sitting in the easy chair, not far from her. And the living room would be full of church folks and relatives. There they sit, in chairs all around the living room, and the night is creeping up outside, but nobody knows it yet. You can see the darkness growing against the windowpanes and you hear the street noises every now and again, or maybe the jangling beat of a tambourine from one of the churches close by, but it's real quiet in the room. For a moment nobody's talking, but every face looks darkening, like the sky outside. And my mother rocks a little from the waist, and my father's eyes are closed. Everyone is looking at something a child can't see. For a minute they've forgotten the children. Maybe a kid is lying on the rug, half asleep. Maybe somebody's got a kid in his lap and is absent-mindedly stroking the kid's head. Maybe there's a kid, quiet and big-eyed, curled up in a big chair in the corner. The silence, the darkness coming, and the darkness in the faces frighten the child obscurely. He hopes that the hand which strokes his forehead will never stop — will never die. He hopes that there will never come a time when the old folks won't be sitting around the living room, talking about where they've come from, and what they've seen, and what's happened to them and their kinfolk.

But something deep and watchful in the child knows that this is bound to end, is already ending. In a moment someone will get up and turn on the light. Then the old folks will remember the children and they won't talk any more that day. And when light fills the room, the child is filled with darkness. He knows that every time this happens he's moved just a little closer to that darkness outside. The darkness outside is what the old folks have been talking about. It's what they've come from. It's what they endure. The child knows that they won't talk any more because if he knows too much about what's happened to *them,* he'll know too much too soon, about what's going to happen to *him.*

The last time I talked to my mother, I remember I was restless. I wanted to get out and see Isabel. We weren't married then and we had a lot to straighten out between us.

There Mama sat, in black, by the window. She was humming an old church song, *Lord, you brought me from a long way off.* Sonny was out somewhere. Mama kept watching the streets.

"I don't know," she said, "if I'll ever see you again, after you go off from here. But I hope you'll remember the things I tried to teach you."

"Don't talk like that," I said, and smiled. "You'll be here a long time yet."

She smiled, too, but she said nothing. She was quiet for a long time. And I said, "Mama, don't you worry about anything. I'll be writing all the time, and you be getting the checks. . . . "

"I want to talk to you about your brother," she said, suddenly. "If anything happens to me he ain't going to have nobody to look out for him."

"Mama," I said, "ain't nothing going to happen to you or Sonny. Sonny's all right. He's a good boy and he's got good sense."

"It ain't a question of his being a good boy," Mama said, "nor of his having good sense. It ain't only the bad ones, nor yet the dumb ones that gets sucked under." She stopped, looking at me. "Your Daddy once had a brother," she said, and she smiled in a way that made me feel she was in pain. "You didn't never know that, did you?"

"No," I said, "I never knew that," and I watched her face.

"Oh, yes," she said, "your Daddy had a brother." She looked out of the window again. "I know you never saw your Daddy cry. But I did — many a time, through all these years."

I asked her, "What happened to his brother? How come nobody's ever talked about him?"

This was the first time I ever saw my mother look old.

"His brother got killed," she said, "when he was just a little younger than you are now. I knew him. He was a fine boy. He was maybe a little full of the devil, but he didn't mean nobody no harm."

Then she stopped and the room was silent, exactly as it had sometimes been on those Sunday afternoons. Mama kept looking out into the streets.

"He used to have a job in the mill," she said, "and, like all young folks, he just liked to perform on Saturday nights. Saturday nights, him and your father would drift around to different places, go to dances and things like that, or just sit around with people they knew, and your father's brother would sing, he had a fine voice, and play along with himself on his guitar. Well, this particular Saturday night, him and your father was coming home from some place, and they were both a little drunk and there was a moon that night, it was bright like day. Your father's brother was feeling kind of good, and he was whistling to himself, and he had his guitar slung over his shoulder. They was coming down a hill and beneath them was a road that turned off from the highway. Well, your father's brother, being always kind of frisky, decided to run down this hill, and he did, with that guitar banging and clanging behind him, and he ran across the road, and he was making water behind a tree. And your father was sort of amused at him and he was still coming down the hill, kind of slow. Then he heard a car motor and that same minute his brother stepped from behind the tree, into the road, in the moonlight. And he started to cross the road. And your father started to run down the hill, he says he don't know why. This car was full of white men. They was all drunk, and when they seen your father's brother they let out a great whoop and holler and they aimed the car straight at him. They was having fun, they just wanted to scare him, the way they do sometimes, you know. But they was drunk. And I guess the boy, being drunk, too, and scared, kind of lost his head. By the time he jumped it was too late. Your father says he heard his brother scream when the car rolled over him, and he heard the wood of that guitar when it give, and he heard them strings go flying, and he heard them white men shouting, and the car kept on a-going and it ain't stopped till this day. And, time your father got down the hill, his brother weren't nothing but blood and pulp."

Tears were gleaming on my mother's face. There wasn't anything I could say.

"He never mentioned it," she said, "because I never let him mention it before you children. Your Daddy was like a crazy man that night and for many a night thereafter. He says he never in his life seen anything as dark as that road after the lights of that car had gone away. Weren't nothin, weren't nobody on that road, just your Daddy and his brother and that busted guitar. Oh, yes. Your Daddy never did really get right again. Till the day he died he weren't sure but that every white man he saw was the man that killed his brother."

She stopped and took out her handkerchief and dried her eyes and looked at me.

"I ain't telling you all this," she said, "to make you scared or bitter or to make you hate nobody. I'm telling you this because you got a brother. And the world ain't changed."

I guess I didn't want to believe this. I guess she saw this in my face. She turned away from me, toward the window again, searching those streets.

"But I praise my Redeemer," she said at last, "that He called your Daddy home before me. I ain't saying it to throw no flowers at myself, but, I declare, it keeps me from feeling too cast down to know I helped your father get safely through this world. Your father always acted like he was the roughest, strongest man on earth. And everybody took him to be like that. But if he hadn't had me there — to see his tears!"

She was crying again. Still, I couldn't move. I said, "Lord, Lord, Mama, I didn't know it was like that."

"Oh, honey," she said, "there's a lot that you don't know. But you are going to find out." She stood up from the window and came over to me. "You got to hold on to your brother," she said, "and don't let him fall, no matter what it looks like is happening to him and no matter how evil you gets with him. You going to be evil with him many a time. But don't you forget what I told you, you hear?"

"I won't forget," I said. "Don't you worry, I won't forget. I won't let nothing happen to Sonny."

My mother smiled as though she were amused at something she saw in my face. Then, "You may not be able to stop nothing from happening. But you got to let him know you's *there.*"

Two days later I was married, and then I was gone. And I had a lot of things on my mind and I pretty well forgot my promise to Mama until I got shipped home on a special furlough for her funeral.

And, after the funeral, with just Sonny and me alone in the empty kitchen, I tried to find out something about him.

"What do you want to do?" I asked him.

"I'm going to be a musician," he said.

For he had graduated, in the time I had been away, from dancing to the juke box to finding out who was playing what, and what they were doing with it, and he had bought himself a set of drums.

"You mean, you want to be a drummer?" I somehow had the feeling that being a drummer might be all right for other people but not for my brother Sonny.

"I don't think," he said, looking at me very gravely, "that I'll ever be a good drummer. But I think I can play a piano."

I frowned. I'd never played the role of the older brother quite so seriously before, had scarcely ever, in fact, *asked* Sonny a damn thing. I sensed myself in the presence of something I didn't really know how to handle, didn't understand. So I made my frown a little deeper as I asked: "What kind of musician do you want to be?"

He grinned. "How many kinds do you think there are?"

"Be *serious,*" I said.

He laughed, throwing his head back, and then looked at me. "I am serious."

"Well, then, for Christ's sake, stop kidding around and answer a serious question. I mean, do you want to be a concert pianist, you want to play classical music and all that, or — or what?" Long before I finished he was laughing again. "For Christ's *sake,* Sonny!"

He sobered, but with difficulty. "I'm sorry. But you sound so — *scared!*" and he was off again.

"Well, you may think it's funny now, baby, but it's not going to be so funny when you have to make your living at it; let me tell you that." I was furious because I knew he was laughing at me and I didn't know why.

"No," he said, very sober now, and afraid, perhaps, that he'd hurt me, "I don't want to be a classical pianist. That isn't what interests me. I mean" — he paused, looking hard at me, as though his eyes would help me to understand, and then gestured helplessly, as though perhaps his hand would help — "I mean, I'll have a lot of studying to do, and I'll have to study everything, but, I mean, I want to play with — jazz musicians." He stopped. "I want to play jazz," he said.

Well, the word had never before sounded as heavy, as real, as it sounded that afternoon in Sonny's mouth. I just looked at him and I was probably frowning a real frown by this time. I simply couldn't see why on earth he'd want to spend his time hanging around nightclubs, clowning around on bandstands, while people pushed each other around a dance floor. It seemed — beneath him, somehow. I had never thought about it before, had never been forced to, but I suppose I had always put jazz musicians in a class with what Daddy called "good-time people."

"Are you *serious*?"

"Hell, *yes,* I'm serious."

He looked more helpless than ever, and annoyed, and deeply hurt.

I suggested, helpfully: "You mean — like Louis Armstrong?"

His face closed as though I'd struck him. "No. I'm not talking about none of that old-time, down home crap."

"Well, look, Sonny. I'm sorry, don't get mad. I just don't altogether get it, that's all. Name somebody — you know, a jazz musician you admire."

"Bird."

"Who?"

"Bird! Charlie Parker! Don't they teach you nothing in the goddamn army?"

I lit a cigarette. I was surprised and then a little amused to discover that I was trembling. "I've been out of touch," I said, "You'll have to be patient with me. Now. Who's this Parker character?"

"He's just one of the greatest jazz musicians alive," said Sonny, sullenly, his hands in his pockets, his back to me. "Maybe *the* greatest," he added, bitterly, "that's probably why you never heard of him."

"All right," I said, "I'm ignorant, I'm sorry. I'll go out and buy all the cat's records right away, all right?"

"It don't," said Sonny, with dignity, "make any difference to me. I don't care what you listen to. Don't do me no favors."

I was beginning to realize that I'd never seen him so upset before. With another part of my mind I was thinking that this would probably turn out to be one of those things kids go through and that I shouldn't make it seem important by pushing it too hard. Still, I didn't think it would do any harm to ask: "Doesn't all this take a lot of time? Can you make a living at it?"

He turned back to me and half leaned, half sat, on the kitchen table. "Everything takes time," he said, "and — well, yes, sure, I can make a living at it. But what I don't seem to be able to make you understand is that it's the only thing I want to do."

"Well, Sonny," I said, gently, "you know people can't always do exactly what they *want* to do — "

"*No,* I don't know that," said Sonny, surprising me. "I think people *ought* to do what they want to do, what else are they alive for?"

"You getting to be a big boy," I said desperately, "it's time you started thinking about your future."

"I'm thinking about my future," said Sonny, grimly. "I think about it all the time."

I gave up. I decided, if he didn't change his mind, that we could always talk about it later. "In the meantime," I said, "you got to finish school." We had already decided that he'd have to move in with Isabel and her folks. I knew this wasn't the ideal arrangement because Isabel's folks are inclined to be dicty and they hadn't especially wanted Isabel to marry me. But I didn't know what else to do. "And we have to get you fixed up at Isabel's."

There was a long silence. He moved from the kitchen table to the window. "That's a terrible idea. You know it yourself."

"Do you have a *better* idea?"

He just walked up and down the kitchen for a minute. He was as tall as I was. He had started to shave. I suddenly had the feeling that I didn't know him at all.

He stopped at the kitchen table and picked up my cigarettes. Looking at me with a kind of mocking, amused defiance, he put one between his lips. "You mind?"

"You smoking already?"

He lit the cigarette and nodded, watching me through the smoke. "I just wanted to see if I'd have the courage to smoke in front of you." He grinned and blew a great cloud of smoke to the ceiling. "It was easy." He looked at my face. "Come on, now. I bet you was smoking at my age, tell the truth."

I didn't say anything but the truth was on my face, and he laughed. But now there was something very strained in his laugh. "Sure. And I bet that ain't all you was doing."

He was frightening me a little. "Cut the crap,"

I said. "We already decided that you was going to go and live at Isabel's. Now what's got into you all of a sudden?"

"*You* decided it," he pointed out. "*I* didn't decide nothing." He stopped in front of me, leaning against the stove, arms loosely folded. "Look, brother. I don't want to stay in Harlem no more, I really don't." He was very earnest. He looked at me, then over toward the kitchen window. There was something in his eyes I'd never seen before, some thoughtfulness, some worry all his own. He rubbed the muscle of one arm. "It's time I was getting out of here."

"Where do you want to *go*, Sonny?"

"I want to join the army. Or the navy. I don't care. If I say I'm old enough, they'll believe me."

Then I got mad. It was because I was so scared. "You must be crazy. You goddamn fool, what the hell do you want to go and join the *army* for?"

"I just told you. To get out of Harlem."

"Sonny, you haven't even finished school. And if you really want to be a musician, how do you expect to study if you're in the army?"

He looked at me, trapped, and in anguish. "There's ways. I might be able to work out some kind of deal. Anyway, I'll have the G.I. Bill when I come out."

"*If* you come out." We stared at each other. "Sonny, please. Be reasonable. I know the setup is far from perfect. But we got to do the best we can."

"I ain't learning nothing in school," he said. "Even when I go." He turned away from me and opened the window and threw his cigarette out into the narrow alley. I watched his back. "At least, I ain't learning nothing you'd want me to learn." He slammed the window so hard I thought the glass would fly out, and turned back to me. "And I'm sick of the stink of these garbage cans!"

"Sonny," I said, "I know how you feel. But if you don't finish school now, you're going to be sorry later that you didn't." I grabbed him by the shoulders. "And you only got another year. It ain't so bad. And I'll come back and I swear I'll help you do *whatever* you want to do. Just try to put up with it till I come back. Will you please do that? For me?"

He didn't answer and he wouldn't look at me.

"Sonny. You hear me?"

He pulled away. "I hear you. But you never hear anything *I* say."

I didn't know what to say to that. He looked out of the window and then back at me. "OK," he said, and sighed. "I'll try."

Then I said, trying to cheer him up a little, "They got a piano at Isabel's. You can practice on it."

And as a matter of fact, it did cheer him up for a minute. "That's right," he said to himself. "I forgot that." His face relaxed a little. But the worry, the thoughtfulness, played on it still, the way shadows play on a face which is staring into the fire.

But I thought I'd never hear the end of that piano. At first, Isabel would write me, saying how nice it was that Sonny was so serious about his music and how, as soon as he came in from school, or wherever he had been when he was supposed to be at school, he went straight to that piano and stayed there until suppertime. And, after supper, he went back to that piano and stayed there until everybody went to bed. He was at the piano all day Saturday and all day Sunday. Then he bought a record player and started playing records. He'd play one record over and over again, all day long sometimes, and he'd improvise along with it on the piano. Or he'd play one section of the record, one chord, one change, one progression, then he'd do it on the piano. Then back to the record. Then back to the piano.

Well, I really don't know how they stood it. Isabel finally confessed that it wasn't like living with a person at all, it was like living with sound. And the sound didn't make any sense to her, didn't make any sense to any of them — naturally. They began, in a way, to be afflicted by this presence that was living in their home. It was as though Sonny were some sort of god, or monster. He moved in an atmosphere which wasn't like theirs at all. They fed him and he ate, he washed himself, he walked in and out of their door; he certainly wasn't nasty or unpleasant or rude, Sonny isn't any of those things; but it was as though he were all wrapped up in some cloud, some fire, some vision all his own; and there wasn't any way to reach him.

At the same time, he wasn't really a man yet, he was still a child, and they had to watch out for him in all kinds of ways. They certainly couldn't throw him out. Neither did they dare to make a great scene about that piano because even they dimly sensed, as I sensed, from so many thousands of miles away, that Sonny was at that piano playing for his life.

But he hadn't been going to school. One day a letter came from the school board and Isabel's mother got it — there had, apparently, been other letters but Sonny had torn them up. This day, when Sonny came in, Isabel's mother showed him the letter and asked where he'd been spending his time. And she finally got it out of him that he'd been down in Greenwich Village, with musicians and other characters, in a white girl's apartment. And this scared her and she started to scream at him and what came up, once she began — though she denies it to this day — was what sacrifices they were making to give Sonny a decent home and how little he appreciated it.

Sonny didn't play the piano that day. By evening, Isabel's mother had calmed down but then there was the old man to deal with, and Isabel herself. Isabel says she did her best to be calm but she broke down and started crying. She says she just watched Sonny's face. She could tell, by watching him, what was happening with him. And what was happening was that they penetrated his cloud, they had reached him. Even if their fingers had been a thousand times more gentle than human fingers ever are, he could hardly help feeling that they had stripped him naked and were spitting on that nakedness. For he also had to see that his presence, that music, which was life or death to him, had been torture for them and that they had endured it, not at all for his sake, but only for mine. And Sonny couldn't take that. He can take it a little better today than he could then but he's still not very good at it and, frankly, I don't know anybody who is.

The silence of the next few days must have been louder than the sound of all the music ever played since time began. One morning, before she went to work, Isabel was in his room for something and she suddenly realized that all of his records were gone. And she knew for certain that he was gone. And he was. He went as far as the navy would carry him. He finally sent me a postcard from some place in Greece and that was the first I knew that Sonny was still alive. I didn't see him any more until we were both back in New York and the war had long been over.

He was a man by then, of course, but I wasn't willing to see it. He came by the house from time to time, but we fought almost every time we met. I didn't like the way he carried himself, loose and dreamlike all the time, and I didn't like his friends and his music seemed to be merely an excuse for the life he led. It sounded just that weird and disordered.

Then we had a fight, a pretty awful fight, and I didn't see him for months. By and by I looked him up, where he was living, in a furnished room in the Village, and I tried to make it up. But there were lots of other people in the room and Sonny just lay on his bed, and he wouldn't come downstairs with me, and he treated these other people as though they were his family and I weren't. So I got mad and then he got mad, and then I told him that he might just as well be dead as live the way he was living. Then he stood up and he told me not to worry about him any more in life, that he *was* dead as far as I was concerned. Then he pushed me to the door and the other people looked on as though nothing were happening, and he slammed the door behind me. I stood in the hallway, staring at the door. I heard somebody laugh in the room and then the tears came to my eyes. I started down the steps, whistling to keep from crying. I kept whistling to myself, *You going to need me, baby, one of these cold, rainy days.*

I read about Sonny's trouble in the spring. Little Grace died in the fall. She was a beautiful little girl. But she only lived a little over two years. She died of polio and she suffered. She had a slight fever for a couple of days, but it didn't seem like anything and we just kept her in bed. And we would certainly have called the doctor, but the fever dropped, she seemed to be all right. So we thought it had just been a cold. Then, one day, she was up, playing, Isabel was in the kitchen fixing lunch for the two boys when they'd come in from school, and she heard Grace fall down in the living room. When you have a lot of children you don't always start running when one of them falls, unless they start screaming or something. And, this time, Gracie was quiet. Yet, Isabel says that when she heard that *thump* and then that silence, something happened to her to make her afraid. And she ran to the living room and there was little Grace on the floor, all twisted up, and the reason she hadn't screamed was that she couldn't get her breath. And when she did scream, it was the worst sound, Isabel says, that she'd ever heard in all her life, and she still hears it sometimes in her dreams. Isabel will sometimes wake me up with a low, moaning, strangling sound and I have to be quick to awaken her and hold her to me and where Isabel is weeping against me seems a mortal wound.

I think I may have written Sonny the very day that little Grace was buried. I was sitting in the living room in the dark, by myself, and I suddenly thought of Sonny. My trouble made his real.

One Saturday afternoon, when Sonny had been living with us, or anyway, been in our house, for nearly two weeks, I found myself wandering aimlessly about the living room, drinking from a can of beer, and trying to work up courage to search Sonny's room. He was out, he was usually out whenever I was home, and Isabel had taken the children to see their grandparents. Suddenly I was standing still in front of the living room window, watching Seventh Avenue. The idea of searching Sonny's room made me still. I scarcely dared to admit to myself what I'd be searching for. I didn't know what I'd do if I found it. Or if I didn't.

On the sidewalk across from me, near the entrance to a barbecue joint, some people were holding an old-fashioned revival meeting. The barbecue cook, wearing a dirty white apron, his conked hair reddish and metallic in the pale sun, and a cigarette between his lips, stood in the doorway, watching them. Kids and older people paused in their errands and stood there, along with some older men and a couple of very tough-looking women who watched everything that happened on the avenue, as though they owned it, or were maybe owned by it. Well, they were watching this, too. The revival was being carried on by three sisters in black, and a brother. All they had were their voices and their Bibles and a tambourine. The brother was testifying and while he testified two of the sisters stood together, seeming to say, amen, and the third sister walked around with the tambourine outstretched and a couple of people dropped coins into it. Then the brother's testimony ended and the sister who had been taking up the collection dumped the coins into her palm and transferred them to the pocket of her long black robe. Then she raised both hands, striking the tambourine against the air, and then against one hand, and she started to sing. And the two sisters and the brother joined in.

It was strange, suddenly, to watch, though I had been seeing these meetings all my life. So, of course, had everybody else down there. Yet, they paused and watched and listened and I stood still at the window. "*'Tis the old ship of Zion,*" they sang, and the sister with the tambourine kept a steady, jangling beat, "*it has rescued many a thousand!*" Not a soul under the sound of their voices was hearing this song for the first time, not one of them had been rescued. Nor had they seen much in the way of rescue work being done around them. Neither did they especially believe in the holiness of the three sisters and the brother, they knew too much about them, knew where they lived, and how. The woman with the tambourine, whose voice dominated the air, whose face was bright with joy, was divided by very little from the woman who stood watching her, a cigarette between her heavy, chapped lips, her hair a cuckoo's nest, her face scarred and swollen from many beatings, and her black eyes glittering like coal. Perhaps they both knew this, which was why, when, as rarely, they addressed each other, they addressed each other as Sister. As the singing filled the air the watching, listening faces underwent a change, the eyes focusing on something within; the music seemed to soothe a poison out of them; and time seemed, nearly, to fall away from the sullen, belligerent, battered faces, as though they were fleeing back to their first condition, while dreaming of their last. The barbecue cook half shook his head and smiled, and dropped his cigarette and disappeared into his joint. A man fumbled in his pockets for change and stood holding it in his hand impatiently, as though he had just remembered a pressing appointment further up the avenue. He looked furious. Then I saw Sonny, standing on the edge of the crowd. He was carrying a wide, flat notebook with a green cover, and it made him look, from where I was standing, almost like a schoolboy. The coppery sun brought out the copper in his skin, he was very faintly smiling, standing very still. Then the singing stopped, the tambourine turned into a collection plate again. The furious man dropped in his coins and vanished, so did a couple of the women, and Sonny dropped some change in the plate, looking directly at the woman with a little smile. He started across the avenue, toward the house. He has a slow, loping walk, something like the way Harlem hipsters walk, only he's imposed on this his own half-beat. I had never really noticed it before.

I stayed at the window, both relieved and apprehensive. As Sonny disappeared from my sight, they began singing again. And they were still singing when his key turned in the lock.

"Hey," he said.

"Hey, yourself. You want some beer?"

"No. Well, maybe." But he came up to the window and stood beside me, looking out. "What a warm voice," he said.

They were singing *If I could only hear my mother pray again!*

"Yes," I said, "and she can sure beat that tambourine."

"But what a terrible song," he said, and laughed. He dropped his notebook on the sofa and disappeared into the kitchen. "Where's Isabel and the kids?"

"I think they went to see their grandparents. You hungry?"

"No." He came back into the living room with his can of beer. "You want to come some place with me tonight?"

I sensed, I don't know how, that I couldn't possibly say no. "Sure. Where?"

He sat down on the sofa and picked up his notebook and started leafing through it. "I'm going to sit in with some fellows in a joint in the Village."

"You mean, you're going to play, tonight?"

"That's right." He took a swallow of his beer and moved back to the window. He gave me a sidelong look. "If you can stand it."

"I'll try," I said.

He smiled to himself and we both watched as the meeting across the way broke up. The three sisters and the brother, heads bowed, were singing *God be with you till we meet again.* The faces around them were very quiet. Then the song ended. The small crowd dispersed. We watched the three women and the lone man walk slowly up the avenue.

"When she was singing before," said Sonny, abruptly, "her voice reminded me for a minute of what heroin feels like sometimes — when it's in your veins. It makes you feel sort of warm and cool at the same time. And distant. And — and sure." He sipped his beer, very deliberately not looking at me. I watched his face. "It makes you feel — in control. Sometimes you've got to have that feeling."

"Do you?" I sat down slowly in the easy chair.

"Sometimes." He went to the sofa and picked up his notebook again. "Some people do."

"In order," I asked, "to play?" And my voice was very ugly, full of contempt and anger.

"Well" — he looked at me with great, troubled eyes, as though, in fact, he hoped his eyes would tell me things he could never otherwise say — "they *think* so. And *if* they think so — !"

"And what do *you* think?" I asked.

He sat on the sofa and put his can of beer on the

floor. "I don't know," he said, and I couldn't be sure if he were answering my question or pursuing his thoughts. His face didn't tell me. "It's not so much to *play*. It's to *stand* it, to be able to make it at all. On any level." He frowned and smiled: "In order to keep from shaking to pieces."

"But these friends of yours," I said. "they seem to shake themselves to pieces pretty goddamn fast."

"Maybe." He played with the notebook. And something told me that I should curb my tongue, that Sonny was doing his best to talk, that I should listen. "But of course you only know the ones that've gone to pieces. Some don't — or at least they haven't *yet* and that's just about all *any* of us can say." He paused. "And then there are some who just live, really, in hell, and they know it and they see what's happening and they go right on. I don't know." He sighed, dropped the notebook and folded his arms. "Some guys, you can tell from the way they play, they on something *all* the time. And you can see that, well, it makes something real for them. But of course," he picked up his beer from the floor and sipped it and put the can down again, "they *want* to, too, you've got to see that. Even some of them that say they don't — *some*, not all."

"And what about you?" I asked — I couldn't help it. "What about you? Do *you* want to?"

He stood up and walked to the window and I remained silent for a long time. Then he sighed. "Me," he said. Then: "While I was downstairs before, on my way here, listening to that woman sing, it struck me all of a sudden how much suffering she must have had to go through — to sing like that. It's *repulsive* to think you have to suffer that much."

I said: "But there's no way not to suffer — is there, Sonny?"

"I believe not," he said and smiled, "but that's never stopped anyone from trying." He looked at me. "Has it?" I realized, with this mocking look, that there stood between us, forever, beyond the power of time or forgiveness, the fact that I had held silence — so long! — when he had needed human speech to help him. He turned back to the window. "No, there's no way not to suffer. But you try all kinds of ways to keep from drowning in it, to keep on top of it, and to make it seem — well, like *you*. Like you did something, all right, and now you're suffering for it. You know?" I said nothing. "Well you know," he said, impatiently, "why *do* people suffer? Maybe it's better to do something to give it a reason, *any* reason."

"But we just agreed," I said, "that there's no way not to suffer. Isn't it better, then, just to — take it?"

"But nobody just takes it," Sonny cried, "that's what I'm telling you! *Everybody* tries not to. You're just hung up on the *way* some people try — it's not *your* way!"

The hair on my face began to itch, my face felt wet. "That's not true," I said, "that's not true. I don't give a damn what other people do, I don't even care how they suffer. I just care how *you* suffer." And he looked at me. "Please believe me," I said, "I don't want to see you — die — trying not to suffer."

"I won't," he said flatly, "die trying not to suffer. At least, not any faster than anybody else."

"But there's no need," I said, trying to laugh, "is there? in killing yourself."

I wanted to say more, but I couldn't. I wanted to talk about will power and how life could be — well, beautiful. I wanted to say that it was all within; but was it? or, rather, wasn't that exactly the trouble? And I wanted to promise that I would never fail him again. But it would all have sounded — empty words and lies.

So I made the promise to myself and prayed that I would keep it.

"It's terrible sometimes, inside," he said, "that's what's the trouble. You walk these streets, black and funky and cold, and there's not really a living ass to talk to, and there's nothing shaking, and there's no way of getting it out — that storm inside. You can't talk to it and you can't make love with it, and when you finally try to get with it and play it, you realize *nobody's* listening. So *you've* got to listen. You got to find a way to listen."

And then he walked away from the window and sat on the sofa again, as though all the wind had suddenly been knocked out of him. "Sometimes you'll do *anything* to play, even cut your mother's throat." He laughed and looked at me. "Or your brother's." Then he sobered. "Or your own." Then: "Don't worry. I'm all right now and I think I'll *be* all right. But I can't forget — where I've been. I don't mean just the physical place I've been, I mean where I've *been*. And *what* I've been."

"What have you been, Sonny?" I asked.

He smiled — but sat sideways on the sofa, his elbow resting on the back, his fingers playing with his mouth and chin, not looking at me. "I've been something I didn't recognize, didn't know I could be. Didn't know anybody could be." He stopped, looking inward, looking helplessly young, looking old. "I'm not talking about it now because I feel *guilty* or anything like that — maybe it would be better if I did, I don't know. Anyway, I can't really talk about it. Not to you, not to anybody," and now he turned and faced me. "Sometimes, you know, and it was actually when I was most *out* of the world, I felt that I was in it, that I was *with* it, really, and I could play or I didn't really have to *play*, it just came out of me, it was there. And I don't know how I played, thinking about it now, but I know I did awful things, those times, sometimes, to people. Or it wasn't that I *did* anything to them — it was that they weren't real." He picked up the beer can; it was empty; he rolled it between his palms: "And other times —

well, I needed a fix, I needed to find a place to lean. I needed to clear a space to *listen* — and I couldn't find it, and I — went crazy, I did terrible things to *me*, I was terrible *for* me." He began pressing the beer can between his hands. I watched the metal begin to give. It glittered, as he played with it like a knife, and I was afraid he would cut himself, but I said nothing. "Oh well, I can never tell you. I was all by myself at the bottom of something, stinking and sweating and crying and shaking, and I smelled it, you know? *my* stink, and I thought I'd die if I couldn't get away from it and yet, all the same, I knew that everything I was doing was just locking me in with it. And I didn't know," he paused, still flattening the beer can, "I didn't know, I still *don't* know, something kept telling me that maybe it was good to smell your own stink, but I didn't think that *that* was what I'd been trying to do — and — who can stand it?" and he abruptly dropped the ruined beer can, looking at me with a small, still smile, and then rose, walking to the window as though it were the lodestone rock. I watched his face, he watched the avenue. "I couldn't tell you when Mama died — but the reason I wanted to leave Harlem so bad was to get away from drugs. And then, when I ran away, that's what I was running from — really. When I came back, nothing had changed, I hadn't changed, I was just — older." And he stopped, drumming with his fingers on the windowpane. The sun had vanished, soon darkness would fall. I watched his face. "It can come again," he said, almost as though speaking to himself. Then he turned to me. "It can come again," he repeated. "I just want you to know that."

"All right," I said, at last. "So it can come again. All right."

He smiled, but the smile was sorrowful. "I had to try to tell you," he said.

"Yes," I said. "I understand that."

"You're my brother," he said, looking straight at me, and not smiling at all.

"Yes," I repeated, "yes. I understand that."

He turned back to the window looking out. "All that hatred down there," he said, "all that hatred and misery and love. It's a wonder it doesn't blow the avenue apart."

We went to the only nightclub on a short, dark street, downtown. We squeezed through the narrow, chattering, jampacked bar to the entrance of the big room, where the bandstand was. And we stood there for a moment, for the lights were very dim in this room and we couldn't see. Then, "Hello, boy," said the voice and an enormous black man, much older than Sonny or myself, erupted out of all that atmospheric lighting and put an arm around Sonny's shoulder. "I been sitting right here," he said, "waiting for you."

He had a big voice, too, and heads in the darkness turned toward us.

Sonny grinned and pulled a little away, and said, "Creole, this is my brother. I told you about him."

Creole shook my hand. "I'm glad to meet you, son," he said, and it was clear that he was glad to meet me *there*, for Sonny's sake. And he smiled, "You got a real musician in your family," and he took his arm from Sonny's shoulder and slapped him, lightly, affectionately, with the back of his hand.

"Well. Now I've heard it all," said a voice behind us. This was another musician, and a friend of Sonny's, a coal-black, cheerful-looking man, built close to the ground. He immediately began confiding to me, at the top of his lungs, the most terrible things about Sonny, his teeth gleaming like a lighthouse and his laugh coming up out of him like the beginning of an earthquake. And it turned out that everyone at the bar knew Sonny, or almost everyone; some were musicians, working there, or nearby, or not working, some were simply hangers-on, and some were there to hear Sonny play. I was introduced to all of them and they were all very polite to me. Yet, it was clear that, for them, I was only Sonny's brother. Here, I was in Sonny's world. Or, rather: his kingdom. Here, it was not even a question that his veins bore royal blood.

They were going to play soon and Creole installed me, by myself, at a table in a dark corner. Then I watched them, Creole, and the little black man, and Sonny, and the others, while they horsed around, standing just below the bandstand. The light from the bandstand spilled just a little short of them and, watching them laughing and gesturing and moving about, I had the feeling that they, nevertheless, were being most careful not to step into that circle of light too suddenly: that if they moved into the light too suddenly, without thinking, they would perish in flame. Then, while I watched, one of them, the small black man, moved into the light and crossed the bandstand and started fooling around with his drums. Then — being funny and being, also, extremely ceremonious — Creole took Sonny by the arm and led him to the piano. A woman's voice called Sonny's name and a few hands started clapping. And Sonny, also being funny and being ceremonious, and so touched, I think, that he could have cried, but neither hiding it nor showing it, riding it like a man, grinned, and put both hands to his heart and bowed from the waist.

Creole then went to the bass fiddle and a lean, very bright-skinned brown man jumped up on the bandstand and picked up his horn. So there they were, and the atmosphere on the bandstand and in the room began to change and tighten. Someone stepped up to the microphone and announced them. Then there were all kinds of murmurs. Some people at the bar shushed others. The waitress ran around, frantically getting in the last orders, guys and chicks got closer to each other, and the lights on the bandstand, on the quartet, turned to a kind of indigo. Then they all looked different there. Creole looked about him for the last time, as though he were making certain that all his chickens were in the coop, and then he — jumped and struck the fiddle. And there they were.

All I know about music is that not many people ever really hear it. And even then, on the rare occasions when something opens within, and the music enters, what we mainly hear, or hear corroborated, are personal, private vanishing evocations. But the man who creates the music is hearing something else, is dealing with the roar rising from the void and imposing order on it as it hits the air. What is evoked in him, then, is of another order, more terrible because it has no words, and triumphant, too, for that same reason. And his triumph, when he triumphs, is ours. I just watched Sonny's face. His face was troubled, he was working hard, but he wasn't with it. And I had the feeling that, in a way, everyone on the bandstand was waiting for him, both waiting for him and pushing him along. But as I began to watch Creole, I realized that it was Creole who held them all back. He had them on a short rein. Up there, keeping the beat with his whole body, wailing on the fiddle, with his eyes half closed, he was listening to everything, but he was listening to Sonny. He was having a dialogue with Sonny. He wanted Sonny to leave the shoreline and strike out for the deep water. He was Sonny's witness that deep water and drowning were not the same thing — he had been there, and he knew. And he wanted Sonny to know. He was waiting for Sonny to do the things on the keys which would let Creole know that Sonny was in the water.

And, while Creole listened, Sonny moved, deep within, exactly like someone in torment. I had never before thought of how awful the relationship must be between the musician and his instrument. He has to fill it, this instrument, with the breath of life, his own. He has to make it do what he wants it to do. And a piano is just a piano. It's made out of so much wood and wires and little hammers and big ones, and ivory. While there's only so much you can do with it, the only way to find this out is to try; to try and make it do everything.

And Sonny hadn't been near a piano for over a year. And he wasn't on much better terms with his life, not the life that stretched before him now. He and the piano stammered, started one way, got scared, stopped; started another way, panicked, marked time, started again; then seemed to have found a direction, panicked again, got stuck. And the face I saw on Sonny I'd never seen before. Everything had been burned out of it, and, at the same time, things usually hidden were being burned in, by the fire and fury of the battle which was occurring in him up there.

Yet, watching Creole's face as they neared the end of the first set, I had the feeling that something had happened, something I hadn't heard. Then they finished, there was scattered applause, and then, without an instant's warning, Creole started into something else, it was almost sardonic, it was *Am I Blue.* And, as though he commanded, Sonny began to play. Something began to happen. And Creole let out the reins. The dry, low, black man said something awful on the drums, Creole answered, and the drums talked back. Then the horn insisted, sweet and high, slightly detached perhaps, and Creole listened, commenting now and then, dry, and driving, beautiful and calm and old. Then they all came together again, and Sonny was part of the family again. I could tell this from his face. He seemed to have found, right there beneath his fingers, a damn brand-new piano. It seemed that he couldn't get over it. Then, for a while, just being happy with Sonny, they seemed to be agreeing with him that brand-new pianos certainly were a gas.

Then Creole stepped forward to remind them that what they were playing was the blues. He hit something in all of them, he hit something in me, myself, and the music tightened and deepened, apprehension began to beat the air. Creole began to tell us what the blues were all about. They were not about anything very new. He and his boys up there were keeping it new, at the risk of ruin, destruction, madness, and death, in order to find new ways to make us listen. For, while the tale of how we suffer, and how we are delighted, and how we may triumph is never new, it always must be heard. There isn't any other tale to tell, it's the only light we've got in all this darkness.

And this tale, according to that face, that body, those strong hands on those strings, has another aspect in every country, and a new depth in every generation. Listen, Creole seemed to saying, listen. Now these are Sonny's blues. He made the little black man on the drums know it, and the bright, brown man on the horn. Creole wasn't trying any longer to get Sonny in the water. He was wishing him Godspeed. Then he stepped back, very slowly, filling the air with the immense suggestion that Sonny speak for himself.

Then they all gathered around Sonny and Sonny played. Every now and again one of them seemed to say, amen. Sonny's fingers filled the air with life, his life. But that life contained so many others. And Sonny went all the way back, he really began with the spare, flat statement of the opening phrase of the song. Then he began to make it his. It was very beautiful because it wasn't hurried and it was no longer a lament. I seemed to hear with what burning he had made it his, with what burning we had yet to make it ours, how we could cease lamenting. Freedom lurked around us and I understood, at last, that he could help us to be free if we would listen, that he would never be free until we did. Yet, there was no battle in his face now, I heard what he had gone through, and would continue to go through until he came to rest in earth. He had made it his: that long line, of which we knew only Mama and Daddy. And he was giving it back, as everything must be given back, so that, passing through death, it can live forever. I saw my mother's face again, and felt, for the first time, how the stones of the road she had walked on must have bruised her feet. I saw the moonlit road where my father's brother died. And it brought something else back to me, and carried me past it, I saw my little girl again and felt Isabel's tears again, and I felt my own tears begin to rise. And I was yet aware that this was only a moment, that the world waited outside, as hungry as a tiger, and that trouble stretched above us, longer than the sky.

Then it was over. Creole and Sonny let out their breath, both soaking wet, and grinning. There was a lot of applause and some of it was real. In the dark, the girl came by and I asked her to take drinks to the bandstand. There was a long pause, while they talked up there in the indigo light and after awhile I saw the girl put a scotch and milk on top of the piano for Sonny. He didn't seem to notice it, but just before they started playing again, he sipped from it and looked toward me, and nodded. Then he put it back on top of the piano. For me, then, as they began to play again, it glowed and shook above my brother's head like the very cup of trembling.

HONORÉ DE BALZAC

La Grande Bretèche

Translated by Sylvia Raphael

About a hundred yards from Vendôme on the banks of the Loir, there is an old, brown house with a very high roof; it is completely isolated for in the neighbourhood there exists neither a foul-smelling tannery nor a miserable inn such as you see on the outskirts of nearly all small towns. In front of this dwelling, stretching down to the river, is a garden where the box hedges, which line the paths and used to be clipped, now grow as they please. Willows with their roots in the Loir have grown quickly, like the boundary hedge, and half conceal the house. Plants which we call weeds adorn the sloping river bank with their beautiful vegetation. The fruit trees, neglected for ten years, produce no more fruit and their shoots form an undergrowth. The climbing plants look like hedgerows. The paths, formerly sanded, are full of purslane, but to tell the truth, not a trace of the paths is left. Looking at it from the top of the hill on which are perched the ruins of the old castle of the Dukes of Vendôme (the only spot from which the eye can penetrate this enclosure), one would say that, at some time which it is difficult to determine, this corner of the world was the delight of a country gentleman who busied himself with roses, with tulip trees, in short with horticulture, but above all who loved good fruit. One can see an arbour, or rather the remnants of an arbour, where there is still a table which time has not entirely consumed. At the sight of the remains of this garden which no longer exists, one can imagine the negative pleasures of the peaceful life enjoyed in the country, just as one can imagine the life of a good businessman on reading the epitaph on his tomb. To crown the sad yet pleasing thoughts which grip the heart, there is, on one of the walls, a sundial decorated with this bourgeois and Christian inscription: ULTINAM COGITA! The roof of the house is horribly dilapidated, the shutters are always closed, the balconies are covered with swallows' nests, the doors are continually shut. Tall grasses have outlined in green the cracks in the doorsteps, and the ironwork is rusty. The moon, the sun, the winter, the summer, the snow have hollowed the woodwork, warped the timbers and eaten away the paint. The dismal silence which reigns there is disturbed only by birds, cats, weasels, rats and mice, free to trot to and fro, to fight and to eat each other. Everywhere an invisible hand has written the word *Mystery*. If, moved by curiosity, you were to go and look at the street side of the house, you would perceive a large door, rounded at the top, in which the children of the district have made numerous holes. I learned later that this door had been boarded up for ten years. Through these irregular gaps you would be able to see the perfect harmony that exists between the frontage on the garden side and that on the courtyard side. The same disorder reigns there. Clumps of grass surround the paving stones. Enormous cracks furrow the walls, whose blackened tops are festooned by a thousand garlands of pellitory. The front steps are loose, the bell rope is rotted, the gutters are broken. What fire from heaven has fallen this way? What court of law has given the order to scatter salt on this dwelling? Has God been insulted here? Has France been betrayed here? These are the questions you ask yourself. The snakes crawl about without giving you a reply. The empty deserted house is an immense riddle to which no one knows the answer. It used to be a little fief and bears the name of La Grande Bretèche. During my stay in Vendôme, where Desplein had left me to look after a rich patient, the sight of this strange dwelling became one of my keenest pleasures. Was it not better than a ruin? Undeniably authentic memories are attached to a ruin, but this house, which was still standing, though gradually being demolished by an avenging hand, contained a secret, an unknown thought; it suggested at least a whim. More than once, in the evening, I got through the overgrown hedge protecting the enclosure. I braved scratches, I went into the garden without a master, into the estate which was no longer either public or private. I stayed there for hours on end, looking at its disorder. I did not want to ask a single question of a loquacious inhabitant of Vendôme, even to reap the reward of learning the story of what had caused this strange sight. There, I made up delightful stories, I succumbed to charming little orgies of melancholy. If I had known the reason, perhaps very ordinary, for this desertion I would have lost the unpublished fictions with which I intoxicated myself. For me, this refuge represented the most varied images of human life, clouded by misfortunes. At times it had the atmosphere of a monastery without the monks, at times the peace of the cemetery without the dead who speak in their epitaphs. Today it is a leper house, tomorrow it will be the house of the Atridae. But, above all, it was provincial life with its meditations and its slow tempo. I have often wept there, I have never laughed there. More than once I have felt involuntary terror as I heard over my head the dull whirring of the wings of some hastening wood-pigeon. The ground there is damp. You have to watch out for lizards, vipers and frogs which disport themselves freely in the wilderness of nature. Above all you must not be afraid of the cold, for in a few moments you can feel a cloak of ice being placed on your shoulders like the Commander's hand on Don Juan's neck. One evening I shivered there. The wind had turned an old rusty weathercock whose creaking was like a moan uttered by the house, just as I was finishing a pretty gruesome tale in explanation of this monument of grief. I came back to my hotel, a prey to melancholy ideas. When I had had my supper, the landlady came into my room with an air of secrecy and said, 'Monsieur, here is Monsieur Regnault.'

'What is Monsieur Regnault?'

'What, you don't know Monsieur Regnault? Oh, that's funny!' she said, leaving the room.

Suddenly there came in a tall, spare man dressed in black, holding his hat in his hand, who introduced himself like a ram ready to butt his rival. He had a receding brow, a little pointed head and a pale face rather like a glass of dirty water. You would have said he was like a minister's door-keeper. This stranger was wearing an old jacket very worn at the seams. But he had a diamond on his shirt ruff and gold rings in his ears.

'Monsieur, to whom have I the honour of speaking?' I asked.

He sat down on a chair, placed himself in front of my fire, put his hat on my table and answered me, rubbing his hands, 'Oh, it is very cold, Monsieur. I am Monsieur Regnault.'

I bowed, saying to myself, '*Il bondo cani!* Seek further.'

'I am a lawyer at Vendôme,' he continued.

'I am delighted to hear it,' I exclaimed, 'but I am not in a position to make my will, for personal reasons.'

'One moment,' he replied, raising his hand as if to silence me. 'Allow me, Monsieur, allow me. I have heard that you sometimes go for a walk in the garden of La Grande Bretèche.'

'Yes, Monsieur.'

'One moment,' he said, repeating his gesture. 'That activity constitutes in fact a trespass. Monsieur, I come in the name of the Comtesse de Merret and as executor of her will to request you to cease your visits. One moment! I am not a Turk and don't want to say you have committed a crime. Besides, you may well not know the circumstances which oblige me to let the most beautiful house in Vendôme fall into ruins. Nevertheless, Monsieur, you appear to be an educated man and ought to know that under pain of severe penalties, the law forbids entry into a closed estate. A hedge is as good as a wall. But the state the house is in may serve as an excuse for your curiosity. I would not ask for anything better than to leave you free to come and go in that house, but as I am obliged to carry out the terms of the will, I have the honour, Monsieur, to ask you not to enter the garden again. Since the will was opened I have not set foot in that house which, as I have had the honour to tell you, is part of the estate of Madame de Merret. We have only counted the number of doors and windows so as to ascertain the taxes, which I pay annually out of funds earmarked for this purpose by the late countess. Oh, my dear sir, her will created a great stir in Vendôme!'

At this point the worthy fellow stopped to blow his nose. I respected his loquacity, realizing perfectly that Madame de Merret's will was the most important event in his life, his whole reputation, his glory, his Restoration. I had to bid farewell to my beautiful daydreams, to my romances. So I had no objection to the pleasure of learning the truth officially.

'Monsieur,' I said, 'would it be indiscreet to ask you the reasons for this eccentricity?' At these words a look, which expressed all the pleasure felt by a man used to riding his hobby-horse, passed over the lawyer's face. He straightened his shirt collar with a kind of self-satisfaction, took out his snuff-box, opened it, offered me some snuff and, when I refused, took a substantial pinch. He was happy! A man without a hobby-horse does not know all the advantages that can be obtained from life. A hobby-horse is exactly half-way between a passion and a monomania. At that moment, I understood the full implication of Sterne's apt expression and I understood completely the joy with which Uncle Toby, helped by Trim, bestrode his war-horse.

'Monsieur,' said Monsieur Regnault, 'I was Monsieur Roguin's head clerk in Paris. It was an excellent practice that you may have heard of? No? Yet an unfortunate bankruptcy made it famous. Since I didn't have enough money to do business in Paris at the price to which practices rose in 1816, I came here and acquired my predecessor's. I had relatives in Vendôme, amongst others a very rich aunt who gave me her daughter in marriage. Monsieur,' he continued after a slight pause, 'three months after being admitted by Monseigneur the Keeper of the Seals, I was summoned one evening, just as I was going to bed (I wasn't yet married), by Madame la Comtesse de Merret to her country house of Merret. Her maid, a good girl who today works in this hotel, was at my door with Madame la Comtesse's carriage. Oh, one moment, I must tell you, Monsieur, that Monsieur le Comte de Merret had gone to Paris and died there two months before I came here. He perished there miserably having indulged in all kinds of excesses. You understand? The day of his departure, Madame la Comtesse had left La Grande Bretèche and taken away the furniture. Some people even claim that she burned the furniture, the hangings, in fact all the usual things which furnished the premises rented at present by the aforesaid party ... (Goodness, what am I saying? Forgive me, I thought I was dictating a lease.) That she burned them,' he continued, 'in the meadow at Merret. Have you been to Merret, Monsieur? No,' he said, replying for me. 'Oh, it's a very beautiful spot. For about three months,' he said, continuing after a slight shake of the head, 'Monsieur le Comte and Madame la Comtesse had lived in a strange manner. They no longer received anyone. Madame lived on the ground floor and Monsieur on the first floor. When Madame la Comtesse was left alone, she was to be seen only at church. Later on, in her own home, at her own house, she refused to see the men and women friends who came to visit her. She was already very altered when she left La Grande Bretèche to go to Merret. That dear lady ... (I say "dear" because she left me this diamond. And I only saw her once!) ... well, this good lady was very ill. She had no doubt despaired of recovery for she died without allowing a doctor to be called. So many of our ladies thought that she was not in possession of her full reason. So, Monsieur, my curisoity was strangely excited when I learned that Madame de Merret needed my services. I wasn't the only one who took an interest in this story. That very evening, although it was late, the whole town knew that I was going to Merret. The maid replied rather vaguely to the questions that I put to her on the way. Nevertheless she told me that her mistress had received the last rites from the Merret curé during the day and that she seemed unlikely to survive the night. I arrived at the house about eleven o'clock. I went up the big staircase. After crossing large, high, dark rooms which were cold and devilishly damp, I reached the state bedroom where Madame la Comtesse was lying. Judging from the rumours which circulated about this lady (Monsieur, I would never finish if I were to repeat to you all the stories which have been told about her!) I imagined her to be a coquette. Can you conceive that I had great difficulty in finding her in the great bed where she was lying? It is true that to light this enormous bedroom with its friezes of the old régime, which were covered with so much dust that it made one sneeze only to look at them, she had one of those old Argant lamps. Oh, but you haven't been to Merret! Well, Monsieur, the bed is one of those old-fashioned ones with a high canopy decorated with flowered chintz. A little table was beside the bed and I saw on it an *Imitation of Christ*, which, by the way, I bought for my wife, as well as the lamp. There was also a large armchair for the confidential attendant and two chairs. What's more, there was no fire. That was all the furniture. It wouldn't have taken up ten lines in an inventory. Oh, my dear sir, if you had seen, as I did then, that enormous room draped with brown tapestries, you would have thought you had been transported into a veritable scene from a novel. It was icy, and worse than that, funereal,' he added, raising his arm with a theatrical gesture and pausing. 'By dint of looking as I came near to the bed, I finally saw Madame de Merret, thanks only to the glow of the lamp whose light shone on to the pillows. Her face was as yellow as wax and looked like two joined hands. Madame la Comtesse had a lace night-cap which revealed beautiful hair, but white as flax. She was sitting up and seemed to have great difficulty in remaining in that position. Her large black eyes, sunken by fever no doubt, and already half dead, scarcely moved under the bones. There,' he said, pointing to the arch of his brows. 'Her brow was damp. Her skeletal hands were like bones covered with a delicate skin. Her veins and muscles were clearly visible. She must have been very beautiful. But at the sight of her an indescribable feeling gripped me. According to those who prepared her for burial, no living creature had ever reached her state of thinness without dying. In short, it was terrible to see! Suffering had gnawed at this woman to such an extent that she was no more than a ghost. Her pale, purple lips seemed not to move when she spoke to me. Although my profession has made me familiar with these sights by sometimes taking me to the bedsides of the dying to record their last wishes, I confess that the families in tears and the deathbed scenes that I have witnessed were nothing compared to this lonely, silent woman in her vast country mansion. I could not hear the slightest sound, I could not see the movement which the sick woman's breathing should have given to the sheets which covered her, and I remained quite motionless, looking at her in a kind of daze. I feel as if I were still there. At last her large eyes moved. She tried to raise her right hand which fell back on the bed and these words issued from her mouth like a breath, for her voice was already no longer a voice: "I have been waiting for you very impatiently." Her cheeks suddenly acquired colour. It was an effort for her to speak, Monsieur. "Madame," I said to her. She signed to me to be silent. At that moment the old housekeeper got up and whispered to me, "Don't speak, Madame la Comtesse is not in a state to hear the slightest sound, and she might be upset by what you would say to her." I sat down. Some moments later, Madame de Merret gathered all the strength that remained to her, to move her right arm and put it, not without infinite difficulty, under her bolster. She paused for a brief moment. Then she made a final effort to withdraw her hand, and when she had picked up a sealed document, beads of sweat fell from her brow. "I entrust my will to you," she said, "Oh, God. Oh!" That was all. She grasped a crucifix which was on her bed, carried it swiftly to her lips and died. The expression of her staring eyes still makes me shudder when I think of it. She must have suffered a lot! There was joy in her final look, a feeling which remained imprinted on her closed eyes. I took away the will and, when it was opened, I saw that Madame de Merret had made me her executor. She left all her property to the Vendôme hospital except for some personal legacies. But these were her arrangements for La Grande Bretèche. She ordered me to leave that house for fifty full years in the state in which it would be at the time of her death. She forbade anyone at all to enter the rooms, she did not allow the slightest repairs to be made and she even earmarked money to pay guards, if necessary, to make sure that her intentions would be fully carried out. At the expiry of this term, if the desire expressed in the will has been fulfilled, the house is to belong to my heirs, for you know, Monsieur, that lawyers cannot accept legacies. Otherwise, La Grande Bretèche will revert to whoever is entitled to it, but on condition that he fulfills the stipulations contained in a codicil added to the will which is to be opened only at the end of the aforesaid fifty years. The will has not been disputed, so ... ' With this, and without finishing his sentence, the elongated lawyer looked at me triumphantly. I made him completely happy by paying him some compliments.

'Monsieur,' I said in conclusion, 'you have made such a great impression on me, that I can almost see that dying woman paler than her sheets. Her gleaming eyes frighten me and I shall dream of her tonight. But you must have made some conjectures about the arrangements contained in this strange will.'

'Monsieur,' he said with a comic reticence, 'I never allow myself to judge the behaviour of people who have honoured me with the gift of a diamond.

I soon loosened the tongue of the scrupulous Vendôme lawyer who communicated to me, not without long digressions, the observations made by the profound politicians of both sexes whose word is law in Vendôme. But these observations were so contradictory and so diffuse, that I almost fell asleep in spite of the interest which I took in this true story. The heavy tone and the monotonous voice of the lawyer, no doubt used to listening to himself and to making his clients or his compatriots listen to him, got the better of my curiosity. Fortunately he went away.

'Oh, Monsieur,' he said on the staircase, 'many people would like to live forty-five years more; but, one moment,' and with a crafty look he placed the first finger of his right hand on his nose as if he wanted to say, 'Pay great attention to this!' 'To go as far as that, you must not be about sixty.'

I closed my door, after being awoken from my apathy by this last remark which the lawyer thought very witty. Then I sat down in my armchair, putting my feet on the two firedogs in my fireplace. I became absorbed in a Radcliffe-like novel, based on the legal information given by Monsieur Regnault, when my door, manipulated by a woman's light hand, turned on its hinges. I saw my landlady come in, a large, cheerful, good-humoured woman who had missed her vocation. She was a Fleming who should have been born in a Teniers picture.

'Well, sir,' she said, 'Monsieur Regnault has no doubt been telling yet again his story of La Grande Bretèche.'

'Yes, my good Madame Lepas.'

'What did he tell you?'

I repeated in a few words the cold, gloomy story of Madame de Merret. At each sentence, my hostess craned forward, looking at me with the perspicacity of an innkeeper, a kind of cross between the instinct of a policeman, the wiliness of a spy, and the cunning of a shopkeeper.

'Madame Lepas, my good woman,' I added as I finished. 'You seem to know more about it, don't you? Otherwise, why did you come up to my room?'

'Oh, on my honour as an honest woman, and as truly as my name is Lepas ... '

'Don't swear. Your eyes are laden with a secret. You knew Monsieur de Merret. What kind of a man was he?'

'Well you see, Monsieur de Merret was a handsome man who was so long that you never saw the end of him, a highly esteemed nobleman from Picardy who, as we say here, was quick to fly off the handle. He paid cash so that he would have no difficulties with anyone. But you see he was hot-tempered. The ladies here found him very agreeable.'

'Because he was hot-tempered?' I asked my landlady.

'Perhaps so,' she said. 'You can imagine, sir, that man must have had good prospects, as they say, to marry Madame de Merret who, with no disrespect to others, was the richest and most beautiful young lady in Vendôme. She had an income of about twenty thousand livres. The whole town was at her wedding. The bride was sweet and charming, a real jewel of a girl. Oh, they made a handsome couple at that time.'

'Was it a happy marriage?'

'Well, yes and no, as far as one can tell, as you can imagine, people like us didn't live cheek by jowl with them. Madame de Merret was a good woman, very nice, who perhaps at times suffered a lot from her husband's bad tempers. But though he was a little proud, we liked him. Bah, that was his situation in life to be like that! When a man is a noble, you see ... '

'But there must have been some catastrophe to make Monsieur and Madame de Merret separate so violently?'

'I didn't say there was a catastrophe, sir. I know nothing about it.'

'Good. I am sure now that you know the whole story.'

'Well sir, I'll tell you everything. When I saw Monsieur Regnault go upstairs to your room, I thought that he would certainly talk to you about Madame de Merret, about La Grande Bretèche. That gave me the idea of asking your advice, sir, for you seem to me a sensible man incapable of betraying a poor woman like me who never harmed anyone and yet is tortured by her conscience. Up till now I never dared unburden myself to the people around here. They are all chatterboxes with sharp tongues. In short, sir, I've never yet had a traveller who has stayed as long as you in my inn and to whom I could tell the story of the fifteen thousand francs ...'

'My good Madame Lepas,' I replied, stopping the flow of her words, 'if your confidence is of a kind that would compromise me, I wouldn't want to be burdened with it for anything in the world.'

'There is nothing to be afraid of,' she said interrupting me, 'you will see.'

This eagerness made me think that I wasn't the only one to whom my good innkeeper had told the secret which I alone was to hear, and I listened.

'Well sir,' she said, 'when the Emperor sent Spanish or other prisoners of war here, I had to put up, at government expense, a young Spaniard who had been sent to Vendôme on parole. In spite of the parole, he went every day to report to the sub-prefect. He was a Spanish grandee! Excuse me a moment. He had a name ending in *os* and in *dia,* like Bagos de Feredia. I have his name on my register; you can read it if you want to. Oh, he was a handsome young man for a Spaniard — they are all said to be ugly. He was barely five feet two or three inches tall, but he was well built. He had little hands that he took great care of. Oh, you should have seen him. He had as many brushes for his hands as a woman has for all her beauty care! He had thick black hair, fiery eyes and a rather copper-coloured complexion which I liked all the same. He wore fine linen such as I've seen on no one else, though I have put up princesses, and amongst others General Bertránd, the Duke and Duchess of Abrantès, Monsieur Decazes and the King of Spain. He didn't eat much, but he had such courteous, kindly manners that one couldn't hold it against him. Oh, I liked him very much, though he didn't say four words a day and it was impossible to have the slightest conversation with him. If you spoke to him, he didn't reply. That's a habit, a mania that they all have, so I'm told. He read his breviary like a priest; he went to Mass and to all the services regularly. Where did he sit in church? (We noticed that later.) Two steps from Madame de Merret's chapel. As he installed himself there the first time he came to church, nobody imagined that he did so intentionally. Besides, he never took his nose out of his prayer book, poor young man! At that time, sir, in the evenings, he used to go for a walk in the hills, in the castle ruins. That was the poor man's only distraction; it reminded him of his own country. They say that it's all mountains in Spain. From the very first days of his detention here, he stayed out late. I was anxious at not seeing him come back till the stroke of midnight. But we all got used to his whim. He took the front-door key, and we didn't wait up for him any more. He lodged in the house that we have in the Rue des Casernes. Then one of our stable boys told us that one evening, as he was taking the horses into the water, he thought he saw the Spanish grandee swimming like a fish far out in the river. When he came back I told him to take care of the weeds. He seemed put out at having been seen in the water.

Finally, sir, one day, or rather one morning, we couldn't find him in his room. He hadn't come back. I rummaged everywhere till I found in his table drawer a letter containing fifty Spanish gold pieces that are called *portugaises* and are worth about five thousand francs; then there were ten thousand francs' worth of diamonds in a little sealed box. His letter said that, in case he didn't return, he left us his money and these diamonds on condition that we founded Masses to thank God for his escape and to pray for his salvation. At that time, I still had my husband and he went off to look for the Spaniard. And here is the queer part of the story. He brought back the Spaniard's clothes which he found under a large stone among some piles on the river bank, on the castle side, almost opposite La Grande Bretèche. My husband had gone there so early in the morning that no one had seen him. He burned the clothes after reading the letter and, according to Count Feredia's wish, we declared that he had escaped. The sub-prefect set the whole police force on his trail. But, lor, they didn't catch him. Lepas thought the Spaniard had been drowned. But, sir, I don't think so. I believe, rather, that he had something to do with Madame de Merret, since Rosalie told me that the crucifix, to which her mistress was so attached that she had it buried with her, was made of ebony and silver. Now when Monsieur Feredia first came to stay here he had one of ebony and silver which I never saw in his possession again. Now, sir, isn't it true that I oughtn't to have any remorse about the Spaniard's fifteen thousand francs, and that they are really mine?'

'Certainly, but haven't you tried to question Rosalie?' I said.

'Oh, I certainly did, sir. But what could I do? That girl, she's like a wall. She knows something but it's impossible to get her to spill the beans.'

After chatting with me for a moment longer, my landlady left me a prey to vague, gloomy thoughts, to a romantic curiosity, to a religious terror rather like the deep feeling which grips us when, at night, we go into a dark church where we can see a faint, distant light under lofty arches; an indeterminate figure glides past, the rustle of a dress or a surplice can be heard ... we have shuddered. La Grande Bretèche and its tall grasses, its condemned windows, its rusty ironwork, its closed doors, its deserted room, suddenly rose fantastically before me. I tried to penetrate the mystery of this dwelling as I searched for the clue of the solemn story, the drama that had killed three people. In my eyes Rosalie was the most interesting person in Vendôme. On looking at her carefully, I discovered the traces of a secret thought, despite the glowing health which beamed from her plump face. She had within her a source of remorse or of hope. Her demeanour suggested that she had a secret, like that of pious women who pray excessively, or of a girl guilty of infanticide who always hears her child's last cry. Yet her manner was ingenuous and uncouth. Her stupid smile had nothing criminal about it and you would have deemed her innocent at the mere sight of the big red and blue check handkerchief covering her strapping bust which was encased, squeezed, parcelled up in a white and purple-striped dress.

'No,' I thought, 'I shall not leave Vendôme without knowing the whole story of La Grande Bretèche. To achieve my aim, I shall become Rosalie's friend, if there is no other way.'

'Rosalie,' I said to her one evening.

'What is it, sir?'

'You are not married?'

She gave a slight start.

'Oh, I won't be short of men when the whim to be unhappy takes hold of me,' she said, with a laugh.

She recovered quickly from her embarrassment, for all women, from the great lady down to and including hotel maids, have a self-possession which is peculiar to them.

'You are young and attractive enough not to be short of lovers. But tell me, Rosalie, why did you become a hotel maid when you left Madame de Merret? Was it because she didn't leave you any income?'

'Oh yes, indeed she did. But, sir, my place is the best in the whole of Vendôme.'

This reply was one of those that judges and lawyers call 'dilatory'. Rosalie seemed to me to have a place in this romantic story like the square in the middle of a chess-board. She was in the very centre of the interest and of the truth. She seemed to me to be tied up in the web. It wasn't an ordinary seduction that I had to attempt. In this girl there was the last chapter of a novel. So, from that moment, Rosalie became the object of my predilection. Through studying this girl, I noticed that, like all women who preoccupy our thoughts, she had a host of good qualities. She was clean, and neat, she was beautiful, that goes without saying. Soon she had all the attractions that our desire lends to women in whatever situation they may be. A fortnight after the lawyer's visit, one evening, or rather, one morning, for it was very early, I said to Rosalie, 'Tell me everything you know about Madame de Merret.'

'Oh,' she replied terrified, 'don't ask me that, Monsieur Horace.' Her beautiful face clouded over, her lively, animated complexion turned pale, and her eyes lost their innocent, moist gleam.

'Well,' she continued, 'since you want me to, I shall tell you. But be sure and keep my secret.'

'Of course, my poor girl, I shall keep all your secrets with a thief's honesty. That's the most dependable there is.'

'If you don't mind,' she said, 'I prefer you to keep them with your own.'

With this, she rearranged her scarf and settled herself as if to tell a tale, for, indeed, a certain attitude of trust and security is neccessary for the telling of a story. The best tales are told at a certain time, as now, when we are all here, at table. No one has ever told a good story standing up, or when they are hungry. But if I had to reproduce word for word Rosalie's diffuse eloquence, a whole volume would scarcely be enough. Now, since the event of which she gave me a jumbled account is situated between the lawyer's and Madame Lepas' gossip as exactly as the middle terms of an arithmetical progression are between their two extremes, it only remains for me to tell it to you in a few words. So I abbreviate.

The room occupied by Madame de Merret at La Bretèche was on the ground floor. She used a little closet about four feet deep as her wardrobe. Three months before the evening whose events I am going to relate, Madame de Merret had been so seriously unwell that her husband left her alone in her room and he slept in a room on the first floor. By one of those chances which are impossible to foresee, that evening, he came back two hours later than usual from the club where he went to read the newspapers and talk politics with the inhabitants of the district. His wife thought that he had come home, gone to bed and fallen asleep. But the invasion of France had been the subject of a very lively discussion, the billiard game had become very keen and he had lost forty francs, an enormous sum at Vendôme where everybody amasses money, and where the style of life is kept within the limits of a praiseworthy modesty which perhaps becomes the source of a true happiness unknown to any Parisian. For some time Monsieur de Merret used to content himself with asking Rosalie if his wife was in bed. She always said 'yes' and, when he heard this, he immediately went to his own room with the complacency that comes from habit and confidence. That evening, when he came in, he took it into his head to go to Madame de Merret's room to tell her of his mishap, perhaps too to console himself for it. During dinner, he had thought that Madame de Merret was very elegantly dressed. As he returned home from the club, he said to himself that his wife was no longer unwell, that her convalescence had improved her looks and he noticed this, as husbands notice everything, a little late. Instead of calling Rosalie, who at that moment was busy in the kitchen watching the cook and the coachman playing a difficult game of bezique, Monsieur de Merret made his way to his wife's room by the light of the lantern that he had put down on the first step of the staircase. His easily recognizable step rang out under the arches of the corridor. Just as the nobleman turned the key of his wife's room, he thought he heard the door of the closet I have mentioned being shut, but when he came in, Madame de Merret was alone, standing in front of the fireplace. The husband thought naïvely that Rosalie was in the closet. However, a suspicion which rang in his ears like the sound of bells, put him on his guard. He looked at his wife and thought he saw an indefinable look of wild distress in her eyes.

'You are very late home,' she said.

Her voice which was usually so pure and gracious seemed to him slightly altered. Monsieur de Merret made no answer, for at this moment Rosalie came in. This was like a thunderbolt for him. He walked up and down the room, going from one window to the other with an even stride and his arms folded.

'Have you had some sad news, or are you not feeling well?' his wife asked apprehensively, while Rosalie undressed her.

He kept silent.

'You may go,' Madame de Merret said to her maid. 'I shall put in my curlers myself.'

She guessed something was wrong, just from the look of her husband's face, and wanted to be alone with him. When Rosalie had gone or when they thought she had gone, for she remained some moments in the corridor, Monsieur de Merret came and stood in front of his wife and said to her coldly, 'Madame, there is someone in your closet!'

She looked at her husband calmly and replied simply, 'No, Monsieur.'

This 'No' was heartbreaking to Monsieur de Merret. He did not believe it, yet his wife had never looked so pure and so devout as she seemed to be at that moment. He got up to go and open the closet. Madame de Merret took him by the hand, stopped him, looked at him sadly and said to him in a voice strangely filled with emotion. 'If you find no one there, you must reflect that everything will be over between us!'

The incredible dignity of his wife's attitude restored Monsieur de Merret's deep esteem for her and suggested to him one of those resolutions which only lack a wider setting to become immortal.

'No, Joséphine,' he said, 'I shan't go. In either case we would be separated for ever. Listen to me. I know how pure your soul is and I know that you lead a saintly life. You would not want to commit a mortal sin at the cost of your life.'

At these words, Madame de Merret looked at her husband with a drawn look on her face.

'Look, here is your crucifix,' he added. 'Swear to me before God that there's no one there. I shall believe you. I shall not open that door.'

Madame de Merret took the crucifix and said, 'I swear.'

'Say it louder,' said her husband, 'and repeat, "I swear before God that there is no one in that closet." ' She repeated the words without embarrassment.

'Good,' Monsieur de Merret said coldly. Then, after a moment's silence, picking up the ebony crucifix inlaid with silver and very artistically carved, he said, 'You have a very beautiful object that I am not familiar with.'

'I found it at Duvivier's. When that group of prisoners passed through Vendôme last year, he bought it from a Spanish priest.'

'Oh,' said Monsieur de Merret, putting the crucifix back on its nail, and he rang the bell. Rosalie didn't keep him waiting. Monsieur de Merret went quickly to meet her, took her into the bay of the window which looks out on to the garden, and said to her in a low voice, 'I know that Gorenflot wants to marry you. Only poverty prevents you from setting up house together, and you have told him that you will not be his wife unless he finds a way of establishing himself as a master mason ... Well, go and find him and tell him to come here with his trowel and his tools. Do it such a way that you don't wake up anyone in the house but him; his fortune will surpass your wishes. Above all, don't gossip when you leave here, otherwise ...'

He frowned. Rosalie set off. He called her back. 'Here's my pass key,' he said. 'Take it.'

'Jean,' shouted Monsieur de Merret in a voice that thundered down the corridor. Jean, who was both his coachman and his man of confidence, left his game of bezique and came.

'Go to bed, all of you,' his master said to him, as he motioned to him to come nearer, and Monsieur de Merret added, but in a low voice, 'When they are all asleep, *asleep* you understand, you will come down and let me know.'

Monsieur de Merret, who had not lost sight of his wife as he gave orders, came back calmly beside her in front of the fire and began to tell her about the events of the billiard game and the discussions at the club. When Rosalie came back, she found Monsieur and Madame de Merret chatting in a friendly manner.

Monsieur de Merret had recently renewed the

ceilings of all his reception rooms on the ground floor. Plaster is very scarce at Vendôme and transport adds considerably to the price; so Monsieur de Merret had ordered quite a large amount, knowing that he would always find purchasers for any that he had left over. This circumstance gave him the idea for the plan that he carried out.

'Monsieur, Gorenflot is here,' Rosalie said quietly.

'Tell him to come in,' replied the Picard nobleman out loud.

Madame de Merret turned slightly pale when she saw the mason.

'Gorenflot,' said her husband, 'go and get some bricks from under the coach house and bring enough to wall up that closet door; use the plaster that I have left over to plaster the wall.' Then drawing Rosalie and the workman aside, he said in a low voice, 'Now listen, Gorenflot, you will sleep here tonight. But, tomorrow morning, you will have a passport to go abroad to a town that I shall name. I shall give you six thousand francs for your journey. You will stay ten years in that town. If you are not happy there, you can settle in another provided that it is in the same country. You will go via Paris where you will wait for me. There, I shall guarantee you by contract six thousand francs more which will be paid to you on your return, if you have fulfilled the conditions of our bargain. For this reward, you will have to maintain absolute silence about what you have done here tonight. As for you, Rosalie, I shall give you ten thousand francs which will be paid to you only on your wedding-day and on condition that you marry Gorenflot. But in order to marry you must say nothing. Otherwise, there will be no dowry.'

'Rosalie,' said Madame de Merret, 'come and do my hair.'

Her husband calmly walked up and down keeping an eye on the door, the mason, and his wife, but without showing any insulting suspicion. Gorenflot could not help making a noise. Madame de Merret took advantage of a moment when the workman was unloading bricks and when her husband was at the other end of the room, to say to Rosalie, 'An income of a thousand francs for you, my dear, if you can tell Gorenflot to leave a crack at the bottom.' Then, out loud, she said to her composedly,

'Go and help him.'

Monsieur and Madame de Merret said nothing during the whole time that Gorenflot took to wall up the door. The husband's silence was intentional as he did not want to give his wife an opportunity of making ambiguous remarks; she was silent either out of caution or pride. When the wall was half-built, the cunning mason took advantage of a moment when the gentleman had his back turned, to break one of the two glass panes of the door with his pick. This action made Madame de Merret realize that Rosalie had spoken to Gorenflot. Then all three of them saw a gloomy, swarthy man's face, black hair, and fiery eyes. Before her husband had turned round, the poor woman had time to sign to the foreigner with movement of the head. For him this sign meant, 'Hope!'

At four o'clock, towards dawn, for it was September, the construction was completed. The mason was put under the guard of Jean, and Monsieur de Merret slept in his wife's room. The next morning, as he got up he said carelessly, 'Oh, what a nuisance, I must go to the town-hall for the passport.'

He put on his hat, took three steps towards the door, came back and took the crucifix.

His wife gave a start of delight. 'He will go to Duvivier's,' she thought.

As soon as Monsieur de Merret had gone out, Madame de Merret rang for Rosalie; then she cried in a terrible voice, 'The pick, the pick. Set to work. I saw yesterday how Gorenflot set about it. We'll have time to make a hole and to fill it up again.'

In the twinkling of an eye, Rosalie brought her mistress a kind of axe. With indescribable energy she began to demolish the wall. She had already dislodged some bricks when, as she prepared to strike a blow even stronger than the others, she saw Monsieur de Merret behind her. She fainted.

'Put Madame on her bed,' said Monsieur de Merret coldly. Foreseeing what would happen during his absence, he had set a trap for his wife. He had quite simply written to the mayor and sent for Duvivier. The jeweller arrived just as the disorder in the room had been tidied up.

'Duvivier,' asked Monsieur de Merret, 'did you buy some crucifixes from Spaniards who passed through the town?'

'No, sir.'

'Good, thank you,' said Monsieur de Merret giving his wife a ferocious look. 'Jean,' he added turning towards his confidential valet, 'have my meals served in Madame de Merret's room. She is ill and I shan't leave her till she is better.'

The cruel nobleman stayed at his wife's side for twenty days. At first, when there were some sounds in the walled-up closet and Joséphine wanted to beg his mercy for the dying stranger, he replied without letting her say a word, 'You swore on the cross that there was no one there.'

JOHN BARTH

Lost in the Funhouse

For whom is the funhouse fun? Perhaps for lovers. For Ambrose it is *a place of fear and confusion.* He has come to the seashore with his family for the holiday, *the occasion of their first visit is Independence Day, the most important secular holiday of the United States of America.* A single straight underline is the manuscript mark for italic type, *which in turn* is the printed equivalent to oral emphasis of words and phrases as well as the customary type for titles of complete works, not to mention. Italics are also employed, in fiction stories especially, for "outside," intrusive, or artificial voices, such as radio announcements, the texts of telegrams and newspaper articles, et cetera. They should be used *sparingly.* If passages originally in roman type are italicized by someone repeating them, it's customary to acknowledge the fact. *Italics mine.*

Ambrose was "at that awkward age." His voice came out high-pitched as a child's if he let himself get carried away; to be on the safe side, therefore, he moved and spoke with *deliberate calm* and *adult gravity.* Talking soberly of unimportant or irrelevant matters and listening consciously to the sound of your own voice are useful habits for maintaining control in this difficult interval. *En route* to Ocean City he sat in the back seat of the family car with his brother Peter, age fifteen, and Magda G--, age fourteen, a pretty girl, an exquisite young lady, who lived not far from them on B-- Street in the town of D--, Maryland. Initials, blanks, or both were often substituted for proper names in nineteenth-century fiction to enhance the illusion of reality. It is as if the author felt it necessary to delete the names for reasons of tact or legal liability. Interestingly, as with other aspects of realism, it is an *illusion* that is being enhanced, by purely artificial means. Is it likely, does it violate the principle of verisimilitude, that a thirteen-year-old boy could make such a sophisticated observation? A girl of fourteen is the *psychological coeval* of a boy of fifteen or sixteen; a thirteen-year-old boy, therefore, even one precocious in some other aspects, might be three years *her emotional junior.*

Thrice a year — on Memorial, Independence, and Labor Days — the family visits Ocean City for the afternoon and evening. When Ambrose and Peter's father was their age, the excursion was made by train, as mentioned in the novel *The 42nd Parallel* by John Dos Passos. Many families from the same neighborhood used to travel together, with dependent relatives and often with Negro servants; schoolfuls of children swarmed through the railway cars; everyone shared everyone else's Maryland fried chicken, Virginia ham, deviled eggs, potato salad, beaten biscuits, iced tea. Nowadays (that is, in 19–, the year of our story) the journey is made by automobile — more comfortably and quickly though without the extra fun though without the *camaraderie* of a general excursion. It's all part of the deterioration of American life, their father declares; Uncle Karl supposes that when the boys take *their* families to Ocean City for the holidays they'll fly in Autogiros. Their mother, sitting in the middle of the front seat like Magda in the second, only with her arms on the seat-back behind the men's shoulders, wouldn't want the good old days back again, the steaming trains and stuffy long dresses; on the other hand she can do without Autogiros, too, if she has to become a grandmother to fly in them.

Description of physical appearance and mannerisms is one of several standard methods of characterization used by writers of fiction. It is also important to "keep the senses operating"; when a detail from one of the five senses, say visual, is "crossed" with a detail from another, say auditory, the reader's imagination is oriented to the scene, perhaps unconsciously. This procedure may be compared to the way surveyors and navigators determine their positions by two or more compass bearings, a process known as triangulation. The brown hair on Ambrose's mother's forearms gleamed in the sun like. Though right-handed, she took her left arm from the seat-back to press the dashboard cigar lighter for Uncle Karl. When the glass bead in its handle glowed red, the lighter was ready for use. The smell of Uncle Karl's cigar smoke reminded one of. The fragrance of the ocean came strong to the picnic ground where they always stopped for lunch, two miles inland from Ocean City. Having to pause for a full hour almost within sound of the breakers was difficult for Peter and Ambrose when they were younger; even at their present age it was not easy to keep their anticipation, *stimulated by the briny spume,* from turning into short temper. The Irish author James Joyce, in his unusual novel entitled *Ulysses,* now available in this country, uses the adjectives *snot-green* and *scrotum-tightening* to describe the sea. Visual, auditory, tactile, olfactory, gustatory.

Peter and Ambrose's father, while steering their black 1936 LaSalle sedan with one hand, could with the other remove the first cigarette from a white pack of Lucky Strikes and, more remarkably, light it with a match forefingered from its book and thumbed against the flint paper without being detached. The matchbook cover merely advertised U.S. War Bonds and Stamps. A fine metaphor, simile, or other figure of speech, in addition to its obvious "first-order" relevance to the thing it describes, will be seen upon reflection to have a second order of significance: it may be drawn from the *milieu* of the action, for example, or be particularly appropriate to the sensibility of the narrator, even hinting to the reader things of which the narrator is unaware; or it may cast further and subtler lights upon the thing it describes, sometimes ironically qualifying the more evident sense of the comparison.

To say that Ambrose's and Peter's mother was *pretty* is to accomplish nothing; the reader may acknowledge the proposition, but his imagination is not engaged. Besides, Magda was also pretty, yet in an altogether different way. Although she lived on B-- Street she had very good manners and did better than average in school. Her figure was very well developed for her age. Her right hand lay casually on the plush upholstery of the seat, very near Ambrose's left leg, on which his own hand rested. The space between their legs, between her right and his left leg, was out of the line of sight of anyone sitting on the other side of Magda, as well as anyone glancing into the rearview mirror. Uncle Karl's face resembled Peter's — rather, vice versa. Both had dark hair and eyes, short husky statures, deep voices. Magda's left hand was probably in a similar position on her left side. The boys' father is difficult to describe; no particular feature of his appearance or manner stood out. He wore glasses and was principal of a T-- County grade school. Uncle Karl was a masonry contractor.

Although Peter must have known as well as Ambrose that the latter, because of his position in the car, would be the first to see the electrical towers of the power plant at V--, the halfway point of their trip, he leaned forward and slightly toward the center of the car and pretended to be looking for them through the flat pinewoods and tuckahoe creeks along the highway. For as long as the boys could remember, "looking for the Towers" had been a feature of the first half of their excursions to Ocean City, "looking for the standpipe" of the second. Though the game was childish, their mother preserved the tradition of rewarding the first to see the Towers with a candy-bar or piece of fruit. She insisted now that Magda play the game; the prize, she said, was "something hard to get nowadays." Ambrose decided not to join in; he sat far back in his seat. Magda, like Peter, leaned forward. Two sets of straps were discernible through the shoulders of her sun dress; the inside right one, a brassiere-strap, was fastened or shortened with a small safety pin. The right armpit of her dress, presumably the left as well, was damp with perspiration. The simple strategy for being first to espy the Towers, which Ambrose had understood by the age of four, was to sit on the right-hand side of the car. Whoever sat there, however, had also to put up with the worst of the sun, and so Ambrose, without mentioning the matter, chose sometimes the one and sometimes the other. Not impossibly Peter had never caught on to the trick, or thought that his brother hadn't simply because Ambrose on occasion preferred shade to a Baby Ruth or tangerine.

The shade-sun situation didn't apply to the front seat, owing to the windshield; if anything the driver got more sun, since the person on the passenger side not only was shaded below by the door and dashboard but might swing down his sunvisor all the way too.

"Is that them?" Magda asked. Ambrose's mother teased the boys for letting Magda win, insinuating that "somebody [had] a girl-friend." Peter and Ambrose's father reached a long thin arm across their mother to butt his cigarette in the dashboard ashtray, under the lighter. The prize this time for seeing the Towers first was a banana. Their mother bestowed it after chiding their father for wasting a half-smoked cigarette when everything else was so scarce. Magda, to take the prize, moved her hand from so near Ambrose's that he could have touched it as though accidentally. She offered to share the prize, things like that were so hard to find; but everyone insisted it was hers alone. Ambrose's mother sang an iambic trimeter couplet from a popular song, femininely rhymed:

"What's good is in the Army;
What's left will never harm me."

Uncle Karl tapped his cigar ash out the ventilator window; some particles were sucked by the slipstream back into the car through the rear window on the passenger side. Magda demonstrated her ability to hold a banana in one hand and peel it with her teeth. She still sat forward; Ambrose pushed his glasses back onto the bridge of his nose with his left hand, which he then negligently let fall to the seat cushion immediately behind her. He even permitted the single hair, gold, on the second joint of his thumb to brush the fabric of her skirt. Should she have sat back at that instant, his hand would have been caught under her.

Plush upholstery prickles uncomfortably through gabardine slacks in the July sun. The function of the *beginning* of a story is to introduce the principal characters, establish their initial relationships, set the scene for the main action, expose the background of the situation if necessary, plant motifs and foreshadowings where appropriate, and initiate the first complication or whatever of the "rising action." Actually, if one imagines a story called "The Funhouse," or "Lost in the Funhouse," the details of the drive to Ocean City don't seem especially relevant. The *beginning* should recount the events between Ambrose's first sight of the funhouse early in the afternoon and his entering it with Magda and Peter in the evening. The *middle* would narrate all relevant events from the time he goes in to the time he loses his way; middles have the double and contradictory function of delaying the climax while at the same time preparing the reader for it and fetching him to it. Then the *ending* would tell what Ambrose does while he's lost, how he finally finds his way out, and what everybody makes of the experience. So far there's been no real dialogue, very little sensory detail, and nothing in the way of a *theme.* And a long time has gone by already without anything happening; it makes a person wonder. We haven't even reached Ocean City yet: we will never get out of the funhouse.

The more closely an author identifies with the narrator, literally or metaphorically, the less advisable it is, as a rule, to use the first-person narrative viewpoint. Once three years previously the young people *aforementioned* played Niggers and Masters in the backyard; when it was Ambrose's turn to be Master and theirs to be Niggers Peter had to go serve his evening papers; Ambrose was afraid to punish Magda alone, but she led him to the whitewashed Torture Chamber between the woodshed and the privy in the Slaves Quarters; there she knelt sweating among bamboo rakes and dusty Mason jars, pleadingly embraced his knees, and while bees droned in the lattice as if on an ordinary summer afternoon, purchased clemency at a surprising price set by herself. Doubtless she remembered nothing of this event; Ambrose on the other hand seemed unable to forget the least detail of his life. He even recalled how, standing beside himself with awed impersonality in the reeky heat, he'd stared the while at an empty cigar box in which Uncle Karl kept stone-cutting chisels: beneath the words *El Producto,* a laureled, loose-toga'd lady regarded the sea from a marble bench; beside her, forgotten or not yet turned to, was a five-stringed lyre. Her shin reposed on the back of her right hand; her left depended negligently from the bencharm. The lower half of scene and lady was peeled away; the words EXAMINED BY- -were inked there into the wood. Nowadays cigar boxes are made of pasteboard. Ambrose wondered what Magda would have done, Ambrose wondered what Magda would do when she sat back on his hand as he resolved she should. Be angry. Make a teasing joke of it. Give no sign at all. For a long time she leaned forward, playing cowpoker with Peter against Uncle Karl and Mother and watching for the first sign of Ocean City. At nearly the same instant, picnic ground and Ocean City standpipe hove into view; an Amoco filling station on their side of the road cost Mother and Uncle Karl fifty cows and the game; Magda bounced back, clapping her right hand on Mother's right arm; Ambrose moved clear "in the nick of time."

At this rate our hero, at this rate our protagonist will remain in the funhouse forever. Narrative ordinarily consists of alternating dramatization and summarization. One symptom of nervous tension, paradoxically, is repeated and violent yawning; neither Peter nor Magda nor Uncle Karl nor Mother reacted in this manner. Although they were no longer small children, Peter and Ambrose were each given a dollar to spend on boardwalk amusements in addition to what money of their own they'd brought along. Magda too, though she protested she had ample spending money. The boys' mother made a little scene out of distributing the bills; she pretended that her sons and Magda were small children and cautioned them not to spend the sum too quickly or in one place. Magda promised with a merry laugh and, having both hands free, took the bill with her left. Peter laughed also and pledged in a falsetto to be a good boy. His imitation of a child was not clever. The boys' father was tall and thin, balding, fair-complexioned. Assertions of that sort are not effective; the reader may acknowledge the proposition, but. We should be much farther along than we are; something has gone wrong; not much of this preliminary rambling seems relevant. Yet everyone begins in the same place; how is it that most go along without difficulty but a few lose their way?

"Stay out from under the boardwalk," Uncle Karl growled from the side of his mouth. The boys' mother pushed his shoulder *in mock annoyance.* They were all standing before Fat May the Laughing Lady who advertised the funhouse. Larger than life, Fat May mechanically shook, rocked on her heels, slapped her thighs while recorded laughter — uproarious, female — came amplified from a hidden loudspeaker. It chuckled, wheezed, wept; tried in vain to catch its breath; tittered, groaned, exploded raucous and anew. You couldn't hear it without laughing yourself, no matter how you felt. Father came back from talking to a Coast-Guardsman on duty and reported that the surf was spoiled with crude oil from tankers recently torpedoed offshore. Lumps of it, difficult to remove, made tarry tidelines on the beach and stuck on swimmers. Many bathed in the surf nevertheless and came out speckled; others paid to use a municipal pool and only sunbathed on the beach. We would do the latter. We would do the latter. We would do the latter.

Under the boardwalk, matchbook covers, grainy other things. What is the story's theme? Ambrose is ill. He perspires in the dark passages; candied apples-on-a-stick, delicious-looking, disappointing to eat. Funhouses need men's and ladies' rooms at intervals. Others perhaps have also vomited in corners and corridors; may even have had bowel movements liable to be stepped in in the dark. The word *fuck* suggests suction and/or and/or flatulence. Mother and Father; grandmothers and grandfathers on both sides; great-grandmothers and great-grandfathers on four sides, et cetera. Count a generation as thirty years: in approximately the year when Lord Baltimore was granted charter to the province of Maryland by Charles I, five hundred twelve women — English, Welsh, Bavarian, Swiss — of every class and character, received into themselves the penises the intromittent organs of five hundred twelve men, ditto, in every circumstance and posture, to conceive the five hundred twelve ancestors of the two hundred fifty-six ancestors of the et cetera et cetera et cetera et cetera et cetera et cetera et cetera et cetera of the author, of the narrator, of this story, *Lost in the Funhouse.* In alleyways, ditches, canopy beds, pinewoods, bridal suites, ships' cabins, coach-and-fours, coaches-and-four, sultry toolsheds; on the cold sand under boardwalks, littered with *El Producto* cigar butts, treasured with Lucky Strike cigarette stubs, Coca-Cola caps, gritty turds, cardboard lollipop sticks, matchbook covers warning that A Slip of the Lip Can Sink a Ship. The shluppish whisper, continuous as seawash round the globe, tidelike falls and rises with the circuit of dawn and dusk.

Magda's teeth. She *was* left-handed. Perspiration. They've gone all the way, through, Magda and Peter, they've been waiting for hours with Mother and Uncle Karl while Father searches for his lost son; they draw french-fried potatoes from a paper cup and shake their heads. They've named the children they'll one day have and bring to Ocean City on holidays. Can spermatozoa properly be thought of as male animalcules when there are no female spermatozoa? They grope through hot, dark windings, past Love's Tunnel's fearsome obstacles. Some perhaps lose their way.

Peter suggested then and there that they do the funhouse; he had been through it before, so had Magda, Ambrose hadn't and suggested, his voice cracking on account of Fat May's laughter, that they swim first. All were chuckling, couldn't help it; Ambrose's father, Ambrose's and Peter's father came up grinning like a lunatic with two boxes of syrup-coated popcorn, one for Mother, one for Magda; the men were to help themselves. Ambrose walked on Magda's right; being by nature lefthanded, she carried the box in her left hand. Up front the situation was reversed.

"What are you limping for?" Magda inquired of Ambrose. He supposed in a husky tone that his foot had gone to sleep in the car. Her teeth flashed. "Pins and needles?" It was the honeysuckle on the lattice of the former privy that drew the bees. Imagine being stung there. How long is this going to take?

The adults decided to forgo the pool; but Uncle Karl insisted they change into swimsuits and do the beach. "He wants to watch the pretty girls," Peter teased, and ducked behind Magda from Uncle Karl's pretended wrath. "You've got all the pretty girls you need right here," Magda declared, and Mother said: "Now that's the gospel truth." Magda scolded Peter, who reached over her shoulder to sneak some popcorn. "Your brother and father aren't getting any." Uncle Karl wondered if they were going to have fireworks that night, what with the shortages. It wasn't the shortages, Mr M-- replied; Ocean City had fireworks from prewar. But it was too risky on account of the enemy submarines, some people thought.

"Don't seem like Fourth of July without fireworks," said Uncle Karl. The inverted tag in dialogue writing is still considered permissible with proper names or epithets, but sounds old-fashioned with personal pronouns. "We'll have 'em again soon enough," predicted the boys' father. Their mother declared she could do without fireworks: they reminded her too much of the real thing. Their father said all the more reason to shoot off a few now and again. Uncle Karl asked *rhetorically* who needed reminding, just look at people's hair and skin.

"The oil, yes," said Mrs. M--.

Ambrose had a pain in his stomach and so didn't swim but enjoyed watching the others. He and his father burned red easily. Magda's figure was exceedingly well developed for her age. She too declined to swim, and got mad, and became angry when Peter attempted to drag her into the pool. She always swam, he insisted; what did she mean not swim? Why did a person come to Ocean City?

"Maybe I want to lay here with Ambrose," Magda teased.

Nobody likes a pedant.

"Aha," said Mother. Peter grabbed Magda by one ankle and ordered Ambrose to grab the other. She squealed and rolled over on the beach blanket. Ambrose pretended to help hold her back. Her tan was darker than even Mother's and Peter's. "Help out, Uncle Karl!" Peter cried. Uncle Karl went to seize the other ankle. Inside the top of her swimsuit, however, you could see the line where the sunburn ended and, when she hunched her shoulders and squealed again, one nipple's auburn edge. Mother made them behave themselves. "*You* should certainly know," she said to Uncle Karl. Archly. "That when a lady says she doesn't feel like swimming, a gentleman doesn't ask questions." Uncle Karl said excuse *him*; Mother winked at Magda; Ambrose blushed; stupid Peter kept saying "Phooey on *feel like!*" and tugging at Magda's ankle; then even he got the point, and cannonballed with a holler into the pool.

"I swear," Magda said, in mock *in feigned* exasperation.

The diving would make a suitable literary symbol. To go off the high board you had to wait in a line along the poolside and up the ladder. Fellows tickled girls and goosed one another and shouted to the little ones at the top to hurry up, or razzed them for bellyfloppers. Once on the springboard some took a great while posing or clowning or deciding on a dive or getting up their nerve; others ran right off. Especially among the younger fellows the idea was to strike the funniest pose or do the craziest stunt as you fell, a thing that got harder to do as you kept on and on. But whether you hollered *Geromino!* or *Sieg heil!*, held your nose or "rode a bicycle," pretended to be shot or did a perfect jackknife or changed your mind halfway down and ended up with nothing, it was over in two seconds, after all that wait. Spring, pose, splash. Spring, neat-o, splash. Spring, aw fooey, splash.

The grown-ups had gone on; Ambrose wanted to converse with Magda; she was remarkably well developed for her age; it was said that that came from rubbing with a turkish towel, and there were other theories. Ambrose could think of nothing to say except how good a diver Peter was, who was showing off for her benefit. You could pretty well tell by looking at their bathing suits and arm muscles how far along the different fellows were. Ambrose was glad he hadn't gone in swimming, the cold water shrank you up so. Magda pretended to be uninterested in the diving; she probably weighed as much as he did. If you knew your way around in the funhouse like your own bedroom, you could wait until a girl came along and then slip away without ever getting caught, even if her boyfriend was right with her. She'd think *he* did it! It would be better to be the boyfriend, and act outraged, and tear the funhouse apart.

Not act; *be.*

"He's a master diver," Ambrose said. In feigned admiration. "You really have to slave away at it to get it that good." What would it matter anyhow if he asked her right out whether she remembered, even teased her with it as Peter would have?

There's no point in going farther; this isn't getting anybody anywhere; they haven't even come to the funhouse yet. Ambrose is off the track, in some new or old part of the place that's not supposed to be used; he strayed into it by some one-in-a-million chance, like the time the roller-coaster car left the tracks in the nineteen-teens against all the laws of physics and sailed over the boardwalk in the dark. And they can't locate him because they don't know where to look. Even the designer and operator have forgotten this other part, that winds around on itself like a whelk shell. That winds around the right part like the snakes on Mercury's caduceus. Some people, perhaps, don't "hit their stride" until their twenties, when the growing-up business is over and women appreciate other things besides wise-cracks and teasing and strutting. Peter didn't have one-tenth the imagination *he* had, not one-tenth. Peter did this naming-their-children thing as a joke, making up names like Aloysius and Murgatroyd, but Ambrose knew *exactly* how it would feel to be married and have children of your own, and be a loving husband and father, and go comfortably to work in the mornings and to bed with your wife at night, and wake up with her there. With a breeze coming through the sash and birds and mockingbirds singing in the Chinese-cigar trees. His eyes watered, there aren't enough ways to say that. He would be quite famous in his line of work. Whether Magda was his wife or not, one evening when he was wise-lined and gray at the temples he'd smile gravely, at a fashionable dinner party, and remind her of his youthful passion. The time they went with his family to Ocean City; the *erotic fantasies* he used to have about her. How long ago it seemed, and childish! Yet tender, too, *n'est-ce pas?* Would she have imagined that the world-famous whatever remembered how many strings were on the bench beside the girl on the label of the cigar box he'd stared at in the toolshed at age ten while she, age eleven. Even then he had felt *wise beyond his years;* he'd stroked her hair and said in his deepest voice and correctest English, as to a dear child: "I shall never forget this moment."

But though he had breathed heavily, groaned as if ecstatic, what he'd really felt throughout was an odd detachment, as though someone else were Master. Strive as he might to be transported, he heard his mind take notes upon the scene: *This is what they call* passion. *I am experiencing it.* Many of the digger machines were out of order in the penny arcades and could not be repaired or replaced for the duration. Moreover the prizes, made now in USA, were less interesting than formerly, pasteboard items for the most part, and some of the machines wouldn't work on white pennies. The gypsy fortune-teller machine might have provided a foreshadowing of the climax of this story if Ambrose had operated it. It was even dilapidateder than most: the silver coating was worn off the brown metal handles, the glass windows around the dummy were cracked and taped, her kerchiefs and silks long-faded. If a man lived by himself, he could take a department-store mannequin with flexible joints and modify her in certain ways. *However:* by the time he was that old he'd have a real woman. There was a machine that stamped your name around a white-metal coin with a star in the middle: *A*--. His son would be the second, and when the lad reached thirteen or so he would put a strong arm around his shoulder and tell him calmly: "It is perfectly normal. We have all been through it. It will not last forever." Nobody knew how to be what they were right. He'd smoke a pipe, teach his son how to fish and softcrab, assure him he needn't worry about himself. Magda would certainly give, Magda would certainly yield a great deal of milk, although guilty of occasional solecisms. It don't taste so bad. Suppose the lights came on now!

The day wore on. You think you're yourself, but there are other persons in you. Ambrose gets hard when Ambrose doesn't want to, *and obversely.* Ambrose watches them disagree; Ambrose watches him watch. In the funhouse mirror-room you can't see yourself go on forever, because no matter how you stand, your head gets in the way. Even if you had a glass periscope, the image of your eye would cover up the thing you really wanted to see. The police will come; there'll be a story in the papers. That must be where it happened. Unless he can find a surprise exit, an unofficial backdoor or escape hatch opening on an alley, say, and then stroll up to the family in front of the funhouse and ask where everybody's been; *he's* been out of the place for ages. That's just where it happened, in that last lighted room: Peter and Magda found the right exit; he found one that you weren't supposed to find and strayed off into the works somewhere. In a perfect funhouse you'd be able to go only one way, like the divers off the highboard; getting lost would be impossible; the doors and halls would work like minnow traps or the valves in veins.

On account of German U-boats, Ocean City was "browned-out": streetlights were shaded on the seaward side; shop-windows and boardwalk amusement places were kept dim, not to silhouette tankers and Liberty-ships for torpedoing. In a short story about Ocean City, Maryland, during World War II, the author could make use of the image of sailors on leave in the penny arcades and shooting galleries, sighting through the crosshairs of toy machine guns at swastika'd subs, while out in the black Atlantic a U-boat skipper squints through his periscope at real ships outlined by the glow of penny arcades. After dinner the family strolled back to the amusement end of the boardwalk. The boys' father had burnt red as always and was masked with Noxzema, a minstrel in reverse. The grownups stood at the end of the boardwalk where the Hurricane of '33 had cut an inlet from the ocean to Assawoman Bay.

"Pronounced with a long *o*," Uncle Karl reminded Magda with a wink. His shirt sleeves were rolled up; Mother punched his brown biceps with the arrowed heart on it and said his mind was naughty. Fat May's laugh came suddenly from the funhouse, as if she'd just got the joke; the family laughed too at the coincidence. Ambrose went under the boardwalk to search for out-of-town matchbook covers with the aid of his pocket flashlight; he looked out from the edge of the North American continent and wondered how far their laughter carried over the water. Spies in rubber rafts; survivors in lifeboats. If the joke had been beyond his understanding, he could have said *"The laughter was over his head."* And let the reader see the serious wordplay on second reading.

He turned the flashlight on and then off at once even before the woman whooped. He sprang away, heart athud, dropping the light. What had the man grunted? Perspiration drenched and chilled him by the time he scrambled up to the family. "See anything?" his father asked. His voice wouldn't come; he shrugged and violently brushed sand from his pants legs.

"Let's ride the old flying horses!" Magda cried. I'll never be an author. It's been forever already, everybody's gone home, Ocean City's deserted, the ghost-crabs are tickling across the beach and down the littered cold streets. And the empty halls of clapboard hotels and abandoned funhouses. A tidal wave; an enemy air raid; a monster-crab swelling like an island from the sea. *The inhabitants fled in terror.* Magda clung to his trouser leg; he alone knew the maze's secret. "He gave his life that we might live," said Uncle Karl with a scowl of pain, as he. The fellow's hands had been tattooed; the woman's legs, the woman's fat white legs had. *An astonishing coincidence.* He yearned to tell Peter. He wanted to throw up for excitement. They hadn't even chased him. He wished he were dead.

One possible ending would be to have Ambrose come across another lost person in the dark. They'd match their wits together against the funhouse, struggle like Ulysses past obstacle after obstacle, help and encourage each other. Or a girl. By the time they found the exit they'd be closest friends, sweethearts if it were a girl; they'd know each other's inmost souls, be bound together by *the cement of shared adventure;* then they'd emerge into the light and it would turn out that his friend was a Negro. A blind girl. President Roosevelt's son. Ambrose's former archenemy.

Shortly after the mirror room he'd groped along a musty corridor, his heart already misgiving him at the absence of phosphorescent arrows and other signs. He'd found a crack of light — not a door, it turned out, but a seam between the plyboard wall panels — and squinting up to it, espied a small old man, *in appearance not unlike* the photographs at home of Ambrose's late grandfather, nodding upon a stool beneath a bare, speckled bulb. A crude panel of toggle- and knife-switches hung beside the open fuse box near his head; elsewhere in the little room were wooden levers and ropes belayed to boat cleats. At the time, Ambrose wasn't lost enough to rap or call; later he couldn't find that crack. Now it seemed to him that he'd possibly dozed off for a few minutes somewhere along the way; certainly he was exhausted from the afternoon's sunshine and the evening's problems; he couldn't be sure he hadn't dreamed part or all of the sight. Had an old black wall fan droned like bees and shimmied two flypaper streamers? Had the funhouse operator — gentle, somewhat sad and tired-appearing, in expression not unlike the photographs at home of Ambrose's late Uncle Konrad — murmured in his sleep? Is there really such a person as Ambrose, or is he a figment of the author's imagination? Was it Assawoman Bay or Sinepuxent? Are there other errors of fact in this fiction? Was there another sound besides the little slap slap of thigh on ham, like water sucking at the chine-boards of a skiff?

When you're lost, the smartest thing to do is stay put till you're found, hollering if necessary. But to holler guarantees humiliation as well as rescue; keeping silent permits some saving of face — you can act surprised at the fuss when your rescuers find you and swear you weren't lost, if they do. What's more you might find your own way yet, *however belatedly.*

"Don't tell me your foot's still asleep!" Magda exclaimed as the three young people walked from the inlet to the area set aside for ferris wheels, carousels, and other carnival rides, they having decided in favor of the vast and ancient merry-go-round instead of the funhouse. What a sentence, everything was wrong from the outset. People don't know what to make of him, he doesn't know what to make of himself, he's only thirteen, *athletically and socially inept,* not astonishingly bright, but there are antennae; he has ... some sort of receivers in his head; things speak to him, he understands more than he should, the world winks at him through its objects, grabs grinning at his coat. Everybody else is in on some secret he doesn't know; they've forgotten to tell him. Through simple *procrastination* his mother put off his baptism until this year. Everyone else had it done as a baby; he'd assumed the same of himself, as had his mother, so she claimed, until it was time for him to join Grace Methodist-Protestant and the oversight came out. He was mortified, but pitched sleepless through his private catechizing, intimidated by the ancient mysteries, a thirteen year old would never say that, resolved to experience conversion like St. Augustine. When the water touched his brow and Adam's sin left him, he contrived by a strain like defecation to bring tears into his eyes — but felt nothing. There was some simple radical difference about him; he hoped it was genius, feared it was madness, devoted himself to amiability and inconspicuousness. Alone on the seawall near his house he was seized by the terrifying transports he'd thought to find in toolshed, in Communion-cup. The grass was alive! The town, the river, himself, were not imaginary; time roared in his ears like wind; the world was *going on!* This part ought to be dramatized. The Irish author James Joyce once wrote. Ambrose M-- is going to scream.

There is no *texture of rendered sensory detail,* for one thing. The faded distorting mirrors beside Fat May; the impossibility of choosing a mount when one had but a single ride on the great carrousel; the *vertigo attendant on his recognition* that Ocean City has worn out, the place of fathers and grandfathers, straw-boatered men and parasoled ladies survived by their amusements. Money spent, the three paused at Peter's insistence beside Fat May to watch the girls get their skirts blown up. The object was to tease Magda, who said: "I swear, Peter M--, you've got a one-track mind! Amby and me aren't *interested* in such things." In the tumbling-barrel, too, just inside the Devil's-mouth entrance to the funhouse, the girls were upended and their boyfriends and others could see up their dresses if they cared to. Which was the whole point, Ambrose realized. Of the entire funhouse! If you looked around, you noticed that almost all the people on the boardwalk were paired off into couples except the small children; in a way, that was the whole point of Ocean City! If you had X-ray eyes and could see everything going on at that instant under the boardwalk and in all the hotel rooms and cars and alleyways, you'd realize that all that normally *showed,* like restaurants and dance halls and clothing and test-your-strength machines, was merely preparation and intermission. Fat May screamed.

Because he watched the goings-on from the corner of his eye, it was Ambrose who spied the half-dollar on the boardwalk near the tumbling-barrel. Losers weepers. The first time he'd heard some people moving through a corridor not far away, just after he'd lost sight of a crack of light, he'd decided not to call to them, for fear they'd guess he was scared and poke fun; it sounded like roughnecks; he'd hoped they'd come by and he could follow in the dark without their knowing. Another time he'd heard just one person, unless he imagined it, bumping along as if on the other side of the plywood; perhaps Peter coming back for him, or Father, or Magda lost too. Or the owner and operator of the funhouse. He'd called out once, as though merrily: "Anybody know where the heck we are?" But the query was too stiff, his voice cracked, when the sounds stopped he was terrified: maybe it was a queer who waited for fellows to get lost, or a longhaired filthy monster that lived in some cranny of the funhouse. He stood rigid for hours it seemed like, scarcely respiring. His future was shockingly clear, in outline. He tried holding his breath to the point of unconsciousness. There ought to be a button you could push to end your life absolutely without pain; disappear in a flick, like turning out a light. He would push it instantly! He despised Uncle Karl. But he despised his father too, for not being what he was supposed to be. Perhaps his father hated *his* father, and so on, and his son would hate him, and so on. Instantly!

Naturally he didn't have nerve enough to ask Magda to go through the funhouse with him. With incredible nerve and to everyone's surprise he invited Magda, quietly and politely, to go through the funhouse with him. "I warn you, I've never been through it before," he added *laughing easily;* "but I reckon we can manage somehow. The important thing to remember, after all, is that it's meant to be a *fun*house; that is, a place of amusement. If people really got lost or injured or too badly frightened in it, the owner'd go out of business. There'd even be lawsuits. No character in a work of fiction can make a speech this long without interruption or acknowledgment from the other characters."

Mother teased Uncle Karl: "Three's a crowd, I always heard." But actually Ambrose was relieved that Peter now had a quarter too. Nothing was what it looked like. Every instant, under the surface of the Atlantic Ocean, millions of living animals devoured one another. Pilots were falling in flames over Europe; women were being forcibly raped in the South Pacific. His father should have taken him aside and said: "There is a simple secret to getting through the funhouse, as simple as being first to see the Towers. Here it is. Peter does not know it; neither does your Uncle Karl. You and I are different. Not surprisingly, you've often wished you weren't. Don't think I haven't noticed how unhappy your childhood has been! But you'll understand, when I tell you, why it had to be kept secret until now. And you won't regret not being like your brother and your uncle. *On the contrary!"* If you knew all the stories behind all the people on the boardwalk, you'd see that *nothing* was what it looked like. Husbands and wives often hated each other; parents didn't necessarily love their children; et cetera. A child took things for granted because he had nothing to compare his life to and everybody acted as if things were as they should be. Therefore each saw himself as the hero of the story, when the truth might turn out to be that he's the villain, or the coward. And there wasn't one thing you could do about it!

Hunchbacks, fat ladies, fools — that no one chose what he was was unbearable. In the movies he'd meet a beautiful young girl in the funhouse; they'd have hairs-breadth escapes from real dangers; he'd do and say the right things; she also; in the end they'd be lovers; their dialogue lines would match up; he'd be perfectly at ease; she'd not only like him well enough, she'd think he was *marvelous;* she'd lie awake thinking about *him,* instead of vice versa — the way *his* face looked in different lights and how he stood and exactly what he'd said — and yet that would be only one small episode in his wonderful life, among many many others. Not a *turning point* at all. What had happened in the toolshed was nothing. He hated, he loathed his parents! One reason for not writing a lost-in-the-funhouse story is that either everybody's felt what Ambrose feels, in which case it goes without saying, or else no normal person feels such things, in which case Ambrose is a freak. "Is anything more tiresome, in fiction, than the problems of sensitive adolescents?" And it's all too long and rambling, as if the author. For all a person knows the first time through, the end could be just around any corner; perhaps *not impossibly* it's been within reach any number of times. On the other hand he may be scarcely past the start, with everything yet to get through, an intolerable idea.

Fill in: His father's raised eyebrows when he announced his decision to do the funhouse with Magda. Ambrose understands now, but didn't then, that his father was wondering whether he knew what the funhouse was *for* — especially since he didn't object, as he should have, when Peter decided to come along too. The ticket-woman, witchlike, mortifying him when inadvertently he gave her his name-coin instead of the half-dollar, then unkindly calling Magda's attention to the birthmark on his temple: "Watch out for him girlie, he's a marked man!" She wasn't even cruel, he understood, only vulgar and insensitive. Somewhere in the world there was a young woman with such splendid understanding that she'd see him entire, like a poem or story, and find his words so valuable after all that when he confessed his apprehensions she would explain why they were in fact the very things that made him precious to her ... and to Western Civilization! There was no such girl, the simple truth being. Violent yawns as they approached the mouth. Whispered advice from an old-timer on a bench near the barrel: "Go crabwise and ye'll get an eyeful without upsetting!" Composure vanished at the first pitch: Peter hollered joyously, Magda tumbled, shrieked, clutched her skirt; Ambrose scrambled crabwise, tight-lipped with terror, was soon out, watched his dropped name-coin slide among the couples. Shame-faced he saw that to get through expeditiously was not the point; Peter feigned assistance in order to trip Magda up, shouted "I see Christmas!" when her legs went flying. The old man, his latest betrayer, cackled approval. A dim hall then of black-thread cobwebs and recorded gibber: he took Magda's elbow to steady her against revolving discs set in the slanted floor to throw your feet out from under, and explained to her in a calm, deep voice his theory that each phase of the funhouse was triggered either automatically, by a series of photoelectric devices, or else manually by operators stationed at peepholes. But he lost his voice thrice as the discs unbalanced him; Magda was anyhow squealing; but at one point she clutched him about the waist to keep from falling, and her right cheek pressed for a moment against his belt-buckle. Heroically he drew her up, it was his chance to clutch her close as if for support and say: "I love you." He even put an arm lightly about the small of her back before a sailor-and-girl pitched into them from behind, sorely treading his left big toe and knocking Magda asprawl with them. The sailor's girl was a string-haired hussy with a loud laugh and light blue drawers; Ambrose realized that he wouldn't have said "I love you" anyhow, and was smitten with self-contempt. How much better it would be to be that common sailor! A wiry little Seaman 3rd, the fellow squeezed a girl to each side and stumbled hilarious into the mirror room, closer to Magda in thirty seconds than Ambrose had got in thirteen years. She giggled at something the fellow said to Peter; she drew her hair from her eyes with a movement so womanly it struck Ambrose's heart; Peter's smacking her backside then seemed particularly coarse. But Magda made a pleased indignant face and cried, "All right for *you*, mister!" and pursued Peter into the maze without a backward glance. The sailor followed after, leisurely, drawing his girl against his hip; Ambrose understood not only that they were all so relieved to be rid of his burdensome company that they didn't even notice his absence, but that he himself shared their relief. Stepping from the treacherous passage at last into the mirror-maze, he saw once again, more clearly than ever, how readily he deceived himself into supposing he was a person. He even foresaw, wincing at his dreadful self-knowledge, that he would repeat the deception, at ever-rarer intervals, all his wretched life, so fearful were the alternatives. Fame, madness, suicide; perhaps all three. It's not believable that so young a boy could articulate that reflection, and in fiction the merely true must always yield to the plausible. Moreover, the symbolism is in places heavy-footed. Yet Ambrose M-- understood, as few adults do, that the famous loneliness of the great was no popular myth but a general truth — furthermore, that it was as much cause as effect.

All the preceding except the last few sentences is exposition that should've been done earlier or interspersed with the present action instead of lumped together. No reader would put up with so much with such *prolixity.* It's interesting that Ambrose's father, though presumably an intelligent man (as indicated by his role as grade-school principal), neither encouraged nor discouraged his sons at all in any way — as if he either didn't care about them or cared all right but didn't know how to act. If this fact should contribute to one of them's becoming a celebrated but wretchedly unhappy scientist, was it a good thing or not? He too might someday face the question; it would be useful to know whether it had tortured his father for years, for example, or never once crossed his mind.

In the maze two important things happened. First, our hero found a name-coin someone else had lost or discarded: *AMBROSE*, suggestive of the famous lightship and of his late grandfather's favorite dessert, which his mother used to prepare on special occasions out of coconut, oranges, grapes, and what else. Second, as he wondered at the endless replication of his image in the mirrors, second, as he *lost himself in the reflection* that the necessity for an observer makes perfect observation impossible, better make him eighteen at least, yet that would render other things unlikely, he heard Peter and Magda chuckling somewhere together in the maze. "Here!" "No, here!" they shouted to each other; Peter said, "Where's Amby?" Magda murmured. "Amb?" Peter called. In a pleased, friendly voice. He didn't reply. The truth was, his brother was a *happy-go-lucky youngster* who'd've been better off with a regular brother of his own, but who seldom complained of his lot and was generally cordial. Ambrose's throat ached; there aren't enough different ways to say that. He stood quietly while the two young people giggled and thumped through the glittering maze, hurrah'd their discovery of its exit, cried out in joyful alarm at what next beset them. Then he set his mouth and followed after, as he supposed, took a wrong turn, strayed into the pass *wherein he lingers yet.*

The action of conventional dramatic narrative may be represented by a diagram called Freitag's Triangle:

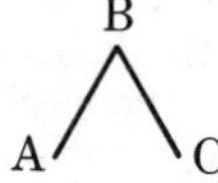

or more accurately by a variant of that diagram:

A B C D

in which *AB* represents the exposition, *B* the introduction of conflict, *BC* the "rising action," complication, or development of the conflict, *C* the climax, or turn of the action, *CD* the dénouement, or resolution of the conflict. While there is no reason to regard this pattern as an absolute necessity, like many other conventions it became conventional because great numbers of people over many years learned by trial and error that it was effective; one ought not to forsake it, therefore, unless one wishes to forsake as well the effect of drama or has clear cause to feel that deliberate violation of the "normal" pattern can better can better effect that effect. This can't go on much longer; it can go on forever. He died telling stories to himself in the dark; years later, when that vast unsuspected area of the funhouse came to light, the first expedition found his skeleton in one of its labyrinthine corridors and mistook it for part of the entertainment. He died of starvation telling himself stories in the dark; but unbeknownst unbeknownst to him, an assistant operator of the funhouse, happening to overhear him, crouched just behind the plyboard partition and wrote down his every word. The operator's daughter, an exquisite young woman with a figure unusually well developed for her age, crouched just behind the partition and transcribed his every word. Though she had never laid eyes on him, she recognized that here was one of Western Culture's truly great imaginations, the eloquence of whose suffering would be an inspiration to unnumbered. And her heart was torn between her love for the misfortunate young man (yes, she loved him, though she had never laid though she knew him only — but how well! — through his words, and the deep, calm voice in which he spoke them) between her love et cetera and her womanly intuition that only in suffering and isolation could he give voice et cetera. Lone dark dying. Quietly she kissed the rough plyboard, and a tear fell upon the page. Where she had written in shorthand *Where she had written in shorthand* Where she had written in shorthand *Where she* et cetera. A long time ago we should have passed the apex of Freitag's Triangle and made brief work of the *dénouement;* the plot doesn't rise by meaningful steps but winds upon itself, digresses, retreats, hesitates, sighs, collapses, expires. The climax of the story must be its protagonist's discovery of a way to get through the funhouse. But he has found none, may have ceased to search.

What relevance does the war have to the story? Should there be fireworks outside or not?

Ambrose wandered, languished, dozed. Now and then he fell into his habit of rehearsing to himself the unadventurous story of his life, narrated from the third-person point of view, from his earliest memory parenthesis of maple leaves stirring in the summer breath of tidewater Maryland end of parenthesis to the present moment. Its principal events, on this telling, would appear to have been *A, B, C,* and *D*.

He imagined himself years hence, successful, married, at ease in the world, the trials of his adolescence far behind him. He has come to the seashore with his family for the holiday: how Ocean City has changed! But at one seldom at one ill-frequented end of the boardwalk a few derelict amusements survive from times gone by: the great carrousel from the turn of the century, with its monstrous griffins and mechanical concert band; the roller coaster rumored since 1916 to have been condemned; the mechanical shooting gallery in which only the image of our enemies changed. His own son laughs with Fat May and wants to know what a funhouse is; Ambrose hugs the sturdy lad close and smiles around his pipestem at his wife.

The family's going home. Mother sits between Father and Uncle Karl, who teases him good-naturedly who chuckles over the fact that the comrade with whom he'd fought his way shoulder to shoulder through the funhouse had turned out to be a blind Negro girl — to their mutual discomfort, as they'd opened their souls. But such are the walls of custom, which even. Whose arm is where? How must it feel. He dreams of a funhouse vaster by far than any yet constructed; but by then they may be out of fashion, like steamboats and excursion trains. Already quaint and seedy: the draperied ladies on the frieze of the carrousel are his father's father's mooncheeked dreams; if he thinks of it more he will vomit his apple-on-a stick.

He wonders: will he become a regular person? Something has gone wrong; his vaccination didn't take; at the Boy-Scout initiation camp-fire he only pretended to be deeply moved, as he pretends to this hour that it is not so bad after all in the funhouse, and that he has a little limp. How long will it last? He envisions a truly astonishing funhouse, incredibly complex yet utterly controlled from a great central switchboard like the console of a pipe organ. Nobody had enough imagination. He could design such a place himself, wiring and all, and he's only thirteen years old. He would be its operator: panel lights would show what was up in every cranny of its cunning of its multifarious vastness; a switch-flick would ease this fellow's way, complicate that's, to balance things out; if anyone seemed lost or frightened, all the operator had to do was.

He wishes he had never entered the funhouse. But he has. Then he wishes he were dead. But he's not. Therefore he will construct funhouses for others and be their secret operator — though he would rather be among the lovers for whom funhouses are designed.

DONALD BARTHELME

The Balloon

The balloon, beginning at a point on Fourteenth Street, the exact location of which I cannot reveal, expanded northward all one night, while people were sleeping, until it reached the Park. There, I stopped it; at dawn the northernmost edges lay over the Plaza; the free-hanging motion was frivolous and gentle. But experiencing a faint irritation at stopping, even to protect the trees, and seeing no reason the balloon should not be allowed to expand upward, over the parts of the city it was already covering, into the "air space" to be found there, I asked the engineers to see to it. This expansion took place throughout the morning, soft imperceptible sighing of gas through the valves. The balloon then covered forty-five blocks north-south and an irregular area east-west, as many as six crosstown blocks on either side of the Avenue in some places. That was the situation, then.

But it is wrong to speak of "situations," implying sets of circumstances leading to some resolution, some escape of tension; there were no situations, simply the balloon hanging there — muted heavy grays and browns for the most part, contrasting with walnut and soft yellows. A deliberate lack of finish, enhanced by skillful installation, gave the surface a rough, forgotten quality; sliding weights on the inside, carefully adjusted, anchored the great, vari-shaped mass at a number of points. Now we have had a flood of original ideas in all media, works of singular beauty as well as significant milestones in the history of inflation, but at that moment there was only *this balloon*, concrete particular, hanging there.

There were reactions. Some people found the balloon "interesting." As a response this seemed inadequate to the immensity of the balloon, the suddenness of its appearance over the city; on the other hand, in the absence of hysteria or other societally-induced anxiety, it must be judged a calm, "mature" one. There was a certain amount of initial argumentation about the "meaning" of the balloon; this subsided, because we have learned not to insist on meanings, and they are rarely even looked for now, except in cases involving the simplest, safest phenomena. It was agreed that since the meaning of the balloon could never be known absolutely, extended discussion was pointless, or at least less purposeful than the activities of those who, for example, hung green and blue paper lanterns from the warm gray underside, in certain streets, or seized the occasion to write messages on the surface, announcing their availability for the performance of unnatural acts, or the availability of acquaintances.

Daring children jumped, especially at those points where the balloon hovered close to a building, so that the gap between balloon and building was a matter of a few inches, or points where the balloon actually made contact, exerting an ever-so-slight pressure against the side of a building, so that balloon and building seemed a unity. The upper surface was so structured that a "landscape" was presented, small valleys as well as slight knolls, or mounds; once atop the balloon, a stroll was possible, or even a trip, from one place to another. There was pleasure in being able to run down an incline, then up the opposing slope, both gently graded, or in making a leap from one side to the other. Bouncing was possible, because of the pneumaticity of the surface, and even falling, if that was your wish. That all these varied motions, as well as others, were within one's possibilities, in experiencing the "up" side of the balloon, was extremely exciting for children, accustomed to the city's flat, hard skin. But the purpose of the balloon was not to amuse children.

Too, the number of people, children and adults, who took advantage of the opportunities described was not so large as it might have been: a certain timidity, lack of trust in the balloon, was seen. There was, furthermore, some hostility. Because we had hidden the pumps, which fed helium to the interior, and because the surface was so vast that the authorities could not determine the point of entry — that is, the point at which the gas was injected — a degree of frustration was evidenced by those city officers into whose province such manifestations normally fell. The apparent purposelessness of the balloon was vexing (as was the fact that it was "there" at all). Had we painted, in great letters, "LABORATORY TESTS PROVE" or "18% MORE EFFECTIVE" on the sides of the balloon, this difficulty would have been circumvented. But I could not bear to do so. On the whole, these officers were remarkably tolerant, considering the dimensions of the anomaly, this tolerance being the result of, first, secret tests conducted by night that convinced them that little or nothing could be done in the way of removing or destroying the balloon, and, secondly, a public warmth that arose (not uncolored by touches of the aforementioned hostility) toward the balloon, from ordinary citizens.

As a single balloon must stand for a lifetime of thinking about balloons, so each citizen expressed, in the attitude he chose, a complex of attitudes. One man might consider that the balloon had to do with the notion *sullied*, as in the sentence *The big balloon sullied the otherwise clear and radiant Manhattan sky.* That is, the balloon was, in this man's view, an imposture, something inferior to the sky that had formerly been there, something interposed between the people and their "sky." But in fact it was January, the sky was dark and ugly; it was not a sky you could look up into, lying on your back in the street, with pleasure, unless pleasure, for you, proceeded from having been threatened, from having been misused. And the underside of the balloon was a pleasure to look up into, we had seen to that, muted grays and browns for the most part, contrasted with walnut and soft, forgotten yellows. And so, while this man was thinking *sullied*, still there was an admixture of pleasurable cognition in his thinking, struggling with the original perception.

Another man, on the other hand, might view the balloon as if it were part of a system of unanticipated rewards, as when one's employer walks in and says, "Here, Henry, take this package of money I have wrapped for you, because we have been doing so well in the business here, and I admire the way you bruise the tulips, without which bruising your department would not be a success, or at least not the success that it is." For this man the balloon might be a brilliantly heroic "muscle and pluck" experience, even if an experience poorly understood.

Another man might say, "Without the example of——, it is doubtful that——would exist today in its present form," and find many to agree with him, or to argue with him. Ideas of "bloat" and "float" were introduced, as well as concepts of dream and responsibility. Others engaged in remarkably detailed fantasies having to do with a wish either to lose themselves in the balloon, or to engorge it. The private character of these wishes, of their origins, deeply buried and unknown, was such that they were not much spoken of; yet there is evidence that they were widespread. It was also argued that what was important was what you felt when you stood under the balloon; some people claimed that they felt sheltered, warmed, as never before, while enemies of the balloon felt, or reported feeling, constrained, a "heavy" feeling.

Critical opinion was divided:

"monstrous pourings"

"harp"

XXXXXXX "certain contrasts with darker portions"

"inner joy"

"large, square corners"

"conservative eclecticism that has so far governed modern balloon design"

::::::: "abnormal vigor"

"warm, soft, lazy passages"

"Has unity been sacrificed for a sprawling quality?"

"Quelle catastrophe!"

"munching"

People began, in a curious way, to locate themselves in relation to aspects of the balloon: "I'll be at that place where it dips down into Forty-seventh Street almost to the sidewalk, near the Alamo Chile House," or, "Why don't we go stand on top, and take the air, and maybe walk about a bit, where it forms a tight, curving line with the façade of the Gallery of Modern Art — " Marginal intersections offered entrances within a given time duration, as well as "warm, soft, lazy passages" in which ... But it is wrong to speak of "marginal intersections," each intersection was crucial, none could be ignored (as if, walking there, you might not find someone capable of turning your attention, in a flash, from old exercises to new exercises, risks and escalations). Each intersection was crucial, meeting of balloon and building, meeting of balloon and man, meeting of balloon and balloon.

It was suggested that what was admired about the balloon was finally this: that it was not limited, or defined. Sometimes a bulge, blister, or subsection would carry all the way east to the river on its own initiative, in the manner of an army's movements on a map, as seen in a headquarters remote from the fighting. Then that part would be, as it were, thrown back again, or would withdraw into new dispositions; the next morning, that part would have made another sortie, or disappeared altogether. This ability of the balloon to shift its shape, to change, was very pleasing, especially to people whose lives were rather rigidly patterned, persons to whom change, although desired, was not available. The balloon, for the twenty-two days of its existence, offered the possibility, in its randomness, of mislocation of the self, in contradistinction to the grid of precise, rectangular pathways under our feet. The amount of specialized training currently needed, and the consequent desirability of long-term commitments, has been occasioned by the steadily growing importance of complex machinery, in virtually all kinds of operations; as this tendency increases, more and more people will turn, in bewildered inadequacy, to solutions for which the balloon may stand as a prototype, or "rough draft."

I met you under the balloon, on the occasion of your return from Norway; you asked if it was mine; I said it was. The balloon, I said, is a spontaneous autobiographical disclosure, having to do with the unease I felt at your absence, and with sexual deprivation, but now that your visit to Bergen has been terminated, it is no longer necessary or appropriate. Removal of the balloon was easy; trailer trucks carried away the depleted fabric, which is now stored in West Virginia, awaiting some other time of unhappiness, sometime, perhaps, when we are angry with one another.

SAUL BELLOW

Looking for Mr. Green

Whatsoever thy hand findeth to do,
do it with thy might....

Hard work? No, it wasn't really so hard. He wasn't used to walking and stair-climbing, but the physical difficulty of his new job was not what George Grebe felt most. He was delivering relief checks in the Negro district, and although he was a native Chicagoan this was not a part of the city he knew much about — it needed a depression to introduce him to it. No, it wasn't literally hard work, not as reckoned in foot-pounds, but yet he was beginning to feel the strain of it, to grow aware of its peculiar difficulty. He could find the streets and numbers, but the clients were not where they were supposed to be, and he felt like a hunter inexperienced in the camouflage of his game. It was an unfavorable day, too — fall, and cold, dark weather, windy. But, anyway, instead of shells in his deep trenchcoat pocket he had the cardboard of checks, punctured for the spindles of the file, the holes reminding him of the holes in player-piano paper. And he didn't look much like a hunter, either; his was a city figure entirely, belted up in his Irish conspirator's coat. He was slender without being tall, stiff in the back, his legs looking shabby in a pair of old tweed pants gone through and fringy at the cuffs. With this stiffness, he kept his head forward, so that his face was red from the sharpness of the weather; and it was an indoors sort of face with gray eyes that persisted in some kind of thought and yet seemed to avoid definiteness of conclusion. He wore sideburns that surprised you somewhat by the tough curl of the blond hair and the effect of assertion in their length. He was not so mild as he looked, nor so youthful; and nevertheless there was no effort on his part to seem what he was not. He was an educated man; he was a bachelor; he was in some ways simple; without lushing, he liked a drink; his luck had not been good. Nothing was deliberately hidden.

He felt that his luck was better than usual today. When he had reported for work that morning he had expected to be shut up in the relief office at a clerk's job, for he had been hired downtown as a clerk, and he was glad to have, instead, the freedom of the streets and welcomed, at least at first, the vigor of the cold and even the blowing of the hard wind. But on the other hand he was not getting on with the distribution of the checks. It was true that it was a city job; nobody expected you to push too hard at a city job. His supervisor, that young Mr. Raynor, had practically told him that. Still, he wanted to do well at it. For one thing, when he knew how quickly he could deliver a batch of checks, he would know also how much time he could expect to clip for himself. And then, too, the clients would be waiting for their money. That was not the most important consideration, though it certainly mattered to him. No, but he wanted to do well, simply for doing-well's sake, to acquit himself decently of a job because he so rarely had a job to do that required just this sort of energy. Of this peculiar energy he now had a superabundance; once it had started to flow, it flowed all too heavily. And, for the time being anyway, he was balked. He could not find Mr. Green.

So he stood in his big-skirted trenchcoat with a large envelope in his hand and papers showing from his pocket, wondering why people should be so hard to locate who were too feeble or sick to come to the station to collect their own checks. But Raynor had told him that tracking them down was not so easy at first and had offered him some advice on how to proceed. "If you can see the postman, he's your first man to ask, and your best bet. If you can't connect with him, try the stores and tradespeople around. Then the janitor and the neighbors. But you'll find the closer you come to your man the less people will tell you. They don't want to tell you anything."

"Because I'm a stranger."

"Because you're white. We ought to have a Negro doing this, but we don't at the moment, and of course you've got to eat, too, and this is public employment. Jobs have to be made. Oh, that holds for me too. Mind you, I'm not letting myself out. I've got three years of seniority on you, that's all. And a law degree. Otherwise, you might be back of the desk and I might be going out into the field this cold day. The same dough pays us both and for the same, exact, identical reason. What's my law degree got to do with it? But you have to pass out these checks, Mr. Grebe, and it'll help if you're stubborn, so I hope you are."

"Yes, I'm fairly stubborn."

Raynor sketched hard with an eraser in the old dirt of his desk, left-handed, and said, "Sure, what else can you answer to such a question. Anyhow, the trouble you're going to have is that they don't like to give information about anybody. They think you're a plain-clothes dick or an installment collector, or summons-server or something like that. Till you've been seen around the neighborhood for a few months and people know you're only from the relief."

It was dark, ground-freezing, pre-Thanksgiving weather; the wind played hob with the smoke, rushing it down, and Grebe missed his gloves, which he had left in Raynor's office. And no one would admit knowing Green. It was past three o'clock and the postman had made his last delivery. The nearest grocer, himself a Negro, had never heard the name Tulliver Green, or said he hadn't. Grebe was inclined to think that it was true, that he had in the end convinced the man that he wanted only to deliver a check. But he wasn't sure. He needed experience in interpreting looks and signs and, even more, the will not to be put off or denied and even the force to bully if need be. If the grocer did know, he had got rid of him easily. But since most of his trade was with reliefers, why should he prevent the delivery of a check? Maybe Green, or Mrs. Green, if there was a Mrs. Green, patronized another grocer. And was there a Mrs. Green? It was one of Grebe's great handicaps that he hadn't looked at any of the case records. Raynor should have let him read files for a few hours. But he apparently saw no need for that, probably considering the job unimportant. Why prepare systematically to deliver a few checks?

But now it was time to look for the janitor. Grebe took in the building in the wind and gloom of the late November day — trampled, frost-hardened lots on one side; on the other an automobile junk yard and then the infinite work of Elevated frames, weak-looking, gaping with rubbish fires; two sets of leaning brick porches three stories high and a flight of cement stairs to the cellar. Descending, he entered the underground passage, where he tried the doors until one opened and he found himself in the furnace room. There someone rose toward him and approached, scraping on the coal grit and bending under the canvas-jacketed pipes.

"Are you the janitor?"

"What do you want?"

"I'm looking for a man who's supposed to be living here. Green."

"What Green?"

"Oh, you maybe have more than one Green?" said Grebe with new, pleasant hope. "This is Tulliver Green."

"I don't think I c'n help you, mister. I don't know any."

"A crippled man."

The janitor stood bent before him. Could it be that he was crippled? Oh, God! what if he was. Grebe's gray eyes sought with excited difficulty to see. But no, he was only very short and stooped. A head awakened from meditation, a strong-haired beard, low, wide shoulders. A staleness of sweat and coal rose from his black shirt and the burlap sack he wore as an apron.

"Crippled how?"

Grebe thought and then answered with the light voice of unmixed candor, "I don't know. I've never seen him." This was damaging, but his only other choice was to make a lying guess, and he was not up to it. "I'm delivering checks for the relief to shut-in cases. If he weren't crippled he'd come to collect himself. That's why I said crippled. Bed-ridden, chair-ridden — is there anybody like that?"

This sort of frankness was one of Grebe's oldest talents, going back to childhood. But it gained him nothing here.

"No suh. I've got four buildin's same as this that I take care of. I don' know all the tenants, leave alone the tenants' tenants. The rooms turn over so fast, people movin' in and out every day. I can't tell you."

The janitor opened his grimy lips but Grebe did not hear him in the piping of the valves and the consuming pull of air to flame in the body of the furnace. He knew, however, what he had said.

"Well, all the same, thanks. Sorry I bothered you. I'll prowl around upstairs again and see if I can turn up someone who knows him."

Once more in the cold air and early darkness he made the short circle from the cellarway to the entrance crowded between the brickwork pillars and began to climb to the third floor. Pieces of plaster ground under his feet; strips of brass tape from which the carpeting had been torn away marked old boundaries at the sides. In the passage, the cold reached him worse than in the street; it touched him to the bone. The hall toilets ran like springs. He thought grimly as he heard the wind burning around the building with a sound like that of the furnace, that this was a great piece of constructed shelter. Then he struck a match in the gloom and searched for names and numbers among the writings and scribbles on the walls. He saw WHOODY-DOODY GO TO JESUS, and zigzags, caricatures, sexual scrawls, and curses. So the sealed rooms of pyramids were also decorated, and the caves of human dawn.

The information on his card was, TULLIVER GREEN — APT 3D. There were no names, however, and no numbers. His shoulders drawn up, tears of cold in his eyes, breathing vapor, he went the length of the corridor and told himself that if he had been lucky enough to have the temperament for it he would bang on one of the doors and bawl out "Tulliver Green!" until he got results. But it wasn't in him to make an uproar and he continued to burn matches, passing the light over the walls. At the rear, in a corner of the hall, he discovered a door he had not seen before and he thought it best to investigate. It sounded empty when he knocked, but a young Negress answered, hardly more than a girl. She opened only a bit, to guard the warmth of the room.

"Yes suh?"

"I'm from the district relief station on Prairie Avenue. I'm looking for a man named Tulliver Green to give him his check. Do you know him?"

No, she didn't; but he thought she had not understood anything of what he had said. She had a dream-bound, dream-blind face, very soft and black, shut off. She wore a man's jacket and pulled the ends together at her throat. Her hair was parted in three directions, at the sides and transversely, standing up at the front in a dull puff.

"Is there somebody around here who might know?"

"I jus' taken this room las' week."

He observed that she shivered, but even her shiver was somnambulistic and there was no sharp consciousness of cold in the big smooth eyes of her handsome face.

"All right, miss, thank you. Thanks," he said, and went to try another place.

Here he was admitted. He was grateful, for the room was warm. It was full of people, and they were silent as he entered — ten people, or a dozen, perhaps more, sitting on benches like a parliament. There was no light, properly speaking, but a tempered darkness that the window gave, and everyone seemed to him enormous, the men padded out in heavy work clothes and winter coats, and the women huge, too, in their sweaters, hats, and old furs. And, besides, bed and bedding, a black cooking range, a piano piled towering to the ceiling with papers, a dining-room table of the old style of prosperous Chicago. Among these people Grebe, with his cold-heightened fresh color and his smaller stature, entered like a schoolboy. Even though he was met with smiles and good will, he knew, before a single word was spoken, that all the currents ran against him and that he would make no headway. Nevertheless he began. "Does anybody here know how I can deliver a check to Mr. Tulliver Green?"

"Green?" It was the man that had let him in who answered. He was in short sleeves, in a checkered shirt, and had a queer, high head, profusely overgrown and long as a shako; the veins entered it strongly from his forehead. "I never heard mention of him. Is this where he live?"

"This is the address they gave me at the station. He's a sick man, and he'll need his check. Can't anybody tell me where to find him?"

He stood his ground and waited for a reply, his crimson wool scarf wound about his neck and drooping outside his trenchcoat, pockets weighted with the block of checks and official forms. They must have realized that he was not a college boy employed afternoons by a bill collector, trying foxily to pass for a relief clerk, recognized that he was an older man who knew himself what need was, who had had more than an average seasoning in hardship. It was evident enough if you looked at the marks under his eyes and at the sides of his mouth.

"Anybody know this sick man?"

"No suh." On all sides he saw heads shaken and smiles of denial. No one knew. And maybe it was true, he considered, standing silent in the earthen, musky human gloom of the place as the rumble continued. But he could never really be sure.

"What's the matter with this man?" said shakohead.

"I've never seen him. All I can tell you is that he can't come in person for his money. It's my first day in this district."

"Maybe they given you the wrong number?"

"I don't believe so. But where else can I ask about him?" He felt that this persistence amused them deeply, and in a way he shared their amusement that he should stand up so tenaciously to them. Though smaller, though slight, he was his own man, he retracted nothing about himself, and he looked back at them, gray-eyed, with amusement and also with a sort of courage. On the bench some man spoke in his throat, the words impossible to catch, and a woman answered with a wild, shrieking laugh, which was quickly cut off.

"Well, so nobody will tell me?"

"Ain't nobody who knows."

"At least, if he lives here, he pays rent to someone. Who manages the building?"

"Greatham Company. That's on Thirty-ninth Street."

Grebe wrote it in his pad. But, in the street again, a sheet of wind-driven paper clinging to his leg while he deliberated what direction to take next, it seemed a feeble lead to follow. Probably this Green didn't rent a flat, but a room. Sometimes there were as many as twenty people in an apartment; the real-estate agent would know only the lessee. And not even the agent could tell you who the renters were. In some places the beds were even used in shifts, watchmen or jitney drivers or short-order cooks in night joints turning out after a day's sleep and surrendering their beds to a sister, a nephew, or perhaps a stranger, just off the bus. There were large numbers of newcomers in this terrific, blight-bitten portion of the city between Cottage Grove and Ashland, wandering from house to house and room to room. When you saw them, how could you know them? They didn't carry bundles on their backs or look picturesque. You only saw a man, a Negro, walking in the street or riding in the car, like everyone else, with his thumb closed on a transfer. And therefore how were you supposed to tell? Grebe thought the Greatham agent would only laugh at his question.

But how much it would have simplified the job

to be able to say that Green was old, or blind, or consumptive. An hour in the files, taking a few notes, and he needn't have been at such a disadvantage. When Raynor gave him the block of checks he asked, "How much should I know about these people?" Then Raynor had looked as though he were preparing to accuse him of trying to make the job more important than it was. He smiled, because by then they were on fine terms, but nevertheless he had been getting ready to say something like that when the confusion began in the station over Staika and her children.

Grebe had waited a long time for this job. It came to him through the pull of an old schoolmate in the Corporation Counsel's office, never a close friend, but suddenly sympathetic and interested — pleased to show, moreover, how well he had done, how strongly he was coming on even in these miserable times. Well, he was coming through strongly, along with the Democratic administration itself. Grebe had gone to see him in City Hall, and they had had a counter lunch or beers at least once a month for a year and finally it had been possible to swing the job. He didn't mind being assigned the lowest clerical grade, nor even being a messenger, though Raynor thought he did.

This Raynor was an original sort of guy and Grebe had taken to him immediately. As was proper on the first day, Grebe had come early, but he waited long, for Raynor was late. At last he darted into his cubicle of an office as though he had just jumped from one of those hurtling huge red Indian Avenue cars. His thin, rough face was wind-stung and he was grinning and saying something breathlessly to himself. In his hat, a small fedora, and his coat, the velvet collar a neat fit about his neck, and his silk muffler that set off the nervous twist of his chin, he swayed and turned himself in his swivel chair, feet leaving the ground; so that he pranced a little as he sat. Meanwhile he took Grebe's measure out of his eyes, eyes of an unusual vertical length and slightly sardonic. So the two men sat for a while, saying nothing, while the supervisor raised his hat from his miscombed hair and put it in his lap. His cold-darkened hands were not clean. A steel beam passed through the little makeshift room, from which machine belts once had hung. The building was an old factory.

"I'm younger than you; I hope you won't find it hard taking orders from me," said Raynor. "But I don't make them up, either. You're how old, about?"

"Thirty-five."

"And you thought you'd be inside doing paper work. But it so happens I have to send you out."

"I don't mind."

"And it's mostly a Negro load we have in this district."

"So. I thought it would be."

"Fine. You'll get along. *C'est un bon boulot.* Do you know French?"

"Some."

"I thought you'd be a university man."

"Have you been in France?" said Grebe.

"No, that's the French of the Berlitz School. I've been at it for more than a year, just as I'm sure people have been, all over the world, office boys in China and braves in Tanganyika. In fact, I damn well know it. Such is the attractive power of civilization. It's overrated, but what do you want? *Que voulez-vous?* I get *Le Rire* and all the spicy papers, just like in Tanganyika. It must be mystifying, out there. But my reason is that I'm aiming at the diplomatic service. I have a cousin who's a courier, and the way he describes it is awfully attractive. He rides the *wagon-lits* and reads books. While we — What did you do before?"

"I sold."

"Where?"

"Canned meat at Stop and Shop. In the basement."

"And before that?"

"Window shades, at Goldblatt's."

"Steady work?"

"No. Thursdays and Saturdays. I also sold shoes."

"You've been a shoe-dog too. Well. And prior to that? Here it is in your folder." He opened the record. "Saint Olaf's College, instructor in classical languages. Fellow, University of Chicago, 1926-27. I've had Latin, too. Let's trade quotations — '*Dum spiro spero.*' "

" '*Da dextram misero.*' "

" '*Alea jacta est.*' "

" '*Excelsior.*' "

Raynor shouted with laughter, and other workers came to look at him over the partition. Grebe also laughed, feeling pleased and easy. The luxury of fun on a nervous morning.

When they were done and no one was watching or listening Raynor said rather seriously, "What made you study Latin in the first place? Was it for the priesthood?"

"No."

"Just for the hell of it? For the culture? Oh, the things people think they can pull!" He made his cry hilarious and tragic. "I ran my pants off so I could study for the bar, and I've passed the bar, so I get twelve dollars a week more than you as a bonus for having seen life straight and whole. I'll tell you, as a man of culture, that even though nothing looks to be real, and everything stands for something else, and that thing for another thing, and that thing for a still further one — there ain't any comparison between twenty-five and thirty-seven dollars a week, regardless of the last reality. Don't you think that was clear to your Greeks? They were a thoughtful people, but they didn't part with their slaves."

This was a great deal more than Grebe had looked for in his first interview with his supervisor. He was too shy to show all the astonishment he felt. He laughed a little, aroused, and brushed at the sunbeam that covered his head with its dust. "Do you think my mistake was so terrible?"

"Damn right it was terrible, and you know it now that you've had the whip of hard times laid on your back. You should have been preparing yourself for trouble. Your people must have been well off to send you to the university. Stop me, if I'm stepping on your toes. Did your mother pamper you? Did your father give in to you? Were you brought up tenderly, with permission to go and find out what were the last things that everything else stands for while everybody else labored in the fallen world of appearances?"

"Well, no, it wasn't exactly like that." Grebe smiled. *The fallen world of appearances!* no less. But now it was his turn to deliver a surprise. "We weren't rich. My father was the last genuine English butler in Chicago — "

"Are you kidding?"

"Why should I be?"

"In a livery?"

"In livery. Up on the Gold Coast."

"And he wanted you to be educated like a gentleman?"

"He did not. He sent me to the Armour Institution to study chemical engineering. But when he died I changed schools."

He stopped himself, and considered how quickly Raynor had reached him. In no time he had your valise on the table and all your stuff unpacked. And afterward, in the streets, he was still reviewing how far he might have gone, and how much he might have been led to tell if they had not been interrupted by Mrs. Staika's great noise.

But just then a young woman, one of Raynor's workers, ran into the cubicle exclaiming, "Haven't you heard all the fuss?"

"We haven't heard anything."

"It's Staika, giving out with all her might. The reporters are coming. She said she phoned the papers, and you know she did."

"But what is she up to?" said Raynor.

"She brought her wash and she's ironing it here, with our current, because the relief won't pay her electric bill. She has her ironing board set up by the admitting desk, and her kids are with her, all six. They never are in school more than once a week. She's always dragging them around with her because of her reputation."

"I don't want to miss any of this," said Raynor, jumping up. Grebe, as he followed with the secretary, said, "Who is this Staika?"

"They call her the 'Blood Mother of Federal Street.' She's a professional donor at the hospitals. I think they pay ten dollars a pint. Of course it's no joke, but she makes a very big thing out of it and she and the kids are in the papers all the time."

A small crowd, staff and clients divided by a plywood barrier, stood in the narrow space of the entrance, and Staika was shouting in a gruff, mannish voice, plunging the iron on the board and slamming it on the metal rest.

"My father and mother came in a steerage, and I was born in our house, Robey by Huron. I'm no dirty immigrant. I'm a U.S. citizen. My husband is a gassed veteran from France with lungs weaker'n paper, that hardly can he go to the toilet by himself. These six children of mine, I have to buy the shoes for their feet with my own blood. Even a lousy little white Communion necktie, that's a couple of drops of blood; a little piece of mosquito veil for my Vadja so she won't be ashamed in church for the other girls, they take my blood for it by Goldblatt. That's how I keep going'. A fine thing if I had to depend on the relief. And there's plenty of people on the rolls — fakes! There's nothin' they can't get, that can go and wrap bacon at Swift and Armour any time. They're lookin' for them by the Yards. They never have to be out of work. Only they rather lay in their lousy beds and eat the public's money." She was not afraid, in a predominantly Negro station, to shout this way about Negroes.

Grebe and Raynor worked themselves forward to get a closer view of the woman. She was flaming with anger and with pleasure at herself, broad and huge, a golden-headed woman who wore a cotton cap laced with pink ribbon. She was barelegged and had on black gym shoes, her Hoover apron was open and her great breasts, not much restrained by a man's undershirt, hampered her arms as she worked at the kid's dress on the ironing board. And the children, silent and white, with a kind of locked obstinacy, in sheepskins and lumberjackets, stood behind her. She had captured the station, and the pleasure this gave her was enormous. Yet her grievances were true grievances. She was telling the truth. But she behaved like a liar. The look of her small eyes was hidden, and while she raged she also seemed to be spinning and planning.

"They send me out college case workers in silk pants to talk me out of what I got comin'. Are they better'n me? Who told them? Fire them. Let 'em go and get married, and then you won't have to cut electric from people's budget."

The chief supervisor, Mr. Ewing, couldn't silence her and he stood with folded arms at the head of his staff, bald, bald-headed, saying to his subordinates like the ex-school principal he was, "Pretty soon she'll be tired and go."

"No she won't," said Raynor to Grebe. "She'll get what she wants. She knows more about the relief even than Ewing. She's been on the rolls for years, and she always gets what she wants because she puts on a noisy show. Ewing knows it. He'll give in soon. He's only saving face. If he gets bad publicity, the Commissioner'll have him on the carpet, downtown. She's got him submerged; she'll submerge everybody in time, and that includes nations and governments."

Grebe replied with his characteristic smile, disagreeing completely. Who would take Staika's orders, and what changes could her yelling ever bring about?

No, what Grebe saw in her, the power that made people listen, was that her cry expressed the war of flesh and blood, perhaps turned a little crazy and certainly ugly, on this place and this condition. And at first, when he went out, the spirit of Staika somehow presided over the whole district for him, and it took color from her; he saw her color, in the spotty curb fires, and the fires under the El, the straight alley of flamy gloom. Later, too, when he went into a tavern for a shot of rye, the sweat of beer, association with West Side Polish streets, made him think of her again.

He wiped the corners of his mouth with his muffler, his handkerchief being inconvenient to reach for, and went out again to get on with the delivery of his checks. The air bit cold and hard and a few flakes of snow formed near him. A train struck by and left a quiver in the frames and a bristling icy hiss over the rails.

Crossing the street, he descended a flight of board steps into a basement grocery, setting off a little bell. It was a dark, long store and it caught you with its stinks of smoked meat, soap, dried peaches, and fish. There was a fire wrinkling and flapping in the little stove, and the proprietor was waiting, an Italian with a long, hollow face and stubborn bristles. He kept his hands warm under his apron.

No, he didn't know Green. You knew people but not names. The same man might not have the same name twice. The police didn't know, either, and mostly didn't care. When somebody was shot or knifed they took the body away and didn't look for the murderer. In the first place, nobody would tell them anything. So they made up a name for the coroner and called it quits. And in the second place, they didn't give a goddamn anyhow. But they couldn't get to the bottom of a thing even if they wanted to. Nobody would get to know even a tenth of what went on among these people. They stabbed and stole, they did every crime and abomination you ever heard of, men and men, women and women, parents and children, worse than the animals. They carried on their own way, and the horrors passed off like a smoke. There was never anything like it in the history of the whole world.

It was a long speech, deepening with every word in its fantasy and passion and becoming increasingly senseless and terrible: a swarm amassed by suggestion and invention, a huge, hugging, despairing knot, a human wheel of heads, legs, bellies, arms, rolling through his shop.

Grebe felt that he must interrupt him. He said sharply, "What are you talking about! All I asked was whether you knew this man."

"That isn't even the half of it. I been here six years. You probably don't want to believe this. But suppose it's true?"

"All the same," said Grebe, "there must be a way to find a person."

The Italian's close-spaced eyes had been queerly concentrated, as were his muscles, while he leaned across the counter trying to convince Grebe. Now he gave up the effort and sat down on his stool. "Oh — I suppose. Once in a while. But I been telling you, even the cops don't get anywhere."

"They're always after somebody. It's not the same thing."

"Well, keep trying if you want. I can't help you."

But he didn't keep trying. He had no more time to spend on Green. He slipped Green's check to the back of the block. The next name on the list was FIELD, WINSTON.

He found the back-yard bungalow without the least trouble; it shared a lot with another house, a few feet of yard between. Grebe knew these two-shack arrangements. They had been built in vast numbers in the days before the swamps were filled and the streets raised, and they were all the same — a boardwalk along the fence, well under street level, three or four ball-headed posts for clotheslines, greening wood, dead shingles, and a long, long flight of stairs to the rear door.

A twelve-year-old boy let him into the kitchen, and there the old man was, sitting by the table in a wheel chair.

"Oh it's d' Government man," he said to the boy when Grebe drew out his checks. "Go bring me my box of papers." He cleared a space on the table.

"Oh, you don't have to go to all that trouble," said Grebe. But Field laid out his papers: Social Security card, relief certification, letters from the state hospital in Manteno, and a naval discharge dated San Diego, 1920.

"That's plenty," Grebe said. "Just sign."

"You got to know who I am," the old man said. "You're from the Government. It's not your check, it's a Government check and you got no business to hand it over till everything is proved."

He loved the ceremony of it, and Grebe made no more objections. Field emptied his box and finished out the circle of cards and letters.

There's everything I done and been. Just the death certificate and they can close book on me." He said this with a certain happy pride and magnificence. Still he did not sign; he merely held the little pen upright on the golden-green corduroy of his thigh. Grebe did not hurry him. He felt the old man's hunger for conversation.

"I got to get better coal," he said. "I send my little gran'son to the yard with my order and they fill his wagon with screening. The stove ain't made for it. It fall through the grate. The order says Franklin County egg-size coal."

"I'll report it and see what can be done."

"Nothing can be done, I expect. You know and I know. There ain't no little ways to make things better, and the only big thing is money. That's the only sunbeams, money. Nothing is black where it shines, and the only place you see black is where it ain't shining. What we colored have to have is our own rich. There ain't no other way."

Grebe sat, his reddened forehead bridged levelly by his close-cut hair and his cheeks lowered in the wings of his collar — the caked fire shone hard within the isinglass-and-iron frames but the room was not comfortable — sat and listened while the old man unfolded his scheme. This was to create one Negro millionaire a month by subscription. One clever, good-hearted young fellow elected every month would sign a contract to use the money to start a business employing Negroes. This would be advertised by chain letters and word of mouth, and every Negro wage earner would contribute a dollar a month. Within five years there would be sixty millionaires.

"That'll fetch respect," he said with a throat-stopped sound that came out like a foreign syllable. "You got to take and organize all the money that gets thrown away on the policy wheel and horse race. As long as they can take it away from you, they got no respect for you. Money, that's d'sun of human kind!" Field was a Negro of mixed blood, perhaps Cherokee, or Natchez; his skin was reddish. And he sounded, speaking about a golden sun in this dark room, and looked, shaggy and slab-headed, with the mingled blood of his face and broad lips, the little pen still upright in his hand, like one of the underground kings of mythology, old judge Minos himself.

And now he accepted the check and signed. Not to soil the slip, he held it down with his knuckles. The table budged and creaked, the center of the gloomy, heathen midden of the kitchen covered with bread, meat, and cans, and the scramble of papers.

"Don't you think my scheme'd work?"

"It's worth thinking about. Something ought to be done. I agree."

"It'll work if people will do it. That's all. That's the only thing any time. When they understand it in the same way, all of them."

"That's true," said Grebe, rising. His glance met the old man's."

"I know you got to go," he said. "Well, God bless you, boy, you ain't been sly with me. I can tell it in a minute."

He went back through the buried yard. Someone nursed a candle in a shed, where a man unloaded kindling wood from a sprawl-wheeled baby buggy and two voices carried on a high conversation. As he came up the sheltered passage he heard the hard boost of the wind in the branches and against the house fronts, and then, reaching the sidewalk, he saw the needle-eye red of cable towers in the open icy height hundreds of feet above the river and the factories — those keen points. From here, his view was obstructed all the way to the South Branch and its timber banks, and the cranes beside the water. Rebuilt after the Great Fire, this part of the city was, not fifty years later, in ruins again, factories boarded up, buildings deserted or fallen, gaps of prairie between. But it wasn't desolation that this made you feel, but rather a faltering of organization that set free a huge energy, an escaped, unattached, unregulated power from the giant raw place. Not only must people feel it but, it seemed to Grebe, they were compelled to match it. In their very bodies. He no less than others, he realized. Say that his parents had been servants in their time, whereas he was not supposed to be one. He thought that they had never done any service like this, which no one visible asked for, and probably flesh and blood could not even perform. Nor could anyone show why it should be performed; or see where the performance would lead. That did not mean that he wanted to be released from it, he realized with a grimly pensive face. On the contrary. He had something to do. To be compelled to feel this energy and yet have no task to do — that was horrible; that was suffering; he knew what that was. It was now quitting time. Six o'clock. He could go home if he liked, to his room, that is, to wash in hot water, to pour a drink, lie down on his quilt, read the paper, eat some liver paste on crackers before going out to dinner. But to think of this actually made him feel a little sick, as though he had swallowed hard air. He had six checks left, and he was determined to deliver at least one of these: Mr. Green's check.

So he started again. He had four or five dark blocks to go, past open lots, condemned houses, old foundations, closed schools, black churches, mounds, and he reflected that there must be many people alive who had once seen the neighborhood rebuilt and new. Now there was a second layer of ruins; centuries of history accomplished through human massing. Numbers had given the place forced growth; enormous numbers had also broken it down. Objects once so new, so concrete that it could have occurred to anyone they stood for other things, had crumbled. Therefore, reflected Grebe, the secret of them was out. It was that they stood for themselves by agreement, and were natural and not unnatural by agreement, and when the things themselves collapsed the agreement became visible. What was it, otherwise, that kept cities from looking peculiar? Rome, that was almost permanent, did not give rise to thoughts like these. And was it abidingly real? But in Chicago, where the cycles were so fast and the familiar died out, and again rose changed, and died again in thirty years, you saw the common agreement or covenant, and you were forced to think about appearances and realities. (He remembered Raynor and he smiled. Raynor was a clever boy.) Once you had grasped this, a great many things became intelligible. For instance, why Mr. Field should conceive such a scheme. Of course, if people were to agree to create a millionaire, a real millionaire would come into existence. And if you wanted to know how Mr. Field was inspired to think of this, why, he had within sight of his kitchen window the chart, the very bones of a successful scheme — the El with its blue and green confetti of signals. People consented to pay dimes and ride the crash-box cars, and so it was a success. Yet how absurd it looked: how little reality there was to start with. And yet Yerkes, the great financier who built it, had known that he could get people to agree to do it. Viewed as itself, what a scheme of a scheme it seemed, how close to an appearance. Then why wonder at Mr. Field's idea? He had grasped a principle. And then Grebe remembered, too, that Mr. Yerkes had established the Yerkes Observatory and endowed it with millions. Now how did the notion come to him in his New York museum of a palace or his Aegean-bound yacht to give money to astronomers? Was he awed by the success of his bizarre enterprise and therefore ready to spend money to find out where in the universe being and seeming were identical? Yes, he wanted to know what abides; and whether flesh is Bible grass; and he offered money to be burned in the fire of suns. Okay, then, Grebe thought further, these things exist because people consent to exist with them — we have got so far — and also there is a reality which doesn't depend on consent but within which consent is a game. But what about need, the need that keeps so many vast thousands in position? You tell me that, you private little gentleman and *decent* soul — he used these words against himself scornfully. Why is the consent given to misery? And why so painfully ugly? Because there is something that is dismal and permanently ugly? Here he sighed and gave it up, and thought it was enough for the present moment that he had a real check in his pocket for a Mr. Green who must be real beyond question. If only his neighbors didn't think they had to conceal him.

This time he stopped at the second floor. He struck a match and found a door. Presently a man answered his knock and Grebe had the check ready and showed it even before he began. "Does Tulliver Green live here? I'm from the relief."

The man narrowed the opening and spoke to someone at his back.

"Does he live here?"

"Uh-uh. No."

"Or anywhere in this building? He's a sick man and he can't come for his dough." He exhibited the check in the light, which was smoky — the air smelled of charred lard — and the man held off the brim of his cap to study it.

"Uh-uh. Never seen the name."

"There's nobody around here that uses crutches?"

He seemed to think, but it was Grebe's impression that he was simply waiting for a decent interval to pass.

"No, suh. Nobody I ever see."

"I've been looking for this man all afternoon" — Grebe spoke out with sudden force — "and I'm going to have to carry this check back to the station. It seems strange not to be able to find a person to *give* him something when you're looking for him for a good reason. I suppose if I had bad news for him I'd find him quick enough."

There was a responsive motion in the other man's face. "That's right, I reckon."

"It almost doesn't do any good to have a name if you can't be found by it. It doesn't stand for anything. He might as well not have any," he went on, smiling. It was as much of a concession as he could make to his desire to laugh.

"Well, now, there's a little old knot-back man I see once in a while. He might be the one you lookin' for. Downstairs."

"Where? Right side or left? Which door?"

"I don't know which. Thin-face little knot-back with a stick."

But no one answered at any of the doors on the first floor. He went to the end of the corridor, searching by matchlight, and found only a stairless exit to the yard, a drop of about six feet. But there was a bungalow near the alley, an old house like Mr. Field's. To jump was unsafe. He ran from the front door, through the underground passage and into the yard. The place was occupied. There was a light through the curtains, upstairs. The name on the ticket under the broken, scoop-shaped mailbox was Green! He exultantly rang the bell and pressed against the locked door. Then the lock clicked faintly and a long staircase opened before him. Someone was slowly coming down — a woman. He had the impression in the weak light that she was shaping her hair as she came, making herself presentable, for he saw her arms raised. But it was for support that they were raised; she was feeling her way downward, down the wall, stumbling. Next he wondered about the pressure of her feet on the treads; she did not seem to be wearing shoes. And it was a freezing stairway. His ring had got her out of bed, perhaps, and she had forgotten to put them on. And then he saw that she was not only shoeless but naked; she was entirely naked, climbing down while she talked to herself, a heavy woman, naked and drunk. She blundered into him. The contact of her breasts, though they touched only his coat, made him go back against the door with a blind shock. See what he had tracked down, in his hunting game!

The woman was saying to herself, furious with insult, "So I cain't — k, huh? I'll show that son-of-a-bitch kin I, cain't I."

What should he do now? Grebe asked himself. Why, he should go. He should turn away and go. He couldn't talk to this woman. He couldn't keep her standing naked in the cold. But when he tried he found himself unable to turn away.

He said, "Is this where Mr. Green lives?"

But she was still talking to herself and did not hear him.

"Is this Mr. Green's house?"

At last she turned her furious drunken glance on him. "What do you want?"

Again her eyes wandered from him; there was a dot of blood in their enraged brilliance. He wondered why she didn't feel the cold.

"I'm from the relief."

"Awright, what?"

"I've got a check for Tulliver Green."

This time she heard him and put out her hand.

"No, no, for *Mr.* Green. He's got to sign," he said. How was he going to get Mr. Green's signature tonight!

"I'll take it. He cain't."

He desperately shook his head, thinking of Mr. Field's precautions about identification. "I can't let you have it. It's for him. Are you Mrs. Green?"

"Maybe I is, and maybe I ain't. Who want to know?"

"Is he upstairs?"

"Awright. Take it up yourself, you goddamn fool."

Sure, he was a goddamn fool. Of course he could not go up because Green would probably be drunk and naked, too. And perhaps he would appear on the landing soon. He looked eagerly upward. Under the light was a high narrow brown wall. Empty! It remained empty!

"Hell with you, then!" he heard her cry. To deliver a check for coal and clothes, he was keeping her in the cold. She did not feel it, but his face was burning with frost and self-ridicule. He backed away from her.

"I'll come tomorrow, tell him."

"Ah, hell with you. Don' never come. What you doin' here in the nighttime? Don' come back." She yelled so that he saw the breadth of her tongue. She stood astride in the long cold box of the hall and held on to the banister and the wall. The bungalow itself was shaped something like a box, a clumsy, high box pointing into the freezing air with its sharp, wintry lights.

"If you are Mrs. Green, I'll give you the check," he said, changing his mind.

"Give here, then." She took the pen offered with it in her left hand, and tried to sign the receipt on the wall. He looked around, almost as though to see whether his madness was being observed, and came near believing that someone was standing on a mountain of used tires in the auto-junking shop next door.

"But are you Mrs. Green?" he thought to ask. But she was already climbing the stairs with the check, and it was too late, if he had made an error, if he was now in trouble, to undo the thing. But he wasn't going to worry about it. Though she might not be Mrs. Green, he was convinced that Mr. Green was upstairs. Whoever she was, the woman stood for Green, whom he was not to see this time. Well, you silly bastard, he said to himself, so you think you found him. So what? Maybe you really did find him — what of it? But it was important that there was a real Mr. Green whom they could not keep him from reaching because he seemed to come as an emissary from hostile appearances. And though the self-ridicule was slow to diminish, and his face still blazed with it, he had, nevertheless, a feeling of elation, too. "For after all," he said, "he *could* be found!"

AMBROSE BIERCE

An Occurrence at Owl Creek Bridge

I

A man stood upon a railroad bridge in Northern Alabama, looking down into the swift waters twenty feet below. The man's hands were behind his back, the wrists bound with a cord. A rope loosely encircled his neck. It was attached to a stout cross-timber above his head, and the slack fell to the level of his knees. Some loose boards laid upon the sleepers supporting the metals of the railway supplied a footing for him and his executioners — two private soldiers of the Federal army, directed by a sergeant, who in civil life may have been a deputy sheriff. At a short remove upon the same temporary platform was an officer in the uniform of his rank, armed. He was a captain. A sentinel at each end of the bridge stood with his rifle in the position known as 'support,' that is to say, vertical in front of the left shoulder, the hammer resting on the forearm thrown straight across the chest — a formal and unnatural position, enforcing an erect carriage of the body. It did not appear to be the duty of these two men to know what was occurring at the centre of the bridge; they merely blockaded the two ends of the foot plank which traversed it.

Beyond one of the sentinels nobody was in sight; the railroad ran straight away into a forest for a hundred yards, then, curving, was lost to view. Doubtless there was an outpost further along. The other bank of the stream was open ground — a gentle acclivity crowned with a stockade of vertical tree trunks, loop-holed for rifles, with a single embrasure through which protruded the muzzle of a brass cannon commanding the bridge. Midway of the slope between bridge and fort were the spectators — a single company of infantry in line, at 'parade rest,' the butts of the rifles on the ground, the barrels inclining slightly backward against the right shoulder, the hands crossed upon the stock. A lieutenant stood at the right of the line, the point of his sword upon the ground, his left hand resting upon his right. Excepting the group of four at the centre of the bridge not a man moved. The company faced the bridge, staring stonily, motionless. The sentinels, facing the banks of the stream, might have been statues to adorn the bridge. The captain stood with folded arms, silent, observing the work of his subordinates but making no sign. Death is a dignitary who, when he comes announced, is to be received with formal manifestations of respect, even by those most familiar with him. In the code of military etiquette silence and fixity are forms of deference.

The man who was engaged in being hanged was apparently about thirty-five years of age. He was a civilian, if one might judge from his dress which was that of a planter. His features were good — a straight nose, firm mouth, broad forehead, from which his long, dark hair was combed straight back, falling behind his ears to the collar of his well-fitting frock coat. He wore a moustache and pointed beard, but no whiskers; his eyes were large and dark grey and had a kindly expression which one would hardly have expected in one whose neck was in the hemp. Evidently this was no vulgar assassin. The liberal military code makes provision for hanging many kinds of people, and gentlemen are not excluded.

The preparations being complete, the two private soldiers stepped aside and each drew away the plank upon which he had been standing. The sergeant turned to the captain, saluted and placed himself immediately behind that officer, who in turn moved apart one pace. These movements left the condemned man and the sergeant standing on the two ends of the same plank, which spanned three of the cross-ties of the bridge. The end upon which the civilian stood almost, but not quite, reached a fourth. This plank had been held in place by the weight of the captain; it was now held by that of the sergeant. At a signal from the former, the latter would step aside, the plank would tilt and the condemend man go down between two ties. The arrangement commended itself to his judgment as simple and effective. His face had not been covered nor his eyes bandaged. He looked a moment at his 'unsteadfast footing,' then let his gaze wander to the swirling water of the stream racing madly beneath his feet. A piece of dancing driftwood caught his attention and his eyes followed it down the current. How slowly it appeared to move! What a sluggish stream!

He closed his eyes in order to fix his last thoughts upon his wife and children. The water, touched to gold by the early sun, the brooding mists under the banks at some distance down the stream, the fort, the soldiers, the piece of drift — all had distracted him. And now he became conscious of a new disturbance. Striking through the thought of his dear ones was a sound which he could neither ignore nor understand, a sharp, distinct, metallic percussion like the stroke of a blacksmith's hammer upon the anvil; it had the same ringing quality. He wondered what it was, and whether immeasurably distant or near by — it seemed both. Its recurrence was regular, but as slow as the tolling of a death knell. He awaited each stroke with impatience and — he knew not why — apprehension. The intervals of silence grew progressively longer; the delays became maddening. With their greater infrequency the sounds increased in strength and sharpness. They hurt his ear like the thrust of a knife; he feared he would shriek. What he heard was the ticking of his watch.

He unclosed his eyes and saw again the water below him. 'If I could free my hands,' he thought, 'I might throw off the noose and spring into the stream. By diving I could evade the bullets, and swimming vigorously, reach the bank, take to the woods, and get away home. My home, thank God, is as yet outside their lines; my wife and little ones are still beyond the invader's farthest advance.'

As these thoughts, which have here to be set down in words, were flashed into the doomed man's brain rather than evolved from it, the captain nodded to the sergeant. The sergeant stepped aside.

II

Peyton Farquhar was a well-to-do planter, of an old and highly respected Alabama family. Being a slave owner, and, like other slave owners, a politician, he was naturally an original secessionist and ardently devoted to the Southern cause. Circumstances of an imperious nature which it is unnecessary to relate here, had prevented him from taking service with the gallant army which had fought the disastrous campaigns ending with the fall of Corinth, and he chafed under the inglorious restraint, longing for the release of his energies, the larger life of the soldier, the opportunity for distinction. That opportunity, he felt, would come, as it comes to all in war time. Meanwhile he did what he could. No service was too humble for him to perform in aid of the South, no adventure too perilous for him to undertake if consistent with the character of a civilian who was at heart a soldier, and who in good faith and without too much qualification assented to at least a part of the frankly villainous dictum that all is fair in love and war.

One evening while Farquhar and his wife were sitting on a rustic bench near the entrance to his grounds, a grey-clad soldier rode up to the gate and asked for a drink of water. Mrs. Farquhar was only too happy to serve him with her own white hands. While she was gone to fetch the water, her husband approached the dusty horseman and inquired eagerly for news from the front.

'The Yanks are repairing the railroads,' said the man, 'and are getting ready for another advance. They have reached the Owl Creek bridge, put it in order, and built a stockade on the other bank. The commandant has issued an order, which is posted everywhere, declaring that any civilian caught interfering with the railroad, its bridges, tunnels or trains, will be summarily hanged. I saw the order.'

'How far is it to the Owl Creek bridge?' Farquhar asked.

'About thirty miles.'

'Is there no force on this side the creek?'

'Only a picket post half a mile out, on the railroad, and a single sentinel at this end of the bridge.'

'Suppose a man — a civilian and student of hanging — should elude the picket post and perhaps get the better of the sentinel,' said Farquhar, smiling, 'what could he accomplish?'

The soldier reflected. 'I was there a month ago,' he replied. 'I observed that the flood of last winter had lodged a great quantity of driftwood against the wooden pier at this end of the bridge. It is now dry and would burn like tow.'

The lady had now brought the water, which the soldier drank. He thanked her ceremoniously, bowed to her husband, and rode away. An hour later, after nightfall, he repassed the plantation, going northward in the direction from which he had come. He was a Federal scout.

III

As Peyton Farquhar fell straight downward through the bridge, he lost consciousness and was as one already dead. From this state he was awakened — ages later, it seemed to him — by the pain of a sharp pressure upon his throat, followed by a sense of suffocation. Keen, poignant agonies seemed to shoot from his neck downward through every fibre of his body and limbs. The pains appeared to flash along well-defined lines of ramification, and to beat with an inconceivably rapid periodicity. They seemed like streams of pulsating fire heating him to an intolerable temperature. As to his head, he was conscious of nothing but a feeling of fullness — of congestion. These sensations were unaccompanied by thought. The intellectual part of his nature was already effaced; he had power only to feel, and feeling was torment. He was conscious of motion. Encompassed in a luminous cloud, of which he was now merely the fiery heart, without material substance, he swung through unthinkable arcs of oscillation, like a vast pendulum. Then all at once, with terrible suddenness, the light about him shot upward with the noise of a loud plash; a frightful roaring was in his ears, and all was cold and dark. The power of thought was restored; he knew that the rope had broken and he had fallen into the stream. There was no additional strangulation; the noose about his neck was already suffocating him, and kept the water from his lungs. To die of hanging at the bottom of a river! — the idea seemed to him ludicrous. He opened his eyes in the blackness and saw above him a gleam of light, but how distant, how inaccessible! He was still sinking, for the light became fainter and fainter until it was a mere glimmer. Then it began to grow and brighten, and he knew that he was rising toward the surface — knew it with reluctance, for he was now very comfortable. 'To be hanged and drowned,' he thought, 'that is not so bad; but I do not wish to be shot. No; I will not be shot; that is not fair.'

He was not conscious of an effort, but a sharp pain in his wrist apprised him that he was trying to free his hands. He gave the struggle his attention, as an idler might observe the feat of a juggler, without interest in the outcome. What splendid effort! — what magnificent, what superhuman strength! Ah, that was a fine endeavour! Bravo! The cord fell away; his arms parted and floated upward, the hands dimly seen on each side in the growing light. He watched them with a new interest as first one and then the other pounced upon the noose at his neck. They tore it away and thrust it fiercely aside, its undulations resembling those of a water-snake. 'Put it back, put it back!' He thought he shouted these words to his hands, for the undoing of the noose had been succeeded by the direst pang which he had yet experienced. His neck ached horribly; his brain was on fire; his heart, which had been fluttering faintly, gave a great leap, trying to force itself out at his mouth. His whole body was racked and wrenched with an insupportable anguish! But his disobedient hands gave no heed to the command. They beat the water vigorously with quick, downward strokes, forcing him to the surface. He felt his head emerge; his eyes were blinded by the sunlight; his chest expanded convulsively, and with a supreme and crowning agony his lungs engulfed a great draught of air, which instantly he expelled in a shriek!

He was now in full possession of his physical senses. They were, indeed, preternaturally keen and alert. Something in the awful disturbance of his organic system had so exalted and refined them that they made record of things never before perceived. He felt the ripples upon his face and heard their separate sounds as they struck. He looked at the forest on the bank of the stream, saw the individual trees, the leaves and the veining of each leaf — saw the very insects upon them, the locusts, the brilliant-bodied flies, the grey spiders stretching their webs from twig to twig. He noted the prismatic colors in all the dewdrops upon a million blades of grass. The humming of the gnats that danced above the eddies of the stream, the beating of the dragon flies' wings, the strokes of the water spiders' legs, like oars which had lifted their boat — all these made audible music. A fish slid along beneath his eyes and he heard the rush of its body parting the water.

He had come to the surface facing down the stream; in a moment the visible world seemed to wheel slowly round, himself the pivotal point, and he saw the bridge, the fort, the soldiers upon the bridge, the captain, the sergeant, the two privates, his executioners. They were in silhouette against the blue sky. They shouted and gesticulated, pointing at him; the captain had drawn his pistol, but did not fire; the others were unarmed. Their movements were grotesque and horrible, their forms gigantic.

Suddenly he heard a sharp report and something struck the water smartly within a few inches of his head, spattering his face with spray. He heard a second report, and saw one of the sentinels with his rifle at his shoulder, a light cloud of blue smoke rising from the muzzle. The man in the water saw the eye of the man on the bridge gazing into his own through the sights of the rifle. He observed that it was a grey eye, and remembered having read that grey eyes were keenest and that all famous marksmen had them. Nevertheless, this one had missed.

A counter swirl had caught Farquhar and turned him half round; he was again looking into the forest on the bank opposite the fort. The sound of a clear, high voice in a monotonous singsong now rang out behind him and came across the water with a distinctness that pierced and subdued all other sounds, even the beating of the ripples in his ears. Although no soldier, he had frequented camps enough to know the dread significance of that deliberate, drawling, aspirated chant; the lieutenant on shore was taking a part in the morning's work. How coldly and pitilessly — with what an even, calm intonation, presaging and enforcing tranquility in the men — with what accurately-measured intervals fell those cruel words:

'Attention, company.... Shoulder arms.... Ready.... Aim.... Fire.'

Farquhar dived — dived as deeply as he could. The water roared in his ears like the voice of Niagara, yet he heard the dulled thunder of the volley, and rising again toward the surface, met shining bits of metal, singularly flattened, oscillating slowly downward. Some of them touched him on the face and hands, then fell away, continuing their descent. One lodged between his collar and neck; it was uncomfortably warm, and he snatched it out.

As he rose to the surface, gasping for breath, he saw that he had been a long time under water; he was perceptibly farther down stream — nearer to safety. The soldiers had almost finished reloading; the metal ramrods flashed all at once in the sunshine as they were drawn from the barrels, turned in the air, and thrust into their sockets.

The two sentinels fired again, independently and ineffectually.

The hunted man saw all this over his shoulder; he was now swimming vigorously with the current. His brain was as energetic as his arms and legs; he thought with the rapidity of lightning.

'The officer,' he reasoned, 'will not make that martinet's error a second time. It is as easy to dodge a volley as a single shot. He has probably already given the command to fire at will. God help me, I cannot dodge them all!'

An appalling splash within two yards of him, followed by a loud rushing sound, *diminuendo,* which seemed to travel back through the air to the fort and died in an explosion which stirred the very river to its deeps! A rising sheet of water, which curved over him, fell down upon him, blinded him, strangled him! The cannon had taken a hand in the game. As he shook his head free from the commotion of the smitten water, he heard the deflected shot humming through the air ahead, and in an instant it was cracking and smashing the branches in the forest beyond.

'They will not do that again,' he thought; 'the next time they will use a charge of grape. I must keep my eye upon the gun; the smoke will apprise me — the report arrives too late; it lags behind the missile. It is a good gun.'

Suddenly he felt himself whirled round and round — spinning like a top. The water, the banks, the forest, the now distant bridge, fort and men — all were commingled and blurred. Objects were represented by their colors only; circular horizontal streaks of color — that was all he saw. He had been caught in a vortex and was being whirled on with a velocity of advance and gyration which made him giddy and sick. In a few moments he was flung upon the gravel at the foot of the left bank of the stream — the southern bank — and behind a projecting point which concealed him from his enemies. The sudden arrest of his motion, the abrasion of one of his hands on the gravel, restored him and he wept with delight. He dug his fingers into the sand, threw it over himself in handfuls and audibly blessed it. It looked like gold, like diamonds, rubies, emeralds; he could think of nothing beautiful which it did not resemble. The trees upon the bank were giant garden plants; he noted a definite order in their arrangement, inhaled the fragrance of their blooms. A strange, roseate light shone through the spaces among their trunks, and the wind made in their branches the music of aeolian harps. He had no wish to perfect his escape, was content to remain in that enchanting spot until retaken.

A whizz and rattle of grapeshot among the branches high above his head roused him from his dream. The baffled cannoneer had fired him a random farewell. He sprang to his feet, rushed up the sloping bank, and plunged into the forest.

All that day he travelled, laying his course by the rounding sun. The forest seemed interminable; nowhere did he discover a break in it, not even a woodman's road. He had not known that he lived in so wild a region. There was something uncanny in the revelation.

By nightfall he was fatigued, footsore, famishing. The thought of his wife and children urged him on. At last he found a road which led him in what he knew to be the right direction. It was as wide and straight as a city street, yet it seemed untravelled. No fields bordered it, no dwelling anywhere. Not so much as the barking of a dog suggested human habitation. The black bodies of the great trees formed a straight wall on both sides, terminating on the horizon in a point, like a diagram in a lesson in perspective. Overhead, as he looked up through this rift in the wood, shone great golden stars looking unfamiliar and grouped in strange constellations. He was sure they were arranged in some order which had a secret and malign significance. The wood on either side was full of singular noises, among which — once, twice, and again — he distinctly heard whispers in an unknown tongue.

His neck was in pain, and, lifting his hand to it, he found it horribly swollen. He knew that it had a circle of black where the rope had bruised it. His eyes felt congested; he could no longer close them. His tongue was swollen with thirst; he relieved its fever by thrusting it forward from between his teeth into the cool air. How softly the turf had carpeted the untravelled avenue! He could no longer feel the roadway beneath his feet!

Doubtless, despite his suffering, he fell asleep while walking, for now he sees another scene — perhaps he has merely recovered from a delirium. He stands at the gate of his own home. All is as he left it, and all bright and beautiful in the morning sunshine. He must have travelled the entire night. As he pushes open the gate and passes up the wide white walk, he sees a flutter of female garments: his wife, looking fresh and cool and sweet, steps down from the verandah to meet him. At the bottom of the steps she stands waiting, with a smile of ineffable joy, an attitude of matchless grace and dignity. Ah, how beautiful she is! He springs forward with extended arms. As he is about to clasp her, he feels a stunning blow upon the back of the neck; a blinding white light blazes all about him, with a sound like the shock of a cannon — then all is darkness and silence!

Peyton Farquhar was dead; his body, with a broken neck, swung gently from side to side beneath the timbers of the Owl Creek bridge.

CLARK BLAISE

Grids and Doglegs

When I was sixteen I could spend whole evenings with a straightedge, a pencil, and a few sheets of unlined construction paper, and with those tools I would lay out imaginary cities along twisting rivers or ragged coastlines. Centuries of expansion and division, terrors of fire and renewal, recorded in the primitive fiction of gaps and clusters, grids and doglegs. My cities were tangles; inevitably, like Pittsburgh. And as I built my cities, I'd keep the Pirates game on (in another notebook I kept running accounts of my team's declining fortune ... "Well, Tony Bartirome, that knocks you down to .188 ... " the pregame averages were never exact enough for me), and during the summers I excavated for the Department of Man, Carnegie Museum. Twice a week during the winter I visited the Casino Burlesque (this a winter pleasure, to counter the loss of baseball). I was a painter too, of sweeping subjects: my paleobotanical murals for the Devonian Fishes Hall are still a model for younger painter-excavators. (Are there others, still, like me, in Pittsburgh? This story is for them.) On Saturdays I lectured to the Junior Amateur Archaeologists and Anthropologists of Western Pennsylvania. I was a high school junior, my parents worked at their new store, and I was, obviously, mostly alone. In the afternoons, winter and summer, I picked up dirty clothes for my father's laundry.

I had — obviously, again — very few friends; there were not many boys like me. Fat, but without real bulk, arrogant but ridiculously shy. Certifiably brilliant but hopelessly unstudious, I felt unallied to even the conventionally bright honor-rollers in my suburban high school. Keith Godwin was my closest friend; I took three meals a week at his house, and usually slept over on Friday night.

Keith's father was a chemist with Alcoa; his mother a pillar of the local United Presbyterian Church, the Women's Club, and the University Women's chapter; and the four children (all but Keith, the oldest), were models of charm, ambition, and beauty. Keith was a moon-faced redhead with freckles and dimples — one would never suspect the depth of his cynicism — with just two real passions: the organ and competitive chess. I have seen him win five simultaneous blindfold games, ten-second moves — against tournament competition. We used to play at the dinner table without the board, calling out our moves while shoveling in the food. Years later, high school atheism behind him, he enrolled in a Presbyterian seminary of Calvinist persuasions and is now a minister somewhere in California. He leads a number of extremist campaigns (crackpot drives, to be exact), against education, books, movies, minorities, pacifists — this, too, was a part of our rebellion, though I've turned the opposite way. But this isn't a story about Keith. He had a sister, Cyndy, one year younger.

She was tall, like her father, about five-eight, an inch taller than I. Hers was the beauty of contrasts: fair skin, dark hair, gray eyes, and the sharpness of features so common in girls who take after their fathers. Progressively I was to desire her as a sister, then wife, and finally as lover; but by then, of course, it was too late. I took a fix on her, and she guided me through high school; no matter how far out I veered, the hope of eventually pleasing Cyndy drove me back.

In the summer of my junior year, I put away the spade, my collection of pots and flints, and took up astronomy. There's a romance to astronomy, an almost courtly type of pain and fascination, felt by all who study it. The excitement: that like a character in the childhood comics, I could shrink myself and dismiss the petty frustrations of school, the indifference of Cyndy and my parents; that I could submit to points of light long burned-out and be rewarded with their cosmic tolerance of my obesity, ridicule from the athletes in the lunch line, and the Pirates' latest losing streak. I memorized all I could from the basic texts at Carnegie Library, and shifted my allegiance from Carnegie Museum to Buhl Planetarium. There was a workshop in the basement just getting going, started for teen-age telescope-builders, and I became a charter member.

Each week I ground out my lens; glass over glass through gritty water, one night a week for at least a year. Fine precise work, never my style, but I stuck with it while most of the charter enthusiasts fell away. The abrasive carborundum grew finer, month by month, from sand, to talc, to rouge — a single fleck of a coarser grade in those final months would have plundered my mirror like a meteorite. Considering the winter nights on which I sacrificed movies and TV for that lens, the long streetcar rides, the aching arches, the insults from the German shop foreman, the meticulous scrubbing-down after each Wednesday session, the temptation to sneak upstairs for the "Skyshow" with one of the chubby compliant girls — my alter egos — from the Jewish high school: *considering all that,* plus the all-important exclusiveness and recognition it granted, that superb instrument was a heavy investment to sell, finally, for a mere three hundred dollars. But I did, in the fine-polishing stage, because, I felt, I owed it to Cyndy. Three hundred dollars, for a new investment in myself.

Astronomy is the moral heavyweight of the physical sciences; it is a humiliating science, a destroyer of pride in human achievements, or shame in human failings. Compared to the vacant dimensions of space — of time, distance, and temperature — what could be felt for Eisenhower's heart attack, Grecian urns, six million Jews, my waddle and shiny gabardines? My parents were nearing separation, their store beginning to falter — what could I care for their silence, their fights, the begging for bigger and bigger loans? The diameter of Antares, the Messier system, the swelling of space into uncreated nothingness — these things mattered because they were large, remote, and perpetual. The Tammany Ring and follies of Hitler, Shakespeare, and the Constitution were dust; the Andromeda galaxy was *worlds.* I took my meals out or with the Godwins, and I thought of these things as I struggled at chess with Keith and caught glimpses of Cyndy as she dried the dishes — if only I'd had dishes to dry!

The arrogance of astronomy, archaeology, chess, burlesque, baseball, science-fiction, everything I cared for: humility and arrogance are often so close (the men I'm writing this for — who once painted murals and played in high school bands just to feel a part of something — they know); it's all the same feeling, isn't it? Nothing matters, except, perhaps, the proper irony. I had that irony once (I wish, in fact, I had it now), and it was something like this:

In the days of the fifties, each home room of each suburban high school started the day with a Bible reading and the pledge of allegiance to the flag. Thirty mumbling souls, one fervent old woman, and me. It had taken me one night, five years earlier, to learn the Lord's Prayer backwards. I had looked up, as well, the Russian pledge and gotten it translated into English: this did for my daily morning ablutions. The lone difficulty had to do with Bible Week, which descended without warning on a Monday morning with the demand that we, in turn, quote a snatch from the Bible. This is fine if one's name is Zymurgy and you've had a chance to memorize everyone else's favorite, or the shortest verse. But I am a Dyer, and preceded often by Cohens and Bernsteins (more on that later): Bible Week often caught me unprepared. So it happened in the winter of my senior year that Marvin Bernstein was excused ("We won't ask Marvin, class, for he is of a different faith. Aren't you, Marvin?") and then a ruffian named Callahan rattled off a quick, "For God so loved the world that he gave his only begotten Son . . . " so fast that I couldn't catch it. A Sheila Cohen, whose white bra straps I'd stared at for one hour a day, five days a week, for three years — Sheila Cohen was excused. And Norman Dyer, I, stood. "Remember, Norman," said the teacher, "I won't have the Lord's Prayer and the Twenty-second Psalm." She didn't like Callahan's rendition either, and knew she'd get thirty more. From me she expected originality. I didn't disappoint.

"Om," I said, and quickly sat. I'd learned it from the Vedanta, something an astronomer studies.

Her smile had frozen. It was her habit, after a recitation, to smile and nod and congratulate us, with, "Ah, yes, Revelations, a lovely choice, Nancy . . . " But gathering her pluckiness she demanded, "Just what is that supposed to mean, Norman?"

"Everything," I said, with an astronomer's shrug. I was preparing a justification, something to do with more people in the world praying "Om" than anything else, but I had never caused trouble before, and she decided to drop it. She called on my alphabetical shadow (a boy who'd stared for three years at my dandruff and flaring ears?), another Catholic, Dykes was his name, and Dykes this time, instead of following Callahan, twisted the knife a little deeper, and boomed out, "Om . . . amen!" Our teacher shut the Bible, caressed the marker, the white leather binding, and then read us a long passage having to do, as I recall, with nothing we had said.

That was the only victory of my high school years.

I imagined a hundred disasters a day that would wash Cyndy Godwin into my arms, grateful and bedraggled. Keith never suspected. My passion had a single outlet — the telephone. Alone in my parents' duplex, the television on, the Pirates game on, I would phone. No need to check the dial, the fingering was instinctive. Two rings at the Godwins'; if anyone but Cyndy answered, I'd hang up immediately. But with Cyndy I'd hold, through her perplexed "Hellos?" till she queried, "Susie, is that you?" "Brenda?" "Who is it, please?" and I would hold until her voice betrayed fear beyond the irritation. Oh, the pleasure of her slightly hysterical voice, "Daddy, it's that *man* again," and I would sniffle menacingly into the mouthpiece. Then I'd hang up and it was over; like a Pirates' loss, nothing to do but wait for tomorrow. Cyndy would answer the phone perhaps twice a week. Added to the three meals a week I took with them, I convinced myself that five sightings or soundings a week would eventually cinch a marriage if I but waited for a sign she'd surely give me. She was of course dating a bright, good-looking boy a year ahead of me (already at Princeton), a conventional sort of doctor-to-be, active in Scouts, Choir, Sports, and Junior Achievement, attending Princeton on the annual Kiwanis Fellowship. A very common type in our school and suburb, easily tolerated and easily dismissed. Clearly, a girl of Cyndy's sensitivity could not long endure his ministerial humor, his mere ignorance disguised as modesty. Everything about him — good looks, activities, athletics, piety, manners — spoke against him. In those years the only competition for Cyndy that I might have feared would have come from someone of my own circle. And that was impossible, for none of us had ever had a date.

And I knew her like a brother! Hours spent with her playing "Scrabble," driving her to the doctor's for curious flaws I was never to learn about ... and, in the summers, accompanying the family to their cabin and at night hearing her breathing beyond a burlap wall ... Like a brother? Not even that, for as I write I remember Keith grabbing her on the stairs, slamming his open hands against her breasts, and Cyndy responding, while I ached to save her, "Keith! What will Normie think?" And this went on for three years, from the first evening I ate with the Godwins when I was in tenth grade, till the spring semester of my senior year; Cyndy was a junior. There was no drama, no falling action, merely a sweet and painful stasis that I aggrandized with a dozen readings of *Cyrano de Bergerac,* and a customizing of his soliloquies ... "This butt that follows me by half an hour ... An ass, you say? Say rather a caboose, a dessert ... " All of this was bound to end, only when I could break the balance.

We are back to the telescope, the three hundred well-earned dollars. Some kids I knew, Keith not included this time, took over the school printing press and ran off one thousand dramatic broadsheets, condemning a dozen teachers for incompetence and Lesbianism (a word that we knew meant more than "an inhabitant of Lesbos," the definition in our high school dictionary). We were caught, we proudly confessed (astronomy again: I sent a copy to *Mad* magazine and they wrote back, *"funny but don't get caught. You might end up working for a joint like this"*). The school wrote letters to every college that had so greedily accepted us a few weeks earlier, calling on them to retract their acceptance until we publicly apologized. Most of us did, for what good it did; I didn't — it made very little difference anyway, since my parents no longer could have afforded Yale. It would be Penn State in September.

I awoke one morning in April — a gorgeous morning — and decided to diet. A doctor in Squirrel Hill made his living prescribing amphetamines by the carload to suburban matrons. I lost thirty pounds in a month and a half, which dropped me into the ranks of the flabby underweights (funny, I'd always believed there was a *hard* me, under the fat, waiting to be sculpted out — there wasn't). And the pills (as a whole new generation is finding out) were marvelous: the uplift, the energy, the ideas they gave me! As though I'd been secretly rewired for a late but normal adolescence.

Tight new khakis and my first sweaters were now a part of the "New Look" Norman Dyer, which I capped one evening by calling the Arthur Murray Studios. I earned a free dance analysis by answering correctly a condescending question from their television quiz the night before. Then, with the three hundred dollars, I enrolled.

I went to three studio parties, each time with the enormous kid sister of my voluptuous instructress. That gigantic adolescent with a baby face couldn't dance a step (and had been brought along for me, I was certain), and her slimmed-down but still ample sister took on only her fellow teachers and some older, lonelier types, much to my relief. I wanted to dance, but not to be noticed. The poor big-little sister, whose name was Almajean, was dropping out of a mill-town high school in a year to become ... what? I can't guess, and she didn't know, even then. We drank a lot of punch, shuffled together when we had to, and I told her about delivering clothes, something she could respect me for, never admitting that my father owned the store.

But I knew what I had to do. For my friends there was a single event in our high school careers that *had,* above all, to be missed. We had avoided every athletic contest, every dance, pep rally, party — everything voluntary and everything mildly compulsory; we had our private insurrections against the flag and God, but all that good work, all that conscientious effort, would be wasted if we attended the flurry of dances in our last two weeks. The Senior Prom was no problem — I'd been barred because of the newspaper caper. But a week later came the Women's Club College Prom, for everyone going on to higher study (92 percent always did). The pressure for a 100 per cent turn-out was stifling. Even the teachers wore WC buttons so we wouldn't forget. Home room teachers managed to find out who was still uninvited (no one to give Sheila Cohen's bra a snap?). The College Prom combined the necessary exclusiveness and sophistication — smoking was permitted on the balcony — to have become the very essence of graduation night. And there was a special feature that we high schoolers had heard about ever since the eighth grade: the sifting of seniors into a few dozen booths, right on the dance floor, to meet local alums of their college-to-be, picking up a few fraternity bids, athletic money, while the band played a medley of privileged alma maters. I recalled the pain I had felt a year before, as I watched Cyndy leave with her then-senior boy friend, and I was still there, playing chess, when they returned around 2 a.m., for punch.

It took three weeks of aborted phone calls before I asked Cyndy to the College Prom. She of course accepted. Her steady boy friend was already at Princeton and ineligible. According to Keith, he'd left instructions: nothing serious. What did *he* know of seriousness, I thought, making my move. I bought a dinner jacket, dancing shoes, shirt, links, studs, cummerbund, and got ten dollars spending money from my astonished father. I was seventeen, and this was my first date.

Cyndy was a beautiful *woman* that night; it was the first time I'd seen her consciously glamorous. The year before she'd been a girl, well turned-out, but a trifle thin and shaky. But not tonight! Despite the glistening car and my flashy clothes, my new near-mesomorphy, I felt like a worm as I slipped the white orchid corsage around her wrist. (I could have had a bosom corsage; when the florist suggested it, I nearly ran from the shop. What if I jabbed her, right *there*?) And I could have cried at the trouble she'd gone to, for *me*: her hair was up, she wore glittering earrings and a pale sophisticated lipstick that made her lips look chapped. And, mercifully, flat heels. The Godwin family turned out for our departure, so happy that I had asked her, so respectful of my sudden self-assurance. Her father told me to stay out as long as we wished. Keith and the rest of my friends were supposedly at the movies, but had long been planning, I knew, for the milkman's matinee at the Casino Burlesque. I appreciated not having to face him — wondering, in fact, how I ever would again. My best-kept secret was out (Oh, the ways they have of getting us kinky people straightened out!), but she was mine tonight, the purest, most beautiful, the *kindest* girl I'd ever met. And for the first time, for the briefest instant, I connected her to those familiar bodies of the strippers I knew so well, and suddenly I felt that I knew what this dating business was all about and why it excited everyone so. I understood how thrilling it must be actually to touch, and kiss, and look at naked, a beautiful woman whom you loved, and who might touch you back.

The ballroom of the Woman's Club was fussily decorated; dozens of volunteers had worked all week. Clusters of spotlights strained through the sagging roof of crepe (the light blue-filtered, something like the Casino), and the couples in formal gowns and dinner jackets seemed suddenly worthy of college and the professional lives they were destined to enter. A few people stared at Cyndy and smirked at me, and I began to feel a commingling of pride and shame, mostly the latter.

We danced a little — rumbas were my best — but mainly talked, drinking punch and nibbling the rich sugar cookies that her mother, among so many others, had helped to bake. We talked soberly, of my enforced retreat from the Ivy League (not even the car stealers and petty criminals on the fringe of our suburban society had been treated as harshly as I), of Keith's preparation for Princeton. Her gray eyes never left me. I talked of other friends, two who were leaving for a summer in Paris, to polish their French before entering Yale. Cyndy listened to it all, with her cool hand on my wrist. "How I wish Keith had taken someone tonight!" she exclaimed.

Then at last came the finale of the dance: everyone to the center of the floor, everyone once by the reviewing stand, while the orchestra struck up a medley of collegiate tunes. "Hail to Pitt!" cried the president of the Woman's Club, and Pitt's incoming freshmen, after whirling past the bandstand, stopped at an adjoining booth, signed a book, and collected their name tags. The rousing music blared on, the fight songs of Yale and Harvard, Duquesne and Carnegie Tech, Penn State, Wash and Jeff, Denison and Weslyan ...

"Come on, Normie, we can go outside," she suggested. We had just passed under the reviewing stand, where the three judges were standing impassively. Something about the King and Queen; nothing I'd been let in on. The dance floor was thinning as the booths filled. I broke the dance-stride and began walking her out, only to be reminded by the WC president, straining above "Going Back to Old Nassau," to keep on dancing, please. The panel of judges — two teachers selected by the students, and Mr. Hartman, husband of the club's president — were already on the dance floor, smiling at the couples and poking their heads into the clogged booths. Cyndy and I were approaching the doors, near the bruisers in my Penn State booth. One of the algebra teachers was racing toward us, a wide grin on his florid face, and Cyndy gave my hand a tug. "Normie," she whispered, "I think something wonderful is about to happen."

The teacher was with us, a man much shorter than Cyndy, who panted, "Congratulations! You're my choice." He held a wreath of roses above her head, and she lowered her head to receive it. "Ah — what is your name?"

"Cyndy Godwin," she said, "Mr. Esposito."

"Keith Godwin's sister?"

"Yes."

"And how are you, Norman — or should I ask?" Mr. Wheeler, my history teacher, shouldered his way over to us; he held out a bouquet of yellow mums. "Two out of three," he grinned, "that should just about do it."

"Do what?" I asked. I wanted to run, but felt too sick. Cyndy squeezed my cold hand; the orchid nuzzled me like a healthy dog. My knees were numb, face burning.

"Cinch it," said Wheeler, "King Dyer."

"If Hartman comes up with someone else, then

there'll be a vote," Esposito explained. "If he hasn't been bribed, then he'll choose this girl too and that'll be it."

I have never prayed harder. Wheeler led us around the main dance floor, by the rows of chairs that were now empty. The musicians suspended the Cornell evening hymn to enable the WC president to announce dramatically, in her most practiced voice, "The Queen approaches."

There was light applause from the far end of the floor. Couples strained from the college booths as we passed, and I could hear the undertone, "... he's a brain in my biology class, Norman something-or-other, but I don't know her ... " I don't *have* to be here, I reminded myself. No one made me bring her. I could have asked one of the girls from the Planetarium who respected me for my wit and memory alone — or I could be home like any other self-respecting intellectual, in a cold sweat over *I Led Three Lives.* The Pirates were playing a twi-nighter and I could have been out there at Forbes Field in my favorite right-field upperdeck, where I'm an expert ... why didn't I ask her out to a baseball game? Or I could have been where I truly belonged, with my friends down at the Casino Burlesque ...

"You'll lead the next dance, of course," Wheeler whispered. Cyndy was ahead of us, with Esposito.

"Couldn't someone else?" I said. "Maybe you — why not you?" Then I said with sudden inspiration, "She's not a senior. I don't think she's eligible, do you?"

"Don't worry, don't worry, Norman." I had been one of his favorite pupils. "Her class hasn't a thing to do with it, just her looks. And Norman" — he smiled confidently — "she's an extraordinarily beautiful girl."

"Yeah," I agreed, had to. I drifted to the stairs by the bandstand, "I'm going to check anyway," I said. I ran to Mrs. Hartman herself. "Juniors aren't eligible to be Queen, are they? I mean, she'll get her own chance next year when she's going to college right?"

Her smile melted as she finally looked at me; she had been staring into the lights, planning her speech. "Is her escort a senior?"

"Yes," I admitted, "but *he* wasn't chosen. Anyway, he's one of those guys who were kept from the Prom. By rights I don't think he should even be here."

"I don't think this has ever come up before." She squinted into the footlights, a well-preserved woman showing strain. "I presume you're a class officer."

"No, I'm her escort."

"Her, *escort*? I'm afraid I don't understand. Do I know the girl?"

"Cyndy Godwin?"

"You don't mean Betsy Godwin's girl? Surely I'm not to take the prize away from that lovely girl, just because — well, just because *why* for heaven's sake?"

The bandleader leaned over and asked if he should start the "Miss America" theme. Mrs. Hartman fluttered her hand. And then from the other side of the stand, the third judge, Mr. Hartman, hissed to his wife. "Here she is," he beamed.

"Oh, dear me," began Mrs. Hartman.

"A vote?" I suggested. "It has to be democratic."

The second choice, a peppy redhead named Paula, innocently followed Mr. Hartman up the stairs and was already smiling like a winner. She was a popular senior, co-vice-president of nearly everything. Oh, poise! Glorious confidence! Already the front rows were applauding the apparent Queen, though she had only Mr. Hartman's slender cluster of roses to certify her. Now the band started up, the applause grew heavy, and a few enthusiasts even whistled. Her escort, a union leader's son, took his place behind her, and I cheerfully backed off the bandstand, joining Cyndy and the teachers at the foot of the steps. Cyndy had returned her flowers, and Mr. Wheeler was standing dejectedly behind her, holding her bouquet. The wreath dangled from his wrist.

"I feel like a damn fool," he said.

"That was very sweet of you, Normie," Cyndy said, and kissed me hard on the cheek.

"I just can't get over it," Wheeler went on, "if anyone here deserves that damn thing, it's you. At least take the flowers."

I took them for her. "Would you like to go?" I asked. She took my arm and we walked out. I left the flowers on an empty chair.

I felt more at ease as we left the school and headed across the street to the car. It was a cool night, and Cyndy was warm at my side, holding my arm tightly. "Let's have something to eat," I suggested, having practiced the line a hundred times, though it still sounded badly acted. I had planned the dinner as well; *filet mignon* on toast at a classy restaurant out on the highway. I hadn't planned it for quite so early in the night, but even so, I was confident. A girl like Cyndy ate out perhaps once or twice a year, and had probably never ordered *filet.* I was more at home in a fancy restaurant than at a family table.

"I think I'd like that," she said.

"What happened in there was silly — just try to forget all about it," I said. "It's some crazy rule or something."

We walked up a side street, past a dozen cars strewn with crepe.

"It's not winning so much," she said, "it's just an embarrassing thing walking up there like that and then being left holding the flowers."

"There's always next year."

"Oh, I won't get it again. There are lots of

prettier girls than me in my class."

An opening, I thought. So easy to tell her that she was a queen, deservedly, any place. But I couldn't even slip my arm around her waist, or take her hand that rested on my sleeve.

"Well, I think you're really pretty." And I winced.

"Thank you, Norman."

"Prettier than anyone I've ever — "

"I understand," she said Then she took my hand and pointed it above the streetlights. "I'll bet you know all those stars, don't you, Normie?"

"Sure."

"You and Keith — you're going to be really something someday."

We came to the car; I opened Cyndy's door and she got in. "Normie?" she said, as she smoothed her skirt before I closed the door, "could we hurry? I've got to use the bathroom."

I held the door open a second. *How dare she,* I thought, that's not what she's supposed to say. This is a date; you're a queen, my own queen. I looked at the sidewalk, a few feet ahead of us, then said suddenly, bitterly, "There's a hydrant up there. Why don't you use it?"

I slapped the headlights as I walked to my side, hoping they would shatter and I could bleed to death.

"That wasn't a very nice thing to say, Norman," she said as I sat down.

"I know."

"A girl who didn't know you better might have gotten offended."

I drove carefully, afraid now on this night of calamity that I might be especially accident-prone. It was all too clear now, why she had gone with me. Lord, protect me from a too-easy forgiveness. In the restaurant parking lot, I told her how sorry I was for everything, without specifying how broad an everything I was sorry for.

"You were a perfect date," she said. "Come on, let's forget about everything, OK?"

Once inside, she went immediately to the powder room. The hostess, who knew me, guided me to a table at the far end of the main dining room. She would bring Cyndy to me. My dinner jacket attracted some attention; people were already turning to look for my date. I sat down; water was poured for two, a salad bowl appeared. When no one was looking, I pounded the table. *Years of this*, I thought: slapping headlights, kicking tables, wanting to scream a memory out of existence, wanting to shrink back into the stars, the quarries, the right-field stands — things that could no longer contain me. A smiling older man from the table across the aisle snapped his fingers and pointed to his cheek, then to mine, and winked. "Lipstick!" he finally whispered, no longer smiling. I had begun to wet the napkin when I saw Cyndy and the hostess approaching — and the excitement that followed in Cyndy's wake. I stood to meet her. She was the Queen, freshly beautiful, and as I walked to her she took a hanky from her purse and pressed it to her lips. Then in front of everyone, she touched the moistened hanky to my cheek, and we turned to take our places.

HEINRICH BÖLL

The Adventure

Translated by Leila Vennewitz

Fink walked over to the side entrance of the church. Right and left of the cracked asphalt were tiny triangular garden plots bordered with black iron railings: sour, gray-black earth and two box shrubs with leaves as tough and desiccated as leather. Leaning his shoulder against the brown padded door, he opened it and found himself in a musty entrance with another padded door ahead. This one he punched open with his fist, and before entering the church he glanced at a notice on a plywood board which read: "Third Order of St. Francis — Announcements. . . ."

The church was filled with a greenish half-light, and on a wall painted a nondescript color Fink saw a white placard showing a hand, done in black, pointing straight down. Above the stiff, exaggeratedly long forefinger were the words: Confessional Bell. Underneath, in brown holders, were bell-pushes of dark ivory, and name plates. He did not bother to decipher the names but pressed one of the buttons at random, and it seemed to him that this act represented something irrevocable, final. Then he listened — not a sound.

He dipped his finger into a pink plaster stoup in the form of a shell; in the dim light it resembled a great artificial palate with a few bits chipped out of it. Slowly he crossed himself and entered the center nave. On either side he saw two dark confessionals, their red curtains drawn shut, and he now noticed that bomb damage had caused the stucco roof between the gothic columns to crumble away: the ugly masonry of yellow brick was laid bare, somehow it reminded him of an old-fashioned public bathhouse. What was once the main entrance had been walled up with rough stones, and squashed in among them was a crooked old window frame from which the white paint had flaked off.

Fink knelt down in the center nave and tried to pray, but over his folded hands he had to keep watching the four confessionals and peering into the dimness so as not to miss the priest who might suddenly appear from somewhere. He would probably come from the sacristy, up front, where in the semi-darkness Fink could make out a brass bell with a red velvet rope next to the perpetual light. Toward the middle the church got lighter, and he now saw that the whole center nave had been repaired: the ruined, jagged walls supported temporary, almost flat rafters boarded up with grimy old planks — some of the planks were dark with floor varnish — and the saints against the columns were all minus their heads, a helpless, pathetic double rank of strange plaster figures with their heads knocked off and their emblems torn from their grasp, somber truncated torsos which seemed to be holding out their mutilated hands to him in supplication.

Fink tried to summon feelings of remorse and contrition, but without success; he found it hard to concentrate, and from within him there arose a welter of stumbling, spasmodic, imploring prayers, interspersed with memories and the ever-recurring desire to get all this over with quickly and leave, get out and away from this town.

He could already sense it: the thing he wanted to confess was starting to become a memory, to acquire luster; imperceptibly it was emerging from the level of the sordid daily grind, and it seemed to him that one day, soon — he would somehow rise above it and look down: a beautiful, sinful adventure, while in reality — and this he knew too — he had simply followed the rules of the game out of a sort of politeness, rules so depressingly casual and so grimly serious that he had been appalled. Even before it happened, he had been seized with disgust, but he had joined in the game, persuading himself that after all it was nothing but a mechanical act, dictated by nature, while in his heart he knew that the arrow, already in the bow, was going to be released, and would strike him unerringly in that invisible something for which he could find no other name than soul.

He sighed, and began to feel impatient; in his mind's eye the images — those which were gradually acquiring a golden patina, and the real ones — were hovering beside, above, below one another, occasionally merging for an instant, and his gaze traveled in agonizing suspense past the headless saints against their columns to that velvet rope beside the bell.

It occurred to him that possibly the bell was not even working, or that the priest whose name he had not bothered to read was not there. He was not familiar with this form of confession; in the old days they used to make jokes about it. He was just about to get up and go over to the bell-pushes again when he saw in the motionless background of the empty church a dark figure which emerged from the sacristy, genuflected before the altar, and crossed over to the confessionals on the right-hand side. His tense gaze followed the monk; he was tall and slight, and the circle of hair left by the tonsure was thick and black.

Fink quickly tried once more to summon a sense of remorse and contrition, he silently intoned the formulas he had known by heart for twenty years, and stood up. As he stepped into the aisle he stumbled; somewhere in the red and white tiles with their pattern of lilies there must be a damaged place; he steadied himself against a prayer stool and heard the priest switch off the tiny light and pull the curtain aside. As he knelt down in the airless, dark and very uncomfortable little space and made out the pale ear behind the grille, he felt his heart pounding in his throat; he was too agitated to speak.

"Praise be to Jesus Christ," said a colorless, detached voice.

He forced out a "For ever and ever Amen" and was silent. The sweat was pouring down his back, making his shirt cling to his skin, closely and relentlessly, as if it had been soaked in water; there seemed to be no room left to breathe. The priest cleared his throat.

"I have committed adultery," stammered Fink, and he knew that with that he had said about all he was capable of saying.

"Are you married?"

"No."

"But the woman is?"

"Yes."

"How many times?" The question brought him instantly to his senses. Everything that had been swimming in front of his vision, this large white ear, which looked enormous to him, and the grille — of a strange, crisp brown like the latticework on an apple pie — all this he now saw quite clearly, in all its reality, and he looked into the drooping sleeve of the priest's propped-up arm, a dark cavity between the monk's habit and the pale skin covered with light hairs.

"Once," and a deep involuntary sigh escaped him.

"When?" The questions came tersely, rapidly, impersonally, like a doctor's during an examination.

"Today," he said. Actually it had already receded far into the past for him, but the word brought it back again before his eyes, like a camera zooming toward its object to fix it for ever. One was compelled to look closely at something one did not want to look at closely.

"Avoid seeing this woman."

Now for the first time Fink realized he would be seeing her again; a pretty little housewife with a firm neck and wearing a red housecoat, with eyes which were both boring and sad, and he pictured her with such intensity that he almost missed the priest's question.

"Do you love her?"

He could not say no; to say yes seemed even more monstrous. He thought about it, while the sweat accumulated hot and burning above his eyebrows. "No," he said quickly, adding: "It will be very difficult to avoid seeing her."

The priest was silent, and for a moment Fink saw the lowered lids jerk up, a pair of very quiet gray eyes.

"I am a salesman for a firm that makes prefabricated houses," he said, "and the — the lady has ordered a house from us."

"And you have that territory?"

"Yes." He thought of how he would have to negotiate with her, present plans, discuss estimates, advise on details — countless details which, if one wanted to, could be dragged out for months.

"You must see that you are transferred."

Fink was silent.

The voice became more forceful. "You must do all you can not to see her again. Habit is strong, very strong. You have the sincere desire and resolve not to see the woman again?"

"Yes," said Fink at once, and he knew that for the first time he was really speaking the truth.

"Try; do everything in your power. Think of the Bible message: If thy left hand offend thee, cut it off. Accept the possibility of material loss." He was silent for a moment. "I know it is not easy, but Hell doesn't make things easy for us."

His voice had lost its personal quality again when he said: "Anything else?"

Fink was startled. He was not familiar with this kind of confession, although by this time he realized it was serious, extremely serious, more serious than that regular mechanical hygiene he underwent at home every three months with the chaplain.

"Anything else?" asked the voice impatiently. "When did you last confess?"

"Eight weeks ago."

"And go to Mass?"

"Four."

In a monotonous voice the priest began to intone the Commandments, the way he did with the penitents he was accustomed to, people who scarcely knew the Creed, whose religious vocabulary consisted of Our Father and Hail Mary. Fink was feeling uncomfortable, he wanted to leave.

"No," he said each time quietly, as far as the fifth Commandment. The priest left out the sixth.

"Stealing," said the priest without emotion, "and lying, the seventh and eight Commandments."

Fink felt his color rising, it surged hot into his ears. For God's sake, he wasn't a thief.

"Have you told a lie?"

Fink said nothing. Never before had anyone asked him whether he had told a lie. In any case it seemed to him he had never confessed before. These crude formulas struck him like hammer blows, and while he was thinking he had never confessed before, he muttered: "Oh well, the houses, our houses are not quite the way they look in the catalogue — I mean, they — people are often disappointed when they actually see them. . . ."

The priest could not suppress an "Aha." He said: "We must be honest about that too, although . . ." he groped for words, "although it seems impossible. But it is a lie to sell something of whose value one is not convinced." He cleared his throat again, and Fink saw the propped-up arm disappear as the priest began to whisper: "Now we will take it all together and fervently beseech Our Lord Jesus Christ to obtain our forgiveness. He died on the Cross to free us from our sins, and each one of our sins nails Him once more to the Cross. Summon remorse and contrition within yourself again, and as a penance recite one decade of the Sorrowful Mystery."

The priest sat up straight in the center of the confessional, murmuring with closed eyes, then he suddenly turned his face toward Fink again, pronounced the *Absolvo te* in a clear voice, and made the sign of the Cross over him.

"Praise be to Jesus Christ — "

"For ever and ever Amen!" said Fink.

He was stiff all over, and he felt as if hours had gone by. He sat down in a pew and pulled out his handkerchief, and as he began to dry the sweat off he noticed the priest disappearing again into the sacristy.

Fink was tired. He tried to pray, but the words tumbled back inside him like a heavy fall of rock, and while he fought against sleep he saw through half-closed lids that in the dark corner next to the side door candles were now burning in front of the altar of the Mother of God: the cheap paraffin tapers flickered restlessly, consuming themselves in feverish haste, and their shimmer swung the silhouette of a small, old woman onto the wall of the center nave, in gigantic and outlandish detail: single hairs protruding from her forehead stood out hard and black on the wall, a childlike nose and the tired slackness of her lips moving silently: a fleeting memorial, towering above the truncated plaster figures and seeming to grow out beyond the edge of the roof.

JORGE LUIS BORGES

The Garden of Forking Paths

Translated by Donald A. Yates

On page 22 of Liddell Hart's *History of World War I* you will read that an attack against the Serre-Mountauban line by thirteen British divisions (supported by 1,400 artillery pieces) planned for the 24th of July, 1916, had to be postponed until the morning of the 29th. The torrential rains, Captain Liddell Hart comments, caused this delay, an insignificant one, to be sure.

The following statement, dictated, reread and sighed by Dr. Yu Tsun, former professor of English at the *Hochschule* at Tsingtao, throws an unsuspected light over the whole affair. The first two pages of the document are missing.

"... and I hung up the receiver. Immediately afterwards, I recognized the voice that had answered in German. It was that of Captain Richard Madden. Madden's presence in Viktor Runeberg's apartment meant the end of our anxieties and — but this seemed, *or should have seemed,* very secondary to me — also the end of our lives. It meant that Runeberg had been arrested or murdered.[1] Before the sun set on the day, I would encounter the same fate. Madden was implacable. Or rather, he was obliged to be so. An Irishman at the service of England, a man accused of laxity and perhaps of treason, how could he fail to seize and be thankful for such a miraculous opportunity; the discovery, capture, maybe even the death of two agents of the German Reich? I went up to my room; absurdly I locked the door and threw myself on my back on the narrow iron cot. Through the window I saw the familiar roofs and the cloud-shaded six o'clock sun. It seemed incredible to me that that day without premonitions or symbols should be the one of my inexorable death. In spite of my dead father, in spite of having been a child in a symmetrical garden of Hai Feng, was I — now — going to die? Then I reflected that everything happens to a man precisely, precisely *now.* Centuries of centuries and only in the present do things happen; countless men in the air, on the face of the earth and the sea, and all that really is happening is happening to me ... The almost intolerable recollection of Madden's horselike face banished these wanderings. In the midst of my hatred and terror (it means nothing to me now to speak of terror, now that I have mocked Richard Madden, now that my throat yearns for the noose) it occurred to me that that tumultuous and doubtless happy warrior did not suspect that I possessed the Secret. The name of the exact location of the new British artillery park on the River Ancre. A bird streaked across the gray sky and blindly I translated it into an airplane and that airplane into many (against the French sky) annihilating the artillery station with vertical bombs. If only my mouth, before a bullet shattered it, could cry out that secret name so it could be heard in Germany ... My human voice was very weak. How might I make it carry to the ear of the Chief? To the ear of that sick and hateful man who knew nothing of Runeberg and me save that we were in Staffordshire and who was waiting in vain for our report in his arid office in Berlin, endlessly examining newspapers ... I said out loud: *I must flee.* I sat up noiselessly, in a useless perfection of silence, as if Madden were already lying in wait for me. Something — perhaps the mere vain ostentation of proving my resources were nil — made me look through my pockets. I found what I knew I would find. The American watch, the nickel chain and the square coin, the key ring with the incriminating useless keys to Runeberg's apartment, the notebook, a letter which I resolved to destroy immediately (and which I did not destroy), a crown, two shillings and a few pence, the red and blue pencil, the handkerchief, the revolver with one bullet. Absurdly, I took it in my hand and weighed it in order to inspire courage within myself. Vaguely I thought that a pistol report can be heard at a great distance. In ten minutes my plan was perfected. The telephone book listed the name of the only person capable of transmitting the message; he lived in a suburb of Fenton, less than a half hour's train ride away.

I am a cowardly man. I say it now, now that I have carried to its end a plan whose perilous nature no one can deny. I know its execution was terrible. I didn't do it for Germany, no. I care nothing for a barbarous country which imposed upon me the abjection of being a spy. Besides, I know of a man from England — a modest man — who for me is no less great than Goethe. I talked with him for scarcely an hour, but during that

1. An hypothesis both hateful and odd. The Prussian spy Hans Rabener, alias Viktor Runeberg, attacked with drawn automatic the bearer of the warrant for his arrest, Captain Richard Madden. The latter, in self-defense, inflicted the wound which brought about Runeberg's death. (Editor's note.)

hour he was Goethe . . . I did it because I sensed that the Chief somehow feared people of my race — for the innumerable ancestors who merge within me. I wanted to prove to him that a yellow man could save his armies. Besides, I had to flee from Captain Madden. His hands and his voice could call at my door at any moment. I dressed silently, bade farewell to myself in the mirror, went downstairs, scrutinized the peaceful street and went out. The station was not far from my home, but I judged it wise to take a cab. I argued that in this way I ran less risk of being recognized; the fact is that in the deserted street I felt myself visible and vulnerable, infinitely so. I remember that I told the cab driver to stop a short distance before the main entrance. I got out with voluntary, almost painful slowness; I was going to the village of Ashgrove but I bought a ticket for a more distant station. The train left within a very few minutes, at eight-fifty. I hurried; the next one would leave at nine-thirty. There was hardly a soul on the platform. I went through the coaches; I remember a few farmers, a woman dressed in mourning, a young boy who was reading with fervor the *Annals* of Tacitus, a wounded and happy soldier. The coaches jerked forward at last. A man whom I recognized ran in vain to the end of the platform. It was Captain Richard Madden. Shattered, trembling, I shrank into the far corner of the seat, away from the dreaded window.

From this broken state I passed into an almost abject felicity. I told myself that the duel had already begun and that I had won the first encounter by frustrating, even if for forty minutes, even if by a stroke of fate, the attack of my adversary. I argued that this slightest of victories foreshadowed a total victory. I argued (no less fallaciously) that my cowardly felicity proved that I was a man capable of carrying out the adventure successfully. From this weakness I took strength that did not abandon me. I foresee that man will resign himself each day to more atrocious undertakings; soon there will be no one but warriors and brigands; I give them this counsel: *The author of an atrocious undertaking ought to imagine that he has already accomplished it, ought to impose upon himself a future as irrevocable as the past.* Thus I proceeded as my eyes of a man already dead registered the elapsing of the day, which was perhaps the last, and the diffusion of the night. The train ran gently along, amid ash trees. It stopped, almost in the middle of the fields. No one announced the name of the station. "Ashgrove?" I asked a few lads on the platform. "Ashgrove," they replied. I got off.

A lamp enlightened the platform but the faces of the boys were in shadow. One questioned me, "Are you going to Dr. Stephen Albert's house?" Without waiting for my answer, another said, "The house is a long way from here, but you won't get lost if you take this road to the left and at every crossroads turn again to your left." I tossed them a coin (my last), descended a few stone steps and started down the solitary road. It went downhill slowly. It was of elemental earth; overhead the branches were tangled; the low, full moon seemed to accompany me.

For an instant, I thought that Richard Madden in some way had penetrated my desperate plan. Very quickly, I understood that that was impossible. The instructions to turn always to the left reminded me that such was the common procedure for discovering the central point of certain labyrinths. I have some understanding of labyrinths: not for nothing am I the great grandson of that Ts'ui Pên who was governor of Yunnan and who renounced worldly power in order to write a novel that might be even more populous than the *Hung Lu Meng* and to construct a labyrinth in which all men would become lost. Thirteen years he dedicated to the heterogeneous tasks, but the hand of a stranger murdered him — and his novel was incoherent and no one found the labyrinth. Beneath English trees I meditated on that lost maze: I imagined it inviolate and perfect at the secret crest of a mountain; I imagined it erased by rice fields or beneath the water; I imagined it infinite, no longer composed of octagonal kiosks and returning paths, but of rivers and provinces and kingdoms . . . I thought of a labyrinth of labyrinths, of one sinuous spreading labyrinth that would encompass the past and the future and in some way involve the stars. Absorbed in these illusory images, I forgot my destiny of one pursued. I felt myself to be, for an unknown period of time, an abstract perceiver of the world. The vague, living countryside, the moon, the remains of the day worked on me, as well as the slope of the road which eliminated any possiblility of weariness. The afternoon was intimate, infinite. The road descended and forked among the now confused meadows. A high-pitched, almost syllabic music approached and receded in the shifting of the wind, dimmed by leaves and distance. I thought that a man can be an enemy of other men, of the moments of other men, but not of a country: not of fireflies, words, gardens, streams of water, sunset. Thus I arrived before a tall, rusty gate. Between the iron bars I made out a poplar grove and a pavilion. I understood suddenly two things, the first trivial, the second almost unbelievable: the music came from the pavilion, and the music was Chinese. For precisely that reason I had openly accepted it without paying it any heed. I do not remember whether there was a bell or whether I knocked with my hand. The sparkling of the music continued.

From the rear of the house within a lantern approached: a lantern that the trees sometimes striped and sometimes eclipsed, a paper lantern that had the form of a drum and the color of the moon. A tall man bore it. I didn't see his face for the light blinded me. He opened the door and said slowly, in my own language: "I see that the pious Hsi P'êng persists in correcting my solitude. You no doubt wish to see the garden?"

I recognized the name of one of our consuls and I replied, disconcerted, "The garden?"

"The garden of forking paths."

Something stirred in my memory and I uttered with incomprehensible certainty, "The garden of my ancestor Ts'ui Pên."

"Your ancestor? Your illustrious ancestor? Come in."

The damp path zigzagged like those of my childhood. We came to a library of Eastern and Western books. I recognized bound in yellow silk several volumes of the Lost Encyclopedia, edited by the Third Emperor of the Luminous Dynasty but never printed. The record on the phonograph revolved next to a bronze phoenix. I also recall a *famille rose* vase and another, many centuries older, of that shade of blue which our craftsmen copied from the potters of Persia ...

Stephen Albert observed me with a smile. He was, as I have said, very tall, sharp-featured, with gray eyes and a gray beard. He told me that he had been a missionary in Tientsin "before aspiring to become a Sinologist."

We sat down — I on a long, low divan, he with his back to the window and a tall circular clock. I calculated that my pursuer, Richard Madden, could not arrive for at least an hour. My irrevocable determination could wait.

"An astounding fate, that of Ts'ui Pên," Stephen Albert said. "Governor of his native province, learned in astronomy, in astrolology and in the tireless interpretation of the canonical books, chess player, famous poet and calligrapher — he abandoned all this in order to compose a book and a maze. He renounced the pleasures of both tyranny and justice, of his populous couch, of his banquets and even of erudition — all to close himself up for thirteen years in the Pavilion of the Limpid Solitude. When he died, his heirs found nothing save chaotic manuscripts. His family, as you may be aware, wished to condemn them to the fire; but his executor — a Taoist or Buddhist monk — insisted on their publication."

"We descendants of Ts'ui Pên," I replied, "continue to curse that monk. Their publication was senseless. The book is an indeterminate heap of contradictory drafts. I examined it once: in the third chapter the hero dies, in the fourth he is alive. As for the other undertaking of Ts'ui Pên, his labyrinth ..."

"Here is Ts'ui Pên's labyrinth," he said, indicating a tall lacquered desk.

"An ivory labyrinth!" I exclaimed. "A minimum labyrinth."

"A labyrinth of symbols," he corrected. "An invisible labyrinth of time. To me, a barbarous Englishman, has been entrusted the revelation of this diaphanous mystery. After more than a hundred years, the details are irretrievable; but it is not hard to conjecture what happened. Ts'ui Pên must have said once: *I am withdrawing to write a book.* And another time: *I am withdrawing to construct a labyrinth.* Every one imagined two works; to no one did it occur that the book and the maze were one and the same thing. The Pavilion of the Limpid Solitude stood in the center of a garden that was perhaps intricate; that circumstance could have suggested to the heirs a physical labyrinth. Hs'ui Pên died; no one in the vast territories that were his came upon the labyrinth; the confusion of the novel suggested to me that *it* was the maze. Two circumstances gave me the correct solution of the problem. One: the curious legend that Ts'ui Pên had planned to create a labyrinth which would be strictly infinite. The other: a fragment of a letter I discovered."

Albert rose. He turned his back on me for a moment; he opened a drawer of the black and gold desk. He faced me and in his hands he held a sheet of paper that had once been crimson, but was now pink and tenuous and cross-sectioned. The fame of Ts'ui Pên as a calligrapher had been justly won. I read, uncomprehendingly and with fervor, these words written with a minute brush by a man of my blood: *I leave to the various futures (not to all) my garden of forking paths.* Wordlessly, I returned the sheet. Albert continued:

"Before unearthing this letter, I had questioned myself about the ways in which a book can be infinite. I could think of nothing other than a cyclic volume, a circular one. A book whose last page was identical with the first, a book which had the possibility of continuing indefinitely. I remembered too that night which is at the middle of the Thousand and One Nights when Scheherazade (through a magical oversight of the copyist) begins to relate word for word the story of the Thousand and One Nights, establishing the risk of coming once again to the night when she must repeat it, and thus on to infinity. I imagined as well a Platonic, hereditary work, transmitted from father to son, in which each new individual adds a chapter or corrects with pious care the pages of his elders. These conjectures diverted me; but none seemed to correspond, not even remotely, to the contradictory chapters of Ts'ui Pên. In the midst of this perplexity, I received from Oxford the manuscript you have examined. I lingered, naturally, on the sentence: *I leave to the various futures (not to all) my garden of forking paths.* Almost instantly, I understood: 'the garden of forking paths' was the chaotic novel; the phrase 'the various futures (not to all)' suggested to me the forking in time, not in space. A broad rereading of the work confirmed the theory. In all fictional works, each time a man is confronted with several alternatives, he chooses one and eliminates the others; in the fiction of Ts'ui Pên, he chooses — simultaneously — all of them. *He creates,* in this way, diverse futures, diverse times which themselves also proliferate and fork. Here, then, is the explanation of the novel's contradictions. Fang, let us say, has a secret; a stranger calls at his door; Fang resolves to kill him. Naturally, there are several possible outcomes: Fang can kill the intruder, the intruder can kill Fang, they both can escape, they both can die, and so forth. In the work of Ts'ui Pên, all possible outcomes occur; each one is the point of departure for other forkings. Sometimes, the paths of this labyrinth converge: for example, you arrive at this house, but in one of the possible pasts you are my enemy, in another, my friend. If you will resign yourself to my incurable pronunciation, we shall read a few pages."

His face, within the vivid circle of the lamplight, was unquestionably that of an old man, but with something unalterable about it, even immortal. He read with slow precision two versions of the same epic chapter. In the first, an army marches to a battle across a lonely mountain; the horror of the rocks and shadows makes the men undervalue their lives and they gain an easy victory. In the second, the same army traverses a palace where a great festival is taking place; the resplendent battle seems to them a continuation of the celebration and they win the victory. I listened with proper veneration to these ancient narratives, perhaps less admirable in themselves than the fact that they had been created by my blood and were being restored to me by a man of a remote empire, in the course of a desperate adventure, on a Western isle. I remember the last words, repeated in each version like a secret commandment: *Thus fought the heroes, tranquil their admirable hearts, violent their swords, resigned to kill and to die.*

From that moment on, I felt about me and within my dark body an invisible, intangible swarming. Not the swarming of the divergent, parallel and finally coalescent armies, but a more inaccessible, more intimate agitation that they in some manner prefigured. Stephen Albert continued:

"I don't believe that your illustrious ancestor played idly with these variations. I don't consider it credible that he would sacrifice thirteen years to the infinite execution of a rhetorical experiment. In your country, the novel is a subsidiary form of literature; in Ts'ui Pên's time it was a despicable form. Ts'ui Pên was a brilliant novelist, but he was also a man of letters who doubtless did not consider himself a mere novelist. The testimony of his contemporaries proclaims — and his life fully confirms — his metaphysical and mystical interests. Philosophic controversy usurps a good part of the novel. I know that of all problems, none disturbed him so greatly nor worked upon him so much as the abysmal problem of time. Now then, the latter is the only problem that does not figure in the pages of the *Garden.* He does not even use the word that signifies *time.* How do you explain this voluntary omission!"

I proposed several solutions — all unsatisfactory. We discussed them. Finally, Stephen Albert said to me:

"In a riddle whose answer is chess, what is the only prohibited word?"

I thought a moment and replied, "The word *chess.*"

"Precisely," said Albert. "*The Garden of Forking Paths* is an enormous riddle, or parable, whose theme is time; this recondite cause prohibits its mention. To omit a word always, to resort to inept metaphors and obvious periphrases, is perhaps the most emphatic way of stressing it. That is the tortuous method preferred, in each of the meanderings of his indefatigable novel, by the oblique Ts'ui Pên. I have compared hundreds of manuscripts, I have corrected the errors that the negligence of the copyists has introduced, I have guessed the plan of this chaos, I have re-established — I believe I have re-established — the primordial organization, I have translated the entire work: it is clear to me that not once does he employ the word 'time.' The explanation is obvious: *The Garden of Forking Paths* is an incomplete, but not false, image of the universe as Ts'ui Pên conceived it. In contrast to Newton and Schopenhauer, your ancestor did not believe in a uniform, absolute time. He believed in an infinite series of times, in a growing, dizzying net of divergent, convergent and parallel times. This network of times which approached one another, forked, broke off, or were unaware of one another for centuries, embraces *all* possibilities of time. We do not exist in the majority of these times; in some you exist, and not I; in others I, and not you; in others, both of us. In the present one, which a favorable fate has granted me, you have arrived at my house; in another, while crossing the garden, you found me dead; in still another, I utter these same words, but I am a mistake, a ghost."

"In every one," I pronounced, not without a tremble to my voice, "I am grateful to you and revere you for your re-creation of the garden of Ts'ui Pên."

"Not in all," he murmured with a smile. "Time forks perpetually toward innumerable futures. In one of them I am your enemy."

Once again I felt the swarming sensation of which I have spoken. It seemed to me that the humid garden that surrounded the house was infinitely saturated with invisible persons. Those persons were Albert and I, secret, busy and multiform in other dimensions of time. I raised my eyes and the tenuous nightmare dissolved. In the yellow and black garden there was only one man; but this man was as strong as a statue . . . this man was approaching along the path and he was Captain Richard Madden.

"The future already exists," I replied, "but I am your friend. Could I see the letter again?"

Albert rose. Standing tall, he opened the drawer of the tall desk; for the moment his back was to me. I had readied the revolver. I fired with extreme caution. Albert fell uncomplainingly, immediately. I swear his death was instantaneous — a lightning stroke.

The rest is unreal, insignificant. Madden broke in, arrested me. I have been condemned to the gallows. I have won out abominably; I have communicated to Berlin the secret name of the city they must attack. They bombed it yesterday; I read it in the same papers that offered to England the mystery of the learned Sinologist Stephen Albert who was murdered by a stranger, one Yu Tsun. The Chief had deciphered this mystery. He knew my problem was to indicate (through the uproar of the war) the city called Albert, and that I found no other means to do so than to kill a man of that name. He does not know (no one can know) my innumerable contrition and weariness."

GEORGE BOWERING

The Elevator

Last night I was thinking: there I sit alone in the dark room with a little portable television — we face each other with the lights of our opposite eyes, lenses bending toward each other, and in the dark I suddenly know what it is coming in rays to my eyes, thru them to my front brain — the blue light of the television, the open end of the set, it is actually a hole out of this darkness, thru all walls, into the open world. It is an extension of my eyes, the television set and the invisible camera somewhere at the other end of the wires. I can sit in my darkened room and see into the world, whichever direction I'm looking at the time. Dip — look into bedroom, young wife in silk to her knees, husband with tie hanging loose in front of him like an Anglican minister thing, talking to each other, and my ear is there too in their room, they are shouting at each other, and I see — my eye looks down at them from the ceiling and the walls have ears.

Till I thought: how still I'm sitting. Sure, so I can watch into the New York bedroom, zoom from airplane over the Riviera to look at bathing suits. No, because I'm necessary there. Can I remember turning the television on? What was I thinking at the time? Did I do it on purpose? I hesitate to think it. Am I annexed by the camera? Part of its action. The brain for its eye. Or worse. It came into the room to look across at me, then stayed there all the time while I came in and went out, it was waiting for me, always there when I came in with bottle of beer and newspaper, turning on the dial, to look at over the top of the news. Come here, fingers.

"You. Television. Who needs you?"

"This is probably the salad oil you're using now."

"Salad oil. Up yours with your salad oil."

The cat jumped down off the wooden table where he'd been licking the dried food on yesterday's plate, and he made that throaty meow as his front feet hit the floor first, then his back ones, then gather, and spring into a slow walk across the floor to me, tail in the air, his eyes now adding to the television, looking at me. What if television looked from a cat's eyes, in the dark? What's in that bedroom then?

The cat walked back and forth in front of me, rubbing his sides against my legs, stepping heavily with one cat foot on my toe. He was hungry. Welcome aboard. Neither of us had eaten since the day before. But for the cat it was sad. I hadn't let him out, and he'd shit in the empty bathtub again, and that was the last food he'd eaten, already hard and black in the white tub. Down the drain with you all — cat, shit, television. I got up and went out. The cat scooted out with me. As he disappeared around the corner of the house his tail went down, crouch already in the back.

"Good hunting, Janet."

Moreover thou hast taken thy sons and thy daughters whom thou hast borne unto me, and these hast thou sacrificed unto them to be devoured. Is this of thy whoredoms a small matter, that thou has slain my children, and delivered them to cause them to pass thru the fire for them?

Ezekial claimed that God said that to Jerusalem, but Zeke had been reading the older prophets, including several false ones, and he knew that's what the folks wanted him to say. They're still saying it, and Jerusalem among others is still doing it. I was one of the lucky children who hadn't passed thru the fire. But I'd always taken precautions. Going down in an elevator, I always flexed my knees in case of a runaway crash. But I had lately got too involved with this too — thinking too hard about a burst blood vessel in the brain can cause a burst blood vessel in the brain. Then where are you?

Outside the house, looking at the snow.

Maybe a couple quarts of fuel in the gas tank, so I started it up in the dark and drove lights out thru the streets, lighted by blue gaslights of Alberta natural gas, shining off the black steel of the car stretched out after the windshield in front of me, till I got downtown in the East End, Eighth Avenue, Sunday night, no stores open, wind in the dark flipping Saturday's paper end over end along the sidewalk till it came flat against dark red 1910 bricks. Cornices two stories higher jutted into the wind like leading edges of aircraft. I stopped the car and got out, thinking I was a professor, professional before I came to Calgary, so I have never walked alone in the East End winery part of town here as I had in Vancouver. And here there were no pigeons on the sidewalk.

The wind was cold, and at select corners it blew up peacock tails of snow, into the face turned the wrong way. I was the only one on the street. It was early March, no end to winter. In Vancouver the crocuses were popping up in people's lawns. I met an old man in a dark coat that came to his heels.

"Cold night," I said.

"You're right there," he said.

Without calling me sonny or young fellow. Here there's not much trouble about differing ages. The old men wear shoes with cracks down the back. The young wear boots that will eventually wear out. In the windows of the second-hand stores there are boots for eleven dollars, bright yellow next to bright yellow guitars and shiny flipdown toasters, and the big jacknife with twenty blades in various degrees of open.

I watched the man walk farther along the sidewalk, his hand up on his bald head, walking carefully so the broken shoes wouldn't fall off his feet, and I noticed he was Chinese, the darkness rushing in to fill the place between us.

What is your name what is your name? Long coat frosted by the wind, moving into the loom of dark East Eighth Avenue, snow blowing into long skidded footprints, collar blown against my chin, something glanced off the side of my head and struck hard downward on my shoulder. I turned and crouched and it was dark there in front of me. I hit out and grabbed at movement, hands sliding in wet darkness as he moved away and came back. It was in his hand at the side, the thing he hit me with. My one arm was numb, hanging useless, but I stepped that way and hit him low in the middle and he spun slightly to my side and I kicked out and missed. The street was gone, the town was gone, the old Chinese man. The thing came at me again, past my face, and I knew my only way was to rush, and I swept him, so he must have been small, against the brick wall, and hit him as fast as I could here out of the wind. I hit and held him against the wall with my body, knee coming up against my thigh, looking for my soft groin. I saw the head for a second and smashed with my fist and back with the back of my hand, and it was hard, bones of my knuckles coming thru skin, I felt his head give way, and it hit the side of the building. He fell into the pile of snow at the base of the wall and I kicked him, but he didn't move. The thing was still in his hand. I walked away hurting, close to the wall, and toward the car. I hadn't seen his face. Old or young, I hadn't seen him. I bounced off the wall as I walked away.

In the car I sat with the engine running and fumbled with cigarettes till I got one in my mouth, the cigarette very little in my thick lips, the cold and the pain taking away all taste. I started the car and drove north, into the wind and snow.

"The temperature in Calgary a chilly three degrees," said the radio.

Chaucer. I've done Chaucer, Shakespeare, Donne, Milton, Blake. Now Pope, Wordsworth, Shelley, Browning. Professor. People outside the university call me Professor. In a town like Calgary — city they like to call it but the railroad tracks still cut it in half, demonstrably, like the small towns that clamp around the tracks from east to west across the prairie. In February of this cold winter dead antelope lay frozen along a hundred miles of Alberta tracks, stiff legs pointing up at CPR passengers rolling by, eating turkey sandwiches with gravy in the dining cars. Calgary is 80 miles from the mountains and hundreds of miles from the nearest city, fed by television towers and the boxcars that carry newsprint. This university now four years old, where teachers from Germany and Chicago and Vancouver speak to inmates of Calgary about far foreign things.

That's where I was going. I had left the apartment where there was no food, and the cafés downtown were closed. Couldn't stay there now, a body lying against the wall dead or alive probably alive, and young or old. Small, with something in his hand. The car drove me out to the old Banff highway, turn left at the university road, around to the bus stop.

Outside the wind was stronger here on the edge of the prairie, blowing in from the Rocky Mountain Trench snow, piled for days waiting for a wind. I kept my collar up and bent over, walking to the library. My office on the fourth floor. All the lights were on; a few students would be there on the coldest night.

"Sir, I've been doing some reading."

"Good."

"I've heard that Blake was crazy. How are we supposed to read his poetry? I mean — "

"As if he was crazy. Do you think Jesus was sane? Don't underestimate Jesus, either."

Jesus tipped against his own dark satanic windmills. The glass front of the library building loomed yellow in the dark wind, snow cutting around the straight corners, glass holding it off from the books. The hole in my right shoe allowed wetness that would dye the bottom of my foot the colour of whatever sock I was wearing. In the library no one needs shoes. Eyes.

The heavy glass door gave way to the wind half open, and I stepped in to sudden heat and stillness and the drifted snow started to melt at my throat. What time is it? Ten o'clock right on. Students — young girls with ski slacks and boys in red poplin jackets — were being rushed out of the building by skinny library women anxious to be home in time for the late show. I rode the elevator upstairs to the fourth floor, my office.

The lights were bright oblongs in the ceiling, this place meant for stacks of books, but now temporarily they said full of cubicles, offices, each with bookshelves, desk, chair on wheels, blackboard, pin-board, piles of papers, ashtrays and curious oblong waste-paper buckets emptied every night by unseen janitors, large windows in a room full of easy chairs, lounge, with west windows, black now, mountains in the distance, snow hissing on the glass.

I was there to do something meaningful. I sat

down and unfolded a lined paper and made marks on it with a red ballpoint pen.

I opened a book and started to read a long poem by Robert Browning, but I stopped after a dozen lines — somebody in Renaissance Italy talking in long lines.

There were no footsteps in the hall. All the other offices were empty. Nobody getting ahead but me.

I smoked a cigarette and carelessly threw the burning end on the floor.

I continued marking papers in the silence that's the same anywhere there's an empty school — numbers nailed to the doors now with no meaning, blackboards within closed rooms, administrating to rows of empty seats. Chalkdust could fill the air without liming any pink lungs, like the silence, in those rooms and halls so used to the fullness of talk. I make my living by being able to talk, me, so shy I couldn't raise my questioning hand in a classroom full of my peers, most of them stupid, afraid of getting a job. I was afraid of getting out of the wide halls and desk-filled rooms. The papers in front of my eyes on the grey-topped desk weren't familiar, I'd never written anything like that when I was a freshman — hesitant, awkwardly trying to fit long nouns from lecture notes into English sentences, with verbs, so shaky, so unsure. It made my heart soft as it always did. I wanted to sit close to each one, boy or girl, shadowy Walt Whitman teacher, and tell them not to try to make sense of the coincidence of bafflement in the schoolbooks of stone university, and the warm fluid that welled threateningly and buried between their soft bellies and seldom-touched thighs.

They could so obviously offer a kind of comfort to me, none of them terrified or bewildered by television; they could sit in partial observance and scrutinize the weekly trials of a blood-hand doctor, and sympathize with his patience for the sudden appearance of bottled salad oil. I was certainly gifted with speech — I could hold them, thirty at a time, and speak slowly as I wanted, authority coming from the verses in my own 170 pounds. But there were a hundred thousand television screens in Calgary, burning chill blue in dark March nights behind heavy window drapes. Could I hold up my end in a face-to-face encounter? I dropped my red pen on the paper and wheeled my chair back to the shelves of books.

There was dried blood on the knuckles of my right hand. Time to get up like the clean-conscious American on the screen, go out and like they say bathe the hand in warm water, then cold water, it closes the bloody pores. It feeds the bloody cat. I got up to leave, grabbing coat from the rack and carefully fingering the thing on the edge of the door, locker of offices, opener of minds, fair friends never met.

BERGEN, Norway (AP) — Norwegian pigs are becoming so idle they are biting each other's tails too much and causing a rise in infectious diseases, a slaughter-house veterinary surgeon has reported.

FALSE TEETH — Chewing Efficiency increased up to 35%.

New, new.

I walked then, head down, to the elevator, flexing my knees experimentaly, slightly, while walking, my worn suede shoes phantom in the empty hall. Push button. Red arrow light. Distant down sounds of lurching machinery. When it came I walked in, looking at the shape of my toes through the suede. The door whisped shut behind me. Then the lights went out, and the elevator stopped going down. My knees flexed without my thinking of it. The liquid in the top of my head dropped abruptly to earlobe level. I composed myself, knowing there was a power failure, ready to wait. I'd seen it happen before; all the bright yellow lights would be gone from the windows, and the eerie spotlights with power batteries would be shining down from the high walls, a selective light in the gloom of stone corridors. My fingers had curled into a fist, slightly opening the cuts again, dab of fresh blood. It was absolutely black in the elevator.

And breathing. A scent, perfume. She was in the black too, I hadn't known there was anyone else in the elevator, someone left after the doors were locked. That had happened before too.

The breathing was right beside me, a hand touched my chin, end of fingers, she was walking slowly in the dark, hand out in front of her, it touched me for just a second, then was snatched away. I stood still. Her breathing was not back where it started from. I was breathing too, and maybe that would make her feel all right. Because I had no idea what she looked like, how old, how big, I had had my head down coming into the elevator.

"What happened?" she whispered. Her voice was very close. I wondered why.

"Power went off," I whispered back, across close darkness. "It's okay. We just have to wait."

"Couldn't we yell or something?"

"Too late at night, nobody would hear us."

There was probably a janitor or a late-working librarian. Well, no sense complicating things. What good would yelling do? No amount of yelling turns on the lights. That had happened before, too. She must have moved quietly because I could feel her arm brush mine. It went away, and came back. I was comfort in the dark, I suppose, the professor. Meek and mild George Delsing puts on his magic necktie, mutters the ancient words of the scroll, and becomes: Professor-Man!

The dark man in the elevator put his arm out slowly, slowly, plunged up to the shoulder in the darkness, around probably behind her, and drew it toward him till it touched. Her. She was wearing a coat for the cold, here unnecessary for the dark, a man could be wearing nothing; teaching in a school for blind girls, walking naked around the room, in and out among the blind, dark alleys of the elevator. The girl, the woman, didn't move. Till I felt her hand on my wrist where I was holding her. I placed my other hand on her, and she came up to my neck, her hair scented under my chin. Then I felt her hands on me, here in the university, all over my body, timidly on the front of my pants, hesitating a moment on the broken skin of the knuckles.

Dew melon dew melon lying half-hidden under the broad green leaves. The earth is rich.

I began taking her clothes from her, beginning with her long coat, and it was easy there in the dark, no sight of awkward lifted elbows, it was as easy as taking the linen drape from a nude sculpture. Her blouse came undone and over her shoulders, and her hands were at her skirt so that it too came off, down, easily, fell to some dark corner of the elevator. A few clasps, a few caresses of my hand on her back, her leg. My fingers went inside her panties and gently pulled them down over the round buttocks. My clothes came off easily, her hair on my naked shoulders, and we eased each other down on the pile of clothes, breath in our faces, moisture in the vales of God's morning, and we fell to the deepest darkness, flowers cascading over the head of the young hero.

When my blood was moving fastest, the knuckles on my hand were hurting. Broken flesh had met broken flesh in the dark.

She whispered: "When the lights come on I'll have my back to you, and you mustn't look at me."

"But who are you?" I asked. "I want to see you again — "

But I did as she bid. As the doors opened on the main floor, she spoke again.

"For all you'll know, I might be one of the people in your class."

I waited as she asked, ten minutes, till she would be completely away from the university. My body was warm, and this would last for a few minutes in the cold night outside. In two days I would meet my class again, and the eyes of all the girls in the class would be looking at me, and they would all be listening to my voice. Wordsworth.

When I got home I had a bag full of groceries, on credit, and among them was a can of cat food. If I had a dog instead, maybe it could have licked my aching knuckles.

ERSKINE CALDWELL

Where the Girls Were Different

Nobody could ever explain exactly why it was, but the girls who lived in all the other parts of Oconee County were different from the ones in our section. All the girls in Woodlawn, which was the name of the town where we lived, were the sassy kind. They were always slapping and biting, too. I suppose all of them were tomboys. That's about the worst thing you can call a girl when she is growing up. But the girls who lived at Macy's Mill, and at Bradford, and especially in Rosemark, were a different kind. We used to talk about it a lot, but nobody knew why it was.

"How are the Rosemark girls different?" I asked Ben, when we were talking about it one day.

"Jiggers," he said, "I don't know exactly."

I never went around like Ben and the other boys did, because I had a girl who lived in town and I went to see her two or three times a week, and that was as many nights as my folks would let me go out. They did not believe in letting me go all over the county to see girls. So I stayed at home and went to see Milly pretty often.

But those girls in other parts of the county were not like the ones at home. The other boys used to go off nearly every night to see girls at Bradford and Macy's Mill and Rosemark, Rosemark especially. I don't know why that was, either. There was just something about those girls down in Rosemark that made a man act kind of funny.

Ben went down to Rosemark three or four nights every week to see girls. The strange part of it was he rarely went to see the same girl more than once. He had a new girl almost every time he went down there. The other boys did the same way, too. They had a new girl every time. Shucks, I had to stay at home and go to see Milly and nobody else.

I asked Ben in a confidential way what it was about the girls down in Rosemark that made them so different from the ones around home.

Ben was my first cousin and I didn't mind asking him personal questions.

"Jumping jiggers!" he said. "You've never been down there to see a Rosemark girl, have you, Fred?"

I told him how it was about Milly. I did not want to go to see her all the time, but I never had a chance to go down to Rosemark like the other boys.

"Well," he said, "you are a fool to go to see her all the time. She's just like all the other girls around here. You've got to go down to Rosemark and see some real girls. They're not like these around Woodlawn."

"What are they like, Ben?" I asked him again. Everybody said they were different, but nobody ever said in what way they were different. "What do they do that's different?"

"Well, that's hard to say. They act just like all girls do — but they are different."

"Tell me about them, Ben."

"I'll tell you this," he said. "You got to be careful down there. Every girl in Rosemark that's got an old man or a brother is watched pretty close. I guess that's because they are pretty wild."

"How are they wild?" I asked him. "What do they do?"

"That's hard to say, too. You can't put your finger on it exactly — they are just different. You've got to go down there."

"But how can I get a date with one of them?"

"Oh, that's easy," he said. "You just go down there some Sunday night and wait outside a church until they come out. Then pick one out and ask her to let you take her home. That's the way to do it."

"Can I do that? Would she let me take her home?"

"Sure. That's one way they are different. You can get any girl you want if you ask her before somebody else does. You go down Sunday night and try it. Jiggers, Fred, you got to see those Rosemark girls! The ones around here aren't fit to fool with."

I hated to tell my folks the next Sunday night that I was going to see Milly when I wasn't, but — gee — I had to go down to see those girls in Rosemark. I drove the old car down and got there just before the churches let out.

I picked out the biggest church I could find and waited outside the door. I figured that the bigger the church the better chance I would have because there would be more girls in it.

Shucks, it wasn't any trouble at all. I asked the first girl that came out by herself if I could take her home and she said, "Sure," just as nice. Gee, this was the way to see girls. Up at home the girls acted sassy about letting you take them home. These Rosemarks girls were different that way.

"Where do you live?" I asked her.

"About five miles out in the country," she said.

She talked nice and soft like all girls would if they knew what was good for themselves. "Do you want to take me?"

"You bet I do," I told her. "I don't care how far it is."

Five miles wasn't anything. It was fine, because I'd have a longer time to find out about her. I could tell right away she was different.

She showed me the way to go and we started out. The old car was running good, but there was no hurry to get there.

"What's your name?" I asked her.

"Betty," she said.

No girl up in Woodlawn had a name like that. I was beginning to see why all the boys at home liked to come down to Rosemark.

Gee, she was different! She sat real close to me and sort of hunched her shoulders forward like she was awfully pleased. I had never seen a girl act so nice in all my life. She put her arm through mine and sort of leaned against me a lot and I had a devil of a time trying to keep our old car in the road.

As soon as we got outside of town a little distance another automobile came up behind us real close. I drew over to the side of the road so it could pass, but whoever was running it wouldn't try to pass. I thought that was funny, because I was driving only about ten miles an hour and making a lot of dust behind, too. The man who was running the other car was crazy not to pass us and go ahead.

Betty sat closer and closer all the time and was so nice I didn't know what to make of it.

"The devil," I said to myself, "I'm going to take a chance and kiss her."

That was a reckless thing to do, because all the girls I know up home were pretty particular about things like that and they didn't mind slapping you good and hard, either.

Gee whiz! I reached down and kissed her and she wouldn't let me stop. The old car rocked from one side of the road to the other as dizzy as a bat. I couldn't see to steer it because Betty wouldn't let me stop kissing her, and I had to wait until we ran into a ditch almost before I knew which way to turn the wheel. Gee whiz! The girls in Rosemark were certainly different, all right.

Finally I got away from her and got back my breath and saw which way to guide the old car.

"Don't you like to kiss me?" she asked, hunching her shoulders forward again like a girl does when she wants to make you feel funny.

Shucks, I couldn't let her get away with that! I reached my right arm around her and kissed her as hard as I could. She didn't mind how rough I was, either. I guess she liked it, because she put both of her arms around my neck and both of her legs across my lap and hugged the life out of me. *Gee whiz!* I didn't know girls did like that! Ben said the girls down in Rosemark were different, but I didn't expect anything like this to happen to me. Holy cats! The girl was sitting on my lap under the steering wheel and I was having a devil of a time trying to kiss her for all I was worth and steer the old car at the same time.

Right then I knew I was coming down to Rosemark again as soon as I could get away. Ben sure knew what he was talking about when he said the girls down here were nothing like the ones at home. Shucks, those old girls up at home were not anything.

By this time we had got to the place where she lived and she looked up just at the right moment to tell me where to turn in. Before I could steer the old car into the driveway the automobile that had been behind us all the time beat me to it and I had to jerk on the brakes to keep from running smack into it.

"Who is that fool?" I asked Betty.

"That's Poppa," she said.

I started to say something pretty mean about him for doing a thing like that but I thought I had better not if I wished to come back to see her. I was going to ask her for a lot of dates as soon as we got in the yard.

She took her arms down and moved over to her side of the seat just as if nothing in the world had happened.

I shut off the engine and reached over and opened the door for her. She jumped out just as nice and I was right behind her. I got as far as the running board when the man who had beaten us to the gate pushed me back into the seat. He shoved me so hard I hurt my spine on the steering wheel.

"Where do you think you're going?" he growled at me. "Start up that car and get away from here and don't ever let me see you again."

He came closer and shoved me again. I then saw for the first time that he had a great big rusty pistol with a barrel about a foot and a half long in his other hand.

"If I ever catch you around Betty again I'll use this gun on you," he said.

I didn't lose any time getting away from there. I hated to go away and not see Betty again, so I could ask her for a lot of dates next week, but it wouldn't do any good to have dates if I couldn't come back.

I drove the old car back home and went to bed. I knew now why Ben never went to see the same girl twice. He knew what he was doing, all right. And I knew why he said the girls down there were different. They sure were different. It was hard to say what the difference was, but if you ever went down there it was easy to feel it all over yourself.

The next morning I saw Ben and told him about going down to Rosemark the night before. After a while I told him about the way Betty kissed me and how she wanted to sit on my lap under the steering wheel.

"What!" he said, his eyes wide open.

I told him about it again, and how she wouldn't let me stop kissing her and how she put her legs across my lap.

"Jumping jiggers, that's funny. None of them ever let me kiss her, and none of them ever sat on my lap."

"Gosh, Ben," I said, "then why did you think they were different?"

"Jumping jiggers!" he said again, frowning all over. "I don't know."

MORLEY CALLAGHAN

Last Spring They Came Over

Alfred Bowles came to Canada from England and got a job on a Toronto paper. He was a young fellow with clear, blue eyes and heavy pimples on the lower part of his face, the son of a Baptist minister whose family was too large for his salary. He got thirty dollars a week on the paper and said it was surprisingly good screw to start. For five a week he got an attic room in a brick house painted brown on Mutual Street. He ate his meals in a quick-lunch near the office. He bought a cane and a light-gray fedora.

He wasn't a good reporter but was inoffensive and obliging. After he had been working two weeks the fellows took it for granted he would be fired in a little while and were nice to him, liking the way the most trifling occurrences surprised him. He was happy to carry his cane on his arm and wear the fedora at a jaunty angle, quite the reporter. He liked to explain that he was doing well. He wrote home about it.

When they put him doing night police he felt important, phoning the fire department, hospitals, and police stations, trying to be efficient. He was getting along all right. It was disappointing when after a week the assistant city editor, Mr. H. J. Brownson, warned him to phone his home if anything important happened, and he would have another man cover it. But Bowles got to like hearing the weary, irritable voice of the assistant city editor called from his bed at three o'clock in the morning. He liked to politely call Mr. Brownson as often and as late as possible, thinking it a bit of good fun.

Alfred wrote long letters to his brother and to his father, the Baptist minister, using a typewriter, carefully tapping the keys, occasionally laughing to himself. In a month's time he had written six letters describing the long city room, the fat belly of the city editor, and the bad words the night editor used when speaking of the Orangemen.

The night editor took a fancy to him because of the astounding puerility of his political opinions. Alfred was always willing to talk pompously of the British Empire policing the world and about all Catholics being aliens, and the future of Ireland and Canada resting with the Orangemen. He flung his arms wide and talked in the hoarse voice of a bad actor, but no one would have thought of taking him seriously. He was merely having a dandy time. The night editor liked him because he was such a nice boy.

Then Alfred's brother came out from the Old Country, and got a job on the same paper. Some of the men started talking about cheap cockney labourers crowding the good guys out of the jobs, but Harry Bowles was frankly glad to get the thirty a week. It never occurred to him that he had a funny idea of good money. With his first pay he bought a derby hat, a pair of spats, and a cane, but he never looked as nice as his younger brother because his heavy nose curved up at the end. The landlady on Mutual Street moved a double bed into Alfred's room and Harry slept with his brother.

The days passed with many good times together. At first it was awkward that Alfred should be working at night and his brother in the daytime, but Harry was pleased to come down to the office every night at eleven and they went down the street to the hotel that didn't bother about Prohibition. They drank a few glasses of good beer. It became a kind of rite that had to be performed carefully. Harry would put his left foot and Alfred his right foot on the rail and leaning an elbow on the bar they would slowly survey the zigzag line of frothing glasses the length of the long bar. Men jostled them for a place at the foot-rail.

And Alfred said: "Well, a bit of luck."

Harry grinning and raising his glass said: "Righto."

"It's the stuff that heals."

"Down she goes."

"It helps the night along."

"Fill them up again."

"Toodleoo."

Then they would walk out of the crowded barroom, vaguely pleased with themselves. Walking slowly and erectly along the street they talked with assurance, a mutual respect for each other's opinion making it merely an exchange of information. They talked of the Englishman in Canada, comparing his lot with that of the Englishman in South Africa and India. They had never travelled but to ask what they knew of strange lands would have made one feel uncomfortable; it was better to take it for granted that the Bowles boys knew all about the ends of the earth and had judged them carefully, for in their eyes was the light of far-away places. Once in a while, after walking a block or two, one of the brothers would say he would damn well like to see India and the other would say it would be simply topping.

After work and on Sundays they took a look at the places they had heard about in the city. One Sunday they got up in good time and took the boat to Niagara. Their father had written asking if they had seen the Falls and would they send some souvenirs. That day they had as nice a time as a man would want to have. Standing near the pipe-rail a little way from the hotel that overlooks the Falls they watched the water-line just before the drop, smooth as a long strip of bevelled glass, and Harry compared it favourably with a cataract in the Himalayas and a giant waterfall in Africa, just above the Congo. They took a car along the gorge and getting off near the whirlpool, picked out a little hollow near a big rock at the top of the embankment where the grass was lush and green. They stretched themselves out with hats tilted over their eyes for sunshades. The river whirled below. They talked about the funny ways of Mr. Brownson and his short fat legs and about the crazy women who fainted at the lifted hand of the faith healer who was in the city for the week. They liked the distant rumble of the Falls. They agreed to try and save a lot of money and go west to the Pacific in a year's time. They never mentioned trying to get a raise in pay.

Afterwards they each wrote home about the trip, sending the souvenirs.

Neither one was doing well on the paper. Harry wasn't much good because he hated writing the plain copy and it was hard for him to be strictly accurate. He liked telling a good tale but it never occurred to him that he was deliberately lying. He imagined a thing and straightway felt it to be true. But it never occurred to Alfred to depart from the truth. He was accurate but lazy, never knowing when he was really working. He was taken off night police and for two weeks helped a man do courts at the City Hall. He got to know the boys at the press gallery, who smiled at his naïve sincerity and thought him a decent chap, without making up their minds about him. Every noon-hour Harry came to the press gallery and the brothers, sitting at typewriters, wrote long letters all about the country and the people, anything interesting, and after exchanging letters, tilted back in their swivel chairs, laughing out loud. Heaven only knows who got the letters in the long run. Neither one when in the press gallery seemed to write anything for the paper.

Some of the men tried kidding Alfred, teasing him about women, asking if he found girls in this country to his liking; but he seemed to enjoy it more than they did. Seriously he explained that he had never met a girl in this country, but they looked very nice. Once Alfred and Bun Brophy, a red-headed fellow with a sharp tongue who did City Hall for the paper, were alone in the gallery. Brophy had in his hands a big picture of five girls in masquerade costumes. Without explaining that he loved one of the girls Brophy asked Bowles which of the lot was the prettiest.

"You want me to settle that," said Alfred, grinning and waving his pipe. He very deliberately selected a demure little girl with a shy smile.

Brophy was disappointed. "Don't you think this one is pretty?" — a colourful, bold-looking girl.

"Well, she's all right in her way, but she's too vivacious. I'll take this one. I like them kittenish," Alfred said.

Brophy wanted to start an argument but Alfred said it was neither here nor there. He really didn't like women.

"You mean to say you never step out?" Brophy said.

"I've never seemed to mix with them," he said, adding that the whole business didn't matter because he liked boys much better.

The men in the press room heard about it and some suggested nasty things to Alfred. It was hard to tease him when he wouldn't be serious. Sometimes they asked if he took Harry out walking in the evenings. Brophy called them the heavy lovers. The brothers didn't mind because they thought the fellows were having a little fun.

In the fall Harry was fired. The editor in a nice note said that he was satisfied Mr. H. W. Bowles could not adapt himself to their methods. But everybody wondered why he hadn't been fired sooner. He was no good on the paper.

The brothers smiled, shrugged their shoulders and went on living together. Alfred still had his job. Every noon-hour in the City Hall press room they were together, writing letters.

Time passed and the weather got cold. Alfred's heavy coat came from the Old Country and he gave his vest and a thin sweater to Harry, who had only a light spring coat. As the weather got colder Harry buttoned his coat higher up on his throat and even though he looked cold he was neat as a pin with his derby and cane.

Then Alfred lost his job. The editor, disgusted, called him a fool. For the first time since coming over last spring he felt hurt, something inside him was hurt and he told his brother about it, wanting to know why people acted in such a way. He said he had been doing night police. On the way over to No. 1 station very late Thursday night he had met two men from other papers. They told him about a big fire earlier in the evening just about the time when Alfred was accustomed to going to the hotel to have a drink with his brother. They were willing to give all the details and Alfred thankfully shook hands with them and hurried back to the office to write the story. Next morning the assistant city editor phoned Alfred and asked how it was the morning papers missed the story. Alfred tried to explain but Mr. Brownson said he was a damn fool for not phoning the police and making sure instead of trying to make the paper look like a pack of fools printing a fake story. The fellows who had kidded him said that too. Alfred kept asking his brother why the fellows had to do it. He seemed to be losing a good feeling for people.

Still the brothers appeared at noontime in the press room. They didn't write so many letters. They were agreeable, cheerful, on good terms with everybody. Bun Brophy every day asked how they were doing and they felt at home there. Harry would stand for a while watching the checker game always in progress, knowing that if he stood staring intently at the black and red squares, watching every deliberate move, he would be asked to sit in when it was necessary that one of the players make the rounds in the hall. Once Brophy gave Harry his place and walked over to the window where Alfred stood watching the fleet of automobiles arranged in a square in the courtyard. The police wagon with a load of drunks was backing toward the cells.

"Say, Alfie, I often wonder how you guys manage," he said.

"Oh, first rate."

"Well, you ought to be in a bad way by now."

"Oh no, we have solved the problem," said Alfred in a grand way, grinning, as if talking about the British Empire.

He was eager to tell how they did it. There was a store in their block where a package of tobacco could be got for five cents; they did their own cooking and were able to live on five dollars a week.

"What about coming over and having tea with us sometimes?" Alfred said. He was decidedly on his uppers but he asked Brophy to visit them and have tea.

Brophy, abashed, suggested the three of them go over to the café and have a little toast. Harry talked volubly on the way over and while having coffee. He was really a better talker than his brother. They sat in an arm-chair lunch, gripped the handles of their thick mugs, and talked about religion. The brothers were sons of a Baptist minister but never thought of going to church. It seemed that Brophy had travelled a lot during war-time and afterward in Asia Minor and India. He was telling about a great golden temple of the Sikhs at Amritsar and Harry listened carefully, asking many questions. Then they talked about newspapers until Harry started talking about the East, slowly feeling his way. All of a sudden he told about standing on a height of land near Amritsar, looking down at a temple. It couldn't have been so but he would have it that Brophy and he had seen the same temple and he described the country in the words Brophy had used. When he talked that way you actually believed that he had seen the temple.

Alfred liked listening to his brother but he said finally: "Religion is a funny business. I tell you it's a funny business." And for the time being no one would have thought of talking seriously about religion. Alfred had a casual way of making a cherished belief or opinion seem unimportant, a way of dismissing even the bright yarns of his brother.

After that afternoon in the café Brophy never saw Harry. Alfred came often to the City Hall but never mentioned his brother. Someone said maybe Harry had a job but Alfred laughed and said no such luck in this country, explaining casually that Harry had a bit of a cold and was resting up. In the passing days Alfred came only once in a while to the City Hall, writing his letter without enthusiasm.

The press men would have tried to help the brothers if they had heard Harry was sick. They were entirely ignorant of the matter. On a Friday afternoon at three-thirty Alfred came into the gallery and, smiling apologetically, told Brophy that his brother was dead; the funeral was to be in three-quarters of an hour; would he mind coming? It was pneumonia, he added. Brophy, looking hard at Alfred, put on his hat and coat and they went out.

It was a poor funeral. The hearse went on before along the way to the Anglican cemetery that overlooks the ravine. One old cab followed behind. There had been a heavy fall of snow in the morning, and the slush on the pavement was thick. Alfred and Brophy sat in the old cab, silent. Alfred was leaning forward, his chin resting on his hands, the cane acting as a support, and the heavy pimples stood out on the lower part of his white face. Brophy was uncomfortable and chilly but he mopped his shinning forehead with a big handkerchief. The window was open and the air was cold and damp.

Alfred politely asked how Mrs. Brophy was doing. Then he asked about Mr. Brownson.

"Oh, he's fine," Brophy said. He wanted to close the window but it would have been necessary to move Alfred so he sat huddled in the corner, shivering.

Alfred asked suddenly if funerals didn't leave a bad taste in the mouth and Brophy, surprised, started talking absently about that golden temple of the Sikhs in India. Alfred appeared interested until they got to the cemetery. He said suddenly he would have to take a look at the temple one fine day.

They buried Harry Bowles in a grave in the paupers' section on a slippery slope of the hill. The earth was hard and chunky and it thumped down on the coffin case. It snowed a little near the end.

On the way along the narrow, slippery footpath up the hill Alfred thanked Brophy for being thoughtful enough to come to the funeral. There was little to say. They shook hands and went different ways.

After a day or two Alfred again appeared in the press room. He watched the checker game, congratulated the winner and then wrote home. The men were sympathetic and said it was too bad about his brother. And he smiled cheerfully and said they were good fellows. In a little while he seemed to have convinced them that nothing important had really happened.

His last cent must have gone to the undertaker, for he was particular about paying bills, but he seemed to get along all right. Occasionally he did a little work for the paper, a story from a night assignment when the editor thought the staff was being overworked.

One afternoon at two-thirty in the press gallery Brophy saw the last of Alfred, who was sucking his pipe, his feet up on a desk, wanting to be amused. Brophy asked if anything had turned up. In a playful, resigned tone, his eye on the big clock, Alfred said he had until three to join the Air Force. They wouldn't take him, he said, unless he let them know by three.

Brophy said, "How will you like that?"

"I don't fancy it."

"But you're going through."

"Well, I'm not sure. Something else may come along." It was a quarter to three and he was sitting there waiting for a job to turn up before three.

No one saw him after that, but he didn't join the Air Force. Someone in the gallery said that wherever he went he probably wrote home as soon as he got there.

ITALO CALVINO

The Count of Monte Cristo

Translated by William Weaver

I

From my cell, I can say little about the construction of this Château d'If where I have been imprisoned for so many years. The tiny barred window is at the end of a shaft that pierces the thickness of the wall: it frames no view; from the greater or lesser luminosity of the sky I can recognize approximately the hours and the seasons; but I do not know if, beneath that window, there is the open sea or the ramparts or one of the inner courtyards of the fortress. The shaft narrows in the form of a chute; to look out I would have to advance, crawling, to the very end; I have tried, it is impossible, even for a man reduced, as I am, to a mere shadow. The opening perhaps is farther than it seems: estimation of the distance is confused by the tunnel-like perspective and by the contrasts of the light.

The walls are so thick they could contain other cells, stairways, casemates, and powder magazines; or else the fortress could be all wall, a full and compact solid, with one live man buried in the middle. The images you summon up when you are imprisoned follow one another without any reciprocal exclusion: the cell, the aperture, the corridors along which the jailer comes twice a day with the soup and the bread could be simply tiny pores in a rock of spongy consistency.

You hear the sea pounding, especially on stormy nights; at times it seems almost that the waves are breaking here against the very wall to which I put my ear; at times they seem to be digging below, under the rocks of the foundations, and my cell seems to be at the top of the tallest tower, and the rumble rises through the prison, a prisoner too, as in the horn of a conch shell.

I prick up my ears: the sounds describe variable, jagged spaces and forms around me. From the jailers' shuffling I try to establish the network of the corridors, the turns, the openings, the straight lines broken by the dragging of the kettle to the threshold of each cell and by the creak of the locks: I succeed only in fixing a succession of points in time, without any correspondence in space. At night the sounds become more distinct, but more uncertain in marking places and distances: somewhere a rat is gnawing, an ill man groans, a boat's siren announces its entry into the Marseilles roads, and Abbé Faria's spade continues digging its way among these stones.

I don't know how many times Abbé Faria has attempted to escape: each time he has worked for months prising up the stone slabs, crumbling the seams of mortar, perforating the rock with rudimentary awls; but at the moment when the pick's last blow should open his way to the rocky shore, he realizes he has come out in a cell that is even deeper in the fortress than the one from which he set out. It requires only a little error of calculation, a slight deviation in the incline of a tunnel and he is penetrating into the prison's viscera with no hope of finding his way again. After every failure, he goes back to correcting the plans and formulas with which he has frescoed the walls of his cell; he goes back to improving his arsenal of improvised tools; and then he resumes his scraping.

II

I too have thought and still think about a method of escape; in fact, I have made so many surmises about the topography of the fortress, about the shortest and surest way to reach the outer bastion and dive into the sea, that I can no longer distinguish between my conjectures and the data based on experience. Working with hypotheses, I can at times construct for myself such a minute and convincing picture of the fortress that in my mind I can move through it completely at my ease; whereas the elements I derive from what I see and what I hear are confused, full of gaps, more and more contradictory.

In the early days of my imprisonment, when my desperate acts of rebellion hadn't yet brought me to rot in this solitary cell, the routine tasks of prison life had caused me to climb up and down stairs and bastions, cross the entrance halls and posterns of the Château d'If; but from all the images retained by my memory, which now I keep arranging and rearranging in my conjectures, there is not one that fits neatly with another, none that helps explain to me the shape of the fortress or the point where I now am. Too many thoughts tormented me then — about how, I, Edmond Dantès, poor but honest sailor, could have run afoul of the law's severity and suddenly lost my freedom — too many thoughts to allow my attention to concern itself with the plan of my surroundings.

The bay of Marseilles and its islands have been familiar to me since boyhood; and every embarkation of my not long life as a sailor, the departures and the arrivals, had this background; but the seaman's eye, every time it encounters the black fort of If, shifts away in an instinctive fear. So when they brought me here chained in a boat filled with gendarmes, and this cliff and the walls then loomed on the horizon, I understood my fate and bowed my head. I didn't see — or I don't remember — the pier where the boat docked, the steps they made me climb, the door that closed behind my back.

Now that, with the passage of years, I have stopped brooding over the chain of infamy and ill-luck that caused my imprisonment, I have come to understand one thing: the only way to escape the prisoner's state is to know how the prison is built.

If I feel no desire to imitate Faria, it is because the very knowledge that someone is seeking an avenue of escape is enough to convince me that such an avenue exists or, at least, that one can set himself the problem of seeking it. So the sound of Faria's digging has become a necessary complement to the concentration of my thoughts. I feel not only that Faria is a man attempting his own escape but also that he is a part of my plan; and not because I am hoping for an avenue to safety opened by him — he has been wrong so many times by now I have lost all faith in his intuition — but because the only information I have concerning this place where I am has come to me from the series of his mistakes.

III

The walls and the vaults have been pierced in every direction by the Abbé's pick, but his itineraries continue to wind around themselves like a ball of yarn, and he constantly goes through my cell as he follows, each time, a different course. He has long since lost his sense of orientations: Faria no longer recognizes the cardinal points, indeed he cannot recognize even the zenith and the nadir. At times I hear scratching at the ceiling; a rain of plaster falls on me; a breach opens; Faria's head appears, upside down. Upside down for me, not for him; he crawls out of his tunnel, he walks head down, while nothing about his person is ruffled, not his white hair, nor his beard green with mold, nor the tatters of sack-cloth that cover his emaciated loins. He walks across the ceiling and the walls like a fly, he sinks his pick into a certain spot, a hole opens; he disappears.

Sometimes he has hardly disappeared through one wall when he pops out again from the wall opposite: he hasn't yet drawn his heel through the hole here when his beard is already appearing over there. He emerges again, more weary, skeletal, aged, as if years had passed since the last time I saw him.

At other times, however, he has hardly slipped into his tunnel when I hear him make the sound of a long aspiration like somebody preparing to sneeze loudly: in the labyrinth of the fortress there is much cold and damp; but the sneeze never comes. I wait: I wait for a week, for a month, for a year; Faria doesn't come back; I persuade myself he is dead. All of a sudden the wall opposite trembles as if shaken by an earthquake; from the shower of stones Faria looks out, completing his sneeze.

We exchange fewer and fewer words; or we continue conversations I cannot remember ever having begun. I realize Faria has trouble distinguishing one cell from another among the many he crosses in his mistaken journeys. Each cell contains a pallet, a pitcher, a wooden slops bucket, a man standing and looking at the sky through a narrow slit. When Faria appears from underground, the prisoner turns around: he always has the same face, the same voice, the same thoughts. His name is the same: Edmond Dantès. The fortress has no favored points: it repeats in space and time always the same combination of figures.

IV

In all my hypotheses of escape, I try to imagine Faria as the protagonist. Not that I tend to identify myself with him: Faria necessarily plays his role so that I can mentally envisage my escape in an objective light, as I could not do if I were living it: I mean, dreaming it in the first person. By now I no longer know if the man I hear digging like a mole is the real Faria opening breaches in the walls of the real fortress of Château d'If or whether it is the hypothesis of a Faria dealing with a hypothetical fortress. It amounts to the same thing in any case: it is the fortress that wins. It is as if, in the contests between Faria and the fortress, I pressed my impartiality so far as to side with the fortress against him ... no, now I am exaggerating: the contest does not take place only in my mind, but between two real contenders, independently of me; my efforts are directed toward seeing it with detachment, in a performance without anguish.

If I can come to observe fortress and Abbé from a perfectly equidistant point of view, I will be able to discern not only the particular errors Faria makes time after time, but also the error in method which continually defeats him and which I, thanks to my correct setting of the problem, will be able to avoid.

Faria proceeds in this way: he becomes aware of a difficulty, he studies a solution, he tries out the solution, encounters a new difficulty, plans a new solution, and so on and on. For him, once all possible errors and unforeseen elements are eliminated, his escape can only be successful: it all lies in planning and carrying out the perfect escape.

I set out from the opposite premise: there exists a perfect fortress from which one cannot escape; escape is possible only if in the planning or building of the fortress some error or oversight was made. While Faria continues taking the fortress apart, sounding out its weak points, I continue putting it back together, conjecturing more and more insuperable barriers.

The images of the fortress that Faria and I create are becoming more and more different: Faria, beginning with a simple figure, is complicating it extremely to include in it each of the single unforeseen elements he encounters in his path; I, setting out from the jumble of these data, see in each isolated obstacle the clue to a system of obstacles, I develop each segment into a regular figure, I fit these figures together as the sides of a solid, polyhedron or hyperpolyhedron, I inscribe these polyhedrons in spheres or hyperspheres, and so the more I enclose the form of the fortress the more I simplify it, defining it in a numerical relation or in an algebraic formula.

But to conceive a fortress in this way I need the Abbé Faria constantly combating landslides of rubble, steel bolts, sewers, sentry boxes, leaps into nothingness, recesses in the sustaining walls, because the only way to reinforce the imagined fortress is to put the real one continuously to the test.

V

Therefore: each cell seems separated from the outside only by the thickness of a wall, but Faria as he excavates discovers that in between there is always another cell, and between this cell and the outside, still another. The image I derive is this: a fortress that grows around us, and the longer we remain shut up in it the more it removes us from the outside. The Abbé digs, digs, but the walls increase in thickness, the battlements and the buttresses are multiplied. Perhaps if he can succeed in advancing faster than the fortress expands, Faria at a certain point will find himself outside unawares. It would be necessary to invert the relative speeds so that the fortress, contracting, would expel the Abbé like a cannonball.

But if the fortress grows with the speed of time, to escape one would have to move even faster, retrace time. The moment in which I would find myself outside would be the same moment I entered here: I look out on the bay at last, and what do I see? A boat full of gendarmes is landing at If; in the midst is Edmond Dantès, in chains.

There, I have gone back to imagining myself as the protagonist of the escape, and I have immediately risked not only my future but my past, my memories. Everything that is unclear in the relationship between an innocent prisoner and his prison continues to cast shadows on images and decisions. If the prison is surrounded by *my* outside, that outside would bring me back inside each time I succeeded in reaching it: the outside is nothing but the past, it is useless to try to escape.

I must conceive of the prison either as a place that is only inside itself without an outside — that is, giving up the idea of leaving it — or I must conceive of it not as *my* prison but as a place with no relation to me inside or outside; that is, I must study an itinerary from inside to outside that precludes the import that "inside" and "outside" have acquired in my emotions; valid, that is, even if instead of "outside" I say "inside" and vice versa.

VI

If outside there is the past, perhaps the future is concentrated at the innermost point of the island of If, in other words the avenue of escape is an avenue toward the inside. In the graffiti with which Abbé Faria covers his walls, two maps with ragged outlines alternate, constellated with arrows and marks: one is meant to be the plan of If, the other of an island of the Tuscan archipelago where a treasure is hidden: Monte Cristo.

It is, in fact, to seek this treasure that Abbé Faria wants to escape. To succeed in his intention he has to draw a line that in the map of the island of If carries him from inside to outside and in the map of the island of Monte Cristo carries him from outside to that point which is farther inland than all the other points, the treasure cave. Between an island he cannot leave and an island he cannot enter there must be a relation: therefore in Faria's hieroglyphics the two maps can be super-imposed and are almost identical.

It is hard for me to understand whether Faria is now digging in order to dive into the open sea or to penetrate the cave full of gold. In either case, if one looks closely, he is tending toward the same point of arrival: the place of the multiplicty of possible things. At times I visualize this multiplicity as concentrated in a gleaming underground cavern, at times I see it as an irradiating explosion. The treasure of Monte Cristo and the escape from If are two phases of the same process, perhaps successive, perhaps periodical as in a pulsation.

The search for the center of If-Monte Cristo does not lead to results that are more sure than those of the march toward its unreachable circumference: in whatever point I find myself the hypersphere stretches out around me in every direction; the center is all around where I am; going deeper means descending into myself. You dig and dig and you do nothing but retrace the same path.

VII

Once he has come into possession of the treasure, Faria intends to liberate the Emperor from Elba, give him the means to put himself again at the head of his army ... The plan of escape-search on the island of If-Monte Cristo is therefore not complete if it does not include also the search-escape of Napoleon from the island where he is confined. Faria digs; he penetrates once again into the cell of Edmond Dantès, he sees the prisoner from behind, looking as usual at the sky through the slit-window; at the sound of the pick the prisoner turns: it is Napoleon Bonaparte. Faria and Dantès-Napoleon together excavate a tunnel in the fortress. The map of If-Monte Cristo-Elba is drawn in such a way that by turning it a certain number of degrees the map of Saint Helena is obtained: the escape is reversed into an exile beyond return.

The confused reasons for which both Faria and Edmond Dantès were imprisoned have, in different ways, something to do with the Bonapartist cause. That hypothetical geometric figure called If-Monte Cristo coincides in certain of its points with another figure called Elba-Saint Helena. There are points of the past and of the future in which Napoleonic history intervenes in our poor prisoners' history, and other points where Faria and I can or could influence a possible return of the Empire.

These intersections make any calculation of predictions even more complicated; there are points where the line that one of us is following bifurcates, ramifies, fans out; each branch can encounter branches that set out from other lines. Along one jagged line Faria goes by, digging: and only a few seconds keep him from bumping into the baggage wagons and cannon of the Imperial Army reconquering France.

We proceed in the dark; only the way our paths twist upon themselves warns us that something has changed in the paths of the others. We may say that Waterloo is the point where the path of Wellington's army might intersect the path of Napoleon; if the two lines meet, the segments beyond that point are cut off; in the map where Faria digs his tunnel, the projection of the Waterloo angle forces him to turn back.

VIII

The intersections of the various hypothetical lines define a series of planes arranged like the pages of a manuscript on a novelist's desk. Let us call Alexandre Dumas the writer who must deliver to his publisher as soon as possible a novel in twelve volumes intitled *The Count of Monte Cristo.* His work proceeds in this fashion: two assistants (Auguste Maquet and P. A. Fiorentino) develop one by one the various alternatives that depart from each single point, and they furnish Dumas with the outline of all the possible variants of an enormous supernovel; Dumas selects, rejects, cuts, pastes, interposes: if a given solution is preferred for well-founded reasons but omits an episode he would find it useful to include, he tries to put together the stub-ends of disparate provenance, he joins them with makeshift links, racks his brain to establish an apparent continuity among divergent segments of future. The final result will be the novel *The Count of Monte Cristo* to be handed to the printer.

The diagrams Faria and I draw on the walls of the prison resemble those Dumas pens on his papers to establish the order of the chosen variants. One bundle of sheets of paper can already be passed for printing: it contains the Marseilles of my youth; moving over the closely written lines I can fight my way onto the docks of the harbor, climb up the Rue de la Canebière in the morning sun, reach the Catalan villaged perched on the hill, see Mercedes again ... Another bundle of papers is awaiting the final touches: Dumas is still revising the chapters of the imprisonment in the Château d'If; Faria and I are stuggling inside there, ink-stained in a tangle of revisions ... At the edges of the desk there are piles of paper, the suggestions for the story's continuation which the two assistants are methodically compiling. In one of them, Dantès escapes from prison, finds Faria's treasure, transforms himself into the Count of Monte Cristo with his ashen, impassive face, devotes his implacable will and his boundless wealth to revenge; and the Machiavellian Villefort, the greedy Danglars, the grim Caderousse pay the price of their foul deeds; just as, for so many years among these walls, I had foreseen in my angry daydreams, in my longings for revenge.

Beside this, other sketches for the future are arranged on the desk. Faria opens a breach in the wall, bursts into the study of Alexandre Dumas, casts an impartial dispassionate look on the expanse of pasts and presents and futures — as I could not do, I who would try to recognize myself with tenderness in the young Dantès just promoted to his captaincy, with pity in the imprisoned Dantès, with delirious grandeur in the Count of Monte Cristo who makes his regal entrance into the proudest salons of Paris; I who in their place would find with dismay so many strangers — Faria takes a page here, a page there, like a monkey he moves his long hairy arms, hunts for the escape chapter, the page without which all the possible continuations of the novel outside the fortress become impossible. The concentric fortress, If-Monte Cristo-Dumas's desk, contains us prisoners, the treasure, and the supernovel *Monte Cristo* with its variants and combinations of variants in the nature of billions of billions but still in a finite number. Faria has set his heart on one page among the many, and he does not despair of finding it; I am interested in seeing the accumulation of rejected sheets increase, the solutions which need not be taken into account, which already form a series of piles, a wall ...

Arranging one after the other all the continuations which allow the story to be extended, probable or improbable as they may be, you obtain the zigzag line of the *Monte Cristo* of Dumas; whereas connecting the circumstances that prevent the story from continuing you outline the spiral of a novel in negative, a *Monte Cristo* preceded by the minus sign. A spiral can wind upon itself toward the inside or toward the outside: if it twists toward the inside of itself, the story closes without any possible development; if it turns in widening curves it could, at every turn, include a segment of the *Monte Cristo* with the plus sign, finally coinciding with the novel Dumas will give to the printer, or perhaps even surpassing it in its wealth of lucky chances. The decisive difference between the two books — sufficient to cause one to be defined as true and the other as false, even if they are identical — lies entirely in the method. To plan a book — or an escape — the first thing to know is what to exclude.

IX

And so we go on dealing with the fortress, Faria sounding out the weak points of the wall and coming up against new obstacles, I reflecting on his unsuccessful attempts in order to conjecture new outlines of walls to add to the plan of my fortress-conjecture.

If I succeed in mentally constructing a fortress from which it is impossible to escape, this conceived fortress either will be the same as the real one — and in this case it is certain we shall never escape from here, but at least we will achieve the serenity of one who knows he is here because he could be nowhere else — or it will be a fortress from which escape is even more impossible than from here — and this, then, is a sign that here an opportunity of escape exists: we have only to identify the point where the imagined fortress does not coincide with the real one and then find it.

ALBERT CAMUS

The Guest

Translated by Justin O'Brien

The schoolmaster was watching the two men climb toward him. One was on horseback, the other on foot. They had not yet tackled the abrupt rise leading to the schoolhouse built on the hillside. They were toiling onward, making slow progress in the snow, among the stones, on the vast expanse of the high, deserted plateau. From time to time the horse stumbled. Without hearing anything yet, he could see the breath issuing from the horse's nostrils. One of the men, at least, knew the region. They were following the trail although it had disappeared days ago under a layer of dirty white snow. The schoolmaster calculated that it would take them half an hour to get onto the hill. It was cold; he went back into the school to get a sweater.

He crossed the empty, frigid classroom. On the blackboard the four rivers of France, drawn with four different colored chalks, had been flowing toward their estuaries for the past three days. Snow had suddenly fallen in mid-October after eight months of drought without the transition of rain, and the twenty pupils, more or less, who lived in the villages scattered over the plateau had stopped coming. With fair weather they would return. Daru now heated only the single room that was his lodging, adjoining the classroom and giving also onto the plateau to the east. Like the class windows, his window looked to the south too. On that side the school was a few kilometers from the point where the plateau began to slope toward the south. In clear weather could be seen the purple mass of the mountain range where the gap opened onto the desert.

Somewhat warmed, Daru returned to the window from which he had first seen the two men. They were no longer visible. Hence they must have tackled the rise. The sky was not so dark, for the snow had stopped falling during the night. The morning had opened with a dirty light which had scarcely become brighter as the ceiling of clouds lifted. At two in the afternoon it seemed as if the day were merely beginning. But still this was better than those three days when the thick snow was falling amidst unbroken darkness with little gusts of wind that rattled the double door of the classroom. Then Daru had spent long hours in his room, leaving it only to go to the shed and feed the chickens or get some coal. Fortunately the delivery truck from Tadjid, the nearest village to the north, had brought his supplies two days before the blizzard. It would return in forty-eight hours.

Besides, he had enough to resist a siege, for the little room was cluttered with bags of wheat that the administration left as a stock to distribute to those of his pupils whose families had suffered from the drought. Actually they had all been victims because they were all poor. Every day Daru would distribute a ration to the children. They had missed it, he knew, during these bad days. Possibly one of the fathers or big brothers would come this afternoon and he could supply them with grain. It was just a matter of carrying them over to the next harvest. Now shiploads of wheat were arriving from France and the worst was over. But it would be hard to forget that poverty, that army of ragged ghosts wandering in the sunlight, the plateaus burned to a cinder month after month, the earth shriveled up little by little, literally scorched, every stone bursting into dust under one's foot. The sheep had died then by thousands and even a few men, here and there, sometimes without anyone's knowing.

In contrast with such poverty, he who lived almost like a monk in his remote schoolhouse, nonetheless satisfied with the little he had and with the rough life, had felt like a lord with his whitewashed walls, his narrow couch, his unpainted shelves, his well, his weekly provision of water and food. And suddenly this snow, without warning, without the foretaste of rain. This is the way the region was, cruel to live in, even without men — who didn't help matters either. But Daru had been born here. Everywhere else, he felt exiled.

He stepped out onto the terrace in front of the schoolhouse. The two men were now halfway up the slope. He recognized the horseman as Balducci, the old gendarme he had known for a long time. Balducci was holding on the end of a rope an Arab who was walking behind him with his hands bound and head lowered. The gendarme waved a greeting to which Daru did not reply, lost as he was in contemplation of the Arab dressed in a faded blue jellaba, his feet in sandals but covered with socks of heavy raw wool, his head surmounted by a narrow, short *chèche.* They were approaching. Balducci was holding back his horse in order not to hurt the Arab, and the group was advancing slowly.

Within earshot, Balducci shouted: "One hour to do the three kilometers from El Ameur!" Daru did not answer. Short and square in his thick sweater, he watched them climb. Not once had the Arab raised his head. "Hello," said Daru when they got up onto the terrace. "Come in and warm up." Balducci painfully got down from his horse without letting go the rope. From under his bristling mustache he smiled at the schoolmaster. His little dark eyes, deep-set under a tanned forehead, and his mouth surrounded with wrinkles made him look attentive and studious. Daru took the bridle, led the horse to the shed, and came back to the two men, who were now waiting for him in the school. He led them into his room. "I am going to heat up the classroom," he said. "We'll be more comfortable there." When he entered the room again, Balducci was on the couch. He had undone the rope tying him to the Arab, who had squatted near the stove. His hands still bound, the *chèche* pushed back on his head, he was looking toward the window. At first Daru noticed only his huge lips, fat, smooth, almost Negroid; yet his nose was straight, his eyes were dark and full of fever. The *chèche* revealed an obstinate forehead and, under the weathered skin now rather discolored by the cold, the whole face had a restless and rebellious look that struck Daru when the Arab, turning his face toward him, looked him straight in the eyes. "Go into the other room," said the schoolmaster, "and I'll make you some mint tea." "Thanks," Balducci said. "What a chore! How I long for retirement." And addressing his prisoner in Arabic: "Come on, you." The Arab got up and, slowly, holding his bound wrists in front of him, went into the classroom.

With the tea, Daru brought a chair. But Balducci was already enthroned on the nearest pupil's desk and the Arab had squatted against the teacher's platform facing the stove, which stood between the desk and the window. When he held out the glass of tea to the prisoner, Daru hesitated at the sight of his bound hands. "He might perhaps be untied." "Sure," said Balducci. "That was for the trip." He started to get to his feet. But Daru, setting the glass on the floor, had knelt beside the Arab. Without saying anything, the Arab watched him with his feverish eyes. Once his hands were free, he rubbed his swollen wrists against each other, took the glass of tea, and sucked up the burning liquid in swift little sips.

"Good," said Daru. "And where are you headed?"

Balducci withdrew his mustache from the tea. "Here, son."

"Odd pupils! And you're spending the night?"

"No. I'm going back to El Ameur. And you will deliver this fellow to Tinguit. He is expected at police headquarters."

Balducci was looking at Daru with a friendly little smile.

"What's this story?" asked the schoolmaster. "Are you pulling my leg?"

"No, son. Those are the orders."

"The orders? I'm not . . ." Daru hesitated, not wanting to hurt the old Corsican. "I mean, that's not my job."

"What! What's the meaning of that? In wartime people do all kinds of jobs."

"Then I'll wait for the declaration of war!"

Balducci nodded.

"O.K. But the orders exist and they concern you too. Things are brewing, it appears. There is talk of a forthcoming revolt. We are mobilized, in a way."

Daru still had his obstinate look.

"Listen, son," Balducci said. "I like you and you must understand. There's only a dozen of us at El Ameur to patrol throughout the whole territory of a small department and I must get back in a hurry. I was told to hand this guy over to you and return without delay. He couldn't be kept there. His village was beginning to stir; they wanted to take him back. You must take him to Tinguit tomorrow before the day is over. Twenty kilometers shouldn't faze a husky fellow like you. After that, all will be over. You'll come back to your pupils and your comfortable life."

Behind the wall the horse could be heard snorting and pawing the earth. Daru was looking out the window. Decidedly, the weather was clearing and the light was increasing over the snowy plateau. When all the snow was melted, the sun would take over again and once more would burn the fields of stone. For days, still, the unchanging sky would shed its dry light on the solitary expanse where nothing had any connection with man.

"After all," he said, turning around toward Balducci, "what did he do?" And, before the gendarme had opened his mouth, he asked: "Does he speak French?"

"No, not a word. We had been looking for him for a month, but they were hiding him. He killed his cousin."

"Is he against us?"

"I don't think so. But you can never be sure."

"Why did he kill?"

"A family squabble, I think. One owed the other grain, it seems. It's not at all clear. In short, he killed his cousin with a billhook. You know, like a sheep, *kreezk!*"

Balducci made the gesture of drawing a blade across his throat and the Arab, his attention attracted, watched him with a sort of anxiety. Daru felt a sudden wrath against the man, against all men with their rotten spite, their tireless hates, their blood lust.

But the kettle was singing on the stove. He served Balducci more tea, hesitated, then served the Arab again, who, a second time, drank avidly. His raised arms made the jellaba fall open and the schoolmaster saw his thin, muscular chest.

"Thanks, kid," Balducci said. "And now, I'm off."

He got up and went toward the Arab, taking a small rope from his pocket.

"What are you doing?" Daru asked dryly.

Balducci, disconcerted, showed him the rope.

"Don't bother."

The old gendarme hesitated. "It's up to you. Of course, you are armed?"

"I have my shotgun."

"Where?"

"In the trunk."

"You ought to have it near your bed."

"Why? I have nothing to fear."

"You're crazy, son. If there's an uprising, no one is safe, we're all in the same boat."

"I'll defend myself. I'll have time to see them coming."

Balducci began to laugh, then suddenly the mustache covered the white teeth.

"You'll have time? O.K. That's just what I was saying. You have always been a little cracked. That's why I like you, my son was like that."

At the same time he took out his revolver and put it on the desk.

"Keep it; I don't need two weapons from here to El Ameur."

The revolver shone against the black paint of the table. When the gendarme turned toward him, the schoolmaster caught the smell of leather and horseflesh.

"Listen, Balducci," Daru said suddenly, "every bit of this disgusts me, and first of all your fellow here. But I won't hand him over. Fight, yes, if I have to. But not that."

The old gendarme stood in front of him and looked at him severely.

"You're being a fool," he said slowly. "I don't like it either. You don't get used to putting a rope on a man even after years of it, and you're even ashamed — yes, ashamed. But you can't let them have their way."

"I won't hand him over," Daru said again.

"It's an order, son, and I repeat it."

"That's right. Repeat to them what I've said to you: I won't hand him over."

Balducci made a visible effort to reflect. He looked at the Arab and at Daru. At last he decided.

"No, I won't tell them anything. If you want to drop us, go ahead; I'll not denounce you. I have an order to deliver the prisoner and I'm doing so. And now you'll just sign this paper for me."

"There's no need. I'll not deny that you left him with me."

"Don't be mean with me. I know you'll tell the truth. You're from hereabouts and you are a man. But you must sign, that's the rule."

Daru opened his drawer, took out a little square bottle of purple ink, the red wooden penholder with the "sergeant-major" pen he used for making models of penmanship, and signed. The gendarme carefully folded the paper and put it into his wallet. Then he moved toward the door.

"I'll see you off," Daru said.

"No," said Balducci. "There's no use being polite. You insulted me."

He looked at the Arab, motionless in the same spot, sniffed peevishly, and turned away toward the door. "Good-by, son," he said. The door shut behind him. Balducci appeared suddenly outside the window and then disappeared. His footsteps were muffled by the snow. The horse stirred on the other side of the wall and several chickens fluttered in fright. A moment later Balducci reappeared outside the window leading the horse by the bridle. He walked toward the little rise without turning around and disappeared from sight with the horse following him. A big stone could be heard bouncing down. Daru walked back toward the prisoner, who, without stirring, never took his eyes off him. "Wait," the schoolmaster said in Arabic and went toward the bedroom. As he was going through the door, he had a second thought, went to the desk, took the revolver, and stuck it in his pocket. Then, without looking back, he went to his room.

For some time he lay on his couch watching the sky gradually close over, listening to the silence. It was this silence that had seemed painful to him during the first days here, after the war. He had requested a post in the little town at the base of the foothills separating the upper plateaus from the desert. There, rocky walls, green and black to the north, pink and lavender to the south, marked the frontier of eternal summer. He had been named to a post farther north, on the plateau itself. In the beginning, the solitude and the silence had been hard for him on these wastelands peopled only by stones. Occasionally, furrows suggested cultivation, but they had been dug to uncover a certain kind of stone good for building. The only plowing here was to harvest rocks. Elsewhere a thin layer of soil accumulated in the hollows would be scraped out to enrich paltry village gardens. This is the way it was: bare rock covered three quarters of the region. Towns sprang up, flourished, then disappeared; men came by, loved one another or fought bitterly, then died. No one in this desert, neither he nor his guest, mattered. And yet, outside this desert neither of them, Daru knew, could have really lived.

When he got up, no noise came from the classroom. He was amazed at the unmixed joy he derived from the mere thought that the Arab might have fled and that he would be alone with no decision to make. But the prisoner was there. He had merely stretched out between the stove and the desk. With eyes open, he was staring at the ceiling. In that position, his thick lips were particularly noticeable, giving him a pouting look. "Come," said Daru. The Arab got up and followed him. In the bedroom, the schoolmaster pointed to a chair near the table under the window. The Arab sat down without taking his eyes off Daru.

"Are you hungry?"

"Yes," the prisoner said.

Daru set the table for two. He took flour and oil, shaped a cake in a frying-pan, and lighted the little stove that functioned on bottled gas. While the cake was cooking, he went out to the shed to get cheese, eggs, dates, and condensed milk. When the cake was done he set it on the window sill to cool, heated some condensed milk diluted with water, and beat up the eggs into an omelette. In one of his motions he knocked against the revolver stuck in his right pocket. He set the bowl down, went into the classroom, and put the revolver in his desk drawer. When he came back to the room, night was falling. He put on the light and served the Arab. "Eat," he said. The Arab took a piece of the cake, lifted it eagerly to his mouth, and stopped short.

"And you?" he asked.

"After you. I'll eat too."

The thick lips opened slightly. The Arab hesitated, then bit into the cake determinedly.

The meal over, the Arab looked at the schoolmaster. "Are you the judge?"

"No, I'm simply keeping you until tomorrow."

"Why do you eat with me?"

"I'm hungry."

The Arab fell silent. Daru got up and went out. He brought back a folding bed from the shed, set it up between the table and the stove, perpendicular to his own bed. From a large suitcase which, upright in a corner, served as a shelf for papers, he took two blankets and arranged them on the camp bed. Then he stopped, felt useless, and sat down on his bed. There was nothing more to do or to get ready. He had to look at this man. He looked at him, therefore, trying to imagine his face bursting with rage. He couldn't do so. He could see nothing but the dark yet shining eyes and the animal mouth.

"Why did you kill him?" he asked in a voice whose hostile tone surprised him.

The Arab looked away.

"He ran away. I ran after him."

He raised his eyes to Daru again and they were full of a sort of woeful interrogation. "Now what will they do to me?"

"Are you afraid?"

He stiffened, turning his eyes away.

"Are you sorry?"

The Arab stared at him openmouthed. Obviously he did not understand. Daru's annoyance was growing. At the same time he felt awkward and self-conscious with his big body wedged between the two beds.

"Lie down there," he said impatiently. "That's your bed."

The Arab didn't move. He called to Daru:

"Tell me!"

The schoolmaster looked at him.

"Is the gendarme coming back tomorrow?"

"I don't know."

"Are you coming with us?"

"I don't know. Why?"

The prisoner got up and stretched out on top of the blankets, his feet toward the window. The light from the electric bulb shone straight into his eyes and he closed them at once.

"Why?" Daru repeated, standing beside the bed.

The Arab opened his eyes under the blinding light and looked at him, trying not to blink.

"Come with us," he said.

In the middle of the night, Daru was still not asleep. He had gone to bed after undressing completely; he generally slept naked. But when he suddenly realized that he had nothing on, he hesitated. He felt vulnerable and the temptation came to him to put his clothes back on. Then he shrugged his shoulders; after all, he wasn't a child and, if need be, he could break his adversary in two. From his bed he could observe him, lying on his back, still motionless with his eyes closed under the harsh light. When Daru turned out the light, the darkness seemed to coagulate all of a sudden. Little by little, the night came back to life in the window where the starless sky was stirring gently. The schoolmaster soon made out the body lying at his feet. The Arab still did not move, but his eyes seemed open. A faint wind was prowling around the schoolhosue. Perhaps it would drive away the clouds and the sun would reappear.

During the night the wind increased. The hens fluttered a little and then were silent. The Arab turned over on his side with his back to Daru, who thought he heard him moan. Then he listened for his guest's breathing, become heavier and more regular. He listened to that breath so close to him and mused without being able to go to sleep. In this room where he had been sleeping alone for a year, this presence bothered him. But it bothered him also by imposing on him a sort of brotherhood he knew well but refused to accept in the present circumstances. Men who share the same rooms, soldiers or prisoners, develop a strange alliance as if, having cast off their armor with their clothing, they fraternized every evening, over and above their differences, in the ancient community of dream and fatigue. But Daru shook himself; he didn't like such musings, and it was essential to sleep.

A little later, however, when the Arab stirred slightly, the schoolmaster was still not asleep. When the prisoner made a second move, he stiffened, on the alert. The Arab was lifting himself slowly on his arms with almost the motion of a sleepwalker. Seated upright in bed, he waited motionless without turning his head toward Daru, as if he were listening attentively. Daru did not stir; it had just occurred to him that the revolver was still in the drawer of his desk. It was better to act at once. Yet he continued to observe the prisoner, who, with the same slithery motion, put his feet on the ground, waited again, then began to stand up slowly. Daru was about to call out to him when the Arab began to walk, in a quite natural but extraordinarily silent way. He was heading toward the door at the end of the room that opened into the shed. He lifted the latch with precaution and went out, pushing the door behind him but without shutting it. Daru had not stirred. "He is running away," he merely thought. "Good riddance!" Yet he listened attentively. The hens were not fluttering; the guest must be on the plateau. A faint sound of water reached him, and he didn't know what it was until the Arab again stood in the doorway, closed the door carefully, and came back to bed without a sound. Then Daru turned his back on him and fell asleep. Still later he seemed, from the depths of his sleep, to hear furtive steps around the schoolhouse. "I'm dreaming! I'm dreaming!" he repeated to himself. And he went on sleeping.

When he awoke, the sky was clear; the loose window let in a cold, pure air. The Arab was asleep, hunched up under the blankets now, his mouth open, utterly relaxed. But when Daru shook him, he started dreadfully, staring at Daru with wild eyes as if he had never seen him and such a frightened expression that the schoolmaster stepped back. "Don't be afraid. It's me. You must eat." The Arab nodded his head and said yes. Calm had returned to his face, but his expression was vacant and listless.

The coffee was ready. They drank it seated together on the folding bed as they munched their pieces of the cake. Then Daru led the Arab under the shed and showed him the faucet where he washed. He went back into the room, folded the blankets and the bed, made his own bed and put the room in order. Then he went through the classroom and out onto the terrace. The sun was already rising in the blue sky; a soft, bright light was bathing the deserted plateau. On the ridge the snow was melting in spots. The stones were about to reappear. Crouched on the edge of the plateau, the schoolmaster looked at the deserted expanse. He thought of Balducci. He had hurt him, for he had sent him off in a way as if he didn't want to be associated with him. He could still hear the gendarme's farewell and, without knowing why, he felt strangely empty and vulnerable. At that moment, from the other side of the schoolhouse, the prisoner coughed. Daru listened to him almost despite himself and then, furious, threw a pebble that whistled through the air before sinking into the snow. That man's stupid crime revolted him, but to hand him over was contrary to honor. Merely thinking of it made him smart with humiliation. And he cursed at one and the same time his own people who had sent him this Arab and the Arab too who had dared to kill and not managed to get away. Daru got up, walked in a circle on the terrace, waited motionless, and then went back into the schoolhouse.

The Arab, leaning over the cement floor of the shed, was washing his teeth with two fingers. Daru looked at him and said: "Come." He went back into the room ahead of the prisoner. He slipped a hunting-jacket on over his sweater and put on walking-shoes. Standing, he waited until the Arab had put on his *chèche* and sandals. They went into the classroom and the schoolmaster pointed to the exit, saying: "Go ahead." The fellow didn't budge. "I'm coming," said Daru. The Arab went out. Daru went back into the room and made a package of pieces of rusk, dates, and sugar. In the classroom, before going out, he hesitated a second in front of his desk, then crossed the threshold and locked the door. "That's the way," he said. He started toward the east, followed by the prisoner. But, a short distance from the schoolhouse, he thought he heard a slight sound behind them. He retraced his steps and examined the surroundings of the house; there was no one there. The Arab watched him without seeming to understand. "Come on," said Daru.

They walked for an hour and rested beside a sharp peak of limestone. The snow was melting faster and faster and the sun was drinking up the puddles at once, rapidly cleaning the plateau, which gradually dried and vibrated like the air itself. When they resumed walking, the ground rang under their feet. From time to time a bird rent the space in front of them with a joyful cry. Daru breathed in deeply the fresh morning light. He felt a sort of rapture before the vast familiar expanse, now almost entirely yellow under its dome of blue sky. They walked an hour more, descending toward the south. They reached a level height made up of crumbly rocks. From there on, the plateau sloped down, eastward, toward a low plain where there were a few spindly trees and, to the south, toward outcroppings of rock that gave the landscape a chaotic look.

Daru surveyed the two directions. There was nothing but the sky on the horizon. Not a man could be seen. He turned toward the Arab, who was looking at him blankly. Daru held out the package to him. "Take it," he said. "There are dates, bread, and sugar. You can hold out for two days. Here are a thousand francs too." The Arab took the package and the money but kept his full hands at chest level as if he didn't know what to do with what was being given him. "Now look," the schoolmaster said as he pointed in the direction of the east, "there's the way to Tinguit. You have a two-hour walk. At Tinguit you'll find the administration and the police. They are expecting you." The Arab looked toward the east, still holding the package and the money against his chest. Daru took his elbow and turned him rather roughly toward the south. At the foot of the height on which they stood could be seen a faint path. "That's the trail across the plateau. In a day's walk from here you'll find pasturelands and the first nomads. They'll take you in and shelter you according to their law." The Arab had now turned toward Daru and a sort of panic was visible in his expression. "Listen," he said. Daru shook his head: "No, be quiet. Now I'm leaving you." He turned his back on him, took two long steps in the direction of the school, looked hesitantly at the motionless Arab, and started off again. For a few minutes he heard nothing but his own step resounding on the cold ground and did not turn his head. A moment later, however, he turned around. The Arab was still there on the edge of the hill, his arms hanging now, and he was looking at the schoolmaster. Daru felt something rise in his throat. But he swore with impatience, waved vaguely, and started off again. He had already gone some distance when he again stopped and looked. There was no longer anyone on the hill.

Daru hesitated. The sun was now rather high in the sky and was beginning to beat down on his head. The schoolmaster retraced his steps, at first somewhat uncertainly, then with decision. When he reached the little hill, he was bathed in sweat. He climbed it as fast as he could and stopped, out of breath, at the top. The rock-fields to the south stood out sharply against the blue sky, but on the plain to the east a steamy heat was already rising. And in that slight haze, Daru, with heavy heart, made out the Arab walking slowly on the road to prison.

A little later, standing before the window of the classroom, the schoolmaster was watching the clear light bathing the whole surface of the plateau, but he hardly saw it. Behind him on the blackboard, among the winding French rivers, sprawled the clumsily chalked-up words he had just read: "You handed over our brother. You will pay for this." Daru looked at the sky, the plateau, and, beyond, the invisible lands stretching all the way to the sea. In this vast landscape he had loved so much, he was alone.

JOHN CHEEVER

The Country Husband

To begin at the beginning, the airplane from Minneapolis in which Francis Weed was traveling East ran into heavy weather. The sky had been a hazy blue, with the clouds below the plane lying so close together that nothing could be seen of the earth. Then mist began to form outside the windows, and they flew into a white cloud of such density that it reflected the exhaust fires. The color of the cloud darkened to gray, and the plane began to rock. Francis had been in heavy weather before, but he had never been shaken up so much. The man in the seat beside him pulled a flask out of his pocket and took a drink. Francis smiled at his neighbor, but the man looked away; he wasn't sharing his pain killer with anyone. The plane began to drop and flounder wildly. A child was crying. The air in the cabin was overheated and stale, and Francis' left foot went to sleep. He read a little from a paper book that he had bought at the airport, but the violence of the storm divided his attention. It was black outside the ports. The exhaust fires blazed and shed sparks in the dark, and, inside, the shaded lights, the stuffiness, and the window curtains gave the cabin an atmosphere of intense and misplaced domesticity. Then the lights flickered and went out. "You know what I've always wanted to do?" the man beside Francis said suddenly. "I've always wanted to buy a farm in New Hampshire and raise beef cattle." The stewardess announced that they were going to make an emergency landing. All but the children saw in their minds the spreading wings of the Angel of Death. The pilot could be heard singing faintly, "I've got sixpence, jolly, jolly sixpence. I've got sixpence to last me all my life . . ." There was no other sound.

The loud groaning of the hydraulic valves swallowed up the pilot's song, and there was a shrieking high in the air, like automobile brakes, and the plane hit flat on its belly in a cornfield and shook them so violently that an old man up forward howled, "Me kidneys! Me kidneys!" The stewardess flung open the door, and someone opened an emergency door at the back, letting in the sweet noise of their continuing mortality — the idle splash and smell of a heavy rain. Anxious for their lives, they filed out of the doors and scattered over the cornfield in all directions, praying that the thread would hold. It did. Nothing happened. When it was clear that the plane would not burn or explode, the crew and the stewardess gathered the passengers together and led them to the shelter of a barn. They were not far from Philadelphia, and in a little while a string of taxis took them into the city. "It's just like the Marne," someone said, but there was surprisingly little relaxation of that suspiciousness with which many Americans regard their fellow travelers.

In Philadelphia, Francis Weed got a train to New York. At the end of that journey, he crossed the city and caught just as it was about to pull out the commuting train that he took five nights a week to his home in Shady Hill.

He sat with Trace Bearden. "You know, I was in that plane that just crashed outside Philadelphia," he said. "We came down in a field . . ." He had traveled faster than the newspapers or the rain, and the weather in New York was sunny and mild. It was a day in late September, as fragrant and shapely as an apple. Trace listened to the story, but how could he get excited? Francis had no powers that would let him re-create a brush with death — particularly in the atmosphere of a commuting train, journeying through a sunny countryside where already, in the slum gardens, there were signs of harvest. Trace picked up his newspaper, and Francis was left alone with his thoughts. He said good night to Trace on the platform at Shady Hill and drove in his secondhand Volkswagen up to the Blenhollow neighborhood, where he lived.

The Weeds' Dutch Colonial house was larger than it appeared to be from the driveway. The living room was spacious and divided like Gaul into three parts. Around an ell to the left as one entered from the vestibule was the long table, laid for six, with candles and a bowl of fruit in the center. The sounds and smells that came from the open kitchen door were appetizing, for Julia Weed was a good cook. The largest part of the living room centered on a fireplace. On the right were some bookshelves and a piano. The room was polished and tranquil, and from the windows that opened to the west there was some late-summer sunlight, brilliant and as clear as water. Nothing here was neglected; nothing had not been burnished. It was not the kind of household where, after prying open a stuck cigarette box, you would find an old shirt button and a tarnished nickel. The hearth was swept, the roses on the piano were reflected in the polish of the broad top, and there was an album of Schubert waltzes on the rack. Louisa Weed, a pretty girl of nine, was looking out the western windows. Her younger brother Henry was standing beside her. Her still younger brother, Toby, was studying the figures of some tonsured monks drinking beer on the polished brass of the woodbox. Francis, taking off his hat and putting down his paper, was not consciously pleased with the scene; he was not that reflective. It was his element, his creation, and he returned to it with that sense of lightness and strength with which any creature returns to his home. "Hi, everybody," he said. "The plane from Minneapolis ..."

Nine times out of ten, Francis would be greeted with affection, but tonight the children are absorbed in their own antagonisms. Francis had not finished his sentence about the plane crash before Henry plants a kick in Louisa's behind. Louisa swings around, saying, "*Damn* you!" Francis makes the mistake of scolding Louisa for bad language before he punishes Henry. Now Louisa turns on her father and accuses him of favoritism. Henry is always right; she is persecuted and lonely; her lot is hopeless. Francis turns to his son, but the boy has justification for the kick — she hit him first; she hit him on the ear, which is dangerous. Louisa agrees with this passionately. She hit him on the ear, and she *meant* to hit him on the ear, because he messed up her china collection. Henry says that this is a lie. Little Toby turns away from the woodbox to throw in some evidence for Louisa. Henry claps his hand over little Toby's mouth. Francis separates the two boys but accidentally pushes Toby into the woodbox. Toby begins to cry. Louisa is already crying. Just then, Julia Weed comes into that part of the room where the table is laid. She is a pretty, intelligent woman, and the white in her hair is premature. She does not seem to notice the fracas. "Hello, darling," she says serenely to Francis. "Wash your hands, everyone. Dinner is ready." She strikes a match and lights the six candles in this vale of tears.

This simple announcement, like the war cries of the Scottish chieftains, only refreshes the ferocity of the combatants. Louisa gives Henry a blow on the shoulder. Henry, although he seldom cries, has pitched nine innings and is tired. He bursts into tears. Little Toby discovers a splinter in his hand and begins to howl. Francis says loudly that he has been in a plane crash and that he is tired. Julia appears again from the kitchen and, still ignoring the chaos, asks Francis to go upstairs and tell Helen that everything is ready. Francis is happy to go; it is like getting back to headquarters company. He is planning to tell his oldest daughter about the airplane crash, but Helen is lying on her bed reading a *True Romance* magazine, and the first thing Francis does is to take the magazine from her hand and remind Helen that he has forbidden her to buy it. She did not buy it, Helen replies. It was given to her by her best friend, Bessie Black. Everybody reads *True Romance.* Bessie Black's father reads *True Romance.* There isn't a girl in Helen's class who doesn't read *True Romance.* Francis expresses his detestation of the magazine and then tells her that dinner is ready — although from the sounds downstairs it doesn't seem so. Helen follows him down the stairs. Julia has seated herself in the candlelight and spread a napkin over her lap. Neither Louisa nor Henry has come to the table. Little Toby is still howling, lying face down on the floor. Francis speaks to him gently: "Daddy was in a plane crash this afternoon, Toby. Don't you want to hear about it?" Toby goes on crying. "If you don't come to the table now, Toby," Francis says, "I'll have to send you to bed without any supper." The little boy rises, gives him a cutting look, flies up the stairs to his bedroom, and slams the door. "Oh dear," Julia says, and starts to go after him. Francis says that she will spoil him. Julia says that Toby is ten pounds underweight and has to be encouraged to eat. Winter is coming, and he will spend the cold months in bed unless he has his dinner. Julia goes upstairs. Francis sits down at the table with Helen. Helen is suffering from the dismal feeling of having read too intently on a fine day, and she gives her father and the room a jaded look. She doesn't understand about the plane crash, because there wasn't a drop of rain in Shady Hill.

Julia returns with Toby, and they all sit down and are served. "Do I have to look at that big, fat slob?" Henry says, of Louisa. Everybody but Toby enters into this skirmish, and it rages up and down the table for five minutes. Toward the end, Henry puts his napkin over his head and, trying to eat that way, spills spinach all over his shirt. Francis asks Julia if the children couldn't have their dinner earlier. Julia's guns are loaded for this. She can't cook two dinners and lay two tables. She paints with lightning strokes that panorama of drudgery in which her youth, her beauty, and her wit have been lost. Francis says that he must be understood; he was nearly killed in an airplane crash, and he doesn't like to come home every night to a battlefield. Now Julia is deeply concerned. Her voice trembles. He doesn't come home every night to a battlefield. The accusation is stupid and mean. Everything was tranquil until he arrived. She stops speaking, puts down her knife and fork, and looks into her plate as if it is a gulf. She begins to cry. "Poor Mummy!" Toby says, and when Julia gets up from the table, drying her tears with a napkin, Toby goes to her side. "Poor Mummy," he says. "Poor Mummy!" And they climb the stairs together. The other children drift away from the battlefield, and Francis goes into the back garden for a cigarette and some air.

It was a pleasant garden, with walks and flower beds and places to sit. The sunset had nearly burned out, but there was still plenty of light.

Put into a thoughtful mood by the crash and the battle, Francis listened to the evening sounds of Shady Hill. "Varmints! Rascals!" old Mr. Nixon shouted to the squirrels in his bird-feeding station. "Avaunt and quit my sight!" A door slammed. Someone was cutting grass. Then Donald Goslin, who lived at the corner, began to play the "Moonlight Sonata." He did this nearly every night. He threw the tempo out the window and played it *rubato* from beginning to end, like an outpouring of tearful petulance, lonesomeness, and self-pity — of everything it was Beethoven's greatness not to know. The music rang up and down the street beneath the trees like an appeal for love, for tenderness, aimed at some lovely housemaid — some fresh-faced, homesick girl from Galway, looking at old snapshots in her third-floor room. "Here, Jupiter, here, Jupiter," Francis called to the Mercers' retriever. Jupiter crashed through the tomato vines with the remains of a felt hat in his mouth.

Jupiter was an anomaly. His retrieving instincts and his high spirits were out of place in Shady Hill. He was as black as coal, with a long, alert, intelligent, rakehell face. His eyes gleamed with mischief, and he held his head high. It was the fierce, heavily collared dog's head that appears in heraldry, in tapestry, and that used to appear on umbrella handles and walking sticks. Jupiter went where he pleased, ransacking wastebaskets, clotheslines, garbage pails, and shoe bags. He broke up garden parties and tennis matches, and got mixed up in the processional at Christ Church on Sunday, barking at the men in red dresses. He crashed through old Mr. Nixon's rose garden two or three times a day, cutting a wide swath through the Condesa de Sastagos, and as soon as Donald Goslin lighted his barbecue fire on Thursday nights, Jupiter would get the scent. Nothing the Goslins did could drive him away. Sticks and stones and rude commands only moved him to the edge of the terrace, where he remained, with his gallant and heraldic muzzle, waiting for Donald Goslin to turn his back and reach for the salt. Then he would spring onto the terrace, lift the steak lightly off the fire, and run away with the Goslins' dinner. Jupiter's days were numbered. The Wrightson's German gardener or the Farquarsons' cook would soon poison him. Even old Mr. Nixon might put some arsenic in the garbage that Jupiter loved. "Here, Jupiter, Jupiter!" Francis called, but the dog pranced off, shaking the hat in his white teeth. Looking at the windows of his house, Francis saw that Julia had come down and was blowing out the candles.

Julia and Francis Weed went out a great deal. Julia was well liked and gregarious, and her love of parties sprang from a most natural dread of chaos and loneliness. She went through her morning mail with real anxiety, looking for invitations, and she usually found some, but she was insatiable, and if she had gone out seven nights a week, it would not have cured her of a reflective look — the look of someone who hears distant music — for she would always suppose that there was a more brilliant party somewhere else. Francis limited her to two week-night parties, putting a flexible interpretation on Friday, and rode through the weekend like a dory in a gale. The day after the airplane crash, the Weeds were to have dinner with the Farquarsons.

Francis got home late from town, and Julia got the sitter while he dressed, and then hurried him out of the house. The party was small and pleasant, and Francis settled down to enjoy himself. A new maid passed the drinks. Her hair was dark, and her face was round and pale and seemed familiar to Francis. He had not developed his memory as a sentimental faculty. Wood smoke, lilac, and other such perfumes did not stir him, and his memory was something like his appendix — a vestigial repository. It was not his limitation at all to be unable to escape the past; it was perhaps his limitation that he had escaped it so successfully. He might have seen the maid at other parties, he might have seen her taking a walk on Sunday afternoons, but in either case he would not be searching his memory now. Her face was, in a wonderful way, a moon face — Norman or Irish — but it was not beautiful enough to account for his feeling that he had seen her before, in circumstances that he ought to be able to remember. He asked Nellie Farquarson who she was. Nellie said that the maid had come through an agency, and that her home was Trenon, in Normandy — a small place with a church and a restaurant that Nellie had once visited. While Nellie talked on about her travels abroad, Francis realized where he had seen the woman before. It had been at the end of the war. He had left a replacement depot with some other men and taken a three-day pass in Trenon. On their second day, they had walked out to a crossroads to see the public chastisement of a young woman who had lived with the German commandant during the Occupation.

It was a cool morning in the fall. The sky was overcast, and poured down onto the dirt crossroads a very discouraging light. They were on high land and could see how like one another the shapes of the clouds and the hills were as they stretched off toward the sea. The prisoner arrived sitting on a three-legged stool in a farm cart. She stood by the cart while the Mayor read the accusation and the sentence. Her head was bent and her face was set in that empty half smile behind which the whipped soul is suspended. When the Mayor was finished, she undid her hair and let it fall across her back. A little man with a gray mustache cut off her hair with shears and dropped it on the ground. Then, with a bowl of soapy water and a straight razor, he shaved her skull clean. A woman approached and began to undo the fastenings of her clothes, but the prisoner pushed her aside and undressed herself. When she pulled her chemise over her head and threw it on the ground, she was naked. The women jeered; the men were still. There was no change in the falseness or the plaintiveness of the prisoner's smile. The cold wind made her white skin rough and hardened the nipples of her breasts. The jeering ended gradually, put down by the recognition of their common humanity. One woman spat on her, but some inviolable grandeur in her nakedness lasted through the ordeal. When the crowd was quiet, she turned — she had begun to cry — and, with nothing on but a pair of worn black shoes and stockings, walked down the dirt road alone away from the village. The round white face had aged a little, but there was no question but that the maid who passed his cocktails and later served Francis his dinner was the woman who had been punished at the crossroads.

The war seemed now so distant and that world where the cost of partisanship had been death or torture so long ago. Francis had lost track of the men who had been with him in Vesey. He could not count on Julia's discretion. He could not tell anyone. And if he had told the story now, at the dinner table, it would have been a social as well as a human error. The people in the Farquarsons' living room seemed united in their tacit claim that there had been no past, no war — that there was no danger or trouble in the world. In the recorded history of human arrangements, this extraordinary meeting would have fallen into place, but the atmosphere of Shady Hill made the memory unseemly and impolite. The prisoner withdrew after passing the coffee, but the encounter left Francis feeling languid; it had opened his memory and his senses, and left them dilated. Julia went into the house. Francis stayed in the car to take the sitter home.

Expecting to see Mrs. Henlein, the old lady who usually stayed with the children, he was surprised when a young girl opened the door and came out onto the lighted stoop. She stayed in the light to count her textbooks. She was frowning and beautiful. Now, the world is full of beautiful young girls, but Francis saw here the difference between beauty and perfection. All those endearing flaws, moles, birthmarks, and healed wounds were missing, and he experienced in his consciousness that moment when music breaks glass, and felt a pang of recognition as strange, deep, and wonderful as anything in his life. It hung from her frown, from an impalpable darkness in her face — a look that impressed him as a direct appeal for love. When she had counted her books, she came down the steps and opened the car door. In the light, he saw that her cheeks were wet. She got in and shut the door.

"You're new," Francis said.

"Yes. Mrs. Henlein is sick. I'm Anne Murchison."

"Did the children give you any trouble?"

"Oh, no, no." She turned and smiled at him unhappily in the dim dashboard light. Her light hair caught in the collar of her jacket, and she shook her head to set it loose.

"You've been crying."

"Yes."

"I hope it was nothing that happened in our house."

"No, no, it was nothing that happened in your house." Her voice was bleak. "It's no secret. Everybody in the village knows. Daddy's an alcoholic, and he just called me from some saloon and gave me a piece of his mind. He thinks I'm immoral. He called just before Mrs. Weed came back."

"I'm sorry."

"Oh *Lord!*" She gasped and began to cry. She turned toward Francis, and he took her in his arms and let her cry on his shoulder. She shook in his embrace, and this movement accentuated his sense of the fineness of her flesh and bone. The layers of their clothing felt thin, and when her shuddering began to diminish, it was so much like a paroxysm of love that Francis lost his head and pulled her roughly against him. She drew away. "I live on Belleview Avenue," she said. "You go down Lansing Street to the railroad bridge."

"All right." He started the car.

"You turn left at that traffic light. ... Now you turn right here and go straight on toward the tracks."

The road Francis took brought him out of his own neighborhood, across the tracks, and toward the river, to a street where the near-poor lived, in houses whose peaked gables and trimmings of wooden lace conveyed the purest feelings of pride and romance, although the houses themselves could not have offered much privacy or comfort, they were all so small. The street was dark, and, stirred by the grace and beauty of the troubled girl, he seemed, in turning into it, to have come into the deepest part of some submerged memory. In the distance, he saw a porch light burning. It was the only one, and she said that the house with the light was where she lived. When he stopped the car, he could see beyond the porch light into a dimly lighted hallway with an old-fashioned clothes tree. "Well, here we are," he said, conscious that a young man would have said something different.

She did not move her hands from the books, where they were folded, and she turned and faced him. There were tears of lust in his eyes. Determinedly — not sadly — he opened the door on his side and walked around to open hers. He took her free hand, letting his fingers in between hers, climbed at her side the two concrete steps, and went up a narrow walk through a front garden where dahlias, marigolds, and roses — things that had withstood the light frosts — still bloomed, and made a bittersweet smell in the night air. At the steps, she freed her hand and then turned and kissed him swiftly. Then she crossed the porch and shut the door. The porch light went out, then the light in the hall. A second later, a light went on upstairs at the side of the house, shining into a tree that was still covered with leaves. It took her only a few minutes to undress and get into bed, and then the house was dark.

Julia was asleep when Francis got home. He opened a second window and got into bed to shut his eyes on that night, but as soon as they were shut — as soon as he had dropped off to sleep — the girl entered his mind, moving with perfect freedom through its shut doors and filling chamber after chamber with her light, her perfume, and the music of her voice. He was crossing the Atlantic with her on the old *Mauretania* and, later, living with her in Paris. When he woke from his dream, he got up and smoked a cigarette at the open window. Getting back into bed, he cast around in his mind for something he desired to do that would injure no one, and he thought of skiing. Up through the dimness in his mind rose the image of a mountain deep in snow. It was late in the day. Wherever his eyes looked, he saw broad and heartening things. Over his shoulder, there was a snow-filled valley, rising into wooded hills where the trees dimmed the whiteness like a sparse coat of hair. The cold deadened all sound but the loud, iron clanking of the lift machinery. The light on the trails was blue, and it was harder than it had been a minute or two earlier to pick the turns, harder to judge — now that the snow was all deep blue — the crust, the ice, the bare spots, and the deep piles of dry powder. Down the mountain he swung, matching his speed against the contours of a slope that had been formed in the first ice age, seeking with ardor some simplicity of feeling and circumstance. Night fell then, and he drank a Martini with some old friend in a dirty country bar.

In the morning, Francis' snow-covered mountain was gone, and he was left with vivid memories of Paris and the *Mauretania*. He had been bitten gravely. He washed his body, shaved his jaws, drank his coffee, and missed the seven-thirty-one. The train pulled out just as he brought his car to the station, and the longing he felt for the coaches as they drew stubbornly away from him reminded him of the humors of love. He waited for the eight-two, on what was now an empty platform. It was a clear morning; the morning seemed thrown like a gleaming bridge of light over his mixed affairs. His spirits were feverish and high. The image of the girl seemed to put him into a relationship to the world that was mysterious and enthralling. Cars were beginning to fill up the parking lot, and he noticed that those that had driven down from the high land above Shady Hill were white with hoarfrost. This first clear sign of autumn thrilled him. An express train — a night train from Buffalo or Albany — came down the tracks between the platforms, and he saw that the roofs of the foremost cars were covered with a skin of ice. Struck by the miraculous physicalness of everything, he smiled at the passengers in the dining car, who could be seen eating eggs and wiping their mouths with napkins as they traveled. The sleeping car compartments, with their soiled bed linen, trailed through the fresh morning like a string of rooming-house windows. Then he saw an extraordinary thing; at one of the bedroom windows sat an unclothed woman of exceptional beauty, combing her golden hair. She passed like an apparition through Shady Hill, combing and combing her hair, and Francis followed her with his eyes until she was out of sight. Then old Mrs. Wrightson joined him on the platform and began to talk.

"Well, I guess you must be surprised to see me here the third morning in a row," she said, "but because of my window curtains I'm becoming a regular commuter. The curtains I bought on Monday I returned on Tuesday, and the curtains I bought Tuesday I'm returning today. On Monday, I got exactly what I wanted — it's a wool tapestry with roses and birds — but when I got them home, I found they were the wrong length. Well, I exchanged them yesterday, and when I got them home, I found they were still the wrong length. Now I'm praying to high heaven that the decorator will have them in the right length, because you know my house, you *know* my living-room windows, and you can imagine what a problem they present. I don't know what to do with them."

"I know what to do with them," Francis said.

"What?"

"Paint them black on the inside, and shut up."

There was a gasp from Mrs. Wrightson, and Francis looked down at her to be sure that she knew he meant to be rude. She turned and walked away from him, so damaged in spirit that she limped. A wonderful feeling enveloped him, as if light were being shaken about him, and he thought again of Venus combing and combing her hair as she drifted through the Bronx. The realization of how many years had passed since he had enjoyed being deliberately impolite sobered him. Among his friends and neighbors, there were brilliant and gifted people — he saw that — but many of them, also, were bores and fools, and he had made the mistake of listening to them all with equal attention. He had confused a lack of discrimination with Christian love, and the confusion seemed general and destructive. He was grateful to the girl for this bracing sensation of independence. Birds were singing — cardinals and the last of the robins. The sky shone like enamel. Even the smell of ink from his morning paper honed his appetite for life, and the world that was spread out around him was plainly a paradise.

If Francis had believed in some hierarchy of love — in spirits armed with hunting bows, in the capriciousness of Venus and Eros — or even in magical potions, philters, and stews, in scapulae and quarters of the moon, it might have explained his susceptibility and his feverish high spirits.

The autumnal loves of middle age are well publicized, and he guessed that he was face to face with one of these, but there was not a trace of autumn in what he felt. He wanted to sport in the green woods, scratch where he itched, and drink from the same cup.

His secretary, Miss Rainey, was late that morning — she went to a psychiatrist three mornings a week — and when she came in, Francis wondered what advice a psychiatrist would have for him. But the girl promised to bring back into his life something like the sound of music. The realization that this music might lead him straight to a trial for statutory rape at the county courthouse collapsed his happiness. The photograph of his four children laughing into the camera on the beach at Gay Head reproached him. On the letterhead of his firm there was a drawing of the Laocoon, and the figure of the priest and his sons in the coils of the snake appeared to him to have the deepest meaning.

He had lunch with Pinky Trabert. At a conversational level, the mores of his friends were robust and elastic, but he knew that the moral card house would come down on them all — on Julia and the children as well — if he got caught taking advantage of a baby-sitter. Looking back over the recent history of Shady Hill for some precedent, he found there was none. There was no turpitude; there had not been a divorce since he lived there; there had not even been a breath of scandal. Things seemed arranged with more propriety even than in the Kingdom of Heaven. After leaving Pinky, Francis went to a jeweler's and bought the girl a bracelet. How happy this clandestine purchase made him, how stuffy and comical the jeweler's clerks seemed, how sweet the women who passed at his back smelled! On Fifth Avenue, passing Atlas with his shoulders bent under the weight of the world, Francis thought of the strenuousness of containing his physicalness within the patterns he had chosen.

He did not know when he would see the girl next. He had the bracelet in his inside pocket when he got home. Opening the door of his house, he found her in the hall. Her back was to him, and she turned when she heard the door close. Her smile was open and loving. Her perfection stunned him like a fine day — a day after a thunderstorm. He seized her and covered her lips with his, and she struggled but she did not have to struggle for long, because just then little Gertrude Flannery appeared from somewhere and said, "Oh, Mr. Weed ..."

Gertrude was a stray. She had been born with a taste for exploration, and she did not have it in her to center her life with her affectionate parents. People who did not know the Flannerys concluded from Gertrude's behavior that she was the child of a bitterly divided family, where drunken quarrels were the rule. This was not true. The fact that little Gertrude's clothing was ragged and thin was her own triumph over her mother's struggle to dress her warmly and neatly. Garrulous, skinny, and unwashed, she drifted from house to house around the Blenhollow neighborhood, forming and breaking alliances based on an attachment to babies, animals, children her own age, adolescents, and sometimes adults. Opening your front door in the morning, you would find Gertrude sitting on your stoop. Going into the bathroom to shave, you would find Gertrude using the toilet. Looking into your son's crib, you would find it empty, and, looking further, you would find that Gertrude had pushed him in his baby carriage into the next village. She was helpful, pervasive, honest, hungry, and loyal. She never went home of her own choice. When the time to go arrived, she was indifferent to all its signs. "Go home, Gertrude," people could be heard saying in one house or another, night after night. "Go home, Gertrude." It's time for you to go home now, Gertrude." "You had better go home and get your supper, Gertrude." "I told you to go home twenty minutes ago, Gertrude." "Your mother will be worrying about you, Gertrude." "Go home, Gertrude, go home."

There are times when the lines around the human eye seem like shelves of eroded stone and when the staring eye itself strikes us with such a wilderness of animal feeling that we are at a loss. The look Francis gave the little girl was ugly and queer, and it frightened her. He reached into his pockets — his hands were shaking — and took out a quarter. "Go home, Gertrude, go home, and don't tell anyone, Gertrude. Don't — " He choked and ran into the living room as Julia called down to him from upstairs to hurry and dress.

The thought that he would drive Anne Murchison home later that night ran like a golden thread through the events of the party that Francis and Julia went to, and he laughed uproariously at dull jokes, dried a tear when Mabel Mercer told him about the death of her kitten, and stretched, yawned, sighed, and grunted like any other man with a rendezvous at the back of his mind. The bracelet was in his pocket. As he sat talking, the smell of grass was in his nose, and he was wondering where he would park the car. Nobody lived in the old Parker mansion, and the driveway was used as a lovers' lane. Townsend Street was a dead end, and he could park there, beyond the last house. The old lane that used to connect Elm Street to the riverbanks was overgrown, but he had walked there with his children, and he could drive his car deep enough into the brushwoods to be concealed.

The Weeds were the last to leave the party, and their host and hostess spoke of their own married happiness while they all stood in the hallway saying good night. "She's my girl," their host said, squeezing his wife. "She's my blue sky. After sixteen years, I still bite her shoulders. She makes me feel like Hannibal crossing the Alps."

The Weeds drove home in silence. Francis brought the car up the driveway and sat still, with the motor running. "You can put the car in the garage," Julia said as she got out. "I told the Murchison girl she could leave at eleven. Someone drove her home." She shut the door, and Francis sat in the dark. He would be spared nothing then, it seemed, that a fool was not spared: ravening lewdness, jealousy, this hurt to his feelings that put tears in his eyes, even scorn — for he could see clearly the image he now presented, his arms spread over the steering wheel and his head buried in them for love.

Francis had been a dedicated Boy Scout when he was young, and, remembering the precepts of his youth, he left his office early the next afternoon and played some round-robin squash, but, with his body toned up by exercise and a shower, he realized that he might better have stayed at his desk. It was a frosty night when he got home. The air smelled sharply of change. When he stepped into the house, he sensed an unusual stir. The children were in their best clothes, and when Julia came down, she was wearing a lavender dress and her diamond sunburst. She explained the stir: Mr. Hubber was coming at seven to take their photograph for the Christmas card. She had put out Francis' blue suit and a tie with some color in it, because the picture was going to be in color this year. Julia was lighthearted at the thought of being photographed for Christmas. It was the kind of ceremony she enjoyed.

Francis went upstairs to change his clothes. He was tired from the day's work and tired with longing, and sitting on the edge of the bed had the effect of deepening his weariness. He thought of Anne Murchison, and the physical need to express himself, instead of being restrained by the pink lamps of Julia's dressing table, engulfed him. He went to Julia's desk, took a piece of writing paper, and began to write on it. "Dear Anne, I love you, I love you, I love you . . ." No one would see the letter, and he used no restraint. He used phrases like "heavenly bliss," and "love nest." He salivated, sighed, and trembled. When Julia called him to come down, the abyss between his fantasy and the practical world opened so wide that he felt it affected the muscles of his heart.

Julia and the children were on the stoop, and the photographer and his assistant had set up a double battery of floodlights to show the family and the architectural beauty of the entrance to their house. People who had come home on a late train slowed their cars to see the Weeds being photographed for their Christmas card. A few waved and called to the family. It took half an hour of smiling and wetting their lips before Mr. Hubber was satisfied. The heat of the lights made an unfresh smell in the frosty air, and when they were turned off, they lingered on the retina of Francis' eyes.

Later that night, while Francis and Julia were drinking their coffee in the living room, the doorbell rang. Julia answered the door and let in Clayton Thomas. He had come to pay for some theatre tickets that she had given his mother some time ago, and that Helen Thomas had scrupulously insisted on paying for, though Julia had asked her not to. Julia invited him in to have a cup of coffee. "I won't have any coffee," Clayton said, "but I will come in for a minute." He followed her into the living room, said good evening to Francis and sat awkwardly in a chair.

Clayton's father had been killed in the war, and the young man's fatherlessness surrounded him like an element. This may have been conspicuous in Shady Hill because the Thomases were the only family that lacked a piece; all the other marriages were intact and productive. Clayton was in his second or third year of college, and he and his mother lived alone in a large house, which she hoped to sell. Clayton had once made some trouble. Years ago, he had stolen some money and run away; he had got to California before they caught up with him. He was tall and homely, wore horn-rimmed glasses, and spoke in a deep voice.

"When do you go back to college, Clayton?" Francis asked.

"I'm not going back," Clayton said. "Mother doesn't have the money, and there's no sense in all this pretense. I'm going to get a job, and if we sell the house, we'll take an apartment in New York."

"Won't you miss Shady Hill?" Julia asked.

"No," Clayton said. "I don't like it."

"Why not?" Francis asked.

"Well, there's a lot here I don't approve of," Clayton said gravely. "Things like the club dances. Last Saturday night, I looked in toward the end and saw Mr. Granner trying to put Mrs. Minot into the trophy case. They were both drunk. I disapprove of so much drinking."

"It was Saturday night," Francis said.

"And all the dovecotes are phony," Clayton said. "And the way people clutter up their lives. I've thought about it a lot, and what seems to me to be really wrong with Shady Hill is that it doesn't have any future. So much energy is spent in perpetuating the place — in keeping out undesirables, and so forth — that the only idea of the future anyone has is just more and more commuting trains and more parties. I don't think that's healthy. I think people ought to be able to dream great dreams."

"It's too bad you couldn't continue with college," Julia said.

"I wanted to go to divinity school," Clayton said.

"What's your church?" Francis asked.

"Unitarian, Theosophist, Transcendentalist, Humanist," Clayton said.

"Wasn't Emerson a transcendentalist?" Julia asked.

"I mean the English transcendentalists," Clayton said. "All the American transcendentalists were goops."

"What kind of job do you expect to get?" Francis asked.

"Well, I'd like to do work for a publisher," Clayton said, "but everyone tells me there's nothing doing. But it's the kind of thing I'm interested in. I'm writing a long verse play about good and evil. Uncle Charlie might get me into a bank, and that would be good for me. I need the discipline. I have a long way to go in forming my character. I have some terrible habits. I talk too much. I think I ought to take vows of silence. I ought to try not to speak for a week, and discipline myself. I've thought of making a retreat at one of the Episcopalian monasteries, but I don't like Trinitarianism."

"Do you have any girl friends?" Francis asked.

"I'm engaged to be married," Clayton said. "Of course, I'm not old enough or rich enough to have my engagement observed or respected or anything, but I bought a simulated emerald for Anne Murchison with the money I made cutting lawns this summer. We're going to be married as soon as she finishes school."

Francis recoiled at the mention of the girl's name. Then a dingy light seemed to emanate from his spirit, showing everything — Julia, the boy, the chairs — in their true colorlessness. It was like a bitter turn of the weather.

"We're going to have a large family," Clayton said. "Her father's a terrible rummy, and I've had my hard times, and we want to have lots of children. Oh, she's wonderful, Mr. and Mrs. Weed, and we have so much in common. We like all the same things. We sent out the same Christmas card last year without planning it, and we both have an allergy to tomatoes, and our eyebrows grow together in the middle. Well, goodnight."

Julia went to the door with him. When she returned, Francis said that Clayton was lazy, irresponsible, affected, and smelly. Julia said that Francis seemed to be getting intolerant; the Thomas boy was young and should be given a chance. Julia had noticed other cases where Francis had been short-tempered. "Mrs. Wrightson has asked everyone in Shady Hill to her anniversary party but us," she said.

"I'm sorry, Julia."

"Do you know why they didn't ask us?"

"Why?"

"Because you insulted Mrs. Wrightson."

"Then you know about it?"

"June Masterson told me. She was standing behind you."

Julia walked in front of the sofa with a small step that expressed, Francis knew, a feeling of anger.

"I did insult Mrs. Wrightson, Julia, and I meant to. I've never liked her parties, and I'm glad she's dropped us."

"What about Helen?"

"How does Helen come into this?"

"Mrs. Wrightson's the one who decides who goes to the assemblies."

"You mean she can keep Helen from going to the dances?"

"Yes."

"I hadn't thought of that."

"Oh. I knew you hadn't thought of it," Julia cried, thrusting hilt-deep into this chink of his armor. "And it makes me furious to see this kind of stupid thoughtlessness wreck everyone's happiness."

"I don't think I've wrecked anyone's happiness."

"Mrs. Wrightson runs Shady Hill and has run it for the last forty years. I don't know what makes you think in a community like this you can indulge every impulse you have to be insulting, vulgar, and offensive."

"I have very good manners," Francis said, trying to give the evening a turn toward the light.

"Damn you, Francis Weed!" Julia cried, and the spit of her words struck him in the face. "I've worked hard for the social position we enjoy in this place, and I won't stand by and see you wreck it. You must have understood when you settled here that you couldn't expect to live like a bear in a cave."

"I've got to express my likes and dislikes."

"You can conceal your dislikes. You don't have to meet everything head on, like a child. Unless you're anxious to be a social leper. It's no accident that we get asked out a great deal! It's no accident that Helen has so many friends. How would you like to spend your Saturday nights at the movies? How would you like to spend your Sundays raking up dead leaves? How would you like it if your daughter spent the assembly nights sitting at her window, listening to the music from the club? How would you like it — " He did something then that was, after all, not so unaccountable, since her words seemed to raise up between them a wall so deadening that he gagged. He struck her full in the face. She staggered and then, a moment later, seemed composed. She went up the stairs to her room. She didn't slam the door. When Francis followed, a few minutes later, he found her packing a suitcase.

"Julia, I'm very sorry."

"It doesn't matter," she said. She was crying.

"Where do you think you're going?"

"I don't know. I just looked at a timetable. There's an eleven-sixteen into New York. I'll take that."

"You can't go, Julia."

"I can't stay. I know that."

"I'm sorry about Mrs. Wrightson, Julia, and I'm — "

"It doesn't matter about Mrs. Wrightson. That isn't the trouble."

"What's the trouble?"

"You don't love me."

"I do love you, Julia."

"No, you don't."

"Julia, I do love you, and I would like to be as we were — sweet and bawdy and dark — but now there are so many people."

"You hate me."

"I don't hate you, Julia."

"You have no idea of how much you hate me. I think it's subconscious. You don't realize the cruel things you've done."

"What cruel things, Julia?"

"The cruel acts your subconscious drives you to in order to express your hatred of me."

"What, Julia?"

"I've never complained."

"Tell me."

"You don't know what you're doing."

"Tell me."

"Your clothes."

"What do you mean?"

"I mean the way you leave your dirty clothes around in order to express your subconscious hatred of me."

"I don't understand."

"I mean your dirty socks and your dirty pajamas and your dirty underwear and your dirty shirts!" She rose from kneeling by the suitcase and faced him, her eyes blazing and her voice ringing with emotion. "I'm talking about the fact that you've never learned to hang up anything. You just leave your clothes all over the floor where they drop, in order to humiliate me. You do it on purpose!" She fell on the bed, sobbing.

"Julia, darling!" he said, but when she felt his hand on her shoulder she got up.

"Leave me alone," she said. "I have to go." She brushed past him to the closet and came back with a dress. "I'm not taking any of the things you've given me," she said. "I'm leaving my pearls and the fur jacket."

"Oh, Julia!" Her figure, so helpless in its self-deceptions, bent over the suitcase made him nearly sick with pity. She did not understand how desolate her life would be without him. She didn't understand the hours that working women have to keep. She didn't understand that most of her friendships existed within the framework of their marriage, and that without this she would find herself alone. She didn't understand about travel, about hotels, about money. "Julia, I can't let you go! What you don't understand, Julia, is that you've come to be dependent on me."

She tossed her head back and covered her face with her hands. "Did you say that *I* was dependent on *you?*" she asked. "Is that what you said? And who is it that tells you what time to get up in the morning and when to go to bed at night? Who is it that prepares your meals and picks up your dirty clothes and invites your friends to dinner? If it weren't for me, your neckties would be greasy and your clothing would be full of moth holes. You were alone when I met you, Francis Weed, and you'll be alone when I leave. When Mother asked you for a list to send out invitations to our wedding, how many names did you have to give her? Fourteen!"

"Cleveland wasn't my home, Julia."

"And how many of your friends came to the church? Two!"

"Cleveland wasn't my home, Julia."

"Since I'm not taking the fur jacket," she said quietly, "you'd better put it back into storage. There's an insurance policy on the pearls that comes due in January. The name of the laundry and the maid's telephone number — all those things are in my desk. I hope you won't drink too much, Francis. I hope that nothing bad will happen to you. If you do get into serious trouble, you can call me."

"Oh, my darling, I can't let you go!" Francis said. "I can't let you go, Julia!" He took her in his arms.

"I guess I'd better stay and take care of you for a little while longer," she said.

Riding to work in the morning, Francis saw the girl walk down the aisle of the coach. He was surprised; he hadn't realized that the school she went to was in the city, but she was carrying books, she seemed to be going to school. His surprise delayed his reaction, but then he got up clumsily and stepped into the aisle. Several people had come between them, but he could see her ahead of him, waiting for someone to open the car door, and then, as the train swerved, putting out her hand to support herself as she crossed the platform into the next car. He followed her through that car and halfway through another before calling her name — "Anne! Anne!" — but she didn't turn. He followed her into still another car, and she sat down in an aisle seat. Coming up to her, all his feelings warm and bent in her direction he put his hand on the back of her seat — even this touch warmed him — and leaning down to speak to her, he saw that it was not Anne. It was an older woman wearing glasses. He went on deliberately into another car, his face red with embarrassment and the much deeper feeling of having his good sense challenged; for if he couldn't tell one person from another, what evidence was there that his life with Julia and the children had as much reality as his dreams of iniquity in Paris or the litter, the grass smell, and the cave-shaped trees in Lovers' Lane.

Late that afternoon, Julia called to remind Francis that they were going out for dinner. A few minutes later, Trace Bearden called. "Look, fellar," Trace said. "I'm calling for Mrs. Thomas. You know? Clayton, that boy of hers, doesn't seem

takes his revenge on Clayton for taking his ideal, dream

able to get a job, and I wondered if you could help. If you'd call Charlie Bell — I know he's indebted to you — and say a good word for the kid, I think Charlie would — "

"Trace, I hate to say this," Francis said, "but I don't feel that I can do anything for that boy. The kid's worthless. I know it's a harsh thing to say, but it's a fact. Any kindness done for him would backfire in everybody's face. He's just a worthless kid, Trace, and there's nothing to be done about it. Even if we got him a job, he wouldn't be able to keep it for a week. I know that to be a fact. It's an awful thing, Trace, and I know it is, but instead of recommending that kid, I'd feel obligated to warn people against him — people who knew his father and would naturally want to step in and do something. I'd feel obliged to warn them. He's a thief ..."

The moment this conversation was finished, Miss Rainey came in and stood by his desk. "I'm not going to be able to work for you any more, Mr. Weed," she said. "I can stay until the seventeenth if you need me, but I've been offered a whirlwind of a job, and I'd like to leave as soon as possible."

She went out, leaving him to face alone the wickedness of what he had done to the Thomas boy. His children in their photograph laughed and laughed, glazed with all the bright colors of summer, and he remembered that they had met a bagpiper on the beach that day and he had paid the piper a dollar to play them a battle song of the Black Watch. The girl would be at the house when he got home. He would spend another evening among his kind neighbors, picking and choosing dead end streets, cart tracks, and the driveways of abandoned houses. There was nothing to mitigate his feeling — nothing that laughter or a game of softball with the children would change and, thinking back over the plane crash, the Farquarsons' new maid, and Anne Murchison's difficulties with her drunken father, he wondered how he could have avoided arriving at just where he was. He was in trouble. He had been lost once in his life, coming back from a trout stream in the north woods, and he had now the same bleak realization that no amount of cheerfulness or hopefulness or valor or perseverance could help him find, in the gathering dark, the path that he'd lost. He smelled the forest. The feeling of bleakness was intolerable, and he saw clearly that he had reached the point where he would have to make a choice.

He could go to a psychiatrist, like Miss Rainey; he could go to church and confess his lusts; he could go to a Danish massage parlor in the West Seventies that had been recommended by a salesman; he could rape the girl or trust that he would somehow be prevented from doing this; or he could get drunk. It was his life, his boat, and, like every other man, he was made to be the father of thousands, and what harm could there be in a tryst that would make them both feel more kindly toward the world? This was the wrong train of thought, and he came back to the first, the psychiatrist. He had the telephone number of Miss Rainey's doctor, and he called and asked for an immediate appointment. He was insistent with the doctor's secretary — it was his manner in business — and when she said that the doctor's schedule was full for the next few weeks, Francis demanded an appointment that day and was told to come at five.

The psychiatrist's office was in a building that was used mostly by doctors and dentists, and the hallways were filled with the candy smell of mouthwash and memories of pain. Francis' character had been formed upon a series of private resolves — resolves about cleanliness, about going off the high diving board or repeating any other feat that challenged his courage, about punctuality, honesty, and virtue. To abdicate the perfect loneliness in which he had made his most vital decisions shattered his concept of character and left him now in a condition that felt like shock. He was stupefied. The scene for his *miserere mei Deus* was, like the waiting room of so many doctors' offices, a crude token gesture toward the sweets of domestic bliss: a place arranged with antiques, coffee tables, potted plants, and etchings of snow-covered bridges and geese in flight, although there were no children, no marriage bed, no stove, even, in this travesty of a house, where no one had ever spent the night and where the curtained windows looked straight onto a dark air shaft. Francis gave his name and address to a secretary and then saw, at the side of the room, a policeman moving toward him. "Hold it, hold it," the policeman said. "Don't move. Keep your hands where they are."

"I think it's all right, Officer," the secretary began. "I think it will be — "

"Let's make sure," the policeman said, and he bagan to slap Francis' clothes, looking for what — pistols, knives, an icepick? Finding nothing, he went off and the secretary began a nervous apology: "When you called on the telephone, Mr. Weed, you seemed very excited, and one of the doctor's patients has been threatening his life, and we have to be careful. If you want to go in now?" Francis pushed open a door connected to an electrical chime, and in the doctor's lair sat down heavily, blew his nose into a handkerchief, searched in his pockets for cigarettes, for matches, for something, and said hoarsely, with tears in his eyes, "I'm in love, Dr. Herzog."

It is a week or ten days later in Shady Hill. The seven-fourteen has come and gone, and here and there dinner is finished and the dishes are in the dish-washing machine. The village hangs, morally and economically, from a thread; but it hangs by its thread in the evening light. Donald Goslin has begun to worry the "Moonlight Sonata" again.

Marcato ma sempre pianissimo! He seems to be wringing out a wet bath towel, but the housemaid does not heed him. She is writing a letter to Arthur Godfrey. In the cellar of his house, Francis Weed is building a coffee table. Dr. Herzog recommends woodwork as a therapy, and Francis finds some true consolation in the simple arithmetic involved and in the holy smell of new wood. Francis is happy. Upstairs, little Toby is crying, because he is tired. He puts off his cowboy hat, gloves, and fringed jacket, unbuckles the belt studded with gold and rubies, the silver bullets and holsters, slips off his suspenders, his checked shirt, and Levi's, and sits on the edge of his bed to pull off his high boots. Leaving this equipment in a heap, he goes to the closet and takes his space suit off a nail. It is a struggle for him to get into the long tights, but he succeeds. He loops the magic cape over his shoulders and, climbing onto the footboard of his bed, he spreads his arms and flies that short distance to the floor, landing with a thump that is audible to everyone in the house but himself.

"Go home, Gertrude, go home," Mrs. Masterson says. "I told you to go home an hour ago, Gertrude. It's way past your suppertime, and your mother will be worried. Go home!" A door on the Babcocks' terrace flies open, and out comes Mrs. Babcock without any clothes on, pursued by a naked husband. (Their children are away at boarding school, and their terrace is screened by a hedge.) Over the terrace they go and in at the kitchen door, as passionate and handsome a nymph and satyr as you will find on any wall in Venice. Cutting the last of the roses in her garden, Julia hears old Mr. Nixon shouting at the squirrels in his bird-feeding station. "Rapscallions! Varmints! Avaunt and quit my sight!" A miserable cat wanders into the garden, sunk in spiritual and physical discomfort. Tied to its head is a small straw hat — a doll's hat — and it is securely buttoned into a doll's dress, from the skirts of which protrudes its long, hairy tail. As it walks, it shakes its feet, as if it had fallen into water.

"Here, pussy, pussy, pussy!" Julia calls.

"Here, pussy, here poor pussy!" But the cat gives her a skeptical look and stumbles away in its skirts. The last to come is Jupiter. He prances through the tomato vines, holding in his generous mouth the remains of an evening slipper. Then it is dark; it is a night where kings in golden suits ride elephants over the mountains.

hum

sexual undertone

ANTON CHEKHOV

The Darling

Translated by Constance Garnett

Olenka, the daughter of the retired collegiate assessor, Plemyanniakov, was sitting in her back porch, lost in thought. It was hot, the flies were persistent and teasing, and it was pleasant to reflect that it would soon be evening. Dark rain-clouds were gathering from the east, and bringing from time to time a breath of moisture in the air.

Kukin, who was the manager of an open-air theatre called the Tivoli, and who lived in the lodge, was standing in the middle of the garden looking at the sky.

"Again!" he observed despairingly. "It's going to rain again! Rain every day, as though to spite me! I might as well hang myself! It's ruin! Fearful losses every day."

He flung up his hands, and went on, addressing Olenka:

"There! that's the life we lead, Olga Semyonovna. It's enough to make one cry. One works and does one's utmost; one wears oneself out, getting no sleep at night, and racks one's brain what to do for the best. And then what happens? To begin with, one's public is ignorant, boorish. I give them the very best operetta, a dainty masque, first-rate music-hall artists. But do you suppose that's what they want! They don't understand anything of that sort. They want a clown; what they ask for is vulgarity. And then look at the weather! Almost every evening it rains. It started on the tenth of May, and it's kept it up all May and June. It's simply awful! The public doesn't come, but I've to pay the rent just the same, and pay the artists."

The next evening the clouds would gather again, and Kukin would say with an hysterical laugh:

"Well, rain away, then! Flood the garden, drown me! Damn my luck in this world and the next! Let the artists have me up! Send me to prison! — to Siberia! — the scaffold! Ha, ha, ha!"

And next day the same thing.

Olenka listened to Kukin with silent gravity, and sometimes tears came into her eyes. In the end his misfortunes touched her; she grew to love him. He was a small thin man, with a yellow face, and curls combed forward on his forehead. He spoke in a thin tenor; as he talked his mouth worked on one side, and there was always an expression of despair on his face; yet he aroused a deep and genuine affection in her. She was always fond of someone, and could not exist without loving. In earlier days she had loved her papa, who now sat in a darkened room, breathing with difficulty; she had loved her aunt who used to come every other year from Bryansk; and before that, when she was at school, she had loved her French master. She was a gentle, soft-hearted, compassionate girl, with mild, tender eyes and very good health. At the sight of her full rosy cheeks, her soft white neck with a little dark mole on it, and the kind, naïve smile, which came into her face when she listened to anything pleasant, men thought, "Yes, not half bad," and smiled too, while lady visitors could not refrain from seizing her hand in the middle of a conversation, exclaiming in a gush of delight, "You darling!"

The house in which she had lived from her birth upwards, and which was left her in her father's will, was at the extreme end of the town, not far from the Tivoli. In the evenings and at night she could hear the band playing, and the crackling and banging of fireworks, and it seemed to her that it was Kukin struggling with his destiny, storming the entrenchments of his chief foe, the indifferent public; there was a sweet thrill at her heart, she had no desire to sleep, and when he returned home at daybreak, she tapped softly at her bedroom window, and showing him only her face and one shoulder through the curtain, she gave him a friendly smile. . . .

He proposed to her, and they were married. And when he had a closer view of her neck and her plump, fine shoulders, he threw up his hands, and said:

"You darling!"

He was happy, but as it rained on the day and night of his wedding, his face still retained an expression of despair.

They got on very well together. She used to sit in his office to look after things in the Tivoli, to put down the accounts and pay the wages. And her rosy cheeks, her sweet, naïve, radiant smile, were to be seen now at the office window, now in the refreshment bar or behind the scenes at the theatre. And already she used to say to her acquaintances that the theatre was the chief and most important thing in life, and that it was only through the drama that one could derive true enjoyment and become cultivated and humane.

"But do you suppose the public understands that?" she used to say. "What they want is a clown. Yesterday we gave 'Faust Inside Out,' and almost all the boxes were empty; but if Vanitchka and I had been producing some vulgar thing, I assure you the theatre would have been packed. To-morrow Vanitchka and I are doing 'Orpheus in Hell.' Do come."

And what Kukin said about the theatre and the actors she repeated. Like him she despised the public for their ignorance and their indifference to art; she took part in the rehearsals, she corrected the actors, she kept an eye on the behaviour of the musicians, and when there was an unfavourable notice in the local paper, she shed tears, and then went to the editor's office to set things right.

The actors were fond of her and used to call her "Vanitchka and I," and "the darling"; she was sorry for them and used to lend them small sums of money, and if they deceived her, she used to shed a few tears in private, but did not complain to her husband.

They got on well in the winter too. They took the theatre in the town for the whole winter, and let it for short terms to a Little Russian company or to a conjurer, or to a local dramatic society. Olenka grew stouter, and was always beaming with satisfaction, while Kukin grew thinner and yellower, and continually complained of their terrible losses, although he had not done badly all the winter. He used to cough at night, and she used to give him hot raspberry tea or lime-flower water, to rub him with eau-de-Cologne and to wrap him in her warm shawls.

"You're such a sweet pet!" she used to say with perfect sincerity, stroking his hair. "You're such a pretty dear!"

Towards Lent he went to Moscow to collect a new troupe, and without him she could not sleep, but sat all night at her window, looking at the stars, and she compared herself with the hens, who are awake all night and uneasy when the cock is not in the hen-house. Kukin was detained in Moscow, and wrote that he would be back at Easter, adding some instructions about the Tivoli. But on the Sunday before Easter, late in the evening, came a sudden ominous knock at the gate; someone was hammering on the gate as though on a barrel — boom, boom, boom! The drowsy cook went flopping with her bare feet through the puddles, as she ran to open the gate.

"Please open," said someone outside in a thick bass. "There is a telegram for you."

Olenka had received telegrams from her husband before, but this time for some reason she felt numb with terror. With shaking hands she opened the telegram and read as follows:

> "Ivan Petrovitch died suddenly to-day.
> Awaiting immate instructions fufuneral
> Tuesday."

That was how it was written in the telegram — "fufuneral," and the utterly incomprehensible word "immate." It was signed by the stage manager of the operatic company.

"My darling!" sobbed Olenka. "Vanitchka, my precious, my darling! Why did I ever meet you! Why did I know you and love you! Your poor heart-broken Olenka is all alone without you!"

Kukin's funeral took place on Tuesday in Moscow, Olenka returned home on Wednesday, and as soon as she got indoors she threw herself on her bed and sobbed so loudly that it could be heard next door, and in the street.

"Poor darling!" the neighbours said, as they crossed themselves. "Olga Semyonovna, poor darling! How she does take on!"

Three months later Olenka was coming home from mass, melancholy and in deep mourning. It happened that one of her neighbours, Vassily Andreitch Pustovalov, returning home from church, walked back beside her. He was the manager at Babakayev's, the timber merchant's. He wore a straw hat, a white waistcoat, and a gold watch-chain, and looked more like a country gentleman than a man in trade.

"Everything happens as it is ordained, Olga Semyonovna," he said gravely, with a sympathetic note in his voice; "and if any of our dear ones die, it must be because it is the will of God, so we ought to have fortitude and bear it submissively."

After seeing Olenka to her gate, he said good-bye and went on. All day afterwards she heard his sedately dignified voice, and whenever she shut her eyes she saw his dark beard. She liked him very much. And apparently she had made an impression on him too, for not long afterwards an elderly lady, with whom she was only slightly acquainted, came to drink coffee with her, and as soon as she was seated at table began to talk about Pustovalov, saying that he was an excellent man whom one could thoroughly depend upon, and that any girl would be glad to marry him. Three days later Pustovalov came himself. He did not stay long, only about ten minutes, and he did not say much, but when he left, Olenka loved him — loved him so much that she lay awake all night in a perfect fever, and in the morning she sent for the elderly lady. The match was quickly arranged, and then came the wedding.

Pustovalov and Olenka got on very well together when they were married.

Usually he sat in the office till dinner-time, then he went out on business, while Olenka took his place, and sat in the office till evening, making up accounts and booking orders.

"Timber gets dearer every year; the price rises twenty per cent" she would say to her customers and friends. "Only fancy we used to sell local timber, and now Vassitchka always has to go for wood to the Mogilev district. And the freight!" she would add, covering her cheeks with her hands in horror. "The freight!"

It seemed to her that she had been in the timber trade for ages and ages, and that the most important and necessary thing in life was timber;

and there was something intimate and touching to her in the very sound of words such as "baulk," "post," "beam," "pole," "scantling," "batten," "lath," "plank," etc.

At night when she was asleep she dreamed of perfect mountains of planks and boards, and long strings of wagons, carting timber somewhere far away. She dreamed that a whole regiment of six-inch beams forty feet high, standing on end, was marching upon the timber-yard; that logs, beams, and boards knocked together with the resounding crash of dry wood, kept falling and getting up again, piling themselves on each other. Olenka cried out in her sleep, and Pustovalov said to her tenderly: "Olenka, what's the matter, darling? Cross yourself!"

Her husband's ideas were hers. If he thought the room was too hot, or that business was slack, she thought the same. Her husband did not care for entertainments, and on holidays he stayed at home. She did likewise.

"You are always at home or in the office," her friends said to her. "You should go to the theatre, darling, or to the circus."

"Vassitchka and I have no time to go to theatres," she would answer sedately. "We have no time for nonsense. What's the use of these theatres?"

On Saturdays Pustovalov and she used to go to the evening service; on holidays to early mass, and they walked side by side with softened faces as they came home from church. There was a pleasant fragrance about them both, and her silk dress rustled agreeably. At home they drank tea, with fancy bread and jams of various kinds, and afterwards they ate pie. Every day at twelve o'clock there was a savoury smell of beetroot soup and of mutton or duck in their yard, and on fast-days of fish, and no one could pass the gate without feeling hungry. In the office the samovar was always boiling, and customers were regaled with tea and cracknels. Once a week the couple went to the baths and returned side by side, both red in the face.

"Yes, we have nothing to complain of, thank God," Olenka used to say to her acquaintances. "I wish everyone were as well off as Vassitchka and I."

When Pustovalov went away to buy wood in the Mogilev district, she missed him dreadfully, lay awake and cried. A young veterinary surgeon in the army, called Smirnin, to whom they had let their lodge, used sometimes to come in in the evening. He used to talk to her and play cards with her, and this entertained her in her husband's absence. She was particularly interested in what he told her of his home life. He was married and had a little boy, but was separated from his wife because she had been unfaithful to him, and now he hated her and used to send her forty roubles a month for the maintenance of their son. And hearing of all of this, Olenka sighed and shook her head. She was sorry for him.

"Well, God keep you," she used to say to him at parting, as she lighted him down the stairs with a candle. "Thank you for coming to cheer me up, and may the Mother of God give you health."

And she always expressed herself with the same sedateness and dignity, the same reasonableness, in imitation of her husband. As the veterinary surgeon was disappearing behind the door below, she would say:

"You know, Vladimir Platonitch, you'd better make it up with your wife. You should forgive her for the sake of your son. You may be sure the little fellow understands."

And when Pustovalov came back, she told him in a low voice about the veterinary surgeon and his unhappy home life, and both sighed and shook their heads and talked about the boy, who, no doubt, missed his father, and by some strange connection of ideas, they went up to the holy ikons, bowed to the ground before them and prayed that God would give them children.

And so the Pustovalovs lived for six years quietly and peaceably in love and complete harmony.

But behold! one winter day after drinking hot tea in the office, Vassily Andreitch went out into the yard without his cap on to see about sending off some timber, caught cold and was taken ill. He had the best doctors, but he grew worse and died after four months' illness. And Olenka was a widow once more.

"I've nobody, now you've left me, my darling," she sobbed, after her husband's funeral. "How can I live without you, in wretchedness and misery! Pity me, good people, all alone in the world!"

She went about dressed in black with long "weepers," and gave up wearing hat and gloves for good. She hardly ever went out, except to church, or to her husband's grave, and led the life of a nun. It was not till six months later that she took off the weepers and opened the shutters of the windows. She was sometimes seen in the mornings, going with her cook to market for provisions, but what went on in her house and how she lived now could only be surmised. People guessed, from seeing her drinking tea in her garden with the veterinary surgeon, who read the newspaper aloud to her, and from the fact that, meeting a lady she knew at the post-office, she said to her:

"There is no proper veterinary inspection in our town, and that's the cause of all sorts of epidemics. One is always hearing of people's getting infection from the milk supply, or catching diseases from horses and cows. The health of domestic animals ought to be as well cared for as the health of human beings."

She repeated the veterinary surgeon's words, and was of the same opinion as he about everything. It was evident that she could not live a year without some attachment, and had found new happiness in the lodge. In anyone else this would have been censured, but no one could think ill of Olenka; everything she did was so natural. Neither she nor the veterinary surgeon said anything to other people of the change in their relations, and tried, indeed, to conceal it, but without success, for Olenka could not keep a secret. When he had visitors, men serving in his regiment, and she poured out tea or served the supper, she would begin talking of the cattle plague, of the foot and mouth disease, and of the municipal slaughter-houses. He was dreadfully embarrassed, and when the guests had gone, he would seize her by the hand and hiss angrily:

"I've asked you before not to talk about what you don't understand. When we veterinary surgeons are talking among ourselves, please don't put your word in. It's really annoying."

And she would look at him with astonishment and dismay, and ask him in alarm: "But, Voloditchka, what *am* I to talk about?"

And with tears in her eyes she would embrace him, begging him not to be angry, and they were both happy.

But this happiness did not last long. The veterinary surgeon departed, departed for ever with his regiment, when it was transferred to a distant place — to Siberia, it may be. And Olenka was left alone.

Now she was absolutely alone. Her father had long been dead, and his arm-chair lay in the attic, covered with dust and lame of one leg. She got thinner and plainer, and when people met her in the street they did not look at her as they used to, and did not smile to her; evidently her best years were over and left behind, and now a new sort of life had begun for her, which did not bear thinking about. In the evening Olenka sat in the porch, and heard the band playing and the fireworks popping in the Tivoli, but now the sound stirred no response. She looked into her yard without interest, thought of nothing, wished for nothing, and afterwards when night came on she went to bed and dreamed of her empty yard. She ate and drank as it were unwillingly.

And what was worst of all, she had no opinions of any sort. She saw the objects about her and understood what she saw, but could not form any opinion about them, and did not know what to talk about. And how awful it is not to have any opinions! One sees a bottle, for instance, or the rain, or a peasant driving in his cart, but what the bottle is for, or the rain, or the peasant, and what is the meaning of it, one can't say, and could not even for a thousand roubles. When she had Kukin, or Pustovalov, or the veterinary surgeon, Olenka could explain everything, and give her opinion about anything you like, but now there was the same emptiness in her brain and in her heart as there was in her yard outside. And it was as harsh and as bitter as wormwood in the mouth.

Little by little the town grew in all directions. The road became a street, and where the Tivoli and the timber-yard had been, there were new turnings and houses. How rapidly time passes! Olenka's house grew dingy, the roof got rusty, the shed sank on one side, and the whole yard was overgrown with docks and stinging-nettles. Olenka herself had grown plain and elderly; in summer she sat in the porch, and her soul, as before, was empty and dreary and full of bitterness. In winter she sat at her window and looked at the snow. When she caught the scent of spring, or heard the chime of the church bells, a sudden rush of memories from the past came over her, there was a tender ache in her heart, and her eyes brimmed over with tears; but this was only for a minute, and then came emptiness again and the sense of the futility of life. The black kitten, Briska, rubbed against her and purred softly, but Olenka was not touched by these feline caresses. That was not what she needed. She wanted a love that would absorb her whole being, her whole soul and reason — that would give her ideas and an object in life, and would warm her old blood. And she would shake the kitten off her skirt and say with vexation:

"Get along; I don't want you!"

And so it was, day after day and year after year, and no joy, and no opinions. Whatever Mavra, the cook, said she accepted.

One hot July day, towards evening, just as the cattle were being driven by, and the whole yard was full of dust, someone suddenly knocked at the gate. Olenka went to open it herself and was dumbfounded when she looked out: she saw Smirnin, the veterinary surgeon, grey-headed, and dressed as a civilian. She suddenly remembered everything. She could not help crying and letting her head fall on his breast without uttering a word, and in the violence of her feeling she did not notice how they both walked into the house and sat down to tea.

"My dear Vladimir Platonitch! What fate has brought you?" she muttered, trembling with joy.

"I want to settle here for good, Olga Semyonovna," he told her. "I have resigned my post, and have come to settle down and try my luck on my own account. Besides, it's time for my boy to go to school. He's a big boy. I am reconciled with my wife, you know."

"Where is she?" asked Olenka.

"She's at the hotel with the boy, and I'm looking for lodgings."

"Good gracious, my dear soul! Lodgings! Why not have my house? Why shouldn't that suit you? Why, my goodness, I wouldn't take any rent!" cried Olenka in a flutter, beginning to cry again. "You live here, and the lodge will do nicely for me. Oh dear! how glad I am!"

Next day the roof was painted and the walls were whitewashed, and Olenka, with her arms akimbo, walked about the yard giving directions. Her face was beaming with her old smile, and she was brisk and alert as though she had waked from a long sleep. The veterinary's wife arrived — a thin, plain lady, with short hair and a peevish expression. With her was her little Sasha, a boy of ten, small for his age, blue-eyed, chubby, with dimples in his cheeks. And scarcely had the boy walked into the yard when he ran after the cat, and at once there was the sound of his gay, joyous laugh.

"Is that your puss, auntie?" he asked Olenka. "When she has little ones, do give us a kitten. Mamma is awfully afraid of mice."

Olenka talked to him, and gave him tea. Her heart warmed and there was a sweet ache in her bosom, as though the boy had been her own child. And when he sat at the table in the evening, going over his lessons, she looked at him with deep tenderness and pity as she murmured to herself:

"You pretty pet!... my precious!... Such a fair little thing, and so clever."

"'An island is a piece of land which is entirely surrounded by water,'" he read aloud.

"An island is a piece of land," she repeated, and this was the first opinion to which she gave utterance with positive conviction after so many years of silence and dearth of ideas.

Now she had opinions of her own, and at supper she talked to Sasha's parents, saying how difficult the lessons were at the high schools, but that yet the high school was better than a commercial one, since with a high school education all careers were open to one, such as being a doctor or an engineer.

Sasha began going to the high school. His mother departed to Harkov to her sister's and did not return; his father used to go off every day to inspect cattle, and would often be away from home for three days together, and it seemed to Olenka as though Sasha was entirely abandoned, that he was not wanted at home, that he was being starved, and she carried him off to her lodge and gave him a little room there.

And for six months Sasha had lived in the lodge with her. Every morning Olenka came into his bedroom and found him fast asleep, sleeping noiselessly with his hands under his cheek. She was sorry to wake him.

"Sashenka," she would say mournfully, "get up, darling. It's time for school."

He would get up, dress and say his prayers, and then sit down to breakfast, drink three glasses of tea, and eat two large cracknels and half a buttered roll. All this time he was hardly awake and a little ill-humoured in consequence.

"You don't quite know your fable, Sashenka," Olenka would say, looking at him as though he were about to set off on a long journey. "What a lot of trouble I have with you! You must work and do your best, darling, and obey your teachers."

"Oh, do leave me alone!" Sasha would say.

Then he would go down the street to school, a little figure, wearing a big cap and carrying a satchel on his shoulder. Olenka would follow him noiselessly.

"Sashenka!" she would call after him, and she would pop into his hand a date or a caramel. When he reached the street where the school was, he would feel ashamed of being followed by a tall, stout woman; he would turn round and say:

"You'd better go home, auntie. I can go the rest of the way alone."

She would stand still and look after him fixedly till he had disappeared at the school-gate.

Ah, how she loved him! Of her former attachments not one had been so deep; never had her soul surrendered to any feeling so spontaneously, so disinterestedly, and so joyously as now that her maternal instincts were aroused. For this little boy with the dimple in his cheek and the big school cap, she would have given her whole life, she would have given it with joy and tears of tenderness. Why? Who can tell why?

When she had seen the last of Sasha, she returned home, contented and serene, brimming over with love; her face, which had grown younger during the last six months, smiled and beamed; people meeting her looked at her with pleasure.

"Good morning, Olga Semyonovna, darling. How are you, darling?"

"The lessons at the high school are very difficult now," she would relate at the market. "It's too much; in the first class yesterday they gave him a fable to learn by heart, and a Latin translation and a problem. You know it's too much for a little chap."

And she would begin talking about the teachers, the lessons, and the school books, saying just what Sasha said.

At three o'clock they had dinner together: in the evening they learned their lessons together and cried. When she put him to bed, she would stay a long time making the cross over him and murmuring a prayer; then she would go to bed and dream of that far-away misty future when Sasha would finish his studies and become a doctor or an engineer, would have a big house of his own with horses and a carriage, would get married and have children.... She would fall asleep still thinking of the same thing, and tears would run down her cheeks from her closed eyes, while the black cat lay purring beside her: "Mrr, mrr, mrr."

Suddenly there would come a loud knock at the gate.

Olenka would wake up breathless with alarm, her heart throbbing. Half a minute later would come another knock.

"It must be a telegram from Harkov," she would think, beginning to tremble from head to foot. "Sasha's mother is sending for him from Harkov.... Oh, mercy on us!"

She was in despair. Her head, her hands, and her feet would turn chill, and she would feel that she was the most unhappy woman in the world. But another minute would pass, voices would be heard: it would turn out to be the veterinary surgeon coming home from the club.

"Well, thank God!" she would think.

And gradually the load in her heart would pass off, and she would feel at ease. She would go back to bed thinking of Sasha, who lay sound asleep in the next room, sometimes crying out in his sleep:

"I'll give it you! Get away! Shut up!"

ARTHUR C. CLARKE

The Star

It is three thousand light-years to the Vatican. Once, I believed that space could have no power over faith, just as I believed that the heavens declared the glory of God's handiwork. Now I have seen that handiwork, and my faith is sorely troubled. I stare at the crucifix that hangs on the cabin wall above the Mark VI Computer, and for the first time in my life I wonder if it is no more than an empty symbol.

I have told no one yet, but the truth cannot be concealed. The facts are there for all to read, recorded on the countless miles of magnetic tape and the thousands of photographs we are carrying back to Earth. Other scientists can interpret them as easily as I can, and I am not one who would condone that tampering with the truth which often gave my order a bad name in the olden days.

The crew are already sufficiently depressed: I wonder how they will take this ultimate irony. Few of them have any religious faith, yet they will not relish using this final weapon in their campaign against me — that private, good-natured, but fundamentally serious, war which lasted all the way from Earth. It amused them to have a Jesuit as chief astrophysicist: Dr. Chandler, for instance, could never get over it (why are medical men such notorious atheists?). Sometimes he would meet me on the observation deck, where the lights are always low so that the stars shine with undiminished glory. He would come up to me in the gloom and stand staring out of the great oval port, while the heavens crawled slowly around us as the ship turned end over end with the residual spin we had never bothered to correct.

"Well, Father," he would say at last, "it goes on forever and forever, and perhaps *Something* made it. But how you can believe that *Something* has a special interest in us and our miserable little world — that just beats me." Then the argument would start, while the stars and nebulae would swing around us in silent, endless arcs beyond the flawlessly clear plastic of the observation port.

It was, I think, the apparent incongruity of my position that caused most amusement to the crew. In vain I would point to my three papers in the *Astrophysical Journal*, my five in the *Monthly Notices of the Royal Astronomical Society.* I would remind them that my order has long been famous for its scientific works. We may be few now, but ever since the eighteenth century we have made contributions to astronomy and geophysics out of all proportion to our numbers. Will my report on the Phoenix Nebula end our thousand years of history? It will end, I fear, much more than that.

I do not know who gave the nebula its name, which seems to me a very bad one. If it contains a prophecy, it is one that cannot be verified for several billion years. Even the word nebula is misleading: this is a far smaller object than those stupendous clouds of mist — the stuff of unborn stars — that are scattered throughout the length of the Milky Way. On the cosmic scale, indeed, the Phoenix Nebula is a tiny thing — a tenuous shell of gas surrounding a single star.

Or what is left of a star . . .

The Rubens engraving of Loyola seems to mock me as it hangs there above the spectrophotometer tracings. What would *you*, Father, have made of this knowledge that has come into my keeping, so far from the little world that was all the universe you knew? Would your faith have risen to the challenge, as mine has failed to do?

You gaze into the distance, Father, but I have traveled a distance beyond any that you could have imagined when you founded our order a thousand years ago. No other survey ship has been so far from Earth: we are at the very frontiers of the explored universe. We set out to reach the Phoenix Nebula, we succeeded, and we are homeward bound with our burden of knowledge. I wish I could lift that burden from my shoulders, but I call to you in vain across the centuries and the light-years that lie between us.

On the book you are holding the words are plain to read. AD MAIOREM DEI GLORIAM, the message runs, but it is a message I can no longer believe. Would you still believe it, if you could see what we have found?

We knew, of course, what the Phoenix Nebula was. Every year, in our galaxy alone, more than a hundred stars explode, blazing for a few hours or days with thousands of times their normal brilliance before they sink back into death and obscurity. Such are the ordinary novae — the commonplace disasters of the universe. I have recorded the spectrograms and light curves of dozens since I started working at the Lunar Observatory.

But three or four times in every thousand years occurs something beside which even a nova pales into total insignificance.

When a star becomes a supernova, it may for a little while outshine all the massed suns of the galaxy. The Chinese astronomers watched this happen in A.D. 1054, not knowing what it was they saw. Five centuries later, in 1572, a supernova blazed in Cassiopeia so brilliantly that it was visible in the daylight sky. There have been three more in the thousand years that have passed since then.

Our mission was to visit the remnants of such a catastrophe, to reconstruct the events that led up to it, and, if possible, to learn its cause. We came slowly in through the concentric shells of gas that had been blasted out six thousand years before, yet were expanding still. They were immensely hot, radiating even now with a fierce violet light, but were far too tenuous to do us any damage. When the star had exploded, its outer layers had been driven upward with such speed that they had escaped completely from its gravitational field. Now they formed a hollow shell large enough to engulf a thousand solar systems, and at its center burned the tiny, fantastic object which the star had now become — a White Dwarf, smaller than the Earth, yet weighing a million times as much.

The glowing gas shells were all around us, banishing the normal night of interstellar space. We were flying into the center of a cosmic bomb that had detonated millennia ago and whose incandescent fragments were still hurtling apart. The immense scale of the explosion, and the fact that the debris already covered a volume of space many billions of miles across, robbed the scene of any visible movement. It would take decades before the unaided eye could detect any motion in these tortured wisps and eddies of gas, yet the sense of turbulent expansion was overwhelming.

We had checked our primary drive hours before, and were drifting slowly toward the fierce little star ahead. Once it had been a sun like our own, but it had squandered in a few hours the energy that should have kept it shining for a million years. Now it was a shrunken miser, hoarding its resources as if trying to make amends for its prodigal youth.

No one seriously expected to find planets. If there had been any before the explosion, they would have been boiled into puffs of vapor, and their substance lost in the greater wreckage of the star itself. But we made the automatic search, as we always do when approaching an unknown sun, and presently we found a single small world circling the star at an immense distance. It must have been the Pluto of this vanished solar system, orbiting on the frontiers of the night. Too far from the central sun ever to have known life, its remoteness had saved it from the fate of all its lost companions.

The passing fires had seared its rocks and burned away the mantle of frozen gas that must have covered it in the days before the disaster. We landed, and we found the Vault.

Its builders had made sure that we would. The monolithic marker that stood above the entrance was now a fused stump, but even the first long-range photographs told us that here was the work of intelligence. A little later we detected the continent-wide pattern of radioactivity that had been buried in the rock. Even if the pylon above the Vault had been destroyed, this would have remained, an immovable and all but eternal beacon calling to the stars. Our ship fell toward this gigantic bull's-eye like an arrow into its target.

The pylon must have been a mile high when it was built, but now it looked like a candle that had melted down into a puddle of wax. It took us a week to drill through the fused rock, since we did not have the proper tools for a task like this. We were astronomers, not archaeologists, but we could improvise. Our original purpose was forgotten: this lonely monument, reared with such labor at the greatest possible distance from the doomed sun, could have only one meaning. A civilization that knew it was about to die had made its last bid for immortality.

It will take us generations to examine all the treasures that were placed in the Vault. They had plenty of time to prepare, for their sun must have given its first warnings many years before the final detonation. Everything that they wished to preserve, all the fruit of their genius, they brought here to this distant world in the days before the end, hoping that some other race would find it and that they would not be utterly forgotten. Would we have done as well, or would we have been too lost in our own misery to give thought to a future we could never see or share?

If only they had had a little more time! They could travel freely enough between the planets of their own sun, but they not yet learned to cross the interstellar gulfs, and the nearest solar system was a hundred light-years away. Yet even had they possessed the secret of the Transfinite Drive, no more than a few millions could have been saved. Perhaps it was better thus.

Even if they had not been so disturbingly human as their sculpture shows, we could not have helped admiring them and grieving for their fate. They left thousands of visual records and the machines for projecting them, together with elaborate pictorial instructions from which it will not be difficult to learn their written language. We have examined many of these records, and brought to life for the first time in six thousand years the warmth and beauty of a civilization that in many ways must have been superior to our own. Perhaps they only showed us the best, and one can hardly blame them. But their worlds were very lovely, and their cities were built with a grace that matches anything of man's. We have watched them at work and play, and listened to their musical speech sounding across the centuries. One scene is still before my eyes — a group of children on a beach of strange blue sand, playing in the waves as children play on Earth. Curious whiplike trees line the shore, and some very large animal is wading in the shadows yet attracting no attention at all.

And sinking into the sea, still warm and friendly and lifegiving, is the sun that will soon turn traitor and obliterate all this innocent happiness.

Perhaps if we had not been so far from home and so vulnerable to loneliness, we would not have been so deeply moved. Many of us had seen the ruins of ancient civilizations on other worlds, but they had never affected us so profoundly. This tragedy was unique. It is one thing for a race to fail and die, as nations and cultures have done on Earth. But to be destroyed so completely in the full flower of its achievement, leaving no survivors — how could that be reconciled with the mercy of God?

My colleagues have asked me that, and I have given what answers I can. Perhaps you could have done better, Father Loyola, but I have found nothing in the *Exercitia Spiritualia* that helps me here. They were not an evil people: I do not know what gods they worshiped, if indeed they worshiped any. But I have looked back at them across the centuries, and have watched while the loveliness they used their last strength to preserve was brought forth again into the light of their shrunken sun. They could have taught us much: why were they destroyed?

I know the answers that my colleagues will give when they get back to Earth. They will say that the universe has no purpose and no plan, that since a hundred suns exploded every year in our galaxy, at this very moment some race is dying in the depths of space. Whether that race has done good or evil during its lifetime will make no difference in the end: there is no divine justice, for there is no God.

Yet, of course, what we have seen proves nothing of the sort. Anyone who argues thus is being swayed by emotion, not logic. God has no need to justify His actions to man. He who built the universe can destroy it when He chooses. It is arrogance — it is perilously near blasphemy — for us to say what He may or may not do.

This I could have accepted, hard though it is to look upon whole worlds and peoples thrown into the furnace. But there comes a point when even the deepest faith must falter, and now, as I look at the calculations lying before me, I know I have reached that point at last.

We could not tell, before we reached the nebula, how long ago the explosion took place. Now, from the astronomical evidence and the record in the rocks of that one surviving planet, I have been able to date it very exactly. I know in what year the light of this colossal conflagration reached our Earth. I know how brilliantly the supernova whose corpse now dwindles behind our speeding ship once shone in terrestrial skies. I know how it must have blazed low in the east before sunrise, like a beacon in that oriental dawn.

There can be no reasonable doubt: the ancient mystery is solved at last. Yet, oh God, there were so many stars you could have used. What was the need to give these people to the fire, that the symbol of their passing might shine above Bethlehem?

SAMUEL CLEMENS (MARK TWAIN)

The Notorious Jumping Frog of Calaveras County

In compliance with the request of a friend of mine, who wrote me from the East, I called on good-natured, garrulous old Simon Wheeler, and inquired about my friend's friend, Leonidas W. Smiley, as requested to do, and I hereunto append the result. I have a lurking suspicion that *Leonidas* W. Smiley is a myth; that my friend never knew such a personage; and that he only conjectured that if I asked old Wheeler about him, it would remind him of his infamous *Jim* Smiley, and he would go to work and bore me to death with some exasperating reminiscence of him as long and as tedious as it should be useless to me. If that was the design, it succeeded.

I found Simon Wheeler dozing comfortably by the bar-room stove of the dilapidated tavern in the decayed mining camp of Angel's and I noticed that he was fat and bald-headed, and had an expression of winning gentleness and simplicity upon his tranquil countenance. He roused up, and gave me good day. I told him that a friend of mine had commissioned me to make some inquiries about a cherished companion of his boyhood named *Leonidas* W. Smiley — *Rev. Leonidas* W. Smiley, a young minister of the Gospel, who he had heard was at one time a resident of Angel's Camp. I added that if Mr. Wheeler could tell me anything about this Rev. Leonidas W. Smiley, I would feel under many obligations to him.

Simon Wheeler backed me into a corner and blockaded me there with his chair, and then sat down and reeled off the monotonous narrative which follows this paragraph. He never smiled, he never frowned, he never changed his voice from the gentle-flowing key to which he tuned his initial sentence, he never betrayed the slightest suspicion of enthusiasm; but all through the interminable narrative there ran a vein of impressive earnestness and sincerity, which showed me plainly that, so far from his imagining that there was anything ridiculous or funny about his story, he regarded it as a really important matter, and admired its two heroes as men of transcendent genius in *finesse.* I let him go on in his own way, and never interrupted him once.

"Rev. Leonidas W. H'm, Reverend Le — well, there was a feller here once by the name of *Jim* Smiley, in the winter of '49 — or maybe it was the spring of '50 — I don't recollect exactly, somehow, though what makes me think it was one or the other is because I remember the big flume warn't finished when he first came to the camp; but anyway, he was the curiousest man about always betting on anything that turned up you ever see, if he could get anybody to bet on the other side; and if he couldn't he'd change sides. Any way that suited the other man would suit *him* — any way just so's he got a bet, *he* was satisfied. But still he was lucky, uncommon lucky; he most always come out winner. He was always ready and laying for a chance; there couldn't be no solit'ry thing mentioned but that feller'd offer to bet on it, and take ary side you please, as I was just telling you. If there was a horse-race, you'd find him flush or you'd find him busted at the end of it; if there was a dog-fight, he'd bet on it; if there was a cat-fight, he'd bet on it; if there was a chicken-fight, he'd bet on it; why, if there was two birds setting on a fence, he would bet you which one would fly first; or if there was a camp-meeting, he would be there reg'lar to bet on Parson Walker, which he judged to be the best exhorter about here, and so he was too, and a good man. If he even see a straddle-bug start to go anywheres, he would bet you how long it would take him to get to — to wherever he was going to, and if you took him, he would foller that straddle-bug to Mexico but what he would find out where he was bound for and how long he was on the road. Lots of the boys here has seen that Smiley, and can tell you about him. Why, it never made no difference to *him* — he'd bet on *any* thing — the dangdest feller. Parson Walker's wife laid very sick once, for a good while, and it seemed as if they warn't going to save her; but one morning he come in, and Smiley up and asked him how she was, and he said she was considerable better — thank the Lord for his inf'nite mercy — and coming on so smart that with the blessing of Prov'dence she'd get well yet; and Smiley, before he thought, says, 'Well, I'll resk two-and-a-half she don't anyway.'

"Thish-yer Smiley had a mare — the boys called her the fifteen-minute nag, but that was only in fun, you know, because of course she was faster than that — and he used to win money on that horse, for all she was so slow and always had the asthma, or the distemper, or the consumption, or something of that kind. They used to give her two or three hundred yards' start, and then pass her under way; but always at the fag end of the race she'd get excited and desperate like, and come cavoting and straddling up, and scattering her legs around limber, sometimes in the air, and sometimes out to one side among the fences, and kicking up m-o-r-e dust and raising m-o-r-e racket with her coughing and sneezing and blowing her nose — and *always* fetch up at the stand just about a neck ahead, as near as you could cipher it down.

"And he had a little small bull-pup, that to look at him you'd think he warn't worth a cent but to set around and look ornery and lay for a chance to steal something. But as soon as money was up on him he was a different dog; his under-jaw'd begin to stick out like the fo'castle of a steamboat, and his teeth would uncover and shine like the furnaces. And a dog might tackle him and bully-rag him, and bite him, and throw him over his shoulder two or three times, and Andrew Jackson — which was the name of the pup — Andrew Jackson would never let on but what *he* was satisfied, and hadn't expected nothing else — and the bets being doubled and doubled on the other side all the time, till the money was all up; and then all of a sudden he would grab that other dog jest by the j'int of his hind leg and freeze to it — not chaw, you understand, but only just grip and hang on till they throwed up the sponge, if it was a year. Smiley always come out winner on that pup, till he harnessed a dog once that didn't have no hind legs, because they'd been sawed off in a circular saw, and when the thing had gone along far enough, and the money was all up, and he come to make a snatch for his pet holt, he see in a minute how he'd been imposed on, and how the other dog had him in the door, so to speak, and he 'peared surprised, and then he looked sorter discouraged-like, and didn't try no more to win the fight, and so he got shucked out bad. He give Smiley a look as much as to say his heart was broke, and it was *his* fault, for putting up a dog that hadn't no hind legs for him to take holt of, which was his main dependence in a fight, and then he limped off a piece and laid down and died. It was a good pup, was that Andrew Jackson, and would have made a name for hisself if he'd lived, for the stuff was in him and he had genius — I know it, because he hadn't no opportunities to speak of, and it don't stand to reason that a dog could make such a fight as he could under them circumstances if he hadn't no talent. It always makes me feel sorry when I think of that last fight of his'n, and the way it turned out.

"Well, thish-yer Smiley had rat-tarriers, and chicken cocks, and tom-cats and all them kind of things, till you couldn't rest, and you couldn't fetch nothing for him to bet on but he'd match you. He ketched a frog one day, and took him home, and said he cal'lated to educate him; and so he never done nothing for three months but set in his back yard and learn that frog to jump. And you bet you he *did* learn him, too. He'd give him a little punch behind, and the next minute you'd see that frog whirling in the air like a doughnut — see him turn one summerset, or maybe a couple, if he got a good start, and come down flat-footed and all right, like a cat. He got him up so in the matter of ketching flies, and kep' him in practice so constant, that he'd nail a fly every time as fur as he could see him. Smiley said all a frog wanted was education, and he could do 'most anything — and I believe him. Why, I've seen him set Dan'l Webster down here on this floor — Dan'l Webster was the name of the frog — and sing out, 'Flies, Dan'l, flies!' and quicker'n you could wink he'd spring straight up and snake a fly off'n the counter there, and flop down on the floor ag'in as solid as a gob of mud, and fall to scratching the side of his head with his hind foot as indifferent as if he hadn't no idea he'd been doin' any more'n any frog might do. You never see a frog so modest and straightfor'ard as he was, for all he was so gifted. And when it come to fair and square jumping on a dead level, he could get over more ground at one straddle than any animal of his breed you ever see. Jumping on a dead level was his strong suit, you understand; and when it come to that, Smiley would ante up money on him as long as he had a red. Smiley was monstrous proud of his frog, and well he might be, for fellers that had traveled and been everywheres, all said he laid over any frog that ever *they* see.

"Well, Smiley kep' the beast in a little lattice box, and he used to fetch him down-town sometimes and lay for a bet. One day a feller — a stranger in the camp, he was — come acrost him and with him box, and says:

"'What might it be that you've got in the box?'

"And Smiley says, sorter indifferent-like, 'It might be a parrot, or it might be a canary, maybe, but it ain't — it's only just a frog.'

"And the feller took it, and looked at it careful, and turned it round this way and that, and says, 'H'm — so 'tis. Well, what's *he* good for?'

"'Well,' Smiley says, easy and careless, 'he's good enough for *one* thing, I should judge — he can outjump any frog in Calaveras County.'

"The feller took the box again, and took another long, particular look, and give it back to Smiley, and says, very deliberate, 'Well,' he says, 'I don't see no p'ints about that frog that's any better'n any other frog.'

"'Maybe you don't,' Smiley says. 'Maybe you understand frogs and maybe you don't understand 'em; maybe you've had experience, and maybe you ain't only a amature, as it were. Anyways, I've got *my* opinion, and I'll resk forty dollars that he can outjump any frog in Calaveras County.'

"And the feller studied a minute, and then says, kinder sadlike 'Well, I'm only a stranger here, and I ain't got no frog; but if I had a frog, I'd bet you.'

"And then Smiley says, 'That's all right — that's all right — if you'll hold my box a minute, I'll go and get you a frog.' And so the feller took the box, and put up his forty dollars along with Smiley's, and set down to wait.

"So he set there a good while thinking and thinking to himself, and then he got the frog out and prized his mouth open and took a teaspoon and filled him full of quail-shot — filled him pretty near up to his chin — and set him on the floor. Smiley he went to the swamp and slopped around in the mud for a long time, and finally he ketched a frog, and fetched him in, and give him to this feller, and says:

"'Now, if you're ready, set him alongside of Dan'l, with his fore paws just even with Dan'l's, and I'll give the word.' Then he says, 'One — two — three — *git!*' and him and the feller touched up the frogs from behind, and the new frog hopped off lively, but Dan'l give a heave, and hysted up his shoulders — so — like a Frenchman, but it warn't no use — he couldn't budge; he was planted as a solid as a church, and he couldn't no more stir than if he was anchored out. Smiley was a good deal surprised, and he was disgusted too, but he didn't have no idea what the matter was, of course.

"The feller took the money and started away; and when he was going out at the door, he sorter jerked his thumb over his shoulder — so — at Dan'l, and says again, very deliberate, 'Well,' he says, '*I* don't see no p'ints about that frog that's any better'n any other frog.'

"Smiley he stood scratching his head and looking down at Dan'l a long time, and at last he says, 'I do wonder what in the nation that frog throw'd off for — I wonder if there ain't something the matter with him — he 'pears to look might baggy, somehow.' And he ketched Dan'l by the nape of the neck, and hefted him, and says, 'Why blame my cats if he don't weigh five pound!'" and turned him upside down and he belched out a double handful of shot. And then he see how it was, and he was the maddest man — he set the frog down and took out after that feller, but he never ketched him. And —"

[Here Simon Wheeler heard his name called from the front yard, and got up to see what was wanted.] And turning to me as he moved away, he said: "Just set where you are, stranger, and rest easy — I ain't going to be gone a second."

But, by your leave, I did not think that a continuation of the history of the enterprising vagabond *Jim* Smiley would be likely to afford me much information concerning the Rev. *Leonidas* W. Smiley, and so I started away.

At the door I met the sociable Wheeler returning, and he button-holed me and recommenced:

"Well, thish-yer Smiley had a yaller one-eyed cow that didn't have no tail, only just a short stump like a bannanner, and —"

However, lacking both time and inclination, I did not wait to hear about the afflicted cow, but took my leave.

ROBERT COOVER

A Pedestrian Accident

Paul stepped off the curb and got hit by a truck. He didn't know what it was that hit him at first, but now, here on his back, under the truck, there could be no doubt. Is it me? he wondered. Have I walked the earth and come here?

Just as he was struck, and while still tumbling in front of the truck and then under the wheels, in a kind of funhouse gambado of pain and terror, he had thought: this has happened before. His neck had sprung, there was a sudden flash of light and a blaze roaring up in the back of his head. The hot — almost fragrant — pain: that was new. It was the *place* he felt he'd returned to.

He lay perpendicular to the length of the truck, under the trailer, just to the rear of the truck's second of three sets of wheels. All of him was under the truck but his head and shoulders. Maybe I'm being born again, he reasoned. He stared straight up, past the side of the truck, toward the sky, pale blue and cloudless. The tops of skyscrapers closed toward the center of his vision; now that he thought about it, he realized it was the first time in years he had looked up at them, and they seemed inclined to fall. The old illusion; one of them anyway. The truck was red with white letters, but his severe angle of vision up the side kept him from being able to read the letters. A capital "K," he could see that — and a number, yes, it seemed to be a "14." He smiled inwardly at the irony, for he had a private fascination with numbers: fourteen! He thought he remembered having had a green light, but it didn't really matter. No way to prove it. It would have changed by now, in any case. The thought, obscurely, troubled him.

"Crazy goddamn fool he just walk right out in fronta me no respect just burstin for a bustin!"

The voice, familiar somehow, guttural, yet falsetto, came from above and to his right. People were gathering to stare down at him, shaking their heads. He felt like one chosen. He tried to turn his head toward the voice, but his neck flashed hot again. Things were bad. Better just to lie still, take no chances. Anyway, he saw now, just in the corner of his eye, the cab of the truck, red like the trailer, and poking out its window, the large head of the truckdriver, wagging in the sunshine. The driver wore a small tweed cap — too small, in fact: it sat just on top of his head.

"Boy I seen punchies in my sweet time but this cookie takes the cake God bless the laboring classes I say and preserve us from the humble freak!"

The truckdriver spoke with broad gestures, bulbous eyes rolling, runty body thrusting itself in and out of the cab window, little hands flying wildly about. Paul worried still about the light. It was important, yet how could he ever know? The world was an ephemeral place, it could get away from you in a minute. The driver had a bent red nose and coarse reddish hair that stuck out like straw. A hard shiny chin, too, like a mirror image of the hooked nose. Paul's eyes wearied of the strain, and he had to stop looking.

"Listen lays and gentmens I'm a good Christian by Judy a decent hardworkin fambly man earnin a honest wage and got a dear little woman and seven yearnin younguns all my own seed a *responsible man* and goddamn that boy what he do but walk right into me and my poor ole truck!"

On some faces Paul saw compassion, or at least a neutral curiosity, an idle amusement, but on most he saw reproach. There were those who winced on witnessing his state and seemed to understand, but there were others — a majority — who jeered.

"He asked for it if you ask me!"

"It's the idler plays the fool and the workingman's to hang for it!"

"Shouldn't allow his kind out to walk the streets!"

"What is the use of running when you are on the wrong road?"

It worsened. Their shouts grew louder and ran together. There were orations and the waving of flags. Paul was wondering: had he been carrying anything? No, no. He had only — *wait!* a book? Very likely, but ... ah well. Perhaps he was carrying it still. There was no feeling in his fingers.

The people were around him like flies, grievances were being aired, sides taken, and there might have been a brawl, but a policeman arrived and broke it up. "All right, everybody! Stand back, please!" he shouted. "Give this man some air! Can't you see he's been injured?"

At last, Paul thought. He relaxed. For a moment, he'd felt himself in a strange and hostile country, but now he felt at home again. He even began to believe he might survive. Though really: had he ever doubted it?

"Everybody back, *back!* The policeman was effective. The crowd grew quiet, and by the sound of their sullen shuffling, Paul guessed they were backing off. Not that he got more or less air by it, but he felt relieved just the same. "Now," said the policeman, gently but firmly, "what has happened here?"

And with that it all started up again, same as before, the clamor, the outrage, the arguments, the learned quotations, but louder and more discordant than ever. I'm hurt, Paul said. No one heard. The policeman cried out for order, and slowly, with his shouts, with his nightstick, with his threats, he reduced them again to silence.

One lone voice hung at the end: "— for the last time, Mister, *stop goosing me!*" Everybody laughed, released.

""Stop goosing her, sir!" the policeman commanded with his chin thrust firmly forward, and everybody laughed again.

Paul almost laughed, but he couldn't, quite. Besides, he'd just, with that, got the picture, and given his condition, it was not a funny one. He opened his eyes and there was the policeman bent down over him. He had a notebook in his hand.

"Now, tell me, son, what happened here?" The policeman's face was thin and pale, like a student's, and he wore a trim little tuft of black moustache under the pinched peak of his nose.

I've just been hit, Paul explained, by this truck, and then he realized that he probably didn't say it at all, that speech was an art no longer his. He cast his eyes indicatively toward the cab of the truck.

"Listen, I asked you what happened here! Cat got your tongue, young man?"

"Crazy goddam fool he just walk right out in fronta me no respect just burstin for a bustin!"

The policeman remained crouched over Paul, but turned his head up to look at the truckdriver. The policeman wore a brilliant blue uniform with large brass buttons. And gold epaulettes.

"Boy I seen punchies in my sweet time but this cookie takes the cake God bless the laboring classes I say and preserve us from the humble freak!"

The policeman looked down at Paul, then back at the truckdriver. "I know about truckdrivers," Paul heard him say.

"Listen lays and gentmens I'm a good Christian by Judy a decent hardworkin fambly man earnin a honest wage and got a dear little woman and seven yearnin younguns all my own seed *a responsible man* and goddamn that boy what he do but walk right into me and my poor ole trike. Truck, I mean."

There was a loose tittering from the crowd, but the policeman's frown and raised stick contained it. "What's your name, lad?" he asked, turning back to Paul. At first, the policeman smiled, he knew who truckdrivers were and he knew who Pauls were, and there was a salvation of sorts in that smile, but gradually it faded. "Come, come, boy! Don't be afraid!" He winked, nudged him gently. "We're here to help you."

Paul, Paul replied. But, no, no doubt about it, it was jammed up in there and he wasn't getting it out.

"Well, if you won't help me, I can't help you," the policeman said pettishly and tilted his nose up. "Anybody here know this man?" he called out to the crowd.

Again a roar, a threatening tumult of words and sounds, shouts back and forth. It was hard to know if none knew him or if they all did. But then one voice, belted out above the others, came through: "O God in heaven! It's Amory! *Amory Westerman!*" The voice, a woman's, hysterical by the sound of it, drew near. "Amory! What... *what* have they *done* to you?"

Paul understood. It was not a mistake. He was astonished by his own acumen.

"Do you know this young man?" the policeman asked, lifting his notebook.

"What? Know him? Did Sarah know Abraham? Did Eve know Cain?"

The policeman cleared his throat uneasily. "Adam," he corrected softly.

"You know who you know, I know who I know," the woman said, and let fly with a low throaty snigger. The crowd responded with a belly laugh.

"But this young man — !" the policeman insisted, flustered.

"Who, you and Amory?" the woman cried. "I can't believe it!" The crowd laughed and the policeman bit his lip. "Amory! What new persecutions are these?" She billowed out above him: old, maybe even seventy, fat and bosomy, pasty-faced with thick red rouges, head haloed by ringlets of sparse orangish hair. "My poor Amory!" And down she came on him. Paul tried to duck, got only a hot flash in his neck for it. Her breath reeked of cheap gin. Help, said Paul.

"Hold, madame! Stop!" the policeman cried, tugging at the woman's sleeve. She stood, threw up her arms before her face, staggered backwards. What more she did, Paul couldn't see, for his view of her face was largely blocked by the bulge of her breasts and belly. There were laughs, though. "Everything in order here," grumped the policeman, tapping his notebook. "Now, what's your name, please ... uh ... miss, madame?"

"My name?" She twirled gracelessly on one dropsied ankle and cried to the crowd: *"Shall I tell?"*

"Tell! Tell! Tell!" shouted the spectators, clapping rhythmically. Paul let himself be absorbed by it; there was, after all, nothing else to do.

The policeman, rapping a pencil against his blue notebook to the rhythm of the chant, leaned down over Paul and whispered: ("I think we've got them on our side now!")

Paul his gaze floating giddily up past the thin white face of the police officer and the red side of the truck into the horizonless blue haze above, wondered if alliance were really the key to it all. What *am* I without them? Could I even die? Suddenly, the whole world seemed to tip: his feet dropped and his head rose. Beneath him the red machine shot grease and muck, the host rioted above his head, the earth pushed him from behind, and out front the skyscrapers pointed, like so many insensate fingers, the path he must walk to oblivion. He squeezed shut his eyes to set right the world again — he was afraid he would slide down beneath the truck to disappear from sight forever.

"*My name — !*" bellowed the woman, and the crowd hushed, tittering softly. Paul opened his eyes. He was on his back again. The policeman stood over him, mouth agape, pencil poised. The woman's puffy face was sequined with sweat. Paul wondered what she'd been doing while he wasn't watching. "My name, officer, is Grundy."

"I beg your pardon?" The policeman, when nervous, had a way of nibbling his moustache with his lowers.

"Mrs. Grundy, dear boy, who did you think I was?" She patted the policeman's thin cheek, tweaked his nose. "But you can call me Charity, handsome!" The policeman blushed. She twiddled her index finger in his little moustache. "Kootchy-kootchy-koo!" There was a roar of laughter from the crowd.

The policeman sneezed. "Please!" he protested.

Mrs. Grundy curtsied and stooped to unzip the officer's fly. "Hello! Anybody home!"

"*Stop that!*" squeaked the policeman through the thunderous laughter and applause. Strange, thought Paul, how much I'm enjoying this.

"Come out, come out, wherever you are!"

"*The story!*" the policeman insisted through the tumult.

"Story? What — ?"

"This young fellow," said the policeman, pointing with his pencil. He zipped up, blew his nose. "Mr., uh, Mr. Westerman ... you said — "

"Mr. Who?" The woman shook her jowls, perplexed. She frowned down at Paul, then brightened. "Oh, yes! Amory!" She paled, seemed to sicken. Paul, if he could've, would've smiled. "Good God!" she rasped, as though appalled at what she saw. Then, once more, she took an operatic grip on her breasts and staggered back a step. "O mortality! O fatal mischief! Done in! A noble man lies stark and stiff! Delenda est Carthago! *Sic transit glans mundi!*"

Gloria, corrected Paul. No, leave it.

"Squashed like a lousy bug!" she cried. "And at the height of his potency!"

"Now, wait a minute!" the policeman protested.

"The final curtain! The last farewell! The journey's end! Over the hill! The last muster!" Each phrase was answered by a happy shout from the mob. "Across the river! The way of all flesh! The last roundup!" She sobbed, then ballooned down on him again, tweaked his ear and whispered: ("How's Charity's weetsie snotkins, enh? Him fall down and bump his little putsy? Mumsy kiss and make well!") And she let him have it on the — well, sort of on the left side of his nose, left cheek, and part of his left eye: one wet enveloping sour blubbering kiss, and this time, sorrily, the policeman did not intervene. He was busy taking notes. Officer, said Paul.

"Hmmm," the policeman muttered, and wrote. "G-R-U-N- ah, ahem, Grundig, Grundig -D, yes, D-I-G. Now what did you — ?"

The woman labored clumsily to her feet, plodded over behind the policeman, and squinted over his shoulder at the notes he was taking. "That's a 'Y' there, buster, a 'Y.'" She jabbed a stubby ruby-tipped finger at the notebook.

"Grundigy?" asked the policeman in disbelief. "What kind of a name is that?"

"No, no!" the old woman whined, her grand manner flung to the winds. "Grundy! Grundy! Without the '-ig,' don't you see? You take off your — "

"Oh, *Grundy!* Now I have it!" The policeman scrubbed the back end of his pencil in the notebook. "Darned eraser. About shot." The paper tore. He looked up irritably. "Can't we just make it Grundig?"

"Grundy," said the woman coldly.

The policeman ripped the page out of his notebook, rumpled it up angrily, and hurled it to the street. "All right, gosh damn it all!" he cried in a rage, scribbling: "Grundy. I have it. Now get on with it, lady!"

"Officer!" sniffed Mrs. Grundy, clasping a handkerchief to her throat. "Remember your place, or I shall have to speak to your superior!" The policeman shrank, blanched, nibbled his lip.

Paul knew what would come. He could read these two like a book. *I'm* the strange one, he thought. He wanted to watch their faces, but his streetlevel view gave him at best a perspective on their underchins. It was their crotches that were prominent. Butts and bellies: the squashed bug's-eye view. And that was strange, too: that he wanted to watch their faces.

The policeman was begging for mercy, wringing his pale hands. There were faint hissing sounds, wriggling out of the crowd like serpents. "Cut the shit, mac," Charity Grundy, said finally, "you're overdoing it." The officer chewed his moustache, stared down at his notebook, abashed. "You wanna know who this poor clown is, right?" The policeman nodded. "Okay, are you ready?" She clasped her bosom again and the crowd grew silent. The police officer held his notebook up, the pencil poised. Mrs. Grundy snuffled, looked down at Paul, winced, turned away and wept. "Officer!" she gasped. "*He was my lover!*"

Halloos and cheers from the crowd, passing to laughter. The policeman started to smile, blinking down at Mrs. Grundy's body, but with a twitch of his moustache, he suppressed it.

"We met ... just one year ago today. O fateful hour!" She smiled bravely, brushing back a tear, her lower lip quivering. Once, her hands clenched woefully before her face, she winked down at Paul. The wink nearly convinced him. Maybe I'm him after all. Why not? "He was selling seachests, door to door. I can see him now as he was then — " She paused to look down at him as he was now, and wrinkles of revulsion swept over her face. Somehow this brought laughter. She looked away, puckered her mouth and bugged her eyes, shook one hand limply from the wrist. The crowd was really with her.

"Mrs. Grundy," the officer whispered, "please ..."

"Yes, there he was, chapfallen and misused, orphaned by the rapacious world, yet pure and undefiled, there: there at my door!" With her baggy arm, flung out, quavering, she indicated the door. "Bent nearly double under his impossible seachest, perspiration illuminating his manly brow, wounding his eyes, wrinkling his undershirt — "

"Careful!" cautioned the policeman nervously, glancing up from his notes. He must have filled twenty or thirty pages by now.

"In short, my heart went out to him!" Gesture of heart going out. "And though — alas! — my need for seachests was limited — "

The spectators somehow discovered something amusing in this and tittered knowingly. Mainly in the way she said it, he supposed. Her story in truth did not bother Paul so much as his own fascination with it. He knew where it would lead, but it didn't matter. In fact, maybe that *was* what fascinated him.

"— I invited him in. Put down that horrid seachest, dear boy, and come in here, I cried, come in to your warm and obedient Charity, love, come in for a cup of tea, come in and rest, rest your pretty little shoulders, your pretty little back, your pretty little ... " Mrs. Grundy paused, smiled with a faint arch of one eyebrow, and the crowd responded with another burst of laughter. "And it *was* pretty little, okay," she grumbled, and again they whooped, while she sniggered throatily.

How was it now? he wondered. In fact, he'd been wondering all along.

"And, well, officer that's what he did, he *did* put down his seachest — alas! sad to tell, right on my unfortunate cat Rasputin, dozing there in the day's brief sun, God rest his soul, his (again, alas!) somewhat homaloidal soul!"

She had a great audience. They never failed her, nor did they now.

The policeman, who had finally squatted down to write on his knee, now stood and shouted for order. "Quiet! *Quiet!*" His moustache twitched. "Can't you see this is a serious matter?" He's the funny one, thought Paul. The crowd thought so, too, for the laughter mounted, then finally died away. "And ... and then what happened?" the policeman whispered. But they heard him anyway and screamed with delight, throwing up a new clamor in which could be distinguished several coarse paraphrases of the policeman's question. The officer's pale face flushed. He looked down at Paul with a brief commiserating smile, shrugged his shoulders, fluttering the epaulettes. Paul made a try at a never-mind kind of gesture, but, he supposed, without bringing it off.

"What happened next, you ask, you naughty boy?" Mrs. Grundy shook and wriggled. Cheers and whistles. She cupped her plump hands under her breasts and hitched her abundant hips heavily to one side. "You don't understand," she told the crowd. "I only wished to be a mother to the lad." Hoohahs and catcalls. "But I had failed to realize, in that fleeting tragic moment when he unburdened himself upon poor Rasputin, how I was wrenching his young and unsullied heart asunder! Oh yes, I know, I know — "

"This is the dumbest story I ever heard," interrupted the policeman finally, but Mrs. Grundy paid him no heed.

"I know I'm old and fat, that I've crossed the Grand Climacteric!" She winked at the crowd's yowls of laughter. "I know the fragrant flush of first flower is gone forever!" she cried, not letting a good thing go, pressing her wrinkled palms down over the soft swoop of her blimp-sized hips, peeking coyly over one plump shoulder at the shrieking crowd. The policeman stamped his foot, but no one noticed except Paul. "I know, I know — *yet:* somehow, face to face with little Charity, a primitive unnameable urgency welled up in his untaught loins, his pretty little — "

"*Stop it!*" cried the policeman, right on cue. "This has gone far enough!"

"And *you* ask what happened next? I shall tell you, officer! For why conceal the truth ... from *you* of all people?" Though uneasy, the policeman seemed frankly pleased that she had put it this way. "Yes, without further discourse, he buried his pretty little head in my bosom — " (Paul felt a distressing sense of suffocation, though perhaps it had been with him all the while) " — and he tumbled me there, yes he did, there on the front porch alongside his seachest and my dying Rasputin, there in the sunlight, before God, before the neighbors, before Mr. Dunlevy the mailman who is hard of hearing, before the children from down the block passing on their shiny little — "

"Crazy goddamn fool he just walk right out in fronta me no respect just burstin for a bustin!" said a familiar voice.

Mrs. Grundy's broad face, now streaked with tears and mottled with a tense pink flush, glowered. There was a long and difficult silence. Then she narrowed her eyes, smiled faintly, squared her shoulders, touched a handkerchief to her eye, plunged the handkerchief back down her bosom, and resumed: " — Before, in short, the whole itchy eyes-agog world, a coupling unequaled in the history of Western concupiscence!" Some vigorous applause, which she acknowledged. "Assaulted, but — yes, I confess it — assaulted, but *aglow,* I reminded him of —

"Boy I seen punchies in my sweet time but this cookie takes the cake God bless the laboring classes I say and preserve us from the humble freak!"

Swiveling his wearying gaze hard right, Paul could see the truckdriver waggling his huge head at the crowd. Mrs. Grundy padded heavily over to him, the back of her thick neck reddening, swung her purse in a great swift arc, but the truckdriver recoiled into his cab, laughing with a taunting cackle. Then, almost in the same instant, he poked his red-beaked head out again, and rolling his eyes, said: "Listen lays and gentmens I'm a good Christian by Judy a decent hardworkin fambly man earnin a honest wage and got a dear little woman and seven yearnin younguns all my own seed *a responsible —"*

"I'll responsible your ass!" hollered Charity Grundy and let fly with her purse again, but once more the driver ducked nimbly inside, cackling obscenely. The crowd, taking sides, was more hysterical than ever. Cheers were raised and bets taken.

Again the driver's waggling head popped out: "— *man* and god — " he began, but this time Mrs. Grundy was waiting for him. Her great lumpish purse caught him square on his bent red nose — *k*a-RAACKK! — and the truckdriver slumped lifelessly over the door of his cab, his stubby little arms dangling limp, reaching just below the top of his head. As best Paul could tell, the tweed cap did not drop off, but since his eyes were cramped with fatigue, he had to stop looking before the truckdriver's head ceased bobbling against the door.

Man and god! he thought. Of course! terrific! What did it mean? Nothing.

The policeman made futile little gestures of interference, but apparently had too much respect for Mrs. Grundy's purse to carry them out. That purse was big enough to hold a bowling ball, and maybe it did.

Mrs. Grundy, tongue dangling and panting furiously, clapped one hand over her heart and, with the handkerchief, fanned herself with the other. Paul saw sweat dripping down her legs. "And so —*foo!* — I . . . I — *puf!* — I reminded him of . . . of the — *whee!* — the cup of tea!" she gasped. She paused, swallowed, mopped her brow, sucked in a deep lungful of air, and exhaled it slowly. She cleared her throat. *"And so I reminded him of the cup of tea!"* she roared with a grand sweep of one powerful arm, the old style recovered. There was a general smattering of complimentary applause, which Mrs. Grundy acknowledged with a short nod of her head. "We went inside. The air was heavy with expectation and the unmistakable aroma of catshit. One might almost be pleased that Rasputin had yielded up the spirit — "

"NOW JUST STOP IT!" cried the policeman. "THIS IS — "

"I poured some tea, we sang the now famous duet, '*¡Ciérrate la bragueta! ¡La braguetta está cerrada!,*' I danced for him, he — "

"ENOUGH, I SAID!" screamed the policeman, his little moustache quivering with indignation. "THIS IS ABSURD!"

You're warm, said Paul. But that's not quite it.

"Absurd?" cried Charity Grundy, aghast. *"Absurd?* You call my dancing *absurd?"*

"I . . . I didn't say — "

"Grotesque, perhaps, and yes, a bit awesome — but *absurd!"* She grabbed him by the lapels, lifting him off the ground. "What to you have against dancing, you worm? *What do you have against grace?"*

"P-please! Put me down!"

"Or is it, you don't believe I *can* dance?" She dropped him.

"N-no!" he sqeaked, brushing himself off, straightening his epaulettes. "No! I — "

"Show him! Show him!" chanted the crowd.

The policeman spun on them. "STOP! IN THE NAME OF THE LAW!" They obeyed. "This man is injured. He may die. He needs help. It's no joking matter. I ask for your cooperation." He paused for effect. "That's better." The policeman stroked his moustache, preening a bit. "Now, ahem, is there a doctor present? A doctor, please?"

"Oh, officer, you're cute! You're *very* cute!" said Mrs. Grundy on a new tack. The crowd snickered. *"Is there a doctor present?"* she mimicked, *"a doctor, please?"*

"Now just cut it out!" the policeman ordered, glaring angrily across Paul's chest at Mrs. Grundy. "Gosh damn it now, you stop it this instant, or . . . or you'll see what'll happen!"

"Aww, you're *jealous!"* cried Mrs. Grundy. "And of poor little supine Rasputin! Amory, I mean." The spectators were in great spirits again, total rebellion threatening, and the police officer was at the end of his rope. "Well, *don't* be jealous, dear boy!" cooed Mrs. Grundy. "Charity tell you a weetsie bitty secret."

"Stop!" sobbed the policeman. Be careful where you step, said Paul below.

Mrs. Grundy leaned perilously out over Paul and got a grip on the policeman's ear. He winced, but no longer attempted escape. "That boy," she said, *"he humps terrible!"*

It carried out to the crowd and broke it up. It was her big line and she wambled about gloriously, her rouged mouth stretched in a flabby toothless grin, retrieving the pennies that people were pitching (Paul knew about them from being hit by them; one landed on his upper lip, stayed there, emitting that familiar dead smell common to pennies the world over), thrusting her chest forward to catch them in the cleft of her bosom. She shook and, shaking, jangled. She grabbed the policeman's hand and pulled him forward to share a bow with her. The policeman smiled awkwardly, twitching his moustache.

"You asked for a doctor," said an old but gentle voice.

The crowd noises subsided. Paul opened his eyes and discovered above him a stooped old man in a rumpled gray suit. His hair was shaggy and white, his face dry, lined with age. He wore rimless glasses, carried a black leather bag. He smiled down at Paul, that easy smile of a man who comprehends and assuages pain, then looked back at the policeman. Inexplicably, a wave of terror shook Paul.

"You wanted a doctor," the old man repeated.

"Yes, *Yes!*" cried the policeman, almost in tears. "Oh, thank God!"

"I'd rather you thanked the profession," the doctor said. "Now what seems to be the problem?

"Oh, doctor, it's awful!" The policeman twisted the notebook in his hands, fairly destroying it. "This man has been struck by this truck, or so it would appear, no one seems to know, it's all a terrible mystery, and there is a woman, but now I don't see — ? and I'm not even sure of his name —"

"No matter," interrupted the doctor with a kindly nod of his old head, "who he is. He is a man and that, I assure you, is enough for me."

"Doctor, that's so good of you to say so!" wept the policeman.

I'm in trouble, thought Paul. Oh boy, I'm really in trouble.

"Well, now, let us just see," said the doctor, crouching down over Paul. He lifted Paul's eyelids with his thumb and peered intently at Paul's eyes; Paul, anxious to assist, rolled them from side to side. "Just relax, son," the doctor said. He opened his black bag, rummaged about in it, withdrew a flashlight. Paul was not sure exactly what the doctor did after that, but he seemed to be looking in his ears. I can't move my head, Paul told him, but the doctor only asked: "Why does he have a penny under his nose?" His manner was not such as to insist upon an answer, and he got none. Gently, expertly, he pried Paul's teeth apart, pinned his tongue down with a wooden depresser and scrutinized his throat. Paul's head was on fire with pain. "Ahh, yes," he mumbled. "Hum, hum."

"How ... how is he, Doctor?" stammered the policeman, his voice muted with dread and respect. "Will ... will he ... ?"

The doctor glared scornfully at the officer, then withdrew a stethoscope from his bag. He hooked it in his ears, slipped the disc inside Paul's shirt and listened intently, his old head inclined to one side like a bird listening for worms. Absolute silence now. Paul could hear the doctor breathing, the policeman whimpering softly. He had the vague impression that the doctor tapped his chest a time or two, but if so, he didn't feel it. His head felt better with his mouth closed. "Humm," said the doctor gravely, "yes ..."

"Oh, please! What *is* it, Doctor?" the policeman cried.

"What is it? *What is it?*" shouted the doctor in a sudden burst of rage. "I'll tell you *what is it!*" He sprang to his feet, nimble for an old man. "I cannot examine this patient while you're hovering over my shoulder and mewling like a goddamn schoolboy, *that's* what *is* it."

"B-but I only — " stammered the officer, staggering backwards.

"And how do you expect me to examine a man half buried under a damned truck?" The doctor was in a terrible temper.

"But I — "

"Damn it! I'll but-I you, you idiot, if you don't remove this truck from the scene so that I can determine the true gravity of this man's injuries! *Have I made myself clear?*"

"Y-yes! But ... but wh-what am I to *do?*" wept the police officer, hands clenched before his mouth. "I'm only a simple policeman, Doctor, doing my duty before God and count — "

"Simple, you said it!" barked the doctor. "I *told* you what to do, you God-and-cunt simpleton — *now get moving!*"

God and cunt! Did it again, thought Paul. Now what?

The policeman, chewing wretchedly on the corners of his notebook, stared first at Paul, then at the truck, at the crowd, back at the truck. Paul felt fairly certain now that the letter following the "K" on the truck's side was an "I." "Shall I ... shall I pull him out from under — ?" the officer began tentatively, thin chin aquiver.

"*Good God, no!*" stormed the doctor, stamping his foot. "This man may have a broken neck! Moving him would *kill* him, don't you see that, you snivelling birdbrain? Now, goddamn it, wipe your wretched nose and go wake up your — your accomplice up there, *and I mean right now!* Tell him to back his truck *off* this poor devil!"

"B-back it off — ! But ... but he'd have to run *over* him again! He —"

"Don't by God run-over-him-again *me* you blackshirt hireling, *or I'll have your badge!*" screamed the doctor, brandishing his stethoscope.

The policeman hesitated but a moment to glance down at Paul's body, then turned and ran to the front of the truck. "Hey! Come on, you!" He whacked the driver on the head with his nightstick. Hollow *thunk!* "Up and at 'em!"

" — DAM THAT BOY WHAT," cried the truckdriver, rearing up wildly and fluttering his head as though lost, "HE DO BUT WALK RIGHT INTO ME AND MY POOR OLE TRICK! TRUCK, I MEAN!" The crowd laughed again, first time in a long time, but the doctor stamped his foot and they quieted right down.

"Now, start up the engine, you, right now! I mean it!" ordered the policeman, stroking his moustache. He was getting a little of his old spit and polish back. He slapped the nightstick in his palm two or three times.

Paul felt the pavement under his back quake as the truckdriver started the motor. The white letters above him joggled in their red fields like butterflies. Beyond, the sky's blue had deepened, but white clouds now flowered in it. The skyscrapers had grayed, as though withdrawing information.

The truck's noise smothered the voices, but Paul did overhear the doctor and the policeman occasionally, the doctor ranting, the policeman imploring, something about and weight and vectors and direction. It was finally decided to go forward, since there were two sets of wheels up front and only one to the rear (a decent kind of humanism maintaining, after all, thought Paul), but the truckdriver apparently misunderstood, because he backed up anyway, and the middle set of wheels rolled up on top of Paul.

"Stop! STOP!" shrieked the police officer, and the truck motor coughed and died. "I ordered you to go *forward,* you pighead, not backward!"

The driver popped his head out the window, bulged his ping-pong-ball eyes at the policeman, then waggled his tiny hands in his ears and brayed. The officer took a fast practiced swing at the driver's big head (epaulettes, or no, he had a skill or two), but the driver deftly dodged it. He clapped his runty hands and bobbed back inside the cab.

"What oh *what* shall we ever do *now?*" wailed the officer. The doctor scowled at him with undisguised disgust. Paul felt like he was strangling, but he could locate no specific pain past his neck. "Dear lord above! There's wheels on each side of him and wheels in the middle!"

"Capital!" the doctor snorted. "Figure that out by yourself, or somebody help you?"

"You're making fun," whimpered the officer.

"AND YOU'RE MURDERING THIS MAN!" bellowed the doctor.

The police officer uttered a short anxious cry, then raced to the front of the truck again. Hostility welling in the crowd, Paul could hear it. "Okay, okay!" cried the officer. "Back up or go forward, *please,* I don't care, but hurry! HURRY!"

The motor started up again, there was a jarring grind of gears abrading, then slowly slowly slowly the middle set of wheels backed down off Paul's body. There was a brief tense interim before the next set climbed up on him, hesitated as a ferris wheel hesitates at the top of its ambit, then sank down off him.

Some time passed.

He opened his eyes.

The truck had backed away, out of sight, out of Paul's limited range of sight anyway. His eyelids weighed closed. He remembered the doctor being huddled over him, shreds of his clothing being peeled away.

Much later, or perhaps not, he opened his eyes once more. The doctor and the policeman were standing over him, some other people too, people he didn't recognize, though he felt somehow he ought to know them. Mrs. Grundy, she was there; in fact, it looked for all the world as though she had set up a ticket booth and was charging admission. Some of the people were holding little children up to see, warm faces, tender, compassionate; more or less. Newsmen were taking his picture. "You'll be famous," one of them said.

"His goddamn body is like a mulligan stew," the doctor was telling a reporter.

The policeman shook his head. He was a bit green. "Do you think — ?"

"Do I think what?" the doctor asked. Then he laughed, a thin raking old man's laugh. "You mean, do I think he's going to *die?*" He laughed again. "Good God, man, you can see for yourself! There's nothing left of him, he's a goddamn gallimaufry, and hardly an appetizing one at that!" He dipped his fingers into Paul, licked them, grimaced. "Foo!"

"I think we should get a blanket for him," the policeman said weakly.

"Of course you should!" snapped the doctor, wiping his stained hands on a small white towel he had brought out of his black bag. He peered down through his rimless spectacles at Paul, smiled. "Still there, eh?" He squatted beside him. "I'm sorry, son. There's not a damn thing I can do. Well, yes, I suppose I can take this penny off your lip. You've little use for it eh?" He laughed softly. "Now, let's see, there's no function for it, is there? No, no, there it is." The doctor started to pitch it away, then pocketed it instead. The eyes, don't they use them for the eyes? "Well, that's better, I'm sure. But let's be honest: it doesn't get to the real problem, does it?" Paul's lip tickled where the penny had been. "No, I'm of all too little use to you there, boy. I can't even prescribe a soporific platitude. Leave that to the goddamn priests, eh? Hee hee hee! Oops, sorry, son! Would you like a priest?"

No thanks, said Paul.

"Can't get it out, eh?" The doctor probed Paul's neck. "Hmmm. No, obviously not." He shrugged. "Just as well. What could you possibly have to say, eh?" He chuckled drily, then looked up at the policeman who still had not left to search out a blanket. "Don't just stand there, man! Get this lad a priest!" The police officer, clutching his mouth, hurried away, out of Paul's eye-reach. "I know it's not easy to accept death," the doctor was saying. He finished wiping his hands, tossed the towel into his black bag, snapped the bag shut. "We all struggle against it, boy, it's part and parcel of being alive, this brawl, this meaningless gutter-fight with death. In fact, let me tell you, son, it's *all* there is to life." He wagged his finger in punctuation, and ended by pressing the tip of it to Paul's nose. "That's the secret, *that's* my happy paregoric! Hee hee hee!"

KI, thought Paul, KI and 14. What could it have been? Never know now. One of those things.

"But death begets life, there's *that* my boy, and don't you ever forget it! Survival and murder are synonyms, son, first flaw of the universe! Hee hee h — oh! Sorry, son! No time for puns! Forget I said it!"

It's okay, said Paul. Listening to the doctor had at least made him forget the tickle on his lip and it was gone.

"New life burgeons out of rot, new mouths consume old organisms, father dies at orgasm, mother dies at birth, only old Dame Mass with her twin dugs of Stuff and Tickle persists, suffering her long slow split into pure light and pure carbon! Hee hee hee! A tender thought! Don't you agree, lad?" The doctor gazed off into space, happily contemplating the process.

I tell you what, said Paul. Let's forget it.

Just then, the policeman returned with a big quilted comforter, and he and the doctor spread it gently over Paul's body, leaving only his face exposed. The people pressed closer to watch.

"Back! *Back!*" shouted the policeman. "Have you no respect for the dying? *Back, I say!*"

"Oh come now," chided the doctor. "Let them watch if they want to. It hardly matters to this poor fellow, and even if it does, it can't matter for much longer. And it will help keep the flies off him."

"Well, doctor, if you think ... " His voice faded away. Paul closed his eyes.

As he lay there among the curious, several odd questions plagued Paul's mind. He knew there was no point to them, but he couldn't rid himself of them. The book, for example: did he have a book? And if he did, what book, and what had happened to it? And what about the stoplight, that lost increment of what men call history, why had no one brought up the matter of the stoplight? And pure carbon he could understand, but as for light: what could its purity consist of? KI 14. That impression that it had happened before. Yes, these were mysteries, all right. His head ached from them.

People approached Paul from time to time to look under the blanket. Some only peeked, then turned away, while others stayed to poke around, dip their hands in the mutilations. There seemed to be more interest in them now that they were covered. There were some arguments and some occasional horseplay, but the doctor and policeman kept things from getting out of hand. If someone arrogantly ventured a Latin phrase, the doctor always put him down with some toilet-wall barbarism; on the other hand, he reserved his purest, most mellifluous toponymy for small children and young girls. He made several medical appointments with the latter. The police officer, though queasy, stayed nearby. Once, when Paul happened to open his eyes after having had them closed some while, the policeman smiled warmly down on him and said: "Don't worry, good fellow. I'm still here. Take it as easy as you can. I'll be here to the very end. You can count on me." Bullshit, thought Paul, though not ungratefully, and he thought he remembered hearing the doctor echo him as he fell off to sleep.

When he awoke, the streets were empty. They had all wearied of it, as he had known they would. It had clouded over, the sky had darkened, it was probably night, and it had begun to rain lightly. He could now see the truck clearly, off to his left. Must have been people in the way before.

MAGIC KISS LIPSTICK

IN

14

DIFFERENT SHADES

Never would have guessed. Only in true life could such things happen.

When he glanced to his right, he was surprised to find an old man sitting near him. Priest, no doubt. He had come after all ... black hat, long grayish beard, sitting in the puddles now forming in the street, legs crossed. Go on, said Paul, don't suffer on my account, don't wait for me, but the old man remained, silent, drawn, rain glistening on his hat, face, beard, clothes: prosopopoeia of patience. The priest. Yet, something about the clothes: well, they were in rags. Pieced together and hanging in tatters. The hat, too, now that he noticed. At short intervals, the old man's head would nod, his eyes would cross, his body would tip, he would catch himself with a start, grunt, glance suspiciously about him, then back down at Paul, would finally relax again and recommence the cycle.

Paul's eyes wearied, especially with the rain splashing into them, so he let them fall closed once more. But he began suffering discomforting visions of the old priest, so he opened them again, squinted off to the left, toward the truck. A small dog, wiry and yellow, padded along in the puddles, hair drooping and bunching up with the rain. It sniffed at the tires of the truck, lifted its legs by one of them, sniffed again, padded on. It circled around Paul, apparently not noticing him, but poking its nose at every object, narrowing the distance between them with every circle. It passed close by the old man, snarled, completed another half-circle, and approached Paul from the left. It stopped near Paul's head — the wet-dog odor was suffocating — and whimpered, licking Paul's face. The old man did nothing, just sat, legs crossed, and passively watched. Of course ... not a priest at all: an old beggar. Waiting for the clothes when he died. If he still had any. Go ahead and take them now, Paul told him, I don't care. But the beggar only sat and stared. Paul felt a tugging sensation from below, heard the dog growl. His whole body seemed to jerk upwards, sending another hot flash through his neck. The dog's hind feet were planted alongside Paul's head, and now and again the right paw would lose its footing, kick nervously at Paul's face, a buffeting counterpoint to the waves of hot pain behind his throat and eyes. Finally, something gave way. The dog shook water out of its yellow coat, and padded away, a fresh piece of flesh between its jaws. The beggar's eyes crossed, his head dipped to his chest, and he started to topple forward, but again he caught himself, took a deep breath, uncrossed his legs, crossed them again, but the opposite way, reached in his pocket and pulled out an old cigarette butt, molded it between his yellow fingers, put it in his mouth, but did not light it. For an instant, the earth upended again, and Paul found himself hung on the street, a target for the millions of raindarts somebody out in the night was throwing at him. There's nobody out there, he reminded himself, and that set the earth right again. The beggar spat. Paul shielded his eyes from the rain with his lids. He thought he heard other dogs. How much longer must this go on? he wondered. How much longer?

STEPHEN CRANE

The Open Boat

A Tale Intended to be after the Fact: Being the Experience of Four Men from the Sunk Steamer Commodore

I

None of them knew the colour of the sky. Their eyes glanced level, and were fastened upon the waves that swept toward them. These waves were of the hue of slate, save for the tops, which were of foaming white, and all of the men knew the colours of the sea. The horizon narrowed and widened, and dipped and rose, and at all times its edge was jagged with waves that seemed thrust up in points like rocks.

Many a man ought to have a bathtub larger than the boat which here rode upon the sea. These waves were most wrongfully and barbarously abrupt and tall, and each frothtop was a problem in small-boat navigation.

The cook squatted in the bottom, and looked with both eyes at the six inches of gunwale which separated him from the ocean. His sleeves were rolled over his fat forearms, and the two flaps of his unbuttoned vest dangled as he bent to bail out the boat. Often he said, "Gawd! that was a narrow clip." As he remarked it he invariably gazed eastward over the broken sea.

The oiler, steering with one of the two oars in the boat, sometimes raised himself suddenly to keep clear of water that swirled in over the stern. It was a thin little oar, and it seemed often ready to snap.

The correspondent, pulling at the other oar, watched the waves and wondered why he was there.

The injured captain, lying in the bow, was at this time buried in that profound dejection and indifference which comes, temporarily at least, to even the bravest and most enduring when, willy-nilly, the firm fails, the army loses, the ship goes down. The mind of the master of a vessel is rooted deep in the timbers of her, though he command for a day or a decade; and this captain had on him the stern impression of a scene in the greys of dawn of seven turned faces, and later a stump of a topmast with a white ball on it, that slashed to and fro at the waves, went low and lower, and down. Thereafter there was something strange in his voice. Although steady, it was deep with mourning, and of a quality beyond oration or tears.

"Keep 'er a little more south, Billie," said he.

"A little more south, sir," said the oiler in the stern.

A seat in this boat was not unlike a seat upon a bucking broncho, and by the same token a broncho is not much smaller. The craft pranced and reared and plunged like an animal. As each wave came, and she rose for it, she seemed like a horse making at a fence outrageously high. The manner of her scramble over these walls of water is a mystic thing, and, moreover, at the top of them were ordinarily these problems in white water, the foam racing down from the summit of each wave requiring a new leap, and a leap from the air. Then, after scornfully bumping a crest, she would slide and race and splash down a long incline, and arrive bobbing and nodding in front of the next menace.

A singular disadvantage of the sea lies in the fact that after successfully surmounting one wave you discover that there is another behind it just as important and just as nervously anxious to do something effective in the way of swamping boats. In a ten-foot dinghy one can get an idea of the resources of the sea in the line of waves that is not probable to the average experience which is never at sea in a dinghy. As each slaty wall of water approached, it shut all else from the view of the men in the boat, and it was not difficult to imagine that this particular wave was the final outburst of the ocean, the last effort of the grim water. There was a terrible grace in the move of the waves, and they came in silence, save for the snarling of the crests.

In the wan light the faces of the men must have been grey. Their eyes must have glinted in strange ways as they gazed steadily astern. Viewed from a balcony, the whole thing would doubtless have been weirdly picturesque. But the men in the boat had no time to see it, and if they had had leisure, there were other things to occupy their minds. The sun swung steadily up the sky, and they knew it was broad day because the colour of the sea changed from slate to emerald green streaked with amber lights, and the foam was like tumbling snow. The process of the breaking day was unknown to them. They were aware only of this effect upon the colour of the waves that rolled toward them.

In disjointed sentences the cook and the correspondent argued as to the difference between a life-saving station and a house of refuge. The cook had said: "There's a house of refuge just north of the Mosquito Inlet Light, and as soon as they see us they'll come off in their boat and pick us up."

"As soon as who see us?" said the correspondent.

"The crew," said the cook.

"Houses of refuge don't have crews," said the correspondent. "As I understand them, they are only places where clothes and grub are stored for the benefit of shipwrecked people. They don't carry crews."

"Oh, yes, they do," said the cook.

"No, they don't," said the correspondent.

"Well, we're not there yet, anyhow," said the oiler, in the stern.

"Well," said the cook, "perhaps it's not a house of refuge that I'm thinking of as being near Mosquito Inlet Light; perhaps it's a life-saving station."

"We're not there yet," said the oiler in the stern.

II

As the boat bounced from the top of each wave the wind tore through the hair of the hatless men, and as the craft plopped her stern down again the spray slashed past them. The crest of each of these waves was a hill, from the top of which the men surveyed for a moment a broad tumultuous expanse, shining and wind-riven. It was probably splendid, it was probably glorious, this play of the free sea, wild with lights of emerald and white and amber.

"Bully good thing it's an on-shore wind," said the cook. "If not, where would we be? Wouldn't have a show."

"That's right," said the correspondent.

The busy oiler nodded his assent.

Then the captain, in the bow, chuckled in a way that expressed humour, contempt, tragedy, all in one. "Do you think we've got much of a show now, boys?" said he.

Whereupon the three were silent, save for a trifle of hemming and hawing. To express any particular optimism at this time they felt to be childish and stupid, but they all doubtless possessed this sense of the situation in their minds. A young man thinks doggedly at such times. On the other hand, the ethics of their condition was decidedly against any open suggestion of hopelessness. So they were silent.

"Oh, well," said the captain, soothing his children, "we'll get ashore all right."

But there was that in his tone which made them think; so the oiler quoth, "Yes! if this wind holds."

The cook was bailing. "Yes! if we don't catch hell in the surf."

Canton-flannel gulls flew near and far. Sometimes they sat down on the sea, near patches of brown seaweed that rolled over the waves with a movement like carpets on a line in a gale. The birds sat comfortably in groups, and they were envied by some in the dinghy, for the wrath of the sea was no more to them than it was to a covey of prairie chickens a thousand miles inland. Often they came very close and stared at the men with black beadlike eyes. At these times they were uncanny and sinister in their unblinking scrutiny, and the men hooted angrily at them, telling them to be gone. One came, and evidently decided to alight on the top of the captain's head. The bird flew parallel to the boat and did not circle, but made short sidelong jumps in the air in chicken-fashion. His black eyes were wistfully fixed upon the captain's head. "Ugly brute," said the oiler to the bird. "You look as if you were made with a jack-knife." The cook and the correspondent swore darkly at the creature. The captain naturally wished to knock it away with the end of the heavy painter, but he did not dare do it, because anything resembling an emphatic gesture would have capsized this freighted boat; and so, with his open hand, the captain gently and carefully waved the gull away. After it had been discouraged from the pursuit the captain breathed easier on account of his hair, and others breathed easier because the bird struck their minds at this time as being somehow gruesome and ominous.

In the meantime the oiler and the correspondent rowed. And also they rowed. They sat together in the same seat, and each rowed an oar. Then the oiler took both oars; then the correspondent took both oars; then the oiler; then the correspondent. They rowed and they rowed. The very ticklish part of the business was when the time came for the reclining one in the stern to take his turn at the oars. By the very last star of truth, it is easier to steal eggs from under a hen than it was to change seats in the dinghy. First the man in the stern slid his hand along the thwart and moved with care, as if he were of Sèvres. Then the man in the rowing-seat slid his hand along the other thwart. It was all done with the most extraordinary care. As the two sidled past each other, the whole party kept watchful eyes on the coming wave, and the captain cried: "Look out, now! Steady, there!"

The brown mats of seaweed that appeared from time to time were like islands, bits of earth. They were travelling, apparently, neither one way nor the other. They were, to all intents, stationary. They informed the men in the boat that it was making progress slowly toward the land.

The captain, rearing cautiously in the bow after the dinghy soared on a great swell, said that he had seen the lighthouse at Mosquito Inlet. Presently the cook remarked that he had seen it. The correspondent was at the oars then, and for some reason he too wished to look at the lighthouse; but his back was toward the far shore, and the waves were important, and for some time he could not seize an opportunity to turn his head. But at last there came a wave more gentle than the others, and when at the crest of it he swiftly scoured the western horizon.

"See it?" said the captain.

"No," said the correspondent, slowly; "I didn't see anything."

"Look again," said the captain. He pointed. "It's exactly in that direction."

At the top of another wave the correspondent did as he was bid, and this time his eyes chanced on a small, still thing on the edge of the swaying horizon. It was precisely like the point of a pin. It took an anxious eye to find a lighthouse so tiny.

"Think we'll make it, Captain?"

"If this wind holds and the boat don't swamp, we can't do much else," said the captain.

The little boat, lifted by each towering sea and splashed viciously by the crests, made progress that in the absence of seaweed was not apparent to those in her. She seemed just a wee thing wallowing, miraculously top up, at the mercy of five oceans. Occasionally a great spread of water, like white flames, swarmed into her.

"Bail her, cook," said the captain, serenely.

"All right, Captain," said the cheerful cook.

III

It would be difficult to describe the subtle brotherhood of men that was here established on the seas. No one said that it was so. No one mentioned it. But it dwelt in the boat, and each man felt it warm him. They were a captain, an oiler, a cook, and a correspondent, and they were friends — friends in a more curiously iron-bound degree than may be common. The hurt captain, lying against the water-jar in the bow, spoke always in a low voice and calmly; but he could never command a more ready and swiftly obedient crew than the motley three of the dinghy. It was more than a mere recognition of what was best for the common safety. There was surely in it a quality that was personal and heart-felt. And after this devotion to the commander of the boat, there was this comradeship, that the correspondent, for instance, who had been taught to be cynical of men, knew even at the time was the best experience of his life. But no one said that it was so. No one mentioned it.

"I wish we had a sail," remarked the captain. "We might try my overcoat on the end of an oar, and give you two boys a chance to rest." So the cook and the correspondent held the mast and spread wide the overcoat; the oiler steered; and the little boat made good way with her new rig. Sometimes the oiler had to scull sharply to keep a sea from breaking into the boat, but otherwise sailing was a success.

Meanwhile the lighthouse had been growing slowly larger. It had now almost assumed colour, and appeared like a little grey shadow on the sky. The man at the oars could not be prevented from turning his head rather often to try for a glimpse of this little grey shadow.

At last, from the top of each wave, the men in the tossing boat could see land. Even as the lighthouse was an upright shadow on the sky, this land seemed but a long black shadow on the sea. It certainly was thinner than paper. "We must be about opposite New Smyrna," said the cook, who had coasted this shore often in schooners. "Captain, by the way, I believe they abandoned that life-saving station there about a year ago."

"Did they?" said the captain.

The wind slowly died away. The cook and the correspondent were not now obliged to slave in order to hold high the oar. But the waves continued their old impetuous swooping at the dinghy, and the little craft, no longer under way, struggled woundily over them. The oiler or the correspondent took the oars again.

Shipwrecks are apropos of nothing. If men could only train for them and have them occur when the men had reached pink condition, there would be less drowning at sea. Of the four in the dinghy none had slept any time worth mentioning for two days and two nights previous to embarking in the dinghy, and in the excitement of clambering about the deck of a foundering ship they had also forgotten to eat heartily.

For these reasons, and for others, neither the oiler nor the correspondent was fond of rowing at this time. The correspondent wondered ingenuously how in the name of all that was sane could there be people who thought it amusing to row a boat. It was not an amusement; it was a diabolical punishment, and even a genius of mental aberrations could never conclude that it was anything but a horror to the muscles and a crime against the back. He mentioned to the boat in general how the amusement of rowing struck him, and the weary-faced oiler smiled in full sympathy. Previously to the foundering, by the way, the oiler had worked double watch in the engine-room of the ship.

"Take her easy now, boys," said the captain. "Don't spend yourselves. If we have to run a surf you'll need all your strength, because we'll sure have to swim for it. Take your time."

Slowly the land arose from the sea. From a black line it became a line of black and a line of white — trees and sand. Finally the captain said that he could make out a house on the shore. "That's the house of refuge, sure," said the cook. "They'll see us before long, and come out after us."

The distant lighthouse reared high. "The keeper ought to be able to make us out now, if he's looking through a glass," said the captain. "He'll notify the life-saving people."

"None of those other boats could have got ashore to give word of the wreck," said the oiler, in a low voice, "else the life-boat would be out hunting us."

Slowly and beautifully the land loomed out of the sea. The wind came again. It had veered from the north-east to the south-east. Finally a new sound struck the ears of the men in the boat. It was the low thunder of the surf on the shore. "We'll never be able to make the lighthouse now," said the captain. "Swing her head a little more north, Billie."

"A little more north, sir," said the oiler.

Whereupon the little boat turned her nose once more down the wind, and all but the oarsman watched the shore grow. Under the influence of this expansion doubt and direful apprehension were leaving the minds of the men. The management of the boat was still most absorbing, but it could not prevent a quiet cheerfulness. In an hour, perhaps, they would be ashore.

Their backbones had become thoroughly used to balancing in the boat, and they now rode this wild colt of a dinghy like circus men. The correspondent thought that he had been drenched to the skin, but happening to feel in the top pocket of his coat, he found therein eight cigars. Four of them were soaked with sea-water; four were perfectly scatheless. After a search, somebody produced three dry matches; and thereupon the four waifs rode impudently in their little boat and, with an assurance of an impending rescue shining in their eyes, puffed at the big cigars, and judged well and ill of all men. Everybody took a drink of water.

IV

"Cook," remarked the captain, "there don't seem to be any signs of life about your house of refuge."

"No," replied the cook. "Funny they don't see us!"

A broad stretch of lowly coast lay before the eyes of the men. It was of low dunes topped with dark vegetation. The roar of the surf was plain, and sometimes they could see the white lip of a wave as it spun up the beach. A tiny house was blocked out black upon the sky. Southward, the slim lighthouse lifted its little grey length.

Tide, wind, and waves were swinging the dinghy northward. "Funny they don't see us," said the men.

The surf's roar was here dulled, but its tone was nevertheless thunderous and mighty. As the boat swam over the great rollers the men sat listening to this roar. "We'll swamp sure," said everybody.

It is fair to say here that there was not a life-saving station within twenty miles in either direction; but the men did not know this fact, and in consequence they made dark and opprobrious remarks concerning the eyesight of the nation's life-savers. Four scowling men sat in the dinghy and surpassed records in the invention of epithets.

"Funny they don't see us."

The light-heartedness of a former time had completely faded. To their sharpened minds it was easy to conjure pictures of all kinds of incompetency and blindness and, indeed, cowardice. There was the shore of the populous land, and it was bitter and bitter to them that from it came no sign.

"Well," said the captain, ultimately, "I suppose we'll have to make a try for ourselves. If we stay out here too long, we'll none of us have strength left to swim after the boat swamps."

And so the oiler, who was at the oars, turned the boat straight for the shore. There was a sudden tightening of muscles. There was some thinking.

"If we don't all get ashore," said the captain — "if we don't all get ashore, I suppose you fellows know where to send news of my finish?"

They then briefly exchanged some addresses and admonitions. As for the reflections of the men, there was a great deal of rage in them. Perchance they might be formulated thus: "If I am going to be drowned — if I am going to be drowned — if I am going to be drowned, why, in the name of the seven mad gods who rule the sea was I allowed to come thus far and contemplate sand and trees? Was I brought here merely to have my nose dragged away as I was about to nibble the sacred cheese of life? It is preposterous. If this old ninny-woman, Fate, cannot do better than this, she should be deprived of the management of men's fortunes. She is an old hen who knows not her intention. If she has decided to drown me, why did she not do it in the beginning, and save me all this trouble? The whole affair is absurd. — But no; she cannot mean to drown me. She dare not drown me. She cannot drown me. Not after all this work." Afterward the man might have had an impulse to shake his fist at the clouds. "Just you drown me, now, and then hear what I call you!"

The billows that came at this time were more formidable. They seemed always just about to break and roll over the little boat in a turmoil of foam. There was a preparatory and long growl in the speech of them. No mind unused to the sea would have concluded that the dinghy could ascend these sheer heights in time. The shore was still afar. The oiler was a wily surfman. "Boys," he said swiftly, "she won't live three minutes more, and we're too far out to swim. Shall I take her to sea again, Captain?"

"Yes; go ahead!" said the captain.

This oiler, by a series of quick miracles and fast and steady oarsmanship, turned the boat in the middle of the surf and took her safely to sea again.

There was a considerable silence as the boat bumped over the furrowed sea to deeper water. Then somebody in gloom spoke: "Well, anyhow, they must have seen us from the shore by now."

The gulls went in slanting flight up the wind toward the grey, desolate east. A squall, marked by dingy clouds and clouds brick-red like smoke from a burning building, appeared from the south-east.

"What do you think of those life-saving people? Ain't they peaches?"

"Funny they haven't seen us."

"Maybe they think we're out here for sport! Maybe they think we're fishin'. Maybe they think we're damned fools."

It was a long afternoon. A changed tide tried to force them southward, but wind and wave said northward. Far ahead, where coast-line, sea, and sky formed their mighty angle, there were little dots which seemed to indicate a city on the shore.

"St. Augustine?"

The captain shook his head. "Too near Mosquito Inlet."

And the oiler rowed, and then the correspondent rowed; then the oiler rowed. It was a weary business. The human back can become the seat of more aches and pains than are registered in books for the composite anatomy of a regiment. It is a limited area, but it can become the theatre of innumerable muscular conflict, tangles, wrenches, knots, and other comforts.

"Did you ever like to row, Billie?" asked the correspondent.

"No," said the oiler; "hang it!"

When one exchanged the rowing-seat for a place in the bottom of the boat, he suffered a bodily depression that caused him to be careless of everything save an obligation to wiggle one finger. There was cold sea-water swashing to and fro in the boat, and he lay in it. His head, pillowed on a thwart, was within an inch of the swirl of a wave-crest, and sometimes a particularly obstreperous sea came aboard and drenched him once more. But these matters did not annoy him. It is almost certain that if the boat had capsized he would have tumbled comfortably out upon the ocean as if he felt sure that it was a great soft mattress.

"Look! There's a man on the shore!"

"Where?"

"There! See 'im?"

"Yes, sure! He's walking along."

"Now he's stopped. Look! He's facing us!"

"He's waving at us!"

"So he is! By thunder!"

"Aha, now we're all right! Now we're all right! There'll be a boat out here for us in half an hour."

"He's going on. He's running. He's going up to that house there."

The remote beach seemed lower than the sea, and it required a searching glance to discern the little black figure. The captain saw a floating stick, and they rowed to it. A bath towel was by some weird chance in the boat, and, tying this on the stick, the captain waved it. The oarsman did not dare turn his head, so he was obliged to ask questions.

"What's he doing now?"

"He's standing still again. He's looking, I think. — There he goes again — toward the house. — Now he's stopped again."

"Is he waving at us?"

"No, not now; he was, though."

"Look. There comes another man!"

"He's running."

"Look at him go, would you!"

"Why, he's on a bicycle. Now he's met the other man. They're both waving at us. Look!"

"There comes something up the beach."

"What the devil is that thing?"

"Why it looks like a boat."

"Why, certainly, it's a boat."

"No; it's on wheels."

"Yes, so it is. Well, that must be the life-boat. They drag them along shore on a wagon."

"That's the life-boat, sure."

"No, by God, it's — it's an omnibus."

"I tell you it's a life-boat."

"It is not! It's an omnibus. I can see it plain. See? One of these big hotel omnibuses."

"By thunder, you're right. It's an omnibus, sure as fate. What do you suppose they are doing with an omnibus? Maybe they are going around collecting the life-crew, hey?"

"That's it, likely. Look! There's a fellow waving a little black flag. He's standing on the steps of the omnibus. There come those other two fellows. Now they're all talking together. Look at the fellow with the flag. Maybe he ain't waving it!"

"That ain't a flag, is it? That's his coat. Why, certainly, that's his coat."

"So it is; it's his coat. He's taken it off and is waving it around his head. But would you look at him swing it!"

"Oh, say, there isn't any life-saving station there. That's just a winter-resort omnibus that has brought over some of the boarders to see us drown."

"What's that idiot with the coat mean? What's he signalling, anyhow?"

"It looks as if he were trying to tell us to go north. There must be a life-saving station up there."

"No; he thinks we're fishing. Just giving us a merry hand. See? Ah, there, Willie!"

"Well, I wish I could make something out of those signals. What do you suppose he means?"

"He don't mean anything; he's just playing."

"Well, if he'd just signal us to try the surf again, or to go to sea and wait, or go north, or go south, or go to hell, there would be some reason in it. But look at him! He just stands there and keeps his coat revolving like a wheel. The ass!"

"There come more people."

"Now there's quite a mob. Look! Isn't that a boat?"

"Where? Oh, I see where you mean. No, that's no boat."

"That fellow is still waving his coat."

"He must think we like to see him do that. Why don't he quit it? It don't mean anything."

"I don't know. I think he is trying to make us go north. It must be that there's a life-saving station there somewhere."

"Say, he ain't tired yet. Look at 'im wave!"

"Wonder how long he can keep that up. He's been revolving his coat ever since he caught sight of us. He's an idiot. Why aren't they getting men to bring a boat out? A fishing-boat — one of those big yawls — could come out here all right. Why don't he do something?"

"Oh, it's all right now."

"They'll have a boat out here for us in less than no time, now that they've seen us."

A faint yellow tone came into the sky over the low land. The shadows on the sea slowly deepened. The wind bore coldness with it, and the men began to shiver.

"Holy smoke!" said one, allowing his voice to express his impious mood, "if we keep on monkeying out here! If we've got to flounder out here all night!"

"Oh, we'll never have to stay here all night! Don't you worry. They've seen us now, and it won't be long before they'll come chasing out after us."

The shore grew dusky. The man waving a coat blended gradually into this gloom, and it swallowed in the same manner the omnibus and the group of people. The spray, when it dashed uproariously over the side, made the voyagers shrink and swear like men who were being branded.

"I'd like to catch the chump who waved the coat. I feel like socking him one, just for luck."

"Why? What did he do?"

"Oh, nothing, but then he seemed so damned cheerful."

In the meantime the oiler rowed, and then the correspondent rowed, and then the oiler rowed. Grey-faced and bowed forward, they mechanically, turn by turn, plied the leaden oars. The form of the lighthouse had vanished from the southern horizon, but finally a pale star appeared, just lifting from the sea. The streaked saffron in the west passed before the all-merging darkness, and the sea to the east was black. The land had vanished, and was expressed only by the low and drear thunder of the surf.

"If I am going to be drowned — if I am going to be drowned — if I am going to be drowned, why, in the name of the seven mad gods who rule the sea, was I allowed to come thus far and contemplate sand and trees? Was I brought here merely to have my nose dragged away as I was about to nibble the sacred cheese of life?"

The patient captain, drooped over the water-jar, was sometimes obliged to speak to the oarsman.

"Keep her head up! Keep her head up!"

"Keep her head up, sir." The voices were weary and low.

This was surely a quiet evening. All save the oarsman lay heavily and listlessly in the boat's bottom. As for him, his eyes were just capable of noting the tall black waves that swept forward in a most sinister silence, save for an occasional subdued growl of a crest.

The cook's head was on a thwart, and he looked without interest at the water under his nose. He was deep in other scenes. Finally he spoke. "Billie," he murmured, dreamfully, "what kind of pie do you like best?"

V

"Pie!" said the oiler and the correspondent, agitatedly. "Don't talk about those things, blast you!"

"Well," said the cook, "I was just thinking about ham sandwiches, and — "

A night on the sea in an open boat is a long night. As darkness settled finally, the shine of the light, lifting from the sea in the south, changed to full gold. On the northern horizon a new light appeared, a small bluish gleam on the edge of the waters. These two lights were the furniture of the world. Otherwise there was nothing but waves.

Two men huddled in the stern, and distances were so magnificent in the dinghy that the rower was enabled to keep his feet partly warm by thrusting them under his companions. Their legs indeed extended far under the rowing-seat until they touched the feet of the captain forward. Sometimes, despite the efforts of the tired oarsman, a wave came piling into the boat, an icy wave of the night, and the chilling water soaked them anew. They would twist their bodies for a moment and groan, and sleep the dead sleep once more, while the water in the boat gurgled about them as the craft rocked.

The plan of the oiler and the correspondent was for one to row until he lost the ability, and then arouse the other from his sea-water couch in the bottom of the boat.

The oiler plied the oars until his head drooped forward and the overpowering sleep blinded him; and he rowed yet afterward. Then he touched a man in the bottom of the boat, and called his name. "Will you spell me for a little while?" he said meekly.

"Sure, Billie," said the correspondent, awaking and dragging himself to a sitting position. They exchanged places carefully, and the oiler, cuddling down in the sea-water at the cook's side, seemed to go to sleep instantly.

The particular violence of the sea had ceased. The waves came without snarling. The obligation of the man at the oars was to keep the boat headed so that the tilt of the rollers would not capsize her, and to preserve her from filling when the crests rushed past. The black waves were silent and hard to be seen in the darkness. Often one was almost upon the boat before the oarsman was aware.

In a low voice the correspondent addressed the captain. He was not sure that the captain was awake, although this iron man seemed to be always awake. "Captain, shall I keep her making for that light north, sir?"

The same steady voice answered him. "Yes. Keep it about two points off the port bow."

The cook had tied a life-belt around himself in order to get even the warmth which this clumsy cork contrivance could donate, and he seemed almost stove-like when a rower, whose teeth invariably chattered wildly as soon as he ceased his labour, dropped down to sleep.

The correspondent, as he rowed, looked down at the two men sleeping underfoot. The cook's arm was around the oiler's shoulders, and, with their fragmentary clothing and haggard faces, they were the babes of the sea — a grotesque rendering of the old babes in the wood.

Later he must have grown stupid at his work, for suddenly there was a growling of water, and a crest came with a roar and a swash into the boat, and it was a wonder that it did not set the cook afloat in his life-belt. The cook continued to sleep, but the oiler sat up, blinking his eyes and shaking with the new cold.

"Oh, I'm awful sorry, Billie," said the correspondent, contritely.

"That's all right, old boy," said the oiler, and lay down again and was asleep.

Presently it seemed that even the captain dozed, and the correspondent thought that he was the one man afloat on all the oceans. The wind had a voice as it came over the waves, and it was sadder than the end.

There was a long, loud swishing astern of the boat, and a gleaming trail of phosphorescence, like blue flame, was furrowed on the black waters. It might have been made by a monstrous knife.

Then there came a stillness, while the correspondent breathed with open mouth and looked at the sea.

Suddenly there was another swish and another long flash of bluish light, and this time it was alongside the boat, and might almost have been reached with an oar. The correspondent saw an enormous fin speed like a shadow through the water, hurling the crystalline spray and leaving the long glowing trail.

The correspondent looked over his shoulder at the captain. His face was hidden, and he seemed to be asleep. He looked at the babes of the sea. They certainly were asleep. So, being bereft of sympathy, he leaned a little way to one side and swore softly into the sea.

But the thing did not then leave the vicinity of the boat. Ahead or astern, on one side or the other, at intervals long or short, fled the long sparkling streak, and there was to be heard the *whirroo* of the dark fin. The speed and power of the thing was greatly to be admired. It cut the water like a gigantic and keen projectile.

The presence of this biding thing did not affect the man with the same horror that it would if he had been a picnicker. He simply looked at the sea dully and swore in an undertone.

Nevertheless, it is true that he did not wish to be alone with the thing. He wished one of his companions to awake by chance and keep him company with it. But the captain hung motionless over the water-jar, and the oiler and the cook in the bottom of the boat were plunged in slumber.

VI

"If I am going to be drowned — if I am going to be drowned — if I am going to be drowned, why, in the name of the seven mad gods who rule the sea, was I allowed to come thus far and contemplate sand and trees?"

During this dismal night, it may be remarked that a man would conclude that it was really the intention of the seven mad gods to drown him, despite the abominable injustice of it. For it was certainly an abominable injustice to drown a man who had worked so hard, so hard. The man felt it would be a crime most unnatural. Other people had drowned at sea since galleys swarmed with painted sails, but still —

When it occurs to a man that nature does not regard him as important, and that she feels she would not maim the universe by disposing of him, he at first wishes to throw bricks at the temple, and he hates deeply the fact that there are no bricks and no temples. Any visible expression of nature would surely be pelleted with his jeers.

Then, if there be no tangible thing to hoot, he feels, perhaps, the desire to confront a personification and indulge in pleas, bowed to one knee, and with hands supplicant, saying, "Yes, but I love myself."

A high cold star on a winter's night is the word he feels that she says to him. Thereafter he knows the pathos of his situation.

The men in the dinghy had not discussed these matters, but each had, no doubt, reflected upon them in silence and according to his mind. There was seldom any expression upon their faces save the general one of complete weariness. Speech was devoted to the business of the boat.

To chime the notes of his emotion, a verse mysteriously entered the correspondent's head. He had even forgotten that he had forgotten this verse, but it suddenly was in his mind.

> A soldier of the Legion lay dying in Algiers;
> There was lack of woman's nursing, there was dearth of woman's tears;
> But a comrade stood beside him, and he took that comrade's hand,
> And he said, "I never more shall see my own, my native land."

In his childhood the correspondent had been made acquainted, with the fact that a soldier of the Legion lay dying in Algiers, but he had never regarded the fact as important. Myriads of his school-fellows had informed him of the soldier's plight, but the dinning had naturally ended by making him perfectly indifferent. He had never considered it his affair that a soldier of the Legion lay dying in Algiers, nor had it appeared to him as a matter for sorrow. It was less to him than the breaking of a pencil's point.

Now, however, it quaintly came to him as a human, living thing. It was no longer merely a picture of a few throes in the breast of a poet, meanwhile drinking tea and warming his feet at the grate; it was an actuality — stern, mournful, and fine.

The correspondent plainly saw the soldier. He lay on the sand with his feet out straight and still. While his pale left hand was upon his chest in an attempt to thwart the going of his life, the blood came between his fingers. In the far Algerian distance, a city of low square forms was set against a sky that was faint with the last sunset hues. The correspondent, plying the oars and dreaming of the slow and slower movements of the lips of the soldier, was moved by a profound and perfectly impersonal comprehension. He was sorry for the soldier of the Legion who lay dying in Algiers.

The thing which had followed the boat and waited had evidently grown bored at the delay. There was no longer to be heard the slash of the cutwater, and there was no longer the flame of the long trail. The light in the north still glimmered, but it was apparently no nearer to the boat. Sometimes the boom of the surf rang in the correspondent's ears, and he turned the craft seaward then and rowed harder. Southward, some one had evidently built a watch-fire on the beach. It was too low and too far to be seen, but it made a shimmering, roseate reflection upon the bluff in back of it, and this could be discerned from the boat. The wind came stronger, and sometimes a wave suddenly raged out like a mountain cat, and there was to be seen the sheen and sparkle of a broken crest.

The captain, in the bow, moved on his water-jar and sat erect. "Pretty long night," he observed to the correspondent. He looked at the shore. "Those life-saving people take their time."

"Did you see that shark playing around?"

"Yes, I saw him. He was a big fellow, all right."

"Wish I had known you were awake."

Later the correspondent spoke into the bottom of the boat.

"Billie!" There was a slow and gradual disentanglement. "Billie, will you spell me?"

"Sure," said the oiler.

As soon as the correspondent touched the cold, comfortable sea-water in the bottom of the boat and had huddled close to the cook's life-belt he was deep in sleep, despite the fact that his teeth played all the popular airs. This sleep was so good to him that it was but a moment before he heard a voice call his name in a tone that demonstrated the last stages of exhaustion. "Will you spell me?"

"Sure, Billie."

The light in the north had mysteriously vanished, but the correspondent took his course from the wide-awake captain.

Later in the night they took the boat farther out to sea, and the captain directed the cook to take one oar at the stern and keep the boat facing the seas. He was to call out if he should hear the thunder of the surf. This plan enabled the oiler and the correspondent to get respite together. "We'll give those boys a chance to get into shape again," said the captain. They curled down and, after a few preliminary chatterings and trembles, slept once more the dead sleep. Neither knew they had bequeathed to the cook the company of another shark, or perhaps the same shark.

As the boat caroused on the waves, spray occasionally bumped over the side and gave them a fresh soaking, but this had no power to break their repose. The ominous slash of the wind and the water affected them as it would have affected mummies.

"Boys," said the cook, with notes of every reluctance in his voice, "she's drifted in pretty close. I guess one of you had better take her to sea again." The correspondent, aroused, heard the crash of the toppled crests.

As he was rowing, the captain gave him some whisky-and-water, and this steadied the chills out of him. "If I ever get ashore and anybody shows me even a photograph of an oar — "

At last there was a short conversation.

"Billie! — Billie, will you spell me?"

"Sure," said the oiler.

VII

When the correspondent again opened his eyes, the sea and the sky were each of the grey hue of the dawning. Later, carmine and gold was painted upon the waters. The morning appeared finally, in its splendour, with a sky of pure blue, and the sunlight flamed on the tips of the waves.

On the distant dunes were set many little black cottages, and a tall white windmill reared above them. No man, nor dog, nor bicycle appeared on the beach. The cottages might have formed a deserted village.

The voyagers scanned the shore. A conference was held in the boat. "Well," said the captain, "if no help is coming, we might better try a run through the surf right away. If we stay out here much longer we will be too weak to do anything for ourselves at all." The others silently acquiesced in this reasoning. The boat was headed for the beach. The correspondent wondered if none ever ascended the tall wind-tower, and if then they never looked seaward. This tower was a giant, standing with its back to the plight of the ants. It represented in a degree, to the correspondent, the serenity of nature amid the struggles of the individual — nature in the wind, and nature in the vision of men. She did not seem cruel to him then, nor beneficent, nor treacherous, nor wise. But she was indifferent, flatly indifferent. It is, perhaps, plausible that a man in this situation, impressed with the unconcern of the universe, should see the innumerable flaws of his life, and have them taste wickedly in his mind, and wish for another chance. A distinction between right and wrong seems absurdly clear to him, then, in this new ignorance of the grave-edge, and he understands that if he were given another opportunity he would mend his conduct and his words, and be better and brighter during an introduction or at a tea.

"Now, boys," said the captain, "she is going to swamp sure. All we can do is to work her in as far as possible, and then when she swamps, pile out and scramble for the beach. Keep cool now, and don't jump until she swamps sure."

The oiler took the oars. Over his shoulders he scanned the surf. "Captain," he said, "I think I'd better bring her about and keep her head-on to the seas and back her in."

"All right, Billie," said the captain. "Back her in." The oiler swung the boat then, and, seated in the stern, the cook and the correspondent were obliged to look over their shoulders to contemplate the lonely and indifferent shore.

The monstrous inshore rollers heaved the boat high until the men were again enabled to see the white sheets of water scudding up the slanted beach. "We won't get in very close," said the captain. Each time a man could wrest his attention from the rollers, he turned his glance toward the shore, and in the expression of the eyes during this contemplation there was a singular quality. The correspondent, observing the others, knew that they were not afraid, but the full meaning of their glances was shrouded.

As for himself, he was too tired to grapple fundamentally with the fact. He tried to coerce his mind into thinking of it, but the mind was dominated at this time by the muscles, and the muscles said they did not care. It merely occurred to him that if he should drown it would be a shame.

There were no hurried words, no pallor, no plain agitation. The men simply looked at the shore. "Now, remember to get well clear of the boat when you jump," said the captain.

Seaward the crest of a roller suddenly fell with a thunderous crash, and the long white comber came roaring down upon the boat.

"Steady now," said the captain. The men were silent. They turned their eyes from the shore to the comber and waited. The boat slid up the incline, leaped at the furious top, bounced over it, and swung down the long back of the wave. Some water had been shipped, and the cook bailed it out.

But the next crest crashed also. The tumbling, boiling flood of white water caught the boat and whirled it almost perpendicular. Water swarmed in from all sides. The correspondent had his hands on the gunwale at this time, and when the water entered at that place he swiftly withdrew his fingers, as if he objected to wetting them.

The little boat, drunken with this weight of water, reeled and snuggled deeper into the sea.

"Bail her out, cook! Bail her out!" said the captain.

"All right, Captain," said the cook.

"Now, boys, the next one will do for us sure," said the oiler. "Mind to jump clear of the boat."

The third wave moved forward, huge, furious, implacable. It fairly swallowed the dinghy, and almost simultaneously the men tumbled into the sea. A piece of life-belt had lain in the bottom of the boat, and as the correspondent went overboard he held this to his chest with his left hand.

The January water was icy, and he reflected immediately that it was colder than he had expected to find it off the coast of Florida. This appeared to his dazed mind as a fact important enough to be noted at the time. The coldness of the water was sad; it was tragic. This fact was somehow mixed and confused with his opinion of his own situation, so that it seemed almost a proper reason for tears. The water was cold.

When he came to the surface he was conscious of little but the noisy water. Afterward he saw his companions in the sea. The oiler was ahead in the race. He was swimming strongly and rapidly. Off to the correspondent's left, the cook's great white and corked back bulged out of the water; and in the rear the captain was hanging with his one good hand to the keel of the overturned dinghy.

There is a certain immovable quality to a shore, and the correspondent wondered at it amid the confusion of the sea.

It seemed also very attractive; but the correspondent knew that it was a long journey, and he paddled leisurely. The piece of life-preserver lay under him, and sometimes he whirled down the incline of a wave as if he were on a hand-sled.

But finally he arrived at a place in the sea where travel was beset with difficulty. He did not pause swimming to inquire what manner of current had caught him, but there his progress ceased. The shore was set before him like a bit of scenery on a stage, and he looked at it and understood with his eyes each detail of it.

As the cook passed, much further to the left, the captain was calling to him, "Turn over on your back, cook! Turn over on your back and use the oar."

"All right, sir." The cook turned on his back, and, paddling with an oar, went ahead as if he were a canoe.

Presently the boat also passed to the left of the correspondent, with the captain clinging with one hand to the keel. He would have appeared like a man raising himself to look over a board fence if it were not for the extraordinary gymnastics of the boat. The correspondent marvelled that the captain could still hold to it.

They passed on nearer to shore — the oiler, the cook, the captain — and following them went the water-jar, bouncing gaily over the seas.

The correspondent remained in the grip of this strange new enemy — a current. The shore, with its white slope of sand and its green bluff topped with little silent cottages, was spread like a picture before him. It was very near to him then, but he was impressed as one who, in a gallery, looks at a scene from Brittany or Algiers.

He thought: "I am going to drown? Can it be possible? Can it be possible? Can it be possible?" Perhaps an individual must consider his own death to be the final phenomenon of nature.

But later a wave perhaps whirled him out of this small deadly current, for he found suddenly that he could again make progress toward the shore. Later still he was aware that the captain, clinging with one hand to the keel of the dinghy, had his face turned away from the shore and toward him, and was calling his name. "Come to the boat! Come to the boat!"

In his struggle to reach the captain and the boat, he reflected that when one gets properly wearied drowning must really be a comfortable arrangement — a cessation of hostilities accompanied by a large degree of relief; and he was glad of it, for the main thing in his mind for some moments had been horror of the temporary agony. He did not wish to be hurt.

Presently he saw a man running along the shore. He was undressing with most remarkable speed. Coat, trousers, shirt, everything flew magically off him.

"Come to the boat!" called the captain.

"All right, Captain." As the correspondent paddled, he saw the captain let himself down to bottom and leave the boat. Then the correspondent performed his one little marvel of the voyage. A large wave caught him and flung him with ease and supreme speed completely over the boat and far beyond it. It struck him even then as an event in gymnastics and a true miracle of the sea. An overturned boat in the surf is not a plaything to a swimming man.

The correspondent arrived in water that reached only to his waist, but his condition did not enable him to stand for more than a moment. Each wave knocked him into a heap, and the undertow pulled at him.

Then he saw the man who had been running and undressing, and undressing and running, come bounding into the water. He dragged ashore the cook, and then waded toward the captain; but the captain waved him away and sent him to the correspondent. He was naked — naked as a tree in winter; but a halo was about his head, and he shone like a saint. He gave a strong pull, and a long drag, and a bully heave at the correspondent's hand. The correspondent, schooled in the minor formulae, said, "Thanks, old man." But suddenly the man cried, "What's that?" He pointed a swift finger. The correspondent said, "Go."

In the shallows, face downward, lay the oiler. His forehead touched sand that was periodically, between each wave, clear of the sea.

The correspondent did not know all that transpired afterward. When he achieved safe ground he fell, striking the sand with each particular part of his body. It was as if he had dropped from a roof, but the thud was grateful to him.

It seems that instantly the beach was populated with men with blankets, clothes, and flasks, and women with coffee-pots and all the remedies sacred to their minds. The welcome of the land to the men from the sea was warm and generous; but a still and dripping shape was carried slowly up the beach, and the land's welcome for it could only be the different and sinister hospitality of the grave.

When it came night, the white waves paced to and fro in the moonlight, and the wind brought the sound of the great sea's voice to the men on the shore, and they felt that they could then be interpreters.

RÉJEAN DUCHARME

The Wedding Gown

Translated by William Kinsley

Talking pessimistically is pleasant. If we were talking pessimistically it wasn't because we were convinced by what we were saying, but because black ideas, like black tulips, are the most beautiful. As we kept walking the sidewalks and talking gloom to each other, something happened which couldn't fail to have consequences, consequences that would occur before we cleared the decks. We were passing by a *haute couture* shop window, and Chateaugué recalled the vow I had made to buy her the most beautiful dress in the world. She stopped in front of the luxuriant display, and planted herself there, fastened herself there. She didn't want to budge.

"That's the one!" she cried. "How beautiful! That's the one I want."

Hands glued to the window like limpets, face flattened against the glass wall, she was experiencing frightful joy, frightening desires. She told me to come over.

"Come here. Closer. Come and see. Come on! Look — that one, there! That's the one, at the end of my finger, that I want to die in."

It was a white dress stitched with stars, a moonlight dress that flowed out from the waist. A dress for a true woman, a woman who hides her feet under her dress, a woman who walks within it secretly.

"You're right out of your mind! That's a wedding gown."

"Sure it's a wedding gown, but that doesn't make any difference. I like it anyway. If you want to buy a dress for me, buy me that one. I've never asked you for anything else."

The wide window bellied inward under the pressure of Chateaugué's covetousness.

"You'll have it. We'll come and steal it."

"When?"

"Tonight."

We played detective. We circled the block. We combed the walls of the five-storey building to see if there was a way of breaking and entering by night. At the back, along a macabre blind alley, we found what we were looking for: a cellar window with a grating held in place by only a few screws.

The grating is only held on by screws. The robbery is set for tonight, not long from now. So it's tonight, this very night, that the consequences of what happened this afternoon will occur. We're waiting for the middle of the night to start out. We, Tate, are cold now; it's cold in our room. Chateaugué is so cold that she has to massage her legs to keep from freezing.

"It's ugly, skin is," she says, rubbing her legs. "It's like poorly made porcelain, not baked enough. It's like dead. It's flabby. It's nothing. It's like paper. You look at it and it doesn't say anything to you."

I look at that skin that doesn't say anything to her, skin that I hear playing the violin. I gather up all my courage. I've had a question to ask Chateaugué ever since we left the restaurant. Whatever happens, I must ask her. At the restaurant we, Tate, were inadvertently seated within earshot of a quartet of horny adolescent schoolboys. They were talking dirty and Chateaugué heard everything they said. She was even listening, ears pricked up, laughing. Besides, I think it was for her benefit that they were talking dirty.

"You know what the Indians call a bra? A tit-rack!"

"I know a girl that has such big ones she has to wear a hammock."

"That's nothing compared to the one that has to buy two parachutes every time because she can't find anything big enough in one piece.

Chateaugué had listened, roaring with laughter, hardly blushing, leaning over to hear better.

I've screwed up all the courage I need.

"Tate, for the first time in our life I want to ask you an embarrassing question. Can I?"

"It's all right with me. I don't believe you."

She seems very much intrigued, but at the same time she's getting ready to have a trick played on her. She holds herself up straight, ready for anything, even the impossible: a revelation.

"Tate, Chateaugué, do you realize ... that ... that you have breasts?"

"That I have what?" she exclaims.

She doesn't understand, not at all. She doesn't have any idea what I'm getting at. She has the impression, since the question was supposed to be embarrassing, that I'm talking about pimples. She tries to look at her own face by lowering her eyes.

"Where?"

"You don't know what they are? I mean ... those ..." Gesturing as I speak, I point to her sheltered little breasts with the end of my finger. Her face suddenly relaxes and lights up.

"Those? Why sure! What an idea! I have them,

you have them, everybody has them. Why shouldn't I realize it?"

She seems relieved that that's all it is. She was a little afraid.

"Me? I don't have them. I'm not like you, I'm not a woman!" I said that cynically, in an outraged voice, strong in the prerogatives of my flat chest.

Chateaugué's face darkens again.

"What do you mean? You do too have them. They aren't like mine, but you have them. Mine are all swelled up like a pig's; yours are tiny like a cat's. But they're the same thing. They're in the same place, so they're the same thing, right?"

"Aw, forget it."

She comes back to it, insistently; her curiosity has been piqued. She probes to find out what I have at the back of my mind. She senses that I'm hiding something from her, that something is going on behind her back. The silly argument excites me so bestially I can't see clearly any more. I want so much to kiss her! She's seeking, waiting, wanting, offering herself. She holds her hand out to me so I can help her climb down into hell. All I'd have to do is pluck her, hold out my hand, and she'd fall to the bottom of the depths from which I'm looking up at her. I want so much to kiss her little breasts that my ears are roaring and it seems as if my lips have already made contact with the red cotton of the blouse that hides those little breasts. Discouraged by the violence of my sensuality, I suddenly let my big head fall and hang against my chest. Chateaugué keeps on talking, but I've stopped listening. Let her talk! Let her go on talking forever! Let her go to the devil with her innocence. Let her spout it forever, that innocence so intent on self-improvement, so eager to change into atrocities, that innocence in such a hurry to change into filth. She has grabbed a handful of my hair and is shaking my head tenderly, awkwardly, hesitantly.

"Mille Milles. Mille Milles? You're all red! Do you feel sick? Are you sick, Mille Milles? Do you want to throw up? Answer me. Answer me!"

"Ivugivic!"

She is standing in front of me. I can feel her face hanging over me, suspended above me like a threat. Right in front of my eyes I have her skirt, with her belly behind it, her belly living behind it, her belly warm behind it. Heedless of everything, I suddenly let my heavy head lean against this belly, sink into the warmth of this belly, and I leave it there, I leave it there to rest. Chateaugué brings her other hand up to join the one already on my head. Now all her hands are moving on my head, or almost aren't moving on my head.

"What's the matter, Mille Milles? Are you hurt? What's the matter? Tell Chateaugué."

She speaks with a catch in her throat. She's afraid of me. Women are afraid of men who lose control of themselves. They're afraid when men get frightened. I seize Chateaugué by the wrists and squeeze, to hurt her, to make her suffer.

"I'll tell you what the matter is! You disgust me! You're not pure, you're just ignorant. You're not chaste, you're stupid. You're only a bloody woman! You're in a big hurry to know how a woman works, eh? You can't wait, eh? It's tough to be a woman, to have all that dirty machinery and not know how to use it, eh? You never *wanted* to be pure, eh? If you *were* pure it wasn't on purpose, eh? You're completely innocent, eh? Grinning from ear to ear whatever happens, eh? You're ready for anything; all you need is for somebody to tell you how to go about it, eh? The first comer, that's what's in store for you. You'll think it's good. You'll think it's funny just like all the others. You'll laugh from ear to ear. You're only a bloody woman, Chateaugué, that's what's the matter! That's what makes me sick."

The idea of evil has never come into her head. What a bloody simpleton! Suddenly I hear someone talking. Suddenly her voice is sombre and grave.

"You mustn't say everything, Tate. You mustn't say everything. Keep your secrets, Tate. Keep yourself to yourself. Don't force things. Don't cause pain."

I feel queer all over. I know what's got hold of me. At the beginning, at the very beginning when I conceived the idea of Chateaugué's purity, I also conceived the idea of her impurity. The more I love her purity, the more I love her impurity. I have chosen the purity, the purity of Chateaugué, the purity of our friendship. But the idea of Chateaugué's impurity keeps asserting itself, trying to force its way into existence. The stronger one idea is, the stronger the opposite. What a lot of words! What a lot of words! What a lot of air! What a lot of water! Chateaugué, I'm a monster, an inveterate dastardurbater, zealously obsessed with sex. If I let myself go I wouldn't stop at caressing Chateaugué. By this time we'd be dead of debauchery. We'd be dead and buried, both of us. All of Tate, all of us would belong to the Plutonian kingdom. That's all she's waiting for, the little whore. I can't wait to die. If I don't leave right away, it will be too late, and I'll look completely ridiculous when I go. I still have a little dignity left. If I keep on waiting I'll lose that. Why this delay before clearing the decks? For whom?

I know why, at bottom. I'm waiting till our friendship has won out, has escaped shining bright from the swamp it's been shoved into; till it stands shining bright on the summit of the white mountain, whiter than the snow of the summit. I'm waiting till our friendship has lost, till it lies defeated in the slimy muddy water, till the green swamp-flies have finished eating its rotted flesh. It's the law of contraries. I have nothing left but our friendship, and I'm waiting till I've committed the commonplace act that will ruin it. I want to die and I want to live. I want to live! I've never wanted to live so much as I have since it's been necessary for me to clear the decks. The desire I feel to take this whole disgusting world into my arms is as strong as the desire to take Chateaugué into my arms. My desire to conquer everything is as strong as my desire to lose everything.

Enough Tate! O you who bring all to pass, please me, let me be nothing but putrefaction and stink. O you who bring all to pass, make me like the corpse of the cat that floats on the slimy water. O you who bring all to pass, make me want to vomit when I look at myself in Chateaugué's face! O you who bring all to pass, change my skin to bronze, swell my chest with light, transform my lukewarmness to ice, make me worthy of myself. Bloody bestialities!

If we must call a spade a spade, the verb love must give over to wantodofilthythingswithyou. Let's conjugate that, the verb wanttodofilthythings withyou. I wanttodofilthythingswithyou, you wantmetodobeastlythingswith you, we wanttododisgustingthingstogether. I love Chateaugué. If I love Chateaugué, I wanttodofilthythingswithher. I don't even have to force myself to admit that I'm disgusting. I'm naturally disgusting. I need to force myself to admit that I'm not disgusting. I love you. You love me. We love each other. We sleep together and we don't do anything bad, but I have to force myself. Sometimes, before we fall asleep, we talk to each other, smoking face to face as if all we had was faces, blowing smoke into each other's face, as if only our wings were jostling together under the covers, as if we were angels. But I have to force myself. To stay pure you need force; you need to force yourself. You need courage; you need to encourage yourself. The most tempting thing about chastity is the courage you need to preserve it. If I'm chaste it's because I've been strong; if I'm strong I'm worthy of myself. I have a right to be proud of myself and climb up onto any pedestal.

"Shall we go?"

"Where?"

"To get my dress. It's two o'clock. It's dark enough, it's dark dark. No one will see us stealing at this hour. You can't even see your hand in front of your face."

"The dress? Oh yes, that's right. I'd forgotten. Let's get going, Boeing."

We aren't going to go skipping across Montreal on foot with a stolen wedding gown under our arm. We decide to take a taxi and hail one that's cruising by, like in a murder mystery. We ask the cabdriver if he has a screwdriver. There's one in the glove compartment. We ask him if he'll lend it to us. He'll lend it to us. We ask him to park at the entrance of the blind alley so as to cover us, and to wait there for us. He says okay.

We plunge into the thick shadows of the alley, which seems like a mountain pass. We plunge in with the screwdriver, thinking of Napoleon crossing the pass of Mont-Cenis. The dark buildings along the alley rise right up into the vault of night. We seem to be at the bottom of an abyss, at the bottom of those structures that stand almost touching, bathing in the volatile black liquid of the night.

The four screws that screw the grating that secures the window are quickly unscrewed. Chateaugué shatters the glass of the window with a kick. Feet first, I work my way between jaws with glass teeth, and jump. It's a long way down; I didn't expect it to be nearly so long. I fall onto a surface cluttered with broken furniture and crack my skull on something. I get up and call Chateaugué. I'm bleeding and in bad shape, but that doesn't bother me. A splinter of glass has pierced my cheek. With a shudder I yank it out. Without seeing me Chateaugué follows, and I go ahead of her without seeing where I put my feet. To get to the show window we have to keep advancing in the direction we're advancing in. I advance. I break down the doors we run into on the way. I find it pleasant to break down doors; it eases the heart. If I didn't have any doors to break down, my heart would explode like a bomb. Chateaugué follows me silently, upsetting everything along the way, touching me to make sure I'm always there ahead of her. She is the cause of the rage that burns in my heart.

The show window is lit up as bright as day. Tate, hidden together silently behind a muslin screen, watches the rare automobiles and the last passersby pass by. Tate holds each other by the hand before crossing the Rubicon. Tate looks each other in the eye and feels sure that after such a burglary there will be no place for Tate in society. We're afraid all of a sudden; we're on the brink of robbery. If we change our mind, our friendship was only a game; if we steal, it wasn't a game; we'd have to clear the decks or go to prison. Will our courage fail us? Are we going to give up at the first real test? Are we going to be terrified and return empty-handed? We won't let ourselves betray Tate. Tate steels ourself to steal.

"Tate, why aren't you a girl like me? Why don't you wear a dress the way I do?"

There's Chateaugué beginning to have ideas. The robbery won't amount to anything. The roots of our friendship are all eaten away by ideas. After examining the situation, we work out a plan. We won't just take away the dress, we'll take the dummy too. We're not going to start undressing the dummy under the eyes of the rare automobiles and the last passersby.

Time passes. The taxi waits. The ten or eleven dummies stand upright on a sort of common pedestal. Well out of sight behind this platform, we crawl along to within reach of the dummy we want to attack and kidnap. We grab her by a foot, turn her upside down and catch her in our arms so she won't get too badly smashed. Then we take off with her, laughing with fear, fleeing on hands and knees. Since the object of our covetousness holds her arms outstretched, she doesn't fit through the opening of the cellar window. We try in vain to think of a way to get her out without amputating. Don't want to ampue Tate. Suddenly there's a haggard head at the window, the cabdriver. I get a spurt of inspiration.

"There's a big tip for you if you don't talk. Take this dummy by the head and pull. We've got to make it or break it. Hey, take it easy! That's not a sack of flour, it's damasked brocade. Hey, don't sweep the street with her! Pick her up and carry her in your arms. She won't bite."

I could go on shouting insults at the driver all night, I'm so mad. At Chateaugué, too. A girl! I should wear a dress! She wishes I was a girl like her! The driver holds the dummy by the head and Chateaugué holds it by the feet. I open the door of the taxi for them. They set it down carefully on the back seat, as if it were a baby. The driver is a real cool cat, singing all the way home. He sings *Mon Pantalon est décousu* to the tune of Rocky Mendelssohn's wedding march.

I give him ten dollars for a tip. His face changes. He looks at my tattered ten-dollar bill as if he wanted to vomit on it. He doesn't think it's enough, and lets us know it. And I bled myself white to please him! He almost runs us down as he leaves, peeling off like a rocket, spinning his rear wheels at top speed and shooting gravel at us. Let him go turn us in! Let him do it, the dirty old wet blanket.

The bride has her forehead torn off and her nose broken; she's missing an arm on one side and three fingers on the other. That's all. She's no worse for wear than that. We don't know where to put her. We put her at the head of our bed, so she can watch us sleep. We put her in place of the orange crate that used to serve as our wall-to-wall bookcase. Her head touches the ceiling, which slopes with the pitch of the roof. We contemplate this calm intruder. We turn our backs on her, then whip around suddenly to surprise her. But she surprises us. We're just not used to having a dummy in our room, a stolen dummy at that. To domesticate it, Chateaugué baptizes it. She smears its face with ink, as she did with the ugly little statue but taking great care not to spatter the dress. The dress isn't as dirty as it might be. But it's not as clean as it was. It has some tears too.

"We have two sculptures, Tate — Bride and Ugly. Here's Bride, who's dead in a living dress, and here's Ugly, who's dead in a dead dress."

"You mean, false in a true dress and false in a false dress."

"No."

The robbery is over. She has her dress. I can breathe. Our friendship, after so many millions of words, has finally made a move, has finally begun to take shape. The day is over, too, since we're sleepy and will have to wait till we've slept to live a little more. Worn out, Tate lies down, side by side. We fall asleep instantly. Our legs interlocked, our eyes closed, looking at each other through our eyelids, we sleep. We look like two angels. Our wings rumple each other under the covers. Tomorrow, in the sun, like flowers, our wings will unrumple. Suddenly, living is so sweet. Suddenly, living is so bitter.

STANLEY ELKIN

A Poetics for Bullies

I'm Push the bully, and what I hate are new kids and sissies, dumb kids and smart, rich kids, poor kids, kids who wear glasses, talk funny, show off, patrol boys and wise guys and kids who pass pencils and water the plants — and cripples, *especially* cripples. I love nobody loved.

One time I was pushing this red-haired kid (I'm a pusher, no hitter, no belter; an aggressor of marginal violence, I hate *real* force) and his mother stuck her head out the window and shouted something I've never forgotten. "*Push,*" she yelled. "*You, Push.* You pick on him because you wish you had his red hair!" It's true; I *did* wish I had his red hair. I wish I were tall, or fat or thin. I wish I had different eyes, different hands, a mother in the supermarket. I wish I were a man, a small boy, a girl in the choir. I'm a coveter, a Boston Blackie of the heart, casing the world. Endlessly I covet and case. (Do you know what makes me cry? The Declaration of Independence. "All men are created equal." That's beautiful.)

If you're a bully like me, you use your head. Toughness isn't enough. You beat them up, they report you. Then where are you? I'm not even particularly strong. (I used to be strong. I used to do exercise, work out, but strength implicates you, and often isn't an advantage anyway — read the judo ads. Besides, your big bullies aren't bullies at all — they're *athletes.* With them, beating guys up is a sport.) But what I lose in size and strength I make up in courage. I'm very brave. That's a lie about bullies being cowards underneath. If you're a coward, get out of the business.

I'm best at torment.

A kid has a toy bow, toy arrows. "Let Push look," I tell him.

He's suspicious, he knows me. "Go way, Push," he says, this mama-warned Push doubter.

"Come on," I say, "come on."

"No, Push. I can't. My mother said I can't."

I raise my arms. I spread them. I'm a bird — slow, powerful, easy, free. I move my head offering profile like something beaked. I'm the Thunderbird. "In the school where I go I have a teacher who teaches me magic," I say. "Arnold Salamancy, give Push your arrows. Give him one, he gives back two. Push is the God of the Neighborhood."

"Go way, Push," the kid says, uncertain.

"Right," Push says, himself again. "Right. I'll disappear. First the fingers." My fingers ball to fists. "My forearms next." They jackknife into my upper arms. "The arms." Quick as bird-blink they snap behind my back, fit between the shoulder blades like a small knapsack. (I am double-jointed, protean.) "My head," I say.

"No, Push," the kid says, terrified. I shudder and everything comes back, falls into place from the stem of self like a shaken puppet.

"The arrow, the arrow. Two where was one." He hands me an arrow.

"*Trouble, trouble, double rubble!*" I snap it and give back the pieces.

Well, sure. There *is* no magic. If there were I would learn it. I would find out the words, the slow turns and strange passes, drain the bloods and get the herbs, do the fires like a vestal. I would look for the main chants. *Then* I'd change things. *Push* would!

But there's only casuistical trick. Sleight-of-mouth, the bully's poetics.

You know the formulas:

"Did you ever see a match burn twice?" you ask. Strike. Extinguish. Jab his flesh with the hot stub.

"Play 'Gestapo'?"

"How do you play?"

"What's your name?"

"It's Morton."

I slap him. "You're lying."

"Adam and Eve and Pinch Me Hard went down to the lake for a swim. Adam and Eve fell in. Who was left?"

"Pinch Me Hard."

I do.

Physical puns, conundrums. Push the punisher, the conundrummer!

But there has to be more than tricks in a bag of tricks.

I don't know what it is. Sometimes I think *I'm* the only new kid. In a room, the school, the playground, the neighborhood, I get the feeling I've just moved in, no one knows me. You know what I like? To stand in crowds. To wait with them at the airport to meet a plane. Someone asks what time it is. I'm the first to answer. Or at the ball park when the vendor comes. He passes the hot dog down the long row. I want *my* hands on it, too. On the dollar going up, the change coming down.

I am ingenious, I am patient.

A kid is going downtown on the elevated train. He's got his little suit on, his shoes are shined, he wears a cap. This is a kid going to the travel bureaus, the foreign tourist offices to get brochures, maps, pictures of the mountains for a unit at his school — a kid looking for extra credit. I follow him. He comes out of the Italian Tourist Information Center. His arms are full. I move from my place at the window. I follow for two blocks and bump into him as he steps from a curb. It's a *collision* — The pamphlets fall from his arms. Pretending confusion, I walk on his paper Florence. I grind my heel in his Riviera. I climb Vesuvius and sack his Rome and dance on the Isle of Capri.

The Industrial Museum is a good place to find children. I cut somebody's five- or six-year-old kid brother out of the herd of eleven- and twelve-year-olds he's come with. "*Quick,*" I say. I pull him along the corridors, up the stairs, through the halls, down to a mezzanine landing. Breathless, I pause for a minute. "I've got some gum. Do you want a stick?" He nods; I stick him. I rush him into an auditorium and abandon him. He'll be lost for hours.

I sidle up to a kid at the movies. "You smacked my brother," I tell him. "After the show — I'll be outside."

I break up games. I hold the ball above my head. "You want it? Take it."

I go into barber shops. There's a kid waiting. "I'm next," I tell him, "understand?"

One day Eugene Kraft rang my bell. Eugene is afraid of me, so he helps me. He's fifteen and there's something wrong with his saliva glands and he drools. His chin is always chapped. I tell him he has to drink a lot because he loses so much water.

"Push? Push," he says. He's wiping his chin with his tissues. "Push, there's this kid —

"Better get a glass of water, Eugene."

"No, Push, no fooling, there's this new kid — he just moved in. You've got to see this kid."

"Eugene, get some water, please. You're drying up. I've never seen you so bad. There are deserts in you, Eugene."

"All right, Push, but then you've got to see — "

"Swallow, Eugene. You better swallow."

He gulps hard.

"Push, this is a kid and a half. Wait, you'll see."

"I'm very concerned about you, Eugene. You're dying of thirst, Eugene. Come into the kitchen with me."

I push him through the door. He's very excited. I've never seen him so excited. He talks at me over his shoulder, his mouth flooding, his teeth like the little stone pebbles at the bottom of a fishbowl. "He's got this sport coat, with a patch over the heart. Like a king, Push. No kidding."

"Be careful of the carpet, Eugene."

I turn on the taps in the sink. I mix in hot water. "Use your tissues, Eugene. Wipe your chin."

He wipes himself and puts the Kleenex in his pocket. All of Eugene's pockets bulge. He looks, with his bulging pockets, like a clumsy smuggler.

"Wipe, Eugene. Swallow, you're drowning."

"He's got this funny accent — you could die." Excited, he tamps at his mouth like a diner, a tubercular.

"Drink some water, Eugene."

"No, Push. I'm not thirsty — really."

"Don't be foolish, kid. That's because your mouth's so wet. Inside where it counts you're drying up. It stands to reason. Drink some water."

"He has this crazy haircut."

"*Drink,*" I command. I shake him. "*Drink!*"

"Push, I've got no glass. Give me a glass at least."

"I can't do that, Eugene. You've got a terrible sickness. How could I let you use our drinking glasses? Lean under the tap and open your mouth."

He knows he'll have to do it, that I won't listen to him until he does. He bends into the sink.

"Push, it's *hot,*" he complains. The water splashes into his nose, it gets on his glasses and for a moment his eyes are magnified, enormous. He pulls away and scrapes his forehead on the faucet.

"Eugene, you touched it. Watch out, please. You're too close to the tap. Lean your head deeper into the sink."

"It's *hot*, Push."

"Warm water evaporates better. With your affliction you've got to evaporate fluids before they get into your glands."

He feeds again from the tap.

"Do you think that's enough?" I ask after a while.

"I do, Push, I really do," he says. He is breathless.

"Eugene," I say seriously, "I think you'd better get yourself a canteen."

"A canteen, Push?"

"That's right. Then you'll always have water when you need it. Get one of those Boy Scout models. The two-quart kind with a canvas strap."

"But you hate the Boy Scouts, Push."

"They make very good canteens, Eugene. *And wear it!* I never want to see you without it. Buy it today."

"All right, Push."

"Promise!"

"All right, Push."

"Say it out."

He made the formal promise that I like to hear.

"Well, then," I said, "let's go see this new kid of yours."

He took me to the schoolyard. "Wait," he said, "you'll see." He skipped ahead.

"Eugene," I said, calling him back. "Let's understand something. No matter what this new kid is like, nothing changes as far as you and I are concerned."

"Aw, Push," he said.

"Nothing, Eugene. I mean it. You don't get out from under me."

"Sure, Push, I know that."

There were some kids in the far corner of the yard, sitting on the ground, leaning up against the wire fence. Bats and gloves and balls lay scattered around them. (It was where they told dirty jokes. Sometimes I'd come by during the little kids' recess and tell them all about what their daddies do to their mommies.)

"There. See? Do you see him?" Eugene, despite himself, seemed hoarse.

"Be quiet," I said, checking him, freezing as a hunter might. I stared.

He was a *prince,* I tell you.

He was tall, tall, even sitting down. His long legs comfortable in expensive wool, the trousers of a boy who had been on ships, jets; who owned a horse, perhaps; who knew Latin — what *didn't* he know? — somebody made up, like a kid in a play with a beautiful mother and a handsome father; who took his breakfast from a sideboard, and picked, even at fourteen and fifteen and sixteen, his mail from a silver plate. He would have hobbies — stamps, stars, things lovely dead. He wore a sport coat, brown as wood, thick as heavy bark. The buttons were leather buds. His shoes seemed carved from horses' saddles, gunstocks. His clothes had once grown in nature. *What it must feel like inside those clothes,* I thought.

I looked at his face, his clear skin, and guessed at the bones, white as beached wood. His eyes had skies in them. His yellow hair swirled on his head like a crayoned sun.

"Look, look at him," Eugene said. "The sissy. Get him, Push."

He was talking to them and I moved closer to hear his voice. It was clear, beautiful, but faintly foreign — like herb-seasoned meat.

When he saw me he paused, smiling. He waved. The others didn't look at me.

"Hello there," he called. "Come over if you'd like. I've been telling the boys about tigers."

"Tigers," I said.

"Give him the 'match burn twice,' Push," Eugene whispered.

"Tigers, is it?" I said. "What do you know about tigers?" My voice was high.

"The 'match burn twice,' Push."

"Not so much as a Master *Tugjah.* I was telling the boys. In India there are men of high caste — *Tugjahs,* they're called. I was apprenticed to one once in the Southern Plains and might perhaps have earned my mastership, but the Red Chinese attacked the northern frontier and ... well, let's just say I had to leave. At any rate, these *Tugjahs* are as intimate with the tiger as you are with dogs. I don't mean they keep them as pets. The relationship goes deeper. Your dog is a service animal, as is your elephant."

"Did you ever see a match burn twice?" I asked suddenly.

"Why no, can you do that? Is it a special match you use?"

"No," Eugene said, "it's an ordinary match. He uses an ordinary match."

"Can you do it with one of mine, do you think?"

He took a matchbook from his pocket and handed it to me. The cover was exactly the material of his jacket, and in the center was a patch with a coat-of-arms identical to the one he wore over his heart.

I held the matchbook for a moment and then gave it back to him. "I don't feel like it," I said.

"Then some other time, perhaps," he said.

Eugene whispered to me. "His accent, Push, his funny *accent."*

"Some other time, perhaps," I said. I am a good mimic. I can duplicate a particular kid's lisp, his stutter, a thickness in his throat. There were two or three here whom I had brought close to tears by holding up my mirror to their voices. I can parody their limps, their waddles, their girlish runs, their clumsy jumps. I can throw as they throw, catch as they catch. I looked around. "Some other time, perhaps," I said again. No one would look at me.

"I'm *so* sorry," the new one said, "we don't know each other's names. You are?"

"I'm so sorry," I said. "You are?"

He seemed puzzled. Then he looked sad, disappointed. No one said anything.

"It don't sound the same," Eugene whispered.

It was true. I sounded nothing like him. I could imitate only defects, only flaws.

A kid giggled.

"Shh," the prince said. He put one finger to his lips.

"Look at that," Eugene said under his breath. "He's a sissy."

He had begun to talk to them again. I squatted, a few feet away. I ran gravel through my loose fists, one bowl in an hour-glass feeding another.

He spoke of jungles, of deserts. He told of ancient trade routes traveled by strange beasts. He described lost cities and a lake deeper than the deepest level of the sea. There was a story about a boy who had been captured by bandits. A woman in the story — it wasn't clear whether she was the boy's mother — had been tortured. His eyes clouded for a moment when he came to this part and he had to pause before continuing. Then he told how the boy escaped — it was cleverly done — and found help, mountain tribesmen riding elephants. The elephants charged the cave in which the mo — the *woman* — was still a prisoner. It might have collapsed and killed her, but one old bull rushed in and, shielding her with his body, took the weight of the crashing rocks. Your elephant is a service animal.

I let a piece of gravel rest on my thumb and flicked it in a high arc above his head. Some of the others who had seen me stared, but the boy kept on talking. Gradually I reduced the range, allowing the chunks of gravel to come closer to his head.

"You see?" Eugene said quietly. "He's afraid. He pretends not to notice."

The arcs continued to diminish. The gravel went faster, straighter. No one was listening to him now, but he kept talking.

" — of magic," he said, "what occidentals call 'a witch doctor.' There are spices that induce these effects. The *Bogdovii* was actually able to stimulate the growth of rocks with the powder. The Dutch traders were ready to go to war for the formula. Well, you can see what it could mean for the Low Countries. Without accessible quarries they've never been able to construct a permanent system of dikes. But with the *Bogdovii's* powder" — he reached out and casually caught the speeding chip as if it had been a ping-pong ball — "they could turn a grain of sand into a pebble, use the pebbles to grow stones, the stones to grow rocks. This little piece of gravel, for example, could be changed into a mountain." He dipped his thumb into his palm as I had and balanced the gravel on his nail. He flicked it; it rose from his nail like a missile and climbed an impossible arc. It disappeared. "The *Bogdovii* never revealed how it was done."

I stood up. Eugene tried to follow me.

"Listen," he said, "you'll get him."

"Swallow," I told him. "Swallow, you pig!"

I have lived my life in pursuit of the vulnerable: Push the chink seeker, wheeler dealer in the flawed cement of the personality, a collapse maker. But what isn't vulnerable, *who* isn't? There is that which is unspeakable, so I speak it, that which is unthinkable, which I think. Me and the devil, we do God's dirty work, after all.

I went home after I left him. I turned once at the gate, and the boys were around him still. The useless Eugene had moved closer. *He* made room for him against the fence.

I ran into Frank the fat boy. He made a move to cross the street, but I had seen him and he went through a clumsy retractive motion. I could tell he thought I would get him for that, but I moved by, indifferent to a grossness in which I had once delighted. As I passed he seemed puzzled, a little hurt, a little — this was astonishing — guilty. *Sure* guilty. Why *not* guilty? The forgiven tire of their exemption. Nothing could ever be forgiven, and I forgave nothing. I held them to the mark. Who else cared about the fatties, about the dummies and slobs and clowns, about the gimps and squares and oafs and fools, the kids with a mouthful of mush, all those shut-ins of the mind and heart, all those losers? Frank the fat boy knew, and passed me shyly. His wide, fat body, stiffened, forced jokishly martial when he saw me, had already become flaccid as he moved by, had already made one more forgiven surrender. Who cared?

The streets were full of failure. Let them. Let them be. There was a paragon, a paragon loose. What could he be doing here, why had he come, what did he want? It was impossible that this hero from India and everywhere had made his home here; that he lived, as Frank the fat boy did, as Eugene did, as *I* did, in an apartment; that he shared our lives.

In the afternoon I looked for Eugene. He was in the park, in a tree. There was a book in his lap. He leaned against the thick trunk.

"Eugene," I called up to him.

"Push, they're closed. It's Sunday, Push. The stores are closed. I looked for the canteen. The stores are closed."

"Where is he?"

"Who, Push? What do you want, Push?"

"*Him.* Your pal. The prince. Where? Tell me, Eugene, or I'll shake you out of that tree. I'll burn you down. I swear it. Where is he?"

"No, Push. I was wrong about that guy. He's nice. He's really nice. Push, he told me about a doctor who could help me. Leave him alone, Push."

"Where, Eugene? *Where?* I count to three."

Eugene shrugged and came down the tree.

I found the name Eugene gave me — funny, foreign — over the bell in the outer hall. The buzzer sounded and I pushed open the door. I stood inside and looked up the carpeted stairs, the angled banisters.

"What is it?" She sounded old, worried.

"The new kid," I called, "the new kid."

"It's for you," I heard her say.

"Yes?" His voice, the one I couldn't mimic. I mounted the first stair. I leaned back against the wall and looked up through the high, boxy banister poles. It was like standing inside a pipe organ.

"Yes?"

From where I stood at the bottom of the stairs I could see only a boot. He was wearing boots.

"Yes? What is it please?"

"*You,*" I roared. "Glass of fashion, mold of form, it's me! It's Push the bully!"

I heard his soft, rapid footsteps coming down the stairs — a springy, spongy urgency. He jingled, the bastard. He had coins — I could see them: rough, golden, imperfectly round; raised, massively gowned goddesses, their heads fingered smooth, their arms gone — and keys to strange boxes, thick doors. I saw his boots. I backed away.

"I brought you down," I said.

"Be quiet, please. There's a woman who's ill. A boy who must study. There's a man with bad bones. An old man needs sleep."

"He'll get it," I said.

"We'll go outside," he said.

"No. Do you live here? What do you do? Will you be in our school? Were you telling the truth?"

"Shh. Please. You're very excited."

"Tell me your name," I said. It could be my campaign, I thought. His *name.* Scratched in new sidewalk, chalked onto walls, written on papers dropped in the street. To leave it behind like so many clues, to give him a fame, to take it away, to slash and cross out, to erase and to smear — my kid's witchcraft. "Tell me your name."

"It's John," he said softly.

"What?"

"It's John."

"John what? Come on now. I'm Push the bully."

"John Williams," he said.

"John Williams? John Williams? Only that? Only John Williams?"

He smiled.

"Who's that on the bell? The name on the box?"

"She needs me," he said.

"Cut it out."

"I help her," he said.

"You stop that."

"There's a man that's in pain. A woman who's old. A husband that's worried. A wife that despairs."

"You're the bully," I said. "Your John Williams is a service animal," I yelled in the hall.

He turned and began to climb the stairs. His calves bloomed in their leather sheathing.

"*Lover,*" I whispered to him.

He turned to me at the landing. He shook his head sadly.

"We'll see," I said.

"We'll see what we'll see," he said.

That night I painted his name on the side of the gymnasium in enormous letters. In the morning it was still there, but it wasn't what I meant. There was nothing incantatory in the huge letters, no scream, no curse. I had never traveled with a gang, there had been no togetherness in my tearing, but this thing on the wall seemed the act of vandals, the low production of ruffians. When you looked at it you were surprised they had gotten the spelling right.

Astonishingly, it was allowed to remain. And each day there was something more celebrational in the giant name, something of increased hospitality, lavish welcome. John Williams might have been a football hero, or someone back from the kidnapers. Finally I had to take it off myself.

Something had changed.

Eugene was not wearing his canteen. Boys didn't break off their conversations when I came up to them. One afternoon a girl winked at me. (Push has never picked on girls. *Their* submissiveness is part of their nature. They are ornamental. Don't get me wrong, please. There is a way in which they function as part of the landscape, like flowers at a funeral. They have a strange cheerfulness. They are the organizers of pep rallies and dances. They put out the Year Book. They are *born* Gray Ladies. I can't bully them.)

John Williams was in the school, but except for brief glimpses in the hall I never saw him. Teachers would repeat the things he had said in their other classes. They read from his papers. In the gym the coach described plays he had made, set shots he had taken. Everyone talked about him, and girls made a reference to him a sort of love signal. If it was suggested that he had smiled at one of them, the girl referred to would blush or, what was worse, look aloofly mysterious. (*Then* I could have punished her, *then* I could.) Gradually his name began to appear on all their notebooks, in the margins of their texts. (It annoyed me to remember what *I* had done on the wall.) The big canvas books, with their careful, elaborate J's and W's, took on the appearance of ancient, illuminated fables. It was the unconscious embroidery of love, hope's bright doodle. Even the administration was aware of him. In Assembly the principal announced that John Williams had broken all existing records in the school's charity drives. She had never seen good citizenship like his before, she said.

It's one thing to live with a bully, another to live with a hero.

Everyone's hatred I understand, no one's love; everyone's grievance, no one's content.

I saw Mimmer. Mimmer should have graduated years ago. I saw Mimmer the dummy.

"Mimmer," I said, "you're in his class."

"He's very smart."

"Yes, but is it fair? You work harder. I've seen you study. You spend hours. Nothing comes. He was born knowing. You could have used just a little of what he's got so much of. It's not fair."

"He's very clever. It's wonderful," Mimmer says.

Slud is crippled. He wears a shoe with a built-up heel to balance himself.

"Ah, Slud," I say "I've seen him run."

"He has beaten the horses in the park. It's very beautiful," Slud says.

"He's handsome, isn't he, Clob?" Clob looks contagious, radioactive. He has severe acne. He is ugly *under* his acne.

"He gets the girls," Clob says.

He gets *everything,* I think. But I'm alone in my envy, awash in my lust. It's as if I were a prophet to the deaf. Schnooks, schnooks, I want to scream, dopes and settlers. What good does his smile do you, of what use is his good heart?

The other day I did something stupid. I went to the cafeteria and shoved a boy out of the way and took his place in the line. It was foolish, but their fear is almost all gone and I felt I had to show the flag. The boy only grinned and let me pass. Then someone called my name. It was *him.* I turned to face him. "Push," he said, "you forgot your silver." He handed it to a girl in front of him and she gave it to the boy in front of her and it came to me down the long line.

I plot, I scheme. Snares, I think; tricks and traps. I remember the old days when there were ways to snap fingers, crush toes, ways to pull noses, twist heads and punch arms — the old-timey Flinch Law I used to impose, the gone bully magic of deceit. But nothing works against him,

I think. How does he know so much? He is bully-prepared, that one, not to be trusted.

It is worse and worse.

In the cafeteria he eats with Frank. "You don't want those potatoes," he tells him. "Not the ice cream, Frank. One sandwich, remember. You lost three pounds last week." The fat boy smiles his fat love at him. John Williams puts his arm around him. He seems to squeeze him thin.

He's helping Mimmer to study. He goes over his lessons and teaches him tricks, short cuts. "I want you up there with me on the Honor Roll, Mimmer."

I see him with Slud the cripple. They go to the gym. I watch from the balcony. "Let's develop those arms, my friend." They work out with weights. Slud's muscles grow, they bloom from his bones.

I lean over the rail. I shout down, "He can bend iron bars. Can he peddle a bike? Can he walk on rough ground? Can he climb up a hill? Can he wait on a line? Can he dance with a girl? Can he go up a ladder or jump from a chair?"

Beneath me the rapt Slud sits on a bench and raises a weight. He holds it at arm's length, level with his chest. He moves it high, higher. It rises above his shoulders, his throat, his head. He bends back his neck to see what he's done. If the weight should fall now it would crush his throat. I stare down into his smile.

I see Eugene in the halls. I stop him. "Eugene, what's he done for you?" I ask. He smiles — he never did this — and I see his mouth's flood. "High tide," I say with satisfaction.

Williams has introduced Clob to a girl. They have double-dated.

A week ago John Williams came to my house to see me! I wouldn't let him in.

"Please open the door, Push. I'd like to chat with you. Will you open the door? Push? I think we ought to talk. I think I can help you to be happier."

I was furious. I didn't know what to say to him. "I don't want to be happier. Go way." It was what little kids used to say to me.

"*Please* let me help you."

"*Please* let me — " I begin to echo. "Please let me alone."

"We ought to be friends, Push."

"No deals." I am choking, I am close to tears. What can I do? *What?* I want to kill him.

I double-lock the door and retreat to my room. He is still out there. I have tried to live my life so that I could keep always the lamb from my door.

He has gone too far this time; and I think sadly, I will have to fight him, I will have to fight him. Push pushed. I think sadly of the pain. Push pushed. I will have to fight him. Not to preserve honor but its opposite. Each time I see him I will have to fight him. And then I think — *of course!* And *I* smile. He has done *me* a favor. I know it at once. If he fights me he fails. He fails if he fights me. *Push pushed pushes!* It's physics! Natural law! I know he'll beat me, but I won't prepare, I won't train, I won't use the tricks I know. It's strength against strength, and my strength is as the strength of ten because my jaw is glass! *He doesn't know everything, not everything he doesn't.* And I think, I could go out now, he's still there, I could hit him in the hall, but I think, No, I want them to see, I want *them* to see!

The next day I am very excited. I look for Williams. He's not in the halls. I miss him in the cafeteria. Afterward I look for him in the schoolyard where I first saw him. (He has them organized now. He teaches them games of Tibet, games of Japan; he gets them to play lost sports of the dead.) He does not disappoint me. He is there in the yard, a circle around him, a ring of the loyal.

I join the ring. I shove in between two kids I have known. They try to change places; they murmur and fret.

Williams sees me and waves. His smile could grow flowers. "Boys," he says, "boys, make room for Push. Join hands, boys." They welcome me to the circle. One takes my hand, then another. I give to each calmly.

I wait. *He doesn't know everything.*

"Boys," he begins, "today we're going to learn a game that the knights of the lords and kings of old France used to play in another century. Now you may not realize it, boys, because today when we think of a knight we think, too, of his fine charger, but the fact is that a horse was a rare animal — not a domestic European animal at all, but Asian. In western Europe, for example, there was no such thing as a work horse until the eighth century. Your horse was just too expensive to be put to heavy labor in the fields. (This explains, incidentally, the prevalence of famine in western Europe, whereas famine is unrecorded in Asia until the ninth century, when Euro-Asian horse trading was at its height.) It wasn't only expensive to purchase a horse, it was expensive to keep one. A cheap fodder wasn't developed in Europe until the tenth century. Then, of course, when you consider the terrific risks that the warrior horse of a knight naturally had to run, you begin to appreciate how expensive it would have been for the lord — unless he was extremely rich — to provide all his knights with horses. He'd want to make pretty certain that the knights who got them knew how to handle a horse. (Only your knights errant — an elite, crack corps — ever had horses. We don't realize that most knights were *home* knights; *chevalier chez* they were called.)

"This game, then, was devised to let the lord, or king, see which of his knights had the skill and strength in his hands to control a horse. Without moving your feet, you must try to jerk the one next to you off balance. Each man has two opponents, so it's very difficult. If a man falls, or if his knee touches the ground, he's out. The circle is diminished but must close up again immediately. Now, once for practice only — "

"Just a minute." I interrupt.

"Yes, Push?"

I leave the circle and walk forward and hit him as hard as I can in the face.

He stumbles backward. The boys groan. He recovers. He rubs his jaw and smiles. I think he is going to let me hit him again. I am prepared for this. He knows what I'm up to and will use his passivity. Either way I win, but I am determined he shall hit me. I am ready to kick him, but as my foot comes up he grabs my ankle and turns it forcefully. I spin in the air. He lets go and I fall heavily on my back. I am surprised at how easy it was, but am content if they understand. I get up and am walking away, but there is an arm on my shoulder. He pulls me around roughly. He hits me.

"*Sic semper tyrannus,*" he exults.

"Where's your other cheek?" I ask, falling backward.

"One cheek for tyrants," he shouts. He pounces on me and raises his fist and I cringe. His anger is terrific. I do not want to be hit again.

"You see? You see?" I scream at the kids, but I have lost the train of my former reasoning. I have in no way beaten him. I can't remember now what I had intended.

He lowers his fist and gets off my chest and they cheer. "Hurrah," they yell. "Hurrah, hurrah." The word seems funny to me.

He offers his hand when I try to rise. It is so difficult to know what to do. Oh God, it is so difficult to know which gesture is the right one. I don't even know this. He knows everything, and I don't even know this. I am a fool on the ground, one hand behind me pushing up, the other not yet extended but itching in the palm where the need is. It is better to give than receive, surely. It is best not to need at all.

Appalled, guessing what I miss, I rise alone.

"Friends?" he asks. He offers to shake.

"Take it, Push." It's Eugene's voice.

"Go ahead, Push." Slud limps forward.

"Push, hatred's so ugly," Clob says, his face shining.

"You'll feel better, Push," Frank, thinner, taller, urges softly.

"Push, don't be foolish," Mimmer says.

I shake my head. I may be wrong. I am probably wrong. All I know at last is what feels good. "Nothing doing," I growl. "No deals." I begin to talk, to spray my hatred at them. They are not an easy target even now. "Only your knights errant — your crack corps — ever have horses. Slud may dance and Clob may kiss but they'll never be good at it. *Push is no service animal.* No. *No.* Can you hear that, Williams? There isn't any magic, but your no is still stronger than your yes, and distrust is where I put my faith." I turn to the boys. "What have you settled for? Only your knights errant ever have horses. *What have you settled for?* Will Mimmer do sums in his head? How do you like your lousy hunger, thin boy? Slud, you can break me but you can't catch me. And Clob will never shave without pain, and ugly, let me tell you, is *still* in the eye of the beholder!"

John Williams mourns for me. He grieves his gamy grief. No one has everything — not even John Williams. He doesn't have *me.* He'll never have me, I think. If my life were only to deny him that, it would almost be enough. I could do his voice now if I wanted. His corruption began when he lost me. "You," I shout, rubbing it in, "*indulger,* dispense me no dispensations. Push the bully hates your heart!"

"Shut him up, somebody," Eugene cries. His saliva spills from his mouth when he speaks.

"Swallow! *Pig, swallow!*"

He rushes toward me.

Suddenly I raise my arms and he stops. I feel a power in me. I am Push, Push the bully, God of the Neighborhood, its incarnation of envy and jealousy and need. I vie, strive, emulate, compete, a contender in every event there is. I didn't make myself. I probably can't save myself, but maybe that's the only need I don't have. I taste my lack and that's how I win — by having nothing to lose. It's not good enough! I want and I want and I will die wanting, but first I will have something. This time I will have something. I say it aloud. "This time I will have something." I step toward them. The power makes me dizzy. It is enormous. They feel it. They back away. They crouch in the shadow of my outstretched wings. It isn't deceit this time but the real magic at last, the genuine thing: the cabala of my hate, of my irreconcilableness.

Logic is nothing. Desire is stronger.

I move toward Eugene. "*I will have something,*" I roar.

"Stand back," he shrieks, "I'll spit in your eye."

"*I will have something.* I will have terror. I will have drought. I bring the dearth. Famine's contagious. Also is thirst. Privation, privation, barrenness, void. I dry up your glands, I poison your well."

He is choking, gasping, chewing furiously. He opens his mouth. It is dry. His throat is parched. There is sand on his tongue.

They moan. They are terrified, but they move up to see. We are thrown together. Slud, Frank, Clob, Mimmer, the others, John Williams, myself. I will not be reconciled, or halve my hate. *It's* what I have, all I can keep. My bully's sour solace. It's enough, I'll make do.

I can't stand them near me. I move against them. I shove them away. I force them off. I press them, thrust them aside. *I push through.*

RALPH ELLISON

King of the Bingo Game

The woman in front of him was eating roasted peanuts that smelled so good that he could barely contain his hunger. He could not even sleep and wished they'd hurry and begin the bingo game. There, on his right, two fellows were drinking wine out of a bottle wrapped in a paper bag, and he could hear soft gurgling in the dark. His stomach gave a low, gnawing growl. "If this was down South," he thought, "all I'd have to do is lean over and say, 'Lady, gimme a few of those peanuts, please ma'am,' and she'd pass me the bag and never think nothing of it." Or he could ask the fellows for a drink in the same way. Folks down South stuck together that way; they didn't even have to know you. But up here it was different. Ask somebody for something, and they'd think you were crazy. Well, I ain't crazy. I'm just broke, 'cause I got no birth certificate to get a job, and Laura 'bout to die 'cause we got no money for a doctor. But I ain't crazy. And yet a pinpoint of doubt was focused in his mind as he glanced toward the screen and saw the hero stealthily entering a dark room and sending the beam of a flashlight along a wall of bookcases. This is where he finds the trapdoor, he remembered. The man would pass abruptly through the wall and find the girl tied to a bed, her legs and arms spread wide, and her clothing torn to rags. He laughed softly to himself. He had seen the picture three times, and this was one of the best scenes.

On his right the fellow whispered wide-eyed to his companion, "Man, look ayonder!"

"Damn!"

"Wouldn't I like to have her tied up like that..."

"Hey! That fool's letting her loose!"

"Aw, man, he loves her."

"Love or no love!"

The man moved impatiently beside him, and he tried to involve himself in the scene. But Laura was on his mind. Tiring quickly of watching the picture he looked back to where the white beam filtered from the projection room above the balcony. It started small and grew large, specks of dust dancing in its whiteness as it reached the screen. It was strange how the beam always landed right on the screen and didn't mess up and fall somewhere else. But they had it all fixed. Everything was fixed. Now suppose when they showed that girl with her dress torn the girl started taking off the rest of her clothes, and when the guy came in he didn't untie her but kept her there and went to taking off his own clothes? *That* would be something to see. If a picture got out of hand like that those guys up there would go nuts. Yeah, and there'd be so many folks in here you couldn't find a seat for nine months! A strange sensation played over his skin. He shuddered. Yesterday he'd seen a bedbug on a woman's neck as they walked out into the bright street. But exploring his thigh through a hole in his pocket he found only goose pimples and old scars.

The bottle gurgled again. He closed his eyes. Now a dreamy music was accompanying the film and train whistles were sounding in the distance, and he was a boy again walking along a railroad trestle down South, and seeing the train coming, and running back as fast as he could go, and hearing the whistle blowing, and getting off the trestle to solid ground just in time, with the earth trembling beneath his feet, and feeling relieved as he ran down the cinder-strewn embankment onto the highway, and looking back and seeing with terror that the train had left the track and was following him right down the middle of the street, and all the white people laughing as he ran screaming...

"Wake up there, buddy! What the hell do you mean hollering like that? Can't you see we trying to enjoy this here picture?"

He stared at the man with gratitude.

"I'm sorry, old man," he said. "I musta been dreaming."

"Well, here, have a drink. And don't be making no noise like that, damn!"

His hands trembled as he tilted his head. It was not wine, but whiskey. Cold rye whiskey. He took a deep swoller, decided it was better not to take another, and handed the bottle back to its owner.

"Thanks, old man," he said.

Now he felt the cold whiskey breaking a warm path straight through the middle of him, growing hotter and sharper as it moved. He had not eaten all day, and it made him light-headed. The smell of the peanuts stabbed him like a knife, and he got up and found a seat in the middle aisle. But no sooner did he sit than he saw a row of intense-faced young girls, and got up again, thinking, "You chicks musta been Lindy-hopping somewhere." He found a seat several rows ahead as the lights came on, and he saw the screen disappear behind a heavy red and gold curtain; then the curtain rising, and the man with the microphone and a uniformed attendant coming on the stage.

He felt for his bingo cards, smiling. The guy at the door wouldn't like it if he knew about his having *five* cards. Well, not everyone played the bingo game; and even with five cards he didn't have much of a chance. For Laura, though, he had to have faith. He studied the cards, each with its different numerals, punching the free center hole in each and spreading them neatly across his lap; and when the lights faded he sat slouched in his seat so that he could look from his cards to the bingo wheel with but a quick shifting of his eyes.

Ahead, at the end of the darkness, the man with the microphone was pressing a button attached to a long cord and spinning the bingo wheel and calling out the number each time the wheel came to rest. And each time the voice rang out his finger read over the cards for the number. With five cards he had to move fast. He became nervous; there were too many cards, and the man went too fast with his grating voice. Perhaps he should just select one and throw the others away. But he was afraid. He became warm. Wonder how much Laura's doctor would cost? Damn that, watch the cards! And with despair he heard the man call three in a row which he missed on all five cards. This way he'd never win ...

When he saw the row of holes punched across the third card, he sat paralyzed and heard the man call three more numbers before he stumbled forward, screaming.

"Bingo! Bingo!"

"Let that fool up there," someone called.

"Get up there, man!"

He stumbled down the aisle and up the steps to the stage into a light so sharp and bright that for a moment it blinded him, and he felt that he had moved into the spell of some strange, mysterious power. Yet it was as familiar as the sun, and he knew it was the perfectly familiar bingo.

The man with the microphone was saying something to the audience as he held out his card. A cold light flashed from the man's finger as the card left his hand. His knees trembled. The man stepped closer, checking the card against the numbers chalked on the board. Suppose he had made a mistake? The pomade on the man's hair made him feel faint, and he backed away. But the man was checking the card over the microphone now, and he had to stay. He stood tense, listening.

"Under the O, forty-four," the man chanted. "Under the I, seven. Under the G, three. Under the B, ninety-six. Under the N, thirteen!"

His breath came easier as the man smiled at the audience.

"Yessir, ladies and gentlemen, he's one of the chosen people!"

The audience rippled with laughter and applause.

"Step right up to the front of the stage."

He moved slowly forward, wishing that the light was not so bright.

"To win to-night's jackpot of $36.90 the wheel must stop between the double zero, understand?"

He nodded, knowing the ritual from the many days and nights he had watched the winners march across the stage to press the button that controlled the spinning wheel and receive the prizes. And now he followed the instructions as though he'd crossed the slippery stage a million prize-winning times.

The man was making some kind of a joke, and he nodded vacantly. So tense had he become that he felt a sudden desire to cry and shook it away. He felt vaguely that his whole life was determined by the bingo wheel; not only that which would happen now that he was at last before it, but all that had gone before, since his birth, and his mother's birth and the birth of his father. It had always been there, even though he had not been aware of it, handing out the unlucky cards and numbers of his days. The feeling persisted, and he started quickly away. I better get down from here before I make a fool of myself, he thought.

"Here, boy," the man called. "You haven't started yet."

Someone laughed as he went hesitantly back.

"Are you all reet?"

He grinned at the man's jive talk, but no words would come, and he knew it was not a convincing grin. For suddenly he knew that he stood on the slippery brink of some terrible embarrassment.

"Where are you from, boy?" the man asked.

"Down South."

"He's from down South, ladies and gentlemen," the man said. "Where from? Speak right into the mike."

"Rocky Mont," he said. "Rock' Mont, North Car'lina."

"So you decided to come down off that mountain to the U.S.," the man laughed. He felt that the man was making a fool of him, but then something cold was placed in his hand, and the lights were no longer behind him.

Standing before the wheel he felt alone, but that was somehow right, and he remembered his plan. He would give the wheel a short quick twirl. Just a touch of the button. He had watched it many times, and always it came close to double zero when it was short and quick. He steeled himself; the fear had left, and he felt a profound sense of promise, as though he were about to be repaid for all the things he'd suffered all his life. Trembling, he pressed the button. There was a whirl of lights, and in a second he realized with finality that though he wanted to, he could not stop. It was as though he held a high-powered line in his naked hand. His nerves tightened. As the wheel increased its speed it seemed to draw him more and more into its power, as though it held his fate; and with it came a deep need to submit, to whirl, to lose himself in its swirl of color. He could not stop it now. So let it be.

The button rested snugly in his palm where the man had placed it. And now he became aware of the man beside him, advising him through the microphone, while behind the shadowy audience hummed with noisy voices. He shifted his feet. There was still that feeling of helplessness within him, making part of him desire to turn back, even now that the jackpot was right in his hand. He squeezed the button until his fist ached. Then, like the sudden shriek of a subway whistle, a doubt tore through his head. Suppose he did not spin the wheel long enough? What could he do, and how could he tell? And then he knew, even as he wondered, that as long as he pressed the button, he could control the jackpot. He and only he could determine whether or not it was to be his. Not even the man with the microphone could do anything about it now. He felt drunk. Then, as though he had come down from a high hill into a valley of people, he heard the audience yelling.

"Come down from there, you jerk?"

"Let somebody else have a chance ..."

"Ole Jack thinks he done found the end of the rainbow ..."

The last voice was not unfriendly, and he turned and smiled dreamily into the yelling mouths. Then he turned his back squarely on them.

"Don't take too long, boy," a voice said.

He nodded. They were yelling behind him. Those folks did not understand what had happened to him. They had been playing the bingo game day in and night out for years, trying to win rent money or hamburger change. But not one of those wise guys had discovered this wonderful thing. He watched the wheel whirling past the numbers and experienced a burst of exaltation: This is God! This is the really truly God! He said it aloud, "This is God!"

He said it with such absolute conviction that he feared he would fall fainting into the footlights. But the crowd yelled so loud that they could not hear. Those fools, he thought. I'm here trying to tell them the most wonderful secret in the world, and they're yelling like they gone crazy. A hand fell upon his shoulder.

"You'll have to make a choice now, boy. You've taken too long."

He brushed the hand violently away.

"Leave me alone, man. I know what I'm doing!"

The man looked surprised and held on to the microphone for support. And because he did not wish to hurt the man's feelings he smiled, realizing with a sudden pang that there was no way of explaining to the man just why he had to stand there pressing the button forever.

"Come here," he called tiredly.

The man approached, rolling the heavy microphone across the stage.

"Anybody can play this bingo game, right?" he said.

"Sure, but ..."

He smiled, feeling inclined to be patient with this slick looking white man with his blue shirt and his sharp gabardine suit.

"That's what I thought," he said. "Anybody can win the jackpot as long as they get the lucky number, right?"

"That's the rule, but after all ..."

"That's what I thought," he said. "And the big prize goes to the man who knows how to win it?"

The man nodded speechlessly.

"Well then, go on over there and watch me win like I want to. I ain't going to hurt nobody," he said, "and I'll show you how to win. I mean to show the whole world how it's got to be done."

And because he understood, he smiled again to let the man know that he held nothing against him for being white and impatient. Then he refused to see the man any longer and stood pressing the button, the voices of the crowd reaching him like sounds in distant streets. Let them yell. All the Negroes down there were just ashamed because he was black like them. He smiled inwardly, knowing how it was. Most of the time he was ashamed of what Negroes did himself. Well, let them be ashamed for something this time. Like him. He was like a long thin black wire that was being stretched and wound upon the bingo wheel; wound until he wanted to scream; wound, but this time himself controlling the winding and the sadness and the shame, and because he did, Laura would be all right. Suddenly the lights flickered. He staggered backwards. Had something gone wrong? All this noise. Didn't they know that although he controlled the wheel, it also controlled him, and unless he pressed the button forever and forever and ever it would stop, leaving him high and dry, dry and high on this hard high slippery hill and Laura dead? There was only one chance; he had to do whatever the wheel demanded. And gripping the button in despair, he discovered with surprise that it imparted a nervous energy. His spine tingled. He felt a certain power.

Now he faced the raging crowd with defiance, its screams penetrating his eardrums like trumpets shrieking from a juke-box. The vague faces glowing in the bingo lights gave him a sense of himself that he had never known before. He was running the show, by God! They had to react to him, for he was their luck. This is *me,* he thought. Let the bastards yell. Then someone was laughing inside him, and he realized that somehow he had forgotten his own name. It was a sad, lost feeling to lose your name, and a crazy thing to do. That name had been given him by the white man who had owned his grandfather a long lost time ago down South. But maybe those wise guys knew his name.

"Who am I?" he screamed.

"Hurry up and bingo, you jerk!"

They didn't know either, he thought sadly. They

didn't even know their own names, they were all poor nameless bastards. Well, he didn't need that old name; he was reborn. For as long as he pressed the button he was The-man-who-pressed-the-button-who-held-the-prize-who-was-the-King-of-Bingo. That was the way it was, and he'd have to press the button even if nobody understood, even though Laura did not understand.

"Live!" he shouted.

The audience quieted like the dying of a huge fan.

"Live, Laura, baby. I got holt of it now, sugar. Live!"

He screamed it, tears streaming down his face. "I got nobody but YOU!"

The screams tore from his very guts. He felt as though the rush of blood to his head would burst out in baseball seams of small red droplets, like a head beaten by police clubs. Bending over he saw a trickle of blood splashing the toe of his shoe. With his free hand he searched his head. It was his nose. God, suppose something has gone wrong? He felt that the whole audience had somehow entered him and was stamping its feet in his stomach and he was unable to throw them out. They wanted the prize, that was it. They wanted the secret for themselves. But they'd never get it; he would keep the bingo wheel whirling forever, and Laura would be safe in the wheel. But would she? It had to be, because if she were not safe the wheel would cease to turn; it could not go on. He had to get away, *vomit* all, and his mind formed an image of himself running with Laura in his arms down the tracks of the subway just ahead of an A train, running desperately *vomit* with people screaming for him to come out but knowing no way of leaving the tracks because to stop would bring the train crushing down upon him and to attempt to leave across the other tracks would mean to run into a hot third rail as high as his waist which threw blue sparks that blinded his eyes until he could hardly see.

He heard singing and the audience was clapping its hands.

Shoot the liquor to him, Jim, boy!
Clap-clap-clap
Well a-calla the cop
He's blowing his top!
Shoot the liquor to him, Jim, boy!

Bitter anger grew within him at the singing. They think I'm crazy. Well let 'em laugh. I'll do what I got to do.

He was standing in an attitude of intense listening when he saw that they were watching something on the stage behind him. He felt weak. But when he turned he saw no one. If only his thumb did not ache so. Now they were applauding. And for a moment he thought that the wheel had stopped. But that was impossible, his thumb still pressed the button. Then he saw them. Two men in uniform beckoned from the end of the stage. They were coming toward him, walking in step, slowly, like a tap-dance team returning for a third encore. But their shoulders shot forward, and he backed away, looking wildly about. There was nothing to fight them with. He had only the long black cord which led to a plug somewhere back stage, and he couldn't use that because it operated the bingo wheel. He backed slowly, fixing the men with his eyes as his lips stretched over his teeth in a tight, fixed grin; moved toward the end of the stage and realizing that he couldn't go much further, for suddenly the cord became taut and he couldn't afford to break the cord. But he had to do something. The audience was howling. Suddenly he stopped dead, seeing the men halt, their legs lifted as in an interrupted step of a slow-motion dance. There was nothing to do but run in the other direction and he dashed forward, slipping and sliding. The men fell back, surprised. He struck out violently going past.

"Grab him!"

He ran, but all too quickly the cord tightened, resistingly, and he turned and ran back again. This time he slipped them, and discovered by running in a circle before the wheel he could keep the cord from tightening. But this way he had to flail his arms to keep the men away. Why couldn't they leave a man alone? He ran, circling.

"Ring down the curtain," someone yelled. But they couldn't do that. If they did the wheel flashing from the projection room would be cut off. But they had him before he could tell them so, trying to pry open his fist, and he was wrestling and trying to bring his knees into the fight and holding on to the button, for it was his life. And now he was down, seeing a foot coming down, crushing his wrist cruelly, down, as he saw the wheel whirling serenely above.

"I can't give it up," he screamed. Then quietly, in a confidential tone, "Boys, I really can't give it up."

It landed hard against his head. And in the blank moment they had it away from him, completely now. He fought them trying to pull him up from the stage as he watched the wheel spin slowly to a stop. Without surprise he saw it rest at double-zero.

"You see," he pointed bitterly.

"Sure, boy, sure, it's O.K.," one of the men said smiling.

And seeing the man bow his head to someone he could not see, he felt very, very happy; he would receive what all the winners received.

But as he warmed in the justice of the man's tight smile he did not see the man's slow wink, nor see the bow-legged man behind him step clear of the swiftly descending curtain and set himself for a blow. He only felt the dull pain exploding in his skull, and he knew even as it slipped out of him that his luck had run out on the stage.

WILLIAM FAULKNER

A Rose for Emily

I

When Miss Emily Grierson died, our whole town went to her funeral: the men through a sort of respectful affection for a fallen monument, the women mostly out of curiosity to see the inside of her house, which no one save an old man-servant — a combined gardener and cook — had seen in at least ten years.

It was a big, squarish frame house that had once been white, decorated with cupolas and spires, and scrolled balconies in the heavily lightsome style of the seventies, set on what had once been our most select street. But garages and cotton gins had encroached and obliterated even the august names of that neighborhood; only Miss Emily's house was left, lifting its stubborn and coquettish decay above the cotton wagons and the gasoline pumps — an eyesore among eyesores. And now Miss Emily had gone to join the representatives of those august names where they lay in the cedar-bemused cemetery among the ranked and anonymous graves of Union and Confederate soldiers who fell at the battle of Jefferson.

Alive, Miss Emily had been a tradition, a duty, and a care; a sort of hereditary obligation upon the town, dating from that day in 1894 when Colonel Sartoris, the mayor — he who fathered the edict that no Negro woman should appear on the street without an apron — remitted her taxes, the dispensation dating from the death of her father on into perpetuity. Not that Miss Emily would have accepted charity. Colonel Sartoris invented an involved tale to the effect that Miss Emily's father had loaned money to the town, which the town, as a matter of business, preferred this way of repaying. Only a man of Colonel Sartoris' generation and thought could have invented it, and only a woman could have believed it.

When the next generation, with its more modern ideas, became mayors and aldermen, this arrangement created some little dissatisfaction. On the first of the year they mailed her a tax notice. February came, and there was no reply. They wrote her a formal letter, asking her to call at the sheriff's office at her convenience. A week later the mayor wrote her himself, offering to call or to send his car for her, and received in reply a note on paper of an archaic shape, in a thin, flowing calligraphy in faded ink, to the effect that she no longer went out at all. The tax notice was also enclosed, without comment.

They called a special meeting of the Board of Aldermen. A deputation waited upon her, knocked at the door through which no visitor had passed since she ceased giving china-painting lessons eight or ten years earlier. They were admitted by the old Negro into a dim hall from which a stairway mounted into still more shadow. It smelled of dust and disuse — a close, dank smell. The Negro led them into the parlor. It was furnished in heavy, leather-covered furniture. When the Negro opened the blinds of one window, they could see that the leather was cracked; and when they sat down, a faint dust rose sluggishly about their thighs, spinning with slow motes in the single sun-ray. On a tarnished gilt easel before the fireplace stood a crayon portrait of Miss Emily's father.

They rose when she entered — a small, fat woman in black, with a thin gold chain descending to her waist and vanishing into her belt, leaning on an ebony cane with a tarnished gold head. Her skeleton was small and spare; perhaps that was why what would have been merely plumpness in another was obesity in her. She looked bloated, like a body long submerged in motionless water, and of the pallid hue. Her eyes, lost in the fatty ridges of her face, looked like two small pieces of coal pressed into a lump of dough as they moved from one face to another while the visitors stated their errand.

She did not ask them to sit. She just stood in the door and listened quietly until the spokesman came to a stumbling halt. Then they could hear the invisible watch ticking at the end of the gold chain.

Her voice was dry and cold. "I have no taxes in Jefferson. Colonel Sartoris explained it to me. Perhaps one of you can gain access to the city records and satisfy yourselves."

"But we have. We are the city authorities, Miss Emily. Didn't you get a notice from the sheriff, signed by him?"

"I received a paper, yes," Miss Emily said. "Perhaps he considers himself the sheriff . . . I have no taxes in Jefferson."

"But there is nothing on the books to show that, you see. We must go by the — "

"See Colonel Sartoris. I have no taxes in Jefferson."

"But Miss Emily — "

"See Colonel Sartoris." (Colonel Sartoris had been dead almost ten years.) "I have no taxes in Jefferson. Tobe!" The Negro appeared. "Show these gentlemen out."

II

So she vanquished them, horse and foot, just as she had vanquished their fathers thirty years before about the smell. That was two years after her father's death and a short time after her sweetheart — the one we believed would marry her — had deserted her. After her father's death she went out very little; after her sweetheart went away, people hardly saw her at all. A few of the ladies had the temerity to call, but were not received, and the only sign of life about the place was the Negro man — a young man then — going in and out with a market basket.

"Just as if a man — any man — could keep a kitchen properly," the ladies said; so they were not surprised when the smell developed. It was another link between the gross, teeming world and the high and mighty Griersons.

A neighbor, a woman, complained to the mayor, Judge Stevens, eighty years old.

"But what will you have me do about it, madam?" he said.

"Why, send her word to stop it," the woman said. "Isn't there a law?"

"I'm sure that won't be necessary," Judge Stevens said. "It's probably just a snake or a rat that nigger of hers killed in the yard. I'll speak to him about it."

The next day he received two more complaints, one from a man who came in diffident deprecation. "We really must do something about it, Judge. I'd be the last one in the world to bother Miss Emily, but we've got to do something." That night the Board of Aldermen met — three graybeards and one younger man, a member of the rising generation.

"It's simple enough," he said. "Send her word to have her place cleaned up. Give her a certain time do it in, and if she don't . . . "

"Dammit, sir," Judge Stevens said, "will you accuse a lady to her face of smelling bad?"

So the next night, after midnight, four men crossed Miss Emily's lawn and slunk about the house like burglars, sniffing along the base of the brickwork and at the cellar openings while one of them performed a regular sowing motion with his hand out of a sack slung from his shoulder. They broke open the cellar door and sprinkled lime there, and in all the outbuildings. As they recrossed the lawn, a window that had been dark was lighted and Miss Emily sat in it, the light behind her, and her upright torso motionless as that of an idol. They crept quietly across the lawn and into the shadow of the locusts that lined the street. After a week or two the smell went away.

That was when people had begun to feel really sorry for her. People in our town, remembering how old lady Wyatt, her great-aunt, had gone completely crazy at last, believed that the Griersons held themselves a little too high for what they really were. None of the young men were quite good enough for Miss Emily and such. We had long thought of them as a tableau, Miss Emily a slender figure in white in the background, her father a spraddled silhouette in the foreground, his back to her and clutching a horsewhip, the two of them framed by the backflung front door. When she got to be thirty and was still single, we were not pleased exactly, but vindicated; even with insanity in the family she wouldn't have turned down all of her chances if they had really materialized.

When her father died, it got about that the house was all that was left to her; and in a way, people were glad. At last they could pity Miss Emily. Being left alone, and a pauper, she had become humanized. Now she too would know the old thrill and the old despair of a penny more or less.

The day after his death all the ladies prepared to call at the house and offer condolence and aid, as is our custom. Miss Emily met them at the door, dressed as usual and with no trace of grief on her face. She told them that her father was not dead. She did that for three days, with the ministers calling on her, and the doctors, trying to persuade her to let them dispose of the body. Just as they were about to resort to law and force, she broke down, and they buried her father quickly.

We did not say she was crazy then. We believed she had to do that. We remembered all the young men her father had driven away, and we knew that with nothing left, she would have to cling to that which had robbed her, as people will.

III

She was sick for a long time. When we saw her again, her hair was cut short, making her look like a girl, with a vague resemblance to those angels in colored church windows — sort of tragic and serene.

The town had just let the contracts for paving the sidewalks, and in the summer after her father's death they began the work. The construction company came with niggers and mules and machinery, and a foreman named Homer Barron, a Yankee — a big, dark, ready man, with a big voice and eyes lighter than his face. The little boys would follow in groups to hear him cuss the niggers, and the niggers singing in time to the rise and fall of picks. Pretty soon he knew everybody in town. Whenever you heard a lot of laughing anywhere about the square, Homer Barron would be in the center of the group. Presently we began to see him and Miss Emily on Sunday afternoons driving in the yellow-wheeled buggy and the matched team of bays from the livery stable.

At first we were glad that Miss Emily would have an interest, because the ladies all said, "Of course a Grierson would not think seriously of a Northerner, a day laborer." But there were still others, older people, who said that even grief could not cause a real lady to forget *noblesse oblige* — without calling it *noblesse oblige.* They just said, "Poor Emily. Her kinsfolk should come to her." She had some kin in Alabama; but years ago her father had fallen out with them over the estate of old lady Wyatt, the crazy woman, and there was no communication between the two families. They had not even been represented at the funeral.

And as soon as the old people said, "Poor Emily," the whispering began. "Do you suppose it's really so?" they said to one another. "Of course it is. What else could ... " This behind their hands; rustling of craned silk and satin behind jalousies closed upon the sun of Sunday afternoon as the thin, swift clop-clop-clop of the matched team passed: "Poor Emily."

She carried her head high enough — even when we believed that she was fallen. It was as if she demanded more than ever the recognition of her dignity as the last Grierson; as if it had wanted that touch of earthiness to reaffirm her imperviousness. Like when she bought the rat poison, the arsenic. That was over a year after they had begun to say "Poor Emily," and while the two female cousins were visiting her.

"I want some poison," she said to the druggist. She was over thirty then, still a slight woman, though thinner than usual, with cold, haughty black eyes in a face the flesh of which was strained across the temples and about the eye-sockets as you imagine a lighthouse-keeper's face ought to look. "I want some poison," she said.

"Yes, Miss Emily. What kind? For rats and such? I'd recom — "

"I want the best you have. I don't care what kind."

The druggist named several. "They'll kill anything up to an elephant. But what you want is —"

"Arsenic," Miss Emily said. "Is that a good one?'

"Is ... arsenic? Yes, ma'am. But what you want —"

"I want arsenic."

The druggist looked down at her. She looked back at him, erect, her face like a strained flag. "Why of course," the druggist said. "If that's what you want. But the law requires you to tell what you are going to use it for."

Miss Emily just stared at him, her head tilted back in order to look him eye for eye, until he looked away and went and got the arsenic and wrapped it up. The Negro delivery boy brought her the package; the druggist didn't come back. When she opened the package at home there was written on the box, under the skull and bones: "For rats."

IV

So the next day we all said, "She will kill herself"; and we said it would be the best thing. When she had first begun to be seen with Homer Barron, we had said, "She will marry him." Then we said, "She will persuade him yet," because Homer himself had remarked — he liked men, and it was known that he drank with the younger men in the Elk's Club — that he was not a marrying man. Later we said, "Poor Emily" behind the jalousies as they passed on Sunday afternoon in the glittering buggy, Miss Emily with her head high and Homer Barron with his hat cocked and cigar in his teeth, reins and whip in a yellow glove.

Then some of the ladies began to say that it was a disgrace to the town and a bad example to the young people. The men did not want to interfere, but at last the ladies forced the Baptist minister — Miss Emily's people were Episcopal — to call upon her. He would never divulge what happened during that interview, but he refused to go back again. The next Sunday they again drove about the streets, and the following day the minister's wife wrote to Miss Emily's relations in Alabama.

So she had blood-kin under her roof again and we sat back to watch developments. At first nothing happened. Then we were sure that they were to be married. We learned that Miss Emily had been to the jeweler's and ordered a man's toilet set in silver, with the letter H. B. on each piece. Two days later we learned that she had bought a complete outfit of men's clothing, including a nightshirt, and we said, "They are married." We were really glad. We were glad because the two female cousins were even more Grierson than Miss Emily had ever been.

So we were not surprised when Homer Barron — the streets had been finished some time since — was gone. We were a little disappointed that there was not a public blowing-off, but we believed that he had gone on to prepare for Miss Emily's coming, or to give her a chance to get rid of the cousins. (By that time it was a cabal, and we were all Miss Emily's allies to help circumvent the cousins.) Sure enough, after another week they departed. And, as we had expected all along, within three days Homer Barron was back in town. A neighbor saw the Negro man admit him at the kitchen door at dusk one evening.

And that was the last we saw of Homer Barron. And of Miss Emily for some time. The Negro man went in and out with the market basket, but the front door remained closed. Now and then we would see her at a window for a moment, as the men did that night when they sprinkled the lime, but for almost six months she did not appear on the streets. Then we knew that this was to be expected too; as if that quality of her father which had thwarted her woman's life so many times had been too virulent and too furious to die.

When we next saw Miss Emily, she had grown fat and her hair was turning gray. During the next few years it grew grayer and grayer until it attained an even pepper-and-salt iron-gray, when it ceased turning. Up to the day of her death at seventy-four it was still that vigorous iron-gray, like the hair of an active man.

From that time on her front door remained closed, save for a period of six or seven years, when she was about forty, during which she gave lessons in china-painting. She fitted up a studio in one of the downstairs rooms, where the daughters and granddaughters of Colonel Sartoris' contemporaries were sent to her with the same regularity and in the same spirit that they were sent to church on Sunday with a twenty-five-cent piece for the collection plate. Meanwhile her taxes had been remitted.

Then the newer generation became the backbone and the spirit of the town, and the painting pupils grew up and fell away and did not send their children to her with boxes of color and tedious brushes and pictures cut from the ladies' magazines. The front door closed upon the last one and remained closed for good. When the town got free postal delivery, Miss Emily alone refused to let them fasten the metal numbers above her door and attach a mailbox to it. She would not listen to them.

Daily, monthly, yearly we watched the Negro grow grayer and more stooped, going in and out with the market basket. Each December we sent her a tax notice, which would be returned by the post office a week later unclaimed. Now and then we would see her in one of the downstairs windows — she had evidently shut up the top floor of the house — like the carven torso of an idol in a niche, looking or not looking at us, we could never tell which. Thus she passed from generation to generation — dear, inescapable, impervious, tranquil, and perverse.

And so she died. Fell ill in the house filled with dust and shadows, with only a doddering Negro man to wait on her. We did not even know she was sick; we had long since given up trying to get any information from the Negro. He talked to no one, probably not even to her, for his voice had grown harsh and rusty, as if from disuse.

She died in one of the downstairs rooms, in a heavy walnut bed with a curtain, her gray head propped on a pillow yellow and moldy with age and lack of sunlight.

V

The Negro met the first of the ladies at the front door and let them in, with their hushed, sibilant voices and their quick, curious glances and then he disappeared. He walked right through the house and out the back and was not seen again.

The two female cousins came at once. They held the funeral on the second day, with the town coming to look at Miss Emily beneath a mass of bought flowers, with the crayon face of her father musing profoundly above the bier and the ladies sibilant and macabre; and the very old men — some in their brushed Confederate uniforms — on the porch and the lawn, talking of Miss Emily as if she had been a contemporary of theirs, believing that they had danced with her and courted her perhaps, confusing time with its mathematical progression, as the old do, to whom all the past is not a diminishing road but, instead, a huge meadow which no winter ever quite touches, divided from them now by the narrow bottle-neck of the most recent decade of years.

Already we knew that there was one room in that region above stairs which no one had seen in forty years, and which would have to be forced. They waited until Miss Emily was decently in the ground before they opened it.

The violence of breaking down the door seemed to fill this room with pervading dust. A thin, acrid pall of the tomb seemed to lie everywhere upon this room decked and furnished as for a bridal: upon the valance curtains of faded rose color, upon the rose-shaded lights, upon the dressing table, upon the delicate array of crystal and the man's toilet things backed with tarnished silver, silver so tarnished that the monogram was obscured. Among them lay a collar and tie, as if they had just been removed, which, lifted, left upon the surface a pale crescent in the dust. Upon a chair hung the suit, carefully folded; beneath it the two mute shoes and the discarded socks.

The man himself lay in the bed.

For a long while we just stood there, looking down at the profound and fleshless grin. The body had apparently once lain in the attitude of an embrace, but now the long sleep that outlasts love, that conquers even the grimace of love, had cuckolded him. What was left of him, rotted beneath what was left of the nightshirt, had become inextricable from the bed in which he lay; and upon him and upon the pillow beside him lay that even coating of the patient and biding dust.

Then we noticed that in the second pillow was the indentation of a head. One of us lifted something from it, and leaning forward, that faint and invisible dust dry and acrid in the nostrils, we saw a long strand of iron-gray hair.

F. SCOTT FITZGERALD

Babylon Revisited

I

"And where's Mr. Campbell?" Charlie asked.

"Gone to Switzerland. Mr. Campbell's a pretty sick man, Mr. Wales."

"I'm sorry to hear that. And George Hardt?" Charlie inquired.

"Back in America, gone to work."

"And where is the Snow Bird?"

"He was in here last week. Anyway, his friend, Mr. Schaeffer, is in Paris."

Two familiar names from the long list of a year and a half ago. Charlie scribbled an address in his notebook and tore out the page.

"If you see Mr. Schaeffer, give him this," he said. "It's my brother-in-law's address. I haven't settled on a hotel yet."

He was not really disappointed to find Paris was so empty. But the stillness in the Ritz bar was strange and portentous. It was not an American bar any more — he felt polite in it, and not as if he owned it. It had gone back into France. He felt the stillness from the moment he got out of the taxi and saw the doorman, usually in a frenzy of activity at this hour, gossiping with a *chasseur* by the servant's entrance.

Passing through the corridor, he heard only a single, bored voice in the once-clamorous women's room. When he turned into the bar he traveled the twenty feet of green carpet with his eyes fixed straight ahead by old habit; and then, with his foot firmly on the rail, he turned and surveyed the room, encountering only a single pair of eyes that fluttered up from a newspaper in the corner. Charlie asked for the head barman, Paul, who in the latter days of the bull market had come to work in his own custom-built car — disembarking, however, with due nicety at the nearest corner. But Paul was at his country house today and Alix giving him information.

"No, no more," Charlie said, "I'm going slow these days."

Alix congratulated him: "You were going pretty strong a couple of years ago."

"I'll stick to it all right," Charlie assured him. "I've stuck to it for over a year and a half now."

"How do you find conditions in America?"

"I haven't been to America for months. I'm in business in Prague, representing a couple of concerns there. They don't know about me down there."

Alix smiled.

"Remember the night of George Hardt's bachelor dinner here?" said Charlie. "By the way, what's become of Claude Fessenden?"

Alix lowered his voice confidentially: "He's in Paris, but he doesn't come here any more. Paul doesn't allow it. He ran up a bill of thirty thousand francs, charging all his drinks and his lunches, and usually his dinner, for more than a year. And when Paul finally told him he had to pay, he gave him a bad check."

Alix shook his head sadly.

"I don't understand it, such a dandy fellow. Now he's all bloated up — " He made a plump apple of his hands.

Charlie watched a group of strident queens installing themselves in a corner.

"Nothing affects them," he thought. "Stocks rise and fall, people loaf or work, but they go on forever." The place oppressed him. He called for the dice and shook with Alix for the drink.

"Here for long, Mr. Wales?"

"I'm here for four or five days to see my little girl."

"Oh-h! You have a little girl?"

Outside, the fire-red, gas-blue, ghost-green signs shone smokily through the tranquil rain. It was late afternoon and the streets were in movement; the *bistros* gleamed. At the corner of the Boulevard des Capucines he took a taxi. The Place de la Concorde moved by in pink majesty; they crossed the logical Seine, and Charlie felt the sudden provincial quality of the Left Bank.

Charlie directed his taxi to the Avenue de l'Opera, which was out of his way. But he wanted to see the blue hour spread over the magnificent façade, and imagine that the cab horns, playing endlessly the first few bars of *Le Plus que Lent*, were the trumpets of the Second Empire. They were closing the iron grill in front of Brentano's Book-store, and people were already at dinner behind the trim little bourgeois hedge of Duval's. He had never eaten at a really cheap restaurant in Paris. Five-course dinner, four francs fifty, eighteen cents, wine included. For some odd reason he wished that he had.

As they rolled on to the Left Bank and he felt its sudden provincialism, he thought. "I spoiled this city for myself. I didn't realize it, but the days came along one after the another, and then two years were gone, and everything was gone, and I was gone."

He was thirty-five, and good to look at. The

Irish mobility of his face was sobered by a deep wrinkle between his eyes. As he rang his brother-in-law's bell in the Rue Palatine, the wrinkle deepened till it pulled down his brows; he felt a cramping sensation in his belly. From behind the maid who opened the door darted a lovely little girl of nine who shrieked "Daddy!" and flew up, struggling like a fish, into his arms. She pulled his head around by one ear and set her cheek against his.

"My old pie," he said.

"Oh, daddy, daddy, daddy, daddy, dads, dads, dads!"

She drew him into the salon, where the family waited, a boy and a girl his daughter's age, his sister-in-law and her husband. He greeted Marion with his voice pitched carefully to avoid feigned enthusiasm or dislike, but her response was more frankly tepid, though she minimized her expression of unalterable distrust by directing her regard toward his child. The two men clasped hands in a friendly way and Lincoln Peters rested his for a moment on Charlie's shoulder.

The room was warm and comfortably American. The three children moved intimately about, playing through the yellow oblongs that led to other rooms; the cheer of six o'clock spoke in the eager smacks of the fire and the sounds of French activity in the kitchen. But Charlie did not relax; his heart sat up rigidly in his body and he drew confidence from his daughter, who from time to time came close to him, holding in her arms the doll he had brought.

"Really extemely well," he declared in answer to Lincoln's question. "There's a lot of business there that isn't moving at all, but we're doing even better than ever. In fact, damn well. I'm bringing my sister over from America next month to keep house for me. My income last year was bigger than it was when I had money. You see, the Czechs — "

His boasting was for a specific purpose; but after a moment, seeing a faint restiveness in Lincoln's eye, he changed the subject:

"Those are fine children of yours, well brought up, good manners."

"We think Honoria's a great little girl too."

Marion Peters came back from the kitchen. She was a tall woman with worried eyes, who had once possessed a fresh American loveliness. Charlie had never been sensitive to it and was always surprised when people spoke of how pretty she had been. From the first there had been an instinctive antipathy between them.

"Well, how do you find Honoria?" she asked.

"Wonderful. I was astonished how much she's grown in ten months. All the children are looking well."

"We haven't had a doctor for a year. How do you like being back in Paris?"

"It seems very funny to see so few Americans around."

"I'm delighted," Marion said vehemently. "Now at least you can go into a store without their assuming you're a millionaire. We've suffered like everybody, but on the whole it's a good deal pleasanter."

"But it was nice while it lasted," Charlie said. "We were a sort of royalty, almost infallible, with a sort of magic around us. In the bar this afternoon" — he stumbled, seeing his mistake — "there wasn't a man I knew."

She looked at him keenly. "I should think you'd have had enough of bars."

"I only stayed a minute. I take one drink every afternoon, and no more."

"Don't you want a cocktail before dinner?" Lincoln asked.

"I take only one drink every afternoon, and I've had that."

"I hope you keep to it," said Marion.

Her dislike was evident in the coldness with which she spoke, but Charlie only smiled; he had larger plans. Her very aggressiveness gave him an advantage, and he knew enough to wait. He wanted them to initiate the discussion of what they knew had brought him to Paris.

At dinner he couldn't decide whether Honoria was most like him or her mother. Fortunate if she didn't combine the traits of both that had brought them to disaster. A great wave of protectiveness went over him. He thought he knew what to do for her. He believed in character; he wanted to jump back a whole generation and trust in character again as the eternally valuable element. Everything else wore out.

He left soon after dinner, but not to go home. He was curious to see Paris by night with clearer and more judicious eyes than those of other days. He bought a *strapontin* for the Casino and watched Josephine Baker go through her chocolate arabesques.

After an hour he left and strolled toward Montmartre, up the Rue Pigalle into the Place Blanche. The rain had stopped and there were a few people in evening clothes disembarking from taxis in front of cabarets, and *cocottes* prowling singly or in pairs, and many Negroes. He passed a lighted door from which issued music, and stopped with the sense of familiarity; it was Bricktop's, where he had parted with so many hours and so much money. A few doors farther on he found another ancient rendezvous and incautiously put his head inside. Immediately an eager orchestra burst into sound, a pair of professional dancers leaped to their feet and a maître d'hôtel swooped toward him, crying, "Crowd just arriving sir!" But he withdrew quickly.

"You have to be damn drunk," he thought.

Zelli's was closed, the bleak and sinister cheap hotels surrounding it were dark; up in the Rue Blanche there was more light and a local, colloquial French crowd. The Poet's Cave had disappeared, but the two great mouths of the Café of

Heaven and the Café of Hell still yawned — even devoured, as he watched, the meager contents of a tourist bus — a German, a Japanese, and an American couple who glanced at him with frightened eyes.

So much for the effort and ingenuity of Montmartre. All the catering to vice and waste was on an utterly childish scale, and he suddenly realized the meaning of the word "dissipate" — to dissipate into thin air; to make nothing out of something. In the little hours of the night every move from place to place was an enormous human jump, an increase of paying for the privilege of slower and slower motion.

He remembered thousand-franc notes given to an orchestra for playing a single number, hundred-franc notes tossed to a doorman for calling a cab.

But it hadn't been given for nothing.

It had been given, even the most wildly squandered sum, as an offering to destiny that he might not remember the things most worth remembering, the things that now he would always remember — his child taken from his control, his wife escaped to a grave in Vermont.

In the glare of a *brasserie* a woman spoke to him. He bought her some eggs and coffee, and then, eluding her encouraging stare, gave her a twenty-franc note and took a taxi to his hotel.

II

He woke upon a fine fall day — football weather. The depression of yesterday was gone and he liked the people on the streets. At noon he sat opposite Honoria at Le Grand Vatel, the only restaurant he could think of not reminiscent of champagne dinners and long luncheons that began at two and ended in a blurred and vague twilight.

"Now, how about vegetables? Oughtn't you to have some vegetables?"

"Well, yes."

"Here's *épinards* and *chou-fleur* and carrots and *haricots.*"

"I'd like *chou-fleur.*"

"Wouldn't you like to have two vegetables?"

"I usually only have one at lunch."

The waiter was pretending to be inordinately fond of children. *"Qu'elle est mignonne la petite! Elle parle exactement comme une Française."*

"How about dessert? Shall we wait and see?"

The waiter disappeared. Honoria looked at her father expectantly.

"What are we going to do?"

"First, we're going to that toy store in the Rue Saint-Honoré and buy you anything you like. And then we're going to the vaudeville at the Empire."

She hesitated. "I like it about the vaudeville, but not the toy store."

"Why not?"

"Well, you brought me this doll." She had it with her. "And I've got lots of things. And we're not rich any more, are we?"

"We never were. But today you are to have anything you want."

"All right," she agreed resignedly.

When there had been her mother and a French nurse he had been inclined to be strict; now he extended himself, reached out for a new tolerance; he must be both parents to her and not shut any of her out of communication.

"I want to get to know you," he said gravely. "First let me introduce myself. My name is Charles J. Wales of Prague."

"Oh, daddy!" her voice cracked with laughter.

"And who are you, please?" he persisted, and she accepted a rôle immediately: "Honoria Wales, Rue Palatine, Paris."

"Married or single?"

"No, not married. Single."

He indicated the doll. "But I see you have a child madame."

Unwilling to disinherit it, she took it to her heart and thought quickly: "Yes, I've been married, but I'm not married now. My husband is dead."

He went on quickly. "And the child's name?"

"Simone. That's after my best friend at school."

"I'm very pleased that you're doing so well at school."

"I'm third this month," she boasted. "Elsie" — that was her cousin — "is only about eighteenth, and Richard is about at the bottom."

"You like Richard and Elsie, don't you?"

"Oh, yes, I like Richard quite well and I like her all right."

Cautiously and casually he asked: "And Aunt Marion and Uncle Lincoln — which do you like best?"

"Oh, Uncle Lincoln, I guess."

He was increasingly aware of her presence. As they came in, a murmur of "... adorable" followed them, and now the people at the next table bent all their silences upon her, staring as if she were something no more conscious than a flower.

"Why don't I live with you?" she asked suddenly. "Because mamma's dead?"

"You must stay here and learn more French. It would have been hard for daddy to take care of you so well."

"I don't really need much taking care of any more. I do everything for myself."

Going out of the restaurant, a man and a woman unexpectedly hailed him.

"Well, the old Wales!"

"Hello there, Lorraine ... Dunc."

Sudden ghosts out of the past: Duncan Schaeffer, a friend from college. Lorraine Quarrles, a lovely, pale blonde of thirty; one of a crowd who had helped them make months into days in the lavish times of three years ago.

"My husband couldn't come this year," she said, in answer to his question. "We're poor as hell.

So he gave me two hundred a month and told me I could do my worst on that . . . This your little girl?"

"What about coming back and sitting down?" Duncan asked.

"Can't do it." He was glad for an excuse. As always, he felt Lorraine's passionate, provocative attraction, but his own rhythm was different now.

"Well, how about dinner?" she asked.

"I'm not free. Give me your address and let me call you."

"Charlie, I believe you're sober," she said judicially. "I honestly believe he's sober, Dunc. Pinch him and see if he's sober."

Charlie indicated Honoria with his head. They both laughed.

"What's your address?" said Duncan skeptically.

He hesitated, unwilling to give the name of the hotel.

"I'm not settled yet. I'd better call you. We're going to see the vaudeville at the Empire."

"There! That's what I want to do," Lorraine said. "I want to see some clowns and acrobats and jugglers. That's just what we'll do, Dunc."

"We've got to do an errand first," said Charlie. "Perhaps we'll see you there."

"All right, you snob . . . Good-by, beautiful little girl."

Honoria bobbed politely.

Somehow, an unwelcome encounter. They liked him because he was functioning, because he was serious; they wanted to see him, because he was stronger than they were now, because they wanted to draw a certain sustenance from his strength.

At the Empire, Honoria proudly refused to sit upon her father's folded coat. She was already an individual with a code of her own, and Charlie was more and more absorbed by the desire of putting a little of himself into her before she crystallized utterly. It was hopeless to try to know her in so short a time.

Between the acts they came upon Duncan and Lorraine in the lobby where the band was playing.

"Have a drink?"

"All right, but not up at the bar. We'll take a table."

"The perfect father."

Listening abstractedly to Lorraine, Charlie watched Honoria's eyes leave their table, and he followed them wistfully about the room, wondering what they saw. He met her glance and she smiled.

"I liked that lemonade," she said.

What had she said? What had he expected? Going home in a taxi afterward, he pulled her over until her head rested against his chest.

"Darling, do you ever think about your mother?"

"Yes, sometimes," she answered vaguely.

"I don't want you to forget her. Have you got a picture of her?"

"Yes, I think so. Anyhow, Aunt Marion has. Why don't you want me to forget her?"

"She loved you very much."

"I loved her too."

They were silent for a moment.

"Daddy, I want to come and live with you," she said suddenly.

His heart leaped; he had wanted it to come like this.

"Aren't you perfectly happy?"

"Yes, but I love you better than anybody. And you love me better than anybody, don't you, now that mummy's dead?"

"Of course I do. But you won't always like me best, honey. You'll grow up and meet somebody your own age and go marry him and forget you ever had a daddy."

"Yes, that's true," she agreed tranquilly.

He didn't go in. He was coming back at nine o'clock and he wanted to keep himself fresh and new for the thing he must say then.

"When you're safe inside, just show yourself in the window."

"All right. Good-by, dads, dads, dads, dads."

He waited in the dark street until she appeared, all warm and glowing in the window above and kissed her fingers out into the night.

III

They were waiting. Marion sat behind the coffee service in a dignified black dinner dress that just faintly suggested mourning. Lincoln was walking up and down with the animation of one who had already been talking. They were as anxious as he was to get into the question. He opened it almost immediately:

"I suppose you know what I want to see you about — why I really came to Paris."

Marion played with the black stars on her necklace and frowned.

"I'm awfully anxious to have a home," he continued. "And, I'm awfully anxious to have Honoria in it. I appreciate your taking in Honoria for her mother's sake, but things have changed now" — he hesitated and then continued more forcibly — "changed radically with me, and I want to ask you to reconsider the matter. It would be silly for me to deny that about three years ago I was acting badly — "

Marion looked up at him with hard eyes.

" — but all that's over. As I told you, I haven't had more than a drink a day for over a year, and I take that drink deliberately, so that the idea of alcohol won't get too big in my imagination. You see the idea?"

"No," said Marion succinctly.

"It's a sort of stunt I set myself. It keeps the matter in proportion."

"I get you," said Lincoln. "You don't want to admit it's got any attraction for you."

"Something like that. Sometimes I forget and don't take it. But I try to take it. Anyhow, I couldn't afford to drink in my position. The people I represent are more than satisfied with what I've done, and I'm bringing my sister over from Burlington to keep house for me, and I want awfully to have Honoria too. You know that even when her mother and I weren't getting along well we never let anything that happened touch Honoria. I know she's fond of me and I know I'm able to take care of her and — well, there you are. How do you feel about it?"

He knew that now he would have to take a beating. It would last an hour or two hours, and it would be difficult, but if he modulated his inevitable resentment to the chastened attitude of the reformed sinner, he might win his point in the end.

Keep your temper, he told himself. You don't want to be justified. You want Honoria.

Lincoln spoke first: "We've been talking it over ever since we got your letter last month. We're happy to have Honoria here. She's a dear little thing, and we're glad to be able to help her, but of course that isn't the question — "

Marion interrupted suddenly. "How long are you going to stay sober, Charlie?" she asked.

"Permanently, I hope."

"How can anybody count on that?"

"You know I never did drink heavily until I gave up business and came over here with nothing to do. Then Helen and I began to run around with — "

"Please leave Helen out of it. I can't bear to hear you talk about her like that."

He stared at her grimly; he had never been certain how fond of each other the sisters were in life.

"My drinking only lasted about a year and a half — from the time we came over until I — collapsed."

"It was time enough."

"It was time enough," he agreed.

"My duty is entirely to Helen," she said. "I try to think what she would have wanted me to do. Frankly, from the night you did that terrible thing you haven't really existed for me. I can't help that. She was my sister."

"Yes."

"When she was dying she asked me to look out for Honoria. If you hadn't been in a sanitarium then, it might have helped matters."

He had no answer.

"I'll never in my life be able to forget the morning when Helen knocked at my door, soaked to the skin and shivering and said you'd locked her out."

Charlied gripped the sides of the chair. This was more difficult than he expected; he wanted to launch out into a long expostulation and explanation, but he only said: "The night I locked her out — " and she interrupted. "I don't feel up to going over that again."

After a moment's silence Lincoln said: "We're getting off the subject. You want Marion to set aside her legal guardianship and give you Honoria. I think the main point for her is whether she has confidence in you or not."

"I don't blame Marion," Charlie said slowly, "but I think she can have entire confidence in me. I had a good record up to three years ago. Of course, it's within human possibilities I might go wrong any time. But if we wait much longer I'll lose Honoria's childhood and my chance for a home." He shook his head, "I'll simply lose her, don't you see?"

"Yes, I see," said Lincoln.

"Why didn't you think of all this before?" Marion asked.

"I suppose I did, from time to time, but Helen and I were getting along badly. When I consented to the guardianship, I was flat on my back in a sanitarium and the market had cleaned me out. I knew I'd acted badly, and I thought if it would bring any peace to Helen, I'd agree to anything. But now it's different. I'm functioning, I'm behaving damn well, so far as — "

"Please don't swear at me," Marion said.

He looked at her, startled. With each remark the force of her dislike became more and more apparent. She had built up all her fear of life into one wall and faced it toward him. This trivial reproof was possibly the result of some trouble with the cook several hours before. Charlie became increasingly alarmed at leaving Honoria in this atmosphere of hostility against himself; sooner or later it would come out, in a word here, a shake of the head there, and some of that distrust would be irrevocably implanted in Honoria. But he pulled his temper down out of his face and shut it up inside him; he had won a point, for Lincoln realized the absurdity of Marion's remark and asked her lightly since when she had objected to the word "damn."

"Another thing," Charlie said: "I'm able to give her certain advantages now. I'm going to take a French governess to Prague with me. I've got a lease on a new apartment — "

He stopped, realizing that he was blundering. They couldn't be expected to accept with equanimity the fact that his income was again twice as large as their own.

"I suppose you can give her more luxuries than we can," said Marion. "When you were throwing away money we were living along watching every ten francs ... I suppose you'll start doing it again."

"Oh, no," he said. "I've learned. I worked hard for ten years, you know — until I got lucky in the market, like so many people. Terribly lucky. It won't happen again."

There was a long silence. All of them felt their nerves straining, and for the first time in a year Charlie wanted a drink. He was sure now that Lincoln Peters wanted him to have his child.

Marion shuddered suddenly; part of her saw that Charlie's feet were planted on the earth now, and her own maternal feeling recognized the naturalness of his desire; but she had lived for a long time with a prejudice — a prejudice founded on a curious disbelief in her sister's happiness, and which, in the shock of one terrible night, had turned to hatred for him. It had all happened at a point in her life where the discouragement of ill health and adverse circumstances made it necessary for her to believe in tangible villainy and a tangible villain.

"I can't help what I think!" she cried out suddenly. "How much you were responsible for Helen's death, I don't know. It's something you'll have to square with your own conscience."

An electric current of agony surged through him; for a moment he was almost on his feet, an unuttered sound echoing in his throat. He hung on to himself for a moment, another moment.

"Hold on there," said Lincoln uncomfortably. "I never thought you were responsible for that."

"Helen died of heart trouble," Charlie said dully.

"Yes, heart trouble." Marion spoke as if the phrase had another meaning for her.

Then, in the flatness that followed her outburst, she saw him plainly and she knew he had somehow arrived at control over the situation. Glancing at her husband, she found no help from him, and as abruptly as if it were a matter of no importance, she threw up the sponge.

"Do what you like!" she cried, springing up from her chair. "She's your child. I'm not the person to stand in your way. I think if it were my child I'd rather see her — " She managed to check herself. "You two decide it. I can't stand this. I'm sick. I'm going to bed."

She hurried from the room; after a moment Lincoln said:

"This has been a hard day for her. You know how strongly she feels — " His voice was almost apologetic: "When a woman gets an idea in her head."

"Of course."

"It's going to be all right. I think she sees now that you — can provide for the child, and we can't very well stand in your way or Honoria's way."

"Thank you, Lincoln."

"I'd better go along and see how she is."

"I'm going."

He was still trembling when he reached the street, but a walk down the Rue Bonaparte to the *quais* set him up, and as he crossed the Seine, fresh and new by the *quai* lamps, he felt exultant. But back in his room he couldn't sleep. The image of Helen haunted him. Helen whom he had loved so until they had senselessly begun to abuse each other's love, tear it into shreds. On that terrible February night that Marion remembered so vividly, a slow quarrel had gone on for hours. There was a scene at the Florida, and then he attempted to take her home, and then she kissed young Webb at a table; after that there was what she had hysterically said. When he arrived home alone he turned the key in the lock in wild anger. How could he know she would arrive an hour later alone, that there would be a snowstorm in which she wandered about in slippers, too confused to find a taxi? Then the aftermath, her escaping pneumonia by a miracle, and all the attendant horror. They were "reconciled," but that was the beginning of the end, as Marion, who had seen with her own eyes and who imagined it to be one of many scenes from her sister's martyrdom, never forgot.

Going over it again brought Helen nearer, and in the white, soft light that steals upon half sleep near morning he found himself talking to her again. She said that he was perfectly right about Honoria and that she wanted Honoria to be with him. She said she was glad he was being good and doing better. She said a lot of other things — very friendly things — but she was in a swing in a white dress, and swinging faster and faster all the time, so that at the end he could not hear clearly all that she said.

IV

He woke up feeling happy. The door of the world was open again. He made plans, vistas, futures for Honoria and himself, but suddenly he grew sad, remembering all the plans he and Helen had made. She had not planned to die. The present was the thing — work to do and someone to love. But not to love too much, for he knew the injury that a father can do to a daughter or a mother to a son by attaching them too closely: afterward, out in the world, the child would seek in the marriage partner the same blind tenderness and, failing probably to find it, turn against love and life.

It was another bright, crisp day. He called Lincoln Peters at the bank where he worked and asked if he could count on taking Honoria when he left for Prague. Lincoln agreed that there was no reason for delay. One thing — the legal guardianship. Marion wanted to retain that a while longer. She was upset by the whole matter, and it would oil things if she felt that the situation was still in her control for another year. Charlie agreed, wanting only the tangible, visible child.

Then the question of a governess. Charles sat in a gloomy agency and talked to a cross Béarnaise and to a buxom Breton peasant, neither of whom he could have endured. There were others whom he would see tomorrow.

He lunched with Lincoln Peters at Griffons, trying to keep down his exultation.

"There's nothing quite like your own child," Lincoln said. "But you understand how Marion feels too."

"She's forgotten how hard I worked for seven years there," Charlie said. "She just remembers one night."

"There's another thing." Lincoln hesitated.

"While you and Helen were tearing around Europe throwing money away, we were just getting along. I didn't touch any of the prosperity because I never got ahead enough to carry anything but my insurance. I think Marion felt there was some kind of injustice in it — you not even working toward the end, and getting richer and richer."

"It went just as quick as it came." said Charlie.

"Yes, a lot of it stayed in the hands of *chasseurs* and saxophone players and maîtres d'hôtel — well, the big party's over now. I just said that to explain Marion's feeling about those crazy years. If you drop in about six o'clock tonight before Marion's too tired, we'll settle the details on the spot."

Back at his hotel, Charlie found a *pneumatique* that had been redirected from the Ritz bar where Charlie had left his address for the purpose of finding a certain man.

"Dear Charlie:

"You were so strange when we saw you the other day that I wondered if I did something to offend you. If so, I'm not conscious of it. In fact, I have thought about you too much for the last year, and it's always been in the back of my mind that I might see you if I came over here. We did have such good times that crazy spring, like the night you and I stole the butcher's tricycle, and the time we tried to call on the president and you had the old derby rim and the wire cane. Everybody seems so old lately, but I don't feel old a bit. Couldn't we get together some time today for old time's sake? I've got a vile hang-over for the moment, but will be feeling better this afternoon and will look for you about five in the sweatshop at the Ritz.

"Always devotedly,
"LORRAINE."

His first feeling was one of awe that he had actually, in his mature years, stolen a tricycle and pedaled Lorraine all over the Étoile between the small hours and dawn. In retrospect it was a nightmare. Locking out Helen didn't fit in with any other act of his life, but the tricycle incident did — it was one of many. How many weeks or months of dissipation to arrive at that condition of utter irresponsibility?

He tried to picture how Lorraine had appeared to him then — very attractive; Helen was unhappy about it, though she said nothing. Yesterday, in the restaurant, Lorraine had seemed trite, blurred, worn away. He emphatically did not want to see her, and he was glad Alix had not given away his hotel address. It was a relief to think, instead, of Honoria, to think of Sundays spent with her and of saying good morning to her and of knowing she was there in his house at night, drawing her breath in the darkness.

At five he took a taxi and bought presents for all the Peters — a piquant cloth doll, a box of Roman soldiers, flowers for Marion, big linen handkerchiefs for Lincoln.

He saw when he arrived in the apartment that Marion had accepted the inevitable. She greeted him now as though he were a recalcitrant member of the family, rather than a menacing outsider. Honoria had been told she was going; Charlie was glad to see that her tact made her conceal her excessive happiness. Only on his lap did she whisper her delight and the question "When?" before she slipped away with the other children.

He and Marion were alone for a minute in the room, and on an impulse he spoke out boldly:

"Family quarrels are bitter things. They don't go according to any rules. They're not like aches or wounds; they're more like splits in the skin that won't heal because there's not enough material. I wish you and I could be on better terms."

"Some things are hard to forget," she answered. "It's a question of confidence." There was no answer to this and presently she asked, "When do you propose to take her?"

"As soon as I can get a governess. I hoped the day after tomorrow."

"That's impossible. I've got to get her things in shape. Not before Saturday."

He yielded. Coming back into the room, Lincoln offered him a drink.

"I'll take my daily whiskey," he said.

It was warm here, it was a home, people together by a fire. The children felt very safe and important; the mother and father were serious, watchful. They had things to do for the children more important than his visit here. A spoonful of medicine was, after all, more important than the strained relations between Marion and himself. They were not dull people, but they were very much in the grip of life and circumstances. He wondered if he couldn't do something to get Lincoln out of his rut at the bank.

A long peal at the door-bell; the *bonne à tout faire* passed through and went down the corridor. The door opened upon another long ring, and then voices, and the three in the salon looked up expectantly; Richard moved to bring the corridor within his range of vision, and Marion rose. Then the maid came back along the corridor, closely followed by the voices, which developed under the light into Duncan Schaeffer and Lorraine Quarrles.

They were gay, they were hilarious, they were roaring with laughter. For a moment Charlie was astounded; unable to understand how they ferreted out the Peters' address.

"Ah-h-h!" Duncan wagged his finger roguishly at Charlie. "Ah-h-h!"

They both slid down another cascade of laughter. Anxious and at a loss, Charlie shook hands with them quickly and presented them to Lincoln and Marion. Marion nodded, scarcely speaking. She had drawn back a step toward the fire; her little girl stood beside her, and Marion put an arm about her shoulder.

With growing annoyance at the intrusion, Charlie waited for them to explain themselves. After some concentration Duncan said:

"We came to invite you out to dinner. Lorraine and I insist that all this shishi, cagy business 'bout your address got to stop."

Charlie came closer to them, as if to force them backward down the corridor.

"Sorry, but I can't. Tell me where you'll be and I'll phone you in half an hour."

This made no impression. Lorraine sat down suddenly on the side of a chair, and focusing her eyes on Richard, cried, "Oh, what a nice little boy! Come here, little boy." Richard glanced at his mother, but did not move. With a perceptible shrug of her shoulders, Lorraine turned back to Charlie.

"Come and dine. Sure your cousins won' mine. See you so sel'om. Or solemn."

"I can't," said Charlie sharply. "You two have dinner and I'll phone you."

Her voice became suddenly unpleasant. "All right, we'll go. But I remember once when you hammered on my door at four a.m. I was enough of a good sport to give you a drink. Come on Dunc."

Still in slow motion, with blurred, angry faces, with uncertain feet, they retired along the corridor.

"Good night," Charlie said.

"Good night!" responded Lorraine emphatically.

When he went back into the salon Marion had not moved, only now her son was standing in the circle of her other arm. Lincoln was still swinging Honoria back and forth like a pendulum from side to side.

"What an outrage!" Charlie broke out. "What an absolute outrage!"

Neither of them answered. Charlie dropped into an armchair, picked up his drink, set it down again and said:

"People I haven't seen for two years having the colossal nerve — "

He broke off. Marion had made the sound "Oh!" in one swift, furious breath, turned her body from him with a jerk and left the room.

Lincoln set down Honoria carefully.

"You children go in and start your soup," he said, and when they obeyed he said to Charlie:

"Marion's not well and she can't stand shocks. That kind of people make her really physically sick."

"I didn't tell them to come here. They wormed your name out of somebody. They deliberately —"

"Well, it's too bad. It doesn't help matters. Excuse me a minute."

Left alone, Charlie sat tense in his chair. In the next room he could hear the children eating, talking in monosyllables, already oblivious to the scene between their elders. He heard a murmur of conversation from a farther room and then the ticking bell of a telephone receiver picked up, and in a panic he moved to the other side of the room and out of earshot.

In a minute Lincoln came back. "Look here, Charlie, I think we'd better call off dinner for tonight. Marion's in bad shape."

"Is she angry with me?"

"Sort of," he said, almost roughly. "She's not strong and — "

"You mean she's changed her mind about Honoria?"

"She's pretty bitter right now. I don't know. You phone me at the bank tomorrow."

"I wish you'd explain to her I never dreamed these people would come here. I'm just as sore as you are."

"I couldn't explain anything to her now."

Charlie got up. He took his coat and hat and started down the corridor. Then he opened the door of the dining room and said in a strange voice, "Good night, children."

Honoria rose and ran around the table to hug him.

"Good night, sweetheart," he said vaguely, and then trying to make his voice more tender, trying to conciliate something, "Good night, dear children."

V

Charlie went directly to the Ritz bar with the furious idea of finding Lorraine and Duncan, but they were not there, and he realized that in any case there was nothing he could do. He had not touched his drink at the Peters, and now he ordered a whisky-and-soda. Paul came over to say hello.

"It's a great change," he said sadly. "We do about half the business we did. So many fellows I hear about back in the States lost everything, maybe not in the first crash, but then in the second. Your friend George Hardt lost every cent, I hear. Are you back in the States?"

"No, I'm in business in Prague."

"I heard that you lost a lot in the crash."

"I did," and he added grimly, "but I lost everything I wanted in the boom."

"Selling short."

"Something like that."

Again the memory of those days swept over him like a nightmare — the people they had met travelling; the people who couldn't add a row of figures or speak a coherent sentence. The little man Helen had consented to dance with at the ship's party, who had insulted her ten feet from the table; the women and girls carried screaming with drinks or drugs out of public places —

— The men who locked their wives out in the snow, because the snow of twenty-nine wasn't real snow. If you didn't want it to be snow, you just paid some money.

He went to the phone and called Peters' apartment; Lincoln answered.

"I called up because this thing is on my mind. Has Marion said anything definite?"

"Marion's sick," Lincoln answered shortly. "I know this thing isn't altogether your fault, but I can't have her go to pieces about it. I'm afraid we'll have to let it slide for six months; I can't take the chance of working her up to this state again."

"I see."

"I'm sorry, Charlie."

He went back to his table. His whisky glass was empty, but he shook his head when Alix looked at it questionably. There wasn't much he could do now except send Honoria some things; he would send her a lot of things tomorrow. He thought rather angrily that this was just money — he had given so many people money . . .

"No, no more," he said to the waiter. "What do I owe you?"

He would come back some day; they couldn't make him pay forever. But he wanted his child, and nothing was much good now, beside that fact. He wasn't young any more, with a lot of nice things and dreams to have by himself. He was absolutely sure Helen wouldn't have wanted him to be so alone.

GUSTAVE FLAUBERT

A Simple Heart

Translated by Robert Baldick

I

For half a century the women of Pont-l'Évêque envied Mme Aubain her maidservant Félicité.

In return for a hundred francs a year she did all the cooking and the housework, the sewing, the washing, and the ironing. She could bridle a horse, fatten poultry, and churn butter, and she remained faithful to her mistress, who was by no means an easy person to get on with.

Mme Aubain had married a young fellow who was good-looking but badly-off, and who died at the beginning of 1809, leaving her with two small children and a pile of debts. She then sold all her property except for the farms of Toucques and Geffosses, which together brought in five thousand francs a year at the most, and left her house at Saint-Melaine for one behind the covered market which was cheaper to run and had belonged to her family.

This house had a slate roof and stood between an alley-way and a lane leading down to the river. Inside there were differences in level which were the cause of many a stumble. A narrow entrance-hall separated the kitchen from the parlour, where Mme Aubain sat all day long in a wicker easy-chair by the window. Eight mahogany chairs were lined up against the white-painted wainscoting, and under the barometer stood an old piano loaded with a pyramid of boxes and cartons. On either side of the chimney-piece, which was carved out of yellow marble in the Louis Quinze style, there was a tapestry-covered arm-chair, and in the middle was a clock designed to look like a temple of Vesta. The whole room smelt a little musty, as the floor was on a lower level than the garden.

On the first floor was 'Madame's' bedroom — very spacious, with a patterned wallpaper of pale flowers and a portrait of 'Monsieur' dressed in what had once been the height of fashion. It opened into a smaller room in which there were two cots, without mattresses. Then came the drawing-room, which was always shut and full of furniture covered with dust-sheets. Next there was a passage leading to the study, where books and papers filled the shelves of a book-case in three sections built round a big writing-table of dark wood. The two end panels were hidden under pen-and-ink drawings, landscapes in gouache, and etchings by Audran, souvenirs of better days and bygone luxury. On the second floor a dormer window gave light to Félicité's room, which looked out over the fields.

Every day Félicité got up at dawn, so as not to miss Mass, and worked until evening without stopping. Then, once dinner was over, the plates and dishes put away, and the door bolted, she piled ashes on the log fire and went to sleep in front of the hearth, with her rosary in her hands. Nobody could be more stubborn when it came to haggling over prices, and as for cleanliness, the shine on her saucepans was the despair of all the other servants. Being of a thrifty nature, she ate slowly, picking up from the table the crumbs from her loaf of bread — a twelve-pound loaf which was baked specially for her and lasted her twenty days.

All the year round she wore a kerchief of printed calico fastened behind with a pin, a bonnet which covered her hair, grey stockings, a red skirt, and over her jacket a bibbed apron such as hospital nurses wear.

Her face was thin and her voice was sharp. At twenty-five she was often taken for forty; once she reached fifty, she stopped looking any age in particular. Always silent and upright and deliberate in her movements, she looked like a wooden doll driven by clock-work.

II

Like everyone else, she had had her love-story.

Her father, a mason, had been killed when he fell off some scaffolding. Then her mother died, and when her sisters went their separate ways, a farmer took her in, sending her, small as she was, to look after the cows out in the fields. She went about in rags, shivering with cold, used to lie flat on the ground to drink water out of the ponds, would be beaten for no reason at all, and was finally turned out of the house for stealing thirty sous, a theft of which she was innocent. She found work at another farm, looking after the poultry, and as she was liked by her employers the other servants were jealous of her.

One August evening — she was eighteen at the time — they took her off to the fête at Colleville. From the start she was dazed and bewildered by the noise of the fiddles, the lamps in the trees, the medley of gaily coloured dresses, the gold crosses and lace, and the throng of people jigging up and down. She was standing shyly on one side when a smart young fellow, who had been leaning on the shaft of a cart, smoking his pipe, came up and asked her to dance. He treated her to cider, coffee, girdle-cake, and a silk neckerchief, and imagining that she knew what he was after, offered to see her home. At the edge of a field of oats, he pushed her roughly to the ground. Thoroughly frightened, she started screaming for help. He took to his heels.

Another night, on the road to Beaumont, she tried to get past a big, slow-moving waggon loaded with hay, and as she was squeezing by she recognized Théodore.

He greeted her quite calmly, saying that she must forgive him for the way he had behaved to her, as 'it was the drink that did it'.

She did not know what to say in reply and felt like running off.

Straight away he began talking about the crops and the notabilities of the commune, saying that his father had left Colleville for the farm at Les Écots, so that they were now neighbours.

'Ah!' she said.

He added that his family wanted to see him settled but that he was in no hurry and was waiting to find a wife to suit his fancy. She lowered her head. Then he asked her if she was thinking of getting married. She answered with a smile that it was mean of him to make fun of her.

'But I'm not making fun of you!' he said. 'I swear I'm not!'

He put his left arm around her waist, and she walked on supported by his embrace. Soon they slowed down. There was a gentle breeze blowing, the stars were shining, the huge load of hay was swaying about in front of them, and the four horses were raising clouds of dust as they shambled along. Then, without being told, they turned off to the right. He kissed her once more and she disappeared into the darkness.

The following week Théodore got her to grant him several rendezvous.

They would meet at the bottom of a farm-yard, behind a wall, under a solitary tree. She was not ignorant of life as young ladies are, for the animals had taught her a great deal; but her reason and an instinctive sense of honour prevented her from giving way. The resistance she put up inflamed Théodore's passion to such an extent that in order to satisfy it (or perhaps out of sheer naïvety) he proposed to her. At first she refused to believe him, but he swore that he was serious.

Soon afterwards he had a disturbing piece of news to tell her: the year before, his parents had paid a man to do his military service for him, but now he might be called up again any day, and the idea of going into the army frightened him. In Félicité's eyes this cowardice of his appeared to be a proof of his affection, and she loved him all the more for it. Every night she would steal out to meet him, and every night Théodore would plague her with his worries and entreaties.

In the end he said that he was going to the Prefecture himself to make inquiries, and that he would come and tell her how matters stood the following Sunday, between eleven and midnight.

At the appointed hour she hurried to meet her sweetheart, but found one of his friends waiting for her instead.

He told her that she would not see Théodore again. To make sure of avoiding conscription, he had married a very rich old woman, Mme Lehoussais of Toucques.

Her reaction was an outburst of frenzied grief. She threw herself on the ground, screaming and calling on God, and lay moaning all alone in the open until sunrise. Then she went back to the farm and announced her intention of leaving. At the end of the month, when she had received her wages, she wrapped her small belongings up in a kerchief and made her way to Pont-l'Évêque.

In front of the inn there, she sought information from a woman in a widow's bonnet, who, as it happened, was looking for a cook. The girl did not know much about cooking, but she seemed so willing and expected so little that finally Mme Aubain ended up by saying: 'Very well, I will take you on.'

A quarter of an hour later Félicité was installed in her house.

At first she lived there in a kind of fearful awe caused by the style of the house, and by the memory of 'Monsieur' brooding over everything. Paul and Virginie, the boy aged seven and the girl barely four, seemed to her to be made of some precious substance. She used to carry them about pick-a-back, and when Mme Aubain told her not to keep on kissing them she was cut to the quick. All the same, she was happy now, for her pleasant surroundings had dispelled her grief.

On Thursdays, a few regular visitors came in to play Boston, and Félicité got the cards and the footwarmers ready beforehand. They always arrived punctually at eight, and left before the clock struck eleven.

Every Monday morning the second-hand dealer who lived down the alley put all his junk out on the pavement. Then the hum of voices began to fill the town, mingled with the neighing of horses, the bleating of lambs, the grunting of pigs, and the rattle of carts in the streets.

About midday, when the market was in full swing, a tall old peasant with a hooked nose and his cap on the back of his head would appear at the door. This was Robelin, the farmer from

Geffosses. A little later, and Liébard, the farmer from Toucques, would arrive — a short, fat, red-faced fellow in a grey jacket and leather gaiters fitted with spurs.

Both men had hens or cheeses they wanted to sell to 'Madame'. But Félicité was up to all their tricks and invariably outwitted them, so that they went away full of respect for her.

From time to time Mme Aubain had a visit from an uncle of hers, the Marquis de Grémanville, who had been ruined by loose living and was now living at Falaise on his last remaining scrap of property. He always turned up at lunch-time, accompanied by a hideous poodle which dirtied all the furniture with its paws. However hard he tried to behave like a gentleman, even going so far as to raise his hat every time he mentioned 'my late father', the force of habit was usually too much for him, for he would start pouring himself one glass after another and telling bawdy stories. Félicité used to push him gently out of the house, saying politely: 'You've had quite enough, Monsieur de Grémanville. See you another time!' and shutting the door on him.

She used to open it with pleasure to M. Bourais, who was a retired solicitor. His white tie and his bald head, his frilled shirt-front and his ample brown frock-coat, the way he had of rounding his arm to take a pinch of snuff, and indeed everything about him made an overwhelming impression on her such as we feel when we meet some outstanding personality.

As he looked after 'Madame's' property, he used to shut himself up with her for hours in 'Monsieur's' study.

He lived in dread of compromising his reputation, had a tremendous respect for the Bench, and laid claim to some knowledge of Latin.

To give the children a little painless instruction, he made them a present of a geography book with illustrations. These represented scenes in different parts of the world, such as cannibals wearing feather head-dresses, a monkey carrying off a young lady, Bedouins in the desert, a whale being harpooned, and so on.

Paul explained these pictures to Félicité, and that indeed was all the education she ever had. As for the children, they were taught by Guyot, a poor devil employed at the Town Hall, who was famous for his beautiful handwriting, and who had a habit of sharpening his penknife on his boots.

When the weather was fine the whole household used to set off early for a day at the Geffosses farm.

The farm-yard there was on a slope, with the house in the middle; and the sea, in the distance, looked like a streak of grey. Félicité would take some slices of cold meat out of her basket, and they would have their lunch in a room adjoining the dairy. It was all the remained of a country house which had fallen into ruin, and the wall-paper hung in shreds, fluttering in the draught. Mme Aubain used to sit with bowed head, absorbed in her memories, so that the children were afraid to talk. 'Why don't you run along and play?' she would say, and away they went.

Paul climbed up into the barn, caught birds, played ducks and drakes on the pond, or banged with a stick on the great casks, which sounded just like drums.

Virginie fed the rabbits, or scampered off to pick cornflowers, showing her little embroidered knickers as she ran.

One autumn evening they came home through the fields. The moon, which was in its first quarter, lit up part of the sky, and there was some mist floating like a scarf over the winding Toucques. The cattle, lying out in the middle of the pasture, looked peacefully at the four people walking by. In the third field a few got up and made a half circle in front of them.

'Don't be frightened!' said Félicité, and crooning softly, she stroked the back of the nearest animal. It turned about and the others did the same. But while they were crossing the next field they suddenly heard a dreadful bellowing. It came from a bull which had been hidden by the mist, and which now came towards the two women.

Mme Aubain started to run.

'No! No!' said Félicité. 'Not so fast!'

All the same they quickened their pace, hearing behind them a sound of heavy breathing which came nearer and nearer. The bull's hooves thudded like hammers on the turf, and they realized that it had broken into a gallop. Turning round, Félicité tore up some clods of earth and flung them at its eyes. It lowered its muzzle and thrust its horns forward, trembling with rage and bellowing horribly.

By now Mme Aubain had got to the end of the field with her two children and was frantically looking for a way over the high bank. Félicité was still backing away from the bull, hurling clods of turf which blinded it, and shouting: 'Hurry! Hurry!'

Mme Aubain got down into the ditch, pushed first Virginie and then Paul up the other side, fell once or twice trying to climb the bank, and finally managed it with a valiant effort.

The bull had driven Félicité back against a gate, and its slaver was spurting into her face. In another second it would have gored her, but she just had time to slip between two of the bars, and the great beast halted in amazement.

This adventure was talked about at Pont-l'Évêque for a good many years, but Félicité never prided herself in the least on what she had done, as it never occurred to her that she had done anything heroic.

Virginie claimed all her attention, for the fright had affected the little girl's nerves, and M. Poupart, the doctor, recommended sea-bathing at Trouville.

In those days the resort had few visitors. Mme

Aubain made inquiries, consulted Bourais, and got everything ready as though for a long journey.

Her luggage went off in Liébard's cart the day before she left. The next morning he brought along two horses, one of which had a woman's saddle with a velvet back, while the other carried a cloak rolled up to make a kind of seat on its crupper. Mme Aubain sat on this, with Liébard in front. Félicité looked after Virginie on the other horse, and Paul mounted M. Lechaptois's donkey, which he had lent them on condition they took great care of it.

The road was so bad that it took two hours to travel the five miles to Toucques. The horses sank into the mud up to their pasterns and had to jerk their hind-quarters to get out; often they stumbled in the ruts, or else they had to jump. In some places, Liébard's mare came to a sudden stop, and while he waited patiently for her to move off again, he talked about the people whose properties bordered the road, adding moral reflexions to each story. For instance, in the middle of Toucques, as they were passing underneath some windows set in a mass of nasturtiums, he shrugged his shoulders and said:

'There's a Madame Lehoussais lives here. Now instead of taking a young man, she ...'

Félicité did not hear the rest for the horses had broken into a trot and the donkey was galloping along. All three turned down a bridle-path, a gate swung open, a couple of boys appeared, and everyone dismounted in front of a manure-heap right outside the farm-house door.

Old Mother Liébard welcomed her mistress with every appearance of pleasure. She served up a sirloin of beef for lunch, with tripe and black pudding, a fricassee of chicken, sparkling cider, a fruit tart and brandy-plums, garnishing the whole meal with compliments to Madame, who seemed to be enjoying better health, to Mademoiselle, who had turned into a 'proper little beauty', and to Monsieur Paul, who had 'filled out a lot'. Nor did she forget their deceased grandparents, whom the Liébards had known personally, having been in the family's service for several generations.

Like its occupants, the farm had an air of antiquity. The ceiling-beams were worm-eaten, the walls black with smoke, and the window-panes grey with dust. There was an oak dresser laden with all sorts of odds and ends — jugs, plates, pewter bowls, wolf-traps, sheep-shears, and an enormous syringe which amused the children. In the three yards outside there was not a single tree without either mushrooms at its base or mistletoe in its branches. Several had been blown down and had taken root again at the middle; all of them were bent under the weight of their apples. The thatched roofs, which looked like brown velvet and varied in thickness, weathered the fiercest winds, but the cart-shed was tumbling down. Mme Aubain said that she would have it seen to, and ordered the animals to be reharnessed.

It took them another half-hour to reach Trouville. The little caravan dismounted to make their way along the Écores, a cliff jutting out over the boats moored below; and three minutes later they got to the end of the quay and entered the courtyard of the Golden Lamb, the inn kept by Mère David.

After the first few days Virginie felt stronger, as a result of the change of air and the sea-bathing. Not having a costume, she went into the water in her chemise and her maid dressed her afterwards in a customs officer's hut which was used by the bathers.

In the afternoons they took the donkey and went off beyond the Roches-Noires, in the direction of Hennequeville. To begin with, the path went uphill between gentle slopes like the lawns in a park, and then came out on a plateau where pastureland and ploughed fields alternated. On either side there were holly-bushes standing out from the tangle of brambles, and here and there a big dead tree spread its zigzag branches against the blue sky.

They almost always rested in the same field, with Deauville on their left, Le Havre on their right, and the open sea in front. The water glittered in the sunshine, smooth as a mirror, and so still that the murmur it made was scarcely audible; unseen sparrows could be heard twittering, and the sky covered the whole scene with its huge canopy. Mme Aubain sat doing her needlework, Virginie plaited rushes beside her, Félicité gathered lavender, and Paul, feeling profoundly bored, longed to get up and go.

Sometimes they crossed the Toucques in a boat and hunted for shells. When the tide went out, sea-urchins, ormers, and jelly-fish were left behind; and the children scampered around, snatching at the foam-flakes carried on the wind. The sleepy waves, breaking on the sand, spread themselves out along the shore. The beach stretched as far as the eye could see, bounded on the land side by the dunes which separated it from the Marais, a broad meadow in the shape of an arena. When they came back that way, Trouville, on the distant hillside, grew bigger at every step, and with its medley of oddly assorted houses seemed to blossom out in gay disorder.

On exceptionally hot days they stayed in their room. The sun shone in dazzling bars of light between the slats of the blind. There was not a sound to be heard in the village, and not a soul to be seen down in the street. Everything seemed more peaceful in the prevailing silence. In the distance caulkers were hammering away at the boats, and the smell of tar was wafted along by a sluggish breeze.

The principal amusement consisted in watching the fishing-boats come in. As soon as they had passed the buoys, they started tacking. With their canvas partly lowered and their foresails blown out like balloons they glided through the splashing waves as far as the middle of the harbour, where they suddenly dropped anchor. Then each boat came alongside the quay, and the crew threw ashore their catch of quivering fish. A line of carts stood waiting, and women in cotton bonnets rushed forward to take the baskets and kiss their men.

One day one of these women spoke to Félicité, who came back to the inn soon after in a state of great excitement. She explained that she had found one of her sisters — and Nastasie Barette, now Leroux, made her appearance, with a baby at her breast, another child holding her right hand, and on her left a little sailor-boy, his arms akimbo and his cap over one ear.

Mme Aubain sent her off after a quarter of an hour. From then on they were forever hanging round the kitchen or loitering about when the family went for a walk, though the husband kept out of sight.

Félicité became quite attached to them. She bought them a blanket, several shirts, and a stove; and it was clear that they were bent on getting all they could out of her.

This weakness of hers annoyed Mme Aubain, who in any event disliked the familiar way in which the nephew spoke to Paul. And so, as Virginie had started coughing and the good weather was over, she decided to go back to Pont-l'Évêque.

M. Bourais advised her on the choice of a school; Caen was considered the best, so it was there that Paul was sent. He said good-bye bravely, feeling really rather pleased to be going to a place where he would have friends of his own.

Mme Aubain resigned herself to the loss of her son, knowing that it was unavoidable. Virginie soon got used to it. Félicité missed the din he used to make, but she was given something new to do which served as a distraction: from Christmas onwards she had to take the little girl to catechism every day.

III

After genuflecting at the door, she walked up the centre aisle under the nave, opened the door of Mme Aubain's pew, sat down, and started looking about her.

The choir-stalls were all occupied, with the boys on the right and the girls on the left, while the curé stood by the lectern. In one of the stained-glass windows in the apse the Holy Ghost looked down on the Virgin; another window showed her kneeling before the Infant Jesus; and behind the tabernacle there was a wood-carving of St Michael slaying the dragon.

The priest began with a brief outline of sacred history. Listening to him, Félicité saw in imagination the Garden of Eden, the Flood, the Tower of Babel, cities burning, peoples dying, and idols being overthrown; and this dazzling vision left her with a great respect for the Almighty and profound fear of His wrath.

Then she wept as she listened to the story of the Passion. Why had they crucified Him, when He loved children, fed the multitudes, healed the blind, and had chosen out of humility to be born among the poor, on the litter of a stable? The sowing of the seed, the reaping of the harvest, the pressing of the grapes — all those familiar things of which the Gospels speak had their place in her life. God had sanctified them in passing, so that she loved the lambs more tenderly for love of the Lamb of God, and the doves for the sake of the Holy Ghost.

She found it difficult, however, to imagine what the Holy Ghost looked like, for it was not just a bird but a fire as well, and sometimes a breath. She wondered whether that was its light she had seen flitting about the edge of the marshes at night, whether that was its breath she had felt driving the clouds across the sky, whether that was its voice she had heard in the sweet music of the bells. And she sat in silent adoration, delighting in the coolness of the walls and the quiet of the church.

Of dogma she neither understood nor even tried to understand anything. The curé discoursed, the children repeated their lesson, and she finally dropped off to sleep, waking up suddenly at the sound of the sabots clattering across the flagstones as they left the church.

It was in this manner, simply by hearing it expounded, that she learnt her catechism, for her religious education had been neglected in her youth. From then on she copied all Virginie's observances, fasting when she did and going to confession with her. On the feast of Corpus Christi the two of them made an altar of repose together.

The preparations for Virginie's first communion caused her great anxiety. She worried over her shoes, her rosary, her missal, and her gloves. And how she trembled as she helped Mme Aubain to dress the child!

All through the Mass her heart was in her mouth. One side of the choir was hidden from her by M. Bourais, but directly opposite her she could see the flock of maidens, looking like a field of snow with their white crowns perched on top of their veils; and she recognized her little darling from a distance by her dainty neck and her rapt attitude. The bell tinkled. Every head bowed low, and there was a silence. Then, to the thunderous accompaniment of the organ, choir and congregation joined in singing the *Agnus Dei.* Next the boys' procession began, and after that the girls got up from their seats. Slowly, their hands joined in prayer, they went towards the brightly lit altar, knelt on the first step, received the Host one by one, and went back to their places in the same order. When it was Virginie's turn, Félicité leant forward to see her, and in one of those imaginative flights born of real affection, it seemed to her that she herself was in the child's place. Virginie's face became her own, Virginie's dress clothed her, Virginie's heart was beating in her breast; and as she closed her eyes and opened her mouth, she almost fainted away.

Early next morning she want to the sacristy and asked M. le Curé to give her communion. She received the sacrament with all due reverence, but did not feel the same rapture as she had the day before.

Mme Aubain wanted her daughter to possess every accomplishment, and since Guyot could not teach her English or music, she decided to send her as a boarder to the Ursuline Convent at Honfleur.

Virginie raised no objection, but Félicité went about sighing at Madame's lack of feeling. Then she thought that perhaps her mistress was right: such matters, after all, lay outside her province.

Finally the day arrived when an old waggonette stopped at their door, and a nun got down from it who had come to fetch Mademoiselle. Félicité hoisted the luggage up on top, gave the driver some parting instructions, and put six pots of jam, a dozen pears, and a bunch of violets in the boot.

At the last moment Virginie burst into a fit of sobbing. She threw her arms around her mother, who kissed her on the forehead, saying: 'Come now, be brave, be brave!' The step was pulled up and the carriage drove away.

Then Mme Aubain broke down, and that evening all her friends, M. and Mme Lormeau, Mme Lechaptois, the Rochefeuille sisters, M. de Houppeville, and Bourais, came in to console her.

To begin with she missed her daughter badly. But she had a letter from her three times a week, wrote back on the other days, walked round her garden, did a little reading, and thus contrived to fill the empty hours.

As for Félicité, she went into Virginie's room every morning from sheer force of habit and looked round it. It upset her not having to brush the child's hair any more, tie her bootlaces, or tuck her up in bed; and she missed seeing her sweet face all the time and holding her hand when they went out together. For want of something to do, she tried making lace, but her fingers were too clumsy and broke the threads. She could not settle to anything, lost her sleep, and, to use her words, was 'eaten up inside'.

To 'occupy her mind', she asked if her nephew Victor might come and see her, and permission was granted.

He used to arrive after Mass on Sunday, his cheeks flushed, his chest bare, and smelling of the countryside through which he had come. She laid a place for him straight away, opposite hers, and they had lunch together. Eating as little as possible herself, in order the save the expense, she stuffed him so full of food that he fell asleep after the meal. When the first bell for vespers rang, she woke him up, brushed his trousers, tied his tie, and set off for church, leaning on his arm with all a mother's pride.

His parents always told him to get something out of her — a packet of brown sugar perhaps, some soap, or a little brandy, sometimes even money. He brought her his clothes to be mended, and she did the work gladly, thankful for anything that would force him to come again.

In August his father took him on a coasting trip. The children's holidays were just beginning, and it cheered her up to have them home again. But Paul was turning capricious and Virginie was getting too old to be addressed familiarly — a state of affairs which put a barrier of constraint between them.

Victor went to Morlais, Dunkirk, and Brighton in turn, and brought her a present after each trip. The first time it was a box covered with shells, the second a coffee cup, the third a big gingerbread man. He was growing quite handsome, with his trim figure, his little moustache, his frank open eyes, and the little leather cap that he wore on the back of his head like a pilot. He kept her amused by telling her stories full of nautical jargon.

One Monday — it was the fourteenth of July 1819, a date she never forgot — Victor told her that he had signed on for an ocean voyage, and that on the Wednesday night he would be taking the Honfleur packet to join his schooner, which was due to sail shortly from Le Havre. He might be away, he said, for two years.

The prospect of such a long absence made Félicité extremely unhappy, and she felt she must bid him godspeed once more. So on the Wednesday evening, when Madame's dinner was over, she put on her clogs and swiftly covered the ten miles between Pont-l'Évêque and Honfleur.

When she arrived at the Calvary she turned right instead of left, got lost in the shipyards, and had to retrace her steps. Some people she spoke to advised her to hurry. She went right round the harbour, which was full of boats, constantly tripping over hawsers. Then the ground fell away, rays of light criss-crossed in front of her, and for a moment she thought she was going mad, for she could see horses up in the sky.

On the quayside more horses were neighing, frightened by the sea. A garnet was hoisting them into the air and dropping them into one of the boats, which was already crowded with passengers elbowing their way between barrels of cider, baskets of cheese, and sacks of grain. Hens were cackling and the captain swearing, while a cabin-boy stood leaning on the cats-head, completely indifferent to it all. Félicité, who had not recognized him, shouted: 'Victor!' and he raised his head. She rushed forward, but at that very moment the gangway was pulled ashore.

The packet moved out of the harbour with women singing as they hauled it along, its ribs creaking and heavy waves lashing its bows. The sail swung round, hiding everyone on board from view, and against the silvery, moonlit sea the boat appeared as a dark shape that grew even fainter, until at last it vanished in the distance.

As Félicité was passing the Calvary, she felt a longing to commend to God's mercy all that she held most dear; and she stood there praying for a long time, her face bathed in tears, her eyes fixed upon the clouds. The town was asleep, except for the customs officers walking up and down. Water was pouring ceaselessly through the holes in the sluice-gate, making as much noise as a torrent. The clocks struck two.

The convent parlour would not be open before daybreak, and Madame would be annoyed if she were late; so, although she would have liked to give a kiss to the other child, she set off for home. The maids at the inn were just waking up as she got to Pont-l'Évêque.

So the poor lad was going to be tossed by the waves for months on end! His previous voyages had caused her no alarm. People came back from England and Brittany; but America, the Colonies, the Islands, were all so far away, somewhere at the other end of the world.

From then on Félicité thought of nothing but her nephew. On sunny days she hoped he was not too thirsty, and when there was a storm she was afraid he would be struck by lightning. Listening to the wind howling in the chimney or blowing slates off the roof, she saw him being buffeted by the very same storm, perched on the top of a broken mast, with his whole body bent backwards under a sheet of foam; or again — and these were reminiscences of the illustrated geography-book — he was being eaten by savages, captured by monkeys in a forest, or dying on a desert shore. But she never spoke of her worries.

Mme Aubain had worries of her own about her daughter. The good nuns said that she was an affectionate child, but very delicate. The slightest emotion upset her, and she had to give up playing the piano.

Her mother insisted on regular letters from the convent. One morning when the postman had not called, she lost patience and walked up and down the room, between her chair and the window. It was really extraordinary! Four days without any news!

Thinking her own example would comfort her, Félicité said:

'I've been six months, Madame, without news.'

'News of whom?'

The servant answered gently:

'Why — of my nephew.'

'Oh, your nephew!' And Mme Aubain started pacing up and down again, with a shrug of her shoulders that seemed to say: 'I wasn't thinking of him — and indeed, why should I? Who cares about a young, good-for-nothing cabin-boy? Whereas my daughter — why, just think!'

Although she had been brought up the hard way, Félicité was indignant with Madame, but she soon forgot. It struck her as perfectly natural to lose one's head where the little girl was concerned. For her, the two children were of equal importance; they were linked together in her heart by a single bond, and their destinies should be the same.

The chemist told her that Victor's ship had arrived at Havana: he had seen this piece of information in a newspaper.

Because of its association with cigars, she imagined Havana as a place where nobody did anything but smoke, and pictured Victor walking about among crowds of Negroes in a cloud of tobacco-smoke. Was it possible, she wondered, 'in case of need' to come back by land? And how far was it from Pont-l'Évêque? To find out she asked M. Bourais.

He reached for his atlas, and launched forth into an explanation of latitudes and longitudes, smiling like the pedant he was at Félicité's bewilderment. Finally he pointed with his pencil at a minute black dot inside a ragged oval patch, saying:

'There it is.'

She bent over the map, but the network of coloured lines meant nothing to her and only tired her eyes. So when Bourais asked her to tell him what was puzzling her, she begged him to show her the house where Victor was living. He threw up his hands, sneezed, and roared with laughter, delighted to come across such simplicity. And Félicité — whose intelligence was so limited that she probably expected to see an actual portrait of her nephew — could not make out why he was laughing.

It was a fortnight later that Liébard came into the kitchen at market-time, as he usually did, and handed her a letter from her brother-in-law. As neither of them could read, she turned to her mistress for help.

Mme Aubain, who was counting the stitches in her knitting, put it down and unsealed the letter. She gave a start, and, looking hard at Félicité, said quietly:

'They have some bad news for you ... Your nephew ...'

He was dead. That was all the letter had to say.

Félicité dropped on to a chair, leaning her head against the wall and closing her eyelids, which suddenly turned pink. Then, with her head bowed, her hands dangling, and her eyes set, she kept repeating:

'Poor little lad! Poor little lad!'

Liébard looked at her and sighed. Mme Aubain was trembling slightly. She suggested that she should go and see her sister at Trouville, but Félicité shook her head to indicate that there was no need for that.

There was a silence. Old Liébard thought it advisable to go.

Then Félicité said:

'It doesn't matter a bit, not to them it doesn't.'

Her head fell forward again, and from time to time she unconsciously picked up the knitting needles lying on the worktable.

Some women went past carrying a tray full of dripping linen.

Catching sight of them through the window, she remembered her own washing; she had passed the lye through it the day before and today it needed rinsing. So she left the room.

Her board and tub were on the bank of the Toucques. She threw a pile of chemises down by the water's edge, rolled up her sleeves, and picked up her battledore. The lusty blows she gave with it could be heard in all the neighbouring gardens.

The fields were empty, the river rippling in the wind; at the bottom long weeds were waving to and fro, like the hair of corpses floating in the water. She held back her grief, and was very brave until the evening; but in her room she gave way to it completely, lying on her mattress with her face buried in the pillow and her fists pressed against her temples.

Long afterwards she learnt the circumstances of Victor's death from the captain of his ship. He had gone down with yellow fever, and they had bled him too much at the hospital. Four doctors had held him at once. He had died straight away, and the chief doctor had said:

'Good! There goes another!'

His parents had always treated him cruelly. She preferred not to see them again, and they made no advances, either because they had forgotten about her or out of the callousness of the poor.

Meanwhile Virginie was growing weaker. Difficulty in breathing, fits of coughing, protracted bouts of fever, and mottled patches on the cheekbones all indicated some deep-seated complaint. M. Poupart had advised a stay in Provence. Mme Aubain decided to follow this suggestion, and, if it had not been the weather at Pont-l'Évêque, she would have brought her daughter home at once.

She arranged with a jobmaster to drive her out to the convent every Tuesday. There was a terrace in the garden, overlooking the Seine, and there Virginie, leaning on her mother's arm, walked up and down over the fallen vine-leaves. Sometimes, while she was looking at the sails in the distance, or at the long stretch of horizon from the Château de Tancarville to the lighthouses of Le Havre, the sun would break through the clouds and make her blink. Afterwards they would rest in the arbour. Her mother had secured a little cask of excellent Malaga, and, laughing at the idea of getting tipsy, Virginie used to drink a thimbleful, but no more.

Her strength revived. Autumn slipped by, and Félicité assured Mme Aubain that there was nothing to fear. But one evening, coming back from some errand in the neighbourhood, she found M. Poupart's gig standing at the door. He was in the hall, and Mme Aubain was tying on her bonnet.

'Give me my foot-warmer, purse, gloves. Quickly now!'

Virginie had pneumonia and was perhaps past recovery.

'Not yet!' said the doctor; and the two of them got into the carriage with snow-flakes swirling around them. Night was falling and it was very cold.

Félicité rushed into the church to light a candle, and then ran after the gig. She caught up with it an hour later, jumped lightly up behind, and hung on to the fringe. But then a thought struck her: the courtyard had not been locked up, and burglars might get in. So she jumped down again.

At dawn the next day she went to the doctor's. He had come home and gone out again on his rounds. Then she waited at the inn, thinking that somebody who was a stranger to the district might call there with a letter. Finally, when it was twilight, she got into the coach for Lisieux.

The convent was at the bottom of a steep lane. When she was half-way down the hill, she heard a strange sound which she recognized as a death-bell tolling.

'It's for somebody else', she thought, as she banged the door-knocker hard.

After a few minutes she heard the sound of shuffling feet, the door opened a little way, and a nun appeared.

The good sister said with an air of compunction that 'she had just passed away'. At that moment the bell of Saint-Léonard was tolled more vigorously than ever.

Félicité went up to the second floor. From the doorway of the room she could see Virginie lying on her back, her hands clasped together, her mouth open, her head tilted back under a black crucifix that leant over her, her face whiter than the curtains that hung motionless on either side. Mme Aubain was clinging to the foot of the bed and sobbing desperately. The Mother Superior stood on the right. Three candlesticks on the chest of drawers added touches of red to the scene, and fog was whitening the windows. Some nuns led Mme Aubain away.

For two nights Félicité never left the dead girl. She said the same prayers over and over again, sprinkled holy water on the sheets, then sat down again to watch. At the end of her first vigil, she noticed that the child's face had gone yellow, the lips were turning blue, the nose looked sharper, and the eyes were sunken. She kissed them several times, and would not have been particularly surprised if Virginie had opened them again: to minds like hers the supernatural is a simple matter. She laid her out, wrapped her in a shroud, put her in her coffin, placed a wreath on her, and spread out her hair. It was fair and amazingly long for her age. Félicité cut off a big lock, half of which she slipped into her bosom, resolving never to part with it.

The body was brought back to Pont-l'Évêque at the request of Mme Aubain, who followed the hearse in a closed carriage.

After the Requiem Mass, it took another three-quarters of an hour to reach the cemetery. Paul walked in front, sobbing. Then came M. Bourais, and after him the principal inhabitants of the town, the women all wearing long black veils, and Félicité. She was thinking about her nephew; and since she had been unable to pay him these last honours, she felt an added grief, just as if they were burying him with Virginie.

Mme Aubain's despair passed all bounds. First of all she rebelled against God, considering it unfair of Him to have taken her daughter from her — for she had never done any harm, and her conscience was quite clear. But was it? She ought to have taken Virginie to the south; other doctors would have saved her life. She blamed herself, wished she could have joined her daughter, and cried out in anguish in her dreams. One dream in particular obsessed her. Her husband, dressed like a sailor, came back from a long voyage, and told her amid tears that he had been ordered to take Virginie away — whereupon they put their heads together to discover somewhere to hide her.

One day she came in from the garden utterly distraught. A few minutes earlier — and she pointed to the spot — father and daughter had appeared to her, doing nothing, but simply looking at her.

For several months she stayed in her room in a kind of stupor. Félicité scolded her gently, telling her that she must take care of herself for her son's sake, and also in remembrance of 'her'.

'Her?' repeated Mme Aubain, as if she were waking from a sleep. 'O, yes, of course! You don't forget her, do you?' This was an allusion to the cemetery, where she herself was strictly forbidden to go.

Félicité went there every day. She would set out on the stroke of four, going past the houses, up the hill, and through the gate, until she came to Virginie's grave. There was a little column of pink marble with a tablet at its base, and a tiny garden enclosed by chains. The beds were hidden under a carpet of flowers. She watered their leaves and changed the sand, going down on her knees to fork the ground thoroughly. The result was that when Mme Aubain was able to come here, she experienced a feeling of relief, a kind of consolation.

Then the years slipped by, each one like the last, with nothing to vary the rhythm of the great festivals: Easter, the Assumption, All Saints' Day. Domestic events marked dates that later served as points of reference. Thus in 1825 a couple of glaziers whitewashed the hall; in 1827 a piece of the roof fell into the courtyard and nearly killed a man; and in the summer of 1828 it was Madame's turn to provide the bread for consecration. About this time Bourais went away in a mysterious fashion; and one by one the old acquaintances disappeared: Guyot, Liébard, Mme Lechaptois, Robelin, and Uncle Grémanville, who had been paralysed for a long time.

One night the driver of the mail-coach brought Pont-l'Évêque news of the July Revolution. A few days later a new sub-prefect was appointed. This was the Baron de Larsonnière, who had been a consul in America, and who brought with him, besides his wife, his sister-in-law and three young ladies who were almost grown-up. They were to be seen on their lawn, dressed in loose-fitting smocks; and they had a Negro servant and a parrot. They paid a call on Mme Aubain, who made a point of returning it. As soon as Félicité saw them coming, she would run and tell her mistress. But only one thing could really awaken her interest, and that was her son's letters.

He seemed to be incapable of following any career and spent all his time in taverns. She paid his debts, but he contracted new ones, and the sighs Mme Aubain heaved as she knitted by the window reached Félicité at her spinning-wheel in the kitchen.

The two women used to walk up and down together beside the espalier, forever talking of Virginie and debating whether such and such a thing would have appealed to her, or what she would have said on such and such an occasion.

All her little belongings were in a cupboard in the children's bedroom. Mme Aubain went through them as seldom as possible. One summer day she resigned herself to doing so, and the moths were sent fluttering out of the cupboard.

Virginie's frocks hung in a row underneath a shelf containing three dolls, a few hoops, a set of toy furniture, and the wash-basin she had used. Besides the frocks, they took out her petticoats, her stockings and her handkerchiefs, and spread them out on the two beds before folding them up again. The sunlight streamed in on these pathetic objects, bringing out the stains and showing up the creases made by the child's movements. The air was warm, the sky was blue, a blackbird was singing, and everything seemed to be utterly at peace.

They found a little chestnut-coloured hat, made of plush with a long nap; but the moths had ruined it. Félicité asked if she might have it. The two women looked at each other and their eyes filled with tears. Then the mistress opened her arms, the maid threw herself into them, and they clasped each other in a warm embrace, satisfying their grief in a kiss which made them equal.

It was the first time that such a thing had happened, for Mme Aubain was not of a demonstrative nature. Félicité was as grateful as if she had received a great favour, and henceforth loved her mistress with dog-like devotion and religious veneration.

Her heart grew softer as time went by.

When she heard the drums of a regiment coming down the street she stood at the door with a jug of cider and offered the soldiers a drink. She looked after the people who went down with cholera. She watched over the Polish refugees, and one of them actually expressed a desire to marry her. But they fell out, for when she came back from the Angelus one morning, she found that he had got into her kitchen and was calmly eating an oil-and-vinegar salad.

After the Poles it was Père Colmiche, an old man who was said to have committed fearful atrocities in '93. He lived by the river in a ruined pig-sty. The boys of the town used to peer at him through the cracks in the walls, and threw pebbles at him which landed on the litter where he lay, constantly shaken by fits of coughing. His hair was extremely long, his eyelids inflamed, and on one arm there was a swelling bigger than his head. Félicité brought him some linen, tried to clean out his filthy hovel, and even wondered if she could install him in the wash-house without annoying Madame. When the tumour had burst, she changed his dressings every day, brought him some cake now and then, and put him out in the sun on a truss of hay. The poor old fellow would thank her in a faint whisper, slavering and trembling all the while, fearful of losing her and stretching his hands out as soon as he saw her moving away.

He died, and she had a Mass said for the repose of his soul.

That same day a great piece of good fortune came her way. Just as she was serving dinner, Mme de Larsonnière's Negro appeared carrying the parrot in its cage, complete with perch, chain, and padlock. The Baroness had written a note informing Mme Aubain that her husband had been promoted to a Prefecture and they were leaving that evening; she begged her to accept the parrot as a keepsake and a token of her regard.

This bird had engrossed Félicité's thoughts for a long time, for it came from America, and that word reminded her of Victor. So she had asked the Negro all about it, and once she had even gone so far as to say:

'How pleased Madame would be if it were hers!'

The Negro had repeated this remark to his mistress, who, unable to take the parrot with her, was glad to get rid of it in this way.

IV

His name was Loulou. His body was green, the tips of his wings were pink, his poll blue, and his breast golden.

Unfortunately he had a tiresome mania for biting his perch, and also used to pull his feathers out, scatter his droppings everywhere, and upset his bath water. He annoyed Mme Aubain, and so she gave him to Félicité for good.

Félicité started training him, and soon he could say: 'Nice boy! Your servant, sir! Hail, Mary!' He was put near the door, and several people who spoke to him said how strange it was that he did not answer to the name of Jacquot, as all parrots were called Jacquot. They likened him to a turkey or a block of wood, and every sneer cut Félicité to the quick. How odd, she thought, that Loulou should be so stubborn, refusing to talk whenever anyone looked at him!

For all that, he liked having people around him, because on Sundays, while the Rochefeuille sisters, M. Houppeville and some new friends — apothecary Onfroy, M. Varin, and Captain Mathieu — were having their game of cards, he would beat on the window-panes with his wings and make such a din that it was impossible to hear oneself speak.

Bourais's face obviously struck him as terribly funny, for as soon as he saw it he was seized with uncontrollable laughter. His shrieks rang round the courtyard, the echo repeated them, and the neighbours came to their windows and started laughing too. To avoid being seen by the bird, M. Bourais used to creep along by the wall, hiding his face behind his hat, until he got to the river, and then come into the house from the garden. The looks he gave the parrot were far from tender.

Loulou had once been cuffed by the butcher's boy for poking his head into his basket; and since then he was always trying to give him a nip through his shirt. Fabu threatened to wring his neck, although he was not a cruel fellow, in spite of his tattooed arms and bushy whiskers. On the contrary, he rather liked the parrot, so much so indeed that in a spirit of jovial camaraderie he tried to teach him a few swear-words. Félicité, alarmed at this development, put the bird in the kitchen. His little chain was removed and he was allowed to wander all over the house.

Coming downstairs, he used to rest the curved part of his beak on each step and then raise first his right foot, then his left; and Félicité was afraid that this sort of gymnastic performance would make him giddy. He fell ill and could neither talk nor eat for there was a swelling under his tongue such as hens sometimes have. She cured him by pulling this pellicule out with her finger-nails. One day M. Paul was silly enough to blow the smoke of his cigar at him; another time Mme Lormeau started teasing him with the end of her parasol, and he caught hold of the ferrule with his beak. Finally he got lost.

Félicité had put him down on the grass in the fresh air, and left him there for a minute. When she came back, the parrot had gone. First of all she looked for him in the bushes, by the river and on the rooftops, paying no attention to her mistress's shouts of: 'Be careful, now! You must be mad!' Next she went over all the gardens in Pont-l'Évêque, stopping passers-by and asking them: 'You don't happen to have seen my parrot by any chance?' Those who did not know him already were given a description of the bird. Suddenly she thought she could make out something green flying about behind the mills at the foot of the hill. But up on the hill there was nothing to be seen. A pedlar told her that he had come upon the parrot a short time before in Mère Simon's shop at Saint-Melaine. She ran all the way there, but no one knew what she was talking about. Finally she came back home, worn out, her shoes falling to pieces, and death in her heart. She was sitting beside Madame on the garden-seat and telling her what she had been doing, when she felt something light drop on her shoulder. It was Loulou! What he had been up to, no one could discover: perhaps he had just gone for a little walk round the town.

Félicité was slow to recover from this fright, and indeed never really got over it.

As the result of a chill she had an attack of quinsy, and soon after that her ears were affected. Three years later she was deaf, and she spoke at the top of her voice, even in church. Although her sins could have been proclaimed over the length and breadth of the diocese without dishonour to her or offence to others, M. le Curé thought it advisable to hear her confession in the sacristy.

Imaginary buzzings in the head added to her troubles. Often her mistress would say: 'Heavens, how stupid you are!' and she would reply: 'Yes, Madame', at the same time looking all around her for something.

The little circle of her ideas grew narrower and narrower, and the pealing of bells and the lowing of cattle went out of her life. Every living thing moved about in a ghostly silence. Only one sound reached her ears now, and that was the voice of the parrot.

As if to amuse her, he would reproduce the click-clack of the turn-spit, the shrill call of a man selling fish, and the noise of the saw at the joiner's across the way; and when the bell rang he would imitate Mme Aubain's 'Félicité! The door, the door!'

They held conversations with each other, he repeating *ad nauseam* the three phrases in his repertory, she replying with words which were just as disconnected but which came from the heart. In her isolation, Loulou was almost a son or a lover to her. He used to climb up her fingers, peck at her lips, and hang on to her shawl; and as she bent over him, wagging her head from side to side as nurses do, the great wings of her bonnet and the wings of the bird quivered in unison.

When clouds banked up in the sky and there was a rumbling of thunder, he would utter piercing cries, no doubt remembering the sudden downpours in his native forests. The sound of the rain falling roused him to frenzy. He would flap excitedly around, shoot up to the ceiling, knocking everything over, and fly out of the window to splash about in the garden. But he would soon come back to perch on one of the firedogs, hopping about to dry his feathers and showing tail and beak in turn.

One morning in the terrible winter of 1837, when she had put him in front of the fire because of the cold, she found him dead in the middle of his cage, hanging head down with his claws caught in the bars. He had probably died of a stroke, but she thought he had been poisoned with parsley, and despite the absence of any proof, her suspicions fell on Fabu.

She wept so much that her mistress said to her: 'Why don't you have him stuffed?'

Félicité asked the chemist's advice, remembering that he had always been kind to the parrot. He wrote to Le Havre, and a man called Fellacher agreed to do the job. As parcels sometimes went astray on the mail-coach, she decided to take the parrot as far as Honfleur herself.

On either side of the road stretched an endless succession of apple-trees, all stripped of their leaves, and there was ice in the ditches. Dogs were barking around the farms; and Félicité, with her hands tucked under her mantlet, her little black sabots and her basket, walked briskly along in the middle of the road.

She crossed the forest, passed Le Haut-Chêne, and got as far as Saint-Gatien.

Behind her, in a cloud of dust, and gathering speed as the horses galloped downhill, a mail-coach swept along like a whirlwind. When he saw this woman making no attempt to get out of the way, the driver poked his head out above the hood, and he and the postillion shouted at her. His four horses could not be held in and galloped faster, the two leaders touching her as they went by. With a jerk of the reins the driver threw them to one side, and then, in a fury, he raised his long whip and gave her such a lash, from head to waist, that she fell flat on her back.

The first thing she did on regaining consciousness was to open her basket. Fortunately nothing had happened to Loulou. She felt her right cheek burning, and when she touched it her hand turned red; it was bleeding.

She sat down on a heap of stones and dabbed her face with her handkerchief. Then she ate a crust of bread which she had taken the precaution of putting in her basket, and tried to forget her wound by looking at the bird.

As she reached the top of the hill at Ecquemauville, she saw the lights of Honfleur twinkling in the darkness like a host of stars, and the shadowy expanse of the sea beyond. Then a sudden feeling of faintness made her stop; and the misery of her childhood, the disappointment of her first love, the departure of her nephew, and the death of Virginie all came back to her at once like the waves of a rising tide, and, welling up in her throat, choked her.

When she got to the boat she insisted on speaking to the captain, and without telling him what was in her parcel, asked him to take good care of it.

Fellacher kept the parrot a long time. Every week he promised it for the next; after six months he announced that a box had been sent off, and nothing more was heard of it. It looked as though Loulou would never come back, and Félicité told herself: 'They've stolen him for sure!'

At last he arrived — looking quite magnificent, perched on a branch screwed into a mahogany base, one foot in the air, his head cocked to one side, and biting a nut which the taxidermist, out of a love of the grandiose, had gilded.

Félicité shut him up in her room.

This place, to which few people were ever admitted, contained such a quantity of religious bric-à-brac and miscellaneous oddments that it looked like a cross between a chapel and a bazaar.

A big wardrobe prevented the door from opening properly. Opposite the window that overlooked the garden was a little round one looking on to the courtyard. There was a table beside the bed, with a water-jug, a couple of combs, and a block of blue soap in a chipped plate. On the walls there were rosaries, medals, several pictures of the Virgin, and a holy-water stoup made out of a coconut. On the chest of drawers, which was draped with a cloth just like an altar, was the shell box Victor had given her, and also a watering-can and a ball, some copy-books, the illustrated geography book, and a pair of ankle-boots. And on the nail supporting the looking-glass, fastened by its ribbons, hung the little plush hat.

Félicité carried this form of veneration to such lengths that she even kept one of Monsieur's frock-coats. All the old rubbish Mme Aubain had no more use for, she carried off to her room. That was how there came to be artificial flowers along the edge of the chest of drawers, and a portrait of the Comte d'Artois in the window-recess.

With the aid of a wall-bracket, Loulou was installed on a chimney-breast that jutted out into the room. Every morning when she awoke, she saw him in the light of the dawn, and then she remembered the old days, and the smallest details of insignificant actions, not in sorrow but in absolute tranquility.

Having no intercourse with anyone, she lived in the torpid state of a sleep-walker. The Corpus Christi processions roused her from this condition, for she would go round the neighbours collecting candlesticks and mats to decorate the altar of repose which they used to set up in the street.

In church she was forever gazing at the Holy Ghost, and one day she noticed that it had something of the parrot about it. This resemblance struck her as even more obvious in a colour-print depicting the baptism of Our Lord. With its red wings and its emerald-green body, it was the very image of Loulou.

She bought the print and hung it in the place of the Comte d'Artois, so that she could include them both in a single glance. They were linked together in her mind, the parrot being sanctified by this connexion with the Holy Ghost, which itself acquired new life and meaning in her eyes. God the Father could not have chosen a dove as a means of expressing Himself, since doves cannot talk, but rather one of Loulou's ancestors. And although Félicité used to say her prayers with her eyes on the picture, from time to time she would turn slightly towards the bird.

She wanted to join the Children of Mary, but Mme Aubain dissuaded her from doing so.

An important event now loomed up — Paul's wedding.

After starting as a lawyer's clerk, he had been in business, in the Customs, and in Inland Revenue, and had even begun trying to get into the Department of Woods and Forests, when, at the age of thirty-six, by some heaven-sent inspiration, he suddenly discovered his real vocation — in the Wills and Probate Department. There he proved so capable that one of the auditors had offered him his daughter in marriage and promised to use his influence on his behalf.

Paul, grown serious-minded, brought her to see his mother. She criticized the way things were done at Pont-l'Évêque, put on airs, and hurt Félicité's feelings. Mme Aubain was relieved to see her go.

The following week came news of M. Bourais's death in an inn in Lower Brittany. Rumours that he had committed suicide were confirmed, and doubts arose as to his honesty. Mme Aubain went over her accounts and was soon conversant with the full catalogue of his misdeeds — embezzlement of interest, secret sales of timber, forged receipts, etc. Besides all this, he was the father of an illegitimate child, and had had 'relations with a person at Dozulé'.

These infamies upset Mme Aubain greatly. In March 1853 she was afflicted with a pain in the chest; her tongue seemed to be covered with a film; leeches failed to make her breathing any easier; and on the ninth evening of her illness she died. She had just reached the age of seventy-two.

She was thought to be younger because of her brown hair, worn in bandeaux round her pale, pock-marked face. There were few friends to mourn her, for she had a haughty manner which put people off. Yet Félicité wept for her as servants rarely weep for their masters. That Madame should die before her upset her ideas, seemed to be contrary to the order of things, monstrous and unthinkable.

Ten days later — the time it took to travel hot-foot from Besançon — the heirs arrived. The daughter-in-law ransacked every drawer, picked out some pieces of furniture and sold the rest; and then back they went to the Wills and Probate Department.

Madame's arm-chair, her pedestal table, her foot-warmer, and the eight chairs had all gone. Yellow squares in the centre of the wall-panels showed where the pictures had hung. They had carried off the two cots with their mattresses, and no trace remained in the cupboard of all Virginie's things. Félicité climbed the stairs to her room, numbed with sadness.

The next day there was a notice on the door, and the apothecary shouted in her ear that the house was up for sale.

She swayed on her feet, and was obliged to sit down.

What distressed her most of all was the idea of leaving her room, which was so suitable for poor Loulou. Fixing an anguished look on him as she appealed to the Holy Ghost, she contracted the idolatrous habit of kneeling in front of the parrot to say her prayers. Sometimes the sun, as it came through the little window, caught his glass eye, so that it shot out a great luminous ray which sent her into ecstasies.

She had a pension of three hundred and eighty francs a year which her mistress had left her. The garden kept her in vegetables. As for clothes, she had enough to last her till the end of her days, and she saved on lighting by going to bed as soon as darkness fell.

She went out as little as possible, to avoid the second-hand dealer's shop, where some of the old furniture was on display. Ever since her fit of giddiness, she had been dragging one leg; and as her strength was failing, Mère Simon, whose grocery business had come to grief, came in every morning to chop wood and pump water for her.

Her eyes grew weaker. The shutters were not opened any more. Years went by, and nobody rented the house and nobody bought it.

For fear of being evicted, Félicité never asked for any repairs to be done. The laths in the roof rotted, all through one winter her bolster was wet. After Easter she began spitting blood.

When this happened Mère Simon called in a doctor. Félicité wanted to know what was the matter with her, but she was so deaf that only one word reached her: 'Pneumonia'. It was a word she knew, and she answered gently: 'Ah! like Madame', thinking it natural that she should follow in her mistress's footsteps.

The time to set up the altars of repose was drawing near.

The first altar was always at the foot of the hill, the second in front of the post office, the third about half-way up the street. There was some argument as to the siting of this one, and finally the women of the parish picked on Mme Aubain's courtyard.

The fever and the tightness of the chest grew worse. Félicité fretted over not doing anything for the altar. If only she could have put something on it! Then she thought of the parrot. The neighbours protested that it would not be seemly, but the curé gave his permission, and this made her so happy that she begged him to accept Loulou, the only thing of value she possessed, when she died.

From Tuesday to Saturday, the eve of Corpus Christi, she coughed more and more frequently. In the evening her face looked pinched and drawn, her lips stuck to her gums, and she started vomiting. At dawn the next day, feeling very low, she sent for a priest.

Three good women stood by her while she was given extreme unction. Then she said that she had to speak to Fabu.

He arrived in his Sunday best, very ill at ease in this funereal atmosphere.

'Forgive me,' she said, making an effort to stretch out her arm. 'I thought it was you who had killed him.'

What could she mean by such nonsense? To think that she had suspected a man like him of murder! He got very indignant and was obviously going to make a scene.

'Can't you see', they said, 'that she isn't in her right mind any more?'

From time to time Félicité would start talking to shadows. The women went away. Mère Simon had her lunch.

A little later she picked Loulou up and held him out to Félicité, saying:

'Come now, say good-bye to him.'

Although the parrot was not a corpse, the worms were eating him up. One of his wings was broken, and the stuffing was coming out of his stomach. But she was blind by now, and she kissed him on the forehead and pressed him against her cheek. Mère Simon took him away from her to put him on the altar.

V

The scents of summer came up from the meadows; there was a buzzing of flies; the sun was glittering in the river and warming the slates of the roof. Mère Simon had come back into the room and was gently nodding off to sleep.

The noise of church bells woke her up; the congregation was coming out from vespers. Félicité's delirium abated. Thinking of the procession, she could see it as clearly as if she had been following it.

All the school-children, the choristers, and the firemen were walking along the pavements, while advancing up the middle of the street came the church officer armed with his halberd, the beadle carrying a great cross, the schoolmaster keeping an eye on the boys, and the nun fussing over her little girls — three of the prettiest, looking like curly-headed angels, were throwing rose-petals into the air. Then came the deacon, with both arms outstretched, conducting the band, and a couple of censer-bearers who turned round at every step to face the Holy Sacrament, which the curé, wearing his splendid chasuble, was carrying under a canopy of poppy-red velvet held aloft by four churchwardens. A crowd of people surged along behind, between the white cloths covering the walls of the houses, and eventually they got to the bottom of the hill.

A cold sweat moistened Félicité's temples. Mère Simon sponged it up with a cloth, telling herself that one day she would have to go the same way.

The hum of the crowd increased in volume, was very loud for a moment, then faded away.

A fusillade shook the window-panes. It was the postilions saluting the monstrance. Félicité rolled her eyes and said as loud as she could: 'Is he all right?' — worrying about the parrot.

She entered into her death-agony. Her breath, coming ever faster, with a rattling sound, made her sides heave. Bubbles of froth appeared at the corners of her mouth, and her whole body trembled.

Soon the booming of the ophicleides, the clear voices of the children, and the deep voices of the men could be heard near at hand. Now and then everything was quiet, and the tramping of feet, deadened by a carpet of flowers, sounded like a flock moving across pasture-land.

The clergy appeared in the courtyard. Mère Simon climbed on to a chair to reach the little round window, from which she had a full view of the altar below.

It was hung with green garlands and adorned with a flounce in English needle-point lace. In the middle was a little frame containing some relics, there were two orange-trees at the corners, and all the way along stood silver candlesticks and china vases holding sunflowers, lilies, peonies, foxgloves, and bunches of hydrangea. This pyramid of bright colours stretched from the first floor right down to the carpet which was spread out over the pavement. Some rare objects caught the eye: a silver-gilt sugar-basin wreathed in violets, some pendants of Alençon gems gleaming on a bed of moss, and two Chinese screens with landscape decorations, Loulou, hidden under roses, showed nothing but his blue poll, which looked like a plaque of lapis lazuli.

The churchwardens, the choristers, and the children lined up along the three sides of the courtyard. The priest went slowly up the steps and placed his great shining gold sun on the lace altar-cloth. Everyone knelt down. There was a deep silence. And the censers, swinging at full tilt, slid up and down their chains.

A blue cloud of incense was wafted up into Félicité's room. She opened her nostrils wide and breathed it in with a mystical, sensuous fervour. Then she closed her eyes. Her lips smiled. Her heart-beats grew slower and slower, each a little fainter and gentler, like a fountain running dry, an echo fading away. And as she breathed her last, she thought she could see, in the opening heavens, a gigantic parrot hovering above her head.

E. M. FORSTER

The Celestial Omnibus

I

The boy who resided at Agathox Lodge, 28, Buckingham Park Road, Surbiton, had often been puzzled by the old sign-post that stood almost opposite. He asked his mother about it, and she replied that it was a joke, and not a very nice one, which had been made many years back by some naughty young men, and that the police ought to remove it. For there were two strange things about this sign-post: firstly, it pointed up a blank alley, and, secondly, it had painted on it, in faded characters, the words, "To Heaven."

"What kind of young men were they?" he asked.

"I think your father told me that one of them wrote verses, and was expelled from the University and came to grief in other ways. Still, it was a long time ago. You must ask your father about it. He will say the same as I do, that it was put up as a joke."

"So it doesn't mean anything at all?"

She sent him up-stairs to put on his best things, for the Bonses were coming to tea, and he was to hand the cake-stand.

It struck him, as he wrenched on his tightening trousers, that he might do worse than ask Mr. Bons about the sign-post. His father, though very kind, always laughed at him — shrieked with laughter whenever he or any other child asked a question or spoke. But Mr. Bons was serious as well as kind. He had a beautiful house and lent one books, he was a churchwarden, and a candidate for the County Council; he had donated to the Free Library enormously, he presided over the Literary Society, and had Members of Parliament to stop with him — in short, he was probably the wisest person alive.

Yet even Mr. Bons could only say that the sign-post was a joke — the joke of a person named Shelley.

"Of course!" cried the mother; "I told you so, dear. That was the name."

"Had you never heard of Shelley?" asked Mr. Bons.

"No," said the boy, and hung his head.

"But is there no Shelley in the house?"

"Why, yes!" exclaimed the lady, in much agitation. "Dear Mr. Bons, we aren't such Philistines as that. Two at the least. One a wedding present, and the other, smaller print, in one of the spare rooms."

"I believe we have seven Shelleys," said Mr. Bons, with a slow smile. Then he brushed the cake crumbs off his stomach, and, together with his daughter, rose to go.

The boy, obeying a wink from his mother, saw them all the way to the garden gate, and when they had gone he did not at once return to the house, but gazed for a little up and down Buckingham Park Road.

His parents lived at the right end of it. After No. 39 the quality of the houses dropped very suddenly, and 64 had not even a separate servants' entrance. But at the present moment the whole road looked rather pretty, for the sun had just set in splendour, and the inequalities of rent were drowned in a saffron afterglow. Small birds twittered, and the breadwinners' train shrieked musically down through the cutting — that wonderful cutting which has drawn to itself the whole beauty out of Surbiton, and clad itself, like any Alpine valley, with the glory of the fir and the silver birch and the primrose. It was this cutting that had first stirred desires within the boy — desires for something just a little different, he knew not what, desires that would return whenever things were sunlit, as they were this evening, running up and down inside him, up and down, up and down, till he would feel quite unusual all over, and as likely as not would want to cry. This evening he was even sillier, for he slipped across the road towards the sign-post and began to run up the blank alley.

The alley runs between high walls — the walls of the gardens of "Ivanhoe" and "Belle Vista" respectively. It smells a little all the way, and is scarcely twenty yards long, including the turn at the end. So not unnaturally the boy soon came to a standstill. "I'd like to kick that Shelley," he exclaimed, and glanced idly at a piece of paper which was pasted on the wall. Rather an odd piece of paper, and he read it carefully before he turned back. This is what he read.

S. AND C. R. C. C.

Alteration in Service.

Owing to lack of patronage the Company are regretfully compelled to suspend the hourly service, and to retain only the

Sunrise and Sunset Omnibuses,

which will run as usual. It is to be hoped that the

public will patronize an arrangement which is intended for their convenience. As an extra inducement, the Company will, for the first time, now issue

Return Tickets!

(available one day only), which may be obtained of the driver. Passengers are again reminded that *no tickets are issued at the other end*, and that no complaints in this connection will receive consideration from the Company. Nor will the Company be responsible for any negligence or stupidity on the part of Passengers, nor for Hailstorms, Lightning, Loss of Tickets, nor for any Act of God.

For the Direction

Now he had never seen this notice before, nor could he imagine where the omnibus went to. S. of course was for Surbiton, and R.C.C. meant Road Car Company. But what was the meaning of the other C.? Coombe and Malden, perhaps, or possibly "City." Yet it could not hope to compete with the South-Western. The whole thing, the boy reflected, was run on hopelessly unbusiness-like lines. Why no tickets from the other end? And what an hour to start! Then he realized that unless the notice was a hoax, an omnibus must have been starting just as he was wishing the Bonses goodbye. He peered at the ground through the gathering dusk, and there he saw what might or might not be the marks of wheels. Yet nothing had come out of the alley. And he had never seen an omnibus at any time in the Buckingham Park Road. No: it must be a hoax, like the sign-posts, like the fairy tales, like the dreams upon which he would wake suddenly in the night. And with a sign he stepped from the alley — right into the arms of his father.

Oh, how his father laughed! "Poor, poor Popsey!" he cried. "Diddums! Diddums! Diddums think he'd walky-palky up to Evvink!" And his mother, also convulsed with laughter, appeared on the steps of Agathox Lodge. "Don't Bob!" she gasped. "Don't be so naughty! Oh, you'll kill me! Oh, leave the boy alone!"

But all the evening the joke was kept up. The father implored to be taken too. Was it a very tiring walk? Need one wipe one's shoes on the door-mat? And the boy went to bed feeling faint and sore, and thankful for only one thing — that he had not said a word about the omnibus. It was a hoax, yet through his dreams it grew more and more real, and the streets of Surbiton, through which he saw it driving, seemed instead to become hoaxes and shadows. And very early in the morning he woke with a cry, for he had had a glimpse of its destination.

He struck a match, and its light fell not only on his watch but also on his calendar, so that he knew it to be half-an-hour to sunrise. It was pitch dark, for the fog had come down from London in the night, and all Surbiton was wrapped in its embraces. Yet he sprang out and dressed himself, for he was determined to settle once for all which was real: the omnibus or the streets. "I shall be a fool one way or the other," he thought, "until I know." Soon he was shivering in the road under the gas lamp that guarded the entrance to the alley.

To enter the alley itself required some courage. Not only was it horribly dark, but he now realized that it was an impossible terminus for an omnibus. If it had not been for a policeman, whom he heard approaching through the fog, he would never have made the attempt. The next moment he had made the attempt and failed. Nothing. Nothing but a blank alley and a very silly boy gaping at its dirty floor. It *was* a hoax. "I'll tell papa and mamma," he decided. "I deserve it. I deserve that they should know. I am too silly to be alive." And he went back to the gate of Agathox Lodge.

There he remembered that his watch was fast. The sun was not risen; it would not rise for two minutes. "Give the bus every chance," he thought cynically, and returned into the alley.

But the omnibus was there.

II

It had two horses, whose sides were still smoking from their journey, and its two great lamps shone through the fog against the alley's walls, changing their cobwebs and moss into tissues of fairyland. The driver was huddled up in a cape. He faced the blank wall, and how he had managed to drive in so neatly and so silently was one of the many things that the boy never discovered. Nor could he imagine how ever he would drive out.

"Please," his voice quavered through the foul brown air, "Please, is that an omnibus?"

"Omnibus est," said the driver, without turning round. There was a moment's silence. The policeman passed, coughing, by the entrance of the alley. The boy crouched in the shadow, for he did not want to be found out. He was pretty sure, too, that it was a Pirate; nothing else, he reasoned, would go from such odd places and at such odd hours.

"About when do you start?" He tried to sound nonchalant.

"At sunrise."

"How far do you go?"

"The whole way."

"And can I have a return ticket which will bring me all the way back?"

"You can."

"Do you know, I half think I'll come." The driver made no answer. The sun must have risen, for he unhitched the brake. And scarcely had the boy jumped in before the omnibus was off.

How? Did it turn? There was no room. Did it go forward? There was a blank wall. Yet it was moving — moving at a stately pace through the fog, which had turned from brown to yellow. The thought of warm bed and warmer breakfast made the boy feel faint. He wished he had not come. His parents would not have approved. He would have gone back to them if the weather had not made it impossible. The solitude was terrible; he was the only passenger. And the omnibus, though well-built, was cold and somewhat musty. He drew his coat round him, and in so doing chanced to feel his pocket. It was empty. He had forgotten his purse.

"Stop!" he shouted. "Stop!" And then, being of a polite disposition, he glanced up at the painted notice-board so that he might call the driver by name. "Mr. Browne! stop; O, do please stop!"

Mr. Browne did not stop, but he opened a little window, and looked in at the boy. His face was a surprise, so kind it was and modest.

"Mr. Browne, I've left my purse behind. I've not got a penny. I can't pay for the ticket. Will you take my watch, please? I am in the most awful hole."

"Tickets on this line," said the driver, "whether single or return, can be purchased by coinage from no terrene mint. And a chronometer, though it had solaced the vigils of Charlemagne, or measured the slumbers of Laura, can acquire by no mutation the double-cake that charms the fangless Cerberus of Heaven!" So saying, he handed in the necessary ticket, and, while the boy said "Thank you," continued: "Titular pretensions, I know it well, are vanity. Yet they merit no censure when uttered on a laughing lip, and in an homonymous world are in some sort useful, since they do serve to distinguish one Jack from his fellow. Remember me, therefore, as Sir Thomas Browne."

"Are you a Sir? Oh, sorry!" He had heard of these gentlemen drivers. "It *is* good of you about the ticket. But if you go on at this rate, however does your bus pay?"

"It does not pay. It was not intended to pay. Many are the faults of my equipage; it is compounded too curiously of foreign woods; its cushions tickle erudition rather than promote repose; and my horses are nourished not on the evergreen pastures of the moment, but on the dried bents and clovers of Latinity. But that it pays! — that error at all events was never intended and never attained."

"Sorry again," said the boy rather hopelessly. Sir Thomas looked sad, fearing that, even for a moment, he had been the cause of sadness. He invited the boy to come up and sit beside him on the box, and together they journeyed on through the fog, which was now changing from yellow to white. There were no houses by the road; so it must be either Putney Heath or Wimbledon Common.

"Have you been a driver always?"

"I was a physician once."

"But why did you stop? Weren't you good?"

"As a healer of bodies I had scant success, and several score of my patients preceded me. But as a healer of the spirit I have succeeded beyond my hopes and my deserts. For though my draughts were not better nor subtler than those of other men, yet, by reason of the cunning goblets wherein I offered them, the queasy soul was ofttimes tempted to sip and be refreshed."

"The queasy soul," he murmured; "if the sun sets with trees in front of it, and you suddenly come strange all over, is that a queasy soul?"

"Have you felt that?"

"Why yes."

After a pause he told the boy a little, a very little, about the journey's end. But they did not chatter much, for the boy, when he liked a person, would as soon sit silent in his company as speak, and this, he discovered, was also the mind of Sir Thomas Browne and of many others with whom he was to be acquainted. He heard, however, about the young man Shelley, who was not quite a famous person, with a carriage of his own, and about some of the other drivers who are in the service of the Company. Meanwhile the light grew stronger, though the fog did not disperse. It was now more like mist than fog, and at times would travel quickly across them, as if it was part of a cloud. They had been ascending, too, in a most puzzling way; for over two hours the horses had been pulling against the collar, and even if it were Richmond Hill they ought to have been at the top long ago. Perhaps it was Epsom, or even the North Downs; yet the air seemed keener than that which blows on either. And as to the name of their destination, Sir Thomas Browne was silent.

Crash!

"Thunder, by Jove!" said the boy, "and not so far off either. Listen to the echoes! It's more like mountains."

He thought, not very vividly, of his father and mother. He saw them sitting down to sausages and listening to the storm. He saw his own empty place. Then there would be questions, alarms, theories, jokes, consolations. They would expect him back at lunch. To lunch he would not come, nor tea, but he would be in for dinner, and so his day's truancy would be over. If he had had his purse he would have bought them presents — not that he should have known what to get them.

Crash!

The peal and the lighting came together. The cloud quivered as if it were alive, and torn streamers of mist rushed past. "Are you afraid?" asked Sir Thomas Browne.

"What is there to be afraid of? Is it much farther?"

The horses of the omnibus stopped just as a ball of fire burst up and exploded with a ringing noise that was deafening but clear, like the noise of a blacksmith's forge. All the cloud was shattered.

"Oh, listen, Sir Thomas Browne! No, I mean look; we shall get a view at last. No, I mean listen; that sounds like a rainbow!"

The noise had died into the faintest murmur, beneath which another murmur grew, spreading stealthily, steadily, in a curve that widened but did not vary. And in widening curves a rainbow was spreading from the horses' feet into the dissolving mists.

"But how beautiful! What colours! Where will it stop? It is more like the rainbows you can tread on. More like dreams."

The colour and the sound grew together. The rainbow spanned an enormous gulf. Clouds rushed under it and were pierced by it, and still it grew, reaching forward, conquering the darkness, until it touched something that seemed more solid than a cloud.

The boy stood up. "What is that out there?" he called. "What does it rest on, out at that other end?"

In the morning sunshine a precipice shone forth beyond the gulf. A precipice — or was it a castle? The horses moved. They set their feet upon the rainbow.

"Oh, look!" the boy shouted. "Oh, listen! Those caves — or are they gateways? Oh, look between those cliffs at those ledges. I see people! I see trees!"

"Look also below," whispered Sir Thomas. "Neglect not the diviner Acheron."

The boy looked below, past the flames of the rainbow that licked against their wheels. The gulf also had cleared, and in its depths there flowed an everlasting river. One sunbeam entered and struck a green pool, and as they passed over he saw three maidens rise to the surface of the pool, singing, and playing with something that glistened like a ring.

"You down in the water —— " he called.

They answered, "You up on the bridge —— " There was a burst of music. "You up on the bridge, good luck to you. Truth in the depth, truth on the height."

"You down in the water, what are you doing?"

Sir Thomas Browne replied: "They sport in the mancipiary possession of their gold"; and the omnibus arrived.

III

The boy was in disgrace. He sat locked up in the nursery of Agathox Lodge, learning poetry for a punishment. His father had said, "My boy! I can pardon anything but untruthfulness," and had caned him, saying at each stroke, "There is *no* omnibus, *no* driver, *no* bridge, *no* mountain; you are a *truant*, a *gutter snipe,* a *liar.*" His father could be very stern at times. His mother had begged him to say he was sorry. But he could not say that. It was the greatest day of his life, in spite of the caning and the poetry at the end of it.

He had returned punctually at sunset — driven not by Sir Thomas Browne, but by a maiden lady who was full of quiet fun. They had talked of omnibuses and also of barouche landaus. How far away her gentle voice seemed now! Yet it was scarcely three hours since he had left her up the alley.

His mother called through the door. "Dear, you are to come down and to bring your poetry with you."

He came down, and found that Mr. Bons was in the smoking-room with his father. It had been a dinner party.

"Here is the great traveller!" said his father grimly. "Here is the young gentleman who drives in an omnibus over rainbows, while young ladies sing to him." Pleased with his wit, he laughed.

"After all," said Mr. Bons, smiling, "there is something a little like it in Wagner. It is odd how, in quite illiterate minds, you will find glimmers of Artistic Truth. The case interests me. Let me plead for the culprit. We have all romanced in our time, haven't we?"

"Hear how kind Mr. Bons is," said his mother, while his father said, "Very well. Let him say his Poem, and that will do. He is going away to my sister on Tuesday, and *she* will cure him of this alley-slopering." (Laughter.) "Say your Poem."

The boy began. "'Standing aloof in giant ignorance.'"

His father laughed again — roared. "One for you, my son! 'Standing aloof in giant ignorance!' I never knew these poets talked sense. Just describes you. Here, Bons, you go in for poetry. Put him through it, will you, while I fetch up the whisky?"

"Yes, give me the Keats," said Mr. Bons. "Let him say his Keats to me."

So for a few moments the wise man and the ignorant boy were left alone in the smoking-room.

"'Standing aloof in giant ignorance, of thee I dream and of the Cyclades, as one who sits ashore and longs perchance to visit —— '"

"Quite right. To visit what?"

"'To visit dolphin coral in deep seas,'" said the boy, and burst into tears.

"Come, come! why do you cry?"

"Because — because all these words that only rhymed before, now that I've come back they're me."

Mr. Bons laid the Keats down. The case was more interesting than he had expected. "*You?*" he exclaimed. "This sonnet, *you?*"

"Yes — and look further on: 'Aye, on the shores of darkness there is light, and precipices show untrodden green.' It *is* so, sir. All these things are true."

"I never doubted it," said Mr. Bons, with closed eyes.

"You — then you believe me? You believe in the

omnibus and the driver and the storm and that return ticket I got for nothing and —— "

"Tut, tut! No more of your yarns, my boy. I meant that I never doubted the essential truth of Poetry. Some day, when you have read more, you will understand what I mean."

"But Mr. Bons, it *is* so. There *is* light upon the shores of darkness. I have seen it coming. Light and a wind."

"Nonsense," said Mr. Bons.

"If I had stopped! They tempted me. They told me to give up my ticket — for you cannot come back if you lose your ticket. They called from the river for it, and indeed I was tempted, for I have never been so happy as among those precipices. But I thought of my mother and father, and that I must fetch them. Yet they will not come, though the road starts opposite our house. It has all happened as the people up there warned me, and Mr. Bons has disbelieved me like every one else. I have been caned. I shall never see that mountain again."

"What's that about me?" said Mr. Bons, sitting up in his chair very suddenly.

"I told them about you, and how clever you were, and how many books you had, and they said, 'Mr. Bons will certainly disbelieve you.'"

"Stuff and nonsense, my young friend. You grow impertinent. I — well — I will settle the matter. Not a word to your father. I will cure you. Tomorrow evening I will myself call here to take you for a walk, and at sunset we will go up this alley opposite and hunt for your omnibus, you silly little boy."

His face grew serious, for the boy was not disconcerted, but leapt about the room singing, "Joy! joy! I told them you would believe me. We will drive together over the rainbow. I told them that you would come." After all, could there be anything in the story? Wagner? Keats? Shelley? Sir Thomas Browne? Certainly the case was interesting.

And on the morrow evening, though it was pouring with rain, Mr. Bons did not omit to call at Agathox Lodge.

The boy was ready, bubbling with excitement, and skipping about in a way that rather vexed the President of the Literary Society. They took a turn down Buckingham Park Road, and then — having seen that no one was watching them — slipped up the alley. Naturally enough (for the sun was setting) they ran straight against the omnibus.

"Good heavens!" exclaimed Mr. Bons. "Good gracious heavens!"

It was not the omnibus in which the boy had driven first, nor yet that in which he had returned. There were three horses — black, gray, and white, the gray being the finest. The driver, who turned round at the mention of goodness and of heaven, was a sallow man with terrifying jaws and sunken eyes. Mr. Bons, on seeing him, gave a cry as if of recognition, and began to tremble violently.

The boy jumped in.

"Is it possible?" cried Mr. Bons. "Is the impossible possible?'

"Sir; come in, sir. It is such a fine omnibus. Oh, here is his name — Dan some one."

Mr. Bons sprang in too. A blast of wind immediately slammed the omnibus door, and the shock jerked down all the omnibus blinds, which were very weak on their springs.

"Dan . . . Show me. Good gracious heavens! we're moving."

"Hooray!" said the boy.

Mr. Bons became flustered. He had not intended to be kidnapped. He could not find the door-handle, nor push up the blinds. The omnibus was quite dark, and by the time he had struck a match, night had come on outside also. They were moving rapidly.

"A strange, a memorable adventure," he said, surveying the interior of the omnibus, which was large, roomy, and constructed with extreme regularity, every part exactly answering to every other part. Over the door (the handle of which was outside) was written, "Lasciate ogni baldanza voi che entrate" — at least, that was what was written, but Mr. Bons said that it was Lashy arty something, and that baldanza was a mistake for speranza. His voice sounded as if he was in church. Meanwhile, the boy called to the cadaverous driver for two return tickets. They were handed in without a word. Mr. Bons covered his face with his hands and again trembled. "Do you know who that is!" he whispered, when the little window had shut upon them. "It is the impossible."

"Well, I don't like him as much as Sir Thomas Browne, though I shouldn't be surprised if he had even more in him."

"More in him?" He stamped irritably. "By accident you have made the greatest discovery of the century, and all you can say is that there is more in this man. Do you remember those vellum books in my library, stamped with red lilies? This — sit still, I bring you stupendous news! — *this is the man who wrote them.*"

The boy sat quite still. "I wonder if we shall see Mrs. Gamp?" he asked, after a civil pause.

"Mrs. —— ?"

"Mrs. Gamp and Mrs. Harris. I like Mrs. Harris. I came upon them quite suddenly. Mrs. Gamp's bandboxes have moved over the rainbow so badly. All the bottoms have fallen out, and two of the pippins off her bedstead tumbled into the stream."

"Out there sits the man who wrote my vellum books!" thundered Mr. Bons, "and you talk to me of Dickens and of Mrs. Gamp?"

"I know Mrs. Gamp so well," he apologized. "I could not help being glad to see her. I recognized her voice. She was telling Mrs. Harris about Mrs. Prig."

"Did you spend the whole day in her elevating company?"

"Oh, no. I raced. I met a man who took me out beyond to a race-course. You run, and there are dolphins out at sea."

"Indeed. Do you remember the man's name?"

"Achilles. No; he was later. Tom Jones."

Mr. Bons sighed heavily. "Well, my lad, you have made a miserable mess of it. Think of a cultured person with your opportunities! A cultured person would have known all these characters and known what to have said to each. He would not have wasted his time with a Mrs. Gamp or a Tom Jones. The creations of Homer, of Shakespeare, and of Him who drives us now, would alone have contented him. He would not have raced. He would have asked intelligent questions."

"But, Mr. Bons," said the boy humbly, "you will be a cultured person. I told them so."

"True, true, and I beg you not to disgrace me when we arrive. No gossiping. No running. Keep close to my side, and never speak to these Immortals unless they speak to you. Yes, and give me the return tickets. You will be losing them."

The boy surrendered the tickets, but felt a little sore. After all, he had found the way to this place. It was hard first to be disbelieved and then to be lectured. Meanwhile, the rain had stopped, and moonlight crept into the omnibus through the cracks in the blinds.

"But how is there to be a rainbow?" cried the boy.

"You distract me," snapped Mr. Bons. "I wish to meditate on beauty. I wish to goodness I was with a reverent and sympathetic person."

The lad bit his lip. He made a hundred good resolutions. He would imitate Mr. Bons all the visit. He would not laugh, or run, or sing, or do any of the vulgar things that must have disgusted his new friends last time. He would be very careful to pronounce their names properly, and to remember who knew whom. Achilles did not know Tom Jones — at least, so Mr. Bons said. The Duchess of Malfi was older than Mrs. Gamp — at least, so Mr. Bons said. He would be self-conscious, reticent, and prim. He would never say he liked any one. Yet, when the blind flew up at a chance touch of his head, all these good resolutions went to the winds, for the omnibus had reached the summit of a moonlit hill, and there was the chasm, and there, across it, stood the old precipices, dreaming, with their feet in the everlasting river. He exclaimed, "The mountain! Listen to the new tune in the water! Look at the camp fires in the ravines," and Mr. Bons, after a hasty glance, retorted, "Water? Camp fires? Ridiculous rubbish. Hold your tongue. There is nothing at all."

Yet, under his eyes, a rainbow formed, compounded not of sunlight and storm, but of moonlight and the spray of the river. The three horses put their feet upon it. He thought it the finest rainbow he had seen, but did not dare say so, since Mr. Bons said that nothing was there. He leant out — the window had opened — and sang the tune that rose from the sleeping waters.

"The prelude to Rhinegold?" said Mr. Bons suddenly. "Who taught you these *leit motifs?*" He, too, looked out of the window. Then he behaved very oddly. He gave a choking cry, and fell back on to the omnibus floor. He writhed and kicked. His face was green.

"Does the bridge make you dizzy?" the boy asked.

"Dizzy!" gasped Mr. Bons. "I want to go back. Tell the driver."

But the driver shook his head.

"We are nearly there," said the boy. "They are asleep. Shall I call? They will be so pleased to see you, for I have prepared them."

Mr. Bons moaned. They moved over the lunar rainbow, which ever and ever broke away behind their wheels. How still the night was! Who would be sentry at the Gate?

"I am coming," he shouted, again forgetting the hundred resolutions. "I am returning — I, the boy."

"The boy is returning," cried a voice to other voices, who repeated, "The boy is returning."

"I am bringing Mr. Bons with me."

Silence.

"I should have said Mr. Bons is bringing me with him."

Profound silence.

"Who stands sentry?"

"Achilles."

And on the rocky causeway, close to the springing of the rainbow bridge, he saw a young man who carried a wonderful shield.

"Mr. Bons, it is Achilles, armed."

"I want to go back," said Mr. Bons.

The last fragment of the rainbow melted, the wheels sang upon the living rock, the door of the omnibus burst open. Out leapt the boy — he could not resist — and sprang to meet the warrior, who, stooping suddenly, caught him on his shield.

"Achilles!" he cried, "let me get down, for I am ignorant and vulgar, and I must wait for that Mr. Bons of whom I told you yesterday."

But Achilles raised him aloft. He crouched on the wonderful shield, on heroes and burning cities, on vineyards graven in gold, on every dear passion, every joy, on the entire image of the Mountain that he had discovered, encircled, like it, with an everlasting stream. "No, no," he protested, "I am not worthy. It is Mr. Bons who must be up here."

But Mr. Bons was whimpering, and Achilles trumpeted and cried, "Stand upright upon my shield!"

"Sir, I did not mean to stand! something made me stand. Sir, why do you delay? Here is only the great Achilles, whom you knew."

Mr. Bons screamed, "I see no one. I see nothing. I want to go back." Then he cried to the driver, "Save me! Let me stop in your chariot. I have honoured you. I have quoted you. I have bound you in vellum. Take me back to my world."

The driver replied, "I am the means and not the end. I am the food and not the life. Stand by yourself, as that boy has stood. I cannot save you. For poetry is a spirit; and they that would worship it must worship in spirit and in truth."

Mr. Bons — he could not resist — crawled out of the beautiful omnibus. His face appeared, gaping horribly. His hands followed, one gripping the step, the other beating the air. Now his shoulders emerged, his chest, his stomach. With a shriek of "I see London," he fell — fell against the hard, moonlit rock, fell into it as if it were water, fell through it, vanished, and was seen by the boy no more.

"Where have you fallen to, Mr. Bons? Here is a procession arriving to honour you with music and torches. Here come the men and women whose names you know. The mountain is awake, the river is awake, over the race-course the sea is awaking those dolphins, and it is all for you. They want you —— "

There was the touch of fresh leaves on his forehead. Some one had crowned him.

ΤΕΛΟΣ

From the *Kingston Gazette*
Surbiton Times,
and *Raynes Park Observer.*

The body of Mr. Septimus Bons has been found in a shockingly mutilated condition in the vicinity of the Bermondsey gas-works. The deceased's pockets contained a sovereign-purse, a silver cigar-case, a bijou pronouncing dictionary, and a couple of omnibus tickets. The unfortunate gentleman had apparently been hurled from a considerable height. Foul play is suspected, and a thorough investigation is pending by the authorities.

MAVIS GALLANT

The Accident

I was tired and did not always understand what they were asking me. I borrowed a pencil and wrote:

PETER HIGGINS
CALGARY 1935 — ITALY 1956

But there was room for more on the stone, and the English clergyman in this Italian town who was doing all he could for me said, "Is there nothing else, child?" Hadn't Pete been my husband, somebody's son? That was what he was asking. It seemed enough. Pete had renounced us, left us behind. His life-span might matter, if anyone cared, but I must have sensed even then that no one would ever ask me what he had been like. His father once asked me to write down what I remembered. He wanted to compose a memorial booklet and distribute it at Christmas, but then his wife died, too, and he became prudent about recollections. Even if I had wanted to, I couldn't have told much — just one or two things about the way Pete died. His mother had some information about him, and I had some, but never enough to describe a life. She had the complete knowledge that puts parents at a loss, finally; she knew all about him except his opinion of her and how he was with me. They were never equals. She was a grown person with part of a life lived and the habit of secrets before he was conscious of her. She said, later, that she and Pete had been friends. How can you be someone's friend if you have had twenty years' authority over him and he has never had one second's authority over you?

He didn't look like his mother. He looked like me. In Italy, on our wedding trip, we were often taken for brother and sister. Our height, our glasses, our soft myopic stares, our assurance, our sloppy comfortable clothes made us seem to the Italians related and somehow unplaceable. Only a North American could have guessed what our families were, what our education amounted to, and where we had got the money to spend on travelling. Most of the time we were just pie-faces, like the tourists in ads though we were not as clean as those couples, and not quite as grown-up. We didn't seem to be married: the honeymoon in hotels, in strange beds, the meals we shared in cheap, bright little restaurants, prolonged the clandestine quality of love before. It was still a game, but now we had infinite time. I became bold, and I dismissed the universe: "It was a rotten little experiment," I said, "and we were given up long ago." I had been brought up by a forcible, pessimistic, widowed mother, and to be able to say aloud "we were given up" shows how far I had come. Pete's assurance was natural, but mine was fragile, and recent, and had grown out of love. Travelling from another direction, he was much more interested in his parents than in God. There was a glorious treason in all our conversations now. Pete wondered about his parents, but I felt safer belittling Creation. My mother had let me know about the strength of the righteous; I still thought the skies would fall if I said too much.

What struck me about these secret exchanges was how we judged our parents from a distance now, as if they were people we had known on a visit. The idea that he and I could be natural siblings crossed my mind. What if I, or Pete, or both, had been adopted? We had been raised in different parts of Canada, but we were only children, and neither of us resembled our supposed parents. Watching him, trapping him almost in mannerisms I could claim, I saw my habit of sprawling, of spreading maps and newspapers on the ground. He had a vast appetite for bread and pastries and sweet desserts. He was easily drunk and easily sick. Yes, we were alike. We talked in hotel rooms, while we drank the drink of the place, the *grappa* or wine or whatever we were given, prone across the bed, the bottle and glasses and the ashtray on the floor. We agreed to live openly, without secrets, though neither of us knew what a secret was. I admired him as I could never have admired myself. I remembered how my mother, the keeper of the castle until now, had said that one day — one treeless, sunless day — real life would overtake me, and then I would realize how spoiled and silly I had always been.

The longest time he and I spent together in one place was three days, in a village up behind the Ligurian coast. I thought that the only success of my life, my sole achievement, would be this marriage. In a dream he came to me with the plans for a house. I saw the white lines on the blue paper, and he showed me the sunny Italian-style loggia that would be built. "It is not quite what we want," he said, "but better than anything we have now." "But we can't afford it, we haven't got the capital," I cried and I panicked, and woke: woke safe, in a room of which the details were dawn, window, sky, first birds of morning, and Pete still sleeping, still in the dark.

The last Italian town of our journey was nothing — just a black beach with sand like soot, and houses shut and dormant because it was the middle of the afternoon. We had come here from our village only to change trains. We were on our way to Nice, then Paris, then home. We left our luggage at the station, with a porter looking after it, and we drifted through empty, baking streets, using up the rest of a roll of film. By now we must have had hundreds of pictures of each other in market squares, next to oleanders, cut in two by broomstick shade, or backed up, squinting, against scaly noonday shutters. Pete now chose to photograph a hotel with a cat on the step, a policeman, and a souvenir stand, as if he had never seen such things in Canada — as if they were monuments. I never once heard him say anything was ugly or dull; for if it was, what were we doing with it? We were often stared at, for we were out of our own background and did not fit into the new. That day, I was eyed more than he was. I was watched by men talking in dark doorways, leaning against the façades of inhospitable shops. I was travelling in shorts and a shirt and rope-soled shoes. I know now that this costume was resented, but I don't know why. There was nothing indecent about my clothes. They were very like Pete's.

He may not have noticed the men. He was always on the lookout for something to photograph, or something to do, and sometimes he missed people's faces. On the steep street that led back to the railway station, he took a careful picture of a bakery, and he bought crescent-shaped bread with a soft, pale crust, and ate it there, on the street. He wasn't hungry; it was a question of using time. Now the closed shutters broke out in the afternoon, and girls appeared — girls with thick hair, smelling of jasmine and honeysuckle. They strolled hand in hand, in light stockings and clean white shoes. Their dresses — blue, lemon, the palest peach — bloomed over rustling petticoats. At home I'd have called them cheap, and made a face at their cheap perfume, but here, in their own place, they were enravishing, and I thought Pete would look at them and at me and compare; but all he remarked was "How do they stand those clothes on a day like this?" So real life, the grey noon with no limits, had not yet begun. I distrusted real life, for I knew nothing about it. It was the middle-aged world without feeling, where no one was loved.

Bored with his bread, he tossed it away and laid his hands on a white Lambretta propped against the curb. He pulled it upright, examining it. He committed two crimes in a second: wasted bread and touched an adored mechanical object belonging to someone else. I knew these were crimes later, when it was no use knowing, no good to either of us. The steering of the Lambretta was locked. He saw a bicycle then, belonging, he thought, to an old man who was sitting in a kitchen chair out on the pavement. "This all right with you?" Pete pointed to the bike, then himself, then down the hill. With a swoop of his hand he tried to show he would come straight back. His pantomime also meant that there was still time before we had to be on the train, that up at the station there was nothing to do, that eating bread, taking pictures of shops, riding a bike downhill and walking it back were all doing, using up your life; yes, it was a matter of living.

The idling old man Pete had spoken to bared his gums. Pete must have taken this for a smile. Later, the old man, who was not the owner of the bike or of anything except the fat sick dog at his feet, said he had cried "Thief!" but I never heard him. Pete tossed me his camera and I saw him glide, then rush away, past the girls who smelled of jasmine, past the bakery, down to the corner, where a policeman in white, under a parasol, spread out one arm and flexed the other and blew hard on a whistle. Pete was standing, as if he were trying to coast to a stop. I saw things meaningless now — for instance that the sun was sifted through leaves. There were trees we hadn't noticed. Under the leaves he seemed under water. A black car, a submarine with Belgian plates, parked at an angle, stirred to life. I saw sunlight deflected from six points on the paint. My view became discomposed, as if the sea were suddenly black and opaque and had splashed up over the policeman and the road, and I screamed, "He's going to open the door!" Everyone said later that I was mistaken, for why would the Belgian have started the motor, pulled out, and *then* flung open the door? He had stopped near a change office; perhaps he had forgotten his sunglasses, or a receipt. He started, stopped abruptly, hurled back the door. I saw that, and then I saw him driving away. No one had taken his number.

Strangers made Pete kneel and then stand, and they dusted the bicycle. They forced him to walk — where? Nobody wanted him. Into a pharmacy, finally. In a parrot's voice he said to the policeman, "Don't touch my elbow." The pharmacist said, "He can't stay here," for Pete was vomiting, but weakly — a weak coughing, like an infant's. I was in a crowd of about twenty people, a spectator with two cameras round my neck. In kind somebody's living room, Pete was placed on a couch with a cushion under his head and another under his dangling arm. The toothless old man turned up now, panting, with his waddling dog, and cried that we had a common thief there before us, and everyone listened and marvelled until the old man spat on the carpet and was turned out.

When I timidly touched Pete, trying to wipe his face with a crumpled Kleenex (all I had), he thought I was one of the strangers. His mouth was a purple color, as if he had been in icy water. His eyes looked at me, but he was not looking out.

"Ambulance," said a doctor who had been fetched by the policeman. He spoke loudly and slowly, dealing with idiots.

"Yes," I heard, in English. "We must have an ambulance."

Everyone now inspected me. I was, plainly, responsible for something. For walking around the streets in shorts? Wasting bread? Conscious of my sweaty hair, my bare legs, my lack of Italian — my nakedness — I began explaining the true error of the day: "The train has gone, and all our things are on it. Our luggage. We've been staying up in that village — oh, what's the name of it, now? Where they make the white wine. I can't remember, no, I can't remember where we've been. I could find it, I could take you there; I've just forgotten what it's called. We were down here waiting for the train. To Nice. We had lots of time. The porter took our things and said he'd put them on the train for us. He said the train would wait here, at the border, that it waited a long time. He was supposed to meet us at the place where you show your ticket. I guess for an extra tip. The train must have gone now. My purse is in the duffelbag up at the ... I'll look in my husband's wallet. Of course that is my husband! Our passports must be on the train, too. Our traveller's checks are in our luggage, his and mine. We were just walking round taking pictures instead of sitting up there in the station. Anyway, there was no place to sit — only the bar, and it was smelly and dark."

No one believed a word of this, of course. Would you give your clothes, your passport, your traveller's checks to a porter? A man you had never seen in your life before? A bandit disguised as a porter, with a stolen cap on his head?

"You could not have taken that train without showing your passport," a careful foreign voice objected.

"What are you two, anyway?" said the man from the change office. His was a tough, old-fashioned movie-American accent. He was puffy-eyed and small, but he seemed superior to us, for he wore an impeccable shirt. Pete, on the sofa, looked as if he had been poisoned, or stepped on. "What are you?" the man from the change office said again. "Students? Americans? No? What, then? Swedes?"

I saw what the doctor had been trying to screen from me: a statue's marble eye.

The tourist who spoke the careful foreign English said, "Be careful of the pillows."

"What? What?" screamed the put-upon person who owned them.

"Blood is coming out of his ears," said the tourist, halting between words. "That is a bad sign." He seemed to search his memory for a better English word. "An *unfortunate* sign," he said, and put his hand over his mouth.

Pete's father and mother flew from Calgary when they had my cable. They made flawless arrangements by telephone, and knew exactly what to bring. They had a sunny room looking onto rusty palms and a strip of beach about a mile from where the accident had been. I sat against one of the windows and told them what I thought I remembered. I looked at the white walls, the white satin bedspreads, at Mrs. Higgins' spotless dressing case, and finally down at my hands.

His parents had not understood, until now, that ten days had gone by since Pete's death.

"What have you been doing, dear, all alone?" said Mrs. Higgins, gently.

"Just waiting, after I cabled you." They seemed to be expecting more. "I've been to the movies," I said.

From this room we could hear the shrieks of children playing on the sand.

"Are they orphans?" asked Mrs. Higgins, for they were little girls, dressed alike, with soft pink sun hats covering their heads.

"It seems to be a kind of summer camp," I said. "I was wondering about them, too."

"It would make an attractive picture," said Pete's mother, after a pause. "The blue sea, and the nuns, and all those bright hats. It would look nice in a dining room."

They were too sick to reproach me. My excuse for not having told them sooner was that I hadn't been thinking, and they didn't ask me for it. I could only repeat what seemed important now. "I don't want to go back home just yet" was an example. I was already in the future, which must have hurt them. "I have a girl friend in the Embassy in Paris. I can stay with her." I scarcely moved my lips. They had to strain to hear. I held still, looking down at my fingers. I was very brown, sun streaks in my hair, more graceful than at my wedding, where I knew they had found me maladroit — a great lump of a Camp Fire Girl. That was how I had seen myself in my father-in-law's eyes. Extremes of shock had brought me near some ideal they had of prettiness. I appeared now much more the kind of girl they'd have wanted as Pete's wife.

So they had come for nothing. They were not to see him, or bury him, or fetch home his bride. All I had to show them was a still unlabelled grave.

When I dared look at them, I saw their way of being was not Pete's. Neither had his soft selective stare. Mr. Higgins' eyes were a fanatic blue. He was thin and sunburned and unused to nonsense. Summer and winter he travelled with his wife in climates that were bad for her skin. She had the fair, papery coloring that requires constant vigilance. All this I knew because of Pete.

They saw his grave at the best time of day, in the late afternoon, with the light at a slant. The cemetery was in a valley between two plaster towns. A flash of the sea was visible, a corner of ultramarine. They saw a stone wall covered with roses, pink and white and near-white, open, without secrets. The hiss of traffic on the road came to us, softer than rain; then true rain came down, and we ran to our waiting taxi through a summer storm. Later they saw the station where Pete had left our luggage but never come back. Like Pete — as Pete had intended to — they were travelling to Nice. Under a glass shelter before the station I paused and said, "That was where it happened, down there." I pointed with my white glove. I was not as elegant as Mrs. Higgins, but I was not a source of embarrassment. I wore gloves, stockings, shoes.

The steep street under rain was black as oil. Everything was reflected upside down. The neon signs of the change office and the pharmacy swam deeply in the pavement.

"I'd like to thank the people who were so kind," said Mrs. Higgins. "Is there time? Shirley, I suppose you got their names?"

"Nobody was kind," I said.

"Shirley! We've met the doctor, and the minister, but you said there was a policeman, and a Dutch gentleman, and a lady — you were in this lady's living room."

"They were all there, but no one was kind."

"The bike's paid for?" asked Mr. Higgins suddenly.

"Yes, I paid. And I paid for having the sofa cushions cleaned."

What sofa cushions? What was I talking about? They seemed petrified, under the glass shelter, out of the rain. They could not take their eyes away from the place I had said was *there.* They never blamed me, never by a word or a hidden meaning. I had explained, more than once, how the porter that day had not put our bags on the train after all but had stood waiting at the customs barrier, wondering what had become of us. I told them how I had found everything intact — passports and checks and maps and sweaters and shoes ... They could not grasp the importance of it. They knew that Pete had chosen me, and gone away with me, and they never saw him again. An unreliable guide had taken them to a foreign graveyard and told them, without evidence, that now he was there.

"I still don't see how anyone could have thought Pete was stealing," said his mother. "What would Pete have wanted with someone's old bike?"

They were flying home from Nice. They loathed Italy now, and they had a special aversion to the sunny room where I had described Pete's death. We three sat in the restaurant at the airport, and they spoke quietly, considerately, because the people at the table next to ours were listening to a football match on a portable radio.

I closed my hand into a fist and let it rest on the table. I imagined myself at home, saying to my mother. "All right, real life has begun. What's your next prophecy?"

I was not flying with them. I was seeing them off. Mrs. Higgins sat poised and prepared in her linen coat, with her large handbag, and her cosmetics and airsickness tablets in her dressing case, and her diamond maple leaf so she wouldn't be mistaken for an American, and her passport ready to be shown to anyone. Pale gloves lay folded over the clasp of the dressing case. "You'll want to go to your own people, I know," she said. "But you have a home with us. You mustn't forget it." She paused. I said nothing, and so she continued, "What are you going to do, dear? I mean, after you have visited your friend. You mustn't be lonely."

I muttered whatever seemed sensible. "I'll have to get a job. I've never had one and I don't know anything much. I can't even type — not properly." Again they gave me this queer impression of expecting something more. What did they want? "Pete said it was no good learning anything if you couldn't type. He said it was the only useful thing he could do."

In the eyes of his parents was the same wound. I have told them something about him they hadn't known.

"Well, I understand," said his mother, presently. "At least, I think I do."

They imagine I want to be near the grave, I supposed. They think that's why I'm staying on the same side of the world. Pete and I had been waiting for a train: now I had taken it without him. I was waiting again. Even if I were to visit the cemetery every day, he would never speak. His last words had not been for me but to a policeman. He would have said something to me, surely, if everyone hadn't been in such a hurry to get him out of the way. His mind was quenched, and his body out of sight. "You don't love with your soul," I had cried to the old clergyman at the funeral — an offensive remark, judging from the look on his face as he turned it aside. Now I was careful. The destination of a soul was of no interest. The death of a voice — now, that was real. The Dutchman suddenly covering his mouth was horror, and a broken elbow was true pain. But I was careful; I kept this to myself.

"You're our daughter now," Pete's father said. "I don't think I want you to have to worry about a job. Not yet." Mr. Higgins happened to know my family's exact status. My father had not left us well off, and my mother had given everything she owned to a sect that did not believe in blood transfusions. She expected the end of the world, and would not eat an egg unless she had first met the hen. That was Mr. Higgins' view. "Shirley must work if that's what she wants to do," Mrs. Higgins said softly.

"I do want to!" I imagined myself, that day, in a river of people pouring into subways.

"I'm fixing something up for you, just the same,"

said Mr. Higgins hurriedly, as if he would not be interrupted by women.

Mrs. Higgins allowed her pale forehead to wrinkle, under her beige veil. Was it not better to struggle and to work, she asked. Wasn't that real life? Would it not keep Shirley busy, take her mind off her loss, her disappointment, her tragedy, if you like (though "tragedy" was not an acceptable way of looking at fate), if she had to think about her daily bread?

"The allowance I'm going to make her won't stop her from working," he said. "I was going to set something up for the kids anyway."

She seemed to approve; she had questioned him only out of some prudent system of ethics.

He said to me. "I always have to remember I could go any minute, just like that. I've got a heart." He tapped it — tapped his light suit. "Meanwhile you better start with this." He gave me the envelope that had been close to his heart until now. He seemed diffident, made ashamed by money, and by death, but it was he and not his wife who had asked if there was a hope that Pete had left a child. No, I had told him. I had wondered, too, but now I was sure. "Then Shirley is all we've got left," he had said to his wife, and I thought they seemed bankrupt, having nothing but me.

"If that's a check on a bank at home, it might take too long to clear," said his wife. "After all Shirley's been through, she needs a fair-sized sum right away."

"She's had that, Betty," said Mr. Higgins, smiling.

I had lived this: three round a table, the smiling parents. Pete had said, "They smile, they go on talking. You wonder what goes on."

"How you manage everything you do without a secretary with you all the time I just don't know," said his wife, all at once admiring him.

"You've been saying that for twenty-two years," he said.

"Twenty-three, now."

With this the conversation came to an end and they sat staring, puzzled, not overcome by life but suddenly lost to it, out of touch. The photograph Pete carried of his mother, that was in his wallet when he died, had been taken before her marriage, with a felt hat all to one side, and an organdie collar, and Ginger Rogers hair. It was easier to imagine Mr. Higgins young — a young Gary Cooper. My father-in-law's blue gaze rested on me now. Never in a million years would he have picked me as a daughter-in-law. I knew that; I understood. Pete was part of him, and Pete, with all the girls he had to choose from, had chosen me. When Mr. Higgins met my mother at the wedding, he thanked God, and was overheard being thankful, that the wedding was not in Calgary. Remembering my mother that day, with her glasses on her nose and a strange borrowed hat on her head, and recalling Mr. Higgins' face, I thought of words that would keep me from laughing. I found, at random, "threesome," "smother," "gambling," "habeas corpus," "sibling." . . .

"How is your mother, Shirley?" said Mrs. Higgins.

"I had a letter . . . She's working with a pendulum now."

"A pendulum?"

"Yes. A weight on a string, sort of. It makes a diagnosis — whether you've got something wrong with your stomach, if it's an ulcer, or what. She can use it to tell when you're pregnant and if the baby will be a girl or a boy. It depends whether it swings north-south or east-west."

"Can the pendulum tell who the father is?" said Mr. Higgins.

"They are useful for people who are afraid of doctors," said Mrs. Higgins, and she fingered her neat gloves, and smiled to herself. "Someone who won't hear the truth from a doctor will listen to any story from a woman with a pendulum or a piece of crystal."

"Or a stone that changes color," I said. "My mother had one of those. When our spaniel had mastoids it turned violet."

She glanced at me then, and caught in her breath, but her husband, by a certain amount of angry fidgeting, made us change the subject. That was the one moment she and I were close to each other — something to do with quirky female humor.

Mr. Higgins did not die of a heart attack, as he had confidently expected, but a few months after this Mrs. Higgins said to her maid in the kitchen, "I've got a terrible pain in my head. I'd better lie down." Pete's father wrote, "She knew what the matter was, but she never said. Typical." I inherited a legacy and some jewelry from her, and wondered why. I had been careless about writing. I could not write the kind of letters she seemed to want. How could I write to someone I hardly knew about someone else who did not exist? Mr. Higgins married the widow of one of his closest friends — a woman six years older than he. They travelled to Europe for their wedding trip. I had a temporary job as an interpreter in a department store. When my father-in-law saw me in a neat suit, with his name, HIGGINS fastened to my jacket, he seemed to approve. He was the only person then who did not say that I was wasting my life and my youth and ought to go home. The new Mrs. Higgins asked to be taken to an English-speaking hairdresser, and there, under the roaring dryer, she yelled that Mr. Higgins may not have been Pete's father. Perhaps he had been, perhaps he hadn't, but one thing he was, and that was a saint. She came out from under the helmet and said in a normal voice. "Martin doesn't know I dye my hair." I wondered if he had always wanted this short, fox-colored woman. The new marriage might for years have been in the maquis of his mind, and of Mrs. Higgins' life. She may have known it as she sat in the airport that day, smiling to herself, touching her unstained gloves. Mr. Higgins had drawn up a new way of life, like a clean will with everyone he loved cut out. I was trying to draw up a will, too, but I was patient, waiting, waiting for someone to tell me what to write. He spoke of Pete conventionally, in a sentimental way that forbade any feeling. Talking that way was easier for both of us. We were both responsible for something — for surviving, perhaps. Once he turned to me and said defiantly, "Well, she and Pete are together now, aren't they? And didn't they leave us here?"

HUGH GARNER

The Yellow Sweater

He stepped on the gas when he reached the edge of town. The big car took hold of the pavement and began to eat up the miles on the straight, almost level, highway. With his elbow stuck through the open window he stared ahead at the shimmering greyness of the road. He felt heavy and pleasantly satiated after his good small-town breakfast, and he shifted his bulk in the seat, at the same time brushing some cigar ash from the front of his salient vest. In another four hours he would be home — a day ahead of himself this trip, but with plenty to show the office for last week's work. He unconsciously patted the wallet resting in the inside pocket of his jacket as he thought of the orders he had taken.

Four thousand units to Slanders ... his second-best line too ... four thousand at twelve percent ... four hundred and eighty dollars! He rolled the sum over in his mind as if tasting it, enjoying its tartness like a kid with a gumdrop.

He drove steadily for nearly an hour, ignorant of the smell of spring in the air, pushing the car ahead with his mind as well as with his foot against the pedal. The success of his trip and the feeling of power it gave him carried him along toward the triumph of his homecoming.

Outside a small village he was forced to slow down for a road repair crew. He punched twice on the horn as he passed them, basking in the stares of the yokels who looked up from their shovels, and smiling at the envy showing on their faces.

A rather down-at-heel young man carrying an army kitbag stepped out from the office of a filling station and gave him the thumb. He pretended not to see the gesture, and pressed down slightly on the gas so that the car began to purr along the free and open road.

It was easy to see that the warm weather was approaching, he thought. The roads were becoming cluttered up once more with hitch-hikers. Why the government didn't clamp down on them was more than he could understand. Why should people pay taxes so that other lazy bums could fritter away their time roaming the country, getting free rides, going God knows where? They were dangerous too. It was only the week before that two of them had beaten up and robbed a man on this very same road. They stood a fat chance of *him* picking them up.

And yet they always thumbed him, or almost always. When they didn't he felt cheated, as a person does when he makes up his mind not to answer another's greeting, only to have them pass by without noticing him.

He glanced at his face in the rear-view mirror. It was a typical middle-aged businessman's face, plump and well-barbered, the shiny skin stretched taut across the cheeks. It was a face that was familiar to him not only from his possession of it, but because it was also the face of most of his friends. What was it the speaker at that service club luncheon had called it? "The physiognomy of success."

As he turned a bend in the road he saw the girl about a quarter of a mile ahead. She was not on the pavement, but was walking slowly along the shoulder of the highway, bent over with the weight of the bag she was carrying. He slowed down, expecting her to turn and thumb him, but she plodded on as though impervious to his approach. He sized her up as he drew near. She was young by the look of her back ... stocking seams straight ... heels muddy but not rundown. As he passed he stared at her face. She was a good-looking kid, probably eighteen or nineteen.

It was the first time in years that he had slowed down for a hiker. His reasons evaded him, and whether it was the feel of the morning, the fact of his going home, or the girl's apparent independence, he could not tell. Perhaps it was a combination of all three, plus the boredom of a long drive. It might be fun to pick her up, to cross-examine her while she was trapped in the seat beside him.

Easing the big car to a stop about fifty yards in front of her he looked back through the mirror. She kept glancing at the car, but her pace had not changed, and she came on as though she had expected him to stop. For a moment he was tempted to drive on again, angered by her indifference. She was not a regular hitch-hiker or she would have waited at the edge of town instead of setting out to walk while carrying such a heavy bag. But there was something about her that compelled him to wait — something which aroused in him an almost forgotten sense of adventure, an eagerness not experienced for years.

She opened the right rear door, saying at the same time, "Thank you very much, sir," in a frightened little voice.

"Put your bag in the back. That's it, on the floor," he ordered, turning towards her with his hand along the back of the seat. "Come and sit up here."

She did as he commanded, sitting very stiff and straight against the door. She was small, almost fragile, with long dark hair that waved where it touched upon the collar of her light-colored top-coat. Despite the warmth of the morning the coat was buttoned, and she held it to her in a way that suggested modesty or fear.

"Are you going very far?" he asked, looking straight ahead through the windshield, trying not to let the question sound too friendly.

"To the city," she answered, with the politeness and eagerness of the recipient of a favor.

"For a job?"

"Well, not exactly — " she began. Then she said, "Yes, for a job."

As they passed the next group of farm buildings she stared hard at them, her head turning with her eyes until they were too far back to be seen.

Something about her reminded him of his eldest daughter, but he shrugged off the comparison. It was silly of him to compare the two, one a hitch-hiking farm skivvy and the other one soon to come home from finishing school. In his mind's eye he could see the photograph of his daughter Shirley that hung on the wall of the living room. It had been taken with a color camera during the Easter vacation, and in it Shirley was wearing a bright yellow sweater.

"Do you live around here?" he asked, switching his thoughts back to the present.

"I was living about a mile down the road from where you picked me up."

"Sick of the farm?" he asked.

"No." She shook her head slowly, seriously.

"Have you anywhere to go in the city?"

"I'll get a job somewhere."

He turned then and got his first good look at her face. She was pretty, he saw, with the country girl's good complexion, her features small and even. "You're young to be leaving home like this," he said.

"That wasn't my home," she murmured. "I was living with my Aunt Bernice and her husband."

He noticed that she did not call the man her uncle.

"You sound as though you don't like the man your aunt is married to?"

"I hate him!" she whispered vehemently.

To change the subject he said, "You've chosen a nice day to leave, anyhow."

"Yes."

He felt a slight tingling along his spine. It was the same feeling he had experienced once when sitting in the darkened interior of a movie house beside a strange yet, somehow, intimate young woman. The feeling that if he wished he had only to let his hand fall along her leg . . .

"You're not very talkative," he said, more friendly now.

She turned quickly and faced him. "I'm sorry. I was thinking about — about a lot of things."

"It's too nice a morning to think of much," he said. "Tell me more about your reasons for leaving home."

"I wanted to get away, that's all."

He stared at her again, letting his eyes follow the contours of her body. "Don't tell me you're in trouble?" he asked.

She lowered her eyes to her hands. They were engaged in twisting the clasp on a cheap black handbag. "I'm not in trouble like that," she said slowly, although the tone of her voice belied her words.

He waited for her to continue. There was a sense of power in being able to question her like this without fear of having to answer any questions himself. He said, "There can't be much else wrong. Was it boy trouble?"

"Yes, that's it," she answered hastily.

"Where's the boy? Is he back there or in the city?"

"Back there," she answered.

He was aware of her nearness, of her young body beside him on the seat. "You're too pretty to worry about one boy," he said, trying to bridge the gap between them with unfamiliar flattery.

She did not answer him, but she smiled nervously in homage to his remark.

They drove on through the morning, and by skillful questioning he got her to tell him more about her life. She had been born near the spot where he had picked her up, she said. She was an orphan, eighteen years old, who for the past three years had been living on her aunt's farm. On his part he told her a little about his job, but not too much. He spoke in generalities, yet let her see how important he was in his field.

They stopped for lunch at a drive-in restaurant outside a small town. While they were eating he noticed that some of the other customers were staring at them. It angered him until he realized that they probably thought she was his mistress. This flattered him and he tried to imagine that it was true. During the meal he became animated, and he laughed loudly at his *risqué* little jokes.

She ate sparingly, politely, not knowing what to do with her hands between courses. She smiled at the things he said, even at the remarks that were obviously beyond her.

After they had finished their lunch he said to her jovially, "Here, we've been travelling together for two hours and we don't even know each other's names yet."

"Mine's Marie. Marie Edwards."

"You can call me Tom," he said expansively.

When he drew out his wallet to pay the check he was careful to cover the initials G. G. M. with the palm of his hand.

As they headed down the highway once again, Marie seemed to have lost some of her timidity and she talked and laughed with him as though he were an old friend. Once he stole a glance at her through the corner of his eye. She was staring ahead as if trying to unveil the future that was being overtaken by the onrushing car.

"A penny for your thoughts, Marie," he said.

"I was just thinking how nice it would be to keep going like this forever."

"Why?" he asked, her words revealing an unsuspected facet to her personality.

"I dunno," she answered, rubbing the palm of her hand along the upholstery of the seat in a gesture that was wholly feminine. "It seems so — safe here, somehow." She smiled as though apologizing for thinking such things. "It seems as if nothing bad could ever catch up to me again."

He gave her a quick glance before staring ahead at the road once more.

The afternoon was beautiful, the warm dampness of the fields bearing aloft the smell of uncovered earth and budding plants. The sun-warmed pavement sang like muted violins beneath the spinning tires of the car. The clear air echoed the sound of life and growth and the urgency of spring.

As the miles clicked off, and they were brought closer to their inevitable parting, an idea took shape in his mind and grew with every passing minute. Why bother hurrying home, he asked himself. After all he hadn't notified his wife to expect him, and he wasn't due back until tomorrow.

He wondered how the girl would react if he should suggest postponing the rest of the trip overnight. He would make it worth her while. There was a tourist camp on the shore of a small lake about twenty miles north of the highway. No one would be the wiser, he told himself. They were both fancy free.

The idea excited him, yet he found himself too timid to suggest it. He tried to imagine how he must appear to the girl. The picture he conjured up was of a mature figure, inclined to stoutness, much older than she was in years but not in spirit. Many men his age had formed liaisons with young women. In fact it was the accepted thing among some of the other salesmen he knew.

But there remained the voicing of the question. She appeared so guileless, so — innocent of his intentions. And yet it was hard to tell; she wasn't as innocent as she let on.

She interrupted his train of thought. "On an afternoon like this I'd like to paddle my feet in a stream," she said.

"I'm afraid the water would be pretty cold."

"Yes, it would be cold, but it'd be nice too. When we were kids we used to go paddling in the creek behind the schoolhouse. The water was strong with the spring freshet, and it would tug at our ankles and send a warm ticklish feeling up to our knees. The smooth pebbles on the bottom would make us twist our feet, and we'd try to grab them with our toes . . . I guess I must sound crazy," she finished.

No longer hesitant he said, "I'm going to turn the car into one of these side roads, Marie. On a long trip I usually like to park for a while under some trees. It makes a little break in the journey."

She nodded her head happily. "That would be nice," she said.

He turned the car off the highway and they travelled north along a road that curved gently between wide stretches of steaming fields. The speed of the car was seemingly increased by the drumming of gravel against the insides of the fenders.

It was time to bring the conversation back to a more personal footing, so he asked, "What happened between you and your boy-friend, Marie?" He had to raise his voice above the noise of the hurtling stones.

"Nothing much," she answered, hesitating as if making up the answer. "We had a fight, that's all."

"Serious?"

"I guess so."

"What happened? Did he try to get a little gay maybe?"

She dropped her head, and he could see the color rising along her neck and into the hair behind her ears.

"Does that embarrass you?" he asked, taking his hand from the wheel and placing it along the collar of her coat.

She tensed herself at his touch and tried to draw away, but he grasped her shoulder and pulled her against him. He could feel the fragility of her beneath his hand and the trembling of her skin beneath the cloth of her coat. The odor of her hair and of some cheap scent filled his nostrils.

She cried, "Don't please!" and broke away from the grip of his hand. She inched herself into the far corner of the seat again.

"You're a little touchy, aren't you?" he asked, trying to cover up his embarrassment at being repulsed so quickly.

"Why did you have to spoil it?"

His frustration kindled a feeling of anger against her. He knew her type all right. Pretending that butter wouldn't melt in her mouth, while all the time she was secretly laughing at him for being the sucker who picked her up, bought her a lunch, and drove her into town. She couldn't fool him; he'd met her type before.

He swung the car down a narrow lane, and they flowed along over the rutted wheel tracks beneath a flimsy ceiling of budding trees.

"Where are we going?" she asked, her voice apprehensive now.

"Along here a piece," he answered, trying to keep his anger from showing.

"Where does this road lead?"

"I don't know. Maybe there's a stream you can paddle in."

There was a note of relief in her voice as she said, "Oh! I didn't mean for us — for you to find a stream."

"You don't seem to know *what* you mean, do you?"

She became silent then and seemed to shrink farther into the corner.

The trees got thicker, and soon they found themselves in the middle of a small wood. The branches of the hardwoods were mottled green, their buds flicking like fingers in the breeze. He brought the car to a stop against the side of the road.

The girl watched him, the corners of her mouth trembling with fear. She slid her hand up the door and grabbed the handle. He tried to make his voice matter-of-fact as he said, "Well, here we are."

Her eyes ate into his face like those of a mesmerized rabbit watching a snake.

He opened a glove compartment and pulled out a package of cigarettes. He offered the package to her, but she shook her head.

"Let's get going," she pleaded.

"What, already? Maybe we should make a day of it."

She did not speak, but the question stood in her eyes. He leaned back against the seat, puffing on his cigarette. "There's a tourist camp on a lake a few miles north of here. We could stay there and go on to the city tomorrow."

She stifled a gasp. "I can't. I didn't think — I had no idea when we — "

He pressed his advantage. "Why can't you stay? Nobody'll know. I may be in a position to help you afterwards. You'll need help, you know."

"No. No, I couldn't," she answered. Her eyes filled with tears.

He had not expected her to cry. Perhaps he had been wrong in his estimation of her. He felt suddenly bored with the whole business, and ashamed of the feelings she had ignited in him.

"Please take me back to the highway," she said, pulling a carefully folded handkerchief from her handbag.

"Sure. In a few minutes." He wanted time to think things out; to find some way of saving face.

"You're just like he was," she blurted out, her words distorted by her handkerchief. "You're all the same."

Her outburst frightened him. "Marie," he said, reaching over to her. He wanted to quiet her, to show her that his actions had been the result of an old man's foolish impulse.

As soon as his hand touched her shoulder she gave a short cry and twisted the door handle. "No. No, please!" she cried.

"Marie, come here!" he shouted, trying to stop her. He grabbed her by the shoulder, but she tore herself from his grasp and fell through the door.

She jumped up from the road and staggered back through the grass into the belt of trees. Her stockings and the bottom of her coat were brown with mud.

"Don't follow me!" she yelled.

"I'm not going to follow you. Come back here and I'll drive you back to the city."

"No you don't! You're the same as he was!" she cried. "I know your tricks!"

He looked about him at the deserted stretch of trees, wondering if anybody could be listening. It would place him in a terrible position to be found with her like this. Pleading with her he said, "Come on Marie, I've got to go."

She began to laugh hysterically, her voice reverberating through the trees.

"Marie, come on," he coaxed. "I won't hurt you."

"No! Leave me alone. Please leave me alone!"

His pleas only seemed to make things worse. "I'm going," he said hurriedly, pulling the car door shut.

"Just leave me alone!" she cried. Then she began sobbing, "Bernice! Bernice!"

What dark fears had been released by his actions of the afternoon he did not know, but they frightened and horrified him. He turned the car around in the narrow lane and let it idle for a moment as he waited, hoping she would change her mind. She pressed herself deeper into the trees, wailing at the top of her voice.

From behind him came a racking noise from down the road, and he looked back and saw a tractor coming around a bend. A man was driving it and there was another riding behind. He put the car in gear and stepped on the gas.

Before the car reached the first turn beneath the trees he looked back. The girl was standing in the middle of the road beside the tractor and she was pointing his way and talking to the men. He wondered if they had his license number, and what sort of a story she was telling them.

He had almost reached the highway again before he remembered her suitcase standing on the floor behind the front seat. His possession of it seemed to tie him to the girl; to make him partner to her terror. He pulled the car to a quick stop, leaned over the back of the seat and picked the suitcase up from the floor. Opening the door he tossed it lightly to the side of the road with a feeling of relief. The frail clasp on the cheap bag opened as it hit the ground and its contents spilled into the ditch. There was a framed photograph, some letters and papers held together with an elastic band, a comb and brush, and some clothing, including a girl's yellow sweater.

"I'm no thief," he said, pushing the car into motion again, trying to escape from the sight of the opened bag. He wasn't to blame for the things that had happened to her. It wasn't his fault that her stupid little life was spilled there in the ditch.

"I've done nothing wrong," he said, as if pleading his case with himself. But there was a feeling of obscene guilt beating in his brain like a reiteration. Something of hers seemed to attach itself to his memory. Then suddenly he knew what it was — the sweater, the damned yellow sweater. His hands trembled around the wheel as he sent the car hurtling towards the safe anonymity of the city.

He tried to recapture his feelings of the morning, but when he looked at himself in the mirror all he saw was the staring face of a fat frightened old man.

WILLIAM H. GASS

In the Heart of the Heart of the Country

A PLACE

So I have sailed the seas and come . . .

to B . . .

a small town fastened to a field in Indiana. Twice there have been twelve hundred people here to answer to the census. The town is outstandingly neat and shady, and always puts its best side to the highway. On one lawn there's even a wood or plastic iron deer.

You can reach us by crossing a creek. In the spring the lawns are green, the forsythia is singing, and even the railroad that guts the town has straight bright rails which hum when the train is coming, and the train itself has a welcome horning sound.

Down the back streets the asphalt crumbles into gravel. There's Westbrook's, with the geraniums, Horsefall's, Mott's. The sidewalk shatters. Gravel dust rises like breath behind the wagons. And I am in retirement from love.

WEATHER

In the Midwest, around the lower Lakes, the sky in the winter is heavy and close, and it is a rare day, a day to remark on, when the sky lifts and allows the heart up. I am keeping count, and as I write this page, it is eleven days since I have seen the sun.

MY HOUSE

There's a row of headless maples behind my house, cut to free the passage of electric wires. High stumps, ten feet tall, remain, and I climb these like a boy to watch the country sail away from me. They are ordinary fields, a little more uneven than they should be, since in the spring they puddle. The topsoil's thin, but only moderately stony. Corn is grown one year, soybeans another. At dusk starlings darken the single tree — a larch — which stands in the middle. When the sky moves, fields move under it. I feel, on my perch, that I've lost my years. It's as though I were living at last in my eyes, as I have always dreamed of doing, and I think then I know why I've come here: to see, and so to go out against new things — oh god how easily — like air in a breeze. It's true there are moments — foolish moments, ecstasy on a tree stump — when I'm all but gone, scattered I like to think like seed, for I'm the sort now in the fool's position of having love left over which I'd like to lose; what good is it now to me, candy ungiven after Halloween?

A PERSON

There are vacant lots on either side of Billy Holsclaw's house. As the weather improves, they fill with hollyhocks. From spring through fall, Billy collects coal and wood and puts the lumps and pieces in piles near his door, for keeping warm is his one work. I see him most often on mild days sitting on his doorsill in the sun. I notice he's squinting a little, which is perhaps the reason he doesn't cackle as I pass. His house is the size of a single garage, and very old. It shed its paint with its youth, and its boards are a warped and weathered gray. So is Billy. He wears a short lumpy faded black coat when it's cold, otherwise he always goes about in the same loose, grease-spotted shirt and trousers. I suspect his galluses were yellow once, when they were new.

WIRES

These wires offend me. Three trees were maimed on their account, and now these wires deface the sky. They cross like a fence in front of me, enclosing the crows with the clouds. I can't reach in, but like a stick, I throw my feelings over. What is it that offends me? I am on my stump, I've built a platform there and the wires prevent my going out. The cut trees, the black wires, all the beyond birds therefore anger me. When I've wormed through a fence to reach a meadow, do I ever feel the same about the field?

THE CHURCH

The church has a steeple like the hat of a witch, and five birds, all doves, perch in its gutters.

MY HOUSE

Leaves move in the windows. I cannot tell you yet how beautiful it is, what it means. But they do move. They move in the glass.

POLITICS

... for all those not in love.

I've heard Batista described as a Mason. A farmer who'd seen him in Miami made this claim. He's as nice a fellow as you'd ever want to meet. Of Castro, of course, no one speaks.

For all those not in love there's law: to rule ... to regulate ... to rectify. I cannot write the poetry of such proposals, the poetry of politics, though sometimes — often — always now — I am in that uneasy peace of equal powers which makes a State; then I communicate by passing papers, proclamations, orders, through my bowels. Yet I was not a State with you, nor were we both together any Indiana. A squad of Pershing Rifles at the moment, I make myself Right Face! Legislation packs the screw of my intestines. Well, king of the classroom's king of the hill. You used to waddle when you walked because my sperm between your legs was draining to a towel. Teacher, poet, folded lover — like the politician, like those drunkards, ill, or those who faucet-off while pissing heartily to preach upon the force and fullness of that stream, or pause from vomiting to praise the purity and passion of their puke — I chant, I beg, I orate, I command, I sing —

Come back to Indiana — not too late!
(Or will you be a ranger to the end?)
Good-bye ... Good-bye ... oh, I shall always wait
You, Larry, traveler —
stranger,
son,
— my friend —

my little girl, my poem by heart, my self, my childhood.

But I've heard Batista described as a Mason. That dries up my pity, melts my hate. Back from the garage where I have overheard it, I slap the mended fender of my car to laugh, and listen to the metal stinging tartly in my hand.

PEOPLE

Their hair in curlers and their heads wrapped in loud scarves, young mothers, fattish in trousers, lounge about in the speedwash, smoking cigarettes, eating candy, drinking pop, thumbing magazines, and screaming at their children above the whir and rumble of the machines.

At the bank a young man freshly pressed is letting himself in with a key. Along the street, delicately teetering, many grandfathers move in a dream. During the murderous heat of summer they perch on window ledges, their feet dangling just inside the narrow shelf of shade the store has made, staring steadily into the street. Where their consciousness has gone I can't say. It's not in the eyes. Perhaps it's diffuse, all temperature and skin, like an infant's, though more mild. Near the corner there are several large overalled men employed in standing. A truck turns to be weighed on the scales at the Feed and Grain. Images drift on the drugstore window. The wind has blown the smell of cattle into town. Our eyes have been driven in like the eyes of the old men. And there's no one to have mercy on us.

VITAL DATA

There are two restaurants here and a tearoom. two bars. one bank. three barbers, one with a green shade with which he blinds his window. two groceries. a dealer in Fords. one drug, one hardware, and one appliance store. several that sell feed, grain, and farm equipment. an antique shop. a poolroom. a laundromat. three doctors. a dentist. a plumber. a vet. a funeral home in elegant repair the color of a buttercup. numerous beauty parlors which open and shut like night-blooming plants. a tiny dime and department store of no width but several floors. a hutch, homemade, where you can order, after lying down or squirming in, furniture that's been fashioned from bent lengths of stainless tubing, glowing plastic, metallic thread, and clear shellac. an American Legion Post and a root beer stand. little agencies for this and that: cosmetics, brushes, insurance, greeting cards and garden produce — anything — sample shoes — which do their business out of hats and satchels, over coffee cups and dissolving sugar. a factory for making paper sacks and pasteboard boxes that's lodged in an old brick building bearing the legend OPERA HOUSE, still faintly golden, on its roof. a library given by Carnegie. a post office. a school. a railroad station. fire station. lumberyard. telephone company. welding shop. garage ... and spotted through the town from one end to the other in a line along the highway, gas stations to the number five.

EDUCATION

In 1833, Colin Goodykoontz, an itinerant preacher with a name from a fairytale, summed up the situation in one Indiana town this way:

Ignorance and her squalid brood. A universal dearth of intellect. Total abstinence from literature is very generally practiced.... There is not a scholar in grammar or geography, or a *teacher capable of instructing* in them, to my knowledge.... Others are supplied a few months of the year with the most antiquated & unreasonable forms of teaching reading, writing & cyphering.... Need I stop to remind you of the host of loathsome reptiles such a stagnant pool is fitted to breed! Croaking jealousy; bloated bigotry; coiling suspicion; wormish blindness; crocodile malice!

Things have changed since then, but in none of the respects mentioned.

BUSINESS

One side section of street is blocked off with sawhorses. Hard, thin, bitter men in blue jeans, cowboy boots and hats, untruck a dinky carnival. The merchants are promoting themselves. There will be free rides, raucous music, parades and coneys, pop, popcorn, candy, cones, awards and drawings, with all you can endure of pinch, push, bawl, shove, shout, scream, shriek, and bellow. Children pedal past on decorated bicycles, their wheels a blur of color, streaming crinkled paper and excited dogs. A little later there's a pet show for a prize — dogs, cats, birds, sheep, ponies, goats — none of which wins. The whirlabouts whirl about. The Ferris wheel climbs dizzily into the sky as far as a tall man on tiptoe might be persuaded to reach, and the irritated operators measure the height and weight of every child with sour eyes to see if they are safe for the machines. An electrical megaphone repeatedly trumpets the names of the generous sponsors. The following day they do not allow the refuse to remain long in the street.

MY HOUSE, THIS PLACE AND BODY

I have met with some mischance, wings withering, as Plato says obscurely, and across the breadth of Ohio, like heaven on a table. I've fallen as far as the poet, to the sixth sort of body, this house in B, in Indiana, with its blue and gray bewitching windows, holy magical insides. Great thick evergreens protect its entry. And I live *in*.

Lost in the corn rows, I remember feeling just another stalk, and thus this country takes me over in the way I occupy myself when I am well . . . completely — to the edge of both my house and body. No one notices, when they walk by, that I am brimming in the doorways. My house, this place and body, I've come in mourning to be born in. To anybody else it's pretty silly: love. Why should I feel a loss? How am I bereft? She was never mine; she was a fiction, always a golden tomgirl, barefoot, with an adolescent's slouch and a boy's taste for sports and fishing, a figure out of Twain, or worse, in Riley. Age cannot be kind.

There's little hand-in-hand here . . . not in B. No one touches except in rage. Occasionally girls will twine their arms about each other and lurch along, school out, toward home and play. I dreamed my lips would drift down your back like a skiff on a river. I'd follow a vein with the point of my finger, hold your bare feet in my naked hands.

THE SAME PERSON

Billy Holsclaw lives alone — how alone it is impossible to fathom. In the post office he talks greedily to me about the weather. His head bobs on a wild flood of words, and I take this violence to be a measure of his eagerness for speech. He badly needs a shave, coal dust has layered his face, he spits when he speaks, and his fingers pick at his tatters. He wobbles out in the wind when I leave him, a paper sack mashed in the fold of his arm, the leaves blowing past him and our encounter drives me sadly home to poetry — where there's no answer. Billy closes his door and carries coal or wood to his fire and closes his eyes, and there's simply no way of knowing how lonely and empty he is or whether he's as vacant and barren and loveless as the rest of us are — here in the heart of the country.

WEATHER

For we're always out of luck here. That's just how it is — for instance in the winter. The sides of the buildings, the roofs, the limbs of the trees are gray. Streets, sidewalks, faces, feelings — they are gray. Speech is gray, and the grass where it shows. Every flank and front, each top is gray. Everything is gray: hair, eyes, window glass, the hawkers bills and touters' posters, lips, teeth, poles and metal signs — they're gray, quite gray. Cars are gray. Boots, shoes, suits, hats, gloves are gray. Horses, sheep, and cows, cats killed in the road, squirrels in the same way, sparrows, doves, and pigeons, all are gray, everything is gray, and everyone is out of luck who lives here.

A similar haze turns the summer sky milky, and the air muffles your head and shoulders like a sweater you've got caught in. In the summer light, too, the sky darkens a moment when you open your eyes. The heat is pure distraction. Steeped in our fluids, miserable in the folds of our bodies, we can scarcely think of anything but our sticky parts. Hot cyclonic winds and storms of dust crisscross the country. In many places, given an indifferent push, the wind will still coast for miles, gathering resource and edge as it goes, cunning and force. According to the season, paper, leaves, field litter, seeds, snow, fill up the fences. Sometimes I think the land is flat because the winds have leveled it, they blow so constantly. In any case, a gale can grow in a field of corn that's as hot as a draft from hell, and to receive it is one of the most dismaying experiences of this life, though the smart of the same wind in winter is more humiliating, and in that sense even worse. But in the spring it rains as well, and the trees fill with ice.

PLACE

Many small Midwestern towns are nothing more than rural slums, and this community could easily become one. Principally during the first decade of the century, though there were many earlier instances, well-to-do farmers moved to town and built fine homes to contain them in their retirement. Others desired a more social life, and so lived in, driving to their fields like storekeepers to their businesses. These houses are now dying like the bereaved who inhabit them; they are slowly losing their senses — deafness, blindness, forgetfulness, mumbling, an insecure gait, an uncontrollable trembling has overcome them. Some kind of Northern Snopes will occupy them next: large-familied, Catholic, Democratic, scrambling, vigorous, poor; and since the parents will work in larger, nearby towns, the children will be loosed upon themselves and upon the hapless neighbors much as the fabulous Khan loosed his legendary horde. These Snopes will undertake makeshift repairs with materials that other people have thrown away; paint halfway round their house, then quit; almost certainly maintain an ugly loud cantankerous dog and underfeed a pair of cats to keep the rodents down. They will collect piles of possibly useful junk in the back yard, park their cars in the front, live largely leaning over engines, give not a hoot for the land, the old community, the hallowed ways, the established clans. Weakening widow ladies have already begun to hire large rude youths from families such as these to rake and mow and tidy the grounds they will inherit.

PEOPLE

In the cinders at the station boys sit smoking steadily in darkened cars, their arms bent out the windows, white shirts glowing behind the glass. Nine o'clock is the best time. They sit in a line facing the highway — two or three or four of them — idling their engines. As you walk by a machine may growl at you or a pair of headlights flare up briefly. In a moment one will pull out, spinning cinders behind it, to stalk impatiently up and down the dark streets or roar half a mile into the country before returning to its place in line and pulling up.

MY HOUSE, MY CAT, MY COMPANY

I must organize myself. I must, as they say, pull myself together, dump this cat from my lap, stir — yes, resolve, move, do. But do what? My will is like the rosy dustlike light in this room: soft, diffuse, and gently comforting. It lets me do ... anything ... nothing. My ears hear what they happen to; I eat what's put before me; my eyes see what blunders into them; my thoughts are not thoughts, they are dreams. I'm empty or I'm full ... depending; and I cannot choose. I sink my claws in Tick's fur and scratch the bones of his back until his rear rises amorously. Mr. Tick, I murmur, I must organize myself. I must pull myself together. And Mr. Tick rolls over on his belly, all ooze.

I spill Mr. Tick when I've rubbed his stomach. Shoo. He steps away slowly, his long tail rhyming with his paws. How beautifully he moves, I think; how beautifully, like you, he commands his loving, how beautifully he accepts. So I rise and wander from room to room, up and down, gazing through most of my forty-one windows. How well this house receives its loving too. Let out like Mr. Tick, my eyes sink in the shrubbery. I am not here; I've passed the glass, passed second-story spaces, flown by branches, brilliant berries, to the ground, grass high in seed and leafage every season; and it is the same as when I passed above you in my aged, ardent body; it's, in short, a kind of love; and I am learning to restore myself, my house, my body, by paying court to gardens, cats, and running water, and with neighbors keeping company.

Mrs. Desmond is my right-hand friend; she's eighty-five. A thin white mist of hair, fine and tangled, manifests the climate of her mind. She is habitually suspicious, fretful, nervous. Burglars break in at noon. Children trespass. Even now they are shaking the pear tree, stealing rhubarb, denting lawn. Flies caught in the screens and numbed by frost awake in the heat to buzz and scrape the metal cloth and frighten her, though she is deaf to me, and consequently cannot hear them. Boards creak, the wind whistles across the chimney mouth, drafts cruise like fish through the hollow rooms. It is herself she hears, her own flesh failing, for only death will preserve her from those daily chores she climbs like stairs, and all that anxious waiting. Is it now, she wonders. No? Then: is it now?

We do not converse. She visits me to talk. My task to murmur. She talks about her grandsons, her daughter who lives in Delphi, her sister or her husband — both gone — obscure friends — dead — obscurer aunts and uncles — lost — ancient neighbors, members of her church or of her clubs — passed or passing on; and in this way she brings the ends of her life together with a terrifying rush: she is a girl, a wife, a mother, widow, all at once. All at once — appalling — but I believe it; I wince in expectation of the clap. Her talk's a fence — a shade drawn, window fastened, door that's locked — for no one dies taking tea in a kitchen; and as her years compress and begin to jumble, I really believe in the brevity of life; I sweat in my wonder; death is the dog down the street, the angry gander, bedroom spider, goblin who's come to get her; and it occurs to me that in my listening posture I'm the boy who suffered the winds of my grandfather with an exactly similar politeness, that I am, right now, all my ages, out in elbows, as angular as badly stacked cards. Thus was I, when I loved you, every man I could be, youth and child

— far from enough — and you, so strangely ambiguous a being, met me, heart for spade, play after play, the whole run of our suits.

Mr. Tick, you do me honor. You not only lie in my lap, but you remain alive there, coiled like a fetus. Through your deep nap, I feel you hum. You are, and are not, a machine. You are alive, alive exactly, and it means nothing to you — much to me. You are a cat — you cannot understand — you are a cat so easily. Your nature is not something you must rise to. You, not I, live in: in house, in skin, in shrubbery. Yes. I think I shall hat my head with a steeple; turn church; devour people. Mr. Tick, though, has a tail he can twitch, he need not fly his Fancy. Claws, not metrical schema, poetry his paws; while smoothing ... smoothing ... smoothing roughly, his tongue laps its neatness. O Mr. Tick, I know you; you are an electrical penis. Go on now, shoo. Mrs. Desmond doesn't like you. She thinks you will tangle yourself in her legs and she will fall. You murder her birds, she knows, and walk upon her roof with death in your jaws. I must gather myself together for a bound. What age is it I'm at right now, I wonder. The heart, don't they always say, keeps the true time. Mrs. Desmond is knocking. Faintly, you'd think, but she pounds. She's brought me a cucumber. I believe she believes I'm a woman. Come in, Mrs. Desmond, thank you, be my company, it looks lovely, and have tea. I'll slice it, crisp, with cream, for luncheon, each slice as thin as me.

POLITICS

O all ye isolate and separate powers, Sing! Sing, and sing in such a way that from a distance it will seem a harmony, a Strindberg play, a friendship ring ... so happy — happy, happy, happy — as here we go hand in handling, up and down. Our union was a singing, though we were silent in the songs we sang like single notes are silent in a symphony. In no sense sober, we barbershopped together and never heard the discords in our music or saw ourselves as dirty, cheap, or silly. Yet cats have worn out better shoes than those thrown through our love songs at us. Hush. Be patient — prudent — politic. Still, Cleveland killed you, Mr. Crane. Were you not politic enough and fond of being beaten? Like a piece of sewage, the city shat you from its stern three hundred miles from history — beyond the loving reach of sailors. Well, I'm not a poet who puts Paris to his temple in his youth to blow himself from Idaho, or — fancy that — Missouri. My god, I said, this is my country, but must my country go so far as Terre Haute or Whiting, go so far as Gary?

When the Russians first announced the launching of their satellite, many people naturally refused to believe them. Later others were outraged that they had sent a dog around the earth. I wouldn't want to take that mutt from out that metal flying thing if he's still living when he lands, our own dog catcher said; anybody knows you shut a dog up by himself to toss around the first thing he'll be setting on to do you let him out is bite somebody.

This Midwest. A dissonance of parts and people, we are a consonance of Towns. Like a man grown fat in everything but heart, we overlabor; our outlook never really urban, never rural either, we enlarge and linger at the same time, as Alice both changed and remained in her story. You are blond. I put my hand upon your belly; feel it tremble from my trembling. We always drive large cars in my section of the country. How could you be a comfort to me now?

MORE VITAL DATA

The town is exactly fifty houses, trailers, stores, and miscellaneous buildings long, but in places no streets deep. It takes on width as you drive south, always adding to the east. Most of the dwellings are fairly spacious farm houses in the customary white, with wide wraparound porches and tall narrow windows, though there are many of the grander kind — fretted, scalloped, turreted, and decorated with clap-boards set at angles or on end, with stained-glass windows at the stair landings and lots of wrought iron full of fancy curls — and a few of these look like castles in their rarer brick. Old stables serve as garages now, and the lots are large to contain them and the vegetable and flower gardens which, ultimately, widows plant and weed and then entirely disappear in. The shade is ample, the grass is good, the sky a glorious fall violet; the apple trees are heavy and red, the roads are calm and empty; corn has sifted from the chains of tractored wagons to speckle the streets with gold and with the russet fragments of the cob, and a man would be a fool who wanted, blessed with this, to live anywhere else in the world.

EDUCATION

Buses like great orange animals move through the early light to school. There the children will be taught to read and warned against Communism. By Miss Janet Jakes. That's not her name. Her name is Helen something — Scott or James. A teacher twenty years. She's now worn fine and smooth, and has a face, Wilfred says, like a mail-order ax. Her voice is hoarse, and she has a cough. For she screams abuse. The children stare, their faces blank. This is the thirteenth week. They are used to it. You will all, she shouts, you will all draw pictures of me. No. She is a Mrs. — someone's missus. And in silence they set to work while Miss Jakes jabs hairpins in her hair. Wilfred says an ax, but she has those rimless tinted glasses, graying hair, an almost dimpled chin. I must concentrate. I must stop making up things. I must give myself to life; let it mold me: that's what they say in *Wisdom's Monthly Digest* every day. Enough, enough — you've been at it long enough; and the children rise formally a row at a time to present their work to her desk. No, she wears rims; it's her chin that's dimple-less. Well, it will take more than a tablespoon of features to sweeten that face. So she grimly shuffles their sheets, examines her reflection crayoned on them. I would not dare ... allow a child ... to put a line around me. Though now and then she smiles like a nick in the blade, in the end these drawings depress her. I could not bear it — how can she ask? — that anyone ... draw me. Her anger's lit. That's why she does it: flame. There go her eyes; the pink in her glasses brightens, dims. She is a pumpkin, and her rage is breathing like the candle in. No, she shouts, no — the cartoon trembling — no, John Mauck, John Stewart Mauck, this will not do. The picture flutters from her fingers. You've made me too muscular.

I work on my poetry. I remember my friends, associates, my students, by their names. Their names are Maypop, Dormouse. Upsydaisy. Their names are Gladiolus, Callow Bladder, Prince and Princess Oleo, Hieronymus, Cardinal Mummum. Mr. Fitchew, The Silken Howdah, Spot. Sometimes you're Tom Sawyer, Huckleberry Finn; it is perpetually summer: your buttocks are my pillow; we are adrift on a raft; your back is our river. Sometimes you are Major Barbara, sometimes a goddess who kills men in battle, sometimes you are soft like a shower of water; you are bread in my mouth.

I do not work on my poetry. I forget my friends, associates, my students, and their names: Gramophone, Blowgun. Pickle. Serenade ... Marge the Barge, Arena, Uberhaupt ... Doctor Dildoe, The Fog Machine. For I am now in B. in Indiana: out of job and out of patience, out of love and time and money, out of bread and out of body, in a temper, Mrs. Desmond, out of tea. So shut your fist up, bitch, you bag of death; go bang another door; go die, my dearie. Die, life-deaf old lady. Spill your breath. Fall over like a frozen board. Gray hair grows from the nose of your mind. You are a skull already — *memento mori* — the foreskin retracts from your teeth. Will your plastic gums last longer than your bones, and color their grinning? And is your twot still hazel-hairy, or are you bald as a ditch? ... bitch ... bitch ... bitch. I wanted to be famous, but you bring me age — my emptiness. Was it *that* which I thought would balloon me above the rest? Love? where are you? ... love me. I want to rise so high, I said, that when I shit I won't miss anybody.

indecent language

BUSINESS

For most people, business is poor. Nearby cities have siphoned off all but a neighborhood trade. Except for feed and grain and farm supplies, you stand a chance to sell only what one runs out to buy. Chevrolet has quit, and Frigidaire. A locker plant has left its afterimage. The lumberyard has been, so far, six months about its going. Gas stations change hands clumsily, a restaurant becomes available, a grocery closes. One day they came and knocked the cornices from the watch repair and pasted campaign posters on the windows. Torn across, by now, by boys, they urge you still to vote for half an orange beblazoned man who as a whole one failed two years ago to win at his election. Everywhere, in this manner, the past speaks, and it mostly speaks of failure. The empty stores, the old signs and dusty fixtures, the debris in alleys, the flaking paint and rusty gutters, the heavy locks and sagging boards: they say the same disagreeable things. What do the sightless windows see, I wonder, when the sun throws a passerby against them? Here a stair unfolds toward the street — dark, rickety, and treacherous — and I always feel, as I pass it, that if I just went carefully up and turned the corner at the landing, I would find myself out of the world. But I've never had the courage.

desperate

THAT SAME PERSON

The weeds catch up with Billy. In pursuit of the hollyhocks, they rise in coarse clumps all around the front of his house. Billy has to stamp down a circle by his door like a dog or cat does turning round to nest up, they're so thick. What particularly troubles me is that winter will find the weeds still standing stiff and tindery to take the sparks which Billy's little mortarless chimney spouts. It's true that fires are fun here. The town whistle, which otherwise only blows for noon (and there's no noon on Sunday), signals the direction of the fire by the length and number of its blasts, the volunteer firemen rush past in their cars and trucks, houses empty their owners along the street every time like an illustration in a children's book. There are many bikes, too, and barking dogs, and sometimes — halleluiah — the fire's right here in town — a vacant lot of weeds and stubble flaming up. But I'd rather it weren't Billy or Billy's lot or house. Quite selfishly I want him to remain the way he is — counting his sticks and logs, sitting on his sill in the soft early sun — though I'm not sure what his presence means to me ... or to anyone. Nevertheless, I keep wondering whether, given time, I might not someday find a figure in our language which would serve him faithfully, and furnish his poverty and loneliness richly out.

uncertainty
vanity

WIRES

Where sparrows sit like fists. Doves fly the steeple. In mist the wires change perspective, rise and twist. If they led to you, I would know what they were. Thoughts passing often, like the starlings who flock these fields at evening to sleep in the trees beyond, would form a family of paths like this; they'd foot down the natural height of air to just about a bird's perch. But they do not lead to you.

Of whose beauty it was sung
She shall make the old man young.

They fasten me.

If I walked straight on, in my present mood, I would reach the Wabash. It's not a mood in which I'd choose to conjure you. Similes dangle like baubles from me. This time of year the river is slow and shallow, the clay banks crack in the sun, weeds surprise the sandbars. The air is moist and I am sweating. It's impossible to rhyme in this dust. Everything — sky, the cornfield, stump, wild daisies, my old clothes and pressless feelings — seem fabricated for installment purchase. Yes. Christ. I am suffering a summer Christmas; and I cannot walk under the wires. The sparrows scatter like handfuls of gravel. Really, wires are voices in thin strips. They are words wound in cables. Bars of connection.

WEATHER

I would rather it were the weather that was to blame for what I am and what my friends and neighbors are — we who live here in the heart of the country. Better the weather, the wind, the pale dying snow . . . the snow — why not the snow? There's never much really, not around the lower Lakes anyway, not enough to boast about, not enough to be useful. My father tells how the snow in the Dakotas would sweep to the roofs of the barns in the old days, and he and his friends could sled on the crust that would form because the snow was so fiercely driven. In Bemidji trees have been known to explode. That would be something — if the trees in Davenport or Francisville or Carbondale or Niles were to go blam some winter — blam! blam! blam! all the way down the gray, cindery, snow-sick streets.

A cold fall rain is blackening the trees or the air is like lilac and full of parachuting seeds. Who cares to live in any season but his own? Still I suspect the secret's in this snow, the secret of our sickness, if we could only diagnose it, for we are all dying like the elms in Urbana. This snow — like our skin it covers the country. Later dust will do it. Right now — snow. Mud presently. But it is snow without any laughter in it, a pale gray pudding thinly spread on stiff toast, and if that seems a strange description, it's accurate all the same. Of course soot blackens everything, but apart from that, we are never sufficiently cold here. The flakes as they come, alive and burning, we cannot retain, for if our temperatures fall, they rise promptly again, just as, in the summer, they bob about in the same feckless way. Suppose though . . . suppose they were to rise some August, climb and rise, and then hang in the hundreds like a hawk through December, what a desert we could make of ourselves — from Chicago to Cairo, from Hammond to Columbus — what beautiful Death Valleys.

PLACE

I would rather it were the weather. It drives us in upon ourselves — an unlucky fate. Of course there is enough to stir our wonder anywhere; there's enough to love, anywhere, if one is strong enough, if one is diligent enough, if one is perceptive, patient, kind enough — whatever it takes; and surely it's better to live in the country, to live on a prairie by a drawing of rivers, in Iowa or Illinois or Indiana, say, than in any city, in any stinking fog of human beings, in any blooming orchard of machines. It ought to be. The cities are swollen and poisonous with people. It ought to be better. Man has never been a fit environment for man — for rats, maybe, rats do nicely, or for dogs or cats and the household beetle.

And how long the street is, nowadays. These endless walls are fallen to keep back the tides of earth. Brick could be beautiful but we have covered it gradually with gray industrial vomits. Age does not make concrete genial, and asphalt is always — like America — twenty-one, until it breaks up in crumbs like stale cake. The brick, the asphalt, the concrete, the dancing signs and garish posters, the feed and excrement of the automobile, the litter of its inhabitants: they compose, they decorate, they line our streets, and there is nowhere, nowadays, our streets can't reach.

A man in the city has no natural thing by which to measure himself. His parks are potted plants. Nothing can live and remain free where he resides but the pigeon, starling, sparrow, spider, cockroach, mouse, moth, fly and weed, and he laments the existence of even these and makes his plans to poison them. The zoo? There *is* the zoo. Through its bars the city man stares at the great cats and dully sucks his ice. Living, alas, among men and their marvels, the city man supposes that his happiness depends on establishing, somehow, a special kind of harmonious accord with others. The novelists of the city, of slums and crowds, they call it love — and break their pens.

Wordsworth feared the accumulation of men in cities. He foresaw their "degrading thirst after outrageous stimulation," and some of their hunger for love. Living in a city, among so many, dwelling in the heat and tumult of incessant movement, a man's affairs are touch and go — that's all. It's not surprising that the novelists of the slums, the cities, and the crowds, should find that sex is but a scratch to ease a tickle, that we're most human when we're sitting on the john, and that the justest image of our life is in full passage through the plumbing.

> That man, immur'd in cities, still retains
> His inborn inextinguishable thirst
> Of rural scenes, compensating his loss
> By supplemental shifts, the best he may.

Come into the country, then. The air nimbly and sweetly recommends itself unto our gentle senses. Here, growling tractors tear the earth. Dust roils up behind them. Drivers sit jouncing under bright umbrellas. They wear refrigerated hats and steer by looking at the tracks they've cut behind them, their transistors blaring. Close to the land, are they? good companions to the soil? Tell me: do they live in harmony with the alternating seasons?

It's a lie of old poetry. The modern husbandman uses chemicals from cylinders and sacks, spike-ball-and-claw machines, metal-sheds, and cost accounting. Nature in the old sense does not matter. It does not exist. Our farmer's only mystical attachment is to parity. And if he does not realize that cows and corn are simply different kinds of chemical engine, he cannot expect to make a go of it.

It isn't necessary to suppose our cows have feelings; our neighbor hasn't as many as he used to have either; but think of it this way a moment, you can correct for the human imputations later: how would it feel to nurse those strange tentacled calves with their rubber, glass, and metal lips, their stainless eyes?

PEOPLE

Aunt Pet's still able to drive her car — a high square Ford — even though she walks with difficulty and a stout stick. She has a watery gaze, a smooth plump face despite her age, and jet black hair in a bun. She has the slowest smile of anyone I ever saw, but she hates dogs, and not very long ago cracked the back of one she cornered in her garden. To prove her vigor she will tell you this, her smile breaking gently while she raises the knob of her stick to the level of your eyes.

HOUSE, MY BREATH AND WINDOW

My window is a grave, and all that lies within it's dead. No snow is falling. There's no haze. It is not still, not silent. Its images are not an animal that waits, for movement is no demonstration. I have seen the sea slack, life bubble through a body without a trace, its spheres impervious as soda's. Downwound, the whore at wagtag clicks and clacks. Leaves wiggle. Grass sways. A bird chirps, pecks the ground. An auto wheel in penning circles keeps its rigid spokes. These images are stones; they are memorials. Beneath this sea lies sea: god rest it . . . rest the world beyond my window, me in front of my reflection, above this page, my shade. Death is not so still, so silent, since silence implies a falling quiet, stillness a stopping, containing, holding in; for death is time in a clock, like Mr. Tick, electric . . . like wind through a windup poet. And my blear floats out to visible against the glass, befog its country and bespill myself. The mist lifts slowly from the fields in the morning. No one now would say: the Earth throws back its covers; it is rising from sleep. Why is the feeling foolish? The image is too Greek. I used to gaze at you so wantonly your body blushed. Imagine: wonder: that my eyes could cause such flowering. Ah, my friend, your face is pale, the weather cloudy; a street has been felled through your chin, bare trees do nothing, houses take root in their rectangles, a steeple stands up in your head. You speak of loving; then give me a kiss. The pane is cold. On icy mornings the fog rises to greet me (as you always did); the barns and other buildings, rather than ghostly, seem all the more substantial for looming, as if they grew in themselves while I watched (as you always did). Oh my approach, I suppose, was like breath in a rubber monkey. Nevertheless, on the road along the Wabash in the morning, though the trees are sometimes obscured by fog, their reflection floats serenely on the river, reasoning the banks, the sycamores in French rows. Magically, the world tips. I'm led to think that only those who grow down live (which will scarcely win me twenty-five from *Wisdom's Monthly Digest*), but I find I write that only those who live down grow; and what I write, I hold, whatever I really know. My every word's inverted, or reversed — or I am. I held you, too, that way. You were so utterly provisional, subject to my change. I could inflate your bosom with a kiss, disperse your skin with gentleness, enter your vagina from within, and make my love emerge like a fresh sex. The pane is cold. Honesty is cold, my inside lover. The sun looks, through the mist, like a plum on the tree of heaven, or a bruise on the slope of your belly. Which? The grass crawls with frost. We meet on this window, the world and I, inelegantly, swimmers of the glass; and swung wrong way round to one another, the world seems in. The world — how grand, how monumental, grave and deadly, that word is: the world, my house and poetry. All poets have their inside lovers. Wee penis does not belong to me, or any of this foggery. It is *his* property which he's thrust through what's womanly of me to set down this. These wooden houses in their squares, gray streets and fallen sidewalks, standing trees, your name I've written sentimentally across my breath into the whitening air, pale birds: they exist in me now because of him. I gazed with what intensity ... A bush in the excitement of its roses could not have bloomed so beautifully as you did then. It was a look I'd like to give this page. For that is poetry: to bring within about, to change.

POLITICS

Sports, politics, and religion are the three passions of the badly educated. They are the Midwest's open sores. Ugly to see, a source of constant discontent, they sap the body's strength. Appalling quantities of money, time, and energy are wasted on them. The rural mind is narrow, passionate, and reckless on these matters. Greed, however shortsighted and direct, will not alone account for it. I have known men, for instance, who for years have voted squarely against their interests. Nor have I ever noticed that their surly Christian views prevented them from urging forward the smithereening, say, of Russia, China, Cuba, or Korea. And they tend to back their country like they back their local team: they have a fanatical desire to win; yelling is their forte; and if things go badly, they are inclined to sack the coach. All in all, then, Birch is a good name. It stands for the bigot's stick, the wild-child-tamer's cane.

Forgetfulness — is that their object?

Oh, I was new, I thought. A fresh start: new cunt, new climate, and new country — there you were, and I was pioneer, and had no history. That language hurts me, too, my dear. You'll never hear it.

FINAL VITAL DATA

The Modern Homemakers' Demonstration Club. The Prairie Home Demonstration Club. The Night-outers' Home Demonstration Club. The IOOF, FFF, VFW, WCTU, WSCS, 4-H, 40 and 8, Psi Iota Chi, and PTA. The Boy and Girl Scouts, Rainbows, Masons, Indians and Rebekah Lodge. Also the Past Noble Grand Club of the Rebekah Lodge. As well as the Moose and the Ladies of the Moose. The Elks, the Eagles, the Jaynettes and the Eastern Star. The Women's Literary Club, the Hobby Club, the Art Club, the Sunshine Society, the Dorcas Society, the Pythian Sisters, the Pilgrim Youth Fellowship, the American Legion, the American Legion Auxiliary, the American Legion Junior Auxiliary, the Gardez Club, the Bridge for Fun Club, the What-can-you-do? Club, the Get Together Club, the Coterie Club, the Worthwhile Club, the Let's Help Our Town Club, the No Name Club, the Forget-me-not Club, the Merry-go-round Club ...

EDUCATION

Has a quarter disappeared from Paula Frosty's pocket book? Imagine the landscape of that face: no crayon could engender it; soft wax is wrong; thin wire in trifling snips might do the trick. Paula Frosty and Christopher Roger accuse the pale and splotchy Cheryl Pipes. But Miss Jakes, I *saw* her. Miss Jakes is so extremely vexed she snaps her pencil. What else is missing? I appoint you a detective, John: search her desk. Gum, candy, paper, pencils, marble, round eraser — whose? A thief. I can't watch her all the time, I'm here to teach. Poor pale fossetted Cheryl, it's determined, can't return the money because she took it home and spent it. Cindy, Janice, John, and Pete — you four who sit around her — you will be detectives this whole term to watch her. A thief. In all my time. Miss Jakes turns, unfists, and turns again. I'll handle you, she cries. To think. A thief. In all my years. Then she writes on the blackboard the name of Cheryl Pipes and beneath that the figure twenty-five with a large sign for cents. Now Cheryl, she says, this won't be taken off until you bring that money out of home, out of home straight up to here, Miss Jakes says, tapping her desk.

Which is three days.

ANOTHER PERSON

I was raking leaves when Uncle Halley introduced himself to me. He said his name came from the comet, and that his mother had borne him prematurely in her fright of it. I thought of Hobbes, whom fear of the Spanish Armada had hurried into birth, and so I believed Uncle Halley to honor the philosopher, though Uncle Halley is a liar, and neither the one hundred twenty-nine nor the fifty-three he ought to be. That fall the leaves had burned themselves out on the trees, the leaf lobes had curled, and now they flocked noisily down the street and were broken in the wires of my rake. Uncle Halley was himself (like Mrs. Desmond and history generally) both deaf and implacable, and he shooed me down his basement stairs to a room set aside there for stacks of newspapers reaching to the ceiling, boxes of leaflets and letters and programs, racks of photo albums, scrapbooks, bundles of rolled-up posters and maps, flags and pennants and slanting piles of dusty magazines devoted mostly to motoring and the Christian ethic. I saw a bird cage, a tray of butterflies, a bugle, a stiff straw boater, and all kinds of tassels tied to a coat tree. He still possessed and had on display the steering level from his first car, a linen duster, driving gloves and goggles, photographs along the wall of himself, his friends, and his various machines, a shell from the first war, a record of "Ramona" nailed through its hole to a post, walking sticks and fanciful umbrellas, shoes of all sorts (his baby shoes, their counters broken, were held in sorrow beneath my nose — they had not been bronzed, but he might have them done someday before he died, he said), countless boxes of medals, pins, beads, trinkets, toys, and keys (I scarcely saw — they flowed like jewels from his palms), pictures of downtown when it was only a path by the railroad station, a brightly colored globe of the world with a dent in Poland, antique guns, belt buckles, buttons, souvenir plates and cups and saucers (I can't remember all of it — I won't), but I recall how shamefully, how rudely, how abruptly, I fled, a good story in my mouth but death in my nostrils; and how afterward I busily, righteously, burned my leaves as if I were purging the world of its years. I still wonder if this town — its life, and mine now — isn't really a record like the one of "Ramona" that I used to crank around on my grandmother's mahogany Victrola through lonely rainy days as a kid.

THE FIRST PERSON

Billy's like the coal he's found: spilled, mislaid, discarded. The sky's no comfort. His house and his body are dying together. His windows are boarded. And now he's reduced to his hands. I suspect he has glaucoma. At any rate he can scarcely see, and weeds his yard of rubble on his hands and knees. Perhaps he's a surgeon cleansing a wound or an ardent and tactile lover. I watch, I must say, apprehensively. Like mine-war detectors, his hands graze in circles ahead of him. Your nipples were the color of your eyes. Pebble. Snarl of paper. Length of twine. He leans down closely, picks up something silvery, holds it near his nose. Foil? cap? coin? He has within him — what, I wonder? Does he know more now because he fingers everything and has to sniff to see? It would be romantic cruelty to think so. He bends the down on your arms like a breeze. You wrote me: something is strange when we don't understand. I write in return: I think when I loved you I fell to my death.

Billy, I could read to you from Beddoes; he's your man perhaps; he held with dying, freed his blood of its arteries; and he said that there were many wretched love-ill fools like me lying alongside the last bone of their former selves, as full of spirit and speech, nonetheless, as Mrs. Desmond, Uncle Halley and the Ferris wheel, Aunt Pet, Miss Jakes, Ramona or the megaphone; yet I reverse him finally, Billy, on no evidence but braggadocio, and I declare that though my inner organs were devoured long ago, the worm which swallowed down my parts still throbs and glows like a crystal palace.

Yes, you were younger. I was Uncle Halley, the museum man and infrequent meteor. Here is my first piece of ass. They weren't so flat in those days, had more round, more juice. And over here's the sperm I've spilled, nicely jarred and clearly labeled. Look at this tape like lengths of intestine where I've stored my spew, the endless worm of words I've written, a hundred million emissions or more: Oh I was quite a man right from the start; even when unconscious in my cradle, from crotch to cranium. I was erectile tissue: though mostly, after the manner approved by Plato, I had intercourse by eye. Never mind, old Holsclaw, you are blind. We pull down darkness when we go to bed; put out like Oedipus the actually offending organ, and train our touch to lies. All cats are gray, says Mr. Tick; so under cover of glaucoma you are sack gray too, and cannot be distinguished from a stallion.

I must pull myself together, get a grip, just as they say, but I feel spilled, bewildered, quite mislaid. I did not restore my house to its youth, but to its age. Hunting, you hitch through the hollyhocks. I'm inclined to say you aren't half the cripple I am, for there is nothing left of me but mouth. However, I resist the impulse. It is another lie of poetry. My organs are all there, though it's there where I fail — at the roots of my experience. Poet of the spiritual, Rilke, weren't you? yet that's what you said. Poetry, like love, is — in and out — a physical caress. I can't tolerate any more of my sophistries about spirit, mind, and breath. Body equals being, and if your weight goes down, you are the less.

HOUSEHOLD APPLES

I knew nothing about apples. Why should I? My country came in my childhood, and I dreamed of sitting among the blooms like the bees. I failed to spray the pear tree too. I doubled up under them at first, admiring the sturdy low branches I should have pruned, and later I acclaimed the blossoms. Shortly after the fruit formed there were falls — not many — apples the size of goodish stones which made me wobble on my ankles when I walked about the yard. Sometimes a piece crushed by a heel would cling on the shoe to track the house. I gathered a few and heaved them over the wires. A slingshot would have been splendid. Hard, an unattractive green, the worms had them. Before long I realized the worms had them all. Even as the apples reddened, lit their tree, they were being swallowed. The birds preferred the pears, which were small — sugar pears I think they're called — with thick skins of graying green that ripen on toward violet. So the fruit fell, and once I made some applesauce by quartering and paring hundreds; but mostly I did nothing, left them, until suddenly, overnight it seemed, in that ugly late September heat we often have in Indiana, my problem was upon me.

My childhood came in the country. I remember, now, the flies on our snowy luncheon table. As we

Destruction, violence

cleared away they would settle, fastidiously scrub themselves and stroll to the crumbs to feed where I would kill them in crowds with a swatter. It was quite a game to catch them taking off. I struck heavily since I didn't mind a few stains; they'd wash. The swatter was a square of screen bound down in red cloth. It drove no air ahead of it to give them warning. They might have thought they'd flown headlong into a summered window. The faint pink dot where they had died did not rub out as I'd supposed, and after years of use our luncheon linen would faintly, pinkly, speckle.

The country became my childhood. Flies braided themselves on the flypaper in my grandmother's house. I can smell the bakery and the grocery and the stables and the dairy in that small Dakota town I knew as a kid; knew as I dreamed I'd know your body, as I've known nothing, before or since; knew as the flies knew, in the honest, unchaste sense: the burned house, hose-wet, which drew a mist of insects like the blue smoke of its smolder, and gangs of boys, moist-lipped, destructive as its burning. Flies have always impressed me; they are so persistenly alive. Now they were coating the ground beneath my trees. Some were ordinary flies; there were the large blue-green ones; there were swarms of fruit flies too, and the red-spotted scavenger beetle; there were a few wasps, several sorts of bees and butterflies — checkers, sulphurs, monarchs, commas, question marks — and delicate dragonflies . . . but principally houseflies and horseflies and bottleflies, flies and more flies in clusters around the rotting fruit. They loved the pears. Inside, they fed. If you picked up a pear, they flew, and the pear became skin and stem. They were everywhere the fruit was: in the tree still — apples like a hive for them — or where the fruit littered the ground, squashing itself as you stepped . . . there was no help for it. The flies droned, feasting on the sweet juice. No one could go near the trees; I could not climb; so I determined at last to labor like Hercules. There were fruit baskets in the barn. Collecting them and kneeling under the branches, I began to gather remains. Deep in the strong rich smell of the fruit, I began to hum myself. The fruit caved in at the touch. Glistening red apples, my lifting disclosed, had families of beetles, flies, and bugs, devouring their rotten undersides. There were streams of flies; there were lakes and cataracts and rivers of flies, seas and oceans. The hum was heavier, higher, than the hum of the bees when they came to the blooms in the spring, though the bees were there, among the flies, ignoring me — ignoring everyone. As my work went on and juice covered my hands and arms, they would form a sleeve, black and moving, like knotty wool. No caress could have been more indifferently complete. Still I rose fearfully, ramming my head in the branches, apples bumping against me before falling, bursting with bugs. I'd snap my hand sharply but the flies would cling to the sweet. I could toss a whole cluster into a basket from several feet. As the pear or apple lit, they would explosively rise, like monads for a moment, windowless, certainly, with respect to one another, sugar their harmony. I had to admit, though, despite my distaste, that my arm had never been more alive, oftener or more gently kissed. Those hundreds of feet were light. In washing them off, I pretended the hose was a pump. What have I missed? Childhood is a lie of poetry.

THE CHURCH

Friday night. Girls in dark skirts and white blouses sit in ranks and scream in concert. They carry funnels loosely stuffed with orange and black paper which they shake wildly, and small megaphones through which, as drilled, they direct and magnify their shouting. Their leaders, barely pubescent girls, prance and shake and whirl their skirts above their bloomers. The young men, leaping, extend their arms and race through puddles of amber light, their bodies glistening. In a lull, though it rarely occurs, you can hear the squeak of tennis shoes against the floor. Then the yelling begins again, and then continues; fathers, mothers, neighbors joining in to form a single pulsing ululation — a cry of the whole community — for in this gymnasium each body becomes the bodies beside it, pressed as they are together, thigh to thigh, and the same shudder runs through all of them, and runs toward the same release. Only the ball moves serenely through this dazzling din. Obedient to law it scarcely speaks but caroms quietly and lives at peace.

BUSINESS

It is the week of Christmas and the stores, to accommodate the rush they hope for, are remaining open in the evening. You can see snow falling in the cones of the street lamps. The roads are filling — undisturbed. Strings of red and green lights droop over the principal highway, and the water tower wears a star. The windows of the stores have been bedizened. Shamelessly they beckon. But I am alone, leaning against a pole — no . . . there is no one in sight. They're all at home, perhaps by their instruments, tuning in on their evenings, and like Ramona, tirelessly playing and replaying themselves. There's a speaker perched in the tower, and through the boughs of falling snow and over the vacant streets, it drapes the twisted and metallic strains of a tune that can barely be distinguished — yes, I believe it's one of the jolly ones, it's "Joy to the World." There's no one to hear the music but myself, and though I'm listening, I'm no longer certain. Perhaps the record's playing something else.

DAVE GODFREY

The Hard-Headed Collector

K'UN

Learn to lessen rancour. When the lake is without water, the greater man can wager his life on joyousness.

In the gloomy valley, no sight but quiet men under bare trees — beware of the abyss and the void.

If, for three years, there is nothing to see, little to say, and oppression while at meat and drink, look inward and prepare sacrifices. Voyage inward slowly. Wait patiently for one who can lead and prepare and forsee. Do not be oppressed by stone walls or lean on thorns and thistles. Voyage firmly for disgrace and danger mean death is near — easy then to lose your woman, hide from her love.

Golden carriages can also oppress; the wealthy suck energetic hitchhikers towards them. Remember then your friends among the people, their needs, their humiliations, and press onward, sing offerings, pour libations. Although they scar your face and amputate your feet, say: "Joy comes softly, joy comes softly." The ministers have forgotten this as they eat their sorrows, but the vines that creep about you both can be easily broken. Never be, like them, a servant to evil, however high the payscale. Do not say to me, like them: "Movement brings remorse." Make a start, damn it, make a firm decision. Strength within leaves the greater man blameless and oppression is changed. Eventually even rancour may be lessened. Good fortune and abundance.

They came through the mountains themselves unscathed, although Piet Catogas nearly tumbled into the gorges beneath Yellowhead Pass when his horse skitthered out from under him. The last horse. When they entered North Battleford they were all seven afoot, but they were well entertained in front of the tent of the bread baker, who kept them amused with juggling tricks and poured them many cups of hot tea in blue galvanized cups filled to the brim then with swirling milk.

The bread baker's final trick was to keep seven round oranges up in the air at once, and when the rotund man had heard enough of their clapping he gave one orange to each man. His own children clustered around and his wife walked back into the tent, so the men were careful to divide, but Pier Dela Ombre, throwing his filthy black hair out of his eyes so that the firelight could blaze back out of his pupils, asked for a second orange from Piet Catagos, the leader, and began to explain to the children why the earth did not fall into the sun. He sang to them.

Katrina, the wife of the bread maker, came out of the tent and said to her husband, "Why not offer Mr. Dela Ombre two loaves of wheat bread every morning so that he will be encouraged to stay here."

The bread maker stated the offer to Piet, but Piet refused. "We are on our way to a strange land and there is not one man that I can afford to lose. We have the return journey on our minds too."

Pier Dela Ombre's orange sun rotated around and around the orange earth held stationary by little Katrina, the bread baker's only daughter. The mother smiled.

At midnight, when all the men except Ole Siuk and Scrop Calla were seated around the fire drinking the white lightning which the Scottish whiskymaker distilled in North Battleford, Katrina came out of the tent with the bread baker.

"We will give you your own tent," she said directly to Pier Dela Ombre. "And a complete set of the *European Encyclopedia,* and after twenty years' service a golden shovel. Which will no doubt help to make you feel glorious as you clear away the blizzards from your door or clean out the many ashes from your stove. Around here we have very little anthracite."

Pier Dela Ombre smiled and said that he needed no time to consider their kindness. "We do not even know how far we now need to travel," he said to the woman, "but we must be there by May and then there is the long journey back before we can really set down to work, and for each stage I will have to learn the new strophe that the good Calla writes. In fact, if he were not out now stealing the settlement's horses, he would probably be putting one together, telling of our dangerous passage through the mountains. I cannot stay."

They both laughed at his humour of the horses and determined even more to persuade him to stay.

"Little Katrina will be disappointed you were unable to explain to her the proportions of the sun and the earth," the woman said. "At times in the summer I have heard her say that they almost seem equal. It does get very hot here in the summer, but we arrange many boat picnics on the Saskatchewan, and of course there is nothing like sawdust to keep the winter's ice safely stored."

They kept after him, gently, until the bread maker fell asleep.

Ole and Scrop came back very early in the morning, before the sun, but little Katrina had risen and was adding yeast to the sugar water for the day's baking.

"If you let him stay long enough to explain the proportions of the earth and the sun," she said to Piet, "I will not awaken my father and tell him that the man with the sunken eyes has taken possession of Elder Clough's grey horse and silver bridle. And six other poorer horses."

Piet nodded to Pier Dela Ombre. He laid the golden orange of the sun on the ashes of last night's fire and took Katrina by the hand.

"If the sun were made that small," Pier said, "let us say about a thousand to one, then the earth would still be so large that in a whole day we could not walk around its edge."

He held her hand more tightly and began walking with her away from the tent and the fire, in the gentle circle of one who is uncaringly lost.

The six men were glad to have the extra horse and the mountains behind them, with the summer not completely gone.

"He'll be in real trouble when they discover the loss," Scrop Calla said to Piet when they next stopped.

"The mother will get him out of it," Piet replied. "If the little girl can't. God, they start them young here. I can't believe there's anywhere they start them so young. Even among the Sasarians."

Why had he decided to present the works to the United States!

"Well, a lot of people wanted it . . . but I couldn't do what I did in any other country. What I did I accomplished here in the United States. It belongs here."

Did he have any comment about President Johnson!

"I told him I've adopted him. I love him."

They went eastward safely for five days across the lush prairie grass until they heard gunfire in the distance ahead and what they thought might be a tornado, a dust storm. Coming over the rise they saw a Nanarian Indian from one of the reserves who shouted at them as he drove his almost collapsing wagon at a dangerous pace towards the west. His wife and children sat on mounds of hay in the back, firing whence they had come. The men rode on, although they knew there was a fire ahead which would block their way.

"We can return later," Piet said, "and cross over the ashes. Or look for the river again."

"I'm sure I can find it if you let me lead," said Torah Black.

He rode back whence they had come — the mountains were invisible — and the others followed, although Piet had said nothing.

The wagon was overturned less than a mile to the west. Besides the wife and the four children there was a milkwhite goat among the hay. "This will save us all," Black said and slit its throat. He held it by the hind legs as it kicked its way to death and circumscribed a large circle around the wagon, the men, the four children, and the woman.

"We had better ride on," Piet said.

After a time the firing started again, and once or twice the five men could distinguish the sound of Torah Black's shotgun. Scrop Calla could see the gold engraving on its stock glittering in the sun.

"What does a gunsmith know about old superstitions," Piet said as they rode back eastward over the powdery black ashes. Looky McLaww nodded sagely.

Mr. Hirshhorn lives with his fourth wife, Olga, in Greenwich. He is the father of six children, two of them adopted, and is a grandfather several times over. He is board chairman of the Callahan Mining Company, and the principal stockholder in Prairie Oil Royalties, a Canadian concern.

He has been trying to follow doctor's orders to take it easy, but finds it a trial. When he appears at Parke-Bernet, the auctioneer knows that he has to keep a sharp eye for the little man with the expressive face who signals vigorously with his program. If there is any doubt, Mr. Hirshhorn lets the auctioneer know what he is up to. He calls out his bids in a loud clear voice.

"He's a tiger," an old, close friend said.

Beyond the death of Torah Black they had no more difficulties until they reached Winnipeg. It was difficult to find a place that would take all of them, for the Leagues were busy, but eventually they found a large old house on the river in St. Vital. All of the girls spoke French so that André was kept busy as a translator; but after all, what is there to say?

"We have made it over the hard part," Piet said. "We have still eight months to go. Let us hope that the winter will be easy. Tonight you may enjoy yourselves; there is no more need of the horses in any case."

The first girl did not satisfy Looky because the pleasure of her body simply filled his head with memories of the wife he had left on Queen Charlotte Island.

"That damn Hunky won't want more than a snack," he said and walked into Ole Siuk's room and threw him out of bed. *"J'ai une qualité inestimable,"* he said to the girl and she shone with delight.

"He is afraid for his wife," Piet said to Ole Siuk. "There are many other carvers and poets on the island. She is a loving model, puts her heart into it."

"Mineur, how's about a free and equal exchange of riches," Looky later said to André. But when André tried his new girl he found her cold and exhausted. She swung a condom full of black beetles over his head and threatened him with death.

Looky took Scrop Calla's girl also, a plumper one than the first three, but when he came to Piet's room he found him gone.

The old woman, the girl provider, still lay in the bed and offered herself to Looky, but she was dark haired and hidden-eyed like Looky's wife and he could not take her.

"There's the matter of the bill," she said, "but that's not important. I have the horses. If you had slept with me those bay-tards would have beaten you to death with horseshoes on the end of pikes and we would have put you out in the stable to freeze until spring, but as it is you will save us the cost of putting an ad in the *Free Press* for some able body to haul our ashes all winter."

"At least McLaww won't have to go about with a gold shovel in his hands," Piet Catogas said to Scrop Calla as the four men trudged on bear-paw snowshoes through the wine-dark snows north of Fort Frances, as the sun fell.

But, with the end of World War I, he guessed wrong on the market and found his fortune had shrunk to $4,000. Mr. Hirshhorn says he has always learned by his mistakes. At any rate, he was back on top in a few years and intuitively got out of the market with $4 million just before it broke in 1929.

When he was a child, Mr. Hirshhorn was attracted to the pictures on the Prudential Life Insurance Company's calendars.

Mr. Hirshhorn was attracted to the possibilities of Canada, bought 470 square miles of land and, by 1950, was mining uranium. His biggest coup occurred in 1952. On the advice of Franc Joubin, a geologist who had little audience elsewhere, Mr. Hirshhorn secretly put together 56,000 square miles of claims in Ontario's Algoma Basin and struck a uranium bonanza in Blind River.

When the four men were only twelve miles from Chapleau, they came across a group of Hémonites at prayers. These had built a great square wall of snowblocks out onto the lake, no more than a foot high, and at intervals, dressed in brown worsted cowls, stood women, men, and the older children, praying into the sky.

"This is a chance for Calla to use his four iamb line," said old Siuk, who had taken over the post of religious cynic since they had lost McLaww.

Piet could see no altar, but in the centre of the square was a tall ancient man standing above a slender circular hole cut deep into the ice down to the dark water below.

"In the summer you can see clear down thirty-two feet," the old man said.

Near him were three boys tending nine blanketed cattle. On a high easel, facing in the direction in which all prayed, was an old lithograph of an Essex County dairy farm, coated in plastic to protect it against the weather but torn in one corner so that the gold of cut hay was stuck to a piece of flapping plastic and glittered in the frosted sunlight.

"No one will do it," the old man said.

"I'm out of grass, acid, and mushrooms," said Scrop Calla, "but I know what you want and I will attempt it."

He stripped himself naked and lowered himself into the water three times so that not only his heavy beard and hair were covered with a silver of ice, but his whole body. It shone.

He held his arms outward in the direction of them all and said loudly and with no sound of rhythm: "I know, I know, I know."

Upon the horizon appeared, as though on the edge of a highly polished silver punch bowl, a simple inverted image of all: the penitents, the wall of snowblocks, the old priest, Scrop Calla, the strangers, and the forests and the snow-covered meadows behind them. With the exception that, in the inverted image, the cows were unblanketed and moved about freely, their udders thick with milk, their coats sleek as threshed grain.

"You're a genius and a half," the old priest said. "You'll have to settle here. In the summer you can see down thirty-two feet and the fishing licence's only two bucks — to natives that is."

"During the war," said Piet to Ole Siuk as they came near French River, "Calla once deserted and tried to find the enemy, but a handful of men went unknowingly after him and became so enthused with their fear that they broke through the lines of the Sasarians and covered themselves with loot and glory."

At night when they stopped now, Ole Siuk read in Calla's leather-bound notebooks and occasionally was seen stamping his left foot heavily and repeatedly on the hard earth of the world.

"Poverty has a bitter taste," Mr. Hirshhorn said years later, recalling how his mother was sent to the hospital when a fire gutted their tenement on Humbolt Street, and the family was dispersed to various homes in the neighborhood. "I ate garbage."

In French River the three men were fed and lodged in a building as tall as the smallest of the foothills they had long left behind them.

"Perhaps we have gone far enough," said André. "That is a building tall enough to house Egsdrull. The tools must be rusty and I long to hear the chips shatter, even a practice stroke."

All of the people there had a small exact circle of soot on each cheek, but they were kind to the voyagers, gave them fat for their stiff-thonged snowshoes, and did not laugh loudly at Ole Siuk's awkward attempts at song.

"You can see God's fish," they said at the end of the recital. "Perhaps then you will stay and teach us to sing."

Inside the tall building sat rows and rows of old men and women, all dressed in heavy blue robes, but seemingly divided into three groups.

Some had two circles of dark soot on their cheeks, so that only the blue robes distinguished them from the guide. These sat reading from a book that was passed slowly down the rows, meditating while they awaited their turn. Others had only one circle of soot, that on their right cheek, and were busy at work benches, hammering tiny marbles of gold into large, almost circular flakes. Their blue robes seemed cumbersome, and many seemed too old for such a task.

The third group had no marks on their cheeks, but on their foreheads was a slightly, larger, more oval, circle of soot. These seemed to be neither reading nor hammering, but once, while the strangers were there, one of the old men among them went up to the forty-foot fish which dominated the entire building, a *mashkinoje*. Only its skeletal frame was finished: the outer covering was not yet half done. The old man laid in place on the others his own interlocking golden scale. Then fire consumed him.

"Each year," said the guide, "we get just about done before the Sasarians come raiding. We've calmed the Nanarians. One year the Sasarians will be awed by God's fish and will allow us to finish. Below God's fish, you will see the coffins of the fifty original scale craftsmen. Each holds an ivory tooth on his breast, and on the day that the Sasarians are awed, they will all arise and the teeth will complete the fish of unity."

When Piet and Ole left, Andre Mineur was talking in Arabic to the God's fish's tail. He was not speaking of their own voyages and their many losses.

"He's a sucker, that Mineur," said Piet Catogas to Ole Siuk as they crossed the St. Lawrence at Three Rivers. "It won't sell. I've seen men making them in Boston, twice the size, every scale machine-polished, and for half the price."

"I think you have the right reason," said Ole Siuk. "Hah, hah, hah." His teeth had all fallen out because of the bad diet they had endured during the winter and he looked very old and ugly.

"It's almost the end of April," he said.

The President added:
"Washington is a city of powerful institutions — the seat of government for the strongest government on earth, the place where democratic ideals are translated into reality. It must also be a place of beauty and learning, and museums should re-

flect a people whose commitment is to the best that is within them to dream. We have the elements of a great capital of beauty and learning, no less impressive than its power."

The two men avoided all contact with the Sasarians, although Piet was certain he could communicate with them if necessary, but when they arrived in Edmundston and stated that they were determined to reach the Bay of Chaleur even though only two of them remained, they ran into the united opposition of all the Town Fathers.

"The *day* of judgement is only possible as a concept because of our notions of the duration of time," the Mayor said. "In reality there is a summary court in perpetual session and we're going to beat your knackers down to your knees."

They turned upon Siuk, stripped off all his clothing, tore away his finger nails with their teeth, gnawed his fingers with the fury of famished dogs, and thrust a sword through one of his hands. They drove the two men between them in a hastily formed aisle, and beat them with clubs and thorny sticks. Then they hung them by the wrists to two of the poles that supported the Town Hall. A woman was commanded to cut off Piet's thumb, which she did; and a thumb of Siuk was also severed, a clam-shell being used as an instrument, in order to increase the pain.

In the morning the children came to castrate them, and then they were set free. Hair was pulled from their beards and their wounds were lacerated before they left.

In the night Ole Siuk wrote out a message for Piet, the leader, although he did not awaken him.

"I guess I've followed Areskoui and that crew long enough. I feel the need of those Edmundston men more than anything. My great-aunt was a nun in the Ukraine, but she was of unsound motives in her religious pursuits. When she was not made Mother Superior at a time she had appointed, she stripped herself naked during a Sunday mass and declared herself to the world as an atheist. The family has had bad luck ever since. Maybe this act of mine will atone in some way. I wouldn't visit us, however, on your way back. I'll probably be married to the woman who collects thumbs."

Piet had no-one to talk to, but he chuckled to himself as he came upon the birch bright sea.

"It's lucky old McLaww didn't make it to that part of the contest. He would have hated me for the rest of his life."

"This is a magnificent day for the nation's capital and for millions of Americans who will visit Washington in the years to come," the President said, smiling at Mr. Hirshhorn at his side.

"Throughout the world," the President said, "Mr. Hirshhorn has sought the great art of our time — those expressions of man's will to make sense of his experience on earth, to find order and meaning in the physical world about him, to render what is familiar in a new way."

It was late June when he arrived at the bay.

"I've come for Egsdrull," said Piet to the manager of the lumber yard. "I'm the carver from Queen Charlotte." He handed him the receipt.

"You're a *little* late," replied the manager. "And as well there's the little matter of the seven terms: shape an axe, sing its joints, engrave its shaft, bless its point, name it in ten tongues, knit soul and intent, determine where lies its enemy."

"I had men who could do all that. Ole Siuk could have shaped it out of brittle rock; Pier Dela Ombre was once with the Scalla; the best man with a graver you ever saw was Torah Black; Looky McLaww would have had a libation for the blade: Andre Mineur knew a baker's-dozen tongues; Scrop Calla would have taught you a thing or two about serpents biting their own tails and how to hoop a barrel hoop. And I, why do you think I came all this way? Put that axe in my hands and show me the tree, show me Egsdrull, and God himself will not be able to catch the bloody chips."

"Terms is terms," the manager said. "The sea probably has fish who could do all that, but you don't see him standing there begging."

Piet could find nothing to say.

"I've got something out behind the slab pile that might do for you," the manager said. "We flooded those ten or twelve years back when we gave up hope on you."

Beyond the slab pile, where a small red fork-lift truck scurried with its swaying load of sixteen- and eighteen-foot slabs, was a scene of desolation. The creek which once had there flowed into the Bay of Chaleur was dammed. Forty feet or more on either side was flooded. All the trees that once had grown there were black stubs. Not ankle high, as a good piece of future meadowland might look waiting for the years to rot the stumps, but man high, totem high; trunks like amputated limbs.

"You're free to make something of one of those if you like," said the manager. "But I don't expect any of them is fit for a trip back the coast. Hollow rotten."

"I did not come all that way," said Piet. He was screaming. "Lose all those men, suffer all that laceration. Father, father, I am a grown man. You promised me Egsdrull. I discovered the Pacific; I fed China for three months; I played poker with Lord Astor; I kissed the dirty Hun's lady. I courted death. You have forsworn me. Thiefman."

"Forsworn you, my ass. Terms is terms. There it is in black and white. Ninth of May or all terms void. Seven terms to be fulfilled before delivery. It's time you earned your daily bread for a change, young fellow. Don't father me. Perhaps we can fit you in on the butt-saw, if you can keep up. You're not so spry as you once were. What do you say, young fellow? Want to try Newfoundland?"

President Johnson formally accepted the Hirshhorn art collection today "on behalf of the American people" in a ceremony at noon in the Rose Garden of the White House.

Piet Catogas lasted a week at work before his death. Not on the butt-saw, which is a skilled task and requires a young and agile man, but out in the yard in the sunlight, sorting the lumber by lengths, widths, and grades.

This was a job for the young or the very old, but he found no sympathy among his comrades and was unable to speak to them of the carvings that he had made before he was half their age, back on the island.

More than one of his wounds was infected, and though he bathed in the warm sea he knew it was futile and awaited his death with great equanimity. At night he wondered if Dela Ombre would have blond sons later with Katrina or what Torah had thought about as he fired into the flame and smoke; he chuckled at the thought of Looky beaten by the horseshoes on pikes and wondered how many winters Calla would survive; he was afraid Mineur had sold out to those madmen and prayed for Ole Siuk.

In the mornings he slept later and later. He would have been fired on the morning he died if ever he had reached the yard where men sorted the sixteen-foot one-by-sixes into four grades without a passing glance at the ship which came for his body.

NICOLAI GOGOL

The Nose

Translated by Constance Garnett

I

An extraordinarily strange incident took place in Petersburg on the twenty-fifth of March. The barber, Ivan Yakovlevich, who lives on Voznesensky Avenue (his surname is lost, and nothing more appears even on his signboard, where a gentleman is depicted with his cheeks covered with soapsuds, together with an inscription "also lets blood") — the barber Ivan Yakovlevich woke up rather early and was aware of a smell of hot bread. Raising himself in bed he saw his wife, a rather portly lady who was very fond of drinking coffee, engaged in taking out of the oven some freshly baked loaves.

"I won't have coffee today, Praskovia Osipovna," said Ivan Yakovlevich. "Instead I would like some hot bread with onions." (The fact is that Ivan Yakovlevich would have liked both, but he knew that it was utterly impossible to ask for two things at once, for Praskovia Osipovna greatly disliked such caprices.)

"Let the fool have bread: so much the better for me," thought his wife to herself. "There will be an extra cup of coffee left," and she flung one loaf on the table.

For the sake of propriety Ivan Yakovlevich put a jacket over his shirt, and, sitting down at the table, sprinkled some salt, peeled two onions, took a knife in his hand and, assuming an air of importance, began to cut the bread. After dividing the loaf into two halves he looked into the middle of it — and to his amazement saw something there that looked white. Ivan Yakovlevich probed at it carefully with his knife and felt it with his finger: "It's solid," he said to himself. "What in the world is it?"

He thrust in his fingers and pulled it out — it was a nose! … Ivan Yakovlevich's hand dropped with astonishment, he rubbed his eyes and felt it: it actually was a nose, and what's more, it looked to him somehow familiar. A look of horror came into Ivan Yakovlevich's face. But that horror was nothing compared to the indignation with which his wife was overcome.

"Where have you cut that nose off, you monster? she cried wrathfully. "You scoundrel, you drunkard, I'll go to the police myself to report you! You villain! I have heard from three men that when you are shaving them you pull at their noses till you almost tug them off."

But Ivan Yakovlevich was more dead than alive: he recognized that the nose belonged to none other than Kovaliov, the collegiate assessor whom he shaved every Wednesday and every Sunday.

"Wait, Praskovia Osipovna! I'll wrap it up in a rag and put it in a corner. Let it stay there for a while; I'll return it later on."

"I won't hear of it! As though I would allow a stray nose to lie about in my room. You dried-up biscuit! He can do nothing but sharpen his razors on the strop, but soon he won't be fit to do his duties at all, the gadabout, the good-for-nothing! As though I were going to answer to the police for you. … Oh, you dirt, you stupid blockhead. Away with it, away with it! Take it where you like! Don't let me set eyes on it again!"

Ivan Yakovlevich stood as though utterly crushed. He thought and thought, and did not know what to think. "The devil only knows how it happened," he said at last, scratching behind his ear. "Did I come home drunk last night or not? I can't say for certain now. But from all signs it seems that something extraordinary must have happened, for bread is a thing that is baked, while a nose is something quite different. I can't make head or tail of it." Ivan Yakovlevich sank into silence. The thought that the police might make a search there for the nose and throw the blame of it on him reduced him to complete prostration. Already the red collar, beautifully embroidered with silver, the saber, hovered before his eyes, and he trembled all over. At last he got his trousers and his boots, pulled on these wretched objects, and, accompanied by the stern approaches of Praskovia Osipovna, wrapped the nose in a rag and went out into the street.

He wanted to thrust it out of sight somewhere, under a gate, or somehow accidentally to drop it and then turn off into a side street, but as ill-luck would have it he kept coming across people he knew, who would at once begin asking: "Where are you going?" or "Whom are you going to shave so early?" so that Ivan Yakovlevich could never find a moment to get rid of it. Another time he really did drop it, but a policeman pointed to it with his halberd from a long way off, saying as he did so: "Pick it up, you have dropped something!" and Ivan Yakovlevich was obliged to pick up the nose and put it in his pocket. He was overcome by despair, especially as the number of people in the street was continually increasing as the shops and stalls began to open.

He made up his mind to go to Isakievsky Bridge in the hope of being able to fling it into the Neva. ... But I am afraid I am a little to blame for not having so far said more about Ivan Yakovlevich, a worthy man in many respects.

Ivan Yakovlevich, like every self-respecting Russian workman, was a terrible drunkard, and though every day he shaved other people's chins, his own went forever unshaven. Ivan Yakovlevich's jacket (he never wore any other shape) was motley, that is, it was black dappled all over with brown and yellow and gray; the collar was shiny, and instead of three buttons there was only one hanging on a thread. Ivan Yakovlevich was a great cynic, and when Kovaliov the collegiate assessor said to him while he was being shaved: "Your hands always stink, Ivan Yakovlevich," the latter would reply with the question: "What should make them stink?" "I can't tell, my good man, but they do stink," the collegiate assessor would say, and, taking a pinch of snuff, Ivan Yakovlevich lathered him for that on his cheeks and under his nose and behind his ears and under his beard — in fact, wherever he chose.

The worthy citizen found himself by now on Isakievsky Bridge. First of all he looked about him, then bent over the parapet as though to look under the bridge to see whether there were a great number of fish racing by, and stealthily flung in the rag with the nose. He felt as though a heavy weight had rolled off his back. Ivan Yakovlevich actually grinned. Instead of going to shave the chins of government clerks, he went to an establishment bearing the inscription "Tea and refreshments" and asked for a glass of punch, when he suddenly observed at the end of the bridge a police inspector of respectable appearance with full whiskers, a three-cornered hat, and a sword. He turned cold, and meanwhile the inspector beckoned to him and said: "Come this way, my good man."

Ivan Yakovlevich, knowing etiquette, took off his hat some way off and, as he approached, said: "I wish your honor good health."

"No, no, old fellow, I am not 'your honor': tell me what you were doing on the bridge?"

"I swear, sir, I was on my way to shave my customers, and I was only looking to see whether the current was running fast."

"That's a lie, that's a lie! You won't get off with that. Kindly answer!"

"I am ready to shave you, gracious sir, two or even three times a week with no conditions whatever," answered Ivan Yakovlevich.

"No, my friend, that is nonsense; I have three barbers to shave me and they think it a great honor, too. But be so kind as to tell me what you were doing there?"

Ivan Yakovlevich turned pale ... but the incident is completely veiled in obscurity, and absolutely nothing is known of what happened next.

II

Kovaliov the collegiate assessor woke up early next morning and made the sound "brrr ..." with his lips as he always did when he woke up, though he could not himself have explained the reason for his doing so. Kovaliov stretched and asked for a little mirror that was standing on the table. He wanted to look at a pimple which had appeared on his nose the previous evening, but to his great astonishment there was a completely flat space where his nose should have been. Frightened, Kovaliov asked for some water and a towel to rub his eyes; there really was no nose. He began feeling with his hand, and pinched himself to see whether he was still asleep: it appeared that he was not. The collegiate assessor jumped out of bed, he shook himself — there was still no nose. ... He ordered his clothes to be given him at once and flew off straight to the police commissioner.

But meanwhile we must say a word about Kovaliov in order that the reader may have some idea of what kind of collegiate assessor he was. Collegiate assessors who receive that title with the aid of academic diplomas cannot be compared with those who are created collegiate assessors in the Caucasus. They are two quite different species. The erudite collegiate assessors ... But Russia is such a wonderful country that, if you say a word about one collegiate assessor, all the collegiate assessors from Riga to Kamchatka would certainly think you are referring to them; and it is the same, of course, with all grades and titles. Kovaliov was a collegiate assessor from the Caucasus. He had only been of that rank for the last two years, and so could not forget it for a moment; and to give himself greater weight and dignity he did not call himself simply collegiate assessor but always spoke of himself as a major. "Listen, my dear," he would usually say when he met a woman in the street selling shirt fronts, "you go to my house; I live in Sadovaya Street; just ask, does Major Kovaliov live here? Anyone will show you." If he met some pretty little baggage he would also give her a secret instruction, adding: "You ask for Major Kovaliov's flat, my love." For this reason we will for the future speak of him as the major.

Major Kovaliov was in the habit of walking every day up and down Nevsky Prospekt. The collar of his shirt front was always extremely clean and well starched. His whiskers were such as one may see nowadays on provincial and district surveyors, on architects and army doctors, also on those employed on special commissions, and in general on all such men as have full ruddy cheeks and are very good hands at a game of boston: these whiskers start from the middle of the cheek and go straight up to the nose. Major Kovaliov used to wear a number of cornelian seals, some with crests on them and others on which were carved Wednesday, Thursday, Monday, and so on. Major Kovaliov had come to Petersburg on business, that is, to look for a post befitting his rank: if he were successful, the post of a vice-governor, and failing that, the situation of an executive clerk in some prominent department. Major Kovaliov was not averse to matrimony, but only on condition he could find a bride with a fortune of two hundred thousand. And so the reader may judge for himself what was the major's position when he saw, instead of a nice-looking, well-proportioned nose, an extremely absurd flat space.

As misfortune would have it, not a cab was to be seen in the street, and he was obliged to walk, wrapping himself in his cloak and hiding his face in his handkerchief, as though his nose were bleeding. "But perhaps it was my imagination: it's impossible: I couldn't have been idiotic enough to lose my nose," he thought, and went into a café to look at himself in the mirror. Fortunately there was no one in the shop; some boys were sweeping the floor and arranging all the chairs; others with sleepy faces were bringing in hot pastries on trays; yesterday's papers covered with coffee stains were lying about on the tables and chairs. "Well, thank God, there is nobody here," he thought; "now I can look." He went timidly up to the mirror and looked. "What the hell's the meaning of it? Damn it!" he said, spitting. "If only there had been something instead of a nose, but there is nothing! ..."

Biting his lips with vexation, he went out of the café and resolved, contrary to his usual practice, not to look or smile at anyone. All at once he stood as though rooted to the spot before the door of a house. Something inexplicable took place before his eyes: a carriage was stopping at the entrance; the carriage door flew open; a gentleman in uniform, bending down, sprang out and ran up the steps. What was the horror and at the same time amazement of Kovaliov when he recognized that this was his own nose! At this extraordinary phenomenon it seemed to him that everything was swimming before his eyes; he felt that he could scarcely stand; but he made up his mind, come what may, to await the gentleman's return to the carriage, and he stood trembling all over as though in a fever. Two minutes later the nose actually did come out. He was in a gold-braided uniform with a high collar; he had on buckskin trousers and at his side was a sword. From his plumed hat it might be inferred that he was of the rank of a civil councilor. Everything showed that he was going somewhere to pay a visit. He looked to both sides, called to the coachman to open the carriage door, got in, and drove off.

Poor Kovaliov almost went out of his mind; he did not know what to think of such a strange occurrence. How was it possible for a nose — which had only yesterday been on his face and could neither drive nor walk — to be in uniform! He ran after the carriage, which luckily did not go far, but stopped before the entrance of Kazansky Cathedral.

He hurried in that direction, made his way through a row of old beggar women with their faces tied up and two slits in place of their eyes at whom he used to laugh so merrily, and went into the church. There were not many people inside the church. Kovaliov felt so upset that he could not pray, and he looked for the gentleman. At last he saw him standing apart from the other worshippers. The nose was hiding his face completely in a high stand-up collar and was saying his prayers in an attitude of complete piety.

"How am I to approach him?" thought Kovaliov. "One can see by everything — from his uniform, from his hat — that he is a civil councilor. Damned if I know how to do it!"

He began by coughing at his side; but the nose never changed his pious attitude for a minute and continued genuflecting.

"Sir," said Kovaliov, inwardly forcing himself to speak confidently. "Sir ..."

"What do you want?" answered the nose, turning around.

"It seems ... strange to me sir. ... You ought to know your proper place, and all at once I find you in church, of all places! You will admit ..."

"Excuse me, I cannot understand what you are talking about. ... Explain."

"How am I to explain to him?" thought Kovaliov, and plucking up his courage he began: "Of course I ... I am a major, by the way. For me to go about without a nose, you must admit, is improper. An old woman selling peeled oranges on Voskresensky Bridge may sit there without a nose; but having prospects of obtaining ... and being besides acquainted with a great many ladies in the families of Chekhtariova the civil councilor and others ... You can judge for yourself ... I don't know, sir" (at this point Major Kovaliov shrugged his shoulders) "... excuse me ... if you look at the matter in accordance with the principles of duty and honor ... you can understand of yourself ..."

"I don't understand a word," said the nose. "Explain it more satisfactorily."

"Sir," said Kovaliov, with a sense of his own dignity, "I don't know how to understand your words. The matter appears to me perfectly obvious ... either you wish ... Why, you are my own nose!"

The nose looked at the major and his eyebrows slightly quivered.

"You are mistaken, sir. I am an independent individual. Moreover, there can be no sort of close relations between us. I see, sir, from the buttons of your uniform, you must be serving in a different department." Saying this, the nose turned away.

Kovaliov was utterly confused, not knowing what to do or even what to think. Meanwhile they heard the agreeable rustle of a lady's dress: an elderly lady was approaching, all decked out in lace, and with her a slim lady in a white dress which looked very charming on her slender figure, in a straw-colored hat as light as a pastry puff. Behind them stood, opening his snuffbox, a tall footman with big whiskers and a dozen collars.

Kovaliov came nearer, pulled out the cambric collar of his shirt front, arranged the seals on his gold watch chain, and smiling from side to side, turned his attention to the ethereal lady who, like a spring flower, faintly swayed forward and put her white hand with its half-transparent fingers to her brow. The smile on Kovaliov's face broadened when he saw under the hat her round, dazzingly white chin and part of her cheek flushed with the hues of the first spring rose; but all at once he skipped away as though he had been scalded. He remembered that he had absolutely nothing on his face in place of a nose, and tears oozed from his eyes. He turned away to tell the gentleman in uniform straight out that he was only pretending to be a civil councilor, that he was a rogue and a scoundrel, and that he was nothing else than his own nose. ... But the nose was no longer there; he had managed to gallop off, probably again to call on someone.

This reduced Kovaliov to despair. He went back and stood for a minute or two under the colonnade, carefully looking in all directions to see whether the nose was anywhere about. He remembered very well that there was plumage in his hat and gold braid on his uniform; but he had not noticed his overcoat nor the color of his carriage, nor his horses, nor even whether he had a footman behind him and if so in what livery. Moreover, such numbers of carriages were driving backwards and forwards and at such a speed that it was difficult even to distinguish them; and if he had distinguished one of them he would have had no means of stopping it. It was a lovely, sunny day. There were masses of people on Nevsky Prospekt; ladies were scattered like a perfect cataract of flowers all over the pavement from Politseysky to the Anichkin Bridge. Here he saw coming toward him a court councilor of his acquaintance whom he used to call "lieutenant colonel," particularly if he were speaking to other people. There he saw Yarygin, a head clerk in the senate, a great friend of his, who always lost points when he went eight at boston. And here was another major who had received the rank of assessor in the Caucasus, beckoning to him....

"Hell!" said Kovaliov. "Hi, cab! drive straight to the police commissioner's."

Kovaliov got into a cab and shouted to the driver:

"Drive like a house on fire."

"Is the commissioner at home?" he cried, going into the hall.

"No," answered the porter, "he has just gone out."

"Well, that's my luck."

"Yes," added the porter, "and he has not been gone so long: if you had come but a tiny minute earlier you might have found him."

Kovaliov, still keeping the handkerchief over his face, got into the cab and shouted in a voice of despair: "Drive on."

"Where?" asked the cabman.

"Drive straight on!"

"How straight on? The street divides here; is it to the right or to the left?"

This question forced Kovaliov to pause, to think, again. In his position he ought first of all to address himself to the department of law and order, not because it had any direct connection with the police but because the intervention of the latter might be far more rapid than any help he could get in other departments. To seek satisfaction from the higher officials of the department in which the nose had announced himself as serving would have been unwise, since from the nose's own answers he had been able to perceive that nothing was sacred to that man and that he might tell lies in this case too, just as he had lied in declaring that he had never seen him before. And so Kovaliov was on the point of telling the cabman to drive to the police station, when again the idea occurred to him that this rogue and scoundrel who had at their first meeting behaved in such a shameless way might seize the opportunity and slip out of town — and then all his searches would be in vain, or might be prolonged, God forbid, for a whole month. At last it seemed that Heaven itself directed him. He decided to go straight to a newspaper office and without loss of time to publish a circumstantial description of the nose, so that anyone meeting it might at once present it to him or at least let him know where it was. And so, deciding upon this course, he told the cabman to drive to the newspaper office, and all the way never stopped hitting him with his fist on the back, saying as he did so, "Faster, you rascal; hurry, you scoundrel!"

"Ugh, sir!" said the cabman, shaking his head and flicking with the reins at the horse, whose coat was as long as a lapdog's. At last the cab stopped and Kovaliov ran panting into a little reception room where a gray-headed clerk in spectacles, wearing an old jacket, was sitting at a table and with a pen between his teeth was counting over some coppers he had before him.

"Who receives inquiries here?" cried Kovaliov. "Ah, good day!"

"I wish you good day," said the gray-headed

clerk, raising his eyes for a moment and then dropping them again on the money lying in heaps on the table.

"I want to insert an advertisement ..."

'Allow me to ask you to wait a minute," the clerk pronounced, with one hand noting a figure on the paper and with the finger of his left hand moving two beads on the abacus. A footman in a braided coat and of rather smart appearance, which betrayed that he had at some time served in an aristocratic family, was standing at the table with a written paper in his hand and thought fit to display his social abilities: "Would you believe it, sir, that the little bitch is not worth eighty kopeks; in fact I wouldn't give eight for it, but the countess is fond of it — my goodness, she is fond of it, and here she will give a hundred rubles to anyone who finds it! To speak politely, as you and I are speaking now, people's tastes are quite incompatible: when a man's a sportsman, then he'll keep a setter or a poodle; he won't mind giving five hundred or a thousand so long as it is a good dog."

The worthy clerk listened to this with a significant air, and at the same time was reckoning the number of letters in the advertisement brought him. Along the sides of the room stood a number of old women, shop assistants, and house porters who had brought advertisements. In one it was announced that a coachman of sober habits was looking for a situation; in the next a secondhand carriage brought from Paris in 1814 was offered for sale; next a maid, aged nineteen, experienced in laundry work and also competent to do other work, was looking for a situation; a strong carriage with only one spring broken was for sale; a spirited, young, dappled gray horse, only seventeen years old, for sale; a new consignment of turnip and radish seed from London; a summer villa with all conveniences, stabling for two horses, and a piece of land that might well be planted with fine birches and pine trees; there was also an appeal to those wishing to purchase old boot soles, inviting such to come for the same every day between eight o'clock in the morning and three o'clock in the afternoon. The room in which all this company was assembled was a small one and the air in it was extremely thick, but the collegiate assessor Kovaliov was incapable of noticing the stench both because he kept his handkerchief over his face and because his nose was goodness knows where.

"Dear sir, allow me to ask you ... my case is very urgent," he said at last impatiently.

"In a minute, in a minute! ... Two rubles, forty-three kopeks! ... This minute! One ruble and sixty-four kopeks!" said the gray-headed gentleman, flinging the old women and house porters the various documents they had bought. "What can I do for you?" he said at last, turning to Kovaliov.

"I want to ask ..." said Kovaliov. "Some robbery or swindle has occurred; I cannot understand it at all. I only want you to advertise that anyone who brings me the scoundrel will receive a handsome reward."

"Allow me to ask what is your surname?"

"No, why put my surname? I cannot give it to you! I have a large circle of acquaintances: Chekhtariova, wife of a civil councilor, Podtochina, widow of an officer ... they will find out. God forbid! You can simply put: 'a collegiate assessor,' or better still, 'a person of major's rank.'"

"Is the runaway your house serf, then?"

"A house serf indeed! that would not be so bad! It's my nose ... has run away from me ... my own nose."

"H'm, what a strange surname! And is it a very large sum this Mr. Nosov has robbed you of?"

"Nosov! ... you are on the wrong track. It is my nose, my own nose that has disappeared. I don't know where. The devil wanted to have a joke at my expense."

"But in what way did it disappear? There is something I can't quite understand."

"And indeed, I can't tell you how it happened; the point is that now it is driving about the town, calling itself a civil councilor. And so I beg you to announce that anyone who catches him must bring him at once to me as quickly as possible. Only think, really, how can I manage without such a conspicuous part of my person? It's not like a little toe, the loss of which I could hide in my boot and no one could say whether it was there or not. I go on Thursdays to Chekhtariova's: Podtochina, an officer's widow, and her very pretty daughter are great friends of mine; and you can judge for yourself what a fix I am in now ... I can't possibly show myself now. ..."

The clerk pondered, a fact which was obvious from the way he compressed his lips.

"No, I can't put an advertisement like that in the paper," he said at last, after a long silence.

"What? Why not?"

"Well. The newspaper might lose its reputation. If everyone is going to write that his nose has run away, why ... As it is, they say we print lots of absurd things and false reports."

"But what is there absurd about this? I don't see anything absurd in it."

"You think there is nothing absurd in it? But last week, now, this was what happened. A government clerk came to me just as you have; he brought an advertisement, it came to two rubles seventy-three kopeks, and all the advertisement amounted to was that a poodle with a black coat had strayed. You wouldn't think that there was anything in that, would you? But it turned out to be libelous: the poodle was the cashier of some department, I don't remember which."

"But I am not asking you to advertise about poodles but about my own nose; that is almost the same as about myself."

"No, such an advertisement I cannot insert."

"But since my nose really is lost!"

"If it is lost that is a matter for the doctor. They say there are people who can fit you with a nose of any shape you like. But I observe you must be a gentleman of merry disposition and are fond of having your little joke."

"I swear as God is holy! If you like, since it has come to that, I will show you."

"I don't want to trouble you," said the clerk, taking a pinch of snuff. "However, if it is no trouble," he added, moved by curiosity, "it might be desirable to have a look."

The collegiate assessor took the handkerchief from his face. "It really is extremely strange," said the clerk, "the place is perfectly flat, like a freshly fried pancake. Yes, it's incredibly smooth."

"Will you dispute it now? You see for yourself I must advertise. I shall be particularly grateful to you and very glad this incident has given me the pleasure of your acquaintance."

The major, as may be seen, made up his mind on this occasion to resort to a little flattery.

"To print such an advertisement is, of course, not such a very great matter," said the clerk. "But I do not foresee any advantage to you from it. If you do want to, put it in the hands of someone with a skillful pen, describe it as a rare freak of nature, and publish the little article in *The Northern Bee*" (at this point he once more took a pinch of snuff) "for the benefit of youth" (at this moment he wiped his nose), "or anyway as a matter of general interest."

The collegiate assessor felt quite hopeless. He dropped his eyes and looked at the bottom of the paper where there was an announcement of a theatrical event; his face was ready to break into a smile as he saw the name of a pretty actress, and his hand went to his pocket to feel whether he had a five-ruble note there, for an officer of his rank ought, in Kovaliov's opinion, to have a seat in the orchestra; but the thought of his nose spoiled it all.

Even the clerk seemed touched by Kovaliov's difficult position. Desirous of relieving his distress in some way, he thought it befitting to express his sympathy in a few words: "I am really very much grieved that such an incident should have occurred to you. Wouldn't you like a pinch of snuff? it relieves headache and dissipates depression; even in intestinal trouble it is of use." Saying this the clerk offered Kovaliov his snuffbox, rather deftly opening the lid with a portrait of a lady in a hat on it.

This thoughtless act exhausted Kovaliov's patience.

"I can't understand how you can think it proper to make a joke of it," he said angrily; "don't you see that I am without just what I need for sniffing? To hell with your snuff! I can't bear the sight of it now, not merely your miserable Berezinsky stuff but even if you were to offer me rappee itself!" Saying this he walked out of the newspaper office, deeply mortified, and went in the direction of the local police inspector.

Kovaliov walked in at the very moment when he was stretching and clearing his throat and saying: "Ah, I should enjoy a couple of hours' nap!" And so it might be foreseen that the collegiate assessor's visit was not very opportune. The police inspector was a great patron of all arts and manufactures; but he preferred money to everything. "That is a thing," he used to say; "there is nothing better than that thing; it does not ask for food, it takes up little space, there is always room for it in the pocket, and if you drop it, it does not break."

The police inspector received Kovaliov rather coldly and said that after dinner was not the time to make an inquiry, that nature itself had ordained that man should rest a little after eating (the collegiate assessor could see from this that the sayings of the ancient sages were not unfamiliar to the local inspector), and that a respectable man does not have his nose pulled off.

This was adding insult to injury. It must be said that Kovaliov was very easily offended. He could forgive anything said about himself, but could never forgive insult to his rank or his calling. He was even of the opinion that any reference to officers of the higher ranks might be allowed to pass in stage plays, but that no attack ought to be made on those of a lower grade. The reception given him by the local inspector so disconcerted him that he tossed his head and said with an air of dignity and a slight gesture of surprise: "I must observe that after observations so insulting on your part I can add nothing more ..." and went out.

He went home hardly conscious of the ground under his feet. By now it was dusk. His lodgings seemed to him melancholy or rather utterly disgusting after all these unsuccessful efforts. Going into his hall he saw his valet, Ivan, lying on his dirty leather sofa; he was spitting on the ceiling and rather successfully aiming at the same spot. The nonchalance of his servant enraged him; he hit him on the forehead with his hat, saying: "You pig, you are always doing something stupid."

Ivan jumped up and rushed headlong to help him off with his cloak.

Going into his room, weary and dejected, the major threw himself into an easy chair, and at last, after several sighs, said:

"My God, my God! Why has this misfortune befallen me? If I had lost an arm or a leg it would have been better; but without a nose a man is goodness knows what: neither fish nor fowl nor human being, good for nothing but to be flung out of the window! And if only it had been cut off in battle or in a duel, or if I had been the cause of it myself, but as it is, it is lost for no cause or reason, it is lost for nothing, absolutely nothing! But no, it cannot be," he added after a moment's thought; "it's incredible that a nose should be lost. It must be a dream or an illusion. Perhaps by some mistake I drank instead of water the vodka I used to rub my chin with after shaving. Ivan, the idiot, did not remove it and very likely I took it." To convince himself that he was not drunk, the major pinched himself so painfully that he shrieked. The pain completely convinced him that he was living and acting in real life. He slowly approached the mirror and at first screwed up his eyes with the idea that maybe his nose would appear in its proper place; but at the same minute sprang back, saying: "What a terrible sight!"

It really was incomprehensible; if a button had been lost or a silver spoon or a watch or anything similar — but to have lost this, and in one's own apartment too! Thinking over all the circumstances, Major Kovaliov reached the supposition that what might be nearest the truth was that the person responsible for this could be no other than Madame Podtochina, who wanted him to marry her daughter. He himself liked flirting with her, but avoided a definite engagement. When the mother had informed him plainly that she wished for the marriage, he had slyly put her off with his compliments, saying that he was still young, that he must serve for five years or so to be exactly forty-two. And that Madame Podtochina had therefore made up her mind, probably out of revenge, to ruin him, and had hired for the purpose some peasant witches, because it was impossible to suppose that the nose had been cut off in any way; no one had come into his room; the barber Ivan Yakovlevich had shaved him on Wednesday, and all Wednesday and even all Thursday his nose had been all right — that he remembered and was quite certain about; besides, he would have felt pain, and there could have been no doubt that the wound could not have healed so soon and been as flat as a pancake. He formed various plans in his mind; either to summon Madame Podtochina formally before the court or to go to her himself and confront her with it. These reflections were interrupted by a light which gleamed through all the cracks of the door and informed him that a candle had been lighted in the hall by Ivan. Soon Ivan himself appeared, holding it before him and lighting up the whole room. Kovaliov's first movement was to snatch up his handkerchief and cover the place where yesterday his nose had been, so that his really stupid servant might not gape at the sight of anything so peculiar in his master.

Ivan had hardly time to retreat to his lair when there was the sound of an unfamiliar voice in the hall, pronouncing the words: "Does the collegiate assessor Kovaliov live here?"

"Come in, Major Kovaliov is here," said Kovaliov, jumping up hurriedly and opening the door.

A police officer walked in. He was of handsome appearance, with whiskers neither too fair nor too dark, and rather fat cheeks, the same officer who at the beginning of our story was standing at the end of Isakievsky Bridge.

"Did you lose your nose, sir?"

"That is so."

"It is now found."

"What are you saying?" cried Major Kovaliov. He could not speak for joy. He stared at the police officer standing before him, on whose full lips and cheeks the flickering light of the candle was brightly reflected. "How?"

"By extraordinary luck: he was caught almost on the road. He had already taken his seat in the stagecoach and was intending to go to Riga, and had already taken a passport in the name of a government clerk. And the strange thing is that I myself took him for a gentleman at first, but fortunately I had my spectacles with me and I soon saw that it was a nose. You know I am shortsighted. And if you stand before me I only see that you have a face, but I don't notice your nose or your beard or anything. My mother-in-law, that is my wife's mother, doesn't see anything either."

Kovaliov was beside himself with joy. "Where? Where? I'll go at once."

"Don't disturb yourself. Knowing that you were in need of it I brought it along with me. And the strange thing is that the man who has had the most to do with the affair is a rascal of a barber on Voznesensky Avenue, who is now in our custody. I have long suspected him of drunkenness and thieving, and only the day before yesterday he carried off a strip of buttons from one shop. Your nose is exactly as it was." With this the police officer put his hand in his pocket and drew out the nose just as it was.

"That's it!" Kovaliov cried. "That's certainly it. You must have a cup of tea with me this evening."

"I should look upon it as a great pleasure, but I can't possibly manage it: I have to go from here to the penitentiary. . . . How the price of food is going up! . . . At home I have my mother-in-law, that is my wife's mother, and my children, the eldest particularly gives signs of great promise, he is a very intelligent child; but we have absolutely no means for his education . . ."

For some time after the policeman's departure the collegiate assessor remained in a state of bewilderment, and it was only a few minutes later that he was capable of feeling and understanding again: so reduced was he to stupefaction by this unexpected good fortune. He took the recovered nose carefully in his two hands, holding them together like a cup, and once more examined it attentively.

"Yes, that's it, it's certainly it," said Major Kovaliov. "There's the pimple that came out on the left side yesterday." The major almost laughed aloud with joy.

But nothing in this world is of long duration, and so his joy was not so great the next moment;

and the moment after, it was still less, and in the end he passed imperceptibly into his ordinary frame of mind, just as a circle on the water caused by a falling stone gradually passes away into the unbroken smoothness of the surface. Kovaliov began to think, and reflected that the business was not finished yet; the nose was found, but it had to be put on, fixed in its proper place.

"And what if it won't stick?" Asking himself this question, the major turned pale.

With a feeling of irrepressible terror he rushed to the table and moved the mirror forward so that he might not put the nose on crooked. His hands trembled. Cautiously and gently he replaced it in its former position. Oh horror, the nose would not stick on! . . . He put it to his lips, slightly warmed it with his breath, and again applied it to the flat space between his two cheeks; but nothing would make the nose stick.

"Come, come, stick on, you fool!" he said to it; but the nose seemed made of wood and fell on the table with a strange sound as though it were a cork. The major's face twisted convulsively.

"Is it possible that it won't grow on again?" But, however often he applied it to the proper place, the attempt was as unsuccessful as before.

He called Ivan and sent him for a doctor who lived in the best apartment on the first floor of the same house. The doctor was a handsome man; he had magnificent pitch-black whiskers, a fresh and healthy wife, ate fresh apples in the morning, and kept his mouth extraordinarily clean, rinsing it out for nearly three-quarters of an hour every morning and cleaning his teeth with five different sorts of brushes. The doctor appeared immediately. Asking how long ago the trouble had occurred, he took Major Kovaliov by the chin and with his thumb gave him a flip on the spot where the nose had been, making the major jerk his head so abruptly that he knocked the back of it against the wall. The doctor said that that did not matter, and, advising him to move a little away from the wall, he told him to bend his head around first to the right, and feeling the place where the nose had been, said, "H'm!" Then he told him to turn his head around to the left side and again said "H'm!" And in conclusion he gave him another flip with his thumb, so that Major Kovaliov threw up his head like a horse when his teeth are being looked at. After making this experiment the doctor shook his head and said:

"No, it's impossible. You had better stay as you are, for it may be made much worse. Of course, it might be stuck on; I could stick it on for you at once, if you like; but I assure you it would be worse for you."

"That's a nice thing to say! How can I stay without a nose?" said Kovaliov. "Thing's can't possibly be worse than now. It's simply beyond everything. Where can I show myself with such a terrible face? I have a good circle of acquaintances. Today, for instance, I ought to be at two evening parties. I know a great many people; Chekhtariova, the wife of a civil councilor, Podtochina, an officer's widow . . . though after the way she has behaved, I'll have nothing more to do with her except through the police. Do me a favor," Kovaliov went on in a supplicating voice; "is there no way to stick it on? Even if it were not neatly done, as long as it would stay on; I could even hold it on with my hand at critical moments. I wouldn't dance in any case for fear of a sudden movement upsetting it. As for remuneration for your services, you may be assured that as far as my means allow . . ."

"Believe me," said the doctor, in a voice neither loud nor low but persuasive and magnetic, "that I never work from mercenary motives; that is opposed to my principles and my science. It is true that I accept a fee for my visits, but that is simply to avoid wounding my patients by refusing it. Of course I could replace your nose; but I assure you on my honor, since you do not believe my word, that it will be much worse for you. You had better wait for the action of nature itself. Wash it frequently with cold water, and I assure you that even without a nose you will be just as healthy as with one. And I advise you to put the nose in a bottle, in spirits or, better still, put two tablespoons of sour vodka on it and heated vinegar — and then you might get quite a sum of money for it. I'd even take it myself, if you don't ask too much for it."

"No, no, I wouldn't sell it for anything," Major Kovaliov cried in despair; "I'd rather it were lost than that!"

"Excuse me!" said the doctor, bowing himself out, "I was trying to be of use to you. . . . Well, there is nothing I can do! Anyway, you see that I have done my best." Saying this the doctor walked out of the room with a majestic air. Kovaliov did not notice his face, and, almost unconscious, saw nothing but the cuffs of his immaculate white shirt peeping out from the sleeves of his black tail coat.

Next day he decided, before lodging a complaint with the police, to write to Madame Podtochina to see whether she would consent to return him what she had taken without a struggle. The letter was as follows:

DEAR MADAM,
ALEKSANDRA GRIGORIEVNA
I cannot understand this strange conduct on your part. You may rest assured that you will gain nothing by what you have done, and you will not get a step nearer forcing me to marry your daughter. Believe me, that business in regard to my nose is no secret, no more than it is that you and no other are the person chiefly responsible. The sudden parting of the same from its natural position, its flight and masquerading, at one time in

the form of a government clerk and finally in its own shape, is nothing less than the consequence of the sorceries engaged by you or by those who are versed in the same honorable arts as you are. For my part I consider it my duty to warn you, if the above-mentioned nose is not in its proper place today, I shall be obliged to resort to the assistance and protection of the law.

I have, however, with complete respect to you, the honor to be

Your respectful servant,
PLATON KOVALIOV

DEAR SIR,
PLATON KUZMICH!
Your letter greatly astonished me. I must frankly confess that I did not expect it, especially in regard to your unjust reproaches. I assure you I have never received the government clerk of whom you speak in my house, neither in masquerade nor in his own attire. It is true that Filipp Ivanovich Potanchikov has been to see me, and although, indeed, he is asking me for my daughter's hand and is a well-conducted, sober man of great learning, I have never encouraged his hopes. You make some reference to your nose also. If you wish me to understand by that that you imagine that I meant to make a long nose at you, that is, to give you a formal refusal, I am surprised that you should speak of such a thing when, as you know perfectly well, I was quite of the opposite way of thinking, and if you are courting my daughter with a view to lawful matrimony I am ready to satisfy you immediately, seeing that has always been the object of my keenest desires, in the hopes of which I remain always ready to be of service to you.

ALEKSANDRA PODTOCHINA

"No," said Kovaliov to himself after reading the letter, "she really is not to blame. It's impossible. The letter is written as it could not be written by anyone guilty of a crime." The collegiate assessor was an expert on this subject, as he had been sent several times to the Caucasus to conduct investigations. "In what way, by what fate, has this happened? Only the devil could understand it!" he said at last, letting his hands fall to his sides.

Meanwhile the rumors of this strange occurrence were spreading all over the town, and of course, not without special additions. Just at that time the minds of all were particularly interested in the marvelous: experiments in the influence of magnetism had been attracting public attention only recently. Moreover, the story of the dancing chair in Koniuchennaya Street was still fresh, and so there is nothing surprising in the fact that people were soon beginning to say that the nose of a collegiate assessor called Kovaliov was walking along Nevsky Prospekt at exactly three in the afternoon. Numbers of inquisitive people flocked there every day. Somebody said that the nose was in Yunker's shop — and near Yunker's there was such a crowd and such a crush that the police were actually obliged to intervene. One speculator, a man of dignified appearance with whiskers, who used to sell all sorts of cakes and tarts at the doors of the theaters, purposely constructed some very strong wooden benches, which he offered to the curious to stand on, for eighty kopeks each. One very worthy colonel left home earlier on account of it, and with a great deal of trouble made his way through the crowd; but to his great indignation, instead of the nose, he saw in the shop windows the usual woolen undershirt and a lithograph depicting a girl pulling up her stocking while a foppish young man, with a cutaway waistcoat and a small beard, peeps at her from behind a tree; a picture which had been hanging in the same place for more than ten years. As he walked away he said with vexation: "How can people be led astray by such stupid and incredible stories!" Then the rumor spread that it was not on Nevsky Prospekt but in Tavrichersky Park that Major Kovaliov's nose took its walks; that it had been there for a long time; that, even when Khozrev-Mirza used to live there, he was greatly surprised at this strange freak of nature. Several students from the Academy of Surgery made their way to the park. One worthy lady of high rank wrote a letter to the superintendent of the park asking him to show her children this rare phenomenon with, if possible, an explanation that should be edifying and instructive for the young.

All the gentlemen who invariably attend social gatherings and like to amuse the ladies were extremely thankful for all these events, for their stock of anecdotes was completely exhausted. A small group of worthy and well-intentioned persons were greatly displeased. One gentleman said with indignation that he could not understand how in the present enlightened age people could spread abroad these absurd stories, and that he was surprised that the government took no notice of it. This gentleman, as may be seen, belonged to the number of those who would like the government to meddle in everything, even in their daily quarrels with their wives. After this ... but here again the whole is lost in fog, and what happened afterward is absolutely unknown.

III

What is utterly absurd happens in the world. Sometimes there is not the slightest semblance of truth to it: all at once that very nose which had been driving about the place in the shape of a civil councilor, and had made such a stir in the town, turned up again as though nothing had happened, in its proper place, that is, precisely between the two cheeks of Major Kovaliov. This took place on the seventh of April. Waking up and casually glancing into the mirror, he sees — his nose! puts up his hands — actually his nose! "Aha!" said Kovaliov, and in his joy he almost danced a jig barefoot about his room; but the entrance of Ivan stopped him. He ordered Ivan to bring him water at once, and as he washed he glanced once more into the mirror — the nose! As he wiped himself with the towel he glanced into the mirror — the nose!

"Look, Ivan, I think I have a pimple on my nose," he said, while he thought: "How horrible it will be if Ivan says, 'No, indeed, sir, there's no pimple and, indeed, there is no nose either!'"

But Ivan said: "There is nothing, there is no pimple: your nose is quite clear!"

"Damn it, that's wonderful!" the major said to himself, and he snapped his fingers.

At that moment Ivan Yakovlevich the barber peeped in at the door, but as timidly as a cat who had just been beaten for stealing the bacon.

"Tell me first: are your hands clean?" Kovaliov shouted to him while he was still some way off.

"Yes."

"You are lying!"

"Upon my word, they are clean, sir."

"Well, be careful."

Kovaliov sat down. Ivan Yakovlevich covered him up with a towel, and in one instant with the aid of his brushes had smothered the whole of his beard and part of his cheek in cream, like that which is served at merchants' name-day parties.

"Look here!" Ivan Yakovlevich said to himself, glancing at the nose and then turning his customer's head on the other side and looking at it sideways. "There it is, sure enough. What can it mean?" He went on pondering, and for a long while he gazed at the nose. At last, lightly, with a cautiousness which may well be imagined, he raised two fingers to take it by the tip. Such was Ivan Yakovlevich's system.

"Now, now, now, careful!" cried Kovaliov. Ivan Yakovlevich let his hands drop, and was flustered and confused as he had never been confused before. At last he began gently tickling him with the razor under his beard, and, although it was difficult and not at all easy for him to shave without holding on to the olfactory portion of the face, yet he did at last somehow, pressing his rough thumb into his cheek and lower jaw, overcome all difficulties, and finish shaving him.

When it was all over, Kovaliov at once made haste to dress, took a cab, and drove to the café. Before he was inside the door he shouted: "Waiter, a cup of chocolate!" and at the same instant peeped at himself in the mirror. The nose was there. He turned around gaily and, with a satirical air, slightly screwing up his eyes, looked at two military men, one of whom had a nose hardly bigger than a vest button. After that he started off for the office of the department, in which he was urging his claims to a post as vice-governor or, failing that, the post of an executive clerk. After crossing the reception room he glanced at the mirror; the nose was there. Then he drove to see another collegiate assessor or major, who was very fond of making fun of people, and to whom he often said in reply to various biting observations: "Ah you! I know you, you are as sharp as a pin!" On the way he thought: "If the major does not split with laughter when he sees me, then it is a sure sign that everything is in its place." But the sarcastic collegiate assessor said nothing. "Good, good, damn it all!" Kovaliov thought to himself. On the way he met Podtochina, the officer's wife, and her daughter; he was profuse in his bows to them and was greeted with exclamations of delight — so there could be nothing wrong with him, he thought. He conversed with them for a long time and, taking out his snuffbox, purposely put a pinch to each nostril while he said to himself: "So much for you, you foolish petticoats, you hens! but I am not going to marry your daughter anyway. This is only *par amour!*"

And from that time forth Major Kovaliov promenaded about, as though nothing had happened, on Nevsky Prospekt, and at the theaters and everywhere. And the nose, too, as though nothing had happened, sat on his face without even a sign of coming off at the sides. And after this Major Kovaliov was always seen in a good humor, smiling, resolutely pursuing all the pretty ladies, and even on one occasion stopping before a shop in the Gostiny Court and buying the ribbon of some order, I cannot say for what purpose, since he was not himself a cavalier of any order.

So this is the strange event that occurred in the northern capital of our spacious empire! Only now, on thinking it all over, we perceive that there is a great deal that is improbable in it. Apart from the fact that it certainly is strange for a nose supernaturally to leave its place and to appear in various places in the guise of a civil councilor — how was it that Kovaliov did not grasp that he could not advertise about his nose in a newspaper office? I do not mean to say that I should think it too expensive to advertise: that is nonsense, and I am by no means a mercenary person: but it is improper, awkward, not nice! And again: how did the nose get into the loaf, and how about Ivan Yakovlevich himself? ... no, that I cannot understand, I am absolutely unable to understand it! But what is stranger, what is more incomprehensible than anything is that authors can choose such subjects. I confess that is quite beyond my grasp, it really is ... No, no! I cannot understand it at all. In the first place, it is absolutely without profit to our country; in the second place ... but in the second place, too, there is no profit. I really do not know what to say of it. ...

And yet, in spite of it all, though of course one may admit the first point, the second and the third ... may even ... but there, are there not absurd things everywhere? — and yet, when you think it over, there really is something in it. Despite what anyone may say, such things do happen— not often, but they do happen.

NATHANIEL HAWTHORNE

My Kinsman, Major Molineux

After the kings of Great Britain had assumed the right of appointing the colonial governors, the measures of the latter seldom met with the ready and generous approbation which had been paid to those of their predecessors, under the original charters. The people looked with most jealous scrutiny to the exercise of power which did not emanate from themselves, and they usually rewarded their rulers with slender gratitude for the compliances by which, in softening their instructions from beyond the sea, they had incurred the reprehension of those who gave them. The annals of Massachusetts Bay will inform us, that of six governors in the space of about forty years from the surrender of the old charter, under James II., two were imprisoned by a popular insurrection; a third, as Hutchinson inclines to believe, was driven from the province by the whizzing of a musket-ball; a fourth, in the opinion of the same historian, was hastened to his grave by continual bickerings with the House of Representatives; and the remaining two, as well as their successors, till the Revolution, were favored with few and brief intervals of peaceful sway. The inferior members of the court party, in times of high political excitement, led scarcely a more desirable life. These remarks may serve as a preface to the following adventures, which chanced upon a summer night, not far from a hundred years ago. The reader, in order to avoid a long and dry detail of colonial affairs, is requested to dispense with an account of the train of circumstances that had caused much temporary inflammation of the popular mind.

It was near nine o'clock of a moonlight evening, when a boat crossed the ferry with a single passenger, who had obtained his conveyance at that unusual hour by the promise of an extra fare. While he stood on the landing-place, searching in either pocket for the means of fulfilling his agreement, the ferryman lifted a lantern, by the aid of which, and the newly risen moon, he took a very accurate survey of the stranger's figure. He was a youth of barely eighteen years, evidently country-bred, and now, as it should seem, upon his first visit to town. He was clad in a coarse gray coat, well worn, but in excellent repair; his under garments were durably constructed of leather, and fitted tight to a pair of serviceable and well-shaped limbs; his stocking of blue yarn were the incontrovertible work of a mother or a sister; and on his head was a three-cornered hat, which in its better days had perhaps sheltered the graver brow of the lad's father. Under his left arm was a heavy cudgel formed of an oak sapling, and retaining a part of the hardened root; and his equipment was completed by a wallet, not so abundantly stocked as to incommode the vigorous shoulders on which it hung. Brown, curly hair, well-shaped features, and bright, cheerful eyes were nature's gifts, and worth all that art could have done for his adornment.

The youth, one of whose names was Robin, finally drew from his pocket the half of a little province bill of five shillings, which, in the depreciation in that sort of currency, did but satisfy the ferryman's demand, with the surplus of a sexangular piece of parchment, valued at three pence. He then walked forward into the town, with as light a step as if his day's journey had not already exceeded thirty miles, and with as eager an eye as if he were entering London city, instead of the little metropolis of a New England colony. Before Robin had proceeded far, however, it occurred to him that he knew not whither to direct his steps; so he paused, and looked up and down the narrow street, scrutinizing the small and mean wooden buildings that were scattered on either side.

"This low hovel cannot be my kinsman's dwelling," thought he, "nor yonder old house, where the moonlight enters at the broken casement; and truly I see none hereabouts that might be worthy of him. It would have been wise to inquire my way of the ferryman, and doubtless he would have gone with me, and earned a shilling from the Mayor for his pains. But the next man I meet will do as well."

He resumed his walk, and was glad to perceive that the street now became wider, and the houses more respectable in their appearance. He soon discerned a figure moving on moderately in advance, and hastened his steps to overtake it. As Robin drew nigh, he saw that the passenger was a man in years, with a full periwig of gray hair, a wide-skirted coat of dark cloth, and silk stockings rolled above his knees. He carried a long and polished cane, which he struck down perpendicularly before him at every step; and at regular intervals he uttered two successive hems, of a peculiarly solemn and sepulchral intonation. Having made these observations, Robin laid hold of the skirt of the old man's coat, just when the light from the open door and windows of a barber's shop fell upon both their figures.

"Good evening to you, honored sir," said he, making a low bow, and still retaining his hold of the skirt. "I pray you tell me whereabouts is the dwelling of my kinsman, Major Molineux."

The youth's question was uttered very loudly; and one of the barbers, whose razor was descending on a well-soaped chin, and another who was dressing a Ramillies wig, left their occupations, and came to the door. The citizen, in the meantime, turned a long-favored countenance upon Robin, and answered him in a tone of excessive anger and annoyance. His two sepulchral hems, however, broke into the very centre of his rebuke, with most singular effect, like a thought of the cold grave obtruding among wrathful passions.

"Let go my garment, fellow! I tell you, I know not the man you speak of. What! I have authority, I have — hem, hem — authority; and if this be the respect you show for your betters, your feet shall be brought acquainted with the stocks by daylight, tomorrow morning!"

Robin released the old man's skirt, and hastened away, pursued by an ill-mannered roar of laughter from the barber's shop. He was at first considerably surprised by the result of his question, but, being a shrewd youth, soon thought himself able to account for the mystery.

"This is some country representative," was his conclusion, "who has never seen the inside of my kinsman's door, and lacks the breeding to answer a stranger civilly. The man is old, or verily — I might be tempted to turn back and smite him on the nose. Ah, Robin, Robin! even the barber's boys laugh at you for choosing such a guide! You will be wiser in time, friend Robin."

He now became entangled in a succession of crooked and narrow streets, which crossed each other, and meandered at no great distance from the water-side. The smell of tar was obvious to his nostrils, the masts of vessels pierced the moonlight above the tops of the buildings, and the numerous signs, which Robin paused to read, informed him that he was near the centre of business. But the streets were empty, the shops were closed, and lights were visible only in the second stories of a few dwelling-houses. At length, on the corner of a narrow lane, through which he was passing, he beheld the broad countenance of a British hero swinging before the door of an inn, whence proceeded the voices of many guests. The casement of one of the lower windows was thrown back, and a very thin curtain permitted Robin to distinguish a party at supper, round a well-furnished table. The fragrance of the good cheer steamed forth into the outer air, and the youth could not fail to recollect that the last remnant of his travelling stock of provision had yielded to his morning appetite, and that noon had found and left him dinnerless.

"Oh, that a parchment three-penny might give me a right to sit down at yonder table!" said Robin, with a sigh. "But the Major will make me welcome to the best of his victuals; so I will even step boldly in, and inquire my way to his dwelling."

He entered the tavern, and was guided by the murmur of voices and the fumes of tobacco to the public-room. It was a long and low apartment, with oaken walls, grown dark in the continual smoke, and a floor which was thickly sanded, but of no immaculate purity. A number of persons — the larger part of whom appeared to be mariners, or in some way connected with the sea — occupied the wooden benches, or leather-bottomed chairs, conversing on various matters, and occasionally lending their attention to some topic of general interest. Three or four little groups were draining as many bowls of punch, which the West Indian trade had long since made a familiar drink in the colony. Others, who had the appearance of men who lived by regular and laborious handicraft, preferred the insulated bliss of an unshared potation, and became more taciturn under its influence. Nearly all, in short, evinced a predilection for the Good Creature in some of its various shapes, for this is a vice to which, as Fast Day sermons of a hundred years ago will testify, we have a long hereditary claim. The only guests to whom Robin's sympathies inclined him were two or three sheepish countrymen, who were using the inn somewhat after the fashion of a Turkish caravansary; they had gotten themselves into the darkest corner of the room, and heedless of the Nicotian atmosphere, were supping on the bread of their own ovens, and the bacon cured in their own chimney-smoke. But though Robin felt a sort of brotherhood with these strangers, his eyes were attracted from them to a person who stood near the door, holding whispered conversation with a group of ill-dressed associates. His features were separately striking almost to grotesqueness, and the whole face left a deep impression on the memory. The forehead bulged out into a double prominence, with a vale between; the nose came boldly forth in an irregular curve, and its bridge was of more than a finger's breadth; the eyebrows were deep and shaggy, and the eyes glowed beneath them like fire in a cave.

While Robin deliberated of whom to inquire respecting his kinsman's dwelling, he was accosted by the innkeeper, a little man in a stained white apron, who had come to pay his professional welcome to the stranger. Being in the second generation from a French Protestant, he seemed to have inherited the courtesy of his parent nation; but no variety of circumstances was ever known to change his voice from the one shrill note in which he now addressed Robin.

"From the country, I presume, sir?" said he, with a profound bow. "Beg leave to congratulate you on your arrival, and trust you intend a long stay with us. Fine town here, sir, beautiful buildings, and much that may interest a stranger. May I hope for the honor of your commands in respect to supper?"

"The man sees a family likeness! the rogue has guessed that I am related to the Major!" thought Robin, who had hitherto experienced little superfluous civility.

All eyes were now turned on the country lad, standing at the door, in his worn three-cornered hat, gray coat, leather breeches, and blue yarn stockings, leaning on an oaken cudgel, and bearing a wallet on his back.

Robin replied to the courteous innkeeper, with such an assumption of confidence as befitted the Major's relative. "My honest friend," he said, "I shall make it a point to patronize your house on some occasion, when" — here he could not help lowering his voice — "when I may have more than a parchment three-pence in my pocket. My present business," continued he, speaking with lofty confidence, "is merely to inquire my way to the dwelling of my kinsman, Major Molineux."

There was a sudden and general movement in the room, which Robin interpreted as expressing the eagerness of each individual to become his guide. But the innkeeper turned his eyes to a written paper on the wall, which he read, or seemed to read, with occasional recurrences to the young man's figure.

"What have we here?" said he, breaking his speech into little dry fragments. "'Left the house of the subscriber, bounden servant, Hezekiah Mudge, — had on, when he went away, gray coat, leather breeches, master's third-best hat. One pound currency reward to whosoever shall lodge him in any jail of the providence.' Better trudge, boy; better trudge!"

Robin had begun to draw his hand towards the lighter end of the oak cudgel, but a strange hostility in every countenance induced him to relinquish his purpose of breaking the courteous innkeeper's head. As he turned to leave the room, he encountered a sneering glance from the bold-featured personage whom he had before noticed; and no sooner was he beyond the door, than he heard a general laugh, in which the innkeeper's voice might be distinguished, like the dropping of small stones into a kettle.

"Now, is it not strange," thought Robin, with his usual shrewdness, — "is it not strange that the confession of an empty pocket should outweigh the name of my kinsman, Major Molineux? Oh, if I had one of those grinning rascals in the woods, where I and my oak sapling grew up together, I would teach him that my arm is heavy though my purse be light!"

On turning the corner of the narrow lane, Robin found himself in a spacious street, with an unbroken line of lofty houses on each side, and a steepled building at the upper end, whence the ringing of a bell announced the hour of nine. The light of the moon, and the lamps from the numerous shop-windows, discovered people promenading on the pavement, and amongst them Robin had hoped to recognize his hitherto inscrutable relative. The result of his former inquiries made him unwilling to hazard another, in a scene of such publicity, and he determined to walk slowly and silently up the street, thrusting his face close to that of every elderly gentleman, in search of the Major's lineaments. In his progress, Robin encountered many gay and gallant figures. Embroidered garments of showy colors, enormous periwigs, gold-laced hats, and silver-hilted swords glided past him and dazzled his optics. Travelled youths, imitators of the European fine gentlemen of the period, trod jauntily along, half dancing to the fashionable tunes which they hummed, and making poor Robin ashamed of his quiet and natural gait. At length, after many pauses to examine the gorgeous display of goods in the shop-windows, and after suffering some rebukes for the impertinence of his scrutiny into people's faces, the Major's kinsman found himself near the steepled building, still unsuccessful in his search. As yet, however, he had seen only one side of the thronged street; so Robin crossed, and continued the same sort of inquisition down the opposite pavement, with stronger hopes than the philosopher seeking an honest man, but with no better fortune. He had arrived about midway towards the lower end, from which his course began, when he overhead the approach of some one who struck down a cane on the flagstones at every step, uttering at regular intervals, two sepulchral hems.

"Mercy on us!" quoth Robin, recognizing the sound.

Turning a corner, which chanced to be close at his right hand, he hastened to pursue his researches in some other part of the town. His patience now was wearing low, and he seemed to feel more fatigue from his rambles since he crossed the ferry, than from his journey of several days on the other side. Hunger also pleaded loudly within him, and Robin began to balance the propriety of demanding, violently, and with lifted cudgel, the necessary guidance from the first solitary passenger whom he should meet. While a resolution to this effect was gaining strength, he entered a street of mean appearance, on either side of which a row of ill-built houses was straggling towards the harbor. The moonlight fell upon no passenger along the whole extent, but in the third domicile which Robin passed there was a half-opened door, and his keen glance detected a woman's garment within.

"My luck may be better here," said he to himself.

Accordingly, he approached the door, and beheld it shut closer as he did so; yet an open space remained, sufficing for the fair occupant to observe the stranger, without a corresponding display on her part. All that Robin could discern was a strip of scarlet petticoat, and the occasional sparkle of an eye, as if the moonbeams were trembling on some bright thing.

"Pretty mistress," for I may call her so with a good conscience, thought the shrewd youth, since I know nothing to the contrary, — "my sweet pretty mistress, will you be kind enough to tell me whereabouts I must seek the dwelling of my kinsman, Major Molineux?"

Robin's voice was plaintive and winning, and the female, seeing nothing to be shunned in the handsome country youth, thrust open the door, and came forth into the moonlight. She was a dainty little figure, with a white neck, round arms, and a slender waist, at the extremity of which her scarlet petticoat jutted out over a hoop, as if she were standing in a balloon. Moreover, her face was oval and pretty, her hair dark beneath the little cap, and her bright eyes possessed a sly freedom, which triumphed over those of Robin.

"Major Molineux dwells here," said this fair woman.

Now, her voice was the sweetest Robin had heard that night, yet he could not help doubting whether that sweet voice spoke Gospel truth. He looked up and down the mean street, and then surveyed the house before which they stood. It was a small, dark edifice of two stories, the second of which projected over the lower floor, and the front apartment had the aspect of a shop for petty commodities.

"Now, truly, I am in luck," replied Robin, cunningly, "and so indeed is my kinsman, the Major, in having so pretty a housekeeper. But I prithee trouble him to step to the door; I will deliver him a message from his friends in the country, and then go back to my lodgings at the inn."

"Nay, the Major has been abed this hour or more," said the lady of the scarlet petticoat; "and it would be to little purpose to disturb him to-night, seeing his evening draught was of the strongest. But he is a kind-hearted man, and it would be as much as my life's worth to let a kinsman of his turn away from the door. You are the good old gentleman's very picture, and I could swear that was his rainy-weather hat. Also he has garments very much resembling those leather small-clothes. But come in, I pray, for I bid you hearty welcome in his name."

So saying, the fair and hospitable dame took our hero by the hand; and the touch was light, and the force was gentleness, and though Robin read in her eyes what he did not hear in her words, yet the slender-waisted woman in the scarlet petticoat proved stronger than the athletic country youth. She had drawn his half-willing footsteps nearly to the threshold, when the opening of a door in the neighborhood startled the Major's housekeeper, and, leaving the Major's kinsman, she vanished speedily into her own domicile. A heavy yawn preceded the appearance of a man, who, like the Moonshine of Pyramus and Thisbe, carried a lantern, needlessly aiding his sister luminary in the heavens. As he walked sleepily up the street, he turned his broad, dull face on Robin, and displayed a long staff, spiked at the end.

"Home, vagabond, home!" said the watchman, in accents that seemed to fall asleep as soon as they were uttered. "Home, or we'll set you in the stocks by peep of day!"

"This is the second hint of the kind," thought Robin, "I wish they would end my difficulties, by setting me there to-night."

Nevertheless, the youth felt an instinctive antipathy towards the guardian of midnight order, which at first prevented him from asking his usual question. But just when the man was about to vanish behind the corner, Robin resolved not to lose the opportunity, and shouted lustily after him, —

"I say, friend! will you guide me to the house of my kinsman, Major Molineux?"

The watchman made no reply, but turned the corner and was gone; yet Robin seemed to hear the sound of drowsy laughter stealing along the solitary street. At that moment, also, a pleasant titter saluted him from the open window above his head; he looked up, and caught the sparkle of a saucy eye; a round arm beckoned to him, and next he heard light footsteps descending the staircase within. But Robin, being of the household of a New England clergyman, was a good youth, as well as a shrewd one; so he resisted temptation, and fled away.

He now roamed desperately, and at random, through the town, almost ready to believe that a spell was on him, like that by which a wizard of his country had once kept three pursuers wandering, a whole winter night, within twenty paces of the cottage which they sought. The streets lay before him, strange and desolate, and the lights were extinguished in almost every house. Twice, however, little parties of men, among whom Robin distinguished individuals in outlandish attire, came hurrying along; but, though on both occasions, they paused to address him, such intercourse did not at all enlighten his perplexity. They did but utter a few words in some language of which Robin knew nothing, and perceiving his inability to answer, bestowed a curse upon him in plain English and hastened away. Finally, the lad determined to knock at the door of every mansion that might appear worthy to be occupied by his kinsman, trusting the perseverance would overcome the fatality that had hitherto thwarted him. Firm in this resolve, he was passing beneath the walls of a church, which formed the corner of the two streets, when, as he turned into the shade of its steeple, he encountered a bulky stranger, muffled in a cloak. The man was proceeding with the speed of earnest business, but Robin planted himself full before him, holding the oak cudgel with both hands across his body as a bar to further passage.

"Halt, honest man, and answer me a question," said he, very resolutely. "Tell me, this instant, whereabouts is the dwelling of my kinsman, Major Molineux!"

"Keep your tongue between your teeth, fool, and let me pass!" said a deep, gruff voice, which Robin partly remembered. "Let me pass, or I'll strike you to the earth!"

"No, no, neighbor!" cried Robin, flourishing his cudgel, and then thrusting its larger end close to the man's muffled face. "No, no, I'm not the fool you take me for, nor do you pass till I have an answer to my question. Whereabouts is the dwelling of my kinsman, Major Molineux?"

The stranger, instead of attempting to force his passage, stepped back into the moonlight, unmuffled his face, and stared full into that of Robin.

"Watch here an hour, and Major Molineux will pass by," said he.

Robin gazed with dismay and astonishment on the unprecedented physiognomy of the speaker. The forehead with its double prominence, the broad hooked nose, the shaggy eyebrows, and fiery eyes were those which he had noticed at the inn, but the man's complexion had undergone a singular, or, more properly, a twofold change. One side of the face blazed an intense red, while the other was black as midnight, the division line being in the broad bridge of the nose; and a mouth which seemed to extend from ear to ear was black or red, in contrast to the color of the cheek. The effect was as if two individual devils, a fiend of fire and a fiend of darkness, had united themselves to form this infernal visage. The stranger grinned in Robin's face, muffled his party-colored features, and was out of sight in a moment.

"Strange things we travellers see!" ejaculated Robin.

He seated himself, however, upon the steps of the church-door, resolving to wait the appointed time for his kinsman. A few moments were consumed in philosophical speculations upon the species of man who had just left him; but having settled this point shrewdly, rationally, and satisfactorily, he was compelled to look elsewhere for his amusement. And first he threw his eyes along the street. It was of more respectable appearance than most of those into which he had wandered; and the moon, creating, like the imaginative power, a beautiful strangeness in familiar objects, gave something of romance to a scene that might not have possessed it in the light of day. The irregular and often quaint architecture of the houses, some of whose roofs were broken into numerous little peaks, while others ascended, steep and narrow, into a single point, and others again were square; the pure snow-white of some of their complexions, the aged darkness of others, and the thousand sparklings, reflected from bright substances in the walls of many; these matters engaged Robin's attention for a while, and then began to grow wearisome. Next he endeavored to define the forms of distant objects, starting away, with almost ghostly indistinctness, just as his eye appeared to grasp them; and finally he took a minute survey of an edifice which stood on the opposite side of the street, directly in front of the church-door, where he was stationed. It was a large, square mansion, distinguished from its neighbors by a balcony, which rested on tall pillars, and by an elaborate Gothic window, communicating therewith.

"Perhaps this is the very house I have been seeking," thought Robin.

Then he strove to speed away the time, by listening to a murmur which swept continually along the street, yet was scarcely audible, except to an unaccustomed ear like his; it was a low, dull, dreamy sound, compounded of many noises, each of which was at too great a distance to be separately heard. Robin marvelled at this snore of a sleeping town, and marvelled more whenever its continuity was broken by now and then a distant shout, apparently loud where it originated. But altogether it was a sleep-inspiring sound, and, to shake off its drowsy influence, Robin arose, and climbed a window-frame, that he might view the interior of the church. There the moonbeams came trembling in, and fell down upon the deserted pews, and extended along the quiet aisles. A fainter yet more awful radiance was hovering around the pulpit, and one solitary ray had dared to rest upon the open page of the great Bible. Had nature, in that deep hour, become a worshipper in the house which man had builded? Or was that heavenly light the visible sanctity of the place, — visible because no earthly and impure feet were within the walls? The scene made Robin's heart shiver with a sensation of loneliness stronger than he had ever felt in the remotest depths of his native woods; so he turned away and sat down again before the door. There were graves around the church, and now an uneasy thought obtruded into Robin's breast. What if the object of his search, which had been so often and so strangely thwarted, were all the time mouldering in his shroud? What if his kinsman should glide through yonder gate, and nod and smile to him in dimly passing by?

"Oh that any breathing thing were here with me!" said Robin.

Recalling his thoughts from this uncomfortable track, he sent them over forest, hill, and stream, and attempted to imagine how that evening of ambiguity and weariness had been spent by his father's household. He pictured them assembled at the door, beneath the tree, the great old tree, which had been spared for its huge twisted trunk and venerable shade, when a thousand leafy brethren fell. There, at the going down of the summer sun, it was his father's custom to perform domestic worship, that the neighbors might come and join with him like brothers of the family, and that the wayfaring man might pause to drink at that fountain, and keep his heart pure by freshening the memory of home. Robin distinguished the seat of every individual of the little audience; he saw the good man in the midst, holding the Scriptures in the golden light that fell from the western clouds; he beheld him close the book and all rise up to pray. He heard the old thanksgiving for daily mercies, the old supplications for their continuance, to which he had so often listened in weariness, but which were now among his dear remembrances. He perceived the slight inequality of his father's voice when he came to speak of the absent one; he noted how his mother turned her face to the broad and knotted trunk; how his elder brother scorned, because the beard was rough upon his upper lip, to permit his features to be moved; how the younger sister drew down a low hanging branch before her eyes; and how the little one of all, whose sports had hitherto broken the decorum of the scene, understood the prayer for her playmate, and burst into clamorous grief. Then he saw them go in at the door; and when Robin would have entered also, the latch tinkled into its place, and he was excluded from his home.

"Am I here, or there?" cried Robin, starting; for all at once, when his thoughts had become visible and audible in a dream, the long, wide, solitary street shone out before him.

He aroused himself, and endeavoured to fix his attention steadily upon the large edifice which he had surveyed before. But still his mind kept vibrating between fancy and reality; by turns, the pillars of the balcony lengthened into the tall, bare stems of pines, dwindled down to human figures, settled again into their true shape and size, and then commenced a new succession of changes. For a single moment, when he deemed himself awake, he could have sworn that a visage — one which he seemed to remember, yet could not absolutely name as his kinsman's — was looking towards him from the Gothic window. A deeper sleep wrestled with and nearly overcame him, but fled at the sound of footsteps along the opposite pavement. Robin rubbed his eyes, discerned a man passing at the foot of the balcony, and addressed him in a loud, peevish, and lamentable cry.

"Hallo, friend! must I wait here all night for my kinsman, Major Molineux?"

The sleeping echoes awoke, and answered the voice; and the passenger, barely able to discern a figure sitting in the oblique shade of the steeple, traversed the street to obtain a nearer view. He was himself a gentleman in his prime, of open, intelligent, cheerful, and altogether prepossessing countenance. Perceiving a country youth, apparently homeless and without friends, he accosted him in a tone of real kindness, which had become strange to Robin's ears.

"Well, my good lad, why are you sitting here?" inquired he. "Can I be of service to you in any way?"

"I am afraid not, sir," replied Robin, despondingly; "yet I shall take it kindly, if you'll answer me a single question. I've been searching, half the night, for one Major Molineux; now, sir, is there really such a person in these parts, or am I dreaming?"

"Major Molineux! The name is not altogether strange to me," said the gentleman, smiling. "Have you any objection to telling me the nature of your business with him?"

Then Robin briefly related that his father was a clergyman, settled on a small salary, at a long distance back in the country, and that he and Major Molineux were brothers' children. The Major, having inherited riches, and acquired civil and military rank, had visited his cousin, in great pomp, a year or two before; had manifested much interest in Robin and an elder brother, and, being childless himself, had thrown out hints respecting the future establishment of one of them in life. The elder brother was destined to succeed to the farm which his father cultivated in the interval of sacred duties; it was therefore determined that Robin should profit by his kinsman's generous intentions, especially as he seemed to be rather the favorite, and was thought to possess other necessary endowments.

"For I have the name of being a shrewd youth," observed Robin, in this part of his story.

"I doubt not you deserve it," replied his new friend, good-naturedly; "but pray proceed."

"Well, sir, being nearly eighteen years old, and well grown, as you see," continued Robin, drawing himself up to his full height, "I thought it high time to begin in the world. So my mother and sister put me in handsome trim, and my father gave me half the remnant of his last year's salary, and five days ago I started for this place, to pay the Major a visit. But, would you believe it, sir! I crossed the ferry a little after dark, and have yet found nobody that would show me the way to his dwelling; only, an hour or two since, I was told to wait here, and Major Molineux would pass by."

"Can you describe the man who told you this?" inquired the gentleman.

"Oh, he was a very ill-favored fellow, sir," replied Robin, "with two great bumps on his forehead, a hook nose, fiery eyes; and, what struck me as the strangest, his face was of two different colors. Do you happen to know such a man, sir?"

"Not intimately," answered the stranger, "but I chanced to meet him a little time previous to your stopping me. I believe you may trust his word, and that the Major will very shortly pass through this street. In the mean time, as I have a singular curiosity to witness your meeting, I will sit down here upon the steps and bear you company."

He seated himself accordingly, and soon engaged his companion in animated discourse. It was but of brief continuance, however, for a noise of shouting, which had long been remotely audible, drew so much nearer that Robin inquired its cause.

"What may be the meaning of this uproar?" asked he. "Truly, if your town be always as noisy, I shall find little sleep while I am an inhabitant."

"Why, indeed, friend Robin, there do appear to be three or four riotous fellows abroad to-night," replied the gentleman. "You must not expect all the stillness of your native woods here in our streets. But the watch will shortly be at the heels of these lads and" —

"Ay, and set them in the stocks by peep of day," interrupted Robin, recollecting his own encounter with the drowsy lantern-bearer. "But, dear sir, if I may trust my ears, an army of watchmen would never make head against such a multitude of rioters. There were at least a thousand voices went up to make that one shout."

"May not a man have several voices, Robin, as well as two complexions?" said his friend.

"Perhaps a man may; but Heaven forbid that a woman should!" responded the shrewd youth, thinking of the seductive tones of the Major's housekeeper.

The sounds of a trumpet in some neighboring street now became so evident and continual, that Robin's curiosity was strongly excited. In addition to the shouts, he heard frequent bursts from many instruments of discord, and a wild and confused laughter filled up the intervals. Robin rose from the steps, and looked wistfully towards a point whither people seemed to be hastening.

"Surely some prodigious merry-making is going on," exclaimed he. "I have laughed very little since I left home, sir, and should be sorry to lose an opportunity. Shall we step round the corner by that darkish house, and take our share of the fun?"

"Sit down again, sit down, good Robin," replied the gentleman, laying his hand on the skirt of the gray coat. "You forget that we must wait here for your kinsman; and there is reason to believe that he will pass by, in the course of a very few moments."

The near approach of the uproar had now disturbed the neighborhood; windows flew open on all sides; and many heads, in the attire of the pillow, and confused by sleep suddenly broken, were protruded to the gaze of whoever had leisure to observe them. Eager voices hailed each other from house to house, all demanding the explanation, which not a soul could give. Half-dressed men hurried towards the unknown commotion, stumbling as they went over the stone steps that thrust themselves into the narrow foot-walk. The shouts, the laughter, and the tuneless bray, the antipodes of music, came onwards with increasing din, till scattered individuals, and then denser bodies, began to appear round a corner at the distance of a hundred yards.

"Will you recognize your kinsman, if he passes in this crowd?" inquired the gentleman.

"Indeed, I can't warrant it, sir; but I'll take my stand here, and keep a bright lookout," answered Robin, descending to the outer edge of the pavement.

A mighty stream of people now emptied into the street, and came rolling slowly towards the church. A single horseman wheeled the corner in the midst of them, and close behind him came a band of fearful wind-instruments, sending forth a fresher discord now that no intervening buildings kept it from the ear. Then a redder light disturbed the moonbeams, and a dense multitude of torches shone along the street, concealing, by their glare, whatever object they illuminated. The single horseman, clad in a military dress, and bearing a drawn sword, rode onward as the leader, and, by his fierce and variegated countenance, appeared like war personified; the red of one cheek was an emblem of fire and sword; the blackness of the other betokened the mourning that attends them. In his train were wild figures in the Indian dress, and many fantastic shapes without a model, giving the whole march a visionary air, as if a dream had broken forth from some feverish brain, and were sweeping visibly through the midnight streets. A mass of people, inactive, except as applauding spectators, hemmed the procession in; and several women ran along the sidewalk, piercing the confusion of heavier sounds with their shrill voices of mirth or terror.

"The double-faced fellow has his eye upon me," muttered Robin, with an indefinite but an uncomfortable idea that he was himself to bear a part in the pageantry.

The leader turned himself in the saddle, and fixed his glance full upon the country youth, as the steed went slowly by. When Robin had freed his eyes from those fiery ones, the musicians were passing before him, and the torches were close at hand; but the unsteady brightness of the latter formed a veil which he could not penetrate. The rattling of wheels over the stones sometimes found its way to his ear, and confused traces of a human form appeared at intervals, and then melted into the vivid light. A moment more, and the leader thundered a command to halt: the trumpets vomited a horrid breath, and then held their peace; the shouts and laughter of the people died away, and there remained only a universal hum, allied to silence. Right before Robin's eyes was an uncovered cart. There the torches blazed the brightest, there the moon shone out like day, and there, in tar-and-feathery dignity, sat his kinsman, Major Molineux!

He was an elderly man, of large and majestic person, and strong, square features, betokening a steady soul; but steady as it was, his enemies had found means to shake it. His face was pale as death, and far more ghastly; the broad forehead was contracted in his agony, so that his eyebrows formed one grizzled line; his eyes were red and wild, and the foam hung white upon his quivering lip. His whole frame was agitated by a quick and continual tremor, which his pride strove to quell, even in those circumstances of overwhelming humiliation. But perhaps the bitterest pang of all was when his eyes met those of Robin; for he evidently knew him on the instant, as the youth stood witnessing the foul disgrace of a head grown gray in honor. They stared at each other in silence, and Robin's knees shook, and his hair bristled, with a mixture of pity and terror. Soon, however, a bewildering excitement began to seize upon his mind; the preceding adventures of the night, the unexpected appearance of the crowd, the torches, the confused din and the hush that followed, the spectre of his kinsman reviled by that great multitude, — all this, and, more than all, a perception of tremendous ridicule in the whole scene, affected him with a sort of mental inebriety. At that moment a voice of sluggish merriment saluted Robin's ears; he turned instinctively, and just behind the corner of the church stood the lantern-bearer, rubbing his eyes, and drowsily enjoying the lad's amazement. Then he heard a peal of laughter like the ringing of silvery bells; a woman twitched his arm, a saucy eye met his, and he saw the lady of the scarlet petticoat. A sharp, dry cachinnation appealed to his memory, and, standing on tiptoe in the crowd, with his white apron over his head, he beheld the courteous little innkeeper. And lastly, there sailed over the heads of the multitude a great, broad laugh, broken in the midst by two sepulchral hems; thus, "Haw, haw, haw — hem, hem, — haw, haw, haw, haw!"

The sound proceeded from the balcony of the opposite edifice, and thither Robin turned his eyes. In front of the Gothic window stood the old citizen, wrapped in a wide gown, his gray periwig exchanged for a nightcap, which was thrust back from his forehead, and his silk stockings hanging about his legs. He supported himself on his polished cane in a fit of convulsive merriment, which manifested itself on his solemn old features like a funny inscription on a tombstone. Then Robin seemed to hear the voices of the barbers, of the guests of the inn, and of all who had made sport of him that night. The contagion was spreading among the multitude when all at once it seized upon Robin, and he sent forth a shout of laughter that echoed through the street, — every man shook his sides, every man emptied his lungs, but Robin's shout was the loudest there. The cloud-spirits peeped from their silvery islands, as the congregated mirth went roaring up the sky! The Man in the Moon heard the far bellow. "Oho," quoth he, "the old earth is frolicsome to-night!"

When there was a momentary calm in that tempestuous sea of sound, the leader gave the sign, the procession resumed its march. On they went, like fiends that throng in mockery around some dead potentate, mighty no more, but majestic still in his agony. On they went, in counterfeited pomp, in senseless uproar, in frenzied merriment, trampling all on an old man's heart. On swept the tumult, and left a silent street behind.

• • •

"Well, Robin, are you dreaming?" inquired the gentleman, laying his hand on the youth's shoulder.

Robin started, and withdrew his arm from the stone post to which he had instinctively clung, as the living stream rolled by him. His cheek was somewhat pale, and his eye not quite as lively as in the earlier part of the evening.

"Will you be kind enough to show me the way to the ferry?" said he, after a moment's pause.

"You have, then, adopted a new subject of inquiry?" observed his companion, with a smile.

"Why, yes, sir," replied Robin, rather dryly. "Thanks to you, and to my other friends, I have at last met my kinsman, and he will scarce desire to see my face again. I begin to grow weary of a town life, sir. Will you show me the way to the ferry?"

"No, my good friend Robin, — not to-night, at least," said the gentleman. "Some few days hence, if you wish it, I will speed you on your journey. Or, if you prefer to remain with us, perhaps, as you are a shrewd youth, you may rise in the world without the help of your kinsman, Major Molineux."

ANNE HÉBERT

The Coral Frock

Translated by Gwendolyn Moore

There were ten girls working in Madame Grospou's shop: ten working-girls, some pretty, others less so, ten chatterboxes, each with her lipstick and her silk stockings, her short dress, each with a sad love story.

And there was little Emilie, whose slight and silent presence was not even noticed.

Emilie had arrived one evening at Madame Grospou's, just like that; all alone, just a child. No one knew where she came from; they hardly remembered her arrival; she had not even spoken, and they had thought her mute.

She had come to the shop, no bigger than a child. But her unlined face, then as now, was ageless; neither youth nor maturity could be discerned in her large eyes, expressionless, devoid of dreams. They were surprising and a little disquieting, those big eyes, as though they had never been used; and unconsciously one told oneself it was better that they had not, for if those enormous eyes were ever filled with the secret power of illumination, it would spread like a sea of fire. But such a thing did not seem likely to happen in this world. Emilie's eyes were too large because they were empty.

Madame Grospou had been immediately ravished by Emilie's skill as a knitter. She seemed never to have done anything else in her life.

And from the beginning Emilie had proven herself an extraordinary worker. She would knit feverishly, all day long, without a break. She made the day the servant of her work, and one would have thought that she was knitting it into her wool.

Each week was spent in this unceasing labour; and on Sunday, when she stopped working, she felt tired, filled with an endless desert, deprived of the only reason for living that she knew. She would wait impatiently for Monday and it never occurred to her to glance back and ask herself what had become of all those days she had knitted.

One afternoon, a strapping young man, back from the lumber-camps, came into the shop. Much fluttering and stirring of hearts among the working girls. He bought some socks, and gave the girls coloured pictures as presents.

Emilie deigned to look at hers, without stopping her work. The picture represented a shepherdess who was knitting, surrounded by her sheep. But horrors! The artist had profanely put only one needle in the hands of his shepherdess. How could he be so ridiculously ignorant of the art of knitting stockings?

No one could remember ever having heard Emilie laugh. However she found this so funny that she began to laugh quite naturally. And as she started to laugh, she began to see *him*, to be conscious of him, as though this laugh were the prelude to a mysterious rite to which she would be summoned.

Emilie never left her knitting; it was a part of her. But this evening, while walking home, casting on her stitches as usual, part of her was elsewhere, on a first and tremulous voyage.

Back in her room, Emilie retired into herself. The piece she was working on was difficult and very delicate. It was a coral frock that a very rich woman had just ordered. The frock had to be finished and delivered within a week.

The living wool slipped over the bone needles; and a dream that was even more alive slipped imperceptibly into the heart of the little worker.

Instead of working until she fell asleep under the burden of her task, this evening Emilie put her wool away sooner than usual.

She did not yet know what she was looking for, but some indispensable object was missing from her room; an object which had not been there before, and yet was missing. Nothing in the room had changed, but Emilie had a desire that day that she did not have the day before.

There was no mirror in the room, but in her imagination Emilie considered her face carefully. Perturbed, she questioned herself, and then another face consoled her, like the apparition of a saint: Gabriel, returning from the woods, his skin tanned, his eyes sparkling like the rivers newly released by the spring break-up.

Emilie kept curling the ends of her hair with her fingers, more compulsively now than ever since they no longer held the needles.

She did two fantastic things before going to bed, but did not seem to be astonished at herself. Over her grey dress, she pinned the coral sleeve she had just finished and, groping with her hands, she put up her hair in clean rags.

That night, she dreamed that her hair was a heap of pale shavings, which Gabriel was cutting with great shears and throwing into the river.

Then, under her frightened eyes, the young man went into the log drive, leaping from one curl to the other with the aid of a hook.

The following morning, her curls were round and silky to the touch. She covered them with a scarf to go to the shop.

Why should she knit on her way to work? That morning nothing seemed urgent. She felt completely occupied doing nothing.

And yet there was a small torment. She would have liked to borrow a mirror from one of the other girls; but she was afraid they would make fun of her.

But what was wrong with the wool? One could scarcely feel it, and yet it intimated strange things. Then from the cover of the wool that the girl was knitting the day came forth like a vein of gold. Into her mind, now free of any burden, came all the days she had ever knitted. She had never before paid attention to anything; but now the dike was broken and life asserted itself.

In her mind Emilie saw the big mirror in the home of Madame Elisabeth, where she had been for a fitting. She also saw the woods where she had played on Sundays as a child. How beautiful the woods had been. How fragrant the leaves. Emilie also remembered that Madame Elisabeth, who was so beautiful, had embraced her one day. It was foolish, but how much Emilie would have liked Madame Elisabeth to hug her again.

The girl laughed to herself amidst the clicking of her needles, and the sound of her laughter gave rise again to a vision of the hardy, sun-burned face. And in evoking those eyes, as sparkling as the rivers, Emilie discovered the mirror she had never owned.

That evening she returned to her garret with two complete sleeves and the front of the bodice. The coral wool glowed richly against her grey dress, and her hair, without the scarf, frothed like champagne.

Emilie leaned out of the window. From outside all that was visible of her was the haloed head and the radiant coral bodice.

That was how she could be seen from below, and that was how Gabriel saw her, for he was listening for her on the grass. But Emilie, high up in her window, was watching the crescent moon which had stopped, miraculously, above the head of the one for whom she waited.

And he sang to her, beneath the silver crescent, to the accompaniment of his accordion. Emilie could scarcely maintain her silence long enough to listen fully to the music. His voice was sweet as he sang. "Lui y'a longtemps que je t'aime," and the accordion continued long after he had finished, "Jamais je ne t'oublierai."

Every evening for a whole week, as the knitting of the dress progressed, the window displayed a little more of Emilie's figure to the young man in the moonlight.

As the image in the pink dress drew nearer Gabriel felt a more acute desire to see all of it, with the small feet at the bottom of the dress, passing through the window.

Then she had finished knitting. She had surpassed herself. The frock was a jewel, exactly her own size, as exquisite as an evening gown, and as simple as long hair.

She had been in such a hurry to finish that she had left ten rows off the length of the skirt.

The accordion music came to an end when Gabriel brought a ladder up to the window and took the trembling young girl in his arms. The whole coral dress was there, with the little girl in it, her delicate limbs showing beneath the shortened gown.

Without having to be taught, Emilie put her arms around Gabriel's neck; descending, he placed her gently on the ground, then took her in his arms again, as though unable to accept that she was still distinct from him as when they had been two separate islands, she at the window, he on the grass below.

He bore her across the fields, leaping over fences and streams, and took her into the forest. She closed her eyes in fear as he ran faster and faster, exalted by the perfume of her hair brushing his cheek.

Following an old road that was used by loggers in the winter, he stopped at last in a clearing, the last outpost of the lumbermen. All around them were red firs and charred trunks. The stumps sat about as though disposed for a council of war of Indian chiefs or fabulous animals.

He had borne her for a long way without tiring; it was the beating of his heart alone which took his breath away.

How light she was, and supple as a taper. It seemed to the young man that he had moulded forever the fragile body to the shape of the arms which had carried it. And the youthful heart of Emilie, held close to that of Gabriel, grew warm and melted like wax brought near a flame.

The young man spread out on the ground a bed of balsam branches, sweet with resin, and over them he laid his mackinaw with its red-and-black checks. Upon this couch he placed Emilie. Her eyes were astonished at nothing, marvelling at everything.

A moment in time may have a certain hue, an aroma, a definite feeling and a luminescence, but it has no contours and no boundaries; it is as unattached as mist.

The rays of the moon, all white between the trees, converged upon the clearing; the pure scent of the balsams permeated Gabriel's mackinaw.

He pressed her to him, and she held him tightly;

each of them without pretence, entirely absorbed in the living moment.

Their tenderness continued throughout the long night.

In the morning only the shadows were stirring. All else was in the same place, including the lovers.

Everything was still possible. The next night could be the same.

The same perfumes, the same hues mingled with the same feelings, and the same illumination, all could be invited to the feast. But Emilie had a vague presentiment that her happiness could no more resist the daylight than could the morning mists when, pierced by the sun, they disappear in evanescent shreds. Moments without shape, which one dreams of grasping.

Emilie shivered despite her woollen dress. Gabriel put on his mackinaw. He had a worried air, and seemed in a hurry to go back.

The young couple walked side by side, but he no longer carried Emilie in his arms, and her feet stumbled in the ruts.

His manner towards her now was distant. It seemed that all he kept of their night together in the forest were the fleeting, star-like marks embossed on his skin by the twigs of the fir branches.

To come back in the cold, damp dawn would have meant nothing if only, in separating, they had taken the time to think a little what this separation might mean, after the intimacy they had shared.

But there was no chance to listen to the presentiments of the heart; it was already time to return to Madame Grospou.

Formerly, Emilie was thought to have no expression. Now that she had given in to her own being, she had to create a new face for herself right away in order to appear again in public — an ordeal, after having been so true to one's self.

Emilie would have preferred to burrow somewhere, never to face her companions. She knew that she would never again pass unnoticed as before. Could they not see the new mouth (reshaped by other lips) and the eyes, which were at last inhabited, but guardedly, like pools whose depths one fears?

Emilie became upset as soon as she entered the shop, and the images in her mind became inconsistent and broken like the reflections in water when the wind blows.

Her companions cornered her, staring at her with avidity and questioning her.

And suddenly Marcelle was holding out a package, and saying:

"Here, this is for you. That boy from the lumber camp just left it here. He is going back to his village. He says if he hangs around any longer he will have no money left to buy his fiancée even a string of cranberries when he gets back."

Laughter fell around Emilie like a storm of hail, fine and hard.

"Let's see what's in the parcel!" demanded Marcelle.

Emilie did not defend herself. There was nothing left to defend — someone had taken it all away.

"Is it true that he was serenading you under your window, in the moonlight? Tell us, Emilie. All this time, we were thinking you were a little saint! You're a good one!"

Emilie did not reply. She had nothing to say, for someone had taken even her voice away.

"It's a mirror. Look, Emilie!"

Emilie shivered. A mirror. She had wanted one so much. But why should she look at herself now, when he no longer wanted to look at her?

Marcelle held out the mirror, and they all crowded in, pushing Emilie with them.

Emilie saw her face for the first time, and she saw that she was crying.

Madame Grospou was a practical soul and resolved to simplify the problem by putting Emilie back to the one thing that suited her — knitting.

"You will have to do this dress all over again. It is ten times too small. And in the future, don't let such a distraction enter again. Knit! You are on this earth to knit!"

Emilie began the coral dress again. One hope remained — perhaps the wool still held within its tight stitches some of the dreams which had accompanied her metamorphosis?

She unravelled the knitting nervously but the stitches yielded nothing. And Emilie realized that in freeing the wool, she was freeing herself.

She did not have the courage to continue this empty task ... nor to knit another dream.

She travelled the roadways, taking farm work. No work seemed too rough to her — laundering, gardening, cutting hay or labouring in the fields.

Her one desire was to exhaust her hands, her whole body, just to achieve an overwhelming weariness. Just to lose herself in the heaviness of the work, after having found herself so painfully for one week — the week of the coral frock.

But when one has once come to life, one does not finish with living so easily.

Although she sought to destroy herself, she could not destroy that first encounter with her soul, when she had found herself crying.

Labour could not undo the workings of the heart. Expectation remained alive within her, and a faith in miracles.

And then, one day, she found that her soul was very tranquil.

And she realized that she was praying.

Autumn 1939

ERNEST HEMINGWAY

The Snows of Kilimanjaro

Kilimanjaro is a snow covered mountain 19,710 feet high, and is said to be the highest mountain in Africa. Its western summit is called the Masai "Ngàje Ngài," the House of God. Close to the western summit there is the dried and frozen carcass of a leopard. No one has explained what the leopard was seeking at that altitude.

"The marvellous thing is that it's painless," he said. "That's how you know when it starts."

"Is it really?"

"Absolutely. I'm awfully sorry about the odor though. That must bother you."

"Don't! Please don't."

"Look at them," he said. "Now is it sight or is it scent that brings them like that?"

The cot the man lay on was in the wide shade of a mimosa tree and as he looked out past the shade onto the glare of the plain there were three of the big birds squatted obscenely, while in the sky a dozen more sailed, making quick-moving shadows as they passed.

"They've been there since the day the truck broke down," he said. "Today's the first time any have lit on the ground. I watched the way they sailed very carefully at first in case I ever wanted to use them in a story. That's funny now."

"I wish you wouldn't," she said.

"I'm only talking," he said. "It's much easier if I talk. But I don't want to bother you."

"You know it doesn't bother me," she said. "It's that I've gotten so very nervous not being able to do anything. I think we might make it as easy as we can until the plane comes."

"Or until the plane doesn't come."

"Please tell me what I can do. There must be something I can do."

"You can take the leg off and that might stop it, though I doubt it. Or you can shoot me. You're a good shot now. I taught you to shoot didn't I?"

"Please don't talk that way. Couldn't I read to you?"

"Read what?"

"Anything in the book bag that we haven't read."

"I can't listen to it," he said. "Talking is the easiest. We quarrel and that makes the time pass."

"I don't quarrel. I never want to quarrel. Let's not quarrel any more. No matter how nervous we get. Maybe they will be back with another truck today. Maybe the plane will come."

"I don't want to move," the man said. "There is no sense in moving now except to make it easier for you."

"That's cowardly."

"Can't you let a man die as comfortably as he can without calling him names? What's the use of slanging me?"

"You're not going to die."

"Don't be silly. I'm dying now. Ask those bastards." He looked over to where the huge, filthy birds sat, their naked heads sunk in the hunched feathers. A fourth planed down, to run quick-legged and then waddle slowly toward the others.

"They are around every camp. You never notice them. You can't die if you don't give up."

"Where did you read that? You're such a bloody fool."

"You might think about some one else."

"For Christ's sake," he said, "That's been my trade."

He lay then and was quiet for a while and looked across the heat shimmer of the plain to the edge of the bush. There were a few Tommies that showed minute and white against the yellow and, far off, he saw a herd of zebra, white against the green of the bush. This was a pleasant camp under big trees against a hill, with good water, and close by, a nearly dry water hole where sand grouse flighted in the mornings.

"Wouldn't you like me to read?" she asked. She was sitting on a canvas chair beside his cot. "There's a breeze coming up."

"No thanks."

"Maybe the truck will come."

"I don't give a damn about the truck."

"I do."

"You give a damn about so many things that I don't."

"Not so many, Harry."

"What about a drink?"

"It's supposed to be bad for you. It said in Black's to avoid all alcohol. You shouldn't drink."

"Molo!" he shouted.

"Yes Bwana."

"Bring whiskey-soda."

"Yes Bwana."

"You shouldn't," she said. "That's what I mean by giving up. It says it's bad for you. I know it's bad for you."

"No," he said. "It's good for me."

So now it was all over, he thought. So now he would never have a chance to finish it. So this was the way it ended in a bickering over a drink. Since the gangrene started in his right leg he had no pain and with the pain the horror had gone and all he felt now was a great tiredness and anger that this was the end of it. For this, that now was coming, he had very little curiosity. For years it had obsessed him; but now it meant nothing in itself. It was strange how easy being tired enough made it.

Now he would never write the things that he had saved to write until he knew enough to write them well. Well, he would not have to fail at trying to write them either. Maybe you could never write them, and that was why you put them off and delayed the starting. Well he would never know, now.

"I wish we'd never come," the woman said. She was looking at him holding the glass and biting her lip. "You never would have gotten anything like this in Paris. You always said you loved Paris. We could have stayed in Paris or gone anywhere. I'd have gone anywhere. I said I'd go anywhere you wanted. If you wanted to shoot we could have gone shooting in Hungary and been comfortable."

"Your bloody money," he said.

"That's not fair," she said. "It was always yours as much as mine. I left everything and I went wherever you wanted to go and I've done what you wanted to do. But I wish we'd never come here."

"You said you loved it."

"I did when you were all right. But now I hate it. I don't see why that had to happen to your leg. What have we done to have that happen to us?"

"I suppose what I did was to forget to put iodine on it when I first scratched it. Then I didn't pay any attention to it because I never infect. Then, later, when it got bad, it was probably using that weak carbolic solution when the other antiseptics ran out that paralyzed the minute blood vessels and started the gangrene." He looked at her, "What else?"

"I don't mean that."

"If we would have hired a good mechanic instead of a half baked kikuyu driver, he would have checked the oil and never burned out that bearing in the truck."

"I don't mean that."

"If you hadn't left your own people, your goddamned Old Westbury, Saratoga, Palm Beach people to take me on ——"

"Why, I loved you. That's not fair. I love you now. I'll always love you. Don't you love me?"

"No," said the man. "I don't think so. I never have."

"Harry, what are you saying? You're out of your head."

"No. I haven't any head to go out of."

"Don't drink that," she said. "Darling, please don't drink that. We have to do everything we can."

"You do it," he said. "I'm tired."

Now in his mind he saw a railway station at Karagatch and he was standing with his pack and that was the headlight of the Simplon-Orient cutting the dark now and he was leaving Thrace then after the retreat. That was one of the things he had saved to write, with, in the morning at breakfast, looking out the window and seeing snow on the mountains in Bulgaria and Nansen's Secretary asking the old man if it were snow and the old man looking at it and saying, No, that's not snow. It's too early for snow. And the Secretary repeating to the other girls, No, you see. It's not snow and them all saying, It's not snow we were mistaken. But it was the snow all right and he sent them on into it when he evolved exchange of populations. And it was snow they tramped along in until they died that winter.

It was snow too that fell all Christmas week that year up in the Gauertal, that year they lived in the woodcutter's house with the big square porcelain stove that filled half the room, and they slept on mattresses filled with beech leaves, the time the deserter came with his feet bloody in the snow. He said the police were right behind him and they gave him woolen socks and held the gendarmes talking until the tracks had drifted over.

In Schrunz, on Christmas day, the snow was so bright it hurt your eyes when you looked out from the weinstube and saw every one coming home from church. That was where they walked up the sleigh-smoothed urine-yellowed road along the river with the steep pine hills, skis heavy on the shoulder, and where they ran that great run down the glacier above the Madlener-haus, the snow as smooth to see as cake frosting and as light as powder and he remembered the noiseless rush the speed made as you dropped down like a bird.

They were snow-bound a week in the Madlener-haus that time in the blizzard playing cards in the smoke by the lantern light and the stakes were higher all the time as Herr Lent lost more. Finally he lost it all. Everything, the skischule money and all the season's profit and then his capital. He could see him with his long nose, picking up the cards and then opening, "Sans Voir." There was always gambling then. When there was no snow you gambled and when there was too much you gambled. He thought of all the time in his life he had spent gambling.

But he had never written a line of that, nor of that cold, bright Christmas day with the mountains showing across the plain that Barker had flown across the lines to bomb the Austrian officers' leave train, machine-gunning them as they scattered and ran. He remembered Barker after-

wards coming into the mess and starting to tell about it. And how quiet it got and then somebody saying, "You bloody murderous bastard."

Those were the same Austrians they killed then that he skied with later. No not the same. Hans, that he skied with all that year, had been in the Kaiser-Jägers and when they went hunting hares together up the little valley above the saw-mill they had talked of the fighting on Pasubio and of the attack on Pertica and Asalone and he had never written a word of that. Nor of Monte Corno, nor the Siete Commum, nor of Arsiedo.

How many winters had he lived in the Voralberg and the Arlberg? It was four and then he remembered the man who had the fox to sell when they had walked into Bludenz, that time to buy presents, and the cherry-pit taste of good kirsch, the fast-slipping rush of running powder-snow on crust, singing "Hi! Ho! said Rolly!" as you ran down the last stretch to the steep drop, taking it straight, then running the orchard in three turns and out across the ditch and onto the icy road behind the inn. Knocking your bindings loose, kicking the skis free and leaning them up against the wooden wall of the inn, the lamplight coming from the window, where inside, in the smoky, new-wine smelling warmth, they were playing the accordion.

"Where did we stay in Paris?" he asked the woman who was sitting by him in a canvas chair now, in Africa.

"At the Crillon. You know that."

"Why do I know that?"

"That's where we always stayed."

"No. Not always."

"There and at the Pavillion Henri-Quatre in St. Germain. You said you loved it there."

"Love is a dunghill," said Harry. "And I'm the cock that gets on it to crow."

"If you have to go away," she said, "is it absolutely necessary to kill off everything you leave behind? I mean do you have to take away everything? Do you have to kill your horse, and your wife and burn your saddle and your armour?"

"Yes," he said. "Your damned money was my armour. My Swift and my Armour."

"Don't."

"All right. I'll stop that. I don't want to hurt you."

"It's a little bit late now."

"All right then. I'll go on hurting you. It's more amusing. The only thing I ever really liked to do with you I can't do now."

"No, that's not true. You liked to do many things and everything you wanted to do I did."

"Oh, for Christ sake top bragging, will you?"

He looked at her and saw her crying.

"Listen," he said. "Do you think that it is fun to do this? I don't know why I'm doing it. It's trying to kill to keep yourself alive, I imagine. I was all right when we started talking. I didn't mean to start this, and now I'm crazy as a coot and being as cruel to you as I can be. Don't pay any attention, darling, to what I say. I love you, really. You know I love you. I've never loved any one else the way I love you."

He slipped into the familiar lie he made his bread and butter by.

"You're sweet to me."

"You bitch," he said. "You rich bitch. That's poetry. I'm full of poetry now. Rot and poetry. Rotten poetry."

"Stop it. Harry, why do you have to turn into a devil now?"

"I don't like to leave anything," the man said." "I don't like to leave things behind."

• • •

It was evening now and he had been asleep. The sun was gone behind the hill and there was a shadow all across the plain and the small animals were feeding close to camp; quick dropping heads and switching tails, he watched them keeping well out away from the bush now. The birds no longer waited on the ground. They were all perched heavily in a tree. There were many more of them. His personal boy was sitting by the bed.

"Memsahib's gone to shoot," the boy said. "Does Bwana want?"

"Nothing."

She had gone to kill a piece of meat and, knowing how he liked to watch the game, she had gone well away so she would not disturb this little pocket of the plain that he could see. She was always thoughtful, he thought. On anything she knew about, or had read, or that she had ever heard.

It was not her fault that when he went to her he was already over. How could a woman know that you meant nothing that you said; that you spoke only from habit and to be comfortable? After he no longer meant what he said, his lies were more successful with women than when he had told them the truth.

It was not so much that he lied as that there was no truth to tell. He had had his life and it was over and then he went on living it again with different people and more money, with the best of the same places, and some new ones.

You kept from thinking and it was all marvellous. You were equipped with good insides so that you did not go to pieces that way, the way most of them had, and you made an attitude that you cared nothing for the work you used to do, now that you could no longer do it. But, in yourself, you said that you would write about these people; about the very rich; that you were really not of them but a spy in their country; that you would leave it and write of it and for once it would be written by some one who knew what he was writing of. But he would never do it, because each day of not writing, of comfort, of being that which he despised, dulled his ability and softened his will to work so that, finally, he did no work at all. The people he knew now were all much more comfortable when he did not work. Africa was where he had been happiest in the good time of his life, so he had come out here to start again. They had made this safari with the minimum of comfort. There was no hardship; but there was no luxury and he had thought that he could get back into training that way. That in some way he could work the fat off his soul the way a fighter went into the mountains to work and train in order to burn it out of his body.

She had liked it. She said she loved it. She loved anything that was exciting, that involved a change of scene, where there were new people and where things were pleasant. And he had felt the illusion of returning strength of will to work. Now if this was how it ended, and he knew it was, he must not turn like some snake biting itself because its back was broken. It wasn't this woman's fault. If it had not been she it would have been another. If he lived by a lie he should try to die by it. He heard a shot beyond the hill.

She shot very well this good, this rich bitch, this kindly caretaker and destroyer of his talent. Nonsense. He had destroyed his talent himself. Why should he blame this woman because she kept him well? He had destroyed his talent by not using it, by betrayals of himself and what he believed in, by drinking so much that he blunted the edge of his perceptions, by laziness, by sloth, and by snobbery, by pride and by prejudice, by hook and by crook. What was this? A catalogue of old books? What was his talent anyway? It was a talent all right but instead of using it, he had traded on it. It was never what he had done, but always what he could do. And he had chosen to make his living with something else instead of a pen or a pencil. It was strange, too, wasn't it, that when he fell in love with another woman, that woman should always have more money than the last one? But when he no longer was in love, when he was only lying, as to this woman, now, who had the most money of all, who had all the money there was, who had had a husband and children, who had taken lovers and been dissatisfied with them, and who loved him dearly as a writer, as a man, as a companion and as a proud possession; it was strange that when he did not love her at all and was lying, that he should be able to give her more for her money than when he had really loved.

We must all be cut out for what we do, he thought. However you make your living is where your talent lies. He had sold vitality, in one form or another, all his life and when your affections are not too involved you give much better value for the money. He had found that out but he would never write that, now, either. No, he would not write that, although it was well worth writing.

Now she came in sight, walking across the open toward the camp. She was wearing jodphurs and carrying her rifle. The two boys had a Tommie slung and they were coming along behind her. She was still a good-looking woman, he thought, and she had a pleasant body. She had a great talent and appreciation for the bed, she was not pretty, but he liked her face, she read enormously, liked to ride and shoot and, certainly, she drank too much. Her husband had died when she was still a comparatively young woman and for a while she had devoted herself to her two just-grown children, who did not need her and were embarrassed at having her about, to her stable of horses, to books, and to bottles. She liked to read in the evening before dinner and she drank Scotch and soda while she read. By dinner she was fairly drunk and after a bottle of wine at dinner she was usually drunk enough to sleep.

That was before the lovers. After she had the lovers she did not drink so much because she did not have to be drunk to sleep. But the lovers bored her. She had been married to a man who had never bored her and these people bored her very much.

Then one of her two children was killed in a plane crash and after that was over she did not want the lovers, and drink being no anaesthetic she had to make another life. Suddenly, she had been acutely frightened of being alone. But she wanted someone that she respected with her.

It had begun very simply. She liked what he wrote and she had always envied the life he led. She thought he did exactly what he wanted to. The steps by which she had acquired him and the way in which she had finally fallen in love with him were all part of a regular progression in which she had built herself a new life and he had traded away what remained of his old life.

He had traded it for security, for comfort too, there was no denying that, and for what else? He did not know. She would have bought him anything he wanted. He knew that. She was a damned nice woman too. He would as soon be in bed with her as any one; rather with her, because she was richer, because she was very pleasant and appreciative and because she never made scenes. And now this life that she had built again was coming to a term because he had not used iodine two weeks ago when a thorn had scratched his knee as they moved forward trying to photograph a herd of waterbuck standing, their heads up, peering while their nostrils searched the air, their ears spread wide to hear the first noise that would send them rushing into the bush. They had bolted, too, before he got the picture.

Here she came now.

He turned his head on the cot to look toward her. "Hello," he said.

"I shot a Tommy ram," she told him. "He'll

make you good broth and I'll have them mash some potatoes with the Klim. How do you feel?"

"Much better."

"Isn't that lovely? You know I thought perhaps you would. You were sleeping when I left."

"I had a good sleep. Did you walk far?"

"No. Just around behind the hill. I made quite a good shot on the Tommy."

"You shoot marvellously, you know."

"I love it. I've loved Africa. Really. If *you're* all right it's the most fun that I've ever had. You don't know the fun it's been to shoot with you. I've loved the country."

"I love it too."

"Darling, you don't know how marvellous it is to see you feeling better. I couldn't stand it when you felt that way. You won't talk to me like that again, will you? Promise me?"

"No," he said. "I don't remember what I said."

"You don't have to destroy me. Do you? I'm only a middle-aged woman who loves you and wants to do what you want to do. I've been destroyed two or three times already. You wouldn't want to destroy me again, would you?"

"I'd like to destroy you a few times in bed," he said.

"Yes. That's the good destruction. That's the way we're made to be destroyed. The plane will be here tomorrow."

"How do you know?"

"I'm sure. It's bound to come. The boys have the wood all ready and the grass to make the smudge. I went down and looked at it again today. There's plenty of room to land and we have the smudges ready at both ends."

"What makes you think it will come tomorrow?"

"I'm sure it will. It's overdue now. Then, in town, they will fix up your leg and then we will have some good destruction. Not that dreadful talking kind."

"Should we have a drink? The sun is down."

"Do you think you should?"

"I'm having one."

"We'll have one together. *Molo, letti dui whiskey-soda!"* she called.

"You'd better put on your mosquito boots," he told her.

"I'll wait till I bathe . . ."

While it grew dark they drank and just before it was dark and there was no longer enough light to shoot, a hyena crossed the open on his way around the hill.

"That bastard crosses there every night," the man said. "Every night for two weeks."

"He's the one makes the noise at night. I don't mind it. They're a filthy animal though."

Drinking together, with no pain now except the discomfort of lying in the one position, the boys lighting a fire, its shadow jumping on the tents, he could feel the return of acquiescence in this life of pleasant surrender. She *was* very good to him. He had been cruel and unjust in the afternoon. She was a fine woman, marvellous really. And just then it occurred to him that he was going to die.

It came with a rush; not as a rush of water nor of wind; but of a sudden evil-smelling emptiness and the odd thing was that the hyena slipped lightly along the edge of it.

"What is it Harry?" she asked him.

"Nothing," he said. "You had better move over to the other side. To windward."

"Did Molo change the dressing?"

"Yes. I'm just using the boric now."

"How do you feel?"

"A little wobbly."

"I'm going in to bathe," she said. "I'll be right out. I'll eat with you and then we'll put the cot in."

So, he said to himself, we did well to stop the quarrelling. He had never quarrelled much with this woman, while with the women that he loved he had quarrelled so much they had finally, always, with the corrosion of the quarrelling, killed what they had together. He had loved too much, demanded too much, and he wore it all out.

He thought about being alone in Constantinople that time, having quarrelled in Paris before he had gone out. He had whored the whole time and then, when that was over, and he had failed to kill his loneliness, but only made it worse, he had written her, the first one, the one who left him, a letter telling her how he had never been able to kill it . . . How when he thought he saw her outside the Regence *one time it made him go all faint and sick inside, and that he would follow a woman who looked like her in some way, along the Boulevard, afraid to see it was not she, afraid to lose the feeling it gave him. How every one he had slept with had only made him miss her more. How what she had done could never matter since he knew he could not cure himself of loving her. He wrote this letter at the Club, cold sober, and mailed it to New York asking her to write him at the office in Paris. That seemed safe. And that night missing her so much it made him feel hollow sick inside, he wandered up past Taxim's, picked a girl up and took her out to supper. He had gone to a place to dance with her afterward, she danced badly, and left her for a hot Armenian slut, that swung her belly against him so it almost scalded. He took her away from a British gunner subaltern after a row. The gunner asked him outside and they fought in the street on the cobbles in the dark. He'd hit him twice, hard, on the side of the jaw and when he didn't go down he knew he was in for a fight. The gunner hit him in the body, then beside his eye. He swung with his left again and landed and the gunner fell on him and grabbed his coat and tore the sleeve off and he clubbed him twice behind the ear and then smashed him with his right as he pushed him away. When the gunner went down his head hit first and he ran with the girl because they heard the M.P.'s coming. They got into a taxi and drove out to Rimmily Hissa along the Bosphorus, and around, and back in the cool night and went to bed and she felt as over-ripe as she looked but smooth, rose-petal, syrupy, smooth-bellied, big-breasted and needed no pillow under her buttocks, and he left her before she was awake looking blousy enough in the first daylight and turned up at the Pera Palace with a black eye, carrying his coat because one sleeve was missing.*

That same night he left for Anatolia and he remembered, later on that trip, riding all day through fields of the poppies that they raised for opium and how strange it made you feel, finally, and all the distances seemed wrong, to where they had made the attack with the newly arrived Constantine officers, that did not know a god-damned thing, and the artillery had fired into the troops and the British observer had cried like a child.

That was the day he'd first seen dead men wearing white ballet skirts and upturned shoes with pompons on them. The Turks had come steadily and lumpily and he had seen the skirted men running and the officers shooting into them and running then themselves and he and the British observer had run too until his lungs ached and his mouth was full of the taste of pennies and they stopped behind some rocks and there were the Turks coming as lumpily as ever. Later he had seen the things that he could never think of and later still he had seen much worse. So when he got back to Paris that time he could not talk about it or stand to have it mentioned. And there in the café as he passed was that American poet with a pile of saucers in front of him and a stupid look on his potato face talking about the Dada movement with a Roumanian who said his name was Tristan Tzara, who always wore a monocle and had a headache, and, back at the apartment with his wife that now he loved again, the quarrel all over, the madness all over, glad to be home, the office sent his mail up to the flat. So then the letter in answer to the one he'd written came in on a platter one morning and when he saw the handwriting he went cold all over and tried to slip the letter underneath another. But his wife said, "Who is that letter from, dear?" and that was the end of the beginning of that.

He remembered the good times with them all, and the quarrels. They always picked the finest places to have the quarrels. And why had they always quarrelled when he was feeling best? He had never written any of that because, at first, he never wanted to hurt any one and then it seemed as though there was enough to write without it. But he had always thought that he would write it finally. There was so much to write. He had seen the world change; not just the events; although he had seen many of them and had watched the people, but he had seen the subtler change and he could remember how the people were at different times. He had been in it and he had watched it and it was his duty to write of it; but now he never would.

"How do you feel?" she said. She had come out from the tent now after her bath.

"All right."

"Could you eat now?" He saw Molo behind her with the folding table and the other boy with the dishes.

"I want to write," he said.

"You ought to take some broth to keep your strength up."

"I'm going to die tonight," he said. "I don't need my strength up."

"Don't be melodramatic, Harry, please," she said.

"Why don't you use your nose? I'm rotted half way up my thigh now. What the hell should I fool with broth for? Molo bring whiskey-soda."

"Please take the broth," she said gently.

"All right."

The broth was too hot. He had to hold it in the cup until it cooled enough to take it and then he just got it down without gagging.

"You're a fine woman," he said. "Don't pay any attention to me."

She looked at him with her well-known, well-loved face from *Spur* and *Town and Country,* only a little the worse for drink, only a little the worse for bed, but *Town and Country* never showed those good breasts and those useful thighs and those lightly small-of-back caressing hands, and as he looked and saw her well known pleasant smile, he felt death come again. This time there was no rush. It was a puff, as of a wind that makes a candle flicker and the flame go tall.

"They can bring my net out later and hang it from the tree and build the fire up. I'm not going in the tent tonight. It's not worth moving. It's a clear night. There won't be any rain."

So this was how you died, in whispers that you did not hear. Well, there would be no more quarrelling. He could promise that. The one experience that he had never had was not going to spoil now. He probably would. You spoiled everything. But perhaps he wouldn't.

"You can't take dictation, can you?"

"I never learned," she told him.

"That's all right."

There wasn't time, of course, although it seemed as though it telescoped so that you might put it all into one paragraph if you could get it right.

There was a log house, chinked white with mortar, on a hill above the lake. There was a bell on a pole by the door to call the people in to meals. Behind the house were fields and behind the fields was the timber. A line of lombardy poplars ran from the house to the dock. Other poplars ran along the point. A road went up to the hills along the edge of the timber and along that road he picked blackberries. Then that log house was burned down and all the guns that had been on deer foot racks above the open fire place were burned and afterwards their barrels, with the lead melted in the magazines, and the stocks burned away, lay out on the heap of ashes that were used to make lye for the big iron soap kettles, and you asked Grandfather if you could have them to play with, and he said, no. You see they were his guns still and he never bought any others. Nor did he hunt any more. The house was rebuilt in the same place out of lumber now and painted white and from its porch you saw the poplars and the lake beyond; but there were never any more guns. The barrels of the guns that had hung on the deer feet on the wall of the log house lay out there on the heap of ashes and no one ever touched them.

In the Black Forest, after the war, we rented a trout stream and there were two ways to walk to it. One was down the valley from Triberg and around the valley road in the shade of the trees that bordered the white road, and then up a side road that went up through the hills past many small farms, with the big Schwarzwald houses, until that road crossed the stream. That was where our fishing began.

The other way was to climb steeply up to the edge of the woods and then go across the top of the hills through the pine woods, and then out to the edge of a meadow and down across this meadow to the bridge. There were birches along the stream and it was not big, but narrow, clear and fast, with pools where it had cut under the roots of the birches. At the Hotel in Triberg the proprietor had a fine season. It was very pleasant and we were all great friends. The next year came the inflation and the money he had made the year before was not enough to buy supplies to open the hotel and he hanged himself.

You could dictate that, but you could not dictate the Place Contrescarpe where the flower sellers dyed their flowers in the street and the dye ran out over the paving where the autobus started and the old men and the women, always drunk on wine and bad marc; and the children with their noses running in the cold; the smell of dirty sweat and poverty and drunkenness at the Café des Amateurs and the whores at the Bal Musette they lived above. The Concierge who entertained the trooper of the Garde Republicaine in her loge, his horse-hair-plumed helmet on a chair. The locataire across the hall whose husband was a bicycle racer and her joy that morning at the Cremerie when she had opened L'Auto and seen where he placed third in Paris-Tours, his first big race. She had blushed and laughed and then gone upstairs crying with the yellow sporting paper in her hand. The husband of the woman who ran the Bal Musette drove a taxi and when he, Harry, had to take an early plane the husband knocked upon the door to wake him and they each drank a glass of white wine at the zinc of the bar before they started. He knew his neighbors in that quarter then because they all were poor.

Around that Place *there were two kinds; the drunkards and the sportifs. The drunkards killed their poverty that way; the sportifs took it out in exercise. They were the descendants of the Communards and it was no struggle for them to know their politics. They knew who had shot their fathers, their relatives, their brothers, and their friends when the Versailles troops came in and took the town after the Commune and executed any one they could catch with calloused hands, or who wore a cap, or carried any other sign he was a working man. And in that poverty, and in that quarter across the street from a Boucherie Chevaline and a wine co-operative he had written the start of all he was to do. There never was another part of Paris that he loved like that, the sprawling trees, the old white plastered houses painted brown below, the long green of the autobus in that round square, the purple flower dye upon the paving, the sudden drop down the hill of the rue Cardinal Lemoine to the River, and the other way the narrow crowded world of the rue Mouffetard. The street that ran up toward the Pantheon and the other that he always took with the bicycle, the only asphalted street in all that quarter, smooth under the tires, with the high narrow houses and the cheap tall hotel where Paul Verlaine had died. There were only two rooms in the apartments where they lived and he had a room on the top floor of that hotel that cost him sixty francs a month where he did his writing, and from it he could see the roofs and chimney pots and all the hills of Paris.*

From the apartment you could only see the wood and coal man's place. He sold wine too, bad wine. The golden horse's head outside the Boucherie Chevaline where the carcasses hung yellow gold and red in the open window, and the green painted co-operative where they bought their wine; good wine and cheap. The rest was plaster walls and the windows of the neighbors. The neighbors who, at night, when some one lay drunk in the street, moaning and groaning in that typical French ivresse *that you were propaganded to believe did not exist, would open their windows and then the murmur of talk.*

"Where is the policeman? When you don't want him the bugger is always there. He's sleeping with some concierge. Get the Agent.*" Till some one threw a bucket of water from a window and the moaning stopped. "What's that? Water. Ah, that's intelligent." And the windows shutting. Marie, his femme de menage, protesting against the eight-hour day saying, "If a husband works until six he gets only a little drunk on the way home and does*

not waste too much. If he works only until five he is drunk every night and one has no money. It is the wife of the working man who suffers from this shortening of hours."

"Wouldn't you like some more broth?" the woman asked him now.

"No, thank you very much. It is awfully good."

"Try just a little."

"I would like a whiskey-soda."

"It's not good for you."

"No. It's bad for me. Cole Porter wrote the words and the music. This knowledge that you're going mad for me."

"You know I like you to drink."

"Oh yes. Only it's bad for me."

When she goes, he thought. I'll have all I want. Not all I want but all there is. Ayee he was tired. Too tired. He was going to sleep a little while. He lay still and death was not there. It must have gone around another street. It went in pairs, on bicycles, and moved absolutely silently on the pavements.

No, he had never written about Paris. Not the Paris that he cared about. But what about the rest that he had never written?

What about the ranch and the silvered gray of the sage brush, the quick, clear water in the irrigation ditches, and the heavy green of the alfalfa. The trail went up into the hills and the cattle in the summer were shy as deer. The bawling and the steady noise and slow moving mass raising a dust as you brought them down in the fall. And behind the mountains, the clear sharpness of the peak in the evening light and, riding down along the trail in the moonlight, bright across the valley. Now he remembered coming down through the timber in the dark holding the horse's tail when you could not see and all the stories that he meant to write.

About the half-wit chore boy who was left at the ranch that time and told not to let any one get any hay, and that old bastard from the Forks who had beaten the boy when he had worked for him stopping to get some feed. The boy refusing and the old man saying he would beat him again. The boy got the rifle from the kitchen and shot him when he tried to come into the barn and when they came back to the ranch he'd been dead a week, frozen in the corral, and the dogs had eaten part of him. But what was left you packed on a sled wrapped in a blanket and roped on and you got the boy to help you haul it, and the two of you took it out over the road on skis, and sixty miles down to town to turn the boy over. He having no idea that he would be arrested. Thinking he had done his duty and that you were his friend and he would be rewarded. He'd helped to haul the old man in so everybody could know how bad the old man had been and how he'd tried to steal some feed that didn't belong to him, and when the sheriff put the handcuffs on the boy he couldn't believe it. Then he'd started to cry. That was one story he had saved to write. He knew at least twenty good stories from out there and he had never written one. Why?

"You tell them why," he said.

"Why what, dear?"

"Why nothing."

She didn't drink so much, now, since she had him. But if he lived he would never write about her, he knew that now. Nor about any of them. The rich were dull and they drank too much, or they played too much backgammon. They were dull and they were repetitious. He remembered poor Julian and his romantic awe of them and how he had started a story once that began, "The very rich are different from you and me." And how some one had said to Julian, Yes, they have more money. But that was not humorous to Julian. He thought they were a special glamourous race and when he found they weren't it wrecked him just as much as any other thing that wrecked him.

He had been contemptuous of those who wrecked. You did not have to like it because you understood it. He could beat anything, he thought, because nothing could hurt him if he did not care.

All right. Now he would not care for death. One thing he had always dreaded was the pain. He could stand pain as well as any man, until it went on too long, and wore him out, but here he had something that had hurt frightfully and just when he had felt it breaking him, the pain had stopped.

He remembered long ago when Williamson, the bombing officer, had been hit by a stick bomb some one in a German patrol had thrown as he was coming in through the wire that night and, screaming, had begged every one to kill him. He was a fat man, very brave, and a good officer, although addicted to fantastic shows. But that night he was caught in the wire, with a flare lighting him up and his bowels spilled out into the wire, so when they brought him in, alive, they had to cut him loose. Shoot me, Harry. For Christ sake shoot me. They had had an argument one time about our Lord never sending you anything you could not bear and some one's theory had been that meant that at a certain time the pain passed you out automatically. But he had always remembered Williamson, that night. Nothing passed out Williamson until he gave him all his morphine tablets that he had always saved to use himself and then they did not work right away.

Still this now, that he had, was very easy; and if it was no worse as it went on there was nothing to worry about. Except that he would rather be in better company.

He thought a little about the company that he would like to have.

No, he thought, when everything you do, you do

too long, and do too late, you can't expect to find the people still there. The people all are gone. The party's over and you are with your hostess now.

I'm getting as bored with dying as with everything else, he thought.

"It's a bore," he said out loud.

"What is, my dear?"

"Anything you do too bloody long."

He looked at her face between him and the fire. She was leaning back in the chair and the firelight shone on her pleasantly lined face and he could see that she was sleepy. He heard the hyena make a noise just outside the range of the fire.

"I've been writing," he said. "But I got tired."

"Do you think you will be able to sleep?"

"Pretty sure. Why don't you turn in?"

"I like to sit here with you."

"Do you feel anything strange?" he asked her.

"No. Just a little sleepy."

"I do," he said.

He had just felt death come by again.

"You know the only thing I've never lost is curiosity," he said to her.

"You've never lost anything. You're the most complete man I've ever known."

"Christ," he said. "How little a woman knows. What is that? Your intuition?"

Because, just then, death had come and rested its head on the foot of the cot and he could smell its breath.

"Never believe any of that about a scythe and a skull," he told her. "It can be two bicycle policemen as easily, or be a bird. Or it can have a wide snout like a hyena."

It had moved up on him now, but it had no shape any more. It simply occupied space.

"Tell it to go away."

It did not go away but moved a little closer.

"You've got a hell of a breath," he told it. "You stinking bastard."

It moved up closer to him still and now he could not speak to it, and when it saw he could not speak it came a little closer, and now he tried to send it away without speaking, but it moved in on him so its weight was all upon his chest, and while it crouched there and he could not move, or speak, he heard the woman say, "Bwana is asleep now. Take the cot up very gently and carry it into the tent."

He could not speak to tell her to make it go away and it crouched now, heavier, so he could not breathe. And then, while they lifted the cot, suddenly it was all right and the weight went from his chest.

It was morning and had been morning for some time and he heard the plane. It showed very tiny and then made a wide circle and the boys ran out and lit the fires, using kerosene, and piled on grass so there were two big smudges at each end of the level place and the morning breeze blew them toward the camp and the plane circled twice more, low this time, and then glided down and levelled off and landed smoothly and, coming walking toward him, was old Compton in slacks, a tweed jacket and a brown felt hat.

"What's the matter, old cock?" Compton said.

"Bad leg," he told him. "Will you have some breakfast?"

"Thanks. I'll just have some tea. It's the Puss Moth you know. I won't be able to take the Memsahib. There's only room for one. Your lorry is on the way."

Helen had taken Compton aside and was speaking to him. Compton came back more cheery than ever.

"We'll get you right in," he said. "I'll be back for the Mem. Now I'm afraid I'll have to stop at Arusha to refuel. We'd better get going."

"What about the tea?"

"I don't really care about it you know."

The boys had picked up the cot and carried it around the green tents and down along the rock and out onto the plain and along past the smudges that were burning brightly now, the grass all consumed, and the wind fanning the fire, to the little plane. It was difficult getting him in, but once in he lay back in the leather seat, and the leg was stuck straight out to one side of the seat where Compton sat. Compton started the motor and got in. He waved to Helen and to the boys and, as the clatter moved into the old familiar roar, they swung around with Compie watching for wart-hog holes and roared, bumping, along the stretch between the fires and with the last bump rose and he saw them all standing below, waving, and the camp beside the hill, flattening now, and the plain spreading, clumps of trees, and the bush flattening, while the game trails ran now smoothly to the dry waterholes, and there was a new water that he had never known of. The zebra, small rounded backs now, and the wildebeeste, big-headed dots seeming to climb as they moved in long fingers across the plain, now scattering as the shadow came toward them, they were tiny now, and the movement had no gallop, and the plain as far as you could see, gray-yellow now and ahead old Compie's tweed back and the brown felt hat. Then they were over the first hills and the wildebeeste were trailing up them, and then they were over mountains with sudden depths of green-rising forest and the solid bamboo slopes, and then the heavy forest again, sculptured into peaks and hollows until they crossed, and hills sloped down and then another plain, hot now, and purple brown, bumpy with heat and Compie looking back to see how he was riding. Then there were other mountains dark ahead.

And then instead of going on to Arusha they turned left, he evidently figured that they had the gas, and looking down he saw a pink sifting cloud, moving over the ground, and in the air, like the first snow in a blizzard, that comes from nowhere, and he knew the locusts were coming up from the South. Then they began to climb and they were going to the East it seemed, and then it darkened and they were in a storm, the rain so thick it seemed like flying through a waterfall, and then they were out and Compie turned his head and grinned and pointed and there, ahead, all he could see, as wide as all the world, great, high, and unbelievably white in the sun, was the square top of Kilimanjaro. And then he knew that there was where he was going.

Just then the hyena stopped whimpering in the night and started to make a strange, human, almost crying sound. The woman heard it and stirred uneasily. She did not wake. In her dream she was at the house on Long Island and it was the night before her daughter's début. Somehow her father was there and he had been very rude. Then the noise the hyena made was so loud she woke and for a moment she did not know where she was and she was very afraid. Then she took the flashlight and shone it on the other cot that they had carried in after Harry had gone to sleep. She could see his bulk under the mosquito bar but somehow he had gotten his leg out and it hung down alongside the cot. The dressings had all come down and she could not look at it.

"Molo," she called, "Molo! Molo!"

Then she said, "Harry, Harry!" Then her voice rising, "Harry! Please, Oh Harry!"

There was no answer and she could not hear him breathing.

Outside the tent the hyena made the same strange noise that had awakened her. But she did not hear him for the beating of her heart.

JACK HODGINS

The Trench Dwellers

Macken this. Macken that. Gerry Mack had had enough. Why should he waste his life riding ferries to weddings and family reunions? There were already too many things you were forced to do in this world whether you liked them or not. "And I've hated those family gatherings for as long as I can remember," he said. "Why else would I move away?"

The problem was that Gerry's Aunt Nora Macken really did believe family was important. She used to tell how the Mackens first settled on the north slope of the valley more than fifty years ago when Black Alex, her father, brought the whole dozen of his children onto the Island in his touring car and started hacking a farm out of what had for centuries been pure timber land. And would tell, too, that by now there was hardly a household left in all the valley that wasn't related to them in one way or another. What Aunt Nora called The Immediate Family had grown to include more than four hundred people, three-quarters of whom were named Smith or O'Brien or Laitenen though she called them all the Mackens.

There wasn't any real substitute for having a lot of relatives, she said. And the people who knew her best, this tall big-footed old maid living out on that useless farm, said that yes, she was right, there was no substitute for family.

And because Nora Macken lived on those three hundred acres of farmland which had gone back already in two generations to second-growth timber, she thought it her duty every time there was a wedding or a funeral to call a reunion of The Immediate Family the day after the ceremony. More than three hundred relatives gathered. The older people, her own generation, spent the day in the house telling each other stories about Black Alex, reassuring one another that he really was as mean and miserable as they remembered, but that it couldn't be denied he was a bit of a character, too, all the same.

The young adults drank beer outside in the grassy yard or on the verandah and talked about their jobs and their houses, and each of them tried to find out how much money the others were earning. The children chased each other between the dead orchard trees and climbed the rickety ladders to the barn mow and fought over the sticky slices of cake Nora Macken put outside on a folding card table in the sun.

As for someone like Gerry Mack, her nephew, who was the only member of the Immediate Family ever to move off Vancouver Island, these events were more than he could bear.

When Gerry was twenty years old he very nearly married Karen O'Brien, a pretty blonde he'd gone all the way through school with. They went to movies together on Saturday nights and sometimes to dances, and afterwards they parked up the gravel road to the city dump to kiss each other until their mouths were raw. But Karen was already a member of The Immediate Family and had half a dozen brothers eager to increase the population. Gerry balked at marriage. He was the son of one of Nora's older brothers and had wished since the time he was six years old that he'd been an orphan.

Soon after dumping Karen O'Brien he met a stoop-shouldered secretary named April Klamp, who was plain-looking and very dull and wore clothes that looked as if they were bought for someone else, perhaps her mother. But she was an only child and had no relatives at all, only a pair of doddering parents who didn't care very much what happened to her. Gerry asked her to marry him a week after their first meeting and of course she accepted. No one before had even given her so much as a second look.

Some member of The Immediate Family had a few words to say about it. It seemed odd, they said, that a young man as vibrant as Gerry couldn't find himself a wife who was more of a match. Aunt Nora, too, thought it was unusual, but she'd given Gerry up long ago as not a real Macken at heart. And besides, she said, it could have been worse. He could have married a church-goer (something no Macken had ever done) or worse still remained a bachelor (something three of her brothers had done and become cranky old grouches as a result). "Just watch him," she said. "He'll cut off his nose to spite his face."

Gerry didn't particularly care what any of them thought. Before his wedding he took two letters off his name and became Gerry Mack. He got no argument from April, of course. She was quick to agree that having too much family was worse than having none at all. She didn't even mind that he insisted on getting married seventy miles down-island by a minister she'd never met so that it would be impossible to have a reception afterwards. And when he told her that they would live on the mainland she merely nodded and said it was about time one of the Mackens showed a little spunk. Personally, she said, she'd always hated living on an island. She agreed with everything that Gerry Mack said and never took her eyes off his face while he spoke. It was clear to everyone that when Gerry married her what he got was not a separate person to live with but an extension of himself. Aunt Nora said he could have gone out and bought a wooden leg if that was all he wanted.

Though she added, "At least they won't ever get into a fight. An extra limb doesn't talk back."

Their intention was to move far inland, but Gerry hadn't driven a hundred miles up the Fraser Valley before he realized he couldn't stand to be away from the coast. They turned back and settled in a little town on the edge of the strait, facing across to the Island, directly across to the valley where he had grown up. They bought a house fifty feet from the beach, with huge plate-glass windows facing west, and began saving their money to buy a small boat of their own so they could fish in the evenings.

Because he was a young man with a good rich voice and many opinions, Gerry had no trouble getting a job as an open-line moderator for the new radio station. He spent the first week voicing as many outlandish ideas as he could think of and being as rude as he dared to people who phoned in, so it didn't take long for him to draw most listeners away from the competing station. Within a month he had a large and faithful following on both sides of the strait. People didn't say they listened to CLCB, they said they listened to Gerry Mack's station.

What pleased him most was knowing that whether they liked it or not, most of The Immediate Family would be listening to him every day. He could imagine them in their houses, cringing whenever he was rude to callers, and hoping no one else realized where he'd come from, and saying Thank goodness he'd had the sense to change his name. He made a habit of saying "So long, Nora" every day as a sign-off but didn't tell anyone what it meant. People in the mainland town guessed that Nora must be his wife's middle name or else the name of a grandmother who'd died when he was a little boy. None of them ever guessed, of course, that Aunt Nora Macken over on the island sat by her radio every morning for the whole time he was on and went red in the face when he signed off, and told herself maybe he was the only real Macken in the lot after all, though she could spank him for his cheek.

And that, he thought, will show you that here's one Macken who has no need for family.

Though he did not know then, of course, that even the most weak-minded and agreeable wife could suddenly find a backbone and will in herself when she became pregnant. He was sitting in the living room with his feet up on the walnut coffee table looking for good controversial topics in the newspaper when she handed him the wedding invitation that had arrived in the mail that morning. "I think we should go," she said.

"The hell you say," he said, and read through the silver script. "We hardly know them. Who's this Peter O'Brien to us?"

"A cousin," she said. "But that doesn't matter. I think we should be there for the reunion the next day."

Gerry put down the newspaper and looked at his wife. She was rubbing a hand over her round swollen belly. "What for?" he said. "I've been to a million of them. They're all the same. I thought we moved over here to get away from all that."

She sat down beside him on the sofa and put her head against his shoulder. "It's been a year since we've even put a foot on the Island. Let's go just for the fun."

He looked down into her plain mousey hair, her white scalp. She had never asked for a thing before. "We'll go," he said, "but only on the condition that we leave the minute I can't stand any more."

They took the two-hour ferry ride across the strait, and though he sat with a book in his lap and tried to read, he found it hard to concentrate and spent a lot of time watching the Island get closer and bigger and more distinct. He hated sitting idle, he was a man who liked to be doing things, and right now he would have preferred to be at work in the radio station or digging in his garden.

Aunt Nora outdid herself. "Lord," she said. "This must be the best reunion ever. There are three hundred and fifty people here, at least, and listen to that racket! When the Mackens get together there's no such thing as a lull in the conversation, there's never a moment when tongues have ceased."

"They do seem to have the gift of the gab," April said.

"A Macken," Aunt Nora said, smiling, "is a sociable person. A Macken enjoys company and conversation."

Macken this Macken that, Gerry thought.

His cousin George Smith put a bottle of beer in his hand and steered him across the yard to lean up against someone's car. He said he couldn't understand why Gerry put up with all the bullshit he had to listen to on his show. He wanted to know why Gerry didn't just threaten to quit his job if people wouldn't smarten up.

Gerry noticed that the whole back yard and orchard were filled with parked cars, and that against nearly every car there was at least one pair leaning and drinking beer and talking. Only the old ones were inside. April was standing straighter than he'd ever seen her, laughing with a bunch of women gathered beside a new Buick. "It doesn't matter a damn to me what they say," he told George Smith. "It's just part of my job to listen. Sometimes I tell them to go take a flying leap, but what the hell? Who cares?"

George told him he'd cleared over fifteen hundred dollars last month, working in the pulp and paper mill, most of it from overtime. He said he couldn't understand why most of the rest of them worked in the logging camp or in stores in town where there was hardly any overtime at all. It was overtime, he said, that made it possible for him to buy this here little baby they were leaning on. He pushed down on the front fender of the sports car and rocked it gently and with great fondness. Then he asked Gerry if a person working for a radio station got paid a salary or a wage, and what kind of car was he driving anyways? Gerry pointed vaguely across the yard and said as far as he was concerned it was just a way of getting places. But George told him if he got enough overtime in in the next few months he intended to buy himself a truck and camper so he could take more weekends off to go fishing up in the lakes. "Everybody's got one," he said. "One time I went up to Gooseneck Lake with Jim and Harriet and there were sixteen truck-and-campers there already. Nine of them were Mackens. Even old Uncle Morris was there, driving a brand-new Chev, and he only makes the minimum wage at *his* job. I told him, I said How could you afford a thing like that? and he said it pays to have a son in the car-selling business. I said I bet you'll be paying for that thing for the rest of your life."

"And he said?" Gerry said.

"Nothing," George said. "He just told me I was jealous. Ha!"

April came across the yard and led Gerry away towards a large group of people sitting in lawn chairs in a circle and doing a lot of laughing. But Aunt Nora, tall Aunt Nora with all her dyed-black hair piled up on top of her head, intercepted them and took them inside so that Uncle Morgan, who had been sick in the hospital the whole time they were engaged, could meet April. "It won't do," she said, "to have strangers in the same family." She pushed them right into her cluttered little living room and made someone get up so April could have a comfortable chair. Gerry leaned against the door frame and wondered if old Black Alex realized when he was alive that the dozen kids he'd hauled onto the Island in his touring car would eventually become these aging wrinkled people.

And of course it was Black Alex they were talking about. Uncle Morris said "I mind the time he said to me Get off that roof boy or I'll stuff you down the chimney!" He laughed so hard at that he had to haul out a handkerchief to wipe the tears off his big red face.

Aunt Nora, too, shrieked. "Oh, that was his favourite! He was always threatening to stuff one of us down the chimney." Though she was careful to explain to April that never in his life did he do any such thing to any of them, that in fact the worst he ever did was apply the toe of his boot to their backsides. "He was a noisy man," she said. "But some of us learned how to handle him."

Then she drew everybody's attention to April and said, "As you can easily see, there's one more little Macken waiting to be born. Boy or girl we wish it luck."

"D'you know?" Uncle Morgan said. "Not one person in the family has ever named a child after Dad."

"No wonder!" Aunt Nora cried. "There could only be one Alex Macken. No one else would dare try to match him."

"Or want to," Aunt Katherine said. "Suppose they got his temper too, along with his name."

"One thing for sure," Aunt Nora said. "He'll have plenty of cousins to play with. He'll never run out of playmates or friends." Then, remembering, she added, "Of course, as long as they keep him isolated over there on the mainland I suppose he'll miss out on everything."

"It's terrible having no one to play with," April said. "Especially if you're too shy to go out making friends on your own. Just ask me, I know. At least with cousins you don't have to start from scratch. Nobody needs to be scared of a relative."

"Right!" Aunt Nora said, and looked right at Gerry. "Though there are some people who think loneliness is a prize to be sought after."

Gerry Mack knew, of course, that something had happened to the wife he thought was a sure bet to remain constant. It came as something of a surprise. After all, who expected an adult's foot to suddenly turn into a hand or start growing off in a new direction? He brooded about it all the way home on the ferry and wouldn't speak to her even while she got ready for bed. He sat in his living room until he was sure she'd gone to sleep, then he tiptoed in to the bedroom and undressed without turning on the light.

The next day he held off the phone calls that came into the station and kept the air waves to himself. From his little sound-booth he could look out across the strait. "From over here," he told his listeners, "from here on the mainland, Vancouver Island is just a pale blue chain of mountains stretched right across your whole range of vision. A jagged-backed wall between us and the open sea. Go have a look. Stop what you're doing for a minute and go to your window." He waited for a while, and thought not of the housewives who were moving to the ocean side of their houses, but of the islanders who were over there listening and wondering what he was up to.

"There it is," he said. "Twenty miles away. I bet you hardly ever notice it there, like a fence that borders the back yard." He drank a mouthful of the coffee he kept with him throughout the show. "Now those of you who've been across on the ferry know that as you get closer those mountains begin to take on shapes and change from blue to green and show big chunks of logged-off sections and zig-zag logging roads like knife-scars up their sides. And closer still, of course, you see that along the edge of the Island, stretched out along the shelf of flatter land, is a chain of farms and fishing villages and towns and tourist resorts and bays full of log booms and peninsulas dotted with summer cabins. All of it, ladies and gentlemen, facing over to us as if those people too think these mountains are nothing but a wall at their backs, holding off the Pacific."

He gulped coffee again and glanced at his watch. He thought of the mainlanders looking across. He thought of the islanders wondering what the hell he was talking about. Then he said, "But the funny thing is this: to those people over there on that island, this mainland they spend most of their lives facing is nothing but a blue chain of jagged mountains stretched across their vision like a wall separating them from the rest of North America. That continent behind us doesn't even exist to some of them. To them we look just the same as they do to us."

Then, just before opening the telephone lines to callers, he said, "What we live in is a trench. Do you suppose trench-dwellers think any different from the rest of the world?"

His line was busy for the rest of the morning. Most wanted to talk about why they liked living in a place like this, some asked him couldn't he think of a more pleasant comparison to make, and a few tried to change the subject to the recent tax increase. One long-distance call came in from the Island, an old man who told him he was jabbering nonsense and ought to be locked up, some place where all he could see would be bars and padded walls. "If you want to live in a trench," he said, "I'll dig you one. Six feet long by six feet deep." Gerry Mack hung up on his cackling laughter and vowed he would never cross that strait again.

But April told him that didn't mean *she* couldn't go across just whenever she felt like it.

So that when the next wedding invitation arrived he was ready for her announcement. Even if he didn't want to go, she said, she was heading across and taking Jimmy with her. He couldn't deprive her for ever of the pleasure of showing off her son to his family. And Jimmy, too, had a right to meet his cousins. She was pregnant again, and there was a new hard glint in her eye. Gerry Mack, when she talked like that to him, felt very old and wondered what life would have been like if he'd married Karen O'Brien. If that's what happened to women, he thought, you might as well marry your own sister.

When she came back she told him the reunion of course was a huge success and everybody asked where he was. She'd stayed right at Aunt Nora's, she said, and it was amazing how much room there was in that old farmhouse when everyone else had gone home. She'd felt right at home there. Jimmy had had a wonderful time, had made friends with dozens of cousins, and could hardly wait for the next time they went over. And oh yes, Aunt Nora sent him a message.

"What is it?" he said, weary.

"She says there's a wonderful new man on *their* radio station. She says she doesn't know of a single Macken who still listens to you. This new fellow plays softer music and isn't nearly so rude to his callers. She says people do appreciate good manners after all and she can't think of one good reason for you not to be at the next wedding."

"At the rate they're marrying," he said, "The Immediate Family will soon swallow up the whole Island."

"The Mackens believe in marriage," she said. "And in sticking together."

Mackens this Mackens that, Gerry thought.

"Nora told me her father used to say being a Macken was like being part of a club. Or a religion."

"Do you know why they call him Black Alex?"

"Why?"

"When he was alive people used to call him Nigger Alex because his hair was so black and you never saw him without dirt on his hands and face. People over there never saw a real black man in those days. But the 'children' decided after his death that Black Alex was politer and what people would've called him if they'd only stopped to think."

"Well at least they called him something," she said. "It shows he was liked. It shows people noticed him. I never heard anyone call you anything but Gerry, an insipid name if I ever heard one. Pretty soon those people over there will forget you even exist."

"That's fine with me," Gerry Mack said, and went outside to sprinkle powder on his rose leaves.

But she followed him. "Sometimes I don't think it's family you're trying to get away from at all. I think it's humanity itself."

"Don't be ridiculous," he said. "If that was what I wanted I'd have become a hermit."

"What else are we?" She was on the verge of tears. "You don't let Jimmy play with anyone else's kids, none of them are good enough for you. And we've hardly any friends ourselves."

"Don't harp," he said. "Don't nag at me."

It passed through his mind to tell her she had no business going against his wishes when it came to bringing up the boy. But he was a strange kid anyway, and Gerry had always been uncomfortable with children. It was easier to let her do what she wanted with him.

When April went across to George Smith's wedding (his second) and took Jimmy and the baby with her, he knew she would not be coming back. He wasn't surprised when she didn't get off the Sunday evening ferry. He didn't even bother watching the ferries coming in during the next week. The only surprise was the sight of Aunt Nora getting out of a taxi the following weekend and throwing herself into the leather armchair in Gerry's living room.

"My God," she said. "It looks as if you could walk across in fifteen minutes but that damn ferry takes for ever."

"Where's April?" he said.

The wedding, she told him, was lovely. Because it was George's second the girl didn't try to make it into too much of a thing, but just as many people turned out for it as for his first. "He's got a real dandy this time," she said. "He's not going to want to spend so much time at his precious pulp mill when he's got this one waiting at home. She's got outdoor teeth of course, but still she is pretty!"

Gerry said George's first wife hadn't been much to look at, but then George was no prize himself.

Then, suddenly, Aunt Nora said, "I think she'll be asking you for a legal separation."

"Who?" he said, stupidly.

"I told her she could live with me. There's too much room in that old house for one person. I'll enjoy the company. I remember Dad saying if a Macken couldn't count on one of his own relatives in times of trouble, who could he count on? That little boy of yours is going to look just like him." She stood up and took off her coat and laid it over the back of her chair. Then she took a cigarette out of her purse and lit it and sat down again.

"If you want to come back with me and try to patch it up, that's all right."

"Patch what up?" he said. "We haven't even had a fight."

But she acted as if she hadn't heard. "I'll tell you something, Gerry, you've got spunk. Maybe you're the only real Macken in the whole kaboodle."

"Ha."

"And if you and April patch it up, if you want to live on the farm, that's all right with me too."

"Why should I want to live there?"

"It's the family homestead," she said, as if it was something he might have forgotten. "It's where your grandfather started out. Where the family began."

Gerry grunted and went to the refrigerator to get himself a bottle of beer.

"Well, somebody will have to take it over some day," she said. "You can see what's happened to the farm with just an old maid living on it. He never should have left it to me in the first place. Except, of course, it's the best place for holding family get-togethers and I know if it was left to anyone else they'd never get done."

"Look," he said. "You got her and my two kids. Three for one. That sounds like a pretty good trade to me."

"I just can't believe you don't care about those children," Aunt Nora said. "Those two little boys. No Macken has ever abandoned his own children. It doesn't seem natural."

"Natural," Gerry Mack said, and tilted up his bottle of beer.

But when she caught the morning ferry home he did not go with her. In fact, he was to make only one more visit to the Island, and that would not be until two years later when he attended his son's funeral. Aunt Nora phoned him in the middle of the day to say the boy had drowned in a swimming accident. The Immediate Family was at the funeral, four hundred or so of them, standing all over the graveyard where Mackens were buried. He'd sat beside April in the chapel but when they got to the graveside she seemed to be surrounded by relatives and he was left alone, on the far side of the ugly hole where they were putting his son. Aunts and cousins were weeping openly, but April in their midst stared straight ahead with her jaw set like stone. She appeared then to have lost all of the slump that was once in her back. Even her mousey brown hair seemed to have taken on more life. When their eyes met she nodded in a way that might have been saying "Thank you" or might have been only a dismissal, or could perhaps have been simply acknowledging that she had noticed his, a stranger's, presence.

Aunt Nora, afterwards, cornered him in her little living room. She seemed smaller now, slightly stooped, getting old. There were deep lines in her face. "Now," she said. "Now do you see where your place is? Now do you see where you belong?"

He turned, tried to find someone to rescue him.

"This whole farm, Gerry, it's yours. Just move here, stay here where you belong."

And it was April who rescued him after all. She came into the room swiftly, her eyes darting with the quick concern of a hostess making sure everything was going well. "Oh Nora!" she said. "Uncle Morris was asking for you. I promised I'd take you to him."

When the old woman stood up to leave, April let her gaze flicker momentarily over him. Her complexion against the black dress looked nearly ivory. Beautiful skin. She would be a beautiful woman yet. "George Smith was wondering where you were," she said. "I told him I thought you'd already gone home."

For several years after that Aunt Nora visited the mainland every summer to report to Gerry on his wife and remaining son and to tell him all about the weddings and reunions he'd missed. April, she told him, had taken over the last reunion completely, did all the planning and most of the work. And some people on the Island were listening to him again she said, now that he was only reading the news, once a day.

But she stopped coming altogether years later when he sold the seaside house and moved in with a woman far up a gravel road behind town, in a junky unpainted house beside a swamp. She had nearly a dozen children from various fathers, some Scandinavian, two Indian, and one Chinese, and her name was Netty Conroy. Which meant, Aunt Nora Macken was soon able to discover after a little investigation, that she was related to more than half the people who lived in that mainland town, not to mention most who lived in the countryside around it. It was a strange thing, she told The Immediate Family, but she still felt closer to Gerry Mack than to any of the rest of them. Perhaps it was because she, too, had had a tendency to cut off her nose to spite her face. Everyone laughed at the notion because of course, they said, Aunt Nora had always had everything just the way she wanted it in this world.

HUGH HOOD

New Country

They'd been staying in a borrowed apartment at the corner of Lawrence so the simplest thing to do was go straight up through Hogg's Hollow and get onto 401 going east from Yonge. Early Saturday afternoon, bright and cold in mid-March, with a rush of wind along the flanks of the car making it judder and fishtail at highway speeds, a light car, bouncy and jumpy and peppy. Lester didn't like to spend money on big cars, always drove a Nova or a Fairmont, changing them every October. He could always rely on his car.

He swung the six-months-old Nova across the service lanes, working his blinker lights and reading the rear-view mirrors expertly, and entered the eastbound through traffic at sixty-five. Molly never spoke while he was executing this manoeuvre. She liked to watch his face as his eyes flicked from the road to the mirror overhead, then to the left window, then across her to the right. He had had extra-large mirrors installed on every car they'd ever owned; you could see almost all the way around behind you if they were properly adjusted. Delivery of a new car each October meant an afternoon spent adjusting the mirrors for maximum visibility to the rear.

She waited for him to say something. When they first used to make this trip he would start to chat, on the way back to Stoverville, somewhere around Morningside Drive where the freeway drew away from the suburbs. These days he took longer to thaw. 401 spanned six full lanes of brisk traffic as far as Oshawa, and was being widened there, strewn with construction signs and warnings, and suddenly disappearing shoulders, arbitrary ramp-closings sprouting where wholly unlooked-for. Lester liked to hold his peace until the traffic thinned perceptibly, often saying little or nothing as far as Ajax or Whitby, then initiating a conversation only to lapse into glum silence as he negotiated the cramped outmoded underpasses of Oshawa.

"Ritson Road," he said suddenly, sighing. They were already almost forty miles along their way home. "Well, and how was she?"

"Brenda?"

"Just a minute till I get around this idiot."

She sat and waited; the seat-back punched powerfully at her shoulders; the blinker arrow came on; the car swayed.

"Brenda."

"Bad. She was bad, Lester. I think it was what we thought. She doesn't know. She didn't say anything about that; all she wanted to do was talk about her fibroids. I wanted to laugh, God forgive me. You know, Lester, I used to have this funny image of fibroids, like little pieces of candy. Like chocolates. I don't know why that was. Women talk about these things all the time and I don't suppose any of us has ever seen one. So you kind of make a picture in your mind of what they look like, and for years I've always imagined fibroids sitting in a row like fancy chocolates in a tray in an expensive candy store. In little crinkled brown paper pants. I think I've been seeing them as a lot of little Laura Secords. And I don't even know what a fibroid is."

"It must be made of fibre, judging by the word."

"I guess it is, but that doesn't tell me a thing. I believe they're little tumours of some kind. 'My fibroids were benign,' she kept saying, and she'd give me this awful grin. I think she suspects. I think it's what we thought. Way inside. I wish you could have seen her. I'd have liked to know what you thought. She had a poor colour, very very pale, very dry skin. And she used to have that lovely skin without a mark or a wrinkle on it. I wanted to cry, but I didn't dare show what I was thinking. All her clothes are two sizes too big for her and the worst thing is she suspects. I mean she sounded so beat-up and awful. She said her gynecologist was just awful to her, wouldn't call her by her first name on account of the feminists; it was Mrs. this, and Mrs. that. Never a friendly word, and the usual comic insults. 'We'll just take a little tuck in it to tighten you up,' he said, poking in her vaginal canal. It was so offensive. She said she felt she was the size of a motorman's glove inside, too big for fun. 'I'm all saggy in there,' she kept saying. 'I'm so ashamed, I'm so lapsed and saggy that Irving can't get any purchase. No wonder he never wants to do it anymore. It isn't that he's too small. I never felt he was too small. I've got a hole in me the size of a circus tent.' Then she started to cry buckets. 'Oh Molly,' she said, 'never let them do it to you. I don't know how I let that man talk me into it. I think he just does them for the money. The government pays, so why not? It's like tonsils; they used to do tonsils routinely but they don't anymore. Now it's hysterectomies. They see a woman fifty years old, and they want to gut her just because it's the in-thing to do. Don't let them try it on you, Molly.

The cure is worse than the disease.' And she laughed. I don't know what disease she was thinking of, maybe pregnancy."

"At least they did have kids."

"They never see the kids now. Neither of the boys visited her in the hospital, and when Arlene came they had a shattering argument, according to Brenda. She said Arlene said she was faking it, can you imagine? I mean the day before, practically, they'd removed the poor woman's womb surgically, and her daughter accuses her of malingering. Maybe she expected to see it in a bottle on the bedside table, for proof. They've never got along, and the boys are off somewhere, and nobody knows where. Irving is worse than useless about it. He can't control them."

"I think Irving has his own problems."

"Yes, and poor Brenda has them to think about while she's lying there. 'They do this routinely,' she kept saying. 'They recommend it for everybody. It wasn't as if there was anything seriously wrong. Wait till I get up and around. I'm too thin. Everybody tells me I'm too thin.' Like that. Now tell me, was she just kidding me? Or herself?"

"I'd say she probably doesn't know for sure."

"Well nobody does."

Lester kept his eyes fixed on the big camper in front of him, a home-on-wheels with a high centre of gravity and a tendency to sway in a crosswind. He eased into the passing lane.

"Lester, did Irving say something to you?"

"Just a second."

He flipped the right blinker on.

"She's my sister. I've got a right to know if anybody does."

"Molly, when they got inside she was like fishnet. All they could do was sew her up and forget about it. I talked to Irving on Thursday night while you were at the hospital."

"My God! Where?"

"Oh everywhere. Liver, womb, ovaries."

"She's younger than I am."

"Yeah, what is it, about two years?"

"I don't think she's fifty yet, honey. I was born in May and she was born in early June. The fifth. The fifth of June. She'll be fifty next June the fifth."

Lester said nothing and Molly quavered, "The poor thing." They covered a short distance in heavy silence. Then the car mounted an elegant rising curve, five miles east of Oshawa along the shoulder of a knoll which overlooks the lake. At this point the shoreline curves in under the hillside, and motorists have a view of the water across a bay or inlet — technically perhaps a bight — which always seems calm. It is the last place on the highway to present a prospect of the water before Kingston, a hundred miles further down. Lester used to enjoy the sight of the lake; today he ignored it.

The car sped inland towards Bowmanville and the Flying Dutchman Motel.

"Sam didn't look any too good either," said Lester. "I don't think he's a well man. His hemorrhoids are a curse, he says, and you know, you can tell from the way he walks. He has this air cushion in the office. I used to think it was funny, but it isn't funny really. All he wants to talk about is his proctologist. I was forty-five before I knew what a proctologist did. Now it's all I hear about. He can't concentrate on the line. How can you talk to buyers when all the time you're afraid to sit down? It's undignified; it's painful; it's on your mind and you wonder if they'll have to cut you. He told me this horror story about some friend who had the operation for hemorrhoids, and was he ever sick? When he woke up he couldn't go to the toilet. Either way. After a couple of days they had to introduce a catheter; otherwise he'd have got kidney-poisoning or uremia or whatever. I'm no doctor. They shove this long tube up through your thing, you know, and it drains off the piss. It hurts like hell. Just from the shock of the operation, it's no picnic. I don't know about Sammy. He hasn't been the same since Phil went. It was Phil who created Style-Made Sportswear. Sam was always really more of the accountant than anything. He doesn't know how to talk to buyers, or dress a display suite; he doesn't have the feel for it. He's anxious all the time and the customers can sense it; they know they've got him over a barrel. He has to do business so he can discount the orders and keep his cash flow in line. If the paper isn't available the bank gets upset. Sam is an accountant; he can judge to a second when the credit man from the bank is going to be on the line. He's always had this line with the Commerce, oh, years and years. Now they say that the industry is going to be phased out. They don't trust what the government says about imports, and nobody knows what the hell is happening. Getting goods into the stores is like a sport; you have to relax and swing easy and not frighten them off by pushing. It's hard to go on shipping to somebody who's in that frame of mind."

"Lester, he's your own brother."

"He's not the same. He hasn't been the same for two years, not since Phil died. Imagine the shock! They were sitting in the office in the factory around ten-thirty in the morning . . ."

"I don't want to hear this again."

". . . and Sammy hears the canteen wagon roll up. He says to Phil, 'What'll I get you?' They used to take turns buying, I mean for thirty years. 'Get me a coffee, no cream, and a roll of plain Tums,' says Phil. 'OK.' Sam goes out, gets the stuff, a doughnut for him and the Tums for Phil, and he goes back into the office and there he is, lying back in the chair with this look on his face. Gone. Like somebody switched out the light, and Sam says he didn't look peaceful. He looked like somebody hit him one hell of a smack on the side of the head. Sammy's standing there with this roll of plain Tums and the coffee getting cold in his hand. It stays in your mind."

Molly said, "It doesn't have to stay in your mind. It's not your affair."

"It's as much my affair as Brenda is your affair. He's my brother."

"You've never been as close as we were."

"He's a big account. Half our production goes to Style-Made. Almost half. Thirty percent anyway. I should have seen it coming. I blame myself."

"What could you have done about it?"

"It was losing that cutter did it. Some people might think I just wanted to unload every possible yard of goods on Style-Made, but it was never like that. You can't be greedy. You've got to supply quality in a good selection of widths; you've got to stay abreast of design trends. I admit it, I hate polyester. It makes me feel cold all the time. But it has definite uses if you're trying to produce sportswear at a price, so we have to be in a position to supply cotton and poly at any time in nice colours and patterns, no matter how I feel about it. I've given the trade maximum convenience and I've had plenty of customers. Maybe I made a mistake by selling so much to Phil and Sammy but they were always right there asking for our product. You don't say to your brother, 'I can only let you have so much this season. I've got you on a quota.' The effect of it is, I'm very tightly linked in with Style-Made, in a tough marketing situation, and they've always got maximum yield from our fabrics. That old man was a wonder."

"Highlands of Hastings," said Molly.

"What?"

"You missed the sign. 'You are now entering the Highlands of Hastings regional vacation area.' "

"Already? We're making good time. We'll be home for dinner."

Molly shrugged her shoulders up and down vigorously, and wound her head on her neck. "It's around three," she said, "it won't be dark for hours and hours; the days are getting longer."

"Old Everett Stapleton. He was a wonder. He could cut more pieces from a length of goods than you'd believe. You never used to see their factory knee-deep in remnants. He could look at a length and see, right in the flat cloth, how many garments could be made up out of it, including sleeves and gussets, like some kind of a sculptor. The designers used to take instructions from him. If the design couldn't be cut economically from the goods, he'd show them how to re-work it. He'd re-do the sketches, right in the cutting room. Phil used to talk about him with tears in his eyes. Then he died, and they've never been able to replace him. After that, their ordering was less precise; they bought more, and I'll bet they produced fewer dozen garments from what they bought. A cutter like that . . . almost an artist, you'd have to say. I think it was losing him that brought on Phil's coronary. It isn't as though Phil was an old man. He was younger than Sam. I think Phil and I were about the same age. He always used to take good care of himself, then to go just like that."

Across the highway above the westbound lanes, a high ridge loomed up in a long centre arc along the roadside, cutting off the view of the sky. They could see a long way ahead, perhaps two miles. Then the eastbound lanes banked down into a valley and were lost from view. The movement of the car and the presence of the high ridge beside them gave the impression that the car was floating idly and slowly towards a whirlpool.

"Highlands of Hastings," said Lester suddenly. "I wonder what the Highlands of Hastings are exactly? I wonder what they look like." He gave a sharp yank at the wheel. The car veered into the passing lane, then back to the right. Molly stared at him doubtfully.

"I've been going up and down the 401 for twenty years," he said discontentedly, "Stoverville to Toronto, Toronto to Stoverville. I've gotten to know this run too damn' well. Glen Miller Road, Wooler, Salmon River. I might as well be on tracks. I never see what's off to the side. I've never had a look at the Highlands of Hastings."

He stared fixedly at the high ground swelling up on the other side of the road.

Molly said, "Keep your eyes on the highway, Lester."

"I wonder what's happening in the Highlands of Hastings tonight. Is there really anybody there? Sometimes I get the impression that big ridge up there is nothing but a canvas drop. Here! Let's go and have a look at what's behind it." They passed a sign which said, *Hwy 30 North-South Brighton Next Exit Only 2 km.*

"Kilometres, kilometres, why couldn't they have left it miles? Messing around with everything. Can't keep their hands off anything." He put on the right blinker and turned onto the exit ramp. The car slowed abruptly, running down to the stop sign at the sideroad, deep in a cupped hollow to one side of 401. They sat at the stop sign, the car idling quietly in neutral, looking around them at the wholly foreign scene.

"Left," said Lester, "we'll go left; we'll have a look at the back country."

"It's past four o'clock."

"You said yourself, it won't be dark till late. It's almost spring — according to the calendar — and the fields seem clear. Come on, we've seen 401 too many times. We'll go up to Highway 7, and go home the back way. It'll be something to do for a change. It doesn't really matter if we get in tonight." He paused, then said as if amazed at the notion, "We could get a motel room; we could go the rest of the way tomorrow. After all, why not?"

A car drew up behind them and honked softly. Lester gave a slight start, then put the car in motion, turning left. The ground began to rise at once; they were climbing up a steep hill as they came out of the underpass on the other side of 401. The highway narrowed abruptly as they came up the hillside, and a tight curve around a spur of high ground concealed the freeway from sight behind them. The motor whined, and Lester shifted into second. He said, "I haven't done that in years." The car continued to climb for some moments.

"We're going up through that ridge," said Molly suddenly. "It isn't a piece of scenery, it's quite real." The road wound slowly upwards to the right for another mile and a half; they might have climbed three hundred and fifty feet. Then it emerged into a terrain which was utterly novel to them, perfectly unlike the open countryside around Toronto or the limestone ridges, the granite shelves and narrow beds of good soil north of Stoverville. This was a central Ontario landscape seen by fewer and fewer people. They felt transported back to the nineteen-thirties. Highway 30 had the grassy ditches and narrow shoulders and Queen's Highway markers, the cracked surfaces and sudden, poorly-marked curves and intersections of the thirties. Molly felt the pace and rhythm of the car slow and adapt itself to the altered driving conditions. She felt no apprehension. Lester was, if anything, a better driver at these speeds than at seventy. She began to enjoy the deliberate motion, staring out into the deserted fields — what she could see of them — with curiosity, and real surprise at their unfamiliar aspect. Shown them in a photograph, perhaps on a postcard, she would not have been able to identify them as any part of the province she knew. She had a vague impression that they resembled some part of France. Even the earth tones in the fields, where small snowbanks lingered in hedges and along the depressions of drainage ditches, seemed darker and more distant, oddly withdrawn. There was a slight peculiarity to the lie of the country which at first perplexed her.

An elderly International pickup, with a homemade stake body rattling loudly, came at them all at once around a curve, passing very near. Its front wheels had a pronounced shimmy. Lester took a quick look over his shoulder, disturbed by the narrow margin for passing. He dropped to forty. "Close enough," he said in a low voice, "maybe even too close. I wonder where we are exactly. Could you dig out the map? There's an Ontario road map in there somewhere."

She opened the glove compartment with an increasingly intense sense of *déjà vu.* When they had been an engaged couple, and for some short time after their marriage, Lester and Molly had made the usual weekend trips around their countryside along the back roads, on picnics and an occasional hayride. She always used to read the map for him, she remembered. She always had the customary comic trouble about re-folding the free road maps from the gas stations. They were no longer free, she reflected. Most stations couldn't be bothered to stock them, and those which did charged a dollar for a map.

"We're going north on Highway 30," she announced a moment later. "In a minute we'll be — no, here it is — we're going through Orland."

They passed a corner where a green arrow pointed eastwards. It said "Wooler."

"My gosh," said Lester, "so that's where Wooler is. I've never actually believed in the existence of Wooler. I wonder if there are five proofs for the existence of Wooler?"

"I'm enjoying this," said Molly. All the same she felt certain distinct qualms. She was not entirely happy with the prospect of the high, short fields. They were curiously broken and folded and they fell away out of view disturbingly, to reveal sudden deeps and shadows. It was still bright afternoon on the upper ground where the highway ran along between the small farms, but to either side the fields slanted away and down into obscurity. Here and there the entire rectangular outline of a field could be seen, a quarter-mile away from the road, lying athwart the pitch of neighbouring small hills, like a wet handkerchief draped on a radiator to dry. These fields had a convoluted up-and-down shape. Nearer the highway the enclosures seemed — and doubtless were — smaller, humped up beside the road. The fields were in work already, most of them, freshly-turned furrows awaiting the seed, perhaps already seeded and concealing new growth from her inexpert eye. There were no people visible in the fields, not so much as a tractor. It's late Saturday afternoon, she thought, and they've all gone into ... into ... she consulted the map. Where would they go on Saturday night? Codrington?

They went through Codrington as this question crossed her mind, and it was at once evident that Codrington was not where the crowds went on Saturday night; there was nobody in town. One or two farmhouse lights began to contest the late sunshine. Soon it would be time for dinner. She thought of Brenda and Sammy and Phil, briefly considered the prospect of reviving that conversation, rejected it, and waited for Lester to say something. He was concentrating on the road.

"My God, what country," he muttered. The car bounced and swerved. "We ought to be out of the high country pretty soon. Isn't Campbellford somewhere around here? I seem to remember ..."

"Just a minute, just a minute." She rearranged the unhandy map. "There isn't room for this thing."

"It ought to be somewhere up ahead. We ought to look for a place to spend the night. I'll tell you, I wouldn't want to come up this way in the dark. I'm having to fight to hold the car steady."

"We go through a place called, just a minute till I get my glasses on, called Meyersberg, that's it. It can't be very big, so you'd better keep an eye open. After that we ought to be down out of these hills — which make me feel uncomfortable. Highlands of Hastings indeed! We ought to hit the Trent system somewhere up around Meyersberg, and after that it can't be more than a few miles to Campbellford. What makes you think of Campbellford particularly?"

"I just happen to remember it's around here. I saw a picture in some book. And there's your precious Meyersberg, look at that! It's a ghost town. I noticed in the paper the other day, last Saturday, an advertisement for a book called *Ghost Towns of Ontario*. It kind of made me think."

Molly folded the map carefully and put it away. She felt the car begin to descend. All at once, off to the right, a long stretch of water came in sight, broadening out as they approached, with huge shadows lying across it. As they came down the side of the hill — in second gear — they lost the sunlight, and the water looked flat and black and very cold.

"It isn't moving at all," Molly whispered.

"Is that a lake or the river?"

"I don't know what it is," she said, "and I'm not going to struggle with that damn' map again. There's no current in that water. Look! Not a ripple."

"We'll be into town in a few minutes," said Lester. "I can see lights ahead. Oh, somebody else I forgot to mention dropped dead in Toronto while we were there. Do you remember Lionel Breitbart?"

"No," she said, "I don't and I don't want to talk about it. What's the matter with you, Lester? Where did the middle of our lives go? When we used to take this trip what we talked about was who was getting engaged. Who was getting married ... having a baby ..."

"We'll find a place," he said through his teeth. He speeded up, heading into a blind curve.

SHIRLEY JACKSON

The Lottery

The morning of June 27th was clear and sunny, with the fresh warmth of a full-summer day; the flowers were blossoming profusely and the grass was richly green. The people of the village began to gather in the square, between the post office and the bank, around ten o'clock; in some towns there were so many people that the lottery took two days and had to be started on June 26th, but in this village, where there were only about three hundred people, the whole lottery took less than two hours, so it could begin at ten o'clock in the morning and still be through in time to allow the villagers to get home for noon dinner.

The children assembled first, of course. School was recently over for the summer, and the feeling of liberty sat uneasily on most of them; they tended to gather together quietly for a while before they broke into boisterous play, and their talk was still of the classroom and the teacher, of books and reprimands. Bobby Martin had already stuffed his pockets full of stones, and the other boys soon followed his example, selecting the smoothest and roundest stones; Bobby and Harry Jones and Dickie Delacroix — the villagers pronounced his name "Dellacroy" — eventually made a great pile of stones in one corner of the square and guarded it against the raids of the other boys. The girls stood aside, talking among themselves, looking over their shoulders at the boys, and the very small children rolled in the dust or clung to the hands of their older brothers or sisters.

Soon the men began to gather, surveying their own children, speaking of planting and rain, tractors and taxes. They stood together, away from the pile of stones in the corner, and their jokes were quiet and they smiled rather than laughed. The women, wearing faded house dresses and sweaters, came shortly after their menfolk. They greeted one another and exchanged bits of gossip as they went to join their husbands. Soon the women, standing by their husbands, began to call to their children, and the children came reluctantly, having to be called four or five times. Bobby Martin ducked under his mother's grasping hand and ran, laughing, back to the pile of stones. His father spoke up sharply, and Bobby came quickly and took his place between his father and his oldest brother.

The lottery was conducted — as were the square dances, the teen-age club, the Halloween program — by Mr. Summers, who had time and energy to devote to civic activities. He was a round-faced, jovial man and he ran the coal business, and people were sorry for him, because he had no children and his wife was a scold. When he arrived in the square, carrying the black wooden box, there was a murmur of conversation among the villagers, and he waved and called, "Little late today, folks." The postmaster, Mr. Graves, followed him, carrying a three-legged stool, and the stool was put in the center of the square and Mr. Summers set the black box down on it. The villagers kept their distance, leaving a space between themselves and the stool, and when Mr. Summers said, "Some of you fellows want to give me a hand?" there was a hesitation before two men, Mr. Martin and his oldest son, Baxter, came forward to hold the box steady on the stool while Mr. Summers stirred up the papers inside it.

The original paraphernalia for the lottery had been lost long ago, and the black box now resting on the stool had been put into use even before Old Man Warner, the oldest man in town, was born. Mr. Summers spoke frequently to the villagers about making a new box, but no one liked to upset even as much tradition as was represented by the black box. There was a story that the present box had been made with some pieces of the box that had preceded it, the one that had been constructed when the first people settled down to make a village here. Every year, after the lottery, Mr. Summers began talking again about a new box, but every year the subject was allowed to fade off without anything's being done. The black box grew shabbier each year; by now it was no longer completely black but splintered badly along one side to show the original wood color, and in some places faded or stained.

Mr. Martin and his oldest son, Baxter, held the black box securely on the stool until Mr. Summers had stirred the papers thoroughly with his hand. Because so much of the ritual had been forgotten or discarded, Mr. Summers had been successful in having slips of paper substituted for the chips of wood that had been used for generations. Chips of wood, Mr. Summers had argued, had been all very well when the village was tiny, but now that the population was more than three hundred and likely to keep on growing, it was necessary to use something that would fit more easily into the black box. The night before the lottery, Mr. Summers and Mr. Graves made up the slips of paper and put them in the box, and it was then taken to the safe of Mr. Summers' coal company and locked up until Mr. Summers was ready to take it to the square next morning. The rest of the year, the box was put away, sometimes one place, sometimes another; it had spent one year in Mr. Graves's barn and another year underfoot in the post office, and sometimes it was set on a shelf in the Martin grocery and left there.

There was a great deal of fussing to be done before Mr. Summers declared the lottery open. There were the lists to make up — of heads of families, heads of households in each family, members of each household in each family. There was the proper swearing-in of Mr. Summers by the postmaster, as the official of the lottery; at one time, some people remembered, there had been a recital of some sort, performed by the official of the lottery, a perfunctory, tuneless chant that had been rattled off duly each year; some people believed that the official of the lottery used to stand just so when he said or sang it, others believed that he was supposed to walk among the people, but years and years ago this part of the ritual had been allowed to lapse. There had been, also, a ritual salute, which the official of the lottery had had to use in addressing each person who came up to draw from the box, but this also had changed with time, until now it was felt necessary only for the official to speak to each person approaching. Mr. Summers was very good at all this; in his clean white shirt and blue jeans, with one hand resting carelessly on the black box, he seemed very proper and important as he talked interminably to Mr. Graves and the Martins.

Just as Mr. Summers finally left off talking and turned to the assembled villagers, Mrs. Hutchinson came hurriedly along the path to the square, her sweater thrown over her shoulders, and slid into place in the back of the crowd. "Clean forgot what day it was," she said to Mrs. Delacroix, who stood next to her and they both laughed softly. "Thought my old man was out back stacking wood," Mrs. Hutchinson went on, "and then I looked out the window and the kids was gone, and then I remembered it was the twenty-seventh and came a-running." She dried her hands on her apron, and Mrs. Delacroix said, "You're in time, though. They're still talking away up there."

Mrs. Hutchinson craned her neck to see through the crowd and found her husband and children standing near the front. She tapped Mrs. Delacroix on the arm as a farewell and began to make her way through the crowd. The people separated good-humoredly to let her through; two or three people said, in voices just loud enough to be heard across the crowd, "Here comes your Missus, Hutchinson," and "Bill, she made it after all." Mrs. Hutchinson reached her husband, and Mr. Summers, who had been waiting, said cheerfully, "Thought we were going to have to get on without you, Tessie," Mrs. Hutchinson said, grinning, "Wouldn't have me leave m'dishes in the sink, now, would you, Joe?," and soft laughter ran through the crowd as the people stirred back into position after Mrs. Hutchinson's arrival.

"Well, now," Mr. Summers said soberly, "guess we better get started, get this over with, so's we can go back to work. Anybody ain't here?"

"Dunbar," several people said. "Dunbar, Dunbar."

Mr. Summers consulted his list. "Clyde Dunbar," he said. "That's right. He's broke his leg, hasn't he? Who's drawing for him?"

"Me, I guess," a woman said, and Mr. Summers turned to look at her. "Wife draws for her husband," Mr. Summers said. "Don't you have a grown boy to do it for you, Janey?" Although Mr. Summers and everyone else in the village knew the answer perfectly well, it was the business of the official of the lottery to ask such questions formally. Mr. Summers waited with an expression of polite interest while Mrs. Dunbar answered.

"Horace's not but sixteen yet," Mrs. Dunbar said regretfully. "Guess I gotta fill in for the old man this year."

"Right," Mr. Summers said. He made a note on the list he was holding. Then he asked, "Watson boy drawing this year?"

A tall boy in the crowd raised his hand. "Here," he said. "I'm drawing for m'mother and me." He blinked his eyes nervously and ducked his head as several voices in the crowd said things like "Good fellow, Jack," and "Glad to see your mother's got a man to do it."

"Well," Mr. Summers said, "guess that's everyone. Old Man Warner make it?"

"Here," a voice said, and Mr. Summers nodded.

A sudden hush fell on the crowd as Mr. Summers cleared his throat and looked at the list. "All ready?" he called. "Now, I'll read the names — heads of families first — and the men come up and take a paper out of the box. Keep the paper folded in your hand without looking at it until everyone has had a turn. Everything clear?"

The people had done it so many times that they only half listened to the directions; most of them were quiet, wetting their lips, not looking around. Then Mr. Summers raised one hand high and said, "Adams." A man disengaged himself from the crowd and came forward. "Hi, Steve," Mr. Summers said, and Mr. Adams said, "Hi, Joe." They grinned at one another humorlessly and nervously. Then Mr. Adams reached into the black box and took out a folded paper. He held it firmly by one corner as he turned and went hastily back to his place in the crowd, where he stood a little apart from his family, not looking down at his hand.

"Allen," Mr. Summers said, "Anderson.... Bentham."

"Seems like there's no time at all between lotteries any more," Mrs. Delacroix said to Mrs.

Graves in the back row. "Seems like we got through with the last one only last week."

"Time sure goes fast," Mrs Graves said.

"Clark.... Delacroix."

"There goes my old man," Mrs. Delacroix said. She held her breath while her husband went forward.

"Dunbar," Mr. Summers said, and Mrs. Dunbar went steadily to the box while one of the women said, "Go on, Janey," and another said, "There she goes."

"We're next," Mrs. Graves said. She watched while Mr. Graves came around from the side of the box, greeted Mr. Summers gravely, and selected a slip of paper from the box. By now, all through the crowd there were men holding the small folded papers in their large hands, turning them over and over nervously. Mrs. Dunbar and her two sons stood together, Mrs. Dunbar holding the slip of paper.

"Harburt.... Hutchinson."

"Get up there, Bill," Mrs. Hutchinson said, and the people near her laughed.

"Jones."

"They do say," Mr. Adams said to Old Man Warner, who stood next to him, "that over in the north village they're talking of giving up the lottery."

Old Man Warner snorted. "Pack of crazy fools," he said. "Listening to the young folks, nothing's good enough for *them*. Next thing you know, they'll be wanting to go back to living in caves, nobody work any more, live *that* way for a while. Used to be a saying about 'Lottery in June, corn be heavy soon.' First thing you know, we'd all be eating stewed chickweed and acorns. There's *always* been a lottery," he added petulantly. "Bad enough to see young Joe Summers up there joking with everybody."

"Some places have already quit lotteries," Mrs. Adams said.

"Nothing but trouble in *that*," Old Man Warner said stoutly. "Pack of young fools."

"Martin." And Bobby Martin watched his father go forward. "Overdyke.... Percy."

"I wish they'd hurry," Mrs. Dunbar said to her older son. "I wish they'd hurry."

"They're almost through," her son said.

"You get ready to run tell Dad," Mrs. Dunbar said.

Mr. Summers called his own name and then stepped forward precisely and selected a slip from the box. Then he called, "Warner."

"Seventy-seventh year I been in the lottery," Old Man Warner said as he went through the crowd. "Seventy-seventh time."

"Watson." The tall boy came awkwardly through the crowd. Someone said, "Don't be nervous, Jack," and Mr. Summers said, "Take your time, son."

"Zanini."

After that, there was a long pause, a breathless pause, until Mr. Summers, holding his slip of paper in the air, said, "All right, fellows." For a minute, no one moved, and then all the slips of paper were opened. Suddenly, all the women began to speak at once, saying, "Who is it?," "Who's got it?," "Is it the Dunbars?," "Is it the Watsons?" Then the voices began to say, "It's Hutchinson. It's Bill," "Bill Hutchinson's got it."

"Go tell you father," Mrs. Dunbar said to her older son.

People began to look around to see the Hutchinsons. Bill Hutchinson was standing quiet, staring down at the paper in his hand. Suddenly, Tessie Hutchinson shouted to Mr. Summers, "You didn't give him time enough to take any paper he wanted. I saw you. It wasn't fair!"

"Be a good sport, Tessie," Mrs. Delacroix called, and Mrs. Graves said, "All of us took the same chance."

"Shut up, Tessie," Bill Hutchinson said.

"Well, everyone," Mr. Summers said, "that was done pretty fast, and now we've got to be hurrying a little more to get done in time." He consulted his next list. "Bill," he said, "you draw for the Hutchinson family. You got any other households in the Hutchinsons?"

"There's Don and Eva," Mrs. Hutchinson yelled. "Make *them* take their chance!"

"Daughters draw with their husbands' families, Tessie," Mr. Summers said gently. "You know that as well as anyone else."

"It wasn't *fair*," Tessie said.

"I guess not, Joe," Bill Hutchinson said regretfully. "My daughter draws with her husband's family, that's only fair. And I've got no other family except the kids."

"Then, as far as drawing for families is concerned, it's you," Mr. Summers said in explanation, "and as far as drawing for households is concerned, that's you, too. Right?"

"Right," Bill Hutchinson said.

"How many kids, Bill?" Mr. Summers asked formally.

"Three," Bill Hutchinson said. "There's Bill Jr., and Nancy, and little Dave. And Tessie and me."

"All right, then," Mr. Summers said. "Harry, you got their tickets back?"

Mr. Graves nodded and held up the slips of paper. "Put them in the box, then," Mr. Summers directed. "Take Bill's and put it in."

"I think we ought to start over," Mrs. Hutchinson said, as quietly as she could. "I tell you it wasn't *fair*. You didn't give him time enough to choose. *Every*body saw that."

Mr. Graves had selected the five slips and put them in the box, and he dropped all the papers but those onto the ground, where the breeze caught them and lifted them off.

"Listen, everybody," Mrs. Hutchinson was saying to the people around her.

"Ready, Bill?" Mr. Summers asked, and Bill Hutchinson, with one quick glance around at his wife and children, nodded.

"Remember," Mr. Summers said, "take the slips and keep them folded until each person has taken one. Harry, you help little Dave." Mr. Graves took the hand of the little boy, who came willingly with him up to the box. "Take a paper out of the box, Davy," Mr. Summers said. Davy put his hand into the box and laughed. "Take just *one* paper," Mr. Summers said. "Harry, you hold it for him." Mr. Graves took the child's hand and removed the folded paper from the tight fist and held it while little Dave stood next to him and looked up at him wonderingly.

"Nancy next," Mr. Summers said. Nancy was twelve, and her school friends breathed heavily as she went forward, switching her skirt, and took a slip daintily from the box. "Bill, Jr.," Mr. Summers said, and Billy, his face red and his feet overlarge, nearly knocked the box over as he got a paper out. "Tessie," Mr. Summers said. She hesitated for a minute, looking around defiantly, and then set her lips and went up to the box. She snatched a paper out and held it behind her.

"Bill," Mr. Summers said, and Bill Hutchinson reached into the box and felt around, bringing his hand out at last with the slip of paper in it.

The crowd was quiet. A girl whispered, "I hope it's not Nancy," and the sound of the whisper reached the edges of the crowd.

"It's not the way it used to be," Old Man Warner said clearly. "People ain't the way they used to be."

"All right," Mr. Summers said. "Open the papers. Harry, you open little Dave's."

Mr. Graves opened the slip of paper and there was a general sigh through the crowd as he held it up and everyone could see that it was blank. Nancy and Bill, Jr., opened theirs at the same time, and both beamed and laughed, turning around to the crowd and holding their slips of paper above their heads.

"Tessie," Mr. Summers said. There was a pause, and then Mr. Summers looked at Bill Hutchinson, and Bill unfolded his paper and showed it. It was blank.

"It's Tessie," Mr. Summers said, and his voice was hushed. "Show us her paper, Bill."

Bill Hutchinson went over to his wife and forced the slip of paper out of her hand. It had a black spot on it, the black spot Mr. Summers had made the night before with the heavy pencil in the coal-company office. Bill Hutchinson held it up, and there was a stir in the crowd.

"All right, folks," Mr. Summers said. "Let's finish quickly."

Although the villagers had forgotten the ritual and lost the original black box, they still remembered to use stones. The pile of stones the boys had made earlier was ready; there were stones on the ground with the blowing scraps of paper that had come out of the box. Mrs. Delacroix selected a stone so large she had to pick it up with both hands and turned to Mrs. Dunbar. "Come on," she said. "Hurry up."

Mrs. Dunbar had small stones in both hands, and she said, gasping for breath, "I can't run at all. You'll have to go ahead and I'll catch up with you."

The children had stones already, and someone gave little Davy Hutchinson a few pebbles.

Tessie Hutchinson was in the center of a cleared space by now, and she held her hands out desperately as the villagers moved in on her. "It isn't fair," she said. A stone hit her on the side of the head.

Old Man Warner was saying, "Come on, come on, everyone." Steve Adams was in the front of the crowd of villagers, with Mrs. Graves beside him.

"It isn't fair, it isn't right," Mrs. Hutchinson screamed, and then they were upon her.

HENRY JAMES

The Tree of Knowledge

I

It was one of the secret opinions, such as we all have, of Peter Brench that his main success in life would have consisted in his never having committed himself about the work, as it was called, of his friend Morgan Mallow. This was a subject on which it was, to the best of his belief, impossible with veracity to quote him, and it was nowhere on record that he had, in the connexion, on any occasion and in any embarrassment, either lied or spoken the truth. Such a triumph had its honour even for a man of other triumphs — a man who had reached fifty, who had escaped marriage, who had lived within his means, who had been in love with Mrs. Mallow for years without breathing it, and who, last not least, had judged himself once for all. He had so judged himself in fact that he felt an extreme and general humility to be his proper portion; yet there was nothing that made him think so well of his parts as the course he had steered so often through the shallows just mentioned. It became thus a real wonder that the friends in whom he had most confidence were just those with whom he had most reserves. He couldn't tell Mrs. Mallow — or at least he supposed, excellent man, he couldn't — that she was the one beautiful reason he had never married; any more than he could tell her husband that the sight of the multiplied marbles in that gentleman's studio was an affliction of which even time had never blunted the edge. His victory, however, as I have intimated, in regard to these productions, was not simply in his not having let it out that he deplored them; it was, remarkably, in his not having kept it in by anything else.

The whole situation, among these good people, was verily a marvel, and there was probably not such another for a long way from the spot that engages us — the point at which the soft declivity of Hampstead began at that time to confess in broken accents to Saint John's Wood. He despised Mallow's statues and adored Mallow's wife, and yet was distinctly fond of Mallow, to whom, in turn, he was equally dear. Mrs. Mallow rejoiced in the statues — though she preferred, when pressed, the busts; and if she was visibly attached to Peter Brench it was because of his affection for Morgan. Each loved the other moreover for the love borne in each case to Lancelot, whom the Mallows respectively cherished as their only child and whom the friend of their fireside identified as the third — but decidedly the handsomest — of his godsons. Already in the old years it had come to that — that no one, for such a relation, could possibly have occurred to any of them, even to the baby itself, but Peter. There was luckily a certain independence, of the pecuniary sort, all round: the Master could never otherwise have spent his solemn *Wanderjahre* in Florence and Rome, and continued by the Thames as well as by the Arno and the Tiber to add unpurchased group to group and model, for what was too apt to prove in the event mere love, fancy-heads of celebrities either too busy or too buried — too much of the age or too little of it — to sit. Neither could Peter, lounging in almost daily, have found time to keep the whole complicated tradition so alive by his presence. He was massive but mild, the depositary of these mysteries — large and loose and ruddy and curly, with deep tones, deep eyes, deep pockets, to say nothing of the habit of long pipes, soft hats and brownish greyish weather-faded clothes, apparently always the same.

He had "written," it was known, but had never spoken, never spoken in particular of that; and he had the air (since, as was believed, he continued to write) of keeping it up in order to have something more — as if he hadn't at the worst enough — to be silent about. Whatever his air, at any rate, Peter's occasional unmentioned prose and verse were quite truly the result of an impulse to maintain the purity of his taste by establishing still more firmly the right relation of fame to feebleness. The little green door of his domain was in a garden-wall on which the discoloured stucco made patches, and in the small detached villa behind it everything was old, the furniture, the servants, the books, the prints, the immemorial habits and the new improvements. The Mallows, at Carrara Lodge, were within ten minutes, and the studio there was on their little land, to which they had added, in their happy faith, for building it. This was the good fortune, if it was not the ill, of her having brought him in marriage a portion that put them in a manner at their ease and enabled them thus, on their side, to keep it up. And they did keep it up — they always had — the infatuated sculptor and his wife, for whom nature had refined on the impossible by relieving them of the sense of the difficult. Morgan had at all events everything of the sculptor but the spirit of Phidias — the brown velvet, the becoming *beretto*, the "plastic" presence, the fine fingers, the beautiful accent in Italian and the old Italian factotum. He seemed to make up for everything when he addressed Egidio with the "tu" and waved him to turn one of the rotary pedestals of which the place was full. They were tremendous Italians at Carrara Lodge, and the secret of the part played by this fact in Peter's life was in a large degree that it gave him, sturdy Briton as he was, just the amount of "going abroad" he could bear. The Mallows were all his Italy, but it was in a measure for Italy he liked them. His one worry was that Lance — to which they had shortened his godson — was, in spite of a public school, perhaps a shade too Italian. Morgan meanwhile looked like somebody's flattering idea of somebody's own person as expressed in the great room provided at the Uffizzi Museum for the general illustration of that idea by eminent hands. The Master's sole regret that he hadn't been born rather to the brush than to the chisel sprang from his wish that he might have contributed to that collection.

It appeared with time at any rate to be to the brush that Lance had been born; for Mrs. Mallow, one day when the boy was turning twenty, broke it to their friend, who shared, to the last delicate morsel, their problems and pains, that it seemed as if nothing would really do but that he should embrace the career. It had been impossible longer to remain blind to the fact that he was gaining no glory at Cambridge, where Brench's own college had for a year tempered its tone to him as for Brench's own sake. Therefore why renew the vain form of preparing him for the impossible? The impossible — it had become clear — was that he should be anything but an artist.

"Oh dear, dear!" said poor Peter.

"Don't you believe in it?" asked Mrs. Mallow, who still, at more than forty, had her violet velvet eyes, her creamy satin skin and her silken chestnut hair.

"Believe in what?"

"Why in Lance's passion."

"I don't know what you mean by 'believing in it.' I've never been unaware, certainly, of his disposition, from his earliest time, to daub and draw; but I confess I've hoped it would burn out."

"But why should it," she sweetly smiled, "with his wonderful heredity? Passion is passion — though of course indeed *you*, dear Peter, know nothing of that. Has the Master's ever burned out?"

Peter looked off a little and, in his familiar formless way, kept up for a moment a sound between a smothered whistle and a subdued hum. "Do you think he's going to be another Master?"

She seemed scarce prepared to go that length, yet she had on the whole a marvellous trust. "I know what you mean by that. Will it be a career to incur the jealousies and provoke the machinations that have been at times almost too much for his father? Well — say it may be, since nothing but clap-trap, in these dreadful days, *can*, it would seem, make its way, and since, with the curse of refinement and distinction, one may easily find one's self begging one's bread. Put it at the worst — say he *has* the misfortune to wing his flight further than the vulgar taste of his stupid countrymen can follow. Think, all the same, of the happiness — the same the Master has had. He'll *know*."

Peter looked rueful. "Ah, but *what* will he know?"

"Quiet joy!" cried Mrs. Mallow, quite impatient and turning away.

II

He had of course before long to meet the boy himself on it and to hear that practically everything was settled. Lance was not to go up again, but to go instead to Paris where, since the die was cast, he would find the best advantages. Peter had always felt he must be taken as he was, but had never perhaps found him so much of that pattern as on this occasion. "You chuck Cambridge then altogether? Doesn't that seem rather a pity?"

Lance would have been like his father, to his friend's sense, had he had less humour, and like his mother had he had more beauty. Yet it was a good middle way for Peter that, in the modern manner, he was, to the eye, rather the young stockbroker than the young artist. The youth reasoned that it was a question of time — there was such a mill to go through, such an awful lot to learn. He had talked with fellows and had judged. "One has got, to-day," he said, "don't you see? to know."

His interlocutor, at this, gave a groan. "Oh hang it, *don't* know!"

Lance wondered. "'Don't'? Then what's the use — ?"

"The use of what?"

"Why of anything. Don't you think I've talent?"

Peter smoked away for a little in silence; then went on: "It isn't knowledge, it's ignorance that — as we've been beautifully told — is bliss."

"Don't you think I've talent?" Lance repeated.

Peter, with his trick of queer kind demonstrations, passed his arm round his godson and held him a moment. "How do I know?"

"Oh," said the boy, "if it's your own ignorance you're defending —!"

Again, for a pause, on the sofa, his godfather smoked. "It isn't. I've the misfortune to be omniscient."

"Oh well," Lance laughed again, "if you know *too* much —!"

"That's what I do, and it's why I'm so wretched."

Lance's gaiety grew. "Wretched? Come, I say!"

"But I forgot," his companion went on —"you're not to know about that. It would indeed for you to make the too much. Only I'll tell you what I'll do." And Peter got up from the sofa. "If you'll go up again I'll pay your way at Cambridge."

Lance stared, a little rueful in spite of being still more amused. "Oh Peter! You disapprove so of Paris?"

"Well, I'm afraid of it."

"Ah I see!"

"No, you don't see — yet. But you will — that is you would. And you mustn't."

The young man thought more gravely. "But one's innocence, already —!"

"Is considerably damaged? Ah that won't matter," Peter persisted — "we'll patch it up here."

"Here? Then you want me to stay at home?"

Peter almost confessed to it. "Well, we're so right — we four together — just as we are. We're so safe. Come, don't spoil it."

The boy, who had turned to gravity, turned from this, on the real pressure in his friend's tone, to consternation. "Then what's a fellow to be?"

"My particular care. Come, old man" — and Peter now fairly pleaded — "I'll look out for you."

Lance, who had remained on the sofa with his legs out and his hands in his pockets, watched him with eyes that showed suspicion. Then he got up. "You think there's something the matter with me — that I can't make a success."

"Well, what do you call a success?"

Lance thought again. "Why the best sort, I suppose, is to please one's self. Isn't that the sort that, in spite of cabals and things, is — in his own peculiar line — the Master's?"

There were so much too many things in this question to be answered at once that they practically checked the discussion, which became particularly difficult in the light of such renewed proof that, though the young man's innocence might, in the course of his studies, as he contended, somewhat have shrunken, the finer essence of it still remained. That was indeed exactly what Peter had assumed and what above all he desired; yet perversely enough it gave him a chill. The boy believed in the cabals and things, believed in the peculiar line, believed, to be brief, in the Master. What happened a month or two later wasn't that he went up again at the expense of his godfather, but that a fortnight after he had got settled in Paris this personage sent him fifty pounds.

He had meanwhile at home, this personage, made up his mind to the worst; and what that might be had never yet grown quite so vivid to him as when, on his presenting himself one Sunday night, as he never failed to do, for supper, the mistress of Carrara Lodge met him with an appeal as to — of all things in the world — the wealth of the Canadians. She was earnest, she was even excited. "Are many of them *really* rich?"

He had to confess he knew nothing about them, but he often thought afterwards of that evening. The room in which they sat was adorned with sundry specimens of the Master's genius, which had the merit of being, as Mrs. Mallow herself frequently suggested, of an unusually convenient size. They were indeed of dimensions not customary in the products of the chisel, and they had the singularity that, if the objects and features intended to be small looked too large, the objects and features intended to be large looked too small. The Master's idea, either in respect to this matter or to any other, had in almost any case, even after years, remained undiscoverable to Peter Brench. The creations that so failed to reveal it stood about on pedestals and brackets, on tables and shelves, a little staring white population, heroic, idyllic, allegoric, mythic, symbolic, in which "scale" had so strayed and lost itself that the public square and the chimney-piece seemed to have changed places, the monumental being all diminutive and the diminutive all monumental; branches at any rate, markedly, of a family in which stature was rather oddly irrespective of function, age and sex. They formed, like the Mallows themselves, poor Brench's own family — having at least to such a degree the note of familiarity. The occasion was one of those he had long ago learnt to know and to name — short flickers of the faint flame, soft gusts of a kinder air. Twice a year regularly the Master believed in his fortune, in addition to believing all the year round in his genius. This time it was to be made by a bereaved couple from Toronto, who had given him the handsomest order for a tomb to three lost children, each of whom they desired to see, in the composition, emblematically and characteristically represented.

Such was naturally the moral of Mrs. Mallow's question: if their wealth was to be assumed, it was clear, from the nature of their admiration, as well as from mysterious hints thrown out (they were a little odd!) as to other possibilities of the same mortuary sort, that their further patronage might be; and not less evident that should the Master become at all known in those climes nothing would be more inevitable than a run of Canadian custom. Peter had been present before at runs of custom, colonial and domestic — present at each of those of which the aggregation had left so few gaps in the marble company round him; but it was his habit never at these junctures to prick the bubble in advance. The fond illusion, while it lasted, eased the wound of elections never won, the long ache of medals and diplomas carried off, on every chance, by every one but the Master; it moreover lighted the lamp that would glimmer through the next eclipse. They lived, however, after all — as it was always beautiful to see — at a height scarce susceptible of ups and downs. They strained a point at times charmingly, strained it to admit that the public was here and there not too bad to buy; but they would have been nowhere without their attitude that the Master was always too good to sell. They were at all events deliciously formed, Peter often said to himself, for their fate; the Master had a vanity, his wife had a loyalty, of which success, depriving these things of innocence, would have diminished the merit and the grace. Any one could be charming under a charm, and as he looked about him at a world of prosperity more void of proportion even than the Master's museum he wondered if he knew another pair that so completely escaped vulgarity.

"What a pity Lance isn't with us to rejoice!" Mrs. Mallow on this occasion sighed at supper.

"We'll drink to the health of the absent," her husband replied, filling his friend's glass and his own and giving a drop to their companion; "but we must hope he's preparing himself for a happiness much less like this of ours this evening — excusable as I grant it to be! — than like the comfort we have always (whatever has happened or has not happened) been able to trust ourselves to enjoy. The comfort," the Master explained, leaning back in the pleasant lamplight and firelight, holding up his glass and looking round at his marble family, quartered more or less, a monstrous brood, in every room — "the comfort of an art in itself!"

Peter looked a little shyly at his wine. "Well — I don't care what you may call it when a fellow doesn't — but Lance must learn to *sell*, you know. I drink to his acquisition of the secret of a base popularity!"

"Oh yes, *he* must sell," the boy's mother, who was still more, however, this seemed to give out, the Master's wife, rather artlessly allowed.

"Ah," the sculptor after a moment confidently pronounced, "Lance *will*. Don't be afraid. He'll have learnt."

"Which is exactly what Peter," Mrs. Mallow gaily returned — "why in the world were you so perverse, Peter? — wouldn't when he told him hear of."

Peter, when this lady looked at him with accusatory affection — a grace on her part not infrequent — could never find a word; but the Master, who was always all amenity and tact, helped him out now as he had often helped him before. "That's his old idea, you know — on which we've so often differed: his theory that the artist should be all impulse and instinct. *I* go in of course for a certain amount of school. Not too much — but a due proportion. There's where his protest came in," he continued to explain to his wife, "as against what *might*, don't you see? be in question for Lance."

"Ah well" — and Mrs. Mallow turned the violet eyes across the table at the subject of this discourse — "he's sure to have meant of course nothing but good. Only that wouldn't have prevented him, if Lance *had* taken his advice, from being in effect horribly cruel."

They had a sociable way of talking to him to his face as if he had been in the clay or — at most — in the plaster, and the Master was unfailingly generous. He might have been waving Egidio to make him revolve. "Ah but poor Peter wasn't so wrong as to what it may after all come to that he *will* learn."

"Oh but nothing artistically bad," she urged — still, for poor Peter, arch and dewy.

"Why just the little French tricks," said the Master: on which their friend had to pretend to admit, when pressed by Mrs. Mallow, that these aesthetic vices had been the objects of his dread.

III

"I know now," Lance said to him the next year, "why you were so much against it." He had come back supposedly for a mere interval and was looking about him at Carrara Lodge, where indeed he had already on two or three occasions since his expatriation briefly reappeared. This had the air of a longer holiday. "Something rather awful has happened to me. It *isn't* so very good to know."

"I'm bound to say high spirits don't show in your face," Peter was rather ruefully forced to confess. "Still, are you very sure you do know?"

"Well, I at least know about as much as I can bear." These remarks were exchanged in Peter's den, and the young man, smoking cigarettes, stood before the fire with his back against the mantel. Something of his bloom seemed really to have left him.

Poor Peter wondered. "You're clear then as to what in particular I wanted you not to go for?"

"In particular?" Lance thought. "It seems to me that in particular there can have been only one thing."

They stood for a little sounding each other. "Are you quite sure?"

"Quite sure I'm a beastly duffer? Quite — by this time."

"Oh!" — and Peter turned away as if almost with relief.

"It's *that* that isn't pleasant to find out."

"Oh I don't care for 'that,'" said Peter, presently coming round again. "I mean I personally don't."

"Yet I hope you can understand a little that I myself should!"

"Well, what do you mean by it?" Peter sceptically asked.

And on this Lance had to explain — how the upshot of his studies in Paris had inexorably proved a mere deep doubt of his means. These studies had so waked him up that a new light was in his eyes; but what the new light did was really to show him too much. "Do you know what's the matter with me? I'm too horribly intelligent. Paris was really the last place for me. I've learnt what I can't do."

Poor Peter stared — it was a staggerer; but even after they had had, on the subject, a longish talk in which the boy brought out to the full the hard truth of his lesson, his friend betrayed less pleasure than usually breaks into a face to the happy tune of "I told you so!" Poor Peter himself made now indeed so little a point of having told him so that Lance broke ground in a different place a day or two after. "What was it then that — before I went — you were afraid I should find out?" This, however, Peter refused to tell him — on the ground that if he hadn't yet guessed perhaps he never would, and that in any case nothing at all for either of them was to be gained by giving the thing a name. Lance eyed him on this an instant with the bold curiosity of youth — with the air indeed of having in his mind two or three names, of which one or other would be right. Peter nevertheless, turning his back again, offered no encouragement, and when they parted afresh it was with some show of impatience on the side of the boy. Accordingly on their next encounter Peter saw at a glance that he had now, in the interval, devined and that, to sound his note, he was only waiting till they should find themselves alone. This he had soon arranged and he then broke straight out. "Do you know your conundrum has been keeping me awake? But in the watches of the night the answer came over me — so that, upon my honour, I quite laughed out. Had you been supposing I had to go to Paris to learn *that*?" Even now, to see him still so sublimely on his guard, Peter's young friend had to laugh afresh. "You won't give a sign till you're sure? Beautiful old Peter!" But Lance at last produced it. "Why, hang it, the truth about the Master."

It made between them for some minutes a lively passage, full of wonder for each at the wonder of the other. "Then how long have you understood —"

"The true value of his work? I understood it," Lance recalled, "as soon as I began to understand anything. But I didn't begin fully to do that, I admit, till I got *là-bas*."

"Dear, dear!" — Peter gasped with retrospective dread.

"But for what have you taken me? I'm a hopeless muff — that I *had* to have rubbed in. But I'm not such a muff as the Master!" Lance declared.

"Then why did you never tell me —?"

"That I hadn't after all" — the boy took him up — "remained such an idiot? Just because I never dreamed *you* knew. But I beg your pardon. I only wanted to spare you. And what I don't now understand is how the deuce then for so long you've managed to keep bottled."

Peter produced his explanation, but only after some delay and with a gravity not void of embarrassment. "It was for your mother."

"Oh!" said Lance.

"And that's the great thing now — since the murder *is* out. I want a promise from you. I mean" — and Peter almost feverishly followed it up — "a vow from you, solemn and such as you owe me here on the spot, that you'll sacrifice anything rather than let her ever guess —"

"That *I've* guessed?" — Lance took it in. "I see." He evidently after a moment had taken in much. "But what is it you've in mind that I may have a chance to sacrifice?"

"Oh one has always something."

Lance looked at him hard. "Do you mean that *you've* had —?" The look he received back, however, so put the question by that he found soon enough another. "Are you really sure my mother doesn't know?"

Peter, after renewed reflexion, was really sure. "If she does she's too wonderful."

"But aren't we all too wonderful?"

"Yes," Peter granted — "but in different ways. The thing's so desperately important because your father's little public consists only, as you know then," Peter developed — "well, of how many?"

"First of all," the Master's son risked, "of himself. And last of all too. I don't quite see of whom else."

Peter had an approach to impatience. "Of your mother, I say — *always*."

Lance cast it all up. "You absolutely feel that?"

"Absolutely."

"Well then with yourself that makes three."

"Oh *me*!" — and Peter, with a wag of his kind old head, modestly excused himself. "The number's at any rate small enough for any individual dropping out to be too dreadfully missed. Therefore, to put it in a nutshell, take care, my boy — that's all — that *you're* not!"

"I've got to keep on humbugging?" Lance wailed.

"It's just to warn you of the danger of your failing of that that I've seized this opportunity."

"And what do you regard in particular," the young man asked, "as the danger?"

"Why this certainty: that the moment your mother, who feels so strongly, should suspect your secret — well," said Peter desperately, "the fat would be on the fire."

Lance for a moment seemed to stare at the blaze. "She'd throw me over?"

"She'd throw *him* over."

"And come round to us?"

Peter, before he answered, turned away. "Come round to *you*." But he had said enough to indicate — and, as he evidently trusted, to avert — the horrid contingency.

IV

Within six months again, none the less, his fear was on more occasions than one all before him. Lance had returned to Paris for another trial; then had reappeared at home and had had, with his father, for the first time in his life, one of the scenes that strike sparks. He described it with much expression to Peter, touching whom (since they had never done so before) it was the sign of a new reserve on the part of the pair at Carrara Lodge that they at present failed, on a matter of intimate interest, to open themselves — if not in joy then in sorrow — to their good friend. This produced perhaps practically between the parties a shade of alienation and a slight intermission of commerce — marked mainly indeed by the fact that to talk at his ease with his old playmate Lance had in general to come to see him. The closest if not quite the gayest relation they had yet known together was thus ushered in. The difficulty for poor Lance was a tension at home — begotten by the fact that his father wished him to be at least the sort of success he himself had been. He hadn't "chucked" Paris — though nothing appeared more vivid to him than that Paris had chucked him: he would go back again because of the fascination in trying, in seeing, in sounding the depths — in learning one's lesson, briefly, even if the lesson were simply that of one's impotence in the presence of one's larger vision. But what did the Master, all aloft in his senseless fluency, know of impotence, and what vision — to be called such — had he in all his blind life ever had? Lance, heated and indignant, frankly appealed to his godparent on this score.

His father, it appeared, had come down on him for having, after so long, nothing to show, and hoped that on his next return this deficiency would be repaired. *The* thing, the Master complacently set forth was — for any artist, however inferior to himself — at least to "do" something. "What can you do? That's all I ask!" *He* had certainly done enough, and there was no mistake about what he had to show. Lance had tears in his eyes when it came thus to letting his old friend know how great the strain might be on the "sacrifice" asked of him. It wasn't so easy to continue humbugging — as from son to parent — after feeling one's self despised for not grovelling in mediocrity. Yet a noble duplicity was what, as they intimately faced the situation, Peter went on requiring; and it was still for a time what his young friend, bitter and sore, managed loyally to comfort him with. Fifty pounds more than once again, it was true, rewarded both in London and in Paris the young friend's loyalty; none the less sensibly, doubtless, at the moment, that the money was a direct advance on a decent sum for which Peter had long since privately prearranged an ultimate function. Whether by these arts or others, at all events, Lance's just resentment was kept for a season — at bay. The day arrived when he warned his companion that he could hold out — or hold in — no longer. Carrara Lodge had had to listen to another lecture delivered from a great height — an infliction really heavier at last than, without striking back or in some way letting the Master have the truth, flesh and blood could bear.

"And what I don't see is," Lance observed with a certain irritated eye for what was after all, if it came to that, owing to himself too; "what I don't see is, upon my honour, how *you*, as things are going, can keep the game up."

"Oh the game for me is only to hold my tongue," said placid Peter. "And I have my reason."

"Still my mother?"

Peter showed a queer face as he had often shown it before — that is by turning it straight away. "What will you have? I haven't ceased to like her."

"She's beautiful — she's a dear of course," Lance allowed; "but what is she to you, after all, and what is it to you that, as to anything whatever, she should or she shouldn't?"

Peter, who had turned red, hung fire a little. "Well — it's all simply what I make of it."

There was now, however, in his young friend a strange, an adopted insistence. "What are you after all to *her*?"

"Oh nothing. But that's another matter."

"She cares only for my father," said Lance the Parisian.

"Naturally — and that's just why."

"Why you've wished to spare her?"

"Because she cares so tremendously much."

Lance took a turn about the room, but with his eyes still on his host. "How awfully — always — you must have liked her!"

"Awfully. Always," said Peter Brench.

The young man continued for a moment to muse — then stopped again in front of him. "Do you know how much she cares?" Their eyes met on it, but Peter, as if his own found something new in Lance's, appeared to hesitate, for the first time in an age, to say he did know. "*I've* only just found out," said Lance. "She came to my room last night, after being present, in silence and only with her eyes on me, at what I had had to take from him: she came — and she was with me an extraordinary hour."

He had paused again and they had again for a while sounded each other. Then something — and it made him suddenly turn pale — came to Peter. "She *does* know?"

"She does know. She let it all out to me — so as to demand of me no more than 'that,' as she said, of which she herself had been capable. She has always known," said Lance without pity.

Peter was silent a long time; during which his companion might have heard him gently breathe, and on touching him might have felt within him the vibration of a long low sound suppressed. By the time he spoke at last he had taken everything in. "Then I do see how tremendously much."

"Isn't it wonderful?" Lance asked.

"Wonderful," Peter mused.

"So that if your original effort to keep me from Paris was to keep me from knowledge —!" Lance exclaimed as if with a sufficient indication of this futility.

It might have been at the futility Peter appeared for a little to gaze. "I think it must have been — without my quite at the time knowing it — to keep *me*!" he replied at last as he turned away.

JAMES JOYCE

Araby

North Richmond Street, being blind, was a quiet street except at the hour when the Christian Brothers' School set the boys free. An uninhabited house of two storeys stood at the blind end, detached from its neighbours in a square ground. The other houses of the street, conscious of decent lives within them, gazed at one another with brown imperturbable faces.

The former tenant of our house, a priest, had died in the back drawing-room. Air, musty from having been long enclosed, hung in all the rooms, and the waste room behind the kitchen was littered with old useless papers. Among these I found a few paper-covered books, the pages of which were curled and damp: *The Abbot,* by Walter Scott, *The Devout Communicant* and *The Memoirs of Vidocq.* I liked the last best because its leaves were yellow. The wild garden behind the house contained a central apple-tree and a few straggling bushes under one of which I found the late tenant's rusty bicycle-pump. He had been a very charitable priest; in his will he had left all his money to institutions and the furniture of his house to his sister.

When the short days of winter came dusk fell before we had well eaten our dinners. When we met in the street the houses had grown sombre. The space of sky above us was the colour of ever-changing violet and towards it the lamps of the street lifted their feeble lanterns. The cold air stung us and we played till our bodies glowed. Our shouts echoed in the silent street. The career of our play brought us through the dark muddy lanes behind the houses where we ran the gantlet of the rough tribes from the cottages, to the back doors of the dark dripping gardens where odours arose from the ashpits, to the dark odorous stables where a coachman smoothed and combed the horse or shook music from the buckled harness. When we returned to the street light from the kitchen windows had filled the areas. If my uncle was seen turning the corner we hid in the shadow until we had seen him safely housed. Or if Mangan's sister came out on the doorstep to call her brother in to his tea we watched her from our shadow peer up and down the street. We waited to see whether she would remain or go in and, if she remained, we left our shadow and walked up to Mangan's steps resignedly. She was waiting for us, her figure defined by the light from the half-opened door. Her brother always teased her before he obeyed and I stood by the railings looking at her. Her dress swung as she moved her body and the soft rope of her hair tossed from side to side.

Every morning I lay on the floor in the front parlour watching her door. The blind was pulled down to within an inch of the sash so that I could not be seen. When she came out on the doorstep my heart leaped. I ran to the hall, seized my books and followed her. I kept her brown figure always in my eye and, when we came near the point at which our ways diverged, I quickened my pace and passed her. This happened morning after morning. I had never spoken to her, except for a few casual words, and yet her name was like a summons to all my foolish blood.

Her image accompanied me even in places the most hostile to romance. On Saturday evenings when my aunt went marketing I had to go to carry some of the parcels. We walked through the flaring streets, jostled by drunken men and bargaining women, amid the curses of labourers, the shrill litanies of shop-boys who stood on guard by the barrels of pigs' cheeks, the nasal chanting of street-singers, who sang a *come-all-you* about O'Donovan Rossa, or a ballad about the troubles in our native land. These noises converged in a single sensation of life for me: I imagined that I bore my chalice safely through a throng of foes. Her name sprang to my lips at moments in strange prayers and praises which I myself did not understand. My eyes were often full of tears (I could not tell why) and at times a flood from my heart seemed to pour itself out into my bosom. I thought little of the future. I did not know whether I would ever speak to her or not or, if I spoke to her, how I could tell her of my confused adoration. But my body was like a harp and her words and gestures were like fingers running upon the wires.

One evening I went into the back drawing-room in which the priest had died. It was a dark rainy evening and there was no sound in the house. Through one of the broken panes I heard the rain impinge upon the earth, the fine incessant needles of water playing in the sodden beds. Some distant lamp or lighted window gleamed below me. I was thankful that I could see so little. All my senses seemed to desire to veil themselves and, feeling that I was about to slip from them, I pressed the palms of my hands together until they trembled, murmuring: *O love! O love!* many times.

At last she spoke to me. When she addressed

the first words to me I was so confused that I did not know what to answer. She asked me was I going to *Araby.* I forgot whether I answered yes or no. It would be a splendid bazaar, she said; she would love to go.

— And why can't you? I asked.

While she spoke she turned a silver bracelet round and round her wrist. She could not go, she said, because there would be a retreat that week in her convent. Her brother and two other boys were fighting for their caps and I was alone at the railings. She held one of the spikes, bowing her head towards me. The light from the lamp opposite our door caught the white curve of her neck, lit up her hair that rested there and, falling, lit up the hand upon the railing. It fell over one side of her dress and caught the white border of a petticoat, just visible as she stood at ease.

— It's well for you, she said.

— If I go, I said, I will bring you something.

What innumerable follies laid waste my walking and sleeping thoughts after that evening! I wished to annihilate the tedious intervening days. I chafed against the work of school. At night in my bedroom and by day in the classroom her image came between me and the page I strove to read. The syllables of the word *Araby* were called to me through the silence in which my soul luxuriated and cast an Eastern enchantment over me. I asked for leave to go to the bazaar on Saturday night. My aunt was surprised and hoped it was not some Freemason affair. I answered few questions in class. I watched my master's face pass from amiability to sternness; he hoped I was not beginning to idle. I could not call my wandering thoughts together. I had hardly any patience with the serious work of life which, now that it stood between me and my desire, seemed to me child's play, ugly monotonous child's play.

On Saturday morning I reminded my uncle that I wished to go to the bazaar in the evening. He was fussing at the hallstand, looking for the hatbrush, and answered me curtly:

— Yes, boy, I know.

As he was in the hall I could not go into the front parlour and lie at the window. I left the house in bad humour and walked slowly towards the school. The air was pitilessly raw and already my heart misgave me.

When I came home to dinner my uncle had not yet been home. Still it was early. I sat staring at the clock for some time and, when its ticking began to irritate me, I left the room. I mounted the staircase and gained the upper part of the house. The high cold empty gloomy rooms liberated me and I went from room to room singing. From the front window I saw my companions playing below in the street. Their cries reached me weakened and indistinct and, leaning my forehead against the cool glass, I looked over at the dark house where she lived. I may have stood there for an hour, seeing nothing but the brown-clad figure cast by my imagination, touched discreetly by the lamplight at the curved neck, at the hand upon the railings and at the border below the dress.

When I came downstairs again I found Mrs Mercer sitting at the fire. She was a old garrulous woman, a pawnbroker's widow, who collected used stamps for some pious purpose. I had to endure the gossip of the tea-table. The meal was prolonged beyond an hour and still my uncle did not come. Mrs Mercer stood up to go: she was sorry she couldn't wait any longer, but it was after eight o'clock and she did not like to be out late, as the night air was bad for her. When she had gone I began to walk up and down the room, clenching my fists. My aunt said:

— I'm afraid you may put off your bazaar for this night of Our Lord.

At nine o'clock I heard my uncle's latchkey in the halldoor. I heard him talking to himself and heard the hallstand rocking when it had received the weight of his overcoat. I could interpret these signs. When he was midway through his dinner I asked him to give me the money to go to the bazaar. He had forgotten.

— The people are in bed and after their first sleep now, he said.

I did not smile. My aunt said to him energetically:

— Can't you give him the money and let him go? You've kept him late enough as it is.

My uncle said he was very sorry he had forgotten. He said he believed in the old saying: *All work and no play makes Jack a dull boy.* He asked me where I was going and, when I had told him a second time he asked me did I know *The Arab's Farewell to his Steed.* When I left the kitchen he was about to recite the opening lines of the piece to my aunt.

I held a florin tightly in my hand as I strode down Buckingham Street towards the station. The sight of the streets thronged with buyers and glaring with gas recalled to me the purpose of my journey. I took my seat in a third-class carriage of a deserted train. After an intolerable delay the train moved out of the station slowly. It crept onward among ruinous houses and over the twinkling river. At Westland Row Station a crowd of people pressed to the carriage doors; but the porters moved them back, saying that it was a special train for the bazaar. I remained alone in the bare carriage. In a few minutes the train drew up beside an improvised wooden platform. I passed out on the road and saw by the lighted dial of a clock that it was ten minutes to ten. In front of me was a large building which displayed the magical name.

I could not find any sixpenny entrance and, fearing that the bazaar would be closed, I passed in quickly through a turnstile, handing a shilling to a weary-looking man. I found myself in a big hall girdled at half its height by a gallery. Nearly all the stalls were closed and the greater part of the hall was in darkness. I recognised a silence like that which pervades a church after a service. I walked into the centre of the bazaar timidly. A few people were gathered about the stalls which were still open. Before a curtain, over which the words *Café Chantant* were written in coloured lamps, two men were counting money on a salver. I listened to the fall of the coins.

Remembering with difficulty why I had come I went over to one of the stalls and examined porcelain vases and flowered tea-sets. At the door of the stall a young lady was talking and laughing with two young gentlemen. I remarked their English accents and listened vaguely to their conversation.

— O, I never said such a thing!
— O, but you did!
— O, but I didn't!
— Didn't she say that?
— Yes. I heard her.
— O, there's a ... fib!

Observing me the young lady came over and asked me did I wish to buy anything. The tone of her voice was not encouraging; she seemed to have spoken to me out of a sense of duty. I looked humbly at the great jars that stood like eastern guards at either side of the dark entrance to the stall and murmured.:

— No, thank you.

The young lady changed the position of one of the vases and went back to the two young men. They began to talk of the same subject. Once or twice the young lady glanced at me over her shoulder.

I lingered before her stall, though I knew my stay was useless, to make my interest in her wares seem the more real. Then I turned away slowly and walked down the middle of the bazaar. I allowed the two pennies to fall against the sixpence in my pocket. I heard a voice call from one end of the gallery that the light was out. The upper part of the hall was now completely dark.

Gazing up into the darkness I saw myself as a creature driven and derided by vanity; and my eyes burned with anguish and anger.

W. P. KINSELLA

Dance Me Outside

Little Margaret Wolfchild got murdered down to Wetaskiwin one Saturday night last fall. She wasn't little like most people would think of little. She already eighteen and she got a baby herself about two years ago. She got called Little Margaret because when she born, Moses Wolfchild, what with ten or eleven kids at home, forgot he got a daughter named Margaret. So she is called Little Margaret and the one they got already is Big Margaret. Big Margaret growed up and moved to Calgary five or six years ago and nobody ever heard of her since.

Margaret, she been to the Blue Quills Dance Hall at Hobbema Crossing on Saturday night and sometime after midnight she left with some white guys in a car. They cut her belly with a knife and sort of stuffed her body in a garbage can. Little Margaret she was pretty too. Her face was round and her arms were chubby and she used to wear her hair in braids down her back. She was Robert Coyote's girlfriend when he wasn't off working in the bush.

"I tell you, Silas, we sure as hell gonna have to kill that guy when he get out," Robert says to me.

I don't disagree with Robert Coyote cause he's bigger and older than me and he also waving a very mean looking hunting knife when he say this. Frank and Charlie Fence-post and Eathen Firstrider, they is all there too, and they say we sure as hell gonna kill Clarence Gaskell when he get out of the jail down to Fort Saskatchewan.

After the murder it don't take the RCMP guys long to catch Clarence. Lots of people saw Little Margaret leave in his car. They arrested two other guys with him but let them go cause they said all they did was sit in the car while Clarence and Little Margaret went in the back seat and messed around. Then Little Margaret said something Clarence didn't like and he got mad and killed her. Everybody know Clarence get mean when he drinks. He put the boots to Billy Bigcharles one time and he'd of killed him too if his friends hadn't stopped him. Billy still got a bad arm from that beating.

I don't know much about law even though I go to the Technical School over to Wetaskiwin and I like to read, especially about Indian history. They only charged Clarence with manslaughter. I guess it because Little Margaret was Indian. If she been white it would of been murder for sure. More for sure if it been an Indian guy killed a white girl.

Clarence's Dad, he own the John Deere tractor store in Wetaskiwin, and he hires a lawyer all the way from Calgary. The lawyer's neck folds down over his collar. The jury is all men from Wetaskiwin and there ain't no Indians on it.

They got Clarence's hair cut and dress him up in a suit and tie. And they even bought him a couple of teeth to fill the hole in his face where he had some teeth knocked out in a fight over to the Alice Hotel beer parlour. When the trial starts, Clarence, he look like one of them religious kids that you see in the park — the ones come from the Lutheran College over to Camrose.

We all went and sat in the back row of the courtroom, wearing our jeans and denim jackets and our hair all blown around cause we had to stand on the highway for a long time every day to hitch a ride into town. Eathen Firstrider, he got a car but he can't take it off the reserve for it don't have no license and neither does Eathen.

That lawyer, he get Clarence to tell his story and he helps him along whenever he gets stuck. It go on for an hour or so and it sound like Clarence a really nice guy and Little Margaret is a bad drunk Indian girl.

The lawyer's words sure sound funny come out of Clarence's mouth, cause everybody who know him know that Clarence he can't say two words together without cursing. I bet he don't even know what half the words he is saying mean.

They are big lawyer's words that come out of Clarence but what he say is that him and Margaret get to mess around in the car but when their clothes is off Margaret is laugh at him, and to him that a good enough reason to take his knife and kill her.

"Did he say what I think he say?" Robert asks.

"He say he kill Little Margaret cause she made fun of his cock," says Frank. "I gonna bring the shotgun tomorrow."

Frank Fence-post, he been wanting all along to bring a shotgun right into court and blast Clarence good, but Robert Coyote say no, if anybody gonna kill Clarence it gonna be him, but we wait and see what the court do first.

The lawyer, he talk to the jury like they is little kids and he the school principal. He tell them it okay for Clarence to do what he done cause he know that any one of them would get mad too if somebody made fun of their *manhood.*

Clarence, he blow his nose, wipe his eyes with a big white cloth handkerchief, and cry and carry on while he tell his story. He end it by saying he sorry he done it and he wish everyone should forgive him for make a bad mistake.

If what he say was true I be the first one to agree with him, but we all know it ain't. Little Margaret is a girl who laugh lots and be friendly with everyone, even bad dudes like Clarence. We had a murder out to the reserve once, Louis Halter got himself killed, but he deserved what he got. He was all drunk up and he said to Eddy Crow, "I fucked your wife." Yelled it right in Eddy's face. "I fucked your wife and she liked it so much she come back for a couple more times." I mean somebody said that to me about my girlfriend Sadie One-wound, and I had a rifle handy, I'd use it too.

Clarence's friends both tell the same story as him and in the lawyer's words too. A Catholic priest and the Anglican minister both say what a good boy Clarence is. I don't think none of the Gaskell family ever been to a church except for weddings and funerals.

The lawyer gets the court to take a recess after Clarence tell his story, and you can tell by look around that most everybody is sure impressed with how true it is especially that lawyer and the jury.

When we out in the hall Eathen say, "Little Margaret, she wouldn't do none of that."

"Yeah, but you think any of them white farmers gonna know that," say Robert.

Frank Fence-post, he took off his jacket the second day of the trial and the court orderly or whatever he is come down the aisle to where we sitting. "Put your jacket on, boy," he says to Frank. "You can't sit in your shirtsleeves in the presence of the Queen."

"I never knew she was here, partner, or I'd of worn my new shirt," says Frank. I figure the guy is gonna throw us all out, but he just look at us like we too ugly to look at and clump back up the aisle.

Since Clarence admit that he done it, the judge tell the jury they got to find him guilty, but when they do they say they recommend mercy.

"Ninety days and a $500 fine," says the judge, and Clarence he smile and shake hands all around before they take him off to jail.

"I'm gonna kill you, you son-of-a-bitch," Robert Coyote says, loud enough for everybody to draw in their breath real sharp and for a second there is silence until Frank Fence-post says, "Me too."

The RCMP guys herd us all down to the highway and tell us to get the fuck back to the reserve and stay there.

Frank Fence-post he ran the mile from Hobbema Crossing, across the slough and up the hill to where our cabins are. "Clarence Gaskell got out today," he puffed.

Robert Coyote wiped his hunting knife on his jeans.

"We still gonna kill him, right?" he ask.

"Right," says Eathen Firstrider, and everybody else including me, finally. I feel kind of tingly all over and kind of sick at the same time. I never been in jail, but Robert Coyote has and he say it ain't so bad except you don't get no women. But he say it warm, the food is good and you don't have to work. I think about how we get maybe twenty years and I feel awful scared.

I guess there never was any question that we were going to kill Clarence Gaskell after he got out of jail. We'd sit around our cabin and talk about it and our girls would try to talk us out of it, or tell us at least to try not get caught.

"We all gonna take our guns," says Robert. "Silas, you go down to the dance at Blue Quills tonight. Just keep your eyes open and see who he come with and how they acting. About midnight the rest of us we come down with our guns. You meet us in the bush behind the hall. Then we figure out how we going to get him outside by himself so we can kill him. We don't want to hurt nobody else except Clarence."

"I get to take his scalp," say Frank Fence-post.

"Be careful," says Bertha Bigcharles. Bertha is slim and pretty and would like to be Robert's girl, but he say he don't have no women until he kill Clarence Gaskell.

Sadie One-wound look at me with scared eyes and say, "I don't want you should go to jail, Silas." Sadie is awful special to me. She not very pretty, I guess. She's skinny and got kind of sharp features, but Sadie like to kiss me, and when she hold herself real close to me it sure make me feel strong and brave. I don't say nothing cause maybe I afraid what my voice sound like, but I try to look very solemn.

Some of his friends told Clarence about how Robert Coyote is still saying he going to kill him when he gets home, but Clarence say he not afraid of no fucking Indians, and he be at Blue Quills for the dance, just like old times.

At the dance Clarence is smiling and is strut around like a turkey. He shakes hands on a lot of people and his friends take him back and forth to their cars for drinks quite often.

I watch the big Pepsi-Cola clock above the stage and wait for midnight. Sadie want me to dance with her but I tell her go away. And she does. Clarence is dancing, even with the Indian girls; they laugh with him a lot and I sure don't like to see that.

Along about 11:30 all hell break loose. Somebody come yelling into the hall that Clarence been killed and for somebody to call the RCMP. All the white people and even some of the Indians is all gathered around him back behind the parking lot. They say pretty ugly things but they don't know who to be mad at for sure. What I can't figure out is why Robert and Eathen and the other guys don't wait for me like they supposed to. I finally walk down to the bush where they supposed to be and find them just get there.

"What's going on?" they all want to know.

"How come you killed him without waiting for me?" I ask like I real disappointed, but inside I am kind of glad they did.

"We just got here," says Robert. He is carry two rifles and he shove one of them into my hands. About then the RCMP come skidding into the parking lot with their red light turning.

"The Indians are down there in the bush," somebody says, "they're the ones said they were going to kill Clarence." And before we know what happening they got their spotlight on us and we all stand there shielding our eyes while they take away our guns and put handcuffs on us.

When we in the back of the police car on the way to Wetaskiwin, the RCMP guys talk about Clarence was stabbed, but first they say he was sexually mutilated. They say what a bunch of bastards we were to do something like that to a white man.

Frank Fence-post, he say, "Does sexually mutilated mean he got his balls cut off?" The RCMP guy reach around and just about knock Frank through the back seat.

"I guess it does," Frank whisper into my shoulder, while his nose bleeds all down the front of his shirt.

"Wasn't he shot?" I ask as polite as I know how.

"You should know," says the RCMP.

They questioned all us guys for most of the night, sometimes alone and sometimes all of us together. There was a lot of blood they say, and they got the jackknife that was used on him and they want to know which one of us owns it.

They stamped our fingerprints and took away all of our clothes and even our boots. They say they going to send our clothes to the crime laboratory in Regina, and they say too, that if there is even so much as one drop of Clarence Gaskell's blood on those clothes, or one fingerprint on the knife, they going to charge us all with murder. And they say they don't give a shit how we get back to the reserve with nothing but shorts on.

I sure hope Frank ain't got the same blood as Clarence, cause his nose splash on all of us in the back of the car there. Frank ain't worried though, he say Indians got eagle's blood, so they be able to tell the difference easy in a laboratory.

If it hadn't been for the Seventh Day Adventist minister, who give us some blankets and a ride, we'd of all froze. We had to promise to come to his church the next Sunday or he wouldn't of helped us. None of us went, although I thought about it.

None of us guys ever got our clothes back from the RCMP but I figure that a pretty cheap way not to get charged with murder. When the tests come back from Regina the RCMP is real disappointed that our clothes and boots don't have none of Clarence's blood on them. They questioned all us guys again a few times, especially Robert Coyote, but about all they do is call us bad names and say what they going to do to the guy who done it when they catch him. Nobody ever got charged and they haven't been around for a long time now.

At the dance that night most everybody is dancing all the time but me. I just sit on the bench along the side of the hall and I must of been the only one who seen that it was Bertha Bigcharles who danced Clarence outside. I even heard him say it. Bertha was pushing herself up close to him and whispering in his ear, and I hear him laugh and say, "Dance me outside, baby," as they go by me. When I look around the hall I see that my Sadie One-wound and some of the other girls are not there too.

When the minister finally brought us home that night, Sadie is waiting at our cabin. I make her burn her jeans and shoes, and she go and has Bertha Bigcharles, Sandra Coyote, and maybe another couple of girls do the same.

"Hold on to me, Silas," Sadie say to me that night, "and don't let me go for a long time," and her body is tremble and it is a very long time before she finally go to sleep in my arms.

RING LARDNER

Haircut

I got another barber that comes over from Carterville and helps me out Saturdays, but the rest of the time I can get along all right alone. You can see for yourself that this ain't no New York City and besides that, the most of the boys works all day and don't have no leisure to drop in here and get themselves prettied up.

You're a newcomer, ain't you? I thought I hadn't seen you round before. I hope you like it good enough to stay. As I say, we ain't no New York City or Chicago, but we have pretty good times. Not as good, though, since Jim Kendall got killed. When he was alive, him and Hod Meyers used to keep this town in an uproar. I bet they was more laughin' done here than any town its size in America.

Jim was comical, and Hod was pretty near a match for him. Since Jim's gone, Hod tries to hold his end up just the same as ever, but it's tough goin' when you ain't got nobody to kind of work with.

They used to be plenty fun in here Saturdays. This place is jampacked Saturdays, from four o'clock on. Jim and Hod would show up right after their supper, round six o'clock. Jim would set himself down in that big chair, nearest the blue spittoon. Whoever had been settin' in that chair, why they'd get up when Jim come in and give it to him.

You'd of thought it was a reserved seat like they have sometimes in a theayter. Hod would generally always stand or walk up and down, or some Saturdays, of course, he'd be settin' in this chair part of the time, gettin' a haircut.

Well, Jim would set there a w'ile without openin' his mouth only to spit, and then finally he'd say to me, "Whitey," — my right name, that is, my right first name, is Dick, but everybody round here calls me Whitey — Jim would say, "Whitey, your nose looks like a rosebud tonight. You must of been drinkin' some of your aw de cologne."

So I'd say, "No, Jim, but you look like you'd been drinkin' somethin' of that kind or somethin' worse."

Jim would have to laugh at that, but then he'd speak up and say, "No, I ain't had nothin' to drink, but that ain't sayin' I wouldn't like somethin'. I wouldn't even mind if it was wood alcohol."

Then Hod Meyers would say, "Neither would your wife." That would set everybody to laughin' because Jim and his wife wasn't on very good terms. She'd of divorced him only they wasn't no chance to get alimony and she didn't have no way to take care of herself and the kids. She couldn't never understand Jim. He *was* kind of rough, but a good fella at heart.

Him and Hod had all kinds of sport with Milt Sheppard. I don't suppose you've seen Milt. Well, he's got an Adam's apple that looks more like a mushmelon. So I'd be shavin' Milt and when I'd start to shave down on his neck, Hod would holler, "Hey, Whitey, wait a minute! Before you cut into it, let's make up a pool and see who can guess closest to the number of seeds."

And Jim would say, "If Milt hadn't of been so hoggish, he'd of ordered a half a cantaloupe instead of a whole one and it might not of stuck in his throat."

All the boys would roar at this and Milt himself would force a smile, though the joke was on him. Jim certainly was a card!

There's his shavin' mug, settin' on the shelf, right next to Charley Vail's. "Charles M. Vail." That's the druggist. He comes in regular for his shave, three times a week. And Jim's is the cup next to Charley's. "James H. Kendall." Jim won't need no shavin' mug no more, but I'll leave it there just the same for old time's sake. Jim certainly was a character!

Years ago, Jim used to travel for a canned goods concern over in Carterville. They sold canned goods. Jim had the whole northern half of the State and was on the road five days out of every week. He'd drop in here Saturdays and tell his experiences for that week. It was rich.

I guess he paid more attention to playin' jokes than makin' sales. Finally the concern let him out and he come right home here and told everybody he'd been fired instead of sayin' he'd resigned like most fellas would of.

It was a Saturday and the shop was full and Jim got up out of that chair and says, "Gentlemen, I got an important announcement to make. I been fired from my job."

Well, they asked him if he was in earnest and he said he was and nobody could think of nothin' to say till Jim finally broke the ice himself. He says, "I been sellin' canned goods and now I'm canned goods myself."

You see, the concern he'd been workin' for was a factory that made canned goods. Over in Carterville. And now Jim said he was canned himself. He was certainly a card!

Jim had a great trick that he used to play w'ile he was travelin'. For instance, he'd be ridin' on a train and they'd come to some little town like, well, like we'll say, like Benton. Jim would look out the train window and read the signs on the stores.

For instance, they'd be a sign, "Henry Smith, Dry Goods." Well, Jim would write down the name and the name of the town and when he got to wherever he was goin' he'd mail back a postal card to Henry Smith at Benton and not sign no name to it, but he'd write on the card, well, somethin' like "Ask your wife about that book agent that spent the afternoon last week," or "Ask your Missus who kept her from gettin' lonesome the last time you was in Carterville." And he'd sign the card, "A Friend."

Of course, he never knew what really come of none of these jokes, but he could picture what *probably* happened and that was enough.

Jim didn't work very steady after he lost his position with the Carterville people. What he did earn, doin' odd jobs round town, why he spent pretty near all of it on gin and his family might of starved if the stores hadn't of carried them along. Jim's wife tried her hand at dressmakin', but they ain't nobody goin' to get rich makin' dresses in this town.

As I say, she'd of divorced Jim, only she seen that she couldn't support herself and the kids and she was always hopin' that some day Jim would cut out his habits and give her more than two or three dollars a week.

They was a time when she would go to whoever he was workin' for and ask them to give her his wages, but after she done this once or twice, he beat her to it by borrowin' most of his pay in advance. He told it all round town, how he had outfoxed his Missus. He certainly was a caution!

But he wasn't satisfied with just outwittin' her. He was sore the way she had acted, tryin' to grab off his pay. And he made up his mind he'd get even. Well, he waited till Evans's Circus was advertised to come to town. Then he told his wife and two kiddies that he was goin' to take them to the circus. The day of the circus, he told them he would get the tickets and meet them outside the entrance to the tent.

Well, he didn't have no intentions of bein' there or buyin' tickets or nothin'. He got full of gin and laid round Wright's poolroom all day. His wife and the kids waited and waited and of course he didn't show up. His wife didn't have a dime with her, or nowhere else, I guess. So she finally had to tell the kids it was all off and they cried like they wasn't never goin' to stop.

Well, it seems, w'ile they was cryin', Doc Stair came along and he asked what was the matter, but Mrs. Kendall was stubborn and wouldn't tell him, but the kids told him and he insisted on takin' them and their mother in the show. Jim found this out afterwards and it was one reason why he had it in for Doc Stair.

Doc Stair come here about a year and a half ago. He's a mighty handsome young fella and his clothes always look like he has them made to order. He goes to Detroit two or three times a year and w'ile he's there he must have a tailor take his measure and then make him a suit to order. They cost pretty near twice as much, but they fit a whole lot better than if you just bought them in a store.

For a w'ile everybody was wonderin' why a young doctor like Doc Stair should come to a town like this where we already got old Doc Gamble and Doc Foote that's both been here for years and all the practice in town was always divided between the two of them.

Then they was a story got round that Doc Stair's gal had throwed him over, a gal up in the Northern Peninsula somewheres, and the reason he come here was to hide himself away and forget it. He said himself that he thought they wasn't nothin' like general practice in a place like ours to fit a man to be a good all round doctor. And that's why he'd came.

Anyways, it wasn't long before he was makin' enough to live on, though they tell me that he never dunned nobody for what they owed him, and the folks here certainly has got the owin' habit, even in my business. If I had all that was comin' to me for just shaves alone, I could go to Carterville and put up at the Mercer for a week and see a different picture every night. For instance, they's old George Purdy — but I guess I shouldn't ought to be gossipin'.

Well, last year, our coroner died, died of the flu. Ken Beatty, that was his name. He was the coroner. So they had to choose another man to be coroner in his place and they picked Doc Stair. He laughed at first and said he didn't want it, but they made him take it. It ain't no job that anybody would fight for and what a man makes out of it in a year would just about buy seeds for their garden. Doc's the kind, though, that can't say no to nothin' if you keep at him long enough.

But I was goin' to tell you about a poor boy we got here in town — Paul Dickson. He fell out of a tree when he was about ten years old. Lit on his head and it done somethin' to him and he ain't never been right. No harm in him, but just silly. Jim Kendall used to call him cuckoo; that's a name Jim had for anybody that was off their head, only he called people's head their bean. That was another of his gags, callin' head bean and callin' crazy people cuckoo. Only poor Paul ain't crazy, but just silly.

You can imagine that Jim used to have all kinds of fun with Paul. He'd send him to the White Front Garage for a left-handed monkey wrench. Of course they ain't no such a thing as a left-handed monkey wrench.

And once we had a kind of a fair here and they was a baseball game between the fats and the leans and before the game started Jim called Paul over and sent him way down to Schrader's hardware store to get a key for the pitcher's box.

They wasn't nothin' in the way of gags that Jim couldn't think up, when he put his mind to it.

Poor Paul, was always kind of suspicious of people, maybe on account of how Jim had kept foolin' him. Paul wouldn't have much to do with anybody only his own mother and Doc Stair and a girl here in town named Julie Gregg. That is, she ain't a girl no more, but pretty near thirty or over.

When Doc first come to town, Paul seemed to feel like here was a real friend and he hung round Doc's office most of the w'ile; the only time he wasn't there was when he'd go home to eat or sleep or when he seen Julie Gregg doin' her shoppin'.

When he looked out Doc's window and seen her, he'd run downstairs and join her and tag along with her to the different stores. The poor boy was crazy about Julie and she always treated him mighty nice and made him feel like he was welcome, though of course it wasn't nothin' but pity on her side.

Doc done all he could to improve Paul's mind and he told me once that he really thought the boy was gettin' better, that they was times when he was as bright and sensible as anybody else.

But I was goin' to tell you about Julie Gregg. Old Man Gregg was in the lumber business, but got to drinkin' and lost the most of his money and when he died, he didn't leave nothin' but the house and just enough insurance for the girl to skimp along on.

Her mother was a kind of a half invalid and didn't hardly ever leave the house. Julie wanted to sell the place and move somewheres else after the old man died, but the mother said she was born here and would die here. It was tough on Julie, as the young people round this town — well, she's too good for them.

She's been away to school and Chicago and New York and different places and they ain't no subject she can't talk on, where you take the rest of the young folks here and you mention anything to them outside of Gloria Swanson or Tommy Meighan and they think you're delirious. Did you see Gloria in Wages of Virtue? You missed somethin'!

Well, Doc Stair hadn't been here more than a week when he came in one day to get shaved and I recognized who he was as he had been pointed out to me, so I told him about my old lady. She's been ailin' for a couple years and either Doc Gamble or Doc Foote, neither one, seemed to be helpin' her. So he said he would come out and see her, but if she was able to get out herself, it would be better to bring her to his office where he could make a completer examination.

So I took her to his office and w'ile I was waitin' for her in the reception room, in come Julie Gregg. When somebody comes in Doc Stair's office, they's a bell that rings in his inside office so as he can tell they's somebody to see him.

So he left my old lady inside and come out to the front office and that's the first time him and Julie met and I guess it was what they call love at first sight. But it wasn't fifty-fifty. This young fella was the slickest lookin' fella she'd ever seen in this town and she went wild over him. To him she was just a young lady that wanted to see the doctor.

She'd came on about the same business I had. Her mother had been doctorin' for years with Doc Gamble and Doc Foote and without no results. So she'd heard they was a new doc in town and decided to give him a try. He promised to call and see her mother that same day.

I said a minute ago that it was love at first sight on her part. I'm not only judgin' by how she acted afterwards but how she looked at him that first day in his office. I ain't no mind reader, but it was wrote all over her face that she was gone.

Now Jim Kendall, besides bein' a jokesmith and a pretty good drinker, well, Jim was quite a lady-killer. I guess he run pretty wild durin' the time he was on the road for them Carterville people, and besides that, he'd had a couple little affairs of the heart right here in town. As I say, his wife could of divorced him, only she couldn't.

But Jim was like the majority of men, and women, too, I guess. He wanted what he couldn't get. He wanted Julie Gregg and worked his head off tryin' to land her. Only he'd of said bean instead of head.

Well, Jim's habits and his jokes didn't appeal to Julie and of course he was a married man, so he didn't have no more chance than, well, than a rabbit. That's an expression of Jim's himself. When somebody didn't have no chance to get elected or somethin', Jim would always say they didn't have no more chance than a rabbit.

He didn't make no bones about how he felt. Right in here, more than once, in front of the whole crowd, he said he was stuck on Julie and anybody that could get her for him was welcome to his house and his wife and kids included. But she wouldn't have nothin' to do with him; wouldn't even speak to him on the street. He finally seen he wasn't gettin' nowheres with his usual line so he decided to try the rough stuff. He went right up to her house one evenin' and when she opened the door he forced his way in and grabbed her. But she broke loose and before he could stop her, she run in the next room and locked the door and phones to Joe Barnes. Joe's the marshal. Jim could hear who she was phonin' to and he beat it before Joe got there.

Joe was an old friend of Julie's pa. Joe went to Jim the next day and told him what would happen if he ever done it again.

I don't know how the news of this little affair leaked out. Chances is that Joe Barnes told his wife and she told somebody else's wife and they told their husband. Anyways, it did leak out and Hod Meyers had the nerve to kid Jim about it, right here in this shop. Jim didn't deny nothin' and kind of laughed it off and said for us all to wait; that lots of people had tried to make a monkey out of him, but he always got even.

Meanw'ile everybody in town was wise to Julie's bein' wild mad over the Doc. I don't suppose she had any idear how her face changed when him and her was together; of course she couldn't of, or she'd of kept away from him. And she didn't know that we was all noticin' how many times she made excuses to go up to his office to see if he was there. I felt sorry for her and so did other people.

Hod Meyers kept rubbin' it into Jim about how the Doc had cut him out. Jim didn't pay no attention to the kiddin' and you could see he was plannin' one of his jokes.

One trick Jim had was the knack of changin' his voice. He could make you think he was a girl talkin' and he could mimic any man's voice. To show you how good he was along this line, I'll tell you the joke he played on me once.

You know, in most towns of any size, when a man is dead and needs a shave, why the barber that shaves him soaks him five dollars for the job; that is, he don't soak *him,* but whoever ordered the shave. I just charge three dollars because personally I don't mind much shavin' a dead person. They lay a whole lot stiller than live customers. The only thing is that you don't feel like talkin' to them and you get kind of lonesome.

Well, about the coldest day we ever had here, two years ago last winter, the phone rang at the house w'ile I was home to dinner and I answered the phone and it was a woman's voice and she said she was Mrs. John Scott and her husband was dead and would I come out and shave him.

Old John had always been a good customer of mine. But they live seven miles out in the country, on the Streeter road. Still I didn't see how I could say no.

So I said I would be there, but would have to come in a jitney and it might cost three or four dollars besides the price of the shave. So she, or the voice, it said that was all right, so I got Frank Abbott to drive me out to the place and when I got there, who should open the door but old John himself! He wasn't no more dead than, well, than a rabbit.

It didn't take no private detective to figure out who had played me this little joke. Nobody could of thought it up but Jim Kendall. He certainly was a card!

I tell you this accident just to show you how he could disguise his voice and make you believe it was somebody else talkin'. I'd of swore it was Mrs. Scott had called me. Anyways, some woman.

Well, Jim waited till he had Doc Stair's voice down pat; then he went after revenge.

He called Julie up on a night when he knew Doc was over in Carterville. She never questioned but what it was Doc's voice. Jim said he must see her that night; he couldn't wait no longer to tell her somethin'. She was all excited and told him to come to the house. But he said he was expecting an important long distance call and wouldn't she please forget her manners for once and come to his office. He said they couldn't nothin' hurt her and nobody would see her and he just *must* talk to her a little w'ile. Well, poor Julie fell for it.

Doc always keeps a night light in his office, so it looked to Julie like they was somebody there.

Meanw'ile Jim Kendall had went to Wright's poolroom, where they was a whole gang amusin' themselves. The most of them had drank plenty of gin, and they was a rough bunch even when sober. They was always strong for Jim's jokes and when he told them to come with him and see some fun they give up their card games and pool games and followed along.

Doc's office is on the second floor. Right outside his door they's a flight of stairs leadin' to the floor above. Jim and his gang hid in the dark behind these stairs.

Well, Julie came up to Doc's door and rung the bell and they was nothin' doin'. She rung it again and she rung it seven or eight times. Then she tried the door and found it locked. Then Jim made some kind of a noise and she heard it and waited a minute, and then she says, "Is that you Ralph?" Ralph is Doc's first name.

They was no answer and it must of came to her all of a sudden that she'd been bunked. She pretty near fell downstairs and the gang after her. They chased her all the way home, hollerin'. "Is that you, Ralph?" and "Oh, Ralphie, dear, is that you?" Jim says he couldn't holler it himself, as he was laughin' too hard.

Poor Julie! She didn't show up here on Main Street for a long, long time afterward.

And of course Jim and his gang told everybody in town, everybody but Doc Stair. They was scared to tell him, and he might of never knowed only for Paul Dickson. The poor cuckoo, as Jim called him, he was here in the shop one night when Jim was still gloatin' yet over what he'd done to Julie. And Paul took in as much of it as he could understand and he run to Doc with the story.

It's a cinch Doc went up in the air and swore he'd make Jim suffer. But it was a kind of a delicate thing, because if it got out that he had beat Jim up, Julie was bound to hear of it and then she'd know that Doc knew and of course knowin' that he knew would make it worse for her than ever. He was goin' to do somethin', but it took a lot of figurin'.

Well, it was a couple days later when Jim was here in the shop again, and so was the cuckoo. Jim was goin' duck-shootin' the next day and had come in lookin' for Hod Meyers to go with him. I happened to know that Hod had went over to Carterville and wouldn't be home till the end of the week. So Jim said he hated to go alone and he guessed he would call it off. Then poor Paul spoke up and said if Jim would take him he would go along. Jim thought a w'ile and then he said, well, he guessed a half-wit was better than nothin'.

I suppose he was plottin' to get Paul out in the boat and play some joke on him, like pushin' him in the water. Anyways, he said Paul could go. He asked him had he ever shot a duck and Paul said no, he'd never even had a gun in his hands. So Jim said he could set in the boat and watch him and if he behaved himself, he might lend him his gun for a couple of shots. They made a date to meet in the mornin' and that's the last I seen of Jim alive.

Next mornin', I hadn't been open more than ten minutes when Doc Stair come in. He looked kind of nervous. He asked me had I seen Paul Dickson. I said no, but I knew where he was, out duck-shootin' with Jim Kendall. So Doc says that's what he heard, and he couldn't understand it because Paul had told him he wouldn't never have no more to do with Jim as long as he lived.

He said Paul had told him about the joke Jim had played on Julie. He said Paul had asked him what he thought of the joke and the Doc had told him that anybody that would do a thing like that ought not to be let live.

I said it had been a kind of a raw thing, but Jim just couldn't resist no kind of a joke, no matter how raw. I said I thought he was all right at heart, but just bubblin' over with mischief. Doc turned and walked out.

At noon he got a phone call from old John Scott. The lake where Jim and Paul had went shootin' is on John's place. Paul had came runnin' up the house a few minutes before and said they'd been an accident. Jim had shot a few ducks and then give the gun to Paul and told him to try his luck. Paul hadn't never handled a gun and he was nervous. He was shakin' so hard that he couldn't control the gun. He let fire and Jim sunk back in the boat, dead.

Doc Stair, bein' the coroner, jumped in Frank Abbott's flivver and rushed out to Scott's farm. Paul and old John was down on the shore of the lake. Paul had rowed the boat to shore, but they'd left the body in it, waitin' for Doc to come.

Doc examined the body and said they might as well fetch it back to town. They was no use leavin' it there or callin' a jury, as it was a plain case of accidental shootin'.

Personally I wouldn't never leave a person shoot a gun in the same boat I was in unless I was sure they knew somethin' about guns. Jim was a sucker to leave a new beginner have his gun, let alone a half-wit. It probably served Jim right, what he got. But still we miss him round here. He certainly was a card!

Comb it wet or dry?

MARGARET LAURENCE

A Bird in the House

The parade would be almost over by now, and I had not gone. My mother had said in a resigned voice, "All right, Vanessa, if that's the way you feel," making me suffer twice as many jabs of guilt as I would have done if she had lost her temper. She and Grandmother MacLeod had gone off, my mother pulling the low boxsleigh with Roddie all dolled up in his new red snowsuit, just the sort of little kid anyone would want people to see. I sat on the lowest branch of the birch tree in our yard, not minding the snowy wind, even welcoming its punishment. I went over my reasons for not going, trying to believe they were good and sufficient, but in my heart I felt I was betraying my father. This was the first time I had stayed away from the Remembrance Day parade. I wondered if he would notice that I was not there, standing on the sidewalk at the corner of River and Main while the parade passed, and then following to the Court House grounds where the service was held.

I could see the whole thing in my mind. It was the same every year. The Manawaka Civic Band always led the way. They had never been able to afford full uniforms, but they had peaked navy-blue caps and sky-blue chest ribbons. The were joined on Remembrance Day by the Salvation Army band, whose uniforms seemed too ordinary for a parade, for they were the same ones the bandsmen wore every Saturday night when they played "Nearer My God to Thee" at the foot of River Street. The two bands never managed to practise quite enough together, so they did not keep in time too well. The Salvation Army band invariably played faster, and afterwards my father would say irritably, "They play those marches just like they do hymns, blast them, as though they wouldn't get to heaven if they didn't hustle up." And my mother, who had great respect for the Salvation Army because of the good work they did, would respond chidingly, "Now, now, Ewen —" I vowed I would never say "Now, now" to my husband or children, not that I ever intended having the latter, for I had been put off by my brother Roderick, who was now two years old with wavy hair, and everyone said what a beautiful child. I was twelve, and no one in their right mind would have said what a beautiful child, for I was big-boned like my Grandfather Connor and had straight lanky black hair like a Blackfoot or Cree.

After the bands would come the veterans. Even thinking of them at this distance, in the white and withdrawn quiet of the birch tree, gave me a sense of painful embarrassment. I might not have minded so much if my father had not been among them. How could he go? How could he not see how they all looked? It must have been a long time since they were soldiers, for they had forgotten how to march in step. They were old — that was the thing. My father was bad enough, being almost forty, but he wasn't a patch on Howard Tully from the drugstore, who was completely grey-haired and also fat, or Stewart MacMurchie, who was bald at the back of his head. They looked to me like imposters, plump or spindly caricatures of past warriors. I almost hated them for walking in that limping column down Main. At the Court House, everyone would sing *Lord God of Hosts, be with us yet, lest we forget, lest we forget.* Will Masterson would pick up his old Army bugle and blow the last Post. Then it would be over and everyone could start gabbling once more and go home.

I jumped down from the birch bough and ran to the house, yelling, making as much noise as I could.

I'm a poor lonesome cowboy
An' a long way from home —

I stepped inside the front hall and kicked off my snow boots. I slammed the door behind me, making the dark ruby and emerald glass shake in the small leaded panes. I slid purposely on the hall rug, causing it to bunch and crinkle on the slippery polished oak of the floor. I seized the newel post, round as a head, and spun myself to and fro on the bottom stair.

I ain't got no father
To buy the clothes I wear.
I'm a poor lonesome —

At this moment my shoulders were firmly seized and shaken by a pair of hands, white and delicate and old, but strong as talons.

"Just what do you think you're doing, young lady?" Grandmother MacLeod enquired, in a voice like frost on a windowpane, infinitely cold and clearly etched.

I went limp and in a moment she took her hands away. If you struggled she would always hold on longer.

"Gee, I never knew you were home yet."

"I would have thought that on a day like this you might have shown a little respect and consideration," Grandmother MacLeod said, "even if you couldn't make the effort to get cleaned up enough to go to the parade."

I realized with surprise that she imagined this to be my reason for not going. I did not try to correct her impression. My real reason would have been even less acceptable.

"I'm sorry," I said quickly.

In some families, *please* is described as the magic word. In our house, however, it was *sorry.*

"This isn't an easy day for any of us," she said.

Her younger son Uncle Roderick, had been killed in the Great War. When my father marched, and when the hymn was sung, and when that unbearably lonely tune was sounded by the one bugle and everyone forced themselves to keep absolutely still, it would be that boy of whom she was thinking. I felt the enormity of my own offence.

"Grandmother — I'm sorry."

"So you said."

I could not tell her I had not really said it before at all. I went into the den and found my father there. He was sitting in the leather-cushioned armchair beside the fireplace. He was not doing anything, just sitting and smoking. I stood beside him, wanting to touch the light-brown hairs on his forearm, but thinking he might laugh at me or pull his arm away if I did.

"I'm sorry," I said, meaning it.

"What for, honey?"

"For not going."

"Oh — that. What was the matter?"

I did not want him to know, and yet I had to tell him, make him see.

"They look silly." I blurted. "Marching like that."

For a minute I thought he was going to be angry. It would have been a relief to me if he had been. Instead, he drew his eyes away from mine and fixed them above the mantelpiece where the sword hung, the handsome and evil-looking crescent in its carved bronze sheath that some ancestor had once brought from the Northern Frontier of India.

"Is that the way it looks to you?" he said.

I felt in his voice some hurt, something that was my fault. I wanted to make everything all right between us, to convince him that I understood, even if I did not. I prayed that Grandmother MacLeod would stay put in her room, and that my mother would take a long time in the kitchen, giving Roddie his lunch. I wanted my father to myself, so I could prove to him that I cared more about him than any of the others did. I wanted to speak in some way that would be more poignant and comprehending than anything of which my mother could possibly be capable. But I did not know how.

"You were right there when Uncle Roderick got killed, weren't you?" I began uncertainly.

"Yes."

"How old was he, Dad?"

"Eighteen," my father said.

Unexpectedly, that day came into intense being for me. He had had to watch his own brother die, not in the antiseptic calm of some hospital, but out in the open, the stretches of mud I had seen in his snapshots. He would not have known what to do. He would just have had to stand there and look at it, whatever that might mean. I looked at my father with a kind of horrified awe, and then I began to cry. I had forgotten about impressing him with my perception. Now I needed him to console me for this unwanted glimpse of the pain he had once known.

"Hey, cut it out, honey," he said, embarrassed. "It was bad, but it wasn't all as bad as that part. There was a few other things."

"Like what?" I said, not believing him.

"Oh — I don't know," he replied evasively. "Most of us were pretty young, you know, I and the boys I joined up with. None of us had ever been away from Manawaka before. Those of us who came back mostly came back here, or else went no further away from town than Winnipeg. So when we were overseas — that was the only time most of us were ever a long way from home."

"Did you want to be?" I asked, shocked.

"Oh well —" my father said uncomfortably. "It was kind of interesting to see a few other places for a change, that's all."

Grandmother MacLeod was standing in the doorway.

"Beth's called you twice for lunch, Ewen. Are you deaf, you and Vanessa?"

"Sorry," my father and I said simultaneously.

Then we went upstairs to wash our hands.

That winter my mother returned to her old job as nurse in my father's medical practice. She was able to do this only because of Noreen.

"Grandmother MacLeod says we're getting a maid," I said to my father, accusingly, one morning. "We're not, are we?"

"Believe you me, on what I'm going to be paying her," my father growled, "she couldn't be called anything as classy as a maid. Hired girl would be more like it."

"Now, now, Ewen," my mother put in, "it's not as if we were cheating her or anything. You know she wants to live in town, and I can certainly see why, stuck out there on the farm, and her father hardly ever letting her come in. What kind of life is that for a girl?"

"I don't like the idea of your going back to work, Beth," my father said. "I know you're fine now, but you're not exactly the robust type."

"You can't afford to hire a nurse any longer. It's all very well to say the Depression won't last forever — probably it won't, but what else can we do for now?"

"I'm damned if I know," my father admitted.

"Beth —"

"Yes?"

They both seemed to have forgotten about me. It was at breakfast, which we always ate in the kitchen, and I sat rigidly on my chair, pretending to ignore and thus snub their withdrawal from me. I glared at the window, but it was so thickly plumed and scrolled with frost that I could not see out. I glanced back to my parents. My father had not replied, and my mother was looking at him in that anxious and half-frowning way she had recently developed.

"What is it, Ewen?" Her voice had the same nervous sharpness it bore sometimes when she would say to me, "For mercy's sake, Vanessa, what is it *now*?" as though whatever was the matter, it was bound to be the last straw.

My father spun his sterling silver serviette ring, engraved with his initials, slowly around on the table.

"I never thought things would turn out like this, did you?"

"Please —" my mother said in a low strained voice, "please, Ewen, let's not start all this again. I can't take it."

"All right," my father said. "Only —"

"The MacLeods used to have money and now they don't," my mother cried. "Well, they're not alone. Do you think all that matters to me, Ewen? What I can't bear is to see you forever reproaching yourself. As if it were your fault."

"I don't think it's the comedown," my father said. "If I were somewhere else, I don't suppose it would matter to me, either, except where you're concerned. But I suppose you'd work too hard wherever you were — it's bred into you. If you haven't got anything to slave away at, you'll sure as hell invent something."

"What do you think I should do, let the house go to wrack and ruin? That would go over well with your mother, wouldn't it?"

"That's just it," my father said. "It's the damned house all the time. I haven't only taken on my father's house, I've taken on everything that goes with it, apparently. Sometimes I really wonder —"

"Well, it's a good thing I've inherited some practicality even if you haven't," my mother said. "I'll say that for the Connors — they aren't given to brooding, thank the Lord. Do you want your egg poached or scrambled?

"Scrambled," my father said. "All I hope is that this Noreen doesn't get married straightaway, that's all."

"She won't," my mother said. "Who's she going to meet who could afford to marry?"

"I marvel at you, Beth," my father said. "You look as though a puff of wind would blow you away. But underneath, by God, you're all hardwood."

"Don't talk stupidly," my mother said. "All I hope is that she won't object to taking your mother's breakfast up on a tray."

"That's right," my father said angrily. "Rub it in."

"Oh Ewen, I'm sorry!" my mother cried, her face suddenly stricken. "I don't know why I say these things. I didn't mean to."

"I know," my father said. "Here, cut it out, honey. Just for God's sake please don't cry."

"I'm sorry," my mother repeated, blowing her nose.

"We're both sorry," my father said. "Not that that changes anything."

After my father had gone, I got down from my chair and went to my mother.

"I don't want you to go back to the office. I don't want a hired girl here. I'll hate her."

My mother sighed, making me feel that I was placing an intolerable burden on her, and yet making me resent having to feel this weight. She looked tired, as she often did these days. Her tiredness bored me, made me want to attack her for it.

"Catch me getting along with a dumb old hired girl," I threatened.

"Do what you like," my mother said abruptly. "What can I do about it?"

And then, of course, I felt bereft, not knowing which way to turn.

• • •

My father need not have worried about Noreen getting married. She was, as it turned out, interested not in boys but in God. My mother was relieved about the boys but alarmed about God.

"It isn't natural," she said, "for a girl of seventeen. Do you think she's all right mentally, Ewen?"

When my parents, along with Grandmother MacLeod, went to the United Church every Sunday, I was made to go to Sunday school in the church basement, where there were small red chairs which humiliatingly resembled kindergarten furniture, and pictures of Jesus wearing a white sheet and surrounded by a whole lot of well-dressed kids whose mothers obviously had not suffered them to come unto Him until every face and ear was properly scrubbed. Our religious observances also included grace at meals, when my father would mumble "For what we are about to receive the Lord make us truly thankful Amen," running the words together as though they were one long word. My mother approved of these rituals, which seemed decent and moderate to her. Noreen's religion, however, was a different matter. Noreen belonged to the Tabernacle of the Risen and Reborn, and she had got up to testify no less than seven times in the past two years, she told us. My mother, who could not imagine anyone's voluntarily making a public spectacle of themselves, was profoundly shocked by this revelation.

"Don't worry," my father soothed her. "She's all right. She's just had kind of a dull life, that's all."

My mother shrugged and went on worrying and trying to help Noreen without hurting her feelings, by tactful remarks about the advisability of modulating one's voice when singing hymns, and the fact that there was plenty of hot water so Noreen really didn't need to hesitate about taking a bath. She even bought a razor and a packet of blades and whispered to Noreen that any girl who wore transparent blouses so much would probably like to shave under her arms. None of these suggestions had the slightest effect on Noreen. She did not cease belting out hymns at the top of her voice, she bathed once a fortnight, and the sorrel-coloured hair continued to bloom like a thicket of Indian paint-brush in her armpits.

Grandmother MacLeod refused to speak to Noreen. This caused Noreen a certain amount of bewilderment until she finally hit on an answer.

"Your poor grandma," she said. "She is deaf as a post. These things are sent to try us here on earth, Vanessa. But if she makes it into Heaven, I'll bet you anything she will hear clear as a bell."

Noreen and I talked about Heaven quite a lot, and also Hell. Noreen had an intimate and detailed knowledge of both places. She not only knew what they looked like — she even knew how big they were. Heaven was seventy-seven thousand miles square and it had four gates, each one made out of a different kind of precious jewel. The Pearl Gate, the Topaz Gate, the Amethyst Gate, the Ruby Gate — Noreen would reel them off, all the gates of Heaven. I told Noreen they sounded like poetry, but she was puzzled by my reaction and said I shouldn't talk that way. If you said poetry, it sounded like it was just made up and not really so, Noreen said.

Hell was larger than Heaven, and when I asked why, thinking of it as something of a comedown for God, Noreen said naturally it had to be bigger because there were a darn sight more people there than in Heaven. Hell was one hundred and ninety million miles deep and was in perpetual darkness, like a cave or under the sea. Even the flames (this was the awful thing) *did not give off any light.*

I did not actually believe in Noreen's doctrines, but the images which they conjured up began to inhabit my imagination. Noreen's fund of exotic knowledge was not limited to religion, although in a way it all seemed related. She could do many things which had a spooky tinge to them. Once when she was making a cake, she found we had run out of eggs. She went outside and gathered a bowl of fresh snow and used it instead. The cake rose like a charm, and I stared at Noreen as though she were a sorceress. In fact, I began to think of her as a sorceress, someone not quite of this earth. There was nothing unearthly about her broad shoulders and hips and her forest of dark red hair, but even these features took on a slightly sinister significance to me. I no longer saw her through the eyes or the expressed opinions of my mother and father, as a girl who had quit school at grade eight and whose life on the farm had been endlessly drab. I knew the truth — Noreen's life had not been drab at all, for she dwelt in a world of violent splendours, a world filled with angels whose wings of delicate light bore real feathers, and saints shining like the dawn, and prophets who spoke in ancient tongues, and the ecstatic souls of the saved, as well as denizens of the lower regions — mean-eyed imps and crooked cloven-hoofed monsters and beasts with the bodies of swine and the human heads of murderers, and lovely depraved jezebels torn by dogs through all eternity. The middle layer of Creation, our earth, was equally full of grotesque presences, for Noreen believed strongly in the visitation of ghosts and the communication with spirits. She could prove this with her Ouija board. We would both place our fingers lightly on the indicator, and it would skim across the board and spell out answers to our questions. I did not believe wholeheartedly in the Ouija board, either, but I was cautious about the kind of question I asked, in case the answer would turn out unfavourable and I would be unable to forget it.

One day Noreen told me she could also make a table talk. We used the small table in my bedroom, and sure enough, it lifted very slightly under our fingertips and tapped once for *Yes*, twice for *No*. Noreen asked if her Aunt Ruthie would get better from the kidney operation, and the table replied *No*. I withdrew my hands.

"I don't want to do it any more."

"Gee, what's the matter, Vanessa?" Noreen's plain placid face creased in a frown. "We only just begun."

"I have to do my homework."

My heart lurched as I said this. I was certain Noreen would know I was lying, and that she would know not by any ordinary perception, either. But her attention had been caught by something else, and I was thankful, at least until I saw what it was.

My bedroom window was not opened in the coldest weather. The storm window, which was fitted outside as an extra wall against the winter, had three small circular holes in its frame so that some fresh air could seep into the house. The sparrow must have been floundering in the new snow on the roof, for it had crawled in through one of these holes and was now caught between the two layers of glass. I could not bear the panic of the trapped bird, and before I realized what I was doing, I had thrown open the bedroom window. I was not releasing the sparrow into any better a situation, I soon saw, for instead of remaining quiet and allowing us to catch it in order to free it, it began flying blindly around the room, hitting the lampshade, brushing against the walls, its wings seeming to spin faster and faster.

I was petrified. I thought I would pass out if those palpitating wings touched me. There was something in the bird's senseless movements that revolted me. I also thought it was going to damage itself, break one of those thin wing-bones, perhaps, and then it would be lying on the floor, dying, like the pimpled and horribly featherless baby birds we saw sometimes on the sidewalks in the spring when they had fallen out of their nests. I was not any longer worried about the sparrow. I wanted only to avoid the sight of it lying broken on the floor. Viciously, I thought that if Noreen said, *God sees the little sparrow fall,* I would kick her in the shins. She did not, however, say this.

"A bird in the house means a death in the house," Noreen remarked.

Shaken, I pulled my glance away from the whirling wings and looked at Noreen.

"What?"

"That's what I've heard said, anyhow."

The sparrow had exhausted itself. It lay on the floor, spent and trembling. I could not bring myself to touch it. Noreen bent and picked it up. She cradled it with great gentleness between her cupped hands. Then we took it downstairs, and when I had opened the back door, Noreen set the bird free.

"Poor little scrap," she said, and I felt struck to the heart, knowing she had been concerned all along about the sparrow, while I, perfidiously, in the chaos of the moment, had been concerned only about myself.

"Wanna do some with the Ouija board, Vanessa?" Noreen asked.

I shivered a little, perhaps only because of the blast of cold air which had come into the kitchen when the door was opened.

"No thanks, Noreen. Like I said, I got my homework to do. But thanks all the same."

"That's okay," Noreen said in her guileless voice. "Any time."

But whenever she mentioned the Ouija board or the talking table, after that, I always found some excuse not to consult these oracles.

"Do you want to come to church with me this evening, Vanessa?" my father said.

"How come you're going to the evening service?" I enquired.

"Well, we didn't go this morning. We went snowshoeing instead, remember? I think your grandmother was a little bit put out about it. She went alone this morning. I guess it wouldn't hurt you and me, to go now."

We walked through the dark, along the white streets, the snow squeaking dryly under our feet. The streetlights were placed at long intervals along the sidewalks, and around each pole the circle of flimsy light created glistening points of blue and crystal on the crusted snow. I would have liked to take my father's hand, as I used to do, but I was too old for that now. I walked beside him, taking long steps so he would not have to walk more slowly on my account.

The sermon bored me, and I began leafing through the Hymnary for entertainment. I must have drowsed, for the next thing I knew, my father was prodding me and we were on our feet for the closing hymn.

Near the Cross, near the Cross,
Be my glory ever,
Till my ransomed soul shall find
Rest beyond the river.

I knew the tune well, so I sang loudly for the first verse. But the music to that hymn is sombre, and all at once the words themselves seemed too dreadful to be sung. I stopped singing, my throat knotted. I thought I was going to cry, but I did not know why, except that the song recalled to me my Grandmother Connor, who had been dead only a year now. I wondered why her soul needed to be ransomed. If God did not think she was good enough just as she was, then I did not have much use for His opinion. *Rest beyond the river* — was that what had happened to her? She had believed in Heaven, but I did not think that rest beyond the river was quite what she had in mind. To think of her in Noreen's flashy Heaven, though — that was even worse. Someplace where nobody ever got annoyed or had to be smoothed down and placated, someplace where there were never any family scenes — that would have suited my Grandmother Connor. Maybe she wouldn't have minded a certain amount of rest beyond the river, at that.

When we had the silent prayer, I looked at my father. He sat with his head bowed and his eyes closed. He was frowning deeply, and I could see the pulse in his temple. I wondered then what he believed. I did not have any real idea what it might be. When he raised his head, he did not look uplifted or anything like that. He merely looked tired. Then Reverend McKee pronounced the benediction, and we could go home.

"What do you think about all that stuff, Dad?" I asked hesitantly, as we walked.

"What stuff, honey?"

"Oh, Heaven and Hell, and like that."

My father laughed. "Have you been listening to Noreen too much? Well, I don't know. I don't think they're actual places. Maybe they stand for something that happens all the time here, or else doesn't happen. It's kind of hard to explain. I guess I'm not so good at explanations."

Nothing seemed to have been made any clearer to me. I reached out and took his hand, not caring that he might think this is a babyish gesture.

"I hate that hymn!"

"Good Lord," my father said in astonishment. "Why, Vanessa?"

But I did not know and so could not tell him.

Many people in Manawaka had flu that winter, so my father and Dr. Cates were kept extremely busy. I had flu myself, and spent a week in bed, vomiting only the first day and after that enjoying poor health, as my mother put it, with Noreen bringing me ginger ale and orange juice, and each evening my father putting a wooden tongue-depressor into my mouth and peering down my throat, then smiling and saying he thought I might live after all.

Then my father got sick himself, and had to stay at home and go to bed. This was such an unusual occurrence that it amused me.

"Doctors shouldn't get sick," I told him.

"You're right," he said. "That was pretty bad management."

"Run along now, dear," my mother said.

That night I woke and heard voices in the upstairs hall. When I went out, I found my mother and Grandmother MacLeod, both in their dressing-gowns. With them was Dr. Cates. I did not go immediately to my mother, as I would have done only a year before. I stood in the doorway of my room, squinting against the sudden light.

"Mother — what is it?"

She turned, and momentarily I saw the look on her face before she erased it and put on a contrived calm.

"It's all right," she said. "Dr. Cates has just come to have a look at Daddy. You go on back to sleep."

The wind was high that night, and I lay and listened to it rattling the storm windows and making the dry and winter-stiffened vines of the Virginia creeper scratch like small persistent claws against the red brick. In the morning, my mother told me that my father had developed pneumonia.

Dr. Cates did not think it would be safe to move my father to the hospital. My mother began sleeping in the spare bedroom, and after she had been there for a few nights, I asked if I could sleep in there too. I thought she would be bound to ask me why, and I did not know what I would say, but she did not ask. She nodded, and in some way her easy agreement upset me.

That night Dr. Cates came again, bringing with him one of the nurses from the hospital. My mother stayed upstairs with them. I sat with Grandmother MacLeod in the living room. That was the last place in the world I wanted to be, but I thought she would be offended if I went off. She sat as straight and rigid as a totem pole, and embroidered away at the needlepoint cushion cover she was doing. I perched on the edge of the chesterfield and kept my eyes fixed on *The White Company* by Conan Doyle, and from time to time I turned a page. I had already read it three times before, but luckily Grandmother MacLeod did not know that. At nine o'clock she looked at her gold brooch watch, which she always wore pinned to her dress, and told me to go to bed, so I did that.

I wakened in darkness. At first, it seemed to me that I was in my own bed, and everything was as usual, with my parents in their room, and Roddie curled up in the crib in his room, and Grandmother MacLeod sleeping with her mouth open in her enormous spool bed, surrounded by half a dozen framed photos of Uncle Roderick and only one of my father, and Noreen snoring fitfully in the room next to mine, with the dark flames of her hair spreading out across the pillow, and the pink and silver motto cards from the Tabernacle stuck with adhesive tape onto the wall beside her bed — *Lean on Him, Emmanuel Is My Refuge, Rock of Ages Cleft for Me*.

Then in the total night around me, I heard a sound. It was my mother, and she was crying, not loudly at all, but from somewhere very deep inside her. I sat up in bed. Everything seemed to have stopped, not only time but my own heart and blood as well. Then my mother noticed that I was awake.

I did not ask her, and she did not tell me anything. There was no need. She held me in her arms, or I held her, I am not certain which. And after a while the first mourning stopped, too, as everything does sooner or later, for when the limits of endurance have been reached, then people must sleep.

In the days following my father's death, I stayed close beside my mother, and this was only partly for my own consoling. I also had the feeling that she needed my protection. I did not know from what, nor what I could possibly do, but something held me there. Reverend McKee called, and I sat with my grandmother and my mother in the living room. My mother told me that I did not need to stay unless I wanted to, but I refused to go. What I thought chiefly was that he would speak of the healing power of prayer, and all that, and it would be bound to make my mother cry again. And in fact, it happened in just that way, but when it actually came, I could not protect her from this assault. I could only sit there and pray my own prayer, which was that he would go away quickly.

My mother tried not to cry unless she was alone or with me. I also tried, but neither of us was entirely successful. Grandmother MacLeod, on the other hand, was never seen crying, not even the day of my father's funeral. But that day, when we had returned to the house and she had taken off her black velvet overshoes and her heavy sealskin coat with its black fur that was the softest thing I had ever touched, she stood in the hallway and for the first time she looked unsteady. When I reached out instinctively towards her, she sighed.

"That's right," she said. "You might just take my arm while I go upstairs, Vanessa."

That was the most my Grandmother MacLeod

ever gave in, to anyone's sight. I left her in her bedroom, sitting on the straight chair beside her bed and looking at the picture of my father that had been taken when he graduated from medical college. Maybe she was sorry now that she had only the one photograph of him, but whatever she felt, she did not say.

I went down into the kitchen. I had scarcely spoken to Noreen since my father's death. This had not been done on purpose. I simply had not seen her. I had not really seen anyone except my mother. Looking at Noreen now, I suddenly recalled the sparrow. I felt physically sick, remembering the fearful darting and plunging of those wings, and the fact that it was I who had opened the window and let it in. Then an inexplicable fury took hold of me, some terrifying need to hurt, burn, destroy. Absolutely without warning, either to her or myself, I hit Noreen as hard as I could. When she swung around, appalled, I hit out at her once more, my arms and legs flailing. Her hands snatched at my wrists, and she held me, but still I continued to struggle, fighting blindly, my eyes tightly closed, as though she were a prison all around me and I was battling to get out. Finally, too shocked at myself to go on, I went limp in her grasp and she let me drop to the floor.

"Vanessa! I never done one single solitary thing to you, and here you are hitting and scratching me like that! What in the world has got into you?"

I began to say I was sorry, which was certainly true, but I did not say it. I could not say anything.

"You're not yourself, what with your dad and everything," she excused me. "I been praying every night that your dad is with God, Vanessa. I know he wasn't actually saved in the regular way, but still and all —"

"Shut up," I said.

Something in my voice made her stop talking. I rose from the floor and stood in the kitchen doorway.

"He didn't need to be saved," I went on coldly, distinctly. "And he is not in Heaven, because there is no Heaven. And it doesn't matter, see? *It doesn't matter!*"

Noreen's face looked peculiarly vulnerable now, her high wide cheekbones and puzzled childish eyes, and the thick russet tangle of her hair. I had not hurt her much before, when I hit her. But I had hurt her now, hurt her in some inexcusable way. Yet I sensed, too, that already she was gaining some satisfaction out of feeling sorrowful about my disbelief.

I went upstairs to my room. Momentarily I felt a sense of calm, almost of acceptance. *Rest beyond the river*. I knew now what that meant. It meant Nothing. It meant only silence, forever.

Then I lay down on my bed and spent the last of my tears, or what seemed then to be the last. Because, despite what I had said to Noreen, it did matter. It mattered, but there was no help for it.

Everything changed after my father's death. The MacLeod house could not be kept up any longer. My mother sold it to a local merchant who subsequently covered the deep red of the brick over with yellow stucco. Something about the house had always made me uneasy — that tower room where Grandmother MacLeod's potted plants drooped in a lethargic and lime-green confusion, those long stairways and hidden places, the attic which I had always imagined to be dwelt in by the spirits of the family dead, that gigantic portrait of the Duke of Wellington at the top of the stairs. It was never an endearing house. And yet when it was no longer ours, and when the Virginia creeper had been torn down and the dark walls turned to a light marigold, I went out of my way to avoid walking past, for it seemed to me that the house had lost the stern dignity that was its very heart.

Noreen went back to the farm. My mother and brother and myself moved into Grandfather Connor's house. Grandmother MacLeod went to live with Aunt Morag in Winnipeg. It was harder for her than for anyone, because so much of her life was bound up with the MacLeod house. She was fond of Aunt Morag, but that hardly counted. Her men were gone, her husband and her sons, and a family whose men are gone is no family at all. The day she left, my mother and I did not know what to say. Grandmother MacLeod looked even smaller than usual in her fur coat and her black velvet toque. She became extremely agitated about trivialities, and fussed about the possibility of the taxi not arriving on time. She had forbidden us to accompany her to the station. About my father, or the house, or anything important, she did not say a word. Then, when the taxi had finally arrived, she turned to my mother.

"Roddie will have Ewen's seal ring, of course, with the MacLeod crest on it," she said. "But there is another seal as well, don't forget, the larger one with the crest and motto. It's meant to be worn on a watch chain. I keep it in my jewelbox. It was Roderick's. Roddie's to have that, too, when I die. Don't let Morag talk you out of it."

During the Second World War, when I was seventeen and in love with an airman who did not love me, and desperately anxious to get away from Manawaka and from my grandfather's house, I happened one day to be going through the old mahogany desk that had belonged to my father. It had a number of small drawers inside, and I accidentally pulled one of these all the way out. Behind it there was another drawer, one I had not known about. Curiously, I opened it. Inside there was a letter written on almost transparent paper in a cramped angular handwriting. It began — *Cher Monsieur Ewen* — That was all I could make out, for the writing was nearly impossible to read and my French was not good. It was dated 1919. With it, there was a picture of a girl, looking absurdly old-fashioned to my eyes, like the faces on long-discarded calendars or chocolate boxes. But beneath the dated quality of the photograph, she seemed neither expensive nor cheap. She looked like what she probably had been — an ordinary middle-class girl, but in another country. She wore her hair in long ringlets, and her mouth was shaped into a sweetly sad posed smile like Mary Pickford's. That was all. There was nothing else in the drawer.

I looked for a long time at the girl, and hoped she had meant some momentary and unexpected freedom. I remembered what he had said to me, after I hadn't gone to the Remembrance Day parade.

"What are you doing, Vanessa?" my mother called from the kitchen.

"Nothing," I replied.

I took the letter and picture outside and burned them. That was all I could do for him. Now that we might have talked together, it was many years too late. Perhaps it would not have been possible anyway. I did not know.

As I watched the smile of the girl turn into scorched paper, I grieved for my father as though he had just died now.

D. H. LAWRENCE

The Rocking-Horse Winner

There was a woman who was beautiful, who started with all the advantages, yet she had no luck. She married for love, and the love turned to dust. She had bonny children, yet she felt they had been thrust upon her, and she could not love them. They looked at her coldly, as if they were finding fault with her. And hurriedly she felt she must cover up some fault in herself. Yet what it was that she must cover up she never knew. Nevertheless, when her children were present, she always felt the centre of her heart go hard. This troubled her, and in her manner she was all the more gentle and anxious for her children, as if she loved them very much. Only she herself knew that at the centre of her heart was a hard little place that could not feel love, no, not for anybody. Everybody else said of her: "She is such a good mother. She adores her children." Only she herself, and her children themselves, knew it was not so. They read it in each other's eyes.

There were a boy and two little girls. They lived in a pleasant house, with a garden, and they had discreet servants, and felt themselves superior to anyone in the neighbourhood.

Although they lived in style, they felt always an anxiety in the house. There was never enough money. The mother had a small income, and the father had a small income, but not nearly enough for the social position which they had to keep up. The father went in to town to some office. But though he had good prospects, these prospects never materialized. There was always the grinding sense of the shortage of money, though the style was always kept up.

At last the mother said: "I will see if I can't make something." But she did not know where to begin. She racked her brains, and tried this thing and the other, but could not find anything successful. The failure made deep lines come into her face. He children were growing up, they would have to go to school. There must be more money, there must be more money. The father, who was always very handsome and expensive in his tastes, seemed as if he never *would* be able to do anything worth doing. And the mother, who had a great belief in herself, did not succeed any better, and her tastes were just as expensive.

And so the house came to be haunted by the unspoken phrase: *There must be more money! There must be more money!* The children could hear it all the time, though nobody said it aloud. They heard it at Christmas, when the expensive and splendid toys filled the nursery. Behind the shining modern rocking-horse, behind the smart doll's-house, a voice would start whispering: "There *must* be more money! There *must* be more money!" And the children would stop playing, to listen for a moment. They would look into each other's eyes to see if they had all heard. And each one saw in the eyes of the other two that they too had heard. "There *must* be more money! There *must* be more money!"

It came whispering from the springs of the still-swaying rocking-horse, and even the horse, bending his wooden, champing head, heard it. The big doll, sitting so pink and smirking in her new pram, could hear it quite plainly, and seemed to be smirking all the more self-consciously because of it. The foolish puppy, too, that took the place of the teddy-bear, he was looking so extraordinarily foolish for no other reason but that he heard the secret whisper all over the house: "There *must* be more money!"

Yet nobody ever said it aloud. The whisper was everywhere, and therefore no one spoke it. Just as no one ever says: "We are breathing!" in spite of the fact that breath is coming and going all the time.

"Mother," said the boy Paul one day, "why don't we keep a car of our own? Why do we always use uncle's, or else a taxi?"

"Because we're the poor members of the family," said the mother.

"But why *are* we, mother?"

"Well — I suppose," she said slowly and bitterly, "it's because your father has no luck."

The boy was silent for some time.

"Is luck money, mother?" he asked rather timidly.

"No, Paul. Not quite. It's what causes you to have money."

"Oh!" said Paul vaguely. "I thought when Uncle Oscar said *filthy lucker*, it meant money."

"*Filthy lucre* does mean money," said the mother. "But it's lucre, not luck."

"Oh!" said the boy. "Then what *is* luck, mother?"

"It's what causes you to have money. If you're lucky you have money. That's why it's better to be born lucky than rich. If you're rich, you may lose your money. But if you're lucky, you will always get more money."

"Oh! Will you? And is father not lucky?"

"Very unlucky, I should say," she said bitterly.

The boy watched her with unsure eyes.

"Why?" he asked.

"I don't know. Nobody ever knows why one person is lucky and another unlucky."

"Don't they? Nobody at all? Does *nobody* know?"

"Perhaps God. But He never tells."

"He ought to, then. And aren't you lucky either, mother?"

"I can't be, if I married an unlucky husband."

"But by yourself, aren't you?"

"I used to think I was, before I married. Now I think I am very unlucky indeed."

"Why?"

"Well — never mind! Perhaps I'm not really," she said.

The child looked at her, to see if she meant it. But he saw, by the lines of her mouth, that she was only trying to hide something from him.

"Well, anyhow," he said stoutly, "I'm a lucky person."

"Why?" said his mother, with a sudden laugh.

He stared at her. He didn't even know why he had said it.

"God told me," he asserted, brazening it out.

"I hope He did, dear!" she said, again with a laugh, but rather bitter.

"He did, mother!"

"Excellent!" said the mother, using one of her husband's exclamations.

The boy saw she did not believe him; or, rather, that she paid no attention to his assertion. This angered him somewhat, and made him want to compel her attention.

He went off by himself, vaguely, in a childish way seeking for the clue to "luck." Absorbed, taking no heed of other people, he went about with a sort of stealth, seeking inwardly for luck. He wanted luck, he wanted it, he wanted it. When the two girls were playing dolls in the nursery, he would sit on his big rocking-horse, charging madly into space, with a frenzy that made the little girls peer at him uneasily. Wildly the horse careered, the waving dark hair of the boy tossed, his eyes had a strange glare in them. The little girls dared not speak to him.

When he had ridden to the end of his mad little journey, he climbed down and stood in front of his rocking-horse, staring fixedly into its lowered face. Its red mouth was slightly open, its big eye was wide and glassy-bright.

"Now!" he would silently command the snorting steed. "Now, take me to where there is luck! Now take me."

And he would slash the horse on the neck with the little whip he had asked Uncle Oscar for. He *knew* the horse could take him to where there was luck, if only he forced it. So he would mount again, and start on his furious ride, hoping at last to get there. He knew he could get there.

"You'll break your horse, Paul!" said the nurse.

"He's always riding like that! I wish he'd leave off!" said his elder sister Joan.

But he only glared down on them in silence. Nurse gave him up. She could make nothing of him. Anyhow he was growing beyond her.

One day his mother and his Uncle Oscar came in when he was on one of his furious rides. He did not speak to them.

"Hallo, you young jockey! Riding a winner?" said his uncle.

"Aren't you growing too big for a rocking-horse? You're not a very little boy any longer, you know," said his mother.

But Paul only gave a blue glare from his big, rather close-set eyes. He would speak to nobody when he was in full tilt. His mother watched him with an anxious expression on her face.

At last he suddenly stopped forcing his horse into the mechanical gallop, and slid down.

"Well, I got there!" he announced fiercely, his blue eyes still flaring, and his sturdy long legs straddling apart.

"Where did you get to?" asked his mother.

"Where I wanted to go," he flared back at her.

"That's right, son!" said Uncle Oscar. "Don't you stop till you get there. What's the horse's name?"

"He doesn't have a name," said the boy.

"Gets on without all right?" asked the uncle.

"Well, he has different names. He was called Sansovino last week."

"Sansovino, eh? Won the Ascot. How did you know his name?"

"He always talks about horse-races with Bassett," said Joan.

The uncle was delighted to find that his small nephew was posted with all the racing news. Bassett, the young gardener, who had been wounded in the left foot in the war and had got his present job through Oscar Cresswell, whose batman he had been, was a perfect blade of the "turf." He lived in the racing events, and the small boy lived with him.

Oscar Cresswell got it all from Bassett.

"Master Paul comes and asks me, so I can't do more than tell him, sir," said Bassett, his face terribly serious, as if he were speaking of religious matters.

"And does he ever put anything on a horse he fancies?"

"Well — I don't want to give him away — he's a young sport, a fine sport, sir. Would you mind asking him himself? He sort of takes pleasure in it, and perhaps he'd feel I was giving him away, sir, if you don't mind.

Bassett was serious as a church.

The uncle went back to his nephew and took him off for a ride in the car.

"Say, Paul, old man, do you ever put anything on a horse?" the uncle asked.

The boy watched the handsome man closely.

"Why, do you think I oughtn't to?" he parried.
"Not a bit of it! I thought perhaps you might give me a tip for the Lincoln."

The car sped on into the country, going down to Uncle Oscar's place in Hampshire.

"Honour bright?" said the nephew.

"Honour bright, son!" said the uncle.

"Well, then, Daffodil."

"Daffodil! I doubt it, sonny. What about Mirza?"

"I only know the winner," said the boy. "That's Daffodil."

"Daffodil, eh?"

There was a pause. Daffodil was an obscure horse comparatively.

"Uncle!"

"Yes, son?"

"You won't let it go any further, will you? I promised Bassett."

"Bassett be damned, old man! What's he got to do with it?"

"We're partners. We've been partners from the first. Uncle, he lent me my first five shillings, which I lost. I promised him, honour bright, it was only between me and him; only you gave me that ten-shilling note I started winning with, so I thought you were lucky. You won't let it go any further, will you?"

The boy gazed at his uncle from those big, hot, blue eyes, set rather close together. The uncle stirred and laughed uneasily.

"Right you are, son! I'll keep your tip private. Daffodil, eh? How much are you putting on him?"

"All except twenty pounds," said the boy. "I keep that in reserve."

The uncle thought it a good joke.

"You keep twenty pounds in reserve, do you, my young romancer? What are you betting, then?"

"I'm betting three hundred," said the boy gravely. "But it's between you and me, Uncle Oscar! Honour bright?"

The uncle burst into a roar of laughter.

"It's between you and me all right, you young Nat Gould," he said, laughing. "But where's your three hundred?"

"Bassett keeps it for me. We're partners."

"You are, are you! And what is Bassett putting on Daffodil?"

"He won't go quite as high as I do, I expect. Perhaps he'll go a hundred and fifty."

"What, pennies?" laughed the uncle.

"Pounds," said the child, with a surprised look at his uncle. "Bassett keeps a bigger reserve than I do."

Between wonder and amazement Uncle Oscar was silent. He pursued the matter no further, but he determined to take his nephew with him to the Lincoln races.

"Now, son," he said, "I'm putting twenty on Mirza, and I'll put five for you on any horse you fancy. What's your pick?"

"Daffodil, uncle."

"No, not the fiver on Daffodil!"

"I should if it was my own fiver," said the child.

"Good! Good! Right you are! A fiver for me and a fiver for you on Daffodil."

The child had never been to a race-meeting before, and his eyes were blue fire. He pursed his mouth tight, and watched. A Frenchman just in front had put his money on Lancelot. Wild with excitement, he flayed his arms up and down, yelling *"Lancelot! Lancelot!"* in his French accent.

Daffodil came in first, Lancelot second, Mirza third. The child, flushed and with eyes blazing, was curiously serene. His uncle brought him four five-pound notes, four to one.

"What am I to do with these?" he cried, waving them before the boy's eyes.

"I suppose we'll talk to Bassett," said the boy. "I expect I have fifteen hundred now; and twenty in reserve; and this twenty."

His uncle studied him for some moments.

"Look here, son!" he said. "You're not serious about Bassett and that fifteen hundred, are you?"

"Yes, I am. But it's between you and me, uncle. Honour bright!"

"Honour bright all right, son! But I must talk to Bassett."

"If you'd like to be a partner, uncle, with Bassett and me, we could all be partners. Only, you'd have to promise, honour bright, uncle, not to let it go beyond us three. Bassett and I are lucky, and you must be lucky, because it was your ten shillings I started winning with. . . ."

Uncle Oscar took both Bassett and Paul into Richmond Park for an afternoon, and there they talked.

"It's like this, you see, sir," Bassett said. "Master Paul would get me talking about racing events, spinning yarns, you know, sir. And he was always keen on knowing if I'd made or if I'd lost. It's about a year since, now, that I put five shilling on Blush of Dawn for him — and we lost. Then the luck turned, with that ten shillings he had from you, that we put on Singhalese. And since that time, it's been pretty steady, all things considering. What do you say, Master Paul?"

"We're all right when we're sure," said Paul. "It's when we're not quite sure that we go down."

"Oh, but we're careful then," said Bassett.

"But when are you *sure?"* smiled Uncle Oscar.

"It's Master Paul, sir," said Bassett, in a secret, religious voice. "It's as if he had it from heaven. Like Daffodil, now, for the Lincoln. That was as sure as eggs."

"Did you put anything on Daffodil?" asked Oscar Cresswell.

"Yes, sir. I made my bit."

"And my nephew?"

Bassett was obstinately silent, looking at Paul.

"I made twelve hundred, didn't I, Bassett?

I told uncle I was putting three hundred on Daffodil."

"That's right," said Bassett, nodding.

"But where's the money?" asked the uncle.

"I keep it safe locked up, sir. Master Paul he can have it any minute he likes to ask for it."

"What, fifteen hundred pounds?"

"And twenty! And *forty,* that is, with the twenty he made on the course."

"It's amazing!" said the uncle.

"If Master Paul offers you to be partners, sir, I would, if I were you; if you'll excuse me," said Bassett.

Oscar Cresswell thought about it.

"I'll see the money," he said.

They drove home again, and sure enough, Bassett came round to the garden-house with fifteen hundred pounds in notes. The twenty pounds reserve was left with Joe Glee, in the Turf Commission deposit.

"You see, it's all right, uncle, when I'm *sure!* Then we go strong, for all we're worth. Don't we, Bassett?"

"We do that, Master Paul."

"And when are you sure?" said the uncle, laughing.

"Oh, well, sometimes I'm *absolutely* sure, like about Daffodil," said the boy; "and sometimes I have an idea; and sometimes I haven't even an idea, have I, Bassett? Then we're careful, because we mostly go down."

"You do, do you! And when you're sure, like about Daffodil, what makes you sure, sonny?"

"Oh, well, I don't know," said the boy uneasily. "I'm sure, you know, uncle; that's all."

"It's as if he had it from heaven, sir," Bassett reiterated.

"I should say so!" said the uncle.

But he became a partner. And when the Leger was coming on, Paul was "sure" about Lively Spark, which was a quite inconsiderable horse. The boy insisted on putting a thousand on the horse, Bassett went for five hundred, and Oscar Cresswell two hundred. Lively Spark came in first, and the betting had been ten to one against him. Paul had made ten thousand.

"You see," he said, "I was absolutely sure of him."

Even Oscar Cresswell had cleared two thousand.

"Look here, son," he said, "this sort of thing makes me nervous."

"It needn't, uncle! Perhaps I shan't be sure again for a long time."

"But what are you going to do with your money?" asked the uncle.

"Of course," said the boy, "I started it for mother. She said she had no luck, because father is unlucky, so I thought if *I* was lucky, it might stop whispering."

"What might stop whispering?"

"Our house. I *hate* our house for whispering."

"What does it whisper?"

"Why — why" — the boy fidgeted — "why, I don't know. But it's always short of money, you know, uncle."

"I know it, son, I know it."

"You know people send mother writs, don't you, uncle?"

"I'm afraid I do," said the uncle.

"And then the house whispers, like people laughing at you behind your back. It's awful, that is! I thought if I was lucky ..."

"You might stop it," added the uncle.

The boy watched him with big blue eyes, that had an uncanny cold fire in them, and he said never a word.

"Well, then!" said the uncle. "What are we doing?"

"I shouldn't like mother to know I was lucky," said the boy.

"Why not, son?"

"She'd stop me."

"I don't think she would."

"Oh!" — and the boy writhed in an odd way — "I *don't* want her to know, uncle."

"All right, son! We'll manage it without her knowing."

They managed it very easily. Paul, at the other's suggestion, handed over five thousand pounds to his uncle, who deposited it with the family lawyer, who was then to inform Paul's mother that a relative had put five thousand pounds into his hands, which sum was to be paid out a thousand pounds at a time, on the mother's birthday, for the next five years.

"So she'll have a birthday present of a thousand pounds for five successive years," said Uncle Oscar. "I hope it won't make it all the harder for her later."

Paul's mother had her birthday in November. The house had been "whispering" worse than ever lately, and, even in spite of his luck, Paul could not bear up against it. He was very anxious to see the effect of the birthday letter, telling his mother about the thousand pounds.

When there were no visitors, Paul now took his meals with his parents, as he was beyond the nursery control. His mother went into town nearly every day. She had discovered that she had an odd knack of sketching furs and dress materials, so she worked secretly in the studio of a friend who was the chief "artist" for the leading drapers. She drew the figures of ladies in furs and ladies in silk and sequins for the newspaper advertisements. This young woman artist earned several thousand pounds a year, but Paul's mother only made several hundreds, and she was again dissatisfied. She so wanted to be first in something, and she did not succeed, even in making sketches for drapery advertisements.

She was down to breakfast on the morning of her birthday. Paul watched her face as she read her letters. He knew the lawyer's letter. As his mother read it, her face hardened and became more expressionless. Then a cold, determined look came on her mouth. She hid the letter under the pile of others, and said not a word about it.

"Didn't you have anything nice in the post for your birthday, mother?" said Paul.

"Quite moderately nice," she said, her voice cold and absent.

She went away to town without saying more.

But in the afternoon Uncle Oscar appeared. He said Paul's mother had had a long interview with the lawyer, asking if the whole five thousand could not be advanced at once, as she was in debt.

"What do you think, uncle?" said the boy.

"I leave it to you, son."

"Oh, let her have it, then! We can get some more with the other," said the boy.

"A bird in the hand is worth two in the bush, laddie!" said Uncle Oscar.

"But I'm sure to *know* for the Grand National; or the Lincolnshire; or else the Derby. I'm sure to know for *one* of them," said Paul.

So Uncle Oscar signed the agreement, and Paul's mother touched the whole five thousand. Then something very curious happened. The voices in the house suddenly went mad, like a chorus of frogs on a spring evening. There were certain new furnishings, and Paul had a tutor. He was *really* going to Eton, his father's school, in the following autumn. There were flowers in the winter, and a blossoming of the luxury Paul's mother had been used to. And yet the voices in the house, behind the sprays of mimosa and almond blossom, and from under the piles of iridescent cushions, simply trilled and screamed in a sort of ecstasy: "There *must* be more money! Oh-h-h; there *must* be more money. Oh, now, now-w! — there *must* be more money! — more than ever! More than ever!"

It frightened Paul terribly. He studied away at his Latin and Greek with his tutors. But his intense hours were spent with Bassett. The Grand National had gone by: he had not "known," and had lost a hundred pounds. Summer was at hand. He was in agony for the Lincoln. But even for the Lincoln he didn't "know," and he lost fifty pounds. He became wild-eyed and strange, as if something were going to explode in him.

"Let it alone, son! Don't you bother about it!" urged Uncle Oscar. But it was as if the boy couldn't really hear what his uncle was saying.

"I've got to know for the Derby! I've got to know for the Derby!" the child reiterated, his big blue eyes blazing with a sort of madness.

His mother noticed how overwrought he was.

"You'd better go to the seaside. Wouldn't you like to go now to the seaside, instead of waiting? I think you'd better," she said, looking down at him anxiously, her heart curiously heavy because of him.

But the child lifted his uncanny blue eyes.

"I couldn't possibly go before the Derby, mother!" he said. "I couldn't possibly!"

"Why not?" she said, her voice becoming heavy when she was opposed. "Why not? You can still go from the seaside to see the Derby with your Uncle Oscar, if that's what you wish. No need for you to wait here. Besides, I think you care too much about these races. It's a bad sign. My family has been a gambling family, and you won't know till you grow up how much damage it has done. But it has done damage. I shall have to send Bassett away, and ask Uncle Oscar not to talk racing to you, unless you promise to be reasonable about it; go away to the seaside and forget it. You're all nerves!"

"I'll do what you like, mother, so long as you don't send me away till after the Derby," the boy said.

"Send you away from where? Just from this house?"

"Yes," he said, gazing at her.

"Why, you curious child, what makes you care about this house so much, suddenly? I never knew you loved it."

He gazed at her without speaking. He had a secret within a secret, something he had not divulged, even to Bassett or to his Uncle Oscar.

But his mother, after standing undecided and a little bit sullen for some moments, said:

"Very well, then! Don't go to the seaside till after the Derby, if you don't wish it. But promise me you won't let your nerves go to pieces. Promise you won't think so much about horse-racing and *events,* as you call them!"

"Oh, no," said the boy casually. "I won't think much about them, mother. You needn't worry. I wouldn't worry, mother, if I were you."

"If you were me and I were you," said his mother, "I wonder what we *should* do!"

"But you know you needn't worry, mother, don't you?" the boy repeated.

"I should be awfully glad to know it," she said wearily.

"Oh, well, you *can,* you know. I mean, you *ought* to know you needn't worry," he insisted.

"Ought I? Then I'll see about it," she said.

Paul's secret of secrets was his wooden horse, that which had no name. Since he was emancipated from a nurse and a nursery-governess, he had had his rocking-horse removed to his own bedroom at the top of the house.

"Surely, you're too big for a rocking-horse!" his mother had remonstrated.

"Well, you see, mother, till I can have a *real* horse, I like to have *some* sort of animal about," had been his quaint answer.

"Do you feel he keeps you company?" she laughed.

"Oh, yes! He's very good, he always keeps me company, when I'm there," said Paul.

So the horse, rather shabby, stood in an arrested prance in the boy's bedroom.

The Derby was drawing near, and the boy grew more and more tense. He hardly heard what was spoken to him, he was very frail, and his eyes were really uncanny. His mother had sudden strange seizures of uneasiness about him. Sometimes, for half-an-hour, she would feel a sudden anxiety about him that was almost anguish. She wanted to rush to him at once, and know he was safe.

Two nights before the Derby, she was at a big party in town, when one of her rushes of anxiety about her boy, her first-born, gripped her heart till she could hardly speak. She fought with the feeling, might and main, for she believed in common sense. But it was too strong. She had to leave the dance and go downstairs to telephone to the country. The children's nursery-governess was terribly surprised and startled at being rung up in the night.

"Are the children all right, Miss Wilmot?"

"Oh, yes, they are quite all right."

"Master Paul? Is he all right?"

"He went to bed as right as a trivet. Shall I run up and look at him?"

"No," said Paul's mother reluctantly. "No! Don't trouble. It's all right. Don't sit up. We shall be home fairly soon." She did not want her son's privacy intruded upon.

"Very good," said the governess.

It was about one o'clock when Paul's mother and father drove up to their house. All was still. Paul's mother went to her room and slipped off her white fur cloak. She had told her maid not to wait up for her. She heard her husband downstairs, mixing a whisky-and-soda.

And then, because of the strange anxiety at her heart, she stole upstairs to her son's room. Noiselessly she went along the upper corridor. Was there a faint noise? What was it?

She stood, with arrested muscles, outside his door, listening. There was a strange, heavy, and yet not loud noise. Her heart stood still. It was a soundless noise, yet rushing and powerful. Something huge, in violent, hushed motion. What was it? What in God's name was it? She ought to know. She felt that she knew the noise. She knew what it was.

Yet she could not place it. She couldn't say what it was. And on and on it went, like a madness.

Softly, frozen with anxiety and fear, she turned the door-handle.

The room was dark. Yet in the space near the window, she heard and saw something plunging to and fro. She gazed in fear and amazement.

Then suddenly she switched on the light, and saw her son, in his green pyjamas, madly surging on the rocking-horse. The blaze of light suddenly lit him up, as he urged the wooden horse, and lit her up, as she stood, blonde, in her dress of pale green and crystal, in the doorway.

"Paul!" she cried. "Whatever are you doing?"

"It's Malabar!" he screamed, in a powerful, strange voice. "It's Malabar!"

His eyes blazed at her for one strange and senseless second, as he ceased urging his wooden horse. Then he fell with a crash to the ground, and she, all her tormented motherhood flooding upon her, rushed to gather him up.

But he was unconscious, and unconscious he remained, with some brain-fever. He talked and tossed, and his mother sat stonily by his side.

"Malabar! It's Malabar! Bassett. Bassett, I *know!* It's Malabar!"

So the child cried, trying to get up and urge the rocking-horse that gave him his inspiration.

"What does he mean by Malabar?" asked the heart-frozen mother.

"I don't know," said the father stonily.

"What does he mean by Malabar?" she asked her brother Oscar.

"It's one of the horses running for the Derby," was the answer.

And in spite of himself, Oscar Cresswell spoke to Bassett, and himself put a thousand on Malabar: at fourteen to one.

The third day of the illness was critical: they were waiting for a change. The boy, with his rather long, curly hair, was tossing ceaselessly on the pillow. He neither slept nor regained consciousness, and his eyes were like blue stones. His mother sat, feeling her heart had gone, turned actually into a stone.

In the evening, Oscar Cresswell did not come, but Bassett sent a message, saying could he come up for one moment, just one moment? Paul's mother was very angry at the intrusion, but on second thought she agreed. The boy was the same. Perhaps Bassett might bring him to consciousness.

The gardener, a shortish fellow with a little brown moustache, and sharp little brown eyes, tip-toed into the room, touched his imaginary cap to Paul's mother, and stole to the bedside, staring with glittering, smallish eyes, at the tossing, dying child.

"Master Paul!" he whispered. "Master Paul! Malabar came in first all right, a clean win. I did as you told me. You've made over seventy thousand pounds, you have; you've got over eighty thousand. Malabar came in all right, Master Paul."

"Malabar! Malabar! Did I say Malabar, mother? Did I say Malabar? Do you think I'm lucky, mother? I knew Malabar, didn't I? Over eighty thousand pounds! I call that lucky, don't you, mother? Over eighty thousand pounds! I knew, didn't I know I knew? Malabar came in all right. If I ride my horse till I'm sure, then I tell you, Bassett, you can go as high as you like. Did you go for all you were worth, Bassett?"

"I went a thousand on it, Master Paul."

"I never told you, mother, that if I can ride my horse, and *get there*, then I'm absolutely sure — oh, absolutely! Mother, did I ever tell you? I *am* lucky!"

"No, you never did," said the mother.

But the boy died in the night.

And even as he lay dead, his mother heard her brother's voice saying to her: "My God, Hester, you're eighty-odd thousand to the good, and a poor devil of a son to the bad. But, poor devil, poor devil, he's best gone out of a life where he rides his rocking-horse to find a winner."

DORIS LESSING

A Room

When I first came into this flat of four small boxlike rooms, the bedroom was painted pale pink, except for the fireplace wall, which had a fanciful pink-and-blue paper. The woodwork was a dark purple, almost black. This paint is sold by a big decorating shop in the West End and is called Bilberry.

Two girls had the flat before me. Very little money, obviously, because the carpeting was going into holes and the walls were decorated with travel posters. The woman upstairs told me they often had parties that lasted all night. "But I liked to hear them, I enjoy the sounds of life." She was reproachful. I don't have parties often enough for her. The girls left no forwarding address, following the tradition for this flat. Over the years it has often happened that the bell rings and people ask for "Angus Ferguson — I thought he lived here?" And the Maitlands? And Mrs. Dowland? And the young Caitsbys? All these people, and probably many others, have lived in this flat, and departed leaving nothing behind. I know nothing about them, nor does anyone else in the building, though some of them have lived here for years.

I found the pink too assertive, and after several mistakes settled on white walls, leaving the plum-colour, or Bilberry, woodwork. First I had grey curtains, then blue ones. My bed is under the window. There is a desk, which I had meant to write on, but it is always too cluttered with papers. So I write in the livingroom or on the kitchen table. But I spend a lot of time in the bedroom. Bed is the best place for reading, thinking, or doing nothing. It is my room; it is where I feel I live, though the shape is bad and there are things about it that can never be anything but ugly. For instance, the fireplace was of iron — a bulging, knobbed, ornamental black. The girls had left it as it was, using a small gas heater in the opening. Its heavy ugliness kept drawing my eyes towards it; and I painted a panel from the ceiling downwards in the dark plum colour, so that the fireplace and the small thick shelf over it would be absorbed. On either side of the panel, since I could not have the whole wall in plum, which at night looks black, were left two panels of the absurd wallpaper which had bright people like birds in pink-and-blue cages. The fireplace seemed less obtrusive, but my fire is a gas fire, a square solid shape of bronze, brought from an earlier flat where it did not look too bad. But it does not fit here at all. So the whole wall doesn't work, it fails to come off.

Another wall, the one beside my bed, is also deformed. Over the bed swells a grainy irregular lump two or more feet across. Someone — Angus Ferguson? The Maitlands? Mrs. Dowland? — attempted to replace falling plaster and made a hash of it. No professional plasterer could have got away with such a protuberance.

On the whole, this wall gives me pleasure: it reminds me of the irregular whitewashed walls of another house I lived in once. Probably I chose to paint this room white because I wanted to have the whitewashed lumpy walls of that early house repeated here in London?

The ceiling is a ceiling: flat, white, plain. It has a plaster border which is too heavy for the room and looks as if it might fall off easily. The whole building has a look of solid ugliness, but it was built cheap, and is not solid at all. For instance, walls, tapped, sound hollow; the plaster, when exposed, at once starts to trickle as if the walls were of loose sand held together by wallpaper. I can hear anything that goes on over my head, where the old woman who likes to hear a bit of life lives with her husband. She is Swedish, gives Swedish lessons. She dresses prettily, and looks a dear respectable old thing. Yet she is quite mad. Her door has four heavy, specially fitted locks inside, as well as bolts and bars. If I knock she opens the door on a chain four inches long and peers through to make sure that I (or they) will not attack her. Inside is a vision of neatness and order. She spends all day cleaning and arranging. When she can't find anything more to do in her flat she posts notices on the stairs saying: "Any person who drops rubbish on these stairs will be reported to the Authorities!" Then she visits every flat in turn (there are eight identical flats, one above the other) and says confidingly: "Of course the notice isn't meant for you."

Her husband works for an export firm and is away a good deal. When she expects him back, she dresses as carefully as a bride and goes off to meet him, blushing. On the nights he comes back from his trips the bed creaks over my head, and I hear them giggling.

They are an orderly couple, bed at eleven every night, up every morning at nine. As for myself, my life has no outward order and I like having them up there. Sometimes, when I've worked late, I hear them getting up and I think through my sleep or half-sleep: Good, the day's started, has it? And I drift back to semiconsciousness blended with their footsteps and the rattling of cups.

Sometimes, when I sleep in the afternoons, which I do because afternoon sleep is more interesting than night sleep, she takes a nap too. I think of her and of myself lying horizontally above each other, as if we were on two shelves.

When I lie down after lunch there is nothing unplanned about it. First I must feel the inner disturbance or alertness that is due to overstimulation, or being a little sick or very tired. Then I darken the room, shut all the doors so the telephone won't wake me (though its distant ringing can be a welcome dream-progenitor) and I get into bed carefully, preserving the mood. It is these sleeps which help me with my work, telling me what to write or where I've gone wrong. And they save me from the fever of restlessness that comes from seeing too many people. I always drift off to sleep in the afternoons with the interest due to a long journey into the unknown, and the sleep is thin and extraordinary and takes me into regions hard to describe in a waking state.

But one afternoon there was no strange journey, nor was there useful information about my work. The sleep was so different from usual that for some time I thought I was awake.

I had been lying in the semidark, the curtains, of varying shades of dark blue, making a purply-moving shade. Outside it was a busy afternoon. I could hear sounds from the market underneath, and there was angry shouting, a quarrel of some kind, a man's voice and a woman's. I was looking at the fireplace and thinking how ugly it was, wondering what sort of person had deliberately chosen such a hideous shape of black iron. Though of course I had painted it over. Yes, whether I could afford it or not, I must get rid of the square bronze gas fire and find a prettier one. I saw the bronze shape had gone; there was a small black iron grate and a small fire in it, smoking. The smoke was coming into the room, and my eyes were sore.

The room was different; I felt chilled and estranged from myself as I looked. The walls had a paper whose general effect was a dingy brown, but looking closely at it I saw a small pattern of brownish-yellow leaves and brown stems. There were stains on it. The ceiling was yellowish and shiny from the smoke. There were some shreds of pinky-brown curtains at the windows with a tear in one so that the bottom edge hung down.

I was no longer lying on the bed, but sitting by the fire across the room, looking at the bed and at the window. Outside a shrill quarrel went on, the voices rising up from the street. I felt cold, I was shivering, and my eyes watered. In the little grate sat three small lumps of shiny coal, smoking dismally. Under me was a cushion or a folded coat, something like that. The room seemed much larger. Yes, it was a largish room. A chest of brown-varnished wood stain stood by the bed, which was low, a good foot lower than mine. There was a red army blanket stretched across the bed's foot. The recesses on either side of the fireplace had shallow wooden shelves down them, holding folded clothes, old magazines, crockery, a brown teapot. These things conveyed an atmosphere of thin poverty.

I was alone in the room, though someone was next door. I could hear sounds that made me unhappy, apprehensive. From upstairs a laugh, hostile to me. Was the old Swedish lady laughing? With whom? Had her husband come back suddenly?

I was desolate with loneliness that felt it would never be assuaged, no one would ever come to comfort me. I sat and looked at the bed which had the cheap red blanket on it that suggested illness, and sniffed because the smoke was tearing at the back of my throat. I was a child, I knew that. And that there was a war, something to do with war, war had something to do with this dream or memory —*whose?* I came back to my own room, lying on my bed, with silence upstairs and next door. I was alone in the flat, watching my soft dark blue curtains softly moving. I was filled with misery.

I left my pretty bedroom and made myself tea; then returned to draw the curtains and let the light in. I switched on the gas heater, which came up hot and red, driving the memory of cold away; and I looked behind its bronze efficiency into a grate that had not had coals in it, I knew, for years.

I have tried to dream myself back into that other room which is under this room, or beside it, or in it, or existing in someone's memory. Which war was it? Whose was the chilly poverty? And I would like to know more about the frightened little child. He (or she) must have been very small for the room to look so big. So far I have failed. Perhaps it was the quarrel outside in the street that . . . that *what?* And why?

ALISTAIR MACLEOD

The Boat

There are times even now, when I awake at four o'clock in the morning with the terrible fear that I have overslept; when I imagine that my father is waiting for me in the room below the darkened stairs or that the shorebound men are tossing pebbles against my window while blowing their hands and stomping their feet impatiently on the frozen steadfast earth. There are times when I am half out of bed and fumbling for socks and mumbling for words before I realize that I am foolishly alone, that no one waits at the base of the stairs and no boat rides restlessly in the waters by the pier.

At such times only the grey corpses on the overflowing ashtray beside my bed bear witness to the extinction of the latest spark and silently await the crushing out of the most recent of their fellows. And then because I am afraid to be alone with death, I dress rapidly, make a great to-do about clearing my throat, turn on both faucets in the sink and proceed to make loud splashing ineffectual noises. Later I go out and walk the mile to the all-night restaurant.

In the winter it is a very cold walk and there are often tears in my eyes when I arrive. The waitress usually gives a sympathetic little shiver and says, "Boy, it must be really cold out there; you got tears in your eyes."

"Yes," I say, "it sure is; it really is."

And then the three or four of us who are always in such places at such times make uninteresting little protective chit-chat until the dawn reluctantly arrives. Then I swallow the coffee which is always bitter and leave with a great busy rush because by that time I have to worry about being late and whether I have a clean shirt and whether my car will start and about all the other countless things one must worry about when he teaches at a great Midwestern university. And I know then that that day will go by as have all the days of the past ten years, for the call and the voices and the shapes and the boat were not really there in the early morning's darkness and I have all kinds of comforting reality to prove it. They are only shadows and echoes, the animals a child's hands make on the wall by lamplight, and the voices from the rain barrel; the cuttings from an old movie made in the black and white of long ago.

I first became conscious of the boat in the same way and at almost the same time that I became aware of the people it supported. My earliest recollection of my father is a view from the floor of gigantic rubber boots and then of being suddenly elevated and having my face pressed against the stubble of his cheek, and of how it tasted of salt and of how he smelled of salt from his red-soled rubber boots to the shaggy whiteness of his hair.

When I was very small, he took me for my first ride in the boat. I rode the half-mile from our house to the wharf on his shoulders and I remember the sound of his rubber boots galumphing along the gravel beach, the tune of the indecent little song he used to sing, and the odour of the salt.

The floor of the boat was permeated with the same odour and in its constancy I was not aware of change. In the harbour we made our little circle and returned. He tied the boat by its painter, fastened the stern to its permanent anchor and lifted me high over his head to the solidity of the wharf. Then he climbed up the little iron ladder that led to the wharf's cap, placed me once more upon his shoulders and galumphed off again.

When we returned to the house everyone made a great fuss over my precocious excursion and asked, "How did you like the boat?" "Were you afraid in the boat?" "Did you cry in the boat?" They repeated "the boat" at the end of all their questions and I knew it must be very important to everyone.

My earliest recollection of my mother is of being alone with her in the mornings while my father was away in the boat. She seemed to be always repairing clothes that were "torn in the boat," preparing food "to be eaten in the boat" or looking for "the boat" through our kitchen window which faced upon the sea. When my father returned about noon, she would ask, "Well, how did things go in the boat today?" It was the first question I remember asking: "Well, how did things go in the boat today?" "Well, how did things go in the boat today?"

The boat in our lives was registered at Port Hawkesbury. She was what Nova Scotians called a Cape Island boat and was designed for the small inshore fishermen who sought the lobsters of the spring and the mackerel of summer and later the cod and haddock and hake. She was thirty-two feet long and nine wide, and was powered by an engine from a Chevrolet truck. She had a marine clutch and a high speed reverse gear and was painted light green with the name *Jenny Lynn* stencilled in black letters on her bow and painted on an oblong plate across her stern. Jenny Lynn had been my mother's maiden name and the boat was called after her as another link in the chain of tradition. Most of the boats that berthed at the wharf bore the names of some female member of their owner's household.

I say this now as if I knew it all then. All at once, all about boat dimensions and engines, and as if on the day of my first childish voyage I noticed the difference between a stencilled name and a painted name. But of course it was not that way at all, for I learned it all very slowly and there was not time enough.

I learned first about our house which was one of about fifty which marched around the horseshoe of our harbour and the wharf which was its heart. Some of them were so close to the water that during a storm the sea spray splashed against their windows while others were built farther along the beach as was the case with ours. The houses and their people, like those of the neighbouring towns and villages, were the result of Ireland's discontent and Scotland's Highland Clearances and America's War of Independence. Impulsive emotional Catholic Celts who could not bear to live with England and shrewd determined Protestant Puritans who, in the years after 1776, could not bear to live without.

The most important room in our house was one of those oblong old-fashioned kitchens heated by a wood- and coal-burning stove. Behind the stove was a box of kindlings and beside it a coal scuttle. A heavy wooden table with leaves that expanded or reduced its dimensions stood in the middle of the floor. There were five wooden home-made chairs which had been chipped and hacked by a variety of knives. Against the east wall, opposite the stove, there was a couch which sagged in the middle and had a cushion for a pillow, and above it a shelf which contained matches, tobacco, pencils, odd fish-hooks, bits of twine, and a tin can filled with bills and receipts. The south wall was dominated by a window which faced the sea and on the north there was a five-foot board which bore a variety of clothes hooks and the burdens of each. Beneath the board there was a jumble of odd footwear, mostly of rubber. There was also, on this wall, a barometer, a map of the marine area and a shelf which held a tiny radio. The kitchen was shared by all of us and was a buffer zone between the immaculate order of ten other rooms and the disruptive chaos of the single room that was my father's.

My mother ran her house as her brothers ran their boats. Everything was clean and spotless and in order. She was tall and dark and powerfully energetic. In later years she reminded me of the women of Thomas Hardy, particularly Eustacia Vye, in a physical way. She fed and clothed a family of seven children, making all of the meals and most of the clothes. She grew miraculous gardens and magnificent flowers and raised broods of hens and ducks. She would walk miles on berry-picking expeditions and hoist her skirts to dig for clams when the tide was low. She was fourteen years younger than my father, whom she had married when she was twenty-six and had been a local beauty for a period of ten years. My mother was of the sea as were all of her people, and her horizons were the very literal ones she scanned with her dark and fearless eyes.

Between the kitchen clothes rack and barometer, a door opened into my father's bedroom. It was a room of disorder and disarray. It was as if the wind which so often clamoured about the house succeeded in entering this single room and after whipping it into turmoil stole quietly away to renew its knowing laughter from without.

My father's bed was against the south wall. It always looked rumpled and unmade because he lay on top of it more than he slept within any folds it might have had. Beside it, there was a little brown table. An archaic goose-necked reading light, a battered table radio, a mound of wooden matches, one or two packages of tobacco, a deck of cigarette papers and an overflowing ashtray cluttered its surface. The brown larvae of tobacco shreds and the grey flecks of ash covered both the table and the floor beneath it. The once-varnished surface of the table was disfigured by numerous black scars and gashes inflicted by the neglected burning cigarettes of many years. They had tumbled from the ashtray unnoticed and branded their statements permanently and quietly into the wood until the odour of their burning caused the snuffing out of their lives. At the bed's foot there was a single window which looked upon the sea.

Against the adjacent wall there was a battered bureau and beside it there was a closet which held his single ill-fitting serge suit, the two or three white shirts that strangled him and the square black shoes that pinched. When he took off his more friendly clothes, the heavy woollen sweaters, mitts and socks which my mother knitted for him and the woollen and doeskin shirts, he dumped them unceremoniously on a single chair. If a visitor entered the room while he was lying on the bed, he would be told to throw the clothes on the floor and take their place upon the chair.

Magazines and books covered the bureau and competed with the clothes for domination of the chair. They further overburdened the heroic little table and lay on top of the radio. They filled a baffling and unknowable cave beneath the bed, and in the corner by the bureau they spilled from the walls and grew up from the floor.

The magazines were the most conventional: *Time, Newsweek, Life, Maclean's, Family Herald, Reader's Digest.* They were the result of various cut-rate subscriptions or of the gift subscriptions associated with Christmas, "the two whole years for only $3.50."

The books were more varied. There were a few hard-cover magnificents and bygone Book-of-the Month wonders and some were Christmas or birthday gifts. The majority of them, however, were used paperbacks which came from those second-hand bookstores which advertise in the backs of magazines: "Miscellaneous Used Paperbacks 10¢ Each." At first he sent for them himself, although my mother resented the expense, but in later years they came more and more often from my sisters who had moved to the cities. Especially at first they were very weird and varied. Mickey Spillane and Ernest Haycox vied with Dostoyevsky and Faulkner, and the Penguin Poets edition of Gerard Manley Hopkins arrived in the same box as a little book on sex technique called *Getting the Most Out of Love.* The former had been assiduously annotated by a very fine hand using a very blue-inked fountain pen while the latter had been studied by someone with very large thumbs, the prints of which were still visible in the margins. At the slightest provocation it would open almost automatically to particularly graphic and well-smudged pages.

When he was not in the boat, my father spent most of his time lying on the bed in his socks, the top two buttons of his trousers undone, his discarded shirt on the ever-ready chair and the sleeves of the woollen Stanfield underwear, which he wore both summer and winter, drawn half way up to his elbows. The pillows propped up the whiteness of his head and the goose-necked lamp illuminated the pages in his hands. The cigarettes smoked and smouldered on the ashtray and on the table and the radio played constantly, sometimes low and sometimes loud. At midnight and at one, two, three and four, one could sometimes hear the radio, his occasional cough, the rustling thud of a completed book being tossed to the corner heap, or the movement necessitated by his sitting on the edge of the bed to roll the thousandth cigarette. He seemed never to sleep, only to doze, and the light shone constantly from his window to the sea.

My mother despised the room and all it stood for and she had stopped sleeping in it after I was born. She despised disorder in rooms and in houses and in hours and in lives, and she had not read a book since high school. There she had read *Ivanhoe* and considered it a colossal waste of time. Still the room remained, like a solid rock of opposition in the sparkling waters of a clear deep harbour, opening off the kitchen where we really lived our lives, with its door always open and its contents visible to all.

The daughters of the room and of the house were very beautiful. They were tall and willowy like my mother and had her fine facial features set off by the reddish copper-coloured hair that had apparently once been my father's before it turned to white. All of them were very clever in school and helped my mother a great deal about the house. When they were young they sang and were very happy and very nice to me because I was the youngest and the family's only boy.

My father never approved of their playing about the wharf like the other children, and they went there only when my mother sent them on an errand. At such times they almost always overstayed, playing screaming games of tag or hide-and-seek in and about the fishing shanties, the piled traps and tubs of trawl, shouting down to the perch that swam languidly about the wharf's algae-covered piles, or jumping in and out of the boats that tugged gently at their lines. My mother was never uneasy about them at such times, and when her husband criticized her she would say, "Nothing will happen to them there," or "They could be doing worse things in worse places."

By about the ninth or tenth grade my sisters one by one discovered my father's bedroom and then the change would begin. Each would go into the room one morning when he was out. She would go with the ideal hope of imposing order or with the more practical objective of emptying the ashtray, and later she would be found spellbound by the volume in her hand. My mother's reaction was always abrupt, bordering on the angry. "Take your nose out of that trash and come and do your work," she would say, and once I saw her slap my youngest sister so hard that the print of her hand was scarletly emblazoned upon her daughter's cheek while the broken-spined paperback fluttered uselessly to the floor.

Thereafter my mother would launch a campaign against what she had discovered but could not understand. At times although she was not overly religious she would bring in God to bolster her arguments, saying, "In the next world God will see to those who waste their lives reading useless books when they should be about their work." Or without theological aid, "I would like to know how books help anyone to live a life." If my father were in, she would repeat the remarks louder than necessary, and her voice would carry into his room where he lay upon his bed. His usual reaction was to turn up the volume of the radio, although that action in itself betrayed the success of the initial thrust.

Shortly after my sisters began to read the books, they grew restless and lost interest in darning socks and baking bread, and all of them eventually went to work as summer waitresses in the Sea Food Restaurant. The restaurant was run by a big American concern from Boston and catered to the tourists that flooded the area during July and August. My mother despised the whole operation. She said the restaurant was not run by "our people," and "our people" did not eat there, and that it was run by outsiders for outsiders.

"Who are these people anyway?" she would ask, tossing back her dark hair, "and what do they, though they go about with their cameras for a hundred years, know about the way it is here, and what do they care about me and mine, and why should I care about them?"

She was angry that my sisters should even conceive of working in such a place and more angry when my father made no move to prevent it, and she was worried about herself and about her family and about her life. Sometimes she would say softly to her sisters, "I don't know what's the matter with my girls. It seems none of them are interested in any of the right things." And sometimes there would be bitter savage arguments. One afternoon I was coming in with three mackerel I'd been given at the wharf when I heard her say, "Well I hope you'll be satisfied when they come home knocked up and you'll have had your way."

It was the most savage thing I'd ever heard my mother say. Not just the words but the way she said them, and I stood there in the porch afraid to breathe for what seemed like the years from ten to fifteen, feeling the damp moist mackerel with their silver glassy eyes growing clammy against my leg.

Through the angle in the screen door I saw my father who had been walking into his room wheel around on one of his rubber-booted heels and look at her with his blue eyes flashing like clearest ice beneath the snow that was his hair. His usually ruddy face was drawn and grey, reflecting the exhaustion of a man of sixty-five who had been working in those rubber boots for eleven hours on an August day, and for a fleeting moment I wondered what I would do if he killed my mother while I stood there in the porch with those three foolish mackerel in my hand. Then he turned and went into his room and the radio blared forth the next day's weather forecast and I retreated under the noise and returned again, stamping my feet and slamming the door too loudly to signal my approach. My mother was busy at the stove when I came in, and did not raise her head when I threw the mackerel in a pan. As I looked into my father's room, I said, "Well how did things go in the boat today?" and he replied, "Oh not too badly, all things considered." He was lying on his back and lighting the first cigarette and the radio was talking about the Virginia coast.

All of my sisters made good money on tips. They bought my father an electric razor which he tried to use for a while and they took out even more magazine subscriptions. They bought my mother a great many clothes of the type she was very fond of, the wide-brimmed hats and the brocaded dresses, but she locked them all in trunks and refused to wear any of them.

On one August day my sisters prevailed upon my father to take some of their restaurant customers for an afternoon ride in the boat. The tourists with their expensive clothes and cameras and sun glasses awkwardly backed down the iron ladder at the wharf's side to where my father waited below, holding the rocking *Jenny Lynn* in snug against the wharf with one hand on the iron ladder and steadying his descending passengers with the other. They tried to look both prim and wind-blown like the girls in the Pepsi-Cola ads and did the best they could, sitting on the thwarts where the newspapers were spread to cover the splattered blood and fish entrails, crowding to one side so that they were in danger of capsizing the boat, taking the inevitable pictures or merely trailing their fingers through the water of their dreams.

All of them liked my father very much and, after he'd brought them back from their circles in the harbour, they invited him to their rented cabins which were located high on a hill overlooking the village to which they were so alien. He proceeded to get very drunk up there with the beautiful view and the strange company and the abundant liquor, and late in the afternoon he began to sing.

I was just approaching the wharf to deliver my mother's summons when he began, and the familiar yet unfamiliar voice that rolled down from the cabins made me feel as I had never felt before in my young life or perhaps as I had always felt without really knowing it, and I was ashamed yet proud, young yet old and saved yet forever lost, and there was nothing I could do to control my legs which trembled nor my eyes which wept for what they could not tell.

The tourists were equipped with tape recorders and my father sang for more than three hours. His voice boomed down the hill and bounced off the surface of the harbour, which was an unearthly blue on that hot August day, and was then reflected to the wharf and the fishing shanties where it was absorbed amidst the men who were baiting their lines for the next day's haul.

He sang all the old sea chanties which had come across from the old world and by which men like him had pulled ropes for generations, and he sang the East Coast sea songs which celebrated the sealing vessels of Northumberland Strait and the long liners of the Grand Banks, and of Anticosti, Sable Island, Grand Manan, Boston Harbor, Nantucket and Block Island. Gradually he shifted to the seemingly unending Gaelic drinking songs with their twenty or more verses and inevitable refrains, and the men in the shanties smiled at the coarseness of some of the verses and at the thought that the singer's immediate audience did not know what they were applauding nor recording to take back to staid old Boston. Later as the sun was setting he switched to the laments and the wild and haunting Gaelic war songs of those spattered

Highland ancestors he had never seen, and when his voice ceased, the savage melancholy of three hundred years seemed to hang over the peaceful harbour and the quiet boats and the men leaning in the doorways of their shanties with their cigarettes glowing in the dusk and the women looking to the sea from their open windows with their children in their arms.

When he came home he threw the money he had earned on the kitchen table as he did with all his earnings but my mother refused to touch it and the next day he went with the rest of the men to bait his trawl in the shanties. The tourists came to the door that evening and my mother met them there and told them that her husband was not in although he was lying on the bed only a few feet away with the radio playing and the cigarette upon his lips. She stood in the doorway until they reluctantly went away.

In the winter they sent him a picture which had been taken on the day of the singing. On the back it said, "To Our Ernest Hemingway" and the "Our" was underlined. There was also an accompanying letter telling how much they had enjoyed themselves, how popular the tape was proving and explaining who Ernest Hemingway was. In a way it almost did look like one of those unshaven, taken-in-Cuba pictures of Hemingway. He looked both massive and incongruous in the setting. His bulky fisherman's clothes were too big for the green and white lawn chair in which he sat, and his rubber boots seemed to take up all of the well-clipped grass square. The beach umbrella jarred with his sunburned face and because he had already been singing for some time, his lips which chapped in the winds of spring and burned in the water glare of summer had already cracked in several places, producing tiny flecks of blood at the corners and onto the whiteness of his teeth. The bracelets of brass chain which he wore to protect his wrists from chafing seemed abnormally large and his broad leather belt had been slackened and his heavy shirt and underwear were open at the throat revealing an uncultivated wilderness of white chest hair bordering on the semi-controlled stubble of his neck and chin. His blue eyes had looked directly into the camera and his hair was whiter than the two tiny clouds which hung over his left shoulder. The sea was behind him and its immense blue flatness stretched out to touch the arching blueness of the sky. It seemed very far away from him or else he was so much in the foreground that he seemed too big for it.

Each year another of my sisters would read the books and work in the restaurant. Sometimes they would stay out quite late on the hot summer nights and when they came up the stairs my mother would ask them many long and involved questions which they resented and tried to avoid. Before ascending the stairs they would go into my father's room and those of us who waited above could hear them throwing his clothes off the chair before sitting on it or the squeak of the bed as they sat on its edge. Sometimes they would talk to him a long time, the murmur of their voices blending with the music of the radio into a mysterious vapour-like sound which floated softly up the stairs.

I say this again as if it all happened at once and as if all of my sisters were of identical ages and like so many lemmings going into another sea and, again, it was of course not that way at all. Yet go they did, to Boston, to Montreal, to New York with the young men they met during the summers and later married in those far-away cities. The young men were very articulate and handsome and wore fine clothes and drove expensive cars and my sisters, as I said, were very tall and beautiful with their copper-coloured hair and were tired of darning socks and baking bread.

One by one they went. My mother had each of her daughters for fifteen years, then lost them for two and finally forever. None married a fisherman. My mother never accepted any of the young men, for in her eyes they seemed always a combination of the lazy, the effeminate, the dishonest and the unknown. They never seemed to do any physical work and she could not comprehend their luxurious vacations and she did not know whence they came nor who they were. And in the end she did not really care, for they were not of her people and they were not of her sea.

I say this now with a sense of wonder at my own stupidity in thinking I was somehow free and would go on doing well in school and playing and helping in the boat and passing into my early teens while streaks of grey began to appear in my mother's dark hair and my father's rubber boots dragged sometimes on the pebbles of the beach as he trudged home from the wharf. And there were but three of us in the house that had at one time been so loud.

Then during the winter that I was fifteen he seemed to grow old and ill at once. Most of January he lay upon the bed, smoking and reading and listening to the radio while the wind howled about the house and the needle-like snow blistered off the ice-covered harbour and the doors flew out of people's hands if they did not cling to them like death.

In February when the men began overhauling their lobster traps he still did not move, and my mother and I began to knit lobster trap headings in the evenings. The twine was as always very sharp and harsh, and blisters formed upon our thumbs and little paths of blood snaked quietly down between our fingers while the seals that had drifted down from distant Labrador wept and moaned like human children on the ice-floes of the Gulf.

In the daytime my mother's brother who had been my father's partner as long as I could remember also came to work upon the gear. He was a year older than my mother and was tall and dark and the father of twelve children.

By March we were very far behind and although I began to work very hard in the evenings I knew it was not hard enough and that there were but eight weeks left before the opening of the season on May first. And I knew that my mother worried and my uncle was uneasy and that all of our very lives depended on the boat being ready with her gear and two men, by the date of May the first. And I knew then that *David Copperfield* and *The Tempest* and all of those friends I had dearly come to love must really go forever. So I bade them all good-bye.

The night after my first full day at home and after my mother had gone upstairs he called me into his room where I sat upon the chair beside his bed. "You will go back tomorrow," he said simply.

I refused then, saying I had made my decision and was satisfied.

"That is no way to make a decision," he said, "and if you are satisfied I am not. It is best that you go back." I was almost angry then and told him as all children do that I wished he would leave me alone and stop telling me what to do.

He looked at me a long time then, lying there on the same bed on which he had fathered me those sixteen years before, fathered me his only son, out of who knew what emotions when he was already fifty-six and his hair had turned to snow. Then he swung his legs over the edge of the squeaking bed and sat facing me and looked into my own dark eyes with his of crystal blue and placed his hand upon my knee. "I am not telling you to do anything," he said softly, "only asking you."

The next morning I returned to school. As I left, my mother followed me to the porch and said, "I never thought a son of mine would choose useless books over the parents that gave him life."

In the weeks that followed he got up rather miraculously and the gear was ready and the *Jenny Lynn* was freshly painted by the last two weeks of April when the ice began to break up and the lonely screaming gulls returned to haunt the silver herring as they flashed within the sea.

On the first day of May the boats raced out as they had always done, laden down almost to the gunwales with their heavy cargoes of traps. They were almost like living things as they plunged through the waters of the spring and manoeuvred between the still floating icebergs of crystal-white and emerald green on their way to the traditional grounds that they sought out every May. And those of us who sat that day in the high school on the hill, discussing the water imagery of Tennyson, watched them as they passed back and forth beneath us until by afternoon the piles of traps which had been stacked upon the wharf were no longer visible but were spread about the bottoms of the sea. And the *Jenny Lynn* went too, all day, with my uncle tall and dark, like a latter-day Tashtego standing at the tiller with his legs wide apart and guiding her deftly between the floating pans of ice and my father in the stern standing in the same way with his hands upon the ropes that lashed the cargo to the deck. And at night my mother asked, "Well, how did things go in the boat today?"

And the spring wore on and the summer came and school ended in the third week of June and the lobster season on July first and I wished that the two things I loved so dearly did not exclude each other in a manner that was so blunt and too clear.

At the conclusion of the lobster season my uncle said he had been offered a berth on a deep sea dragger and had decided to accept. We all knew that he was leaving the *Jenny Lynn* forever and that before the next lobster season he would buy a boat of his own. He was expecting another child and would be supporting fifteen people by the next spring and could not chance my father against the family that he loved.

I joined my father then for the trawling season, and he made no protest and my mother was quite happy. Through the summer we baited the tubs of trawl in the afternoon and set them at sunset and revisited them in the darkness of the early morning. The men would come tramping by our house at four A.M. and we would join them and walk with them to the wharf and be on our way before the sun rose out of the ocean where it seemed to spend the night. If I was not up they would toss pebbles to my window and I would be very embarrassed and tumble downstairs to where my father lay fully clothed atop his bed, reading his book and listening to his radio and smoking his cigarette. When I appeared he would swing off his bed and put on his boots and be instantly ready and then we would take the lunches my mother had prepared the night before and walk off toward the sea. He would make no attempt to wake me himself.

It was in many ways a good summer. There were few storms and we were out almost every day and we lost a minimum of gear and seemed to land a maximum of fish and I tanned dark and brown after the manner of my uncles.

My father did not tan — he never tanned — because of his reddish complexion, and the salt water irritated his skin as it had for sixty years. He burned and reburned over and over again and his lips still cracked so that they bled when he smiled, and his arms, especially the left, still broke out into the oozing salt-water boils as they had ever since as a child I had first watched him soaking and bathing them in a variety of ineffectual solutions. The chafe-preventing bracelets of brass linked chain that all the men wore about their wrists in early spring were his the full season and he shaved but painfully and only once a week.

And I saw them, that summer, many things that I had seen all my life as if for the first time and I thought that perhaps my father had never been intended for a fisherman either physically or mentally. At least not in the manner of my uncles; he had never really loved it. And I remembered that, one evening in his room when we were talking about *David Copperfield,* he had said that he had always wanted to go to the university and I had dismissed it then in the way one dismisses his father's saying he would like to be a tightrope walker, and we had gone on to talk about the Peggottys and how they loved the sea.

And I thought then to myself that there were many things wrong with all of us and all our lives and I wondered why my father, who was himself an only son, had not married before he was forty and then I wondered why he had. I even thought that perhaps he had had to marry my mother and checked the dates on the flyleaf of the Bible where I learned that my oldest sister had been born a prosaic eleven months after the marriage, and I felt myself then very dirty and debased for my lack of faith and for what I had thought and done.

And then there came into my heart a very great love for my father and I thought it was very much braver to spend a life doing what you really do not want rather than selfishly following forever your own dreams and inclinations. And I knew then that I could never leave him alone to suffer the iron-tipped harpoons which my mother would forever hurl into his soul because he was a failure as a husband and a father who had retained none of his own. And I felt that I had been very small in a little secret place within me and that even the completion of high school was for me a silly shallow selfish dream.

So I told him one night very resolutely and very powerfully that I would remain with him as long as he lived and we would fish the sea together. And he made no protest but only smiled through the cigarette smoke that wreathed his bed and replied, "I hope you will remember what you've said."

The room was now so filled with books as to be almost Dickensian, but he would not allow my mother to move or change them and he continued to read them, sometimes two or three a night. They came with great regularity now, and there were more hard covers, sent by my sisters who had gone so long ago and now seemed so distant and so prosperous, and sent also pictures of small red-haired grandchildren with baseball bats and dolls which he placed upon his bureau and which my mother gazed at wistfully when she thought no one would see. Red-haired grandchildren with baseball bats and dolls who would never know the sea in hatred or in love.

And so we fished through the heat of August and into the cooler days of September when the water was so clear we could almost see the bottom and the white mists rose like delicate ghosts in the early morning dawn. And one day my mother said to me, "You have given added years to his life."

And we fished on into October when it began to roughen and we could no longer risk night sets but took our gear out each morning and returned at the first sign of the squalls; and on into November when we lost three tubs of trawl and the clear blue water turned to a sullen grey and the trochoidal waves rolled rough and high and washed across our bows and decks as we ran within their troughs. We wore heavy sweaters now and the awkward rubber slickers and the heavy woollen mitts which soaked and froze into masses of ice that hung from our wrists like the limbs of gigantic monsters until we thawed them against the exhaust pipe's heat. And almost every day we would leave for home before noon, driven by the blasts of the northwest wind, coating our eyebrows with ice and freezing our eyelids closed as we leaned into a visibility that was hardly there, charting our course from the compass and the sea, running with the waves and between them but never confronting their towering might.

And I stood at the tiller now, on these homeward lunges, stood in the place and in the manner of my uncle, turning to look at my father and to shout over the roar of the engine and the slop of the sea to where he stood in the stern, drenched and dripping with the snow and the salt and the spray and his bushy eyebrows caked in ice. But on November twenty-first, when it seemed we might be making the final run of the season, I turned and he was not there and I knew even in that instant that he would never be again.

On November twenty-first the waves of the grey Atlantic are very very high and the waters are very cold and there are no signposts on the surface of the sea. You cannot tell where you have been five minutes before and in the squalls of snow you cannot see. And it takes longer than you would believe to check a boat that has been running before a gale and turn her ever so carefully in a wide and stupid circle, with timbers creaking and straining, back into the face of storm. And you know that it is useless and that your voice does not carry the length of the boat and that even if you knew the original spot, the relentless waves would carry such a burden perhaps a mile or so by the time you could return. And you know also, the final irony, that your father, like your uncles and all the men that form your past, cannot swim a stroke.

The lobster beds off the Cape Breton coast are still very rich and now, from May to July, their offerings are packed in crates of ice, and thundered by the gigantic transport trucks, day and night, through New Glasgow, Amherst, Saint John and

Bangor and Portland and into Boston where they are tossed still living into boiling pots of water, their final home.

And though the prices are higher and the competition tighter, the grounds to which the *Jenny Lynn* once went remain untouched and unfished as they have for the last ten years. For if there are no signposts on the sea in storm there are certain ones in calm and the lobster bottoms were distributed in calm before any of us can remember and the grounds my father fished were those his father fished before him and there were others before and before and before. Twice the big boats have come from forty and fifty miles, lured by the promise of the grounds, and strewn the bottom with their traps and twice they have returned to find their buoys cut adrift and their gear lost and destroyed. Twice the Fisheries Officer and the Mounted Police have come and asked many long and involved questions and twice they have received no answers from the men leaning in the doors of their shanties and the women standing at their windows with their children in their arms. Twice they have gone away saying: "There are no legal boundaries in the Marine area"; "No one can own the sea"; "Those grounds don't wait for anyone."

But the men and the women, with my mother dark among them, do not care for what they say, for to them the grounds are sacred and they think they wait for me.

It is not an easy thing to know that your mother lives alone on an inadequate insurance policy and that she is too proud to accept any other aid. And that she looks through her lonely window onto the ice of winter and the hot flat calm of summer and the rolling waves of fall. And that she lies awake in the early morning's darkness when the rubber boots of the men scrunch upon the gravel as they pass beside her house on their way down to the wharf. And she knows that the footsteps never stop, because no man goes from her house, and she alone of all the Lynns has neither son nor son-in-law that walks toward the boat that will take him to the sea. And it is not an easy thing to know that your mother looks upon the sea with love and on you with bitterness because the one has been so constant and the other so untrue.

But neither is it easy to know that your father was found on November twenty-eighth, ten miles to the north and wedged between two boulders at the base of the rockstrewn cliffs where he had been hurled and slammed so many many times. His hands were shredded ribbons as were his feet which had lost their boots to the suction of the sea, and his shoulders came apart in our hands when we tried to move him from the rocks. And the fish had eaten his testicles and the gulls had pecked out his eyes and the white-green stubble of his whiskers had continued to grow in death, like the grass on graves, upon the purple, bloated mass that was his face. There was not much left of my father, physically, as he lay there with the brass chain on his wrists and the seaweed in his hair.

BERNARD MALAMUD

The Magic Barrel

Not long ago there lived in uptown New York, in a small almost meager room, though crowded with books, Leo Finkle, a rabbinical student in the Yeshivah University. Finkle, after six years of study, was to be ordained in June and had been advised by an acquaintance that he might find it easier to win himself a congregation if he were married. Since he had no present prospects of marriage, after two tormented days of turning it over in his mind, he called in Pinye Salzman, a marriage broker whose two-line advertisement he had read in the *Forward.*

The matchmaker appeared one night out of the dark fourth-floor hallway of the graystone rooming house where Finkle lived, grasping a black, strapped portfolio that had been worn thin with use. Salzman, who had been long in the business, was of slight but dignified build, wearing an old hat, and an overcoat too short and tight for him. He smelled frankly of fish, which he loved to eat, and although he was missing a few teeth, his presence was not displeasing, because of an amiable manner curiously contrasted with mournful eyes. His voice, his lips, his wisp of beard, his bony fingers were animated, but give him a moment of repose and his mild blue eyes revealed a depth of sadness, a characteristic that put Leo a little at ease although the situation, for him, was inherently tense.

He at once informed Salzman why he had asked him to come, explaining that his home was in Cleveland, and that but for his parents, who had married comparatively late in life, he was alone in the world. He had for six years devoted himself almost entirely to his studies, as a result of which, understandably, he had found himself without time for a social life and the company of young women. Therefore he thought it the better part of trial and error — of embarrassing fumbling — to call in an experienced person to advise him on these matters. He remarked in passing that the function of the marriage broker was ancient and honorable, highly approved in the Jewish community, because it made practical the necessary without hindering joy. Moreover, his own parents had been brought together by a matchmaker. They had made, if not a financially profitable marriage — since neither had possessed any worldly goods to speak of — at least a successful one in the sense of their everlasting devotion to each other. Salzman listened in embarrassed surprise, sensing a sort of apology. Later, however, he experienced a glow of pride in his work, an emotion that had left him years ago, and he heartily approved of Finkle.

The two went to their business. Leo had led Salzman to the only clear place in the room, a table near a window that overlooked the lamp-lit city. He seated himself at the matchmaker's side but facing him, attempting by an act of will to suppress the unpleasant tickle in his throat. Salzman eagerly unstrapped his portfolio and removed a loose rubber band from a thin packet of much-handled cards. As he flipped through them, a gesture and sound that physically hurt Leo, the student pretended not to see and gazed steadfastly out the window. Although it was still February, winter was on its last legs, signs of which he had for the first time in years begun to notice. He now observed the round white moon, moving high in the sky through a cloud menagerie, and watched with half-open mouth as it penetrated a huge hen, and dropped out of her like an egg laying itself. Salzman, though pretending through eyeglasses he had just slipped on, to be engaged in scanning the writing on the cards, stole occasional glances at the young man's distinguished face, noting with pleasure the long, severe scholar's nose, brown eyes heavy with learning, sensitive yet ascetic lips, and a certain, almost hollow quality of the dark cheeks. He gazed around at shelves upon shelves of books and let out a soft, contented sigh.

When Leo's eyes fell upon the cards, he counted six spread out in Salzman's hand.

"So few?" he asked in disappointment.

"You wouldn't believe me how much cards I got in my office," Salzman replied. "The drawers are already filled to the top, so I keep them now in a barrel, but is every girl good for a new rabbi?"

Leo blushed at this, regretting all he had revealed of himself in a curriculum vitae he had sent to Salzman. He had thought it best to acquaint him with his strict standards and specifications, but in having done so, felt he had told the marriage broker more than was absolutely necessary.

He hesitantly inquired, "Do you keep photographs of your clients on file?"

"First comes family, amount of dowry, also what kind promises." Salzman replied, unbuttoning his tight coat and settling himself in the chair. "After comes pictures, rabbi."

"Call me Mr. Finkle. I'm not yet a rabbi."

Salzman said he would, but instead called him doctor, which he changed to rabbi when Leo was not listening too attentively.

Salzman adjusted his horn-rimmed spectacles, gently cleared his throat and read in an eager voice the contents of the top card:

"Sophie P. Twenty four years. Widow one year. No children. Educated high school and two years college. Father promises eight thousand dollars. Has wonderful wholesale business. Also real estate. On the mother's side comes teachers, also one actor. Well known on Second Avenue."

Leo gazed up in surprise. "Did you say a widow?"

"A widow don't mean spoiled, rabbi. She lived with her husband maybe four months. He was a sick boy she made a mistake to marry him."

"Marrying a widow has never entered my mind."

"This is because you have no experience. A widow, especially if she is young and healthy, like this girl, is a wonderful person to marry. She will be thankful to you the rest of her life. Believe me if I was looking now for a bride, I would marry a widow."

Leo reflected, then shook his head.

Salzman hunched his shoulders in an almost imperceptible gesture of disappointment. He placed the card down on the wooden table and began to read another:

"Lily H. High school teacher. Regular. Not a substitute. Has savings and new Dodge car. Lived in Paris one year. Father is successful dentist thirty-five years. Interested in professional man. Well Americanized family. Wonderful opportunity."

"I knew her personally," said Salzman. "I wish you could see this girl. She is a doll. Also very intelligent. All day you could talk to her about books and theyater and what not. She also knows current events."

"I don't believe you mentioned her age?"

"Her age?" Salzman said, raising his brows. "Her age is thirty-two years."

Leo said after a while, "I'm afraid that seems a little too old."

Salzman let out a laugh. "So how old are you, rabbi?"

"Twenty-seven."

"So what is the difference, tell me, between twenty-seven and thirty-two? My own wife is seven years older than me. So what did I suffer? — Nothing. If Rothschild's a daughter wants to marry you, would you say on account her age, no?"

"Yes," Leo said dryly.

Salzman shook off the no in the yes. "Five years don't mean a thing. I give you my word that when you will live with her for one week you will forget her age. What does it mean five years — that she lived more and knows more than somebody who is younger? On this girl, God bless her, years are not wasted. Each one that it comes makes better the bargain."

"What subject does she teach in high school?"

"Languages. If you heard the way she speaks French, you will think it is music. I am in the business twenty-five years, and I recommend her with my whole heart. Believe me, I know what I'm talking, rabbi."

"What's on the next card?" Leo said abruptly.

Salzman reluctantly turned up the third card:

"Ruth K. Nineteen years. Honor student. Father offers thirteen thousand cash to the right bridegroom. He is a medical doctor. Stomach specialist with marvelous practice. Brother-in-law owns own garment business. Particular people."

Salzman looked as if he had read his trump card.

"Did you say nineteen?" Leo asked with interest.

"On the dot."

"Is she attractive?" He blushed. "Pretty?"

Salzman kissed his finger tips. "A little doll. On this I give you my word. Let me call the father tonight and you will see what means pretty."

But Leo was troubled. "You're sure she's that young?"

"This I am positive. The father will show you the birth certificate."

"Are you positive there isn't something wrong with her?" Leo insisted.

"Who says there is wrong?"

"I don't understand why an American girl her age should go to a marriage broker."

A smile spread over Salzman's face.

"So for the same reason you went, she comes."

Leo flushed. "I am pressed for time."

Salzman, realizing he had been tactless, quickly explained. "The father came, not her. He wants she should have the best, so he looks around himself. When we will locate the right boy he will introduce him and encourage. This makes a better marriage than if a young girl without experience takes for herself. I don't have to tell you this."

"But don't you think this young girl believes in love?" Leo spoke uneasily.

Salzman was about to guffaw but caught himself and said soberly, "Love comes with the right person, not before."

Leo parted dry lips but did not speak. Noticing that Salzman had snatched a glance at the next card, he cleverly asked, "How is her health?"

"Perfect," Salzman said, breathing with difficulty. "Of course, she is a little lame on her right foot from an auto accident that it happened to her when she was twelve years, but nobody notices on account she is so brilliant and also beautiful."

Leo got up heavily and went to the window. He felt curiously bitter and upbraided himself for having called in the marriage broker. Finally, he shook his head.

"Why not?" Salzman persisted, the pitch of his voice rising.

"Because I detest stomach specialists."

"So what do you care what is his business? After you marry her do you need him? Who says he must come every Friday night in your house?"

Ashamed of the way the talk was going, Leo dismissed Salzman, who went home with heavy, melancholy eyes.

Though he had felt only relief at the marriage broker's departure, Leo was in low spirits the next day. He explained it as arising from Salzman's failure to produce a suitable bride for him. He did not care for his type of clientele. But when Leo found himself hesitating whether to seek out another matchmaker, one more polished than Pinye, he wondered if it could be — his protestations to the contrary, and although he honored his father and mother — that he did not, in essence, care for the matchmaking institution? This thought he quickly put out of mind yet found himself still upset. All day he ran around in the woods — missed an important appointment, forgot to give out his laundry, walked out of a Broadway cafeteria without paying and had to run back with the ticket in his hand; had even not recognized his landlady in the street when she passed with a friend and courteously called out, "A good evening to you, Doctor Finkle." By nightfall, however, he had regained sufficient calm to sink his nose into a book and there found peace from his thoughts.

Almost at once there came a knock on the door. Before Leo could say enter, Salzman, commercial cupid, was standing in the room. His face was gray and meager, his expression hungry, and he looked as if he would expire on his feet. Yet the marriage broker managed by some trick of the muscles, to display a broad smile.

"So good evening. I am invited?"

Leo nodded, disturbed to see him again, yet unwilling to ask the man to leave.

Beaming still, Salzman laid his portfolio on the table. "Rabbi, I got for you tonight good news."

"I've asked you not to call me rabbi. I'm still a student."

"Your worries are finished. I have for you a first-class bride."

"Leave me in peace concerning this subject." Leo pretended lack of interest.

"The world will dance at your wedding."

"Please. Mr. Salzman, no more."

"But first must come back my strength," Salzman said weakly. He fumbled with the portfolio straps and took out of the leather case an oily paper bag, from which he extracted a hard, seeded roll and a small, smoked white fish. With a quick motion of his hand he stripped the fish out of its skin and began ravenously to chew. "All day in a rush," he muttered.

Leo watched him eat.

"A sliced tomato you have maybe?" Salzman hesitantly inquired.

"No."

The marriage broker shut his eyes and ate. When he had finished he carefully cleaned up the crumbs and rolled up the remains of the fish, in the paper bag. His spectacled eyes roamed the room until he discovered, amid some piles of books, a one-burner gas stove. Lifting his hat he humbly asked, "A glass tea you got, rabbi?"

Conscience-striken, Leo rose and brewed the tea. He served it with a chunk of lemon and two cubes of lump sugar, delighting Salzman.

After he had drunk his tea, Salzman's strength and good spirits were restored.

"So tell me, rabbi," he said amiably, "you considered some more the three clients I mentioned yesterday?"

"There was no need to consider."

"Why not?"

"None of them suits me."

"What then suits you?"

Leo let it pass because he could give only a confused answer.

Without waiting for a reply, Salzman asked, "You remember this girl I talked to you — the high school teacher?"

"Age thirty-two?"

But surprisingly, Salzman's face lit in a smile. "Age twenty-nine."

Leo shot him a look. "Reduced from thirty-two?"

"A mistake," Salzman avowed. "I talked today with the dentist. He took me to his safety deposit box and showed me the birth certificate. She was twenty-nine years last August. They made her a party in the mountains where she went for her vacation. When her father spoke to me the first time I forgot to write the age and I told you thirty-two, but now I remember this was a different client, a widow."

"The same one you told me about? I thought she was twenty-four?"

"A different. Am I responsible that the world is filled with widows?"

"No, but I'm not interested in them, nor for that matter, in school teachers."

Salzman pulled his clasped hands to his breast. Looking at the ceiling he devoutly exclaimed, "Yiddishe kinder, what can I say to somebody that he is not interested in high school teachers? So what then you are interested?"

Leo flushed but controlled himself.

"In what else will you be interested," Salzman went on, "if you not interested in this fine girl that she speaks four languages and has personally in the bank ten thousand dollars? Also her father guarantees further twelve thousand. Also she has a new car, wonderful clothes, talks on all subjects, and she will give you a first-class home and children. How near do we come in our life to paradise?"

"If she's so wonderful, why wasn't she married ten years ago?"

"Why?" said Salzman with a heavy laugh. " — Why? because she is *partikiler.* This is why. She wants the *best.*"

Leo was silent, amused at how he had entangled himself. But Salzman had aroused his interest in Lily H., and he began seriously to consider calling on her. When the marriage broker observed how intently Leo's mind was at work on the facts he had supplied, he felt certain they would soon come to an agreement.

Late Saturday afternoon, conscious of Salzman, Leo Finkle walked with Lily Hirschorn along Riverside Drive. He walked briskly and erectly, wearing with distinction the black fedora he had that morning taken with trepidation out of the dusty hat box on his closet shelf, and the heavy black Saturday coat he had thoroughly whisked clean. Leo also owned a walking stick, a present from a distant relative, but quickly put temptation aside and did not use it. Lily, petite and not unpretty, had on something signifying the approach of spring. She was au courant, animatedly, with all sorts of subjects, and he weighed her words and found her surprisingly sound — score another for Salzman, whom he uneasily sensed to be somewhere around, hiding perhaps high in a tree along the street, flashing the lady signals with a pocket mirror; or perhaps a cloven-hoofed Pan, piping nuptial ditties as he danced his invisible way before them, strewing wild buds on the walk and purple grapes in their path, symbolizing fruit of a union, though there was of course still none.

Lily startled Leo by remarking, "I was thinking of Mr. Salzman, a curious figure, wouldn't you say?"

Not certain what to answer, he nodded.

She bravely went on, blushing, "I for one am grateful for his introducing us. Aren't you?"

He courteously replied, "I am."

"I mean," she said with a little laugh — and it was all in good taste, or at least gave the effect of being not in bad — "do you mind that we came together so?"

He was not displeased with her honesty, recognizing that she meant to set the relationship aright, and understanding that it took a certain amount of experience in life, and courage, to want to do it quite that way. One had to have some sort of past to make that kind of beginning.

He said that he did not mind. Salzman's function was traditional and honorable — valuable for what it might achieve, which, he pointed out, was frequently nothing.

Lily agreed with a sigh. They walked on for a while and she said after a long silence, again with a nervous laugh, "Would you mind if I asked you something a little bit personal? Frankly, I find the subject fascinating." Although Leo shrugged, she went on half embarrassedly, "How was it that you came to your calling? I mean was it a sudden passionate inspiration?"

Leo, after a time, slowly replied, "I was always interested in the Law."

"You saw revealed in it the presence of the Highest?"

He nodded and changed the subject. "I understand that you spent a little time in Paris, Miss Hirschorn?"

"Oh, did Mr. Salzman tell you, Rabbi Finkle?" Leo winced but she went on, "It was ages ago and almost forgotten. I remember I had to return for my sister's wedding."

And Lily would not be put off. "When," she asked in a trembly voice, "did you become enamored of God?"

He stared at her. Then it came to him that she was talking not about Leo Finkle, but of a total stranger, some mystical figure, perhaps even passionate prophet that Salzman had dreamed up for her — no relation to the living or dead. Leo trembled with rage and weakness. The trickster had obviously sold her a bill of goods, just as he had him, who'd expected to become acquainted with a young lady of twenty-nine, only to behold, the moment he laid eyes upon her strained and anxious face, a woman past thirty-five and aging rapidly. Only his self control had kept him this long in her presence.

"I am not," he said gravely, "a talented religious person," and in seeking words to go on, found himself possessed by shame and fear. "I think," he said in a strained manner, "that I came to God not because I loved Him, but because I did not."

This confession he spoke harshly because its unexpectedness shook him.

Lily wilted. Leo saw a profusion of loaves of bread go flying like ducks high over his head, not unlike the winged loaves by which he had counted himself to sleep last night. Mercifully, then, it snowed, which he would not put past Salzman's machinations.

He was infuriated with the marriage broker and swore he would throw him out of the room the minute he reappeared. But Salzman did not come that night, and when Leo's anger had subsided, an unaccountable despair grew in its place. At first he thought this was caused by his disappointment in Lily, but before long it became evident that he had involved himself with Salzman without a true knowledge of his own intent. He gradually realized — with an emptiness that seized him with six hands — that he had called in the broker to find him a bride because he was incapable of doing it himself. This terrifying insight he had derived as a result of his meeting and conversation with Lily Hirschorn. Her probing questions had somehow irritated him into revealing — to himself more than her — the true nature of his relationship to

God, and from that it had come upon him, with shocking force, that apart from his parents, he had never loved anyone. Or perhaps it went the other way, that he did not love God so well as he might, because he had not loved man. It seemed to Leo that his whole life stood starkly revealed and he saw himself for the first time as he truly was — unloved and loveless. This bitter but somehow not fully unexpected revelation brought him to a point of panic, controlled only by extraordinary effort. He covered his face with his hands and cried.

The week that followed was the worst of his life. He did not eat and lost weight. His beard darkened and grew ragged. He stopped attending seminars and almost never opened a book. He seriously considered leaving the Yeshivah, although he was deeply troubled at the thought of the loss of all his years of study — saw them like pages torn from a book, strewn over the city — and at the devastating effect of this decision upon his parents. But he had lived without knowledge of himself, and never in the Five Books and all the Commentaries — mea culpa — had the truth been revealed to him. He did not know where to turn, and in all this desolating loneliness there was no *to whom,* although he often thought of Lily but not once could bring himself to go downstairs and make the call. He became touchy and irritable, especially with his landlady, who asked him all manner of personal questions; on the other hand, sensing his own disagreeableness, he waylaid her on the stairs and apologized abjectly, until mortified, she ran from him. Out of this, however, he drew the consolation that he was a Jew and that a Jew suffered. But gradually, as the long and terrible week drew to a close, he regained his composure and some idea of purpose in life: to go on as planned. Although he was imperfect, the ideal was not. As for his quest of a bride, the thought of continuing afflicted him with anxiety and heartburn, yet perhaps with this new knowledge of himself he would be more successful than in the past. Perhaps love would now come to him and a bride to that love. And for this sanctified seeking who needed a Salzman?

The marriage broker, a skeleton with haunted eyes, returned that very night. He looked, withal, the picture of frustrated expectancy — as if he had steadfastly waited the week at Miss Lily Hirschorn's side for a telephone call that never came.

Casually coughing, Salzman came immediately to the point: "So how did you like her?"

Leo's anger rose and he could not refrain from chiding the matchmaker: "Why did you lie to me, Salzman?"

Salzman's pale face went dead white, the world had snowed on him.

"Did you not state that she was twenty-nine?" Leo insisted.

"I give you my word — "

"She was thirty-five, if a day. *At least* thirty-five."

"Of this don't be too sure. Her father told me —"

"Never mind. The worst of it was that you lied to her."

"How did I lie to her, tell me?"

"You told her things about me that weren't true. You made me out to be more, consequently less than I am. She had in mind a totally different person, a sort of semimystical Wonder Rabbi."

"All I said, you was a religious man."

"I can imagine."

Salzman sighed. "This is my weakness that I have," he confessed. "My wife says to me I shouldn't be a salesman, but when I have two fine people that they would be wonderful to be married, I am so happy that I talk too much." He smiled wanly. "This is why Salzman is a poor man."

Leo's anger left him. "Well, Salzman, I'm afraid that's all."

The marriage broker fastened hungry eyes on him.

"You don't want any more a bride?"

"I do," said Leo, "but I have decided to seek her in a different way. I am no longer interested in an arranged marriage. To be frank, I now admit the necessity of premarital love. That is, I want to be in love with the one I marry."

"Love?" said Salzman, astounded. After a moment he remarked. "For us, our love is our life, not for the ladies. In the ghetto they — "

"I know, I know," said Leo. "I've thought of it often. Love, I have said to myself, should be a by-product of living and worship rather than its own end. Yet for myself I find it necessary to establish the level of my need and fulfill it."

Salzman shrugged but answered, "Listen, rabbi, if you want love, this I can find for you also. I have such beautiful clients that you will love them the minute your eyes will see them."

Leo smiled unhappily. "I'm afraid you don't understand."

But Salzman hastily unstrapped his portfolio and withdrew a manila packet from it.

"Pictures," he said, quickly laying the envelope on the table.

Leo called after him to take the pictures away, but as if on the wings of the wind, Salzman had disappeared.

March came, Leo had returned to his regular routine. Although he felt not quite himself yet — lacked energy — he was making plans for a more active social life. Of course it would cost something, but he was an expert in cutting corners; and when there were no corners left he would make circles rounder. All the while Salzman's pictures had lain on the table, gathering dust. Occasionally as Leo sat studying, or enjoying a cup of tea, eyes fell on the manila envelope, but he never opened it.

The days went by and no social life to speak of developed with a member of the opposite sex — it was difficult, given the circumstances of his situation. One morning Leo toiled up the stairs to his room and stared out the window at the city. Although the day was bright his view of it was dark. For some time he watched the people in the street below hurrying along and then turned with a heavy heart to his little room. On the table was the packet. With a sudden relentless gesture he tore it open. For a half-hour he stood by the table in a state of excitement, examining the photographs of the ladies Salzman had included. Finally, with a deep sigh he put them down. There were six, of varying degrees of attractiveness, but look at them long enough and they all became Lily Hirschorn: all past their prime, all starved behind bright smiles, not a true personality in the lot. Life, despite their frantic yoohooings, had passed them by; they were pictures in a briefcase that stank of fish. After a while, however, as Leo attempted to return the photographs into the envelope, he found in it another, a snapshot of the type taken by a machine for a quarter. He gazed at it a moment and let out a cry.

Her face deeply moved him. Why, he could at first not say. It gave him the impression of youth — spring flowers, yet age — a sense of having been used to the bone, wasted; this came from the eyes, which were hauntingly familiar, yet absolutely strange. He had a vivid impression that he had met her before, but try as he might he could not place her although he could almost recall her name, as if he had read it in her own handwriting. No, this couldn't be; he would have remembered her. It was not, he affirmed, that she had an extraordinary beauty — no, though her face was attractive enough; it was that *something* about her moved him. Feature for feature, even some of the ladies of the photographs could do better; but she leaped forth to his heart — had *lived* or wanted to — more than just wanted, perhaps regretted how she had lived — had somehow deeply suffered: it could be seen in the depths of those reluctant eyes, and from the way the light enclosed and shone from her, and within her, opening realms of possibility: this was her own. Her he desired. His head ached and eyes narrowed with the intensity of his gazing, then as if an obscure fog had blown up in the mind, he experienced fear of her and was aware that he had received an impression, somehow, of evil. He shuddered, saying softly, it is thus with us all. Leo brewed some tea in a small pot and sat sipping it without sugar, to calm himself. But before he had finished drinking, again with excitement he examined the face and found it good: good for Leo Finkle. Only such a one could understand him and help him seek whatever he was seeking. She might, perhaps, love him. How she had happened to be among the discards in Salzman's barrel he could never guess, but he knew he must urgently go find her.

Leo rushed downstairs, grabbed up the Bronx telephone book, and searched for Salzman's home address. He was not listed, nor was his office. Neither was he in the Manhattan book. But Leo remembered having written down the address on a slip of paper after he had read Salzman's advertisement in the "personals" column of the *Forward.* He ran up to his room and tore through his papers, without luck. It was exasperating. Just when he needed the matchmaker he was nowhere to be found. Fortunately Leo remembered to look in his wallet. There on a card he found his name written and a Bronx address. No phone number was listed, the reason — Leo now recalled — he had originally communicated with Salzman by letter. He got on his coat, put a hat on over his skull cap and hurried to the subway station. All the way to the far end of the Bronx he sat on the edge of his seat. He was more than once tempted to take out the picture and see if the girl's face was as he remembered it, but he refrained, allowing the snapshot to remain in his inside coat pocket, content to have her so close. When the train pulled into the station he was waiting at the door and bolted out. He quickly located the street Salzman had advertised.

The building he sought was less than a block from the subway, but it was not an office building, nor even a loft, nor a store in which one could rent office space. It was a very old tenement house. Leo found Salzman's name in pencil on a soiled tag under the bell and climbed three dark flights to his apartment. When he knocked, the door was opened by a thin, asthmatic, gray-haired woman, in felt slippers.

"Yes?" she said, expecting nothing. She listened without listening. He could have sworn he had seen her, too, before but knew it was an illusion.

"Salzman — does he live here? Pinye Salzman," he said, "the matchmaker?"

She stared at him a long minute. "Of course."

He felt embarrassed. "Is he in?"

"No." Her mouth, though left open, offered nothing more.

"The matter is urgent. Can you tell me where his office is?"

"In the air." She pointed upward.

"You mean he has no office?" Leo asked.

"In his socks."

He peered into the apartment. It was sunless and dingy, one large room divided by a half-open curtain, beyond which he could see a sagging metal bed. The near side of a room was crowded with rickety chairs, old bureaus, a three-legged table, racks of cooking utensils, and all the apparatus of a kitchen. But there was no sign of Salzman or his magic barrel, probably also a figment of the imagination. An odor of frying fish made Leo weak to the knees.

"Where is he?" he insisted. "I've got to see your husband."

At length she answered, "So who knows where he is? Every time he thinks a new thought he runs to a different place. Go home, he will find you."

"Tell him Leo Finkle."

She gave no sign she had heard.

He walked downstairs, depressed.

But Salzman, breathless, stood waiting at his door.

Leo was astounded and overjoyed. "How did you get here before me?"

"I rushed."

"Come inside."

They entered. Leo fixed tea, and a sardine sandwich for Salzman. As they were drinking he reached behind him for the packet of pictures and handed them to the marriage broker.

Salzman put down his glass and said expectantly, "You found somebody you like?"

"Not among these."

The marriage broker turned away.

"Here is the one I want." Leo held forth the snapshot.

Salzman slipped on his glasses and took the picture into his trembling hand. He turned ghastly and let out a groan.

"What's the matter?" cried Leo.

"Excuse me. Was an accident this picture. She isn't for you."

Salzman frantically shoved the manila packet into his portfolio. He thrust the snapshot into his pocket and fled down the stairs.

Leo, after momentary paralysis, gave chase and cornered the marriage broker in the vestibule. The landlady made hysterical outcries but neither of them listened.

"Give me back the picture, Salzman."

"No." The pain in his eyes was terrible.

"Tell me who she is then."

"This I can't tell you. Excuse me."

He made to depart, but Leo, forgetting himself, seized the matchmaker by his tight coat and shook him frenziedly.

"Please," sighed Salzman. "*Please.*"

Leo ashamedly let him go. "Tell me who she is," he begged. "It's very important for me to know."

"She is not for you. She is a wild one — wild, without shame. This is not a bride for a rabbi."

"What do you mean wild?"

"Like an animal. Like a dog. For her to be poor was a sin. This is why to me she is dead now."

"In God's name, what do you mean?"

"Her I can't introduce to you," Salzman cried.

"Why are you so excited?"

"Why, he asks," Salzman said, bursting into tears. "This is my baby, my Stella, she should burn in hell."

Leo hurried up to bed and hid under the covers. Under the covers he thought his life through. Although he soon fell asleep he could not sleep her out of his mind. He woke, beating his breast. Though he prayed to be rid of her, his prayers went unanswered. Through days of torment he endlessly struggled not to love her; fearing success, he escaped it. He then concluded to convert her to goodness, himself to God. The idea alternately nauseated and exalted him.

He perhaps did not know that he had come to a final decision until he encountered Salzman in a Broadway cafeteria. He was sitting alone at a rear table, sucking the bony remains of a fish. The marriage broker appeared haggard, and transparent to the point of vanishing.

Salzman looked up at first without recognizing him. Leo had grown a pointed beard and his eyes were weighted with wisdom.

"Salzman," he said, "love has at last come to my heart."

"Who can love from a picture?" mocked the marriage broker.

"It is not impossible."

"If you can love her, then you can love anybody. Let me show you some new clients that they just sent me their photographs. One is a little doll."

"Just her I want," Leo murmured.

"Don't be a fool, doctor. Don't bother with her."

"Put me in touch with her, Salzman," Leo said humbly. "Perhaps I can be of service."

Salzman had stopped eating and Leo understood with emotion that it was now arranged.

Leaving the cafeteria, he was, however, afflicted by a tormenting suspicion that Salzman had planned it all to happen this way.

Leo was informed by letter that she would meet him on a certain corner, and she was there one spring night, waiting under a street lamp. He appeared, carrying a small bouquet of violets and rosebuds. Stella stood by the lamp post, smoking. She wore white with red shoes, which fitted his expectations, although in a troubled moment he had imagined the dress red, and only the shoes white. She waited uneasily and shyly. From afar he saw that her eyes — clearly her father's — were filled with desperate innocence. He pictured, in her, his own redemption. Violins and lit candles revolved in the sky. Leo ran forward with flowers outthrust.

Around the corner, Salzman leaning against a wall, chanted prayers for the dead.

KATHERINE MANSFIELD

The Fly

"Y'are very snug in here," piped old Mr. Woodifield, and he peered out of the great, green leather armchair by his friend the boss's desk as a baby peers out of its pram. His talk was over; it was time for him to be off. But he did not want to go. Since he had retired, since his . . . stroke, the wife and the girls kept him boxed up in the house every day of the week except Tuesday. On Tuesday he was dressed up and brushed and allowed to cut back to the City for the day. Though what he did there the wife and girls couldn't imagine. Made a nuisance of himself to his friends, they supposed . . . Well, perhaps so. All the same, we cling to our last pleasures as the tree clings to its last leaves. So there sat old Woodifield, smoking a cigar and staring almost greedily at the boss, who rolled in his office chair, stout, rosy, five years older than he, and still going strong, still at the helm. It did one good to see him.

Wistfully, admiringly, the old voice added, "It's snug in here, upon my word!"

"Yes, it's comfortable enough," agreed the boss, and he flipped the *Financial Times* with a paper-knife. As a matter of fact he was proud of his room; he liked to have it admired, especially by old Woodifield. It gave him a feeling of deep, solid satisfaction to be planted there in the midst of it in full view of that frail old figure in the muffler.

"I've had it done up lately," he explained, as he had explained for the past — how many? — weeks. "New carpet," and he pointed to the bright red carpet with a pattern of large white rings. "New furniture," and he nodded towards the massive bookcase and the table with legs like twisted treacle. "Electric heating!" He waved almost exultantly towards the five transparent, pearly sausages glowing so softly in the tilted copper pan.

But he did not draw old Woodifield's attention to the photograph over the table of a grave-looking boy in uniform standing in one of those spectral photographers' parks with photographers' storm-clouds behind him. It was not new. It had been there for over six years.

"There was something I wanted to tell you," said old Woodifield, and his eyes grew dim remembering. "Now what was it? I had it in my mind when I started out this morning." His hands began to tremble, and patches of red showed above his beard.

Poor old chap, he's on his last pins, thought the boss. And, feeling kindly, he winked at the old man, and said jokingly, "I tell you what. I've got a little drop of something here that'll do you good before you go out into the cold again. It's beautiful stuff. It wouldn't hurt a child." He took a key off his watch-chain, unlocked a cupboard below his desk, and drew forth a dark, squat bottle. "That's the medicine," said he. "And the man from whom I got it told me on the strict Q.T. it came from the cellars at Windsor Cassel."

Old Woodifield's mouth fell open at the sight. He couldn't have looked more surprised if the boss had produced a rabbit.

"It's whisky, ain't it?" he piped, feebly.

The boss turned the bottle and lovingly showed him the label. Whisky it was.

"D'you know," said he, peering up at the boss wonderingly, "they won't let me touch it at home." And he looked as though he was going to cry.

"Ah, that's where we know a bit more than the ladies," cried the boss, swooping across for two tumblers that stood on the table with the water-bottle, and pouring a generous finger into each. "Drink it down. It'll do you good. And don't put any water with it. It's sacrilege to tamper with stuff like this. Ah!" He tossed off his, pulled out his handkerchief, hastily wiped his moustaches, and cocked an eye at old Woodifield, who was rolling his in his chaps.

The old man swallowed, was silent a moment, and then said faintly, "It's nutty!"

But it warmed him; it crept into his chill old brain — he remembered.

"That was it," he said, heaving himself out of his chair. "I thought you'd like to know. The girls were in Belgium last week having a look at poor Reggie's grave, and they happened to come across your boy's. They're quite near each other, it seems."

Old Woodifield paused, but the boss made no reply. Only a quiver in his eyelids showed that he heard.

"The girls were delighted with the way the place is kept," piped the old voice. "Beautifully looked after. Couldn't be better if they were at home. You've not been across, have yer?"

"No, no!" For various reasons the boss had not been across.

"There's miles of it," quavered old Woodifield, "and it's all as neat as a garden. Flowers growing on all the graves. Nice broad paths." It was plain from his voice how much he liked a nice broad path.

The pause came again. Then the old man brightened wonderfully.

"D'you know what the hotel made the girls pay for a pot of jam?" he piped. "Ten francs! Robbery, I call it. It was a little pot, so Gertrude says, no bigger than a half-crown. And she hadn't taken more than a spoonful when they charged her ten francs. Gertrude brought the pot away with her to teach 'em a lesson. Quite right, too; it's trading on our feelings. They think because we're over there having a look around we're ready to pay anything. That's what it is." And he turned towards the door.

"Quite right, quite right!" cried the boss, though what was quite right he hadn't the least idea. He came round by his desk, followed the shuffling footsteps to the door, and saw the old fellow out. Woodifield was gone.

For a long moment the boss stayed, staring at nothing, while the grey-haired office messenger, watching him, dodged in and out of his cubbyhole like a dog that expects to be taken for a run. Then: "I'll see nobody for half an hour, Macey," said the boss.
"Understand? Nobody at all."

"Very good, sir."

The door shut, the firm heavy steps recrossed the bright carpet, the fat body plumped down in the spring chair, and leaning forward, the boss covered his face with his hands. He wanted, he intended, he had arranged to weep ...

It had been a terrible shock to him when old Woodifield sprang that remark upon him about the boy's grave. It was exactly as though the earth had opened and he had seen the boy lying there with Woodifield's girls staring down at him. For it was strange. Although over six years had passed away, the boss never thought of the boy except as lying unchanged, unblemished in his uniform, asleep for ever. "My son!" groaned the boss. But no tears came yet. In the past, in the first months and even years after the boy's death, he had only to say those words to be overcome by such grief that nothing short of a violent fit of weeping could relieve him. Time, he had declared then, he had told everybody, could make no difference. Other men perhaps might recover, might live their loss down, but not he. How was it possible? His boy was an only son. Ever since his birth the boss had worked at building up this business for him; it had no other meaning if it was not for the boy. Life itself had come to have no other meaning. How on earth could he have slaved, denied himself, kept going all those years without the promise forever before him of the boy's stepping into his shoes and carrying on where he left off?

And that promise had been so near being fulfilled. The boy had been in the office learning the ropes for a year before the war. Every morning they had started off together; they had come back by the same train. And what congratulations he had received as the boy's father! No wonder; he had taken to it marvellously. As to his popularity with the staff, every man jack of them down to old Macey couldn't make enough of the boy. And he wasn't in the least spoilt. No, he was just his bright, natural self, with the right word for everybody, with that boyish look and his habit of saying, "Simply splendid!"

But all that was over and done with as though it never had been. The day had come when Macey had handed him the telegram that brought the whole place crashing about his head. "Deeply regret to inform you ... " And he had left the office a broken man, with his life in ruins.

Six years ago, six years ... How quickly time passed! It might have happened yesterday. The boss took his hands from his face; he was puzzled. Something seemed to be wrong with him. He wasn't feeling as he wanted to feel. He decided to get up and have a look at the boy's photograph. But it wasn't a favorite photograph of his; the expression was unnatural. It was cold, even stern-looking. The boy had never looked like that.

At that moment the boss noticed that a fly had fallen into his broad inkpot, and was trying feebly but desperately to clamber out again. Help! help! said those struggling legs. But the sides of the inkpot were wet and slippery; it fell back again and began to swim. The boss took up a pen, picked the fly out of the ink, and shook it on to a piece of blotting-paper. For a fraction of a second it lay still on the dark patch that oozed round it. Then the front legs waved, took hold, and, pulling its small sodden body up it began the immense task of cleaning the ink from its wings. Over and under, over and under, went a leg along a wing, as the stone goes over and under the scythe. Then there was a pause, while the fly, seeming to stand on the tips of its toes, tried to expand first one wing and then the other. It succeeded at last, and, sitting down, it began, like a minute cat, to clean its face. Now one could imagine that the little front legs rubbed against each other lightly, joyfully. The horrible danger was over; it had escaped; it was ready for life again.

But just then the boss had an idea. He plunged his pen back into the ink, leaned his thick wrist on the blotting paper, and as the fly tried its wings down came a great heavy blot. What would it make of that? What indeed! The little beggar seemed absolutely cowed, stunned, and afraid to move because of what would happen next. But then, as if painfully, it dragged itself forward. The front legs waved, caught hold, and, more slowly this time, the task began from the beginning.

He's a plucky little devil, thought the boss, and he felt a real admiration for the fly's courage. That was the way to tackle things; that was the right spirit. Never say die; it was only a question of ... But the fly had again finished its laborious task, and the boss had just time to refill his pen, to shake fair and square on the new-cleaned body yet another dark drop. What about it this time? A painful moment of suspense followed. But behold, the front legs were again waving; the boss felt a rush of relief. He leaned over the fly and said to it tenderly, "You artful little b . . . " And he actually had the brilliant notion of breathing on it to help the drying process. All the same, there was something timid and weak about its efforts now, and the boss decided that this time should be the last, as he dipped the pen into the inkpot.

It was. The last blot on the soaked blotting-paper, and the draggled fly lay in it and did not stir. The back legs were stuck to the body; the front legs were not to be seen.

"Come on," said the boss. "Look sharp!" And he stirred it with his pen — in vain. Nothing happened or was likely to happen. The fly was dead.

The boss lifted the corpse on the end of the paper-knife and flung it into the waste-paper basket. But such a grinding feeling of wretchedness seized him that he felt positively frightened. He started forward and pressed the bell for Macey.

"Bring me some fresh blotting-paper," he said, sternly, "and look sharp about it." And while the old dog padded away he fell to wondering what it was he had been thinking about before. What was it? It was . . . He took out his handkerchief and passed it inside his collar. For the life of him he could not remember.

- woodifield to the boss is comparable to the fly.

GABRIEL GARCÍA MÁRQUEZ

A Very Old Man with Enormous Wings

A TALE FOR CHILDREN

Translated by Gregory Rabassa

On the third day of rain they had killed so many crabs inside the house that Pelayo had to cross his drenched courtyard and throw them into the sea, because the newborn child had a temperature all night and they thought it was due to the stench. The world had been sad since Tuesday. Sea and sky were a single ash-gray thing and the sands of the beach, which on March nights glimmered like powdered light, had become a stew of mud and rotten shellfish. The light was so weak at noon that when Pelayo was coming back to the house after throwing away the crabs, it was hard for him to see what it was that was moving and groaning in the rear of the courtyard. He had to go very close to see that it was an old man, a very old man, lying face down in the mud, who, in spite of his tremendous efforts, couldn't get up, impeded by his enormous wings.

Frightened by that nightmare, Pelayo ran to get Elisenda, his wife, who was putting compresses on the sick child, and he took her to the rear of the courtyard. They both looked at the fallen body with mute stupor. He was dressed like a ragpicker. There were only a few faded hairs left on his bald skull and very few teeth in his mouth, and his pitiful condition of a drenched great-grandfather had taken away any sense of grandeur he might have had. His huge buzzard wings, dirty and half-plucked, were forever entangled in the mud. They looked at him so long and so closely that Pelayo and Elisenda very soon overcame their surprise and in the end found him familiar. Then they dared speak to him, and he answered in an incomprehensible dialect with a strong sailor's voice. That was how they skipped over the inconvenience of the wings and quite intelligently concluded that he was a lonely castaway from some foreign ship wrecked by the storm. And yet, they called in a neighbor woman who knew everything about life and death to see him, and all she needed was one look to show them their mistake.

"He's an angel," she told them. "He must have been coming for the child, but the poor fellow is so old that the rain knocked him down."

On the following day everyone knew that a flesh-and-blood angel was held captive in Pelayo's house. Against the judgment of the wise neighbor woman, for whom angels in those times were the fugitive survivors of a celestial conspiracy, they did not have the heart to club him to death. Pelayo watched over him all afternoon from the kitchen, armed with his bailiff's club, and before going to bed he dragged him out of the mud and locked him up with the hens in the wire chicken coop. In the middle of the night, when the rain stopped, Pelayo and Elisenda were still killing crabs. A short time afterward the child woke up without a fever and with a desire to eat. Then they felt magnanimous and decided to put the angel on a raft with fresh water and provisions for three days and leave him to his fate on the high seas. But when they went out into the courtyard with the first light of dawn, they found the whole neighborhood in front of the chicken coop having fun with the angel, without the slightest reverence, tossing him things to eat through the openings in the wire as if he weren't a supernatural creature but a circus animal.

Father Gonzaga arrived before seven o'clock, alarmed at the strange news. By that time onlookers less frivolous than those at dawn had already arrived and they were making all kinds of conjectures concerning the captive's future. The simplest among them thought that he should be named mayor of the world. Others of sterner mind felt that he should be promoted to the rank of five-star general in order to win all wars. Some visionaries hoped that he could be put to stud in order to implant on earth a race of winged wise men who could take charge of the universe. But Father Gonzaga, before becoming a priest, had been a robust woodcutter. Standing by the wire, he reviewed his catechism in an instant and asked them to open the door so that he could take a close look at that pitiful man who looked more like a huge decrepit hen among the fascinated chickens. He was lying in a corner drying his open wings in the sunlight among the fruit peels and breakfast leftovers that the early risers had thrown him. Alien to the impertinences of the world, he only lifted his antiquarian eyes and murmured something in his dialect when Father Gonzaga went into the chicken coop and said good morning to him in Latin. The parish priest had his first suspicion of an imposter when he saw that he did not understand the language of God or know how to greet His ministers. Then he noticed that seen close up he was much too human: he had an unbearable smell of the outdoors, the back side of his wings was strewn with parasites and his main feathers had been mistreated by terrestrial winds, and nothing about him measured up to the proud dignity of angels. Then he came out of the chicken coop and in a brief sermon warned the curious against the risks of being ingenuous. He reminded them that the devil had the bad habit of making use of carnival tricks in order to confuse the unwary. He argued that if wings were not the essential element in determining the difference between a hawk and an airplane, they were even less so in the recognition of angels. Nevertheless, he promised to write a letter to his bishop so that the latter would write to his primate so that the latter would write to the Supreme Pontiff in order to get the final verdict from the highest courts.

His prudence fell on sterile hearts. The news of the captive angel spread with such rapidity that after a few hours the courtyard had the bustle of a marketplace and they had to call in troops with fixed bayonets to disperse the mob that was about to knock the house down. Elisenda, her spine all twisted from sweeping up so much marketplace trash, then got the idea of fencing in the yard and charging five cents admission to see the angel.

The curious came from far away. A traveling carnival arrived with a flying acrobat who buzzed over the crowd several times, but no one paid any attention to him because his wings were not those of an angel but, rather, those of a sidereal bat. The most unfortunate invalids on earth came in search of health: a poor woman who since childhood had been counting her heartbeats and had run out of numbers; a Portuguese man who couldn't sleep because the noise of the stars disturbed him; a sleepwalker who got up at night to undo the things he had done while awake; and many others with less serious ailments. In the midst of that shipwreck disorder that made the earth tremble, Pelayo and Elisenda were happy with fatigue, for in less than a week they had crammed their rooms with money and the line of pilgrims waiting their turn to enter still reached beyond the horizon.

The angel was the only one who took no part in his own act. He spent his time trying to get comfortable in his borrowed nest, befuddled by the hellish heat of the oil lamps and sacramental candles that had been placed along the wire. At first they tried to make him eat some mothballs, which, according to the wisdom of the wise neighbor woman, were the food prescribed for angels. But he turned them down, just as he turned down the papal lunches that the penitents brought him, and they never found out whether it was because he was an angel or because he was an old man that in the end he ate nothing but eggplant mush. His only supernatural virtue seemed to be patience. Especially during the first days, when the hens pecked at him, searching for the stellar parasites that proliferated in his wings, and the cripples pulled out feathers to touch their defective parts with, and even the most merciful threw stones at him, trying to get him to rise so they could see him standing. The only time they succeeded in arousing him was when they burned his side with an iron for branding steers, for he had been motionless for so many hours that they thought he was dead. He awoke with a start, ranting in his hermetic language and with tears in his eyes, and he flapped his wings a couple of times, which brought on a whirlwind of chicken dung and lunar dust and a gale of panic that did not seem to be of this world. Although many thought that his reaction had been one not of rage but of pain, from then on they were careful not to annoy him, because the majority understood that his passivity was not that of a hero taking his ease but that of a cataclysm in repose.

Father Gonzaga held back the crowd's frivolity with formulas of maidservant inspiration while awaiting the arrival of a final judgment on the nature of the captive. But the mail from Rome showed no sense of urgency. They spent their time finding out if the prisoner had a navel, if his dialect had any connection with Aramaic, how many times he could fit on the head of a pin, or whether he wasn't just a Norwegian with wings. Those meager letters might have come and gone until the end of time if a providential event had not put an end to the priest's tribulations.

It so happened that during those days, among so many other carnival attractions, there arrived in town the traveling show of the woman who had been changed into a spider for having disobeyed her parents. The admission to see her was not only less than the admission to see the angel, but people were permitted to ask her all manner of questions about her absurd state and to examine her up and down so that no one would ever doubt the truth of her horror. She was a frightful tarantula the size of a ram and with the head of a sad maiden. What was most heart-rending, however, was not her outlandish shape but the sincere affliction with which she recounted the details of her misfortune. While still practically a child she had sneaked out of her parents' house to go to a dance, and while she was coming back through the woods after having danced all night without permission, a fearful thunderclap rent the sky in two and through the crack came the lightning bolt of brimstone that changed her into a spider. Her only nourishment came from the meatballs that charitable souls chose to toss into her mouth. A spectacle like that, full of so much human truth and with such a fearful lesson, was bound to defeat without even trying that of a haughty angel who scarcely deigned to look at mortals. Besides, the few miracles attributed to the angel showed a certain mental disorder, like the blind man who didn't recover his sight but grew three new teeth, or the paralytic who didn't get to walk but almost won the lottery, and the leper whose sores sprouted sunflowers. Those consolation miracles, which were more like mocking fun, had already ruined the angel's reputation when the woman who had been changed into a spider finally crushed him completely. That was how Father Gonzaga was cured forever of his insomnia and Pelayo's courtyard went back to being as empty as during the time it had rained for three days and crabs walked through the bedrooms.

The owners of the house had no reason to lament. With the money they saved they built a two-story mansion with balconies and gardens and high netting so that crabs wouldn't get in during the winter, and with iron bars on the windows so that angels wouldn't get in. Pelayo also set up a rabbit warren close to town and gave up his job as bailiff for good, and Elisenda bought some satin pumps with high heels and many dresses of iridescent silk, the kind worn on Sunday by the most desirable women in those times. The chicken coop was the only thing that didn't receive any attention. If they washed it down with creolin and burned tears of myrrh inside it every so often, it was not in homage to the angel but to drive away the dungheap stench that still hung everywhere like a ghost and was turning the new house into an old one. At first, when the child learned to walk, they were careful that he not get too close to the chicken coop. But then they began to lose their fears and got used to the smell, and before the child got his second teeth he'd gone inside the chicken coop to play, where the wires were falling apart. The angel was no less standoffish with him than with other mortals, but he tolerated the most ingenious infamies with the patience of a dog who had no illusions. They both came down with chicken pox at the same time. The doctor who took care of the child couldn't resist the temptation to listen to the angel's heart, and he found so much whistling in the heart and so many sounds in his kidneys that it seemed impossible for him to be alive. What surprised him most, however, was the logic of his wings. They seemed so natural on that completely human organism that he couldn't understand why other men didn't have them too.

When the child began school it had been some time since the sun and rain had caused the collapse of the chicken coop. The angel went dragging himself about here and there like a stray dying man. They would drive him out of the bedroom with a broom and a moment later find him in the kitchen. He seemed to be in so many places at the same time that they grew to think that he'd been duplicated, that he was reproducing himself all through the house, and the exasperated and unhinged Elisenda shouted that it was awful living in that hell full of angels. He could scarcely eat and his antiquarian eyes had also become so foggy that he went about bumping into posts. All he had left were the bare cannulae of his last feathers. Pelayo threw a blanket over him and extended him the charity of letting him sleep in the shed, and only then did they notice that he had a temperature at night, and was delirious with the tongue twisters of an old Norwegian. That was one of the few times they became alarmed, for they thought he was going to die and not even the wise neighbor woman had been able to tell them what to do with dead angels.

And yet he not only survived his worst winter, but seemed improved with the first sunny days. He remained motionless for several days in the farthest corner of the courtyard, where no one would see him, and at the beginning of December some large, stiff feathers began to grow on his wings, the feathers of a scarecrow, which looked more like another misfortune of decrepitude. But he must have known the reason for those changes, for he was quite careful that no one should notice them, that no one should hear the sea chanteys that he sometimes sang under the stars. One morning Elisenda was cutting some bunches of onions for lunch when a wind that seemed to come from the high seas blew into the kitchen. Then she went to the window and caught the angel in his first attempts at flight. They were so clumsy that his fingernails opened a furrow in the vegetable patch and he was on the point of knocking the shed down with the ungainly flapping that slipped on the light and couldn't get a grip on the air. But he did manage to gain altitude. Elisenda let out a sigh of relief, for herself and for him, when she saw him pass over the last houses, holding himself up in some way with the risky flapping of a senile vulture. She kept watching him even when she was through cutting the onions and she kept on watching until it was no longer possible for her to see him, because then he was no longer an annoyance in her life but an imaginary dot on the horizon of the sea.

GUY DE MAUPASSANT

The Necklace

Translated by Marjorie Laurie

She was one of those pretty and charming girls who are sometimes, as if by a mistake of destiny, born in a family of clerks. She had no dowry, no expectations, no means of being known, understood, loved, wedded by any rich and distinguished man; and she let herself be married to a little clerk at the Ministry of Public Instruction.

She dressed plainly because she could not dress well, but she was as unhappy as though she had really fallen from her proper station since with women there is neither caste nor rank: and beauty, grace, and charm act instead of family and birth. Natural fineness, instinct for what is elegant, suppleness of wit, are the sole hierarchy, and make from women of the people the equals of the very greatest ladies.

She suffered ceaselessly, feeling herself born for all the delicacies and all the luxuries. She suffered from the poverty of her dwelling, from the wretched look of the walls, from the worn-out chairs, from the ugliness of the curtains. All those things, of which another woman of her rank would never even have been conscious, tortured her and made her angry. The sight of the little Breton peasant who did her humble housework aroused in her regrets which were despairing, and distracted dreams. She thought of the silent ante-chambers hung with Oriental tapestry, lit by tall bronze candelabra, and of the two great footmen in knee breeches who sleep in the big armchairs, made drowsy by the heavy warmth of the hot-air stove. She thought of the long salons fitted up with ancient silk, of the delicate furniture carrying priceless curiosities, and of the coquettish perfumed boudoirs made for talks at five o'clock with intimate friends, with men famous and sought after, whom all women envy and whose attention they all desire.

When she sat down to dinner, before the round table covered with a tablecloth three days old, opposite her husband, who uncovered the soup tureen and declared with an enchanted air, "Ah, the good *pot-au-feu*! I don't know anything better than that," she thought of dainty dinners, of shining silverware, of tapestry which peopled the walls with ancient personages and with strange birds flying in the midst of a fairy forest; and she thought of delicious dishes served on marvelous plates, and of the whispered gallantries which you listen to with a sphinxlike smile, while you are eating the pink flesh of a trout or the wings of a quail.

She had no dresses, no jewels, nothing. And she loved nothing but that; she felt made for that. She would so have liked to please, to be envied, to be charming, to be sought after.

She had a friend, a former schoolmate at the convent, who was rich, and whom she did not like to go and see any more, because she suffered so much when she came back.

But one evening, her husband returned home with a triumphant air, and holding a large envelope in his hand.

"There," said he. "Here is something for you."

She tore the paper sharply, and drew out a printed card which bore these words:

"The Minister of Public Instruction and Mme. Georges Ramponneau request the honor of M. and Mme. Loisel's company at the palace of the Ministry on Monday evening, January eighteenth."

Instead of being delighted, as her husband hoped, she threw the invitation on the table with disdain, murmuring:

"What do you want me to do with that?"

"But, my dear, I thought you would be glad. You never go out, and this is such a fine opportunity. I had awful trouble to get it. Everyone wants to go; it is very select, and they are not giving many invitations to clerks. The whole official world will be there."

She looked at him with an irritated glance, and said, impatiently:

"And what do you want me to put on my back?"

He had not thought of that; he stammered:

"Why, the dress you go to the theater in. It looks very well, to me."

He stopped, distracted, seeing his wife was crying. Two great tears descended slowly from the corners of her eyes toward the corners of her mouth. He stuttered:

"What's the matter? What's the matter?"

But, by violent effort, she had conquered her grief, and she replied, with a calm voice, while she wiped her wet cheeks:

"Nothing. Only I have no dress and therefore I can't go to this ball. Give your card to some colleague whose wife is better equipped than I."

He was in despair. He resumed:

"Come, let us see, Mathilde. How much would it cost, a suitable dress, which you could use on other occasions. Something very simple?"

She reflected several seconds, making her calculations and wondering also what sum she could ask without drawing on herself an immediate refusal and a frightened exclamation from the economical clerk.

Finally, she replied, hesitatingly:

"I don't know exactly, but I think I could manage it with four hundred francs."

He had grown a little pale, because he was laying aside just that amount to buy a gun and treat himself to a little shooting next summer on the plain of Nanterre, with several friends who went to shoot larks down there, of a Sunday.

But he said:

"All right. I will give you four hundred francs. And try to have a pretty dress."

The day of the ball drew near, and Mme. Loisel seemed sad, uneasy, anxious. Her dress was ready, however. Her husband said to her one evening:

"What is the matter? Come, you've been so queer these last three days."

And she answered:

"It annoys me not to have a single jewel, not a single stone, nothing to put on. I shall look like distress. I should almost rather not go at all."

He resumed:

"You might wear natural flowers. It's very stylish at this time of the year. For ten francs you can get two or three magnificent roses."

She was not convinced.

"No; there's nothing more humiliating than to look poor among other women who are rich."

But her husband cried:

"How stupid you are! Go look up your friend Mme. Forestier, and ask her to lend you some jewels. You're quite thick enough with her to do that."

She uttered a cry of joy:

"It's true. I never thought of it."

The next day she went to her friend and told of her distress.

Mme. Forestier went to a wardrobe with a glass door, took out a large jewel-box, brought it back, opened it, and said to Mme. Loisel:

"Choose, my dear."

She saw first of all some bracelets, then a pearl necklace, then a Venetian cross, gold and precious stones of admirable workmanship. She tried on the ornaments before the glass, hesitated, could not make up her mind to part with them, to give them back. She kept asking:

"Haven't you any more?"

"Why, yes. Look. I don't know what you like."

All of a sudden she discovered, in a black satin box, a superb necklace of diamonds, and her heart began to beat with an immoderate desire. Her hands trembled as she took it. She fastened it around her throat, outside her high-necked dress, and remained lost in ecstacy at the sight of herself.

Then she asked, hesitating, filled with anguish:

"Can you lend me that, only that?"

"Why, yes, certainly."

She sprang upon the neck of her friend, kissed her passionately, then fled with her treasure.

The day of the ball arrived. Mme. Loisel made a great success. She was prettier than them all, elegant, gracious, smiling, and crazy with joy. All the men looked at her, asked her name, endeavored to be introduced. All the attachés of the Cabinet wanted to waltz with her. She was remarked by the minister himself.

She danced with intoxication, with passion, made drunk by pleasure, forgetting all, in the triumph of her beauty, in the glory of her success, in a sort of cloud of happiness composed of all this homage, of all this admiration, of all these awakened desires, and of that sense of complete victory which is so sweet to a woman's heart.

She went away about four o'clock in the morning. Her husband had been sleeping since midnight, in a little deserted anteroom, with three other gentlemen whose wives were having a very good time. He threw over her shoulders the wraps which he had brought, modest wraps of common life, whose poverty contrasted with the elegance of the ball dress. She felt this, and wanted to escape so as not to be remarked by the other women, who were enveloping themselves in costly furs.

Loisel held her back.

"Wait a bit. You will catch cold outside. I will go and call a cab."

But she did not listen to him, and rapidly descended the stairs. When they were in the street they did not find a carriage; and they began to look for one, shouting after the cabmen whom they saw passing by at a distance.

They went down toward the Seine, in despair, shivering with cold. At last they found on the quay one of those ancient noctambulant coupés which, exactly as if they were ashamed to show their misery during the day, are never seen round Paris until after nightfall.

It took them to their door in the Rue des Martyrs, and once more, sadly, they climbed up homeward. All was ended, for her. And as to him, he reflected that he must be at the Ministry at ten o'clock.

She removed the wraps which covered her shoulders, before the glass, so as once more to see herself in all her glory. But suddenly she uttered a cry. She no longer had the necklace around her neck!

Her husband, already half undressed, demanded:

"What is the matter with you?"

She turned madly towards him:

"I have — I have — I've lost Mme. Forestier's necklace."

He stood up, distracted.

"What! — how? — impossible!"

And they looked in the folds of her dress, in the folds of her cloak, in her pockets, everywhere. They did not find it.

He asked:

"You're sure you had it on when you left the ball?"

"Yes, I felt it in the vestibule of the palace."

"But if you had lost it in the street we should have heard it fall. It must be in the cab."

"Yes. Probably. Did you take his number?"

"No. And you, didn't you notice it?"

"No."

They looked, thunderstruck, at one another. At last Loisel put on his clothes.

"I shall go back on foot," said he, "over the whole route which we have taken to see if I can find it."

And he went out. She sat waiting on a chair in her ball dress, without strength to go to bed, overwhelmed, without fire, without a thought

Her husband came back about seven o'clock. He had found nothing.

He went to Police Headquarters, to the newspaper offices, to offer a reward; he went to the cab companies — everywhere, in fact, whither he was urged by the least suspicion of hope.

She waited all day, in the same condition of mad fear before this terrible calamity.

Loisel returned at night with a hollow, pale face; he had discovered nothing.

"You must write to your friend," said he, "that you have broken the clasp of her necklace and that you are having it mended. That will give us time to turn round."

She wrote at his dictation.

At the end of a week they had lost all hope.

And Loisel, who had aged five years, declared:

"We must consider how to replace that ornament."

The next day they took the box which had contained it, and they went to the jeweler whose name was found within. He consulted his books.

"It was not I, madame, who sold that necklace; I must simply have furnished the case."

Then they went from jeweler to jeweler, searching for a necklace like the other, consulting their memories, sick both of them with chagrin and anguish.

They found, in a shop at the Palais Royal, a string of diamonds which seemed to them exactly like the one they looked for. It was worth forty thousand francs. They could have it for thirty-six.

So they begged the jeweler not to sell it for three days yet. And they made a bargain that he should buy it back for thirty-four thousand francs, in case they found the other one before the end of February.

Loisel possessed eighteen thousand francs which his father had left him. He would borrow the rest.

He did borrow, asking a thousand francs of one, five hundred of another, five louis here, three louis there. He gave notes, took up ruinous obligations, dealt with usurers and all the race of lenders. He compromised all the rest of his life, risked his signature without even knowing if he could meet it; and, frightened by the pains yet to come, by the black misery which was about to fall upon him, by the prospect of all the physical privation and of all the moral tortures which he was to suffer, he went to get the new necklace, putting down upon the merchant's counter thirty-six thousand francs.

When Mme. Loisel took back the necklace, Mme. Forestier said to her, with a chilly manner:

"You should have returned it sooner; I might have needed it."

She did not open the case, as her friend had so much feared. If she had detected the substitution, what would she have thought, what would she have said? Would she not have taken Mme. Loisel for a thief?

Mme. Loisel now knew the horrible existence of the needy. She took her part, moreover, all of a sudden, with heroism. That dreadful debt must be paid. She would pay it. They dismissed their servant; they changed their lodgings; they rented a garret under the roof.

She came to know what heavy housework meant and the odious cares of the kitchen. She washed the dishes, using her rosy nails on the greasy pots and pans. She washed the dirty linen, the shirts, and the dishcloths, which she dried upon a line; she carried the slops down to the street every morning, and carried up the water, stopping for breath at every landing. And, dressed like a woman of the people, she went to the fruiterer, the grocer, the butcher, her basket on her arm, bargaining, insulted, defending her miserable money sou by sou.

Each month they had to meet some notes, renew others, obtain more time.

Her husband worked in the evening making a fair copy of some tradesman's accounts, and late at night he often copied manuscript for five sous a page.

And this life lasted for ten years.

At the end of ten years, they had paid everything, everything, with the rates of usury, and the accumulations of the compound interest.

Mme. Loisel looked old now. She had become the woman of impoverished households — strong and hard and rough. With frowsy hair, skirts askew, and red hands, she talked loud while washing the floor with great swishes of water. But sometimes, when her husband was at the office, she sat down near the window, and she thought of that gay evening of long ago, of that ball where she had been so beautiful and so fêted.

What would have happened if she had not lost that necklace? Who knows? Who knows? How life is strange and changeful! How little a thing is needed for us to be lost or to be saved!

But, one Sunday, having gone to take a walk in the Champs Elysées to refresh herself from the labor of the week, she suddenly perceived a woman who was leading a child. It was Mme. Forestier, still young, still beautiful, still charming.

Mme. Loisel felt moved. Was she going to speak to her? Yes, certainly. And now that she had paid, she was going to tell her all about it. Why not?

She went up.

"Good-day, Jeanne."

The other, astonished to be familiarly addressed by this plain goodwife, did not recognize her at all, and stammered:

"But — madam! — I do not know — You must be mistaken."

"No. I am Mathilde Loisel."

Her friend uttered a cry.

"Oh, my poor Mathilde! How you are changed!"

"Yes, I have had days hard enough, since I have seen you, days wretched enough — and that because of you!"

"Of me! How so?"

"Do you remember that diamond necklace which you lent me to wear at the ministerial ball?"

"Yes. Well?"

"Well, I lost it."

"What do you mean? You brought it back."

"I brought you back another just like it. And for this we have been ten years paying. You can understand that it was not easy for us, us who had nothing. At last it is ended, and I am very glad."

Mme. Forestier had stopped.

"You say that you bought a necklace of diamonds to replace mine?"

"Yes. You never noticed it, then! They were very like."

And she smiled with a joy which was proud and naïve at once.

Mme. Forestier, strongly moved, took her two hands.

"Oh, my poor Mathilde! Why, my necklace was paste. It was worth at most five hundred francs!"

CARSON McCULLERS

A Tree, a Rock, a Cloud

It was raining that morning, and still very dark. When the boy reached the streetcar café he had almost finished his route and he went in for a cup of coffee. The place was an all-night café owned by a bitter and stingy man called Leo. After the raw, empty street the café seemed friendly and bright: along the counter there were a couple of soldiers, three spinners from the cotton mill, and in a corner a man who sat hunched over with his nose and half his face down in a beer mug. The boy wore a helmet such as aviators wear. When he went into the café he unbuckled the chin strap and raised the right flap up over his pink little ear; often as he drank his coffee someone would speak to him in a friendly way. But this morning Leo did not look into his face and none of the men were talking. He paid and was leaving the café when a voice called out to him:

'Son! Hey Son!'

He turned back and the man in the corner was crooking his finger and nodding to him. He had brought his face out of the beer mug and he seemed suddenly very happy. The man was long and pale, with a big nose and faded orange hair.

'Hey Son!'

The boy went toward him. He was an undersized boy of about twelve, with one shoulder drawn higher than the other because of the weight of the paper sack. His face was shallow, freckled, and his eyes were round child eyes.

'Yeah Mister?'

The man laid one hand on the paper boy's shoulders, then grasped the boy's chin and turned his face slowly from one side to the other. The boy shrank back uneasily.

'Say! What's the big idea?'

The boy's voice was shrill; inside the café it was suddenly very quiet.

The man said slowly: 'I love you.'

All along the counter the men laughed. The boy, who had scowled and sidled away, did not know what to do. He looked over the counter at Leo, and Leo watched him with a weary, brittle jeer. The boy tried to laugh also. But the man was serious and sad.

'I did not mean to tease you, Son,' he said. 'Sit down and have a beer with me. There is something I have to explain.'

Cautiously, out of the corner of his eye, the paper boy questioned the men along the counter to see what he should do. But they had gone back to their beer or their breakfast and did not notice him. Leo put a cup of coffee on the counter and a little jug of cream.

'He is a minor,' Leo said.

The paper boy slid himself up onto the stool. His ear beneath the upturned flap of the helmet was very small and red. The man was nodding at him soberly. 'It is important,' he said. Then he reached in his hip pocket and brought out something which he held up in the palm of his hand for the boy to see.

'Look very carefully,' he said.

The boy stared, but there was nothing to look at very carefully. The man held in his big, grimy palm a photograph. It was the face of a woman, but blurred, so that only the hat and the dress she was wearing stood out clearly.

'See?' the man asked.

The boy nodded and the man placed another picture in his palm. The woman was standing on a beach in a bathing suit. The suit made her stomach very big, and that was the main thing you noticed.

'Got a good look?' He leaned over closer and finally asked: 'You ever seen her before?'

The boy sat motionless, staring slantwise at the man. 'Not so I know of.'

'Very well.' The man blew on the photographs and put them back into his pocket. 'That was my wife.'

'Dead?' the boy asked.

Slowly the man shook his head. He pursed his lips as though about to whistle and answered in a long-drawn way: 'Nuuu —' he said. 'I will explain.'

The beer on the counter before the man was in a large brown mug. He did not pick it up to drink. Instead he bent down and, putting his face over the rim, he rested there for a moment. Then with both hands he tilted the mug and sipped.

'Some night you'll go to sleep with your nose in a mug and drown,' said Leo. 'Prominent transient drowns in beer. That would be a cute death.'

The paper boy tried to signal to Leo. While the man was not looking he screwed up his face and worked his mouth to question soundlessly: 'Drunk?' But Leo only raised his eyebrows and turned away to put some pink strips of bacon on the grill. The man pushed the mug away from him, straightened himself, and folded his loose crooked hands on the counter. His face was sad as he looked at the paper boy. He did not blink, but from time to time the lids closed down with delicate gravity over his pale green eyes. It was nearing dawn and the boy shifted the weight of the paper sack.

'I am talking about love,' the man said. 'With me it is a science.'

The boy half slid down from the stool. But the man raised his forefinger, and there was something about him that held the boy and would not let him go away.

'Twelve years ago I married the woman in the photograph. She was my wife for one year, nine months, three days, and two nights. I loved her. Yes . . .' He tightened his blurred, rambling voice and said again: 'I loved her. I thought also that she loved me. I was a railroad engineer. She had all home comforts and luxuries. It never crept into my brain that she was not satisfied. But do you know what happened?'

'Mgneeow!' said Leo.

The man did not take his eyes from the boy's face. 'She left me. I came in one night and the house was empty and she was gone. She left me.'

'With a fellow?' the boy asked.

Gently the man placed his palm down on the counter. 'Why naturally, Son. A woman does not run off like that alone.'

The café was quiet, the soft rain black and endless in the street outside. Leo pressed down the frying bacon with the prongs of his long fork. 'So you have been chasing the floozie for eleven years. You frazzled old rascal!'

For the first time the man glanced at Leo. 'Please don't be vulgar. Besides, I was not speaking to you.' He turned back to the boy and said in a trusting and secretive undertone: 'Let's not pay any attention to him. O.K.?'

The paper boy nodded doubtfully.

'It was like this,' the man continued. 'I am a person who feels many things. All my life one thing after another has impressed me. Moonlight. The leg of a pretty girl. One thing after another. But the point is that when I had enjoyed anything there was a peculiar sensation as though it was laying around loose in me. Nothing seemed to finish itself up or fit in with the other things. Women? I had my portion of them. The same. Afterwards laying around loose in me. I was a man who had never loved.'

Very slowly he closed his eyelids, and the gesture was like a curtain drawn at the end of a scene in a play. When he spoke again his voice was excited and the words came fast — the lobes of his large, loose ears seemed to tremble.

'Then I met this woman. I was fifty-one and she was thirty. I met her at a filling station and we were married within three days. And do you know what it was like? I just can't tell you. All I had ever felt was gathered together around this woman. Nothing lay loose in me any more but was finished up by her.'

The man stopped suddenly and stroked his long nose. His voice sank down to a steady and reproachful undertone: 'I'm not explaining this right. What happened was this. There were these beautiful feelings and loose little pleasures inside me. And this woman was something like an assembly line for my soul. I run these little pieces of myself through her and I come out complete. Now do you follow me?'

'What was her name?' the boy asked.

'Oh,' he said. 'I called her Dodo. But that is immaterial.'

'Did you try to make her come back?'

The man did not seem to hear. 'Under the circumstances you can imagine how I felt when she left me.'

Leo took the bacon from the grill and folded two strips of it between a bun. He had a gray face, with slitted eyes, and a pinched nose saddled by faint blue shadows. One of the mill workers signaled for more coffee and Leo poured it. He did not give refills on coffee free. The spinner ate breakfast there every morning, but the better Leo knew his customers the stingier he treated them. He nibbled his own bun as though he grudged it to himself.

'And you never got hold of her again?'

The boy did not know what to think of the man, and his child's face was uncertain with mingled curiosity and doubt. He was new on the paper route; it was still strange to him to be out in the town in the black, queer early morning.

'Yes,' the man said. 'I took a number of steps to get her back. I went around trying to locate her. I went to Tulsa where she had folks. And to Mobile. I went to every town she had ever mentioned to me, and I hunted down every man she had formerly been connected with. Tulsa, Atlanta, Chicago, Cheehaw, Memphis. . . . For the better part of two years I chased around the country trying to lay hold of her.'

'But the pair of them had vanished from the face of the earth!' said Leo.

'Don't listen to him,' the man said confidentially. 'And also just forget those two years. They are not important. What matters is that around the third year a curious thing begun to happen to me.'

'What?' the boy asked.

The man leaned down and tilted his mug to take a sip of beer. But as he hovered over the mug his nostrils fluttered slightly; he sniffed the staleness of the beer and did not drink. 'Love is a curious thing to begin with. At first I thought only of getting her back. It was a kind of mania. But then as time went on I tried to remember her. But do you know what happened?'

'No,' the boy said.

'When I laid myself down on a bed and tried to think about her my mind became a blank. I couldn't see her. I would take out her pictures and look. No good. Nothing doing. A blank. Can you imagine it?'

'Say Mac!' Leo called down the counter. 'Can you imagine this bozo's mind a blank!'

Slowly, as though fanning away flies, the man waved his hand. His green eyes were concentrated and fixed on the shallow little face of the paper boy.

'But a sudden piece of glass on a sidewalk. Or a nickel tune in a music box. A shadow on a wall at night. And I would remember. It might happen in a street and I would cry or bang my head against a lamppost. You follow me?'

'A piece of glass . . .' the boy said.

'Anything. I would walk around and I had no power of how and when to remember her. You think you can put up a kind of shield. But remembering don't come to a man face forward — it corners around sideways. I was at the mercy of everything I saw and heard. Suddenly instead of me combing the countryside to find her she begun to chase me around in my very soul. *She* chasing *me,* mind you! And in my soul.'

The boy asked finally: 'What part of the country were you in then?'

'Ooh,' the man groaned. 'I was a sick mortal. It was like smallpox. I confess, Son, that I boozed. I fornicated. I committed any sin that suddenly appealed to me. I am loath to confess it but I will do so. When I recall that period it is all curdled in my mind, it was so terrible.'

The man leaned his head down and tapped his forehead on the counter. For a few seconds he stayed bowed over in this position, the back of his stringy neck covered with orange furze, his hands with their long warped fingers held palm to palm in an attitude of prayer. Then the man straightened himself; he was smiling and suddenly his face was bright and tremulous and old.

'It was in the fifth year that it happened,' he said. 'And with it I started my science.'

Leo's mouth jerked with a pale, quick grin. 'Well none of we boys are getting any younger,' he said. Then with sudden anger he balled up a dishcloth he was holding and threw it down hard on the floor. 'You draggle-tailed old Romeo!'

'What happened?' the boy asked.

The old man's voice was high and clear: 'Peace,' he answered.

'Huh?'

'It is hard to explain scientifically, Son,' he said. 'I guess the logical explanation is that she and I had fleed around from each other for so long that finally we just got tangled up together and lay down and quit. Peace. A queer and beautiful blankness. It was spring in Portland and the rain came every afternoon. All evening I just stayed there on my bed in the dark. And that is how the science come to me.'

The windows in the streetcar were pale blue with light. The two soldiers paid for their beers and opened the door — one of the soldiers combed his hair and wiped off his muddy puttees before they went outside. The three mill workers bent silently over their breakfasts. Leo's clock was ticking on the wall.

'It is this. And listen carefully. I meditated on love and reasoned it out. I reasoned it out. I realized what is wrong with us. Men fall in love for the first time. And what do they fall in love with?'

The boy's soft mouth was partly open and he did not answer.

'A woman,' the old man said. 'Without science, with nothing to go by, they undertake the most dangerous and sacred experience in God's earth. They fall in love with a woman. Is that correct, Son?'

'Yeah,' the boy said faintly.

'They start at the wrong end of love. They begin at the climax. Can you wonder it is so miserable? Do you know how men should love?'

The old man reached over and grasped the boy by the collar of his leather jacket. He gave him a gentle little shake and his green eyes gazed down unblinking and grave.

'Son, do you know how love should be begun?'

The boy sat small and listening and still. Slowly he shook his head. The old man leaned closer and whispered:

'A tree. A rock. A cloud.'

It was still raining outside in the street: a mild, gray, endless rain. The mill whistle blew for the six o'clock shift and the three spinners paid and went away. There was no one in the café but Leo, the old man, and the little paper boy.

'The weather was like this in Portland,' he said. 'At the time my science was begun. I meditated and I started very cautious. I would pick up something from the street and take it home with me. I bought a goldfish and I concentrated on the goldfish and I loved it. I graduated from one thing to another. Day by day I was getting this technique. On the road from Portland to San Diego — '

'Aw shut up!' screamed Leo suddenly. 'Shut up! Shut up!'

The old man still held the collar of the boy's jacket; he was trembling and his face was earnest and bright and wild. 'For six years now I have gone around by myself and built up my science. And now I am a master. Son. I can love anything. No longer do I have to think about it even. I see a street full of people and a beautiful light comes in me. I watch a bird in the sky. Or I meet a traveler on the road. Everything, Son. And anybody. All stranger and all loved! Do you realize what a science like mine can mean?'

The boy held himself stiffly, his hands curled tight around the counter edge. Finally he asked: 'Did you ever really find that lady?'

'What? What say, Son?'

'I mean,' the boy asked timidly. 'Have you fallen in love with a woman again?'

The old man loosened his grasp on the boy's collar. He turned away and for the first time his green eyes had a vague and scattered look. He lifted the mug from the counter, drank down the yellow beer. His head was shaking slowly from side to side. Then finally he answered: 'No, Son. You see that is the last step in my science. I go cautious. And I am not quite ready yet.'

'Well!' said Leo. 'Well well well!'

The old man stood in the open doorway. 'Remember,' he said. Framed there in the gray damp light of the early morning he looked shrunken and seedy and frail. But his smile was bright. 'Remember I love you,' he said with a last nod. And the door closed quietly behind him.

The boy did not speak for a long time. He pulled down the bangs on his forehead and slid his grimy little forefinger around the rim of his empty cup. Then without looking at Leo he finally asked:

'Was he drunk?'

'No,' said Leo shortly.

The boy raised his clear voice higher. 'Then was he a dope fiend?'

'No.'

The boy looked up at Leo, and his flat little face was desperate, his voice urgent and shrill. 'Was he crazy? Do you think he was a lunatic?' The paper boy's voice dropped suddenly with doubt. 'Leo? Or not?'

But Leo would not answer him. Leo had run a night café for fourteen years, and he held himself to be a critic of craziness. There were the town characters and also the transients who roamed in from the night. He knew the manias of all of them. But he did not want to satisfy the questions of the waiting child. He tightened his pale face and was silent.

So the boy pulled down the right flap of his helmet and as he turned to leave he made the only comment that seemed safe to him, the only remark that could not be laughed down and despised:

'He sure has done a lot of traveling.'

YUKIO MISHIMA

Patriotism

Translated by Geoffrey W. Sargent

On the twenty-eighth of February, 1936 (on the third day, that is, of the February 26 Incident), Lieutenant Shinji Takeyama of the Konoe Transport Battalion — profoundly disturbed by the knowledge that his closest colleagues had been with the mutineers from the beginning, and indignant at the imminent prospect of Imperial troops attacking Imperial troops — took his officer's sword and ceremonially disemboweled himself in the eight-mat room of his private residence in the sixth block of Aoba-chō, in Yotsuya Ward. His wife, Reiko, followed him, stabbing herself to death. The lieutenant's farewell note consisted of one sentence: "Long live the Imperial Forces." His wife's, after apologies for her unfilial conduct in thus preceding her parents to the grave, concluded: "The day which, for a soldier's wife, had to come, has come. . . ." The last moments of this heroic and dedicated couple were such as to make the gods themselves weep. The lieutenant's age, it should be noted, was thirty-one, his wife's twenty-three; and it was not half a year since the celebration of their marriage.

II

Those who saw the bride and bridegroom in the commemorative photograph — perhaps no less than those actually present at the lieutenant's wedding — had exclaimed in wonder at the bearing of this handsome couple. The lieutenant, majestic in military uniform, stood protectively beside his bride, his right hand resting upon his sword, his officer's cap held at his left side. His expression was severe, and his dark brows and wide-gazing eyes well conveyed the clear integrity of youth. For the beauty of the bride in her white over-robe no comparisons were adequate. In the eyes, round beneath soft brows, in the slender, finely shaped nose, and in the full lips, there was both sensuousness and refinement. One hand, emerging shyly from a sleeve of the over-robe, held a fan, and the tips of the fingers clustering delicately, were like the bud of a moonflower.

After the suicide, people would take out this photograph and examine it, and sadly reflect that too often there was a curse on these seemingly flawless unions. Perhaps it was no more than imagination, but looking at the picture after the tragedy it almost seemed as if the two young people before the gold-lacquered screen were gazing, each with equal clarity, at the deaths which lay before them.

Thanks to the good offices of their go-between, Lieutenant General Ozeki, they had been able to set themselves up in a new home at Aoba-chō in Yotsuya. "New home" is perhaps misleading. It was an old three-room rented house backing onto a small garden. As neither the six- nor the four-and-a-half-mat room downstairs was favored by the sun, they used the upstairs eight-mat room as both bedroom and guest room. There was no maid, so Reiko was left alone to guard the house in her husband's absence.

The honeymoon trip was dispensed with on the grounds that these were times of national emergency. The two of them had spent the first night of their marriage at this house. Before going to bed, Shinji, sitting erect on the floor with his sword laid before him, had bestowed upon his wife a soldierly lecture. A woman who had become the wife of a soldier should know and resolutely accept that her husband's death might come at any moment. It could be tomorrow. It could be the day after. But, no matter when it came — he asked — was she steadfast in her resolve to accept it? Reiko rose to her feet, pulled open a drawer of the cabinet, and took out what was the most prized of her new possessions, the dagger her mother had given her. Returning to her place, she laid the dagger without a word on the mat before her, just as her husband had laid his sword. A silent understanding was achieved at once, and the lieutenant never again sought to test his wife's resolve.

In the first few months of her marriage Reiko's beauty grew daily more radiant, shining serene like the moon after rain.

As both were possessed of young, vigorous bodies, their relationship was passionate. Nor was this merely a matter of the night. On more than one occasion, returning home straight from maneuvers, and begrudging even the time it took to remove his mud-splashed uniform, the lieutenant had pushed his wife to the floor almost as soon as he had entered the house. Reiko was equally ardent in her response. For a little more or a little less than a month, from the first night of their marriage Reiko knew happiness, and the lieutenant, seeing this, was happy too.

Reiko's body was white and pure, and her swelling breasts conveyed a firm and chaste refusal; but, upon consent, those breasts were lavish with their intimate, welcoming warmth. Even in bed these two were frighteningly and awesomely serious. In the very midst of wild, intoxicating passions, their hearts were sober and serious.

By day the lieutenant would think of his wife in the brief rest periods between training; and all day long, at home, Reiko would recall the image of her husband. Even when apart, however, they had only to look at the wedding photograph for their happiness to be once more confirmed. Reiko felt not the slightest surprise that a man who had been a complete stranger until a few months ago should now have become the sun about which her whole world revolved.

All these things had a moral basis, and were in accordance with the Education Rescript's injunction that "husband and wife should be harmonious." Not once did Reiko contradict her husband, nor did the lieutenant ever find reason to scold his wife. On the god shelf below the stairway, alongside the tablet from the Great Ise Shrine, were set photographs of their Imperial Majesties, and regularly every morning, before leaving for duty, the lieutenant would stand with his wife at this hallowed place and together they would bow their heads low. The offering water was renewed each morning, and the sacred sprig of *sasaki* was always green and fresh. Their lives were lived beneath the solemn protection of the gods and were filled with an intense happiness which set every fiber in their bodies trembling.

III

Although Lord Privy Seal Saitō's house was in their neighborhood, neither of them heard any noise of gunfire on the morning of February 26. It was a bugle, sounding muster in the dim, snowy dawn, when the ten-minute tragedy had already ended, which first disrupted the lieutenant's slumbers. Leaping at once from his bed, and without speaking a word, the lieutenant donned his uniform, buckled on the sword held ready for him by his wife, and hurried swiftly out into the snow-covered streets of the still darkened morning. He did not return until the evening of the twenty-eighth.

Later, from the radio news, Reiko learned the full extent of this sudden eruption of violence. Her life throughout the subsequent two days was lived alone, in complete tranquillity, and behind locked doors.

In the lieutenant's face, as he hurried silently out into the snowy morning, Reiko had read the determination to die. If her husband did not return, her own decision was made: she too would die. Quietly she attended to the disposition of her personal possessions. She chose her sets of visiting kimonos as keepsakes for friends of her schooldays, and she wrote a name and address on the stiff paper wrapping in which each was folded. Constantly admonished by her husband never to think of the morrow, Reiko had not even kept a diary and was now denied the pleasure of assiduously rereading her record of the happiness of the past few months and consigning each page to the fire as she did so. Ranged across the top of the radio were a small china dog, a rabbit, a squirrel, a bear, and a fox. There were also a small vase and a water pitcher. These comprised Reiko's one and only collection. But it would hardly do, she imagined, to give such things as keepsakes. Nor again would it be quite proper to ask specifically for them to be included in the coffin. It seemed to Reiko, as these thoughts passed through her mind, that the expressions on the small animals' faces grew even more lost and forlorn.

Reiko took the squirrel in her hand and looked at it. And then, her thoughts turning to a realm far beyond these child-like affections, she gazed up into the distance at the great sunlike principle which her husband embodied. She was ready, and happy, to be hurtled along to her destruction in that gleaming sun chariot — but now, for these few moments of solitude, she allowed herself to luxuriate in this innocent attachment to trifles. The time when she had genuinely loved these things, however, was long past. Now she merely loved the memory of having once loved them, and their place in her heart had been filled by more intense passions, by a more frenzied happiness.... For Reiko had never, even to herself, thought of those soaring joys of the flesh as a mere pleasure. The February cold, and the icy touch of the china squirrel, had numbed Reiko's slender fingers; yet, even so, in her lower limbs, beneath the ordered repetition of the pattern which crossed the skirt of her trim *meisen* kimono, she could feel now, as she thought of the lieutenant's powerful arms reaching out toward her, a hot moistness of the flesh which defied the snows.

She was not in the least afraid of the death hovering in her mind. Waiting alone at home, Reiko firmly believed that everything her husband was feeling or thinking now, his anguish and distress, was leading her — just as surely as the power in his flesh — to a welcome death. She felt as if her body could melt away with ease and be transformed to the merest fraction of her husband's thought.

Listening to the frequent announcements on the radio, she heard the names of several of her husband's colleagues mentioned among those of the insurgents. This was news of death. She followed the developments closely, wondering anxiously, as the situation became daily more irrevocable, why no Imperial ordinance was sent down, and watching what had at first been taken as a movement to restore the nation's honor come gradually to be branded with the infamous name of mutiny. There was no communication from the regiment. At any moment, it seemed, fighting might commence in the city streets, where the remains of the snow still lay.

Toward sundown on the twenty-eighth Reiko was startled by a furious pounding on the front door. She hurried downstairs. As she pulled with fumbling fingers at the bolt, the shape dimly outlined beyond the frosted-glass panel made no sound, but she knew it was her husband. Reiko had never known the bolt on the sliding door to be so stiff. Still it resisted. The door just would not open.

In a moment, almost before she knew she had succeeded, the lieutenant was standing before her on the cement floor inside the porch, muffled in a khaki greatcoat, his top boots heavy with slush from the street. Closing the door behind him, he returned the bolt once more to its socket. With what significance, Reiko did not understand.

"Welcome home."

Reiko bowed deeply, but her husband made no response. As he had already unfastened his sword and was about to remove his greatcoat, Reiko moved around behind to assist. The coat, which was cold and damp and had lost the odor of horse dung it normally exuded when exposed to the sun, weighed heavily upon her arm. Draping it across a hanger, and cradling the sword and leather belt in her sleeves, she waited while her husband removed his top boots and then followed behind him into the "living room." This was the six-mat room downstairs.

Seen in the clear light from the lamp, her husband's face, covered with a heavy growth of bristle, was almost unrecognizably wasted and thin. The cheeks were hollow, their luster and resilience gone. In his normal good spirits he would have changed into old clothes as soon as he was home and have pressed her to get supper at once, but now he sat before the table still in his uniform, his head drooping dejectedly. Reiko refrained from asking whether she should prepare the supper.

After an interval the lieutenant spoke.

"I knew nothing. They hadn't asked me to join. Perhaps out of consideration, because I was newly married. Kanō, and Homma too, and Yamaguchi."

Reiko recalled momentarily the faces of high-spirited young officers, friends of her husband, who had come to the house occasionally as guests.

"There may be an Imperial ordinance sent down tomorrow. They'll be posted as rebels, I imagine. I shall be in command of a unit with orders to attack them.... I can't do it. It's impossible to do a thing like that."

He spoke again.

"They've taken me off guard duty, and I have permission to return home for one night. Tomorrow morning, without question, I must leave to join the attack. I can't do it, Reiko."

Reiko sat erect with lowered eyes. She understood clearly that her husband had spoken of his death. The lieutenant was resolved. Each word, being rooted in death, emerged sharply and with powerful significance against this dark, unmovable background. Although the lieutenant was speaking of his dilemma, already there was no room in his mind for vacillation.

However, there was a clarity, like the clarity of a stream fed from melting snows, in the silence which rested between them. Sitting in his own home after the long two-day ordeal, and looking across at the face of his beautiful wife, the lieutenant was for the first time experiencing true peace of mind. For he had at once known, though she said nothing, that his wife divined the resolve which lay beneath his words.

"Well, then ..." The lieutenant's eyes opened wide. Despite his exhaustion they were strong and clear, and now for the first time they looked straight into the eyes of his wife. "To-night I shall cut my stomach."

Reiko did not flinch.

Her round eyes showed tension, as taut as the clang of a bell.

"I am ready," she said. "I ask permission to accompany you."

The lieutenant felt almost mesmerized by the strength in those eyes. His words flowed swiftly and easily, like the utterances of a man in delirium, and it was beyond his understanding how permission in a matter of such weight could be expressed so casually.

"Good. We'll go together. But I want you as a witness, first, for my own suicide. Agreed?"

When this was said a sudden release of abundant happiness welled up in both their hearts. Reiko was deeply affected by the greatness of her husband's trust in her. It was vital for the lieutenant, whatever else might happen, that there should be no irregularity in his death. For that reason there had to be a witness. The fact that he had chosen his wife for this was the first mark of his trust. The second, and even greater mark, was that though he had pledged that they should die together he did not intend to kill his wife first — he had deferred her death to a time when he would no longer be there to verify it. If the lieutenant had been a suspicious husband, he would doubtless, as in the usual suicide pact, have chosen to kill his wife first.

When Reiko said, "I ask permission to accompany you," the lieutenant felt these words to be the final fruit of the education which he had himself given his wife, starting on the first night of their marriage, and which had schooled her, when the moment came, to say what had to be said without a shadow of hesitation. This flattered the lieutenant's opinion of himself as a self-reliant man. He was not so romantic or conceited as to imagine that the words were spoken spontaneously, out of love for her husband.

With happiness welling almost too abundantly in their hearts, they could not help smiling at each other. Reiko felt as if she had returned to her wedding night.

Before her eyes was neither pain nor death. She seemed to see only a free and limitless expanse opening out into vast distances.

"The water is hot. Will you take your bath now?"

"Ah yes, of course."

"And supper . . .?"

The words were delivered in such level, domestic tones that the lieutenant came near to thinking, for the fraction of a second, that everything had been a hallucination.

"I don't think we'll need supper. But perhaps you could warm some sake?"

"As you wish."

As Reiko rose and took a *tanzen* gown from the cabinet for after the bath, she purposely directed her husband's attention to the opened drawer. The lieutenant rose, crossed to the cabinet, and looked inside. From the ordered array of paper wrappings he read, one by one, the addresses of the keepsakes. There was no grief in the lieutenant's response to this demonstration of heroic resolve. His heart was filled with tenderness. Like a husband who is proudly shown the childish purchases of a young wife, the lieutenant, overwhelmed by affection, lovingly embraced his wife from behind and implanted a kiss upon her neck.

Reiko felt the roughness of the lieutenant's unshaven skin against her neck. This sensation, more than being just a thing of this world, was for Reiko almost the world itself, but now — with the feeling that it was soon to be lost forever — it had freshness beyond all her experience. Each moment had its own vital strength, and the senses in every corner of her body were reawakened. Accepting her husband's caresses from behind, Reiko raised herself on the tips of her toes, letting the vitality seep through her entire body.

"First the bath, and then, after some sake . . . lay out the bedding upstairs, will you?"

The lieutenant whispered the words into his wife's ear. Reiko silently nodded.

Flinging off his uniform, the lieutenant went to the bath. To faint background noises of slopping water Reiko tended the charcoal brazier in the living room and began the preparations for warming the sake.

Taking the *tanzen,* a sash, and some underclothes, she went to the bathroom to ask how the water was. In the midst of a coiling cloud of steam the lieutenant was sitting cross-legged on the floor, shaving, and she could dimly discern the rippling movements of the muscles on his damp, powerful back as they responded to the movement of his arms.

There was nothing to suggest a time of any special significance. Reiko, going busily about her tasks, was preparing side dishes from odds and ends in stock. Her hands did not tremble. If anything, she managed even more efficiently and smoothly than usual. From time to time, it is true, there was a strange throbbing deep within her breast. Like distant lightning, it had a moment of sharp intensity and then vanished without trace. Apart from that, nothing was in any way out of the ordinary.

The lieutenant, shaving in the bathroom, felt his warmed body miraculously healed at last of the desperate tiredness of the days of indecision and filled — in spite of the death which lay ahead — with pleasurable anticipation. The sound of his wife going about her work came to him faintly. A healthy physical craving, submerged for two days, reasserted itself.

The lieutenant was confident there had been no impurity in that joy they had experienced when resolving upon death. They had both sensed at that moment — though not, of course, in any clear and conscious way — that those permissible pleasures which they shared in private were once more beneath the protection of Righteousness and Divine Power, and of a complete and unassailable morality. On looking into each other's eyes and discovering there an honorable death, they had felt themselves safe once more behind steel walls which none could destroy, encased in an impenetrable armor of Beauty and Truth. Thus, so far from seeing any inconsistency or conflict between the urges of his flesh and the sincerity of his patriotism, the lieutenant was even able to regard the two as parts of the same thing.

Thrusting his face close to the dark, cracked, misted wall mirror, the lieutenant shaved himself with great care. This would be his death face. There must be no unsightly blemishes. The clean-shaven face gleamed once more with a youthful luster, seeming to brighten the darkness of the mirror. There was a certain elegance, he even felt, in the association of death with this radiantly healthy face.

Just as it looked now, this would become his death face! Already, in fact, it had half departed from the lieutenant's personal possession and had become the bust above a dead soldier's memorial. As an experiment he closed his eyes tight. Everything was wrapped in blackness, and he was no longer a living, seeing creature.

Returning from the bath, the traces of the shave glowing faintly blue beneath his smooth cheeks, he seated himself beside the now well-kindled charcoal brazier. Busy though Reiko was, he noticed, she had found time to lightly touch up her face.

Her cheeks were gay and her lips moist. There was no shadow of sadness to be seen. Truly, the lieutenant felt, as he saw this mark of his young wife's passionate nature, he had chosen the wife he ought to have chosen.

As soon as the lieutenant had drained his sake cup he offered it to Reiko. Reiko had never before tasted sake, but she accepted without hesitation and sipped timidly.

"Come here," the lieutenant said.

Reiko moved to her husband's side and was embraced as she leaned backward across his lap. Her breast was in violent commotion, as if sadness, joy, and the potent sake were mingling and reacting within her. The lieutenant looked down into his wife's face. It was the last face he would see in this world, the last face he would see of his wife. The lieutenant scrutinized the face minutely, with the eyes of a traveler bidding farewell to splendid vistas which he will never revisit. It was a face he could not tire of looking at — the features regular yet not cold, the lips lightly closed with a soft strength. The lieutenant kissed those lips, unthinkingly. And suddenly, though there was not the slightest distortion of the face into the unsightliness of sobbing, he noticed that tears were welling slowly from beneath the long lashes of the closed eyes and brimming over into a glistening stream.

When, a little later, the lieutenant urged that they should move to the upstairs bedroom, his wife replied that she would follow after taking a bath. Climbing the stairs alone to the bedroom, where the air was already warmed by the gas heater, the lieutenant lay down on the bedding with arms outstretched and legs apart. Even the time at which he lay waiting for his wife to join him was no later and no earlier than usual.

He folded his hands beneath his head and gazed at the dark boards of the ceiling in the dimness beyond the range of the standard lamp. Was it death he was now waiting for? Or a wild ecstasy of the senses? The two seemed to overlap, almost as if the object of this bodily desire was death itself. But, however that might be, it was certain that never before had the lieutenant tasted such total freedom.

There was the sound of a car outside the window. He could hear the screech of its tires skidding in the snow piled at the side of the street. The sound of its horn re-echoed from near-by walls. ... Listening to these noises he had the feeling that this house rose like a solitary island in the ocean of a society going as restlessly about its business as ever. All around, vastly and untidily, stretched the country for which he grieved. He was to give his life for it. But would that great country, with which he was prepared to remonstrate to the extent of destroying himself, take the slightest heed of his death? He did not know; and it did not matter. His was a battlefield without glory, a battlefield where none could display deeds of valor: it was the front line of the spirit.

Reiko's footsteps sounded on the stairway. The steep stairs in this old house creaked badly. There were fond memories in that creaking, and many a time, while waiting in bed, the lieutenant had listened to its welcome sound. At the thought that he would hear it no more he listened with intense concentration, striving for every corner of every moment of this precious time to be filled with the sound of those soft footfalls on the creaking stairway. The moments seemed transformed to jewels, sparkling with inner light.

Reiko wore a Nagoya sash about the waist of her *yukata,* but as the lieutenant reached toward it, its redness sobered by the dimness of the light, Reiko's hand moved to his assistance and the sash fell away, slithering swiftly to the floor. As she stood before him, still in her *yukata,* the lieutenant inserted his hands through the side slits beneath each sleeve, intending to embrace her as she was; but at the touch of his finger tips upon the warm naked flesh, and as the armpits closed gently about his hands, his whole body was suddenly aflame.

In a few moments the two lay naked before the glowing gas heater.

Neither spoke the thought, but their hearts, their bodies, and their pounding breasts blazed with the knowledge that this was the very last time. It was as if the words "The Last Time" were spelled out, in invisible brushstrokes, across every inch of their bodies.

The lieutenant drew his wife close and kissed her vehemently. As their tongues explored each other's mouths, reaching out into the smooth, moist interior, they felt as if the still-unknown agonies of death had tempered their senses to the keenness of red-hot steel. The agonies they could not yet feel, the distant pains of death, had refined their awareness of pleasure.

"This is the last time I shall see your body," said the lieutenant. "Let me look at it closely." And, tilting the shade on the lampstand to one side, he directed the rays along the full length of Reiko's outstretched form.

Reiko lay still with her eyes closed. The light from the low lamp clearly revealed the majestic sweep of her white flesh. The lieutenant, not without a touch of egocentricity, rejoiced that he would never see this beauty crumble in death.

At his leisure, the lieutenant allowed the unforgettable spectacle to engrave itself upon his mind. With one hand he fondled the hair, with the other he softly stroked the magnificent face, implanting kisses here and there where his eyes lingered. The quiet coldness of the high, tapering forehead, the closed eyes with their long lashes beneath faintly etched brows, the set of the finely shaped nose, the gleam of teeth glimpsed between full, regular lips, the soft cheeks and the small, wise chin ... these things conjured up in the lieutenant's mind the vision of a truly radiant death face, and again and again he pressed his lips tight against the white throat — where Reiko's own hand was soon to strike — and the throat reddened faintly beneath his kisses. Returning to the mouth he laid his lips against it with the gentlest of pressures, and moved them rhythmically over Reiko's with the light rolling motion of a small boat. If he closed his eyes, the world became a rocking cradle.

Wherever the lieutenant's eyes moved his lips faithfully followed. The high, swelling breasts, surmounted by nipples like the buds of a wild cherry, hardened as the lieutenant's lips closed about them. The arms flowed smoothly downward from each side of the breast, tapering toward the wrists, yet losing nothing of their roundness or symmetry, and at their tips were those delicate fingers which had held the fan at the wedding ceremony. One by one, as the lieutenant kissed them, the fingers withdrew behind their neighbor as if in shame. ... The natural hollow curving between the bosom and the stomach carried in its lines a suggestion not only of softness but of resilient strength, and while it gave forewarning of the rich curves spreading outward from here to the hips it had, in itself, an appearance only of restraint and proper discipline. The whiteness and richness of the stomach and hips was like milk brimming in a great bowl, and the sharply shadowed dip of the navel could have been the fresh impress of a raindrop, fallen there that very moment. Where the shadows gathered more thickly, hair clustered, gentle and sensitive, and as the agitation mounted in the now no longer passive body there hung over this region a scent like the smoldering of fragrant blossoms, growing steadily more pervasive.

At length, in a tremulous voice, Reiko spoke.

"Show me.... Let me look too, for the last time."

Never before had he heard from his wife's lips so strong and unequivocal a request. It was as if something which her modesty had wished to keep hidden to the end had suddenly burst its bonds of constraint. The lieutenant obediently lay back and surrendered himself to his wife. Lithely she raised her white, trembling body, and — burning with an innocent desire to return to her husband what he had done for her — placed two white fingers on the lieutenant's eyes, which gazed fixedly up at her, and gently stroked them shut.

Suddenly overwhelmed by tenderness, her cheeks flushed by a dizzying uprush of emotion, Reiko threw her arms about the lieutenant's close-cropped head. The bristly hairs rubbed painfully against her breast, the prominent nose was cold as it dug into her flesh, and his breath was hot. Relaxing her embrace, she gazed down at her husband's masculine face. The severe brows, the closed eyes, the splendid bridge of the nose, the shapely lips drawn firmly together ... the blue, clean-shaven cheeks reflecting the light and gleaming smoothly. Reiko kissed each of these. She kissed the broad nape of the neck, the strong, erect shoulders, the powerful chest with its twin circles like shields and its russet nipples. In the armpits, deeply shadowed by the ample flesh of the shoulders and chest, a sweet and melancholy odor emanated from the growth of hair, and in the sweetness of this odor was contained, somehow, the essence of young death. The lieutenant's naked skin glowed like a field of barley, and everywhere the muscles showed in sharp relief, converging on the lower abdomen about the small, unassuming navel. Gazing at the youthful, firm stomach, modestly covered by a vigorous growth of hair, Reiko thought of it as it was soon to be, cruelly cut by the sword, and she laid her head upon it, sobbing in pity, and bathed it with kisses.

At the touch of his wife's tears upon his stomach the lieutenant felt ready to endure with courage the cruelest agonies of his suicide.

What ecstasies they experienced after these tender exchanges may well be imagined. The lieutenant raised himself and enfolded his wife in a powerful embrace, her body now limp with exhaustion after her grief and tears. Passionately they held their faces close, rubbing cheek against cheek. Reiko's body was trembling. Their breasts, moist with sweat, were tightly joined, and every inch of the young and beautiful bodies had become so much one with the other that it seemed impossible there should ever again be a separation. Reiko cried out. From the heights they plunged into the abyss, and from the abyss they took wing and soared once more to dizzying heights. The lieutenant panted like the regimental standard-bearer on a route march. ... As one cycle ended, almost immediately a new wave of passion would be generated, and together — with no trace of fatigue — they would climb again in a single breathless movement to the very summit.

IV

When the lieutenant at last turned away, it was not from weariness. For one thing, he was anxious not to undermine the considerable strength he would need in carrying out his suicide. For another, he would have been sorry to mar the sweetness of these last memories by over-indulgence.

Since the lieutenant had clearly desisted, Reiko too, with her usual compliance, followed his example. The two lay naked on their backs, with fingers interlaced, staring fixedly at the dark ceiling. The room was warm from the heater, and even when the sweat had ceased to pour from their bodies they felt no cold. Outside, in the hushed night, the sounds of passing traffic had ceased. Even the noises of the trains and streetcars around Yotsuya station did not penetrate this far. After echoing through the region bounded by the moat, they were lost in the heavily wooded park fronting the broad driveway before Akasaka Palace. It was hard to believe in the tension gripping this whole quarter, where the two factions of the bitterly divided Imperial Army now confronted each other, poised for battle.

Savoring the warmth glowing within themselves, they lay still and recalled the ecstasies they had just known. Each moment of the experience was relived. They remembered the taste of kisses which had never wearied, the touch of naked flesh, episode after episode of dizzying bliss. But already, from the dark boards of the ceiling, the face of death was peering down. These joys had been final, and their bodies would never know them again. Not that joy of this intensity — and the same thought had occurred to them both — was ever likely to be reexperienced, even if they should live on to old age.

The feel of their fingers intertwined — this too would soon be lost. Even the wood-grain patterns they now gazed at on the dark ceiling boards would be taken from them. They could feel death edging in, nearer and nearer. There could be no hesitation now. They must have the courage to reach out to death themselves, and to seize it.

"Well, let's make our preparations," said the lieutenant. The note of determination in the words was unmistakable, but at the same time Reiko had never heard her husband's voice so warm and tender.

After they had risen, a variety of tasks awaited them.

The lieutenant, who had never once before helped with the bedding, now cheerfully slid back the door of the closet, lifted the mattress across the room by himself, and stowed it away inside.

Reiko turned off the gas heater and put away the lamp standard. During the lieutenant's absence she had arranged this room carefully, sweeping and dusting it to a fresh cleanness, and now — if one overlooked the rosewood table drawn into one corner — the eight-mat room gave all the appearance of a reception room ready to welcome an important guest.

"We've seen some drinking here, haven't we? With Kanō and Homma and Noguchi . . ."

"Yes, they were great drinkers, all of them."

"We'll be meeting them before long, in the other world. They'll tease us, I imagine, when they find I've brought you with me."

Descending the stairs, the lieutenant turned to look back into this calm, clean room, now brightly illuminated by the ceiling lamp. There floated across his mind the faces of the young officers who had drunk there, and laughed, and innocently bragged. He had never dreamed then that he would one day cut open his stomach in this room.

In the two rooms downstairs husband and wife busied themselves smoothly and serenely with their respective preparations. The lieutenant went to the toilet, and then to the bathroom to wash. Meanwhile Reiko folded away her husband's padded robe, placed his uniform tunic, his trousers, and a newly cut bleached loincloth in the bathroom, and set out sheets of paper on the living-room table for the farewell notes. Then she removed the lid from the writing box and began rubbing ink from the ink tablet. She had already decided upon the wording of her own note.

Reiko's fingers pressed hard upon the cold gilt letters of the ink tablet, and the water in the shallow well at once darkened, as if a black cloud had spread across it. She stopped thinking that this repeated action, this pressure from her fingers, this rise and fall of faint sound, was all and solely for death. It was a routine domestic task, a simple paring away time until death should finally stand before her. But somehow, in the increasingly smooth motion of the tablet rubbing on the stone, and in the scent from the thickening ink, there was unspeakable darkness.

Neat in his uniform, which he now wore next to his skin, the lieutenant emerged from the bathroom. Without a word he seated himself at the table, bolt upright, took a brush in his hand, and stared undecidedly at the paper before him.

Reiko took a white silk kimono with her and entered the bathroom. When she reappeared in the living room, clad in the white kimono and with her face lightly made up, the farewell note lay completed on the table beneath the lamp. The thick black brushstrokes said simply:

"Long Live the Imperial Forces — Army Lieutenant Takeyama Shinji."

While Reiko sat opposite him writing her own note, the lieutenant gazed in silence, intensely serious, at the controlled movement of his wife's pale fingers as they manipulated the brush.

With their respective notes in their hands — the lieutenant's sword strapped to his side, Reiko's small dagger thrust into the sash of her white kimono — the two of them stood before the god shelf and silently prayed. Then they put out all the downstairs lights. As he mounted the stairs the lieutenant turned his head and gazed back at the striking, white-clad figure of his wife, climbing behind him, with lowered eyes, from the darkness beneath.

The farewell notes were laid side by side in the alcove of the upstairs room. They wondered whether they ought not to remove the hanging scroll, but since it had been written by their go-between, Lieutenant General Ozeki, and consisted, moreover, of two Chinese characters signifying "Sincerity," they left it where it was. Even if it were to become stained with splashes of blood, they felt that the lieutenant general would understand.

The lieutenant, sitting erect with his back to the alcove, laid his sword on the floor before him.

Reiko sat facing him, a mat's width away. With the rest of her so severely white the touch of rouge on her lips seemed remarkably seductive.

Across the dividing mat they gazed intently into each other's eyes. The lieutenant's sword lay before his knees. Seeing it, Reiko recalled their first night and was overwhelmed with sadness. The lieutenant spoke, in a hoarse voice:

"As I have no second to help me I shall cut deep. It may look unpleasant, but please do not panic. Death of any sort is a fearful thing to watch. You must not be discouraged by what you see. Is that all right?"

"Yes."

Reiko nodded deeply.

Looking at the slender white figure of his wife the lieutenant experienced a bizarre excitement. What he was about to perform was an act in his public capacity as a soldier, something he had never previously shown his wife. It called for a resolution equal to the courage to enter battle; it was a death of no less degree and quality than death in the front line. It was his conduct on the battlefield that he was now to display.

Momentarily the thought led the lieutenant to a strange fantasy. A lonely death on the battlefield, a death beneath the eyes of his beautiful wife ... in the sensation that he was now to die in these two dimensions, realizing an impossible union of them both, there was sweetness beyond words. This must be the very pinnacle of good fortune, he thought. To have every moment of his death observed by those beautiful eyes — it was like being borne to death on a gentle, fragrant breeze. There was some special favor here. He did not understand precisely what it was, but it was a domain unknown to others: a dispensation granted to no one else had been permitted to himself. In the radiant, bridelike figure of his white-robed wife the lieutenant seemed to see a vision of all those things he had loved and for which he was to lay down his life — the Imperial Household, the Nation, the Army Flag. All these, no less than the wife who sat before him, were presences observing him closely with clear and never-faltering eyes.

Reiko too was gazing intently at her husband, so soon to die, and she thought that never in this world had she seen anything so beautiful. The lieutenant always looked well in uniform, but now, as he contemplated death with severe brows and firmly closed lips, he revealed what was perhaps masculine beauty at its most superb.

"It's time to go," the lieutenant said at last.

Reiko bent her body low to the mat in a deep bow. She could not raise her face. She did not wish to spoil her make-up with tears, but the tears could not be held back.

When at length she looked up she saw hazily through the tears that her husband had wound a white bandage around the blade of his now unsheathed sword, leaving five or six inches of naked steel showing at the point.

Resting the sword in its cloth wrapping on the mat before him, the lieutenant rose from his knees, resettled himself crosslegged, and unfastened the hooks of his uniform collar. His eyes no longer saw his wife. Slowly, one by one he undid the flat brass buttons. The dusky brown chest was revealed, and then the stomach. He unclasped his belt and undid the buttons of his trousers. The pure whiteness of the thickly coiled loincloth showed itself. The lieutenant pushed the cloth down with both hands, further to ease his stomach, and then reached for the white-bandaged blade of his sword. With his left hand he massaged his abdomen, glancing downward as he did so.

To reassure himself on the sharpness of his sword's cutting edge the lieutenant folded back the left trouser flap, exposing a little of his thigh, and lightly drew the blade across his skin. Blood welled up in the wound at once, and several streaks of red trickled downward, glistening in the strong light.

It was the first time Reiko had ever seen her husband's blood, and she felt a violent throbbing in her chest. She looked at her husband's face. The lieutenant was looking at the blood with calm appraisal. For a moment — though thinking at the same time that it was hollow comfort — Reiko experienced a sense of relief.

The lieutenant's eyes fixed his wife with an intense, hawk-like stare. Moving the sword around to his front, he raised himself slightly on his hips and let the upper half of his body lean over the sword point. That he was mustering his whole strength was apparent from the angry tension of the uniform at his shoulders. The lieutenant aimed to strike deep into the left of his stomach. His sharp cry pierced the silence of the room.

Despite the effort he had himself put into the blow, the lieutenant had the impression that someone else had struck the side of his stomach agonizingly with a thick rod of iron. For a second or so his head reeled and he had no idea what had happened. The five or six inches of naked point had vanished completely into his flesh, and the white bandage, gripped in his clenched fist, pressed directly against his stomach.

He returned to consciousness. The blade had certainly pierced the wall of the stomach, he thought. His breathing was difficult, his chest thumped violently, and in some far deep region, which he could hardly believe was a part of himself, a fearful and excruciating pain came welling up as if the ground had split open to disgorge a boiling stream of molten rock. The pain came suddenly nearer, with terrifying speed. The lieutenant bit his lower lip and stifled an instinctive moan.

Was this *seppuku?* — he was thinking. It was a sensation of utter chaos, as if the sky had fallen on his head and the world was reeling drunkenly. His will power and courage, which had seemed so robust before he made the incision, had now dwindled to something like a single hairlike thread of steel, and he was assailed by the uneasy feeling that he must advance along this thread, clinging to it with desperation. His clenched fist had grown moist. Looking down, he saw that both his hand and the cloth about the blade were drenched in blood. His loincloth too was dyed a deep red. It struck him as incredible that, amidst this terrible agony, things which could be seen could still be seen, and existing things existed still.

The moment the lieutenant thrust the sword into his left side and she saw the deathly pallor fall across his face, like an abruptly lowered curtain, Reiko had to struggle to prevent herself from rushing to his side. Whatever happened, she must watch. She must be a witness. That was the duty her husband had laid upon her. Opposite her, a mat's space away, she could clearly see her husband biting his lip to stifle the pain. The pain was there, with absolute certainty, before her eyes. And Reiko had no means of rescuing him from it.

The sweat glistened on her husband's forehead. The lieutenant closed his eyes, and then opened them again, as if experimenting. The eyes had lost their luster, and seemed innocent and empty like the eyes of a small animal.

The agony before Reiko's eyes burned as strong as the summer sun, utterly remote from the grief which seemed to be tearing herself apart within. The pain grew steadily in stature, stretching upward. Reiko felt that her husband had already become a man in a separate world, a man whose whole being had been resolved into pain, a prisoner in a cage of pain where no hand could reach out to him. But Reiko felt no pain at all. Her grief was not pain. As she thought about this, Reiko began to feel as if someone had raised a cruel wall of glass high between herself and her husband.

Ever since her marriage her husband's existence had been her own existence, and every breath of his had been a breath drawn by herself. But now, while her husband's existence in pain was a vivid reality, Reiko could find in this grief of hers no certain proof at all of her own existence.

With only his right hand on the sword the lieutenant began to cut sideways across his stomach. But as the blade became entangled with the entrails it was pushed constantly outward by their soft resilience; and the lieutenant realized that it would be necessary, as he cut, to use both hands to keep the point pressed deep into his stomach. He pulled the blade across. It did not cut as easily as he had expected. He directed the strength of his whole body into his right hand and pulled again. There was a cut of three or four inches.

The pain spread slowly outward from the inner depths until the whole stomach reverberated. It was like the wild clanging of a bell. Or like a thousand bells which jangled simultaneously at every breath he breathed and every throb of his pulse, rocking his whole being. The lieutenant could no longer stop himself from moaning. But by now the blade had cut its way through to below the navel, and when he noticed this he felt a sense of satisfaction, and a renewal of courage.

The volume of blood had steadily increased, and now it spurted from the wound as if propelled by the beat of the pulse. The mat before the lieutenant was drenched red with splattered blood, and more blood overflowed onto it from pools which gathered in the folds of the lieutenant's khaki trousers. A spot, like a bird, came flying across to Reiko and settled on the lap of her white silk kimono.

By the time the lieutenant had at last drawn the sword across to the right side of his stomach, the blade was already cutting shallow and had revealed its naked tip, slippery with blood and grease. But, suddenly stricken by a fit of vomiting, the lieutenant cried out hoarsely. The vomiting made the fierce pain fiercer still, and the stomach, which had thus far remained firm and compact, now abruptly heaved, opening wide its wound, and the entrails burst through, as if the wound too were vomiting. Seemingly ignorant of their master's suffering, the entrails gave an impression of robust health and almost disagreeable vitality as they slipped smoothly out and spilled over into the crotch. The lieutenant's head drooped, his shoulders heaved, his eyes opened to narrow slits, and a thin trickle of saliva dribbled from his mouth. The gold markings on his epaulettes caught the light and glinted.

Blood was scattered everywhere. The lieutenant was soaked in it to his knees, and he sat now in a crumpled and listless posture, one hand on the floor. A raw smell filled the room. The lieutenant, his head drooping, retched repeatedly, and the movement showed vividly in his shoulders. The blade of the sword, now pushed back by the entrails and exposed to its tip, was still in the lieutenant's right hand.

It would be difficult to imagine a more heroic sight than that of the lieutenant at this moment, as he mustered his strength and flung back his head. The movement was performed with sudden violence, and the back of his head struck with a sharp crack against the alcove pillar. Reiko had been sitting until now with her face lowered, gazing in fascination at the tide of blood advancing toward her knees, but the sound took her by surprise and she looked up.

The lieutenant's face was not the face of a living man. The eyes were hollow, the skin parched, the once so lustrous cheeks and lips the color of dried mud. The right hand alone was moving.

Laboriously gripping the sword, it hovered shakily in the air like the hand of a marionette and strove to direct the point at the base of the lieutenant's throat. Reiko watched her husband make this last, most heart-rending, futile exertion. Glistening with blood and grease, the point was thrust at the throat again and again. And each time it missed its aim. The strength to guide it was no longer there. The straying point struck the collar and the collar badges. Although its hooks had been unfastened, the stiff military collar had closed together again and was protecting the throat.

Reiko could bear the sight no longer. She tried to go to her husband's help, but she could not stand. She moved through the blood on her knees, and her white skirts grew deep red. Moving to the rear of her husband, she helped no more than by loosening the collar. The quivering blade at last contacted the naked flesh of the throat. At that moment Reiko's impression was that she herself had propelled her husband forward; but that was not the case. It was a movement planned by the lieutenant himself, his last exertion of strength. Abruptly he threw his body at the blade, and the blade pierced his neck, emerging at the nape. There was a tremendous spurt of blood and the lieutenant lay still, cold blue-tinged steel protruding from his neck at the back.

V

Slowly, her socks slippery with blood, Reiko descended the stairway. The upstairs room was now completely still.

Switching on the ground-floor lights, she checked the gas jet and the main gas plug and poured water over the smoldering, half-buried charcoal in the brazier. She stood before the upright mirror in the four-and-a-half mat room and held up her skirts. The bloodstains made it seem as if a bold, vivid pattern was printed across the lower half of her white kimono. When she sat down before the mirror, she was conscious of the dampness and coldness of her husband's blood in the region of her thighs, and she shivered. Then, for a long while, she lingered over her toilet preparations. She applied the rouge generously to her cheeks, and her lips too she painted heavily. This was no longer make-up to please her husband. It was make-up for the world which she would leave behind, and there was a touch of the magnificent and the spectacular in her brush-work. When she rose, the mat before the mirror was wet with blood. Reiko was not concerned about this.

Returning from the toilet, Reiko stood finally on the cement floor of the porchway. When her husband had bolted the door here last night it had been in preparation for death. For a while she stood immersed in the consideration of a simple problem. Should she now leave the bolt drawn? If she were to lock the door, it could be that the neighbors might not notice their suicide for several days. Reiko did not relish the thought of their two corpses putrefying before discovery. After all, it seemed, it would be best to leave it open.... She released the bolt, and also drew open the frosted-glass door a fraction. ... At once a chill wind blew in. There was no sign of anyone in the midnight streets, and stars glittered ice-cold through the trees in the large house opposite.

Leaving the door as it was, Reiko mounted the stairs. She had walked here and there for some time and her socks were no longer slippery. About halfway up, her nostrils were already assailed by a peculiar smell.

The lieutenant was lying on his face in a sea of blood. The point protruding from his neck seemed to have grown even more prominent than before. Reiko walked heedlessly across the blood. Sitting beside the lieutenant's corpse, she stared intently at the face, which lay on one cheek on the mat. The eyes were opened wide, as if the lieutenant's attention had been attracted by something. She raised the head, folding it in her sleeve, wiped the blood from the lips, and bestowed a last kiss.

Then she rose and took from the closet a new white blanket and a waist cord. To prevent any derangement of her skirts, she wrapped the blanket about her waist and bound it there firmly with the cord.

Reiko sat herself on a spot about one foot distant from the lieutenant's body. Drawing the dagger from her sash, she examined its dully gleaming blade intently, and held it to her tongue. The taste of the polished steel was slightly sweet.

Reiko did not linger. When she thought how the pain which had previously opened such a gulf between herself and her dying husband was now to become a part of her own experience, she saw before her only the joy of herself entering a realm her husband had already made his own. In her husband's agonized face there had been something inexplicable which she was seeing for the first time. Now she would solve that riddle. Reiko sensed that at last she too would be able to taste the true bitterness and sweetness of that great moral principle in which her husband believed. What had until now been tasted only faintly through her husband's example she was about to savor directly with her own tongue.

Reiko rested the point of the blade against the base of her throat. She thrust hard. The wound was only shallow. Her head blazed, and her hands shook uncontrollably. She gave the blade a strong pull sideways. A warm substance flooded into her mouth, and everything before her eyes reddened, in a vision of spouting blood. She gathered her strength and plunged the point of the blade deep into her throat.

ALICE MUNRO

The Found Boat

At the end of Bell Street, McKay Street, Mayo Street, there was the Flood. It was the Wawanash River, which every spring overflowed its banks. Some springs, say one in every five, it covered the roads on that side of town and washed over the fields, creating a shallow choppy lake. Light reflected off the water made everything bright and cold, as it is in a lakeside town, and woke or revived in people certain vague hopes of disaster. Mostly during the late afternoon and early evening, there were people straggling out to look at it, and discuss whether it was still rising, and whether this time it might invade the town. In general, those under fifteen and over sixty-five were most certain that it would.

Eva and Carol rode out on their bicycles. They left the road — it was the end of Mayo Street, past any houses — and rode right into a field, over a wire fence entirely flattened by the weight of the winter's snow. They coasted a little way before the long grass stopped them, then left their bicycles lying down and went to the water.

"We have to find a log and ride on it," Eva said.

"Jesus, we'll freeze our legs off."

"Jesus, we'll freeze our legs off!" said one of the boys who were there too at the water's edge. He spoke in a sour whine, the way boys imitated girls although it was nothing like the way girls talked. These boys — there were three of them — were all in the same class as Eva and Carol at school and were known to them by name (their names being Frank, Bud and Clayton), but Eva and Carol, who had seen and recognized them from the road, had not spoken to them or looked at them or, even yet, given any sign of knowing they were there. The boys seemed to be trying to make a raft, from lumber they had salvaged from the water.

Eva and Carol took off their shoes and socks and waded in. The water was so cold it sent pain up their legs, like blue electric sparks shooting through their veins, but they went on, pulling their skirts high, tight behind and bunched so they could hold them in front.

"Look at the fat-assed ducks in wading."

"Fat-assed fucks."

Eva and Carol, of course, gave no sign of hearing this. They laid hold of a log and climbed on, taking a couple of boards floating in the water for paddles. There were always things floating around in the Flood — branches, fence-rails, logs, road signs, old lumber; sometimes boilers, washtubs, pots and pans, or even a car seat or stuffed chair, as if somewhere the Flood had got into the dump.

They paddled away from the shore, heading out into the cold lake. The water was perfectly clear, they could see the brown grass swimming along the bottom. Suppose it was the sea, thought Eva. She thought of drowned cities and countries. Atlantis. Suppose they were riding in a Viking boat — Viking boats on the Atlantic were more frail and narrow than this log on the Flood — and they had miles of clear sea beneath them, then a spired city, intact as a jewel irretrievable on the ocean floor.

"This is a Viking boat," she said. "I am the carving on the front." She stuck her chest out and stretched her neck, trying to make a curve, and she made a face, putting out her tongue. Then she turned and for the first time took notice of the boys.

"Hey, you sucks!" she yelled at them. "You'd be scared to come out here, this water is ten feet deep!"

"Liar," they answered without interest, and she was.

They steered the log around a row of trees, avoiding floating barbed wire, and got into a little bay created by a natural hollow of the land. Where the bay was now, there would be a pond full of frogs later in the spring, and by the middle of summer there would be no water visible at all, just a low tangle of reeds and bushes, green, to show that mud was still wet around their roots. Larger bushes, willows, grew around the steep bank of this pond and were still partly out of the water. Eva and Carol let the log ride in. They saw a place where something was caught.

It was a boat, or part of one. An old rowboat with most of one side ripped out, the board that had been the seat just dangling. It was pushed up among the branches, lying on what would have been its side, if it had a side, the prow caught high.

Their idea came to them without consultation, at the same time:

"You guys! Hey, you guys!"

"We found you a boat!"

"Stop building your stupid raft and come and look at the boat!"

What surprised them in the first place was that the boys really did come, scrambling overland, half running, half sliding down the bank, wanting to see.

"Hey, where?"

"Where is it, I don't see no boat."

What surprised them in the second place was that when the boys did actually see what boat was meant, this old flood-smashed wreck held up in the branches, they did not understand that they had been fooled, that a joke had been played on them. They did not show a moment's disappointment, but seemed as pleased at the discovery as if the boat had been whole and new. They were already barefoot, because they had been wading in the water to get lumber, and they waded in here without a stop, surrounding the boat and appraising it and paying no attention even of an insulting kind to Eva and Carol who bobbed up and down on their log. Eva and Carol had to call to them.

"How do you think you're going to get it off?"

"It won't float anyway."

"What makes you think it will float?"

"It'll sink. Glub-blub-blub, you'll all be drownded."

The boys did not answer, because they were too busy walking around the boat, pulling at it in a testing way to see how it could be got off with the least possible damage. Frank, who was the most literate, talkative and inept of the three, began referring to the boat as *she,* an affectation which Eva and Carol acknowledged with fish-mouths of contempt.

"She's caught two places. You got to be careful not to tear a hole in her bottom. She's heavier than you'd think."

It was Clayton who climbed up and freed the boat, and Bud, a tall fat boy, who got the weight of it on his back to turn it into the water so that they could half float, half carry it to shore. All this took some time. Eva and Carol abandoned their log and waded out of the water. They walked overland to get their shoes and socks and bicycles. They did not need to come back this way but they came. They stood at the top of the hill, leaning on their bicycles. They did not go on home, but they did not sit down and frankly watch, either. They stood more or less facing each other, but glancing down at the water and at the boys struggling with the boat, as if they had just halted for a moment out of curiosity, and staying longer than they intended, to see what came of this unpromising project.

About nine o'clock, or when it was nearly dark — dark to people inside the houses, but not quite dark outside — they all returned to town, going along Mayo Street in a sort of procession. Frank and Bud and Clayton came carrying the boat, upside-down, and Eva and Carol walked behind, wheeling their bicycles. The boys' heads were almost hidden in the darkness of the overturned boat, with its smell of soaked wood, cold swampy water. The girls could look ahead and see the street lights in their tin reflectors, a necklace of lights climbing Mayo Street, reaching all the way up to the standpipe. They turned onto Burns Street heading for Clayton's house, the nearest house belonging to any of them. This was not the way home for Eva or for Carol either, but they followed along. The boys were perhaps too busy carrying the boat to tell them to go away. Some younger children were still out playing, playing hopscotch on the sidewalk though they could hardly see. At this time of year the bare sidewalk was still such a novelty and delight. These children cleared out of the way and watched the boat go by with unwilling respect; they shouted questions after it, wanting to know where it came from and what was going to be done with it. No one answered them. Eva and Carol as well as the boys refused to answer or even look at them.

The five of them entered Clayton's yard. The boys shifted weight, as if they were going to put the boat down.

"You better take it round to the back where nobody can see it," Carol said. That was the first thing any of them had said since they came into town.

The boys said nothing but went on, following a mud path between Clayton's house and a leaning board fence. They let the boat down in the back yard.

"It's a stolen boat, you know," said Eva, mainly for the effect. "It must've belonged to somebody. You stole it."

"You was the ones who stole it then," Bud said, short of breath. "It was you seen it first."

"It was you took it."

"It was all of us then. If one of us gets in trouble then all of us does."

"Are you going to tell anybody on them?" said Carol as she and Eva rode home, along the streets which were dark between the lights now and potholed from winter.

"It's up to you. I won't if you won't."

"I won't if you won't."

They rode in silence, relinquishing something, but not discontented.

The board fence in Clayton's back yard had every so often a post which supported it, or tried to, and it was on these posts that Eva and Carol spent several evenings sitting, jauntily but not very comfortably. Or else they just leaned against the fence while the boys worked on the boat. During the first couple of evenings neighborhood children attracted by the sound of hammering tried to get into the yard to see what was going on, but Eva and Carol blocked their way.

"Who said you could come in here?"

"Just us can come in this yard."

These evenings were getting longer, the air milder. Skipping was starting on the sidewalks. Further along the street there was a row of hard maples that had been tapped. Children drank the sap as fast as it could drip into the buckets. The old man and woman who owned the trees, and who hoped to make syrup, came running out of the house making noises as if they were trying to scare away crows. Finally, every spring, the old man would come out on his porch and fire his shotgun into the air, and then the thieving would stop.

None of those working on the boat bothered about stealing sap, though all had done so last year.

The lumber to repair the boat was picked up here and there, along back lanes. At this time of year things were lying around — old boards and branches, sodden mitts, spoons flung out with the dishwater, lids of pudding pots that had been set in the snow to cool, all the debris that can sift through and survive winter. The tools came from Clayton's cellar — left over, presumably, from the time when his father was alive — and though they had nobody to advise them the boys seemed to figure out more or less the manner in which boats are built, or rebuilt. Frank was the one who showed up with diagrams from books and *Popular Mechanics* magazines. Clayton looked at these diagrams and listened to Frank read the instructions and then went ahead and decided in his own way what was to be done. Bud was best at sawing. Eva and Carol watched everything from the fence and offered criticism and thought up names. The names for the boat that they thought of were: Water Lily, Sea Horse, Flood Queen, and Caro-Eve, after them because they had found it. The boys did not say which, if any, of these names they found satisfactory.

The boat had to be tarred. Clayton heated up a pot of tar on the kitchen stove and brought it out and painted slowly, his thorough way, sitting astride the overturned boat. The other boys were sawing a board to make a new seat. As Clayton worked, the tar cooled and thickened so that finally he could not move the brush any more. He turned to Eva and held out the pot and said, "You can go in and heat this on the stove."

Eva took the pot and went up the back steps. The kitchen seemed black after outside, but it must be light enough to see in, because there was Clayton's mother standing at the ironing board, ironing. She did that for a living, took in wash and ironing.

"Please may I put the tar pot on the stove?" said Eva, who had been brought up to talk politely to parents, even wash-and-iron ladies, and who for some reason especially wanted to make a good impression on Clayton's mother.

"You'll have to poke up the fire then," said Clayton's mother, as if she doubted whether Eva would know how to do that. But Eva could see now, and she picked up the lid with the stove-lifter, and took the poker and poked up a flame. She stirred the tar as it softened. She felt privileged. Then and later. Before she went to sleep a picture of Clayton came to her mind; she saw him sitting astride the boat, tar-painting, with such concentration, delicacy, absorption. She thought of him speaking to her, out of his isolation, in such an ordinary peaceful taking-for-granted voice.

• • •

On the twenty-fourth of May, a school holiday in the middle of the week, the boat was carried out of town, a long way now, off the road over fields and fences that had been repaired, to where the river flowed between its normal banks. Eva and Carol, as well as the boys, took turns carrying it. It was launched in the water from a cow-trampled spot between willow bushes that were fresh out in leaf. The boys went first. They yelled with triumph when the boat did float, when it rode amazingly down the river current. The boat was painted black, and green inside, with yellow seats, and a strip of yellow all the way around the outside. There was no name on it, after all. The boys could not imagine that it needed any name to keep it separate from the other boats in the world.

Eva and Carol ran along the bank, carrying bags full of peanut butter-and-jam sandwiches, pickles, bananas, chocolate cake, potato chips, graham crackers stuck together with corn syrup and five bottles of pop to be cooled in the river water. The bottles bumped against their legs. They yelled for a turn.

"If they don't let us they're bastards," Carol said, and they yelled together, "We found it! We found it!"

The boys did not answer, but after a while they brought the boat in, and Carol and Eva came crashing, panting down the bank.

"Does it leak?"

"It don't leak yet."

"We forgot a bailing can," wailed Carol, but nevertheless she got in, with Eva, and Frank pushed them off, crying, "Here's to the Watery Grave!"

And the thing about being in a boat was that it was not solidly bobbing, like a log, but was cupped in the water, so that riding in it was not like being on something in the water, but like being in the water itself. Soon they were all going out in the boat in mixed-up turns, two boys and a girl, two girls and a boy, a girl and a boy, until things were so confused it was impossible to tell whose turn came next, and nobody cared anyway. They went down the river — those who weren't riding, running along the bank to keep up. They passed under two bridges, one iron, one cement. Once they saw a big carp just resting, it seemed to smile at them, in the bridge-shaded water. They did not know how far they had gone on the river, but things had changed — the water had got shallower, and the land flatter. Across an open field they saw a building that looked like a house, abandoned. They dragged the boat up on the bank and tied it and set out across the field.

"That's the old station," Frank said. "That's Pedder Station." The others had heard this name but he was the one who knew, because his father was the station agent in town. He said that this was a station on a branch line that had been torn up, and that there had been a sawmill here, but a long time ago.

Inside the station it was dark, cool. All the windows were broken. Glass lay in shards and in fairly big pieces on the floor. They walked around finding the larger pieces of glass and tramping on them, smashing them, it was like cracking ice on puddles. Some partitions were still in place, you could see where the ticket window had been. There was a bench lying on its side. People had been here, it looked as if people came here all the time, though it was so far from anywhere. Beer bottles and pop bottles were lying around, also cigarette packages, gum and candy wrappers, the paper from a loaf of bread. The walls were covered with dim and fresh pencil and chalk writings and carved with knives.

I LOVE RONNIE COLES

I WANT TO FUCK

KILROY WAS HERE

RONNIE COLES IS AN ASS-HOLE

WHAT ARE YOU DOING HERE?

WAITING FOR A TRAIN

DAWNA   MARY-LOU   BARBARA   JOANNE

It was exciting to be inside this large, dark, empty place, with the loud noise of breaking glass and their voices ringing back from the underside of the roof. They tipped the old beer bottles against their mouths. That reminded them that they were hungry and thirsty and they cleared a place in the middle of the floor and sat down and ate the lunch. They drank the pop just as it was, lukewarm. They ate everything there was and licked the smears of peanut butter and jam off the bread-paper in which the sandwiches had been wrapped.

They played Truth or Dare.

"I dare you to write on the wall, I am a Stupid Ass, and sign your name."

"Tell the truth — what is the worst lie you ever told?"

"Did you ever wet the bed?"

"Did you ever dream you were walking down the street without any clothes on?"

"I dare you to go outside and pee on the railway sign."

It was Frank who had to do that. They could not see him, even his back, but they knew he did it, they heard the hissing sound of his pee. They all sat still, amazed, unable to think of what the next dare would be.

"I dare everybody," said Frank from the doorway, "I dare — Everybody."

"What?"

"Take off all our clothes."

Eva and Carol screamed.

"And anybody who won't do it has to walk — has to *crawl* — around this floor on their hands and knees."

They were all quiet, till Eva said, almost complacently, "What first?"

"Shoes and socks."

"Then we have to go outside, there's too much glass here."

They pulled off their shoes and socks in the doorway, in the sudden blinding sun. The field before them was bright as water. They ran across where the tracks used to go.

"That's enough, that's enough," said Carol. "Watch out for thistles!"

"Tops! Everybody take off their tops!"

"I won't! We won't, will we, Eva?"

But Eva was whirling round and round in the sun where the track used to be. "I don't care, I don't care! Truth or Dare! Truth or Dare!"

She unbuttoned her blouse as she whirled, as if she didn't know what her hand was doing, she flung it off.

Carol took off hers. "I wouldn't have done it, if you hadn't!"

"Bottoms!"

Nobody said a word this time, they all bent and stripped themselves. Eva, naked first, started running across the field, and then all the others ran, all five of them running bare through the knee-high hot grass, running towards the river. Not caring now about being caught but in fact leaping and yelling to call attention to themselves, if there was anybody to hear or see. They felt as if they were going to jump off a cliff and fly. They felt that something was happening to them different from anything that had happened before, and it had to do with the boat, the water, the sunlight, the dark ruined station, and each other. They thought of each other now hardly as names or people, but as echoing shrieks, reflections, all bold and white and loud and scandalous, and as fast as arrows. They went running without a break into the cold water and when it came almost to the tops of their legs they fell on it and swam. It stopped their noise. Silence, amazement, came over them in a rush. They dipped and floated and separated, sleek as mink.

Eva stood up in the water her hair dripping, water running down her face. She was waist deep. She stood on smooth stones, her feet fairly wide apart, water flowing between her legs. About a yard away from her Clayton also stood up, and they were blinking the water out of their eyes, looking at each other. Eva did not turn or try to hide; she was quivering from the cold of the water, but also with pride, shame, boldness, and exhilaration.

Clayton shook his head violently, as if he wanted

to bang something out of it, then bent over and took a mouthful of river water. He stood up with his cheeks full and made a tight hole of his mouth and shot the water at her as if it was coming out of a hose, hitting her exactly, first one breast and then the other. Water from his mouth ran down her body. He hooted to see it, a loud self-conscious sound that nobody would have expected, from him. The others looked up from wherever they were in the water and closed in to see.

Eva crouched down and slid into the water, letting her head go right under. She swam, and when she let her head out, downstream, Carol was coming after her and the boys were already on the bank, already running into the grass, showing their skinny backs, their white, flat buttocks. They were laughing and saying things to each other but she couldn't hear, for the water in her ears.

"What did he do?" said Carol.

"Nothing."

They crept in to shore. "Let's stay in the bushes till they go," said Eva. "I hate them anyway. I really do. Don't you hate them?"

"Sure," said Carol, and they waited, not very long, until they heard the boys still noisy and excited coming down to the place a bit upriver where they had left the boat. They heard them jump in and start rowing.

"They've got all the hard part, going back," said Eva, hugging herself and shivering violently. "Who cares? Anyway. It never was our boat."

"What if they tell?" said Carol.

"We'll say it's a lie."

Eva hadn't thought of this solution until she said it, but as soon as she did she felt almost light-hearted again. The ease and scornfulness of it did make them both giggle, and slapping themselves and splashing out of the water they set about developing one of those fits of laughter in which, as soon as one showed signs of exhaustion, the other would snort and start up again, and they would make helpless — soon genuinely helpless — faces at each other and bend over and grab themselves as if they had the worst pain.

VLADIMIR NABOKOV

Signs and Symbols

I

For the fourth time in as many years they were confronted with the problem of what birthday present to bring a young man who was incurably deranged in his mind. He had no desires. Manmade objects were to him either hives of evil, vibrant with a malignant activity that he alone could perceive, or gross comforts for which no use could be found in his abstract world. After eliminating a number of articles that might offend him or frighten him (anything in the gadget line for instance was taboo), his parents chose a dainty and innocent trifle: a basket with ten different fruit jellies in ten little jars.

At the time of his birth they had been married already for a long time; a score of years had elapsed, and now they were quite old. Her drab gray hair was done anyhow. She wore cheap black dresses. Unlike other women of her age (such as Mrs. Sol, their next-door neighbor, whose face was all pink and mauve with paint and whose hat was a cluster of brookside flowers), she presented a naked white countenance to the fault-finding light of spring days. Her husband, who in the old country had been a fairly successful businessman, was now wholly dependent on his brother Isaac, a real American of almost forty years standing. They seldom saw him and had nick-named him "the Prince."

That Friday everything went wrong. The underground train lost its current between two stations, and for a quarter of an hour one could hear nothing but the dutiful beating of one's heart and the rustling of newspapers. The bus they had to take next kept them waiting for ages; and when it did come, it was crammed with garrulous high-school children. It was raining hard as they walked up the brown path leading to the sanitarium. There they waited again; and instead of their boy shuffling into the room as he usually did (his poor face blotched with acne, ill-shaven, sullen, and confused), a nurse they knew, and did not care for, appeared at last and brightly explained that he had again attempted to take his life. He was all right, she said, but a visit might disturb him. The place was so miserably understaffed, and things got mislaid or mixed up so easily, that they decided not to leave their present in the office but to bring it to him next time they came.

She waited for her husband to open his umbrella and then took his arm. He kept clearing his throat in a special resonant way he had when he was upset. They reached the bus-stop shelter on the other side of the street and he closed his umbrella. A few feet away, under a swaying and dripping tree, a tiny half-dead unfledged bird was helplessly twitching in a puddle.

During the long ride to the subway station, she and her husband did not exchange a word; and every time she glanced at his old hands (swollen veins, brown-spotted skin), clasped and twitching upon the handle of his umbrella, she felt the mounting pressure of tears. As she looked around trying to hook her mind onto something, it gave her a kind of soft shock, a mixture of compassion and wonder, to notice that one of the passengers, a girl with dark hair and grubby red toenails, was weeping on the shoulder of an older woman. Whom did that woman resemble? She resembled Rebecca Borisovna, whose daughter had married one of the Soloveichiks — in Minsk, years ago.

The last time he had tried to do it, his method had been, in the doctor's words, a masterpiece of inventiveness; he would have succeeded, had not an envious fellow patient thought he was learning to fly — and stopped him. What he really wanted to do was to tear a hole in his world and escape.

The system of his delusions had been the subject of an elaborate paper in a scientific monthly, but long before that she and her husband had puzzled it out for themselves. "Referential mania," Herman Brink had called it. In these very rare cases the patient imagines that everything happening around him is a veiled reference to his personality and existence. He excludes real people from the conspiracy — because he considers himself to be so much more intelligent than other men. Phenomenal nature shadows him wherever he goes. Clouds in the staring sky transmit to one another, by means of slow signs, incredibly detailed information regarding him. His inmost thoughts are discussed at nightfall, in manual alphabet, by darkly gesticulating trees. Pebbles or stains or sun flecks form patterns representing in some awful way messages which he must intercept. Everything is a cipher and of everything he is the theme. Some of the spies are detached observers, such are glass surfaces and still pools; others, such as coats in store windows, are prejudiced witnesses, lynchers at heart; others again (running water, storms) are hysterical to the point of insanity, have a distorted opinion of him and grotesquely misinterpret his actions. He must be always on his guard and devote every minute and module of life to the decoding of the undulation of things. The very air he exhales is indexed and filed away. If only the interest he provokes were limited to his immediate surroundings — but alas it is not! With distance the torrents of wild scandal increase in volume and volubility. The silhouettes of his blood corpuscles, magnified a million times, flit over vast plains; and still farther, great mountains of unbearable solidity and height sum up in terms of granite and groaning firs the ultimate truth of his being.

II

When they emerged from the thunder and foul air of the subway, the last dregs of the day were mixed with the street lights. She wanted to buy some fish for supper, so she handed him the basket of jelly jars, telling him to go home. He walked up to the third landing and then remembered he had given her his keys earlier in the day.

In silence he sat down on the steps and in silence rose when some ten minutes later she came, heavily trudging upstairs, wanly smiling, shaking her head in deprecation of her silliness. They entered their two-room flat and he at once went to the mirror. Straining the corners of his mouth apart by means of his thumbs, with a horrible masklike grimace, he removed his new hopelessly uncomfortable dental plate and severed the long tusks of saliva connecting him to it. He read his Russian-language newspaper while she laid the table. Still reading, he ate the pale victuals that needed no teeth. She knew his moods and was also silent.

When he had gone to bed, she remained in the living room with her pack of soiled cards and her old albums. Across the narrow yard where the rain tinkled in the dark against some battered ash cans, windows were blandly alight and in one of them a black-trousered man with his bare elbows raised could be seen lying supine on an untidy bed. She pulled the blind down and examined the photographs. As a baby he looked more surprised than most babies. From a fold in the album, a German maid they had had in Leipzig and her fat-faced fiancé fell out. Minsk, the Revolution, Leipzig, Berlin, Leipzig, a slanting house front badly out of focus. Four years old, in a park: moodily, shyly, with puckered forehead, looking away from an eager squirrel as he would from any other stranger. Aunt Rosa, a fussy, angular, wild-eyed old lady, who had lived in a tremulous world of bad news, bankruptcies, train accidents, cancerous growths — until the Germans put her to death, together with all the people she had worried about. Age six — that was when he drew wonderful birds with human hands and feet, and suffered from insomnia like a grown-up man. His cousin, now a famous chess player. He again, aged about eight, already difficult to understand, afraid of the wallpaper in the passage, afraid of a certain picture in a book which merely showed an idyllic landscape with rocks on a hillside and an old cart wheel hanging from the branch of a leafless tree. Aged ten: the year they left Europe. The shame, the pity, the humiliating difficulties, the ugly, vicious, backward children he was with in that special school. And then came a time in his life, coinciding with a long convalescence after pneumonia, when those little phobias of his which his parents had stubbornly regarded as the eccentricities of a prodigiously gifted child hardened as it were into a dense tangle of logically interacting illusions, making him totally inaccessible to normal minds.

This, and much more, she accepted — for after all living did mean accepting the loss of one joy after another, not even joys in her case — mere possibilities of improvement. She thought of the endless waves of pain that for some reason or other she and her husband had to endure; of the invisible giants hurting her boy in some unimaginable fashion; of the incalculable amount of tenderness contained in the world; of the fate of this tenderness, which is either crushed, or wasted, or transformed into madness; of neglected children humming to themselves in unswept corners; of beautiful weeds that cannot hide from the farmer and helplessly have to watch the shadow of his simian stoop leave mangled flowers in its wake, as the monstrous darkness approaches.

III

It was past midnight when from the living room she heard her husband moan; and presently he staggered in, wearing over his nightgown the old overcoat with astrakhan collar which he much preferred to the nice blue bathrobe he had.

"I can't sleep," he cried.

"Why," she asked, "why can't you sleep? You were so tired."

"I can't sleep because I am dying," he said and lay down on the couch.

"Is it your stomach? Do you want me to call Dr. Solov?"

"No doctors, no doctors," he moaned, "To the devil with doctors! We must get him out of there quick. Otherwise we'll be responsible. Responsible!" he repeated and hurled himself into a sitting position, both feet on the floor, thumping his forehead with his clenched fist.

"All right," she said quietly, "we shall bring him home tomorrow morning."

"I would like some tea," said her husband and retired to the bathroom.

Bending with difficulty, she retrieved some playing cards and a photograph or two that had slipped from the couch to the floor: knave of hearts, nine of spades, ace of spades, Elsa and her bestial beau.

He returned in high spirits, saying in a loud voice:

"I have it all figured out. We will give him our bedroom. Each of us will spend part of the night near him and the other part on this couch. By turns. We will have the doctor see him at least twice a week. It does not matter what the Prince says. He won't have to say much anyway because it will come out cheaper."

The telephone rang. It was an unusual hour for their telephone to ring. His left slipper had come off and he groped for it with his heel and toe as he stood in the middle of the room, and childishly, toothlessly, gaped at his wife. Having more English than he did, it was she who attended to calls.

"Can I speak to Charlie," said a girl's dull little voice.

"What number you want? No. That is not the right number."

The receiver was gently cradled. Her hand went to her old tired heart.

"It frightened me," she said.

He smiled a quick smile and immediately resumed his excited monologue. They would fetch him as soon as it was day. Knives would have to be kept in a locked drawer. Even at his worst he presented no danger to other people.

The telephone rang a second time. The same toneless anxious young voice asked for Charlie.

"You have the incorrect number. I will tell you what you are doing: you are turning the letter O instead of the zero."

They sat down to their unexpected festive midnight tea. The birthday present stood on the table. He sipped noisily; his face was flushed; every now and then he imparted a circular motion to his raised glass so as to make the sugar dissolve more thoroughly. The vein on the side of his bald head where there was a large birthmark stood out conspicuously and, although he had shaved that morning, a silvery bristle showed on his chin. While she poured him another glass of tea, he put on his spectacles and re-examined with pleasure the luminous yellow, green, red little jars. His clumsy moist lips spelled out their eloquent labels: apricot, grape, beech plum, quince. He had got to crab apple, when the telephone rang again.

V. S. NAIPAUL

A Christmas Story

Though it is Christmas Eve my mind is not on Christmas. I look forward instead to the day after Boxing Day, for on that day the inspectors from the Audit Department in Port-of-Spain will be coming down to the village where the new school has been built. I await their coming with calm. There is still time, of course, to do all that is necessary. But I shall not do it, though my family, from whom the spirit of Christmas has, alas, also fled, have been begging me to lay aside my scruples, my new-found faith, and to rescue us all from disgrace and ruin. It is in my power to do so, but there comes a time in every man's life when he has to take a stand. This time, I must confess, has come very late for me.

It seems that everything has come late to me. I continued a Hindu, though of that religion I saw and knew little save meaningless and shameful rites, until I was nearly eighteen. Why I continued I cannot explain. Perhaps it was the inertia with which that religion deadens its devotees. It did not, after all, require much intelligence to see that Hinduism, with its animistic rites, its idolatry, its emphasis on mango leaf, banana leaf and — the truth is the truth — cowdung, was a religion little fitted for the modern world. I had only to contrast the position of the Hindus with that of the Christians. I had only to consider the differing standards of dress, houses, food. Such differences have today more or less disappeared, and the younger generation will scarcely understand what I mean. I might even be reproached with laying too great a stress on the superficial. What can I say? Will I be believed if I say that to me the superficial has always symbolized the profound? But it is enough, I feel, to state that at eighteen my eyes were opened. I did not have to be 'converted' by the Presbyterians of the Canadian Mission. I had only to look at the work they were doing among the backward Hindus and Moslems of my district. I had only to look at their schools, to look at the houses of the converted.

My Presbyterianism, then, though late in coming, affected me deeply. I was interested in teaching — there was no other thing a man of my limited means and limited education could do — and my Presbyterianism was a distinct advantage. It gave me a grace in the eyes of my superiors. It also enabled me to be a good teacher, for between what I taught and what I felt there was no discordance. How different the position of those who, still unconverted, attempted to teach in Presbyterian schools!

And now that the time for frankness has come, I must also remark on the pleasure my new religion gave me. It was a pleasure to hear myself called Randolph, a name of rich historical associations, a name, I feel, thoroughly attuned to the times in which we live and to the society in which I found myself, and to forget that once — I still remember it with shame — I answered, with simple instinct, to the name of Choonilal. That, however, is so much in the past. I have buried it. Yet I remember it now, not only because the time for frankness has come, but because only two weeks ago my son Winston, going through some family papers — clearly the boy had no right to be going through my private papers, but he shares his mother's curiosity — came upon the name. He teased, indeed reproached me, with it, and in a fit of anger, for which I am now grievously sorry and for which I must make time, while time there still is, to apologize to him, in a fit of anger I gave him a sound thrashing, such as I often gave in my school-teaching days to those pupils whose persistent shortcomings were matched by the stupidity and backwardness of their parents. Backwardness has always roused me to anger.

As much as by the name Randolph, pleasure was given me by the stately and *clean* — there is no other word for it — rituals sanctioned by my new religion. How agreeable, for instance, to rise early on a Sunday morning, to bathe and breakfast and then, in the most spotless of garments, to walk along the still quiet and cool roads to our place of worship, and there to see the most respectable and respected, all dressed with a similar purity, addressing themselves to the devotions in which I myself could participate, after for long being an outsider, someone to whom the words *Christ* and *Father* meant no more than *winter* or *autumn* or *daffodil.* Such of the unconverted village folk who were energetic enough to be awake and alert at that hour gaped at us as we walked in white procession to our church. And though their admiration was sweet, I must confess that at the same time it filled me with shame to reflect that not long before I too formed part of the gaping crowd. To walk past their gaze was peculiarly painful to me, for I, more perhaps than anyone in that slow and stately procession, *knew* — and by my silence had for nearly eighteen years condoned — the practices those people indulged in in the name of religion. My attitude towards them was somewhat stern, and it gave me some little consolation to know that though we were in some ways alike, we were distinguished from them not only by our names, which after all no man carries pinned to his lapel, but also by our dress. On these Sundays of which I speak the men wore trousers and jackets of white drill, quite unlike the leg-revealing dhoti which it still pleased those others to wear, a garment which I have always felt makes the wearer ridiculous. I even sported a white solar topee. The girls and ladies wore the short frocks which the others held in abhorrence; they wore hats; in every respect, I am pleased to say, they resembled their sisters who had come all the way from Canada and other countries to work among our people. I might be accused of laying too much stress on superficial things. But I ought to say in my own defence that it is my deeply held conviction that progress is not a matter of outward show, but an attitude of mind; and it was this that my religion gave me.

It might seem from what I have so far said that the embracing of Presbyterianism conferred only benefits and pleasure. I wish to make no great fuss of the trials I had to endure, but it is sufficient to state that, while at school and in other associations my fervent adherence to my new faith was viewed with favour, I had elsewhere to put up with the constant ridicule of those of my relations who continued, in spite of my example, in the ways of darkness. They spoke my name, Randolph, with accents of the purest mockery. I bore this with fortitude. It was what I expected, and I was greatly strengthened by my faith, as a miser is by the thought of his gold. In time, when they saw that their ridiculing of my name had not the slightest effect on me — on the contrary, whereas before I had in my signature suppressed my first name behind the blank initial C, now I spelt out Randolph in full — in time they desisted.

But that was not the end of my trials. I had up to that time eaten with my fingers, a manner of eating which is now so repulsive to me, so ugly, so unhygienic, that I wonder how I managed to do it until my eighteenth year. Yet I must now confess that at that time food never tasted as sweet as when eaten with the fingers, and that my first attempts to eat with the proper implements of knife and fork and spoon were almost in the nature of shameful experiments, furtively carried out; and even when I was by myself I could not get rid of the feeling of self-consciousness. It was easier to get used to the name of Randolph than to knife and fork.

Eating, then, in my determined manner one Sunday lunchtime, I heard that I had a visitor. It was a man; he didn't knock, but came straight into my room, and I knew at once that he was a relation. These people have never learned to knock or to close doors behind them.

I must confess I felt somewhat foolish to be caught with those implements in my hand.

'Hello, Randolph,' the boy Hori said, pronouncing the name in a most offensive manner.

'Good afternoon, *Hori.*'

He remained impervious to my irony. This boy, Hori, was the greatest of my tormentors. He was also the grossest. He strained charity. He was a great lump of a man and he gloried in his brutishness. He fancied himself a debater as well, and many were the discussions and arguments we had had, this lout — he strained charity, as I have said — insisting that to squat on the ground and eat off banana leaves was hygienic and proper, that knives and forks were dirty because used again and again by various persons, whereas the fingers were personal and could always be made thoroughly clean by washing. But he never had *his* fingers clean, that I knew.

'Eating, Randolph?'

'I am having my lunch, *Hori.*'

'Beef, Randolph. You are progressing, Randolph.'

'I am glad you note it, *Hori.*"

I cannot understand why these people should persist in this admiration for the cow, which has always seemed to me a filthy animal, far filthier than the pig, which they abhor. Yet it must be stated that this eating of beef was the most strenuous of my tests. If I persevered it was only because I was strengthened by my faith. But to be found at this juncture — I was in my Sunday suit of white drill, my prayer book was on the table, my white solar topee on the wall, and I was eating beef with a knife and fork — to be found thus by Hori was a trifle embarrassing. I must have looked the picture of the over-zealous convert.

My instinct was to ask him to leave. But it occurred to me that that would have been too easy, too cowardly a way out. Instead, I plied my knife and fork with as much skill as I could command at that time. He sat, not on a chair, but on the table, just next to my plate, the lout, and gazed at me while I ate. Ignoring his smile, I ate, as one might eat of sacrificial food. He crossed his fat legs, leaned back on his palms and examined me. I paid no attention. Then he took one of the forks that were about and began picking his teeth with it. I was angry and revolted. Tears sprang to my eyes. I rose, pushed away my plate, pushed back my chair, and asked him to leave. The violence of my reaction surprised him, and he did as I asked. As soon as he had gone I took the fork he had handled and bent it and stamped on it and threw it out of the window.

Progress, as I have said, is an attitude of mind. And if I relate this trifling incident with such feeling, it is because it demonstrates how difficult that attitude of mind is to acquire, for there are hundreds who are ready to despise and ridicule those who they think are getting above themselves. And let people say what they will, the contempt even of the foolish is hard to bear. Let no one think, therefore, that my new religion did not bring its share of trials and tribulations. But I was sufficiently strengthened by my faith to bear them all with fortitude.

My life thereafter was a lonely one. I had cut myself off from my family, and from those large family gatherings which had hitherto given me so much pleasure and comfort, for always, I must own, at the back of my mind there had been the thought that in the event of real trouble there would be people to whom I could turn. Now I was deprived of this solace. I stuck to my vocation with a dedication which surprised even myself. To be a teacher it is necessary to be taught; and after much difficulty I managed to have myself sent to the Training College in Port-of-Spain. The competition for these places was fierce, and for many years I was passed over, because there were many others who were more fitting. Some indeed had been born of Presbyterian parents. But my zeal, which ever mounted as the failures multiplied, eventually was rewarded. I was twenty-eight when I was sent to the Training College, considerably older than most of the trainees.

It was no pleasure to me to note that during those ten years the boy Hori had been prospering. He had gone into the trucking business and he had done remarkably well. He had bought a second truck, then a third, and it seemed that to his success there could be no limit, while my own was always restricted to the predictable contents of the brown-paper pay-packet at the end of the month. The clothes in which I had taken such pride at first became less resplendent, until I felt it as a disgrace to go to church in them. But it became clear to me that this was yet another of the trials I was called upon to undergo, and I endured it, until I almost took pleasure in the darns on my sleeves and elbows.

At this time I was invited to the wedding of Hori's son, Kedar. They marry young, these people! It was an occasion which surmounted religious differences, and it was a distinct pleasure to me to be again with the family, for their attitude had changed. They had become reconciled to my Presbyterianism and indeed treated me with respect for my profession, a respect which, I fear, was sometimes missing in the attitude of my superiors and even my pupils. The marriage rites distressed me. The make-shift though beautiful tent, the coconut-palm arches hung with clusters of fruit, the use of things like mango leaves and grass and saffron, the sacrificial fire, all these things filled me with shame rather than delight. But the rites were only a small part of the celebrations. There was much good food, strictly vegetarian but somehow extremely tempting; and after a period of distaste for Indian food, I had come back to it again. The food, I say, was rich. The music and the dances were thrilling. The tent and the illuminations had a charm which not even our school hall had on concert nights, though the marriage ceremony did not of course have the grace and dignity of those conducted, as proper marriages should be, in a church.

Kedar received a fabulous dowry, and his bride, of whose face I had just a glimpse when her silk veil was parted, was indeed beautiful. But such beauty has always appeared to me skin deep. Beauty in women is a disturbing thing. But beyond the beauty it is always necessary to look for the greater qualities of manners and — a thing I always remind Winston of — no one is too young or too old to learn — manners and *ways*. She was beautiful. It was sad to think of her joined to Kedar for life, but she was perhaps fitted for nothing else. No need to speak of the resplendent regalia of Kedar himself: his turban, the crown with tassels and pendant glass, his richly embroidered silk jacket, and all those other adornments which for that night concealed so well the truck-driver that he was.

I left the wedding profoundly saddened. I could not help reflecting on my own position and contrasting it with Hori's or even Kedar's. I was now over forty, and marriage, which in the normal way would have come to me at the age of twenty or thereabouts, was still far from me. This was my own fault. Arranged marriages like Kedar's had no part in my scheme of things. I wished to marry, as the person says in *The Vicar of Wakefield,* someone who had qualities that would wear well. My choice was severely restricted. I wished to marry a Presbyterian lady who was intelligent, well brought up and educated, and wished to marry me. This last condition, alas, I could find few willing to fulfil. And indeed I had little to offer. Among Hindus it would have been otherwise. There might have been men of substance who would have been willing to marry their daughters to a teacher, to acquire respectability and the glamour of a learned profession. Such a position has its strains, of course, for it means that the daughter remains, as it were, subject to her family; but the position is not without its charms.

You might imagine — and you would be correct — that at this time my faith was undergoing its severest strain. How often I was on the point of reneging I shudder to tell. I felt myself about to yield; I stiffened in my devotions and prayers. I reflected on the worthlessness of worldly things, but this was a reflection I found few to share. I might add here, in parenthesis and without vanity, that I had had several offers from the fathers of unconverted daughters, whose only condition was the one, about my religion, which I could not accept; for my previous caste had made me acceptable to many.

In this situation of doubt, of nightly wrestling with God, an expression whose meaning I came only then fully to understand, my fortune changed. I was appointed a headmaster. Now I can speak! How many people know of the tribulations, the pettiness, the intrigue which schoolteachers have to undergo to obtain such promotion? Such jockeying, such jealousy, such ill-will comes into play. What can I say of the advances one has to make, the rebuffs one has to suffer in silence, the waiting, the undoing of the unworthy who seek to push themselves forward for positions which they are ill-qualified to fill but which, by glibness and all the outward shows of respectability and efficiency and piety, they manage to persuade our superiors that they alone can fill? I too had my adversaries. My chief rival — but let him rest in peace! I am, I trust, a Christian, and will do no man the injustice of imagining him to persist in error even after we have left this vale of tears.

In my fortune, so opportune, I saw the hand of God. I speak in all earnestness. For without this I would surely have lapsed into the ways of darkness, for who among us can so steel himself as to resist temptation for all time? In my gratitude I applied myself with renewed dedication to my task. And it was this that doubtless evoked the gratification of my superiors which was to lead to my later elevation. For at a time when most men, worn out by the struggle, are content to relax, I showed myself more eager than before. I instituted prayers four times a day. I insisted on attendance at Sunday School. I taught Sunday School myself, and with the weight of my influence persuaded the other teachers to do likewise, so that Sunday became another day for us, a day of rest which we consumed with work for the Lord.

And I did not neglect the educational side. The blackboards all now sparkled with diagrams in chalks of various colours, projects which we had in hand. Oh, the school was such a pretty sight then! I instituted a rigid system of discipline, and forbade indiscriminate flogging by pupil teachers. All flogging I did myself on Friday afternoons, sitting in impartial judgment, as it were, on the school, on pupils as well as teachers. It is surely a better system, and I am glad to say that it has now been adopted throughout the island. The most apt pupils I kept after school, and for some trifling extra fee gave them private lessons. And the school became so involved with work as an ideal that had to be joyously pursued and not as something that had to be endured, that the usefulness of these private lessons was widely appreciated, and soon larger numbers than I could cope with were staying after school for what they affectionately termed their 'private.'

And I married. It was now in my power to marry virtually anyone I pleased, and there were among the Sunday School staff not a few who made their attachment to me plain. I am not such a bad-looking fellow! But I wished to marry someone who had qualities that would wear well. I was nearly fifty. I did not wish to marry someone who was much younger than myself. And it was my good fortune at this juncture to receive an offer — I hesitate to use this word, which sounds so much like the Hindu custom and reminds one of the real estate business, but here I must be frank — from no less a person than a schools inspector, who had an unmarried daughter of thirty-five, a woman neglected by the men of the island because of her attainments — yes, you read right — which were considerable, but not of the sort that proclaims itself to the world. In our attitude to women much remains to be changed! I have often, during these past days, reflected on marriage. Such a turning, a point in time whence so many consequences flow. I wonder what Winston, poor boy, will do when his time comes.

My establishment could not rival Hori's or Kedar's for splendour, but within it there was peace and culture such as I had long dreamed of. It was a plain wooden house, but well built, built to last, unlike so many of these modern monstrosities which I see arising these days; and it was well ordered. We had simple bentwood chairs with cane bottoms. No marble-topped tables with ball-fringed lace! No glass cabinets! I hung my treasured framed teaching diploma on the wall, with my religious pictures and some scenes of the English countryside. It was also my good fortune at this time to get an old autographed photograph of one of our first missionaries. In the decoration of our humble home my wife appeared to release all the energy and experience of her thirty-five years which had so far been denied expression.

To her, as to myself, everything came late. It was our fear, confirmed by the views of many friends who behind their expressions of goodwill concealed as we presently saw much uncharitableness, that we would be unable to have children, considering our advanced years. But they, and we, underestimated the power of prayer, for within a year of our marriage Winston was born.

The birth of Winston came to us as a grace and a blessing. Yet it also filled me with anxiety, for I could not refrain from assessing the difference between our ages. It occurred to me, for instance, that he would be thirty when I was eighty. It was a disturbing thought, for the companionship of children is something which, perhaps because of my profession, I hold very dear. My anxiety had another reason. It was that Winston, in his most formative years, would be without not only guidance — for what guidance can a man of seventy give to a lusty youngster of twenty? — but also without my financial support.

The problem of money, strange as it might appear, considering my unexpected elevation and all its accruing benefits, was occupying the minds of both my wife and myself. For my retirement was drawing near, and my pension would scarcely be more than what I subsisted on as a simple pupil teacher. It seemed then that like those pilgrims, whose enthusiasm I admire but cannot share, I was advancing towards my goal by taking two steps forward and one step back, though in my case a likelier simile might be that I was always taking one step forward and one step back. So success always turns to ashes in the mouth of those who seek it as ardently as I had! And if I had the vision and the depth of faith which I now have, I might have seen even then how completely false are the things of this world, how much they flatter only to deceive.

We were both, as I say, made restless. And now the contemplation of baby Winston was a source of much pain to both of us, for the poor innocent creature could scarcely know what anguish awaited him when we would both be withdrawn from this vale of tears. His helplessness, his dependence tortured me. I was past the age when the taking out of an insurance policy was a practicable proposition; and during my days as a simple teacher I never had the resources to do so. It seemed, then, that I was being destroyed by my own good fortune, by the fruits of all my endeavour. Yet I did not heed this sign.

I continued while I could giving private lessons. I instituted a morning session as well, in addition to the afternoon one. But I did so with a heavy heart, tormented by the thought that in a few years this privilege and its small reward would be denied me, for private lessons, it must be understood, are considered the prerogative of a headmaster: in this way he stamps his character on the school. My results in the exhibition examinations for boys under twelve continued to be heartening; they far surpassed those of many other country schools. My religious zeal continued unabated; and it was this zeal which, burning in those years when most men in my position would have relaxed — they, fortunate souls, having their children fully grown — it was this surprising zeal, I say, which also contributed, I feel, to my later elevation which, as you will see from the plain narration of these events, I did not seek.

My retirement grew nearer. I became fiercer at school. I wished all the boys under me could grow up at once. I was merciless towards the backward. My wife, poor creature, could not control her anxiety with as much success as myself. She had no occupation, no distracting vocation, in which her anxiety might have been consumed. She had only Winston, and this dear infant continually roused her to fears about his future. For his sake she would, I believe, have sacrificed her own life! It was not easy for her. And it required but the exercise of the mildest Christian charity to see that the reproaches she flung with increased acerbity and frequency at my head were but expressions of her anxiety. Sometimes, I must confess, I failed! And then my own unworthiness would torment me, as it torments me now.

We confided our problems to my wife's father, the schools inspector. Though we felt it unfair to let another partake of our troubles, it is none the less a recognized means of lightening any load which the individual finds too heavy to bear. But he, poor man, though as worried on his daughter's behalf as she was on Winston's, could offer only sympathy and little practical help. He reported that the authorities were unwilling to give me an extension of my tenure as headmaster. My despondency found expression in a display of temper, which he charitably forgave; for though he left the house, promising not to do another thing for us, he presently returned, and counselled patience.

So patient we were. I retired. I could hardly bear to remain at home, so used had I been to the daily round, the daily trials. I went out visiting, for no other reason than that I was afraid to be alone at home. My zeal, I believe, was remarked upon, though I took care to avoid the school, the scene of my late labours. I sought to take in for private lessons two or three pupils whose progress had deeply interested me. But my methods were no longer the methods that found favour! The parents of these children reported that the new headmaster had expressed himself strongly, and to my great disfavour, on the subject, to such a degree, in fact, that the progress of their children at school was being hampered. So I desisted; or rather, since the time has come for frankness, they left me.

The schools inspector, a regular visitor now at our humble, sad home, continued to counsel patience. I have so far refrained in this narrative from permitting my wife to speak directly; for I wish to do nothing that might increase the load she will surely have to bear, for my wife, though of considerable attainments, has not had the advantages of a formal education on which so much stress is nowadays laid. So I will refrain from chronicling the remark with which she greeted this advice of her father's. Suffice it to say that she spoke a children's rhyme without any great care for its metre or rhyme, the last of which indeed she destroyed by accidentally, in her haste, pulling down a vase from the centre-table on to the floor, where the water ran like one of the puddles which our baby Winston so lately made. After this incident relations between my wife and her father underwent a perceptible strain; and I took care to be out of the house as often as possible, and indeed it was pleasant to forget one's domestic troubles and walk abroad and be greeted as 'Headmaster' by the simple village folk.

Then, as it appears has happened so regularly throughout my life, the clouds rolled away and the sky brightened. I was appointed a School Manager. The announcement was made in the most heart-warming way possible, by the schools inspector himself, anticipating the official notification by a week or so. And the occasion became a family reunion. It was truly good to see the harassed schools inspector relaxing at last, and to see father and daughter reasonably happy with one another. My delight in this was almost as great as the delight in my new dignity.

For a school managership is a good thing to come to a man in the evening of his days. It permits an exercise of the most benign power imaginable. It permits a man at a speech day function to ask for a holiday for the pupils; and nothing is as warming as the lusty and sincere cheering that follows such a request. It gives power even over headmasters, for one can make surprise visits and it is in one's power to make reports to the authorities. It is a position of considerable responsibility as well, for a school manager manages a school as much as a managing director manages a company. It is in his power to decide whether the drains, say, need to be remade entirely or need simply be plastered over to look as new; whether one coat of paint or two are needed; whether a ceiling can be partially renovated and painted over or taken out altogether and replaced. He orders the number of desks and blackboards which he considers necessary, and the chalks and the stationery. It is, in short, a dignity ideally suited to one who has led an active life and is dismayed by the prospect of retirement. It brings honour as well as reward. It has the other advantage that school managers are like civil servants; they are seldom dismissed; and their honours tend to increase rather than diminish.

I entered on my new tasks with zeal, and once again all was well at our home. My wife's father visited us regularly, as though, poor man, anxious to share the good fortune for which he was to a large measure responsible. I looked after the school, the staff, the pupils. I visited all the parents of the pupils under my charge and spoke to them of the benefits of education, the dangers of absenteeism, and so on. I know I will be forgiven if I add that from time to time, whenever the ground appeared ripe, I sowed the seed of Presbyterianism or at any rate doubt among those who continued in the ways of darkness. Such zeal was unknown among school managers. I cannot account for it myself. It might be that my early austerity and ambition had given me something of the crusading zeal. But it was inevitable that such zeal should have been too much for some people to stomach.

For all his honour, for all the sweet cheers that greet his request for a holiday for the pupils, the school manager's position is one that sometimes attracts adverse and malicious comment. It is the fate of anyone who finds himself in a position of power and financial responsibility. The rumours persisted; and though they did not diminish the esteem in which I was so clearly held by the community — at the elections, for example, I was approached by all five candidates and asked to lend my voice to their cause, a situation of peculiar difficulty, which I resolved by promising all five to remain neutral, for which they were effusively grateful — it is no good thing for a man to walk among people who every day listen eagerly — for flesh is frail, and nothing attracts our simple villagers as much as scurrilous gossip — to slanders against himself. It was beneath my dignity, or rather, the dignity of my position, to reply to such attacks; and in this situation I turned, as I was turning with growing frequency, to my wife's father for advice. He suggested that I should relinquish one of my managerships, to indicate my disapproval of the gossip and the little esteem in which I held worldly honour. For I had so far succeeded in my new functions that I was now the manager of three schools, which was the maximum number permitted.

I followed his advice. I relinquished the managership of a school which was in a condition so derelict that not even repeated renovations could efface the original gimcrackery of its construction. This school had been the cause of most of the rumours, and my relinquishing of it attracted widespread comment and was even mentioned in the newspapers. It remained dear to me, but I was willing for it to go into other hands. This action of mine had the effect of stilling rumours and gossip. And the action proved to have its own reward, for some months later my wife's father, ever the bearer of good tidings, intimated that there was a possibility of a new school being put up in the area. I was thoroughly suited for its management; and he, the honest broker between the authorities and myself, said that my name was being mentioned in this connection. I was at that time manager of only two schools; I was entitled to a third. He warmly urged me to accept. I hesitated, and my hesitations were later proved to be justified. But the thought of a new school fashioned entirely according to my ideas and principles was too heady. I succumbed to temptation. If now I could only go back and withdraw that acceptance! The good man hurried back with the news; and within a fortnight I received the official notification.

I must confess that during the next few months I lost sight of my doubts in my zeal and enthusiasm for the new project. My two other schools suffered somewhat. For if there is a thing to delight the heart of the school manager, it is the management of a school not yet built. But, alas! We are at every step reminded of the vanity of worldly things. How often does it happen that a person, placed in the position he craves, a position which he is in every way suited to fill, suddenly loses his grip! Given the opportunity for which he longs, he is unable to make use of it. The effort goes all into the striving.

So now it happened with me. Nearly everything I touched failed to go as it should. I, so careful and correct in assessments and estimates, was now found repeatedly in error. None of my calculations were right. There were repeated shortages and stoppages. The school progressed far more slowly than I would have liked. And it was no consolation to me to find that in this moment I was alone, in this long moment of agony! Neither to my wife nor to her father could I turn for comfort. They savoured the joy of my managership of a new school without reference to me. I had my great opportunity; they had no doubt I would make use of it; and I could not bear disillusioning them or breaking into their happiness with my worries.

My errors attracted other errors. My errors multiplied, I tell you! To cover up one error I had to commit twenty acts of concealment, and these twenty had to be concealed. I felt myself caught in a curious inefficiency that seemed entirely beyond my control, something malignant, powered by forces hostile to myself. Until at length it seemed that failure was staring me in the face, and that my entire career would be forgotten in this crowning failure. The building went up, it is true. It had a respectable appearance. It looked a building. But it was far from what I had visualized. I had miscalculated badly, and it was too late to remedy the errors. Its faults, its weaknesses would be at once apparent even to the scantily trained eye. And now night after night I was tormented by this failure of mine. With the exercise of only a little judgment it could so easily have been made right. Yet now the time for that was past! Day after day I was drawn to the building, and every day I hoped that by some miracle it would have been effaced during the night. But there it always stood, a bitter reproach.

Matters were not made easier for me by the reproaches of my wife and her father. They both rounded on me and said with justice that my failure would involve them all. And the days went by! I could not — I have never liked bickering, the answering of insult with insult — I could not reproach them with having burdened me with such an enterprise at the end of my days. I did it for their glory, for I had acquired sufficient to last me until the end of my days. I did it it for my wife and her father, and for my son Winston. But who will believe me? Who will believe that a man works for the glory of others, except he work for the glory of God? They reproached me. They stood aside from me. In this moment of need they deserted me.

They were bitter days. I went for long walks through our villages in the cool of the evening. The children ran out to greet me. Mothers looked up from their cooking, fathers from their perches on the roadside culverts, and greeted me, 'Headmaster!' And soon my failure would be apparent even to the humblest among them. I had to act quickly. Failures should be destroyed. The burning down of a school is an unforgiveable thing, but there are surely occasions when it can be condoned, when it is the only way out. Surely this was such an occasion! It is a drastic step. But it is one that has been taken more than once in this island. So I argued with myself. And always the answer was there: my failure had to be destroyed, not only for my own sake, but for the sake of all those, villagers included, whose fates were involved with mine.

Once I had made up my mind, I acted with decision. It was that time of year, mid-November, when people are beginning to think of Christmas to the exclusion of nearly everything else. This served my purpose well. I required — with what shame I now confess it — certain assistants, for it was necessary for me to be seen elsewhere on the day of the accident. Much money, much of what we had set aside for the future of our son Winston, had to go on this. And already it had been necessary to seal the lips of certain officials who had rejoiced in my failure and were willing to proclaim it to the world. But at last it was ready. On Boxing Day we would go to Port-of-Spain, to the races. When we returned the following day, the school would be no more. I say 'we', though my wife had not been apprised of my intentions.

With what fear, self-reproach, and self-disgust I waited for the days to pass! When I heard the Christmas carols, ever associated for me with the indefinable sweetness of Christmas Eve — which I now once more feel, thanks to my decision, though underneath there is a sense of doom and destruction, deserved, but with their own inevitable reward — when I heard carols and Christmas commercials on the radio, my heart sank; for it seemed that I had cut myself off from all about me, that once more I had become a stranger to the faith which I profess. So these days passed in sorrow, in nightly frenzies of prayer and self-castigation. Regret assailed me. Regret for what might have been, regret for what was to come. I was sinking, I felt, into a pit of defilement whence I could never emerge.

Of all this my wife knew nothing. But then she

asked one day, 'What have you decided to do?' and, without waiting for my reply, at once drew up such a detailed plan, which corresponded so closely to what I had myself devised, that my heart quailed. For if, in this moment of my need, when the deepest resource was needed, I could devise a plan which might have been devised by anyone else, then discovery was certain. And to my shame, Winston, who only two or three days before had been teasing me with my previous unbaptized name, Winston took part in this discussion, with no appearance of shame on his face, only thrill and — sad am I to say it — a pride in me greater than I had ever seen the boy display.

How can one tell of the workings of the human heart? How can one speak of the urge to evil — an urge of which Christians more than anyone else are so aware — and of the countervailing urge to good? You must remember that this is the season of good will. And goodwill it was. For goodwill was what I was feeling towards all. At every carol my heart melted. Whenever a child rushed towards me and cried, 'Headmaster!' I was tormented by grief. For the sight of the unwashed creatures, deprived so many of them of schooling, which matters so much in those early years, and the absence of which ever afterwards makes itself felt, condemning a human being to an animal-like existence, the sight of these creatures, grateful towards me who had on so many evenings gone among them propagating the creed with what energy I could, unmanned me. They were proud of their new school. They were even prouder of their association with the man who had built it.

Everywhere I felt rejected. I went to church as often as I could, but even there I found rejection. And as the time drew nearer the enormity of what I proposed grew clearer to me. It was useless to tell myself that what I was proposing had been often done. The carols, the religious services, the talk of birth and life, they all unmanned me.

I walked among the children as one who had it in his power to provide or withhold blessing, and I thought of that other Walker, who said of those among whom I walked that they were blessed, and that theirs was the kingdom of heaven. And as I walked it seemed that at last I had seized the true essence of the religion I had adopted, and whose worldly success I had with such energy promoted. So that it seemed that these trials I was undergoing had been reserved to the end of my days, so that only then I could have a taste of the ecstasy about which I had so far only read. With this ecstasy I walked. It was Christmas Eve. It is Christmas Eve. My head felt drawn out of my body. I had difficulty in assessing the size and distance of objects. I felt myself tall. I felt myself part of the earth and yet removed.

And: 'No!' I said to my wife at teatime. 'No, I will not disgrace myself by this action of cowardice. Rather, I will proclaim my failure to the world and ask for my due punishment.'

She behaved as I expected. She had been busy putting up all sorts of Christmas decorations, expensive ones from the United States, which are all the rage now, so unlike the simple decorations I used to see in the homes of our early missionaries before the war. But how changed is the house to which we moved! How far has simplicity vanished and been replaced by show! And I gloried in it!

She begged me to change my mind. She summoned Winston to her help. They both wept and implored me to go through with our plan. But I was firm. I do believe that if the schools inspector were alive, he would also have been summoned to plead with me. But he, fortunate man, passed away some three weeks ago, entrusting his daughter and grandson to my care; and this alone is my fear, that by gaining glory for myself I might be injuring them. But I was firm. And then there started another of those scenes with which I had become only too familiar, and the house which that morning was filled with the enthusiasm of Winston was changed into one of mourning. Winston sobbed, tears running down his plump cheeks and down his well-shaped nose to his firm top lip, pleading with me to burn the school down, and generally behaving as though I had deprived him of a bonfire. And then a number of things were destroyed by his mother, and she left the house with Winston, vowing never to see me again, never to be involved in the disgrace which was sure to come.

And so here I sit, waiting not for Christmas, but in this house where the autographed photograph of one of our earliest missionaries gazes down at me through his rich beard and luxuriant eyebrows, and where the walls carry so many reminders of my past life of endeavour and hardship and struggle and triumph and also, alas, final failure, I wait for the day after Boxing Day, after the races to which we were to have gone, for the visit of the inspectors of the Audit Department. The house is lonely and dark. The radios play the Christmas songs. I am very lonely. But I am strong. And here I lay down my pen. My hand tires; the beautiful letters we were taught to fashion at the mission school have begun to weaken and to straggle untidily over the ruled paper; and someone is knocking.

December 27. How can one speak of the ways of the world, how can one speak of the tribulations that come one's way? Even expiation is denied me. For even as I wrote the last sentence of the above account, there came a knocking at my door, and I went to open unto him who knocked. And lo, there was a boy, bearing tidings. And behold, towards the west the sky had reddened, and the boy informed me that the school was ablaze. What could I do? My world fell about my ears. Even final expiation, final triumph, it seemed, was denied me. Certain things are not for me. In this moment of anguish and despair my first thought was for my wife. Where had she gone? I went out to seek her. When I returned, after a fruitless errand, I discovered that she and Winston had come back to seek me. Smiling through our tears, we embraced. So it was Christmas after all for us. And, with lightened heart, made heavy only by my wrestling with the Lord, we went to the races on Boxing Day, yesterday. We did not gamble. It is against our principles. The inspectors from the Audit Department sent word today that they would not, after all, come.

ALDEN NOWLAN

Miracle at Indian River

This is the story of how mates were chosen for all the marriageable young men and women in the congregation of the Fire-Baptized Tabernacle of the Living God in Indian River, New Brunswick. It is a true story, more or less, and whether it is ridiculous or pathetic or even oddly beautiful depends a good deal on the mood you're in when you read it.

Indian River is one of those little places that don't really exist, except in the minds of their inhabitants. Passing through it as a stranger you might not even notice that it is there. Or if you did notice it, you'd think it was no different from thousands of other little backwoods communities in Canada and the United States. But you'd be wrong. Indian River, like every community large and small, has a character all its own.

The inhabitants of Indian River are pure Dutch, although they don't know it. Their ancestors settled in New Amsterdam more than three hundred years ago and migrated to New Brunswick after the American Revolution. But they've always been isolated, always intermarried, so that racially they're probably more purely Dutch than most of the Dutch in Holland, even though they've long ago forgotten the language and few of them could locate the Netherlands on a map.

The village contains a railway station which hasn't been used since 1965 when the CNR discontinued passenger service in that part of northwestern New Brunswick, a one-room school that was closed five years ago when the government began using buses to carry local children to the regional school in Cumberland Centre, a general store and two churches: St. Edward's Anglican, which used to be attended by the station agent, the teacher and the storekeeper, and the Fire-Baptized Tabernacle of the Living God, attended by practically everyone else in Indian River.

The tabernacle, formerly a barracks, was bought from the Department of National Defence and brought in on a flatcar. "Jesus Saves" is painted in big red letters over the door. A billboard beside the road warns drivers to prepare to meet their God. There is an evergreen forest to the north, a brook full of speckled trout to the west and, in the east, a pasture in which a dozen Holstein cattle and a team of Clydesdale horses graze together. The pastor, Rev. Horace Zwicker, his wife, Myrtle, and their five children live in a flat behind the pulpit.

Pastor Zwicker was born in Indian River and, before he was called of God to the ministry, was a door-to-door salesman of magazine subscriptions and patent medicines, chauffeur for a chiropractor, and accordionist in a hillbilly band that toured the Maritime Provinces and Maine.

Services are held in the tabernacle Wednesday night, Sunday morning and Sunday night. During the summer evangelists arrive, usually from Alabama, Georgia or Tennessee, and then there are services every night of the week. Almost every one of the evangelists has some sort of speciality, like painting a pastel portrait of Christ as he delivers his sermon or playing "The Old Rugged Cross" on an instrument made from empty whiskey bottles. Once there was a man with a long black beard and shoulder-length hair who claimed to have gone to school with Hitler; another time a professed ex-convict named Bent-Knee Benjamin preached in striped pajamas, a ball and chain fastened to his leg.

Fire-Baptized people worry a good deal about sin — mostly innocent little rural sins like smoking, drinking, watching television and going to the movies. Fire-Baptized women, of whom there are several thousands in northwestern New Brunswick, are easy to identify on the streets of towns like Woodstock and Fredericton because they don't use cosmetics and wear their hair in a sort of Oregon Trail bun at the backs of their necks. Fire-Baptized girls are made to dress somewhat the way Elizabeth dressed before she met Philip. There is a legend, invented presumably by Anglicans and Catholics, that Fire-Baptized girls are extraordinarily agreeable and inordinately passionate.

A few years ago there happened to be an unusually large number of unmarried young men and women in Indian River.

Pastor Zwicker frequently discussed this matter with his Lord.

"Lord," he said, "You know as well as I do that it isn't good to have a pack of hot young bucks and fancy-free young females running around loose. Like Paul says, those who don't marry are apt to burn, and when they've burned long enough they'll do just about anything to put the fire out. Now, tell me straight, Lord, what do You figure I should do about it?"

The Lord offered various suggestions and Pastor Zwicker tried them all.

He had long and prayerful conversations with

each young man and woman. He told Harris Brandt, for example, that Rebecca Vaneyck was not only a sweet Christian girl, pure and obedient, she made the best blueberry pie of any cook her age in Connaught County. "Never cared much for blueberries myself, Pastor," Harris said. He told Rebecca that Harris was a stout Christian youth who wouldn't get drunk, except perhaps if he were sorely tempted of the devil on election day, and wouldn't beat her unless she really deserved it. And she replied: "But, Pastor, he has such bad teeth!"

His conversations with the others were equally fruitless. The Lord advised stronger methods.

"Look here, Brother," the pastor admonished young Francis Witt's father, "it's time that young fellow of yours settled down and got himself a wife. I was talking it over with the Lord just the other night. Now, as you're well aware, Brother, the Scriptures tell us that a son should be obedient to his father. So if I was you — "

"Need the boy," replied the father. "Couldn't run this place without him. Talked to the Lord about it myself. Wife did too. Lord said maybe Francis wouldn't ever get married. Might be an old bachelor like his Uncle Ike. Nothing wrong in that, Lord said."

Other parents made other excuses. If even one couple had responded favorably to his efforts, Pastor Zwicker might have decided that he was worrying himself and the Lord needlessly. But to be met everywhere by disinterest! It was unnatural. Was the devil turning his flock into a herd of Papist celibates?

He had talked once with an escapee from a nunnery in Ireland. A tunnel to the rectory. Lecherous old men, naked under their black nightgowns. Babies' bones in the walls.

His body trembled and his soul — although he did not know this and would have been horrified had he known — made the sign of the cross. What was there left for a man of God to do?

God moves in a mysterious way His wonders to perform. The following Sunday night the power of the Holy Ghost shook the tabernacle to its very foundations. The Day of Pentecost described in the Acts of the Apostles was reenacted with more fervour than ever before in Indian River.

Pastor Zwicker had summoned a guitarist from Houlton, Maine, and a fiddler from Fredericton. He himself played the accordion and his wife the Jew's harp. Old Sister Rossa was at the piano and little Billy Wagner was sent home to fetch his harmonica and mandolin.

There was music — music even as the pastor laid aside his accordion and preached, music and singing and, as the service progressed, a Jericho dance up and down the aisle.

Later, old men said it was the best sermon they had ever heard. "Brother Zwicker just opened his mouth and let the Lord fill it," they said.

His theme was the sins of the flesh. As near as Woodstock, as near as Fredericton, as near as Presque Isle, half-naked women with painted faces and scented bodies prowled the streets seeking whom they might devour. He had looked upon their naked thighs, observed the voluptuous movements of their rumps, had noted that their nipples were visible through their blouses. In King Square in Saint John he had stepped aside to allow a young lady to precede him onto a bus and had discovered to his horrified amazement that she was not wearing drawers. Saint John was another Babylon where before long men and women would be dancing together naked in the streets.

There was much more of the same kind of thing, interspersed, of course, with many quotations from the Bible, particularly from Genesis, Leviticus and Revelation. The Bible was almost the only book that Pastor Zwicker had ever read and he knew great stretches of it by heart.

"Praise the Lord!" the people shouted. "Hallelujah! Thank you, Jesus!"

Old Ike Witt stood on his chair and danced.

"Oh, diddly-doe-dum, diddly-dee-doe-dee," he sang. "Oh, too-row-lou-row-tiddly-lou-do-dee! Glory to Jesus! Diddly-day-dum! Glory to Jesus! Tiddly-lee-tum-tee!"

Matilda Rega threw herself on the floor, laughing and crying, yelling: "Oh, Jesus! Christ Almighty! Oh, sweet Jesus! God Almighty! Oh, Jesus!"

She began crawling down the aisle toward the altar.

The Jericho dancers leapt back and forth across her wriggling body:

We are marching to Zion!
Beautiful, beautiful Zion!
We are marching to Zion,
The beautiful City of God!

Kneeling before the altar, Timothy Fairvort whimpered and slapped his own face, first one cheek, then the other.

"I have sinned," he moaned.

SLAP!

"I have lusted in my heart."

SLAP!

"I will burn in hell if I am not saved."

SLAP!

"Oh, help me, Jesus."

SLAP!

The Jericho dancers sang:

Joy, Joy, Joy, There is joy in my heart!
Joy in my heart! Joy in my heart!
Joy, Joy, Joy, There is joy in my heart!
Joy in my heart TODAY!

It was as if the midway of the Fredericton Exhibition, Hank Snow and the Rainbow Ranch Boys, Oral Roberts, Billy Graham, a Salvation Army band, Lester Flatt and Earl Scruggs, Garner Ted Armstrong and a Tory leadership convention were somehow all rolled into one and compressed into the lobby of the Admiral Beatty Hotel in Saint John.

Then it happened.

Sister Zwicker began speaking in an unknown tongue.

"Elohim!" she yelled. "Elohim, angaro metalani negat! Gonolariski motono etalo bene! Wanga! Wanga! Angaro talans fo do easta analandanoro!"

"Listen!" roared the pastor. "Listen!"

The Jericho dancers sang:

When the saints go marching in!
When the saints go marching in!
How I long to be in that company
When the saints go marching in!

"Elohim!" screamed Myrtle Zwicker. "Wanga! Ortoro ortoro clana estanatoro! Wanga!"

"Listen!" bellowed the pastor. "Listen!"

Others took up the cry. At last the Jericho dancers returned to their seats, exhausted, sweat pouring down their hot, red faces. The music faded away. Old Ike Witt climbed down from his chair. Matilda Rega lay still, quietly sobbing, at the foot of the altar. Timothy Fairvort put his jacket over his head, like a criminal in a newspaper photograph. There was silence except for the voices of the pastor and his wife.

"The Lord is talking to us!" shouted the pastor, who had by now taken off his jacket and tie and unbuttoned his shirt to the waist. "Harken to the voice of the Lord!"

"Elohim!" cried his wife. "Naro talaro eganoto wanga! Tao laro matanotalero. Wanga!"

"It is Egyptian," the pastor explained. "The Lord is addressing us in the language of Pharaoh, the tongue that Joseph spoke when he was a prisoner in the land of Egypt."

"Egyptian," murmured the congregation. "Thank you, Jesus."

"Taro wanga sundaro —"

"The Lord is telling us that His heart is saddened."

"Metizo walla toro delandonaro —"

"His heart is saddened by the disobedience of His people."

"Crena wontano meta kleva sancta danco —"

"The disobedience and perversity of His young people is heavy upon His heart."

"Zalanto wanga —"

"For they have refused to marry and multiply and be fruitful and replenish the earth, as He has commanded them."

"Toronalanta wanga —"

"In His mercy He has chosen to give them one more chance to escape the just punishment for their disobedience."

"Praise His name! Thank you, Jesus!"

"Willo morto innitaro —"

"It is His will that His handmaiden, Rebecca Vaneyck, should become the bride of —"

"Altaro mintanaro —"

"Yes, yes, the bride of Harris Brandt. This is the will of the God of Abraham and of Isaac and of Jacob, for it was He who brought you out of the land of Egypt."

"Yes, yes," chanted the congregation. "It is the Lord's will. Let it be done. Hallelujah!"

Rebecca and Harris were led to the altar. They looked at one another with dazed, wondering faces. After a moment he reached out and took her hand.

Within half an hour, three other couples stood with them. The Lord had revealed His will. Puny mortals such as they had no say in the matter.

The Jericho dancers leapt and cavorted in thanksgiving. So did Ike Witt and Timothy Fairvort, whose face was still hidden by his jacket. He stumbled blindly around the tabernacle, knocking over chairs, singing behind his jacket:

When the roll is called up yonder!
When the roll is called up yonder!
When the roll is called up yonder!
When the roll is called up yonder,
I'll be there!

Pastor Zwicker fanned himself with a copy of *The Fire Baptized Quarterly.* Next week there would be four marriages in his tabernacle. The Lord's will had been accomplished.

"Thank you, Jesus," he murmured.

Then he remembered Ike Witt and Matilda Rega, the old bachelor and the old maid. Could it be the Lord's will that they, too, should be joined together? He would discuss it with Myrtle. Perhaps next Sunday the Lord would reveal His thoughts about the matter.

JOYCE CAROL OATES omniscient / 1 person

How I Contemplated the World from the Detroit House of Correction and Began My Life Over Again

NOTES FOR AN ESSAY FOR AN ENGLISH CLASS AT BALDWIN COUNTRY DAY SCHOOL; POKING AROUND IN DEBRIS; DISGUST AND CURIOSITY; A REVELATION OF THE MEANING OF LIFE; A HAPPY ENDING . . .

I
EVENTS

1. The girl (myself) is walking through Branden's, that excellent store. Suburb of a large famous city that is a symbol for large famous American cities. The event sneaks up on the girl, who believes she is herding it along with a small fixed smile, a girl of fifteen, innocently experienced. She dawdles in a certain style by a counter of costume jewelry. Rings, earrings, necklaces. Prices from $5 to $50, all within reach. All ugly. She eases over to the glove counter, where everything is ugly too. In her close-fitted coat with its black fur collar she contemplates the luxury of Branden's, which she has known for many years: its many mild pale lights, easy on the eye and the soul, its elaborate tinkly decorations, its women shoppers with their excellent shoes and coats and hairdos, all dawdling gracefully, in no hurry.

Who was ever in a hurry here?

2. The girl seated at home. A small library, paneled walls of oak. Someone is talking to me. An earnest, husky, female voice drives itself against my ears, nervous, frightened, groping around my heart, saying, "If you wanted gloves, why didn't you say so? Why didn't you ask for them?" That store, Branden's, is owned by Raymond Forrest who lives on Du Maurier Drive. We live on Sioux Drive. Raymond Forrest. A handsome man? An ugly man? A man of fifty or sixty, with gray hair, or a man of forty with earnest, courteous eyes, a good golf game; who is Raymond Forrest, this man who is my salvation? Father has been talking to him. Father is not his physician; Dr. Berg is his physician. Father and Dr. Berg refer patients to each other. There is a connection. Mother plays bridge with . . . On Mondays and Wednesdays our maid Billie works at . . . The strings draw together in a cat's cradle, making a net to save you when you fall. . . .

3. *Harriet Arnold's.* A small shop, better than Branden's. Mother in her black coat, I in my close-fitted blue coat. Shopping. Now look at this, isn't this cute, do you want this, why don't you want this, try this on, take this with you to the fitting room, take this also, what's wrong with you, what can I do for you, why are you so strange . . .? "I wanted to steal but not to buy," I don't tell her. The girl droops along in her coat and gloves and leather boots, her eyes scan the horizon, which is pastel pink and decorated like Branden's, tasteful walls and modern ceilings with graceful glimmering lights.

4. Weeks later, the girl at a bus stop. Two o'clock in the afternoon, a Tuesday; obviously she has walked out of school.

5. The girl stepping down from a bus. Afternoon, weather changing to colder. Detroit. Pavement and closed-up stores; grillwork over the windows of a pawnshop. What is a pawnshop, exactly?

II
CHARACTERS

1. The girl stands five feet five inches tall. An ordinary height. Baldwin Country Day School draws them up to that height. She dreams along the corridors and presses her face against the Thermoplex glass. No frost or steam can ever form on that glass. A smudge of grease from her forehead . . . could she be boiled down to grease? She wears her hair loose and long and straight in suburban

teen-age style, 1968. Eyes smudged with pencil, dark brown. Brown hair. Vague green eyes. A pretty girl? An ugly girl? She sings to herself under her breath, idling in the corridor, thinking of her many secrets (the thirty dollars she once took from the purse of a friend's mother, just for fun, the basement window she smashed in her own house just for fun) and thinking of her brother who is at Susquehanna Boys' Academy, an excellent preparatory school in Maine, remembering him unclearly ... he has long manic hair and a squeaking voice and he looks like one of the popular teen-age singers of 1968, one of those in a group, *The Certain Forces, The Way Out, The Maniacs Responsible.* The girl in her turn looks like one of those fieldsful of girls who listen to the boys' singing, dreaming and mooning restlessly, breaking into high sullen laughter, innocently experienced.

2. The mother. A Midwestern woman of Detroit and suburbs. Belongs to the Detroit Athletic Club. Also the Detroit Golf Club. Also the Bloomfield Hills Country Club. The Village Women's Club at which lectures are given each winter on Genet and Sartre and James Baldwin, by the Director of the Adult Education Program at Wayne State University.... The Bloomfield Art Association. Also the Founders Society of the Detroit Institute of Arts. Also ... Oh, she is in perpetual motion, this lady, hair like blown-up gold and finer than gold, hair and fingers and body of inestimable grace. Heavy weighs the gold on the back of her hairbrush and hand mirror. Heavy heavy the candlesticks in the dining room. Very heavy is the big car, a Lincoln, long and black, that on one cool autumn day split a squirrel's body in two unequal parts.

3. The father. Dr. ______. He belongs to the same clubs as = 2. A player of squash and golf; he has a golfer's umbrella of stripes. Candy stripes. In his mouth nothing turns to sugar, however; saliva works no miracles here. His doctoring is of the slightly sick. The sick are sent elsewhere (to Dr. Berg?), the deathly sick are sent back for more tests and their bills are sent to their homes, the unsick are sent to Dr. Coronet (Isabel, a lady), an excellent psychiatrist for unsick people who angrily believe they are sick and want to do something about it. If they demand a male psychiatrist, the unsick are sent by Dr. ______ (my father) to Dr. Lowenstein, a male psychiatrist, excellent and expensive, with a limited practice.

4. Clarita. She is twenty, twenty-five, she is thirty or more? Pretty, ugly, what? She is a woman lounging by the side of a road, in jeans and a sweater, hitchhiking, or she is slouched on a stool at a counter in some roadside diner. A hard line of jaw. Curious eyes. Amused eyes. Behind her eyes processions move, funeral pageants, cartoons. She says, "I never can figure out why girls like you bum around down here. What are you looking for anyway?" An odor of tobacco about her. Unwashed underclothes, or no underclothes, unwashed skin, gritty toes, hair long and falling into strands, not recently washed.

5. Simon. In this city the weather changes abruptly, so Simon's weather changes abruptly. He sleeps through the afternoon. He sleeps through the morning. Rising, he gropes around for something to get him going, for a cigarette or a pill to drive him out to the street, where the temperature is hovering around 35°. Why doesn't it drop? Why, why doesn't the cold clean air come down from Canada; will he have to go up into Canada to get it? will he have to leave the Country of his Birth and sink into Canada's frosty fields ...? Will the F.B.I. (which he dreams about constantly) chase him over the Canadian border on foot, hounded out in a blizzard of broken glass and horns ...?

"Once I was Huckleberry Finn," Simon says, "but now I am Roderick Usher." Beset by frenzies and fears, this man who makes my spine go cold, he takes green pills, yellow pills, pills of white and capsules of dark blue and green ... he takes other things I may not mention, for what if Simon seeks me out and climbs into my girl's bedroom here in Bloomfield Hills and strangles me, what then ...? (As I write this I begin to shiver. Why do I shiver? I am now sixteen and sixteen is not an age for shivering.) It comes from Simon, who is always cold.

III
WORLD EVENTS

Nothing.

IV
PEOPLE & CIRCUMSTANCES CONTRIBUTING TO THIS DELINQUENCY

Nothing.

V
SIOUX DRIVE

George, Clyde G. 240 Sioux. A manufacturer's representative; children, a dog, a wife. Georgian with the usual columns. You think of the White House, then of Thomas Jefferson, then your mind goes blank on the white pillars and you think of nothing. Norris, Ralph W. 246 Sioux. Public relations. Colonial. Bay window, brick, stone, concrete, wood, green shutters, sidewalk, lantern, grass, trees, blacktop drive, two children, one of them my classmate Esther (Esther Norris) at Baldwin. Wife, cars. Ramsey, Michael D. 250 Sioux. Colonial. Big living room, thirty by twenty-five, fireplaces in living room, library, recreation room, paneled walls wet bar five bathrooms five bedrooms two lavatories central air conditioning automatic sprinkler automatic garage door three children one wife two cars a breakfast room a patio a large fenced lot fourteen trees a front door with a brass knocker never knocked. Next is our house. Classic contemporary. Traditional modern. Attached garage, attached Florida room, attached patio, attached pool and cabana, attached roof. A front door mail slot through which pour *Time Magazine, Fortune, Life, Business Week, the Wall Street Journal, the New York Times, the New Yorker, the Saturday Review, M.D., Modern Medicine, Disease of the Month* . . . and also. . . . And in addition to all this, a quiet sealed letter from Baldwin saying: *Your daughter is not doing work compatible with her performance on the Stanford Binet*. . . . And your son is not doing well, not well at all, very sad. Where is your son anyway? Once he stole trick-and-treat candy from some six-year-old kids, he himself being a robust ten. The beginning. Now your daughter steals. In the Village Pharmacy she made off with, yes she did, don't deny it, she made off with a copy of *Pageant Magazine* for no reason, she swiped a roll of Life Savers in a green wrapper and was in no need of saving her life or even in need of sucking candy; when she was no more than eight years old she stole, don't blush, she stole a package of Tums only because it was out on the counter and available, and the nice lady behind the counter (now dead) said nothing. . . . Sioux Drive. Maples, oaks, elms. Diseased elms cut down. Sioux Drive runs into Roosevelt Drive. Slow, turning lanes, not streets, all drives and lanes and ways and passes. A private police force. Quiet private police, in unmarked cars. Cruising on Saturday evenings with paternal smiles for the residents who are streaming in and out of houses, going to and from parties, a thousand parties, slightly staggering, the women in their furs alighting from automobiles bought of Ford and General Motors and Chrysler, very heavy automobiles. No foreign cars. Detroit. In 275 Sioux, down the block in that magnificent French-Normandy mansion, lives   himself, who has the C   account itself, imagine that! Look at where he lives and look at the enormous trees and chimneys, imagine his many fireplaces, imagine his wife and children, imagine his wife's hair, imagine her fingernails, imagine her bathtub of smooth clean glowing pink, imagine their embraces, his trouser pockets filled with odd coins and keys and dust and peanuts, imagine their ecstasy on Sioux Drive, imagine their income tax returns, imagine their little boy's pride in his experimental car, a scaled-down C   , as he roars around the neighborhood on the sidewalks frightening dogs and Negro maids, oh imagine all these things, imagine everything, let your mind roar out all over Sioux Drive and Du Maurier Drive and Roosevelt Drive and Ticonderoga Pass and Burning Bush Way and Lincolnshire Pass and Lois Lane.

When spring comes, its winds blow nothing to Sioux Drive, no odors of hollyhocks or forsythia, nothing Sioux Drive doesn't already possess, everything is planted and performing. The weather vanes, had they weather vanes, don't have to turn with the wind, don't have to contend with the weather. There is no weather.

VI
DETROIT

There is always weather in Detroit. Detroit's temperature is always 32°. Fast-falling temperatures. Slow-rising temperatures. Wind from the north-northeast four to forty miles an hour, small-craft warnings, partly cloudy today and Wednesday changing to partly sunny through Thursday . . . small warnings of frost, soot warnings, traffic warnings, hazardous lake conditions for small craft and swimmers, restless Negro gangs, restless cloud formations, restless temperatures aching to fall out the very bottom of the thermometer or shoot up over the top and boil everything over in red mercury.

Detroit's temperature is 32°. Fast-falling temperatures. Slow-rising temperatures. Wind from the north-northeast four to forty miles an hour. . . .

VII
EVENTS

1. The girl's heart is pounding. In her pocket is a pair of gloves! In a plastic bag! Airproof breathproof plastic bag, gloves selling for twenty-five dollars on Branden's counter! In her pocket! Shoplifted! . . . In her purse is a blue comb, not very clean. In her purse is a leather billfold (a birthday present from her grandmother in Philadelphia) with snapshots of the family in clean plastic windows, in the billfold are bills, she doesn't know how many bills. . . . In her purse is an ominous note from her friend Tykie *What's this about Joe H. and the kids hanging around at Louise's Sat. night? You heard anything?* . . . passed in French class. In her purse is a lot of dirty yellow Kleenex, her mother's heart would break to see such very dirty Kleenex, and at the bottom of her purse are brown hairpins and safety pins and a broken pencil and a ballpoint pen (blue) stolen from somewhere forgotten and a purse-size compact of Cover Girl Make-Up, Ivory Rose. . . . Her lipstick is Broken Heart, a corrupt pink; her fingers are trembling like crazy; her teeth are beginning to chatter; her insides are alive; her eyes glow in her head; she is saying to her mother's astonished face *I want to steal but not to buy.*

2. At Clarita's. Day or night? What room is this? A bed, a regular bed, and a mattress on the floor nearby. Wallpaper hanging in strips. Clarita says she tore it like that with her teeth. She was fighting a barbaric tribe that night, high from some pills; she was battling for her life with men wearing helmets of heavy iron and their faces no more than Christian crosses to breathe through, every one of those bastards looking like her lover Simon, who seems to breathe with great difficulty through the slits of mouth and nostrils in his face. Clarita has never heard of Sioux Drive. Raymond Forrest cuts no ice with her, nor does the C   account and its millions; Harvard Business School could be at the corner of Vernor and 12th Street for all she cares, and Vietnam might have sunk by now into the Dead Sea under its tons of debris, for all the amazement she could show ... her face is overworked, overwrought, at the age of twenty (thirty?) it is already exhausted but fanciful and ready for a laugh. Clarita says mournfully to me *Honey somebody is going to turn you out let me give you warning.* In a movie shown on late television Clarita is not a mess like this but a nurse, with short neat hair and a dedicated look, in love with her doctor and her doctor's patients and their diseases, enamored of needles and sponges and rubbing alcohol.... Or no: she is a private secretary. Robert Cummings is her boss. She helps him with fantastic plots, the canned audience laughs, no, the audience doesn't laugh because nothing is funny, instead her boss is Robert Taylor and they are not boss and secretary but husband and wife, she is threatened by a young starlet, she is grim, handsome, wifely, a good companion for a good man.... She is Claudette Colbert. Her sister too is Claudette Colbert. They are twins, identical. Her husband Charles Boyer is a very rich handsome man and her sister, Claudette Colbert, is plotting her death in order to take her place as the rich man's wife, no one will know because they are *twins*.... All these marvelous lives Clarita might have lived, but she fell out the bottom at the age of thirteen. At the age when I was packing my overnight case for a slumber party at Toni Deshield's she was tearing filthy sheets off a bed and scratching up a rash on her arms.... Thirteen is uncommonly young for a white girl in Detroit, Miss Brock of the Detroit House of Correction said in a sad newspaper interview for the *Detroit News;* fifteen and sixteen are more likely. Eleven, twelve, thirteen are not surprising in colored ... they are more precocious. What can we do? Taxes are rising and the tax base is falling. The temperature rises slowly but falls rapidly. Everything is falling out the bottom. Woodward Avenue is filthy, Livernois Avenue is filthy! Scraps of paper flutter in the air like pigeons, dirt flies up and hits you right in the eye, oh Detroit is breaking up into dangerous bits of newspaper and dirt, watch out....

Clarita's apartment is over a restaurant. Simon her lover emerges from the cracks at dark. Mrs. Olesko, a neighbor of Clarita's, an aged white wisp of a woman, doesn't complain but sniffs with contentment at Clarita's noisy life and doesn't tell the cops, hating cops, when the cops arrive. I should give more fake names, more blanks, instead of telling all these secrets. I myself am a secret; I am a minor.

3. My father reads a paper at a medical convention in Los Angeles. There he is, on the edge of the North American continent, when the unmarked detective put his hand so gently on my arm in the aisle of Branden's and said, "Miss, would you like to step over here for a minute?"

And where was he when Clarita put her hand on my arm, that wintry dark sulphurous aching day in Detroit, in the company of closed-down barber shops, closed-down diners, closed-down movie houses, homes, windows, basements, faces ... she put her hand on my arm and said, "Honey, are you looking for somebody down here?"

And was he home worrying about me, gone for two weeks solid, when they carried me off ...? It took three of them to get me in the police cruiser, so they said, and they put more than their hands on my arm.

4. I work on this lesson. My English teacher is Mr. Forest, who is from Michigan State. Not handsome, Mr. Forest, and his name is plain, unlike Raymond Forrest's, but he is sweet and rodentlike, he has conferred with the principal and my parents, and everything is fixed ... treat her as if nothing has happened, a new start, begin again, only sixteen years old, what a shame, how did it happen? — nothing happened, nothing could have happened, a slight physiological modification known only to a gynecologist or to Dr. Coronet. I work on my lesson. I sit in my pink room. I look around the room with my sad pink eyes. I sigh, I dawdle, I pause, I eat up time, I am limp and happy to be home, I am sixteen years old suddenly, my head hangs heavy as a pumpkin on my shoulders, and my hair has just been cut by Mr. Faye at the Crystal Salon and is said to be very becoming.

(Simon too put his hand on my arm and said, "Honey, you have got to come with me," and in his six-by-six room we got to know each other. Would I go back to Simon again? Would I lie down with him in all that filth and craziness? Over and over again.

a Clarita is being betrayed as in front of a Cunningham Drug Store she is nervously eying a colored man who may or may not have money, or a nervous white boy of twenty with sideburns and an Appalachian look, who may or may not have a knife hidden in his jacket pocket, or a husky red-faced man of friendly countenance who may or may not be a member of the Vice Squad out for an early twilight walk.)

I work on my lesson for Mr. Forest. I have filled up eleven pages. Words pour out of me and won't stop. I want to tell everything ... what was the song Simon was always humming, and who was Simon's friend in a very new trench coat with an old high school graduation ring on his finger ...? Simon's bearded friend? When I was down too low for him, Simon kicked me out and gave me to him for three days, I think, on Fourteenth Street in Detroit, an airy room of cold cruel drafts with newspapers on the floor.... Do I really remember that or am I piecing it together from what they told me? Did they tell the truth? Did they know much of the truth?

VIII
CHARACTERS

1. Wednesdays after school, at four; Saturday mornings at ten. Mother drives me to Dr. Coronet. Ferns in the office, plastic or real, they look the same. Dr. Coronet is queenly, an elegant nicotine-stained lady who would have studied with Freud had circumstances not prevented it, a bit of a Catholic, ready to offer you some mystery if your teeth will ache too much without it. Highly recommended by Father! Forty dollars an hour, Father's forty dollars! Progress! Looking up! Looking better! That new haircut is so becoming, says Dr. Coronet herself, showing how normal she is for a woman with an I.Q. of 180 and many advanced degrees.

2. Mother. A lady in a brown suede coat. Boots of shiny black material, black gloves, a black fur hat. She would be humiliated could she know that of all the people in the world it is my ex-lover Simon who walks most like her ... self-conscious and unreal, listening to distant music, a little bow-legged with craftiness....

3. Father. Tying a necktie. In a hurry. On my first evening home he put his hand on my arm and said, "Honey, we're going to forget all about this."

4. Simon. Outside, a plane is crossing the sky, in here we're in a hurry. Morning. It must be morning. The girl is half out of her mind, whimpering and vague; Simon her dear friend is wretched this morning ... he is wretched with morning itself ... he forces her to give him an injection with that needle she knows is filthy, she has a dread of needles and surgical instruments and the odor of things that are to be sent into the blood, thinking somehow of her father.... This is a bad morning, Simon says that his mind is being twisted out of shape, and so he submits to the needle that he usually scorns and bites his lip with his yellowish teeth, his face going very pale. *Ah baby!* he says in his soft mocking voice, which with all women is a mockery of love, *do it like this — Slowly —* And the girl, terrified, almost drops the precious needle but manages to turn it up to the light from the window ... is it an extension of herself then? She can give him this gift then? *I wish you wouldn't do this to me,* she says, wise in her terror, because it seems to her that Simon's danger — in a few minutes he may be dead — is a way of pressing her against him that is more powerful than any other embrace. She has to work over his arm, the knotted corded veins of his arm, her forehead wet with perspiration as she pushes and releases the needle, staring at that mixture of liquid now stained with Simon's bright blood.... When the drug hits him she can feel it herself, she feels that magic that is more than any woman can give him, striking the back of his head and making his face stretch as if with the impact of a terrible sun.... She tries to embrace him but he pushes her aside and stumbles to his feet. *Jesus Christ,* he says....

5. Princess, a Negro girl of eighteen. What is her charge? She is closed-mouthed about it, shrewd and silent, you know that no one had to wrestle her to the sidewalk to get her in here; she came with dignity. In the recreation room she sits reading *Nancy Drew and the Jewel Box Mystery,* which inspires in her face tiny wrinkles of alarm and interest: what a face! Light brown skin, heavy shaded eyes, heavy eyelashes, a serious sinister dark brow, graceful fingers, graceful wristbones, graceful legs, lips, tongue, a sugar-sweet voice, a leggy stride more masculine than Simon's and my mother's, decked out in a dirty white blouse and dirty white slacks; vaguely nautical is Princess' style.... At breakfast she is in charge of clearing the table and leans over me, saying, *Honey you sure you ate enough?*

6. The girl lies sleepless, wondering. Why here, why not there? Why Bloomfield Hills and not jail? Why jail and not her pink room? Why downtown Detroit and not Sioux Drive? What is the difference? Is Simon all the difference? The girl's head is a parade of wonders. She is nearly sixteen, her breath is marvelous with wonders, not long ago she was coloring with crayons and now she is smearing the landscape with paints that won't come off and won't come off her fingers either. She says to the matron *I am not talking about anything,* not because everyone has warned her not to talk but because, because she will not talk; because she won't say anything about Simon, who is her secret. And she says to the matron, *I won't go home,* up until that night in the lavatory when everything was changed.... "No, I won't go home I want to stay here," she says, listening to her

own words with amazement, thinking that weeds might climb everywhere over that marvelous $180,000 house and dinosaurs might return to muddy the beige carpeting, but never never will she reconcile four o'clock in the morning in Detroit with eight o'clock breakfasts in Bloomfield Hills.... oh, she aches still for Simon's hands and his caressing breath, though he gave her little pleasure, he took everything from her (five-dollar bills, ten-dollar bills, passed into her numb hands by men and taken out of her hands by Simon) until she herself was passed into the hands of other men, police, when Simon evidently got tired of her and her hysteria.... *No, I won't go home, I don't want to be bailed out.* The girl thinks as a *Stubborn and Wayward Child* (one of several charges lodged against her), and the matron understands her crazy white-rimmed eyes that are seeking out some new violence that will keep her in jail, should someone threaten to let her out. Such children try to strangle the matrons, the attendants, or one another... they want the locks locked forever, the doors nailed shut ... and this girl is no different up until that night her mind is changed for her....

IX
THAT NIGHT

Princess and Dolly, a little white girl of maybe fifteen, hardy however as a sergeant and in the House of Correction for armed robbery, corner her in the lavatory at the farthest sink and the other girls look away and file out to bed, leaving her. God, how she is beaten up! Why is she beaten up? Why do they pound her, why such hatred? Princess vents all the hatred of a thousand silent Detroit winters on her body, this girl whose body belongs to me, fiercely she rides across the Midwestern plains on this girl's tender bruised body ... revenge on the oppressed minorities of America! revenge on the slaughtered Indians! revenge on the female sex, on the male sex, revenge on Bloomfield Hills, revenge revenge....

X
DETROIT

In Detroit, weather weighs heavily upon everyone. The sky looms large. The horizon shimmers in smoke. Downtown the buildings are imprecise in the haze. Perpetual haze. Perpetual motion inside the haze. Across the choppy river is the city of Windsor, in Canada. Part of the continent has bunched up here and is bulging outward, at the tip of Detroit; a cold hard rain is forever falling on the expressways.... Shoppers shop grimly, their cars are not parked in safe places, their windshields may be smashed and graceful ebony hands may drag them out through their shatterproof smashed windshields, crying, *Revenge for the Indians!* Ah, they all fear leaving Hudson's and being dragged to the very tip of the city and thrown off the parking roof of Cobo Hall, that expensive tomb, into the river....

XI
CHARACTERS WE ARE FOREVER ENTWINED WITH

1. Simon drew me into his tender rotting arms and breathed gravity into me. Then I came to earth, weighed down. He said, *You are such a little girl,* and he weighed me down with his delight. In the palms of his hands were teeth marks from his previous life experiences. He was thirty-five, they said. Imagine Simon in this room, in my pink room: he is about six feet tall and stoops slightly, in a feline cautious way, always thinking, always on guard, with his scuffed light suede shoes and his clothes that are anyone's clothes, slightly rumpled ordinary clothes that ordinary men might wear to not-bad jobs. Simon has fair long hair, curly hair, spent languid curls that are like ... exactly like the curls of wood shavings to the touch, I am trying to be exact ... and he smells of unheated mornings and coffee and too many pills coating his tongue with a faint green-white scum.... Dear Simon, who would be panicked in this room and in this house (right now Billie is vacuuming next door in my parents' room; a vacuum cleaner's roar is a sign of all good things), Simon who is said to have come from a home not much different from this, years ago, fleeing all the carpeting and the polished banisters ... Simon has a deathly face, only desperate people fall in love with it. His face is bony and cautious, the bones of his cheeks prominent as if with the rigidity of his ceaseless thinking, plotting, for he has to make money out of girls to whom money means nothing, they're so far gone they can hardly count it, and in a sense money means nothing to him either except as a way of keeping on with his life. *Each Day's Proud Struggle,* the title of a novel we could read at jail.... Each day he needs a certain amount of money. He devours it. It wasn't love he uncoiled in me with his hollowed-out eyes and his courteous smile, that remnant of a prosperous past, but a dark terror that needed to press itself flat against him, or against another man ... but he was the first, he came over to me and took my arm, a claim. We struggled on the stairs and I said, *Let me loose, you're hurting my neck, my face,* it was such a surprise that my skin hurt where he rubbed it, and afterward we lay face to face and he breathed everything into me. In the end I think he turned me in.

2. Raymond Forrest. I just read this morning that Raymond Forrest's father, the chairman of

the board at   , died of a heart attack on a plane bound for London. I would like to write Raymond Forrest a note of sympathy. I would like to thank him for not pressing charges against me one hundred years ago, saving me, being so generous ... well, men like Raymond Forrest are generous men, not like Simon. I would like to write him a letter telling of my love, or of some other emotion that is positive and healthy. Not like Simon and his poetry, which he scrawled down when he was high and never changed a word ... but when I try to think of something to say, it is Simon's language that comes back to me, caught in my head like a bad song, it is always Simon's language:

There is no reality only dreams
Your neck may get snapped when you wake
My love is drawn to some violent end
She keeps wanting to get away
My love is heading downward
And I am heading upward
She is going to crash on the sidewalk
And I am going to dissolve into the clouds

XII
EVENTS

1. Out of the hospital, bruised and saddened and converted, with Princess' grunts still tangled in my hair ... and Father in his overcoat looking like a prince himself, come to carry me off. Up the expressway and out north to home. Jesus Christ, but the air is thinner and cleaner here. Monumental houses. Heartbreaking sidewalks, so clean.

2. Weeping in the living room. The ceiling is two stories high and two chandeliers hang from it. Weeping, weeping, though Billie the maid is *probably listening.* I will never leave home again. Never. Never leave home. Never leave this home again, never.

3. Sugar doughnuts for breakfast. The toaster is very shiny and my face is distorted in it. Is that my face?

first persona

4. The car is turning in the driveway. Father brings me home. Mother embraces me. Sunlight breaks in movieland patches on the roof of our traditional-contemporary home, which was designed for the famous automotive stylist whose identity, if I told you the name of the famous car he designed, you would all know, so I can't tell you because my teeth chatter at the thought of being sued ... or having someone climb into my bedroom window with a rope to strangle me.... The car turns up the blacktop drive. The house opens to me like a doll's house, so lovely in the sunlight, the big living room beckons to me with its walls falling away in a delirium of joy at my return, Billie the maid is *no doubt* listening from the kitchen as I burst into tears and the hysteria Simon got so sick of. Convulsed in Father's arms, I say I will never leave again, never, why did I leave, where did I go, what happened, my mind is gone wrong, my body is one big bruise, my backbone was sucked dry, it wasn't the men who hurt me and Simon never hurt me but only those girls ... my God, how they hurt me ... I will never leave home again.... The car is perpetually turning up the drive and I am perpetually breaking down in the living room and we are perpetually taking the right exit from the expressway (Lahser Road) and the wall of the rest room is perpetually banging against my head and perpetually are Simon's hands moving across my body and adding everything up and so too are Father's hands on my shaking bruised back, far from the surface of my skin on the surface of my good blue cashmere coat (drycleaned for my release).... I weep for all the money here, for God in gold and beige carpeting, for the beauty of chandeliers and the miracle of a clean polished gleaming toaster and faucets that run both hot and cold water, and I tell them, *I will never leave home, this is my home, I love everything here, I am in love with everything here....*

I am home.

new sense of identity
will to live

FLANNERY O'CONNOR

A Good Man Is Hard to Find

The grandmother didn't want to go to Florida. She wanted to visit some of her connections in east Tennessee and she was seizing at every chance to change Bailey's mind. Bailey was the son she lived with, her only boy. He was sitting on the edge of his chair at the table, bent over the orange sports section of the *Journal.* "Now look here, Bailey," she said, "see here, read this," and she stood with one hand on her thin hip and the other rattling the newspaper at his bald head. "Here this fellow that calls himself The Misfit is aloose from the Federal Pen and headed toward Florida and you read here what it says he did to these people. Just you read it. I wouldn't take my children in any direction with a criminal like that aloose in it. I couldn't answer to my conscience if I did."

Bailey didn't look up from his reading so she wheeled around then and faced the children's mother, a young woman in slacks, whose face was as broad and innocent as a cabbage and was tied around with a green head-kerchief that had two points on the top like a rabbit's ears. She was sitting on the sofa, feeding the baby his apricots out of a jar. "The children have been to Florida before," the old lady said. "You all ought to take them somewhere else for a change so they would see different parts of the world and be broad. They never have been to east Tennessee."

The children's mother didn't seem to hear her but the eight-year-old boy, John Wesley, a stocky child with glasses, said, "If you don't want to go to Florida, why dontcha stay at home?" He and the little girl, June Star, were reading the funny papers on the floor.

"She wouldn't stay at home to be queen for a day," June Star said without raising her yellow head.

"Yes and what would you do if this fellow, The Misfit, caught you?" the grandmother asked.

"I'd smack his face," John Wesley said.

"She wouldn't stay at home for a million bucks," June Star said. "Afraid she'd miss something. She has to go everywhere we go."

"All right, Miss," the grandmother said. "Just remember that the next time you want me to curl your hair."

June Star said her hair was naturally curly.

The next morning the grandmother was the first one in the car, ready to go. She had her big black valise that looked like the head of a hippopotamus in one corner, and underneath it she was hiding a basket with Pitty Sing, the cat, in it. She didn't intend for the cat to be left alone in the house for three days because he would miss her too much and she was afraid he might brush against one of the gas burners and accidentally asphyxiate himself. Her son, Bailey, didn't like to arrive at a motel with a cat.

She sat in the middle of the back seat with John Wesley and June Star on either side of her. Bailey and the children's mother and the baby sat in front and they left Atlanta at eight forty-five with the mileage on the car at 55890. The grandmother wrote this down because she thought it would be interesting to say how many miles they had been when they got back. It took them twenty minutes to reach the outskirts of the city.

The old lady settled herself comfortably, removing her white cotton gloves and putting them up with her purse on the shelf in front of the back window. The children's mother still had on slacks and still had her head tied up in a green kerchief, but the grandmother had on a navy blue straw sailor hat with a bunch of white violets on the brim and a navy blue dress with a small white dot in the print. Her collars and cuffs were white organdy trimmed with lace and at her neckline she had pinned a purple spray of cloth violets containing a sachet. In case of an accident, anyone seeing her dead on the highway would know at once that she was a lady.

She said she thought it was going to be a good day for driving, neither too hot nor too cold, and she cautioned Bailey that the speed limit was fifty-five miles an hour and that the patrolmen hid themselves behind billboards and small clumps of trees and sped out after you before you had a chance to slow down. She pointed out interesting details of the scenery: Stone Mountain; the blue granite that in some places came up to both sides of the highway; the brilliant red clay banks slightly streaked with purple; and the various crops that made rows of green lace-work on the ground. The trees were full of silver-white sunlight and the meanest of them sparkled. The children were reading comic magazines and their mother had gone back to sleep.

"Let's go through Georgia fast so we won't have to look at it much," John Wesley said.

"If I were a little boy," said the grandmother, "I wouldn't talk about my native state that way.

Tennessee has the mountains and Georgia has the hills."

"Tennessee is just a hillbilly dumping ground," John Wesley said, "and Georgia is a lousy state too."

"You said it," June Star said.

"In my time," said the grandmother, folding her thin veined fingers, "children were more respectful of their native states and their parents and everything else. People did right then. Oh look at the cute little pickaninny!" she said and pointed to a Negro child standing in the door of a shack. "Wouldn't that make a picture, now?" she asked and they all turned and looked at the little Negro out of a back window. He waved.

"He didn't have any britches on," June Star said.

"He probably didn't have any," the grandmother explained. "Little niggers in the country don't have things like we do. If I could paint, I'd paint that picture," she said.

The children exchanged comic books.

The grandmother offered to hold the baby and the children's mother passed him over the front seat to her. She set him on her knee and bounced him and told him about the things they were passing. She rolled her eyes and screwed up her mouth and stuck her leathery thin face into his smooth bland one. Occasionally he gave her a faraway smile. They passed a large cotton field with five or six graves fenced in the middle of it, like a small island. "Look at the graveyard!" the grandmother said, pointing it out. "That was the old family burying ground. That belonged to the plantation."

"Where's the plantation?" John Wesley asked.

"Gone With the Wind," said the grandmother. "Ha. Ha."

When the children finished all the comic books they had brought, they opened the lunch and ate it. The grandmother ate a peanut butter sandwich and an olive and would not let the children throw the box and the paper napkins out the window. When there was nothing else to do they played a game by choosing a cloud and making the other two guess what shape it suggested. John Wesley took one the shape of a cow and June Star guessed a cow and John Wesley said, no, an automobile, and June Star said he didn't play fair, and they began to slap each other over the grandmother.

The grandmother said she would tell them a story if they would keep quiet. When she told a story, she rolled her eyes and waved her head and was very dramatic. She said once when she was a maiden lady she had been courted by a Mr. Edgar Atkins Teagarden from Jasper, Georgia. She said he was a very good-looking man and a gentleman and that he brought her a watermelon every Saturday afternoon with his initials cut in it, E. A. T. Well, one Saturday, she said, Mr. Teagarden brought the watermelon and there was nobody at home and he left it on the front porch and returned in his buggy to Jasper, but she never got the watermelon, she said, because a nigger boy ate it when he saw the initials, E. A. T.! This story tickled John Wesley's funny bone and he giggled and giggled but June Star didn't think it was any good. She said she wouldn't marry a man that just brought her a watermelon on Saturday. The grandmother said she would have done well to marry Mr. Teagarden because he was a gentleman and had bought Coca-Cola stock when it first came out and that he had died only a few years ago, a very wealthy man.

They stopped at The Tower for barbecued sandwiches. The Tower was a part stucco and part wood filling station and dance hall set in a clearing outside of Timothy. A fat man named Red Sammy Butts ran it and there were signs stuck here and there on the building and for miles up and down the highway saying, TRY RED SAMMY'S FAMOUS BARBECUE. NONE LIKE FAMOUS RED SAMMY'S! RED SAM! THE FAT BOY WITH THE HAPPY LAUGH! A VETERAN! RED SAMMY'S YOUR MAN!

Red Sammy was lying on the bare ground outside The Tower with his head under a truck while a gray monkey about a foot high, chained to a small chinaberry tree, chattered nearby. The monkey sprang back into the tree and got on the highest limb as soon as he saw the children jump out of the car and run toward him.

Inside, The Tower was a long dark room with a counter at one end and tables at the other and dancing space in the middle. They all sat down at a board table next to the nickelodeon and Red Sam's wife, a tall burnt-brown woman with hair and eyes lighter than her skin, came and took their order. The children's mother put a dime in the machine and played "The Tennessee Waltz," and the grandmother said that tune always made her want to dance. She asked Bailey if he would like to dance but he only glared at her. He didn't have a naturally sunny disposition like she did and trips made him nervous. The grandmother's brown eyes were very bright. She swayed her head from side to side and pretended she was dancing in her chair. June Star said play something she could tap to so the children's mother put in another dime and played a fast number and June Star stepped out onto the dance floor and did her tap routine.

"Ain't she cute?" Red Sam's wife said, leaning over the counter. "Would you like to come be my little girl?"

"No I certainly wouldn't," June Star said. "I wouldn't live in a broken-down place like this for a million bucks!" and she ran back to the table.

"Ain't she cute?" the woman repeated, stretching her mouth politely.

"Aren't you ashamed?" hissed the grandmother.

Red Sam came in and told his wife to quit lounging on the counter and hurry up with these people's order. His khaki trousers reached just to his hip bones and his stomach hung over them like a sack of meal swaying under his shirt. He came over and sat down at a table nearby and let out a combination sigh and yodel. "You can't win," he said. "You can't win," and he wiped his sweating red face off with a gray handkerchief. "These days you don't know who to trust." he said. "Ain't that the truth?"

"People are certainly not nice like they used to be," said the grandmother.

"Two fellers come in here last week," Red Sammy said, "driving a Chrysler. It was a old beat-up car but it was a good one and these boys looked all right to me. Said they worked at the mill and you know I let them fellers charge the gas they bought? Now why did I do that?"

"Because you're a good man!" the grandmother said at once.

"Yes'm, I suppose so," Red Sam said as if he were struck with this answer.

His wife brought the orders, carrying the five plates all at once without a tray, two in each hand and one balanced on her arm. "It isn't a soul in this green world of God's that you can trust," she said. "And I don't count nobody out of that, not nobody," she repeated, looking at Red Sammy.

"Did you read about that criminal, The Misfit, that's escaped?" asked the grandmother.

"I wouldn't be a bit surprised if he didn't attack this place right here," said the woman. "If he hears about it being here, I wouldn't be none surprised to see him. If he hears it's two cent in the cash register, I wouldn't be a tall surprised if he . . ."

"That'll do." Red Sam said. "Go bring these people their Co'-Colas," and the woman went off to get the rest of the order.

"A good man is hard to find," Red Sammy said. "Everything is getting terrible. I remember the day you could go off and leave your screen door unlatched. Not no more."

He and the grandmother discussed better times. The old lady said that in her opinion Europe was entirely to blame for the way things were now. She said the way Europe acted you would think we were made of money and Red Sam said it was no use talking about it, she was exactly right. The children ran outside into the white sunlight and looked at the monkey in the lacy chinaberry tree. He was busy catching fleas on himself and biting each one carefully between his teeth as if it were a delicacy.

They drove off again into the hot afternoon. The grandmother took cat naps and woke up every few minutes with her own snoring. Outside of Toombsboro she woke up and recalled an old plantation that she had visited in this neighborhood once when she was a young lady. She said the house had six white columns across the front and that there was an avenue of oaks leading up to it and two little wooden trellis arbors on either side in front where you sat down with your suitor after a stroll in the garden. She recalled exactly which road to run off to get to it. She knew that Bailey would not be willing to lose any time looking at an old house, but the more she talked about it, the more she wanted to see it once again and find out if the little twin arbors were still standing. "There was a secret panel in this house," she said craftily, not telling the truth but wishing that she were, "and the story went that all the family silver was hidden in it when Sherman came through but it was never found . . ."

"Hey!" John Wesley said. "Let's go see it! We'll find it! We'll poke all the woodwork and find it! Who lives there? Where do you turn off at? Hey Pop, can't we turn off there?"

"We never have seen a house with a secret panel!" June Star shrieked. "Let's go to the house with the secret panel! Hey Pop, can't we go see the house with the secret panel!"

"It's not far from here, I know," the grandmother said. "It wouldn't take over twenty minutes."

Bailey was looking straight ahead. His jaw was as rigid as a horseshoe. "No," he said.

The children began to yell and scream that they wanted to see the house with the secret panel. John Wesley kicked the back of the front seat and June Star hung over her mother's shoulder and whined desperately into her ear that they never had any fun even on their vacation, that they could never do what THEY wanted to do. The baby began to scream and John Wesley kicked the back of the seat so hard that his father could feel the blows in his kidney.

"All right!" he shouted and drew the car to a stop at the side of the road. "Will you all shut up? Will you all just shut up for one second? If you don't shut up, we won't go anywhere."

"It would be very educational for them," the grandmother murmured.

"All right," Bailey said, "but get this: this is the only time we're going to stop for anything like this. This is the one and only time."

"The dirt road that you have to turn down is about a mile back," the grandmother directed. "I marked it when we passed."

"A dirt road," Bailey groaned.

After they had turned around and were headed toward the dirt road, the grandmother recalled other points about the house, the beautiful glass over the front doorway and the candle-lamp in the hall. John Wesley said that the secret panel was probably in the fireplace.

"You can't go inside this house," Bailey said. "You don't know who lives there."

"While you all talk to the people in front, I'll run around behind and get in a window," John Wesley suggested.

"We'll all stay in the car," his mother said.

They turned onto the dirt road and the car raced roughly along in a swirl of pink dust. The grandmother recalled the times when there were no paved roads and thirty miles was a day's journey. The dirt road was hilly and there were sudden washes in it and sharp curves on dangerous embankments. All at once they would be on a hill, looking down over the blue tops of trees for miles around, then the next minute, they would be in a red depression with the dust-coated trees looking down on them.

"This place had better turn up in a minute," Bailey said, "or I'm going to turn around."

The road looked as if no one had traveled on it in months.

"It's not much farther," the grandmother said and just as she said it, a horrible thought came to her. The thought was so embarrassing that she turned red in the face and her eyes dilated and her feet jumped up, upsetting her valise in the corner. The instant the valise moved, the newspaper top she had over the basket under it rose with a snarl and Pitty Sing, the cat, sprang onto Bailey's shoulder.

The children were thrown to the floor and their mother, clutching the baby, was thrown out the door onto the ground; the old lady was thrown into the front seat. The car turned over once and landed right-side-up in a gulch off the side of the road. Bailey remained in the driver's seat with the cat — gray-striped with a broad white face and an orange nose — clinging to his neck like a caterpillar.

As soon as the children saw they could move their arms and legs, they scrambled out of the car, shouting, "We've had an ACCIDENT!" The grandmother was curled up under the dashboard, hoping she was injured so that Bailey's wrath would not come down on her all at once. The horrible thought she had had before the accident was that the house she had remembered so vividly was not in Georgia but in Tennessee.

Bailey removed the cat from his neck with both hands and flung it out the window against the side of a pine tree. Then he got out of the car and started looking for the children's mother. She was sitting against the side of the red gutted ditch, holding the screaming baby, but she only had a cut down her face and a broken shoulder. "We've had an ACCIDENT!" the children screamed in a frenzy of delight.

"But nobody's killed," June Star said with disappointment as the grandmother limped out of the car, her hat still pinned to her head but the broken front brim standing up at a jaunty angle and the violet spray hanging off the side. They all sat down in the ditch, except the children, to recover from the shock. They were all shaking.

"Maybe a car will come along," said the children's mother hoarsely.

"I believe I have injured an organ," said the grandmother, pressing her side, but no one answered her. Bailey's teeth were clattering. He had on a yellow sport shirt with bright blue parrots designed in it and his face was as yellow as the shirt. The grandmother decided that she would not mention that the house was in Tennessee.

The road was about ten feet above and they could see only the tops of the trees on the other side of it. Behind the ditch they were sitting in there were more woods, tall and dark and deep. In a few minutes they saw a car some distance away on top of a hill, coming slowly as if the occupants were watching them. The grandmother stood up and waved both arms dramatically to attract their attention. The car continued to come on slowly, disappeared around a bend and appeared again, moving even slower, on top of the hill they had gone over. It was a big black battered hearse-like automobile. There were three men in it.

It came to a stop just over them and for some minutes, the driver looked down with a steady expressionless gaze to where they were sitting, and didn't speak. Then he turned his head and muttered something to the other two and they got out. One was a fat boy in black trousers and a red sweat shirt with a silver stallion embossed on the front of it. He moved around on the right side of them and stood staring, his mouth partly open in a kind of loose grin. The other had on khaki pants and a blue striped coat and a gray hat pulled down very low, hiding most of his face. He came around slowly on the left side. Neither spoke.

The driver got out of the car and stood by the side of it, looking down at them. He was an older man than the other two. His hair was just beginning to gray and he wore silver-rimmed spectacles that gave him a scholarly look. He had a long creased face and didn't have on any shirt or undershirt. He had on blue jeans that were too tight for him and was holding a black hat and a gun. The two boys also had guns.

"We've had an ACCIDENT!" the children screamed.

The grandmother had the peculiar feeling that the bespectacled man was someone she knew. His face was as familiar to her as if she had known him all her life but she could not recall who he was. He moved away from the car and began to come down the embankment, placing his feet carefully so that he wouldn't slip. He had on tan and white shoes and no socks, and his ankles were red and thin. "Good afternoon," he said. "I see you all had you a little spill."

"We turned over twice!" said the grandmother.

"Oncet," he corrected. "We seen it happen. Try their car and see will it run, Hiram," he said quietly to the boy with the gray hat.

"What you got that gun for?" John Wesley asked. "Whatcha gonna do with that gun?"

"Lady," the man said to the children's mother, "would you mind calling them children to sit down by you? Children make me nervous. I want all you all to sit down right together there where you're at."

"What are you telling US what to do for?" June Star asked.

Behind them the line of woods gaped like a dark open mouth. "Come here," said their mother.

"Look here now," Bailey began suddenly, "we're in a predicament! We're in . . ."

The grandmother shrieked. She scrambled to her feet and stood staring. "You're The Misfit!" she said. "I recognized you at once!"

"Yes'm," the man said, smiling slightly as if he were pleased in spite of himself to be known, "but it would have been better for all of you, lady, if you hadn't of reckernized me."

Bailey turned his head sharply and said something to his mother that shocked even the children. The old lady began to cry and The Misfit reddened.

"Lady," he said, "don't you get upset. Sometimes a man says things he don't mean. I don't reckon he meant to talk to you thataway."

"You wouldn't shoot a lady, would you?" the grandmother said and removed a clean handkerchief from her cuff and began to slap at her eyes with it.

The Misfit pointed the toe of his shoe into the ground and made a little hole and then covered it up again. "I would hate to have to," he said.

"Listen," the grandmother almost screamed, "I know you're a good man. You don't look a bit like you have common blood. I know you must come from nice people!"

"Yes mam," he said, "finest people in the world." When he smiled he showed a row of strong white teeth. "God never made a finer woman than my mother and my daddy's heart was pure gold," he said. The boy with the red sweat shirt had come around behind them and was standing with his gun at his hip. The Misfit squatted down on the ground. "Watch them children, Bobby Lee," he said. "You know they make me nervous." He looked at the six of them huddled together in front of him and he seemed to be embarrassed as if he couldn't think of anything to say. "Ain't a cloud in the sky," he remarked, looking up at it. "Don't see no sun but don't see no cloud neither.

"Yes, it's a beautiful day," said the grandmother. "Listen," she said, "you shouldn't call yourself The Misfit because I know you're a good man at heart. I can just look at you and tell."

"Hush!" Bailey yelled. "Hush! Everybody shut up and let me handle this!" He was squatting in the position of a runner about to sprint forward but he didn't move.

"I pre-chate that, lady," The Misfit said and drew a little circle in the ground with the butt of his gun.

"It'll take a half a hour to fix this here car," Hiram called, looking over the raised hood of it.

"Well, first you and Bobby Lee get him and that little boy to step over yonder with you," The Misfit said, pointing to Bailey and John Wesley. "The boys want to ast you something," he said to Bailey. "Would you mind stepping back in them woods there with them?"

"Listen," Bailey began, "we're in a terrible predicament! Nobody realizes what this is," and his voice cracked. His eyes were as blue and intense as the parrots in his shirt and he remained perfectly still.

The grandmother reached up to adjust her hat brim as if she were going to the woods with him but it came off in her hand. She stood staring at it and after a second she let it fall on the ground. Hiram pulled Bailey up by the arm as if he were assisting an old man. John Wesley caught hold of his father's hand and Bobby Lee followed. They went off toward the woods and just as they reached the dark edge, Bailey turned and supporting himself against a gray naked pine trunk, he shouted, "I'll be back in a minute, Mamma, wait on me!"

"Come back this instant!" his mother shrilled but they all disappeared into the woods.

"Bailey Boy!" the grandmother called in a tragic voice but she found she was looking at The Misfit squatting on the ground in front of her. "I just know you're a good man," she said desperately. "You're not a bit common!"

"Nome, I ain't a good man," The Misfit said after a second as if he had considered her statement carefully, "but I ain't the worst in the world neither. My daddy said I was a different breed of dog from my brothers and sisters. 'You know,' Daddy said, 'it's some that can live their whole life out without asking about it and it's others has to know why it is, and this boy is one of the latters. He's going to be into everything!' " He put on his black hat and looked up suddenly and then away deep into the woods as if he were embarrassed again. "I'm sorry I don't have on a shirt before you ladies," he said, hunching his shoulders slightly. "We buried our clothes that we had on when we escaped and we're just making do until we can get better. We borrowed these from some folks we met," he explained.

"That's perfectly all right," the grandmother said. "Maybe Bailey has an extra shirt in his suitcase."

"I'll look and see terrectly," The Misfit said.

"Where are they taking him?" the children's mother screamed.

"Daddy was a card himself," The Misfit said. "You couldn't put anything over on him. He never got in trouble with the Authorities though. Just had the knack of handling them."

"You could be honest too if you'd only try," said the grandmother. "Think how wonderful it would be to settle down and live a comfortable life and not have to think about somebody chasing you all the time."

The Misfit kept scratching in the ground with the butt of his gun as if he were thinking about it. "Yes'm, somebody is always after you," he murmured.

The grandmother noticed how thin his shoulder blades were just behind his hat because she was standing up looking down on him. "Do you ever pray?" she asked.

He shook his head. All she saw was the black hat wiggle between his shoulder blades. "Nome," he said.

There was a pistol shot from the woods, followed closely by another. Then silence. The old lady's head jerked around. She could hear the wind move through the tree tops like a long satisfied insuck of breath. "Bailey Boy!" she called.

"I was a gospel singer for a while," The Misfit said. "I been most everything. Been in the arm service, both land and sea, at home and abroad, been twict married, been an undertaker, been with the railroads, plowed Mother Earth, been in a tornado, seen a man burnt alive oncet," and looked up at the children's mother and the little girl who were sitting close together, their faces white and their eyes glassy; "I even seen a woman flogged," he said.

"Pray, pray," the grandmother began, "pray, pray . . ."

"I never was a bad boy that I remember of," The Misfit said in an almost dreamy voice, "but somewheres along the line I done something wrong and got sent to the penitentiary. I was buried alive," and he looked up and held her attention to him by a steady stare.

"That's when you should have started to pray," she said. "What did you do to get sent to the penitentiary that first time?"

"Turn to the right, it was a wall," The Misfit said, looking up again at the cloudless sky. "Turn to the left, it was a wall. Look up it was a ceiling, look down it was a floor. I forget what I done, lady. I set there and set there, trying to remember what it was I done and I ain't recalled it to this day. Oncet in a while, I would think it was coming to me, but it never come."

"Maybe they put you in by mistake," the old lady said vaguely.

"Nome," he said. "It wasn't no mistake. They had the papers on me."

"You must have stolen something," she said.

The Misfit sneered slightly. "Nobody had nothing I wanted," he said. "It was a head-doctor at the penitentiary said what I had done was kill my daddy but I known that for a lie. My daddy died in nineteen ought nineteen of the epidemic flu and I never had a thing to do with it. He was buried in the Mount Hopewell Baptist churchyard and you can go there and see for yourself."

"If you would pray," the old lady said, "Jesus would help you."

"That's right," The Misfit said.

"Well then, why don't you pray?" she asked trembling with delight suddenly.

"I don't want no hep," he said. "I'm doing all right by myself."

Bobby Lee and Hiram came ambling back from the woods. Bobby Lee was dragging a yellow shirt with bright blue parrots in it.

"Throw me that shirt, Bobby Lee," The Misfit said. The shirt came flying at him and landed on his shoulder and he put it on. The grandmother couldn't name what the shirt reminded her of. "No, lady," The Misfit said while he was buttoning it up, "I found out the crime don't matter. You can do one thing or you can do another, kill a man or take a tire off his car, because sooner or later you're going to forget what it was you done and just be punished for it."

The children's mother had begun to make heavier noises as if she couldn't get her breath. "Lady," he asked, "would you and that little girl like to step off yonder with Bobby Lee and Hiram and join your husband?"

"Yes, thank you," the mother said faintly. Her left arm dangled helplessly and she was holding the baby, who had gone to sleep, in the other. "Hep that lady up, Hiram," The Misfit said as she struggled to climb out of the ditch, "and Bobby Lee, you hold onto that little girl's hand."

"I don't want to hold hands with him," June Star said. "He reminds me of a pig."

The fat boy blushed and laughed and caught her by the arm and pulled her off into the woods after Hiram and her mother.

Alone with The Misfit, the grandmother found that she had lost her voice. There was not a cloud in the sky nor any sun. There was nothing around her but woods. She wanted to tell him that he must pray. She opened and closed her mouth several times before anything came out. Finally she found herself saying, "Jesus, Jesus," meaning, Jesus will help you, but the way she was saying it, it sounded as if she might be cursing.

"Yes'm," The Misfit said as if he agreed. "Jesus thown everything off balance. It was the same case with Him as with me except He hadn't committed any crime and they could prove I had committed one because they had the papers on me. Of course," he said, "they never shown me my papers. That's why I sign myself now. I said long ago, you get you a signature and sign everything you do and keep a copy of it. Then you'll know what you done and you can hold up the crime to the punishment and see do they match and in the end you'll have something to prove you ain't been treated right. I call myself The Misfit," he said, "because I can't make what all I done wrong fit what all I gone through in punishment."

There was a piercing scream from the woods, followed closely by a pistol report. "Does it seem right to you, lady, that one is punished a heap and another ain't punished at all?"

"Jesus!" the old lady cried. "You've got good blood! I know you wouldn't shoot a lady! I know you come from nice people! Pray! Jesus, you ought not to shoot a lady. I'll give you all the money I've got!"

"Lady," The Misfit said, looking beyond her far into the woods, "there never was a body that give the undertaker a tip."

There were two more pistol reports and the grandmother raised her head like a parched old turkey hen crying for water and called, "Bailey Boy, Bailey Boy!" as if her heart would break.

"Jesus was the only One that ever raised the dead," The Misfit continued, "and He shouldn't have done it. He thrown everything off balance. If He did what He said, then it's nothing for you to do but throw away everything and follow Him, and if He didn't, then it's nothing for you to do but enjoy the few minutes you got left the best way you can — by killing somebody or burning down his house or doing some other meanness to him. No pleasure but meanness," he said and his voice had become almost a snarl.

"Maybe He didn't raise the dead," the old lady mumbled, not knowing what she was saying and feeling so dizzy that she sank down in the ditch with her legs twisted under her.

"I wasn't there so I can't say He didn't," The Misfit said. "I wisht I had of been there," he said, hitting the ground with his fist. "It ain't right I wasn't there because if I had of been there I would of known. Listen lady," he said in a high voice, "if I had of been there I would of known and I wouldn't be like I am now." His voice seemed about to crack and the grandmother's head cleared for an instant. She saw the man's face twisted close to her own as if he were going to cry and she murmured, "Why you're one of my babies. You're one of my own children!" She reached out and touched him on the shoulder. The Misfit sprang back as if a snake had bitten him and shot her three times through the chest. Then he put his gun down on the ground and took off his glasses and began to clean them.

Hiram and Bobby Lee returned from the woods and stood over the ditch, looking down at the grandmother who half sat and half lay in a puddle of blood with her legs crossed under her like a child's and her face smiling up at the cloudless sky.

Without his glasses, The Misfit's eyes were red-rimmed and pale and defenseless-looking. "Take her off and throw her where you thrown the others," he said, picking up the cat that was rubbing itself against his leg.

"She was a talker, wasn't she?" Bobby Lee said, sliding down the ditch with a yodel.

"She would of been a good woman," The Misfit said, "if it had been somebody there to shoot her every minute of her life."

"Some fun!" Bobby Lee said.

"Shut up, Bobby Lee," The Misfit said. "It's no real pleasure in life."

TILLIE OLSEN

I Stand Here Ironing

I stand here ironing, and what you asked me moves tormented back and forth with the iron.

"I wish you would manage the time to come in and talk with me about your daughter. I'm sure you can help me understand her. She's a youngster who needs help and whom I'm deeply interested in helping."

"Who needs help." Even if I came, what good would it do? You think because I am her mother I have a key, or that in some way you could use me as a key? She has lived for nineteen years. There is all that life that has happened outside of me, beyond me.

And when is there time to remember, to sift, to weigh, to estimate, to total? I will start and there will be an interruption and I will have to gather it all together again. Or I will become engulfed with all I did or did not do, with what should have been and what cannot be helped.

She was a beautiful baby. The first and only of our five that was beautiful at birth. You do not guess how new and uneasy her tenancy in her now-loveliness. You did not know her all those years she was thought homely, or see her poring over her baby pictures, making me tell her over and over how beautiful she had been — and would be, I would tell her — and was now, to the seeing eye. But the seeing eyes were few or non-existent. Including mine.

I nursed her. They feel that's important nowadays. I nursed all the children, but with her, with all the fierce rigidity of first motherhood, I did like the books then said. Though her cries battered me to trembling and my breasts ached with swollenness, I waited till the clock decreed.

Why do I put that first? I do not even know if it matters, or if it explains anything.

She was a beautiful baby. She blew shining bubbles of sound. She loved motion, loved light, loved color and music and textures. She would lie on the floor in her blue overalls patting the surface so hard in ecstasy her hands and feet would blur. She was a miracle to me, but when she was eight months old I had to leave her daytimes with the woman downstairs to whom she was no miracle at all, for I worked or looked for work and for Emily's father, who "could no longer endure" (he wrote in his good-bye note) "sharing want with us."

I was nineteen. It was the pre-relief, pre-WPA world of the depression. I would start running as soon as I got off the streetcar, running up the stairs, the place smelling sour, and awake or asleep to startle awake, when she saw me she would break into a clogged weeping that could not be comforted, a weeping I can hear yet.

After a while I found a job hashing at night so I could be with her days, and it was better. But it came to where I had to bring her to his family and leave her.

It took a long time to raise the money for her fare back. Then she got chicken pox and I had to wait longer. When she finally came, I hardly knew her, walking quick and nervous like her father, looking like her father, thin, and dressed in a shoddy red that yellowed her skin and glared at the pockmarks. All the baby loveliness gone.

She was two. Old enough for nursery school they said, and I did not know then what I know now — the fatigue of the long day, and the lacerations of group life in the kinds of nurseries that are only parking places for children.

Except that it would have made no difference if I had known. It was the only place there was. It was the only way we could be together, the only way I could hold a job.

And even without knowing, I knew. I knew the teacher that was evil because all these years it has curdled into my memory, the little boy hunched in the corner, her rasp, "why aren't you outside, because Alvin hits you? that's no reason, go out, scaredy." I knew Emily hated it even if she did not clutch and implore "don't go Mommy" like the other children, mornings.

She always had a reason why we should stay home. Momma, you look sick, Momma. I feel sick. Momma, the teachers aren't there today, they're sick. Momma, we can't go, there was a fire there last night. Momma, it's a holiday today, no school, they told me.

But never a direct protest, never rebellion. I think of our others in their three, four-year-oldness — the explosions, the tempers, the denunciations, the demands — and I feel suddenly ill. I put the iron down. What in me demanded that goodness in her? And what was the cost, the cost to her of such goodness?

The old man living in the back once said in his gentle way: "You should smile at Emily more when you look at her." What *was* in my face when I looked at her? I loved her. There were all the acts of love.

It was only with the others I remembered what he said, and it was the face of joy, and not of care or tightness or worry I turned to them — too late for Emily. She does not smile easily, let alone almost always as her brothers and sisters do. Her face is closed and sombre, but when she wants, how fluid. You must have seen it in her pantomimes, you spoke of her rare gift for comedy on the stage that rouses a laughter out of the audience so dear they applaud and applaud and do not want to let her go.

Where does it come from, that comedy? There was none of it in her when she came back to me that second time, after I had had to send her away again. She had a new daddy now to learn to love, and I think perhaps it was a better time.

Except when we left her alone nights, telling ourselves she was old enough.

"Can't you go some other time, Mommy, like tomorrow?" she would ask. "Will it be just a little while you'll be gone? Do you promise?"

The time we came back, the front door open, the clock on the floor in the hall. She rigid awake. "It wasn't just a little while. I didn't cry. Three times I called you, just three times, and then I ran downstairs to open the door so you could come faster. The clock talked loud. I threw it away, it scared me what it talked."

She said the clock talked loud again that night I went to the hospital to have Susan. She was delirious with the fever that comes before red measles, but she was fully conscious all the week I was gone and the week after we were home when she could not come near the new baby or me.

She did not get well. She stayed skeleton thin, not wanting to eat, and night after night she had nightmares. She would call for me, and I would rouse from exhaustion to sleepily call back: "You're all right, darling, go to sleep, it's just a dream," and if she still called, in a sterner voice, "now go to sleep, Emily, there's nothing to hurt you." Twice, only twice, when I had to get up for Susan anyhow, I went in to sit with her.

Now when it is too late (as if she would let me hold and comfort her like I do the others) I get up and go to her at once at her moan or restless stirring. "Are you awake, Emily? Can I get you something?" And the answer is always the same: "No, I'm all right, go back to sleep, Mother."

They persuaded me at the clinic to send her away to a convalescent home in the country where "she can have the kind of food and care you can't manage for her, and you'll be free to concentrate on the new baby." They still send children to that place. I see pictures on the society page of sleek young women planning affairs to raise money for it, or dancing at the affairs, or decorating Easter eggs or filling Christmas stockings for the children.

They never have a picture of the children so I do not know if the girls still wear those gigantic red bows and the ravaged looks on the every other Sunday when parents can come to visit "unless otherwise notified" — as we were notified the first six weeks.

Oh it is a handsome place, green lawns and tall trees and fluted flower beds. High up on the balconies of each cottage the children stand, the girls in their red bows and white dresses, the boys in white suits and giant red ties. The parents stand below shrieking up to be heard and the children shriek down to be heard, and between them the invisible wall "Not To Be Contaminated by Parental Germs or Physical Affection."

There was a tiny girl who always stood hand in hand with Emily. Her parents never came. One visit she was gone. "They moved her to Rose College," Emily shouted in explanation. "They don't like you to love anybody here."

She wrote once a week, the labored writing of a seven-year-old. "I am fine. How is the baby. If I write my leter nicly I will have a star. Love." There never was a star. We wrote every other day, letters she could never hold or keep but only hear read — once. "We simply do not have room for children to keep any personal possessions," they patiently explained when we pieced one Sunday's shrieking together to plead how much it would mean to Emily, who loved so to keep things, to be allowed to keep her letters and cards.

Each visit she looked frailer. "She isn't eating," they told us.

(They had runny eggs for breakfast or mush with lumps, Emily said later, I'd hold it in my mouth and not swallow. Nothing ever tasted good, just when they had chicken.)

It took us eight months to get her released home, and only the fact that she gained back so little of her seven lost pounds convinced the social worker.

I used to try to hold and love her after she came back, but her body would stay stiff, and after a while she'd push away. She ate little. Food sickened her, and I think much of life too. Oh she had physical lightness and brightness, twinkling by on skates, bouncing like a ball up and down up and down over the jump rope, skimming over the hill; but these were momentary.

She fretted about her appearance, thin and dark and foreign-looking at a time when every little girl was supposed to look or thought she should look a chubby blonde replica of Shirley Temple. The doorbell sometimes rang for her, but no one seemed to come and play in the house or be a best friend. Maybe because we moved so much.

There was a boy she loved painfully through two school semesters. Months later she told me how she had taken pennies from my purse to buy him candy. "Licorice was his favorite and I brought him some every day, but he still liked Jennifer better'n me. Why, Mommy?" The kind of question for which there is no answer.

School was a worry to her. She was not glib or quick in a world where glibness and quickness were easily confused with ability to learn. To her overworked and exasperated teachers she was an over-conscientious "slow learner" who kept trying to catch up and was absent entirely too often.

I let her be absent, though sometimes the illness was imaginary. How different from my now-strictness about attendance with the others. I wasn't working. We had a new baby, I was home anyhow. Sometimes, after Susan grew old enough, I would keep her home from school, too, to have them all together.

Mostly Emily had asthma, and her breathing, harsh and labored, would fill the house with a curiously tranquil sound. I would bring the two old dresser mirrors and her boxes of collections to her bed. She would select beads and single earrings, bottle tops and shells, dried flowers and pebbles, old postcards, and scraps, all sorts of oddments; then she and Susan would play Kingdom, setting up landscapes and furniture, peopling them with action.

Those were the only times of peaceful companionship between her and Susan. I have edged away from it, that poisonous feeling between them, that terrible balancing of hurts and needs I had to do between the two, and did so badly, those earlier years.

Oh there are conflicts between the others too, each one human, needing, demanding, hurting, taking — but only between Emily and Susan, no, Emily toward Susan that corroding resentment. It seems so obvious on the surface, yet it is not obvious. Susan, the second child, Susan, golden- and curly-haired and chubby, quick and articulate and assured, everything in appearance and manner Emily was not; Susan, not able to resist Emily's precious things, losing or sometimes clumsily breaking them; Susan telling jokes and riddles to company for applause while Emily sat silent (to say to me later: that was *my* riddle, Mother, I told it to Susan); Susan, who for all the five years' difference in age was just a year behind Emily in developing physically.

I am glad for that slow physical development that widened the difference between her and her contemporaries, though she suffered over it. She was too vulnerable for that terrrible world of youthful competition, of preening and parading, of constant measuring of yourself against every other, of envy, "If I had that copper hair," "If I had that skin ..." She tormented herself enough about not looking like the others, there was enough of the unsureness, the having to be conscious of words before you speak, the constant caring — what are they thinking of me? without having it all magnified by the merciless physical drives.

Ronnie is calling. He is wet and I change him. It is rare there is such a cry now. That time of motherhood is almost behind me when the ear is not one's own but must always be racked and listening for the child cry, the child call. We sit for a while and I hold him, looking out over the city spread in charcoal with its soft aisles of light. "*Shoogily*," he breathes and curls closer. I carry him back to bed, asleep. *Shoogily.* A funny word, a family word, inherited from Emily, invented by her to say: *comfort.*

In this and other ways she leaves her seal, I say aloud. And startle at my saying it. What do I mean? What did I start to gather together, to try and make coherent? I was at the terrible, growing years. War years. I do not remember them well. I was working, there were four smaller ones now, there was not time for her. She had to help be a mother, and housekeeper, and shopper, She had to set her seal. Mornings of crisis and near hysteria trying to get lunches packed, hair combed, coats and shoes found, everyone to school or Child Care on time, the baby ready for transportation. And always the paper scribbled on by a smaller one, the book looked at by Susan then mislaid, the homework not done. Running out to that huge school where she was one, she was lost, she was a drop; suffering over the unpreparedness, stammering and unsure in her classes.

There was so little time left at night after the kids were bedded down. She would struggle over books, always eating (it was in those years she developed her enormous appetite that is legendary in our family) and I would be ironing, or preparing food for the next day, or writing V-mail to Bill, or tending the baby. Sometimes, to make me laugh, or out of her despair, she would imitate happenings or types at school.

I think I said once: "Why don't you do something like this in the school amateur show?" One morning she phoned me at work, hardly understandable through the weeping: "Mother, I did it. I won, I won; they gave me first prize; they clapped and clapped and wouldn't let me go."

Now suddenly she was Somebody, and as imprisoned in her difference as she had been in anonymity.

She began to be asked to perform at other high schools, even in colleges, then at city and statewide affairs. The first one we went to, I only recognized her that first moment when thin, shy, she almost drowned herself into the curtains. Then: Was this Emily? The control, the command, the convulsing and deadly clowning, the spell, then the roaring, stamping audience, unwilling to let this rare and precious laughter out of their lives.

Afterwards: You ought to do something about her with a gift like that — but without money or knowing how, what does one do? We have left it all to her, and the gift has as often eddied inside, clogged and clotted, as been used and growing.

She is coming. She runs up the stairs two at a

time with her light graceful step, and I know she is happy tonight. Whatever it was that occasioned your call did not happen today.

"Aren't you ever going to finish the ironing, Mother? Whistler painted his mother in a rocker. I'd have to paint mine standing over an ironing board." This is one of her communicative nights and she tells me everything and nothing as she fixes herself a plate of food out of the icebox.

She is so lovely. Why did you want me to come in at all? Why were you concerned? She will find her way.

She starts up the stairs to bed. "Don't get me up with the rest in the morning." "But I thought you were having midterms." "Oh, those," she comes back in, kisses me, and says quite lightly," in a couple of years when we'll all be atom-dead they won't matter a bit."

She has said it before. She *believes* it. But because I have been developing the past, and all that compounds a human being is so heavy and meaningful in me, I cannot endure it tonight.

I will never total it all. I will never come in to say: She was a child seldom smiled at. Her father left me before she was a year old. I had to work her first six years when there was work, or I sent her home and to his relatives. There were years she had care she hated. She was dark and thin and foreign-looking in a world where the prestige went to blondeness and curly hair and dimples, she was slow where glibness was prized. She was a child of anxious, not proud, love. We were poor and could not afford for her the soil of easy growth. I was a young mother, I was a distracted mother. There were the other children pushing up, demanding. Her younger sister seemed all that she was not. There were years she did not let me touch her. She kept too much in herself, her life was such she had to keep too much in herself. My wisdom came too late. She has much to her and probably little will come of it. She is a child of her age, of depression, of war, of fear.

Let her be. So all that is in her will not bloom — but in how many does it? There is still enough left to live by. Only help her to know — help make it so there is cause for her to know — that she is more than this dress on the ironing board, helpless before the iron.

EDGAR ALLAN POE

The Fall of the House of Usher

Son coeur est un luth suspendu;
Sitôt qu'on le touche il rèsonne.
De Béranger[1]

During the whole of a dull, dark, and soundless day in the autumn of the year, when the clouds hung oppressively low in the heavens, I had been passing alone, on horseback, through a singularly dreary tract of country; and at length found myself, as the shades of the evening drew on, within view of the melancholy House of Usher. I know not how it was — but, with the first glimpse of the building, a sense of insufferable gloom pervaded my spirit. I say insufferable; for the feeling was unrelieved by any of that half-pleasurable, because poetic, sentiment, with which the mind usually receives even the sternest natural images of the desolate or terrible. I looked upon the scene before me — upon the mere house, and the simple landscape features of the domain — upon the bleak walls — upon the vacant eye-like windows — upon a few rank sedges — and upon a few white trunks of decayed trees — with an utter depression of soul which I can compare to no earthly sensation more properly than to the after-dream of the reveller upon opium — the bitter lapse into everyday life — the hideous dropping off of the veil. There was an iciness, a sinking, a sickening of the heart — an unredeemed dreariness of thought which no goading of the imagination could torture into aught of the sublime. What was it — I paused to think — what was it that so unnerved me in the contemplation of the House of Usher? It was a mystery all insoluble; nor could I grapple with the shadowy fancies that crowded upon me as I pondered. I was forced to fall back upon the unsatisfactory conclusion, that while, beyond doubt, there *are* combinations of very simple natural objects which have the power of thus affecting us, still the analysis of this power lies among considerations beyond our depth. It was possible, I reflected, that a mere different arrangement of the particulars of the scene, of the details of the picture, would be sufficient to modify, or perhaps to annihilate its capacity for sorrowful impression; and, acting upon this idea, I reined my horse to the precipitous brink of a black and lurid tarn that lay in unruffled lustre by the dwelling, and gazed down — but with a shudder even more thrilling than before — upon the remodelled and inverted images of the gray sedge, and the ghastly tree-stems, and the vacant and eye-like windows.

Nevertheless, in this mansion of gloom I now proposed to myself a sojourn of some weeks. Its proprietor, Roderick Usher, had been one of my boon companions in boyhood; but many years had elapsed since our last meeting. A letter, however, had lately reached me in a distant part of the country — a letter from him — which, in its wildly importunate nature, had admitted of no other than a personal reply. The MS. gave evidence of nervous agitation. The writer spoke of acute bodily illness — of a mental disorder which oppressed him — and of an earnest desire to see me, as his best, and indeed his only personal friend, with a view of attempting, by the cheerfulness of my society, some alleviation of his malady. It was the manner in which all this, and much more, was said — it was the apparent *heart* that went with his request — which allowed me no room for hesitation; and I accordingly obeyed forthwith what I still considered a very singular summons.

Although, as boys, we had been even intimate associates, yet I really knew little of my friend. His reserve had been always excessive and habitual. I was aware, however, that his very ancient family had been noted, time out of mind, for a peculiar sensibility of temperament, displaying itself, through long ages, in many works of exalted art, and manifested, of late, in repeated deeds of munificent yet unobtrusive charity, as well as in a passionate devotion to the intricacies, perhaps even more than to the orthodox and easily recognisable beauties, of musical science. I had learned, too, the very remarkable fact, that the stem of the Usher race, all time-honored as it was, had put forth, at no period, any enduring branch; in other words, that the entire family lay in the direct line of descent, and had always, with very trifling and very temporary variation, so lain. It was this deficiency, I considered, while running over in thought the perfect keeping of the character of the premises with the accredited character of the people, and while speculating upon the possible influence which the one, in the long lapse of cen-

1. 'His heart is a hanging lute; As soon as it is touched it resounds.'

turies, might have exercised upon the other — it was this deficiency, perhaps, of collateral issue, and the consequent undeviating transmission, from sire to son, of the patrimony with the name, which had, at length, so identified the two as to merge the original title of the estate in the quaint and equivocal appellation of the 'House of Usher' — an appellation which seemed to include, in the minds of the peasantry who used it, both the family and the family mansion.

I have said that the sole effect of my somewhat childish experiment — that of looking down within the tarn — had been to deepen the first singular impression. There can be no doubt that the consciousness of the rapid increase of my superstition — for why should I not so term it? — served mainly to accelerate the increase itself. Such, I have long known, is the paradoxical law of all sentiments having terror as a basis. And it might have been for this reason only, that, when I again uplifted my eyes to the house itself, from its image in the pool, there grew in my mind a strange fancy — a fancy so ridiculous, indeed, that I but mention it to show the vivid force of the sensations which oppressed me. I had so worked upon my imagination as really to believe that about the whole mansion and domain there hung an atmosphere peculiar to themselves and their immediate vicinity — an atmosphere which had no affinity with the air of heaven, but which had reeked up from the decayed trees, and the gray wall, and the silent tarn — a pestilent and mystic vapor, dull, sluggish, faintly discernible, and leaden-hued.

Shaking off from my spirit what *must* have been a dream, I scanned more narrowly the real aspect of the building. Its principal feature seemed to be that of an excessive antiquity. The discoloration of ages had been great. Minute fungi overspread the whole exterior, hanging in a fine tangled web-work from the eaves. Yet all this was apart from any extraordinary dilapidation. No portion of the masonry had fallen; and there appeared to be a wild inconsistency between its still perfect adaptation of parts, and the crumbling condition of the individual stones. In this there was much that reminded me of the specious totality of old wood-work which has rotted for long years in some neglected vault, with no disturbance from the breath of the external air. Beyond this indication of extensive decay, however, the fabric gave little token of instability. Perhaps the eye of a scrutinizing observer might have discovered a barely perceptible fissure, which, extending from the roof of the building in front, made its way down the wall in a zigzag direction, until it became lost in the sullen waters of the tarn.

Noticing these things, I rode over a short causeway to the house. A servant in waiting took my horse, and I entered the Gothic archway of the hall. A valet, of stealthy step, thence conducted me, in silence, through many dark and intricate passages in my progress to the *studio* of his master. Much that I encountered on the way contributed, I know not how, to heighten the vague sentiments of which I have already spoken. While the objects around me — while the carvings of the ceilings, the sombre tapestries of the walls, the ebon blackness of the floors, and the phantasmagoric armorial trophies which rattled as I strode, were but matters to which, or to such as which, I had been accustomed from my infancy — while I hesitated not to acknowledge how familiar was all this — I still wondered to find how unfamiliar were the fancies which ordinary images were stirring up. On one of the staircases, I met the physician of the family. His countenance, I thought, wore a mingled expression of low cunning and perplexity. He accosted me with trepidation and passed on. The valet now threw open a door and ushered me into the presence of his master.

The room in which I found myself was very large and lofty. The windows were long, narrow, and pointed, and at so vast a distance from the black oaken floor as to be altogether inaccessible from within. Feeble gleams of encrimsoned light made their way through the trellissed panes, and served to render sufficiently distinct the more prominent objects around; the eye, however, struggled in vain to reach the remoter angles of the chamber, or the recesses of the vaulted and fretted ceiling. Dark draperies hung upon the walls. The general furniture was profuse, comfortless, antique, and tattered. Many books and musical instruments lay scattered about, but failed to give any vitality to the scene. I felt that I breathed an atmosphere of sorrow. An air of stern, deep, and irredeemable gloom hung over and pervaded all.

Upon my entrance, Usher arose from a sofa on which he had been lying at full length, and greeted me with a vivacious warmth which had much in it, I at first thought, of an overdone cordiality — of the constrained effort of the *ennuyé* man of the world. A glance, however, at his countenance, convinced me of his perfect sincerity. We sat down; and for some moments, while he spoke not, I gazed upon him with a feeling half of pity, half of awe. Surely, man had never before so terribly altered, in so brief a period, as had Roderick Usher! It was with difficulty that I could bring myself to admit the identity of the wan being before me with the companion of my early boyhood. Yet the character of his face had been at all times remarkable. A cadaverousness of complexion; an eye large, liquid, and luminous beyond comparison; lips somewhat thin and very pallid, but of a surpassingly beautiful curve; a nose of a delicate Hebrew model, but with a breadth of nostril unusual in similar formations; a finely moulded chin, speaking, in its want of prominence, of a want of moral energy; hair of a more than web-like softness and tenuity; these features, with an inordinate expansion above the regions of the temple, made up altogether a countenance not easily to be forgotten. And now in the mere exaggeration of the prevailing character of these features, and of the expression they were wont to convey, lay so much of change that I doubted to whom I spoke. The now ghastly pallor of the skin, and the now miraculous lustre of the eye, above all things startled and even awed me. The silken hair, too, had been suffered to grow all unheeded, and as, in its wild gossamer texture, it floated rather than fell about the face, I could not, even with effort, connect its Arabesque expression with any idea of simple humanity.

In the manner of my friend I was at once struck with an incoherence — an inconsistency; and I soon found this to arise from a series of feeble and futile struggles to overcome an habitual trepidancy — an excessive nervous agitation. For something of this nature I had indeed been prepared, no less by his letter, than by reminiscences of certain boyish traits, and by conclusions deduced from his peculiar physical conformation and temperament. His action was alternately vivacious and sullen. His voice varied rapidly from a tremulous indecision (when the animal spirits seemed utterly in abeyance) to that species of energetic concision — that abrupt, weighty, unhurried, and hollow-sounding enunciation — that leaden, self-balanced and perfectly modulated guttural utterance, which may be observed in the lost drunkard, or the irreclaimable eater of opium, during the periods of his most intense excitement.

It was thus that he spoke of the object of my visit, of his earnest desire to see me, and of the solace he expected me to afford him. He entered, at some length, into what he conceived to be the nature of his malady. It was, he said, a constitutional and a family evil, and one for which he despaired to find a remedy — a mere nervous affection, he immediately added, which would undoubtedly soon pass off. It displayed itself in a host of unnatural sensations. Some of these, as he detailed them, interested and bewildered me; although, perhaps, the terms, and the general manner of the narration had their weight. He suffered much from a morbid acuteness of the senses; the most insipid food was alone endurable; he could wear only garments of certain texture; the odors of all flowers were oppressive; his eyes were tortured by even a faint light; and there were but peculiar sounds, and these from stringed instruments, which did not inspire him with horror.

To an anomalous species of terror I found him a bounden slave. 'I shall perish,' said he, 'I *must* perish in this deplorable folly. Thus, thus, and not otherwise, shall I be lost. I dread the events of the future, not in themselves, but in their results. I shudder at the thought of any, even the most trivial, incident, which may operate upon this intolerable agitation of soul. I have, indeed, no abhorrence of danger, except in its absolute effect — in terror. In this unnerved — in this pitiable condition — I feel that the period will sooner or later arrive when I must abandon life and reason together, in some struggle with the grim phantasm, FEAR.'

I learned, moreover, at intervals, and through broken and equivocal hints, another singular feature of his mental condition. He was enchained by certain superstitious impressions in regard to the dwelling which he tenanted, and whence, for many years, he had never ventured forth — in regard to an influence whose supposititious force was conveyed in terms too shadowy here to be restated — an influence which some peculiarities in the mere form and substance of his family mansion, had, by dint of long sufferance, he said, obtained over his spirit — an effect which the *physique* of the gray walls and turrets, and of the dim tarn into which they all looked down, had, at length, brought about upon the *morale* of his existence.

He admitted, however, although with hesitation, that much of the peculiar gloom which thus afflicted him could be traced to a more natural and far more palpable origin — to the severe and long-continued illness — indeed to the evidently approaching dissolution — of a tenderly beloved sister — his sole companion for long years — his last and only relative on earth. 'Her decease,' he said, with a bitterness which I can never forget, 'would leave him (him the hopeless and the frail) the last of the ancient race of the Ushers.' While he spoke, the lady Madeline (for so was she called) passed slowly through a remote portion of the apartment, and, without having noticed my presence, disappeared. I regarded her with an utter astonishment not unmingled with dread — and yet I found it impossible to account for such feelings. A sensation of stupor oppressed me, as my eyes followed her retreating steps. When a door, at length, closed upon her, my glance sought instinctively and eagerly the countenance of the brother — but he had buried his face in his hands, and I could only perceive that a far more than ordinary wanness had overspread the emaciated fingers through which trickled many passionate tears.

The disease of the lady Madeline had long baffled the skill of her physicians. A settled apathy, a gradual wasting away of the person, and frequent although transient affections of a partially cataleptical character, were the unusual diagnosis. Hitherto she had steadily borne up against the pressure of her malady, and had not betaken herself finally to bed; but, on the closing in of the evening of my arrival at the house, she succumbed (as her brother told me at night with inexpressible agitation) to the prostrating power of the destroyer; and I learned that the glimpse I had obtained of her person would thus probably be the last I should obtain — that the lady, at least while living, would be seen by me no more.

For several days ensuing, her name was unmentioned by either Usher or myself: and during this period I was busied in earnest endeavors to alleviate the melancholy of my friend. We painted and read together; or I listened, as if in a dream, to the wild improvisations of his speaking guitar. And thus, as a closer and still closer intimacy admitted me more unreservedly into the recesses of his spirit, the more bitterly did I perceive the futility of all attempt at cheering a mind from which darkness, as if an inherent positive quality, poured forth upon all objects of the moral and physical universe, in one unceasing radiation of gloom.

I shall ever bear about me a memory of the many solemn hours I thus spent alone with the master of the House of Usher. Yet I should fail in any attempt to convey an idea of the exact character of the studies, or of the occupations, in which he involved me, or led me the way. An excited and highly distempered ideality threw a sulphureous lustre over all. His long improvised dirges will ring forever in my ears. Among other things, I hold painfully in mind a certain singular perversion and amplification of the wild air of the last waltz of Von Weber. From the paintings over which his elaborate fancy brooded, and which grew, touch by touch, into vaguenesses at which I shuddered the more thrillingly, because I shuddered knowing not why; — from these paintings (vivid as their images now are before me) I would in vain endeavor to educe more than a small portion which should lie within the compass of merely written words. By the utter simplicity, by the nakedness of his designs, he arrested and overawed attention. If ever mortal painted an idea, that mortal was Roderick Usher. For me at least — in the circumstances then surrounding me — there arose out of the pure abstractions which the hypochondriac contrived to throw upon his canvass, an intensity of intolerable awe, no shadow of which felt I ever yet in the contemplation of the certainly glowing yet too concrete reveries of Fuseli.

One of the phantasmagoric conceptions of my friend, partaking not so rigidly of the spirit of abstraction, may be shadowed forth, although feebly, in words. A small picture presented the interior of an immensely long and rectangular vault or tunnel, with low walls, smooth, white, and without interruption or device. Certain accessory points of the design served well to convey the idea that this excavation lay at an exceeding depth below the surface of the earth. No outlet was observed in any portion of its vast extent, and no torch, or other artificial source of light was discernible; yet a flood of intense rays rolled throughout, and bathed the whole in a ghastly and inappropriate splendor.

I have just spoken of that morbid condition of the auditory nerve which rendered all music intolerable to the sufferer, with the exception of certain effects of stringed instruments. It was, perhaps, the narrow limits to which he thus confined himself upon the guitar, which gave birth, in great measure, to the fantastic character of his performances. But the fervid *facility* of his *impromptus* could not be so accounted for. They must have been, and were, in the notes, as well as in the words of his wild fantasias (for he not unfrequently accompanied himself with rhymed verbal improvisations), the result of that intense mental collectedness and concentration to which I have previously alluded as observable only in particular moments of the highest artificial excitement. The words of one of these rhapsodies I have easily remembered. I was, perhaps, the more forcibly impressed with it, as he gave it, because, in the under or mystic current of its meaning, I fancied that I perceived, and for the first time, a full consciousness on the part of Usher, of the tottering of his lofty reason upon her throne. The verses, which were entitled 'The Haunted Palace,' ran very nearly, if not accurately, thus:

I

In the greenest of our valleys,
  By good angels tenanted,
Once a fair and stately palace —
  Radiant palace — reared its head.
In the monarch Thought's dominion —
  It stood there!
Never seraph spread a pinion
  Over fabric half so fair.

II

Banners yellow, glorious, golden,
  On its roof did float and flow;
(This — all this — was in the olden
  Time long ago)
And every gentle air that dallied,
  In that sweet day,
Along the ramparts plumed and pallid,
  A winged odor went away.

III

Wanderers in that happy valley
  Through two luminous windows saw
Spirits moving musically
  To a lute's well-tunéd law,
Round about a throne, where sitting
  (Porphyrogene!)
In state his glory well befitting,
  The ruler of the realm was seen.

IV

And all with pearl and ruby glowing
  Was the fair palace door,
Through which came flowing, flowing, flowing,
  And sparkling evermore,
A troop of Echoes whose sweet duty

Was but to sing,
In voices of surpassing beauty,
The wit and wisdom of their king.

V

But evil things, in robes of sorrow,
Assailed the monarch's high estate;
(Ah, let us mourn, for never morrow
Shall dawn upon him, desolate!)
And, round about his home, the glory
That blushed and bloomed
Is but a dim-remembered story
Of the old time entombed.

VI

And travellers now within that valley,
Through the red-litten windows, see
Vast forms that move fantastically
To a discordant melody;
While, like a rapid ghastly river,
Through the pale door,
A hideous throng rush out forever,
And laugh — but smile no more.

I well remember that suggestions arising from this ballad, led us into a train of thought wherein there became manifest an opinion of Usher's which I mention not so much on account of its novelty, (for other men have thought thus,) as on account of the pertinacity with which he maintained it. This opinion, in its general form, was that of the sentience of all vegetable things. But, in his disordered fancy, the idea had assumed a more daring character, and trespassed, under certain conditions, upon the kingdom of inorganization. I lack words to express the full extent, or the earnest *abandon* of his persuasion. The belief, however, was connected (as I have previously hinted) with the gray stones of the home of his forefathers. The conditions of the sentience had been here, he imagined, fulfilled in the method of collocation of these stones — in the order of their arrangement, as well as in that of the many *fungi* which overspread them, and of the decayed trees which stood around — above all, in the long undisturbed endurance of this arrangement, and in its reduplication in the still waters of the tarn. Its evidence — the evidence of the sentience — was to be seen, he said, (and I here started as he spoke,) in the gradual yet certain condensation of an atmosphere of their own about the waters and the walls. The result was discoverable, he added, in that silent, yet importunate and terrible influence which for centuries had moulded the destinies of his family, and which made *him* what I now saw him — what he was. Such opinions need no comment, and I will make none.

Our books — the books which, for years, had formed no small portion of the mental existence of the invalid — were, as might be supposed, in strict keeping with this character of phantasm. We pored together over such works as the Ververt et Chartreuse of Gresset; the Belphegor of Machiavelli; the Heaven and Hell of Swedenborg; the Subterranean Voyage of Nicholas Klimm by Holberg; the Chiromancy of Robert Flud, of Jean D'Indaginé, and of De la Chambre; the Journey into the Blue Distance of Tieck; and the City of the Sun of Campanella. One favorite volume was a small octavo edition of the *Directorium Inquisitorium*, by the Dominican Eymeric de Gironne; and there were passages in Pomponius Mela, about the old African Satyrs and Ægipans, over which Usher would sit dreaming for hours. His chief delight, however, was found in the perusal of an exceedingly rare and curious book in quarto Gothic — the manual of a forgotten church — the *Vigiliae Mortuorum secundum Chorum Ecclesiae Maguntinae*.

I could not help thinking of the wild ritual of this work, and of its probable influence upon the hypochondriac, when, one evening, having informed me abruptly that the lady Madeline was no more, he stated his intention of preserving her corpse for a fortnight, (previously to its final interment,) in one of the numerous vaults within the main walls of the building. The worldly reason, however, assigned for this singular proceeding, was one which I did not feel at liberty to dispute. The brother had been led to his resolution (so he told me) by consideration of the unusual character of the malady of the deceased, of certain obtrusive and eager inquiries on the part of her medical men, and of the remote and exposed situation of the burial-ground of the family. I will not deny that when I called to mind the sinister countenance of the person whom I met upon the staircase, on the day of my arrival at the house, I had no desire to oppose what I regarded as at best but a harmless, and by no means an unnatural, precaution.

At the request of Usher, I personally aided him in the arrangements for the temporary entombment. The body having been encoffined, we two alone bore it to its rest. The vault in which we placed it (and which had been so long unopened that our torches, half smothered in its oppressive atmosphere, gave us little opportunity for investigation) was small, damp, and entirely without means of admission for light; lying, at great depth, immediately beneath that portion of the building in which was my own sleeping apartment. It had been used, apparently, in remote feudal times, for the worst purposes of a donjon-keep, and, in later days, as a place of deposit for powder, or some other highly combustible substance, as a portion of its floor, and the whole interior of a long archway through which we reached it, were carefully sheathed with copper. The door, of massive iron, had been, also, similarly protected. Its immense weight caused an unusually sharp grating sound, as it moved upon its hinges.

Having deposited our mournful burden upon tressels within this region of horror, we partially turned aside the yet unscrewed lid of the coffin, and looked upon the face of the tenant. A striking similitude between the brother and sister now first arrested my attention; and Usher, divining, perhaps, my thoughts, murmured out some few words from which I learned that the deceased and himself had been twins, and that sympathies of a scarcely intelligible nature had always existed between them. Our glances, however, rested not long upon the dead — for we could not regard her unawed. The disease which had thus entombed the lady in the maturity of youth, had left, as usual in all maladies of a strictly cataleptical character, the mockery of a faint blush upon the bosom and the face, and that suspiciously lingering smile upon the lip which is so terrible in death. We replaced and screwed down the lid, and, having secured the door of iron, made our way, with toil, into the scarcely less gloomy apartments of the upper portion of the house.

And now, some days of bitter grief having elapsed, an observable change came over the features of the mental disorder of my friend. His ordinary manner had vanished. His ordinary occupations were neglected or forgotten. He roamed from chamber to chamber with hurried, unequal, and objectless step. The pallor of his countenance had assumed, if possible, a more ghastly hue — but the luminousness of his eye had utterly gone out. The once occasional huskiness of his tone was heard no more; and a tremulous quaver, as if of extreme terror, habitually characterized his utterance. There were times, indeed, when I thought his unceasingly agitated mind was laboring with some oppressive secret, to divulge which he struggled for the necessary courage. At times, again, I was obliged to resolve all into the mere inexplicable vagaries of madness, for I beheld him gazing upon vacancy for long hours, in an attitude of the profoundest attention, as if listening to some imaginary sound. It was no wonder that his condition terrified — that it infected me. I felt creeping upon me, by slow yet certain degrees, the wild influences of his own fantastic yet impressive superstitions.

It was, especially, upon retiring to bed late in the night of the seventh or eighth day after the placing of the lady Madeline within the donjon, that I experienced the full power of such feelings. Sleep came not near my couch — while the hours waned and waned away. I struggled to reason off the nervousness which had dominion over me. I endeavored to believe that much, if not all of what I felt, was due to the bewildering influence of the gloomy furniture of the room — of the dark and tattered draperies, which, tortured into motion by the breath of a rising tempest, swayed fitfully to and fro upon the walls, and rustled uneasily about the decorations of the bed. But my efforts were fruitless. An irrepressible tremor gradually pervaded my frame; and, at length, there sat upon my very heart an incubus of utterly causeless alarm. Shaking this off with a gasp and a struggle, I uplifted myself upon the pillows, and, peering earnestly within the intense darkness of the chamber, harkened — I know not why, except that an instinctive spirit prompted me — to certain low and indefinite sounds which came, through the pauses of the storm, at long intervals, I knew not whence. Overpowered by an intense sentiment of horror, unaccountable yet unendurable, I threw on my clothes with haste (for I felt that I should sleep no more during the night), and endeavored to arouse myself from the pitiable condition into which I had fallen, by pacing rapidly to and fro through the apartment.

I had taken but few turns in this manner, when a light step on an adjoining staircase arrested my attention. I presently recognised it as that of Usher. In an instant afterward he rapped, with a gentle touch, at my door, and entered, bearing a lamp. His countenance was, as usual, cadaverously wan — but, moreover, there was a species of mad hilarity in his eyes — an evidently restrained *hysteria* in his whole demeanor. His air appalled me — but anything was preferable to the solitude which I had so long endured, and I even welcomed his presence as a relief.

'And you have not seen it?' he said abruptly, after having stared about him for some moments in silence — 'you have not then seen it? — but, stay! you shall.' Thus speaking, and having carefully shaded his lamp, he hurried to one of the casements, and threw it freely open to the storm.

The impetuous fury of the entering gust nearly lifted us from our feet. It was, indeed, a tempestuous yet sternly beautiful night, and one wildly singular in its terror and its beauty. A whirlwind had apparently collected its force in our vicinity; for there were frequent and violent alterations in the direction of the wind; and the exceeding density of the clouds (which hung so low as to press upon the turrets of the house) did not prevent our perceiving the life-like velocity with which they flew careering from all points against each other, without passing away into the distance. I say that even their exceeding density did not prevent our perceiving this — yet we had no glimpse of the moon or stars — nor was there any flashing forth of the lightning. But the under surfaces of the huge masses of agitated vapor, as well as all terrestrial objects immediately around us, were glowing in the unnatural light of a faintly luminous and distinctly visible gaseous exhalation which hung about and enshrouded the mansion.

'You must not — you shall not behold this!' said

I, shudderingly, to Usher, as I led him, with a gentle violence, from the window to a seat. 'These appearances, which bewilder you, are merely electrical phenomena not uncommon — or it may be that they have their ghastly origin in the rank miasma of the tarn. Let us close this casement; — the air is chilling and dangerous to your frame. Here is one of your favorite romances. I will read, and you shall listen; — and so we will pass away this terrible night together.'

The antique volume which I had taken up was the 'Mad Trist' of Sir Launcelot Canning; but I had called it a favorite of Usher's more in sad jest than in earnest; for, in truth, there is little in its uncouth and unimaginative prolixity which could have had interest for the lofty and spiritual ideality of my friend. It was, however, the only book immediately at hand; and I indulged a vague hope that the excitement which now agitated the hypochondriac, might find relief (for the history of mental disorder is full of similar anomalies) even in the extremeness of the folly which I should read. Could I have judged, indeed, by the wild overstrained air of vivacity with which he harkened, or apparently harkened, to the words of the tale, I might well have congratulated myself upon the success of my design.

I had arrived at that well-known portion of the story where Ethelred, the hero of the Trist, having sought in vain for peaceable admission into the dwelling of the hermit, proceeds to make good an entrance by force. Here, it will be remembered, the words of the narrative run thus:

'And Ethelred, who was by nature of a doughty heart, and who was now mighty withal, on account of the powerfulness of the wine which he had drunken, waited no longer to hold parley with the hermit, who, in sooth, was of an obstinate and maliceful turn, but, feeling the rain upon his shoulders, and fearing the rising of the tempest, uplifted his mace outright, and, with blows, made quickly room in the plankings of the door for his gauntleted hand; and now pulling therewith sturdily, he so cracked, and ripped, and tore all asunder, that the noise of the dry and hollow-sounding wood alarummed and reverberated throughout the forest.'

At the termination of this sentence I started, and for a moment, paused; for it appeared to me (although I at once concluded that my excited fancy had deceived me) — it appeared to me that, from some very remote portion of the mansion, there came, indistinctly, to my ears, what might have been, in its exact similarity of character, the echo (but a stifled and dull one certainly) of the very cracking and ripping sound which Sir Launcelot had so particularly described. It was, beyond doubt, the coincidence alone which had arrested my attention; for, amid the rattling of the sashes of the casements, and the ordinary commingled noises of the still increasing storm, the sound, in itself, had nothing, surely, which should have interested or disturbed me. I continued the story:

'But the good champion Ethelred, now entering within the door, was sore enraged and amazed to perceive no signal of the maliceful hermit; but, in the stead thereof, a dragon of a scaly and prodigious demeanor, and of a fiery tongue, which sate in guard before a palace of gold, with a floor of silver; and upon the wall there hung a shield of shining brass with this legend enwritten —

Who entereth herein, a conqueror hath bin;
Who slayeth the dragon, the shield he shall win;

And Ethelred uplifted his mace, and struck upon the head of the dragon, which fell before him, and gave up his pesty breath, with a shriek so horrid and harsh, and withal so piercing, that Ethelred had fain to close his ears with his hands against the dreadful noise of it, the like whereof was never before heard.'

Here again I paused abruptly, and now with a feeling of wild amazement — for there could be no doubt whatever that, in this instance, I did actually hear (although from what direction it proceeded I found it impossible to say) a low and apparently distant, but harsh, protracted, and most unusual screaming or grating sound — the exact counterpart of what my fancy had already conjured up for the dragon's unnatural shriek as described by the romancer.

Oppressed, as I certainly was, upon the occurrence of this second and most extraordinary coincidence, by a thousand conflicting sensations, in which wonder and extreme terror were predominant, I still retained sufficient presence of mind to avoid exciting, by any observation, the sensitive nervousness of my companion. I was by no means certain that he had noticed the sounds in question; although, assuredly, a strange alteration had, during the last few minutes, taken place in his demeanor. From a position fronting my own, he had gradually brought round his chair, so as to sit with his face to the door of the chamber; and thus I could but partially perceive his features, although I saw that his lips trembled as if he were murmuring inaudibly. His head had dropped upon his breast — yet I knew that he was not asleep, from the wide and rigid opening of the eye as I caught a glance of it in profile. The motion of his body, too, was at variance with this idea — for he rocked from side to side with a gentle yet constant and uniform sway. Having rapidly taken notice of all this, I resumed the narrative of Sir Launcelot, which thus proceeded:

'And now, the champion, having escaped from the terrible fury of the dragon, bethinking himself of the brazen shield, and of the breaking up of the enchantment which was upon it, removed the carcass from out of the way before him, and approached valorously over the silver pavement of the castle to where the shield was upon the wall; which in sooth tarried not for his full coming, but fell down at his feet upon the silver floor, with a mighty great and terrible ringing sound.'

No sooner had these syllables passed my lips, than — as if a shield of brass had indeed, at the moment fallen heavily upon a floor of silver — I became aware of a distinct, hollow, metallic, and clangorous, yet apparently muffled reverberation. Completely unnerved, I leaped to my feet; but the measured rocking movement of Usher was undisturbed. I rushed to the chair in which he sat. His eyes were bent fixedly before him, and throughout his whole countenance there reigned a stony rigidity. But, as I placed my hand upon his shoulder, there came a strong shudder over his whole person; a sickly smile quivered about his lips; and I saw that he spoke in a low, hurried, and gibbering murmur, as if unconscious of my presence. Bending closely over him, I at length drank in the hideous import of his words.

'Not hear it? — yes, I hear it, and *have* heard it. Long — long — long — many minutes, many hours, many days, have I heard it — yet I dared not — oh, pity me, miserable wretch that I am! — I dared not — I *dared* not speak! *We have put her living in the tomb!* Said I not that my senses were acute? I *now* tell you that I heard her first feeble movements in the hollow coffin. I heard them — many, many days ago — yet I dared not — *I dared not speak!* And now — to-night — Ethelred — ha! ha! — the breaking of the hermit's door, and the death-cry of the dragon, and the clangor of the shield! — say, rather, the rending of her coffin, and the grating of the iron hinges of her prison, and her struggles within the coppered archway of the vault! Oh whither shall I fly? Will she not be here anon? Is she not hurrying to upbraid me for my haste? Have I not heard her footstep on the stair? Do I not distinguish that heavy and horrible beating of her heart? Madman!' — here he sprang furiously to his feet, and shrieked out his syllables, as if in the effort he were giving up his soul — *'Madman! I tell you that she now stands without the door!'*

As if in the superhuman energy of his utterance there had been found the potency of a spell — the huge antique pannels to which the speaker pointed, threw slowly back, upon the instant, their ponderous and ebony jaws. It was the work of the rushing gust — but then without those doors there *did* stand the lofty and enshrouded figure of the lady Madeline of Usher. There was blood upon her white robes, and the evidence of some bitter struggle upon every portion of her emaciated frame. For a moment she remained trembling and reeling to and fro upon the threshold — then, with a low moaning cry, fell heavily inward upon the person of her brother, and in her violent and now final death-agonies, bore him to the floor a corpse, and a victim to the terrors he had anticipated.

From that chamber, and from that mansion, I fled aghast. The storm was still abroad in all its wrath as I found myself crossing the old causeway. Suddenly there shot along the path a wild light, and I turned to see whence a gleam so unusual could have issued; for the vast house and its shadows were alone behind me. The radiance was that of the full, setting, and blood-red moon, which now shone vividly through that once barely-discernible fissure, of which I have before spoken as extending from the roof of the building, in a zigzag direction, to the base. While I gazed, this fissure rapidly widened — there came a fierce breath of the whirlwind — the entire orb of the satellite burst at once upon my sight — my brain reeled as I saw the mighty walls rushing asunder — there was a long tumultuous shouting sound like the voice of a thousand waters — and the deep and dank tarn at my feet closed sullenly and silently over the fragments of the '*House of Usher*.'

KATHERINE ANNE PORTER

The Grave

The grandfather, dead for more than thirty years, had been twice disturbed in his long repose by the constancy and possessiveness of his widow. She removed his bones first to Louisiana and then to Texas as if she had set out to find her own burial place, knowing well she would never return to the places she had left. In Texas she set up a small cemetery in a corner of her first farm, and as the family connection grew, and oddments of relations came over from Kentucky to settle, it contained at last about twenty graves. After the grandmother's death, part of her land was to be sold for the benefit of certain of her children, and the cemetery happened to lie in the part set aside for sale. It was necessary to take up the bodies and bury them again in the family plot in the big new public cemetery, where the grandmother had been buried. At last her husband was to lie beside her for eternity, as she had planned.

The family cemetery had been a pleasant small neglected garden of tangled rose bushes and ragged cedar trees and cypress, the simple flat stones rising out of uncropped sweet-smelling wild grass. The graves were lying open and empty one burning day when Miranda and her brother Paul, who often went together to hunt rabbits and doves, propped their twenty-two Winchester rifles carefully against the rail fence, climbed over and explored among the graves. She was nine years old and he was twelve.

They peered into the pits all shaped alike with such purposeful accuracy, and looking at each other with pleased adventurous eyes, they said in solemn tones: "These were graves!" trying by words to shape a special, suitable emotion in their minds, but they felt nothing except an agreeable thrill of wonder: they were seeing a new sight, doing something they had not done before. In them both there was also a small disappointment at the entire commonplaceness of the actual spectacle. Even if it had once contained a coffin for years upon years, when the coffin was gone a grave was just a hole in the ground. Miranda leaped into the pit that had held her grandfather's bones. Scratching around aimlessly and pleasurably as any young animal, she scooped up a lump of earth and weighed it in her palm. It had a pleasantly sweet, corrupt smell, being mixed with cedar needles and small leaves, and as the crumbs fell apart, she saw a silver dove no larger than a hazel nut, with spread wings and a neat fan-shaped tail. The breast had a deep round hollow in it. Turning it up to the fierce sunlight, she saw that the inside of the hollow was cut in little whorls. She scrambled out, over the pile of loose earth that had fallen back into one end of the grave, calling to Paul that she had found something, he must guess what . . . His head appeared smiling over the rim of another grave. He waved a closed hand at her. "I've got something too!" They ran to compare treasures, making a game of it, so many guesses each, all wrong, and a final show-down with opened palms. Paul had found a thin wide gold ring carved with intricate flowers and leaves. Miranda was smitten at sight of the ring and wished to have it. Paul seemed more impressed by the dove. They made a trade, with some little bickering. After he had got the dove in his hand, Paul said, "Don't you know what this is? This is a screw head for a *coffin!* . . . I'll bet nobody else in the world has one like this!"

Miranda glanced at it without covetousness. She had the gold ring on her thumb; it fitted perfectly. "Maybe we ought to go now," she said. "Maybe one of the niggers'll see us and tell somebody." They knew the land had been sold, the cemetery was no longer theirs, and they felt like trespassers. They climbed back over the fence, slung their rifles loosely under their arms — they had been shooting at targets with various kinds of firearms since they were seven years old — and set out to look for the rabbits and doves or whatever small game might happen along. On these expeditions Miranda always followed at Paul's heels along the path, obeying instructions about handling her gun when going through fences; learning how to stand it up properly so it would not slip and fire unexpectedly; how to wait her time for a shot and not just bang away in the air without looking, spoiling shots for Paul, who really could hit things if given a chance. Now and then, in her excitement at seeing birds whizz up suddenly before her face, or a rabbit leap across her very toes, she lost her head, and almost without sighting she flung her rifle up and pulled the trigger. She hardly ever hit any sort of mark. She had no proper sense of hunting at all. Her brother would be often completely disgusted with her. "You don't care whether you get your bird or not," he said. "That's no way to hunt." Miranda could not understand his indignation. She had seen him smash his hat and yell with fury when he had missed his aim. "What I like about shooting," said Miranda, with exasperating inconsequence, "is pulling the trigger and hearing the noise."

"Then, by golly," said Paul, "whyn't you go back to the range and shoot at bulls-eyes?"

"I'd just as soon," said Miranda, "only like this, we walk around more."

"Well, you just stay behind and stop spoiling my shots," said Paul, who, when he made a kill, wanted to be certain he had made it. Miranda, who alone brought down a bird once in twenty rounds, always claimed as her own any game they got when they fired at the same moment. It was tiresome and unfair and her brother was sick of it.

"Now, the first dove we see, or the first rabbit, is mine," he told her. "And the next will be yours. Remember that and don't get smarty."

"What about snakes?" asked Miranda idly. "Can I have the first snake?"

Waving her thumb gently and watching her gold ring glitter, Miranda lost interest in shooting. She was wearing her summer roughing outfit: dark blue overalls, a light blue shirt, a hired-man's straw hat, and thick brown sandals. Her brother had the same outfit except his was a sober hickory-nut color. Ordinarily Miranda preferred her overalls to any other dress, though it was making rather a scandal in the countryside, for the year was 1903, and in the back country the law of female decorum had teeth in it. Her father had been criticized for letting his girls dress like boys and go careering around astride barebacked horses. Big sister Maria, the really independent and fearless one, in spite of her rather affected ways, rode at a dead run with only a rope knotted around her horse's nose. It was said the motherless family was running down, with the grandmother no longer there to hold it together. It was known that she had discriminated against her son Harry in her will, and that he was in straits about money. Some of his old neighbors reflected with vicious satisfaction that now he would probably not be so stiff-necked, nor have any more high-stepping horses either. Miranda knew this, though she could not say how. She had met along the road old women of the kind who smoked corn-cob pipes, who had treated her grandmother with most sincere respect. They slanted their gummy old eyes side-ways at the granddaughter and said, "Ain't you ashamed of yoself, Missy? It's aginst the Scriptures to dress like that. Whut yo Pappy thinkin about?" Miranda, with her powerful social sense, which was like a fine set of antennae radiating from every pore of her skin, would feel ashamed because she knew well it was rude and ill-bred to shock anybody, even bad-tempered old crones, though she had faith in her father's judgment and was perfectly comfortable in the clothes. Her father had said, "They're just what you need, and they'll save your dresses for school ..." This sounded quite simple and natural to her. She had been brought up in rigorous economy. Wastefulness was vulgar. It was also a sin. These were truths; she had heard them repeated many times and never once disputed.

Now the ring, shining with the serene purity of fine gold on her rather grubby thumb, turned her feelings against her overalls and sockless feet, toes sticking through the thick brown leather straps. She wanted to go back to the farmhouse, take a good cold bath, dust herself with plenty of Maria's violet talcum powder — provided Maria was not present to object, of course — put on the thinnest, most becoming dress she owned, with a big sash, and sit in a wicker chair under the trees ... These things were not all she wanted, of course; she had vague stirrings of desire for luxury and a grand way of living which could not take precise form in her imagination but were founded on family legend of past wealth and leisure. These immediate comforts were what she could have, and she wanted them at once. She lagged rather far behind Paul, and once she thought of just turning back without a word and going home. She stopped, thinking that Paul would never do that to her, and so she would have to tell him. When a rabbit leaped, she let Paul have it without dispute. He killed it with one shot.

When she came up with him, he was already kneeling, examining the wound, the rabbit trailing from his hands. "Right through the head," he said complacently, as if he had aimed for it. He took out his sharp, competent bowie knife and started to skin the body. He did it very cleanly and quickly. Uncle Jimbilly knew how to prepare the skins so that Miranda always had fur coats for her dolls, for though she never cared much for her dolls she liked seeing them in fur coats. The children knelt facing each other over the dead animal. Miranda watched admiringly while her brother stripped the skin away as if he were taking off a glove. The flayed flesh emerged dark scarlet, sleek, firm; Miranda with thumb and finger felt the long fine muscles with the silvery flat strips binding them to the joints. Brother lifted the oddly bloated belly. "Look," he said, in a low amazed voice. "It was going to have young ones."

Very carefully he slit the thin flesh from the center ribs to the flanks, and a scarlet bag appeared. He slit again and pulled the bag open, and there lay a bundle of tiny rabbits, each wrapped in a thin scarlet veil. The brother pulled these off and there they were, dark gray, their sleek wet down lying in minute even ripples, like a baby's head just washed, their unbelievably small delicate ears folded close, their little blind faces almost featureless.

Miranda said, "Oh, I want to *see*," under her breath. She looked and looked — excited but not frightened, for she was accustomed to the sight of animals killed in hunting — filled with pity and astonishment and a kind of shocked delight in the wonderful little creatures for their own sakes, they were so pretty. She touched one of them ever so carefully, "Ah, there's blood running over them," she said and began to tremble without knowing why. Yet she wanted most deeply to see and to know. Having seen, she felt at once as if she had known all along. The very memory of her former ignorance faded, she had always known just this. No one had ever told her anything outright, she had been rather unobservant of the animal life around her because she was so accustomed to animals. They seemed simply disorderly and unaccountably rude in their habits, but altogether natural and not very interesting. Her brother had spoken as if he had known about everything all along. He may have seen all this before. He had never said a word to her, but she knew now a part at least of what he knew. She understood a little of the secret, formless intuitions in her own mind and body, which had been clearing up, taking form, so gradually and so steadily she had not realized that she was learning what she had to know. Paul said cautiously, as if he were talking about something forbidden: "They were just about ready to be born." His voice dropped on the last word. "I know," said Miranda, "like kittens. I know, like babies." She was quietly and terribly agitated, standing again with her rifle under her arm, looking down at the bloody heap. "I don't want the skin," she said, "I won't have it." Paul buried the young rabbits again in their mother's body, wrapped the skin around her, carried her to a clump of sage bushes, and hid her away. He came out again at once and said to Miranda, with an eager friendliness, a confidential tone quite unusual in him, as if he were taking her into an important secret on equal terms: "Listen now. Now you listen to me, and don't ever forget. Don't you ever tell a living soul that you saw this. Don't tell a soul. Don't tell Dad because I'll get into trouble. He'll say I'm leading you into things you ought not to do. He's always saying that. So now don't you go and forget and blab out sometime the way you're always doing ... Now, that's a secret. Don't you tell."

Miranda never told, she did not even wish to tell anybody. She thought about the whole worrisome affair with confused unhappiness for a few days. Then it sank quietly into her mind and was heaped over by accumulated thousands of impressions, for nearly twenty years. One day she was picking her path among the puddles and crushed refuse of a market street in a strange city of a strange country, when without warning, plain and clear in its true colors as if she looked through a frame upon a scene that had not stirred nor changed since the moment it happened, the episode of that far-off day leaped from its burial place before her mind's eye. She was so reasonlessly horrified she halted suddenly staring, the scene before her eyes dimmed by the vision back of them. An Indian vendor had held up before her a tray of dyed sugar sweets, in the shapes of all kinds of small creatures: birds, baby chicks, baby rabbits, lambs, baby pigs. They were in gay colors and smelled of vanilla, maybe. ... It was a very hot day and the smell in the market, with its piles of raw flesh and wilting flowers, was like the mingled sweetness and corruption she had smelled that other day in the empty cemetery at home: the day she had remembered always until now vaguely as the time she and her brother had found treasure in the opened graves. Instantly upon this thought the dreadful vision faded, and she saw clearly her brother, whose childhood face she had forgotten, standing again in the blazing sunshine, again twelve years old, a pleased sober smile in his eyes, turning the silver dove over and over in his hands.

LEON ROOKE

Standing in for Nita

When my hostess that evening said, "And you, Nita, what will you have?" I should have corrected her then. But I didn't, others were milling around, all in high excitement from the performance we'd just seen, and it didn't strike me as important. "James," she told her husband, "that will be one whisky, two gin and tonics, and a vodka screwdriver for Nita." I couldn't correct her then either, I was feeling good too, a drink was all I needed, so I felt, and they could have called me — oh I don't know — Sinbad the Sailor for all I cared. A few minutes later her husband came into the room with drinks on a tray, deposited them with their various owners, and arrived in front of me to say, "And a vodka screwdriver for you, Nita."

Everyone present heard him call me Nita. I thought one of them might have corrected him, they might have said, "No, that isn't Nita, thank God, no, that's Mona," but no one did. Of course I might have done so myself that time, but he was looking at me in a peculiar way and saying something about shoes, about what he always looked at first on a woman was her shoes — which was odd, I thought, since he apparently meant it — and my chance simply passed. The conversation heated up, we were talking about the new Bastion Theatre production and it seemed they had finally done something we appreciated, something *worth* doing, and everyone was eager to put in her or his two cents worth, including me. They were all being catty too, gossipy in a way that fascinated me, and since most of them knew the performers or knew people who knew them, a lot of interesting remarks were being made about who was doing what to who and so forth.

My host and hostess continued to address me as Nita. It seemed to me they were mentioning that name all the time and staring at me with their flinty blue eyes and hanging on to everything I said. I was clearly the centre of attention for them, if not for the others who knew I wasn't Nita, and I thought: *so this is what it's like to be Nita.*

I liked it.

At one point James sat very close to me on the sofa and touched me a few times, though it seemed harmless enough and maybe even — so I thought then — accidental. He made an intense speech about the ideal relationship of the business community and the arts which didn't interest me in the least, though I pretended it did, and he finished this up by taking my hands in his and saying, very seriously and with deep passion, "Nita, you're a sweetheart, you're not at all the way I imagined you would be, I forgive you for *everything!*" Then he kissed my fingers and got up to go get someone a drink before I could tell him he'd be better off making that speech to the real Nita.

My friend Tessie was giving us the fisheye, but she didn't say anything either. Tessie and I had met by chance at the theatre, and it was after the show, drifting through the lobby and trying to decide where we wanted to go for a drink, that we'd become attached to this small group the Simcoes had eventually invited over.

I told Tessie then that I thought James Simcoe was quite good-looking. She had said, "Fine, dear, but don't let him know it."

Tessie came over on the sofa and sat with me, though she didn't say anything about my being Nita, she only wanted to talk about her painting, a subject I find boring.

The party broke up about one in the morning.

When I got in my car to drive home, it wouldn't start. The motor would turn over, it would catch for a second or two, then it would die out again. Finally it wouldn't turn over at all. I sat fuming, wondering what I should do. Everyone else had already gone, and one by one the lights went out in the Simcoe house. I caught a glimpse of the wife once or twice as she passed a window, and once I thought I saw him at the front door peering out, but I suppose he was just locking up.

I could have walked home, of course, it isn't far, but I was wearing evening shoes and wouldn't have got a hundred yards before the heels fell off. And I didn't want to ruin my new pantyhose or take them off there on the road in front of their house. Actually they live on a narrow twisty lane, the houses scattered, and everything very dark because there are no streetlights.

I stood out in their yard a long time, looking at their house, not wanting to disturb them but not knowing what else I could do.

I finally did take off my pantyhose and started walking but the road was all gravel and hurt my feet and I couldn't see where I was walking in the first place. So I came back.

I was hoping she would come to the door but it was him, James.

I told him what had happened but he didn't understand right away. We stood in the doorway, both of us whispering, and finally he reached inside and turned off the entrance lights. Then he stepped outside with me, closing the door gently behind him, and guiding me down the steps. He kept whispering, "No trouble, no trouble, don't worry about it, I'm only surprised you're *in* trouble, I thought nothing ever buffaloed Nita." He was wearing a dressing gown of soft velour and his feet were bare. He was guiding me, saying "This way, this way" because it was so dark, but he couldn't see either and in a minute we found ourselves walking on grass and both of us broke out in a kind of hushed giggle, as if we imagined we were doing something secretive and illegal. "It's frost," he said, "there's frost on the ground," and I said I knew, that I wasn't wearing shoes either, and he said, "Let me see," and stooped down, and a second or two later his hands were running up to my legs and his head was under my coat kissing my bare stomach.

I was afraid his wife would get uneasy and come to the door and turn on all the lights, but he said no, she was asleep. He was naked under the gown and I was practically naked myself and it was easy, in a couple of minutes it was all over.

"God, it's cold," he said, and I laughed, and that hurt his feelings, I suppose, because he started gloating, he even turned vicious, asking if I had got what I wanted, saying that now I was acting like the Nita he'd heard so much about.

I didn't say anything. I already regretted what had happened, I didn't like him, and I was beginning to think that all those people who went around criticizing Nita and gossiping about her were themselves worse than she could possibly be. That was our trouble in the first place, I thought, we were quick to pigeonhole people and to believe the worst of them. It seemed to me he was as guilty as the rest and that argument he'd been giving me earlier about how the arts and the business community would never get together because the artists held themselves so aloof and superior and how their art just dragged good people down and tended to make something rotten of them and *that's* why the business community avoided supporting the arts, that was all a lot of nonsense and excuse-making on his part for the simple truth was that the business world just *preferred* to spend their money building another golf course and could just care less about life's more noble endeavours.

He said he bet there was nothing at all wrong with my car.

He climbed in to give it a try and naturally the motor caught the instant he turned on the ignition. "Goddammit," he said, "Nita, you take the cake," and he laughed, very pleased with himself, as if he thought he had just uncovered and proved some dark and evil point about the mysterious Nita.

"It wouldn't start for me," I snapped back, "probably there was moisture under the distributor cap, I've had that trouble before."

"I suppose you're an authority on cars the way you are on everything else."

I called him a bastard, I said "You bastard" under my breath.

Then the motor conked out and he had to admit he was wrong, he even managed a fairly convincing apology.

He got his keys from the house and put on some clothes and drove me home in his car. "Sit over here," he said, patting a spot next to him, and I slid over. He put his hand on my thigh, and for the rest of the short drive was nice, talking about my artistic talent, meaning Nita's, how she was a magician with a camera, a true genius, and that this to his mind excused a lot of things, that I could do whatever I wanted, or Nita could, and I would never hear him running me (Nita) down. He said I was a very exciting woman, I breathed sensuality, that the rumours were accurate on that score. "But for Godsake," he said, "I hope you'll keep what happened tonight to yourself, you don't have anything to gain by spreading this story around."

He asked if he could trust me, and I assured him he could.

I asked what else he'd heard about Nita.

"Listen," he said, "not to beat around the bush, everyone agrees Nita Riley is a bitch. They say you really hate men, that you're out to get them any way you can."

"I'm not like that," I said.

"Sure," he laughed, "I can see nobody knows a goddamn thing, you're more a mystery than ever."

I should have straightened out the whole identity business then, I could easily have done so, but I felt just too lazy and comfortable to bother with it. He was talking and his hand was moving between my legs and I felt nice and warm and happy with matters just as they were. My head was lodged against his shoulder, his neck was hot and smoothshaven and smelling kind of sweet, and all in all it had been a grand night for me.

When we got out of his car in front of my apartment building he shook my hand. "It's been my real pleasure meeting you after all these years," he said. Then he said, "Good night, Nita," but as I was stepping around him he seemed to change his mind or decided he wanted something a little extra, and backed me up against the car fender and began feeling me up. I let him go on with it for a minute or two, not liking it but not really caring either, although finally I pushed him away and told him he could come up to the apartment with me if he wanted to, that I wouldn't mind but that if I fell asleep on him he'd just have to forgive me.

He thought about it, then said no, he'd better get back home.

"I'll see you around," he said, "take care of yourself."

"Bye-bye," I said.

The next day, Sunday, Tessie telephoned. She wanted to know whether I had a good time and what I thought of the Simcoes. I said they had seemed all right.

"*She* is," Tessie said, "but you'd best watch out for him. He's got an ego big as Superman's and he's out to get what he can. I can't stand him, and not many people can. What was that *Nita* game you were playing with him?"

I asked her what James did.

"For a living? He's in investments, something like that. Makes heaps of money, I suppose. He's said to be a big promoter of the arts, though I didn't see any sign of it last night. Did you get a good look at their walls? I've seen better paintings on fire hydrants."

She asked if I wanted to drop over and see her latest work but I begged off. In the year I've known Tessie she's done perhaps five hundred paintings and except for size they are all exactly alike and about as interesting as a vase of dead flowers.

Nita Riley, I've heard, thinks Tessie is very good.

She thanked me for my enthusiasm, and hung up.

I took a long shower and did my nails. Then I tried out a new hairstyle from *Chatelaine's Make Yourself Beautiful* book, something they call Pyramid with Crinkles, which calls for about one hundred pipe cleaners to be wound around small strands right up to the scalp while the hair is still damp, then later on blow-drying this on low heat so that you finish up with a high profile of cascading ripples that take the shape of a pyramid. The style is supposed to be very good for women with long necks, and the model did in fact look smashing.

It took ages.

I put on a black silk blouse with good decolletage, and black silk bloomer trousers tapered to the ankle. I didn't have any shoes to go with this outfit so I went barefoot.

I popped a bottle of Asti and sat down to paint my toenails and wait.

He dropped by around three. The buzzer sounded and I heard his voice in the intercom box like a wounded bird saying, *"Nita? Nita? Are you there, Nita?"*

I asked who it was.

"Are you alone?" he asked, "is this Nita?" and for ten seconds I said nothing, I let him wonder, then I punched the button unlocking the downstairs door. I checked myself in the mirror, I sprayed on fresh perfume; by that time he was knocking on my door.

The first thing he said after looking me over was "Who is Mona, why is her name on your buzzer?" but I turned my back to him and didn't have to answer, I spread my arms wide and said, "How do you like it?"

"The apartment is just another apartment," he said, "but God, Nita, you look terrific."

I told him thanks.

He came up behind me, nuzzling, putting his arms around me, his hands on my breast. "Good God," he sighed, "you're a siren, an absolute siren." He looked at the Asti and the spread of crackers and Camembert: "I guess you were expecting me."

"Not you exactly," I murmured, "but someone."

He let me go quickly. "You're sure no one else is here? You're alone? Who is this Mona, why isn't your name on the buzzer?"

I poured him his drink. I was on the verge of telling him everything, I meant to and really wanted to, I had the words on my tongue, but then he came at me again, he sat on the floor under me, sloshing his Asti over the carpet, and he started stroking my legs and looking me in the eye and gradually he came up to meet me, pushing me over on the sofa and sliding his body over mine.

This time it lasted a little longer, about five minutes, not long enough, not nearly.

Afterwards, he talked. Some men seem to need to, and it doesn't matter to them what they talk about. They seem peculiarly mortal at such moments, lonely and weak and unweaned, maybe they are even thinking back to their boyhood days when they were ignorant and tortured by their ignorance and their deceits, their bravado, boasting all the time of the girls they have had or what they would do if they had one. A disoriented air seems to claim them, but since this is weakness too they try to disguise it, they light up a cigarette and kick back the sheets if sheets are where they are, and they stare out as if across empty space, as if it's the emptiness of space that threatens them, and they talk, all the time sounding a little like they must have sounded before their voices changed, before they ever slept with a girl, the way they would have sounded at age twelve or thirteen if one could have been invisible and able to sit with them in a room when they were alone and admitting to themselves that they were innocent, that they knew nothing, and doubting in every breath that they ever would.

I nodded, murmuring the occasional assent or disagreement, distracted myself because he was casually stroking my breast, his fingers toying with my nipples which were very erect. I squirmed out from under him and got back into my clothes. I passed him the Asti glass and he lay stretched out, holding it and sucking calmly on his cigarette, blowing smoke towards the open window.

"A plumcake," he said, "that's what you remind me of, a delicious plumcake."

I passed him the Camembert and he said no, then a second later reached down for a wedge. "My God," he said, "now that's a weird effect," and I thought he was speaking of the cheese which was beautifully ripe and delicious, but he was pointing at my feet where I had painted my toenails black. "That's Nita for you," he said, "God, you take the cake." He stared at my toes, shaking his head as if he thought all the world's difficulties would be removed if Nita Riley stopped painting her toenails black.

"I went to that last exhibition of yours, by the way, the one at Leafhill. I hadn't known before that you only do people. It struck me that all your portraits, all your subjects, are grotesques, why is that? Your camera does something to them, I mean, distorts them somehow, so that the feeling I had was — well, I don't know, do you know what I mean?"

I smiled, inviting him to go on.

"I mean, your subjects start out perhaps as ordinary people, but you do something with them, maybe it's in the darkroom, and by the time we see the finished work you have transformed them into something quite bizarre, you've caught the essence of a certain horror that *is* them but *isn't* them, if you follow me."

I hadn't been to the Leafhill exhibit, but I had read the local reviews and they had said just what he was saying, that Nita Riley was the country's most brilliant photographer but wasn't it a shame she was so enthralled by the grotesque.

"Where do you do your work?" he asked. "Why don't you have any of your photographs around here?"

I mentioned something about having a studio somewhere. I said that it would unnerve me to have that bleak, depressing stuff where I lived. I was speaking quietly, I didn't know if he heard me.

He got up, adjusted his trousers, and came towards me. I had been sitting apart from him, in the corner, in the shadows made by the blue drapes pulled shut over the balcony's sliding door.

"My wife has been going on about you all day. She says you're not at all like you're reputed to be: none of the *crème de la crème* business, none of that *ghoul at the altar* business. She says you're malleable, quick-changing, that you're strange but not too strange. I think she liked you."

He asked what I thought of his wife's assessment.

"I don't know," I said. "I'll have to think about it." I was thinking of the one time I had seen Nita Riley, at a gallery opening for another artist's work. She was dressed in a black suit cut like an undertaker's and she had hard black eyes that never smiled at the man she was talking to and when the man had turned on his heels in a rage over something she had said she had laughed at him.

My phone rang. It was Tessie.

"He's there, isn't he?" she said. "James Simcoe is there and that's why you couldn't come over."

I asked her what gave her that idea.

"If you must know, I called their home, I wanted to thank them for the lovely time last night. She said she was glad I called, that she was bored because James had to run down to his office. But he's with you, isn't he?"

I said no. I said I'd talk to her later, and hung up.

James wanted to know if that was Mona.

I said yes, that she was on her way over. "Only for a few minutes," I said, "to pick up some of her things. Then she's off again, mostly she's out of town, which is why I have the use of her apartment."

He said he'd better go, and started scrambling.

At the door he embraced me, he looked up and down the hall, and said: "Shall we go on like this? Are you really interested in me?"

I wriggled out of his arms, smiled neither a yes or a no, and closed the door on him.

Over the next week he dropped by each afternoon for a half hour or an hour, sometimes longer, and what he liked best after the lovemaking was to tell me how much he admired and had come to respect me and how totally different I was from the image everyone had of me. He said my name cropped up frequently in conversations he had with his friends and invariably he was struck by how wide of the mark their evaluations were, it was almost as if they were speaking of another person.

"Jesus, you've got to protect yourself, you really ought to hire a press agent or a team of lawyers. The other day for instance there was this guy over at our house from the Rehabilitation Board for the provincial prisons, and he said you'd gone into this prison, William Head I guess it was, to instruct the guys on darkroom techniques or something like that and you'd lost your temper and called them goons and deadbeats, you'd said you wouldn't climb into the sack with any of them and that they all ought to be hung. Why would you do a thing like that, you could have caused a riot? Is it true, did you do it?"

I said no, no, I hadn't.

"And last night, to give another example, last night my wife and I were dining at The Coach and Four and I heard this party at another table discussing you. One of them remarked that Nita Riley would have less hangups and would stop trying to prove she was a femme fatale in addition to being one of the world's great photographers if somehow she could lose thirty pounds. Isn't that outrageous? You're a stringpole, you're not an ounce overweight."

I shook my head, grinning, not knowing how to reply.

"How do you do it?" he asked. "Create all this mystique, all this fever over which one of your various personalities is the true Nita Riley?"

I shrugged, I said I couldn't understand it.

"Extraordinary tales!" he said. "For instance,

this guy at the table was saying that your house was filled with skulls, spiders in and out of jars, bones by your fireplace, bowls of blood and excrement everywhere. That's what he was saying. I wanted to punch the man out, to tell him that you didn't live in a house on the beach in Sooke in the first place, but in a very conventional apartment here in town, that if you worshipped spider *or* bone I had yet to see it. But of course I couldn't, I'm not supposed to know you very well."

I laughed, thinking how easily I could clear up the puzzle for him, how with a few well-chosen words I could make him forget Nita and decide that Mona was the crazy one.

"How do you explain," he asked, "what's behind all this?"

I said I was me, that's all, that I wasn't responsible for what people said.

"But you do encourage it, don't you? I've heard three people say and read it in the paper that you kicked a university trustee in the nuts because he allegedly had said the Woman's Study Program ought to be cut back. Isn't that story true?"

I couldn't look at him, or reply. I knew it had to come out soon, I'd have to confess that I wasn't Nita, famous photographer, but Mona Graham, part-time hostess at The Imperial Inn's Ali Baba Lounge and Dining Room.

On the day we had this talk I suddenly broke out in tears, I decided I really liked him and that it was cheap and unfair of me to go on deceiving him. "It's the strain I'm under," I told him, "I can't go on living like this," and I went on weeping.

"That's exactly what I mean," he declared, slapping his hands together, "people simply would not believe it if I told them you sat here crying over all the terrible things they'd said about you. You're an enigma, God, it's incredible, I've never been involved in such a weird business."

I saw the situation was hopeless so I soon cheered up. I told myself he was just another man and that I was taking all this too seriously.

"Am I the first one," I asked, "or do you have these extramarital affairs all the time?"

He turned quite tender, he held me and kissed me and insisted I was the first, absolutely. It pleased me he said so, although it was apparent to me he was lying.

He brought me a present the next day, something very small wrapped in a blue foil box, and inside was a gold watch, a pendant watch on a beautiful diamond cut rope chain; on the watch's backside he had had the jeweler inscribe

FOR DARLING NITA
THE TIME IS HOURS

I clasped it to me, I kissed it, I felt such a fool. I felt I had to tell him my real name, but he was putting on his clothes already, he said he didn't have time to chat today, that he was on the run.

Tessie called up several times, sounding very distant and disapproving. She had heard *rumours,* she said, and if we were going to engage in this shoddy nonsense we ought at least to be discreet; I pretended not to know what she was talking about. It's true that I had told a few people what was going on, but only after they had pestered me and sworn themselves to utter secrecy.

Tessie said that if I was going to treat my best friend this way then she would damn well leave me to fry in my own oil.

That week too the Ali Baba people kept calling, two or three conventions were in town, and I had to work the evening shift three nights running.

Tips were good, I cleared over a hundred.

On the weekend, a Sunday, James came over, very excited. His wife had gone to Manitoba, he said, to visit her sister, leaving him free to spend the night with me. "No more of those stolen moments," he said. I got excited too, I told him I would make him a great dinner, we would have a celebration. I went into the kitchen to get us a bottle of Asti. When I came back a few minutes later I found him standing by my coffee table, his face red as a lantern. He was reading my mail. I had dropped it there in a little wicker basket and forgot about it, and he apparently had seen these letters in blue envelopes all addressed to Mona and all of them ripped open, and I guess he had simply picked one up and started reading without much thinking about it.

He turned to me, looking suspicious and mad or embarrassed and not quite sure of what he had discovered.

"That's Mona's mail," I screeched, and tried to yank them from him, "you have no right to be reading her mail!"

He backed up, pushing me away, holding the letters out of reach.

"It says here that Mona has got herself entangled with a married man named James and doesn't know how to get herself out of it. What the hell *is* this?" he asked, shaking a sheet in my face and getting more disturbed by the moment, shoving me roughly back each time I grabbed. "What does it mean here when the writer says he thinks Mona is someone else?"

I lost my temper and began screaming at him to give me the letters.

"What is it? Why are you getting so excited? You mean to tell me this Mona is also involved with a man named James? What the hell?"

I went weak all over, I wilted and just gave up. Whatever happens can just happen, I decided, it's too late for me to do anything about it.

He read one letter through, then he read the second, taking his time, and then he turned back to the first.

"That's incredible," he finally said. "Mona's mother really gave it to her, didn't she?"

I realized he still hadn't caught on.

"Come on," he said, appealing to me, "I apologize for reading this junk, but you read them too, so why get so upset with me?"

I blew my nose and wiped my eyes dry with my fingers. "Mona asked me to," I said. "I'm supposed to go through her mail and send her anything important that comes in."

He said "Oh," but I was unsure whether he believed me.

He poured the Asti, he asked if the watch was keeping good time, he tried steering the subject to trivial matters, and after a while we half-way made up, though I knew I wasn't out of the woods yet, that the guillotine was apt to fall at any moment. I would catch him eyeing me, examining me with suspicion, his manner detached, much as if he was measuring me against someone else, measuring our whole relationship, and deciding I came off on the short end of the stick. He asked a lot of questions about Mona, when she was coming back, what she was like, how long we had known each other, whether I had met her friend James. He asked me how my work was going.

I asked him if he wanted to go to bed yet. He said no, not now, maybe in a little while.

"Are you sure?" I asked. He said yes, he was sure.

Then he relaxed back on the sofa, crossed his legs, and fixed a determined gaze on me: "I met one of your old lovers today," he said.

I barked, "*Who*?" — at that moment genuinely baffled because I have had no lovers in Victoria, I've lived here for an entire year but until he came along I had no luck in meeting anyone I wanted to take up with.

"Jason Mole," he said.

I looked blank, I couldn't think what in God's name he was talking about.

"The architect!" he declared, getting angry. "Of Peake, Dibbs, and Mole!"

I still looked dumb. He strode upon me, shaking my shoulders, roaring: "*Jason Mole, you're telling me you don't remember Jason Mole? Hell, you went with him for a year, you almost drove the man crazy!*"

I shook my head.

"Christ, what line are you shooting me, do you think I'm stupid? You broke up the man's home, practically ruined him, got him to leave his wife and then dumped him! You actually expect me to believe you remember nothing of this?"

It was as if someone suddenly floated in a flag in front of me with her name on it: Nita's.

"How about the others? Have you forgotten them too? I've heard of a dozen homes you've wrecked."

"I don't want to talk about it," I said. "I've got a headache."

His fingers unrolled and one by one he ticked off names of people I, Nita, had been involved with and apparently destroyed.

"I'm next, is that it? Is that your plan?"

I fled into the bedroom.

He hammered at the door, cursing and shouting out all the other terrible things Nita had done.

When finally I came out it was with the idea that he had gone and I had seen the last of him. But he was seated in front of the TV, drunk, the Asti bottle on its side by the easy chair, a gin bottle between his legs. He'd kicked off his shoes and thrown his suit coat on the floor, and he waked grunting as I came up beside him and ran my fingers through his hair.

"I'm not Nita," I said, "I'm Mona."

"Sure," he mumbled. "Hi there, Mona." He kicked the Asti bottle, giggling as it did a fast spin and roll across the floor. "Glad to meet you," he said, laughing, but the laugh turned into a fit of coughing and a dead cigarette fell from his hand.

"Lean on me," I told him, "I'll help you to the bed."

"Good old Nita," he said.

I slept with my arms around him. From time to time during the night he'd come out of sleep and half rise looking around as if he didn't know where he was, then he'd sink down again and snore.

In the morning I waked as he was coming out of the shower. I watched him examine his wrinkled suit and shake his head ruefully, and he studied his face in the vanity mirror, scowling. He put his trousers on, the left leg and then the right and then he stuffed in his shirt. Each time he looked my way I quickly closed my eyes.

I didn't know what he would call me, Nita or Mona, or whether he'd wake me at all.

He left the bedroom and a few minutes afterwards I heard the kettle whistling.

My entrance door opened and I thought he was going, but then it closed and I realized he was only bringing in the paper.

He brought it in and a cup of coffee and placed both on the bedside table. Then he gently shook me.

"I've got to go," he said, "I'm afraid it's another Monday. There's coffee. Thanks for looking after me last night. I hope I wasn't a bore."

I sat up, blinking, leaning back against the pillows.

He sat down on the edge of the bed. He said: "I don't think it's going to work, do you?"

"What do you mean?"

He took my hand and stroked it, then passed the coffee to me.

"I'm only an ordinary businessman," he said. "I don't understand anything that has happened between us since that first moment on the grass. I don't know how you people think."

I said: "We could take a breather for a few days, if you wanted to. We don't necessarily have to call it quits."

He sighed. His eyes were a little bloodshot and he had cut himself shaving. "You know, I think that underneath all the insanity you are a very nice woman."

I told him that I tried to be.

He stood up. He started to speak, but hesitated. Then he left the room, coming back the next minute with his attaché case. "I want to show you something," he said. He opened the case and pulled a photograph from one of its compartments. He passed it to me. It was a picture of him. On the back was stamped the credit line, *by Nita Riley.*

"You took that years ago. I never knew you'd done so until I came across it in your last book. I could have sued you, I suppose, since I signed no release form — but, well, it's an interesting picture."

In the photo he was seated on a bench and it *was* him, although Nita had caught him while he was tying his shoe laces, one ankle resting awkwardly over his knee, his mouth open like an imbecile as he stared out at something in the distance.

"All week I've thought you might remember, though of course you've taken thousands of pictures, and wouldn't."

It was shameful, criminal, what she had made of him.

"You keep it," he said. "Remembrance of me."

Then he left, giving a sad look over his shoulder as I called to him.

That same day, in the afternoon, I had a visitor. She sat in my blue chair with her cameras strapped over her shoulders like so many handbags. She never batted an eye, her face severe, her lips painted on thin as matchsticks, scarlet, her eyes boring, her manner contemptuous, as if she had been forced to visit me out of some sense of loathsome duty. As perhaps she had been.

"Why did you come?" I asked, but she refused to answer, refused to say much of anything except in a brittle voice at the beginning, "No, I don't want any of your coffee, I have only one question and that is whether you are worth a picture."

So she sat studying me, looking stern and beautiful in my chair, indomitable, a portrait of evil. Eventually she removed her cameras from the cases, she began testing light and angles and textures, sighting through first one peephole and then another and drifting from this corner to that, crouching and leaning, her Nikon going *click click click* and *click click click* while I sought to give back the same as she gave, letting her know that I saw through her, saw in her the same corruption and ugliness, the same ignorance and self-deceit and grotesquery that she searched so diligently for in others; telling myself that I didn't care if she found it in me, that I knew it was there, had been, but at the same time I knew now I could defeat it, that I'd be a better person the minute she left; vowing to myself that from this date I would *try* to be better, reminding myself that it had taken me a long time to wake up to the kind of person I did not want to be but that, yes, I was waked up now.

"Good," she said at last, satisfied and smiling, patting my head. "Not bad at all. Oh you're a fine subject. The best. Imitation Woman. Bargain-basement Nita."

SINCLAIR ROSS

The Painted Door

Straight across the hills it was five miles from John's farm to his father's. But in winter, with the roads impassable, a team had to make a wide detour and skirt the hills, so that from five the distance was more than trebled to seventeen.

"I think I'll walk," John said at breakfast to his wife. "The drifts in the hills wouldn't hold a horse, but they'll carry me all right. If I leave early I can spend a few hours helping him with his chores, and still be back by suppertime."

She went to the window, and thawing a clear place in the frost with her breath, stood looking across the snowswept farmyard to the huddle of stables and sheds. "There was a double wheel around the moon last night," she countered presently. "You said yourself we could expect a storm. It isn't right to leave me here alone. Surely I'm as important as your father."

He glanced up uneasily, then drinking off his coffee tried to reassure her. "But there's nothing to be afraid of — even supposing it does start to storm. You won't need to go near the stable. Everything's fed and watered now to last till night. I'll be back at the latest by seven or eight."

She went on blowing against the frosted pane, carefully elongating the clear place until it was oval-shaped and symmetrical. He watched her a moment or two longer, then more insistently repeated, "I say you won't need to go near the stable. Everything's fed and watered, and I'll see that there's plenty of wood in. That will be all right, won't it?"

"Yes — of course — I heard you —" It was a curiously cold voice now, as if the words were chilled by their contact with the frosted pane. "Plenty to eat — plenty of wood to keep me warm — what more could a woman ask for?"

"But he's an old man — living there all alone. What is it, Ann? You're not like yourself this morning."

She shook her head without turning. "Pay no attention to me. Seven years a farmer's wife — it's time I was used to staying alone."

Slowly the clear place on the glass enlarged: oval, then round, then oval again. The sun was risen above the frost mists now, so keen and hard a glitter on the snow that instead of warmth its rays seemed shedding cold. One of the two-year-old colts that had cantered away when John turned the horses out for water stood covered with rime at the stable door again, head down and body hunched, each breath a little plume of steam against the frosty air. She shivered, but did not turn.

In the clear, bitter light the long white miles of prairie landscape seemed a region alien to life. Even the distant farmsteads she could see served only to intensify a sense of isolation. Scattered across the face of so vast and bleak a wilderness it was difficult to conceive them as a testimony of human hardihood and endurance. Rather they seemed futile, lost, to cower before the implacibility of snow-swept earth and clear pale sun-chilled sky.

And when at last she turned from the window there was a brooding stillness in her face as if she had recognized this mastery of snow and cold. It troubled John. "If you're really afraid," he yielded, "I won't go today. Lately it's been so cold, that's all. I just wanted to make sure he's all right in case we do have a storm."

"I know — I'm not really afraid." She was putting in a fire now, and he could no longer see her face. "Pay no attention. It's ten miles there and back, so you'd better get started."

"You ought to know by now I wouldn't stay away," he tried to brighten her. "No matter how it stormed. Before we were married — remember? Twice a week I never missed and we had some bad blizzards that winter too."

He was a slow, unambitious man, content with his farm and cattle, naïvely proud of Ann. He had been bewildered by it once, her caring for a dull-witted fellow like him; then assured at last of her affection he had relaxed against it gratefully, unsuspecting it might ever be less constant than his own. Even now, listening to the restless brooding in her voice, he felt only a quick, unformulated kind of pride that after seven years his absence for a day should still concern her. While she, his trust and earnestness controlling her again:

"I know. It's just that sometimes when you're away I get lonely.... There's a long cold tramp in front of you. You'll let me fix a scarf around your face."

He nodded. "And on my way I'll drop in at Steven's place. Maybe he'll come over tonight for a game of cards. You haven't seen anybody but me for the last two weeks."

She glanced up sharply, then busied herself clearing the table. "It will mean another two miles if you do. You're going to be cold and tired enough as it is. When you're gone I think I'll paint the kitchen woodwork. White this time — you remember we got the paint last fall. It's going to make the room a lot lighter. I'll be too busy to find the day long."

"I will though," he insisted, "and if a storm gets up you'll feel safer, knowing that he's coming. That's what you need, maybe — someone to talk to besides me."

She stood at the stove motionless a moment, then turned to him uneasily. "Will you shave then, John — now — before you go?"

He glanced at her questioningly, and avoiding his eyes she tried to explain, "I mean — he may be here before you're back — and you won't have a chance then."

"But it's only Steven — we're not going anywhere."

"He'll be shaved, though — that's what I mean — and I'd like you too to spend a little time on yourself."

He stood up, stroking the heavy stubble on his chin. "Maybe I should — only it softens up the skin too much. Especially when I've got to face the wind."

She nodded and began to help him dress, bringing heavy socks and a big woollen sweater from the bedroom, wrapping a scarf around his face and forehead. "I'll tell Steven to come early," he said, as he went out. "In time for supper. Likely there'll be chores for me to do, so if I'm not back by six don't wait."

From the bedroom window she watched him nearly a mile along the road. The fire had gone down when at last she turned away, and already through the house there was an encroaching chill. A blaze sprang up again when the draughts were opened, but as she went on clearing the table her movements were furtive and constrained. It was the silence weighing upon her — the frozen silence of the bitter fields and sun-chilled sky — lurking outside as if alive, relentlessly in wait, mile-deep between her now and John. She listened to it, suddenly tense, motionless. The fire crackled and the clock ticked. Always it was there. "I'm a fool," she whispered, rattling the dishes in defiance, going back to the stove to put in another fire. "Warm and safe — I'm a fool. It's a good chance when he's away to paint. The day will go quickly. I won't have time to brood."

Since November now the paint had been waiting warmer weather. The frost in the walls on a day like this would crack and peel it as it dried, but she needed something to keep her hands occupied, something to stave off the gathering cold and loneliness. "First of all," she said aloud, opening the paint and mixing it with a little turpentine, "I must get the house warmer. Fill up the stove and open the oven door so that all the heat comes out. Wad something along the window sills to keep out the draughts. Then I'll feel brighter. It's the cold that depresses."

She moved briskly, performing each little task with careful and exaggerated absorption, binding her thoughts to it, making it a screen between herself and the surrounding snow and silence. But when the stove was filled and the windows sealed it was more difficult again. Above the quiet, steady swishing of her brush against the bedroom door the clock began to tick. Suddenly her movements became precise, deliberate, her posture self-conscious, as if someone had entered the room and were watching her. It was the silence again, aggressive, hovering. The fire spit and crackled at it. Still it was there. "I'm a fool," she repeated. "All farmers' wives have to stay alone. I mustn't give in this way. I mustn't brood. A few hours now and they'll be here."

The sound of her voice reassured her. She went on: "I'll get them a good supper — and for coffee after cards bake some of the little cakes with raisins that he likes. ... Just three of us, so I'll watch, and let John play. It's better with four, but at least we can talk. That's all I need — someone to talk to. John never talks. He's stronger — doesn't need to. But he likes Steven — no matter what the neighbours say. Maybe he'll have him come again, and some other young people too. It's what we need, both of us, to help keep young ourselves. ... And then before we know it we'll be into March. It's cold still in March sometimes, but you never mind the same. At least you're beginning to think about spring."

She began to think about it now. Thoughts that outstripped her words, that left her alone again with herself and the ever-lurking silence. Eager and hopeful first, then clenched, rebellious, lonely. Windows open, sun and thawing earth again, the urge of growing, living things. Then the days that began in the morning at half-past four and lasted till ten at night; the meals at which John gulped his food and scarcely spoke a word; the brute-tired stupid eyes he turned on her if ever she mentioned town or visiting.

For spring was drudgery again. John never hired a man to help him. He wanted a mortgage-free farm; then a new house and pretty clothes for her. Sometimes, because with the best of crops it was going to take so long to pay off anyway, she wondered whether they mightn't better let the mortgage wait a little. Before they were worn out, before their best years were gone. It was something of life she wanted, not just a house and furniture; something of John, not pretty clothes when she would be too old to wear them. But John of course couldn't understand. To him it seemed only right that she should have the clothes — only right that he, fit for nothing else, should slave away fifteen hours a day to give them to her. There was in his devotion a baffling, insurmountable humility that made him feel the need of sacrifice. And when his muscles ached, when his feet dragged stolidly with weariness, then it seemed that in some measure at least he was making amends for his big hulking body and simple mind. Year after year their lives went on in the same little groove. He drove his horses in the field; she milked the cows and hoed potatoes. By dint of his drudgery he saved a few months' wages, added a few dollars more each fall to his payments on the mortgage; but the only real difference that it all made was to deprive her of his companionship, to make him a little duller, older, uglier than he might otherwise have been. He never saw their lives objectively. To him it was not what he actually accomplished by means of the sacrifice that mattered, but the sacrifice itself, the gesture — something done for her sake.

And she, understanding, kept her silence. In such a gesture, however futile, there was a graciousness not to be shattered lightly. "John," she would begin sometimes, "you're doing too much. Get a man to help you — just for a month —" but smiling down at her he would answer simply, "I don't mind. Look at the hands on me. They're made for work." While in his voice there would be a stalwart ring to tell her that by her thoughtfulness she had made him only the more resolved to serve her, to prove his devotion and fidelity.

They were useless, such thoughts. She knew. It was his very devotion that made them useless, that forbade her to rebel. Yet over and over, sometimes hunched still before their bleakness, sometimes her brush making swift sharp strokes to pace the chafe and rancour that they brought, she persisted in them.

This now, the winter, was their slack season. She could sleep sometimes till eight, and John till seven. They could linger over their meals a little, read, play cards, go visiting the neighbours. It was the time to relax, to indulge and enjoy themselves; but instead, fretful and impatient, they kept on waiting for the spring. They were compelled now, not by labour, but by the spirit of labour. A spirit that pervaded their lives and brought with idleness a sense of guilt. Sometimes they did sleep late, sometimes they did play cards, but always uneasily, always reproached by the thought of more important things that might be done. When John got up at five to attend to the fire he wanted to stay up and go out to the stable. When he sat down to a meal he hurried his food and pushed his chair away again, from habit, from sheer work-instinct, even though it was only to put more wood in the stove, or go down cellar to cut up beets and turnips for the cows.

And anyway, sometimes she asked herself, why sit trying to talk with a man who never talked? Why talk when there was nothing to talk about but crops and cattle, the weather and the neighbours? The neighbours, too — why go visiting them when still it was the same — crops and cattle, the weather and the other neighbours? Why go to the dances in the schoolhouse to sit among the older women, one of them now, married seven years, or to waltz with the work-bent, tired old farmers to a squeaky fiddle tune? Once she had danced with Steven six or seven times in the evening, and they had talked about it for as many months. It was easier to stay at home. John never danced or enjoyed himself. He was always uncomfortable in his good suit and shoes. He didn't like shaving in the cold weather oftener than once or twice a week. It was easier to stay at home, to stand at the window staring out across the bitter fields, to count the days and look forward to another spring.

But now, alone with herself in the winter silence, she saw the spring for what it really was. This spring — next spring — all the springs and summers still to come. While they grew old, while their bodies warped, while their minds kept shrivelling dry and empty like their lives. "I mustn't," she said aloud again. "I married him — and he's a good man. I mustn't keep on this way. It will be noon before long, and then time to think about supper. . . . Maybe he'll come early — and as soon as John is finished at the stable we can all play cards."

It was getting cold again, and she left her painting to put in more wood. But this time the warmth spread slowly. She pushed a mat up to the outside door, and went back to the window to pat down the woollen shirt that was wadded along the sill. Then she paced a few times round the room, then poked the fire and rattled the stove lids, then paced again. The fire crackled, the clock ticked. The silence now seemed more intense than ever, seemed to have reached a pitch where it faintly moaned. She began to pace on tiptoe, listening, her shoulders drawn together, not realizing for a while that it was the wind she heard, thin-strained and whimpering through the eaves.

Then she wheeled to the window, and with quick short breaths thawed the frost to see again. The glitter was gone. Across the drifts sped swift and snakelike little tongues of snow. She could not follow them, where they sprang from, or where they disappeared. It was as if all across the yard the snow were shivering awake — roused by the warnings of the wind to hold itself in readiness for the impending storm. The sky had become a sombre, whitish grey. It, too, as if in readiness, had shifted and lay close to earth. Before her as she watched a mane of powdery snow reared up breast-high against the darker background of the stable, tossed for a moment angrily, and then subsided again as if whipped down to obedience and restraint. But another followed, more reckless and impatient than the first. Another reeled and dashed itself against the window where she watched. Then ominously for a while there were only the angry little snakes of snow. The wind rose, creaking the troughs that were wired beneath the eaves. In the distance, sky and prairie now were merged into one another linelessly. All round her it was gathering; already in its press and whimpering there strummed a boding of eventual fury. Again she saw a mane of snow spring up, so dense and high this time that all the sheds and stables were obscured. Then others followed, whirling fiercely out of hand; and, when at last they cleared, the stables seemed in dimmer outline than before. It was the snow beginning, long lancet shafts of it, straight from the north, borne almost level by the straining wind. "He'll be there soon," she whispered, "and coming home it will be in his back. He'll leave again right away. He saw the double wheel — he knows the kind of storm there'll be."

She went back to her painting. For a while it was easier, all her thoughts half-anxious ones of John in the blizzard, struggling his way across the hills; but petulantly again she soon began, "I knew we were going to have a storm — I told him so — but it doesn't matter what I say. Big stubborn fool — he goes his own way anyway. It doesn't matter what becomes of me. In a storm like this he'll never get home. He won't even try. And while he sits keeping his father company I can look after his stable for him, go ploughing through snowdrifts up to my knees — nearly frozen —"

Not that she meant or believed her words. It was just an effort to convince herself that she did have a grievance, to justify her rebellious thoughts, to prove John responsible for her unhappiness. She was young still, eager for excitement and distractions; and John's steadfastness rebuked her vanity, made her complaints seem weak and trivial. She went on, fretfully, "If he'd listen to me sometimes and not be so stubborn we wouldn't still be living in a house like this. Seven years in two rooms — seven years and never a new stick of furniture. . . . There — as if another coat of paint could make it different anyway."

She cleaned her brush, filled up the stove again, and went back to the window. There was a void white moment that she thought must be frost formed on the window pane; then, like a fitful shadow through the whirling snow, she recognized the stable roof. It was incredible. The sudden, maniac raging of the storm struck from her face all its pettishness. Her eyes glazed with fear a little; her lips blanched. "If he starts for home now," she whispered silently — "But he won't — he knows I'm safe — he knows Steven's coming. Across the hills he would never dare."

She turned to the stove, holding out her hands to the warmth. Around her now there seemed a constant sway and tremor, as if the air were vibrating with the shudderings of the walls. She stood quite still, listening. Sometimes the wind struck with sharp, savage blows. Sometimes it bore down in a sustained, minute-long blast, silent with effort and intensity; then with a foiled shriek of threat wheeled away to gather and assault again. Always the eave-troughs creaked and sawed. She stared towards the window again, then detecting the morbid trend of her thoughts, prepared fresh coffee and forced herself to drink a few mouthfuls. "He would never dare," she whispered again. "He wouldn't leave the old man anyway in such a storm. Safe in here — there's nothing for me to keep worrying about. It's after one already. I'll do my baking now, and then it will be time to get supper ready for Steven."

Soon, however, she began to doubt whether Steven would come. In such a storm even a mile was enough to make a man hesitate. Especially Steven, who was hardly the one to face a blizzard for the sake of someone else's chores. He had a stable of his own to look after anyway. It would be only natural for him to think that when the storm blew up John had turned again for home. Another man would have — would have put his wife first.

But she felt little dread or uneasiness at the prospect of spending the night alone. It was the first time she had been left like this on her own resources, and her reaction, now that she could face and appraise her situation calmly, was gradually to feel it a kind of adventure and responsibility. It stimulated her. Before nightfall she must go to the stable and feed everything. Wrap up in some of John's clothes — take a ball of string in her hand, one end tied to the door, so that no matter how blinding the storm she could at least find her way back to the house. She had heard of people having to do that. It appealed to her now because suddenly it made life dramatic. She had not felt the storm yet, only watched it for a minute through the window.

It took nearly an hour to find enough string, to choose the right socks and sweaters. Long before it was time to start out she tried on John's clothes, changing and rechanging, striding around the room to make sure there would be play enough for pitching hay and struggling over snowdrifts; then she took them off again, and for a while busied herself baking the little cakes with raisins that he liked.

Night came early. Just for a moment on the doorstep she shrank back, uncertain. The slow dimming of the light clutched her with an illogical sense of abandonment. It was like the covert withdrawal of an ally, leaving the alien miles unleashed and unrestrained. Watching the hurricane of writhing snow rage past the little house she forced herself, "They'll never stand the night unless I get them fed. It's nearly dark already, and I've work to last an hour."

Timidly, unwinding a little of the string, she crept out from the shelter of the doorway. A gust of wind spun her forward a few yards, then plunged her headlong against a drift that in the dense white whirl lay invisible across her path. For nearly a minute she huddled still, breathless and dazed. The snow was in her mouth and nostrils, inside her scarf and up her sleeves. As she tried to straighten a smothering scud flung itself against her face, cutting off her breath a second time. The wind struck from all sides, blustering and furious. It was as if the storm had discovered her, as if all its forces were concentrated upon her extinction. Seized with panic suddenly she threshed out a moment with her arms, then stumbled back and sprawled her length across the drift.

But this time she regained her feet quickly, roused by the whip and batter of the storm to retaliative anger. For a moment her impulse was to face the wind and strike back blow for blow; then, as suddenly as it had come, her frantic strength gave way to limpness and exhaustion. Suddenly, a comprehension so clear and terrifying that it struck all thoughts of the stable from her mind, she realized in such a storm her puniness. And the realization gave her new strength, stilled this time to a desperate persistence. Just for a moment the wind held her, numb and swaying in its vise; then slowly, buckled far forward she groped her way again towards the house.

Inside, leaning against the door, she stood tense and still a while. It was almost dark now. The top of the stove glowed a deep, dull red. Heedless of the storm, self-absorbed and self-satisfied, the clock ticked on like a glib little idiot. "He shouldn't have gone," she whispered silently. "He saw the double-wheel — he knew. He shouldn't have left me here alone."

For so fierce now, so insane and dominant did the blizzard seem, that she could not credit the safety of the house. The warmth and lull around her was not real yet, not to be relied upon. She was still at the mercy of the storm. Only her body pressing hard like this against the door was staving it off. She didn't dare move. She didn't dare ease the ache and strain. "He shouldn't have gone," she repeated, thinking of the stable again, reproached by her helplessness. "They'll freeze in their stalls — and I can't reach them. He'll say it's all my fault. He won't believe I tried."

Then Steven came. Quickly, startled to quietness and control, she let him in and lit the lamp. He stared at her a moment, then flinging off his cap crossed to where she stood by the table and seized her arms. "You're so white — what's wrong? Look at me —" It was like him in such little situations to be masterful. "You should have known better — for a while I thought I wasn't going to make it here myself —"

"I was afraid you wouldn't come — John left early, and there was the stable —"

But the storm had unnerved her, and suddenly at the assurance of his touch and voice the fear that had been gripping her gave way to an hysteria of relief. Scarcely aware of herself she seized his arm and sobbed against it. He remained still a moment unyielding, then slipped his other arm around her shoulder. It was comforting and she relaxed against it, hushed by a sudden sense of lull and safety. Her shoulders trembled with the easing of the strain, then fell limp and still. "You're shivering," — he drew her gently towards the stove. "It's all right — nothing to be afraid of. I'm going to see to the stable."

It was a quiet sympathetic voice, yet with an undertone of insolence, a kind of mockery even, that made her draw away quickly and busy herself putting in a fire. With his lips drawn in a little smile he watched her till she looked at him again. The smile too was insolent, but at the same time companionable; Steven's smile, and therefore difficult to reprove. It lit up his lean, still-boyish face with a peculiar kind of arrogance: features and smile that were different from John's, from other men's — wilful and derisive, yet naïvely so — as if it were less the difference itself he was conscious of, than the long-accustomed privilege that thereby fell his due. He was erect, tall, square-shouldered. His hair was dark and trim, his lips curved soft and full. While John, she made the comparison swiftly, was thickset, heavy-jowled, and stooped. He always stood before her helpless, a kind of humility and wonderment in his attitude. And Steven now smiled on her appraisingly with the worldly-wise assurance of one for whom a woman holds neither mystery nor illusion.

"It was good of you to come, Steven," she responded, the words running into a sudden, empty laugh. "Such a storm to face — I suppose I should feel flattered."

For his presumption, his misunderstanding of what had been only a momentary weakness, instead of angering quickened her, roused from latency and long disuse all the instincts and resources of her femininity. She felt eager, challenged. Something was at hand that hitherto had always eluded her, even in the early days with John, something vital, beckoning, meaningful. She didn't understand, but she knew. The texture of the moment was satisfyingly dreamlike: an incredibility perceived as such, yet acquiesced in. She was John's wife — she knew — but also she knew that Steven standing here was different from John. There was no thought or motive, no understanding of herself as the knowledge persisted. Wary and poised round a sudden little core of blind excitement she evaded him, "But it's nearly dark — hadn't you better hurry if you're going to do the chores? Don't trouble — I can get them off myself —"

An hour later when he returned from the stable she was in another dress, hair rearranged, a little flush of colour in her face. Pouring warm water for him from the kettle into the basin she said evenly, "By the time you're washed supper will be ready. John said we weren't to wait for him."

He looked at her a moment, "You don't mean you're expecting John tonight? The way it's blowing —"

"Of course." As she spoke she could feel the

colour deepening in her face. "We're going to play cards. He was the one that suggested it."

He went on washing, and then as they took their places at the table, resumed, "So John's coming. When are you expecting him?"

"He said it might be seven o'clock — or a little later." Conversation with Steven at other times had always been brisk and natural, but now all at once she found it strained. "He may have work to do for his father. That's what he said when he left. Why do you ask, Steven?"

"I was just wondering — it's a rough night."

"You don't know John. It would take more than a storm to stop him."

She glanced up again and he was smiling at her. The same insolence, the same little twist of mockery and appraisal. It made her flinch, and ask herself why she was pretending to expect John — why there should be this instinct of defence to force her. This time, instead of poise and excitement, it brought a reminder that she had changed her dress and rearranged her hair. It crushed in a sudden silence, through which she heard the whistling wind again, and the creaking saw of the eaves. Neither spoke now. There was something strange, almost frightening, about this Steven and his quiet, unrelenting smile; but strangest of all was the familiarity: the Steven she had never seen or encountered, and yet had always known, always expected, always waited for. It was less Steven himself that she felt than his inevitability. Just as she had felt the snow, the silence and the storm. She kept her eyes lowered, on the window past his shoulder, on the stove, but his smile now seemed to exist apart from him, to merge and hover with the silence. She clinked a cup — listened to the whistle of the storm — always it was there. He began to speak, but her mind missed the meaning of his words. Swiftly she was making comparisons again; his face so different to John's, so handsome and young and clean-shaven. Swiftly, helplessly, feeling the imperceptible and relentless ascendancy that thereby he was gaining over her, sensing sudden menace in this new, more vital life, even as she felt drawn towards it.

The lamp between them flickered as an onslaught of the storm sent shudderings through the room. She rose to build up the fire again and he followed her. For a long time they stood close to the stove, their arms almost touching. Once as the blizzard creaked the house she spun around sharply, fancying it was John at the door; but quietly he intercepted her. "Not tonight — you might as well make up your mind to it. Across the hills in a storm like this — it would be suicide to try."

Her lips trembled suddenly in an effort to answer, to parry the certainty in his voice, then set thin and bloodless. She was afraid now. Afraid of his face so different from John's — of his smile, of her own helplessness to rebuke it. Afraid of the storm, isolating her here alone with him. They tried to play cards, but she kept starting up at every creak and shiver of the walls. "It's too rough a night," he repeated. "Even for John. Just relax a few minutes — stop worrying and pay a little attention to me."

But in his tone there was a contradiction to his words. For it implied that she was not worrying — that her only concern was lest it really might be John at the door.

And the implication persisted. He filled up the stove for her, shuffled the cards — won — shuffled — still it was there. She tried to respond to his conversation, to think of the game, but helplessly into her cards instead she began to ask, Was he right? Was that why he smiled? Why he seemed to wait, expectant and assured?

The clock ticked, the fire crackled. Always it was there. Furtively for a moment she watched him as he deliberated over his hand. John, even in the days before they were married, had never looked like that. Only this morning she had asked him to shave. Because Steven was coming — because she had been afraid to see them side by side — because deep within herself she had known even then. The same knowledge, furtive and forbidden, that was flaunted now in Steven's smile. "You look cold," he said at last, dropping his cards and rising from the table. "We're not playing, anyway. Come over to the stove for a few minutes and get warm."

"But first I think we'll hang blankets over the door. When there's a blizzard like this we always do." It seemed that in sane, commonplace activity there might be release, a moment or two in which to recover herself. "John has nails to put them on. They keep out a little of the draught."

He stood on a chair for her, and hung the blankets that she carried from the bedroom. Then for a moment they stood silent, watching the blankets sway and tremble before the blade of wind that spurted around the jamb. "I forgot," she said at last, "that I painted the bedroom door. At the top there, see — I've smeared the blankets."

He glanced at her curiously, and went back to the stove. She followed him, trying to imagine the hills in such a storm, wondering whether John would come. "A man couldn't live in it," suddenly he answered her thoughts, lowering the oven door and drawing up their chairs one on each side of it. "He knows you're safe. It isn't likely that he'd leave his father, anyway."

"The wind will be in his back," she persisted. "The winter before we were married — all the blizzards that we had that year — and he never missed —"

"Blizzards like this one? Up in the hills he wouldn't be able to keep his direction for a hundred yards. Listen to it a minute and ask yourself."

His voice seemed softer, kindlier now. She met his smile a moment, its assured little twist of appraisal, then for a long time sat silent, tense, careful again to avoid his eyes.

Everything now seemed to depend on this. It was the same as a few hours ago when she braced the door against the storm. He was watching her, smiling. She dared not move, unclench her hands, or raise her eyes. The flames crackled, the clock ticked. The storm wrenched the walls as if to make them buckle in. So rigid and desperate were all her muscles set, withstanding, that the room around her seemed to swim and reel. So rigid and strained that for relief at last, despite herself, she raised her head and met his eyes again.

Intending that it should be for only an instant, just to breathe again, to ease the tension that had grown unbearable — but in his smile now, instead of the insolent appraisal that she feared, there seemed a kind of warmth and sympathy. An understanding that quickened and encouraged her — that made her wonder why but a moment ago she had been afraid. It was as if the storm had lulled, as if she had suddenly found calm and shelter.

Or perhaps, the thought seized her, perhaps instead of his smile it was she who had changed. She who, in the long, wind-creaked silence, had emerged from the increment of codes and loyalties to her real, unfettered self. She who now felt his air of appraisal as nothing more than an understanding of the unfulfilled woman that until this moment had lain within her brooding and unadmitted, reproved out of consciousness by the insistence of an outgrown, routine fidelity.

For there had always been Steven. She understood now. Seven years — almost as long as John — ever since the night they first danced together.

The lamp was burning dry, and through the dimming light, isolated in the fastness of silence and storm, they watched each other. Her face was white and struggling still. His was handsome, clean-shaven, young. Her eyes were fanatic, believing desperately, fixed upon him as if to exclude all else, as if to find justification. His were cool, bland, drooped a little with expectancy. The light kept dimming, gathering the shadows round them, hushed, conspiratorial. He was smiling still. Her hands again were clenched up white and hard.

"But he always came," she persisted. "The wildest, coldest nights — even such a night as this. There was never a storm —"

"Never a storm like this one." There was a quietness in his smile now, a kind of simplicity almost, as if to reassure her. "You were out in it yourself for a few minutes. He'd have it for five miles, across the hills. .. I'd think twice myself, on such a night before risking even one."

Long after he was asleep she lay listening to the storm. As a check on the draught up the chimney they had left one of the stovelids partly off, and through the open bedroom door she could see the flickerings of flame and shadow on the kitchen wall. They leaped and sank fantastically. The longer she watched the more alive they seemed to be. There was one great shadow that struggled towards her threateningly, massive and black and engulfing all the room. Again and again it advanced, about to spring, but each time a little whip of light subdued it to its place among the others on the wall. Yet though it never reached her still she cowered, feeling that gathered there was all the frozen wilderness, its heart of terror and invincibility.

Then she dozed a while, and the shadow was John. Interminably he advanced. The whips of light still flickered and coiled, but now suddenly they were the swift little snakes that this afternoon she had watched twist and shiver across the snow. And they too were advancing. They writhed and vanished and came again. She lay still, paralysed. He was over her now, so close that she could have touched him. Already it seemed that a deadly tightening hand was on her throat. She tried to scream but her lips were locked. Steven beside her slept on heedlessly.

Until suddenly as she lay staring up at him a gleam of light revealed his face. And in it was not a trace of threat or anger — only calm, and stonelike hopelessness.

That was like John. He began to withdraw, and frantically she tried to call him back. "It isn't true — not really true — listen, John —" but the words clung frozen to her lips. Already there was only the shriek of wind again, the sawing eaves, the leap and twist of shadow on the wall.

She sat up, startled now and awake. And so real had he seemed there, standing close to her, so vivid the sudden age and sorrow in his face, that at first she could not make herself understand she had been only dreaming. Against the conviction of his presence in the room it was necessary to insist over and over that he must still be with his father on the other side of the hills. Watching the shadows she had fallen asleep. It was only her mind, her imagination, distorted to a nightmare by the illogical and unadmitted dread of his return. But he wouldn't come. Steven was right. In such a storm he would never try. They were safe, alone. No one would ever know. It was only fear, morbid and irrational; only the sense of guilt that even her new-found and challenged womanhood could not entirely quell.

She knew now. She had not let herself understand or acknowledge it as guilt before, but gradually through the wind-torn silence of the night his face compelled her. The face that had watched her from the darkness with its stonelike sorrow — the face that was really John — John more than his features of mere flesh and bone could ever be.

She wept silently. The fitful gleam of light began

to sink. On the ceiling and wall at last there was only a faint dull flickering glow. The little house shuddered and quailed, and a chill crept in again. Without wakening Steven she slipped out to build up the fire. It was burned to a few spent embers now, and the wood she put on seemed a long time catching light. The wind swirled through the blankets they had hung around the door, and then, hollow and moaning, roared up the chimney again, as if against its will drawn back to serve still longer with the onrush of the storm.

For a long time she crouched over the stove, listening. Earlier in the evening, with the lamp lit and the fire crackling, the house had seemed a stand against the wilderness, a refuge of feeble walls wherein persisted the elements of human meaning and survival. Now, in the cold, creaking darkness, it was strangely extinct, looted by the storm and abandoned again. She lifted the stove lid and fanned the embers till at last a swift little tongue of flame began to lick around the wood. Then she replaced the lid, extended her hands, and as if frozen in that attitude stood waiting.

It was not long now. After a few minutes she closed the draughts, and as the flames whirled back upon each other, beating against the top of the stove and sending out flickers of light again, a warmth surged up to relax her stiffened limbs. But shivering and numb it had been easier. The bodily well-being that the warmth induced gave play again to an ever more insistent mental suffering. She remembered the shadow that was John. She saw him bent towards her, then retreating, his features pale and overcast with unaccusing grief. She re-lived their seven years together and, in retrospect, found them to be years of worth and dignity. Until crushed by it all at last, seized by a sudden need to suffer and atone, she crossed to where the draught was bitter, and for a long time stood unflinching on the icy floor.

The storm was close here. Even through the blankets she could feel a sift of snow against her face. The eaves sawed, the walls creaked, and the wind was like a wolf in howling flight.

And yet, suddenly she asked herself, hadn't there been other storms, other blizzards? And through the worst of them hadn't he always reached her?

Clutched by the thought she stood rooted a minute. It was hard now to understand how she could have so deceived herself — how a moment of passion could have quieted within her not only conscience, but reason and discretion too. John always came. There could never be a storm to stop him. He was strong, inured to the cold. He had crossed the hills since his boyhood, knew every creek-bed and gully. It was madness to go on like this — to wait. While there was still time she must waken Steven, and hurry him away.

But in the bedroom again, standing at Steven's side, she hesitated. In his detachment from it all, in his quiet, even breathing, there was such sanity, such realism. For him nothing had happened, nothing would. If she wakened him he would only laugh and tell her to listen to the storm. Already it was long past midnight; either John had lost his way or not set out at all. And she knew that in his devotion there was nothing foolhardy. He would never risk a storm beyond his endurance, never permit himself a sacrifice likely to endanger her lot or future. They were both safe. No one would ever know. She must control herself — be sane like Steven.

For comfort she let her hand rest a while on Steven's shoulder. It would be easier were he awake now, with her, sharing her guilt; but gradually as she watched his handsome face in the glimmering light she came to understand that for him no guilt existed. Just as there had been no passion, no conflict. Nothing but the same appraisal of their situation, nothing but the expectant little smile, and the arrogance of features that were different from John's. She winced deeply, remembering how she had fixed her eyes on those features, how she had tried to believe that so handsome and young, so different from John's, they must in themselves be her justification.

In the flickering light they were still young, still handsome. No longer her justification — she knew now — John was the man — but wistfully still, wondering sharply at their power and tyranny, she touched them a moment with her fingertips again.

She could not blame him. There had been no passion, no guilt; therefore there could be no responsibility. Looking down at him as he slept, half-smiling still, his lips relaxed in the conscienceless complacency of his achievement, she understood that thus he was revealed in his entirety — all there ever was or ever could be. John was the man. With him lay all the future. For tonight, slowly and contritely through the day and years to come, she would try to make amends.

Then she stole back to the kitchen, and without thought, impelled by overwhelming need again, returned to the door where the draught was bitter still. Gradually towards morning the storm began to spend itself. Its terror blast became a feeble, worn-out moan. The leap of light and shadow sank, and a chill crept in again. Always the eaves creaked, tortured with wordless prophecy. Heedless of it all the clock ticked on in idiot content.

They found him the next day, less than a mile from home. Drifting with the storm he had run against his own pasture fence and overcome had frozen there, erect still, both hands clasping fast the wire.

"He was south of here," they said wonderingly when she told them how he had come across the hills. "Straight south — you'd wonder how he could have missed the buildings. It was the wind last night, coming every way at once. He shouldn't have tried. There was a double wheel around the moon."

She looked past them a moment, then as if to herself said simply, "If you knew him, though — John would try."

It was later, when they had left her a while to be alone with him, that she knelt and touched his hand. Her eyes dimmed, it was still such a strong and patient hand; then, transfixed, they suddenly grew wide and clear. On the palm, white even against its frozen whiteness, was a little smear of paint.

PHILIP ROTH

Defender of the Faith

In May of 1945, only a few weeks after the fighting had ended in Europe, I was rotated back to the States, where I spent the remainder of the war with a training company at Camp Crowder, Missouri. We had been racing across Germany so swiftly during the late winter and spring that when I boarded the plane that drizzly morning in Berlin, I couldn't believe our destination lay to the west. My mind might inform me otherwise, but there was an inertia of the spirit that told me we were flying to a new front where we would disembark and continue our push eastward — eastward until we'd circled the globe, marching through villages along whose twisting, cobbled streets crowds of the enemy would watch us take possession of what up till then they'd considered their own. I had changed enough in two years not to mind the trembling of the old people, the crying of the very young, the uncertain fear in the eyes of the once-arrogant. After two years I had been fortunate enough to develop an infantryman's heart which, like his feet, at first aches and swells, but finally grows horny enough for him to travel the weirdest paths without feeling a thing.

Captain Paul Barrett was to be my C.O. at Camp Crowder. The day I reported for duty he came out of his office to shake my hand. He was short, gruff, and fiery, and indoors or out he wore his polished helmet liner down on his little eyes. In Europe he had received a battlefield commission and a serious chest wound, and had been returned to the States only a few months before. He spoke easily to me, but was, I thought, unnecessarily abusive towards the troops. At the evening formation, he introduced me.

"Gentlemen," he called. "Sergeant Thurston, as you know, is no longer with this Company. Your new First Sergeant is Sergeant Nathan Marx here. He is a veteran of the European theater and consequently will take no shit."

I sat up late in the orderly room that evening, trying halfheartedly to solve the riddle of duty rosters, personnel forms, and morning reports. The CQ slept with his mouth open on a mattress on the floor. A trainee stood reading the next day's duty roster, which was posted on the bulletin board directly inside the screen door. It was a warm evening and I could hear the men's radios playing dance music over in the barracks.

The trainee, who I knew had been staring at me whenever I looked groggily into the forms, finally took a step in my direction.

"Hey, Sarge — we having a G.I. party tomorrow night?" A G.I. party is a barracks-cleaning.

"You usually have them on Friday nights?"

"Yes," and then he added mysteriously, "that's the whole thing."

"Then you'll have a G.I. party."

He turned away and I heard him mumbling. His shoulders were moving and I wondered if he was crying.

"What's your name, soldier?" I asked.

He turned, not crying at all. Instead his green-speckled eyes, long and narrow, flashed like fish in the sun. He walked over to me and sat on the edge of my desk.

He reached out a hand. "Sheldon," he said.

"Stand on your own two feet, Sheldon."

Climbing off the desk, he said, "Sheldon Grossbart." He smiled wider at the intimacy into which he'd led me.

"You against cleaning the barracks Friday night, Grossbart? Maybe we shouldn't have G.I. parties — maybe we should get a maid." My tone startled me: I felt like a Charlie McCarthy, with every top sergeant I had ever known as my Edgar Bergen.

"No, Sergeant." He grew serious, but with a seriousness that seemed only to be the stifling of a smile. "It's just G.I. parties on Friday night, of all nights . . ."

He slipped up to the corner of the desk again — not quite sitting, but not quite standing either. He looked at me with those speckled eyes flashing and then made a gesture with his hand. It was very slight, no more than a rotation back and forth of the wrist, and yet it managed to exclude from our affairs everything else in the orderly room, to make the two of us the center of the world. It seemed, in fact, to exclude everything about the two of us except our hearts. "Sergeant Thurston was one thing," he whispered, an eye flashing to the sleeping CQ, "but we thought with you here, things might be a little different."

"We?"

"The Jewish personnel."

"Why?" I said, harshly.

He hesitated a moment, and then, uncontrollably, his hand went up to his mouth. "I mean . . ." he said.

"What's on your mind?" Whether I was still

angry at the "Sheldon" business or something else, I hadn't a chance to tell — but clearly I was angry.

"... we thought you ... Marx, you know, like Karl Marx. The Marx brothers. Those guys are all ... M-A-R-X, isn't that how you spell it, Sergeant?"

"M-A-R-X."

"Fishbein said —" He stopped. "What I mean to say, Sergeant —" His face and neck were red, and his mouth moved but no words came out. In a moment, he raised himself to attention, gazing down at me. It was as though he had suddenly decided he could expect no more sympathy from me than from Thurston, the reason being that I was of Thurston's faith and not his. The young man had managed to confuse himself as to what my faith really was, but I felt no desire to straighten him out. Very simply, I didn't like him.

When I did nothing but return his gaze, he spoke, in an altered tone. "You see, Sergeant," he explained to me, "Friday nights, Jews are supposed to go to services."

"Did Sergeant Thurston tell you you couldn't go to them when there was a G.I. party?"

"No."

"Did he say you had to stay and scrub the floors?"

"No, Sergeant."

"Did the Captain say you had to stay and scrub the floors?"

"That isn't it, Sergeant. It's the other guys in the barracks." He leaned toward me. "They think we're goofing off. But we're not. That's when Jews go to services, Friday night. We have to."

"Then go."

"But the other guys make accusations. They have no right."

"That's not the Army's problem, Grossbart. It's a personal problem you'll have to work out yourself."

"But it's un*fair*."

I got up to leave. "There's nothing I can do about it," I said.

Grossbart stiffened in front of me. "But this is a matter of *religion,* sir."

"Sergeant."

"I mean 'Sergeant,"' he said, almost snarling.

"Look, go see the chaplain. The I.G. You want to see Captain Barrett, I'll arrange an appointment."

"No, no. I don't want to make trouble, Sergeant. That's the first thing they throw up to you. I just want my rights!"

"Damn it, Grossbart, stop whining. You have your rights. You can stay and scrub floors or you can go to *shul* —"

The smile swam in again. Spittle gleamed at the corners of his mouth. "You mean church, Sergeant."

"I mean *shul,* Grossbart!" I walked past him and outside. Near me I heard the scrunching of a guard's boots on gravel. In the lighted windows of the barracks the young men in T-shirts and fatigue pants were sitting on their bunks, polishing their rifles. Suddenly there was a light rustling behind me. I turned and saw Grossbart's dark frame fleeing back to the barracks, racing to tell his Jewish friends that they were right — that like Karl and Harpo, I was one of them.

The next morning, while chatting with the Captain, I recounted the incident of the previous evening, as if to unburden myself of it. Somehow in the telling it seemed to the Captain that I was not so much explaining Grossbart's position as defending it.

"Marx, I'd fight side by side with a nigger if the fellow proved to me he was a man. I pride myself," the Captain said looking out the window, "that I've got an open mind. Consequently, Sergeant, nobody gets special treatment here, for the good *or* the bad. All a man's got to do is prove himself. A man fires well on the range, I give him a weekend pass. He scores high in PT, he gets a weekend pass. He *earns* it." He turned from the window and pointed a finger at me. "You're a Jewish fellow, am I right, Marx?"

"Yes, sir."

"And I admire you. I admire you because of the ribbons on your chest, not because you had a hem stitched on your dick before you were old enough to even know you had one. I judge a man by what he shows me on the field of battle, Sergeant. It's what he's got *here*," he said, and then, though I expected he would point to his heart, he jerked a thumb towards the buttons straining to hold his blouse across his belly. "Guts," he said.

"Okay, sir, I only wanted to pass on to you how the men felt."

"Mr. Marx, you're going to be old before your time if you worry about how the men feel. Leave that stuff to the Chaplain — pussy, the clap, church picnics with the little girls from Joplin, that's all his business, not yours. Let's us train these fellas to shoot straight. If the Jewish personnel feels the other men are accusing them of goldbricking ... well, I just don't know. Seems awful funny how suddenly the Lord is calling so loud in Private Grossman's ear he's just got to run to church."

"Synagogue," I said.

"Synagogue is right, Sergeant. I'll write that down for handy reference. Thank you for stopping by."

That evening, a few minutes before the company gathered outside the orderly room for the chow formation, I called the CQ, Corporal Robert LaHill, in to see me. LaHill was a dark burly fellow whose hair curled out of his clothes wherever it could. He carried a glaze in his eyes that made one think of caves and dinosaurs. "LaHill," I said, "when you take the formation, remind the men that they're free to attend church services *whenever* they are held, provided they report to the orderly room before they leave the area."

LaHill didn't flicker; he scratched his wrist, but gave no indication that he'd heard or understood.

"LaHill," I said, "*church*. You remember? Church, priest, Mass, confession ..."

He curled one lip into a ghastly smile; I took it for a signal that for a second he had flickered back up into the human race.

"Jewish personnel who want to attend services this evening are to fall out in front of the orderly room at 1900." And then I added, "By order of Captain Barrett."

A little while later, as a twilight softer than any I had seen that year dropped over Camp Crowder, I heard LaHill's thick, inflectionless voice outside my window: "Give me your ears, troopers. Toppie says for me to tell you that at 1900 hours all Jewish personnel is to fall out in front here if they wants to attend the Jewish Mass."

At seven o'clock, I looked out of the orderly-room window and saw three soldiers in starched khakis standing alone on the dusty quadrangle. They looked at their watches and fidgeted while they whispered back and forth. It was getting darker, and alone on the deserted field they looked tiny. When I walked to the door I heard the noises of the G.I. party coming from the surrounding barracks — bunks being pushed to the wall, faucets pounding water into buckets, brooms whisking at the wooden floors. In the windows big puffs of cloth moved round and round, cleaning the dirt away for Saturday's inspection. I walked outside and the moment my foot hit the ground I thought I heard Grossbart, who was now in the center, call to the other two, "Ten-*hut!*" Or maybe when they all three jumped to attention, I imagined I heard the command.

At my approach, Grossbart stepped forward. "Thank you, sir," he said.

"Sergeant, Grossbart," I reminded him. "You call officers 'Sir.' I'm not an officer. You've been in the Army three weeks — you know that."

He turned his palms out at his sides to indicate that, in truth, he and I lived beyond convention. "Thank you, anyway," he said.

"Yes," the tall boy behind him said. "Thanks a lot."

And the third whispered, "Thank you," but his mouth barely fluttered so that he did not alter by more than a lip's movement, the posture of attention.

"For what?" I said.

Grossbart snorted, happily. "For the announcement before. The Corporal's announcement. It helped. It made it ..."

"Fancier." It was the tall boy finishing Grossbart's sentence.

Grossbart smiled. "He means formal, sir. Public," he said to me. "Now it won't seem as though we're just taking off, goldbricking, because the work has begun."

"It was by order of Captain Barrett," I said.

"Ahh, but you pull a little weight ... " Grossbart said. "So we thank you." Then he turned to his companions. "Sergeant Marx, I want you to meet Larry Fishbein."

The tall boy stepped forward and extended his hand. I shook it. "You from New York?" he asked.

"Yes."

"Me too." He had a cadaverous face that collapsed inward from his cheekbone to his jaw, and when he smiled — as he did at the news of our communal attachment — revealed a mouthful of bad teeth. He blinked his eyes a good deal, as though he were fighting back tears. "What borough?" he asked.

I turned to Grossbart. "It's five after seven. What time are services?"

"*Shul,*" he smiled, "is in ten minutes. I want you to meet Mickey Halpern. This is Nathan Marx, our Sergeant."

The third boy hopped forward. "Private Michael Halpern." He saluted.

"Salute officers, Halpern." The boy dropped his hand, and in his nervousness checked to see if his shirt pockets were buttoned on the way down.

"Shall I march them over, sir?" Grossbart asked, "or are you coming along?"

From behind Grossbart, Fishbein piped up. "Afterwards they're having refreshments. A Ladies' Auxiliary from St. Louis, the rabbi told us last week."

"The chaplain," whispered Halpern.

"You're welcome to come along," Grossbart said.

To avoid his plea, I looked away, and saw, in the windows of the barracks, a cloud of faces staring out at the four of us.

"Look, hurry out of here, Grossbart."

"Okay, then," he said. He turned to the others. "Double time, *march!*" and they started off, but ten feet away Grossbart spun about, and running backwards he called to me, "Good *shabus,* sir." And then the three were swallowed into the Missouri dusk.

Even after they'd disappeared over the parade grounds, whose green was now a deep twilight blue, I could hear Grossbart singing the double-time cadence, and as it grew dimmer and dimmer it suddenly touched some deep memory — as did the slant of light — and I was remembering the shrill sounds of a Bronx playground, where years ago, beside the Grand Concourse, I had played on long spring evenings such as this. Those thin fading sounds ... It was a pleasant memory for a young man so far from peace and home, and it brought so very many recollections with it that I began to grow exceedingly tender about myself. In fact, I indulged myself to a reverie so strong that I felt within as though a hand had opened and was reaching down inside. It had to reach so very far to touch me. It had to reach past those days in the forests of Belgium and the dying I'd refused to weep over; past the nights in those German farmhouses whose books we'd burned to warm us, and which I couldn't bother to mourn; past those endless stretches when I'd shut off all softness I might feel for my fellows, and managed even to deny myself the posture of a conqueror — the swagger that I, as a Jew, might well have worn as my boots whacked against the rubble of Münster, Braunschweig, and finally Berlin.

But now one night noise, one rumor of home and time past, and memory plunged down through all I had anesthetized and came to what I suddenly remembered to be myself. So it was not altogether curious that in search of more of me I found myself following Grossbart's tracks to Chapel No. 3 where the Jewish services were being held.

I took a seat in the last row, which was empty. Two rows in front sat Grossbart, Fishbein, and Halpern, each holding a little white dixie cup. Fishbein was pouring the contents of his cup into Grossbart's, and Grossbart looked mirthful as the liquid drew a purple arc between his hand and Fishbein's. In the glary yellow light, I saw the chaplain on the pulpit chanting the first line of the responsive reading. Grossbart's prayerbook remained closed on his lap; he swished the cup around. Only Halpern responded in prayer. The fingers of his right hand were spread wide across the cover of the book, and his cap was pulled down low onto his brow so that it was round like a *yarmulke* rather than long and pointed. From time to time, Grossbart wet his lips at the cup's edge; Fishbein, his long yellow face, a dying light bulb, looked from here to there, leaning forward at the neck to catch sight of the faces down the row, in front — then behind. He saw me and his eyelids beat a tattoo. His elbow slid into Grossbart's side, his neck inclined towards his friend, and then, when the congregation responded, Grossbart's voice was among them. Fishbein looked into his book now too; his lips, however, didn't move.

Finally it was time to drink the wine. The chaplain smiled down at them as Grossbart swigged in one long gulp, Halpern sipped, meditating, and Fishbein faked devotion with an empty cup.

At last the chaplain spoke: "As I look down amongst the congregation —" he grinned at the word, "this night, I see many new faces, and I want to welcome you to Friday night services here at Camp Crowder. I am Major Leo Ben Ezra, your chaplain . . ." Though an American, the chaplain spoke English very deliberately, syllabically almost, as though to communicate, above all, to the lip-readers in the audience. "I have only a few words to say before we adjourn to the refreshment room where the kind ladies of the Temple Sinai, St. Louis, Missouri, have a nice setting for you."

Applause and whistling broke out. After a momentary grin, the chaplain raised his palms to the congregation, his eyes flicking upward a moment, as if to remind the troops where they were and Who Else might be in attendance. In the sudden silence that followed, I thought I heard Grossbart's cackle — "Let the goyim clean the floors!" Were those the words? I wasn't sure, but Fishbein, grinning, nudged Halpern. Halpern looked dumbly at him, then went back to his prayerbook, which had been occupying him all through the rabbi's talk. One hand tugged at the black kinky hair that stuck out under his cap. His lips moved.

The rabbi continued. "It is about the food that I want to speak to you for a moment. I know, I know, I know," he intoned, wearily, "how in the mouths of most of you the *trafe* food tastes like ashes. I know how you gag, some of you, and how your parents suffer to think of their children eating foods unclean and offensive to the palate. What can I tell you? I can only say close your eyes and swallow as best you can. Eat what you must to live and throw away the rest. I wish I could help more. For those of you who find this impossible, may I ask that you try and try, but then come to see me in private where, if your revulsion is such, we will have to seek aid from those higher up."

A round of chatter rose and subsided; then everyone sang "Ain Kelohanoh", after all those years I discovered I still knew the words.

Suddenly, the service over, Grossbart was upon me. "Higher up? He means the General?"

"Hey, Shelly," Fishbein interrupted, "he means God." He smacked his face and looked at Halpern. "How high can you go!"

"Shhh!" Grossbart said. "What do you think, Sergeant?"

"I don't know. You better ask the chaplain."

"I'm going to. I'm making an appointment to see him in private. So is Mickey."

Halpern shook his head. "No, no, Sheldon . . ."

"You have rights, Mickey. They can't push us around."

"It's okay. It bothers my mother, not me . . ."

Grossbart looked at me. "Yesterday he threw up. From the hash. It was all ham and God knows what else."

"I have a cold — that was why," Halpern said. He pushed his *yamalkah* back into a cap.

"What about you, Fishbein?" I asked. "You kosher too?"

He flushed, which made the yellow more gray than pink. "A little. But I'll let it ride. I have a very strong stomach. And I don't eat a lot anyway . . ." I continued to look at him, and he held up his wrist to re-enforce what he'd just said. His watch was tightened to the last hole and he pointed that out to me. "So I don't mind."

"But services are important to you?" I asked him.

He looked at Grossbart. "Sure, sir."

"Sergeant."

"Not so much at home," said Grossbart, coming between us, "but away from home it gives one a sense of his Jewishness."

"We have to stick together," Fishbein said.

I started to walk towards the door; Halpern stepped back to make way for me.

"That's what happened in Germany," Grossbart was saying, loud enough for me to hear. "They didn't stick together. They let themselves get pushed around."

I turned. "Look, Grossbart, this is the Army, not summer camp."

He smiled. "So?" Halpern tried to sneak off, but Grossbart held his arm. "So?" he said again.

"Grossbart," I asked, "how old are you?"

"Nineteen."

"And you?" I said to Fishbein.

"The same. The same month even."

"And what about him?" I pointed to Halpern, who'd finally made it safely to the door.

"Eighteen," Grossbart whispered. "But he's like he can't tie his shoes or brush his teeth himself. I feel sorry for him."

"I feel sorry for all of us, Grossbart, but just act like a man. Just don't overdo it."

"Overdo what, sir?"

"The sir business. Don't overdo that," I said, and I left him standing there. I passed by Halpern but he did not look up. Then I was outside, black surrounded me — but behind I heard Grossbart call, "Hey, Mickey, *liebschen,* come on back. Refreshments!"

Liebschen! My grandmother's word for me!

One morning, a week later, while I was working at my desk, Captain Barrett shouted for me to come into his office. When I entered, he had his helmet liner squashed down so that I couldn't even see his eyes. He was on the phone, and when he spoke to me, he cupped one hand over the mouthpiece.

"Who the fuck is Grossbart?"

"Third platoon, Captain," I said. "A trainee."

"What's all this stink about food? His mother called a goddam congressman about the food . . ." He uncovered the mouthpiece and slid his helmet up so I could see the curl of his bottom eyelash. "Yes, sir," he said into the phone. "Yes, sir. I'm still here, sir. I'm asking Marx here right now . . ."

He covered the mouthpiece again and looked back to me. "Lightfoot Harry's on the phone," he said, between his teeth. "This congressman calls General Lyman who calls Colonel Sousa who calls the Major who calls me. They're just dying to stick this thing on me. What's a matter," he shook the phone at me, "I don't feed the troops? What the hell is this?"

"Sir, Grossbart is strange . . ." Barrett greeted that with a mockingly indulgent smile. I altered my approach. "Captain, he's a very orthodox Jew and so he's only allowed to eat certain foods."

"He throws up, the congressman said. Every time he eats something his mother says he throws up!"

"He's accustomed to observing the dietary laws, Captain."

"So why's his old lady have to call the White House!"

"Jewish parents, sir, they're apt to be more protective than you expect. I mean Jews have a very close family life. A boy goes away from home, sometimes the mother is liable to get very upset. Probably the boy *mentioned* something in a letter and his mother misinterpreted."

"I'd like to punch him one right in the mouth. There's a goddam war on and he wants a silver platter!"

"I don't think the boy's to blame, sir. I'm sure we can straighten it out by just asking him. Jewish parents worry —"

"*All* parents worry, for Christ sake. But they don't get on their high horses and start pulling strings —"

I interrupted, my voice higher, tighter than before. "The home life, Captain, is so very important . . . but you're right, it may sometimes get out of hand. It's a very wonderful thing, Captain, but because it's so close, this kind of thing —"

He didn't listen any longer to my attempt to present both myself and Lightfoot Harry with an explanation for the letter. He turned back to the phone. "Sir?" he said. "Sir, Marx here tells me Jews have a tendency to be pushy. He says he thinks he can settle it right here in the Company . . . Yes, sir . . . I *will* call back, sir, soon as I can . . ." He hung up. "Where are the men, Sergeant?"

"On the range."

With a whack on the top, he crushed his helmet over his eyes, and charged out of his chair. "We're going for a ride."

The Captain drove and I sat beside him. It was a hot spring day and under my newly starched fatigues it felt as though my armpits were melting down onto my sides and chest. The roads were dry and by the time we reached the firing range, my teeth felt gritty with dust though my mouth had been shut the whole trip. The Captain slammed the brakes on and told me to get the hell out and find Grossbart.

I found him on his belly, firing wildly at the 500 feet target. Waiting their turns behind him were Halpern and Fishbein. Fishbein, wearing a pair of rimless G.I. glasses I hadn't seen on him before, gave the appearance of an old peddler who would gladly have sold you the rifle and cartridges that were slung all over him. I stood back by the ammo boxes, waiting for Grossbart to finish spraying the distant targets. Fishbein straggled back to stand near me.

"Hello, Sergeant Marx."

"How are you?" I mumbled.

"Fine, thank you. Sheldon's really a good shot."

"I didn't notice."

"I'm not so good, but I think I'm getting the hang of it now ... Sergeant, I don't mean to, you know, ask what I shouldn't ..." The boy stopped. He was trying to speak intimately but the noise of the shooting necessitated that he shout at me.

"What is it?" I asked. Down the range I saw Captain Barrett standing up in the jeep, scanning the line for me and Grossbart.

"My parents keep asking and asking where we're going. Everybody says the Pacific. I don't care, but my parents ... If I could relieve their minds I think I could concentrate more on my shooting."

"I don't know where, Fishbein. Try to concentrate anyway."

"Sheldon says you might be able to find out —"

"I don't know a thing, Fishbein. You just take it easy, and don't let Sheldon —"

"*I'm* taking it easy, Sergeant. It's at home —"

Grossbart had just finished on the line and was dusting his fatigues with one hand. I left Fishbein's sentence in the middle.

"Grossbart, the Captain wants to see you."

He came toward us. His eyes blazed and twinkled. "Hi!"

"Don't point that goddam rifle!"

"I wouldn't shoot you, Sarge." He gave me a smile wide as a pumpkin as he turned the barrel aside.

"Damn you, Grossbart — this is no joke! Follow me."

I walked ahead of him and had the awful suspicion that behind me Grossbart was *marching,* his rifle on his shoulder, as though he were a one-man detachment.

At the jeep he gave the Captain a rifle salute. "Private Sheldon Grossbart, sir."

"At ease, Grossman." The captain slid over to the empty front seat, and crooking a finger invited Grossbart closer.

"Bart, sir. Sheldon Gross*bart.* It's a common error." Grossbart nodded to me — *I* understand, he indicated. I looked away, just as the mess truck pulled up the range, disgorging a half dozen K.P.'s with rolled-up sleeves. The mess sergeant screamed at them while they set up the chow line equipment.

"Grossbart, your mama wrote some congressman that we don't feed you right. Do you know that?" the Captain said.

"It's was my father, sir. He wrote to Representative Franconi that my religion forbids me to eat certain foods."

"What religion is that, Grossbart?"

"Jewish."

"Jewish, *sir,*" I said to Grossbart.

"Excuse me, sir. 'Jewish, sir.' "

"What have you been living on?" the Captain asked. "You've been in the Army a month already. You don't look to me like you're falling to pieces."

"I eat because I have to, sir. But Sergeant Marx will testify to the fact that I don't eat one mouthful more than I need to in order to survive."

"Marx," Barrett asked, "is that so?"

"I've never seen Grossbart eat, sir," I said.

"But you heard the rabbi," Grossbart said. "He told us what to do, and I listened."

The Captain looked at me. "Well, Marx?"

"I still don't know what he eats and doesn't eat, sir."

Grossbart raised his rifle, as though to offer it to me. "But, Sergeant —"

"Look, Grossbart, just answer the Captain's questions!" I said sharply.

Barrett smiled at me and I resented it. "All right, Grossbart," he said, "What is it you want? The little piece of paper? You want out?"

"No, sir. Only to be allowed to live as a Jew. And for the others, too."

"What others?"

"Fishbein, sir, and Halpern."

"They don't like the way we serve either?"

"Halpern throws up, sir. I've seen it."

"I thought *you* throw up."

"Just once, sir. I didn't know the sausage was sausage."

"We'll give menus, Grossbart. We'll show training films about the food, so you can identify when we're trying to poison you."

Grossbart did not answer. Out before me, the men had been organized into two long chow lines. At the tail end of one I spotted Fishbein — or rather, his glasses spotted me. They winked sunlight back at me like a friend. Halpern stood next to him, patting inside his collar with a khaki handkerchief. They moved with the line as it began to edge up towards the food. The mess sergeant was still screaming at the K.P.'s, who stood ready to ladle out the food, bewildered. For a moment I was actually terrorized by the thought that somehow the mess sergeant was going to get involved in Grossbart's problem.

"Come over here, Marx," the Captain said to me. "Marx, you're a Jewish fella, am I right?"

I played straight man. "Yes, sir."

"How long you been in the Army? Tell this boy."

"Three years and two months."

"A year in combat, Grossbart. Twelve goddam months in combat all through Europe. I admire this man," the Captain said, snapping a wrist against my chest. "But do you hear him peeping about the food? Do you? I want an answer, Grossbart. Yes or no."

"No, sir."

"And why not? He's a Jewish fella."

"Some things are more important to some Jews than other things to other Jews."

Barrett blew up. "Look, Grossbart, Marx here is a good man, a goddam *hero.* When you were sitting on your sweet ass in high school, Sergeant Marx was killing Germans. Who does more for the Jews, you by throwing up over a lousy piece of sausage, a piece of firstcut meat — or Marx by killing those Nazi bastards? If I was a Jew, Grossbart, I'd kiss this man's feet. He's a goddam hero, you know that? And *he* eats what we give him. Why do you have to cause trouble is what I want to know! What is it you're buckin' for, a discharge?"

"No, sir."

"I'm talking to a *wall!* Sergeant, get him out of my way." Barrett pounced over to the driver's seat. "I'm going to see the chaplain!" The engine roared, the jeep spun around, and then, raising a whirl of dust, the Captain was headed back to camp.

For a moment, Grossbart and I stood side by side, watching the jeep. Then he looked at me and said, "I don't want to start trouble. That's the first thing they toss up to us."

When he spoke I saw that his teeth were white and straight, and the sight of them suddenly made me understand that Grossbart actually did have parents: that once upon a time someone had taken little Sheldon to the dentist. He was someone's son. Despite all the talk about his parents, it was hard to believe in Grossbart as a child, an heir — as related by blood to anyone, mother, father, or, above all, to me. This realization led me to another.

"What does your father do, Grossbart?" I asked, as we started to walk back towards the chow line.

"He's a tailor."

"An American?"

"Now, yes. A son in the Army," he said, jokingly.

"And your mother?" I asked.

He winked. "A *ballabusta* — she practically sleeps with a dustcloth in her hand."

"She's also an immigrant?"

"All she talks is Yiddish, still."

"And your father too?"

"A little English. 'Clean,' 'Press,' 'Take the pants in ...' That's the extent of it. But they're good to me ..."

"Then Grossbart —" I reached out and stopped him. He turned towards me and when our eyes met his seemed to jump back, shiver in their sockets. He looked afraid. "Grossbart, then you were the one who wrote that letter, weren't you?"

It took only a second or two for his eyes to flash happy again. "Yes." He walked on, and I kept pace. "It's what my father *would* have written if he had known how. It was his name, though. *He* signed it. He even mailed it. I sent it home. For the New York postmark."

I was astonished, and he saw it. With complete seriousness, he thrust his right arm in front of me. "Blood is blood, Sergeant," he said, pinching the blue vein in his wrist.

"What the hell *are* you trying to do, Grossbart? I've seen you eat. Do you know that? I told the Captain I don't know what you eat, but I've seen you eat like a hound at chow."

"We work hard, Sergeant. We're in training. For a furnace to work, you've got to feed it coal."

"If you wrote the letter, Grossbart, then why did you say you threw up all the time?"

"I was really talking about Mickey there. But he would never write, Sergeant, though I pleaded with him. He'll waste away to nothing if I don't help. Sergeant, I used my name, my father's name, but it's Mickey and Fishbein too I'm watching out for."

"You're a regular Messiah, aren't you?"

We were at the chow line now.

"That's a good one, Sergeant." He smiled. "But who knows? Who can tell? Maybe you're the Messiah ... a little bit. What Mickey says is the Messiah is a collective idea. He went to Yeshivah, Mickey, for a while. He says together we're the Messiah. Me a little bit, you a little bit.... You should hear that kid talk, Sergeant, when he gets going."

"Me a little bit, you a little bit. You'd like to believe that, wouldn't you, Grossbart? That makes everything so clean for you."

"It doesn't seem too bad a thing to believe, Sergeant. It only means we should all give a little, is all ..."

I walked off to eat my rations with the other noncoms.

Two days later a letter addressed to Captain Barrett passed over my desk. It had come through the chain of command — from the office of Congressman Franconi, where it had been received, to General Lyman, to Colonel Sousa, to Major Lamont, to Captain Barrett. I read it over twice while the Captain was at the officer's mess. It was dated May 14th, the day Barrett had spoken with Grossbart on the rifle range.

Dear Congressman:
First let me thank you for your interest in behalf of my son, Private Sheldon Grossbart. Fortunately, I was able to speak with Sheldon on the phone the other night, and I think I've been able to solve our problem. He is, as I mentioned in my letter, a very religious boy, and it was only with the greatest difficulty that I could persuade him that the religious thing to do — what God Himself would want Sheldon to do — would be to suffer the pangs of religious remorse for the good of his country and all mankind. It took some doing, Congressman, but finally he saw the light. In fact, what he said

(and I wrote down the words on a scratch pad so as never to forget), what he said was, "I guess you're right, Dad. So many millions of my fellow Jews gave up their lives to the enemy, the least I can do is live for a while minus a bit of my heritage so as to help end this struggle and regain for all the children of God dignity and humanity." That, Congressman, would make any father proud.

By the way, Sheldon wanted me to know — and to pass on to you — the name of a soldier who helped him reach this decision: SERGEANT NATHAN MARX. Sergeant Marx is a combat veteran who is Sheldon's First Sergeant. This man has helped Sheldon over some of the first hurdles he's had to face in the Army, and is in part responsible for Sheldon's changing his mind about the dietary laws. I know Sheldon would appreciate any recognition Marx could receive.

Thank you and good luck. I look forward to seeing your name on the next election ballot.

Respectfully,
Samuel E. Grossbart

Attached to the Grossbart communiqué was a communiqué addressed to General Marshall Lyman, the post commander, and signed by Representative Charles E. Franconi of the House of Representatives. The communiqué informed General Lyman that Sergeant Nathan Marx was a credit to the U.S. Army and the Jewish people.

What was Grossbart's motive in recanting? Did he feel he'd gone too far? Was the letter a strategic retreat — a crafty attempt to strengthen what he considered our alliance? Or had he actually changed his mind, via an imaginary dialogue between Grossbart *père* and *fils*? I was puzzled, but only for a few days — that is, only until I realized that whatever his reasons, he had actually decided to disappear from my life: he was going to allow himself to become just another trainee. I saw him at inspection but he never winked; at chow formations but he never flashed me a sign; on Sundays, with the other trainees, he would sit around watching the noncoms' softball team, for whom I pitched, but not once did he speak an unnecessary or unusual word to me. Fishbein and Halpern retreated from sight too, at Grossbart's command I was sure. Apparently he'd seen that wisdom lay in turning back before he plunged us over into the ugliness of privilege undeserved. Our separation allowed me to forgive him our past encounters, and, finally, to admire him for his good sense.

Meanwhile, free of Grossbart, I grew used to my job and my administrative tasks. I stepped on a scale one day and discovered I had truly become a noncombatant: I had gained seven pounds. I found patience to get past the first three pages of a book. I thought about the future more and more, and wrote letters to girls I'd known before the war — I even got a few answers. I sent away to Columbia for a Law School catalogue. I continued to follow the war in the Pacific, but it was not my war and I read of bombings and battles like a civilian. I thought I could see the end in sight and sometimes at night I dreamed that I was walking on the streets of Manhattan — Broadway, Third Avenue, and 116th Street, where I had lived those three years I'd attended Columbia College. I curled myself around these dreams and I began to be happy.

And then one Saturday when everyone was away and I was alone in the orderly room reading a month-old copy of *The Sporting News*, Grossbart reappeared.

"You a baseball fan, Sergeant?"

I looked up. "How are you?"

"Fine," Grossbart said. "They're making a soldier out of me."

"How are Fishbein and Halpern?"

"Coming along," he said. "We've got no training this afternoon. They're at the movies."

"How come you're not with them?"

"I wanted to come over and say hello."

He smiled — a shy, regular-guy smile, as though he and I well knew that our friendship drew its sustenance from unexpected visits, remembered birthdays, and borrowed lawnmowers. At first it offended me, and then the feeling was swallowed by the general uneasiness I felt at the thought that everyone on the post was locked away in a dark movie theater and I was here alone with Grossbart. I folded my paper.

"Sergeant," he said, "I'd like to ask a favor. It is a favor and I'm making no bones about it."

He stopped, allowing me to refuse him a hearing — which, of course, forced me into a courtesy I did not intend. "Go ahead."

"Well, actually it's two favors."

I said nothing.

"The first one's about the rumors. Everybody says we're going to the Pacific."

"As I told your friend Fishbein, I don't know. You'll just have wait to find out. Like everybody else."

"You think there's a chance of any of us going East?"

"Germany," I said, "maybe."

"I meant New York."

"I don't think so, Grossbart. Offhand."

"Thanks for the information, Sergeant," he said.

"It's not information, Grossbart. Just what I surmise."

"It certainly would be good to be near home. My parents ... you know." He took a step towards the door and then turned back. "Oh the other thing. May I ask the other?"

"What is it?"

"The other thing is — I've got relatives in St. Louis and they say they'll give me a whole Passover dinner if I can get down there. God, Sergeant, that'd mean an awful lot to me."

I stood up. "No passes during basic, Grossbart."

"But we're off from now till Monday morning, Sergeant. I could leave the post and no one would even know."

"I'd know. You'd know."

"But that's all. Just the two of us. Last night I called my aunt and you should have heard her. 'Come, come,' she said. 'I got gefilte fish, *chrain,* the works!' Just a day, Sergeant, I'd take the blame if anything happened."

"The captain isn't here to sign a pass."

"You could sign."

"Look, Grossbart —"

"Sergeant, for two months practically I've been eating *trafe* till I want to die."

"I thought you'd made up your mind to live with it. To be minus a little bit of heritage."

He pointed a finger at me. "You!" he said. "That wasn't for you to read!"

"I read it. So what."

"That letter was addressed to a congressman."

"Grossbart, don't feed me any crap. You *wanted* me to read it."

"Why are you persecuting me, Sergeant?"

"Are you kidding!"

"I've run into this before," he said, "but never from my own!"

"Get out of here, Grossbart! Get the hell out of my sight!"

He did not move. "Ashamed, that's what you are. So you take it out on the rest of us. They say Hitler himself was half a Jew. Seeing this, I wouldn't doubt it!"

"What are you trying to do with me, Grossbart? What are you after? You want me to give you special privileges, to change the food, to find out about your orders, to give you weekend passes."

"You even talk like a goy!" Grossbart shook his fist. "Is this a weekend pass I'm asking for? Is a Seder sacred or not?"

Seder! It suddenly occurred to me that Passover had been celebrated weeks before. I confronted Grossbart with the fact.

"That's right," he said. "Who says no? A month ago, and *I* was in the field eating hash! And now all I ask is a simple favor — a Jewish boy I thought would understand. My aunt's willing to go out of her way — to make a Seder a month later —" He turned to go, mumbling.

"Come back here!" I called. He stopped and looked at me. "Grossbart, why can't you be like the rest? Why do you have to stick out like a sore thumb? Why do you beg for special treatment?"

"Because I'm a Jew, Sergeant. I *am* different. Better, maybe not. But different."

"This is a war, Grossbart. For the time being *be* the same."

"I refuse."

"What?"

"I refuse. I can't stop being me, that's all there is to it." Tears came to his eyes. "It's a hard thing to be a Jew. But now I see what Mickey says — it's a harder thing to stay one." He raised a hand sadly toward me. "Look at you."

"Stop crying!"

"Stop this, stop that, stop the other thing! You stop, Sergeant. Stop closing your heart to your own!" And wiping his face with his sleeve, he ran out the door. "The least we can do for one another . . . the least . . ."

An hour later I saw Grossbart headed across the field. He wore a pair of starched khakis and carried only a little leather ditty bag. I went to the door and from the outside felt the heat of the day. It was quiet — not a soul in sight except over by the mess hall four K.P.'s sitting round a pan, sloped forward from the waists, gabbing and peeling potatoes in the sun.

"Grossbart!" I called.

He looked toward me and continued walking.

"Grossbart, get over here!"

He turned and stepped into his shadow. Finally he stood before me.

"Where are you going?" I said.

"St. Louis. I don't care."

"You'll get caught without a pass."

"So I'll get caught without a pass."

"You'll go to the stockade."

"I'm in the stockade." He made an about-face and headed off.

I let him go only a step: "Come back here," I said, and he followed me into the office, where I typed out a pass and signed the Captain's name and my own initials after it.

He took the pass from me and then, a moment later, he reached out and grabbed my hand. "Sergeant, you don't know how much this means to me."

"Okay. Don't get in any trouble."

"I wish I could show you how much this means to me."

"Don't do me any favors. Don't write any more congressmen for citations."

Amazingly, he smiled. "You're right. I won't. But let me do something."

"Bring me a piece of that gefilte fish. Just get out of here."

"I will! With a slice of carrot and a little horseradish. I won't forget."

"All right. Just show your pass at the gate. And don't tell *anybody.*"

"I won't. It's a month late, but a good Yom Tov to you."

"Good Yom Tov, Grossbart," I said.

"You're a good Jew, Sergeant. You like to think you have a hard heart, but underneath you're a fine decent man. I mean that."

Those last three words touched me more than any words from Grossbart's mouth had the right to. "All right, Grossbart. Now call me 'sir' and get the hell out of here."

He ran out the door and was gone. I felt very

pleased with myself — it was a great relief to stop fighting Grossbart. And it had cost me nothing. Barrett would never find out, and if he did, I could manage to invent some excuse. For a while I sat at my desk, comfortable in my decision. Then the screen door flew back and Grossbart burst in again. "Sergeant!" he said. Behind him I saw Fishbein and Halpern, both in starched khakis, both carrying ditty bags exactly like Grossbart's.

"Sergeant, I caught Mickey and Larry coming out of the movies. I almost missed them."

"Grossbart, did I say tell no one?"

"But my aunt said I could bring friends. That I should, in fact."

"I'm the Sergeant, Grossbart — not your aunt!"

Grossbart looked at me in disbelief; he pulled Halpern up by his sleeve. "Mickey, tell the Sergeant what this would mean to you."

"Grossbart, for God's sake, spare us —"

"Tell him what you told me, Mickey. How much it would mean."

Halpern looked at me and, shrugging his shoulders, made his admission. "A lot."

Fishbein stepped forward without prompting. "This would mean a great deal to me and my parents, Sergeant Marx."

"No!" I shouted.

Grossbart was shaking his head. "Sergeant, I could see you denying me, but how you can deny Mickey, a Yeshivah boy, that's beyond me."

"I'm not denying Mickey anything. You just pushed a little too hard, Grossbart. *You* denied him."

"I'll give him my pass, then," Grossbart said. "I'll give him my aunt's address and a little note. At least let him go."

In a second he had crammed the pass into Halpern's pants' pocket. Halpern looked at me, Fishbein too. Grossbart was at the door, pushing it open. "Mickey, bring me a piece of gefilte fish at least." And then he was outside again.

The three of us looked at one another and then I said, "Halpern, hand that pass over."

He took it from his pocket and gave it to me. Fishbein had now moved to the doorway, where he lingered. He stood there with his mouth slightly open and then pointed to himself. "And me?" he asked.

His utter ridiculousness exhausted me. I slumped down in my seat and felt pulses knocking at the back of my eyes. "Fishbein," I said, "you understand I'm not trying to deny you anything, don't you? If it was my Army I'd serve gefilte fish in the mess hall. I'd sell kugel in the PX, honest to God."

Halpern smiled.

"You understand don't you, Halpern?"

"Yes, Sergeant."

"And you, Fishbein? I don't want enemies. I'm just like you — I want to serve my time and go home. I miss the same things you miss."

"Then, Sergeant," Fishbein interrupted, "Why don't you come too?"

"Where?"

"To St. Louis. To Shelley's aunt. We'll have a regular Seder. Play hide-the-matzah." He gave a broad, black-toothed smile.

I saw Grossbart in the doorway again, on the other side of the screen.

"Psst!" He waved a piece of paper. "Mickey, here's the address. Tell her I couldn't get away."

Halpern did not move. He looked at me and I saw the shrug moving up his arms into his shoulders again. I took the cover off my typewriter and made out passes for him and Fishbein. "Go," I said, "the three of you."

I thought Halpern was going to kiss my hand.

That afternoon, in a bar in Joplin, I drank beer and listened with half an ear to the Cardinal game. I tried to look squarely at what I'd become involved in, and began to wonder if perhaps the struggle with Grossbart wasn't as much my fault as his. What was I that I had to *muster* generous feelings? Who was I to have been feeling so grudging, so tight-hearted? After all, I wasn't being asked to move the world. Had I a right, then, or a reason, to clamp down on Grossbart, when that meant clamping down on Halpern, too? And Fishbein, that ugly agreeable soul, wouldn't he suffer in the bargain also? Out of the many recollections that had tumbled over me these past few days, I heard from some childhood moment my grandmother's voice: "What are you making a *tsimas?*" It was what he would ask my mother when, say, I had cut myself with a knife and her daughter was busy bawling me out. I would need a hug and a kiss and my mother would moralize! But my grandmother knew — mercy overrides justice. I should have known it, too. Who was Nathan Marx to be such a pennypincher with kindness? Surely, I thought, the Messiah himself — if he should ever come — won't niggle over nickels and dimes. God willing, he'll hug and kiss.

The next day, while we were playing softball over on the Parade Grounds, I decided to ask Bob Wright, who was noncom in charge over at Classification and Assignment, where he thought our trainees would be sent when their cycle ended in two weeks. I asked casually, between innings, and he said, "They're pushing them all into the Pacific. Shulman cut the orders on your boys the other day."

The news shocked me, as though I were father to Halpern, Fishbein, and Grossbart.

That night I was just sliding into sleep when someone tapped on the door. "What is it?"

"Sheldon."

He opened the door and came in. For a moment

I felt his presence without being able to see him. "How was it?" I asked, as though to the darkness.

He popped into sight before me. "Great, Sergeant." I felt my springs sag; Grossbart was sitting on the edge of the bed. I sat up.

"How about you?" he asked. "Have a nice weekend?"

"Yes."

He took a deep paternal breath. "The others went to sleep . . ." We sat silently for a while, as a homey feeling invaded my ugly little cubicle: the door was locked, the cat out, the children safely in bed.

"Sergeant, can I tell you something? Personal?"

I did not answer and he seemed to know why. "Not about me. About Mickey. Sergeant, I never felt for anybody like I feel for him. Last night I heard Mickey in the bed next to me. He was crying so, it could have broken your heart. Real sobs."

"I'm sorry to hear that."

"I had to talk to him to stop him. He held my hand, Sergeant — he wouldn't let it go. He was almost hysterical. He kept saying if he only knew where we were going. Even if he knew it *was* the Pacific, that would be better than nothing. Just to know."

Long ago, someone had taught Grossbart the sad law that only lies can get the truth. Not that I couldn't believe in Halpern's crying — his eyes *always* seemed red-rimmed. But, fact or not, it became a lie when Grossbart uttered it. He was entirely strategic. But then — it came with the force of indictment — so was I! There are strategies of aggression, but there are strategies of retreat, as well. And so, recognizing that I, myself, had not been without craft and guile, I told him what I knew. "It is the Pacific."

He let out a small gasp, which was not a lie. "I'll tell him. I wish it was otherwise."

"So do I."

He jumped on my words. "You mean you think you could do something? A change maybe?"

"No, I couldn't do a thing."

"Don't you know anybody over at C & A?"

"Grossbart, there's nothing I can do. If your orders are for the Pacific then it's the Pacific."

"But Mickey."

"Mickey, you, me — everybody, Grossbart. There's nothing to be done. Maybe the war'll end before you go. Pray for a miracle."

"But —"

"Good night, Grossbart." I settled back, and was relieved to feel the springs unbend again as Grossbart rose to leave. I could see him clearly now; his jaw had dropped and he looked like a dazed prizefighter. I noticed for the first time a little paper bag in his hand.

"Grossbart" — I smiled — "my gift?"

"Oh, yes, Sergeant. Here, from all of us." He handed me the bag. "It's egg roll."

"Egg roll?" I accepted the bag and felt a damp grease spot on the bottom. I opened it, sure that Grossbart was joking.

"We thought you'd probably like it. You know, Chinese egg roll. We thought you'd probably have a taste for —"

"Your aunt served egg roll?"

"She wasn't home."

"Grossbart, she invited you. You told me she invited you and your friends."

"I know. I just reread the letter. *Next* week."

I got out of bed and walked to the window. It was black as far off as I could see. "Grossbart," I said. But I was not calling him.

"What?"

"What are you, Grossbart? Honest to God, what are you?"

I think it was the first time I'd asked him a question for which he didn't have an immediate answer.

"How can you do this to people?" I asked.

"Sergeant, the day away did us all a world of good. Fishbein, you should see him, he *loves* Chinese food."

"But the Seder," I said.

"We took second best, Sergeant."

Rage came charging at me. I didn't sidestep — I grabbed it, pulled it in, hugged it to my chest.

"Grossbart, you're a liar! You're a schemer and a crook! You've got no respect for anything! Nothing at all! Not for me, for the truth, not even for poor Halpern! You use us all —"

"Sergeant, Sergeant, I feel for Mickey, honest to God, I do. I *love* Mickey. I try —"

"You try! You feel!" I lurched towards him and grabbed his shirt front. I shook him furiously. "Grossbart, get out. Get out and stay the hell away from me! Because if I see you, I'll make your life miserable. *You understand that?*"

"Yes."

I let him free, and when he walked from the room I wanted to spit on the floor where he had stood. I couldn't stop the fury from rising in my heart. It engulfed me, owned me, till it seemed I could only rid myself of it with tears or an act of violence. I snatched from the bed the bag Grossbart had given me and with all my strength threw it out the window. And the next morning, as the men policed the area around the barracks, I heard a great cry go up from one of the trainees who'd been anticipating only his morning handful of cigarette butts and candy wrappers. "Egg roll!" he shouted. "Holy Christ, Chinese goddam egg roll!"

A week later when I read the orders that had come down from C & A I couldn't believe my eyes. Every single trainee was to be shipped to Camp Stoneham, California, and from there to the Pacific. Every trainee but one: Private Sheldon Grossbart was to be sent to Fort Monmouth, New

Jersey. I read the mimeographed sheet several times. Dee, Farrell, Fishbein, Fuselli, Fylypowycz, Glinicki, Gromke, Gucwa, Halpern, Hardy, Helebrandt . . . right down to Anton Zygadlo, all were to be headed West before the month was out. All except Grossbart. He had pulled a string and I wasn't it.

I lifted the phone and called C & A.

The voice on the other end said smartly, "Corporal Shulman, sir."

"Let me speak to Sergeant Wright."

"Who is this calling, sir?"

"Sergeant Marx."

And to my surprise, the voice said, *"Oh."* Then: "Just a minute, Sergeant."

Shulman's *oh* stayed with me while I waited for Wright to come to the phone. Why *oh?* Who was Shulman? And then, so simply, I knew I'd discovered the string Grossbart had pulled. In fact, I could hear Grossbart the day he'd discovered Shulman, in the PX, or the bowling alley, or maybe even at services. "Glad to meet you. Where are you from? Bronx? Me too. Do you know so-and-so? And so-and-so? Me too! You work at C & A? Really? Hey, how's chances of getting East? Could you do something? Change something? Swindle, cheat, lie? We gotta help each other, you know . . . if the Jews in Germany . . ."

At the other end Bob Wright answered. "How are you, Nate? How's the pitching arm?"

"Good. Bob, I wonder if you could do me a favor." I heard clearly my own words and they so reminded me of Grossbart that I dropped more easily than I could have imagined into what I had planned. "This may sound crazy, Bob, but I got a kid here on orders to Monmouth who wants them changed. He had a brother killed in Europe and he's hot to go to the Pacific. Says he'd feel like a coward if he wound up stateside. I don't know, Bob, can anything be done? Put somebody else in the Monmouth slot?"

"Who?" he asked cagily.

"Anybody. First guy on the alphabet. I don't care. The kid just asked if something could be done."

"What's his name?"

"Grossbart, Sheldon."

Wright didn't answer.

"Yeah," I said, "he's a Jewish kid, so he thought I could help him out. You know."

"I guess I can do something," he finally said. "The Major hasn't been around here for weeks — TDY to the golf course. I'll try, Nate that's all I can say."

"I'd appreciate it, Bob. See you Sunday," and I hung up, perspiring.

And the following day the corrected orders appeared: Fishbein, Fuselli, Fylypowycz, Glinicki, Grossbart, Gucwa, Halpern, Hardy . . . Lucky Private Harley Alton was to go to Fort Monmouth, New Jersey, where for some reason or other, they wanted an enlisted man with infantry training.

After chow that night I stopped back at the orderly room to straighten out the guard duty roster. Grossbart was waiting for me. He spoke first.

"You son of a bitch!"

I sat down at my desk and while he glared down at me I began to make the necessary alterations in the duty roster.

"What do you have against me?" he cried. "Against my family? Would it kill you for me to be near my father, God knows how many months he has left to him."

"Why?"

"His heart," Grossbart said. "He hasn't had enough troubles in a lifetime, you've got to add to them. I curse the day I ever met you, Marx! Shulman told me what happened over there. There's no limit to your anti-Semitism, is there! The damage you've done here isn't enough. You have to make a special phone call! You really want me dead!"

I made the last few notations in the duty roster and got up to leave. "Good night, Grossbart."

"You owe me an explanation!" He stood in my path.

"Sheldon, you're the one who owes explanations."

He scowled. "To *you*?"

"To me, I think so, yes. Mostly to Fishbein and Halpern."

"That's right, twist things around. I owe nobody nothing, I've done all I could do for them. Now I think I've got the right to watch out for myself."

"For each other we have to learn to watch out, Sheldon. You told me yourself."

"You call this watching out for me, what you did?"

"No. For all of us."

I pushed him aside and started for the door. I heard his furious breathing behind me, and it sounded like steam rushing from the engine of his terrible strength.

"You'll be all right," I said from the door. And, I thought, so would Fishbein and Halpern be all right, even in the Pacific, if only Grossbart could continue to see in the obsequiousness of the one, the soft spirituality of the other, some profit for himself.

I stood outside the orderly room, and I heard Grossbart weeping behind me. Over in the barracks, in the lighted windows, I could see the boys in their T-shirts sitting on their bunks talking about their orders, as they'd been doing for the past two days. With a kind of quiet nervousness, they polished shoes, shined belt buckles, squared away underwear, trying as best they could to accept their fate. Behind me, Grossbart swallowed hard, accepting his. And then, resisting with all my will an impulse to turn and seek pardon for my vindictiveness, I accepted my own.

GABRIELLE ROY

My Aunt Thérésina Veilleux

Translated by Henry Binsse

My aunt Thérésina Veilleux was born in our cold province of Manitoba, and to her it was a misfortune. She suffered from asthma, and the wind that blows in our parts was one of the most malign for her; the very air harmed her ... except when it was gentle and scented by the wild rose, as happens in the month of June. Then my aunt could breathe without too much fear.

She spent her youth reading love stories. Given the bent later assumed by her character, I think she might have preferred to read other things, but she had no choice; in the countryside where she dwelt, there then circulated only popular almanacs, or papers containing serial stories, to which a few simple souls subscribed and which were passed on from hand to hand. My aunt Thérésina read hundreds of them, even though she complained at seeing them end in so improbable a manner, poor and unlikely young girls always on the last page achieving the hand of some Hungarian or Serbian prince.

A few years later, when my aunt had children, she gave them names as uncommon among us as Serge, Maxence, Clarisse, Léopold ... and we guessed that she had remembered them from her reading during her days as a shut-in. However that may be, my aunt was proud to have found for her children names that one certainly did not encounter frequently along our Manitoba dirt roads; and at least there was that much romance in her life.

At the period when she was reading her novelettes, nothing could have led a person to foresee that one day she would marry. "Poor Thérésina! Whoever would have her with her asthma?" people said of her, half regretfully, while pointing out that she was still young.

She had been unable to go to school — a little school between the wheat fields, two miles from her home — except for a day or two now and then; and even during the mildest seasons of the year, it happens that a shower will break or a harsh wind blow up ... so it was often necessary for someone to undertake to see safely back home this sick child, whom they propped up in a miniature carriage drawn by a good old collie, long Thérésina's best friend.

At twenty she sometimes went to evening parties, when they were held in houses very warmly heated and tight-walled; while the others danced the polka or sang their lungs out, my aunt Thérésina remained seated, a mauve shawl around her shoulders, from time to time touching her lips with a lawn handkerchief. Thus did my uncle Majorique see her, and he loved her at once — my aunt Thérésina — beyond any possibility of change of heart. It seems that she then had very beautiful eyes, perhaps made brilliant by illness. Indeed, between attacks, above all when she had none for a whole week, Thérésina acquired a lively expression, pleasing and a trifle shy, as though she were more observant than the others, and my uncle Majorique, thinking that this young girl must be intelligent, liked her thus. It was long said that he saw in her a resemblance to Emily Brontë, of whom, wholly by accident, he had chanced to see a photograph; yet his imagination must have led my uncle a bit astray, for if Thérésina had a rather long face and Emily's high forehead, her eyes were wholly innocent of any of that fullness of passion immured alive.

All the same, within our family, we had warned my uncle against marriage to this young woman. "Majorique, have you given a thought to the sort of life it would involve?"

He married her during one of the hottest months in the year, so that Thérésina was able to go to the church in muslin, without a coat, having even for that day forsworn her pretty shawl of soft wool. But later on, when Thérésina's children came into the world, I remember having heard whispers and sighs, having detected looks of consternation; I remember an atmosphere of reproach, as though, each time my aunt gave birth to a child, it amounted to a real misfortune. Then, too, I was much astonished in those days that, too ill to care for her children herself, my aunt was not ill enough to avoid passing most of her time bringing them into the world. But at my age then, could anyone understand that life is furiously concerned to propagate itself, even under the most painful circumstances? And indeed, at a later age, does one understand much better?

II

After eight years, they came to settle in our city, or rather right next to us in Winnipeg. My uncle claimed that the winter must be easier to endure in a city like Winnipeg, with its streets laid out in ranks, than in regions where the farms are at least a mile apart. He likewise thought he would find in town doctors who might try something more for Thérésina than old tags of advice: always keep dry and warm, avoid rain. . . .

Having sold his farm, my uncle went into watch and clock repairing in Winnipeg. When anyone manifested a certain astonishment at his choice of this trade, my uncle laughed a little and said that we were still far indeed from conceiving all the things he knew how to do and could undertake. He explained that the city was short precisely of such repairmen; he had noticed it the very first day, as he wandered about the streets, and he had reached the conclusion that he would earn a very good living at putting clocks and watches in order. In our neighborhood, he hinted, there must be many timepieces in bad shape; they would not agree, and how many appointments that must make people miss! Beneath his joking exterior, my uncle was a man whom you eventually discovered to be full of common sense. And, in fact, he became quite skillful at his new trade.

Unfortunately, my aunt was not helped by this move made in her behalf. I recall how, when we went to see her of a January evening, we had to hasten to close behind us the heavy storm door, and then the inside door with its felt weatherstrip. Sometimes, even, thanks to excess of quickness, we caught the tails of our coats in this door. And then a straw mat must at once be thrust over the crack of the threshold. . . . Yet however speedily we observed these regulations, a bit of glacial night must have slipped into the house and reached the tiny sealed room at the end of a hallway, where my aunt kept herself snug, for very often the moment we came in, what we heard was Thérésina's gasping, terrible cough.

You did not go visit her in clothing that might still exhale something of the snow and frost; first of all you warmed yourself in front of the big stove always stuffed with logs and purring evenly; there my uncle, who never lost his gaiety, would tell us about the amusing clients he received in his Main Street shop, and he would make us laugh.

When, later on, you presented yourself before my aunt Thérésina, it did not mean that you saw her face. My aunt was still fearful of the cold air through which we had come, and of which some whiff might remain upon us, in our hair, upon our outer skins. For a year or two she had been living hooded and muffled, wrapped in a complex of blankets, and deep in a horrible sweet and sickish haze, for the Winnipeg doctors made my aunt smoke medicated cigarettes. A shawl thrown over her head, the edge of which she occasionally raised to peer at us, sheltered her like a tent; in its depths you could make out something that shone — probably Thérésina's eyes, the blue eyes my uncle Majorique had loved. A long thin hand hid the rest of the face. My aunt now breathed only from behind her hand, as though not to inhale the least bit more air than was absolutely needed. Never have I seen a person breathe with such care, prudence, and even terror.

We children, having greeted my aunt, always hastened to return to my uncle, who would sing us something or suggest a game of dominoes. To us it seemed impossible that to this huge package of skirts and wool and shawls which was my aunt you might talk, recount your enthusiasms, smile; that toward her you might become affectionate and trusting. My mother, however, carried on real conversations with the odd bundle seated on the edge of the bed, and she must even have inspired it to laughter, for at times the whole mass of blankets would shake in a motion at once funny and frightening. But soon a wheezing would emerge from it, the motion would change aspect, and everyone would rush to help my aunt regain her breath, gently tap her back, hold her up, try to forestall an attack. In fact, laughing was even more baneful to my aunt than breathing. And hence not often were amusing or witty things recounted to my aunt Thérésina. Moreover, even on such occasions, she showed preference for people with afflictions . . . and in this department my mother spoiled her, telling her for a whole evening long about a veritable crowd of wretched beings who aroused my aunt's interest. She would nod and conclude, "Yes, indeed! There are those worse off than we!"

Meanwhile, my mother always claimed that during those long winter nights she herself learned a great deal from my aunt, for if Thérésina was incapable of sewing or cooking herself, she knew very well how one must go about it to succeed in all things. Remote from any practical knowledge, she had accumulated very sound theories about everything — a trifle harsh and authoritarian, but most sound, Maman insisted. Then, too, having a great deal of time to watch people make mistakes, commit serious blunders, my aunt had acquired a remarkable capacity for criticism; she could put her finger on exactly the spot where others went wrong. It was even a truly extraordinary thing that, never venturing forth, living immured and beyond movement, she should have been able to run her house very efficiently, know everything that went on, not only in her own home, but in almost every part of the city. She was the first to inform my mother of the behavior of our cousin Yvonne — her parents had entrusted her to mine so that she might finish her schooling in our city — our cousin Yvonne, whom we thought very devout, since every evening she went to church, but who, in fact, used this as a cover for her meetings with a certain Monsieur Belleau, a newcomer, especially worrisome because no one knew anything about his antecedents. And this time my mother was truly incensed — more against

Thérésina, indeed, than against Yvonne.

But my aunt Thérésina's real passion, far more than for criticism, was, above all else, for geraniums. She had some of a shade of red so unsullied, so bright, that I have never seen the like since. When she was not too indisposed, my aunt would come look at them in the small pots lined up along her windows. She would dust them — I can still see the way she did it! — with the tip of her finger, delicately cleaning off their leaves, and she would say, "You must not leave dust on the leaves of plants; plants breathe through their leaves; plants need good air." And she was still overjoyed to be alive when the month of June came round and she could set her geraniums out in the open. My uncle would offer to do this task for her. He pointed out to her that by going close to the still damp, cool soil, she would lay herself open to aggravating her malady. But, protected by three or four sweaters, a small trowel in her hand, one fine day my aunt would herself emerge to set out her plants.

Alas, the Manitoba summer is very short. With the first autumn rains, Thérésina had to return to her tiny overheated room, reeking with the smell of the dreadful cigarettes which she began once more to smoke. And my uncle Majorique would begin to say that Manitoba did not in the least suit Thérésina's illness, that she needed a wholly different land... California, for instance... yes, why not California?

"She, who so loves plants," my uncle would say, "does it make any sense that she can only see them and enjoy them for two months in the year?..." And he sent to a travel agency for pamphlets and all sorts of information about California.

Thus it was, by means of brochures and vividly colored post cards — they were thought to be overvivid — that California loomed up for us on the frozen prairie horizon, not too far off, and wonderfully real, with small white houses basking in the sun!

From this medley of cards sent to my uncle, my aunt chose one that showed geraniums — no longer mere plants, but almost trees! — covered with huge and glorious flowers. My aunt folded this bit of paper and preserved it between the pages of her prayer book, alongside pictures of the Pope and mementos of the dead bearing the words "In Memoriam." Thus, from the start, did my aunt show sympathy for California.

She would look at the little white stucco houses on the post cards and would say, "See! They're pretty as places to live!"

She already knew that inside these small dwellings there is a garden which is called a "patio."

And finally she invited my mother to come visit her someday in California.

"When we get there," explained my aunt, "you'll come, Eveline. I'll make you come. You, with your rheumatism — it will do you good, too!"

In our family all of us were far from taking too seriously my uncle's new idea. We spoke of it as a silly scheme. Silly? ... Yes ... certainly ... if you thought of the distance, of the money required. All the same, my uncle had looked into the matter seriously: the American government would allow him to establish himself with his family in the United States, but in view of the fact that my aunt was incurable, only on condition of his possessing a capital sum of ten thousand dollars. Apart from that, as far as the warmer air and sunlight were concerned, wasn't the plan the most reasonable thing in the world? Of course, my uncle was far from possessing the capital required by the government of the United States.

So, for want of anything better, and since he had heard that the Saskatchewan climate was auspicious for bronchial infections, my uncle left our city and took all his family to live in Gravelbourg.

III

In Saskatchewan, not only does it blow in winter, but almost all summer, and perhaps the summer wind there is more noxious than the winter. We used to be told — we who had never seen the desert, nor a great deal of Saskatchewan — that the wind blowing there felt as though it came off the Sahara. Yet, through such comparisons, our imaginations heard from afar the Gravelbourg wind, that sad, hot, desiccating wind; all day it sucked up the poor soil, reducing it to wandering, miserable dust. Thus, particle by particle, the best of the land disappeared. My aunt Thérésina wrote us a short and very sad letter, in which she said, "Dear Eveline: I take my pen in hand to tell you that here all goes well enough, except that I cannot go out, even in midsummer. The wind chokes me ... the cattle perish ... the wells are drying up. ..."

Out there my uncle had found too much competition in his trade as watch repairer — or rather, better opportunities for prosperity in another. He became a lumber merchant; in those days a new house was being completed in Gravelbourg every week. The first year he sold I know not how many thousands of board feet. Nevertheless, since the climate was not exactly what suited Thérésina, my uncle was already seeking a buyer for all the wood remaining on his hands. My aunt drew on her reserves of patience. She retained her faith in the California plan, and henceforth ended her letters with such phrases as: "We have got a little closer, it's true, to California, but not so much so, when you think it over. ... It must come soon, because, before long, I shan't even have the strength to leave this dreadful Gravelbourg. ..."

Then we learned that my uncle Majorique, after four and one half years spent at Gravelbourg, had turned even farther west. The family had made its move; the letter bearing us the news was posted from North Battleford.

Whatever could have induced my uncle to select this town? Gravelbourg might do in a pinch! It was a French Canadian center relatively toward the south, and when the family arrived there, they had run into a few acquaintances; but North Battleford! That ugly pioneer town established in mud, at the moment resounding from dawn to dusk with the racket of hammers, passing through a turbulent boom, like the towns of the Klondike during the gold rush! We have long thought that my uncle's sole motive for deciding upon this stop along his way was to acquire some money there. He was able to revert to his former trade, to which he added that of jeweler. "Two things that go together," wrote my uncle, "for here there are many rich, and I feel I can sell them without trouble small diamonds for engagement rings and other odds and ends of precious stones — not too costly — for anniversaries. . . ."

At about this time, however, while my uncle was going full steam ahead, my aunt began to withdraw her confidence. She would henceforth refer to him as "the Utopian!" or "the Dreamer!" and things even less flattering. "You know your brother," she wrote to Maman, "full of wild fancies and unstable! . . . I go bouncing from town to town; scarcely have we time to unpack our things when our fine Majorique wants to move again. . . . California! Yes! Talk about California! At the rate we're going, one of these days we'll end up in Alaska! When you get right down to it, I wonder whether your brother hasn't made an excuse out of this California scheme to satisfy his fidgets. . . ."

For his own part, my uncle Majorique complained to us a little about my aunt Thérésina. "The poor woman is becoming quite ill tempered. I know it is her dreadful illness that makes her this way, and I myself don't mind too much . . . but the children are growing up . . . and they don't like to be scolded all the time. I'm afraid we shall not keep Maxence and Clarisse at home with us much longer."

Obviously to my aunt Thérésina, cheerfulness, bustle, songs, dancing — all such things seemed less and less natural. We heard that she was strict with her daughters and her grown sons. However, what she deplored the most was that Serge had retraced his steps to Gravelbourg, where he was managing the lumber business. Then she had Clarisse to regret; she had found a match — a wealthy one, according to my uncle — at North Battleford.

"We leave children in every town through which we pass," my aunt wrote; "we soon shall not have a single one left . . . what a diaspora!" And she reverted, making it responsible for all these misfortunes, to that stupid scheme of going to California. "We should indeed have stayed home," she told us. And now there could be no vestige of doubt that, through time's weird alchemy — that transformation in our memories which it alone is capable of effecting — the years spent in Manitoba, and even the stifling little Winnipeg room, had become for my aunt the best part of her life.

It was sixteen years after they had left us that we learned they had reached Edmonton.

"Good Lord!" exclaimed my mother. "Think of choosing Edmonton! The northernmost city in Canada! Poor Thérésina, she's good and far from California now!" Suffering more and more from rheumatism, my mother had reached the point of wishing as much for herself as for my aunt that she might see them at last settled in California, since the invitation to pay them a visit there in orange blossom time had never been withdrawn. And nothing seemed more surprising to me in those days than this eagerness to get away manifested by the older people among us. Just the opposite of what happens elsewhere, where it is the young who want to journey forth, here it was the poor souls weary of the cold, the sick, the arthritic, all those who were beset with age or feeling poorly. Why, we young people were keen about the tingling winter, the snow crunching under our feet, our breath freezing as it left our lips, the droll fringes of frost over our lashes, and, overhead, the blue sheen of the stars, as well as, on occasion, the great far-flung play of the aurora borealis!

From Edmonton we received only one single brief letter from Thérésina, which began saying, "I take my pen in hand to tell you that today the thermometer registers fifty-five below zero. . . . Even the horses can't go out. I thought I used to know what cold is like; my mistake was to have complained of it too soon. . . ." Toward the end she told us: "That fine fellow Majorique finds Edmonton a city of the future. . . . He speaks of the future as though we were still twenty years old. . . . As for me, I must be drawing near my end. . . . It was not God's will that I go down to the South. God's will be done."

Later on she was too wretched to give us news. We heard of them through Noémi, who became a trained nurse, settled in Edmonton, and refused to leave when the rest of the family moved on toward Vancouver.

My aunt had become so pessimistic, so thoroughly certain that she would go on forever from cold to colder, that in British Columbia she long refused to believe the air was soft and agreeable. One day, however, having taken a few steps out of doors, my aunt, who believed that she was still living in a region where nature was cruel, saw roses in bloom. She sent us some of their dried petals, telling my mother, "Maybe you won't believe it — I picked them on the twenty-eighth day of February, while I thought of you, my dear Eveline. . . ." A little joy, we saw with pleasure, was rebuilding feelings of affection in our poor aunt's heart.

But the coastal fogs did her asthma no good. Eventually my aunt shut herself up out there in a stifling little room, as she had done almost all her life, be it here or be it there, and — when you came down to it, as she said — how much had she seen of so many cities, of the many weary miles she had traveled, of the almost entire continent she had traversed?

At that juncture my uncle was setting up a laundry business. Ever young, alert, and enterprising, he had certainly just discovered that in this city there were too few laundrymen. This undertaking flourished so mightily that within two or three years he had a string of branch stores and his third son, Léopold, could take over its management. This son of his was to remain in Vancouver; and so, even today, almost all across the country there are children of my aunt Thérésina and my uncle Majorique, as though to prove once and for all that these constant moves, their unbelievable wanderings, were no mere figment of the imagination. As for my uncle, at last we realized to how great an extent, despite all appearances, he had been a man of one set idea... that if he had taken a northern route to go south and then had veered west, he had all the same been making his way toward his goal. In any case, relying upon the good faith of a real-estate agent, he bought a parcel of land in California. It was said that he arranged the purchase before leaving in order the better to make up my aunt's mind, for had the money not been invested and the place ready to receive Thérésina, almost certainly she would have been unwilling, despite the fog, to set off once more.

It lay very close to a small village called Buena Vista or Bella Vista. The property included an orchard containing principally orange and avocado trees. A little withdrawn from the coast, it had a view over the ocean, and one could also glimpse, but very far off, mountains covered with snow. A small house stood waiting for my uncle and aunt. The garden was completely sheltered from the wind, with exposure to the best sunshine of the day. For the moment, however, the most distressing question was whether my aunt Thérésina would be able to stand the trip. Her heart was much weakened. And that winter the rest of us back in Manitoba would ask ourselves, from day to day, "Is Thérésina ever going to arrive in California?"

"Often," my mother would say, "it is at the very moment when one's lifetime desire lies within reach that it is suddenly snatched away!"

IV

She got there, but shaken by the trip, stubborn, already old — true enough — and she refused, as it were, to believe she was there. None the less, she at last began to shed her sweaters, her heavy quilted and interlined skirts, her headband, an old gray muffler that had traveled with her from Manitoba.

And her last and dear child, Rachel, whom we had never seen, wrote us: "We had believed — we had all believed — that Maman was a fairly stout person, on the well-rounded side, eh! Well! When we had taken off the flannel garments which she wore over very nearly all parts of her body, the knitted clothing, and then still more layers of flannel and knit goods, oh, Aunt Eveline! We then realized that of Maman herself there remained almost nothing!..."

But, without letting on too much, they watched how this tiny old woman would react when she saw a nature, a country, a sky that would not be hostile to her, that — quite the opposite — had been made to her order. My uncle, Rachel, Roberto, all were eager to see my aunt's face when she really became aware of God's creation. But they gave no hint of it: my aunt was put out of sorts whenever anyone noticed the brief moments during which she was still a little joyful.

The day came at last when my aunt dared venture into the open air with her hands and face uncovered.

And if the tiny kingdom of God then before her eyes in the least resembled the post card view of it that we received, it must be granted that it was a fine summary of what God could create when His preoccupation was to rejoice the eyes of men.

To the left there was a path bordered with eucalyptus, and the air was made wholly pure by their big, disheveled leaves. On the other side there were bushy rhododendrons and poinsettias. And then, beyond other masses of plants, far away, my aunt surely could glimpse the sea. They told her that this was the Pacific Ocean, that here it deserved its name, and that its langorous waves washed up on the beaches shells from distant isles, perhaps from Hawaii. They led my aunt toward a garden chair so placed that Thérésina could see the valley and water merely by moving her eyes a little. Above her armchair waved syringa branches in bloom.

Two or three times she came back to sit beneath the syringas. They found her there one day, her eyes wide open and staring fixedly forever. And in Thérésina's blue eyes, there was a deep questioning, as though in leaving this world my poor aunt's soul had asked itself, "Why? But why?"

About the meaning of this "why," though, we never agreed in our family. Some claimed that my aunt must have asked God why she should die now that she had arrived; others felt that, looking at the snowy mountains, it was Manitoba that she saw once again, loved and sorrowed for, perhaps, as always; and thus that she had asked herself why she was here, and not there, in her own land, to die.

There cannot exist a better place to abide in than the tiny cemetery attached to the old Spanish mission of San Juan Capistrano. A wind as light as a child's breath stirs a little the wild leaves of the eucalyptus. The pepper trees trail, delicate as the shroud covering the body of a dead young girl, their long, fine foliage. Of no great height, and the color of Mexican pottery jars, a wall of baked earth surrounds this garden; this primitive masonry is called "adobe"; transpose two of its letters and you get "abode," a dwelling place. And here indeed is the habitation of thousands of swallows.

Every year, on the seventeenth of March exactly, and at a set hour as well, they arrive there. Spectators who have taken their places near at hand somewhat ahead of time, await the squadron. At the appointed hour, the sky darkens toward the sea; the whirlwind of birds takes shape, and, on the dot, the swallows dive into their home in the cemetery.

But when my aunt died, there had long been no free space in the San Juan Capistrano cemetery.

My uncle offered a large sum to the prior, yet he refused all the same. Every inch of this garden had been taken for many years, said he; moreover, the famous enclosure, said he, was in the process of becoming a sort of museum.

Then patiently, maybe with a few tears — he imagined that he had caused his wife's death by dragging her to California — my uncle briefly told Thérésina's strange story; how she was born in one of Canada's coldest provinces; how, as a little girl, she had never been able to go to school more than a few days at a time, even though she would have liked to acquire book learning; how, at parties during her youth, she could not dance, which later on had made dancing seem to her frivolous and reprehensible; in short, my uncle pleaded so well that the prior of San Juan Capistrano grew perplexed. While gently moving the branch of a pepper tree, he seemed to be considering the extraordinary destiny of my aunt, born Thérésina Veilleux, and even the coldness there had been all through that life! ...

Then he hinted that perhaps ... perhaps they might dig a grave above another very ancient one; there were some dating back to Spanish days, two hundred years before — maybe even longer — thus, the prior was saying, the family of this dead person, most likely extinct, could not take offense, or the dead person either, reduced as he was to a few dry bits of bone. ... He himself, the prior, in his white robes, seemed to imagine very well that for this dead Manitoba woman there could exist no better burial than within these walls so long baked by the sun.

And this is why, over the grave of my aunt Thérésina Veilleux, all day long the birds sing.

IRWIN SHAW

The Girls in Their Summer Dresses

Fifth Avenue was shining in the sun when they left the Brevoort and started walking toward Washington Square. The sun was warm, even though it was November and everything looked like Sunday morning — the buses, and the well-dressed people walking slowly in couples and the quiet buildings with the windows closed.

Michael held Frances' arm tightly as they walked downtown in the sunlight. They walked lightly, almost smiling, because they had slept late and had a good breakfast and it was Sunday. Michael unbuttoned his coat and let it flap around him in the mild wind. They walked, without saying anything, among the young and pleasant-looking people who somehow seem to make up most of the population of that section of New York City.

"Look out," Frances said, as they crossed Eighth Street. "You'll break your neck."

Michael laughed and Frances laughed with him.

"She's not so pretty, anyway," Frances said. "Anyway, not pretty enough to take a chance breaking your neck looking at her."

Michael laughed again. He laughed louder this time, but not as solidly. "She wasn't a bad-looking girl. She had a nice complexion. Country-girl complexion. How did you know I was looking at her?"

Frances cocked her head to one side and smiled at her husband under the tip-tilted brim of her hat. "Mike, darling ..." she said.

Michael laughed, just a little laugh this time. "O.K.," he said. "The evidence is in. Excuse me. It was the complexion. It's not the sort of complexion you see much in New York. Excuse me."

Frances patted his arm lightly and pulled him along a little faster toward Washington Square.

"This is a nice morning," she said. "This is a wonderful morning. When I have breakfast with you it makes me feel good all day."

"Tonic," Michael said. "Morning pick-up. Rolls and coffee with Mike and you're on the alkali side, guaranteed."

"That's the story. Also, I slept all night, wound around you like a rope."

"Saturday night," he said. "I permit such liberties only when the week's work is done."

"You're getting fat," she said.

"Isn't it the truth? The lean man from Ohio."

"I love it," she said, "an extra five pounds of husband."

"I love it, too," Michael said gravely.

"I have an idea," Frances said.

"My wife has an idea. That pretty girl."

"Let's not see anybody all day," Frances said. "Let's just hang around with each other. You and me. We're always up to our neck in people, drinking their Scotch, or drinking our Scotch, we only see each other in bed ..."

"The Great Meeting Place," Michael said. "Stay in bed long enough and everybody you ever knew will show up there."

"Wise guy," Frances said. "I'm talking serious."

"O.K., I'm listening serious."

"I want to go out with my husband all day long. I want him to talk only to me and listen only to me."

"What's to stop us?" Michael asked. "What party intends to prevent me from seeing my wife alone on Sunday? What party?"

"The Stevensons. They want us to drop by around one o'clock and they'll drive us into the country."

"The lousy Stevensons," Mike said. "Transparent. They can whistle. They can go driving in the country by themselves. My wife and I have to stay in New York and bore each other tête-à-tête."

"Is is a date?"

"It's a date."

Frances leaned over and kissed him on the tip of the ear.

"Darling," Michael said. "This is Fifth Avenue."

"Let me arrange a program," Frances said. "A planned Sunday in New York for a young couple with money to throw away."

"Go easy."

"First let's go see a football game. A professional football game," Frances said, because she knew Michael loved to watch them. "The Giants are playing. And it'll be nice to be outside all day today and get hungry and later we'll go down to Cavanagh's and get a steak as big as a blacksmith's apron, with a bottle of wine, and after that, there's a new French picture at the Filmarte that everybody says ... Say, are you listening to me?"

"Sure," he said. He took his eyes off the hatless girl with the dark hair, cut dancer-style, like a helmet, who was walking past him with the self-conscious strength and grace dancers have. She was walking without a coat and she looked very solid and strong and her belly was flat, like a boy's, under her skirt, and her hips swung boldly because she was a dancer and also because she knew Michael was looking at her. She smiled a little to herself as she went past and Michael noticed all these things before he looked back at his wife. "Sure," he said, "we're going to watch the Giants and we're going to eat steak and we're going to see a French picture. How do you like that?"

"That's it," Frances said flatly. "That's the program for the day. Or maybe you'd just rather walk up and down Fifth Avenue."

"No," Michael said carefully. "Not at all."

"You always look at other women," Frances said. "At every damn woman in the City of New York."

"Oh, come now," Michael said, pretending to joke. "Only pretty ones. And, after all, how many pretty women *are* there in New York? Seventeen?"

"More. At least you seem to think so. Wherever you go."

"Not the truth. Occasionally, maybe, I look at a woman as she passes. In the street. I admit, perhaps in the street I look at a woman once in a while . . ."

"Everywhere," Frances said. "Every damned place we go. Restaurants, subways, theaters, lectures, concerts."

"Now, darling," Michael said, "I look at everything. God gave me eyes and I look at women and men and subway excavations and moving pictures and the little flowers of the field. I casually inspect the universe."

"You ought to see the look in your eye," Frances said, "as you casually inspect the universe on Fifth Avenue."

"I'm a happily married man." Michael pressed her elbow tenderly, knowing what he was doing. "Example for the whole twentieth century, Mr. and Mrs. Mike Loomis."

"You mean it?"

"Frances, baby . . ."

"Are you *really* happily married?"

"Sure," Michael said, feeling the whole Sunday morning sinking like lead inside him. "Now what the hell is the sense in talking like that?"

"I would like to know." Frances walked faster now, looking straight ahead, her face showing nothing, which was the way she always managed it when she was arguing or feeling bad.

"I'm wonderfully happily married," Michael said patiently. "I am the envy of all men between the ages of fifteen and sixty in the State of New York."

"Stop kidding," Frances said.

"I have a fine home," Michael said. "I got nice books and a phonograph and nice friends. I live in a town I like the way I like and I do the work I like and I live with the woman I like. Whenever something good happens, don't I run to you? When something bad happens, don't I cry on your shoulder?"

"Yes," Frances said. "You look at every woman that passes."

"That's an exaggeration."

"Every woman." Frances took her hand off Michael's arm. "If she's not pretty you turn away fairly quickly. If she's half pretty you watch her for about seven steps . . ."

"My lord, Frances!"

"If she's pretty you practically break your neck . . ."

"Hey, let's have a drink," Michael said, stopping.

"We just had breakfast."

"Now, listen, darling," Mike said, choosing his words with care, "it's a nice day and we both feel good and there's no reason why we have to break it up. Let's have a nice Sunday."

"I could have a fine Sunday if you didn't look as though you were dying to run after every skirt on Fifth Avenue."

"Let's have a drink," Michael said.

"I don't want a drink."

"What do you want, a fight?"

"No," Frances said so unhappily that Michael felt terribly sorry for her. "I don't want a fight. I don't know why I started this. All right, let's drop it. Let's have a good time."

They joined hands consciously and walked without talking among the baby carriages and the old Italian men in their Sunday clothes and the young women with Scotties in Washington Square Park.

"I hope it's a good game today," Frances said after a while, her tone a good imitation of the tone she had used at breakfast and at the beginning of their walk. "I like professional football games. They hit each other as though they're made out of concrete. When they tackle each other," she said, trying to make Michael laugh, "they make divots. It's very exciting."

"I want to tell you something," Michael said very seriously. "I have not touched another woman. Not once. In all the five years."

"All right," Frances said.

"You believe that, don't you?"

They walked between the crowded benches, under the scrubby city park trees.

"I try not to notice it," Frances said, as though she were talking to herself. "I try to make believe it doesn't mean anything. Some men're like that, I tell myself, they have to see what they're missing."

"Some women're like that, too," Michael said. "In my time I've seen a couple of ladies."

"I haven't even looked at another man," Frances said, walking straight ahead, "since the second time I went out with you."

"There's no law," Michael said.

"I feel rotten inside, in my stomach, when we pass a woman and you look at her and I see that look in your eye and that's the way you looked at me the first time, in Alice Maxwell's house. Standing there in the living room, next to the radio, with a green hat on and all those people."

"I remember the hat," Michael said.

"The same look," Frances said. "And it makes me feel bad. It makes me feel terrible."

"Sssh, please, darling, sssh . . ."

"I think I would like a drink now," Frances said.

They walked over to a bar on Eighth Street, not saying anything, Michael automatically helping her over curbstones, and guiding her past automobiles. He walked, buttoning his coat, looking thoughtfully at his neatly shined heavy brown shoes as they made the steps toward the bar. They sat near a window in the bar and the sun streamed in, and there was a small cheerful fire in the fireplace. A little Japanese waiter came over and put down some pretzels and smiled happily at them.

"What do you order after breakfast?" Michael asked.

"Brandy, I suppose," Frances said.

"Courvoisier," Michael told the waiter. "Two Courvoisier."

The waiter came with the glasses and they sat drinking the brandy, in the sunlight. Michael finished half his and drank a little water.

"I look at women," he said. "Correct. I don't say it's wrong or right, I look at them. If I pass them on the street and I don't look at them, I'm fooling you, I'm fooling myself."

"You look at them as though you want them," Frances said, playing with her brandy glass. "Every one of them."

"In a way," Michael said, speaking softly and not to his wife, "in a way that's true. I don't do anything about it, but it's true.

"I know it. That's why I feel bad."

"Another brandy," Michael called. "Waiter, two more brandies."

"Why do you hurt me?" Frances asked. "What're you doing?"

Michael sighed and closed his eyes and rubbed them gently with his fingertips. "I love the way women look. One of the things I like best about New York is the battalions of women. When I first came to New York from Ohio that was the first thing I noticed, the million wonderful women, all over the city. I walked around with my heart in my throat."

"A kid," Frances said. "That's a kid's feeling."

"Guess again," Michael said. "Guess again. I'm older now, I'm a man getting near middle age, putting on a little fat and I still love to walk along Fifth Avenue at three o'clock on the east side of the street between Fiftieth and Fifty-seventh Streets, they're all out then, making believe they're shopping, in their furs and their crazy hats, everything all concentrated from all over the world into eight blocks, the best furs, the best clothes, the handsomest women, out to spend money and feeling good about it, looking coldly at you, making believe they're not looking at you as you go past."

The Japanese waiter put the two drinks down, smiling with great happiness.

"Everything is all right?" he asked.

"Everything is wonderful," Michael said.

"If it's just a couple of fur coats," Frances said, "and forty-five-dollar hats . . ."

"It's not the fur coats. Or the hats. That's just the scenery for that particular kind of woman. Understand," he said, "you don't have to listen to this."

"I want to listen."

"I like the girls in the offices. Neat, with their eyeglasses, smart, chipper, knowing what everything is about, taking care of themselves all the time." He kept his eye on the people going slowly past outside the window. "I like the girls on Forty-fourth Street at lunch time, the actresses, all dressed up on nothing a week, talking to the good-looking boys, wearing themselves out being young and vivacious outside Sardi's, waiting for producers to look at them. I like the salesgirls in Macy's, paying attention to you first because you're a man, leaving lady customers waiting, flirting with you over socks and books and phonograph needles. I got all this stuff accumulated in me because I've been thinking about it for ten years and now you've asked for it and here it is."

"Go ahead," Frances said.

"When I think of New York City, I think of all the girls, the Jewish girls, the Italian girls, the Irish, Polack, Chinese, German, Negro, Spanish, Russian girls, all on parade in the city. I don't know whether it's something special with me or whether every man in the city walks around with the same feeling inside him, but I feel as though I'm at a picnic in this city. I like to sit near the women in the theaters, the famous beauties who've taken six hours to get ready and look it. And the young girls at the football games, with the red cheeks, and when the warm weather comes, the girls in their summer dresses . . ." He finished his drink. "That's the story. You asked for it, remember. I can't help but look at them. I can't help but want them."

"You want them," Frances repeated without expression. "You said that."

"Right," Michael said, being cruel now and not caring, because she had made him expose himself. "You brought this subject up for discussion, we will discuss it fully."

Frances finished her drink and swallowed two or three times extra. "You say you love me?"

"I love you, but I also want them. O.K."

"I'm pretty, too," Frances said. "As pretty as any of them."

"You're beautiful," Michael said, meaning it.

"I'm good for you," Frances said, pleading. "I've made a good wife, a good housekeeper, a good friend. I'd do any damn thing for you."

"I know," Michael said. He put his hand out and grasped hers.

"You'd like to be free to ..." Frances said.

"Sssh."

"Tell the truth." She took her hand away from under his.

Michael flicked the edge of his glass with his finger. "O.K.," he said gently. "Sometimes I feel I would like to be free."

"Well," Frances said defiantly, drumming on the table, "anytime you say ..."

"Don't be foolish." Michael swung his chair around to her side of the table and patted her thigh.

She began to cry, silently, into her handkerchief, bent over just enough so that nobody else in the bar would notice. "Some day," she said crying, "you're going to make a move ..."

Michael didn't say anything. He sat watching the bartender slowly peel a lemon.

"Aren't you?" Frances asked harshly. "Come on, tell me. Talk. Aren't you?"

"Maybe," Michael said. He moved his chair back again "How the hell do I know?"

"You know," Frances persisted. "Don't you know?"

"Yes," Michael said after a while, "I know."

Frances stopped crying then. Two or three snuffles into the handkerchief and she put it away and her face didn't tell anything to anybody. "At least do me one favor," she said.

"Sure."

"Stop talking about how pretty this woman is, or that one. Nice eyes, nice breasts, a pretty figure, good voice," she mimicked his voice. "Keep it to yourself. I'm not interested."

"Excuse me." Michael waved to the waiter. "I'll keep it to myself."

Frances flicked the corner of her eyes. "Another brandy," she told the waiter.

"Two," Michael said.

"Yes, ma'am, yes, sir," said the waiter, backing away.

Frances regarded him coolly across the table. "Do you want me to call the Stevensons?" she asked. "It'll be nice in the country."

"Sure," Michael said. "Call them up."

She got up from the table and walked across the room toward the telephone. Michael watched her walk, thinking, what a pretty girl, what nice legs.

ISAAC BASHEVIS SINGER

Gimpel the Fool

Translated by Saul Bellow

I

I am Gimpel the fool. I don't think myself a fool. On the contrary. But that's what folks call me. They gave me the name while I was still in school. I had seven names in all: imbecile, donkey, flax-head, dope, glump, ninny, and fool. The last name stuck. What did my foolishness consist of? I was easy to take in. They said, "Gimpel, you know the rabbi's wife has been brought to childbed?" So I skipped school. Well, it turned out to be a lie. How was I supposed to know? She hadn't had a big belly. But I never looked at her belly. Was that really so foolish? The gang laughed and hee-hawed, stomped and danced and chanted a good-night prayer. And instead of the raisins they give when a woman's lying in, they stuffed my hand full of goat turds. I was no weakling. If I slapped someone he'd see all the way to Cracow. But I'm really not a slugger by nature. I think to myself: Let it pass. So they take advantage of me.

I was coming home from school and heard a dog barking. I'm not afraid of dogs, but of course I never want to start up with them. One of them may be mad, and if he bites there's not a Tartar in the world who can help you. So I made tracks. Then I looked around and saw the whole market place wild with laughter. It was no dog at all but Wolf-Leib the Thief. How was I supposed to know it was he? It sounded like a howling bitch.

When the pranksters and leg-pullers found that I was easy to fool, every one of them tried his luck with me. "Gimpel, the Czar is coming to Frampol; Gimpel, the moon fell down in Turbeen; Gimpel, little Hodel Furpiece found a treasure behind the bathhouse." And I like a golem believed everyone. In the first place, everything is possible, as it is written in the Wisdom of the Fathers, I've forgotten just how. Second, I had to believe when the whole town came down on me! If I ever dared to say, "Ah, you're kidding!" there was trouble. People got angry. "What do you mean! You want to call everyone a liar?" What was I to do? I believed them, and I hope at least that did them some good.

I was an orphan. My grandfather who brought me up was already bent toward the grave. So they turned me over to a baker, and what a time they gave me there! Every woman or girl who came to bake a batch of noodles had to fool me at least once. "Gimpel, there's a fair in heaven; Gimpel, the rabbi gave birth to a calf in the seventh month; Gimpel, a cow flew over the roof and laid brass eggs." A student from the yeshiva came once to buy a roll, and he said, "You, Gimpel, while you stand here scraping with your baker's shovel the Messiah has come. The dead have arisen." "What do you mean?" I said. "I heard no one blowing the ram's horn!" He said, "Are you deaf?" And all began to cry, "We heard it, we heard!" Then in came Rietze the Candle-dipper and called out in her hoarse voice, "Gimpel, your father and mother have stood up from the grave. They're looking for you."

To tell the truth, I knew very well that nothing of the sort had happened, but all the same, as folks were talking, I threw on my wool vest and went out. Maybe something had happened. What did I stand to lose by looking? Well, what a cat music went up! And then I took a vow to believe nothing more. But that was no go either. They confused me so that I didn't know the big end from the small.

I went to the rabbi to get some advice. He said, "It is written, better to be a fool all your days than for one hour to be evil. You are not a fool. They are the fools. For he who causes his neighbor to feel shame loses Paradise himself." Nevertheless the rabbi's daughter took me in. As I left the rabbinical court she said, "Have you kissed the wall yet?" I said, "No; what for?" She answered, "It's the law; you've got to do it after every visit." Well, there didn't seem to be any harm in it. And she burst out laughing. It was a fine trick. She put one over on me, all right.

I wanted to go off to another town, but then everyone got busy matchmaking, and they were after me so they nearly tore my coat tails off. They talked at me and talked until I got water on the ear. She was no chaste maiden, but they told me she was virgin pure. She had a limp, and they said it was deliberate, from coyness. She had a bastard, and they told me the child was her little brother. I cried, "You're wasting your time. I'll never marry that whore." But they said indignantly, "What a way to talk! Aren't you ashamed of yourself? We can take you to the rabbi and have you fined for giving her a bad name." I saw then that I wouldn't escape them so easily and I thought: They're set on making me their butt. But when you're married the husband's the master, and if that's all right with her it's agreeable to me too. Besides, you can't pass through life unscathed, nor expect to.

I went to her clay house, which was built on the sand, and the whole gang, hollering and chorusing, came after me. They acted like bear-baiters. When we came to the well they stopped all the same. They were afraid to start anything with Elka. Her mouth would open as if it were on a hinge, and she had a fierce tongue. I entered the house. Lines were strung from wall to wall and clothes were drying. Barefoot she stood by the tub, doing the wash. She was dressed in a worn hand-me-down gown of plush. She had her hair put up in braids and pinned across her head. It took my breath away, almost, the reek of it all.

Evidently she knew who I was. She took a look at me and said, "Look who's here! He's come, the drip. Grab a seat."

I told her all; I denied nothing. "Tell me the truth," I said, "are you really a virgin, and is that mischievous Yechiel actually your little brother? Don't be deceitful with me, for I'm an orphan."

"I'm an orphan myself," she answered, "and whoever tries to twist you up, may the end of his nose take a twist. But don't let them think they can take advantage of me. I want a dowry of fifty guilders, and let them take up a collection besides. Otherwise they can kiss my you-know-what." She was very plainspoken. I said, "It's the bride and not the groom who gives a dowry." Then she said, "Don't bargain with me. Either a flat 'yes' or a flat 'no' — Go back where you came from."

I thought: No bread will ever be baked from *this* dough. But ours is not a poor town. They consented to everything and proceeded with the wedding. It so happened that there was a dysentery epidemic at the time. The ceremony was held at the cemetery gates, near the little corpse-washing hut. The fellows got drunk. While the marriage contract was being drawn up I heard the most pious high rabbi ask, "Is the bride a widow or a divorced woman?" And the sexton's wife answered for her, "Both a widow and divorced." It was a black moment for me. But what was I to do, run away from under the marriage canopy?

There was singing and dancing. An old granny danced opposite me, hugging a braided white *chalah*. The master of revels made a "God 'a mercy" in memory of the bride's parents. The schoolboys threw burrs, as on Tishe b'Av fast day. There were a lot of gifts after the sermon: a noodle board, a kneading trough, a bucket, brooms, ladles, household articles galore. Then I took a look and saw two strapping young men carrying a crib. "What do you need this for?" I asked. So they said, "Don't rack your brains about it. It's all right, it'll come in handy." I realized I was going to be rooked. Take it another way though, what did I stand to lose? I reflected: I'll see what comes of it. A whole town can't go altogether crazy.

II

At night I came where my wife lay, but she wouldn't let me in. "Say, look here, is this what they married us for?" I said. And she said, "My monthly has come." "But yesterday they took you to the ritual bath, and that's afterward, isn't it supposed to be?" "Today isn't yesterday," said she, "and yesterday's not today. You can beat if if you don't like it." In short, I waited.

Nor four months later she was in childbed. The townsfolk hid their laughter with their knuckles. But what could I do? She suffered intolerable pains and clawed at the walls. "Gimpel," she cried, "I'm going. Forgive me!" The house filled with women. They were boiling pans of water. The screams rose to the welkin.

The thing to do was to go to the House of Prayer to repeat Psalms, and that was what I did.

The townsfolk liked that, all right. I stood in a corner saying Psalms and prayers, and they shook their heads at me. "Pray, pray!" they told me. "Prayer never made any woman pregnant." One of the congregation put a straw to my mouth and said, "Hay for the cows." There was something to that too, by God!

She gave birth to a boy. Friday at the synagogue the sexton stood up before the Ark, pounded on the reading table, and announced, "The wealthy Reb Gimpel invites the congregation to a feast in honor of the birth of a son." The whole House of Prayer rang with laughter. My face was flaming. But there was nothing I could do. After all, I *was* the one responsible for the circumcision honors and rituals.

Half the town came running. You couldn't wedge another soul in. Women brought peppered chick-peas, and there was a keg of beer from the tavern. I ate and drank as much as anyone, and they all congratulated me. Then there was a circumcision, and I named the boy after my father, may he rest in peace. When all were gone and I was left with my wife alone, she thrust her head through the bed-curtain and called me to her.

"Gimpel," said she "why are you silent? Has your ship gone and sunk?"

"What shall I say?" I answered. "A fine thing you've done to me! If my mother had known of it she'd have died a second time."

She said, "Are you crazy, or what?"

"How can you make such a fool," I said, "of one who should be the lord and master?"

"What's the matter with you?" she said. "What have you taken it into your head to imagine?"

I saw that I must speak bluntly and openly. "Do you think this is the way to use an orphan?" I said. "You have borne a bastard."

She answered, "Drive this foolishness out of your head. The child is yours."

"How can he be mine?" I argued. "He was born seventeen weeks after the wedding."

She told me then that he was premature. I said, "Isn't he a little too premature?" She said, she had had a grandmother who carried just as short a time and she resembled this grandmother of hers as one drop of water does another. She swore to it with such oaths that you would have believed a peasant at the fair if he had used them. To tell the plain truth, I didn't believe her; but when I talked it over next day with the schoolmaster he told me that the very same thing had happened to Adam and Eve. Two they went up to bed, and four they descended.

"There isn't a woman in the world who is not the granddaughter of Eve," he said.

That was how it was; they argued me dumb. But then, who really knows how such things are?

I began to forget my sorrow. I loved the child madly, and he loved me too. As soon as he saw me he'd wave his little hands and want me to pick him up, and when he was colicky I was the only one who could pacify him. I bought him a little bone teething ring and a little gilded cap. He was forever catching the evil eye from someone, and then I had to run to get one of those abracadabras for him that would get him out of it. I worked like an ox. You know how expenses go up when there's an infant in the house. I don't want to lie about it; I didn't dislike Elka either, for that matter. She swore at me and cursed, and I couldn't get enough of her. What strength she had! One of her looks could rob you of the power of speech. And her orations! Pitch and sulphur, that's what they were full of, and yet somehow also full of charm. I adored her every word. She gave me bloody wounds though.

In the evening I brought her a white loaf as well as a dark one, and also poppyseed rolls I baked myself. I thieved because of her and swiped everything I could lay hands on: macaroons, raisins, almonds, cakes. I hope I may be forgiven for stealing from the Saturday pots the women left to warm in the baker's oven. I would take out scraps of meat, a chunk of pudding, a chicken leg or head, a piece of tripe, whatever I could nip quickly. She ate and became fat and handsome.

I had to sleep away from home all during the week, at the bakery. On Friday nights when I got home she always made an excuse of some sort. Either she had heartburn, or a stitch in the side, or hiccups, or headaches. You know what women's excuses are. I had a bitter time of it. It was rough. To add to it, this little brother of hers, the bastard, was growing bigger. He'd put lumps on me, and when I wanted to hit back she'd open her mouth and curse so powerfully I saw a green haze floating before my eyes. Ten times a day she threatened to divorce me. Another man in my place would have taken French leave and disappeared. But I'm the type that bears it and says nothing. What's one to do? Shoulders are from God, and burdens too.

One night there was a calamity in the bakery; the oven burst, and we almost had a fire. There was nothing to do but go home, so I went home. Let me, I thought, also taste the joy of sleeping in bed in mid-week. I didn't want to wake the sleeping mite and tiptoed into the house. Coming in, it seemed to me that I heard not the snoring of one but, as it were, a double snore, one a thin enough snore and the other like the snoring of a slaughtered ox. Oh, I didn't like that! I didn't like it at all. I went up to the bed, and things suddenly turned black. Next to Elka lay a man's form. Another in my place would have made an uproar, and enough noise to rouse the whole town, but the thought occurred to me that I might wake the child. A little thing like that — why frighten a little swallow, I thought. All right then, I went back to the bakery and stretched out on a sack of flour and till morning I never shut an eye. I shivered as if I had malaria. "Enough of being a donkey," I said to myself. "Gimpel isn't going to be a sucker all his life. There's a limit even to the foolishness of a fool like Gimpel."

In the morning I went to the rabbi to get advice, and it made a great commotion in the town. They sent the beadle for Elka right away. She came, carrying the child. And what do you think she did? She denied it, denied everything, bone and stone! "He's out of his head," she said. "I know nothing of dreams or divinations." They yelled at her, warned her, hammered on the table, but she stuck to her guns: it was a false accusation, she said.

The butchers and the horse-traders took her part. One of the lads from the slaughterhouse came by and said to me, "We've got our eye on you, you're a marked man." Meanwhile the child started to bear down and soiled itself. In the rabbinical court there was an Ark of the Covenant, and they couldn't allow that, so they sent Elka away.

I said to the rabbi, "What shall I do?"

"You must divorce her at once," said he.

"And what if she refuses?" I asked.

He said. "You must serve the divorce. That's all you'll have to do."

I said, "Well, all right, Rabbi. Let me think about it."

"There's nothing to think about," said he. "You mustn't remain under the same roof with her."

"And if I want to see the child?" I asked.

"Let her go, the harlot," said he, "and her brood of bastards with her."

The verdict he gave was that I mustn't even

cross her threshold — never again, as long as I should live.

During the day it didn't bother me so much. I thought: It was bound to happen, the abscess had to burst. But at night when I stretched out upon the sacks I felt it all very bitterly. A longing took me, for her and for the child. I wanted to be angry, but that's my misfortune exactly, I don't have it in me to be really angry. In the first place — this was how my thoughts went — there's bound to be a slip sometimes. You can't live without errors. Probably that lad who was with her led her on and gave her presents and what not, and women are often long on hair and short on sense, and so he got around her. And then since she denies it so, maybe I was only seeing things? Hallucinations do happen. You see a figure or a mannikin or something, but when you come up closer it's nothing, there's not a thing there. And if that's so, I'm doing her an injustice. And when I got so far in my thoughts I started to weep. I sobbed so that I wet the flour where I lay. In the morning I went to the rabbi and told him that I had made a mistake. The rabbi wrote on with his quill, and he said that if that were so he would have to reconsider the whole case. Until he had finished I wasn't to go near my wife, but I might send her bread and money by messenger.

III

Nine months passed before all the rabbis could come to an agreement. Letters went back and forth. I hadn't realized that there could be so much erudition about a matter like this.

Meanwhile Elka gave birth to still another child, a girl this time. On the Sabbath I went to the synagogue and invoked a blessing on her. They called me up to the Torah, and I named the child for my mother-in-law — may she rest in peace. The louts and loudmouths of the town who came into the bakery gave me a going over. All Frampol refreshed its spirits because of my trouble and grief. However, I resolved that I would always believe what I was told. What's the good of *not* believing? Today it's your wife you don't believe; tomorrow it's God Himself you won't take stock in.

By an apprentice who was her neighbor I sent her daily a corn or a wheat loaf, or a piece of pastry, rolls or bagels, or, when I got a chance, a slab of pudding, a slice of honeycake, or wedding strudel — whatever came my way. The apprentice was a goodhearted lad, and more than once he added something on his own. He had formerly annoyed me a lot, plucking my nose and digging me in the ribs, but when he started to be a visitor to my house he became kind and friendly. "Hey, you, Gimpel," he said to me, "you have a very decent little wife and two fine kids. You don't deserve them."

"But the things people say about her," I said.

"Well, they have long tongues," he said, "and nothing to do with them but babble. Ignore it as you ignore the cold of last winter."

One day the rabbi sent for me and said, "Are you certain, Gimpel, that you were wrong about your wife?"

I said, "I'm certain."

"Why, but look here! You yourself saw it."

"It must have been a shadow," I said.

"The shadow of what?"

"Just of one of the beams, I think."

"You can go home then. You owe thanks to the Yanover rabbi. He found an obscure reference in Maimonides that favored you."

I seized the rabbi's hand and kissed it.

I wanted to run home immediately. It's no small thing to be separated for so long a time from wife and child. Then I reflected: I'd better go back to work now, and go home in the evening. I said nothing to anyone, although as far as my heart was concerned it was like one of the Holy Days. The women teased and twitted me as they did every day, but my thought was: Go on, with your loose talk. The truth is out, like the oil upon the water. Maimonides says it's right, and therefore it is right!

At night, when I had covered the dough to let it rise, I took my share of bread and a little sack of flour and started homeward. The moon was full and the stars were glistening, something to terrify the soul. I hurried onward, and before me darted a long shadow. It was winter, and a fresh snow had fallen. I had a mind to sing, but it was growing late and I didn't want to wake the householders. Then I felt like whistling, but I remembered that you don't whistle at night because it brings the demons out. So I was silent and walked as fast as I could.

Dogs in the Christian yards barked at me when I passed, but I thought: Bark your teeth out! What are you but mere dogs? Whereas I am a man, the husband of a fine wife, the father of promising children.

As I approached the house my heart started to pound as though it were the heart of a criminal. I felt no fear, but my heart went thump! thump! Well, no drawing back. I quietly lifted the latch and went in. Elka was asleep. I looked at the infant's cradle. The shutter was closed, but the moon forced its way through the cracks. I saw the newborn child's face and loved it as soon as I saw it — immediately — each tiny bone.

Then I came nearer to the bed. And what did I see but the apprentice there beside Elka. The moon went out all at once. It was utterly black, and I trembled. My teeth chattered. The bread fell from my hands, and my wife waked and said, "Who is that, ah?"

I muttered, "It's me."

"Gimpel?" she asked. "How come you're here? I thought it was forbidden."

"The rabbi said," I answered and shook as with a fever.

"Listen to me, Gimpel," she said, "go out to the shed and see if the goat's all right. It seems she's been sick." I have forgotten to say that we had a goat. When I heard she was unwell I went into the yard. The nannygoat was a good little creature. I had a nearly human feeling for her.

With hesitant steps I went up to the shed and opened the door. The goat stood there on her four feet. I felt her everywhere, drew her by the horns, examined her udders, and found nothing wrong. She had probably eaten too much bark. "Good night, little goat," I said. "Keep well." And the little beast answered with a "Maa" as though to thank me for the good will.

I went back. The apprentice had vanished.

"Where," I asked, "is the lad?"

"What lad?" my wife answered.

"What do you mean?" I said. "The apprentice. You were sleeping with him."

"The things I have dreamed this night and the night before," she said, "may they come true and lay you low, body and soul! An evil spirit has taken root in you and dazzles your sight." She screamed out, "You hateful creature! You moon calf! You spook! You uncouth man! Get out, or I'll scream all Frampol out of bed!"

Before I could move, her brother sprang out from behind the oven and struck me a blow on the back of the head. I thought he had broken my neck. I felt that something about me was deeply wrong, and I said, "Don't make a scandal. All that's needed now is that people should accuse me of raising spooks and *dybbuks*." For that was what she had meant. "No one will touch bread of my baking."

In short, I somehow calmed her.

"Well," she said, "that's enough. Lie down, and be shattered by wheels."

Next morning I called the apprentice aside. "Listen here, brother!" I said. And so on and so forth. "What do you say?" He stared at me as though I had dropped from the roof or something.

"I swear," he said, "you'd better go to an herb doctor or some healer. I'm afraid you have a screw loose, but I'll hush it up for you." And that's how the thing stood.

To make a long story short, I lived twenty years with my wife. She bore me six children, four daughters and two sons. All kinds of things happened, but I neither saw nor heard. I believed, and that's all. The rabbi recently said to me, "Belief in itself is beneficial. It is written that a good man lives by his faith."

Suddenly my wife took sick. It began with a trifle, a little growth upon the breast. But she evidently was not destined to live long; she had no years. I spent a fortune on her. I have forgotten to say that by this time I had a bakery of my own and in Frampol was considered to be something of a rich man. Daily the healer came, and every witch doctor in the neighborhood was brought. They decided to use leeches, and after that to try cupping. They even called a doctor from Lublin, but it was too late. Before she died she called me to her bed and said, "Forgive me, Gimpel."

I said, "What is there to forgive? You have been a good and faithful wife."

"Woe, Gimpel!" she said. "It was ugly how I deceived you all these years. I want to go clean to my Maker, and so I have to tell you that the children are not yours."

If I had been clouted on the head with a piece of wood it couldn't have bewildered me more.

"Whose are they?" I asked.

"I don't know," she said. "There were a lot ... but they're not yours." And as she spoke she tossed her head to the side, her eyes turned glassy, and it was all up with Elka. On her whitened lips there remained a smile.

I imagined that, dead as she was, she was saying, "I deceived Gimpel. That was the meaning of my brief life."

IV

One night, when the period of mourning was done, as I lay dreaming on the flour sacks, there came the Spirit of Evil himself and said to me, "Gimpel, why do you sleep?"

I said, "What should I be doing? Eating *kreplach*?"

"The whole world deceives you," he said, "and you ought to deceive the world in your turn."

"How can I deceive all the world?" I asked him.

He answered, "You might accumulate a bucket of urine every day and at night pour it into the dough. Let the sages of Frampol eat filth."

"What about the judgment in the world to come?" I said.

"There is no world to come," he said. "They've sold you a bill of goods and talked you into believing you carried a cat in your belly. What nonsense!"

"Well then," I said, "and is there a God?"

He answered, "There is no God either."

"What," I said, "*is* there, then?"

"A thick mire."

He stood before my eyes with a goatish beard and horn, long-toothed, and with a tail. Hearing such words, I wanted to snatch him by the tail, but I tumbled from the flour sacks and nearly broke a rib. Then it happened that I had to answer the call of nature, and, passing, I saw the risen dough, which seemed to say to me, "Do it!" In brief, I let myself be persuaded.

At dawn the apprentice came. We kneaded the bread, scattered caraway seeds on it, and set it to bake. Then the apprentice went away, and I was left sitting in the little trench by the oven, on a pile of rags. Well, Gimpel, I thought, you've revenged yourself on them for all the shame they've put on you. Outside the frost glittered, but it was warm beside the oven. The flames heated my face. I bent my head and fell into a doze.

I saw in a dream, at once, Elka in her shroud. She called to me, "What have you done, Gimpel?"

I said to her, "It's all your fault," and started to cry.

"You fool!" she said. "You fool! Because I was false is everything false too? I never deceived anyone but myself. I'm paying for it all, Gimpel. They spare you nothing here."

I looked at her face. It was black; I was startled and waked, and remained sitting dumb. I sensed that everything hung in the balance. A false step now and I'd lose Eternal Life. But God gave me His help. I seized the long shovel and took out the loaves, carried them into the yard, and started to dig a hole in the frozen earth.

My apprentice came back as I was doing it. "What are you doing boss?" he said, and grew pale as a corpse.

"I know what I'm doing," I said, and I buried it all before his very eyes.

Then I went home, took my hoard from its hiding place, and divided it among the children. "I saw your mother tonight," I said. "She's turning black, poor thing."

They were so astounded they couldn't speak a word.

"Be well," I said, "and forget that such a one as Gimpel ever existed." I put on my short coat, a pair of boots, took the bag that held my prayer shawl in one hand, my stock in the other, and kissed the *mezzuzah.* When people saw me in the street they were greatly surprised.

"Where are you going?" they said.

I answered, "Into the world." And so I departed from Frampol.

I wandered over the land, and good people did not neglect me. After many years I became old and white; I heard a great deal, many lies and falsehoods, but the longer I lived the more I understood that there were really no lies. Whatever doesn't really happen is dreamed at night. It happens to one if it doesn't happen to another, tomorrow if not today, or a century hence if not next year. What difference can it make? Often I heard tales of which I said, "Now this is a thing that cannot happen." But before a year had elapsed I heard that it actually had come to pass somewhere.

Going from place to place, eating at strange tables, it often happens that I spin yarns — improbable things that could never have happened — about devils, magicians, windmills, and the like. The children run after me, calling, "Grandfather, tell us a story." Sometimes they ask for particular stories, and I try to please them. A fat young boy once said to me, "Grandfather, it's the same story you told us before." The little rogue, he was right.

So it is with dreams too. It is many years since I left Frampol, but as soon as I shut my eyes I am there again. And whom do you think I see? Elka. She is standing by the washtub, as at our first encounter, but her face is shining and her eyes are as radiant as the eyes of a saint, and she speaks outlandish words to me, strange things. When I wake I have forgotten it all. But while the dream lasts I am comforted. She answers all my queries, and what comes out is that all is right. I weep and implore, "Let me be with you." And she consoles me and tells me to be patient. The time is nearer than it is far. Sometimes she strokes and kisses me and weeps upon my face. When I awaken I feel her lips and taste the salt of her tears.

No doubt the world is entirely an imaginary world, but it is only once removed from the true world. At the door of the hovel where I lie, there stands the plank on which the dead are taken away. The gravedigger Jew has his spade ready. The grave waits and the worms are hungry; the shrouds are prepared — I carry them in my beggar's sack. Another *shnorrer* is waiting to inherit my bed of straw. When the time comes I will go joyfully. Whatever may be there, it will be real, without complication, without ridicule, without deception. God be praised: there even Gimpel cannot be deceived.

JOHN STEINBECK

The Chrysanthemums

The high gray-flannel fog of winter closed off the Salinas Valley from the sky and from all the rest of the world. On every side it sat like a lid on the mountains and made of the great valley a closed pot. On the broad, level land floor the gang plows bit deep and left the black earth shining like metal where the shares had cut. On the foothill ranches across the Salinas River, the yellow stubble fields seemed to be bathed in pale cold sunshine, but there was no sunshine in the valley now in December. The thick willow scrub along the river flamed with sharp and positive yellow leaves.

It was a time of quiet and of waiting. The air was cold and tender. A light wind blew up from the southwest so that the farmers were mildly hopeful of a good rain before long; but fog and rain do not go together.

Across the river, on Henry Allen's foothill ranch there was little work to be done, for the hay was cut and stored and the orchards were plowed up to receive the rain deeply when it should come. The cattle on the higher slopes were becoming shaggy and rough-coated.

Elisa Allen, working in her flower garden, looked down across the yard and saw Henry, her husband, talking to two men in business suits. The three of them stood by the tractor shed, each man with one foot on the side of the little Fordson. They smoked cigarettes and studied the machine as they talked.

Elisa watched them for a moment and then went back to her work. She was thirty-five. Her face was lean and strong and her eyes were as clear as water. Her figure looked blocked and heavy in her gardening costume, a man's black hat pulled low down over her eyes, clodhopper shoes, a figured print dress almost completely covered by a big corduroy apron with four big pockets to hold the snips, the trowel and scratcher, the seeds and the knife she worked with. She wore heavy leather gloves to protect her hands while she worked.

She was cutting down the old year's chrysanthemum stalks with a pair of short and powerful scissors. She looked down toward the men by the tractor shed now and then. Her face was eager and mature and handsome; even her work with the scissors was over-eager, over-powerful. The chrysanthemum stems seemed too small and easy for her energy.

She brushed a cloud of hair out of her eyes with the back of her glove, and left a smudge of earth on her cheek in doing it. Behind her stood the neat white farm house with red geraniums close-banked around it as high as the windows. It was a hard-swept looking little house, with hard-polished windows, and a clean mud-mat on the front steps.

Elisa cast another glance toward the tractor shed. The strangers were getting into their Ford coupe. She took off a glove and put her strong fingers down into the forest of new green chrysanthemum sprouts that were growing around the old roots. She spread the leaves and looked down among the close-growing stems. No aphids were there, no sowbugs or snails or cutworms. Her terrier fingers destroyed such pests before they could get started.

Elisa started at the sound of her husband's voice. He had come near quietly, and he leaned over the wire fence that protected her flower garden from cattle and dogs and chickens.

"At it again," he said. "You've got a strong new crop coming."

Elisa straightened her back and pulled on the gardening glove again. "Yes. They'll be strong this coming year." In her tone and on her face there was a little smugness.

"You've got a gift with things," Henry observed. "Some of those yellow chrysanthemums you had this year were ten inches across. I wish you'd work out in the orchard and raise some apples that big."

Her eyes sharpened. "Maybe I could do it, too. I've a gift with things, all right. My mother had it. She could stick anything in the ground and make it grow. She said it was having planters' hands that knew how to do it."

"Well, it sure works with flowers," he said.

"Henry, who were those men you were talking to?"

"Why, sure, that's what I came to tell you. They were from the Western Meat Company. I sold those thirty head of three-year-old steers. Got nearly my own price, too."

"Good," she said. "Good for you."

"And I thought," he continued, "I thought how it's Saturday afternoon, and we might go into Salinas for dinner at a restaurant, and then to a picture show — to celebrate, you see."

"Good," she repeated. "Oh, yes. That will be good."

Henry put on his joking tone. "There's fights

tonight. How'd you like to go to the fights?"

"Oh, no," she said breathlessly. "No, I wouldn't like fights."

"Just fooling, Elisa. We'll go to a movie. Let's see. It's two now. I'm going to take Scotty and bring down those steers from the hill. It'll take us maybe two hours. We'll go in town about five and have dinner at the Cominos Hotel. Like that?"

"Of course I'll like it. It's good to eat away from home."

"All right, then. I'll go get up a couple of horses."

She said, "I'll have plenty of time to transplant some of these sets, I guess."

She heard her husband calling Scotty down by the barn. And a little later she saw the two men ride up the pale yellow hillside in search of the steers.

There was a little square bed kept for rooting the chrysanthemums. With her trowel she turned the soil over and over, and smoothed it and patted it firm. Then she dug ten parallel trenches to receive the sets. Back at the chrysanthemum bed she pulled out the little crisp shoots, trimmed off the leaves of each one with her scissors and laid it on a small orderly pile.

A squeak of wheels and plod of hoofs came from the road. Elisa looked up. The country road ran along the dense bank of willows and cottonwoods that bordered the river, and up this road came a curious vehicle, curiously drawn. It was an old spring-wagon, with a round canvas top on it like the cover of a prairie schooner. It was drawn by an old bay horse and a little gray-and-white burro. A big stubble-bearded man sat between the cover flaps and drove the crawling team. Underneath the wagon, between the hind wheels, a lean and rangy mongrel dog walked sedately. Words were painted on the canvas, in clumsy, crooked letters. "Pots, pans, knives, sisors, lawn mores, Fixed." Two rows of articles, and the triumphantly definitive "Fixed" below. The black paint had run down in little sharp points beneath each letter.

Elisa, squatting on the ground, watched to see the crazy, loose-jointed wagon pass by. But it didn't pass. It turned into the farm road in front of her house, crooked old wheels skirling and squeaking. The rangy dog darted from between the wheels and ran ahead. Instantly the two ranch shepherds flew out at him. Then all three stopped, and with stiff and quivering tails, with taut straight legs, with ambassadorial dignity, they slowly circled, sniffing daintily. The caravan pulled up to Elisa's wire fence and stopped. Now the newcomer dog, feeling out-numbered, lowered his tail and retired under the wagon with raised hackles and bared teeth.

The man on the wagon seat called out, "That's a bad dog in a fight when he gets started."

Elisa laughed. "I see he is. How soon does he generally get started?"

The man caught up her laughter and echoed it heartily. "Sometimes not for weeks and weeks," he said. He climbed stiffly down, over the wheel. The horse and the donkey drooped like unwatered flowers.

Elisa saw that he was a very big man. Although his hair and beard were graying, he did not look old. His worn black suit was wrinkled and spotted with grease. The laughter had disappeared from his face and eyes the moment his laughing voice ceased. His eyes were dark, and they were full of the brooding that gets in the eyes of teamsters and of sailors. The calloused hands he rested on the wire fence were cracked, and every crack was a black line. He took off his battered hat.

"I'm off my general road, ma'am," he said. "Does this dirt road cut over across the river to the Los Angeles highway?"

Elisa stood up and shoved the thick scissors in her apron pocket. "Well, yes, it does, but it winds around and then fords the river. I don't think your team could pull through the sand."

He replied with some asperity, "It might surprise you what them beasts can pull through."

"When they get started?" she asked.

He smiled for a second. "Yes. When they get started."

"Well," said Elisa, "I think you'll save time if you go back to the Salinas road and pick up the highway there."

He drew a big finger down the chicken wire and made it sing. "I ain't in any hurry, ma'am. I go from Seattle to San Diego and back every year. Takes all my time. About six months each way. I aim to follow nice weather."

Elisa took off her gloves and stuffed them in the apron pocket with the scissors. She touched the under edge of her man's hat, searching for fugitive hairs. "That sounds like a nice kind of a way to live," she said.

He leaned confidentially over the fence. "Maybe you noticed the writing on my wagon. I mend pots and sharpen knives and scissors. You got any of them things to do?"

"Oh, no," she said quickly. "Nothing like that." Her eyes hardened with resistance.

"Scissors is the worst thing," he explained. "Most people just ruin scissors trying to sharpen 'em, but I know how. I got a special tool. It's a little bobbit kind of thing, and patented. But it sure does the trick."

"No. My scissors are all sharp."

"All right, then. Take a pot," he continued earnestly, "a bent pot, or a pot with a hole. I can make it like new so you don't have to buy no new ones. That's saving for you."

"No," she said shortly. "I tell you I have nothing like that for you to do."

His face fell to an exaggerated sadness. His voice took on a whining undertone. "I ain't had a thing to do today. Maybe I won't have no supper tonight. You see I'm off my regular road. I know folks on the highway clear from Seattle to San Diego. They save their things for me to sharpen up because they know I do it so good and save them money."

"I'm sorry," Elisa said irritably. "I haven't anything for you to do."

His eyes left her face and fell to searching the ground. They roamed about until they came to the chrysanthemum bed where she had been working. "What's them plants, ma'am?"

The irritation and resistance melted from Elisa's face. "Oh, those are chrysanthemums, giant whites and yellows. I raise them every year, bigger than anybody around here."

"Kind of a long-stemmed flower? Looks like a quick puff of colored smoke?" he asked.

"That's it. What a nice way to describe them."

"They smell kind of nasty till you get used to them," he said.

"It's a good bitter smell," she retorted, "not nasty at all."

He changed his tone quickly. "I like the smell myself."

"I had ten-inch blooms this year," she said.

The man leaned farther over the fence. "Look. I know a lady down the road a piece, has got the nicest garden you ever seen. Got nearly every kind of flower but no chrysantheums. Last time I was mending a copper-bottom washtub for her (that's a hard job but I do it good), she said to me, 'If you ever run acrost some nice chrysantheums I wish you'd try to get me a few seeds.' That's what she told me."

Elisa's eyes grew alert and eager. "She couldn't have known much about chrysanthemums. You *can* raise them from seed, but it's much easier to root the little sprouts you see there."

"Oh," he said. "I s'pose I can't take none to her, then."

"Why yes you can," Elisa cried. "I can put some in damp sand, and you can carry them right along with you. They'll take root in the pot if you keep them damp. And then she can transplant them."

"She'd sure like to have some, ma'am. You say they're nice ones?"

"Beautiful," she said. "Oh, beautiful." Her eyes shone. She tore off the battered hat and shook out her dark pretty hair. "I'll put them in a flower pot, and you can take them right with you. Come into the yard."

While the man came through the picket gate Elisa ran excitedly along the geranium-bordered path to the back of the house. And she returned carrying a big red flower pot. The gloves were forgotten now. She kneeled on the ground by the starting bed and dug up the sandy soil with her fingers and scooped it into the bright new flower pot. Then she picked up the little pile of shoots she had prepared. With her strong fingers she pressed them into the sand and tamped around them with her knuckles. The man stood over her. "I'll tell you what to do," she said. "You remember so you can tell the lady."

"Yes, I'll try to remember."

"Well, look. These will take root in about a month. Then she must set them out, about a foot apart in good rich earth like this, see?" She lifted a handful of dark soil for him to look at. "They'll grow fast and tall. Now remember this: In July tell her to cut them down, about eight inches from the ground."

"Before they bloom?" he asked.

"Yes, before they bloom." Her face was tight with eagerness. "They'll grow right up again. About the last of September the buds will start."

She stopped and seemed perplexed. "It's the budding that takes the most care," she said hesitantly. "I don't know how to tell you." She looked deep into his eyes, searchingly. Her mouth opened a little, and she seemed to be listening. "I'll try to tell you," she said. "Did you ever hear of planting hands?"

"Can't say I have, ma'am."

"Well, I can only tell you what it feels like. It's when you're picking off the buds you don't want. Everything goes right down into your fingertips. You watch your fingers work. They do it themselves. You can feel how it is. They pick and pick the buds. They never make a mistake. They're with the plant. Do you see? Your fingers and the plant. You can feel that, right up your arm. They know. They never make a mistake. You can feel it. When you're like that you can't do anything wrong. Do you see that? Can you understand that?"

She was kneeling on the ground looking up at him. Her breast swelled passionately.

The man's eyes narrowed. He looked away self-consciously. "Maybe I know," he said. "Sometimes in the night in the wagon there —"

Elisa's voice grew husky. She broke in on him, "I've never lived as you do, but I know what you mean. When the night is dark — why, the stars are sharp-pointed, and there's quiet. Why, you rise up and up! Every pointed star gets driven into your body. It's like that. Hot and sharp and — lovely."

Kneeling there, her hand went out toward his legs in the greasy black trousers. Her hesitant fingers almost touched the cloth. Then her hand dropped to the ground. She crouched low like a fawning dog.

He said, "It's nice, just like you say. Only when you don't have no dinner, it ain't."

She stood up, then, very straight, and her face was ashamed. She held the flower pot out to him and placed it gently in his arms. "Here. Put it in your wagon, on the seat, where you can watch it. Maybe I can find something for you to do."

At the back of the house she dug in the can pile

and found two old and battered aluminum saucepans. She carried them back and gave them to him. "Here, maybe you can fix these."

His manner changed. He became professional. "Good as new I can fix them." At the back of his wagon he set a little anvil, and out of an oily tool box dug a small machine hammer. Elisa came through the gate to watch him while he pounded out the dents in the kettles. His mouth grew sure and knowing. At a difficult part of the work he sucked his under-lip.

"You sleep right in the wagon?" Elisa asked.

"Right in the wagon, ma'am. Rain or shine I'm dry as a cow in there."

"It must be nice," she said. "It must be very nice. I wish women could do such things."

"It ain't the right kind of a life for a woman."

Her upper lip raised a little, showing her teeth. "How do you know? How can you tell?" she said.

"I don't know, ma'am," he protested. "Of course I don't know. Now here's your kettles, done. You don't have to buy no new ones."

"How much?"

"Oh, fifty cents'll do. I keep my prices down and my work good. That's why I have all them satisfied customers up and down the highway."

Elisa brought him a fifty-cent piece from the house and dropped it in his hand. "You might be surprised to have a rival some time. I can sharpen scissors, too. And I can beat the dents out of little pots. I could show you what a woman might do."

He put his hammer back in the oily box and shoved the little anvil out of sight. "It would be a lonely life for a woman, ma'am, and a scarey life, too, with animals creeping under the wagon all night." He climbed over the singletree, steadying himself with a hand on the burro's white rump. He settled himself in the seat, picked up the lines. "Thank you kindly, ma'am," he said. "I'll do like you told me; I'll go back and catch the Salinas road."

"Mind," she called, "if you're long in getting there, keep the sand damp."

"Sand, ma'am? ... Sand? Oh, sure. You mean around the chrysantheums. Sure I will." He clucked his tongue. The beasts leaned luxuriously into their collars. The mongrel dog took his place between the back wheels. The wagon turned and crawled out the entrance road and back the way it had come, along the river.

Elisa stood in front of her wire fence watching the slow progress of the caravan. Her shoulders were straight, her head thrown back, her eyes half-closed, so that the scene came vaguely into them. Her lips moved silently, forming the words "Good-bye — good-bye." Then she whispered, "That's a bright direction. There's a glowing there." The sound of her whisper startled her. She shook herself free and looked about to see whether anyone had been listening. Only the dogs had heard. They lifted their heads toward her from their sleeping in the dust, and then stretched out their chins and settled asleep again. Elisa turned and ran hurriedly into the house.

In the kitchen she reached behind the stove and felt the water tank. It was full of hot water from the noonday cooking. In the bathroom she tore off her soiled clothes and flung them into the corner. And then she scrubbed herself with a little block of pumice, legs and thighs, loins and chest and arms, until her skin was scratched and red. When she had dried herself she stood in front of a mirror in her bedroom and looked at her body. She tightened her stomach and threw out her chest. She turned and looked over her shoulder at her back.

After a while she began to dress, slowly. She put on her newest underclothing and her nicest stockings and the dress which was the symbol of her prettiness. She worked carefully on her hair, penciled her eyebrows and rouged her lips.

Before she was finished she heard the little thunder of hoofs and the shouts of Henry and his helper as they drove the red steers into the corral. She heard the gate bang shut and set herself for Henry's arrival.

His step sounded on the porch. He entered the house calling, "Elisa, where are you?"

"In my room, dressing. I'm not ready. There's hot water for your bath. Hurry up. It's getting late."

When she heard him splashing in the tub, Elisa laid his dark suit on the bed, and shirt and socks and tie beside it. She stood his polished shoes on the floor beside the bed. Then she went to the porch and sat primly and stiffly down. She looked toward the river road where the willow-line was still yellow with frosted leaves so that under the high gray fog they seemed a thin band of sunshine. This was the only color in the gray afternoon. She sat unmoving for a long time. Her eyes blinked rarely.

Henry came banging out of the door, shoving his tie inside his vest as he came. Elisa stiffened and her face grew tight. Henry stopped short and looked at her. "Why — why, Elisa, You look so nice!"

"Nice? You think I look nice? What do you mean by 'nice'?"

Henry blundered on. "I don't know. I mean you look different, strong and happy."

"I am strong? Yes, strong. What do you mean 'strong'?"

He looked bewildered. "You're playing some kind of a game," he said helplessly. "It's a kind of a play. You look strong enough to break a calf over your knee, happy enough to eat it like a watermelon."

For a second she lost her rigidity. "Henry! Don't talk like that. You didn't know what you said." She grew complete again. "I'm strong," she boasted. "I never knew before how strong."

Henry looked down toward the tractor shed, and when he brought his eyes back to her, they were his own again.

"I'll get out the car. You can put on your coat while I'm starting."

Elisa went into the house. She heard him drive to the gate and idle down his motor, and then she took a long time to put on her hat. She pulled it here and pressed it there. When Henry turned the motor off she slipped into her coat and went out.

The little roadster bounced along on the dirt road by the river, raising the birds and driving the rabbits into the brush. Two cranes flapped heavily over the willow-line and dropped into the river-bed.

Far ahead on the road Elisa saw a dark speck. She knew.

She tried not to look as they passed it, but her eyes would not obey. She whispered to herself sadly, "He might have thrown them off the road. That wouldn't have been much trouble, not very much. But he kept the pot," she explained. "He had to keep the pot. That's why he couldn't get them off the road."

The roadster turned a bend and she saw the caravan ahead. She swung full around toward her husband so she could not see the little covered wagon and the mismatched team as the car passed them.

In a moment it was over. The thing was done. She did not look back.

She said loudly, to be heard above the motor, "It will be good, tonight, a good dinner."

"Now you're changed again," Henry complained. He took one hand from the wheel and patted her knee. "I ought to take you in to dinner oftener. It would be good for both of us. We get so heavy out on the ranch."

"Henry," she asked, "could we have wine at dinner?"

"Sure we could. Say! That will be fine."

She was silent for a while; then she said, "Henry, at those prize fights, do the men hurt each other very much?"

"Sometimes a little, not often. Why?"

"Well, I've read how they break noses, and blood runs down their chests. I've read how the fighting gloves get heavy and soggy with blood."

He looked around at her. "What's the matter, Elisa? I didn't know you read things like that." He brought the car to a stop, then turned to the right over the Salinas River bridge.

"Do any women ever go to the fights?" she asked.

"Oh, sure, some. What's the matter, Elisa? Do you want to go? I don't think you'd like it, but I'll take you if you really want to go."

She relaxed limply in the seat. "Oh, no. No. I don't want to go. I'm sure I don't." Her face was turned away from him. "It will be enough if we can have wine. It will be plenty." She turned up her coat collar so he could not see that she was crying weakly — like an old woman.

AUDREY THOMAS

Xanadu

In the beginning it was hardly paradise. That first night, "the night of the dreadful overture," as she was to call it later, when they had arrived at last at the house, bones aching from the long drive up from the harbor (over a road so pock-marked with holes it looked, as her husband said, "as though an army had blown it up as they retreated"), heads reeling from that first sensuous shock which Africa invariably delivers to the European consciousness, only to discover that the house was in utter darkness and the steward who had been engaged for them by the university was dead drunk on the front veranda (had quite literally stumbled upon this last discovery and experienced a thrill of horror, thinking, for a moment, that the man was dead, not drunk); when they had solved the mysteries of hanging mosquito nets and sent the children off to bed with the remains of the picnic lunch inside ("we couldn't find so much as a can opener"); when she had inhaled the general atmosphere of damp and decay (which even two Bufferin tablets and a large whiskey failed to dispel), had succumbed to self-pity and despair and anger, she did the only sensible thing a woman can do in such circumstances — put her head in her hands and wept. "The whole thing seemed a vast conspiracy," she said to her friends later, "and I felt, somehow, that a large and highly organized 'unwelcoming committee' had been at work." Then she would add, with a small laugh at her own idiosyncrasies, "I attach great importance to beginnings, to signs and portents you might say. My Irish ancestry I suppose." What made it worse was the fact that her husband insisted upon treating the whole thing as a joke, an adventure. "Jason seemed to find it all so interesting, so novel. He kept sticking his head out the door and sniffing — like a great dog who wanted to be let out, or a child on his first night of vacation. I honestly think that if I had been the violent sort — " (a pause while she impishly regarded her listeners and smiled the delightful smile which had made her such a favorite with both men and women) "—if I had been the violent sort I would have killed him on the spot. There is nothing more irritating," she would continue in a half-humorous, half-philosophic tone, "than the sight of another person enjoying a situation which you yourself find absolutely intolerable. *He* couldn't wait for daylight because he wanted to explore. *I* couldn't wait for daylight because I wanted to find the way to the nearest travel office."

Yes, it made for an amusing tale, in retrospect, but it could hardly be called an auspicious beginning. The next morning, in spite of the terrible and tiring events of the day before, she awoke early; and being unable to return to sleep or to endure the sight of her husband's peaceful face on the pillow beside her, she dressed quickly and went down to the kitchen. She was surveying with distaste a platoon of small ants who were breakfasting off the dirty dishes of the night before when she heard a light tap, tap ("almost like a discreet cough") on the kitchen door. Thinking it might be someone from the university, someone who would apologize for their not having been met; for their having to arrive in the dark, the pouring rain, alone and helpless; for the drunken steward, the missing can opener, the musty sheets, for the whole initial fiasco, she flung open the door "as full of righteous indignation as a balloon about to pop." There on the stoop stood a large black man, the blackest man she had ever seen. He was clad only in a pair of khaki shorts and a tattered string vest. She was still in that state, not at all unusual for a European, when all Africans look alike; so, although she had seen the steward of the night before, had seen him clearly in the light of her husband's torch, she did not realize at first that the two men bore very little resemblance to one another and she immediately assumed that they were the same. Naturally she was furious, and she spoke to him very sharply. ("I nearly sent him away!")

"I thought my husband made it very clear to you last night that your services would no longer be required. And if you think you're getting any wages for yesterday's performance you're very much mistaken." He watched her, impassive yet without hostility, and waited politely until she had finished. "There was I, screaming at the poor man like some fishwife, and he never moved a muscle; never even, as I recall, batted an eye." (Of course she was elaborating a little here. In actual fact she had never raised her voice, was furiously calm, spoke slowly and methodically as though, with each word, she were giving him a sharp but precise blow from an unseen hammer. But it made a better story the other way, and she enjoyed the picture she created in her listeners' minds, enjoyed the implication that she, who seemed the mildest of women, had been, at the outset, the typical European bitch. "I was positively archetypal," she would cry, and wrinkle her delightful nose with laughter and pretended self-distaste.) Yet when she had finished her little speech, the man did not go away as she expected and she spoke to him again. "Well? What is it you want? You can hardly expect us to give you a reference, can you?"

"No, Madame. Please, Madame, I know nothin' about yesterday. I have only just arrived. Do you want a steward, Madame?" It was then that she looked at him closely, *really* looked at him, and realized her terrible mistake, her awful blunder.

"I'm terribly sorry," she said, and smiled her brilliant smile — the smile that had endeared her to countless cabdrivers, milkmen and meter-readers (not to mention her wide circle of friends) back home. "I thought you were someone else. Our steward, I mean the steward engaged for us, was drunk when we arrived. We sent him away, and I thought you were he. I've been very rude to you. Forgive me." She found herself offering an apology where no apology had, in fact, been demanded. Perhaps precisely because none had been asked for, not even hinted at in the man's impassive but polite silence; or perhaps because the awareness of centuries of what one might call, euphemistically, European bad manners made her feel that an apology was due and overdue. He accepted the apology in the same way in which he had accepted the accusations — with a polite silence. Yet this very silence seemed to comfort her, seemed to indicate that he understood and approved first, the anger, and second, the apology. But all he did, verbally, was to repeat, "Please, Madame, do you need a steward?"

"Can you cook?" she asked. He could.

"Can you read and write?" He could do this as well. ("Although why I asked that question, then, when all I needed, all I was desperate for, was someone who could clean and scrub and make the wretched stove light, who could bring domestic order out of the chaos into which we had been plunged, I'll never know." She did not remember that she had overheard a woman on the boat say that it was a tremendous advantage if "they" could read and write.)

"Well, then," she said, "you're hired."

"Just like that?" her listeners would ask in wonder and admiration. "Just like that," she would reply with a laugh. "Call it instinct, call it what you will; I somehow felt that he was what we wanted, what we needed, and that it would be ridiculous to ask for letters of reference, or his job book, with all those ants crawling around and the children about to wake up and want their breakfast. It was as though I had rubbed a lamp and the genie had appeared. One doesn't," she added with a laugh, "ask a genie for his testimonials."

And indeed, it did seem like magic. In minutes the dishes were done, the kitchen swept ("the broom seemed to appear from nowhere") and a large pan of bacon and eggs was frying merrily on the stove. Full of excitement she ran up the stairs which she had descended with such foreboding just half an hour before. She found her husband in the children's room, searching through suitcases for clean underwear and socks, for dry sandals (the eldest had managed to step in a puddle the night before), and a missing Teddy bear. The room was in chaos, and for a moment she experienced a renewal of despair as she glanced at the disorder and the all-too-obvious grime of the room itself. But then she remembered her errand, her news, "Listen, Jason, we've got a steward." "We had a steward, you mean," he replied from the corner, where he was trying to persuade the eldest that one brown sandal and one red would look very gay.

"No," she shook her head slowly, triumphantly, "we've got one — a new one. I just hired him."

"Good," he said. And that was all. No questions were asked — nothing. It seemed to him the most natural thing in the world that a steward should appear out of nowhere, and that his wife should hire him on the spot. She was a little put out, a little irritated, that her announcement did not, somehow, seem worthy of blaring trumpets and waving flags. Something (it couldn't have been spite) made her ask, "What if he isn't any good?"

"He'll be good," said her husband. And he was. By the time they all trooped down to breakfast, the sitting room had been swept, the ashtrays emptied, and the table laid with an almost military precision. A pot of coffee stood ready (a hot pad placed carefully under it, she noted with approval), a bowl of fruit was waiting at each place, and she settled herself at the head of the table with a shy, triumphant smile — like a soldier modestly returning home, his erect back and grave smile bearing mute witness to battles won and obstacles endured. Everything was delicious: crisp bacon, solid but not solidified eggs, a veritable regiment of toast lined up for their inspection. And all the time the steward moving to and fro, his sandals slapping efficiently on the terrazzo floor. Plates were whisked away and clean plates substituted; a second rack of toast appeared, more steaming coffee: all this done so quickly, so quietly that the large black man might have been another Ariel with hosts of spirits at his command. The children were delighted, intrigued.

"Did *he* get the breakfast, Mommy? What's his name?" It came as a shock to her, almost as a sensation of good manners breached, that she had, in fact, forgotten to ask him his name. So when he appeared again she turned her shy, brilliant smile on him once more, extended her smile to him, offered it, the way a friend will convey apology with the soft pressure of a hand.

"I'm terribly sorry. I forgot to ask you your name."

"Joseph, Madame." And then, a bit confused as to how to end the brief interview (for she had never dealt with servants before), she simply played her smile over his face once more and reached for the marmalade.

By noon, when they had all returned from an exploratory trip around the compound, had met the registrar and gracefully accepted his equally graceful apologies for thinking that their ship was due in on the tenth, not the ninth; had explained to him about the drunken steward and the lack of electricity; had been assured that the man, if he could be found, would be dealt with, and had been informed, again with a graceful apology, that the electricity was always off on Thursday evenings; when they had collected their mail and bought a few things at the little shop, they discovered that the chaos of the bedrooms had disappeared. Suitcases had been unpacked and set out on the upstairs veranda to air, the children's clothes had been carefully sorted and put away, beds had been stripped of thier musty sheets, and mattresses laid outside to absorb the sun. They discovered Joseph in the bathroom, kneeling over the tub and methodically kneading dirt out of the mosquito nets. Even the missing Teddy bear had been found. And later, after a (by now) predictably delicious lunch, as she lay on her immaculate bed in a state of happy exhaustion and listened to the laughter of the children, who were taking turns on an ancient swing which her husband had discovered at the bottom of the garden, she decided that things had, after all, turned out for the best. She felt, somehow, that she almost owed that miserable creature of the night before a vote of thanks. For it they hadn't had to send him away, then she, in turn, would have sent Joseph away that morning. A bad beginning, she reflected philosophically, just before she dozed off, does not necessarily imply a bad ending.

Thus the days slipped by, each one like some perfect, exotic jewel set carefully and expertly into her golden chalice of contentment. What of mosquitoes? Joseph examined the nets each day, and sprayed the lounge each evening after dinner while they sipped a cup of coffee on the veranda. What of the rains? At the first tentative rumble Joseph ran swiftly through the house, shutting the louvres, bringing in the washing, checking that the candlesticks were ready if the electricity should go off and remain off after dark. What of the orange lady, the bean man, the itinerant traders — the steady stream of merchandise which arrived each day? Joseph took care of it all — made certain that only the biggest oranges at the smallest price, the choicest beans, the largest bunch of bananas, the most serious traders, ever passed her threshold. For the first time in more years than she cared to remember she felt "caught up" with the sheer mass of business necessary to maintaining a comfortable, well-run home. For the first time she could wake up in the morning without a moral hangover, a sense of things left undone or done too hastily, of buttons still missing or unmatched socks. Instead, at six o'clock came the gentle, cough-like knock announcing the arrival of morning tea. Then they dressed, and while her husband shaved and collected the books he would need that morning, she dressed the children for school. By six-thirty breakfast was on the table; by seven her husband had left; by seven-thirty the eldest child had been picked up by the little school bus which traveled the compound. She read and played games with the little one until it was eight-fifteen and his turn to be picked up for nursery school. How strange it seemed, at first, to take her coffee out on the veranda and contemplate the day before her, the day that would unroll like a red carpet under her feet, to choose what she wanted to do, to ignore unmade beds and dirty dishes, washing and ironing, what to serve for lunch. She felt almost as though she were a convalescent who was now recovering slowly but happily, aware perhaps for the first time of the small beauties of the world, the large beauty of being alive at all. Joseph took care of everything — everyone; moved swiftly and noiselessly in and out of their days, a dark brown shuttle weaving a gay-colored carpet for her delight.

Yet with all this idleness, this new and unaccustomed leisure she wasn't bored — not for a minute. She embarked, first of all, on a plan of self-improvement, sent away for books which she had always meant to read, decided to brush up on her French, to begin German. "After all," she said to Jason one evening as they sat on the veranda observing the strange, almost embarrassed pink of the tropical sunset, "I may never have this chance again."

"Which chance is that?"

"The chance to spread my intellectual wings a bit, to grow — as a person, I mean."

"Begin," he said with a teasing smile, "by keeping still and watching that sky."

But his teasing never bothered her, and she was perceptive enough to realize that even the most sympathetic of husbands could not possibly understand what it was like to be suddenly released from all the never-ending pressures of housework, the domestic cares that had always, since the birth of their first child, hovered over her like a swarm of angry bees. "It was not that I had really minded, of course, at the time. I'm old-fashioned enough to believe that a woman's place *is* in the home, not in the office. It's just that one gets so run down, spiritually as well, without even noticing it — without having *time* to notice it I should say." Now, for the first time in many years, she could read a magazine through from cover to cover if she felt like it, at one sitting; she could have friends in for dinner without being conscious, as the evening wore on, of the great stack of unwashed dishes which would have to be dealt with when the final good-byes had been said. Now, while the guests sipped their coffee on the veranda she could hear, as one hears a delightful, far-off tune, the sound of Joseph washing up in the kitchen. And every evening, before the children were bathed and put to bed (always clean pajamas, always a fresh and spotless towel), she sat down with them and read a story: one that they chose, however long, and not one that she had chosen because it was short and quickly gotten through. This hour with the children became very precious to her, and she would even linger over it, as one lingers over a delicious meal, asking the children questions about the characters, reading favorite bits again. The children responded gaily, affectionately, giggling with delight as she changed her voice and became the wicked old witch, the dwarfs, the three bears. She felt like a flower that had been tightly curled and suddenly, in the embrace of the sun, begins to expand.

Then too, there were the coffee mornings when she met the other faculty wives and discussed the advantages and disadvantages of life in the tropics; how difficult it was to get butter and tea, how easy to get fresh fruit. And, of course, they discussed the stewards. It took several weeks before she realized just how lucky they had been. Tales of broken crockery, sullenness, petty thievery; gradually it dawned on her that Joseph was something of a miracle, a paragon. Each week some new disaster was reported. One steward had been caught wearing his master's vests, another had burned a large hole in an heirloom tablecloth. Yet another had disappeared for five days and returned with no explanation at all (and was duly sacked). One woman, who had arrived only three months before, was on her eleventh boy, and *he* didn't seem at all satisfactory. She would come away from these coffee mornings feeling like a healthy woman who has just been regaled with stories of ghastly operations; she found it all hard to believe. But there was, of course, the initial experience, that first night, and almost as though she felt it necessary to defend herself, to justify her good fortune, she would recall her own lurid introduction and speculate with her friends on what would have happened if — ? For she could, in truth, find no fault with Joseph at all. "As a matter of fact," she confided shyly to her new friends, "he is far better at managing a household than I am." Then she would smile her delightful smile and throw up her hands in a pretty gesture of mock despair. It was as though they had all been panning for gold and she, the lucky one, had by chance discovered the richest hoard, the deepest vein, was carrying Joseph's virtues around in her pocket like a sack of golden pebbles. Every Tuesday, early, before the sun had begun to beat down in earnest, she and Joseph would set off in the station wagon for town. Wandering from shop to shop, a gay straw basket on her arm, she did the weekly marketing. (And always Joseph behind her like a cool black shadow.) She enjoyed these Tuesday mornings, enjoyed the colorful pageantry of the busy town, the gay clothes of the men and women — "black Romans in bright togas. How pale and insipid they make the Europeans look." She enjoyed bargaining with the boys who came rushing up with grapefruit, limes, oranges; enjoyed haggling with the "Mammys" over vegetables. Sometimes they would go to the large open-air market where it was her turn to wait quietly while Joseph quickly bargained for yams and sweet potatoes, bananas and pineapples. (He had explained to her, very politely, that the prices were raised for a white woman, and he could therefore obtain more value for the money if he bargained for her; said all this in a manner which indicated full recognition of this deplorable practice and yet somehow managed to convey the idea that such bargaining would be a pleasure for him because it would serve her and "the Master.") Although she could not understand what he said to the various traders, she accepted his prices as absolute and would never dream of interfering in these sometimes long and rather tedious harangues. And if she needed something at the end of the week, she did not hesitate to send him off alone, knowing that her money would be well spent and that he would not add on a sixpence here or a shilling there, as was the practice of many of her friends' boys. "There is something almost regal about him," she commented once to her husband. "It is as though everything that he does for me, for us, is done because he genuinely likes us, because he accepts us as people and not as employers. He serves without being servile — if you know what I mean."

They became fimiliar figures in the town, the small, fair woman in the straw hat and the huge black man. Even when she refused a purchase she would flash her smile and the sting was taken out of the refusal. And when the chattering, the crowding around became too much, she had only to turn to Joseph with a smiling, half-despairing look; a few sharp words in the vernacular and the vegetable boys, the fruit boys, the little crowd of beggars and loungers, would scatter like so many dark birds. It was wonderful to feel so protected, so well-looked-after. And of course, as though to keep her ever mindful of just exactly how wonderful it all was, there were always the Sundays — Joseph's day off. On Sunday morning there was no welcoming cup of tea, no immaculately laid breakfast table, no strong brown arms to deal with the tidying and washing up. On Sundays the magic world, her enchanted island as it were, disappeared. Joseph, like a huge black Prospero, retired to his cell, and she was left to work her own miracles. Strangely enough, in spite of the fact that she was rested and content, things always went wrong for her on Sundays. As though she were a bride of a few months, she found herself burning toast, overcooking eggs, dropping a precious jar of marmalade on the floor. Jason and the children were really quite brutal about it, teased her unmercifully. "Who's Joseph's stand-in?" her husband would say to the eldest child. "I think she might do for a small-boy, don't you, but she'll never make a cook-steward." At first she entered into the game, dropping serviettes on purpose, laying the table backwards, making faces and muttering, "Yes, Master, yes, Master," under her breath, or "Sorry, Master." But after a while it began to hurt a bit, this patronizing attitude of theirs, and one Sunday, when the youngest had wept bitter tears because Joseph wasn't there to chop up the eggs in a special way, she left the table in anger and wept a few bitter tears of her own. After all, in the terrible heat, with a cantankerous stove, they could hardly expect her to be perfect. However, they all filed shyly up to apologize and she soon forgave them with her brilliant, if this time somewhat watery, smile. Nevertheless, although she may have forgotten and forgiven, something remained at the back of her consciousness, something unnamed, unobserved, as infinitesimal as a grain of sand in an oyster, as quiet as the hum of a solitary mosquito. Monday came, Joseph returned to work and everything seemed, on the surface, to be back to normal. If a bit of the old magic was gone, she would have been the last person to admit it, perhaps the last person to understand why. And except for the incident of the snake, things might have gone on, indefinitely, very much as before.

However, one morning, as she made her way across the courtyard with a small basket of wet clothes (for she refused to allow Joseph to wash out her underthings, felt, somehow, that this was too much to ask a man to do), a large python sluggishly uncurled itself from the clothes pole not three feet away from her. For the space of a heartbeat she stood rooted to the spot, hypnotized with terror. Then she ran, screaming, into the house. She was still locked in the farthest bedroom when her husband and the children came home for lunch. When she had been assured that the snake had been killed, she ventured forth and allowed herself to be led to the table. The children were very excited, for apparently Joseph had killed the snake and it was stretched out on a pole behind his quarters. Already a group of admiring neighbors had been to see it and marveled over its length and ugliness. It appeared that the eldest child knew all about snakes. "A python won't bite you, Mother. It crushes you to death. Or anyway, it crushes animals and things." He gazed at her with a condescending smile. But the terror of the morning was still so great in her mind that she scarcely heard the child, and his words bounced off her consciousness without wounding. She ate and drank mechanically and then, at her husband's insistence, went back upstairs to lie down. She had not yet spoken to Joseph, had not yet thanked him for killing the snake. To tell the truth, she was somewhat embarrassed about the whole thing. It was not that anyone would blame her for running away, for screaming, or even for hysterically locking herself in the bedroom. She knew that most people, men as well as women, have a violent reaction to snakes whatever their size. No, she was all right there, and her hasty retreat could hardly be called a social blunder. (As a matter of fact, the one woman on the compound who did show an interest in reptiles was thought by many of the others to be a bit "queer" and certainly slightly unfeminine.) Her embarrassment had to do with Joseph. Lying on the immaculate bed, shutters drawn against the glare, she faced up to the unpleasant fact that she did not want to thank her steward; that in fact she wished the snake had managed to get away. Now she was somehow in his debt, owed something to this dark man who could cope with anything. ("Something?" whispered a voice in her ear. "Everything.") She felt, for the first time, that she belonged to Joseph and not Joseph to her. And yet, the more she thought about it, the more she realized that the incident of the snake was just one example of the way in which Joseph had gradually made himself indispensable. Suddenly she heard the voices of her husband and the children, directly below the window. They must be coming back from viewing the snake, and the littlest child was obviously a bit frightened. "Will Joseph kill all the snakes, Daddy?" she heard him ask in an anxious voice. "Of course. That's what he keeps the big stick for." "But what will we do on Sundays?" said the child, and began to cry. "I'll tell you what," said his father, trying to jolly the child and unaware, of course, that he was being overheard. "On Sundays, if we see any snakes we'll take some of Mummy's toast and hit them right between the eyes. I should think they wouldn't come around here a second time." The child began to giggle, and all three moved around the corner and out of earshot. This was the crowning blow. Not only had Joseph made himself a necessity in their household, but he was making her a family joke. Each time that he increased in importance, she diminished. It was unbearable. She felt stifled, afraid. All the little helps which Joseph had performed for her, all the larger duties which he had removed from her weary shoulders — each act now seemed like a golden thread binding her tighter and tighter to a conception of herself as a totally incompetent, albeit delightful, woman. She felt as though she had been tricked out of her rights, deceived. She lit a cigarette and lay, smoking, while she examined the problem, explored the wound the way a child will explore with his tongue the raw hole where a tooth should be. By tea time she had come to a decision.

The next morning, after her husband had left, after the children had been kissed and put on the bus, she gave Joseph a pound note and asked him to go into the market for some fruits and vegetables. She stood at the window for a long time, watching his erect figure grow smaller and smaller until he turned the bend in the road and disappeared. Almost regretfully she opened the silver chest and selected three coffee spoons, holding the heavy silver in her hands for a moment, hating to part with it for even a few hours. Then, with the spoons in her pocket, she made her way slowly, determinedly, across the courtyard toward the servants' quarters at the back of the house.

JAMES THURBER

The Catbird Seat

Mr. Martin bought the pack of Camels on Monday night in the most crowded cigar store on Broadway. It was theater time and seven or eight men were buying cigarettes. The clerk didn't even glance at Mr. Martin, who put the pack in his overcoat pocket and went out. If any of the staff at F & S had seen him buy the cigarettes, they would have been astonished, for it was generally known that Mr. Martin did not smoke, and never had. No one saw him.

It was just a week to the day since Mr. Martin had decided to rub out Mrs. Ulgine Barrows. The term "rub out" pleased him because it suggested nothing more than the correction of an error — in this case an error of Mr. Fitweiler. Mr. Martin had spent each night of the past week working out his plan and examining it. As he walked home now he went over it again. For the hundredth time he resented the element of imprecision, the margin of guesswork that entered into the business. The project as he had worked it out was casual and bold, the risks were considerable. Something might go wrong anywhere along the line. And therein lay the cunning of his scheme. No one would ever see in it the cautious, painstaking hand of Erwin Martin, head of the filing department at F & S, of whom Mr. Fitweiler had once said, "Man is fallible but Martin isn't." No one would see his hand, that is, unless it were caught in the act.

Sitting in his apartment, drinking a glass of milk, Mr. Martin reviewed his case against Mrs. Ulgine Barrows, as he had every night for seven nights. He began at the beginning. Her quacking voice and braying laugh had first profaned the halls of F & S on March 7, 1941 (Mr. Martin had a head for dates). Old Roberts, the personnel chief, had introduced her as the newly appointed special adviser to the president of the firm, Mr. Fitweiler. The woman had appalled Mr. Martin instantly, but he hadn't shown it. He had given her his dry hand, a look of studious concentration, and a faint smile. "Well," she had said, looking at the papers on his desk, "are you lifting the oxcart out of the ditch?" As Mr. Martin recalled that moment, over his milk, he squirmed slightly. He must keep his mind on her crimes as a special adviser, not on her peccadillos as a personality. This he found difficult to do, in spite of entering an objection and sustaining it. The faults of the woman as a woman kept chattering on in his mind like an unruly witness. She had, for almost two years now, baited him. In the halls, in the elevator, even in his own office, into which she romped now and then like a circus horse, she was constantly shouting these silly questions at him. "Are you lifting the oxcart out of the ditch? Are you tearing up the pea patch? Are you hollering down the rain barrel? Are you scraping around the bottom of the pickle barrel? Are you sitting in the catbird seat?"

It was Joey Hart, one of Mr. Martin's two assistants, who had explained what the gibberish meant. "She must be a Dodger fan," he had said. "Red Barber announces the Dodger games over the radio and he uses those expressions — picked 'em up down South." Joey had gone on to explain one or two. "Tearing up the pea patch" meant going on a rampage; "sitting in the catbird seat" meant sitting pretty, like a batter with three balls and no strikes on him. Mr. Martin dismissed all this with an effort. It had been annoying, it had driven him near to distraction, but he was too solid a man to be moved to murder by anything so childish. It was fortunate, he reflected as he passed on to the important charges against Mrs. Barrows, that he had stood up under it so well. He had maintained always an outward appearance of polite tolerance. "Why, I even believe you like the woman," Miss Paird, his other assistant, had once said to him. He had simply smiled.

A gavel rapped in Mr. Martin's mind and the case proper was resumed. Mrs. Ulgine Barrows stood charged with willful, blatant, and persistent attempts to destroy the efficiency and system of F & S. It was competent, material, and relevant to review her advent and rise to power. Mr. Martin had got the story from Miss Paird, who seemed always able to find things out. According to her, Mrs. Barrows had met Mr. Fitweiler at a party, where she had rescued him from the embraces of a powerfully built drunken man who had mistaken the president of F & S for a famous retired Middle Western football coach. She had led him to a sofa and somehow worked upon him a monstrous magic. The aging gentleman had jumped to the conclusion there and then that this was a woman of singular attainments, equipped to bring out the best in him and in the firm. A week later he had introduced her into F & S as his special adviser. On that day confusion got its foot in the door. After Miss Tyson, Mr. Brundage, and Mr. Bartlett had been fired and Mr. Munson had taken his hat and stalked out, mailing in his resignation later, old Roberts had been emboldened to speak to Mr. Fitweiler. He mentioned that Mr. Munson's department had been "a little disrupted" and hadn't they perhaps better resume the old system there? Mr. Fitweiler had said certainly not. He had the greatest faith in Mrs. Barrows' ideas. "They require a little seasoning, a little seasoning, is all," he had added. Mr. Roberts had given it up. Mr. Martin reviewed in detail all the changes wrought by Mrs. Barrows. She had begun chipping at the cornices of the firm's edifice and now she was swinging at the foundation stones with a pickaxe.

Mr. Martin came now, in his summing up, to the afternoon of Monday, November 2, 1942 — just one week ago. On that day, at 3 P.M., Mrs. Barrows had bounced into his office. "Boo!" she had yelled. "Are you scraping around the bottom of the pickle barrel?" Mr. Martin had looked at her from under his green eyeshade, saying nothing. She had begun to wander about the office, taking it in with her great, popping eyes. "Do you really need *all* these filing cabinets?" she had demanded suddenly. Mr. Martin's heart had jumped. "Each of these files," he had said, keeping his voice even, "plays an indispensable part in the system of F & S." She had brayed at him, "Well, don't tear up the pea patch!" and gone to the door. From there she had bawled, "But you sure have got a lot of fine scrap in here!" Mr. Martin could no longer doubt that the finger was on his beloved department. Her pickaxe was on the upswing, poised for the first blow. It had not come yet; he had received no blue memo from the enchanted Mr. Fitweiler bearing nonsensical instructions deriving from the obscene woman. But there was no doubt in Mr. Martin's mind that one would be forthcoming. He must act quickly. Already a precious week had gone by. Mr. Martin stood up in his living room, still holding his milk glass. "Gentlemen of the jury," he said to himself, "I demand the death penalty for this horrible person."

The next day Mr. Martin followed his routine, as usual. He polished his glasses more often and once sharpened an already sharp pencil, but not even Miss Paird noticed. Only once did he catch sight of his victim; she swept past him in the hall with a patronizing "Hi!" At five-thirty he walked home, as usual, and had a glass of milk, as usual. He had never drunk anything stronger in his life — unless you could count ginger ale. The late Sam Schlosser, the S of F & S, had praised Mr. Martin at a staff meeting several years before for his temperate habits. "Our most efficient worker neither drinks nor smokes," he had said. "The results speak for themselves." Mr. Fitweiler had sat by, nodding approval.

Mr. Martin was still thinking about that red-letter day as he walked over to Schrafft's on Fifth Avenue near Forty-sixth Street. He got there, as he always did, at eight o'clock. He finished his dinner and the financial page of the *Sun* at a quarter to nine, as he always did. It was his custom after dinner to take a walk. This time he walked down Fifth Avenue at a casual pace. His gloved hands felt moist and warm, his forehead cold. He transferred the Camels from his overcoat to a jacket pocket. He wondered, as he did so, if they did not represent an unnecessary note of strain. Mrs. Barrows smoked only Luckies. It was his idea to puff a few puffs on a Camel (after the rubbing-out), stub it out in the ashtray holding her lipstick-stained Luckies, and thus drag a small red herring across the trail. Perhaps it was not a good idea. It would take time. He might even choke, too loudly.

Mr. Martin had never seen the house on West Twelfth Street where Mrs. Barrows lived, but he had a clear enough picture of it. Fortunately, she had bragged to everybody about her ducky first-floor apartment in the perfectly darling three-story red-brick. There would be no doorman or other attendants; just the tenants of the second and third floors. As he walked along, Mr. Martin realized that he would get there before nine-thirty. He had considered walking north on Fifth Avenue from Schrafft's to a point from which it would take him until ten o'clock to reach the house. At that hour people were less likely to be coming in or going out. But the procedure would have made an awkward loop in the straight thread of his casualness, and he had abandoned it. It was impossible to figure when people would be entering or leaving the house, anyway. There was a great risk at any hour. If he ran into anybody, he would simply have to place the rubbing-out of Ulgine Barrows in the inactive file forever. The same thing would hold true if there were someone in her apartment. In that case he would just say that he had been passing by, recognized her charming house and thought to drop in.

It was eighteen minutes after nine when Mr. Martin turned into Twelfth Street. A man passed him, and a man and a woman talking. There was no one within fifty paces when he came to the house, halfway down the block. He was up the steps and in the small vestibule in no time, pressing the bell under the card that said "Mrs. Ulgine Barrows." When the clicking in the lock started, he jumped forward against the door. He got inside fast, closing the door behind him. A bulb in a lantern hung from the hall ceiling on a chain seemed to give a monstrously bright light. There was nobody on the stair, which went up ahead of him along the left wall. A door opened down the hall in the wall on the right. He went toward it swiftly, on tiptoe.

"Well, for God's sake, look who's here!" bawled Mrs. Barrows, and her braying laugh rang out like the report of a shotgun. He rushed past her like a football tackle, bumping her. "Hey, quit shoving!" she said, closing the door behind them. They were in her living room, which seemed to Mr. Martin to be lighted by a hundred lamps. "What's after you?" she said. "You're as jumpy as a goat." He found he was unable to speak. His heart was wheezing in his throat. "I — yes," he finally brought out. She was jabbering and laughing as she started to help him off with his coat. "No, no," he said. "I'll put it here." He took it off and put it on a chair near the door. "Your hat and gloves, too," she said. "You're in a lady's house." He put his hat on top of the coat. Mrs. Barrows seemed larger than he had thought. He kept his gloves on. "I was passing by," he said. "I recognized — is there anyone here?" She laughed louder than ever. "No," she said, "we're all alone. You're as white as a sheet, you funny man. Whatever *has* come over you? I'll mix you a toddy." She started toward a door across the room. "Scotch-and-soda be all right? But say, you don't drink, do you?" She turned and gave him her amused look. Mr. Martin pulled himself together. "Scotch-and-soda will be all right," he heard himself say. He could hear her laughing in the kitchen.

Mr. Martin looked quickly around the living room for the weapon. He had counted on finding one there. There were andirons and a poker and something in a corner that looked like an Indian club. None of them would do. It couldn't be that way. He began to pace around. He came to a desk. On it lay a metal paper knife with an ornate handle. Would it be sharp enough? He reached for it and knocked over a small brass jar. Stamps spilled out of it and it fell to the floor with a clatter. "Hey," Mrs. Barrows yelled from the kitchen, "are you tearing up the pea patch?" Mr. Martin gave a strange laugh. Picking up the knife, he tried its point against his left wrist. It was blunt. It wouldn't do.

When Mrs. Barrows reappeared, carrying two highballs, Mr. Martin, standing there with his gloves on, became actually conscious of the fantasy he had wrought. Cigarettes in his pocket, a drink prepared for him — it was all too grossly improbable. It was more than that; it was impossible. Somewhere in the back of his mind a vague idea stirred, sprouted. "For heaven's sake, take off those gloves," said Mrs. Barrows. "I always wear them in the house," said Mr. Martin. The idea began to bloom, strange and wonderful. She put the glasses on a coffee table in front of a sofa and sat on the sofa. "Come over here, you odd little man," she said. Mr. Martin went over and sat beside her. It was difficult getting a cigarette out of the pack of Camels, but he managed it. She held a match for him, laughing. "Well," she said handing him his drink, "this is perfectly marvelous. You with a drink and a cigarette."

Mr. Martin puffed, not too awkwardly, and took a gulp of the highball. "I drink and smoke all the time," he said. He clinked his glass against hers. "Here's nuts to that old windbag, Fitweiler," he said, and gulped again. The stuff tasted awful, but he made no grimace. "Really, Mr. Martin," she said, her voice and posture changing, "you are insulting our employer." Mrs. Barrows was now all special adviser to the president. "I am preparing a bomb," said Mr. Martin, "which will blow the old goat higher than hell." He had only had a little of the drink, which was not strong. It couldn't be that. "Do you take dope or something?" Mrs. Barrows asked coldly. "Heroin," said Mr. Martin. "I'll be coked to the gills when I bump that old buzzard off." "Mr. Martin!" she shouted, getting to her feet. "That will be all of that. You must go at once." Mr. Martin took another swallow of his drink. He tapped his cigarette out in the ashtray and put the pack of Camels on the coffee table. Then he got up. She stood glaring at him. He walked over and put on his hat and coat. "Not a word about this," he said, and laid an index finger against his lips. All Mrs. Barrows could bring out was "Really!" Mr. Martin put his hand on the doorknob. "I'm sitting in the catbird seat," he said. He stuck his tongue out at her and left. Nobody saw him go.

Mr. Martin got to his apartment, walking, well before eleven. No one saw him go in. He had two glasses of milk after brushing his teeth, and he felt elated. It wasn't tipsiness, because he hadn't been tipsy. Anyway, the walk had worn off all effects of the whisky. He got in bed and read a magazine for a while. He was asleep before midnight.

Mr. Martin got to the office at eight-thirty the next morning, as usual. At a quarter to nine, Ulgine Barrows, who had never before arrived at work before ten, swept into his office. "I'm reporting to Mr. Fitweiler now!" she shouted. "If he turns you over to the police, it's no more than you deserve!" Mr. Martin gave her a look of shocked surprise. "I beg your pardon?" he said. Mrs. Barrows snorted and bounced out of the room, leaving Miss Paird and Joey Hart staring after her. "What's the matter with that old devil now?" asked Miss Paird. "I have no idea," said Mr. Martin, resuming his work. The other two looked at him and then at each other. Miss Paird got up and went out. She walked slowly past the closed door of Mr. Fitweiler's office. Mrs. Barrows was yelling inside, but she was not braying. Miss Paird could not hear what the woman was saying. She went back to her desk.

Forty-five minutes later, Mrs. Barrows left the president's office and went into her own, shutting the door. It wasn't until half an hour later that Mr. Fitweiler sent for Mr. Martin. The head of the filing department, neat, quiet, attentive, stood in front of the old man's desk. Mr. Fitweiler was pale and nervous. He took his glasses off and twiddled them. He made a small, bruffing sound in his throat. "Martin," he said, "you have been with us more than twenty years." "Twenty-two, sir," said Mr. Martin. "In that time," pursued the president, "your work and your — uh — manner have been exemplary." "I trust so, sir," said Mr. Martin. "I have understood, Martin," said Mr. Fitweiler, "that you have never taken a drink or smoked." "That is correct, sir," said Mr. Martin. "Ah, yes." Mr. Fitweiler polished his glasses. "You may describe what you did after leaving the office yesterday, Martin," he said. Mr. Martin allowed less than a second for his bewildered pause. "Certainly, sir," he said. "I walked home. Then I went to Schrafft's for dinner. Afterward I walked home again. I went to bed early, sir, and read a magazine for a while. I was asleep before eleven." "Ah, yes," said Mr. Fitweiler again. He was silent for a moment, searching for the proper words to say to the head of the filing department. "Mrs. Barrows," he said finally, "Mrs. Barrows has worked hard, Martin, very hard. It grieves me to report that she has suffered a severe breakdown. It had taken the form of a persecution complex accompanied by distressing hallucinations." "I am very sorry, sir," said Mr. Martin. "Mrs. Barrows is under the delusion," continued Mr. Fitweiler, "that you visited her last evening and behaved yourself in an — uh — unseemly manner." He raised his hand to silence Mr. Martin's little pained outcry. "It is the nature of these psychological diseases," Mr. Fitweiler said, "to fix upon the least likely and most innocent party as the — uh — source of persecution. These matters are not for the lay mind to grasp, Martin. I've just had my psychiatrist, Dr. Fitch, on the phone. He would not, of course, commit himself, but he made enough generalizations to substantiate my suspicions. I suggested to Mrs. Barrows when she had completed her — uh — story to me this morning, that she visit Dr. Fitch, for I suspected a condition at once. She flew, I regret to say, into a rage, and demanded — uh — requested that I call you on the carpet. You may not know, Martin, but Mrs. Barrows had planned a reorganization of your department — subject to my approval, of course, subject to my approval. This brought you, rather than anyone else, to her mind — but again that is a phenomenon for Dr. Fitch and not for us. So, Martin, I am afraid Mrs. Barrows' usefulness here is at an end." "I am dreadfully sorry, sir," said Mr. Martin.

It was at this point that the door to the office blew open with the suddenness of a gas-main explosion and Mrs. Barrows catapulted through it. "Is the little rat denying it?" she screamed. "He can't get away with that!" Mr. Martin got up and moved discreetly to a point beside Mr. Fitweiler's chair. "You drank and smoked at my apartment," she bawled at Mr. Martin, "and you know it! You called Mr. Fitweiler an old windbag and said you were going to blow him up when you got coked to the gills on your heroin!" She stopped yelling to catch her breath and a new glint came into her popping eyes. "If you weren't such a drab, ordinary little man," she said, "I'd think you'd planned it all. Sticking your tongue out at me, saying you were sitting in the catbird seat, because you thought no one would believe me when I told it! My God, it's really too perfect!" She brayed loudly and hysterically, and the fury was on her again. She glared at Mr. Fitweiler. "Can't you see how he has tricked us, you old fool? Can't you see his little game?" But Mr. Fitweiler had been surreptitiously pressing all the buttons under the top of his desk and employees of F & S began pouring into the room. "Stockton," said Mr. Fitweiler, "you and Fishbein will take Mrs. Barrows to her home. Mrs. Powell, you will go with them." Stockton, who had played a little football in high school, blocked Mrs. Barrows as she made for Mr. Martin. It took him and Fishbein together to force her out of the door into the hall, crowded with stenographers and office boys. She was still screaming imprecations at Mr. Martin, tangled and contradictory imprecations. The hubbub finally died out down the corridor.

"I regret that this has happened," said Mr. Fitweiler. "I shall ask you to dismiss it from your mind, Martin." "Yes, sir," said Mr. Martin, anticipating his chief's "That will be all" by moving to the door. "I will dismiss it." He went out and shut the door, and his step was light and quick in the hall. When he entered his department he had slowed down to his customary gait, and he walked quietly across the room to the W20 file, wearing a look of studious concentration.

IVAN TURGENEV

A Country Doctor

Translated by Bernard Guilbert Guerney

Once, in autumn, on my way back from a remote field, I caught a cold and had to take to my bed. Fortunately, the fever came upon me in the district capital, at a hotel; I sent for a doctor. Half an hour later the general practitioner for the district appeared, a man of no great height, rather thin and with black hair. He prescribed the usual sudorific, ordered a mustard plaster to be applied, quite deftly thrust the five-ruble note into the cuff of his coat sleeve -- during which, however, he gave a dry little cough and looked aside — and was just about to go on about his affairs, but somehow got to talking and stayed. My high temperature was tormenting me; I foresaw a sleepless night and was glad to have a chance of chatting with a kindhearted person. Tea was served. My doctor launched into talk. He was far from being a foolish fellow, expressing himself briskly and quite amusingly. Strange things befall in this world: you may live a long time with some man and be on terms of friendship with him, yet not even once get to talking with him frankly, from the very soul; with some other, however, you have barely had time to become acquainted when, first thing you know, you have either spilled your innermost secrets to him or he has spilled his to you, as if at confessional. I don't know how I had earned the confidence of my new friend, but the fact remains that he "upped" (as they say) and, for no particular reason, told me a rather remarkable incident, and so I now bring his story to the attention of the well-disposed reader. I will try to express myself in the doctor's own words.

"You haven't the pleasure of knowing —" he began in a strained and quavering voice (such is the effect of straight Berezovsky tobacco), "you haven't the pleasure of knowing Mylov, Paul Lukich — our local judge? You haven't that pleasure.... However, it doesn't matter." He coughed to clear his throat and wiped his eyes. "Well, you see, this affair took place about — when shall I say? I wouldn't want to give you a wrong date — it was during Lent, at the height of the thaw. I was sitting at his house — the judge's house, that is — and playing preference whist. Our judge is a fine man, and he's a great hand for playing preference. Suddenly" — my medical friend used the word "suddenly" often — "they tell me: 'There's a man asking for you.' I asked them what he wanted. 'He's brought a note,' they told me, 'must be from someone who's sick.' — 'Let's have the note,' said I. Sure enough: it was about someone who was sick. Well and good: that sort of thing is, you understand, our bread and butter. Here's the thing in a nutshell: a certain landed proprietress, a widow, wrote me that her daughter was dying, now: 'Come, for the sake of Our Lord God Himself; I have even sent the horses to fetch you!' Well, that part of it wasn't so bad — but she lived fifteen miles out of town, and it was night, and the state of the roads was simply unspeakable! Then, too, she herself was struggling with poverty: you couldn't expect more than a couple of silver rubles from her, mind you, and even that was doubtful, for all the chances were you'd have to do the best you could with a piece of homespun linen and whatever crumbs might come your way. However, duty comes first of all, you understand: there was a human being dying. I suddenly handed my cards over to Kalliopin, the permanent councilman, and set out for home.

"I look, and there's a wretched little cart before my entrance; it's drawn by plow horses, with bellies on them ever so big, and the wool on them like downright felt, while the driver, to show his respect, is bareheaded up on his box. 'Well,' I thought, 'I can see, brother, that your masters aren't exactly rolling in wealth!' It pleases you to laugh, and yet I'll tell you this — those of our fraternity are usually poor: they have to take everything into consideration. If the driver is sitting up there like a lord, and doesn't doff his cap, and on top of that sort of sneers through his beard and keeps flicking his dainty whip — it's a safe bet to count on two lovely bank notes of the higher denominations. But here, I saw, things weren't shaping up that way. 'However,' I reflected, 'there's no help for it: duty comes first of all.' I picked up the most necessary medicines and set out. Would you believe it, it was all we could do to drag ourselves there. The road was hellish: swollen streams, snow, mire, washouts, or, all of a sudden, a dam breaking up — what trouble!

"However, get there I did. The house was ever so small, straw-thatched. There was light in the windows, which meant they were waiting for me.

A little old woman came out to meet me — most venerable, she was, in a headdress. 'Save her!' said she. 'She's dying!' — 'Please don't upset yourself,' I told her. 'Where's the patient?' — 'Come right this way, please.'

"I looked about me: a neat little room, a holy lamp in a corner, a girl in bed — about twenty, unconscious. You could feel she was simply burning up with high temperature; she was breathing heavily: obviously in a fever. There were two other girls right there — her sisters — thoroughly frightened, all in tears. 'There,' they told me, 'yesterday she was perfectly well and eating with appetite; this morning she complained about her head, while toward evening, all of a sudden — there, you see the state she's in.'

"I told them once more: 'Please don't upset yourselves' — a doctor's duty that, you know — and began attending to her. I let her blood, ordered mustard plasters to be applied, prescribed a mixture. In the meanwhile I kept looking and looking at her, don't you know: well, by God, never yet had I seen such a face — a beauty, and that's all there was to it! Pity was simply rending me apart. The features so pleasing, and such eyes.... Well, glory be to God, she quieted down at last; perspiration appeared, she seemed to regain her senses, looked about her, smiled, passed her hand over her face. 'Well,' I told them, 'now we ought to let the patient rest.' And so we all tiptoed out; only a maid remained, against any contingency.

"And in the parlor a samovar was already standing on the table, and a bottle of Jamaica rum as well: in our work you can't get around things like that. They gave me tea, begging me to stay for the night; I agreed — how could one travel then! The little old lady kept oh'ing all the time. 'Why do you act like that?' I told her. 'She'll live; please don't upset yourself; it would be better if you were to get a little rest yourself — it's going on two in the morning.' — 'But you'll leave orders to wake me up if anything happens?' — 'I will, I will.' The old woman retired, and the girls also went to their room; a bed was made up for me in the parlor. Well, I lay down; the only thing was, I couldn't sleep — and that was something to wonder at! There, one might think, I'd had enough to tucker me out. Just couldn't get my patient off my mind. Finally I wasn't able to hold out any longer, and got up, all of a sudden: 'There,' I thought, 'I'll go and have a look how my patient is doing.' And, as it happened, her bedroom was right next to the parlor. Well, I got up, opened her door, ever so quietly — but my heart was simply pounding.

"I looked: the maid was asleep, her mouth open and actually snoring, the low-down animal, while the sick woman was lying with her face toward me and had flung out her arms, the poor thing! I approached ... when all of a sudden she opened her eyes and stared at me! 'Who is it? Who is it?' I became embarrassed. 'Don't be frightened, ma'am,' I told her, 'I'm the doctor; I've dropped in to see how you're feeling.' — 'You're the doctor?' — 'I am, I am. Your mother sent to town after me; we have let your blood, ma'am; now go to sleep, if you please, and in a couple of days or so, God willing, we'll have you up on your feet.' — 'Ah, yes, yes, Doctor — don't let me die ... please, please!' — 'Whatever are you saying? God be with you!'

"'And yet she's running a high temperature again,' I said to myself; I felt her pulse: she had high temperature, sure enough. She gave me a look, and then just gripped my arm, all of a sudden: 'I'll tell you why I don't want to die — I'll tell you, I'll tell you ... we're all by ourselves now — only, please, don't tell anybody ... listen —' I leaned toward her; she put her lips to my very ear, her hair touching my cheek — I confess my own head started spinning — and fell to whispering. I couldn't understand a thing. Ah, yes, she was raving! She kept whispering and whispering, and so fast, at that, and just as if in some foreign language; when she had done she shuddered, dropped her head on the pillow, and shook her finger at me. 'Watch out, now, Doctor — not a word to anybody....' Somehow or other I calmed her down, gave her a drink, woke up the maid, and went out."

At this point the doctor again took a pinch of snuff like a hardened addict, and for a moment seemed to be in a catalepsy.

"However," he went on, "the next day, contrary to my expectations, my patient felt no relief. I considered, considered, and suddenly decided to stay on, even though I had other patients expecting me. And, as you know, one can't afford to neglect such things: the practice suffers thereby. But, in the first place, the sick woman really was in a desperate state and, in the second, I must tell you the truth: I myself felt powerfully disposed toward her. Besides that, I had taken a liking to the whole family. Even though they were folks who hadn't much, they were nevertheless cultured — to a rare degree, one may say. The father, now, had been a man of learning, a writer; he had died in poverty, of course, but he had succeeded in imparting an excellent education to his children; he had also left them a lot of books. Whether it was because I attended with such zeal to the sick woman, or for some other reasons, still, I will venture to say, they had come to love me in that household as if I were one of the family.

"Meanwhile, the roads had become frightful — all communications had been cut off, so to speak; even the medicines could be brought back from town only with difficulty. The sick woman wasn't getting any better — day after day, day after day. But now, sir ... at this point, sir...." The doctor was silent for a while. "Really, I don't know how to put the matter to you." He took snuff anew, grunted, and had a sip of tea. "I'll tell you without beating about the bush — my patient ... how am I to put it? Well, she fell in love with me, sort of. Or no; it wasn't that she fell in love with me, exactly ... well, anyway ... really, now, how can I put it, sir —"

The doctor cast down his eyes and turned red.

"No," he went on with animation, "how can one call it falling in love? After all, one should know one's worth. She was an educated young lady, clever, well read, whereas I'd forgotten even my Latin — forgotten it altogether, I may say. As far as my physique is concerned" — the doctor looked at himself with a smile — "I've nothing to brag about, either. But the Lord God hadn't put me on this earth as a fool, at that; I wouldn't call black white — even I know a thing or two. I had, for instance, grasped thoroughly that it wasn't love which Alexandra Andreievna — they called her Alexandra Andreievna — had come to feel for me, but a friendly inclination, so to say, an esteem, or something of that sort. Even though she herself was mistaken in that respect — but then, judge for yourself what her situation was. However," added the doctor, who had uttered all these impetuous speeches without pausing for breath and with evident embarrassment, "I think I've strayed a little too far in my explanations. That way you won't understand anything. But now, if you'll permit me, I'll tell you everything in order."

He finished his glass of tea and began speaking in a calmer voice:

"Very well, then; very well, sir. My patient was getting worse — ever worse. You aren't a medico, my dear sir; you cannot understand what goes on in the soul of one of our fraternity, especially at first, when one begins to surmise that it is the ailment which is getting the upper hand over him. Wherever does one's self-confidence go to, then? You suddenly become so timid that you can't even put it in words. It seems to you that you've simply forgotten not only everything you ever knew, but that the patient, now, has no confidence in you, and that by this time all the others as well are beginning to notice that you've lost your head — and they tell you the symptoms unwillingly, they look at you from under their brows, they whisper; eh, but things are in a bad way! For there is a remedy against this ailment, you keep thinking — all you have to do is find it. There, isn't this it, by chance? You try it out — no, that's not it! You don't give the medicine time to work as it should — you clutch now at this straw, now at that. You'd pick up your pharmaceutical handbook — surely, you think, the remedy is here; it's bound to be here! Upon my word, now and then you'd open the book at random: Maybe fate will decide, you think to yourself. Yet in the meanwhile there's a human being dying — and yet another doctor might save him. 'It will be necessary to have a consultation,' you say. 'I do not take any responsibility upon myself.' And what a fool you look on such occasions!

"Well, in time, you get hardened — it wasn't your fault: you acted according to the rules. But here's something else that's still more agonizing: you see a blind confidence in you, yet you yourself feel that you're unable to help. There, it was precisely such confidence which Alexandra Andreievna's whole family had acquired — they even forgot to think that one of the daughters was in danger. I, too, assured them for my part that, now, it really was nothing — yet at the same time my heart was in my boots.

"To crown the misfortune, the condition of the roads became such that the coachman had to take all of a day to get the medicine. But I didn't set foot out of the sickroom, couldn't tear myself away, kept on telling her all sorts of funny little stories, don't you know, and playing cards with her. I sat there whole nights through. The little old woman thanked me with tears, but I was saying to myself all the time: 'I don't deserve your gratitude.'

"I confess to you frankly — there's no use in concealing anything now — I'd fallen in love with my patient. And Alexandra Andreievna had become attached to me: there were times when she wouldn't let anybody into her room but me. She would start talking with me, questioning me as to where I had studied, how I was getting along, who my kin were, whom I called upon socially. And I felt it wasn't right for her to talk, yet to forbid her — forbid her, in such a positive manner, you know — was something I couldn't do.

"There were times when I'd clutch my head: 'What are you up to, you cutthroat?' Or else she'd take my hand and hold it, looking at me for a long while — then she'd turn away, sigh, and say: 'What a kind man you are!' Her hands were so hot; her eyes huge, languishing. 'Yes,' she would say, 'you're a kind, a fine man; you aren't at all like our neighbors. No, you aren't like that. How is it I hadn't known you up to now!' — 'Alexandra Andreievna,' I'd say, 'do calm down. Believe me, I sympathize; I don't know how I have merited this — but do calm down; calm down, for God's sake; everything will come out right, you will be well.' Yet at the same time, I must tell you," added the doctor, bending forward and raising his eyebrows, "that the reason they had so little to do with their neighbors was because the lesser ones didn't come up to them, whereas pride forbade them to mingle with those who were rich. It was an extraordinarily cultured family, I tell you, and therefore I felt flattered, you know. She would take the medicine only from my hands: she'd raise herself a little with my help, the poor thing, take the medicine, and give me a look — and my heart would simply sink. For at the same time she was getting worse, ever worse. 'She's going to die,' I reflected, 'she's bound to die.' Would you believe it: I felt like lying down in a coffin myself — but there were her mother, her sisters observing me, looking into my eyes — and their confidence was passing. 'Well, how is she?' — 'It's nothing, ma'am, nothing!' — and yet that 'nothing' was of such a nature that it was enough to drive you out of your mind.

"Well, sir, one night I was sitting there, again all by myself, near the sick woman. The maid was sitting right there too, and snoring her fool head off. Well, there was no use calling the wretched wench to account — she, too, had become all tuckered out. As for Alexandra Andreievna, she had felt quite bad all evening; her high temperature had exhausted her. She kept on tossing all the time, right up to midnight; at last she seemed to have fallen asleep — at least she didn't as much as stir as she lay there. There was a holy lamp burning before the images. I was sitting there, you know, my eyes fixed on the floor; I, too, was dozing. All of a sudden, just as though someone had nudged me in the ribs, I turned around. Oh Lord, my God! Alexandra Andreievna was staring at me with all her might — her lips were open, her cheeks simply flaming.

"'What is the matter with you?' — 'Doctor, I'm going to die, am I not?' — 'God forbid!' — 'No, Doctor, no, please don't tell me I'm going to live — don't! If you but knew — listen, for God's sake: don't conceal my condition from me!' — and at the same time she's breathing ever so fast. 'If I knew with certainty that I must die ... I'd tell you everything, then — everything!' — 'Alexandra Andreievna, do be reasonable!' — 'Look — why, I wasn't sleeping at all; I've been watching you a long while. For God's sake ... I have faith in you, you're a kindhearted man, you're a man of honesty: I appeal to you, in the name of everything that is most sacred in this world — tell me the truth! If you but knew of what importance this is to me.... Tell me, Doctor, for God's sake: am I in danger?' — 'What am I to tell you, Alexandra Andreievna? Do be reasonable!' — 'For God's sake — I implore you!' — 'I can't conceal it from you, Alexandra Andreievna — you are, it's true, in danger, but God is merciful.' — 'I'm going to die, I'm going to die —' and it seemed as if she were actually rejoicing, so blithe had her face become: I was frightened. 'Oh, don't be afraid, don't be afraid; death does not terrify me in the least.' She suddenly raised herself and leaned on her elbow. 'Now ... well, now I can tell you that I am grateful to you with all my soul, that you're a kind, a fine man, that I love you —'

"I was staring at her as if I'd gone daft; I felt eerie, you know. 'Do you hear me? I love you....' — 'Alexandra Andreievna, how have I merited this!' — 'No, no, you don't understand me —' and then, speaking to me as to an intimate: 'You don't understand me.' And suddenly she held out her arms, seized my head, and kissed me. Would you believe it, I all but cried out; I threw myself on my knees and buried my head in the pillows. She was silent; her fingers, plunged in my hair, were trembling; I heard her weeping.

"I began to comfort her, to reassure her — really, now, I don't know just what it was I told her. 'Wake up the wench, Alexandra Andreievna,' I told her. 'I thank you ... believe me, I do ... calm yourself.' — 'Oh, that will do, now — that will do,' she kept repeating. 'God be with them all; well, they'll wake up, and they'll come — what does it matter? For I'm going to die, after all. Yes, and why are you losing heart — what are you afraid of? Lift up your head. Or, perhaps, you do not love me; I have deceived myself ... in that case, excuse me.' — 'Alexandra Andreievna, whatever are you saying? I love you, Alexandra Andreievna.' She looked straight into my eyes and opened her arms: 'Take me around, then —'

"I'll be frank with you: I can't understand how I did not lose my mind that night. I felt that my patient was killing herself; I saw that she wasn't quite in her senses; I also grasped that, if she hadn't considered herself at death's door, she would never have thought of me; for, surely, no matter what they say, it's dreadful to be dying at twenty-five, without having loved anyone: for that was what was torturing her, that was why she had, in despair, clutched even at me — do you understand now? But still she wouldn't release me from her arms.

"'Spare me, Alexandra Andreievna — and spare yourself, too,' I told her. 'What for?' she said. 'What's the sense in pity? For, after all, I am bound to die —' She kept repeating that, without cease. 'There, if I knew I'd live on, and again be one of those respectable young ladies, I'd be ashamed ... ashamed, true enough ... but the way things are, what does it matter?' — 'But whoever told you that you would die?' — 'Oh, no, that'll do — you won't deceive me, you don't know how to lie — just look at yourself!' — 'You're going to live, Alexandra Andreievna; I'm going to make you well; we'll ask your mother's blessing ... we'll be joined in wedlock, we'll be happy —' — 'No, no, I have your word — I must die — you promised me ... you told me.' I felt bitter — bitter on many accounts. Why, just judge for yourself — here's the sort of odd things which befall you sometimes: they would seem to be nothing, and yet they hurt. It came into her head to ask me what my name was — not my family name, that is, but my given name. And it would have to be such a miserable one — it so happens that they call me Triphon. Yes sir, yes sir, they call me Triphon — Triphon Ivanovich. In my house, now, they all addressed me as Doctor. There was no help for it: 'It's Triphon, ma'am,' I told her. She narrowed her eyes, shook her head, and whispered something in French — oh, but it was something not at all complimentary — and then started in laughing, and that laugh, too, wasn't anything good.

"Well, that's how I passed almost the whole night with her. Toward morning I went out, just as though I were in a daze from charcoal fumes; when I came into her room again it was in the daytime, when tea was already over. My God, my God! You couldn't recognize her — a corpse laid out in a coffin couldn't have looked worse. I swear to you upon my honor, I can't understand now — I absolutely can't — how I stood up under that torture.

"For three days more, and three nights, did my patient linger on ... and what nights they were! The things she said to me! And on the last night, now — just imagine this to yourself — I was sitting near her, and by that time there was just one thing I was begging God for: 'Take her now, as quickly as possible — and me with her!' Suddenly her old mother dashed into the room. For I'd already told her the evening before that, now, there was but little hope, and it mightn't be amiss to send for the priest. Soon as the sick woman saw her mother, she said: 'Well, now, it's a good thing you've come ... look at us: we love each other, we have exchanged vows.' — 'What's she saying, Doctor — what's she saying?' I was stunned. 'She's in delirium, ma'am,' said I. 'Running a high temperature.' But the sick woman spoke up: 'That'll do, that'll do — you were telling me something altogether different just now, and accepted a betrothal ring from me. Why are you pretending? My mother is a kindhearted woman; she'll forgive us, she'll understand. As for me, I'm dying — there's no reason for me to lie; give me your hand —' I jumped up and dashed out of the room. The little old woman surmised everything, naturally.

"However, I'm not going to depress you with this any longer — and besides, I confess, I myself find it painful to recall all this. My patient died the very next day. May the kingdom of Heaven be hers!" The doctor added this in a patter and with a sigh. "Before her death she asked all her folks to go out of the room and leave me alone with her. 'Forgive me,' said she, 'perhaps I am at fault before you — it's due to my illness. But believe me ... I have never loved anyone more than you. Don't forget me — take care of my ring —'"

The doctor turned away; I took his hand.

"Eh," said he, "let's talk of something else — or would you like to have a go at preference, for small stakes? Those of our fraternity oughtn't, don't you know, to yield to such exalted sentimentalizings. Those of our fraternity ought to have but one thing in mind: to keep the little ones from squalling and the wife from scolding. For since then I've managed to enter into what they call lawful matrimony. How else ... I took a merchant's daughter: with a dowry of seven thousand. They call her Akulina: just the very thing for a Triphon. A female, I must tell you, with a vile temper — she sleeps all day, though, and that's a blessing.... Well, what about preference?"

We sat down to preference for kopeck stakes. Triphon Ivanych won two rubles and a half from me — and left late, quite satisfied with his victory.

JOHN UPDIKE

A & P

In walks these three girls in nothing but bathing suits. I'm in the third checkout slot, with my back to the door, so I don't see them until they're over by the bread. The one that caught my eye first was the one in the plaid green two-piece. She was a chunky kid, with a good tan and a sweet broad soft-looking can with those two crescents of white just under it, where the sun never seems to hit, at the top of the backs of her legs. I stood there with my hand on a box of HiHo crackers trying to remember if I rang it up or not. I ring it up again and the customer starts giving me hell. She's one of these cash-register-watchers, a witch about fifty with rouge on her cheekbones and no eyebrows, and I know it made her day to trip me up. She'd been watching cash registers for fifty years and probably never seen a mistake before.

By the time I got her feathers smoothed and her goodies into a bag — she gives me a little snort in passing, if she'd been born at the right time they would have burned her over in Salem — by the time I get her on her way the girls had circled around the bread and were coming back, without a pushcart, back my way along the counters, in the aisle between the checkouts and the Special bins. They didn't even have shoes on. There was this chunky one, with the two-piece — it was bright green and the seams on the bra were still sharp and her belly was still pretty pale so I guessed she just got it (the suit) — there was this one, with one of those chubby berry-faces, the lips all bunched together under her nose, this one, and a tall one, with black hair that hadn't quite frizzed right, and one of these sunburns right across under the eyes, and a chin that was too long — you know, the kind of girl other girls think is very "striking" and "attractive" but never quite makes it, as they very well know, which is why they like her so much — and then the third one, that wasn't quite so tall. She was the queen. She kind of led them, the other two peeking around and making their shoulders round. She didn't look around, not this queen, she just walked straight on slowly, on these long white prima-donna legs. She came down a little hard on her heels, as if she didn't walk in her bare feet that much, putting down her heels and then letting the weight move along to her toes as if she was testing the floor with every step, putting a little deliberate extra action into it. You never know for sure how girls' minds work (do you really think it's a mind in there or just a little buzz like a bee in a glass jar?) but you got the idea she had talked the other two into coming in here with her, and now she was showing them how to do it, walk slow and hold yourself straight.

She had on a kind of dirty-pink — beige maybe, I don't know — bathing suit with a little nubble all over it and, what got me, the straps were down. They were off her shoulders looped loose around the cool tops of her arms, and I guess as a result the suit had slipped a little on her, so all around the top of the cloth there was this shining rim. If it hadn't been there you wouldn't have known there could have been anything whiter than those shoulders. With the straps pushed off, there was nothing between the top of the suit and the top of her head except just *her*, this clean bare plane of the top of her chest down from the shoulder bones like a dented sheet of metal tilted in the light. I mean, it was more than pretty.

She had sort of oaky hair that the sun and salt had bleached, done up in a bun that was unravelling, and a kind of prim face. Walking into the A & P with your straps down, I suppose it's the only kind of face you *can* have. She held her head so high her neck, coming up out of those white shoulders, looked kind of stretched, but I didn't mind. The longer her neck was, the more of her there was.

She must have felt in the corner of her eye me and over my shoulder Stokesie in the second slot watching, but she didn't tip. Not this queen. She kept her eyes moving across the racks, and stopped, and turned so slow it made my stomach rub the inside of my apron, and buzzed to the other two, who kind of huddled against her for relief, and then they all three of them went up the cat-and-dog-food-breakfast-cereal-macaroni-rice-raisins-seasonings-spreads-spaghetti-soft-drinks-crackers-and-cookies aisle. From the third slot I look straight up this aisle to the meat counter, and I watched them all the way. The fat one with the tan sort of fumbled with the cookies, but on second thought she put the package back. The sheep pushing their carts down the aisle — the girls were walking against the usual traffic (not that we have one-way signs or anything) — were pretty hilarious. You could see them, when Queenie's white shoulders dawned on them, kind of jerk, or hop, or hiccup, but their eyes snapped back to their own baskets and on they pushed. I bet you could set off dynamite in an A & P and the people would by and large keep reaching and checking oatmeal off their lists and muttering "Let me see, there was a third thing, began with A, asparagus, no, ah, yes, applesauce!" or whatever it is they do mutter. But there was no doubt, this jiggled them. A few houseslaves in pin curlers even looked around after pushing their carts past to make sure what they had seen was correct.

You know, it's one thing to have a girl in a bathing suit down on the beach, where what with the glare nobody can look at each other much anyway, and another thing in the cool of the A & P, under the fluorescent lights, against all those stacked packages, with her feet paddling along naked over our checkerboard green-and-cream rubber-tile floor.

"Oh Daddy," Stokesie said beside me. "I feel so faint."

"Darling," I said. "Hold me tight." Stokesie's married, with two babies chalked up on his fuselage already, but as far as I can tell that's the only difference. He's twenty-two, and I was nineteen this April.

"Is it done?" he asks, the responsible married man finding his voice. I forgot to say he thinks he's going to be manager some sunny day, maybe in 1990 when it's called the Great Alexandrov and Petrooshki Tea Company or something.

What he meant was, our town is five miles from a beach, with a big summer colony out on the Point, but we're right in the middle of town, and the women generally put on a shirt or shorts or something before they get out of the car into the street. And anyway these are usually women with six children and varicose veins mapping their legs and nobody, including them, could care less. As I say, we're right in the middle town, and if you stand at our front doors you can see two banks and the Congregational church and the newspaper store and three real-estate offices and about twenty-seven old freeloaders tearing up Central Street because the sewer broke again. It's not as if we're on the Cape; we're north of Boston and there's people in this town haven't seen the ocean for twenty years.

The girls had reached the meat counter and were asking McMahon something. He pointed, they pointed, and they shuffled out of sight behind a pyramid of Diet Delight peaches. All that was left for us to see was old McMahon patting his mouth and looking after them sizing up their joints. Poor kids, I began to feel sorry for them, they couldn't help it.

• • •

Now here comes the sad part of the story, at least my family says it's sad, but I don't think it's so sad myself. The store's pretty empty, it being Thursday afternoon, so there was nothing much to do except lean on the register and wait for the girls to show up again. The whole store was like a pinball machine and I didn't know which tunnel they'd come out of. After a while they come around out of the far aisle, around the light bulbs, records at discount of the Caribbean Six or Tony Martin Sings or some such gunk you wonder they waste the wax on, sixpacks of candy bars, and plastic toys done up in cellophane that fall apart when a kid looks at them anyway. Around they come, Queenie still leading the way, and holding a little gray jar in her hand. Slots Three through Seven are unmanned and I could see her wondering between Stokes and me, but Stokesie with his usual luck draws an old party in baggy gray pants who stumbles up with four giant cans of pineapple juice (what do these bums *do* with all that pineapple juice? I've often asked myself) so the girls come to me. Queenie puts down the jar and I take it into my fingers icy cold. Kingfish Fancy Herring Snacks in Pure Sour Cream: 49¢. Now her hands are empty, not a ring or a bracelet, bare as God made them, and I wonder where the money's coming from. Still with that prim look she lifts a folded dollar bill out of the hollow at the center of her nubbled pink top. The jar went heavy in my hand. Really, I thought that was so cute.

Then everybody's luck begins to run out. Lengel comes in from haggling with a truck full of cabbages on the lot and is about to scuttle into that door marked MANAGER behind which he hides all day when the girls touch his eye. Lengel's pretty dreary, teaches Sunday school and the rest, but he doesn't miss that much. He comes over and says, "Girls, this isn't the beach."

Queenie blushes, though maybe it's just a brush of sunburn I was noticing for the first time, now that she was so close. "My mother asked me to pick up a jar of herring snacks." Her voice kind of startled me, the way voices do when you see the people first, coming out so flat and dumb yet kind of tony, too, the way it ticked over "pick up" and "snacks." All of a sudden I slid right down her voice into her living room. Her father and the other men were standing around in ice-cream coats and bow ties and the women were in sandals picking up herring snacks on toothpicks off a big glass plate and they were all holding drinks the color of water with olives and sprigs of mint in them. When my parents have somebody over they get lemonade and if it's a real racy affair Schlitz in tall glasses with "They'll Do It Every Time" cartoons stencilled on.

"That's all right," Lengel said. "But this isn't the beach." His repeating this struck me as funny, as if it had just occurred to him, and he had been thinking all these years the A & P was a great big dune and he was the head lifeguard. He didn't like my smiling — as I say he doesn't miss much — but he concentrates on giving the girls that sad Sunday-school superintendent stare.

Queenie's blush is no sunburn now, and the plump one in plaid, that I liked better from the back — a really sweet can — pipes up. "We weren't doing any shopping. We just came in for the one thing."

"That makes no difference," Lengel tells her, and I could see from the way his eyes went that he hadn't noticed she was wearing a two-piece before. "We want you decently dressed when you come in here."

"We *are* decent," Queenie says suddenly, her lower lip pushing, getting sore now that she remembers her place, a place from which the crowd that runs the A & P must look pretty crummy. Fancy Herring Snacks flashed in her very blue eyes.

"Girls, I don't want to argue with you. After this come in here with your shoulders covered. It's our policy." He turns his back. That's policy for you. Policy is what the kingpins want. What the others want is juvenile delinquency.

All this while, the customers had been showing up with their carts but, you know, sheep, seeing a scene, they had all bunched up on Stokesie, who shook open a paper bag as gently as peeling a peach, not wanting to miss a word. I could feel in the silence everybody getting nervous, most of all Lengel, who asks me, "Sammy, have you rung up their purchase?"

I thought and said "No" but it wasn't about that I was thinking. I go through the punches, 4, 9, GROC, TOT — it's more complicated than you think, and after you do it often enough, it begins to make a little song, that you hear words to, in my case "Hello *(bing)* there, you *(gung)* hap-py *pee*-pul *(splat)*!" — the *splat* being the drawer flying out. I uncrease the bill, tenderly as you may imagine, it just having come from between the two smoothest scoops of vanilla I had ever known were there, and pass a half and a penny into her narrow pink palm, and nestle the herrings in a bag and twist its neck and hand it over, all the time thinking.

The girls, and who'd blame them, are in a hurry to get out, so I say "I quit" to Lengel quick enough for them to hear, hoping they'll stop and watch me, their unsuspected hero. They keep right on going, into the electric eye; the door flies open and they flicker across the lot to their car, Queenie and Plaid and Big Tall Goony-Goony (not that as raw material she was so bad), leaving me with Lengel and a kink in his eyebrow.

"Did you say something, Sammy?"

"I said I quit."

"I thought you did."

"You didn't have to embarrass them."

"It was they who were embarrassing us."

I started to say something that came out "Fiddle-de-doo." It's a saying of my grandmother's, and I know she would have been pleased.

"I don't think you know what you're saying," Lengel said.

"I know you don't, "I said. "But I do." I pull the bow at the back of my apron and start shrugging it off my shoulders. A couple customers that had been heading for my slot begin to knock against each other, like scared pigs in a chute.

Lengel sighs and begins to look very patient and old and gray. He's been a friend of my parents for years. "Sammy, you don't want to do this to your Mom and Dad," he tells me. It's true, I don't. But it seems to me that once you begin a gesture it's fatal not to go through with it. I fold the apron, "Sammy" stitched in red on the pocket, and put it on the counter, and drop the bow tie on top of it. The bow tie is theirs, if you've ever wondered. "You'll feel this for the rest of your life," Lengel says, and I know that's true, too, but remembering how he made that pretty girl blush makes me so scrunchy inside I punch the No Sale tab and the machine whirs "pee-pul" and the drawer splats out. One advantage to this scene taking place in summer, I can follow this up with a clean exit, there's no fumbling around getting your coat and galoshes, I just saunter into the electric eye in my white shirt that my mother ironed the night before, and the door heaves itself open, and outside the sunshine is skating around on the asphalt.

I look around for my girls, but they're gone, of course. There wasn't anybody but some young married screaming with her children about some candy they didn't get by the door of a powder-blue Falcon station wagon. Looking back in the big windows, over the bags of peat moss and aluminum lawn furniture stacked on the pavement, I could see Lengel in my place in the slot, checking the sheep through. His face was dark gray and his back stiff, as if he'd just had an injection of iron, and my stomach kind of fell as I felt how hard the world was going to be to me hereafter.

W. D. VALGARDSON

Red Dust

If Orville had not been so intent on owning Zeke and Lester's lemon-and-white hound, he would have fought harder against his sister-in-law's daughter coming to live with them. As it was, when he heard the news, he started up like his spine had been jabbed with a cattle prod.

"I won't have it!" he exclaimed, his round jaw thrust forward. His broad face glistened like it had been rubbed with lard. Bending over, he leaned one pudgy hand on the table and waved his fork in his wife's face. She hunched over, her lips squeezed shut, her eyes fixed on her piece of pork hock.

"I won't have it, I tell you. We can't hardly get enough to feed ourselves. And where'll we put her? And what about clothes?" His wife didn't answer so he dropped back into his chair. "Let her go somewhere else."

Angrily, he stabbed his pork knuckle. It skittered across the table and fell to the floor. He snatched it up, wiped it off with his fingers and put it back on his plate. Because of the heat, all he wore was a pair of faded bib overalls and a brown panama hat with a collapsed brim. His arms, back and the part of his chest that showed were hairless and sleek. His skin looked as though it had been formed from the red clay outside the door.

"She's got no place else to go," Minnie said. She was so thin that her skin seemed wrapped tightly around her bones. Her face was long and sloping, descending in a straight line until just above her mouth then, suddenly, it spread outward. The effect was that of a wedge of bread dough that has been held upright and dropped on a bench so that the bottom is forced out. "There was just me and Ellie."

"Are you making so much from eggs that you can afford to keep her?"

Minnie nursed 90 or 100 chickens from one year to the next, fending off black snakes and raccoons with a hoe. When her chickens got sick she kept them in a box beside the stove and fed them vitamins from an eye-dropper until they got well or died. If they quit laying eggs, she cut off their heads and threw them into a pot and boiled them until they were tender enough to eat. Their bones she beat with a mallet and used for fertilizer. Every Saturday, except when he was hunting, Orville drove her to the town square so she could sell eggs and produce. In the fall, she made watermelon pickles and, after a hard frost, persimmon jam to sell, and he cut some of his hardwood to offer to people with fireplaces.

"She's my kin. I got an obligation to my only kin."

"How much?" he asked but he was distracted by his own problems and his mind was already elsewhere. He leaned over his plate, forking up white beans and brooding. "That dog," he said, at last, "ain't worth a hundred dollars of nobody's money."

Ever since Orville's best dog, True Blue, had been hit by a car and left to die, he had been frantic to get another. It was not that he didn't have dogs. Half-a-dozen hounds lay in holes they had dug beside the house but not one of them was a leader. True Blue had been the best hunter in the county.

"Her mother," Minnie said slyly, "has probably left some money to take care of her. She had a good job at the grocery store."

Orville's hand hovered over his plate. He picked up the pork hock and began to chew on it, his eyes thoughtful.

"You know city folk," Minnie added. "They all got money."

The next Saturday they got up before dawn. Minnie had no proper crates so she packed the eggs in cardboard boxes she had scavenged from behind Piggly Wiggly. First, she put down a layer of moss she had pulled from the trees, then she set down six rows of eggs and covered them with another layer of moss. When she had four layers completed, she carried the box to the truck and set it on the floor. She filled four boxes.

Their house sat on a slope that had been stripped bare of trees and planted with beans. The house itself was of two colours, grey and green. The walls were weathered until, from a distance, the house looked like it might have been carved from a single block of stone. Orville had painted the west wall and the bottom third of the south wall green, then had stopped, leaving a ragged, unfinished line that sloped downward to the far corner. Just above head height there was a round window somewhat bigger than a porthole. It was made of stained glass. During the day, with the sun against it, the window was as impenetrable as lead but, as it turned dark outside and lights inside were switched on, there could be seen a circle of blue enclosing a single columbine.

A narrow track led from the clay road to the house. On the other side of the track, there was a series of sheds and a barn. The bottom half of the barn was made of stone, the top half of heavy beams and thick planks cut when the area was still dense forest. Halters, bridles and single-plows hung from pegs set in the walls. Equipment was heaped on the floor. At the rear, three stalls were filled with sacks of grain for the chickens.

Bean rows fanned out from the house, making endless green lines on the red earth. Directly before the front wall, there was an enclosure of chicken wire decked out with aluminum foil to keep the blackbirds away. Here, Minnie kept her garden. After packing the eggs, she methodically walked up and down the rows, one eye watching for ripe vegetables and the other for copperheads. The snakes liked to curl under the leaves and their mottled bodies blended dangerously with the earth. She picked a dozen summer squash and cut a waterpail full of okra. When she reached the first watermelon, she leaned her head to one side like a new mother listening to her child's breathing and scraped gently on the striped rind. She collected eight good-sized watermelons and hefted them onto the back of the truck.

For the trip into town, she always dressed up, putting on a high-necked, long-sleeved dress that fitted her like a tube. There was a white ruffle at the neck and wrists. Today, because she was meeting her niece, she took her good hat as well as her bonnet. She had constructed the hat by covering the round lid of a cereal box with a remnant from her grey dress. Since she had only one good hat, she kept three sprays of dried berries, one red, one white and one black. She wore the black to funerals. Because today something new was going to happen, she made her hat gay by pinning on the red berries. Orville wore his overalls and a white shirt.

It was twenty miles into town. All of it except the last mile on a dirt road. Their truck, a Ford so old that it had a high, square cab of fading green, could only go 30 miles an hour. The trip, what with starts and stops at crossroads and having to slow for washouts and single-lane bridges, took over an hour.

During the trip they never spoke. Because of the eggs, Minnie sat with her legs angled against the door. She wondered what the girl would be like. Minnie had only visited her sister once and what she remembered most about the city was neither her sister nor the child but the bright pink indoor plumbing and the miracle of the air-conditioning.

Orville watched the road for hubcaps and bottles, chewed on a cigarette and thought about Sheba, Zeke and Lester's dog. True Blue had been faster, his voice sweeter but with him buried behind the barn, the lemon-and-white bitch was best. Since True Blue's death, Zeke had taken over the Saturday gatherings in front of the hardware store.

There had been no rain during the winter. The little that had fallen had done no more than speckle the dust and, as a result, the countryside through which they travelled was brown and brittle. Only in deep hollows were there patches of green. Even in the strip pits, the water was so low that, in places, the bottom was visible and catfish could be caught by wading into a pool and beating the surface with a stick. The water, instead of being blue, was a brown stain. The mounds of tailings were grey. Sumac crowded the roadsides but instead of a glossy green, the leaves were wilted and dull like the tongues of old shoes.

As they neared the town, they could see the top of the courthouse rising above the sycamore trees. The yellowed sandstone loomed like the turret of a castle. At the utmost peak of the red-tile roof, there stood a weather vane in the shape of blind justice. Her arms held outright, supporting the scales, told the direction of the wind. At one time, no-one was certain just when, a bolt of lightning had severed her head and, either for lack of the necessary craftsmanship or because of the height, it had never been replaced.

When they arrived, the square was still empty. The courthouse sat at the centre, surrounded by a thin strip of lawn and a scattering of redbud trees. Because the four streets surrounding the courthouse were so wide, there was one-way traffic allowed close to the inner curb, then there was diagonal parking, two-way traffic and, finally, diagonal parking against the outer curb. The outer curb was shunned because it was controlled by parking meters and was regarded as the property of townspeople and businessmen. The farmers used the free parking spaces in the middle of the streets, parking their vehicles with the backs facing the outer sidewalk so that anyone passing could see what goods were for sale.

Orville slipped the truck into its accustomed spot close to the southeast corner. They had chosen this place because, while it meant their getting the late-morning sun, it also meant that, just after one o'clock, they were in the shadow of the courthouse. Directly across the street there was a long red-brick building divided into stores. Sections of clay drain-pipe cemented together supported a metal canopy that sheltered the sidewalk.

Minnie dragged a card table off the truck, spread a white plastic table-cloth over it, then set out a watermelon and a long knife. As the day grew hotter, she would sell slices for ten cents each. Finally, she unfolded a wooden chair, placed a pillow on it and seated herself.

Orville strolled to the sidewalk and sat in one of the rusting chairs lined up against the storefront. More vehicles appeared. Within three quarters of an hour, the square was jammed with cars and trucks. Every space was taken except for Zeke and Lester's. Although some people had to park in the metered area, no-one attempted to take the space in the middle of the block.

Zeke and Lester turned up at ten, pulling across the traffic and blocking it as Zeke manoeuvred their truck into its slot. Immediately, Zeke swaggered over to join the group on the sidewalk. He was over six feet tall with a thick, heavy body and a belly that pulled his purple shirt taut and sagged over his belt, forcing the buckle down between his thighs. Although he was 40 or more, he still fancied himself as a lady's man. His head was narrow and his brown hair, parted at the right and pulled sideways, was greased until it sat stiffly in place. His nose was long and hooked and the flesh under his eyes was creased with dark lines. Lester was standing directly behind him, his mouth drawn up in a loose grin. Lester smiled all the time but his face was as still as a trap.

The brothers had a small coal seam on their farm and, now and again, when they needed cash, they took a pickaxe and chopped out a load. Because they had no woman to mind their truck, once business picked up, they had to take turns, one sitting on the sidewalk, the other staying with the coal.

Although they owned a quarter-section, instead of farming they let their land grow over with scrub brush and spent their time hunting and fishing. They came to town every Saturday, spending the day on the square and the night in the bars that were hidden away among the warehouses and small factories in the south end of town. Because they were aggressive and quick to take offence, most people avoided them. Although they had never been convicted of anything serious enough to be sent to prison, their reputation was such that anyone who ran afoul of them watched his silos and outbuildings with care and kept the number of the fire department handy.

"You decided to give me $50 for the bitch?" Zeke asked. He had raised his voice so everyone could hear him but his pale eyes watched Orville's face. "Cash on the line."

Orville had been describing, for the group's benefit, the hunt they had been planning. Once fall was under way, they gathered at least once for a coon supper. It and the mountain-oyster dinner at the VFW were the social events of the year.

"I guess I'd give you $50," he admitted. He had not had $50 all at once for three years but he knew Minnie had burying money and he expected that, if he had to, he could get her to part with some of it.

Zeke held out his large hand with its black nails and coating of coal dust. Orville heaved himself up, found himself less than an inch from Zeke's stomach and, to give himself room, shifted sideways. As they shook hands, Zeke pressed close, forcing Orville to back away. When he released Orville's hand, Zeke had the empty chair beside him. He sat down.

Zeke put his hands behind his head and smiled at Orville, who was standing, his face shocked at losing his place.

"Well, Orville, now that you've purchased the hind quarters, what are you offering Lester for the front?"

There was smothered laughter. Orville's normally red skin darkened and his broad face stiffened like congealing wax.

"You made a deal," he said.

Zeke gave a grave, exaggerated nod. "Sold my interest but I can't sell what isn't mine. That's against the law. If the back half's worth $50, what do you figure's a fair price for the front?"

"You made a deal," Orville repeated doggedly. Normally, he was careful, waiting for an advantage before pressing anyone, but his desire for the dog and his humiliation made him reckless. "You said a hundred last week. There's no dog worth it but I'll give you $50 and trade for the rest."

Zeke turned his head first to one side, then the other, his cheeks pulled back in anticipation of laughing and Orville realized he was being made to look like a fool. Zeke winked at the nearest man and said, "Now, what would you trade me that's worth $50? A hundred chickens?"

Orville jerked his eyes around to the square. He knew that behind his back they called Minnie the Chicken Woman. He wouldn't have minded that so much but that made him the husband of the Chicken Woman.

"I gotta go take care of the truck," he said.

They couldn't take the truck to the train station for fear of losing their place. They had used the same space for years, but it was still first come, first served. Everyone looked out for himself. Orville went over to where Minnie was sitting, staring at the passersby as if she was going to hypnotize them into buying. She had traded a slice of watermelon for an apple and was surreptitiously peeling it with a pocketknife and popping the pieces into her mouth. Because her teeth hurt her, she had slipped them into the pocket of her apron and was mashing the apple between her gums.

"Git," he said, "and git back."

He had meant to say more about being saddled with her relatives, but he was so disheartened that the words were too much effort. She stood to take off her apron and he sat down, leaning his chin on his breastbone and staring resentfully at the ground. Their poverty was not, he felt, their fault. There had been one bad year after another, forcing him to cut his hardwood trees and sell off his bottom land bit by bit. His father had sold the coal and the company that had bought the rights had ripped the earth apart, leaving so little behind that he was hard pressed to sort out enough coal from the rock to satisfy their own needs. At night, following the hounds, listening to True Blue's clear voice ringing through the frosty air like a bell, he owed nothing to anybody. It was as though his skin had been hollow and was suddenly filled up.

Minnie fussed around the table, seeing that everything was set out properly. Her morning's profit she stuffed into her drawstring purse. She disliked leaving Orville alone with her goods but there was no use trying to get him to meet the train. She was just glad he was co-operative. She had expected him to be in a rage for days. When his dog had been killed, he had wandered around the farm, stiff-legged, striking out at random, at walls, at her, at equipment. From inside the house, she had watched him kick at a bean row until the heat and his own emotion had caused him to buckle at the knees and drop helplessly into the dirt.

If she had had someplace to go, she would have left then, but her sister was dying and she had no close friends. The people on the square were casual acquaintances. Sundays, she and Orville drove to Service and Wednesdays, to Bible Study, but after all these years they were still strangers. At church, they sat in the rear pew. At Bible Study, they sat at the farthest edge of the circle and Orville bolted from his seat the moment the final prayer was done.

The heat had hardened until the glare from the pavement burned her thin ankles. The buildings reflected heat like foil set before a fire. She walked slowly, stopping to rest at the end of each block, for the heat blurred the edge of her vision and made her head feel weightless.

As she walked, because she was afraid of being run down, she kept well away from the road and hesitated at curbs. When she crossed the street, she took two deep breaths, held her chin high, lifted her dress with both hands, and kicked her feet out flatly from the knees.

The station was six blocks from the square in a rundown section of town where she knew everybody was poor because they never threw anything away. Some of them had so many broken plastic children's horses in their yards that their fences might have been corrals. Because she didn't want anyone driving by their place to know that they were poor, Minnie never kept anything that was broken and never let anything lie about their yard. Once she had no use for an object, she took it out to the persimmon grove and left it there. Any items that would fit, she stuffed into one of the car bodies so that, if she ever needed them, she could get them again.

Before she climbed the three stairs to the platform, she rested, her thin fist pressed to her chest. Her heart, strained by the heat, fluttered like a butterfly with an injured wing. She had never been strong but she had persevered, surviving through a tornado, the croup, the loss of two children, a constant night paralysis of her leg, which threatened to creep into her heart while she slept, and marriage. She had persevered, she reminded herself, because she had let nothing distract her from her purpose.

She had only been to the railway station three times before. Each time had been to pick up a shipment of chicks. Now, she kept a rooster with one eye. When she needed more layers, she let him in among the hens. The eggs were hatched in the oven of an old stove.

After 50 years of hardscrabble living, she feared nothing except dying and that she feared because her preparations were incomplete. Her burying money, $223, was wrapped in tight rolls, knotted with thread and stuffed into a vertical rod in the brass bed in which she and Orville slept.

Once she had $457, she was going to walk into town while Orville was away hunting, pick out a coffin with brass handles, leave her good dress and her good shoes to be stored in it, pay for her lot and a dozen lilies. When that was done, she intended to let herself succumb to the first thing that came along.

The cinders were sharp as thorns through her shoes. She mounted the stairs. The platform was deserted. Passengers seldom came anymore. Yellow grass sprouted from between the heavy beams. Made bold by not seeing anyone else about, she went to a bench that sat in the shade of the eaves and perched on the edge of it. Surreptitiously, she took a small handkerchief from her sleeve and dabbed at her face and neck.

"Y'all waiting for someone, honey?"

A fat woman in a short red dress, which bulged around the waist like she was wearing an inner tube beneath it, had appeared from inside the station. In her hand was a yellow ticket. Minnie shied nervously.

"My sister's girl."

"Hot time to visit." The fat woman took off her red hat and fanned her face vigorously. "Better to come in the fall." Her face was as pink as the underbelly of a scrubbed pig.

"She's come to stay," Minnie explained. She so seldom had news, that, when she did, she felt a desperate need to tell it. One of the women at the Bible Study had said news that couldn't be told was not news. It was like a cake not meant for eating. Minnie thought it was the truest thing she had ever heard. "Her mother died of cancer."

"Glory be," the fat woman said, plopping herself down so that her short legs shot straight out. "The tribulations that are put upon us."

Minnie nodded gravely. "It took six months. She had been a heavy woman but at the end they said she was just 67 pounds. No more than a child."

"We never know when good'll turn bad," she intoned. "We are assaulted from without."

They both paused and stared down the track as though to find a confirmation of this profound truth, but the steel rails were two lines of white fire leading to an empty horizon.

"I'm an egg lady," Minnie said. The other woman stared. "I sell eggs."

The fat woman sighed. "Everybody sells something these days. What you sell depends on what you got. I used to be on the stage." In spite of the heat, she twisted her shoulders, made her eyes big and struck a flirtatious pose. "Temporarily, I'm selling magazines." She turned her head and nodded at a brown valise. She panted with the heat and fanned herself more vigorously. "The way things are, it's a wonder they let you sell eggs."

Minnie had never thought anybody let her sell eggs. The work was so hard, the rewards so small that she never considered that anyone else had any say in the matter. Across the track on a long, low tin building, someone had painted *The meek shall inherit the earth.* The letters sloped every which way so that the message seemed to have been painted by a child or an idiot.

The fat woman rolled from cheek to cheek to unstick herself from the bench. Her skirt climbed her thigh, revealing nylons held up by tattered white garters. "At least it's a girl and she can help you around the house. Boys are nothing but trouble. There's no controlling them. What age is she?

"Fourteen," Minnie answered. "She'll have to earn her keep all right. We don't have enough to give and not get."

"This is a coincidence!" the woman cried. "I knew a case just like it except it was the daughter who died of cancer. She was 35."

"You waiting on someone?"

The woman waved her ticket. "Tulsa's my next stop. I was selling magazines just fine but the sheriff, he said I had to stop. Sheriffs," she confided, "are not Christian. I offered him a two years' free subscription to *The Lord's Shepherd* but he said he couldn't read." As she mentioned the title, she eyed Minnie hopefully.

Just then the train came into view. There was only one passenger who got off. It was a young girl with a long, tapered face which, because she was young, was pretty. Her dark hair was cut so that it brushed her shoulders. Although Minnie had expected someone not so grown, the girl had full breasts and hips and long legs. She was wearing a white dress belted at the waist and a white straw hat that was too old for her and looked like her mother's.

"Why!" the fat woman exclaimed, "she's as pretty as a picture."

The girl, unsure of who was her aunt, stood awkwardly, holding onto an ivory suitcase with both hands.

"Lorraine," Minnie said. "I'm your mother's sister."

Orville was disappointed when he saw his wife's niece. He had hoped she would be bigger and able to help with the heavy chores. Standing in the crowd, she looked lost and awkward. He stood still for his wife to introduce them, then hurried back across the street. He was still smarting from Zeke's joke but he hated to be away from the sidewalk for fear he might miss something.

The square had gradually filled. Cars crept forward inches at a time, their drivers leaning out to visit friends. There were knots of buyers around the displays. Occasionally, men would stop to speak to Lester and he would shovel coal into a gunnysack for them or write down an order. Women who passed, however, seemed to swerve instinctively like water around a hidden obstruction. If there had been any wind, a spectator would have said they were afraid of getting coal-dust on their clothes.

At six, all Minnie's goods were sold. The three of them crowded into the cab. As Orville eased past Lester and Zeke, he said, "I'd like to make you a trade."

To his surprise, Zeke nodded and replied, "We can talk about it."

On Sunday they went to church and on Wednesday to Bible Study. Thursday morning while they were weeding the bean rows below the house, the mailman stopped and sounded his horn. Orville dropped his hoe and went down to the box. They seldom got anything in the mail except tax and mortgage notices, so they were apprehensive about letters. The return address was Lovel, Brown and Associates, Kansas City. He tore the end off the envelope and stood, studying the letter until he understood every word of it.

"It's for you," he said resentfully, thrusting the letter at Minnie. "There ain't going to be any money. The lawyer gets to execute the will and that means he took it for himself."

Zeke and Lester arrived an hour later. They strolled along the road, kicking up pink dust with every step. They did not bother to open the gate but climbed over it, then wandered up the track.

Zeke had on an old grey hat with a crow's tail-feather set slantways in the brim. His shirt was the colour of a barely ripe prune plum and was too small in the arms. It had four white pearl buttons on each cuff. Lester trailed behind, his heavy lips turned up in a grin. He was wearing the same khaki shirt and pants that he had on on Saturday. His pants pockets extended to his knees.

Instead of walking all the way up to where Orville was working, they stopped and sat on a tuft of grass that grew along the ruts from the car tires and waited for Orville to work his way down to them. While they waited, they watched with the critical interest of supervisors.

"I see you got some help," Zeke said as Orville reached him.

Lorraine was in the row next to Minnie, awkwardly trying to chop weeds, but the handle of the hoe kept getting in her way. She had on shorts and a white blouse and her white straw hat. Pink dust had settled on the brim. Along the circumference of the crown, the dust was so thick it made a red band. Her blouse was stained with sweat under the arms and down the back and dust had gathered in all the creases.

Lester squatted at the edge of the road and watched Lorraine. His eyes were large but the lids sagged, covering half the iris. It made him look half asleep but Orville wasn't fooled. Lester's eyes were green and clear as glass and always watching with a patient slyness that made Orville think of a coyote.

"If you don't get some rain," Zeke said, poking his finger in the dust, "you ain't going to get many beans."

Orville leaned on his hoe. Heat devils rose over the field.

"Nobody's got a hundred dollars for a dog," he said, watching Zeke out of the corner of his eye.

"Strod's gonna. He's got himself a job at the new factory in town. Regular pay. He'll have it in a week."

"Strod!" Orville felt his throat constrict. He had heard that the factory on the edge of town was hiring but he hadn't believed that anybody would go. "What's he want a dog for? He's working for somebody else, he won't have time to hunt."

Zeke and Lester said nothing. They sat and watched him as if expecting to see him rise from the ground or turn his hoe into a snake.

"He don't know nothin' about dogs," Orville complained. "He let his best one die of worms."

After the brothers had gone, Orville went inside to look for Minnie's jar. He pulled the floorboard loose and reached the change jar out. He had known for a long time where she kept that. Unscrewing the lid, he dumped the contents on the bed. There were sixteen quarters, five dimes, five nickels and twenty-five pennies.

Angrily, he paced about the room testing boards and poking into corners. He took out his penkife and tried to pry up floorboards. Some came loose but there was nothing under them but darkness and clay. He was afraid to poke around too much because of the copperheads he had seen going in and out under the house in search of rats. When he finished with the floor, he started on the walls. A check behind the wooden cross and the calendar beside it that had the picture of a different breed of pig every month turned up nothing.

Snatching up the broom, he went to the porch and called his wife. As he waited, he shifted his grip so that he held the broom just above the straw. Minnie walked slowly toward him and stopped just out of reach. Except for her hands and feet, her body was covered in a grey dress. On her head she wore a grey bonnet, the brim of which curved down the sides of her face and projected forward for six inches.

"You heard what he said?" Orville asked.

Minnie cradled one arm in the other. Her eyes stared out from the tunnel created by her bonnet. Orville was standing slightly above her on the porch. Once, when they'd had a good year, Orville had started to build a porch so they could have a swing to sit in during the long summer evenings, but only the floor had got built and six uprights put in place. The uprights were eight-foot lengths of wood turned on a lathe so that they resembled giant spindles. They were nailed from the bottom and weren't attached to each other or the roof. They stood like the columns of some ancient ruin, the yellow sky huge behind them. They gave the house an unfinished look. She couldn't remember the date of the porch because that year, bright green, the vines and trees entangled with new growth, the flowers, wild bachelor buttons, iris, star flowers, carpeting even the stony places, had become a fixed time before and after which events were reckoned.

"Come here," he ordered.

She shuffled forward reluctantly. He cupped his hand at her and she shuffled forward again, the red dust rising in small puffs like smoke. Orville's hand jerked and the broom snapped out. Struck, she hopped sideways as though beginning a fast dance, but having hopped once she stopped and clutched her arm. Orville's face was wiped clean of expression. It was not the first time he had beaten her but always before it had been a flurry of blows struck in a fit of rage. At those times, she ran and hid in the persimmon thicket until his anger passed. His present calmness frightened her.

"I gotta have that money." Only his lips moved. His eyes were unblinking.

"I've got my faith to sustain me," she replied.

The broom handle leapt out again, striking the other arm. Her mouth dropped open so suddenly that a spring might have been released, but she made no sound. She glanced over her shoulder, thinking about how far it was to the thicket.

"It won't do you no good," he said quietly. "I never come after you before. I'll come after you this time."

She covered her bruises with her hands. Quietly, intensely, she said, "I won't have them sneak me out of town as though I was of no account. I've never had nothing done proper. I'm going to be buried like somebody, with a real service and a casket with brass handles and boughten flowers."

The broom sprang out again, catching her on the point of her hip. She gasped with pain. "I can leave." Her face had receded farther into the tunnel created by her bonnet as though her head, like an angry, frightened cat, had found a hole and was crowding back into the smallest possible space.

For the first time, Minnie began to be afraid. Anger never lasted long and the pain could be borne if it was sure to end, but constant, unrelenting pain that would go on and on was not something she had considered.

"I can hold out for a week," she muttered.

He regarded her sternly. "Strod'll buy her and he'll just want a bigger price to sell her to me, that's all. Instead of a hundred, it'll be $150, maybe two. It'll just take that much longer for you to make it up."

When she did not reply, he shifted his attack.

"That girl of yours, she's afflicted."

"There's nothing wrong with her," Minnie answered defensively.

"Not right out, maybe, but it's inside. That day she came, you told me you asked her to make change and she couldn't do it right. She's broke a dish. She can't work a hoe."

"It's all new."

He shook his head slowly. "I've bin watching. Her hands and feet ain't right. They don't work together. She's like them Edgells. They all got something wrong with them. It's like a car with its timing out." He jabbed at the dirt with the broom handle, making a cluster of concave indentations.

"She does what I tell her and she doesn't complain."

"There ain't going to be any money. She can't work proper. Who's going to pay for her?"

While Orville had talked, Minnie had been thinking about Strod's buying the dog and raising the price. The logic of what Orville had said weighed upon her, making her weak like when she got too much sun.

"I'll dish out supper," she said.

As she passed, he spoke to her back, his voice low and determined. "I don't count for nothing without that dog."

They sat facing each other. Lorraine sat between them. Every time she closed her fingers over her fork, she flinched. Blisters had formed on the soft inside flesh of her fingers. Her cheeks were bright pink from the heat and her blouse was stained as red as if it had been tie-dyed. She had tried to brush the dust off and had only succeeded in working it into the cloth.

They ate in rigid silence. Just as they were finishing, there was a sharp knock at the door. Orville grunted, "Come in," and a white hound with pale yellow and black patches scrambled eagerly into the kitchen, her nails scraping on the wooden floor as she strained at her lead.

Zeke followed, clutching at the rope. Lester was right on his heels. For a moment, they seemed to fill the kitchen until there was hardly room to breathe.

Minnie and Lorraine cleared the table. The brothers sat down and the dog flopped on the floor.

"We brought Sheba. Better you have her than Strod. If you can pay for her."

Orville shifted uncomfortably in his chair. "I ain't got it but I'm getting it." He leaned over and while caressing the dog's head, checked its ears and eyes with his fingers.

"She's got a sweet voice," Zeke said.

"I heard her."

The smell of bourbon drifted from Zeke. He and Lester ran a still deep in the strip pits and drank most of what they produced.

Outside, the light was fading. The cicadas began their dry, endless song. Their sound was high, loud, harsh, a thousand thin wires strained to breaking, then beaten.

"We got a good life," Zeke said with satisfaction. "We get up when we want. We eat when we want. We shoot something nearly every day."

"I'll get your money directly," Orville said.

Lorraine was pressing clothes. Her shorts were made from tight, cut-off jeans. She wore no shoes and the red dust coated her feet like slippers.

Minnie was washing dishes with stiff deliberation, her jaw clenched tight as a fist. She washed the dishes and stacked them without looking down. She kept her back to the men.

"Minnie'll give me what you want." Orville mopped his face with a red handkerchief the size of a dishtowel. Sweat beaded along his hairline and ran down his face.

"We're not missing much," Zeke said. He sat with his black workboots planted on either side of the chair, his stomach resting like a soft melon on his legs.

"There's not much we can't provide for ourselves. Used to be we'd go to town Friday night and that'd do us for a week. Sometimes we paid five dollars," he stopped to grin at Orville, "and sometimes we didn't. Now, we can't go back for quite some Fridays."

"I heard about the trouble," Orville replied. "They'll forget."

"A man's a man," Zeke said. "There's things he needs."

Lester sprawled on his chair, his feet straight out in front of him. He fished in his knee pocket for a glass flask, unscrewed the top and took a drink.

"We don't allow no liquor here," Minnie said. She had been watching their reflection in the window. They never paid her any attention. "We don't allow no liquor here," she repeated but her voice trailed away until she was the only one who heard the last word.

"This is the last chance you got," Zeke said. He studied the top of the dog's head. "You know what you're losing if you don't take it."

"I'll take it." Orville's voice was full of anger.

"Trade's good as cash. With trade, you know what you're getting. Cash, who knows what you got? Prices can change tomorrow and then your dollar doesn't buy so much."

"I ain't got nothing you'd want. Not for a hundred dollars." He had been so intent on the dog that he had not been watching Zeke, but now he looked up and saw both Zeke and Lester staring at Lorraine. All at once, he understood Zeke's willingness to make a deal. Normally, Zeke would not oblige a blind man by stepping aside.

Lorraine was standing behind the ironing-board, her hair hanging forward so that her face seemed hidden by the sides of an open door. She was having a difficult time getting out the wrinkles in a shirt and as she worked, she pulled her lips together. They were full and naturally pink. Her stained shirt was open at the neck and her breasts, with each forward movement, pressed together.

"Lorraine," Orville said, "I must have left my makings in the barn. Would you go and look for them? They could have fallen between the feed sacks so you may have to search some."

After Lorraine went out, Lester slipped to the door and watched her cross the yard. The sky was pale red. Bending forward, with the light against him, Lester looked as thick and dangerous as a bull.

"Minnie," Orville said, turning to look at his wife, "he needs a hundred dollars."

Minnie had finished at the sink and was trying to watch Zeke and Lester at the same time.

"Me and Lester, we both own halves," Zeke said. He shifted in his chair and moved the rope closer to Orville's hand.

Minnie looked from Orville to Zeke. Without taking her eyes from them she stepped to the ironing-board and picked up the iron. Outside, the yard was empty except for the insistent rise and fall of the cicadas. Shadows filled the door of the barn.

"Minnie," Orville said. "He needs a hundred dollars."

Minnie took a half-step forward, her body leaning toward the bedroom. Her face twisted, as though she was, with great effort, trying to lift her foot off the floor. Then, all at once, as Zeke and Orville sat, tensed, as though waiting for a sound, she pulled back, hunched over the ironing-board and began to vigorously iron the shirt that lay before her.

Outside, the red sky and the red ground blended. The barn settled into its own shadows, became suddenly heavier. Orville thought he could hear the girl's feet scuffing the dust as she returned but it was only the dog's leg brushing the floor. Zeke laid the rope against Orville's hand. Orville extended his fingers and scraped the rope toward him.

With that, Lester rushed out the door. Through the window, they could see him half run and half walk to the barn. At the entrance, he hesitated briefly and then, for no discernible reason, stretched his arms over his head. His arms and legs reached to the corners of the doorway, looking like thick khaki ropes. With a sudden movement, he disappeared into the darkness.

Zeke stood up. He glanced toward the door as if he, too, were in a hurry but didn't wish to leave so abruptly as to be impolite.

"Lester," he said apologetically, "he can't wait for anything . He's the same about his food."

Orville's eyes were fixed on a knot in the floor that had risen up as the surrounding wood had been worn away, a hard permanent swirl of lines that would still remain when the rest of the floor had crumbled to nothing. He squeezed the rope and drew it against his chest.

"Everybody's got to earn his keep," he said.

KURT VONNEGUT, JR.

Report on the Barnhouse Effect

Let me begin by saying that I don't know any more about where Professor Arthur Barnhouse is hiding than anyone else does. Save for one short, enigmatic message left in my mailbox on Christmas Eve, I have not heard from him since his disappearance a year and a half ago.

What's more, readers of this article will be disappointed if they expect to learn how *they* can bring about the so-called "Barnhouse Effect." If I were able and willing to give away that secret, I would certainly be something more important than a psychology instructor.

I have been urged to write this report because I did research under the professor's direction and because I was the first to learn of his astonishing discovery. But while I was his student I was never entrusted with knowledge of how the mental forces could be released and directed. He was unwilling to trust anyone with that information.

I would like to point out that the term "Barnhouse Effect" is a creation of the popular press, and was never used by Professor Barnhouse. The name he chose for the phenomenon was *"dynamopsychism,"* or *force of the mind.*

I cannot believe that there is a civilized person yet to be convinced that such a force exists, what with its destructive effects on display in every national capital. I think humanity has always had an inkling that this sort of force does exist. It has been common knowledge that some people are luckier than others with inanimate objects like dice. What Professor Barnhouse did was to show that such "luck" was a measurable force, which in his case could be enormous.

By my calculation, the professor was about fifty-five times more powerful than a Nagasaki-type atomic bomb at the time he went into hiding. He was not bluffing when, on the eve of "Operation Brainstorm," he told General Honus Barker: "Sitting here at the dinner table, I'm pretty sure I can flatten anything on earth — from Joe Louis to the Great Wall of China."

There is an understandable tendency to look upon Professor Barnhouse as a supernatural visitation. The First Church of Barnhouse in Los Angeles has a congregation numbering in the thousands. He is godlike in neither appearance nor intellect. The man who disarms the world is single, shorter than the average American male, stout, and averse to exercise. His I.Q. is 143, which is good but certainly not sensational. He is quite mortal, about to celebrate his fortieth birthday, and in good health. If he is alone now, the isolation won't bother him too much. He was quiet and shy when I knew him, and seemed to find more companionship in books and music than in his associations at the college.

Neither he nor his powers fall outside the sphere of Nature. His dynamopsychic radiations are subject to many known physical laws that apply in the field of radio. Hardly a person has not now heard the snarl of "Barnhouse static" on his home receiver. The radiations are affected by sunspots and variations in the ionosphere.

However, they differ from ordinary broadcast waves in several important ways. Their total energy can be brought to bear on any single point the professor chooses, and that energy is undiminished by distance. As a weapon, then, dynamopsychism has an impressive advantage over bacteria and atomic bombs, beyond the fact that it costs nothing to use: it enables the professor to single out critical individuals and objects instead of slaughtering whole populations in the process of maintaining international equilibrium.

As General Honus Barker told the House Military Affairs Committee: "Until someone finds Barnhouse, there is no defense against the Barnhouse Effect." Efforts to "jam" or block the radiations have failed. Premier Slezak could have saved himself the fantastic expense of his "Barnhouse-proof" shelter. Despite the shelter's twelve-foot-thick lead armor, the premier has been floored twice while in it.

There is talk of screening the population for men potentially as powerful dynamopsychically as the professor. Senator Warren Foust demanded funds for this purpose last month, with the passionate declaration: "He who rules the Barnhouse Effect rules the world!" Commissar Kropotnik said much the same thing, so another costly armaments race, with a new twist, has begun.

This race at least has its comical aspects. The world's best gamblers are being coddled by governments like so many nuclear physicists. There may be several hundred persons with dynamopsychic talent on earth, myself included. But, without knowledge of the professor's technique, they can never be anything but dice-table despots. With the secret, it would probably take them ten years to become dangerous weapons. It took the professor that long. He who rules the Barnhouse Effect is Barnhouse and will be for some time.

Popularly, the "Age of Barnhouse" is said to have begun a year and a half ago, on the day of Operation Brainstorm. That was when dynamopsychism became significant politically. Actually, the phenomenon was discovered in May, 1942, shortly after the professor turned down a direct commission in the Army and enlisted as an artillery private. Like X-rays and vulcanized rubber, dynamopsychism was discovered by accident.

From time to time Private Barnhouse was invited to take part in games of chance by his barrack mates. He knew nothing about the games, and usually begged off. But one evening, out of social grace, he agreed to shoot craps. It was terrible or wonderful that he played, depending upon whether or not you like the world as it now is.

"Shoot sevens, Pop," someone said.

So "Pop" shot sevens — ten in a row to bankrupt the barracks. He retired to his bunk and, as a mathematical exercise, calculated the odds against his feat on the back of a laundry slip. His chances of doing it, he found, were one in almost ten million! Bewildered, he borrowed a pair of dice from the man in the bunk next to his. He tried to roll sevens again, but got only the usual assortment of numbers. He lay back for a moment, then resumed his toying with the dice. He rolled ten more sevens in a row.

He might have dismissed the phenomenon with a low whistle. But the professor instead mulled over the circumstances surrounding his two lucky streaks. There was one single factor in common: on both occasions, *the same thought train had flashed through his mind just before he threw the dice.* It was that thought train which aligned the professor's brain cells into what has since become the most powerful weapon on earth.

The soldier in the next bunk gave dynamopsychism its first token of respect. In an understatement certain to bring wry smiles to the faces of the world's dejected demagogues, the soldier said, "You're hotter'n a two-dollar pistol, Pop." Professor Barnhouse was all of that. The dice that did his bidding weighed but a few grams, so the forces involved were minute; but the unmistakable fact that there were such forces was earthshaking.

Professional caution kept him from revealing his discovery immediately. He wanted more facts and a body of theory to go with them. Later, when the atomic bomb was dropped on Hiroshima, it was fear that made him hold his peace. At no time were his experiments, as Premier Slezak called them, "a bourgeois plot to shackle the true democracies of the world." The professor didn't know where they were leading.

In time, he came to recognize another startling feature of dynamopsychism: *its strength increased with use.* Within six months, he was able to govern dice thrown by men the length of a barracks distant. By the time of his discharge in 1945, he could knock bricks loose from chimneys three miles away.

Charges that Professor Barnhouse could have won the last war in a minute, but did not care to do so, are perfectly senseless. When the war ended, he had the range and power of a 37-millimeter cannon, perhaps — certainly no more. His dynamopsychic powers graduated from the small-arms class only after his discharge and return to Wyandotte College.

I enrolled in the Wyandotte Graduate School two years after the professor had rejoined the faculty. By chance, he was assigned as my thesis adviser. I was unhappy about the assignment, for the professor was, in the eyes of both colleagues and students, a somewhat ridiculous figure. He missed classes or had lapses of memory during lectures. When I arrived, in fact, his shortcomings had passed from the ridiculous to the intolerable.

"We're assigning you to Barnhouse as a sort of temporary thing," the dean of social studies told me. He looked apologetic and perplexed. "Brilliant man, Barnhouse, I guess. Difficult to know since his return, perhaps, but his work before the war brought a great deal of credit to our little school."

When I reported to the professor's laboratory for the first time, what I saw was more distressing than the gossip. Every surface in the room was covered with dust; books and apparatus had not been disturbed for months. The professor sat napping at his desk when I entered. The only signs of recent activity were three overflowing ashtrays, a pair of scissors, and a morning paper with several items clipped from its front page.

As he raised his head to look at me, I saw that his eyes were clouded with fatigue, "Hi," he said, "just can't seem to get my sleeping done at night." He lighted a cigarette, his hands trembling slightly. "You the young man I'm supposed to help with a thesis?"

"Yes, sir," I said. In minutes he converted my misgivings to alarm.

"You an overseas veteran?" he asked.

"Yes, sir."

"Not much left over there, is there?" He frowned, "Enjoy the last war?"

"No, sir."

"Look like another war to you?"

"Kind of, sir."

"What can be done about it?"

I shrugged, "Looks pretty hopeless."

He peered at me intently. "Know anything about international law, the U.N. and all that?"

"Only what I pick up from the papers."

"Same here," he sighed. He showed me a fat scrapbook packed with newspaper clippings. "Never used to pay any attention to international politics. Now I study them the way I used to study rats in mazes. Everybody tells me the same thing — 'Looks hopeless.' "

"Nothing short of a miracle —" I began.

"Believe in magic?" he asked sharply. The professor fished two dice from his vest pocket. "I will try to roll twos," he said. He rolled twos three times in a row. "One chance in about 47,000 of that happening. There's a miracle for you." He beamed for an instant, then brought the interview to an end, remarking that he had a class which had begun ten minutes ago.

He was not quick to take me into his confidence, and he said no more about his trick with the dice. I assumed they were loaded, and forgot about them. He set me the task of watching male rats cross electrified metal strips to get to food or female rats — an experiment that had been done to everyone's satisfaction in the nineteen-thirties. As though the pointlessness of my work were not bad enough, the professor annoyed me further with irrelevant questions. His favorites were: "Think we should have dropped the atomic bomb on Hiroshima?" and "Think every new piece of scientific information is a good thing for humanity?"

However, I did not feel put upon for long. "Give those poor animals a holiday," he said one morning, after I had been with him only a month. "I wish you'd help me look into a more interesting problem — namely, my sanity."

I returned the rats to their cages.

"What you must do is simple," he said, speaking softly. "Watch the inkwell on my desk. If you see nothing happen to it, say so, and I'll go quietly — relieved, I might add — to the nearest sanitarium."

I nodded uncertainly.

He locked the laboratory door and drew the blinds, so that we were in twilight for a moment. "I'm odd, I know," he said. "It's fear of myself that's made me odd."

"I've found you somewhat eccentric, perhaps, but certainly not —"

"If nothing happens to that inkwell, 'crazy as a bedbug' is the only description of me that will do," he interrupted, turning on the overhead lights. His eyes narrowed. "To give you an idea of how crazy, I'll tell you what's been running through my mind when I should have been sleeping. I think maybe I can save the world. I think maybe I can make every nation a *have* nation, and do away with war for good. I think maybe I can clear roads through jungles, irrigate deserts, build dams overnight."

"Yes, sir."

"Watch the inkwell!"

Dutifully and fearfully I watched. A high-pitched humming seemed to come from the inkwell; then it began to vibrate alarmingly, and finally to bound about the top of the desk, making two noisy circuits. It stopped, hummed again, glowed red, then popped in splinters with a blue-green flash.

Perhaps my hair stood on end. The professor laughed gently. "Magnets?" I managed to say at last.

"Wish to heaven it were magnets," he murmured. It was then that he told me of dynamopsychism. He knew only that there was such a force; he could not explain it. "It's me and me alone — and it's awful."

"I'd say it was amazing and wonderful!" I cried.

"If all I could do was make inkwells dance, I'd be tickled silly with the whole business." He shrugged disconsolately. "But I'm no toy, my boy. If you like, we can drive around the neighborhood, and I'll show you what I mean." He told me about pulverized boulders, shattered oaks, and abandoned farm buildings demolished within a fifty-mile radius of the campus. "Did every bit of it sitting right here, just thinking — not even thinking hard."

He scratched his head nervously. "I have never dared to concentrate as hard as I can for fear of the damage I might do. I'm to the point where a mere whim is a blockbuster." There was a depressing pause. "Up until a few days ago, I've thought it best to keep my secret for fear of what use it might be put to," he continued. "Now I realize that I haven't any more right to it than a man has a right to own an atomic bomb."

He fumbled through a heap of papers. "This says about all that needs to be said. I think." He handed me a draft of a letter to the Secretary of State.

Dear Sir:

I have discovered a new force which costs nothing to use, and which is probably more important than atomic energy. I should like to see it used most effectively in the cause of peace, and am, therefore, requesting your advice as to how this might best be done.

Yours truly,
A. Barnhouse.

"I have no idea what will happen next," said the professor.

There followed three months of perpetual nightmare, wherein the nation's political and military great came at all hours to watch the professor's tricks.

We were quartered in an old mansion near Charlottesville, Virginia, to which we had been whisked five days after the letter was mailed. Surrounded by barbed wire and twenty guards, we were labeled "Project Wishing Well," and were classified as Top Secret.

For companionship we had General Honus Barker and the State Department's William K. Cuthrell.

For the professor's talk of peace-through-plenty they had indulgent smiles and much discourse on practical measures and realistic thinking. So treated, the professor, who had at first been almost meek, progressed in a matter of weeks toward stubbornness.

He had agreed to reveal the thought train by means of which he aligned his mind into a dynamopsychic transmitter. But, under Cuthrell's and Barker's nagging to do so, he began to hedge. At first he declared that the information could be passed on simply by word of mouth. Later he said that it would have to be written up in a long report. Finally, at dinner one night, just after General Barker had read the secret orders for Operation Brainstorm, the professor announced, "The report may take as long as five years to write." He looked fiercely at the general. "Maybe twenty."

The dismay occasioned by this flat announcement was offset somewhat by the exciting anticipation of Operation Brainstorm. The general was in a holiday mood. "The target ships are on their way to the Caroline Islands at this very moment," he declared ecstatically. "One hundred and twenty of them! At the same time, ten V-2s are being readied for firing in New Mexico, and fifty radio-controlled jet bombers are being equipped for a mock attack on the Aleutians. Just think of it!" Happily he reviewed his orders. "At exactly 1100 hours next Wednesday, I will give you the order to *concentrate*; and you, professor, will think as hard as you can about sinking the target ships, destroying the V-2s before they hit the ground, and knocking down the bombers before they reach the Aleutians! Think you can handle it?"

The professor turned gray and closed his eyes. "As I told you before, my friend, I don't know what I can do." He added bitterly, "As for this Operation Brainstorm, I was never consulted about it, and it strikes me as childish and insanely expensive."

General Barker bridled. "Sir," he said, "your field is psychology, and I wouldn't presume to give you advice in that field. Mine is national defense. I have had thirty years of experience and success, Professor, and I'll ask you not to criticize my judgment."

The professor appealed to Mr. Cuthrell. "Look," he pleaded, "isn't it war and military matters we're all trying to get rid of? Wouldn't it be a whole lot more significant and lots cheaper for me to try moving cloud masses into drought areas, and things like that? I admit I know next to nothing about international politics, but it seems reasonable to suppose that nobody would want to fight wars if there were enough of everything to go around. Mr. Cuthrell, I'd like to try running generators where there isn't any coal or water power, irrigating deserts, and so on. Why, you could figure out what each country needs to make the most of its resources, and I could give it to them without costing American taxpayers a penny."

"Eternal vigilance is the price of freedom," said the general heavily.

Mr. Cuthrell threw the general a look of mild distaste. "Unfortunately, the general is right in his own way," he said. "I wish to heaven the world were ready for ideals like yours, but it simply isn't. We aren't surrounded by brothers, but by enemies. It isn't a lack of food or resources that has us on the brink or war — it's a struggle for power. Who's going to be in charge of the world, our kind of people or theirs?"

The professor nodded in reluctant agreement and arose from the table. "I beg your pardon, gentlemen. You are, after all, better qualified to judge what is best for the country. I'll do whatever you say." He turned to me. "Don't forget to wind the restricted clock and put the confidential cat out," he said gloomily, and ascended the stairs to his bedroom.

For reasons of national security, Operation Brainstorm was carried on without the knowledge of the American citizenry which was paying the bill. The observers, technicians, and military men involved in the activity knew that a test was under way — a test of what, they had no idea. Only thirty-seven key men, myself included, knew what was afoot.

In Virginia, the day of Operation Brainstorm was unseasonably cool. Inside, a log fire crackled in the fireplace, and the flames were reflected in the polished metal cabinets that lined the living room. All that remained of the room's lovely old furniture was a Victorian love seat, set squarely in the center of the floor, facing three television receivers. One long bench had been brought in for ten of us privileged to watch. The television screens showed, from left to right, the stretch of desert which was the rocket target, the guinea-pig fleet, and a section of the Aleutian sky through which the radio-controlled bomber formation would roar.

Ninety minutes before H-hour the radios announced that the rockets were ready, that the observation ships had backed away to what was thought to be a safe distance, and that the bombers were on their way. The small Virginia audience lined up on the bench in order of rank, smoked a great deal, and said little. Professor Barnhouse was in his bedroom. General Barker bustled about the house like a woman preparing Thanksgiving dinner for twenty.

At ten minutes before the H-hour the general came in, shepherding the professor before him. The professor was comfortably attired in sneakers, gray flannels, a blue sweater, and white shirt open at the neck. The two of them sat side by side on the love seat. The general was rigid and perspiring; the professor was cheerful. He looked at each of the screens, lighted a cigarette and settled back.

"Bombers sighted!" cried the Aleutian observers.

"Rockets away!" barked the New Mexico radio operator.

All of us looked quickly at the big electric clock over the mantel, while the professor, a half-smile on his face, continued to watch the television sets. In hollow tones, the general counted away the seconds remaining. "Five . . . four . . . three . . . two . . . one . . . *Concentrate!*"

Professor Barnhouse closed his eyes, pursed his lips, and stroked his temples. He held the position for a minute. The television images were scrambled, and the radio signals were drowned in the din of Barnhouse static. The professor sighed, opened his eyes, and smiled confidently.

"Did you give it everything you had?" asked the general dubiously.

"I was wide open," the professor replied.

The television images pulled themselves together, and mingled cries of amazement came over the radios tuned to the observers. The Aleutian sky was streaked with the smoke trails of bombers screaming down in flames. Simultaneously, there appeared high over the rocket target a cluster of white puffs, followed by faint thunder.

General Barker shook his head happily. "By George!" he crowed. "Well, sir, by George, by George!"

"Look!" shouted the admiral seated next to me. The fleet — it wasn't touched!"

"The guns seem to be drooping," said Mr. Cuthrell.

We left the bench and clustered about the television sets to examine the damage more closely. What Mr. Cuthrell had said was true. The ships' guns curved downward, their muzzles resting on the steel decks. We in Virginia were making such a hullabaloo that it was impossible to hear the radio reports. We were so engrossed, in fact, that we didn't miss the professor until two short snarls of Barnhouse static shocked us into sudden silence. The radios went dead.

We looked around apprehensively. The professor was gone. A harassed guard threw open the front door from the outside to yell that the professor had escaped. He brandished his pistol in the direction of the gates, which hung open, limp and twisted. In the distance, a speeding government station wagon topped a ridge and dropped from sight into the valley beyond. The air was filled with choking smoke, for every vehicle on the grounds was ablaze. Pursuit was impossible.

"What in God's name got into him?" bellowed the general.

Mr. Cuthrell, who had rushed out onto the front porch, now slouched back into the room, reading a penciled note as he came. He thrust the note into my hands. "The good man left this billet-doux under the door knocker. Perhaps our young friend will be kind enough to read it to you gentlemen, while I take a restful walk through the woods."

"*Gentlemen,*" I read aloud, "*As the first superweapon with a conscience, I am removing myself from your national defense stockpile. Setting a new precedent in the behavior of ordinance, I have humane reasons for going off. A. Barnhouse.*"

Since that day, of course, the professor has been systematically destroying the world's armaments, until there is now little with which to equip an army other than rocks and sharp sticks. His activities haven't exactly resulted in peace, but have, rather, precipitated a bloodless and entertaining sort of war that might be called the "War of the Tattletales." Every nation is flooded with enemy agents whose sole mission is to locate military equipment, which is promptly wrecked when it is brought to the professor's attention in the press.

Just as every day brings news of more armaments pulverized by dynamopsychism, so has it brought rumors of the professor's whereabouts. During last week alone, three publications carried articles proving variously that he was hiding in an Inca ruin in the Andes, in the sewers of Paris, and in the unexplored lower chambers of Carlsbad Caverns. Knowing the man, I am inclined to regard such hiding places as unnecessarily romantic and uncomfortable. While there are numerous persons eager to kill him, there must be millions who would care for him and hide him. I like to think he is in the home of such a person.

One thing is certain: at this writing, Professor Barnhouse is not dead. Barnhouse static jammed broadcasts not ten minutes ago. In the eighteen months since his disappearance, he has been reported dead some half-dozen times. Each report has stemmed from the death of an unidentified man resembling the professor, during a period free of the static. The first three reports were followed at once by renewed talk of rearmament and recourse to war. The saber-rattlers have learned how imprudent premature celebrations of the professor's demise can be.

Many a stouthearted patriot has found himself prone in the tangled bunting and timbers of a smashed reviewing stand, seconds after having announced that the arch-tyranny of Barnhouse was at an end. But those who would make war if they could, in every country in the world, wait in sullen silence for what must come — the passing of Professor Barnhouse.

To ask how much longer the professor will live is to ask how much longer we must wait for the blessings of another world war. He is of short-lived stock: his mother lived to be fifty-three, his father to be forty-nine; and the life-spans of his grandparents on both sides were of the same order. He might be expected to live, then, for perhaps fifteen years more, if he can remain hidden from his enemies. When one considers the number and vigor of these enemies, however, fifteen years seems an extraordinary length of time, which might better be revised to fifteen days, hours, or minutes.

The professor knows that he cannot live much longer. I say this because of the message left in my mailbox on Christmas Eve. Unsigned, typewritten on a soiled scrap of paper, the note consisted of ten sentences. The first nine of these, each a bewildering tangle of psychological jargon and references to obscure texts made no sense to me at first reading. The tenth, unlike the rest, was simply constructed and contained no large words — but its irrational content made it the most puzzling and bizarre sentence of all. I nearly threw the note away, thinking it a colleague's warped notion of a practical joke. For some reason, though, I added it to the clutter on top of my desk, which included, among other mementos, the professor's dice.

It took me several weeks to realize that the message really meant something, that the first nine sentences, when unsnarled, could be taken as instructions. The tenth still told me nothing. It was only last night that I discovered how it fitted in with the rest. The sentence appeared in my thoughts last night, while I was toying absently with the professor's dice.

I promised to have this report on its way to the publishers today. In view of what has happened, I am obliged to break that promise, or release the report incomplete. The delay will not be a long one, for one of the few blessings accorded a bachelor like myself is the ability to move quickly from one abode to another, or from one way of life to another. What property I want to take with me can be packed in a few hours. Fortunately, I am not without substantial private means, which may take as long as a week to realize in liquid and anonymous form. When this is done, I shall mail the report.

I have just returned from a visit to my doctor, who tells me my health is excellent. I am young, and, with any luck at all, I shall live to a ripe old age indeed, for my family on both sides is noted for longevity.

Briefly, I propose to vanish.

Sooner or later, Professor Barnhouse must die. But long before then I shall be ready. So, to the saber-rattlers of today — and even, I hope, of tomorrow — I say: Be advised. Barnhouse will die. But not the Barnhouse Effect.

Last night I tried once more to follow the oblique instructions on the scrap of paper. I took the professor's dice, and then, with the last, nightmarish sentence flitting through my mind, I rolled fifty consecutive sevens.

Good-by.

EUDORA WELTY

Powerhouse

Powerhouse is playing!

He's here on tour from the city — "Powerhouse and His Keyboard" — "Powerhouse and His Tasmanians" — think of the things he calls himself! There's no one in the world like him. You can't tell what he is. "Nigger man"? — he looks more Asiatic, monkey, Jewish, Babylonian, Peruvian, fanatic, devil. He has pale gray eyes, heavy lids, maybe horny like a lizard's, but big glowing eyes when they're open. He has African feet of the greatest size, stomping, both together, on each side of the pedals. He's not coal black — beverage colored — looks like a preacher when his mouth is shut, but then it opens — vast and obscene. And his mouth is going every minute: like a monkey's when it looks for something. Improvising, coming on a light and childish melody — *smooch* — he loves it with his mouth.

Is it possible that he could be this! When you have him there performing for you, that's what you feel. You know people on a stage — and people of a darker race — so likely to be marvelous, frightening.

This is a white dance. Powerhouse is not a show-off like the Harlem boys, not drunk, not crazy — he's in a trance; he's a person of joy, a fanatic. He listens as much as he performs, a look of hideous, powerful rapture on his face. Big arched eyebrows that never stop traveling, like a Jew's — wandering-Jew eyebrows. When he plays he beats down piano and seat and wears them away. He is in motion every moment — what could be more obscene? There he is with his great head, fat stomach, and little round piston legs, and long yellow-sectioned strong big fingers, at rest about the size of bananas. Of course you know how he sounds — you've heard him on records — but still you need to see him. He's going all the time, like skating around the skating rink or rowing a boat. It makes everybody crowd around, here in this shadowless steel-trussed hall with the rose-like posters of Nelson Eddy and the testimonial for the mind-reading horse in handwriting magnified five hundred times. Then all quietly he lays his finger on a key with the promise and serenity of a sibyl touching the book.

Powerhouse is so monstrous he sends everybody into oblivion. When any group, any performers, come to town, don't people always come out and hover near, leaning inward about them, to learn what it is? What is it? Listen. Remember how it was with the acrobats. Watch them carefully, hear the least word, especially what they say to one another, in another language — don't let them escape you; it's the only time for hallucination, the last time. They can't stay. They'll be somewhere else this time tomorrow.

Powerhouse has as much as possible done by signals. Everybody, laughing as if to hide a weakness, will sooner or later hand him up a written request. Powerhouse reads each one, studying with a secret face: that is the face which looks like a mask — anybody's; there is a moment when he makes a decision. Then a light slides under his eyelids, and he says, "92!" or some combination of figures — never a name. Before a number the band is all frantic, misbehaving, pushing, like children in a classroom, and he is the teacher getting silence. His hands over the keys, he says sternly, "You-all ready? You-all ready to do some serious walking?" — waits — then, STAMP. Quiet. STAMP, for the second time. This is absolute. Then a set of rhythmic kicks against the floor to communicate the tempo. Then, O Lord! say the distended eyes from beyond the boundary of the trumpets, Hello and good-bye, and they are all down the first note like a waterfall.

This note marks the end of any known discipline. Powerhouse seems to abandon them all — he himself seems lost — down in the song, yelling up like somebody in a whirlpool — not guiding them — hailing them only. But he knows, really. He cries out, but he must know exactly. "Mercy! ... What I say! ... Yeah!" And then drifting, listening — "Where that skin beater?" — wanting drums, and starting up and pouring it out in the greatest delight and brutality. On the sweet pieces such a leer for everybody! He looks down so benevolently upon all our faces and whispers the lyrics to us. And if you could hear him at his moment on "Marie, the Dawn is Breaking"! He's going up the keyboard with a few fingers in some very derogatory triplet-routine, he gets higher and higher, and then he looks over the end of the piano, as if over a cliff. But not in a show-off way — the song makes him do it.

He loves the way they all play, too — all those next to him. The far section of the band is all studious, wearing glasses, every one — they don't count. Only those playing around Powerhouse are the real ones. He has a bass fiddler from Vicksburg, black as pitch, named Valentine, who plays with his eyes shut and talking to himself, very young: Powerhouse has to keep encouraging him. "Go on, go on, give it up, bring it on out there!" When you heard him like that on records, did you know he was really pleading?

He calls Valentine to take a solo.

"What you going to play?" Powerhouse looks out kindly from behind the piano; he opens his mouth and shows his tongue, listening.

Valentine looks down, drawing against his instrument, and says without a lip movement, "Honeysuckle Rose."

He has a clarinet player named Little Brother, and loves to listen to anything he does. He'll smile and say, "Beautiful!" Little Brother takes a step forward when he plays and stands at the very front, with the whites of his eyes like fishes swimming. Once when he played a low note, Powerhouse muttered a dirty praise, "He went clear downstairs to get that one!"

After a long time, he holds up the number of fingers to tell the band how many choruses still to go — usually five. He keeps his directions down to signals.

It's a bad night outside. It's a white dance, and nobody dances, except a few straggling jitterbugs and two elderly couples. Everybody just stands around the band and watches Powerhouse. Sometimes they steal glances at one another, as if to say, Of course, you know how it is with *them* — Negroes — band leaders — they would play the same way, giving all they've got, for an audience of one. . . . When somebody, no matter who, gives everything, it makes people feel ashamed for him.

Late at night they play the one waltz they will ever consent to play — by request, "Pagan Love Song." Powerhouse's head rolls and sinks like a weight between his waving shoulders. He groans, and his fingers drag into the keys heavily, holding on to the notes, retrieving. It is a sad song.

"You know what happened to me?" says Powerhouse.

Valentine hums a response, dreaming at the bass.

"I got a telegram my wife is dead," says Powerhouse, with wandering fingers.

"Uh-huh?"

His mouth gathers and forms a barbarous O while his fingers walk up straight, unwillingly, three octaves.

"Gypsy? Why how come her to die, didn't you just phone her up in the night last night long distance?"

"Telegram say — here the words: Your wife is dead." He puts 4/4 over the 3/4.

"Not but four works?" This is the drummer, an unpopular boy named Scoot, a disbelieving maniac.

Powerhouse is shaking his vast cheeks. "What the hell was she trying to do? What was she up to?"

"What name has it got signed, if you got a telegram?" Scoot is spitting away with those wire brushes.

Little Brother, the clarinet player, who cannot now speak, glares and tilts back.

"Uranus Knockwood is the name signed." Powerhouse lifts his eyes open. "Ever heard of him?" A bubble shoots out on his lip like a plate on a counter.

Valentine is beating slowly on with his palm and scratching the strings with his long blue nails. He is fond of a waltz, Powerhouse interrupts him.

"I don't know him. Don't know who he is." Valentine shakes his head with the closed eyes.

"Say it agin."

"Uranus Knockwood."

"That ain't Lenox Avenue."

"It ain't Broadway."

"Ain't ever seen it wrote out in any print, even for horse racing."

"Hell, that's on a star, boy, ain't it?" Crash of the cymbals.

"What the hell was she up to?" Powerhouse shudders. "Tell me, tell me, tell me." He makes triplets, and begins a new chorus. He holds three fingers up.

"You say you got a telegram." This is Valentine, patient and sleepy, beginning again.

Powerhouse is elaborate. "Yas, the time I go out, go way downstairs along a long cor-ri-dor to where they puts us: coming back along the cor-ri-dor: steps out and hands me a telegram: Your wife is dead."

"Gypsy?" The drummer like a spider over his drums.

"Aaaaaaaaa!" shouts Powerhouse, flinging out both powerful arms for three whole beats to flex his muscles, then kneading a dough of bass notes. His eyes glitter. He plays the piano like a drum sometimes — why not?

"Gypsy? Such a dancer?"

"Why you don't hear it straight from your agent? Why it ain't come from headquarters? What you been doing, getting telegrams in the *corridor*, signed nobody?"

They all laugh. End of that chorus.

"What time is it?" Powerhouse calls. "What the hell place is this? Where is my watch and chain?"

"I hang it on you," whimpers Valentine. "It still there."

There it rides on Powerhouse's great stomach, down where he can never see it.

"Sure did hear some clock striking twelve while ago. Must be *midnight*."

"It going to be intermission," Powerhouse

declares, lifting up his finger with the signet ring.

He draws the chorus to an end. He pulls a big Northern hotel towel out of the deep pocket in his vast, special-cut tux pants and pushes his forehead into it.

"If she went and killed herself!" he says with a hidden face. "If she up and jumped out that window!" He gets to his feet, turning vaguely, wearing the towel on his head.

"Ha, ha!"

"Sheik, sheik!"

"She wouldn't do that." Little Brother sets down his clarinet like a precious vase, and speaks. He still looks like an East Indian queen, implacable, divine, and full of snakes. "You ain't going to expect people doing what they says over long distance."

"Come on!" roars Powerhouse. He is already at the back door, he has pulled it wide open, and with a wild, gathered-up face is smelling the terrible night.

Powerhouse, Valentine, Scoot and Little Brother step outside into the drenching rain.

"Well, they emptying buckets," says Powerhouse in a modified voice. On the street he holds his hands out and turns up the blanched palms like sieves.

A hundred dark, ragged, silent, delighted Negroes have come around from under the eaves of the hall, and follow wherever they go.

"Watch out Little Brother don't shrink," says Powerhouse. "You just the right size now, clarinet don't suck you in. You got a dry throat, Little Brother, you in the desert?" He reaches into the pocket and pulls out a paper of mints. "Now hold 'em in your mouth — don't chew 'em. I don't carry around nothing without limit."

"Go in that joint and have beer," says Scoot, who walks ahead.

"Beer? Beer? You know what beer is? What do they say is beer? What's beer? Where I been?"

"Down yonder where it say World Café — that do?" They are in Negrotown now.

Valentine patters over and holds open a screen door warped like a sea shell, bitter in the wet, and they walk in, stained darker with the rain and leaving footprints. Inside, sheltered dry smells stand like screens around a table covered with a red-checkered cloth, in the center of which flies hang onto an obelisk-shaped ketchup bottle. The midnight walls are checkered again with admonishing "Not Responsible" signs and black-figured, smoky calendars. It is a waiting, silent, limp room. There is a burned-out-looking nickelodeon and right beside it a long-necked wall instrument labeled "Business Phone, Don't Keep Talking." Circled phone numbers are written up everywhere. There is a worn-out peacock feather hanging by a thread to an old, thin, pink, exposed light bulb, where it slowly turns around and around, whoever breathes.

A waitress watches.

"Come here, living statue, and get all this big order of beer we fixing to give."

"Never seen you before anywhere." The waitress moves and comes forward and slowly shows little gold leaves and tendrils over her teeth. She shoves up her shoulders and breasts. "How I going to know who you might be? Robbers? Coming in out of the black of night right at midnight, setting down so big at my table?"

"Boogers," says Powerhouse, his eyes opening lazily as in a cave.

The girl screams delicately with pleasure. O Lord, she likes talk and scares.

"Where you going to find enough beer to put on this here table?"

She runs to the kitchen with bent elbows and sliding steps.

"Here's a million nickels," says Powerhouse, pulling his hand out of his pocket and sprinkling coins out, all but the last one, which he makes vanish like a magician.

Valentine and Scoot take the money over to the nickelodeon, which looks as battered as a slot machine, and read all the names of the records out loud.

"Whose 'Tuxedo Junction'?" asks Powerhouse.

"You know whose."

"Nickelodeon, I request you please to play 'Empty Red Blues' and let Bessie Smith sing."

Silence: they hold it like a measure.

"Bring me all those nickels on back here," says Powerhouse. "Look at that! What you tell me the name of this place?"

"White dance, week night, raining, Alligator, Mississippi, long ways from home."

"Uh-huh."

"Sent for You Yesterday and Here You Come Today" plays.

The waitress, setting the tray of beer down on a back table, comes up taut and apprehensive as a hen. "Says in the kitchen, back there putting their eyes to little hole peeping out, that you is Mr. Powerhouse ... They knows from a picture they seen."

"They seeing right tonight, that is him" says Little Brother.

"You him?"

"That is him in the flesh," says Scoot.

"Does you wish to touch him?" asks Valentine. "Because he don't bite."

"You passing through?"

"Now you got everything right."

She waits like a drop, hands languishing together in front.

"Little-Bit, ain't you going to bring the beer?"

She brings it, and goes behind the cash register and smiles, turning different ways. The little fillet of gold in her mouth is gleaming.

"The Mississippi River's here," she says once.

Now all the watching Negroes press in gently and bright-eyed through the door, as many as can get in. One is a little boy in a straw sombrero which has been coated with aluminum paint all over.

Powerhouse, Valentine, Scoot and Little Brother drink beer, and their eyelids come together like curtains. The wall and the rain and the humble beautiful waitress waiting on them and the other Negroes watching enclose them.

"Listen!" whispers Powerhouse, looking into the ketchup bottle and slowly spreading his performer's hands over the damp, wrinkling cloth with the red squares. "Listen how it is. My wife gets missing me. Gypsy. She goes to the window. She looks out and sees you know what. Street. Sign saying Hotel. People walking. Somebody looks up. Old man. She looks down, out the window. Well? ... *Sssssst! Plooey!* What she do? Jump out and burst her brains all over the world."

He opens his eyes.

"That's it," agrees Valentine. "You gets a telegram."

"Sure she misses you," Little Brother adds.

"No, it's night time." How softly he tells them! "Sure. It's the night time. She say, What do I hear? Footsteps walking up the hall? That him? Footsteps go on off. It's not me. I'm in Alligator, Mississippi, she's crazy. Shaking all over. Listens till her ears and all grow out like old music-box horns but still she can't hear a thing. She says, All right! I'll jump out the window then. Got on her nightgown. I know that nightgown, and her thinking there. Says, Ho hum, all right, and jumps out the window. Is she mad at me! Is she crazy! She don't leave *nothing* behind her!"

"Ya! Ha!"

"Brains and insides everywhere, Lord, Lord."

All the watching Negroes stir in their delight and to their higher delight he says affectionately, "Listen! Rats in here."

"That must be the way, boss."

"Only, naw, Powerhouse, that ain't true. That sound too *bad*."

"Does I even know who finds her," cries Powerhouse. "That no-good pussy-footed crooning creeper, that creeper that follow around after me, coming up like weeds behind me, following around after me everything I do and messing around on the trail I leave. Bets my numbers, sings my songs, gets close to my agent like a Betsy-bug; when I going out he just coming in. I got him now! I got my eye on him."

"Know who he is?"

"Why, it's that old Uranus Knockwood!"

"Ya! Ha!"

"Yeah, and he coming now, he going to find Gypsy. There he is, coming around that corner, and Gypsy kadoodling down, oh-oh, watch out! *Sssssst! Plooey!* See, there she is in her little old nightgown, and her insides and brains all scattered round."

A sigh fills the room.

"Hush about her brains. Hush about her insides."

"Ya! Ha! You talking about her brains and insides — old Uranus Knockwood," says Powerhouse, "look down and say Jesus! He say, Look here what I'm walking round in!"

They all burst into halloos of laughter. Powerhouse's face looks like a big hot iron stove.

"Why, he picks her up and carries her off!" he says.

"Ya! Ha!"

"Carries her *back* around the corner ..."

"Oh, Powerhouse!"

"You know him."

"Uranus Knockwood!"

"Yeahhh!"

"He take our wives when we gone!"

"He come in when we goes out!"

"Uh-huh!"

"He go out when we comes in!"

"Yeahhh!"

"He standing behind the door!"

"Old Uranus Knockwood."

"You know him."

"Middle-size man."

"Wears a hat."

"That's him."

Everybody in the room moans with pleasure. The little boy in the fine silver hat opens a paper and divides out a jelly roll among his followers.

And out of the breathless ring somebody moves forward like a slave, leading a great logy Negro with bursting eyes, and says, "This here is Sugar-Stick Thompson, that dove down to the bottom of July Creek and pulled up all those drownded white people fall out of a boat. Last summer, pulled up fourteen."

"Hello," says Powerhouse, turning and looking around at them all with his great daring face until they nearly suffocate.

Sugar-Stick, their instrument, cannot speak; he can only look back at the others.

"Can't even swim. Done it by holding his breath," says the fellow with the hero.

Powerhouse looks at him seekingly.

"I his half brother," the fellow puts in.

They step back.

"Gypsy say," Powerhouse rumbles gently again, looking at *them*, " 'What is the use? I'm gonna jump out so far — so far. . . .' *Sssst —!*"

"Don't, boss, don't do it again," says Little Brother.

"It's awful," says the waitress. "I hates that Mr. Knockwoods. All that the truth?"

"Want to see the telegram I got from him?" Powerhouse's hand goes to the vast pocket.

"Now wait, now wait, boss." They all watch him.

"It must be the real truth," says the waitress, sucking in her lower lip, her luminous eyes turning sadly, seeking the windows.

"No, babe, it ain't the truth." His eyebrows fly up, and he begins to whisper to her out of his vast oven mouth. His hand stays in his pocket. "Truth is something worse, I ain't said what, yet. It's something hasn't come to me, but I ain't saying it won't. And when it does, then want me to tell you?" He sniffs all at once, his eyes come open and turn up, almost too far. He is dreamily smiling.

"Don't, boss, don't, Powerhouse!"

"Oh!" the waitress screams.

"Go on get out of here!" bellows Powerhouse, taking his hand out of his pocket and clapping after her red dress.

The ring of watchers breaks and falls away.

"*Look* at that! Intermission is up," says Powerhouse.

He folds money under a glass, and after they go out, Valentine leans back in and drops a nickel in the nickelodeon behind them, and it lights up and begins to play "The Goona Goo." The feather dangles still.

"Take a telegram!" Powerhouse shouts suddenly up into the rain over the street. "Take a answer. Now what was the name?"

They get a little tired.

"Uranus Knockwood."

"You ought to know."

"Yas? Spell it to me."

They spell it all the ways it could be spelled. It puts them in a wonderful humor.

"Here's the answer. I got it right here. 'What in the hell you talking about? Don't make any difference: I gotcha.' Name signed: Powerhouse."

"That going to reach him, Powerhouse?" Valentine speaks in a maternal voice.

"Yas, yas."

All hushing, following him up the dark street at a distance, like old rained-on black ghosts, the Negroes are afraid they will die laughing.

Powerhouse throws back his vast head into the streaming rain, and a look of hopeful desire seems to blow somehow like a vapor from his own dilated nostrils over his face and bring a mist to his eyes.

"Reach him and come out the other side."

"That's it, Powerhouse, that's it. You got him now."

Powerhouse lets out a long sigh.

"But ain't you going back there to call up Gypsy long distance, the way you did last night in that other place? I seen a telephone.... Just to see if she there at home?"

There is a measure of silence. That is one crazy drummer that's going to get his neck broken some day.

"No," growls Powerhouse. "No! How many thousands times tonight I got to say No?"

He holds up his arm in the rain.

"You sure-enough unroll your voice some night, it about reach up yonder to her," says Little Brother, dismayed.

They go on up the street, shaking the rain off and on them like birds.

Back in the dance hall, they play "San" (99). The jitterbugs start up like windmills stationed over the floor, and in their orbits — one circle, another, a long stretch and a zigzag — dance the elderly couples with old smoothness, undisturbed and stately.

When Powerhouse first came back from intermission, no doubt full of beer, they said, he got the band tuned up again in his own way. He didn't strike the piano keys for pitch — he simply opened his mouth and gave falsetto howls — in A, D and so on — they tuned by him. Then he took hold of the piano, as if he saw it for the first time in his life, and tested it for strength, hit it down in the bass, played an octave with his elbow, lifted the top, looked inside, and leaned against it with all his might. He sat down and played it for a few minutes with outrageous force and got it under his power — a bass deep and coarse as a sea net — then produced something glimmering and fragile, and smiled. And who could ever remember any of the things he says? They are just inspired remarks that roll out of his mouth like smoke.

They've requested "Somebody Loves Me," and he's already done twelve or fourteen choruses, piling them up nobody knows how, and it will be a wonder if he ever gets through. Now and then he calls and shouts. " 'Somebody loves me! Somebody loves me, I wonder who!' " His mouth gets to be nothing but a volcano. "I wonder who!"

"Maybe . . ." He uses all his right hand on a trill.

"Maybe . . ." He pulls back his spread fingers and looks out upon the place where he is. A vast, impersonal and yet furious grimace transfigures his wet face.

" . . . Maybe it's you!"

RUDY WIEBE

Where Is the Voice Coming From?

Almighty Voice (1874-97), a Cree Indian, was arrested in 1895 for slaughtering a cow on a reserve near Duck Lake, N.W.T. He escaped, shot and killed a North West Mounted Police officer who was pursuing him, and became a hero to the Crees before he was finally killed by the police.

The problem is to make the story.

One difficulty of this making may have been excellently stated by Teilhard de Chardin: 'We are continually inclined to isolate ourselves from the things and events which surround us ... as though we were spectators, not elements, in what goes on.' Arnold Toynbee does venture, 'For all that we know, Reality is the undifferentiated unity of the mystical experience,' but that need not here be considered. This story ended long ago; it is one of finite acts, of orders, of elemental feelings and reactions, of obvious legal restrictions and requirements.

Presumably all the parts of the story are themselves available. A difficulty is that they are, as always, available only in bits and pieces. Though the acts themselves seem quite clear, some written reports of the acts contradict each other. As if these acts were, at one time, too well known; as if the original nodule of each particular fact had from somewhere received non-factual accretions; or even more, as if, since the basic facts were so clear perhaps there were a larger number of facts than any one reporter, or several, or even any reporter had ever attempted to record. About facts that are still simply told by this mouth to that ear, of course, even less can be expected.

An affair seventy-five years old should acquire some of the shiny transparency of an old man's skin. It should.

Sometimes it would seem that it would be enough — perhaps more than enough — to hear the names only. The grandfather One Arrow; the mother Spotted Calf; the father Sounding Sky; the wife (wives rather, but only one of them seems to have a name, though their fathers are Napaise, Kapahoo, Old Dust, The Rump) — the one wife named, of all things, Pale Face; the cousin Going-Up-To-Sky; the brother-in-law (again, of all things) Dublin. The names of the police sound very much alike; they all begin with Constable or Corporal or Sergeant, but here and there an Inspector, then a Superintendent and eventually all the resonance of an Assistant Commissioner echoes down. More. Herself: Victoria, by the Grace of God etc., etc., QUEEN, defender of the Faith, etc., etc.; and witness 'Our Right Trusty and Right Well-beloved Cousin and Councillor the Right Honorable Sir John Campbell Hamilton-Gordon, Earl of Aberdeen; Viscount Formartine, Baron Haddo, Methlic, Tarves and Kellie, in the Peerage of Scotland; Viscount Gordon of Aberdeen, County of Aberdeen, in the Peerage of the United Kingdom; Baronet of Nova Scotia, Knight Grand Cross of Our Most Distinguished Order of Saint Michael and Saint George, etc., Governor General of Canada'. And of course himself: in the award proclamation named 'Jean-Baptiste' but otherwise known only as Almighty Voice.

But hearing cannot be enough; not even hearing all the thunder of A Proclamation: 'Now Hear Ye that a reward of FIVE HUNDRED DOLLARS will be paid to any person or persons who will give such information as will lead ... (etc., etc.) this Twentieth day of April, in the year of Our Lord one thousand eight hundred and ninety-six, and the Fifty-ninth year of Our Reign ... ' etc. and etc.

Such hearing cannot be enough. The first item to be seen is the piece of white bone. It is almost triangular, slightly convex — concave actually as it is positioned at this moment with its corners slightly raised — graduating from perhaps a strong eighth to a weak quarter of an inch in thickness, its scattered pore structure varying between larger and smaller on its perhaps polished, certainly shiny surface. Precision is difficult since the glass showcase is at least thirteen inches deep and therefore an eye cannot be brought as close as the minute inspection of such a small, though certainly quite adequate, sample of skull would normally require. Also, because of the position it cannot be determined whether the several hairs, well over a foot long, are still in some manner attached or not.

The seven-pounder cannon can be seen standing almost shyly between the showcase and the interior wall. Officially it is known as a gun, not a cannon, and clearly its bore is not large enough to admit a large man's fist. Even if it can be believed that this gun was used in the 1885 Rebellion and that on the evening of Saturday, May 29, 1897 (while the nine-pounder, now unidentified, was in the process of arriving with the police on the special train from Regina), seven shells (all that were available in Prince Albert at that time) from it were sent shrieking into the poplar bluffs as night fell, clearly such shelling could not and would not disembowel the whole earth. Its carriage is now nicely lacquered, the perhaps oak spokes of its petite wheels (little higher than a knee) have been recently scraped, puttied and varnished; the brilliant burnish of its brass breeching testifies with what meticulous care charmen and women have used nationally-advertised cleaners and restorers.

Though it can also be seen, even a careless glance reveals that the same concern has not been expended on the one (of two) .44 calibre 1866 model Winchesters apparently found at the last in the pit with Almighty Voice. It also is preserved in a glass case; the number 1536735 is still, though barely, distinguishable on the brass cartridge section just below the brass saddle ring. However, perhaps because the case was imperfectly sealed at one time (though sealed enough not to warrant disturbance now), or because of simple neglect, the rifle is obviously spotted here and there with blotches of rust and the brass itself reveals discolorations almost like mildew. The rifle bore, the three long strands of hair themselves, actually bristle with clots of dust. It may be that this museum cannot afford to be as concerned as the other; conversely, the disfiguration may be something inherent in the items themselves.

The small building which was the police guardroom at Duck Lake, Saskatchewan Territory, in 1895 may also be seen. It had subsequently been moved from its original place and used to house small animals, chickens perhaps, or pigs — such as a woman might be expected to have under her responsibility. It is, of course, now perfectly empty, and clean so that the public may enter with no more discomfort than a bend under the doorway and a heavy encounter with disinfectant. The doorjamb has obviously been replaced; the bar network at one window is, however, said to be original; smooth still, very smooth. The logs inside have been smeared again and again with whitewash, perhaps paint, to an insistent point of identity-defying characterlessness. Within the small rectangular box of these logs not a sound can be heard from the streets of the, probably dead, town.

Hey Injun you'll get hung for stealing that
steer
Hey Injun for killing that government cow
you'll get three
weeks on the woodpile Hey Injun

The place named Kinistino seems to have disappeared from the map but the Minnechinass Hills have not. Whether they have ever been on a map is doubtful but they will, of course, not disappear from the landscape as long as the grass grows and the rivers run. Contrary to general report and belief, the Canadian prairies are rarely, if ever, flat and the Minnechinass (spelled five different ways and translated sometimes as 'The Outside Hill', sometimes as 'Beautiful Bare Hills') are dissimilar from any other of the numberless hills that everywhere block out the prairie horizon. They are bare; poplars lie tattered along their tops, almost black against the straw-pale grass and sharp green against the grey soil of the plowing laid in half-mile rectangular blocks upon their western slopes. Poles holding various wires stick out of the fields, back down the bend of the valley; what was once a farmhouse is weathering into the cultivated earth. The poplar bluff where Almighty Voice made his stand has, of course, disappeared.

The policemen he shot and killed (not the ones he wounded, of course) are easily located. Six miles east, thirty-nine miles north in Prince Albert, the English Cemetery. Sergeant Colin Campbell Colebrook, North West Mounted Police Registration Number 605, lies presumably under a gravestone there. His name is seventeenth in a very long 'list of non-commissioned officers and men who have died in the service since the inception of the force.' The date is October 29, 1895, and the cause of death is anonymous: 'Shot by escaping Indian prisoner near Prince Albert.' At the foot of this grave are two others: Constable John R. Kerr, No. 3040, and Corporal C.H.S. Hockin, No. 3106. Their cause of death on May 28, 1897 is even more anonymous, but the place is relatively precise: 'Shot by Indians at Min-etch-inass Hills, Prince Albert District.'

The gravestone, if he has one, of the fourth man Almighty Voice killed is more difficult to locate. Mr Ernest Grundy, postmaster at Duck Lake in 1897, apparently shut his window the afternoon of Friday, May 28, armed himself, rode east twenty miles, participated in the second charge into the bluff at about 6:30 p.m., and on the third sweep of that charge was shot dead at the edge of the pit. It would seem that he thereby contributed substantially not only to the Indians' bullet supply, but his clothing warmed them as well.

The burial place of Dublin and Going-Up-To-Sky is unknown, as is the grave of Almighty Voice. It is said that a Métis named Henry Smith lifted the latter's body from the pit in the bluff and gave it to Spotted Calf. The place of burial is not, of course, of ultimate significance. A gravestone is always less evidence than a triangular piece of skull, provided it is large enough.

Whatever further evidence there is to be gathered may rest on pictures. There are, presumably, almost numberless pictures of the policemen in the case, but the only one with direct bearing is one of Sergeant Colebrook who apparently insisted on advancing to complete an arrest after being warned three times that if he took another step he would be shot. The picture must have been taken before he joined the force; it reveals him a large-eared young man, hair brush-cut and ascot tie, his eyelids slightly drooping, almost hooded under thick brows. Unfortunately a picture of Constable R. C. Dickson, into whose charge Almighty Voice was apparently committed in that guardroom and who after Colebrook's death was convicted of negligence, sentenced to two months hard labour and discharged, does not seem to be available.

There are no pictures to be found of either Dublin (killed early by rifle fire) or Going-Up-To-Sky (killed in the pit), the two teenage boys who gave their ultimate fealty to Almighty Voice. There is, however, one said to be of Almighty Voice, Junior. He may have been born to Pale Face during the year, two hundred and twenty-one days that his father was a fugitive. In the picture he is kneeling before what could be a tent, he wears striped denim overalls and displays twin babies whose sex cannot be determined from the double-laced dark bonnets they wear. In the supposed picture of Spotted Calf and Sounding Sky, Sounding Sky stands slightly before his wife; he wears a white and striped blanket folded over his left shoulder in such a manner that the arm in which he cradles a long rifle cannot be seen. His head is thrown back; the rim of his hat appears as a black half-moon above eyes that are pressed shut in, as it were, profound concentration; above a mouth clenched thin in a downward curve. Spotted Calf wears a long dress, a sweater which could also be a man's dress coat, and a large fringed and embroidered shawl which would appear distinctly Dukhobour in origin if the scroll patterns on it were more irregular. Her head is small and turned slightly towards her husband so as to reveal her right ear. There is what can only be called a quizzical expression on her crumpled face; it may be she does not understand what is happening and that she would have asked a question, perhaps of her husband, perhaps of the photographers, perhaps even of anyone, anywhere in the world if such questioning were possible for an Indian lady.

There is one final picture. That is one of Almighty Voice himself. At least it is purported to be of Almighty Voice himself. In the Royal Canadian Mounted Police Museum on the Barracks Grounds just off Dewdney Avenue in Regina, Saskatchewan, it lies in the same showcase, as a matter of fact immediately beside, that triangular piece of skull. Both are unequivocally labelled, and it must be assumed that a police force with a world-wide reputation would not label *such* evidence incorrectly. But here emerges an ultimate problem in making the story.

There are two official descriptions of Almighty Voice. The first reads: 'Height about five feet, ten inches, slight build, rather good looking, a sharp hooked nose with a remarkably flat point. Has a bullet scar on the left side of his face about 1½ inches long running from near corner of mouth towards ear. The scar cannot be noticed when his face is painted but otherwise is plain. Skin fair for an Indian.' The second description is on the Award Proclamation: 'About twenty-two years old, five feet ten inches in height, weight about eleven stone, slightly erect, neat small feet and hands; complexion inclined to be fair, wavey dark hair to shoulders, large dark eyes, broad forehead, sharp features and parrot nose with flat tip, scar on left cheek running from mouth towards ear, feminine appearance.'

So run the descriptions that were, presumably, to identify a well-known fugitive in so precise a manner than an informant could collect five hundred dollars — a considerable sum when a police constable earned between one and two dollars a day. The nexus of the problems appears when these supposed official descriptions are compared to the supposed official picture. The man in the picture is standing on a small rug. The fingers of his left hand touch a curved Victorian settee, behind him a photographer's backdrop of scrolled patterns merges to vaguely paradisiacal trees and perhaps a sky. The moccasins he wears make it impossible to deduce whether his feet are 'neat small'. He may be five feet, ten inches tall, may weigh eleven stone, he certainly is 'rather good looking' and, though it is a frontal view, it may that the point of his long and flaring nose could be 'remarkably flat'. The photograph is slightly over-illuminated and so the unpainted complexion could be 'inclined to be fair'; however, nothing can be seen of a scar, the hair is not wavy and shoulder-length but hangs almost to the waist in two thick straight braids worked through with beads, fur, ribbons and cords. The right hand that holds the corner of the blanket-like coat in position is large and, even in the high illumination, heavily veined. The neck is concealed under coiled beads and the forehead seems more low than 'broad.'

Perhaps, somehow, these picture details could be reconciled with the official description if the face as a whole were not so devastating.

On a cloth-backed sheet two feet by two and one-half feet in size, under the Great Seal of the Lion and the Unicorn, dignified by the names of the Deputy of the Minister of Justice, the Secretary of State, the Queen herself and all the heaped detail of her 'Right Trusty and Right Well Beloved Cousin', this description concludes: 'feminine appearance'. But the pictures: any face of history, any believed face that the world acknowledges as *man* — Socrates, Jesus, Attila, Genghis Khan, Mahatma Gandi, Joseph Stalin — no believed face is more *man* than this face. The mouth, the nose, the clenched brows, the eyes — the eyes are large, yes, and dark, but even in this watered-down reproduction of unending reproductions of that original, a steady look into those eyes cannot be endured. It is a face like an axe.

It is now evident that the de Chardin statement quoted at the beginning has relevance only as it proves itself inadequate to explain what has happened. At the same time, the inadequacy of Aristotle's much more famous statement becomes evident: 'The true difference [between the historian and the poet] is that one relates what *has* happened, the other what *may* happen.' These statements cannot explain the storyteller's activity since, despite the most rigid application of impersonal investigation, the elements of the story have now run me aground. If ever I could, I can no longer pretend to objective, omnipotent disinterestedness. I am no longer *spectator* of what *has* happened or what *may* happen: I am become *element* in what is happening at this very moment.

For it is, of course, I myself who cannot endure the shadows on that paper which are those eyes. It is I who stand beside this broken veranda post where two corner shingles have been torn away, where barbed wire tangles the dead weeds on the edge of this field. The bluff that sheltered Almighty Voice and his two friends has not disappeared from the slope of the Minnechinass, no more than the sound of Constable Dickson's voice in that guardhouse is silent. The sound of his speaking is there even if it has never been recorded in an official report:

hey injun you'll get
hung
for stealing that steer
hey injun for killing that government
cow you'll get three
weeks on the woodpile hey injun

The unknown contradictory words about an unprovable act that move a boy to defiance, an implacable Cree warrior long after the three-hundred-and-fifty-year war is ended, a war already lost the day the Cree watch Cartier hoist his gun ashore at Hochelaga and they begin the long retreat west; these words of incomprehension, of threatened incomprehensible law are there to be heard just as the unmoving tableau of the three-day siege is there to be seen on the slopes of the Minnechinass. Sounding Sky is somewhere not there, under arrest, but Spotted Calf stands on a shoulder of the Hills a little to the left, her arms upraised to the setting sun. Her mouth is open. A horse rears, riderless, above the scrub willow at the edge of the bluff, smoke puffs, screams tangle in rifle barrage, there are wounds, somewhere. The bluff is so green this spring, it will not burn and the ragged line of seven police and two civilians is staggering through, faces twisted in rage, terror, and rifles sputter. Nothing moves. There is no sound of frogs in the night; twenty-seven policeman and five civilians stand in cordon at thirty-yard intervals and a body also lies in the shelter of a gully. Only a voice rises from the bluff:

We have fought well
You have died like braves
I have worked hard and am hungry
Give me food

but nothing moves. The bluff lies, a bright green island on the grassy slope surrounded by men hunched forward rigid over their long rifles, men clumped out of rifle-range, thirty-five men dressed as for fall hunting on a sharp spring day, a small gun positioned on a ridge above. A crow is falling out of the sky into the bluff, its feathers sprayed as by an explosion. The first gun and the second gun are in position, the beginning and end of the bristling surround of thirty-five Prince Albert Volunteers, thirteen civilians and fifty-six policemen in position relative to the bluff and relative to the unnumbered whites astride their horses, standing up in their carts, staring and pointing across the valley, in position relative to the bluff and the unnumbered Indians squatting silent along the higher ridges of the Hills, motionless mounds, faceless against the Sunday morning sunlight edging between and over them down along the tree tips, down into the shadows of the bluff. Nothing moves. Beside the second gun the red-coated officer has flung a handful of grass into the motionless air, almost to the rim of the red sun.

And there is a voice. It is an incredible voice that rises from among the young poplars ripped of their spring bark, from among the dead somewhere lying there, out of the arm-deep pit shorter than a man; a voice rises over the exploding smoke and thunder of guns that reel back in their positions, worked over, serviced by the grimed motionless men in bright coats and glinting buttons, a voice so high and clear, so unbelievably high and strong in its unending wordless cry.

The voice of 'Gitchie-Manitou Wayo' — interpreted as 'voice of the Great Spirit' — that is, The Almighty Voice. His death chant no less incredible in its beauty than in its incomprehensible happiness.

I say 'wordless cry' because that is the way it sounds to me. I could be more accurate if I had a reliable interpreter who would make a reliable interpretation. For I do not, of course, understand the Cree myself.

VIRGINIA WOOLF

The New Dress

Mabel had her first serious suspicion that something was wrong as she took her cloak off and Mrs. Barnet, while handing her the mirror and touching the brushes and thus drawing her attention, perhaps rather markedly, to all the appliances for tidying and improving hair, complexion, clothes, which existed on the dressing table, confirmed the suspicion — that it was not right, not quite right, which growing stronger as she went upstairs and springing at her, with conviction as she greeted Clarissa Dalloway, she went straight to the far end of the room, to a shaded corner where a looking-glass hung and looked. No! It was not *right*. And at once the misery which she always tried to hide, the profound dissatisfaction — the sense she had had, ever since she was a child, of being inferior to other people — set upon her, relentlessly, remorselessly, with an intensity which she could not beat off, as she would when she woke at night at home, by reading Borrow or Scott; for oh these men, oh these women, all were thinking — "What's Mabel wearing? What a fright she looks! What a hideous new dress!" — their eyelids flickering as they came up and then their lids shutting rather tight. It was her own appalling inadequacy; her cowardice; her mean, water-sprinkled blood that depressed her. And at once the whole of the room where, for ever so many hours, she had planned with the little dressmaker how it was to go, seemed sordid, repulsive; and her own drawing-room so shabby, and herself, going out, puffed up with vanity as she touched the letters on the hall table and said: "How dull!" to show off — all this now seemed unutterably silly, paltry, and provincial. All this had been absolutely destroyed, shown up, exploded, the moment she came into Mrs. Dalloway's drawing-room.

What she had thought that evening when, sitting over the teacups, Mrs. Dalloway's invitation came, was that, of course, she could not be fashionable. It was absurd to pretend it even — fashion meant cut, meant style, meant thirty guineas at least — but why not be original? Why not be herself, anyhow? And, getting up, she had taken that old fashion book of her mother's, a Paris fashion book of the time of the Empire, and had thought how much prettier, more dignified, and more womanly they were then, and so set herself — oh, it was foolish — trying to be like them, pluming herself in fact, upon being modest and old-fashioned and very charming, giving herself up, no doubt about it, to an orgy of self-love, which deserved to be chastised, and so rigged herself out like this.

But she dared not look in the glass. She could not face the whole horror — the pale yellow, idiotically old-fashioned silk dress with its long skirt and its high sleeves and its waist and all the things that looked so charming in the fashion book, but not on her, not among all these ordinary people. She felt like a dressmaker's dummy standing there, for young people to stick pins into.

"But, my dear, it's perfectly charming!" Rose Shaw said, looking her up and down with that little satirical pucker of the lips which she expected — Rose herself being dressed in the height of the fashion, precisely like everybody else, always.

We are all like flies trying to crawl over the edge of the saucer, Mabel thought, and repeated the phrase as if she were crossing herself, as if she were trying to find some spell to annul this pain, to make this agony endurable. Tags of Shakespeare, lines from books she had read ages ago, suddenly came to her when she was in agony, and she repeated them over and over again. "Flies trying to crawl," she repeated. If she could say that over often enough and make herself see the flies, she would become numb, chill, frozen, dumb. Now she could see flies crawling slowly out of a saucer of milk with their wings stuck together; and she strained and strained (standing in front of the looking-glass, listening to Rose Shaw) to make herself see Rose Shaw and all the other people there are flies, trying to hoist themselves out of something, or into something, meagre, insignificant, toiling flies. But she could not see them like that, not other people. She saw herself like that — she was a fly, but the others were dragonflies, butterflies, beautiful insects, dancing, fluttering, skimming, while she alone dragged herself up out of the saucer. (Envy and spite, the most detestable of the vices, were her chief faults.)

"I feel like some dowdy, decrepit, horribly dingy old fly," she said, making Robert Haydon stop just to hear her say that, just to reassure herself by furbishing up a poor weak-kneed phrase and so showing how detached she was, how witty, that she did not feel in the least out of anything. And, of course, Robert Haydon answered something quite polite, quite insincere, which she saw through instantly, and said to herself, directly he went (again from some book), "Lies, lies, lies!" For a party makes things either much more real, or much less real, she thought; she saw in a flash to the bottom of Robert Haydon's heart; she saw through everything. She saw the truth. *This* was true, this drawing-room, this self, and the other false. Miss Milan's little workroom was really terribly hot, stuffy, sordid. It smelt of clothes and cabbage cooking; and yet, when Miss Milan put the glass in her hand, and she looked at herself with the dress on, finished, an extraordinary bliss shot through her heart. Suffused with light, she sprang into existence. Rid of cares and wrinkles, what she had dreamed of herself was there — a beautiful woman. Just for a second (she had not dared look longer, Miss Milan wanted to know about the length of the skirt), there looked at her, framed in the scrolloping mahogany, a grey-white, mysteriously smiling, charming girl, the core of herself, the soul of herself; and it was not vanity only, not only self-love that made her think it good, tender, and true. Miss Milan said that the skirt could not well be longer; if anything the skirt, said Miss Milan, puckering her forehead, considering with all her wits about her, must be shorter; and she felt, suddenly, honestly, full of love for Miss Milan, much, much fonder of Miss Milan than of any one in the whole world, and could have cried for pity that she should be crawling on the floor with her mouth full of pins, and her face red and her eyes bulging — that one human being should be doing this for another, and she saw them all as human beings merely, and herself going off to her party, and Miss Milan pulling the cover over the canary's cage, or letting him pick a hemp-seed from between her lips, and the thought of it, of this side of human nature and its patience and its endurance and its being content with such miserable, scanty, sordid, little pleasures filled her eyes with tears.

And now the whole thing had vanished. The dress, the room, the love, the pity, the scrolloping looking-glass, and the canary's cage — all had vanished, and here she was in a corner of Mrs. Dalloway's drawing-room, suffering tortures, woken wide awake to reality.

But it was all so paltry, weak-blooded, and petty-minded to care so much at her age with two children, to be still so utterly dependent on people's opinions and not have principles or convictions, not to be able to say as other people did, "There's Shakespeare! There's death! We're all weevils in a captain's biscuit" — or whatever it was that people did say.

She faced herself straight in the glass; she pecked at her left shoulder; she issued out into the room, as if spears were thrown at her yellow dress from all sides. But instead of looking fierce or tragic, as Rose Shaw would have done — Rose would have looked like Boadicea — she looked foolish and self-conscious, and simpered like a schoolgirl and slouched across the room, positively slinking, as if she were a beaten mongrel, and looked at a picture, an engraving. As if one went to a party to look at a picture! Everybody knew why she did it — it was from shame, from humiliation.

"Now the fly's in the saucer," she said to herself, "right in the middle, and can't get out, and the milk," she thought, rigidly staring at the picture, "is sticking its wings together."

"It's so old-fashioned," she said to Charles Burt, making him stop (which by itself he hated) on his way to talk to some one else.

She meant, or she tried to make herself think that she meant, that it was the picture and not her dress, that was old-fashioned. And one word of praise, one word of affection from Charles would have made all the difference to her at the moment. If he had only said, "Mabel, you're looking charming to-night!" it would have changed her life. But then she ought to have been truthful and direct. Charles said nothing of the kind, of course. He was malice itself. He always saw through one, especially if one were feeling particularly mean, paltry, or feeble-minded.

"Mabel's got a new dress!" he said, and the poor fly was absolutely shoved into the middle of the saucer. Really, he would like her to drown, she believed. He had no heart, no fundamental kindness, only a veneer of friendliness. Miss Milan was much more real, much kinder. If only one could feel that and stick to it, always. "Why," she asked herself — replying to Charles much too pertly, letting him see that she was out of temper, or "ruffled" as he called it ("Rather ruffled?" he said and went on to laugh at her with some woman over there) — "Why," she asked herself, "can't I feel one thing always, feel quite sure that Miss Milan is right, and Charles wrong and stick to it, feel sure about the canary and pity and love and not be whipped all round in a second by coming into a room full of people?" It was her odious, weak, vacillating character again, always giving at the critical moment and not being seriously interested in conchology, etymology, botany, archeology, cutting up potatoes and watching them fructify like Mary Dennis, like Violet Searle.

Then Mrs. Holman, seeing her standing there, bore down upon her. Of course a thing like a dress was beneath Mrs. Holman's notice, with her family always tumbling downstairs or having the scarlet fever. Could Mabel tell her if Elmthorpe was ever let for August and September? Oh, it was a conversation that bored her unutterably! — it made her furious to be treated like a house agent or a messenger boy, to be made use of. Not to have value, that was it, she thought, trying to grasp something hard, something real, while she tried to answer sensibly about the bathroom and the south aspect and the hot water to the top of the house; and all the time she could see little bits of her yellow dress in the round looking-glass which made them all the size of boot-buttons or tadpoles; and it was amazing to think how much humiliation and agony and self-loathing and effort and passionate ups and downs of feeling were contained in a thing the size of a threepenny bit. And what was still odder, this thing, this Mabel Waring, was separate, quite disconnected; and though Mrs. Holman (the black button) was leaning forward and telling her how her eldest boy had strained his heart running, she could see her, too, quite detached in the looking-glass, and it was impossible that the black dot, leaning forward, gesticulating, should make the yellow dot, sitting solitary, self-centred, feel what the black dot was feeling, yet they pretended.

"So impossible to keep boys quiet" — that was the kind of thing one said.

And Mrs. Holman, who could never get enough sympathy and snatched what little there was greedily, as if it were her right (but she deserved much more for there was her little girl who had come down this morning with a swollen knee-joint), took this miserable offering and looked at it suspiciously, grudgingly, as if it were a halfpenny when it ought to have been a pound and put it away in her purse, must put up with it, mean and miserly though it was, times being hard, so very hard; and on she went, creaking, injured Mrs. Holman, about the girl with the swollen joints. Ah, it was tragic, this greed, this clamour of human beings, like a row of cormorants, barking and flapping their wings for sympathy — it was tragic, could one have felt it and not merely pretended to feel it!

But in her yellow dress to-night she could not wring out one drop more; she wanted it all, all for herself. She knew (she kept on looking into the glass, dipping into that dreadfully showing-up blue pool) that she was condemned, despised, left like this in a backwater, because of her being like this a feeble, vacillating creature; and it seemed to her that the yellow dress was a penance which she had deserved, and if she had been dressed like Rose Shaw, in lovely, clinging green with a ruffle of swansdown, she would have deserved that; and she thought that there was no escape for her — none whatever. But it was not her fault altogether, after all. It was being one of a family of ten; never having money enough, always skimping and paring; and her mother carrying great cans, and the linoleum worn on the stair edges, and one sordid little domestic tragedy after another — nothing catastrophic, the sheep farm failing, but not utterly; her eldest brother marrying beneath him but not very much — there was no romance, nothing extreme about them all. They petered out respectably in seaside resorts; every watering-place had one of her aunts even now asleep in some lodging with the front windows not quite facing the sea. That was so like them — they had to to squint at things always. And she had done the same — she was just like her aunts. For all her dreams of living in India, married to some hero like Sir Henry Lawrence, some empire builder (still the sight of a native in a turban filled her with romance), she had failed utterly. She had married Hubert, with his safe, permanent underling's job in the Law Courts, and they managed tolerably in a smallish house, without proper maids, and hash when she was alone or just bread and butter, but now and then — Mrs. Holman was off, thinking her the most dried-up, unsympathetic twig she had ever met, absurdly dressed, too, and would tell every one about Mabel's fantastic appearance — now and then, thought Mabel Waring, left alone on the blue sofa, punching the cushion in order to look occupied, for she would not join Charles Burt and Rose Shaw, chattering like magpies and perhaps laughing at her by the fireplace — now and then, there did come to her delicious moments, reading the other night in bed, for instance, or down by the sea on the sand in the sun, at Easter — let her recall it — a great tuft of pale sand-grass standing all twisted like a shock of spears against the sky, which was blue like a smooth china egg, so firm, so hard, and then the melody of the waves — "Hush, hush," they said, and the children's shouts paddling — yes, it was a divine moment, and there she lay, she felt, in the hand of the Goddess who was the world; rather a hard-hearted, but very beautiful Goddess, a little lamb laid on the alter (one did think these silly things, and it didn't matter so long as one never said them). And also with Hubert sometimes she had quite unexpectedly — carving the mutton for Sunday lunch, for no reason, opening a letter, coming into a room — divine moments, when she said to herself (for she would never say this to anybody else), "This is it. This has happened. This is it!" And the other way about it was equally surprising — that is, when everything was arranged — music, weather, holidays, every reason for happiness was there — then nothing happened at all. One wasn't happy. It was flat, just flat, that was all.

Her wretched self again, no doubt! She had always been a fretful, weak, unsatisfactory mother, a wobbly wife, lolling about in a kind of twilight existence with nothing very clear or very bold, or more one thing than other, like all her brothers and sisters, except perhaps Herbert — they were all the same poor water-veined creatures who did nothing. Then in the midst of this creeping, crawling life, suddenly she was on the crest of a wave. That wretched fly — where had she read the story that kept coming into her mind about the fly and the saucer? — struggled out. Yes, she had those moments. But now that she was forty, they might come more and more seldom. By degrees she would cease to struggle any more. But that was deplorable! That was not to be endured! That made her feel ashamed of herself!

She would go to the London Library to-morrow. She would find some wonderful, helpful, astonishing book, quite by chance, a book by a clergyman, by an American no one had ever heard of; or she would walk down the Strand and drop, accidentally, into a hall where a miner was telling about the life in the pit, and suddenly she would become a new person. She would be absolutely transformed. She would wear a uniform; she would be called Sister Somebody; she would never give a thought to clothes again. And for ever after she would be perfectly clear about Charles Burt and Miss Milan and this room and that room; and it would be always, day after day, as if she were lying in the sun or carving the mutton. It would be it!

So she got up from the blue sofa, and the yellow button in the looking-glass got up too, and she waved her hand to Charles and Rose to show them she did not depend on them one scrap, and the yellow button moved out of the looking-glass, and all the spears were gathered into her breast as she walked towards Mrs. Dalloway and said, "Good night."

"But it's too early to go," said Mrs. Dalloway, who was always so charming.

"I'm afraid I must," said Mabel Waring. "But," she added in her weak, wobbly voice which only sounded ridiculous when she tried to strengthen it, "I have enjoyed myself enormously."

"I have enjoyed myself," she said to Mr. Dalloway, whom she met on the stairs.

"Lies, lies, lies!" she said to herself, going downstairs, and "Right in the saucer!" she said to herself as she thanked Mrs. Barnet for helping her and wrapped herself, round and round and round, in the Chinese cloak she had worn these twenty years.

RICHARD WRIGHT

The Man Who Was Almost a Man

Dave struck out across the fields, looking homeward through paling light. Whut's the use talking wid em niggers in the field? Anyhow, his mother was putting supper on the table. Them niggers can't understan nothing. One of these days he was going to get a gun and practice shooting, then they couldn't talk to him as though he were a little boy. He slowed, looking at the ground. Shucks, Ah ain scareda them even ef they are biggern me! Aw, Ah know whut Ahma do. Ahm going by ol Joe's sto n git that Sears Roebuck catlog n look at them guns. Mebbe Ma will lemme buy one when she gits mah pay from ol man Hawkins. Ahma beg her t gimme some money. Ahm ol ernough to hava gun. Ahm seventeen. Almost a man. He strode, feeling his long loose-jointed limbs. Shucks, a man oughta hava little gun aftah he done worked hard all day.

He came in sight of Joe's store. A yellow lantern glowed on the front porch. He mounted steps and went through the screen door, hearing it bang behind him. There was a strong smell of coal oil and mackerel fish. He felt very confident until he saw fat Joe walk in through the rear door, then his courage began to ooze.

"Howdy, Dave! Whutcha want?"

"How yuh, Mistah Joe? Aw, Ah don wanna buy nothing. Ah jus wanted t see ef yuhd lemme look at tha catlog erwhile."

"Sure! You wanna see it here?"

"Nawsuh. Ah wans t take it home wid me. Ah'll bring it back termorrow when Ah come in from the fiels."

"You plannin on buying something?"

"Yessuh."

"Your ma lettin you have your own money now?"

"Shucks. Mistah Joe, Ahm gittin t be a man like anybody else!"

Joe laughed and wiped his greasy white face with a red bandanna.

"Whut you plannin on buyin?"

Dave looked at the floor, scratched his head, scratched his thigh, and smiled. Then he looked up shyly.

"Ah'll tell yuh, Mistah Joe, ef yuh promise yuh won't tell."

"I promise."

"Waal, Ahma buy a gun."

"A gun? Whut you want with a gun?"

"Ah wanna keep it."

"You ain't nothing but a boy. You don't need a gun."

"Aw, lemme have the catlog, Mistah Joe. Ah'll bring it back."

Joe walked through the rear door. Dave was elated. He looked around at barrels of sugar and flour. He heard Joe coming back. He craned his neck to see if he were bringing the book. Yeah, he's got it. Gawddog, he's got it!

"Here, but be sure you bring it back. It's the only one I got."

"Sho, Mistah Joe."

"Say, if you wanna buy a gun, why don't you buy one from me? I gotta gun to sell."

"Will it shoot?"

"Sure it'll shoot."

"Whut kind is it?"

"Oh, it's kinda old ... a left-hand Wheeler. A pistol. A big one."

"Is it got bullets in it?"

"It's loaded."

"Kin Ah see it?"

"Where's your money?"

"Whut yuh wan fer it?"

"I'll let you have it for two dollars."

"Just two dollahs? Shucks, Ah could buy tha when Ah git mah pay."

"I'll have it here when you want it."

"Awright, suh. Ah be in fer it."

He went through the door, hearing it slam again behind him. Ahma git some money from Ma n buy me a gun! Only two dollahs! He tucked the thick catalogue under his arm and hurried.

"Where yuh been, boy?" His mother held a steaming dish of black-eyed peas.

"Aw, Ma, Ah jus stopped down the road t talk wid the boys."

"Yuh know bettah t keep suppah waitin."

He sat down, resting the catalogue on the edge of the table.

"Yuh git up from there and git to the well n wash yoself! Ah ain feedin no hogs in mah house!"

She grabbed his shoulder and pushed him. He stumbled out of the room, then came back to get the catalogue.

"Whut this?"

"Aw, Ma, it's jusa catlog."

"Who yuh git it from?"

"From Joe, down at the sto."

"Waal, thas good. We kin use it in the outhouse."

"Naw, Ma." He grabbed for it. "Gimme ma catlog, Ma."

She held onto it and glared at him.

"Quit hollerin at me! Whut's wrong wid yuh? Yuh crazy?"

"But Ma, please. It ain mine! It's Joe's! He tol me t bring it back t im termorrow."

She gave up the book. He stumbled down the back steps, hugging the thick book under his arm. When he had splashed water on his face and hands, he groped back to the kitchen and fumbled in a corner for the towel. He bumped into a chair; it clattered to the floor. The catalogue sprawled at his feet. When he had dried his eyes he snatched up the book and held it again under his arm. His mother stood watching him.

"Now, ef yuh gonna act a fool over that ol book, Ah'll take it n burn it up."

"Naw, Ma, please."

"Waal, set down n be still!"

He sat down and drew the oil lamp close. He thumbed page after page, unaware of the food his mother set on the table. His father came in. Then his small brother.

"Whutcha got there, Dave? his father asked.

"Jusa catlog," he answered, not looking up.

"Yeah, here they is!" His eyes glowed at blue-and-black revolvers. He glanced up, feeling sudden guilt. His father was watching him. He eased the book under the table and rested it on his knees. After the blessing was asked, he ate. He scooped up peas and swallowed fat meat without chewing. Buttermilk helped to wash it down. He did not want to mention money before his father. He would do much better by cornering his mother when she was alone. He looked at his father uneasily out of the edge of his eye.

"Boy, how come yuh don quit foolin wid tha book n eat yo suppah?"

"Yessuh."

"How you n ol man Hawkins gitten erlong?"

"Suh?"

"Can't yuh hear? Why don yuh lissen? Ah ast yu how wuz yuh n ol man Hawkins gittin erlong?"

"Oh, swell, Pa. Ah plows mo lan than anybody over there."

"Waal, yuh oughta keep yo mind on whut yuh doin."

"Yessuh."

He poured his plate full of molasses and sopped it up slowly with a chunk of cornbread. When his father and brother had left the kitchen, he still sat and looked again at the guns in the catalogue, longing to muster courage enough to present his case to his mother. Lawd, ef Ah only had tha pretty one! He could almost feel the slickness of the weapon with his fingers. If he had a gun like that he would polish it and keep it shining so it would never rust. N Ah'd keep it loaded, by Gawd!

"Ma?" His voice was hesitant.

"Hunh?"

"Ol man Hawkins give yuh mah money yit?"

"Yeah, but ain no usa yuh thinking bout throwin nona it erway. Ahm keepin tha money sos yuh kin have cloes t go to school this winter."

He rose and went to her side with the open catalogue in his palms. She was washing dishes, her head bent low over a pan. Shyly he raised the book. When he spoke, his voice was husky, faint.

"Ma, Gawd knows Ah wans one of these."

"One of whut?" she asked, not raising her eyes.

"One of these," he said again, not daring even to point. She glanced up at the page, then at him with wide eyes.

"Nigger, is yuh gone plumb crazy?"

"Aw, Ma —"

"Git outta here! Don yuh talk t me bout no gun! Yuh a fool!"

"Ma, Ah kin buy one fer two dollahs."

"Not ef Ah knows it, yuh ain!"

"But yuh promised me one —"

"Ah don care whut Ah promised! Yuh ain nothing but a boy yit!"

"Ma, ef yuh lemme buy one Ah'll *never* ast yuh fer nothing no mo."

"Ah tol yuh t git outta here! Yuh ain gonna toucha penny of tha money fer no gun! Thas how come Ah has Mistah Hawkins t pay yo wages t me, cause Ah knows yuh ain got no sense."

"But, Ma, we needa gun. Pa ain got no gun. We needa gun in the house. Yuh kin never tell whut might happen."

"Now don yuh try to maka fool outta me, boy! Ef we did hava gun, yuh wouldn't have it!"

He laid the catalogue down and slipped his arm around her waist.

"Aw, Ma, Ah done worked hard alla summer n ain ast yuh fer nothin, is Ah, now?"

"Thas whut yuh spose t do!"

"But Ma, Ah wans a gun. Yuh kin lemme have two dollahs outta mah money. Please, Ma. I kin give it to Pa ... Please, Ma! Ah loves yuh, Ma."

When she spoke her voice came soft and low.

"Whut yu wan wida gun, Dave? Yuh don need no gun. Yuh'll git in trouble. N ef yo pa jus thought Ah let yuh have money t buy a gun he'd hava fit."

"Ah'll hide it, Ma. It ain but two dollahs."

"Lawd, chil, whut's wrong wid yuh?"

"Ain nothin wrong, Ma. Ahm almos a man now. Ah wans a gun."

"Who gonna sell yuh a gun?"

"Ol Joe at the sto."

"N it don cos but two dollahs?"

"Thas all, Ma. Jus two dollahs. Please, Ma."

She was stacking the plates away; her hands moved slowly, reflectively. Dave kept an anxious silence. Finally, she turned to him.

"Ah'll let yuh git that gun ef yuh promise me one thing."

"Whut's tha, Ma?"

"Yuh bring it straight back t me, yuh hear? It be fer Pa."

"Yessum! Lemme go now, Ma."

She stooped, turned slightly to one side, raised the hem of her dress, rolled down the top of her stocking, and came up with a slender wad of bills.

"Here," she said. "Lawd knows yuh don need no gun. But yer pa does. Yuh bring it right back t me, yuh hear? Ahma put it up. Now ef yuh don, Ahma have yuh pa lick yuh so hard yuh won fergit it."

"Yessum."

He took the money, ran down the steps, and across the yard.

"Dave! Yuuuuuh Daaaaave!"

He heard, but he was not going to stop now. "Naw, Lawd!"

The first movement he made the following morning was to reach under his pillow for the gun. In the gray light of dawn he held it loosely, feeling a sense of power. Could kill a man with a gun like this. Kill anybody, black or white. And if he were holding his gun in his hand, nobody could run over him; they would have to respect him. It was a big gun, with a long barrel and a heavy handle. He raised and lowered it in his hand, marveling at its weight.

He had not come straight home with it as his mother had asked; instead he had stayed out in the fields, holding the weapon in his hand, aiming it now and then at some imaginary foe. But he had not fired it; he had been afraid that his father might hear. Also he was not sure he knew how to fire it.

To avoid surrendering the pistol he had not come into the house until he knew that they were all asleep. When his mother had tiptoed to his bedside late that night and demanded the gun, he had first played possum; then he had told her that the gun was hidden outdoors, that he would bring it to her in the morning. Now he lay turning it slowly in his hands. He broke it, took out the cartridges, felt them, and then put them back.

He slid out of bed, got a long strip of old flannel from a trunk, wrapped the gun in it, and tied it to his naked thigh while it was still loaded. He did not go in to breakfast. Even though it was not yet daylight, he started for Jim Hawkins' plantation. Just as the sun was rising he reached the barns where the mules and plows were kept.

"Hey! That you, Dave?"

He turned. Jim Hawkins stood eying him suspiciously.

"What're yuh doing here so early?"

"Ah didn't know Ah wuz gittin up so early, Mistah Hawkins. Ah wuz fixin t hitch up ol Jenny n take her t the fiels."

"Good. Since you're so early, how about plowing that stretch down by the woods?"

"Suits me, Mistah Hawkins."

"O.K. Go to it!"

He hitched Jenny to a plow and started across the fields. Hot dog! This was just what he wanted. If he could get down by the woods, he could shoot his gun and nobody would hear. He walked behind the plow, hearing the traces creaking, feeling the gun tied tight to his thigh.

When he reached the woods, he plowed two whole rows before he decided to take out the gun. Finally, he stopped, looked in all directions, then untied the gun and held it in his hand. He turned to the mule and smiled.

"Know whut this is, Jenny? Naw, yuh wouldn know! Yuhs jusa ol mule! Anyhow, this is a gun, n it kin shoot, by Gawd!"

He held the gun at arm's length. Whut t hell, Ahma shoot this thing! He looked at Jenny again. "Lissen here, Jenny! When Ah pull this ol trigger, Ah don wan yuh t run n acka fool now!"

Jenny stood with head down, her short ears pricked straight. Dave walked off about twenty feet, held the gun far out from him at arm's length, and turned his head. Hell, he told himself, Ah ain afraid. The gun felt loose in his fingers; he waved it wildly for a moment. Then he shut his eyes and tightened his forefinger. Bloom! A report half deafened him and he thought his right hand was torn from his arm. He heard Jenny whinnying and galloping over the field, and he found himself on his knees, squeezing his fingers hard between his legs. His hand was numb; he jammed it into his mouth, trying to warm it, trying to stop the pain. The gun lay at his feet. He did not quite know what had happened. He stood up and stared at the gun as though it were a living thing. He gritted his teeth and kicked the gun. Yuh almos broke mah arm! He turned to look for Jenny; she was far over the fields, tossing her head and kicking wildly.

"Hol on there, ol mule!"

When he caught up with her she stood trembling, walling her big white eyes at him. The plow was far away; the traces had broken. Then Dave stopped short, looking, not believing. Jenny was bleeding. Her left side was red and wet with blood. He went closer. Lawd, have mercy! Wondah did Ah shoot this mule? He grabbed for Jenny's mane. She flinched, snorted, whirled, tossing her head.

"Hol on now! Hol on."

Then he saw the hole in Jenny's side, right between the ribs. It was round, wet red. A crimson stream streaked down the front leg, flowing fast. Good Gawd! Ah wuzn't shootin at tha mule. He felt panic. He knew he had to stop that blood, or Jenny would bleed to death. He had never seen so much blood in all his life. He chased the mule for half a mile, trying to catch her. Finally she stopped, breathing hard, stumpy tail half arched.

He caught her mane and led her back to where the plough and gun lay. Then he stooped and grabbed handfuls of damp black earth and tried to plug the bullet hole. Jenny shuddered, whinnied, and broke from him.

"Hol on! Hol on now!"

He tried to plug it again, but blood came anyhow. His fingers were hot and sticky. He rubbed dirt into his palms, trying to dry them. Then again he attempted to plug the bullet hole, but Jenny shied away, kicking her heels high. He stood helpless. He had to do something. He ran at Jenny; she dodged him. He watched a red stream of blood flow down Jenny's leg and form a bright pool at her feet.

"Jenny ... Jenny," he called weakly.

His lips trembled. She's bleeding t death! He looked in the direction of home, wanting to go back, wanting to get help. But he saw the pistol lying in the damp black clay. He had a queer feeling that if he only did something, this would not be; Jenny would not be there bleeding to death.

When he went to her this time, she did not move. She stood with sleepy, dreamy eyes; and when he touched her she gave a low-pitched whinny and knelt to the ground, her front knees slopping in blood.

"Jenny ... Jenny ..." he whispered.

For a long time she held her neck erect; then her head sank, slowly. Her ribs swelled with a mighty heave and she went over.

Dave's stomach felt empty, very empty. He picked up the gun and held it gingerly between his thumb and forefinger. He buried it at the foot of a tree. He took a stick and tried to cover the pool of blood with dirt — but what was the use? There was Jenny lying with her mouth open and her eyes walled and glassy. He could not tell Jim Hawkins he had shot his mule. But he had to tell something. Yeah, Ah'll tell em Jenny started gittin wil n fell on the joint of the plow.... But that would hardly happen to a mule. He walked across the field slowly, head down.

It was sunset. Two of Jim Hawkins' men were over near the edge of the woods digging a hole in which to bury Jenny. Dave was surrounded by a knot of people, all of whom were looking down at the dead mule.

"I don't see how in the world it happened," said Jim Hawkins for the tenth time.

The crowd parted and Dave's mother, father, and small brother pushed into the center.

"Where Dave?" his mother called.

"There he is," said Jim Hawkins.

His mother grabbed him.

"Whut happened, Dave? Whut yuh done?"

"Nothin."

"C mon, boy, talk," his father said.

Dave took a deep breath and told the story he knew nobody believed.

"Waal," he drawled. "Ah brung ol Jenny down here sos Ah could do mah plowin. Ah plowed bout two rows, just like yuh see." He stopped and pointed at the long rows of upturned earth. "Then somethin musta been wrong wid ol Jenny. She wouldn ack right a-tall. She started snortin n kickin her heels. Ah tried t hol her, but she pulled erway, rearin n goin in. Then when the point of the plow was sticking up in the air, she swung erroun n twisted herself back on it ... She stuck herself n started t bleed. N fo Ah could do anything, she wuz dead."

"Did you ever hear of anything like that in all your life?" asked Jim Hawkins.

There were white and black standing in the crowd. They murmured. Dave's mother came close to him and looked hard into his face. "Tell the truth, Dave," she said.

"Looks like a bullet hole to me," said one man.

"Dave, whut yuh do wid the gun?" his mother asked.

The crowd surged in, looking at him. He jammed his hands into his pockets, shook his head slowly from left to right, and backed away. His eyes were wide and painful.

"Did he hava gun?" asked Jim Hawkins.

"By Gawd, Ah tol yuh tha wuz a gun wound," said a man, slapping his thigh.

His father caught his shoulders and shook him till his teeth rattled.

"Tell whut happened, yuh rascal! Tell whut ..."

Dave looked at Jenny's stiff legs and began to cry.

"Whut yuh do wid tha gun?" his mother asked.

"Whut wuz he doin wida gun?" his father asked.

"Come on and tell the truth," said Hawkins. "Ain't nobody going to hurt you ..."

His mother crowded close to him.

"Did yuh shoot tha mule, Dave?"

Dave cried, seeing blurred white and black faces.

"Ahh ddinn gggo tt sshooot hher ... Ah ssswear ffo Gawd Ahh ddin.... Ah wuz a-tryin t sssee ef the old gggun would sshoot —"

"Where yuh git the gun from?" his father asked.

"Ah got it from Joe, at the sto."

"Where yuh git the money?"

"Ma give it t me."

"He kept worryin me, Bob. Ah had t. Ah tol im t bring the gun right back t me ... It was fer yuh, the gun."

"But how yuh happen to shoot that mule?" asked Jim Hawkins.

"Ah wuzn shootin at the mule, Mistah Hawkins. The gun jumped when Ah pulled the trigger ... N fo Ah knowed anythin Jenny was there a-bleedin."

Somebody in the crowd laughed. Jim Hawkins walked close to Dave and looked into his face.

"Well, looks like you have bought you a mule, Dave."

"Ah swear fo Gawd, Ah didn go t kill the mule, Mistah Hawkins!"

"But you killed her!"

All the crowd was laughing now. They stood on tiptoe and poked heads over one another's shoulders.

"Well, boy, looks like yuh done bought a dead mule! Hahaha!"

"Ain tha ershame."

"Hohohohoho."

Dave stood, head down, twisting his feet in the dirt.

"Well, you needn't worry about it, Bob," said Jim Hawkins to Dave's father. "Just let the boy keep on working and pay me two dollars a month."

"Whut yuh wan fer yo mule, Mistah Hawkins?"

Jim Hawkins screwed up his eyes.

"Fifty dollars."

"Whut yuh do wid tha gun?" Dave's father demanded.

Dave said nothing.

"Yuh wan me t take a tree n beat yuh till yuh talk!"

"Nawsuh!"

"Whut yuh do wid it?"

"Ah throwed it erway."

"Where?"

"Ah ... Ah throwed it in the creek."

"Waal, c mon home. N firs thing in the mawnin git to tha creek n fin tha gun."

"Yessuh."

"Whut yuh pay fer it?"

"Two dollahs."

"Take tha gun n git yo money back n carry it t Mistah Hawkins, yuh hear? N don fergit Ahma lam you black bottom good fer this! Now march yosef on home, suh!"

Dave turned and walked slowly. He heard people laughing. Dave glared, his eyes welling with tears. Hot anger bubbled in him. Then he swallowed and stumbled on.

That night Dave did not sleep. He was glad that he had gotten out of killing the mule so easily, but he was hurt. Something hot seemed to turn over inside him each time he remembered how they had laughed. He tossed on his bed, feeling his hard pillow. N Pa says he's gonna beat me ... He remembered other beatings, and his back quivered. Naw, naw, Ah sho don wan im t beat me tha way no mo. Dam em all! Nobody ever gave him anything. All he did was work. They treat me like a mule, n then they beat me. He gritted his teeth. N Ma had t tell on me.

Well, if he had to, he would take old man Hawkins that two dollars. But that meant selling the gun. And he wanted to keep that gun. Fifty dollars for a dead mule.

He turned over, thinking how he had fired the gun. He had an itch to fire it again. Ef other men kin shoota gun, by Gawd, Ah kin! He was still, listening. Mebbe they all sleepin now. The house was still. He heard the soft breathing of his brother. Yes, now! He would go down and get that gun and see if he could fire it! He eased out of bed and slipped into overalls.

The moon was bright. He ran almost all the way to the edge of the woods. He stumbled over the ground, looking for the spot where he had buried the gun. Yeah, here it is. Like a hungry dog scratching for a bone, he pawed it up. He puffed his black cheeks and blew dirt from the trigger and barrel. He broke it and found four cartridges unshot. He looked around; the fields were filled with silence and moonlight. He clutched the gun stiff and hard in his fingers. But, as soon as he wanted to pull the trigger, he shut his eyes and turned his head. Naw, Ah can't shoot wid mah eyes closed n mah head turned. With effort he held his eyes open; then he squeezed. *Blooooom!* He was stiff, not breathing. The gun was still in his hands. Dammit, he'd done it! He fired again. *Blooooom!* He smiled. *Blooooom! Blooooom! Click, click.* There! It was empty. If anybody could shoot a gun, he could. He put the gun into his hip pocket and started across the fields.

When he reached the top of a ridge he stood straight and proud in the moonlight, looking at Jim Hawkins' big white house, feeling the gun sagging in his pocket. Lawd, ef Ah had just one mo bullet Ah'd taka shot at tha house. Ah'd like t scare ol man Hawkins jusa little ... Jusa enough t let im know Dave Saunders is a man.

To his left the road curved, running to the tracks of the Illinois Central. He jerked his head, listening. From far off came a faint *hoooof-hoooof; hoooof-hoooof; hoooof-hoooof*.... He stood rigid. Two dollahs a mont. Les see now ... Tha means it'll take bout two years. Shucks! Ah'll be dam!

He started down the road, toward the tracks. Yeah, here she comes! He stood beside the track and held himself stiffly. Here she comes, erroun the ben ... C mon, yuh slow poke! C mon! He had his hand on his gun; something quivered in his stomach. Then the train thundered past, the gray and brown box cars rumbling and clinking. He gripped the gun tightly; then he jerked his hand out of his pocket. Ah betcha Bill wouldn't do it! Ah betcha ... The cars slid past, steel grinding upon steel. Ahm ridin yuh ternight, so hep me Gawd! He was hot all over. He hesitated just a moment; then he grabbed, pulled atop of a car, and lay flat. He felt his pocket; the gun was still there. Ahead the long rails were glinting in the moonlight, stretching away, away to somewhere, somewhere where he could be a man ...

Novellas

JOSEPH CONRAD

Heart of Darkness

The *Nellie*, a cruising yawl, swung to her anchor without a flutter of the sails, and was at rest. The flood had made, the wind was nearly calm, and being bound down the river, the only thing for it was to come to and wait for the turn of the tide.

The sea-reach of the Thames stretched before us like the beginning of an interminable waterway. In the offing the sea and the sky were welded together without a joint, and in the luminous space the tanned sails of the barges drifting up with the tide seemed to stand still in red clusters of canvas sharply peaked, with gleams of varnished spirits. A haze rested on the low shores that ran out to sea in vanishing flatness. The air was dark above Gravesend, and farther back still seemed condensed into a mournful gloom, brooding motionless over the biggest, and the greatest, town on earth.

The Director of Companies was our captain and our host. We four affectionately watched his back as he stood in the bows looking to seaward. On the whole river there was nothing that looked half so nautical. He resembled a pilot, which to a seaman is trustworthiness personified. It was difficult to realize his work was not out there in the luminous estuary, but behind him, within the brooding gloom.

Between us there was, as I have already said somewhere, the bond of the sea. Besides holding our hearts together through long periods of separation, it had the effect of making us tolerant of each other's yarns — and even convictions. The lawyer — the best of old fellows — had, because of his many years and many virtues, the only cushion on deck, and was lying on the only rug. The accountant had brought out already a box of dominoes, and was toying architecturally with the bones. Marlow sat cross-legged right aft, leaning against the mizzenmast. He had sunken cheeks, a yellow complexion, a straight back, an ascetic aspect, and, with his arms dropped, the palms of hands outwards, resembled an idol. The director, satisfied the anchor had good hold, made his way aft and sat down amongst us. We exchanged a few words lazily. Afterwards there was silence on board the yacht. For some reason or other we did not begin that game of dominoes. We felt meditative, and fit for nothing but placid staring. The day was ending in a serenity of still and exquisite brilliance. The water shone pacifically; the sky, without a speck, was a benign immensity of unstained light; the very mist on the Essex marshes was like a gauzy and radiant fabric, hung from the wooded rises inland, and draping the low shores in diaphanous folds. Only the gloom to the west, brooding over the upper reaches, became more somber every minute, as if angered by the approach of the sun.

And at last, in its curved and imperceptible fall, the sun sank low, and from glowing white changed to a dull red without rays and without heat, as if about to go out suddenly, stricken to death by the touch of that gloom brooding over a crowd of men.

Forthwith a change came over the waters, and the serenity became less brilliant but more profound. The old river in its broad reach rested unruffled at the decline of day, after ages of good service done to the race that peopled its banks, spread out in the tranquil dignity of a waterway leading to the uttermost ends of the earth. We looked at the venerable stream not in the vivid flush of a short day that comes and departs forever, but in the august light of abiding memories. And indeed nothing is easier for a man who has, as the phrase goes, "followed the sea" with reverence and affection, than to evoke the great spirit of the past upon the lower reaches of the Thames. The tidal current runs to and fro in its unceasing service, crowded with memories of men and ships it had borne to the rest of home or to the battles of the sea. It had known and served all the men of whom the nation is proud, from Sir Francis Drake to Sir John Franklin, knights all, titled and untitled — the great knights-errant of the sea. It had borne all the ships whose names are like jewels flashing in the night of time, from the *Golden Hind* returning with her round flanks full of treasure, to be visited by the Queen's Highness and thus pass out of the gigantic tale, to the *Erebus* and *Terror*, bound on other conquests — and that never returned. It had known the ships and the men. They had sailed from Deptford, from Greenwich, from Erith — the adventurers and the settlers; kings' ships and the ships of men on 'Change; captains, admirals, the dark "interlopers" of the Eastern trade, and the commissioned "generals" of East India fleets. Hunters for gold or pursuers of fame, they all had gone out on that stream, bearing the sword, and often the torch, messengers of the might within the land, bearers of a spark from the sacred fire. What greatness had not floated on the ebb of that river into the mystery of an unknown earth! . . . The dreams of men, the seed of commonwealths, the germs of empires.

The sun set; the dusk fell on the stream, and lights began to appear along the shore. The Chapman lighthouse, a three-legged thing erect on a mud-flat, shone strongly. Lights of ships moved in the fairway — a great stir of lights going up and going down. And farther west on the upper reaches the place of the monstrous town was still marked ominously on the sky, a brooding gloom in sunshine, a lurid glare under the stars.

"And this also," said Marlow suddenly, "has been one of the dark places of the earth."

He was the only man of us who still "followed the sea." The worse that could be said of him was that he did not represent his class. He was a seaman, but he was a wanderer, too, while most seamen lead, if one may so express it, a sedentary life. Their minds are of the stay-at-home order, and their home is always with them — the ship; and so is their country — the sea. One ship is very much like another, and the sea is always the same. In the immutability of their surroundings the foreign shores, the foreign faces, the changing immensity of life, glide past, veiled not by a sense of mystery but by a slightly disdainful ignorance; for there is nothing mysterious to a seaman unless it be the sea itself, which is the mistress of his existence and as inscrutable as destiny. For the rest, after his hours of work, a casual stroll or a casual spree on shore suffices to unfold for him the secret of a whole continent, and generally he finds the secret not worth knowing. The yarns of seamen have a direct simplicity, the whole meaning of which lies within the shell of a cracked nut. But Marlow was not typical (if his propensity to spin yarns be excepted), and to him the meaning of an episode was not inside like a kernel but outside, enveloping the tale which brought it out only as a glow brings out a haze, in the likeness of one of these misty halos that sometimes are made visible by the spectral illumination of moonshine.

His remark did not seem at all surprising. It was just like Marlow. It was accepted in silence. No one took the trouble to grunt even; and presently he said, very slow:

"I was thinking of very old times, when the Romans first came here, nineteen hundred years ago — the other day. . . . Light came out of this river since — you say knights? Yes; but it is like a running blaze on a plain, like a flash of lightning in the clouds. We live in the flicker — may it last as long as the old earth keeps rolling! But darkness was here yesterday. Imagine the feelings of a commander of a fine — what d'ye call 'em? — trireme in the Mediterranean, ordered suddenly to the north; run overland across the Gauls in a hurry; put in charge of one of these craft the legionaries — a wonderful lot of handy men they must have been, too — used to build, apparently by the hundred, in a month or two, if we may believe what we read. Imagine him here — the very end of the world, a sea the color of lead, a sky the color of smoke, a kind of ship about as rigid as a concertina — and going up this river with stores, or orders, or what you like. Sandbanks, marshes, forests, savages — precious little to eat fit for a civilized man, nothing but Thames water to drink. No Falernian wine here, no going ashore. Here and there a military camp lost in a wilderness, like a needle in a bundle of hay — cold, fog, tempests, disease, exile, and death — death skulking in the air, in the water, in the bush. They must have been dying like flies here. Oh, yes — he did it. Did it very well, too, no doubt, and without thinking much about it either, except afterwards to brag of what he had gone through in his time, perhaps. They were men enough to face the darkness. And perhaps he was cheered by keeping his eye on a chance of promotion to the fleet at Ravenna by and by, if he had good friends in Rome and survived the awful climate. Or think of a decent young citizen in a toga — perhaps too much dice, you know — coming out here in the train of some prefect, or tax-gatherer, or trader even, to mend his fortunes. Land in a swamp, march through the woods, and in some inland post feel the savagery, the utter savagery, had closed round him — all that mysterious life of the wilderness that stirs in the forest, in the jungles, in the hearts of wild men. There's no initiation either into such mysteries. He has to live in the midst of the incomprehensible, which is also detestable. And it has a fascination, too, that goes to work upon him. The fascination of the abomination — you know, imagine the growing regrets, the longing to escape, the powerless disgust, the surrender, the hate."

He paused.

"Mind," he began again, lifting one arm from the elbow, the palm of the hand outwards, so that, with his legs folded before him, he had the pose of a Buddha preaching in European clothes and without a lotus flower — "Mind, none of us would feel exactly like this. What saves us is efficiency — the devotion to efficiency. But these chaps were not much account, really. They were no colonists; their administration was merely a squeeze, and nothing more, I suspect. They were conquerors, and for that you want only brute force — nothing to boast of, when you have it, since your strength is just an accident arising from the weakness of others. They grabbed what they could get for the sake of what was to be got. It was just robbery with violence, aggravated murder on a great scale, and men going at it blind — as is very proper for those who tackle a darkness. The conquest of the earth, which mostly means the taking it away from those who have a different complexion or slightly flatter noses than ourselves, is not a pretty thing when you look into it too much. What redeems it is the idea only. An idea at the back of it; not a sentimental pretence but an idea; and an unselfish belief in the idea — something you can set up, and bow down before, and offer a sacrifice to. . . ."

He broke off. Flames glided in the river, small green flames, red flames, white flames, pursuing, overtaking, joining, crossing each other — then separating slowly or hastily. The traffic of the great city went on in the deepening night upon the sleepless river. We looked on, waiting patiently — there was nothing else to do till the end of the flood; but it was only after a long silence, when he said, in a hesitating voice, "I suppose you fellows remember I did once turn fresh-water sailor for a bit," that we knew we were fated, before the ebb began to run, to hear about one of Marlow's inconclusive experiences.

"I don't want to bother you much with what happened to me personally," he began, showing in this remark the weakness of many tellers of tales who seem so often unaware of what their audience would best like to hear; "yet to understand the effect of it on me you ought to know how I got out there, what I saw, how I went up that river to the place where I first met the poor chap. It was the farthest point of navigation and the culminating point of my experience. It seemed somehow to throw a kind of light on everything about me — and into my thoughts. It was somber enough, too — and pitiful — not extraordinary in any way — not very clear either. No, not very clear. And yet it seemed to throw a kind of light.

"I had then, as you remember, just returned to London after a lot of Indian Ocean, Pacific, China Seas — a regular dose of the East — six years or so, and I was loafing about, hindering you fellows in your work and invading your homes, just as though I had got a heavenly mission to civilize you. It was very fine for a time, but after a bit I did get tired of resting. Then I began to look for a ship — I should think the hardest work on earth. But the ships wouldn't even look at me. And I got tired of that game, too.

"Now when I was a little chap I had a passion for maps. I would look for hours at South America, or Africa, or Australia, and lose myself in all the glories of exploration. At that time there were many blank spaces on the earth, and when I saw one that looked particularly inviting on a map (but they all look that) I would put my finger on it and say, 'When I grow up I will go there.' The North Pole was one of these places, I remember. Well, I haven't been there yet, and shall not try now. The glamor's off. Other places were scattered about the Equator, and in every sort of latitude all over the two hemispheres. I have been in some of them, and . . . well, we won't talk about that. But there was one yet — the biggest, the most blank, so to speak — that I had a hankering after.

"True, by this time it was not a blank space any more. It had got filled since my boyhood with rivers and lakes and names. It had ceased to be a blank space of delightful mystery — a white patch for a boy to dream gloriously over. It had become a place of darkness. But there was in it one river especially, a mighty big river, that you could see on the map, resembling an immense snake uncoiled, with its head in the sea, its body at rest curving afar over a vast country, and its tail lost in the depths of the land. And as I looked at the map of it in a shop window, it fascinated me as a snake would a bird — a silly little bird. Then I remembered there was a big concern, a company for trade on that river. Dash it all! I thought to myself, they can't trade without using some kind of craft on that lot of fresh water — steamboats! Why shouldn't I try to get charge of one? I went on along Fleet Street, but could not shake off the idea. The snake had charmed me.

"You understand it was a continental concern, that trading society; but I have a lot of relations living on the continent, because it's cheap and not so nasty as it looks, they say.

"I am sorry to own I began to worry them. This was already a fresh departure for me. I was not used to get things that way, you know. I always went my own road and on my own legs where I had a mind to go. I wouldn't have believed it of myself; but, then — you see — I felt somehow I must get there by hook or by crook. So I worried them. The men said 'My dear fellow,' and did nothing. Then — would you believe it? — I tried the women. I, Charlie Marlow, set the women to work — to get a job. Heavens! Well, you see, the notion drove me. I had an aunt, a dear enthusiastic soul. She wrote: 'It will be delightful. I am ready to do anything, anything for you. It is a glorious idea. I know the wife of a very high personage in the administration, and also a man who has lots of influence with,' etc., etc. She was determined to make no end of fuss to get me appointed skipper of a river steamboat, if such was my fancy.

"I got my appointment — of course; and I got it very quick. It appears the company had received news that one of their captains had been killed in a scuffle with the natives. This was my chance, and it made me the more anxious to go. It was only months and months afterwards, when I made the attempt to recover what was left of the body, that I heard the original quarrel arose from a misunderstanding about some hens. Yes, two black hens. Fresleven — that was the fellow's name, a Dane — thought himself wronged somehow in the bargain, so he went ashore and started to hammer the chief of the village with a stick. Oh, it didn't surprise me in the least to hear this, and at the same time to be told that Fresleven was the gentlest, quietest creature that ever walked on two legs. No doubt he was; but he had been a couple of years already out there engaged in the noble cause, you know, and he probably felt the need at last of asserting his self-respect in some way. Therefore he whacked the old nigger mercilessly, while a big crowd of his people watched him, thunderstruck, till some man — I was told the chief's son — in desperation at hearing the old chap yell, made a tentative jab with a spear at the white man — and of course it went quite easy between the shoulder blades. Then the whole population cleared into the forest, expecting all kinds of calamities to happen, while, on the other hand, the steamer Fresleven commanded left also in a bad panic, in charge of the engineer, I believe. Afterwards nobody seemed to trouble much about Fresleven's remains, till I got out and stepped into his shoes. I couldn't let it rest, though; but when an opportunity offered at last to meet my predecessor, the grass growing through his ribs was tall enough to hide his bones. They were all there. The supernatural being had not been touched after he fell. And the village was deserted, the huts gaped black, rotting, all askew within the fallen enclosures. A calamity had come to it, sure enough. The people had vanished. Mad terror had scattered them, men, women, and children, through the bush, and they had never returned. What became of the hens I don't know either. I should think the cause of progress got them, anyhow. However, through this glorious affair I got my appointment, before I had fairly begun to hope for it.

"I flew around like mad to get ready, and before forty-eight hours I was crossing the Channel to show myself to my employers, and sign the contract. In a very few hours I arrived in a city that always makes me think of a whited sepulcher. Prejudice no doubt. I had no difficulty in finding the company's offices. It was the biggest thing in the town, and everybody I met was full of it. They were going to run an oversea empire, and make no end of coin by trade.

"A narrow and deserted street in deep shadow, high houses, innumerable windows with venetian blinds, a dead silence, grass sprouting between the stones, imposing carriage archways right and left, immense double doors standing ponderously ajar. I slipped through one of these cracks, went up a swept and ungarnished staircase, as arid as a desert, and opened the first door I came to. Two women, one fat and the other slim, sat on straw-bottomed chairs, knitting black wool. The slim one got up and walked straight at me — still knitting with downcast eyes — and only just as I began to think of getting out of her way, as you would for a somnambulist, stood still, and looked up. Her dress was as plain as an umbrella-cover, and she turned round without a word and preceded me into a waiting room. I gave my name, and looked about. Deal table in the middle, plain chairs all round the walls, on one end a large shining map, marked with all the colors of a rainbow. There was a vast amount of red — good to see at any time, because one knows that some real work is done in there, a deuce of a lot of blue, a little green, smears of orange, and, on the East Coast, a purple patch, to show where the jolly pioneers of progress drink the jolly lager beer. However, I wasn't going into any of these. I was going into the yellow. Dead in the center. And the river was there — fascinating — deadly — like a snake. Ough! A door opened, a white-haired secretarial head, but wearing a compassionate expression, appeared, and a skinny forefinger beckoned me into the sanctuary. Its light was dim, and a heavy writing desk squatted in the middle. From behind that structure came out an impression of pale plumpness in a frock coat. The great man himself. He was five feet six, I should judge, and had his grip on the handle-end of ever so many millions. He shook hands, I fancy, murmured vaguely, was satisfied with my French. *Bon voyage.*

"In about forty-five seconds I found myself again in the waiting room with the compassionate secretary, who, full of desolation and sympathy, made me sign some document. I believe I undertook amongst other things not to disclose any trade secrets. Well, I am not going to.

"I began to feel slightly uneasy. You know I am not used to such ceremonies, and there was something ominous in the atmosphere. It was just as though I had been let into some conspiracy — I don't know — something not quite right; and I was glad to get out. In the outer room the two women knitted black wool feverishly. People were arriving, and the younger one was walking back and forth introducing them. The old one sat on her chair. Her flat cloth slippers were propped up on a foot-warmer, and a cat reposed on her lap. She wore a starched white affair on her head, had a wart on one cheek, and silver-rimmed spectacles hung on the tip of her nose. She glanced at me above the glasses. The swift and indifferent placidity of that look troubled me. Two youths with foolish and cheery countenances were being piloted over, and she threw at them the same quick glance of unconcerned wisdom. She seemed to know all about them and about me, too. An eerie feeling came over me. She seemed uncanny and fateful. Often far away there I thought of these two, guarding the door of darkness, knitting black wool as for a warm pall, one introducing, introducing continuously to the unknown, the other scrutinizing the cheery and foolish faces with unconcerned old eyes. *Ave!* Old knitter of black wool. *Morituri te salutant.* Not many of those she looked at ever saw her again — not half, by a long way.

"There was yet a visit to the doctor. 'A simple formality,' assured me the secretary, with an air of taking an immense part in all my sorrows. Accordingly a young chap wearing his hat over the left eyebrow, some clerk I suppose — there must have been clerks in the business, though the house was as still as a house in a city of the dead — came from somewhere upstairs, and led me forth. He was shabby and careless, with inkstains on the sleeves of his jacket, and his cravat was large and billowy, under a chin shaped like the toe of an old boot. I was a little too early for the doctor, so I proposed a drink, and thereupon he developed a vein of joviality. As we sat over our vermouths he glorified the company's business, and by and by I expressed casually my surprise at him not going out there. He became very cool and collected all at once. 'I am not such a fool as I look, quoth Plato to his disciples,' he said sententiously, emptied his glass with great resolution, and we rose.

"The old doctor felt my pulse, evidently thinking of something else the while. 'Good, good for there,' he mumbled, and then with a certain eagerness asked me whether I would let him measure my head. Rather surprised, I said 'yes,' when he produced a thing like calipers and got the dimensions back and front and every way, taking notes carefully. He was an unshaven little man in a threadbare coat like a gabardine, with his feet in slippers, and I thought him a harmless fool. 'I always ask leave, in the interests of science, to measure the crania of those going out there,' he said. 'And when they come back, too?' I asked. 'Oh, I never see them,' he remarked; 'and, moreover, the changes take place inside, you know.' He smiled, as if at some quiet joke. 'So you are going out there. Famous. Interesting, too.' He gave me a searching glance, and made another note. 'Ever any madness in your family?' he asked, in a matter-of-fact tone. I felt very annoyed. 'Is that question in the interests of science, too?' 'It would be,' he said, without taking notice of my irritation, 'interesting for science to watch the mental changes of individuals, on the spot, but ...' 'Are you an alienist?' I interrupted. 'Every doctor should be — a little,' answered that original, imperturbably. 'I have a little theory which you messieurs who go out there must help me to prove. This is my share in the advantages my country shall reap from the possession of such a magnificent dependency. The mere wealth I leave to others. Pardon my questions, but you are the first Englishman coming under my observation. ...' I hastened to assure him I was not in the least typical. 'If I were,' said I, 'I wouldn't be talking like this with you.' 'What you say is rather profound, and probably erroneous,' he said, with a laugh. 'Avoid irritation more than exposure to the sun. Adieu. How do you English say, eh? Good-by. Ah! Good-by. Adieu. In the tropics one must before everything keep calm.'... He lifted a warning forefinger.... '*Du calme, du calme. Adieu.*'

"One thing more remained to do — say good-by to my excellent aunt. I found her triumphant. I had a cup of tea — the last decent cup of tea for many days — and in a room that most soothingly looked just as you would expect a lady's drawing room to look, we had a long quiet chat by the fireside. In the course of these confidences it became quite plain to me I had been represented to the wife of the high dignitary, and goodness knows to how many more people besides, as an exceptional and gifted creature — a piece of good fortune for the company — a man you don't get hold of every day. Good heavens! and I was going to take charge of a two-penny-half-penny river steamboat with a penny whistle attached! It appeared, however, I was also one of the Workers, with a capital — you know. Something like an emissary of light, something like a lower sort of apostle. There had been a lot of such rot let loose in print and talk just about that time, and the excellent woman, living right in the rush of all that humbug, got carried off her feet. She talked about 'weaning those ignorant millions from their horrid ways,' till, upon my word, she made me quite uncomfortable. I ventured to hint that the company was run for profit.

" 'You forget, dear Charlie, that the laborer is worthy of his hire,' she said, brightly. It's queer how out of touch with truth women are. They live in a world of their own, and there had never been anything like it, and never can be. It is too beautiful altogether, and if they were to set it up it would go to pieces before the first sunset. Some confounded fact we men have been living contentedly with ever since the day of creation would start up and knock the whole thing over.

"After this I got embraced, told to wear flannel, be sure to write often, and so on — and I left. In the street — I don't know why — a queer feeling came to me that I was an impostor. Odd thing that I, who used to clear out for any part of the world at twenty-four hours' notice, with less thought than most men give to the crossing of a street, had a moment — I won't say of hesitation, but of startled pause, before this commonplace affair. The best way I can explain it to you is by saying that, for a second or two, I felt as though, instead of going to the center of a continent, I were about to set off for the center of the earth.

"I left in a French steamer, and she called in every blamed port they have out there, for, as far as I could see, the sole purpose of landing soldiers and customhouse officers. I watched the coast. Watching a coast as it slips by the ship is like thinking about an enigma. There it is before you — smiling, frowning, inviting, grand, mean, insipid, or savage, and always mute with an air of whispering. Come and find out. This one was almost featureless, as if still in the making, with an aspect of monotonous grimness. The edge of a colossal jungle, so dark-green as to be almost black, fringed with white surf, ran straight, like a ruled line, far, far away along a blue sea whose glitter was blurred by a creeping mist. The sun was fierce, the land seemed to glisten and drip with steam. Here and there grayish-whitish specks showed up clustered inside the white surf, with a flag flying above them perhaps. Settlements some centuries old, and still no bigger than pinheads on the untouched expanse of their background. We pounded along, stopped, landed soldiers; went on, landed customhouse clerks to levy toll in what looked like a God-forsaken wilderness, with a tin shed and a flagpole lost in it; landed more soldiers — to take care of the customhouse clerks, presumably. Some, I heard, got drowned in the surf; but whether they did or not, nobody seemed particularly to care. They were just flung out there, and on we went. Every day the coast looked the same, as though we had not moved; but we passed various places — trading places — with names like Gran' Bassam, Little Popo; names that seemed to belong to some sordid farce acted in front of a sinister back-cloth. The idleness of a passenger, my isolation amongst all these men with whom I had no point of contact, the oily and languid sea, the uniform somberness of the coast, seemed to keep me away from the truth of things, within the toil of a mournful and senseless delusion. The voice of the surf heard now and then was a positive pleasure, like the speech of a brother. It was something natural, that had its reason, that had a meaning. Now and then a boat from the shore gave one a momentary contact with reality. It was paddled by black fellows. You could see from afar the white of their eyeballs glistening. They shouted, sang; their bodies streamed with perspiration; they had faces like grotesque masks — these chaps; but they had bone, muscle, a wild vitality, an intense energy of movement, that was as natural and true as the surf along their coast. They wanted no excuse for being there. They were a great comfort to look at. For a time I would feel I belonged still to a world of straightforward facts; but the feeling would not last long. Something would turn up to scare it away. Once, I remember, we came upon a man-of-war anchored off the coast. There wasn't even a shed there, and she was shelling the bush. It appears the French had one of their wars going on thereabouts. Her ensign dropped limp like a rag; the muzzles of the long six-inch guns stuck out all over the low hull; the greasy, slimy swell swung her up lazily and let her down, swaying her thin masts. In the empty immensity of earth, sky, and water, there she was, incomprehensible, firing into a continent. Pop, would go one of the six-inch guns; a small flame would dart and vanish, a little white smoke would disappear, a tiny projectile would give a feeble screech — and nothing happened. Nothing could happen. There was a touch of insanity in the proceeding, a sense of lugubrious drollery in the sight; and it was not dissipated by somebody on board assuring me earnestly there was a camp of natives — he called them enemies! — hidden out of sight somewhere.

"We gave her her letters (I heard the men in that lonely ship were dying of fever at the rate of three a day) and went on. We called at some more places with farcical names, where the merry dance of death and trade goes on in a still and earthly atmosphere as of an overheated catacomb; all along the formless coast bordered by dangerous surf, as if Nature herself had tried to ward off intruders; in and out of rivers, streams of death in life, whose banks were rotting into mud, whose waters, thickened into slime, invaded the contorted mangroves, that seemed to writhe at us in the extremity of an impotent despair. Nowhere did we stop long enough to get a particularized impression, but the general sense of vague and oppressive wonder grew upon me. It was like a weary pilgrimage amongst hints for nightmares.

"It was upward of thirty days before I saw the mouth of the big river. We anchored off the seat of the government. But my work would not begin till some two hundred miles farther on. So as soon as I could I made a start for a place thirty miles higher up.

"I had my passage on a little seagoing steamer. Her captain was a Swede, and knowing me for a seaman, invited me on the bridge. He was a young man, lean, fair, and morose, with lanky hair and a shuffling gait. As we left the miserable little wharf, he tossed his head contemptuously at the shore. 'Been living there?' he asked. I said, 'Yes.' 'Fine lot these government chaps — are they not?' he went on, speaking English with great precision and considerable bitterness. 'It is funny what some people will do for a few francs a month. I wonder what becomes of that kind when it goes up country?' I said to him I expected to see that soon. 'So-o-o!' he exclaimed. He shuffled athwart, keeping one eye ahead vigilantly. 'Don't be too sure,' he continued. 'The other day I took up a man who hanged himself on the road. He was a Swede, too.' 'Hanged himself! Why, in God's name?' I cried. He kept on looking out watchfully. 'Who knows? The sun too much for him, or the country perhaps.'

"At last we opened a reach. A rocky cliff appeared, mounds of turned-up earth by the shore, houses on a hill, others with iron roofs, amongst a waste of excavations, or hanging to the declivity. A continuous noise of the rapids above hovered over this scene of inhabited devastation. A lot of people, mostly black and naked, moved about like ants. A jetty projected into the river. A blinding sunlight drowned all this at times in a sudden recrudescence of glare. 'There's your company's station,' said the Swede, pointing to three wooden barrack-like structures on the rocky slope. 'I will send your things up. Four boxes did you say? So. Farewell.'

"I came upon a boiler wallowing in the grass, then found a path leading up the hill. It turned aside for the boulders, and also for an undersized railway truck lying there on its back with its wheels in the air. One was off. The thing looked as dead as the carcass of some animal. I came upon more pieces of decaying machinery, a stack of rusty rails. To the left a clump of trees made a shady spot, where dark things seemed to stir feebly.

I blinked, the path was steep. A horn tooted to the right, and I saw the black people run. A heavy and dull detonation shook the ground, a puff of smoke came out of the cliff, and that was all. No change appeared on the face of the rock. They were building a railway. The cliff was not in the way or anything; but this objectless blasting was all the work going on.

"A slight clinking behind me made me turn my head. Six black men advanced in a file, toiling up the path. They walked erect and slow, balancing small baskets full of earth on their heads, and the clink kept time with their footsteps. Black rags were wound round their loins, and the short ends behind waggled to and fro like tails. I could see every rib, the joints of their limbs were like knots in a rope; each had an iron collar on his neck, and all were connected together with a chain whose bights swung between them, rhythmically clinking. Another report from the cliff made me think suddenly of that ship of war I had seen firing into a continent. It was the same kind of ominous voice; but these men could by no stretch of imagination be called enemies. They were called criminals, and the outraged law, like the bursting shells, had come to them, an insoluble mystery from the sea. All their meager breasts panted together, the violently dilated nostrils quivered, the eyes stared stonily uphill. They passed me within six inches, without a glance, with that complete, deathlike indifference of unhappy savages. Behind this raw matter one of the reclaimed, the product of the new forces at work, strolled despondently, carrying a rifle by its middle. He had a uniform jacket with one button off, and seeing a white man on the path, hoisted his weapon to his shoulder with alacrity. This was simple prudence, white men being so much alike at a distance that he could not tell who I might be. He was speedily reassured, and with a large, white, rascally grin, and a glance at his charge, seemed to take me into partnership in his exalted trust. After all, I also was a part of the great cause of these high and just proceedings.

"Instead of going up, I turned and descended to the left. My idea was to let that chain gang get out of sight before I climbed the hill. You know I am not particularly tender; I've had to strike and to fend off. I've had to resist and to attack sometimes — that's only one way of resisting — without counting the exact cost, according to the demands of such sort of life as I had blundered into. I've seen the devil of violence, and the devil of greed, and the devil of hot desire; but, by all the stars! these were strong, lusty, red-eyed devils, that swayed and drove men — men, I tell you. But as I stood on this hillside, I foresaw that in the blinding sunshine of that land I would become acquainted with a flabby, pretending, weak-eyed devil of a rapacious and pitiless folly. How insidious he could be, too, I was only to find out several months later and a thousand miles farther. For a moment I stood appalled, as though by a warning. Finally I descended the hill, obliquely, towards the trees I had seen.

"I avoided a vast artificial hole somebody had been digging on the slope, the purpose of which I found it impossible to divine. It wasn't a quarry or a sandpit, anyhow. It was just a hole. It might have been connected with the philanthropic desire of giving the criminals something to do. I don't know. Then I nearly fell into a very narrow ravine, almost no more than a scar in the hillside. I discovered that a lot of imported drainage pipes for the settlement had been tumbled in there. There wasn't one that was not broken. It was a wanton smashup. At last I got under the trees. My purpose was to stroll into the shade for a moment; but no sooner within than it seemed to me I had stepped into the gloomy circle of some inferno. The rapids were near, and an uninterrupted, uniform, headlong, rushing noise filled the mournful stillness of the grove, where not a breath stirred, not a leaf moved, with a mysterious sound — as though the tearing pace of the launched earth had suddenly become audible.

"Black shapes crouched, lay, sat between the trees leaning against the trunks, clinging to the earth, half coming out, half effaced within the dim light, in all the attitudes of pain, abandonment, and despair. Another mine on the cliff went off, followed by a slight shudder of the soil under my feet. The work was going on. The work! And this was the place where some of the helpers had withdrawn to die.

"They were dying slowly — it was very clear. They were not enemies, they were not criminals, they were nothing earthly now, nothing but black shadows of disease and starvation, lying confusedly in the greenish gloom. Brought from all the recesses of the coast in all the legality of time contracts, lost in uncongenial surroundings, fed on unfamiliar food, they sickened, became inefficient, and were then allowed to crawl away and rest. These moribund shapes were free as air — and nearly as thin. I began to distinguish the gleam of the eyes under the trees. Then, glancing down, I saw a face near my hand. The black bones reclined at full length with one shoulder against the tree, and slowly the eyelids rose and the sunken eyes looked up at me, enormous and vacant, a kind of blind, white flicker in the depths of the orbs, which died out slowly. The man seemed young — almost a boy — but you know with them it's hard to tell. I found nothing else to do but to offer him one of my good Swede's ship's biscuits I had in my pocket. The fingers closed slowly on it and held — there was no other movement and no other glance. He had tied a bit of white worsted round his neck — Why? Where did he get it? Was it a badge — an ornament — a charm — a propitiatory act? Was there any idea at all connected with it? It looked startling round his black neck, this bit of white thread from beyond the seas.

"Near the same tree two more bundles of acute angles sat with their legs drawn up. One, with his chin propped on his knees, stared at nothing, in an intolerable and appalling manner: his brother phantom rested its forehead, as if overcome with a great weariness; and all about others were scattered in every pose of contorted collapse, as in some picture of a massacre or a pestilence. While I stood horror-struck, one of these creatures rose to his hands and knees, and went off on all fours towards the river to drink. He lapped out of his hand, then sat up in the sunlight, crossing his shins in front of him, and after a time let his wooly head fall on his breastbone.

"I didn't want any more loitering in the shade, and I made haste towards the station. When near the buildings I met a white man, in such an unexpected elegance of getup that in the first moment I took him for a sort of vision. I saw a high starched collar, white cuffs, a light alpaca jacket, snowy trousers, a clear necktie, and varnished boots. No hat. Hair parted, brushed, oiled, under a green-lined parasol held in a big white hand. He was amazing, and had a penholder behind his ear.

"I shook hands with this miracle, and I learned he was the company's chief accountant, and that all the bookkeeping was done at this station. He had come out for a moment, he said, 'to get a breath of fresh air.' The expression sounded wonderfully odd, with its suggestion of sedentary desk life. I wouldn't have mentioned the fellow to you at all, only it was from his lips that I first heard the name of the man who is so indissolubly connected with the memories of that time. Moreover, I respected the fellow. Yes; I respected his collars, his vast cuffs, his brushed hair. His appearance was certainly that of a hairdresser's dummy; but in the great demoralization of the land he kept up his appearance. That's backbone. His starched collars and got-up shirt fronts were achievements of character. He had been out nearly three years; and, later, I could not help asking him how he managed to sport such linen. He had just the faintest blush, and said modestly, 'I've been teaching one of the native women about the station. It was difficult. She had a distaste for the work.' Thus this man had truly accomplished something. And he was devoted to his books, which were in apple-pie order.

"Everything else in the station was in a muddle — heads, things, buildings. Strings of dusty niggers with splay feet arrived and departed; a stream of manufactured goods, rubbishy cottons, beads, and brass wire set into the depths of darkness, and in return came a precious trickle of ivory.

"I had to wait in the station for ten days — an eternity. I lived in a hut in the yard, but to be out of the chaos I would sometimes get into the accountant's office. It was built of horizontal planks, and so badly put together that, as he bent over his high desk, he was barred from neck to heels with narrow strips of sunlight. There was no need to open the big shutter to see. It was hot there, too; big flies buzzed fiendishly, and did not sting, but stabbed. I sat generally on the floor, while, of faultless appearance (and even slightly scented), perching on a high stool, he wrote, he wrote. Sometimes he stood up for exercise. When a truckle bed with a sick man (some invalid agent from upcountry) was put in there, he exhibited a gentle annoyance. 'The groans of this sick person,' he said, 'distract my attention. And without that it is extremely difficult to guard against clerical errors in this climate.'

"One day he remarked, without lifting his head, 'In the interior you will no doubt meet Mr. Kurtz.' On my asking who Mr. Kurtz was, he said he was a first-class agent; and seeing my disappointment at this information, he added slowly, laying down his pen, 'He is a very remarkable person.' Further questions elicited from him that Mr. Kurtz was at present in charge of a trading post, a very important one, in the true ivory-country, at 'the very bottom of there. Sends in as much ivory as all the others put together. . . .' He began to write again. The sick man was too ill to groan. The flies buzzed in a great peace.

"Suddenly there was a growing murmur of voices and a great tramping of feet. A caravan had come in. A violent babble of uncouth sounds burst out on the other side of the planks. All the carriers were speaking together, and in the midst of the uproar the lamentable voice of the chief agent was heard 'giving it up' tearfully for the twentieth time that day. . . . He rose slowly. 'What a frightful row,' he said. He crossed the room gently to look at the sick man, and returning, said to me, 'He does not hear.' 'What! Dead?' I asked, startled. 'No, not yet,' he answered, with great composure. Then, alluding with a toss of the head to the tumult in the station yard, 'When one has got to make correct entries, one comes to hate those savages — hate them to the death.' He remained thoughtful for a moment. 'When you see Mr. Kurtz,' he went on, 'tell him from me that everything here' — he glanced at the desk — 'is very satisfactory. I don't like to write to him — with those messengers of ours you never know who may get hold of your letter — at that Central Station.' He stared at me for a moment with his mild, bulging eyes. 'Oh, he will go far, very far,' he began again. 'He will be a somebody in the administration before long. They, above — the council in Europe, you know — mean him to be.'

"He turned to his work. The noise outside had ceased, and presently in going out I stopped at the door. In the steady buzz of flies the homeward-bound agent was lying flushed and insensible; the other, bent over his books, was making correct entries of perfectly correct transactions; and fifty feet below the doorstep I could see the still treetops of the grove of death.

"Next day I left that station at last, with a caravan of sixty men, for a two-hundred-mile tramp.

"No use telling you much about that. Paths, paths, everywhere; a stamped-in network of paths spreading over the empty land, through long grass, through burnt grass, through thickets, down and up chilly ravines, up and down stony hills ablaze with heat; and a solitude, a solitude, nobody, not a hut. The population had cleared out a long time ago. Well, if a lot of mysterious niggers armed with all kinds of fearful weapons suddenly took to traveling on the road between Deal and Gravesend, catching the yokels right and left to carry heavy loads for them, I fancy every farm and cottage thereabouts would get empty very soon. Only here the dwellings were gone, too. Still I passed through several abandoned villages. There's something pathetically childish in the ruins of grass walls. Day after day, with the stamp and shuffle of sixty pair of bare feet behind me, each pair under a sixty-lb. load. Camp, cook, sleep, strike camp, march. Now and then a carrier dead in harness, at rest in the long grass near the path, with an empty water gourd and his long staff lying by his side. A great silence around and above. Perhaps on some quiet night the tremor of far-off drums, sinking, swelling, a tremor vast, faint; a sound weird, appealing, suggestive, and wild — and perhaps with as profound a meaning as the sound of bells in a Christian country. Once a white man in an unbuttoned uniform, camping on the path with an armed escort of lank Zanzibaris, very hospitable and festive — not to say drunk. Was looking after the upkeep of the road he declared. Can't say I saw any road or any upkeep, unless the body of a middle-aged Negro, with a bullethole in the forehead, upon which I absolutely stumbled three miles farther on, may be considered as a permanent improvement. I had a white companion, too, not a bad chap, but rather too fleshy and with the exasperating habit of fainting on the hot hillsides, miles away from the last bit of shade and water. Annoying, you know, to hold your own coat like a parasol over a man's head while he is coming to. I couldn't help asking him once what he meant by coming there at all. 'To make money, of course. What do you think?' he said, scornfully. Then he got fever, and had to be carried in a hammock slung under a pole. As he weighed 224 pounds I had no end of rows with the carriers. They jibbed, ran away, sneaked off with their loads in the night — quite a mutiny. So, one evening, I made a speech in English with gestures, not one of which was lost to the sixty pairs of eyes before me, and the next morning I started the hammock off in front all right. An hour afterwards I came upon the whole concern wrecked in a bush — man, hammock, groans, blankets, horrors. The heavy pole had skinned his poor nose. He was very anxious for me to kill somebody, but there wasn't the shadow of a carrier near. I remember the old doctor, 'It would be interesting for science to watch the mental changes of individuals, on the spot.' I felt I was becoming scientifically interesting. However, all that is to no purpose. On the fifteenth day I came in sight of the big river again, and hobbled into the Central Station. It was on a back water surrounded by scrub and forest, with a pretty border of smelly mud on one side, and on the three others enclosed by a crazy fence of rushes. A neglected gap was all the gate it had, and the first glance at the place was enough to let you see the flabby devil was running that show. White men with long staves in their hands appeared languidly from amongst the buildings, strolling up to take a look at me, and then retired out of sight somewhere. One of them, a stout, excitable chap with black mustaches, informed me with great volubility and many digressions, as soon as I told him who I was, that my steamer was at the bottom of the river. I was thunderstruck. What, how, why? Oh, it was 'all right.' The 'manager himself' was there. All quite correct. 'Everybody had behaved splendidly! splendidly!' — 'you must,' he said in agitation, 'go and see the general manager at once. He is waiting!'

"I did not see the real significance of that wreck at once. I fancy I see it now, but I am not sure — not at all. Certainly the affair was too stupid — when I think of it — to be altogether natural. Still ... But at the moment it presented itself simply as a confounded nuisance. The steamer was sunk. They had started two days before in a sudden hurry up the river with the manager on board, in charge of some volunteer skipper, and before they had been out three hours they tore the bottom out of her on stones, and she sank near the south bank. I asked myself what I was to do there, now my boat was lost. As a matter of fact, I had plenty to do in fishing my command out of the river. I had to set about it the very next day. That, and the repairs when I brought the pieces to the station, took some months.

"My first interview with the manager was curious. He did not ask me to sit down after my twenty-mile walk that morning. He was commonplace in complexion, in feature, in manners, and in voice. He was of middle size and of ordinary build. His eyes, of the usual blue, were perhaps remarkably cold, and he certainly could make his glance fall on one as trenchant and heavy as an axe. But even at these times the rest of his person seemed to disclaim the intention. Otherwise there was only an indefinable, faint expression of his lips, something stealthy — a smile — not a smile — I remember it, but I can't explain. It was unconscious, this smile was, though just after he had said something it got intensified for an instant. It came at the end of his speeches like a seal applied on the words to make the meaning of the commonest phrase appear absolutely inscrutable. He was a common trader, from his youth up employed in these parts — nothing more. He was obeyed, yet he inspired neither love nor fear, nor even respect. He inspired uneasiness. That was it — Uneasiness. Not a definite mistrust — just uneasiness — nothing more. You have no idea how effective such a ... a ... faculty can be. He had no genius for organizing, for initiative, or for order even. That was evident in such things as the deplorable state of the station. He had no learning, and no intelligence. His position had come to him — why? Perhaps because he was never ill ... He had served three terms of three years out there. ... Because triumphant health in the general rout of constitutions is a kind of power in itself. When he went home on leave he rioted on a large scale — pompously. Jack ashore — with a difference — in externals only. This one could gather from his casual talk. He originated nothing, he could keep the routine going — that's all. But he was great. He was great by this little thing that it was impossible to tell what could control such a man. He never gave that secret away. Perhaps there was nothing within him. Such a suspicion made one pause — for out there there were no external checks. Once when various tropical diseases had laid low almost every 'agent' in the station, he was heard to say, 'Men who come out here should have no entrails.' He sealed the utterance with that smile of his, as though it had been a door opening into a darkness he had in his keeping. You fancied you had seen things — but the seal was on. When annoyed at mealtimes by the constant quarrels of the white men about precedence, he ordered an immense round table to be made, for which a special house had to be built. This was the station's messroom. Where he sat was the first place — the rest were nowhere. One felt this to be his unalterable conviction. He was neither civil nor uncivil. He was quiet. He allowed his 'boy' — an overfed young Negro from the coast — to treat the white men, under his very eyes, with provoking insolence.

"He began to speak as soon as he saw me. I had been very long on the road. He could not wait. Had to start without me. The up-river stations had to be relieved. There had been so many delays already that he did not know who was dead and who was alive, and how they got on — and so on, and so on. He paid no attention to my explanations, and, playing with a stick of sealing wax, repeated several times that the situation was 'very grave, very grave.' There were rumors that a very important station was in jeopardy, and its chief, Mr. Kurtz, was ill. Hoped it was not true. Mr. Kurtz was ... I felt weary and irritable. Hang Kurtz, I thought. I interrupted him by saying I had heard of Mr. Kurtz on the coast. 'Ah! So they talk of him down there,' he murmured to himself. Then he began again, assuring me Mr. Kurtz was the best agent he had, an exceptional man, of the greatest importance to the company; therefore I could understand his anxiety. He was, he said, 'very, very uneasy.' Certainly he fidgeted on his chair a good deal, exclaimed, 'Ah, Mr. Kurtz!' broke the stick of sealing wax and seemed dumfounded by the accident. Next thing he wanted to know 'how long it would take to' ... I interrupted him again. Being hungry, you know, and kept on my feet, too, I was getting savage. 'How could I tell?' I said. 'I hadn't even seen the wreck yet — some months, no doubt.' All this talk seemed to me so futile. 'Some months,' he said. 'Well, let us say three months before we can make a start. Yes. That ought to do the affair.' I flung out of his hut (he lived all alone in a clay hut with a sort of veranda) muttering to myself my opinion of him. He was a chattering idiot. Afterwards I took it back when it was borne in upon me startlingly with what extreme nicety he had estimated the time requisite for the 'affair.'

"I went to work the next day, turning, so to speak, my back on that station. In that way only it seemed to me I could keep my hold on the redeeming facts of life. Still, one must look about sometimes; and then I saw this station, these men strolling aimlessly about in the sunshine of the yard. I asked myself sometimes what it all meant. They wandered here and there with their absurd long staves in their hands, like a lot of faithless pilgrims bewitched inside a rotten fence. The word 'ivory' rang in the air, was whispered, was sighed. You would think they were praying to it. A taint of imbecile rapacity blew through it all, like a whiff from some corpse. By Jove! I've never seen anything so unreal in my life. And outside, the silent wilderness surrounding this cleared speck on the earth struck me as something great and invincible, like evil or truth, waiting patiently for the passing away of this fantastic invasion.

"Oh, these months! Well, never mind. Various things happened. One evening a grass shed full of calico, cotton prints, beads, and I don't know what else, burst into a blaze so suddenly that you would have thought the earth had opened to let an avenging fire consume all that trash. I was smoking my pipe quietly by my dismantled steamer, and saw them all cutting capers in the light, with their arms lifted high, when the stout man with mustaches came tearing down to the river, a tin pail in his hand, assured me that everybody was 'behaving splendidly, splendidly,' dipped about a quart of water and tore back again. I noticed there was a hole in the bottom of his pail.

"I strolled up. There was no hurry. You see the thing had gone off like a box of matches. It had been hopeless from the very first. The flame had leaped high, driven everybody back, lighted up everything — and collapsed. The shed was already a heap of embers glowing fiercely. A nigger was being beaten near by. They said he had caused the fire in some way; be that as it may, he was screeching most horribly. I saw him, later, for several days, sitting in a bit of shade looking very sick and trying to recover himself: afterwards he arose and went out — and the wilderness without a sound took him into its bosom again. As I approached the glow from the dark I found myself at the back of two men, talking. I heard the name of Kurtz pronounced, then the words 'take advantage of this unfortunate accident.' One of the men was the manager. I wished him a good evening. 'Did you ever see anything like it — eh? It is incredible,' he said, and walked off. The other man remained. He was a first-class agent, young, gentlemanly, a bit reserved, with a forked little beard and a hooked nose. He was standoffish with the other agents, and they on their side said he was the manager's spy upon them. As to me, I had hardly ever spoken to him before. We got into talk, and by and by we strolled away from the hissing ruins. Then he asked me to his room, which was in the main building of the station. He struck a match, and I perceived that this young aristocrat had not only a silver-mounted dressing case but also a whole candle all to himself. Just at that time the manager was the only man supposed to have any right to candles. Native mats covered the clay walls; a collection of spears, assagais, shields, knives was hung up in trophies. The business intrusted to this fellow was the making of bricks — so I had been informed; but there wasn't a fragment of a brick anywhere in the station, and he had been there more than a year — waiting. It seems he could not make bricks without something, I don't know what — straw maybe. Anyways, it could not be found there, and as it was not likely to be sent from Europe, it did not appear clear to me what he was waiting for. An act of special creation perhaps. However, they were all waiting — all the sixteen or twenty pilgrims of them — for something; and upon my word it did not seem an uncongenial occupation, from the way they took it, though the only thing that ever came to them was disease — as far as I could see. They beguiled the time by backbiting and intriguing against each other in a foolish kind of way. There was an air of plotting about that station, but nothing came of it, of course. It was as unreal as everything else — as the philanthropic pretense of the whole concern, as their talk, as their government, as their show of work. The only real feeling was a desire to get appointed to a trading post where ivory was to be had, so that they could earn percentages. They intrigued and slandered and hated each other only on that account, but as to effectually lifting a little finger — oh, no. By heavens! There is something after all in the world allowing one man to steal a horse while another must not look at a halter. Steal a horse straight out. Very well. He has done it. Perhaps he can ride. But there is a way of looking at a halter that would provoke the most charitable of saints into a kick.

"I had no idea why he wanted to be sociable, but as we chatted in there it suddenly occurred to me the fellow was trying to get at something — in fact, pumping me. He alluded constantly to Europe, to the people I was supposed to know there — putting leading questions as to my acquaintances in the sepulchral city, and so on. His little eyes glittered like mica discs — with curiosity — though he tried to keep up a bit of superciliousness. At first I was astonished, but very soon I became awfully curious to see what he would find out from me. I couldn't possibly imagine what I had in me to make it worth his while. It was very pretty to see how he baffled himself, for in truth my body was full only of chills, and my head had nothing in it but that wretched steamboat business. It was evident he took me for a perfectly shameless prevaricator. At last he got angry, and, to conceal a movement of furious annoyance, he yawned. I rose. Then I noticed a small sketch in oils, on a panel, representing a woman, draped and blindfolded, carrying a lighted torch. The background was somber — almost black. The movement of the woman was stately, and the effect of the torchlight on the face was sinister.

"It arrested me, and he stood by civilly, holding an empty half-pint champagne bottle (medical comforts) with the candle stuck in it. To my question he said Mr. Kurtz had painted this — in this very station more than a year ago — while waiting for means to go to his trading post. 'Tell me, pray,' said I, 'who is this Mr. Kurtz?'

" 'The chief of the Inner Station,' he answered in a short tone, looking away. 'Much obliged,' I said, laughing. 'And you are the brickmaker of the Central Station. Everyone knows that.' He was silent for a while. 'He is a prodigy,' he said at last. 'He is an emissary of pity, and science, and progress, and devil knows what else. We want,' he began to declaim suddenly, 'for the guidance of the cause intrusted to us by Europe, so to speak, higher intelligence, wide sympathies, a singleness of purpose.' 'Who says that?' I asked. 'Lots of them,' he replied. 'Some even write that; and so *he* comes here, a special being, as you ought to know.' 'Why ought I to know?' I interrupted, really surprised. He paid no attention. 'Yes. Today he is chief of the best station, next year he will be assistant manager, two years more and ... but I daresay you know what he will be in two years' time. You are of the new gang — the gang of virtue. The same people who sent him specially also recommended you. Oh, don't say no. I've my own eyes to trust.' Light dawned upon me. My dear aunt's influential acquaintances were producing an unexpected effect upon that young man. I nearly burst into a laugh. 'Do you read the company's confidential correspondence?' I asked. He hadn't a word to say. It was great fun. 'When Mr. Kurtz,' I continued, severely, 'is general manager, you won't have the opportunity.'

"He blew the candle out suddenly, and we went outside. The moon had risen. Black figures strolled about listlessly, pouring water on the glow, whence proceeded a sound of hissing; steam ascended in the moonlight, the beaten nigger groaned somewhere. 'What a row the brute makes!' said the indefatigable man with the mustaches, appearing near us. 'Serve him right. Transgression — punishment — bang! Pitiless, pitiless. That's the only way. This will prevent all conflagrations for the future. I was just telling the manager ...' He noticed my companion, and became crestfallen all at once. 'Not in bed yet,' he said, with a kind of servile heartiness; 'it's so natural. Ha! Danger — agitation.' He vanished. I went on to the river side, and the other followed me. I heard a scathing murmur at my ear, 'Heap of muffs — go to.' The pilgrims could be seen in knots gesticulating, discussing. Several had still their staves in their hands. I truly believe they took these sticks to bed with them. Beyond the fence the forest stood up spectrally in the moonlight, and through the dim stir, through the faint sounds of that lamentable courtyard, the silence of the land went home to one's very heart — its mystery, its greatness, the amazing reality of its concealed life. The hurt nigger moaned feebly somewhere near by, and then fetched a deep sigh that made me mend my pace away from there. I felt a hand introducing itself under my arm. 'My dear sir,' said the fellow, 'I don't want to be misunderstood, and especially by you, who will see Mr. Kurtz long before I can have that pleasure. I wouldn't like him to get a false idea of my disposition. ...'

"I let him run on, this papier-mâché Mephistopheles, and it seemed to me that if I tried I could poke my forefinger through him, and would find nothing inside but a little loose dirt, maybe. He, don't you see, had been planning to be assistant manager by and by under the present man, and I could see that the coming of that Kurtz had upset them both not a little. He talked precipitately, and I did not try to stop him. I had my shoulders against the wreck of my steamer, hauled up on the slope like a carcass of some big river animal. The smell of mud, of primeval mud, by Jove! was in my nostrils, the high stillness of primeval forest was before my eyes; there were shiny patches on the black creek. The moon had spread over everything a thin layer of silver — over the rank grass, over the mud, upon the wall of matted vegetation standing higher than the wall of a temple, over the great river I could see through a somber gap glittering, glittering, as it flowed broadly by without a murmur. All this was great, expectant, mute, while the man jabbered about himself. I wondered whether the stillness on the face of the immensity looking at us two were meant as an appeal or as a menace. What were we who had strayed in here? Could we handle that dumb thing, or would it handle us? I felt how big, how confoundedly big, was that thing that couldn't talk, and perhaps was deaf as well. What was in there? I could see a little ivory coming out from there, and I had heard Mr. Kurtz was in there. I had heard enough about it, too — God knows! Yet somehow it didn't bring any image with it — no more than if I had been told an angel or a fiend was in there. I believed it in the same way one of you might believe there are inhabitants in the planet Mars. I knew once a Scotch sailmaker who was certain, dead sure, there were people in Mars. If you asked him for some idea how they looked and behaved, he would get shy and mutter something about 'walking on all fours.' If you as much as smiled, he would — though a man of sixty — offer to fight you. I would not have gone so far as to fight for Kurtz, but I went for him near enough to a lie. You know I hate, detest, and can't bear a lie, not because I am straighter than the rest of us, but simply because it appalls me. There is a taint of death, a flavor of mortality in lies — which is exactly what I hate and detest in the world — what I want to forget. It makes me miserable and sick, like biting something rotten would do. Temperament, I suppose. Well, I went near enough to it by letting the young fool there believe anything he liked to imagine as to my influence in Europe. I became in an instant as much of a pretense as the rest of the bewitched pilgrims. This simply because I had a notion it somehow would be of help to that Kurtz whom at the time I did not see — you understand. He was just a word for me. I did not see the man in the name any more than you do. Do you see him? Do you see the story? Do you see anything? It seems to me I am trying to tell you a dream — making a vain attempt, because no relation of a dream can convey the dream-sensation, that commingling of absurdity, surprise, and bewilderment in a tremor of struggling revolt, that notion of being captured by the incredible which is of the very essence of dreams. ..."

He was silent for a while.

"... No, it is impossible; it is impossible to convey the life-sensation of any given epoch of one's existence — that which makes its truth, its meaning — its subtle and penetrating essence. It is impossible. We live, as we dream — alone. ..."

He paused again as if reflecting, then added:

"Of course in this you fellows see more than I could then. You see me, whom you know. ..."

It had become so pitch dark that we listeners could hardly see one another. For a long time already he, sitting apart, had been no more to us than a voice. There was not a word from anybody. The others might have been asleep, but I was awake. I listened, I listened on the watch for the sentence, for the word, that would give me the clue to the faint uneasiness inspired by this narrative that seemed to shape itself without human lips in the heavy night air of the river.

"... Yes — I let him run on," Marlow began again, "and think what he pleased about the powers that were behind me. I did! And there was nothing behind me! There was nothing but that wretched, old, mangled steamboat I was leaning against, while he talked fluently about 'the necessity for every man to get on.' 'And when one comes out here, you conceive, it is not to gaze at the moon.' Mr. Kurtz was a 'universal genius,' but even a genius would find it easier to work with 'adequate tools — intelligent men.' He did not make bricks — why, there was a physical impossibility in the way — as I was well aware; and if he did secretarial work for the manager, it was because 'no sensible man rejects wantonly the confidence of his superiors.' Did I see it? I saw it. What more did I want? What I really wanted was rivets, by heaven! Rivets. To get on with the work — to stop the hole. Rivets I wanted. There were cases of them down at the coast — cases — piled up — burst — split! You kicked a loose rivet at every second step in that station yard on the hillside. Rivets had rolled into the grove of death. You could fill your pockets with rivets for the trouble of stooping down — and there wasn't one rivet to be found where it was wanted. We had plates that would do, but nothing to fasten them with. And every week the messenger, a lone Negro, letter bag on shoulder and staff in hand, left our station for the coast. And several times a week a coast caravan came in with trade goods — ghastly glazed calico that made you shudder only to look at it, glass beads, value about a penny a quart, confounded spotted cotton handkerchiefs. And no rivets. Three carriers could have brought all that was wanted to set that steamboat afloat.

"He was becoming confidential now, but I fancy my unresponsive attitude must have exasperated him at last, for he judged it necessary to inform me he feared neither God nor devil, let alone any mere man. I said I could see that very well, but what I wanted was a certain quantity of rivets — and rivets were what really Mr. Kurtz wanted, if he had only known it. Now letters went to the coast every week. ... 'My dear sir,' he cried, 'I wrote from dictation. I demanded rivets. There was a way — for an intelligent man.' He changed his manner; became very cold, and suddenly began to talk about a hippopotamus; wondered whether sleeping on board the steamer (I stuck to my salvage night and day) I wasn't disturbed. There was an old hippo that had the bad habit of getting out on the bank and roaming at night over the station grounds. The pilgrims used to turn out in a body and empty every rifle they could lay hands on at him. Some even had sat up o' nights for him. All this energy was wasted, though. 'That animal has a charmed life,' he said; 'but you can say this only of brutes in this country. No man — you apprehend me? — no man here bears a charmed life.' He stood there for a moment in the moonlight with his delicate hooked nose set a little askew, and his mica eyes glittering without a wink, then, with a curt good night, he strode off. I could see he was disturbed and considerably puzzled, which made me feel more hopeful than I had been for days. It was a great comfort to turn from that chap to my influential friend, the battered, twisted, ruined, tinpot steamboat. I clambered on board. She rang under my feet like an empty Huntley and Palmer biscuit tin kicked along a gutter; she was nothing so solid in make, and rather less pretty in shape, but I had expended enough hard work on her to make me love her. No influential friend would have served me better. She had given me a chance to come out a bit — to find out what I could do. No, I don't like work. I had rather laze about and think of all the fine things that can be done. I don't like work — no man does — but I like what is in the work, the chance to find yourself. Your own reality — for yourself, not for others — what no other man can ever know. They can only see the mere show, and never can tell what it really means.

"I was not surprised to see somebody sitting aft, on the deck, with his legs dangling over the mud. You see I rather chummed with the few mechanics there were in that station, whom the other pilgrims naturally despised — on account of their imperfect manners, I suppose. This was the foreman — a boilermaker by trade — a good worker. He was a lank, bony, yellow-faced man, with big intense eyes. His aspect was worried, and his head was as bald as the palm of my hand; but his hair in falling seemed to have stuck to his chin, and had prospered in the new locality, for his beard hung down to his waist. He was a widower with six young children (he had left them in charge of a sister of his to come out there), and the passion of his life was pigeon flying. He was an enthusiast and a connoisseur. He would rave about pigeons. After work hours he used sometimes to come over from his hut for a talk about his children and his pigeons; at work, when he had to crawl in the mud under the bottom of the steamboat, he would tie up that beard of his in a kind of white serviette he brought for the purpose. It had loops to go over his ears. In the evening he could be seen squatted on the bank rinsing that wrapper in the creek with great care, then spreading it solemnly on a bush to dry.

"I slapped him on the back and shouted 'We shall have rivets!' He scrambled to his feet exclaiming 'No! Rivets!' as though he couldn't believe his ears. Then in a low voice, 'You ... eh?' I don't know why we behaved like lunatics. I put my finger to the side of my nose and nodded mysteriously. 'Good for you!' he cried, snapped his fingers above his head, lifting one foot. I tried a jig. We capered on the iron deck.

A frightful clatter came out of that hulk, and the virgin forest on the other bank of the creek sent it back in a thundering roll upon the sleeping station. It must have made some of the pilgrims sit up in their hovels. A dark figure obscured the lighted doorway of the manager's hut, vanished, then, a second or so after, the doorway itself vanished, too. We stopped, and the silence driven away by the stamping of our feet flowed back again from the recesses of the land. The great wall of vegetation, an exuberant and entangled mass of trunks, branches, leaves, boughs, festoons, motionless in the moonlight, was like a rioting invasion of soundless life, a rolling wave of plants, piled up, crested, ready to topple over the creek, to sweep every little man of us out of his little existence. And it moved not. A deadened burst of mighty splashes and snorts reached us from afar, as though an ichthyosaurus had been taking a bath of glitter in the great river. 'After all,' said the boilermaker in a reasonable tone, 'why shouldn't we get the rivets?' Why not, indeed! I did not know of any reason why we shouldn't. 'They'll come in three weeks,' I said, confidently.

"But they didn't. Instead of rivets there came an invasion, an infliction, a visitation. It came in sections during the next three weeks, each section headed by a donkey carrying a white man in new clothes and tan shoes, bowing from that elevation right and left to the impressed pilgrims. A quarrelsome band of footsore sulky niggers trod on the heels of the donkey; a lot of tents, campstools, tin boxes, white cases, brown bales would be shot down in the courtyard, and the air of mystery would deepen a little over the muddle of the station. Five such instalments came, with their absurd air of disorderly flight with the loot of innumerable outfit shops and provision stores, that, one would think, they were lugging, after a raid, into the wilderness for equitable division. It was an inextricable mess of things decent in themselves but that human folly made look like spoils of thieving.

"This devoted band called itself the Eldorado Exploring Expedition, and I believe they were sworn to secrecy. Their talk, however, was the talk of sordid buccaneers: it was reckless without hardihood, greedy without audacity, and cruel without courage; there was not an atom of foresight or of serious intention in the whole batch of them, and they did not seem aware these things are wanted for the work of the world. To tear treasure out of the bowels of the land was their desire, with no more moral purpose at the back of it than there is in burglars breaking into a safe. Who paid the expenses of the noble enterprise I don't know; but the uncle of our manager was leader of that lot.

"In exterior he resembled a butcher in a poor neighborhood, and his eyes had a look of sleepy cunning. He carried his fat paunch with ostentation on his short legs, and during the time his gang infested the station spoke to no one but his nephew. You could see these two roaming about all day long with their heads close together in an everlasting confab.

"I had given up worrying myself about the rivets. One's capacity for that kind of folly is more limited than you would suppose. I said Hang! — and let things slide. I had plenty of time for meditation, and now and then I would give some thought to Kurtz. I wasn't very interested in him. No. Still, I was curious to see whether this man, who had come out equipped with moral ideas of some sort, would climb to the top after all and how he would set about his work when there."

II

"One evening as I was lying flat on the deck of my steamboat, I heard voices approaching — and there were the nephew and the uncle strolling along the bank. I laid my head on my arm again, and had nearly lost myself in a doze, when somebody said in my ear, as it were: 'I am as harmless as a little child, but I don't like to be dictated to. Am I the manager — or am I not? I was ordered to send him there. It's incredible.' . . . I became aware that the two were standing on the shore alongside the forepart of the steamboat, just below my head. I did not move; it did not occur to me to move: I was sleepy. 'It *is* unpleasant,' grunted the uncle. 'He has asked the administration to be sent there,' said the other, 'with the idea of showing what he could do; and I was instructed accordingly. Look at the influence that man must have. Is it not frightful?' They both agreed it was frightful, then made several bizarre remarks: 'Make rain and fine weather — one man — the council — by the nose' — bits of absurd sentences that got the better of my drowsiness, so that I had pretty near the whole of my wits about me when the uncle said, 'The climate may do away with this difficulty for you. Is he alone there?' 'Yes,' answered the manager; 'he sent his assistant down the river with a note to me in these terms: "Clear this poor devil out of the country, and don't bother sending more of that sort. I had rather be alone than have the kind of men you can dispose of with me." It was more than a year ago. Can you imagine such impudence!' 'Anything since then?' asked the other, hoarsely. 'Ivory,' jerked the nephew; 'lots of it — prime sort — lots — most annoying, from him.' 'And with that?' questioned the heavy rumble. 'Invoice,' was the reply fired out, so to speak. Then silence. They had been talking about Kurtz.

"I was broad awake by this time, but, lying perfectly at ease, remained still, having no inducement to change my position. 'How did that ivory come all this way?' growled the elder man, who seemed very vexed. The other explained that it had come with a fleet of canoes in charge of an English half-caste clerk Kurtz had with him; that Kurtz had apparently intended to return himself, the station being by that time bare of goods and stores, but after coming three hundred miles, had suddenly decided to go back, which he started to do alone in a small dugout with four paddlers, leaving the half-caste to continue down the river with the ivory. The two fellows there seemed astounded at anybody attempting such a thing. They were at a loss for an adequate motive. As to me, I seemed to see Kurtz for the first time. It was a distinct glimpse: the dugout, four paddling savages, and the lone white man turning his back suddenly on the headquarters, on relief, on thoughts of home — perhaps; setting his face towards the depths of the wilderness, towards his empty and desolate station. I did not know the motive. Perhaps he was just simply a fine fellow who stuck to his work for its own sake. His name, you understand, had not been pronounced once. He was 'that man.' The half-caste, who, as far as I could see, had conducted a difficult trip with great prudence and pluck, was invariably alluded to as 'that scoundrel.' The 'scoundrel' had reported that the 'man' had been very ill — had recovered imperfectly. ... The two below me moved away then a few paces, and strolled back and forth at some little distance. I heard: 'Military post — doctor — two hundred miles — quite alone now — unavoidable delays — nine months — no news — strange rumors.' They approached again, just as the manager was saying, 'No one, as far as I know, unless a species of wandering trader — a pestilential fellow, snapping ivory from the natives.' Who was it they were talking about now? I gathered in snatches that this was some man supposed to be in Kurtz's district, and of whom the manager did not approve. 'We will not be free from unfair competition till one of these fellows is hanged for an example,' he said. 'Certainly,' grunted the other; 'get him hanged! Why not? Anything — anything can be done in this country. That's what I say; nobody here, you understand, *here*, can endanger your position. And why? You stand the climate — you outlast them all. The danger is in Europe; but there before I left I took care to — ' They moved off and whispered, then their voices rose again. 'The extraordinary series of delays is not my fault. I did my best.' The fat man sighed. 'Very sad.' 'And the pestiferous absurdity of his talk,' continued the other; 'he bothered me enough when he was here. "Each station should be like a beacon on the road towards better things, a center for trade of course, but also for humanizing, improving, instructing." Conceive you — that ass! And he wants to be manager! No, it's — ' Here he got choked by excessive indignation, and I lifted my head the least bit. I was surprised to see how near they were — right under me. I could have spat upon their hats. They were looking on the ground, absorbed in thought. The manager was switching his leg with a slender twig; his sagacious relative lifted his head. 'You have been well since you came out this time?' he asked. The other gave a start. 'Who? I? Oh! Like a charm — like a charm. But the rest — oh, my goodness! All sick. They die so quick, too, that I haven't the time to send them out of the country — it's incredible!' 'H'm. Just so,' grunted the uncle. 'Ah! my boy, trust to this — I say, trust to this.' I saw him extend his short flipper of an arm for a gesture that took in the forest, the creek, the mud, the river — seemed to beckon with a dishonoring flourish before the sunlit face of the land a treacherous appeal to the lurking death, to the hidden evil, to the profound darkness of its heart. It was so startling that I leaped to my feet and looked back at the edge of the forest, as though I had expected an answer of some sort to that black display of confidence. You know the foolish notions that come to one sometimes. The high stillness confronted these two figures with its ominous patience, waiting for the passing away of a fantastic invasion.

"They swore aloud together — out of sheer fright, I believe — then pretending not to know anything of my existence, turned back to the station. The sun was low: and leaning forward side by side, they seemed to be tugging painfully uphill their two ridiculous shadows of unequal length, that trailed behind them slowly over the tall grass without bending a single blade.

"In a few days the Eldorado Expedition went into the patient wilderness, that closed upon it as the sea closes over a diver. Long afterwards the news came that all the donkeys were dead. I know nothing as to the fate of the less valuable animals. They, no doubt, like the rest of us, found what they deserved. I did not inquire. I was then rather excited at the prospect of meeting Kurtz very soon. When I say very soon I mean it comparatively. It was just two months from the day we left the creek when we came to the bank below Kurtz's station.

"Going up that river was like traveling back to the earliest beginnings of the world, when vegetation rioted on the earth and the big trees were kings. An empty stream, a great silence, an impenetrable forest. The air was warm, thick, heavy, sluggish. There was no joy in the brilliance of sunshine. The long stretches of the waterway ran on, deserted, into the gloom of overshadowed distances. On silvery sandbanks hippos and alligators sunned themselves side by side. The broadening waters flowed through a mob of wooded islands; you lost your way on that river as you would in a desert and butted all day long against shoals, trying to find the channel, till you thought yourself bewitched and cut off forever from everything you had known once — somewhere — far away — in another existence perhaps. There were moments when one's past came back to one, as it will sometimes when you have not a moment to spare to yourself; but it came in the shape of an unrestful and noisy dream, remembered with wonder amongst the overwhelming realities of this strange world of plants and water, and silence. And this stillness of life did not in the least resemble a peace. It was the stillness of an implacable force brooding over an inscrutable intention. It looked at you with a vengeful aspect. I got used to it afterwards; I did not see it any more; I had no time. I had to keep guessing at the channel; I had to discern, mostly by inspiration, the signs of hidden banks; I watched for sunken stones; I was learning to clap my teeth smartly before my heart flew out, when I shaved by a fluke some infernal sly old snag that would have ripped the life out of the tin-pot steamboat and drowned all the pilgrims; I had to keep a lookout for the signs of dead wood we could cut up in the night for next day's steaming. When you have to attend to things of that sort, to the mere incidents of the surface, the reality — the reality, I tell you — fades. The inner truth is hidden — luckily, luckily. But I felt it all the same; I felt often its mysterious stillness watching me at my monkey tricks, just as it watches you fellows performing on your respective tightropes for — what is it? a half crown a tumble — "

"Try to be civil, Marlow," growled a voice, and I knew there was at least one listener awake besides myself.

"I beg your pardon. I forgot the heartache which makes up the rest of the price. And indeed what does the price matter, if the trick be well done? You do your tricks very well. And I didn't do badly either, since I managed not to sink that steamboat on my first trip. It's a wonder to me yet. Imagine a blindfolded man set to drive a van over a bad road. I sweated and shivered over that business considerably, I can tell you. After all, for a seaman, to scrape the bottom of the thing that's supposed to float all the time under his care is the unpardonable sin. No one may know of it, but you never forget the thump — eh? A blow on the very heart. You remember it, you dream of it, you wake up at night and think of it — years after — and go hot and cold all over. I don't pretend to say that steamboat floated all the time. More than once she had to wade for a bit, with twenty cannibals splashing around and pushing. We had enlisted some of these chaps on the way for a crew. Fine fellows — cannibals — in their place. They were men one could work with, and I am grateful to them. And, after all, they did not eat each other before my face: they had brought along a provision of hippo meat which went rotten, and made the mystery of the wilderness stink in my nostrils. Phoo! I can sniff it now. I had the manager on board and three or four pilgrims with their staves — all complete. Sometimes we came upon a station close by the bank, clinging to the skirts of the unknown, and the white men rushing out of a tumbledown hovel, with great gestures of joy and surprise and welcome, seemed very strange — had the appearance of being held there captive by a spell. The word ivory would ring in the air for a while — and on we went again into the silence, along empty reaches, round the still bends, between the high walls of our winding way, reverberating in hollow claps the ponderous beat of the stern wheel. Trees, trees, millions of trees, massive, immense, running up high; and at their foot, hugging the bank against the stream, crept the little begrimed steamboat, like a sluggish beetle crawling on the floor of a lofty portico. It made you feel very small, very lost, and yet it was not altogether depressing, that feeling. After all, if you were small, the grimy beetle crawled on — which was just what you wanted it to do. Where the pilgrims imagined it crawled to I don't know. To some place where they expected to get something, I bet! For me it crawled towards Kurtz — exclusively; but when the steam pipes started leaking we crawled very slow. The reaches opened before us and closed behind, as if the forest had stepped leisurely across the water to bar the way for our return. We penetrated deeper and deeper into the heart of darkness. It was very quiet there. At night sometimes the roll of drums behind the curtain of trees would run up the river and remain sustained faintly, as if hovering in the air high over our heads, till the first break of day. Whether it meant war, peace, or prayer we could not tell. The dawns were heralded by the descent of a chill stillness; the woodcutters slept, their fires burned low; the snapping of a twig would make you start. We were wanderers on prehistoric earth, on an earth that wore the aspect of an unknown planet. We could have fancied ourselves the first of men taking possession of an accursed inheritance, to be subdued at the cost of profound anguish and of excessive toil. But suddenly, as we struggled round a bend, there would be a glimpse of rush walls, of peaked grass roofs, a burst of yells, a whirl of black limbs, a mass of hands clapping, of feet stamping, of bodies swaying, of eyes rolling, under the droop of heavy and motionless foliage. The steamer toiled along slowly on the edge of a black and incomprehensible frenzy. The prehistoric man was cursing us, praying to us, welcoming us — who could tell? We were cut off from the comprehension of our surroundings; we glided past like phantoms, wondering and secretly appalled, as sane men would be before an enthusiastic outbreak in a madhouse. We could not understand because we were too far and could not remember, because we were traveling in the night of first ages, of those ages that are gone, leaving hardly a sign — and no memories.

"The earth seemed unearthly. We are accustomed to look upon the shackled form of a conquered monster, but there — there you could look at a thing monstrous and free. It was unearthly, and the men were — No, they were not inhuman. Well, you know, that was the worst of it — this suspicion of their not being inhuman. It would come slowly to one. They howled and leaped, and spun, and made horrid faces; but what thrilled you was just the thought of their humanity — like yours — the thought of your remote kinship with this wild and passionate uproar. Ugly. Yes, it was ugly enough; but if you were man enough you would admit to yourself that there was in you just the faintest trace of a response to the terrible frankness of that noise, a dim suspicion of there being a meaning in it which you — you so remote from the night of first ages — could comprehend. And why not? The mind of man is capable of anything — because everything is in it, all the past as well as all the future. What was there after all? Joy, fear, sorrow, devotion, valor, rage — who can tell? — but truth — truth stripped of its cloak of time. Let the fool gape and shudder — the man knows, and can look on without a wink. But he must at least be as much of a man as these on the shore. He must meet that truth with his own true stuff — with his own inborn strength. Principles won't do. Acquisitions, clothes, pretty rags — rags that would fly off at the first good shake. No; you want a deliberate belief. An appeal to me in this fiendish row — is there? Very well; I hear; I admit, but I have a voice, too, and for good or evil mine is the speech that cannot be silenced. Of course, a fool, what with sheer fright and fine sentiments, is always safe. Who's that grunting? You wonder I didn't go ashore for a howl and a dance? Well, no — I didn't. Fine sentiments, you say? Fine sentiments, be hanged! I had no time. I had to mess about with white lead and strips of woolen blanket helping to put bandages on those leaky steam pipes — I tell you. I had to watch the steering, and circumvent those snags, and get the tin-pot along by hook or by crook. There was surface truth enough in these things to save a wiser man. And between whiles I had to look after the savage who was fireman. He was an improved specimen; he could fire up a vertical boiler. He was there below me, and, upon my word, to look at him was as edifying as seeing a dog in a parody of breeches and a feather hat, walking on his hind legs. A few months of training had done for that really fine chap. He squinted at the steam gauge and at the water gauge with an evident effort of intrepidity — and he had filed teeth, too, the poor devil, and the wool of his pate shaved into queer patterns, and three ornamental scars on each of his cheeks. He ought to have been clapping his hands and stamping his feet on the bank, instead of which he was hard at work, a thrall to strange witchcraft, full of improving knowledge. He was useful because he had been instructed; and what he knew was this — that should the water in that transparent thing disappear, the evil spirit inside the boiler would get angry through the greatness of his thirst, and take a terrible vengeance. So he sweated and fired up and watched the glass fearfully (with an impromptu charm, made of rags, tied to his arm, and a piece of polished bone, as big as a watch, stuck flatways through his lower lip), while the wooded banks slipped past us slowly, the short noise was left behind, the interminable miles of silence — and we crept on, towards Kurtz. But the snags were thick, the water was treacherous and shallow, the boiler seemed indeed to have a sulky devil in it, and thus neither that fireman nor I had any time to peer into our creepy thoughts.

"Some fifty miles below the Inner Station we came upon a hut of reeds, an inclined and melancholy pole, with the unrecognizable tatters of what had been a flag of some sort flying from it, and a neatly stacked wood pile. This was unexpected. We came to the bank, and on the stack of firewood found a flat piece of board with some faded pencil writing on it. When deciphered it said: 'Wood for you. Hurry up. Approach cautiously.' There was a signature, but it was illegible — not Kurtz — a much longer word. Hurry up. Where? Up the river? 'Approach cautiously.' We had not done so. But the warning could not have been meant for the place where it could be only found after approach. Something was wrong above. But what — and how much? That was the question. We commented adversely upon the imbecility of that telegraphic style. The bush around said nothing, and would not let us look very far, either. A torn curtain of red twill hung in the doorway of the hut, and flapped sadly in our faces. The dwelling was dismantled; but we could see a white man had lived there not very long ago. There remained a rude table — a plank on two posts; a heap of rubbish reposed in a dark corner, and by the door I picked up a book. It had lost its covers, and the pages had been thumbed into a state of extremely dirty softness; but the back had been lovingly stitched afresh with white cotton thread, which looked clean yet. It was an extraordinary find. Its title was, *An Inquiry into Some Points of Seamanship*, by a man Tower, Towson — some such name — Master in his Majesty's Navy. The matter looked dreary reading enough, with illustrative diagrams and repulsive tables of figures, and the copy was sixty years old. I handled this amazing antiquity with the greatest possible tenderness, lest it should dissolve in my hands. Within, Towson or Towser was inquiring earnestly into the breaking strain of ships' chains and tackle, and other such matters. Not a very enthralling book; but at the first glance you could see there a singleness of intention, an honest concern for the right way of going to work, which made these humble pages, thought out so many years ago, luminous with another than a professional light. The simple old sailor, with his talk of chains and purchases, made me forget the jungle and the pilgrims in a delicious sensation of having come upon something unmistakably real. Such a book being there was wonderful enough; but still more astounding were the notes penciled in the margin, and plainly referring to the text. I couldn't believe my eyes! They were in cipher! Yes, it looked like cipher. Fancy a man lugging with him a book of that description into this nowhere and studying it — and making notes — in cipher at that! It was an extravagant mystery.

"I had been dimly aware for some time of a worrying noise, and when I lifted my eyes I saw the wood pile was gone, and the manager, aided by all the pilgrims, was shouting at me from the river side. I slipped the book into my pocket. I assure you to leave off reading was like tearing myself away from the shelter of an old and solid friendship.

"I started the lame engine ahead. 'It must be this miserable trader — this intruder,' exclaimed the manager, looking back malevolently at the place we had left. 'He must be English,' I said. 'It will not save him from getting into trouble if he is not careful,' muttered the manager darkly. I observed with assumed innocence that no man was safe from trouble in this world.

"The current was more rapid now, the steamer seemed at her last gasp, the stern wheel flopped languidly, and I caught myself listening on tiptoe for the next beat of the boat, for in sober truth I expected the wretched thing to give up every moment. It was like watching the last flickers of a life. But still we crawled. Sometimes I would pick out a tree a little way ahead to measure our progress towards Kurtz by, but I lost it invariably before we got abreast. To keep the eyes so long on one thing was too much for human patience. The manager displayed a beautiful resignation. I fretted and fumed and took to arguing with myself whether or not I would talk openly with Kurtz; but before I could come to any conclusion it occurred to me that my speech or my silence, indeed any action of mine, would be a mere futility. What did it matter what anyone knew or ignored? What did it matter who was manager? One gets sometimes such a flash of insight. The essentials of this affair lay deep under the surface, beyond my reach, and beyond my power of meddling.

"Towards the evening of the second day we judged ourselves about eight miles from Kurtz's station. I wanted to push on; but the manager looked grave, and told me the navigation up there was so dangerous that it would be advisable, the sun being very low already, to wait where we were till next morning. Moreover, he pointed out that if the warning to approach cautiously were to be followed, we must approach in daylight — not at dusk, or in the dark. This was sensible enough. Eight miles meant nearly three hours' steaming for us, and I could also see suspicious ripples at the upper end of the reach. Nevertheless, I was annoyed beyond expression at the delay, and most unreasonably, too, since one night more could not matter much after so many months. As we had plenty of wood, and caution was the word, I brought up in the middle of the stream. The reach was narrow, straight, with high sides like a railway cutting. The dusk came gliding into it long before the sun had set. The current ran smooth and swift, but a dumb immobility sat on the banks. The living trees, lashed together by the creepers and every living bush of the undergrowth, might have been changed into stone, even to the slenderest twig, to the lightest leaf. It was not sleep — it seemed unnatural, like a state of trance. Not the faintest sound of any kind could be heard. You looked on amazed, and began to suspect yourself of being deaf — then the night came suddenly, and struck you blind as well. About three in the morning some large fish leaped, and the loud splash made me jump as though a gun had been fired. When the sun rose there was a white fog, very warm and clammy, and more blinding than the night. It did not shift or drive; it was just there, standing all round you like something solid. At eight or nine, perhaps, it lifted as a shutter lifts. We had a glimpse of the towering multitude of trees, of the immense matted jungle, with the blazing little ball of the sun hanging over it — all perfectly still — and then the white shutter came down again, smoothly, as if sliding in greased grooves. I ordered the chain, which we had begun to heave in, to be paid out again. Before it stopped running with a muffled rattle, a cry, a very loud cry, as of infinite desolation, soared slowly in the opaque air. It ceased. A complaining clamor, modulated in savage discords, filled our ears. The sheer unexpectedness of it made my hair stir under my cap. I don't know how it struck the others: to me it seemed as though the mist itself had screamed, so suddenly, and apparently from all sides at once, did this tumultuous and mournful uproar arise. It culminated in a hurried outbreak of almost intolerably excessive shrieking, which stopped short, leaving us stiffened in a variety of silly attitudes, and obstinately listening to the nearly as appalling and excessive silence. 'Good God! What is the meaning — ' stammered at my elbow one of the pilgrims, a little fat man, with sandy hair and red whiskers, who wore sidespring boots, and pink pajamas tucked into his socks. Two others remained openmouthed a whole minute, then dashed into the little cabin, to rush out incontinently and stand darting scared glances, with Winchesters at 'ready' in their hands. What we could see was just the steamer we were on, her outlines blurred as though she had been on the point of dissolving, and a misty strip of water, perhaps two feet broad, around her — and that was all. The rest of the world was nowhere, as far as our eyes and ears were concerned. Just nowhere. Gone, disappeared; swept off without leaving a whisper or a shadow behind.

"I went forward, and ordered the chain to be hauled in short, so as to be ready to trip the anchor and move the steamboat at once if necessary. 'Will they attack?' whispered an awed voice. 'We will be all butchered in this fog,' murmured another. The faces twitched with the strain, the hands trembled slightly, the eyes forgot to wink. It was very curious to see the contrast of expressions of the white men and of the black fellows of our crew, who were as much strangers to that part of the river as we, though their homes were only eight hundred miles away. The whites, of course greatly discomposed, had besides a curious look of being painfully shocked by such an outrageous row. The others had an alert, naturally interested expression; but their faces were essentially quiet, even those of the one or two who grinned as they hauled at the chain. Several exchanged short, grunting phrases, which seemed to settle the matter to their satisfaction. Their headman, a young, broad-chested black, severely draped in dark-blue fringed cloths, with fierce nostrils and his hair all done up artfully in oily ringlets, stood near me. 'Aha!' I said, just for good fellowship's sake. 'Catch 'im,' he snapped, with a bloodshot widening of his eyes and a flash of sharp teeth — 'catch 'im. Give 'im to us.' 'To you, eh?' I asked; 'what would you do with them?' 'Eat 'im!' he said, curtly, and, leaning his elbow on the rail, looked out into the fog in a dignified and profoundly pensive attitude. I would no doubt have been properly horrified, had it not occurred to me that he and his chaps must be very hungry: that they must have been growing increasingly hungry for at least this month past. They had been engaged for six months (I don't think a single one of them had any clear idea of time, as we at the end of countless ages have. They still belonged to the beginnings of time — had no inherited experience to teach them as it were), and of course, as long as there was a piece of paper written over in accordance with some farcical law or other made down the river, it didn't enter anybody's head to trouble how they would live. Certainly they had brought with them some rotten hippo meat, which couldn't have lasted very long, anyway, even if the pilgrims hadn't, in the midst of a shocking hullabaloo, thrown a considerable quantity of it overboard. It looked like a high-handed proceeding; but it was really a case of legitimate self-defense. You can't breathe dead hippo waking, sleeping, and eating, and at the same time keep your precarious grip on existence. Besides that, they had given them every week three pieces of brass wire, each about nine inches long; and the theory was they were to buy their provisions with that currency in river-side villages. You can see how *that* worked. There were either no villages, or the people were hostile, or the director, who like the rest of us fed out of tins, with an occasional old he-goat thrown in, didn't want to stop the steamer for some more or less recondite reasons. So, unless they swallowed the wire itself, or made loops of it to snare the fishes with, I don't see what good their extravagant salary could be to them. I must say it was paid with a regularity worthy of a large and honorable trading company. For the rest, the only thing to eat — though it didn't look eatable in the least — I saw in their possession was a few lumps of some stuff like half-cooked dough, of a dirty lavender color, they kept wrapped in leaves, and now and then swallowed a piece of, but so small that it seemed done more for the looks of the thing than for any serious purpose of sustenance. Why in the name of all the gnawing devils of hunger they didn't go for us — they were thirty to five — and have a good tuck in for once, amazes me now when I think of it. They were big powerful men, with not much capacity to weigh the consequences, with courage, with strength, even yet, though their skins were no longer glossy and their muscles no longer hard. And I saw that something restraining, one of those human secrets that baffle probability, had come into play there. I looked at them with a swift quickening of interest — not because it occurred to me I might be eaten by them before very long, though I own to you that just then I perceived — in a new light, as it were — how unwholesome the pilgrims looked, and I hoped, yes, I positively hoped, that my aspect was not so — what shall I say? — so — unappetizing: a touch of fantastic vanity which fitted well with the dream-sensation that pervaded all my days at that time. Perhaps I had a little fever, too. One can't live with one's finger everlastingly on one's pulse. I had often 'a little fever,' or a little touch of other things — the playful paw-strokes of the wilderness, the preliminary trifling before the more serious onslaught which came in due course. Yes; I looked at them as you would on any human being, with a curiosity of their impulses, motives, capacities, weaknesses, when brought to the test of an inexorable physical necessity. Restraint! What possible restraint? Was it superstition, disgust, patience, fear — or some kind of primitive honor? No fear can stand up to hunger, no patience can wear it out, disgust simply does not exist where hunger is; and as to superstition, beliefs, and what you may call principles, they are less than chaff in a breeze. Don't you know the devilry of lingering starvation, its exasperating torment, its black thoughts, its somber and brooding ferocity? Well, I do. It takes a man all his inborn strength to fight hunger properly. It's really easier to face bereavement, dishonor, and the perdition of one's soul — than this kind of prolonged hunger. Sad, but true. And these chaps, too, had no earthly reason for any kind of scruple. Restraint! I would just as soon have expected restraint from a hyena prowling amongst the corpses of a battlefield. But there was the fact facing me — the fact dazzling, to be seen, like the foam on the depths of the sea, like a ripple on an unfathomable enigma, a mystery greater — when I thought of it — than the curious, inexplicable note of desperate grief in this savage clamor that had swept by us on the river bank, behind the blind whiteness of the fog.

"Two pilgrims were quarreling in hurried whispers as to which bank. 'Left.' 'No, no; how can you? Right, right, of course.' 'It is very serious,' said the manager's voice behind me; 'I would be desolated if anything should happen to Mr. Kurtz before we came up.' I looked at him, and had not the slightest doubt he was sincere. He was just the kind of man who would wish to preserve appearances. That was his restraint. But when he muttered something about going on at once, I did not even take the trouble to answer him. I knew, and he knew, that it was impossible. Were we to let go our hold of the bottom, we would be absolutely in the air — in space. We wouldn't be able to tell where we were going to — whether up- or downstream, or across — till we fetched against one bank or the other, and then we wouldn't know at first which it was. Of course I made no move. I had no mind for a smashup. You couldn't imagine a more deadly place for a shipwreck. Whether drowned at once or not, we were sure to perish speedily in one way or another. 'I authorize you to take all the risks,' he said, after a short silence. 'I refuse to take any,' I said, shortly; which was just the answer he expected, though its tone might have surprised him. 'Well, I must defer to your judgment. You are captain,' he said, with marked civility. I turned my shoulder to him in sign of my appreciation, and looked into the fog. How long would it last? It was the most hopeless lookout. The approach to this Kurtz grubbing for ivory in the wretched bush was beset by as many dangers as though he had been an enchanted princess sleeping in a fabulous castle. "Will they attack, do you think?" asked the manager, in a confidential tone.

"I did not think they would attack, for several obvious reasons. The thick fog was one. If they left the bank in their canoes they would get lost in it, as we would be if we attempted to move. Still, I had also judged the jungle of both banks quite impenetrable — and yet eyes were in it, eyes that had seen us. The riverside bushes were certainly very thick; but the undergrowth behind was evidently penetrable. However, during the short lift I had seen no canoes anywhere in the reach — certainly not abreast of the steamer. But what made the idea of attack inconceivable to me was the nature of the noise — of the cries we had heard. They had not the fierce character boding of immediate hostile intention. Unexpected, wild, and violent as they had been, they had given me an irresistible impression of sorrow. The glimpse of the steamboat had for some reason filled those savages with unrestrained grief. The danger, if any, I expounded, was from our proximity to a great human passion let loose. Even extreme grief may ultimately vent itself in violence — but more generally takes the form of apathy.

"You should have seen the pilgrims stare! They had no heart to grin, or even to revile me: but I believe they thought me gone mad — with fright, maybe. I delivered a regular lecture. My dear boys, it was no good bothering. Keep a lookout? Well, you may guess I watched the fog for the signs of lifting as a cat watches a mouse; but for anything else our eyes were of no more use to us than if we had been buried miles deep in a heap of cotton-wool. It felt like it, too — choking, warm, stifling. Besides, all I said, though it sounded extravagant, was absolutely true to fact. What we afterwards alluded to as an attack was really an attempt at repulse. The action was very far from being aggressive — it was not even defensive, in the usual sense: it was undertaken under the stress of desperation, and in its essence was purely protective.

"It developed itself, I should say, two hours after the fog lifted, and its commencement was at a spot, roughly speaking, about a mile and a half below Kurtz's station. We had just floundered and flopped round a bend, when I saw an islet, a mere grassy hummock of bright green, in the middle of the stream. It was the only thing of the kind; but as we opened the reach more, I perceived it was the head of a long sandbank, or rather of a chain of shallow patches stretching down the middle of the river. They were discolored, just awash, and the whole lot was seen just under the water, exactly as a man's backbone is seen running down the middle of his back under the skin. Now, as far as I did see, I could go to the right or to the left of this. I didn't know either channel, of course. The banks looked pretty well alike, the depth appeared the same; but as I had been informed the station was on the west side, I naturally headed for the western passage.

"No sooner had we fairly entered it than I became aware it was much narrower than I had supposed. To the left of us there was the long uninterrupted shoal, and to the right a high, steep bank heavily overgrown with bushes. Above the bush the trees stood in serried ranks. The twigs overhung the current thickly, and from distance to distance a large limb of some tree projected rigidly over the stream. It was then well on in the afternoon, the face of the forest was gloomy, and a broad strip of shadow had already fallen on the water. In this shadow we steamed up — very slowly, as you may imagine. I sheered her well inshore — the water being deepest near the bank, as the sounding pole informed me.

"One of my hungry and forbearing friends was sounding in the bows just below me. This steamboat was exactly like a decked scow. On the deck, there were two little teakwood houses, with doors and windows. The boiler was in the fore-end, and the machinery right astern. Over the whole there was a light roof, supported on stanchions. The funnel projected through that roof, and in front of the funnel a small cabin built of light planks served for a pilot house. It contained a couch, two camp-stools, a loaded Martini-Henry leaning in one corner, a tiny table, and the steering wheel. It had a wide door in front and a broad shutter at each side. All these were always thrown open, of course. I spent my days perched up there on the extreme fore-end of that roof, before the door. At night I slept, or tried to, on the couch. An athletic black belonging to some coast tribe, and educated by my poor predecessor, was the helmsman. He sported a pair of brass earrings, wore a blue cloth wrapper from the waist to the ankles, and thought all the world of himself. He was the most unstable kind of fool I had ever seen. He steered with no end of a swagger while you were by; but if he lost sight of you, he became instantly the prey of an abject funk, and would let that cripple of a steamboat get the upper hand of him in a minute.

"I was looking down at the sounding pole, and feeling much annoyed to see at each try a little more of it stick out of that river, when I saw my poleman give up the business suddenly, and stretch himself flat on the deck, without even taking the trouble to haul his pole in. He kept hold on it though, and it trailed in the water. At the same time the fireman, whom I could also see below me, sat down abruptly before his furnace and ducked his head. I was amazed. Then I had to look at the river mighty quick, because there was a snag in the fairway. Sticks, little sticks, were flying about — thick: they were whizzing before my nose, dropping below me, striking behind me against my pilot house. All this time the river, the shore, the woods, were very quiet — perfectly quiet. I could only hear the heavy splashing thump of the stern wheel and the patter of these things. We cleared the snag clumsily. Arrows, by Jove! We were being shot at! I stepped in quickly to close the shutter on the land side. That fool helmsman, his hands on the spokes, was lifting his knees high, stamping his feet, champing his mouth, like a reined-in horse. Confound him! And we were staggering within ten feet of the bank. I had to lean right out to swing the heavy shutter, and I saw a face amongst the leaves on the level with my own, looking at me very fierce and steady; and then suddenly, as though a veil had been removed from my eyes, I made out, deep in the tangled gloom, naked breasts, arms, legs, glaring eyes — the bush was swarming with human limbs in movement, glistening, of bronze color. The twigs shook, swayed, and rustled, the arrows flew out of them, and then the shutter came to. 'Steer her straight,' I said to the helmsman. He held his head rigid, face forward; but his eyes rolled, he kept on, lifting and setting down his feet gently, his mouth foamed a little. 'Keep quiet!' I said in a fury. I might just as well have ordered a tree not to sway in the wind. I darted out. Below me there was a great scuffle of feet on the iron deck; confused exclamations; a voice screamed, 'Can you turn back?' I caught sight of a V-shaped ripple on the water ahead. What? Another snag! A fusillade burst out under my feet. The pilgrims had opened with their Winchesters, and were simply squirting lead into that bush. A deuce of a lot of smoke came up and drove slowly forward. I swore at it. Now I couldn't see the ripple or the snag either. I stood in the doorway, peering, and the arrows came in swarms. They might have been poisoned, but they looked as though they wouldn't kill a cat. The bush began to howl. Our woodcutters raised a warlike whoop; the report of a rifle just at my back deafened me. I glanced over my shoulder, and the pilot house was yet full of noise and smoke when I made a dash at the wheel. The fool nigger had dropped everything, to throw the shutter open and let off that Martini-Henry. He stood before the wide opening, glaring, and I yelled at him to come back, while I straightened the sudden twist out of that steamboat. There was no room to turn even if I had wanted to, the snag was somewhere very near ahead in that confounded smoke, there was no time to lose, so I just crowded her into the bank — right into the bank, where I knew the water was deep.

"We tore slowly along the overhanging bushes in a whirl of broken twigs and flying leaves. The fusillade below stopped short, as I had foreseen it would when the squirts got empty. I threw my head back to a glinting whizz that traversed the pilot house, in at one shutter-hole and out at the other. Looking past that mad helmsman, who was shaking the empty rifle and yelling at the shore, I saw vague forms of men running bent double, leaping, gliding, distinct, incomplete, evanescent. Something big appeared in the air before the shutter, the rifle went overboard, and the man stepped back swiftly, looked at me over his shoulder in an extraordinary, profound, familiar manner, and fell upon my feet. The side of his head hit the wheel twice, and the end of what appeared a long cane clattered round and knocked over a little camp-stool. It looked as though after wrenching that thing from somebody ashore he had lost his balance in the effort. The thin smoke had blown away, we were clear of the snag, and looking ahead I could see that in another hundred yards or so I would be free to sheer off, away from the bank; but my feet felt so very warm and wet that I had to look down. The man had rolled on his back and stared straight up at me; both his hands clutched that cane. It was the shaft of a spear that, either thrown or lunged through the opening, had caught him in the side just below the ribs; the blade had gone in out of sight, after making a frightful gash; my shoes were full; a pool of blood lay very still, gleaming dark-red under the wheel; his eyes shone with an amazing luster. The fusillade burst out again. He looked at me anxiously, gripping the spear like something precious, with an air of being afraid I would try to take it away from him. I had to make an effort to free my eyes from his gaze and attend to the steering. With one hand I felt above my head for the line of the steam whistle, and jerked out screech after screech hurriedly. The tumult of angry and warlike yells was checked instantly, and then from the depths of the woods went out such a tremulous and prolonged wail of mournful fear and utter despair as may be imagined to follow the flight of the last hope from the earth. There was a great commotion in the bush; the shower of arrows stopped, a few dropping shots rang out sharply — then silence, in which the languid beat of the stern wheel came plainly to my ears. I put the helm hard a-starboard at the moment when the pilgrim in pink pajamas, very hot and agitated, appeared in the doorway. 'The manager sends me — ' he began in an official tone, and stopped short. 'Good God!' he said, glaring at the wounded man.

"We two whites stood over him, and his lustrous and inquiring glance enveloped us both. I declare it looked as though he would presently put to us some question in an understandable language; but he died without uttering a sound, without moving a limb, without twitching a muscle. Only in the very last moment, as though in response to some sign we could not see, to some whisper we could not hear, he frowned heavily, and that frown gave to his black death mask an inconceivably somber, brooding, and menacing expression. The luster of inquiring glance faded swiftly into vacant glassiness. 'Can you steer?' I asked the agent eagerly. He looked very dubious; but I made a grab at his arm, and he understood at once I meant him to steer whether or no. To tell you the truth, I was morbidly anxious to change my shoes and socks. 'He is dead,' murmured the fellow, immensely impressed. 'No doubt about it,' said I, tugging like mad at the shoelaces. 'And by the way, I suppose Mr. Kurtz is dead as well by this time.'

"For the moment that was the dominant thought. There was a sense of extreme disappointment, as though I had found out I had been striving after something altogether without a substance. I couldn't have been more disgusted if I had traveled all this way for the sole purpose of talking with Mr. Kurtz. Talking with ... I flung one shoe overboard, and became aware that that was exactly what I had been looking forward to — a talk with Kurtz. I made the strange discovery that I had never imagined him as doing, you know, but as discoursing. I didn't say to myself, 'Now I will never see him,' or 'Now I will never shake him by the hand,' but, 'now I will never hear him.' The man presented himself as a voice. Not of course that I did not connect him with some sort of action. Hadn't I been told in all the tones of jealousy and admiration that he had collected, bartered, swindled, or stolen more ivory than all the other agents together? That was not the point. The point was in his being a gifted creature, and that of all his gifts the one that stood out pre-eminently, that carried with it a sense of real presence, was his ability to talk, his words — the gift of expression, the bewildering, the illuminating, the most exalted and the most contemptible, the pulsating stream of light, or the deceitful flow from the heart of an impenetrable darkness.

"The other shoe went flying unto the devil-god of that river. I thought, by Jove! it's all over. We are too late; he has vanished — the gift has vanished, by means of some spear, arrow, or club. I will never hear that chap speak after all, and my sorrow had a startling extravagance of emotion, even such as I had noticed in the howling sorrow of these savages in the bush. I couldn't have felt more of lonely desolation somehow, had I been robbed of a belief or had missed my destiny in life. ... Why do you sigh in this beastly way, somebody? Absurd? Well, absurd. Good Lord! mustn't a man ever — Here, give me some tobacco." ...

There was a pause of profound stillness, then a match flared, and Marlow's lean face appeared, worn, hollow, with downward folds and dropped eyelids, with an aspect of concentrated attention; and as he took vigorous draws at his pipe, it seemed to retreat and advance out of the night in the regular flicker of the tiny flame. The match went out.

"Absurd!" he cried. "This is the worst of trying to tell. ... Here you all are, each moored with two good addresses, like a hulk with two anchors, a butcher round one corner, a policeman round another, excellent appetites, and temperature normal — you hear — normal from year's end to year's end. And you say, Absurd! Absurd be — exploded! Absurd! My dear boys, what can you expect from a man who out of sheer nervousness had just flung overboard a pair of new shoes! Now I think of it, it is amazing I did not shed tears. I am, upon the whole, proud of my fortitude. I was cut to the quick at the idea of having lost the inestimable privilege of listening to the gifted Kurtz. Of course I was wrong. The privilege was waiting for me. Oh, yes, I heard more than enough. And I was right, too. A voice. He was very little more than a voice. And I heard — him — it — this voice — other voices — all of them were so little more than voices — and the memory of that time itself lingers around me, impalpable, like a dying vibration of one immense jabber, silly, atrocious, sordid, savage, or simply mean, without any kind of sense. Voices, voices — even the girl herself — now — "

He was silent for a long time.

"I laid the ghost of his gifts at last with a lie," he began, suddenly. "Girl! What? Did I mention a girl? Oh, she is out of it — completely. They — the women I mean — are out of it — should be out of it. We must help them to stay in that beautiful world of their own, lest ours gets worse. Oh, she had to be out of it. You should have heard the disinterred body of Mr. Kurtz saying, 'My Intended.' You would have perceived directly then how completely she was out of it. And the lofty frontal bone of Mr. Kurtz! They say the hair goes on growing sometimes, but this — ah — specimen, was impressively bald. The wilderness had patted him on the head, and, behold, it was like a ball — an ivory ball; it had caressed him, and — lo! — he had withered; it had taken him, loved him, embraced him, got into his veins, consumed his flesh, and sealed his soul to its own by the inconceivable ceremonies of some devilish initiation. He was its spoiled and pampered favorite. Ivory? I should think so. Heaps of it, stacks of it. The old mud shanty was bursting with it. You would think there was not a single tusk left either above or below the ground in the whole country. 'Mostly fossil,' the manager had remarked, disparagingly. It was no more fossil than I am; but they call it fossil when it is dug up. It appears these niggers do bury the tusks sometimes — but evidently they couldn't bury this parcel deep enough to save the gifted Mr. Kurtz from his fate. We filled the steamboat with it, and had to pile a lot on the deck. Thus he could see and enjoy as long as he could see, because the appreciation of his favor had remained with him to the last. You should have heard him say, 'My ivory.' Oh yes, I heard him. 'My Intended, my ivory, my station, my river, my — ' everything belonged to him. It made me hold my breath in expectation of hearing the wilderness burst into a prodigious peal of laughter that would shake the fixed stars in their places. Everything belonged to him — but that was a trifle. The thing was to know what he belonged to, how many powers of darkness claimed him for their own. That was the reflection that made you creepy all over. It was impossible — it was not good for one either — trying to imagine. He had taken a high seat amongst the devils of the land — I mean literally. You can't understand. How could you? — with solid pavement under your feet, surrounded by kind neighbors ready to cheer you or to fall on you, stepping delicately between the butcher and the policeman, in the holy terror of scandal and gallows and lunatic asylums — how can you imagine what particular region of the first ages a man's untrammeled feet may take him into by the way of solitude — utter solitude without a policeman — by the way of silence — utter silence, where no warning voice of a kind neighbor can be heard whispering of public opinion? These little things make all the great difference. When they are gone you must fall back upon your own innate strength, upon your own capacity for faithfulness. Of course you may be too much of a fool to go wrong — too dull even to know you are being assaulted by the powers of darkness. I take it, no fool ever made a bargain for his soul with the devil: the fool is too much of a fool, or the devil too much of a devil — I don't know which. Or you may be such a thunderingly exalted creature as to be altogether deaf and blind to anything but heavenly sights and sounds. Then the earth for you is only a standing place — and whether to be like this is your loss or your gain I won't pretend to say. But most of us are neither one nor the other. The earth for us is a place to live in, where we must put up with sights, with sounds, with smells, too, by Jove! — breathe dead hippo, so to speak, and not be contaminated. And there, don't you see? Your strength comes in, the faith in your ability for the digging of unostentatious holes to bury the stuff in — your power of devotion, not to yourself, but to an obscure, back-breaking business. And that's difficult enough. Mind, I am not trying to excuse or even explain — I am trying to account to myself for — for — Mr. Kurtz — for the shade of Mr. Kurtz. This initiated wraith from the back of Nowhere honored me with its amazing confidence before it vanished altogether. This was because it could speak English to me. The original Kurtz had been educated partly in England, and — as he was good enough to say himself — his sympathies were in the right place. His mother was half-English, his father was half-French. All Europe contributed to the making of Kurtz; and by and by I learned that, most appropriately, the International Society for the Suppression of Savage Customs had intrusted him with the making of a report, for its future guidance. And he had written it, too. I've seen it. I've read it. It was eloquent, vibrating with eloquence, but too high-strung, I think. Seventeen pages of close writing he had found time for! But this must have been before his — let us say — nerves, went wrong, and caused him to preside at certain midnight dances ending with unspeakable rites, which — as far as I reluctantly gathered from what I heard at various times — were offered up to him — do you understand? — to Mr. Kurtz himself. But it was a beautiful piece of writing. The opening paragraph, however, in the light of later information, strikes me now as ominous. He began with the argument that we whites, from the point of development we had arrived at, 'must necessarily appear to them [savages] in the nature of supernatural beings — we approach them with the might as of a deity,' and so on, and so on. 'By the simple exercise of our will we can exert a power for good practically unbounded,' etc., etc. From that point he soared and took me with him. The peroration was magnificent, though difficult to remember, you know. It gave me the notion of an exotic Immensity ruled by an august Benevolence. It made me tingle with enthusiasm. This was the unbounded power of eloquence — of words — of burning noble words. There were no practical hints to interrupt the magic current of phrases, unless a kind of note at the foot of the last page, scrawled evidently much later, in an unsteady hand, may be regarded as the exposition of a method. It was very simple, and at the end of that moving appeal to every altruistic sentiment it blazed at you, luminous and terrifying, like a flash of lightning in a serene sky: 'Exterminate all the brutes!' The curious part was that he had apparently forgotten all about that valuable postscriptum, because, later on, when he in a sense came to himself, he repeatedly entreated me to take good care of 'my pamphet' (he called it), as it was sure to have in the future a good influence upon his career. I had full information about all these things, and, besides, as it turned out, I was to have the care of his memory. I've done enough for it to give me the indisputable right to lay it, if I choose, for an everlasting rest in the dust bin of progress, amongst all the sweepings and, figuratively speaking, all the dead cats of civilization. But then, you see, I can't choose. He won't be forgotten. Whatever he was, he was not common. He had the power to charm or frighten rudimentary souls into an aggravated witch dance in his honor; he could also fill the small souls of the pilgrims with bitter misgivings: he had one devoted friend at least, and he had conquered one soul in the world that was neither rudimentary nor tainted with self-seeking. No; I can't forget him, though I am not prepared to affirm the fellow was exactly worth the life we lost in getting to him. I missed my late helmsman awfully — I missed him even while his body was still lying in the pilot house. Perhaps you will think it passing strange this regret for a savage who was no more account than a grain of sand in a black Sahara. Well, don't you see, he had done something, he had steered; for months I had him at my back — a help — an instrument. It was a kind of partnership. He steered for me — I had to look after him, I worried about his deficiencies, and thus a subtle bond had been created, of which I only became aware when it was suddenly broken. And the intimate profundity of that look he gave me when he received his hurt remains to this day in my memory — like a claim of distant kinship affirmed in a supreme moment.

"Poor fool! If he had only left that shutter alone. He had no restraint, no restraint — just like Kurtz — a tree swayed by the wind. As soon as I had put on a dry pair of slippers, I dragged him out, after first jerking the spear out of his side, which operation I confess I performed with my eyes shut tight. His heels leaped together over the little doorstep; his shoulders were pressed to my breast; I hugged him from behind desperately. Oh! he was heavy, heavy; heavier than any man on earth, I should imagine. Then without more ado I tipped him overboard. The current snatched him as though he had been a wisp of grass, and I saw the body roll over twice before I lost sight of it forever. All the pilgrims and the manager were then congregated on the awning deck about the pilot house, chattering at each other like a flock of excited magpies, and there was a scandalized murmur at my heartless promptitude. What they wanted to keep that body hanging about for I can't guess. Embalm it, maybe. But I had also heard another, and a very ominous, murmur on the deck below. My friends the woodcutters were likewise scandalized, and with a better show of reason — though I admit that the reason itself was quite inadmissible. Oh, quite! I had made up my mind that if my late helmsman was to be eaten, the fishes alone should have him. He had been a very second-rate helmsman while alive, but now he was dead he might have become a first-class temptation, and possibly cause some startling trouble. Besides, I was anxious to take the wheel, the man in pink pajamas showing himself a hopeless duffer at the business.

"This I did directly the simple funeral was over. We were going half-speed, keeping right in the middle of the stream, and I listened to the talk about me. They had given up Kurtz, they had given up the station; Kurtz was dead, and the station had been burnt — and so on — and so on. The red-haired pilgrim was beside himself with the thought that at least this poor Kurtz had been properly avenged. 'Say! We must have made a glorious slaughter of them in the bush. Eh? What do you think? Say?' He positively danced, the bloodthirsty little gingery beggar. And he had nearly fainted when he saw the wounded man! I could not help saying, 'You made a glorious lot of smoke, anyhow.' I had seen, from the way the tops of the bushes rustled and flew, that almost all the shots had gone too high. You can't hit anything unless you take aim and fire from the shoulder; but these chaps fired from the hip with their eyes shut. The retreat, I maintained — and I was right — was caused by the screeching of the steam whistle. Upon this they forgot Kurtz, and began to howl at me with indignant protests.

"The manager stood by the wheel murmuring confidentially about the necessity of getting well away down the river before dark at all events, when I saw in the distance a clearing on the river side and the outlines of some sort of building. 'What's this?' I asked. He clapped his hands in wonder. 'That station!' he cried. I edged in at once, still going half-speed.

"Through my glasses I saw the slope of a hill interspersed with rare trees and perfectly free from undergrowth. A long decaying building on the summit was half buried in the high grass; the large holes in the peaked roof gaped black from afar; the jungle and the woods made a background. There was no enclosure or fence of any kind; but there had been one apparently, for near the house half-a-dozen slim posts remained in a row, roughly trimmed, and with their upper ends ornamented with round carved balls. The rails, or whatever there had been between, had disappeared. Of course the forest surrounded all that. The river bank was clear, and on the water side I saw a white man under a hat like a cart wheel beckoning persistently with his whole arm. Examining the edge of the forest above and below, I was almost certain I could see movements — human forms gliding here and there. I steamed past prudently, then stopped the engines and let her drift down. The man on the shore began to shout, urging us to land. 'We have been attacked,' screamed the manager. 'I know — I know. It's all right,' yelled back the other, as cheerful as you please. 'Come along. It's all right. I am glad.'

"His aspect reminded me of something I had seen — something funny I had seen somewhere. As I maneuvered to get alongside, I was asking myself, 'What does this fellow look like?' Suddenly I got it. He looked like a harlequin. His clothes had been made of some stuff that was brown holland probably, but it was covered with patches all over, with bright patches, blue, red, and yellow — patches on the back, patches on the front, patches on elbows, on knees; colored binding around his jacket, scarlet edging at the bottom of his trousers; and the sunshine made him look extremely gay and wonderfully neat withal, because you could see how beautifully all this patching had been done. A beardless, boyish face, very fair, no features to speak of, nose peeling, little blue eyes, smiles and frowns chasing each other over that open countenance like sunshine and shadow on a wind-swept plain. 'Look out, captain!' he cried; 'there's a snag lodged in here last night.' What! Another snag? I confess I swore shamefully. I had nearly holed my cripple, to finish off that charming trip. The harlequin on the bank turned his little pug nose up to me. 'You English?' he asked, all smiles. 'Are you?' I shouted from the wheel. The smiles vanished, and he shook his head as if sorry for my disappointment. Then he brightened up. 'Never mind!' he cried, encouragingly. 'Are we in time?' I asked. 'He is up there,' he replied, with a toss of the head up the hill, and becoming gloomy all of a sudden. His face was like the autumn sky, overcast one moment and bright the next.

"When the manager, escorted by the pilgrims, all of them armed to the teeth, had gone to the house this chap came on board. 'I say, I don't like this. These natives are in the bush,' I said. He assured me earnestly it was all right. 'They are simple people,' he added; 'well, I am glad you came. It took me all my time to keep them off.' 'But you said it was all right,' I cried. 'Oh, they meant no harm,' he said; and as I stared he corrected himself, 'Not exactly.' Then vivaciously, 'My faith, your pilot house wants a clean-up!' In the next breath he advised me to keep enough steam on the boiler to blow the whistle in case of any trouble. 'One good screech will do more for you than all your rifles. They are simple people,' he repeated. He rattled away at such a rate he quite overwhelmed me. He seemed to be trying to make up for lots of silence, and actually hinted, laughing, that such was the case. 'Don't you talk with Mr. Kurtz?' I said. 'You don't talk with that man — you listen to him,' he exclaimed with severe exaltation. 'But now — ' He waved his arm, and in the twinkling of an eye was in the uttermost depths of despondency. In a moment he came up again with a jump, possessed himself of both my hands, shook them continuously, while he gabbled: 'Brother sailor ... honor ... pleasure ... delight ... introduce myself ... Russian ... son of an arch-priest ... Government of Tambov ... What? Tobacco! English tobacco; the excellent English tobacco! Now, that's brotherly. Smoke? Where's a sailor that does not smoke?'

"The pipe soothed him, and gradually I made out he had run away from school, had gone to sea in a Russian ship; ran away again; served some time in English ships; was now reconciled with the arch-priest. He made a point of that. 'But when one is young one must see things, gather experience, ideas; enlarge the mind.' 'Here!' I interrupted. 'You can never tell! Here I met Mr. Kurtz,' he said, youthfully solemn and reproachful. I held my tongue after that. It appears he had persuaded a Dutch trading house on the coast to fit him out with stores and goods, and had started for the interior with a light heart, and no more idea of what would happen to him than a baby. He had been wandering about that river for nearly two years alone, cut off from everybody and everything. 'I am not so young as I look. I am twenty-five,' he said. 'At first old Van Shuyten would tell me to go to the devil,' he narrated with keen enjoyment; 'but I stuck to him, and talked and talked, till at last he got afraid I would talk the hind leg off his favorite dog, so he gave me some cheap things and a few guns, and told me he hoped he would never see my face again. Good old Dutchman, Van Shuyten. I've sent him one small lot of ivory a year ago, so that he can't call me a little thief when I get back. I hope he got it. And for the rest I don't care. I had some wood stacked for you. That was my old house. Did you see?'

"I gave him Towson's book. He made as though he would kiss me, but restrained himself. 'The only book I had left, and I thought I had lost it,' he said, looking at it ecstatically. 'So many accidents happen to a man going about alone, you know. Canoes get upset sometimes — and sometimes you've got to clear out so quick when the people get angry.' He thumbed the pages. 'You made notes in Russian?' I asked. He nodded. 'I thought they were written in cipher,' I said. He laughed, then became serious. 'I had lots of trouble to keep these people off,' he said. 'Did they want to kill you?' I asked. 'Oh, no!' he cried, and checked himself. 'Why did they attack us?' I pursued. He hesitated, then said shamefacedly, 'They don't want him to go.' 'Don't they?' I said, curiously. He nodded a nod full of mystery and wisdom. 'I tell you,' he cried, 'this man has enlarged my mind.' He opened his arms wide, staring at me with his little blue eyes that were perfectly round."

III

"I looked at him, lost in astonishment. There he was before me, in motley, as though he had absconded from a troupe of mimes, enthusiastic, fabulous. His very existence was improbable, inexplicable, and altogether bewildering. He was an insoluble problem. It was inconceivable how he had existed, how he had succeeded in getting so far, how he had managed to remain — why he did not instantly disappear. 'I went a little farther,' he said, 'then still a little farther — till I had gone so far that I don't know how I'll ever get back. Never mind. Plenty time. I can manage. You take Kurtz away quick — quick — I tell you.' The glamor of youth enveloped his parti-colored rags, his destitution, his loneliness, the essential desolation of his futile wanderings. For months — for years — his life hadn't been worth a day's purchase; and there he was gallantly, thoughtlessly alive, to all appearance indestructible solely by the virtue of his few years and of his unreflecting audacity. I was seduced into something like admiration — like envy. Glamor urged him on, glamor kept him unscathed. He surely wanted nothing from the wilderness but space to breathe in and to push on through. His need was to exist, and to move onwards at the greatest possible risk, and with a maximum of privation. If the absolutely pure, uncalculating, unpractical spirit of adventure had ever ruled a human being, it ruled this bepatched youth. I almost envied him the possession of this modest and clear flame. It seemed to have consumed all thought of self so completely, that even while he was talking to you, you forgot that it was he — the man before your eyes — who had gone through these things. I did not envy him his devotion to Kurtz, though. He had not meditated over it. It came to him, and he accepted it with a sort of eager fatalism. I must say that to me it appeared about the most dangerous thing in every way he had come upon so far.

"They had come together unavoidably, like two ships becalmed near each other, and lay rubbing sides at last. I suppose Kurtz wanted an audience, because on a certain occasion, when encamped in the forest, they had talked all night, or more probably Kurtz had talked. 'We talked of everything,' he said, quite transported at the recollection. 'I forgot there was such a thing as sleep. The night did not seem to last an hour. Everything! Everything! . . . Of love, too.' 'Ah, he talked to you of love!' I said, much amused. 'It isn't what you think,' he cried, almost passionately. 'It was in general. He made me see things — things.'

"He threw his arms up. We were on deck at the time, and the headman of my woodcutters, lounging near by, turned upon him his heavy and glittering eyes. I looked around, and I don't know why, but I assure you that never, never before, did this land, this river, this jungle, the very arch of this blazing sky, appear to me so hopeless and so dark, so impenetrable to human thought, so pitiless to human weakness. 'And, ever since, you have been with him, of course?' I said.

"On the contrary. It appears their intercourse had been very much broken by various causes. He had, as he informed me proudly, managed to nurse Kurtz through two illnesses (he alluded to it as you would to some risky feat), but as a rule Kurtz wandered alone, far in the depths of the forest. 'Very often coming to this station, I had to wait days and days before he would turn up,' he said. 'Ah, it was worth waiting for! — sometimes.' 'What was he doing? Exploring or what?' I asked. 'Oh, yes, of course'; he had discovered lots of villages, a lake, too — he did not know exactly in what direction; it was dangerous to inquire too much — but mostly his expeditions had been for ivory. 'But he had no goods to trade with by that time,' I objected. 'There's a good lot of cartridges left even yet,' he answered, looking away. 'To speak plainly, he raided the country,' I said. He nodded. 'Not alone, surely!' He muttered something about the villages round that lake. 'Kurtz got the tribe to follow him, did he?' I suggested. He fidgeted a little. 'They adored him,' he said. The tone of these words was so extraordinary that I looked at him searchingly. It was curious to see his mingled eagerness and reluctance to speak of Kurtz. The man filled his life, occupied his thoughts, swayed his emotions. 'What can you expect?' he burst out; 'he came to them with thunder and lightning, you know — and they had never seen anything like it — and very terrible. He could be very terrible. You can't judge Mr. Kurtz as you would an ordinary man. No, no, no! Now — just to give you an idea — I don't mind telling you, he wanted to shoot me, too, one day — but I don't judge him.' 'Shoot you!' I cried. 'What for?' 'Well, I had a small lot of ivory the chief of that village near my house gave me. You see I used to shoot game for them. Well, he wanted it, and wouldn't hear reason. He declared he would shoot me unless I gave him the ivory and then cleared out of the country, because he could do so, and had a fancy for it, and there was nothing on earth to prevent him killing whom he jolly well pleased. And it was true, too. I gave him the ivory. What did I care! But I didn't clear out. No, no. I couldn't leave him. I had to be careful, of course, till we got friendly again for a time. He had his second illness then. Afterwards I had to keep out of the way; but I didn't mind. He was living for the most part in those villages on the lake. When he came down to the river, sometimes he would take to me, and sometimes it was better for me to be careful. This man suffered too much. He hated all this, and somehow he couldn't get away. When I had a chance I begged him to try and leave while there was time; I offered to go back with him. And he would say yes, and then he would remain; go off on another ivory hunt; disappear for weeks; forget himself amongst these people — forget himself — you know.' 'Why! he's mad,' I said. He protested indignantly. Mr. Kurtz couldn't be mad. If I had heard him talk, only two days ago, I wouldn't dare hint at such a thing. . . . I had taken up my binoculars while we talked, and was looking at the shore, sweeping the limit of the forest at each side and at the back of the house. The consciousness of there being people in that bush, so silent, so quiet — as silent and quiet as the ruined house on the hill — made me uneasy. There was no sign on the face of nature of this amazing tale that was not so much told as suggested to me in desolate exclamations, completed by shrugs, in interrupted phrases, in hints ending in deep sighs. The woods were unmoved, like a mask — heavy, like the closed door of a prison — they looked with their air of hidden knowledge, of patient expectation, of unapproachable silence. The Russian was explaining to me that it was only lately that Mr. Kurtz had come down to the river, bringing along with him all the fighting men of that lake tribe. He had been absent for several months — getting himself adored, I suppose — and had come down unexpectedly, with the intention to all appearances of making a raid either across the river or downstream. Evidently the appetite for more ivory had got the better of the — what shall I say? — less material aspirations. However he had got much worse suddenly. 'I heard he was lying helpless, and so I came up — took my chance,' said the Russian. 'Oh, he is bad, very bad.' I directed my glass to the house. There were no signs of life, but there was the ruined roof, the long mud wall peeping above the grass, with three little square window holes, no two of the same size; all this brought within reach of my hand, as it were. And then I made a brusque movement, and one of the remaining posts of that vanished fence leaped up in the field of my glass. You remember I told you I had been struck at the distance by certain attempts at ornamentation, rather remarkable in the ruinous aspect of the place. Now I had suddenly a nearer view, and its first result was to make me throw my head back as if before a blow. Then I went carefully from post to post with my glass, and I saw my mistake. These round knobs were not ornamental but symbolic; they were expressive and puzzling, striking and disturbing — food for thought and also for the vultures if there had been any looking down from the sky; but at all events for such ants as were industrious enough to ascend the pole. They would have been even more impressive, those heads on the stakes, if their faces had not been turned to the house. Only one, the first I had made out, was facing my way. I was not so shocked as you may think. The start back I had given was really nothing but a movement of surprise. I had expected to see a knob of wood there, you know. I returned deliberately to the first I had seen — and there it was, black, dried, sunken, with closed eyelids, a head that seemed to sleep at the top of that pole, and, with the shrunken dry lips showing a narrow white line of the teeth, was smiling, too, smiling continuously at some endless and jocose dream of that eternal slumber.

"I am not disclosing any trade secrets. In fact, the manager said afterwards that Mr. Kurtz's methods had ruined the district. I have no opinion on that point, but I want you clearly to understand that there was nothing exactly profitable in these heads being there. They only showed that Mr. Kurtz lacked restraint in the gratification of his various lusts, that there was something wanting in him — some small matter which, when the pressing need arose, could not be found under his magnificent eloquence. Whether he knew of this deficiency himself I can't say. I think the knowledge came to him at last — only at the very last. But the wilderness had found him out early, and had taken on him a terrible vengeance for the fantastic invasion. I think it had whispered to him things about himself which he did not know, things of which he had no conception till he took counsel with this great solitude — and the whisper had proved irresistibly fascinating. It echoed loudly within him because he was hollow at the core. . . . I put down the glass, and the head that had appeared near enough to be spoken to seemed at once to have leaped away from me into inaccessible distance.

"The admirer of Mr. Kurtz was a bit crestfallen. In a hurried, indistinct voice he began to assure me he had not dared to take these — say, symbols — down. He was not afraid of the natives; they would not stir till Mr. Kurtz gave the word. His ascendancy was extraordinary. The camps of these people surrounded the place, and the chiefs came every day to see him. They would crawl. . . . 'I don't want to know anything of the ceremonies used when approaching Mr. Kurtz,' I shouted. Curious, this feeling that came over me that such details would be more intolerable than those heads drying on the stakes under Mr. Kurtz's windows. After all, that was only a savage sight, while I seemed at one bound to have been transported into some lightless region of subtle horrors, where pure, uncomplicated savagery was a positive relief, being something that had a right to exist — obviously — in the sunshine. The young man looked at me with surprise. I suppose it did not occur to him that Mr. Kurtz was no idol of mine. He forgot I hadn't heard any of these splendid monologues on, what was it? On love, justice, conduct of life — or whatnot. If it had come to crawling before Mr. Kurtz, he crawled as much as the veriest savage of them all. I had no idea of the conditions, he said: these heads were the heads of rebels. I shocked him excessively by laughing. Rebels! What would be the next definition I was to hear? There had been enemies, criminals, workers — and these were rebels. Those rebellious heads looked very subdued to me on their sticks. 'You don't know how such a life tries a man like Kurtz,' cried Kurtz's last disciple. 'Well, and you?' I said. 'I! I! I am a simple man. I have no great thoughts. I want nothing from anybody. How can you compare me to?. . .' His feelings were too much for speech, and suddenly he broke down. 'I don't understand,' he groaned. 'I've been doing my best to keep him alive, and that's enough. I had no hand in all this. I have no abilities. There hasn't been a drop of medicine or a mouthful of invalid food for months here. He was shamefully abandoned. A man like this, with such ideas. Shamefully! Shamefully! I — I — haven't slept for the last ten nights. . . .'

"His voice lost itself in the calm of the evening. The long shadows of the forest had slipped downhill while we talked, had gone far beyond the ruined hovel, beyond the symbolic row of stakes. All this was in the gloom, while we down there were yet in the sunshine, and the stretch of the river abreast of the clearing glittered in a still and dazzling splendor, with a murky and overshadowed bend above and below. Not a living soul was seen on the shore. The bushes did not rustle.

"Suddenly round the corner of the house a group of men appeared, as though they had come up from the ground. They waded waist-deep in the grass, in a compact body, bearing an improvised stretcher in their midst. Instantly, in the emptiness of the landscape, a cry arose whose shrillness pierced the still air like a sharp arrow flying straight to the very heart of the land; and, as if by enchantment, streams of human beings — of naked human beings — with spears in their hands, with bows, with shields, with wild glances and savage movements, were poured into the clearing by the dark-faced and pensive forest. The bushes shook, the grass swayed for a time, and then everything stood still in attentive immobility.

" 'Now, if he does not say the right thing to them we are all done for,' said the Russian at my elbow. The knot of men with the stretcher had stopped, too, halfway to the steamer, as if petrified. I saw the man on the stretcher sit up, lank and with an uplifted arm, above the shoulders of the bearers. 'Let us hope that the man who can talk so well of love in general will find some particular reason to spare us this time,' I said. I resented bitterly the absurd danger of our situation, as if to be at the mercy of that atrocious phantom had been a dishonoring necessity. I could not hear a sound, but through my glasses I saw the thin arm extended commandingly, the lower jaw moving, the eyes of that apparition shining darkly far in its bony head that nodded with grotesque jerks. Kurtz — Kurtz — that means short in German — don't it? Well, the name was as true as everything else in his life — and death. He looked at least seven feet long. His covering had fallen off, and his body emerged from it pitiful and appalling as from a winding sheet. I could see the cage of his ribs all astir, the bones of his arm waving. It was as though an animated image of death carved out of old ivory had been shaking its hand with menaces at a motionless crowd of men made of dark and glittering bronze. I saw him open his mouth wide — it gave him a weirdly voracious aspect, as though he had wanted to swallow all the air, all the earth, all the men before him. A deep voice reached me faintly. He must have been shouting. He fell back suddenly. The stretcher shook as the bearers staggered forward again, and almost at the same time I noticed that the crowd of savages was vanishing without any perceptible movement of retreat, as if the forest that had ejected these beings so suddenly had drawn them in again as the breath is drawn in a long aspiration.

"Some of the pilgrims behind the stretcher carried his arms — two shotguns, a heavy rifle, and a light revolver carbine — the thunderbolts of that pitiful Jupiter. The manager bent over him murmuring as he walked beside his head. They laid him down in one of the little cabins — just a room for a bedplace and a campstool or two, you know. We had brought his belated correspondence, and a lot of torn envelopes and open letters littered his bed. His hand roamed feebly amongst these papers. I was struck by the fire of his eyes and the composed languor of his expression. It was not so much the exhaustion of disease. He did not seem in pain. This shadow looked satiated and calm, as though for the moment it had had its fill of all the emotions.

"He rustled one of the letters, and looking straight in my face said, 'I am glad.' Somebody had been writing to him about me. These special recommendations were turning up again. The volume of tone he emitted without effort, almost without the trouble of moving his lips, amazed me. A voice! a voice! It was grave, profound, vibrating, while the man did not seem capable of a whisper. However, he had enough strength in him — factitious no doubt — to very nearly make an end of us, as you shall hear directly.

"The manager appeared silently in the doorway; I stepped out at once and he drew the curtain after me. The Russian, eyed curiously by the pilgrims, was staring at the shore. I followed the direction of his glance.

"Dark human shapes could be made out in the distance, flitting indistinctly against the gloomy border of the forest, and near the river two bronze figures, leaning on tall spears, stood in the sunlight under fantastic headdresses of spotted skins, warlike and still in statuesque repose. And from right to left along the lighted shore moved a wild and gorgeous apparition of a woman.

"She walked with measured steps, draped in striped and fringed cloths, treading the earth proudly, with a slight jingle and flash of barbarous ornaments. She carried her head high; her hair was done in the shape of a helmet; she had brass leggings to the knee, brass wire gauntlets to the elbow, a crimson spot on her tawny cheek, innumerable necklaces of glass beads on her neck; bizarre things, charms, gifts of witch men, that hung about her, glittered and trembled at every step. She must have had the value of several elephant tusks upon her. She was savage and superb, wild-eyed and magnificent; there was something ominous and stately in her deliberate progress. And in the hush that had fallen suddenly upon the whole sorrowful land, the immense wilderness, the colossal body of the fecund and mysterious life seemed to look at her, pensive, as though it had been looking at the image of its own tenebrous and passionate soul.

"She came abreast of the steamer, stood still, and faced us. Her long shadow fell to the water's edge. Her face had a tragic and fierce aspect of wild sorrow and of dumb pain mingled with the fear of some struggling, half-shaped resolve. She stood looking at us without a stir, and like the wilderness itself, with an air of brooding over an inscrutable purpose. A whole minute passed, and then she made a step forward. There was a low jingle, a glint of yellow metal, a sway of fringed draperies, and she stopped as if her heart had failed her. The young fellow by my side growled. The pilgrims murmured at my back. She looked at us all as if her life had depended upon the unswerving steadiness of her glance. Suddenly she opened her bared arms and threw them up rigid above her head, as though in an uncontrollable desire to touch the sky, and at the same time the swift shadows darted out on the earth, swept around on the river, gathering the steamer into a shadowy embrace. A formidable silence hung over the scene.

"She turned away slowly, walked on, following the bank, and passed into the bushes to the left. Once only her eyes gleamed back at us in the dusk of the thickets before she disappeared.

" 'If she had offered to come aboard I really think I would have tried to shoot her,' said the man of patches, nervously. 'I had been risking my life every day for the last fortnight to keep her out of the house. She got in one day and kicked up a row about those miserable rags I picked up in the storeroom to mend my clothes with. I wasn't decent. At least it must have been that, for she talked like a fury to Kurtz for an hour, pointing at me now and then. I don't understand the dialect of this tribe. Luckily for me, I fancy Kurtz felt too ill that day to care, or there would have been mischief. I don't understand. . . . No — it's too much for me. Ah, well, it's all over now.'

"At this moment I heard Kurtz's deep voice behind the curtain: 'Save me! — save the ivory, you mean. Don't tell me. Save *me*! Why, I've had to save you. You are interrupting my plans now. Sick! Sick! Not so sick as you would like to believe. Never mind. I'll carry my ideas out yet — I will return. I'll show you what can be done. You with your little peddling notions — you are interfering with me. I will return. I . . .'

"The manager came out. He did me the honor to take me under the arm and lead me aside. 'He is very low, very low,' he said. He considered it necessary to sigh, but neglected to be consistently sorrowful. 'We have done all we could for him — haven't we? But there is no disguising the fact, Mr. Kurtz has done more harm than good to the Company. He did not see the time was not ripe for vigorous action. Cautiously, cautiously — that's my principle. We must be cautious yet. The district is closed to us for a time. Deplorable! Upon the whole, the trade will suffer. I don't deny there is a remarkable quantity of ivory — mostly fossil. We must save it, at all events — but look how precarious the position is — and why? Because the method is unsound.' 'Do you,' said I, looking at the shore, 'call it "unsound method?" ' 'Without doubt,' he exclaimed, hotly. 'Don't you?' . . .

" 'No method at all,' I murmured after a while. 'Exactly,' he exulted. 'I anticipated this. Shows a complete want of judgment. It is my duty to point it out in the proper quarter.' 'Oh,' said I, 'that fellow — what's his name? — the brickmaker, will make a readable report for you.' He appeared confounded for a moment. It seemed to me I had never breathed an atmosphere so vile, and I turned mentally to Kurtz for relief — positively for relief. 'Nevertheless I think Mr. Kurtz is a remarkable man,' I said with emphasis. He started, dropped on me a cold heavy glance, said very quietly, 'he *was*,' and turned his back on me. My hour of favor was over; I found myself lumped along with Kurtz as a partisan of methods for which the time was not ripe: I was unsound! Ah! but it was something to have at least a choice of nightmares.

"I had turned to the wilderness really, not to Mr. Kurtz, who, I was ready to admit, was as good as buried. And for a moment it seemed to me as if I also were buried in a vast grave full of unspeakable secrets. I felt an intolerable weight oppressing my breast, the smell of the damp earth, the unseen presence of victorious corruption, the darkness of an impenetrable night.... The Russian tapped me on the shoulder. I heard him mumbling and stammering something about 'brother seaman — couldn't conceal — knowledge of matters that would affect Mr. Kurtz's reputation.' I waited. For him evidently Mr. Kurtz was not in his grave; I suspect that for him Mr. Kurtz was one of the immortals. 'Well!' said I at last, 'speak out. As it happens, I am Mr. Kurtz's friend — in a way.'

"He stated with a good deal of formality that had we not been 'of the same profession,' he would have kept the matter to himself without regard to consequences. 'He suspected there was an active ill will towards him on the part of these white men that — ' 'You are right,' I said, remembering a certain conversation I had overheard. 'The manager thinks you ought to be hanged.' He showed a concern at this intelligence which amused me at first. 'I had better get out of the way quietly,' he said, earnestly. 'I can do no more for Kurtz now, and they would soon find some excuse. What's to stop them? There's a military post three hundred miles from here.' 'Well, upon my word,' said I, 'perhaps you had better go if you have any friends amongst the savages near by.' 'Plenty,' he said. 'They are simple people — and I want nothing, you know.' He stood biting his lip, then: 'I don't want any harm to happen to these whites here, but of course I was thinking of Mr. Kurtz's reputation — but you are a brother seaman and — ' 'All right,' said I, after a time. 'Mr. Kurtz's reputation is safe with me.' I did not know how truly I spoke.

"He informed me, lowering his voice, that it was Kurtz who had ordered the attack to be made on the steamer. 'He hated sometimes the idea of being taken away — and then again... But I don't understand these matters. I am a simple man. He thought it would scare you away — that you would give it up, thinking him dead. I could not stop him. Oh, I had an awful time of it this last month.' 'Very well,' I said. 'He is all right now.' 'Ye-e-es,' he muttered, not very convinced apparently. 'Thanks,' said I; 'I shall keep my eyes open.' 'But quiet — eh?' he urged, anxiously. 'It would be awful for his reputation if anybody here — ' I promised a complete discretion with great gravity. 'I have a canoe and three black fellows waiting not very far. I am off. Could you give me a few Martini-Henry cartridges?' I could, and did, with proper secrecy. He helped himself, with a wink at me, to a handful of my tobacco. 'Between sailors — you know — good English tobacco.' At the door of the pilot house he turned round — 'I say, haven't you a pair of shoes you could spare?' He raised one leg. 'Look.' The soles were tied with knotted strings sandalwise under his bare feet. I rooted out an old pair, at which he looked with admiration before tucking it under his left arm. One of his pockets (bright red) was bulging with cartridges, from the other (dark blue) peeped 'Towson's Inquiry,' etc., etc. He seemed to think himself excellently well equipped for a renewed encounter with the wilderness. 'Ah! I'll never, never meet such a man again. You ought to have heard him recite poetry — his own, too, it was, he told me. Poetry!' He rolled his eyes at the recollection of these delights. 'Oh, he enlarged my mind!' 'Good-by,' said I. He shook hands and vanished in the night. Sometimes I ask myself whether I had ever really seen him — whether it was possible to meet such a phenomenon!...

"When I woke up shortly after midnight his warning came to my mind with its hint of danger that seemed, in the starred darkness, real enough to make me get up for the purpose of having a look round. On the hill a big fire burned, illuminating fitfully a crooked corner of the station house. One of the agents with a picket of a few of our blacks, armed for the purpose, was keeping guard over the ivory; but deep within the forest, red gleams that wavered, that seemed to sink and rise from the ground amongst confused columnar shapes of intense blackness, showed the exact position of the camp where Mr. Kurtz's adorers were keeping their uneasy vigil. The monotonous beating of a big drum filled the air with muffled shocks and a lingering vibration. A steady droning sound of many men chanting each to himself some weird incantation came out from the black, flat wall of the woods as the humming of bees comes out of a hive, and had a strange narcotic effect upon my half-awake senses. I believed I dozed off leaning over the rail, till an abrupt burst of yells, an overwhelming outbreak of a pent-up and mysterious frenzy, woke me up in a bewildered wonder. It was cut short all at once, and the low droning went on with an effect of audible and soothing silence. I glanced casually into the little cabin. A light was burning within, but Mr. Kurtz was not there.

"I think I would have raised an outcry if I had believed my eyes. But I didn't believe them at first — the thing seemed so impossible. The fact is I was completely unnerved by a sheer blank fright, pure abstract terror, unconnected with any distinct shape of physical danger. What made this emotion so overpowering was — how shall I define it? — the moral shock I received, as if something altogether monstrous, intolerable to thought and odious to the soul, had been thrust upon me unexpectedly. This lasted of course the merest fraction of a second, and then the usual sense of commonplace, deadly danger, the possibility of a sudden onslaught and massacre, or something of the kind, which I saw impending, was positively welcome and composing. It pacified me, in fact, so much, that I did not raise an alarm.

"There was an agent buttoned up inside an ulster and sleeping on a chair on deck within three feet of me. The yells had not awakened him; he snored very slightly; I left him to his slumbers and leaped ashore. I did not betray Mr. Kurtz — it was ordered I should never betray him — it was written I should be loyal to the nightmare of my choice. I was anxious to deal with this shadow by myself alone — and to this day I don't know why I was so jealous of sharing with anyone the peculiar blackness of that experience.

"As soon as I got on the bank I saw a trail — a broad trail through the grass. I remember the exultation with which I said to myself, 'He can't walk — he is crawling on all fours — I've got him.' The grass was wet with dew. I strode rapidly with clenched fists. I fancy I had some vague notion of falling upon him and giving him a drubbing. I don't know. I had some imbecile thoughts. The knitting old woman with the cat obtruded herself upon my memory as a most improper person to be sitting at the other end of such an affair. I saw a row of pilgrims squirting lead in the air out of Winchesters held to the hip. I thought I would never get back to the steamer, and imagined myself living alone and unarmed in the woods to an advanced age. Such silly things — you know. And I remember I confounded the beat of the drum with the beating of my heart, and was pleased at its calm regularity.

"I kept to the track though — then stopped to listen. The night was very clear; a dark blue space, sparkling with dew and starlight, in which black things stood very still. I thought I could see a kind of motion ahead of me. I was strangely cocksure of everything that night. I actually left the track and ran in a wide semicircle (I truly believe chuckling to myself) so as to get in front of that stir, of that motion I had seen — if indeed I had seen anything. I was circumventing Kurtz as though it had been a boyish game.

"I came upon him, and, if he had not heard me coming, I would have fallen over him, too, but he got up in time. He rose, unsteady, long, pale, indistinct, like a vapor exhaled by the earth, and swayed slightly, misty and silent before me; while at my back the fires loomed between the trees, and the murmur of many voices issued from the forest. I had cut him off cleverly; but when actually confronting him I seemed to come to my senses, I saw the danger in its right proportion. It was by no means over yet. Suppose he began to shout? Though he could hardly stand, there was still plenty of vigor in his voice. 'Go away — hide yourself,' he said, in that profound tone. It was very awful. I glanced back. We were within thirty yards from the nearest fire. A black figure stood up, strode on long black legs, waving long black arms, across the glow. It had horns — antelope horns, I think — on its head. Some sorcerer, some witch man, no doubt: it looked fiend-like enough. 'Do you know what you are doing?' I whispered. 'Perfectly,' he answered, raising his voice for that single word: it sounded to me far off and yet loud, like a hail through a speaking trumpet. If he makes a row we are lost, I thought to myself. This clearly was not a case for fisticuffs, even apart from the very natural aversion I had to beat that Shadow — this wandering and tormented thing. 'You will be lost,' I said — 'utterly lost.' One gets sometimes such a flash of inspiration, you know. I did say the right thing, though indeed he could not have been more irretrievably lost than he was at this very moment, when the foundations of our intimacy were being laid — to endure — to endure — even to the end — even beyond.

"'I had immense plans,' he muttered irresolutely. 'Yes,' said I; 'but if you try to shout I'll smash your head with — ' There was not a stick or a stone near. 'I will throttle you for good,' I corrected myself. 'I was on the threshold of great things,' he pleaded, in a voice of longing, with a wistfulness of tone that made my blood run cold. 'And now for this stupid scoundrel — ' 'Your success in Europe is assured in any case,' I affirmed, steadily. I did not want to have the throttling of him, you understand — and indeed it would have been very little use for any practical purpose. I tried to break the spell — the heavy, mute spell of the wilderness — that seemed to draw him to its pitiless breast by the awakening of forgotten and brutal instincts, by the memory of gratified and monstrous passions. This alone, I was convinced, had driven him out to the edge of the forest, to the bush, towards the gleam of fires, the throb of drums, the drone of weird incantations; this alone had beguiled his unlawful soul beyond the bounds of permitted aspirations. And, don't you see, the terror of the position was not in being knocked on the head — though I had a very lively sense of that danger, too — but in this, that I had to deal with a being to whom I could not appeal in the name of anything high or low. I had, even like the niggers, to invoke him — himself — his own exalted and incredible degradation. There was nothing either above or below him, and I knew it. He had kicked himself loose of the earth. Confound the man! he had kicked the very earth to pieces. He was alone, and I before him did not know whether I stood on the ground or floated in the air. I've been telling you what we said — repeating the phrases we pronounced — but what's the good? They were common everyday words — the familiar, vague sounds exchanged on every waking day of life. But what of that? They had behind them, to my mind, the terrific suggestiveness of words heard in dreams, of phrases spoken in nightmares. Soul! If anybody had ever struggled with a soul, I am the man. And I wasn't arguing with a lunatic either. Believe me or not, his intelligence was perfectly clear — concentrated, it is true, upon himself with horrible intensity, yet clear; and therein was my only chance — barring, of course, the killing him there and then, which wasn't so good, on account of unavoidable noise. But his soul was mad. Being alone in the wilderness, it had looked within itself, and, by heavens! I tell you, it had gone mad. I had — for my sins, I suppose — to go through the ordeal of looking into it myself. No eloquence could have been so withering to one's belief in mankind as his final burst of sincerity. He struggled with himself, too. I saw it, I heard it. I saw the inconceivable mystery of a soul that knew no restraint, no faith, and no fear, yet struggling blindly with itself. I kept my head pretty well; but when I had him at last stretched on the couch, I wiped my forehead, while my legs shook under me as though I had carried half a ton on my back down that hill. And yet I had only supported him, his bony arm clasped round my neck — and he was not much heavier than a child.

"When next day we left at noon, the crowd, of whose presence behind the curtain of trees I had been acutely conscious all the time, flowed out of the woods again, filled the clearing, covered the slope with a mass of naked, breathing, quivering, bronze bodies. I steamed up a bit, then swung downstream, and two thousand eyes followed the evolutions of the splashing, thumping, fierce river-demon beating the water with its terrible tail and breathing black smoke into the air. In front of the first rank, along the river, three men, plastered with bright red earth from head to foot, strutted to and fro restlessly. When we came abreast again, they faced the river, stamped their feet, nodded their horned heads, swayed their scarlet bodies; they shook towards the fierce river-demon a bunch of black feathers, a mangy skin with a pendent tail — something that looked like a dried gourd; they shouted periodically together strings of amazing words that resembled no sounds of human language; and the deep murmurs of the crowd, interrupted suddenly, were like the responses of some satanic litany.

"We had carried Kurtz into the pilot house: there was more air there. Lying on the couch, he stared through the open shutter. There was an eddy in the mass of human bodies, and the woman with helmeted head and tawny cheeks rushed out to the very brink of the stream. She put out her hands, shouted something, and all that wild mob took up the shout in a roaring chorus of articulated, rapid, breathless utterance.

"Do you understand this?" I asked.

"He kept on looking out past me with fiery, longing eyes, with a mingled expression of wistfulness and hate. He made no answer, but I saw a smile, a smile of indefinable meaning, appear on his colorless lips that a moment after twitched convulsively. 'Do I not?' he said slowly, gasping, as if the words had been torn out of him by a supernatural power.

"I pulled the string of the whistle, and I did this because I saw the pilgrims on deck getting out their rifles with an air of anticipating a jolly lark. At the sudden screech there was a movement of abject terror through that wedged mass of bodies. 'Don't! Don't you frighten them away,' cried someone on deck disconsolately. I pulled the string time after time. They broke and ran, they leaped, they crouched, they swerved, they dodged the flying terror of the sound. The three red chaps had fallen flat, face down on the shore, as though they had been shot dead. Only the barbarous and superb woman did not so much as flinch, and stretched tragically her bare arms after us over the somber and glittering river.

"And then that imbecile crowd down on the deck started their little fun, and I could see nothing more for smoke.

"The brown current ran swiftly out of the heart of darkness, bearing us down towards the sea with twice the speed of our upward progress; and Kurtz's life was running swiftly, too, ebbing, ebbing out of his heart into the sea of inexorable time. The manager was very placid, he had no vital anxieties now, he took us both in with a comprehensive and satisfied glance: the 'affair' had come off as well as could be wished. I saw the time approaching when I would be left alone of the party of 'unsound method.' The pilgrims looked upon me with disfavor. I was, so to speak, numbered with the dead. It is strange how I accepted this unforeseen partnership, this choice of nightmares forced upon me in the tenebrous land invaded by these mean and greedy phantoms.

"Kurtz discoursed. A voice! a voice! It rang deep to the very last. It survived his strength to hide in the magnificent folds of eloquence the barren darkness of his heart. Oh, he struggled! he struggled! The wastes of his weary brain were haunted by shadowy images now — images of wealth and fame revolving obsequiously round his unextinguishable gift of noble and lofty expression. My Intended, my station, my career, my ideas — these were the subjects for the occasional utterances of elevated sentiments. The shade of the original Kurtz frequented the bedside of the hollow sham, whose fate it was to be buried presently in the mold of primeval earth. But both the diabolic love and the unearthly hate of the mysteries it had penetrated fought for the possession of that soul satiated with primitive emotions, avid of lying fame, of sham distinction, of all the appearances of success and power.

"Sometimes he was contemptibly childish. He desired to have kings meet him at railway stations on his return from some ghastly Nowhere, where he intended to accomplish great things. 'You show them you have in you something that is really profitable, and then there will be no limits to the recognition of your ability,' he would say. 'Of course you must take care of the motives — right motives — always.' The long reaches that were like one and the same reach, monotonous bends that were exactly alike, slipped past the steamer with their multitude of secular trees looking patiently after this grimy fragment of another world, the forerunner of change, of conquest, of trade, of massacres, of blessings. I looked ahead — piloting. 'Close the shutter,' said Kurtz suddenly one day; 'I can't bear to look at this.' I did so. There was a silence. 'Oh, but I will wring your heart yet!' he cried at the invisible wilderness.

"We broke down — as I had expected — and had to lie-up for repairs at the head of an island. This delay was the first thing that shook Kurtz's confidence. One morning he gave me a packet of papers and a photograph — the lot tied together with a shoestring. 'Keep this for me,' he said. 'This noxious fool' (meaning the manager) 'is capable of prying into my boxes when I am not looking.' In the afternoon I saw him. He was lying on his back with closed eyes, and I withdrew quietly, but I heard him mutter, 'Live rightly, die, die. . . .' I listened. There was nothing more. Was he rehearsing some speech in his sleep, or was it a fragment of a phrase from some newspaper article? He had been writing for the papers and meant to do so again, 'for the furthering of my ideas. It's a duty.'

"His was an impenetrable darkness. I looked at him as you peer down at a man who is lying at the bottom of a precipice where the sun never shines. But I had not much time to give him, because I was helping the engine driver to take to pieces the leaky cylinders, to straighten a bent connecting rod, and in other such matters. I lived in an infernal mess of rust, filings, nuts, bolts, spanners, hammers, ratchet drills — things I abominate, because I don't get on with them. I tended the little forge we fortunately had aboard; I toiled wearily in a wretched scrapheap — unless I had the shakes too bad to stand.

"One evening coming in with a candle I was startled to hear him say a little tremulously, 'I am lying here in the dark waiting for death.' The light was within a foot of his eyes. I forced myself to murmur, 'Oh, nonsense!' and stood over him as if transfixed.

"Anything approaching the change that came over his features I have never seen before, and hope never to see again. Oh, I wasn't touched. I was fascinated. It was as though a veil had been rent. I saw on that ivory face the expression of somber pride, of ruthless power, of craven terror — of an intense and hopeless despair. Did he live his life again in every detail of desire, temptation, and surrender during that supreme moment of complete knowledge? He cried in a whisper at some image, at some vision — he cried out twice, a cry that was no more than a breath: 'The horror! The horror!'

"I blew the candle out and left the cabin. The pilgrims were dining in the messroom, and I took my place opposite the manager, who lifted his eyes to give me a questioning glance, which I successfully ignored. He leaned back, serene, with that peculiar smile of his sealing the unexpressed depths of his meanness. A continuous shower of small flies streamed upon the lamp, upon the cloth, upon our hands and faces. Suddenly the manager's boy put his insolent black head in the doorway, and said in a tone of scathing contempt —

"'Mistah Kurtz — he dead.'

"All the pilgrims rushed out to see. I remained, and went on with my dinner. I believe I was considered brutally callous. However, I did not eat much. There was a lamp in there — light, don't you know — and outside it was so beastly, beastly dark. I went no more near the remarkable man who had pronounced a judgment upon the adventures of his soul on this earth. The voice was gone. What else had been there? But I am of course aware that next day the pilgrims buried something in a muddy hole.

"And then they very nearly buried me.

"However, as you see, I did not go to join Kurtz there and then. I did not. I remained to dream the nightmare out to the end, and to show my loyalty to Kurtz once more. Destiny. My destiny! Droll thing life is — that mysterious arrangement of merciless logic for a futile purpose. The most you can hope from it is some knowledge of yourself — that comes too late — a crop of unextinguishable regrets. I have wrestled with death. It is the most unexciting contest you can imagine. It takes place in an impalpable grayness, with nothing underfoot, with nothing around, without spectators, without clamor, without glory, without the great desire of victory, without the great fear of defeat, in a sickly atmosphere of tepid skepticism, without much belief in your own right, and still less in that of your adversary. If such is the form of ultimate wisdom, then life is a greater riddle than some of us think it to be. I was within a hair's-breadth of the last opportunity for pronouncement, and I found with humiliation that probably I would have nothing to say. This is the reason why I affirm that Kurtz was a remarkable man. He had something to say. He said it. Since I had peeped over the edge myself, I understand better the meaning of his stare, that could not see the flame of the candle, but was wide enough to embrace the whole universe, piercing enough to penetrate all the hearts that beat in the darkness. He had summed up — he had judged. 'The horror!' He was a remarkable man. After all, this was the expression of some sort of belief; it had candor, it had conviction, it had a vibrating note of revolt in its whisper, it had the appalling face of a glimpsed truth — the strange commingling of desire and hate. And it is not my own extremity I remember best — a vision of grayness without form filled with physical pain, and a careless contempt for the evanescence of all things — even of this pain itself. No! It is his extremity that I seem to have lived through. True, he had made that last stride, he had stepped over the edge, while I had been permitted to draw back my hesitating foot. And perhaps in this is the whole difference; perhaps all the wisdom, and all truth, and all sincerity, are just compressed into that inappreciable moment of time in which we step over the threshold of the invisible. Perhaps! I like to think my summing-up would not have been a word of careless contempt. Better his cry — much better. It was an affirmation, a moral victory paid for by innumerable defeats, by abominable terrors, by abominable satisfactions. But it was a victory! That is why I have remained loyal to Kurtz to the last, and even beyond, when a long time after I heard once more, not his own voice, but the echo of his magnificent eloquence thrown to me from a soul as translucently pure as a cliff of crystal.

"No, they did not bury me, though there is a period of time which I remember mistily, with a shuddering wonder, like a passage through some inconceivable world that had no hope in it and no desire. I found myself back in the sepulchral city resenting the sight of people hurrying through the streets to filch a little money from each other, to devour their infamous cookery, to gulp their unwholesome beer, to dream their insignificant and silly dreams. They trespassed upon my thoughts. They were intruders whose knowledge of life was to me an irritating pretense, because I felt so sure they could not possibly know the things I knew. Their bearing, which was simply the bearing of commonplace individuals going about their business in the assurance of perfect safety, was offensive to me like the outrageous flauntings of folly in the face of a danger it is unable to comprehend. I had no particular desire to enlighten them, but I had some difficulty in restraining myself from laughing in their faces, so full of stupid importance. I daresay I was not very well at that time. I tottered about the streets — there were various affairs to settle — grinning bitterly at perfectly respectable persons. I admit my behavior was inexcusable, but then my temperature was seldom normal in these days. My dear aunt's endeavors to 'nurse up my strength' seemed altogether beside the mark. It was not my strength that wanted nursing, it was my imagination that wanted soothing. I kept the bundle of papers given me by Kurtz, not knowing exactly what to do with it. His mother had died lately, watched over, as I was told, by his Intended. A clean-shaved man, with an official manner and wearing gold-rimmed spectacles, called on me one day and made inquiries, at first circuitous, afterwards suavely pressing, about what he was pleased to denominate certain 'documents.' I was not surprised, because I had had two rows with the manager on the subject out there. I had refused to give up the smallest scrap out of that package, and I took the same attitude with the spectacled man. He became darkly menacing at last, and with much heat argued that the company had the right to every bit of information about its 'territories.' And said he, 'Mr. Kurtz's knowledge of unexplored regions must have been necessarily extensive and peculiar — owing to his great abilities and to the deplorable circumstances in which he had been placed: therefore — ' I assured him Mr. Kurtz's knowledge, however extensive, did not bear upon the problems of commerce or administration. He invoked then the name of science. 'It would be an incalculable loss if,' etc., etc. I offered him the report on the 'Suppression of Savage Customs,' with the postscriptum torn off. He took it up eagerly, but ended by sniffing at it with an air of contempt. 'This is not what we had a right to expect,' he remarked. 'Expect nothing else,' I said. 'There are only private letters.' He withdrew upon some threat of legal proceedings, and I saw him no more; but another fellow, calling himself Kurtz's cousin, appeared two days later, and was anxious to hear all the details about his dear relative's last moments. Incidentally he gave me to understand that Kurtz had been essentially a great musician. 'There was the making of an immense success,' said the man, who was an organist, I believe, with lank gray hair flowing over a greasy coat collar. I had no reason to doubt his statement; and to this day I am unable to say what was Kurtz's profession, whether he ever had any — which was the greatest of his talents. I had taken him for a painter who wrote for the papers, or else for a journalist who could paint — but even the cousin (who took snuff during the interview) could not tell me what he had been — exactly. He was a universal genius — on that point I agreed with the old chap, who thereupon blew his nose noisily into a large cotton handkerchief and withdrew in senile agitation, bearing off some family letters and memoranda without importance. Ultimately a journalist anxious to know something of the fate of his 'dear colleague' turned up. This visitor informed me Kurtz's proper sphere ought to have been politics 'on the popular side.' He had furry straight eyebrows, bristly hair cropped short, an eyeglass on a broad ribbon, and, becoming expansive, confessed his opinion that Kurtz really couldn't write a bit — 'but heavens! how that man could talk. He electrified large meetings. He had faith — don't you see? — he had the faith. He could get himself to believe anything — anything. He would have been a splendid leader of an extreme party.' 'What party?' I asked. 'Any party,' answered the other. 'He was an — an — extremist.' Did I not think so? I assented. Did I know, he asked, with a sudden flash of curiosity, 'what it was that had induced him to go out there?' 'Yes,' said I, and forthwith handed him the famous report for publication, if he thought fit. He glanced through it hurriedly, mumbling all the time, judged 'it would do,' and took himself off with this plunder.

"Thus I was left at last with a slim packet of letters and the girl's portrait. She struck me as beautiful — I mean she had a beautiful expression. I know that the sunlight can be made to lie, too, yet one felt that no manipulation of light and pose could have conveyed the delicate shade of truthfulness upon those features. She seemed ready to listen without mental reservation, without suspicion, without a thought for herself. I concluded I would go and give her back her portrait and those letters myself. Curiosity? Yes; and also some other feeling perhaps. All that had been Kurtz's had passed out of my hands: his soul, his body, his station, his plans, his ivory, his career. There remained only his memory and his Intended — and I wanted to give that up, too, to the past, in a way — to surrender personally all that remained of him with me to that oblivion which is the last word of our common fate. I don't defend myself. I had no clear perception of what it was I really wanted. Perhaps it was an impulse of unconscious loyalty, or the fulfilment of one of these ironic necessities that lurk in the facts of human existence. I don't know. I can't tell. But I went.

"I thought his memory was like the other memories of the dead that accumulate in every man's life — a vague impress on the brain of shadows that had fallen on it in their swift and final passage; but before the high and ponderous door, between the tall houses of a street as still and decorous as a well-kept alley in a cemetery, I had a vision of him on the stretcher, opening his mouth voraciously, as if to devour all the earth with all its mankind. He lived then before me; he lived as much as he had ever lived — a shadow insatiable of splendid appearances, of frightful realities; a shadow darker than the shadow of the night, and draped nobly in the folds of a gorgeous eloquence. The vision seemed to enter the house with me — the stretcher, the phantom-bearers, the wild crowd of obedient worshipers, the gloom of the forests, the glitter of the reach between the murky bends, the beat of the drum, regular and muffled like the beating of a heart — the heart of a conquering darkness. It was a moment of triumph for the wilderness, an invading and vengeful rush which, it seemed to me, I would have to keep back alone for the salvation of another soul. And the memory of what I had heard him say afar there, with the horned shapes stirring at my back, in the glow of fires, within the patient woods, those broken phrases came back to me, were heard again in their ominous and terrifying simplicity. I remembered his abject pleading, his abject threats, the colossal scale of his vile desires, the meanness, the torment, the tempestuous anguish of his soul. And later on I seemed to see his collected languid manner, when he said one day, 'This lot of ivory now is really mine. The company did not pay for it. I collected it myself at a very great personal risk. I am afraid they will try to claim it as theirs though. H'm. It is a difficult case. What do you think I ought to do — resist? Eh? I want no more than justice.'... He wanted no more than justice — no more than justice. I rang the bell before a mahogany door on the first floor, and while I waited he seemed to stare at me out of the glassy panel — stare with that wide and immense stare embracing, condemning, loathing all the universe. I seemed to hear the whispered cry, 'The horror! The horror!'

"The dusk was falling. I had to wait in a lofty drawing room with three long windows from floor to ceiling that were like three luminous and bedraped columns. The bent gilt legs and backs of the furniture shone in indistinct curves. The tall marble fireplace had a cold and monumental whiteness. A grand piano stood massively in a corner; with dark gleams on the flat surfaces like a somber and polished sarcophagus. A high door opened — closed. I rose.

"She came forward, all in black, with a pale head, floating towards me in the dusk. She was in mourning. It was more than a year since his death, more than a year since the news came; she seemed as though she would remember and mourn forever. She took both my hands in hers and murmured, 'I had heard you were coming.' I noticed she was not very young — I mean not girlish. She had a mature capacity for fidelity, for belief, for suffering. The room seemed to have grown darker, as if all the sad light of the cloudy evening had taken refuge on her forehead. This fair hair, this pale visage, this pure brow, seemed surrounded by an ashy halo from which the dark eyes looked out at me. Their glance was guileless, profound, confident, and trustful. She carried her sorrowful head as though she were proud of that sorrow, as though she would say, I — I alone know how to mourn for him as he deserves. But while we were still shaking hands, such a look of awful desolation came upon her face that I perceived she was one of those creatures that are not the playthings of Time. For her he had died only yesterday. And, by Jove! the impression was so powerful that for me, too, he seemed to have died only yesterday — nay, this very minute. I saw her and him in the same instant of time — his death and her sorrow — I saw her sorrow in the very moment of his death. Do you understand? I saw them together — I heard them together. She had said, with a deep catch of the breath, 'I have survived' while my strained ears seemed to hear distinctly, mingled with her tone of despairing regret, the summing-up whisper of his eternal condemnation. I asked myself what I was doing there, with a sensation of panic in my heart as though I had blundered into a place of cruel and absurd mysteries not fit for a human being to behold. She motioned me to a chair. We sat down. I laid the packet gently on the little table, and she put her hand over it. ... 'You knew him well,' she murmured, after a moment of mourning silence.

" 'Intimacy grows quickly out there,' I said. 'I

knew him as well as it is possible for one man to know another.'

" 'And you admired him,' she said. 'It was impossible to know him and not to admire him. Was it?'

" 'He was a remarkable man,' I said, unsteadily. Then before the appealing fixity of her gaze, that seemed to watch for more words on my lips, I went on, 'It was impossible not to — '

" 'Love him,' she finished eagerly, silencing me into an appalled dumbness. 'How true! how true! But when you think that no one knew him so well as I! I had all his noble confidence. I knew him best.'

" 'You knew him best,' I repeated. And perhaps she did. But with every word spoken the room was growing darker, and only her forehead, smooth and white, remained illumined by the unextinguishable light of belief and love.

" 'You were his friend,' she went on. 'His friend,' she repeated, a little louder. 'You must have been if he had given you this, and sent you to me. I feel I can speak to you — and oh! I must speak. I want you — you who have heard his last words — to know I have been worthy of him. ... It is not pride. ... Yes! I am proud to know I understood him better than anyone on earth — he told me so himself. And since his mother died I have had no one — no one — to — to — '

"I listened. The darkness deepened. I was not even sure whether he had given me the right bundle. I rather suspect he wanted me to take care of another batch of his papers which, after his death, I saw the manager examining under the lamp. And the girl talked, easing her pain in the certitude of my sympathy; she talked as thirsty men drink. I had heard that her engagement with Kurtz had been disapproved by her people. He wasn't rich enough or something. And indeed I don't know whether he had not been a pauper all his life. He had given me some reason to infer that it was his impatience of comparative poverty that drove him out there.

" '... Who was not his friend who had heard him speak once?' she was saying. 'He drew men towards him by what was best in them.' She looked at me with intensity. 'It is the gift of the great,' she went on, and the sound of her low voice seemed to have the accompaniment of all the other sounds, full of mystery, desolation, and sorrow, I had ever heard — the ripple of the river, the soughing of the trees swayed by the wind, the murmurs of the crowds, the faint ring of incomprehensible words cried from afar, the whisper of a voice speaking from beyond the threshold of an eternal darkness. 'But you have heard him! You know!' she cried.

" 'Yes, I know,' I said with something like despair in my heart, but bowing my head before the faith that was in her, before that great and saving illusion that shone with an unearthly glow in the darkness, in the triumphant darkness from which I could not have defended her — from which I could not even defend myself.

" 'What a loss to me — to us!' — she corrected herself with beautiful generosity; then added in a murmur, 'To the world.' By the last gleams of twilight I could see the glitter of her eyes, full of tears — of tears that would not fall.

" 'I have been very happy — very fortunate — very proud,' she went on. 'Too fortunate. Too happy for a little while. And now I am unhappy for — for life."

"She stood up; her fair hair seemed to catch all the remaining light in a glimmer of gold. I rose, too.

" 'And of all this,' she went on, mournfully, 'of all his promise, and of all his greatness, of his generous mind, of his noble heart, nothing remains — nothing but a memory. You and I — '

" 'We shall always remember him,' I said, hastily.

" 'No!' she cried. 'It is impossible that all this should be lost — that such a life should be sacrificed to leave nothing — but sorrow. You know what vast plans he had. I knew of them, too — I could not perhaps understand — but others knew of them. Something must remain. His words, at least, have not died.'

" 'His words will remain,' I said.

" 'And his example,' she whispered to herself. 'Men looked up to him — his goodness shone in every act. His example — '

" 'True,' I said; 'his example, too. Yes, his example. I forgot that.'

" 'But I do not. I cannot — I cannot believe — not yet. I cannot believe that I shall never see him again, that nobody will see him again, never, never, never.'

"She put out her arms as if after a retreating figure, stretching them black and with clasped pale hands across the fading and narrow sheen of the window. Never see him! I saw him clearly enough then. I shall see this eloquent phantom as long as I live, and I shall see her, too, a tragic and familiar Shade, resembling in this gesture another one, tragic also, and bedecked with powerless charms, stretching bare brown arms over the glitter of the infernal stream, the stream of darkness. She said suddenly very low, 'He died as he lived.'

" 'His end,' said I, with dull anger stirring in me, 'was in every way worthy of his life.'

" 'And I was not with him,' she murmured. My anger subsided before a feeling of infinite pity.

" 'Everything that could be done — ' I mumbled.

" 'Ah, but I believed in him more than anyone on earth — more than his own mother, more than — himself. He needed me! Me! I would have treasured every sigh, every word, every sign, every glance.'

"I felt like a chill grip on my chest. 'Don't,' I said, in a muffled voice.

" 'Forgive me. I — I — have mourned so long in silence — in silence. ... You were with him — to the last? I think of his loneliness. Nobody near to understand him as I would have understood. Perhaps no one to hear. . . .'

" 'To the very end,' I said, shakily. 'I heard his very last words. . . .' I stopped in a fright.

" 'Repeat them,' she murmured in a heart-broken tone. 'I want — I want — something — something — to — to live with.'

"I was on the point of crying at her, 'Don't you hear them?' The dusk was repeating them in a persistent whisper all around us, in a whisper that seemed to swell menacingly like the first whisper of a rising wind. 'The horror! the horror!'

" 'His last word — to live with,' she insisted. 'Don't you understand I loved him — I loved him — I loved him!'

"I pulled myself together and spoke slowly.

" 'The last word he pronounced was — your name.'

"I heard a light sigh and then my heart stood still, stopped dead short by an exulting and terrible cry, by the cry of inconceivable triumph and of unspeakable pain. 'I knew it — I was sure!' . . . She knew. She was sure. I heard her weeping; she had hidden her face in her hands. It seemed to me that the house would collapse before I could escape, that the heavens would fall upon my head. But nothing happened. The heavens do not fall for such a trifle. Would they have fallen, I wonder, if I had rendered Kurtz that justice which was his due? Hadn't he said he wanted only justice? But I couldn't. I could not tell her. It would have been too dark — too dark altogether. . . ."

Marlow ceased, and sat apart, indistinct and silent, in the pose of a meditating Buddha. Nobody moved for a time. "We have lost the first of the ebb," said the director, suddenly. I raised my head. The offing was barred by a black bank of clouds, and the tranquil waterway leading to the uttermost ends of the earth flowed somber under an overcast sky — seemed to lead into the heart of an immense darkness.

FRANZ KAFKA

The Metamorphosis

Translated by Edwin and Willa Muir

I

As Gregor Samsa awoke one morning from uneasy dreams he found himself transformed in his bed into a gigantic insect. He was lying on his hard, as it were armor-plated, back and when he lifted his head a little he could see his dome-like brown belly divided into stiff arched segments on top of which the bed quilt could hardly keep in position and was about to slide off completely. His numerous legs, which were pitifully thin compared to the rest of his bulk, waved helplessly before his eyes.

What has happened to me? he thought. It was no dream. His room, a regular human bedroom, only rather too small, lay quiet between the four familiar walls. Above the table on which a collection of cloth samples was unpacked and spread out — Samsa was a commercial traveler — hung the picture which he had recently cut out of an illustrated magazine and put into a pretty gilt frame. It showed a lady, with a fur cap on and a fur stole, sitting upright and holding out to the spectator a huge fur muff into which the whole of her forearm had vanished!

Gregor's eyes turned next to the window, and the overcast sky — one could hear rain drops beating on the window gutter — made him quite melancholy. What about sleeping a little longer and forgetting all this nonsense, he thought, but it could not be done, for he was accustomed to sleep on his right side and in his present condition he could not turn himself over. However violently he forced himself towards his right side he always rolled on to his back again. He tried it at least a hundred times, shutting his eyes to keep from seeing his struggling legs, and only desisted when he began to feel in his side a faint dull ache he had never experienced before.

Oh God, he thought, what an exhausting job I've picked on! Traveling about day in, day out. It's much more irritating work than doing the actual business in the office, and on top of that there's the trouble of constant traveling, of worrying about train connections, the bed and irregular meals, casual acquaintances that are always new and never become intimate friends. The devil take it all! He felt a slight itching up on his belly; slowly pushed himself on his back nearer to the top of the bed so that he could lift his head more easily; identified the itching place which was surrounded by many small white spots the nature of which he could not understand and made to touch it with a leg, but drew the leg back immediately, for the contact made a cold shiver run through him.

He slid down again into his former position. This getting up early, he thought, makes one quite stupid. A man needs his sleep. Other commercials live like harem women. For instance, when I come back to the hotel of a morning to write up the orders I've got, these others are only sitting down to breakfast. Let me just try that with my chief; I'd be sacked on the spot. Anyhow, that might be quite a good thing for me, who can tell? If I didn't have to hold my hand because of my parents I'd have given notice long ago, I'd have gone to the chief and told him exactly what I think of him. That would knock him endways from his desk! It's a queer way of doing, too, this sitting on high at a desk and talking down to employees, especially when they have to come quite near because the chief is hard of hearing. Well, there's still hope; once I've saved enough money to pay back my parents' debts to him — that should take another five or six years — I'll do it without fail. I'll cut myself completely loose then. For the moment, though, I'd better get up, since my train goes at five.

He looked at the alarm clock ticking on the chest. Heavenly Father! he thought. It was half-past six o'clock and the hands were quietly moving on, it was even past the half-hour, it was getting on toward a quarter to seven. Had the alarm clock not gone off? From the bed one could see that it had been properly set for four o'clock; of course it must have gone off. Yes, but was it possible to sleep quietly through that ear-splitting noise? Well, he had not slept quietly, yet apparently all the more soundly for that. But what was he to do now? The next train went at seven o'clock, to catch that he would need to hurry like mad and his samples weren't even packed up, and he himself wasn't feeling particularly fresh and active. And even if he did catch the train he wouldn't avoid a row with the chief, since the firm's porter would have been waiting for the five o'clock train and would have long since reported his failure to turn up. The porter was a creature of the chief's, spineless and stupid. Well, supposing he were to say he was sick? But that would be most unpleasant and would look suspicious, since during his five years' employment he had not been ill once. The chief himself would be sure to come with the sick-insurance doctor, would reproach his parents with their son's laziness and would cut all excuses short by referring to the insurance doctor, who of course regarded all mankind as perfectly healthy malingerers. And would he be so far wrong on this occasion? Gregor really felt quite well, apart from a drowsiness that was utterly superfluous after such a long sleep, and he was even unusually hungry.

As all this was running through his mind at top speed without his being able to decide to leave his bed — the alarm clock had just struck a quarter to seven — there came a cautious tap at the door behind the head of his bed. "Gregor," said a voice — it was his mother's — "it's a quarter to seven. Hadn't you a train to catch?" That gentle voice! Gregor had a shock as he heard his own voice answering hers, unmistakably his own voice, it was true, but with a persistent horrible twittering squeak behind it like an undertone, that left the words in their clear shape only for the first moment and then rose up reverberating round them to destroy their sense, so that one could not be sure one had heard them rightly. Gregor wanted to answer at length and explain everything, but in the circumstances he confined himself to saying: "Yes, yes, thank you, Mother, I'm getting up now." The wooden door between them must have kept the change in his voice from being noticeable outside, for his mother contented herself with this statement and shuffled away. Yet this brief exchange of words had made the other members of the family aware that Gregor was still in the house, as they had not expected, and at one of the side doors his father was already knocking, gently, yet with his fist. "Gregor, Gregor," he called, "what's the matter with you?" And after a little while he called again in a deeper voice: "Gregor! Gregor!" At the other side door his sister was saying in a low, plaintive tone: "Gregor? Aren't you well? Are you needing anything?" He answered them both at once: "I'm just ready," and did his best to make his voice sound as normal as possible by enunciating the words very clearly and leaving long pauses between them. So his father went back to his breakfast, but his sister whispered: "Gregor, open the door, do." However, he was not thinking of opening the door, and felt thankful for the prudent habit he had acquired in traveling of locking all doors during the night, even at home.

His immediate intention was to get up quietly without being disturbed, to put on his clothes and above all eat his breakfast, and only then to consider what else was to be done, since in bed, he was well aware, his meditations would come to no sensible conclusion. He remembered that often enough in bed he had felt small aches and pains, probably caused by awkward postures, which had proved purely imaginary once he got up, and he looked forward eagerly to seeing this morning's delusions gradually fall away. That the change in his voice was nothing but the precursor of a severe chill, a standing ailment of commercial travelers, he had not the least possible doubt.

To get rid of the quilt was quite easy; he had only to inflate himself a little and it fell off by itself. But the next move was difficult, especially because he was so uncommonly broad. He would have needed arms and hands to hoist himself up; instead he had only the numerous little legs which never stopped waving in all directions and which he could not control in the least. When he tried to bend one of them it was the first to stretch itself straight; and did he succeed at last in making it do what he wanted, all the other legs meanwhile waved the more wildly in a high degree of unpleasant agitation. "But what's the use of lying idle in bed," said Gregor to himself.

He thought that he might get out of bed with the lower part of his body first, but this lower part, which he had not yet seen and of which he could form no clear conception, proved too difficult to move; it shifted so slowly; and when finally, almost wild with annoyance, he gathered his forces together and thrust out recklessly, he had miscalculated the direction and bumped heavily against the lower end of the bed, and the stinging pain he felt informed him that precisely this lower part of his body was at the moment probably the most sensitive.

So he tried to get the top part of himself out first, and cautiously moved his head towards the edge of the bed. That proved easy enough, and despite its breadth and mass the bulk of his body at last slowly followed the movement of his head. Still, when he finally got his head free over the edge of the bed he felt too scared to go on advancing, for after all if he let himself fall in this way it would take a miracle to keep his head from being injured. And at all costs he must not lose consciousness now, precisely now; he would rather stay in bed.

But when after a repetition of the same efforts he lay in his former position again, sighing, and watched his little legs struggling against each other more wildly than ever, if that were possible, and saw no way of bringing any order into this arbitrary confusion, he told himself again that it was impossible to stay in bed and that the most sensible course was to risk everything for the smallest hope of getting away from it. At the same time he did not forget meanwhile to remind himself that cool reflection, the coolest possible, was much better than desperate resolves. In such moments he focused his eyes as sharply as possible on the window, but, unfortunately, the prospect of the morning fog, which muffled even the other side of the narrow street, brought him little encouragement and comfort. "Seven o'clock already," he said to himself when the alarm clock chimed again, "seven o'clock already and still such a thick fog." And for a little while he lay quiet, breathing lightly, as if perhaps expecting such complete repose to restore all things to their real and normal condition.

But then he said to himself: "Before it strikes a quarter past seven I must be quite out of this bed, without fail. Anyhow, by that time someone will have come from the office to ask for me, since it opens before seven." And he set himself to rocking his whole body at once in a regular rhythm, with the idea of swinging it out of the bed. If he tipped himself out in that way he could keep his head from injury by lifting it at an acute angle when he fell. His back seemed to be hard and was not likely to suffer from a fall on the carpet. His biggest worry was the loud crash he would not be able to help making, which would probably cause anxiety, if not terror, behind all the doors. Still, he must take the risk.

When he was already half out of the bed — the new method was more a game than an effort, for he needed only to hitch himself across by rocking to and fro — it struck him how simple it would be if he could get help. Two strong people — he thought of his father and the servant girl — would be amply sufficient; they would only have to thrust their arms under his convex back, lever him out of the bed, bend down with their burden and then be patient enough to let him turn himself right over on to the floor, where it was to be hoped his legs would then find their proper function. Well, ignoring the fact that the doors were all locked, ought he really to call for help? In spite of his misery he could not suppress a smile at the very idea of it.

He had got so far that he could barely keep his equilibrium when he rocked himself strongly, and he would have to nerve himself very soon for the final decision since in five minutes' time it would be a quarter past seven — when the front door bell rang. "That's someone from the office," he said to himself, and grew almost rigid, while his little legs only jigged about all the faster. For a moment everything stayed quiet. "They're not going to open the door," said Gregor to himself, catching at some kind of irrational hope. But then of course the servant girl went as usual to the door with her heavy tread and opened it. Gregor needed only to hear the first good morning of the visitor to know immediately who it was — the chief clerk himself. What a fate, to be condemned to work for a firm where the smallest omission at once gave rise to the gravest suspicion! Were all employees in a body nothing but scoundrels, was there not among them one single loyal devoted man who, had he wasted only an hour or so of the firm's time in a morning, was so tormented by conscience as to be driven out of his mind and actually incapable of leaving his bed? Wouldn't it really have been sufficient to send an apprentice to inquire — if any inquiry were necessary at all — did the chief clerk himself have to come and thus indicate to the entire family, an innocent family, that this suspicious circumstance could be investigated by no one less versed in affairs than himself? And more through the agitation caused by these reflections than through any act of will Gregor swung himself out of bed with all his strength. There was a loud thump, but it was not really a crash. His fall was broken to some extent by the carpet, his back, too, was less stiff than he thought, and so there was merely a dull thud, not so very startling. Only he had not lifted his head carefully enough and had hit it; he turned it and rubbed it on the carpet in pain and irritation.

"That was something falling down in there," said the chief clerk in the next room to the left. Gregor tried to suppose to himself that something like what had happened to him today might some day happen to the chief clerk; one really could not deny that it was possible. But as if in brusque reply to this supposition the chief clerk took a couple of firm steps in the next-door room and his patent leather boots creaked. From the right-hand room his sister was whispering to inform him of the situation: "Gregor, the chief clerk's here." "I know," muttered Gregor to himself; but he didn't dare to make his voice loud enough for his sister to hear it.

"Gregor," said his father now from the left-hand room, "the chief clerk has come and wants to know why you didn't catch the early train. We don't know what to say to him. Besides, he wants to talk to you in person. So open the door, please. He will be good enough to excuse the untidiness of your room." "Good morning, Mr. Samsa," the chief clerk was calling amiably meanwhile. "He's not well," said his mother to the visitor, while his father was still speaking through the door, "he's not well, sir, believe me. What else would make him miss a train! The boy thinks about nothing but his work. It makes me almost cross the way he never goes out in the evenings; he's been here the last eight days and has stayed at home every single evening. He just sits there quietly at the table reading a newspaper or looking through railway timetables. The only amusement he gets is doing fretwork. For instance, he spent two or three evenings cutting out a little picture frame; you would be surprised to see how pretty it is; it's hanging in his room; you'll see it in a minute when Gregor opens the door. I must say I'm glad you've come, sir; we should never have got him to unlock the door by ourselves; he's so obstinate; and I'm sure he's unwell, though he wouldn't have it to be so this morning." "I'm just coming," said Gregor slowly and carefully, not moving an inch for fear of losing one word of the conversation. "I can't think of any other explanation, madam," said the chief clerk, "I hope it's nothing serious. Although on the other hand I must say that we men of business — fortunately or unfortunately — very often simply have to ignore any slight indisposition, since business must be attended to." "Well, can the chief clerk come in now?" asked Gregor's father impatiently, again knocking on the door. "No," said Gregor. In the left-hand room a painful silence followed this refusal, in the right-hand room his sister began to sob.

Why didn't his sister join the others? She was probably newly out of bed and hadn't even begun to put on her clothes yet. Well, why was she crying? Because he wouldn't get up and let the chief clerk in, because he was in danger of losing his job, and because the chief would begin dunning his parents again for the old debts? Surely these were things one didn't need to worry about for the present. Gregor was still at home and not in the least thinking of deserting the family. At the moment, true, he was lying on the carpet and no one who knew the condition he was in could seriously expect him to admit the chief clerk. But for such a small discourtesy, which could plausibly be explained away somehow later on, Gregor could hardly be dismissed on the spot. And it seemed to Gregor that it would be much more sensible to leave him in peace for the present than to trouble him with tears and entreaties. Still, of course, their uncertainty bewildered them all and excused their behavior.

"Mr. Samsa," the chief clerk called now in a louder voice, "what's the matter with you? Here you are, barricading yourself in your room, giving only 'yes' and 'no' for answers, causing your parents a lot of unnecessary trouble and neglecting — I mention this only in passing — neglecting your business duties in an incredible fashion. I am speaking here in the name of your parents and of your chief, and I beg you quite seriously to give me an immediate and precise explanation. You amaze me, you amaze me. I thought you were a quiet, dependable person, and now all at once you seem bent on making a disgraceful exhibition of yourself. The chief did hint to me early this morning a possible explanation for your disappearance — with reference to the cash payments that were entrusted to you recently — but I almost pledged my solemn word of honor that this could not be so. But now that I see how incredibly obstinate you are, I no longer have the slightest desire to take your part at all. And your position in the firm is not so unassailable. I came with the intention of telling you all this in private, but since you are wasting my time so needlessly I don't see why your parents shouldn't hear it too. For some time past your work has been most unsatisfactory; this is not the season of the year for a business boom, of course, we admit that, but a season of the year for doing no business at all, that does not exist, Mr. Samsa, must not exist."

"But, sir," cried Gregor, beside himself and in his agitation forgetting everything else, "I'm just going to open the door this very minute. A slight illness, an attack of giddiness, has kept me from getting up. I'm still lying in bed. But I feel all right again. I'm getting out of bed now. Just give me a moment or two longer! I'm not quite so well as I thought. But I'm all right, really. How a thing like that can suddenly strike one down! Only last night I was quite well, my parents can tell you, or rather I did have a slight presentiment. I must have showed some sign of it. Why didn't I report it at the office! But one always thinks that an indisposition can be got over without staying in the house. Oh sir, do spare my parents! All that you're reproaching me with now has no foundation; no one has ever said a word to me about it. Perhaps you haven't looked at the last orders I sent in. Anyhow, I can still catch the eight o'clock train, I'm much the better for my few hours' rest. Don't let me detain you here, sir; I'll be attending to business very soon, and do be good enough to tell the chief so and to make my excuses to him!"

And while all this was tumbling out pell-mell and Gregor hardly knew what he was saying, he had reached the chest quite easily, perhaps because of the practice he had had in bed, and was now trying to lever himself upright by means of it. He meant actually to open the door, actually to show himself and speak to the chief clerk; he was eager to find out what the others, after all their insistence, would say at the sight of him. If they were horrified then the responsibility was no longer his and he could stay quiet. But if they took it calmly, then he had no reason either to be upset, and could really get to the station for the eight o'clock train if he hurried. At first he slipped down a few times from the polished surface of the chest, but at length with a last heave he stood upright; he paid no more attention to the pains in the lower part of his body, however they smarted. Then he let himself fall against the back of a near-by chair, and clung with his little legs to the edges of it. That brought him into control of himself again and he stopped speaking, for now he could listen to what the chief clerk was saying.

"Did you understand a word of it?" the chief clerk was asking; "surely he can't be trying to make fools of us?" "Oh dear," cried his mother, in tears, "perhaps he's terribly ill and we're tormenting him. Grete! Grete!" she called out then. "Yes Mother?" called his sister from the other side. They were calling to each other across Gregor's room. "You must go this minute for the doctor. Gregor is ill. Go for the doctor, quick. Did you hear how he was speaking?" "That was no human voice," said the chief clerk in a voice noticeably low beside the shrillness of the mother's. "Anna! Anna!"

his father was calling through the hall to the kitchen, clapping his hands, "get a locksmith at once!" And the two girls were already running through the hall with a swish of skirts — how could his sister have got dressed so quickly? — and were tearing the front door open. There was no sound of its closing again; they had evidently left it open, as one does in houses where some great misfortune has happened.

But Gregor was now much calmer. The words he uttered were no longer understandable, apparently, although they seemed clear enough to him, even clearer than before, perhaps because his ear had grown accustomed to the sound of them. Yet at any rate people now believed that something was wrong with him, and were ready to help him. The positive certainty with which these first measures had been taken comforted him. He felt himself drawn once more into the human circle and hoped for great and remarkable results from both the doctor and the locksmith, without really distinguishing precisely between them. To make his voice as clear as possible for the decisive conversation that was now imminent he coughed a little, as quietly as he could, of course, since this noise too might not sound like a human cough for all he was able to judge. In the next room meanwhile there was complete silence. Perhaps his parents were sitting at the table with the chief clerk, whispering, perhaps they were all leaning against the door and listening.

Slowly Gregor pushed the chair towards the door, then let go of it, caught hold of the door for support — the soles at the end of his little legs were somewhat sticky — and rested against it for a moment after his efforts. Then he set himself to turning the key in the lock with his mouth. It seemed, unhappily, that he hadn't really any teeth — what could he grip the key with? — but on the other hand his jaws were certainly very strong; with their help he did manage to set the key in motion, heedless of the fact that he was undoubtedly damaging them somewhere, since a brown fluid issued from his mouth, flowed over the key and dripped on the floor. "Just listen to that," said the chief clerk next door; "he's turning the key." That was a great encouragement to Gregor; but they should all have shouted encouragement to him, his father and mother too: "Go on, Gregor," they should have called out, "keep going, hold on to that key!" And in the belief that they were all following his efforts intently, he clenched his jaws recklessly on the key with all the force at his command. As the turning of the key progressed he circled round the lock, holding on now only with his mouth, pushing on the key, as required, or pulling it down again with all the weight of his body. The louder click of the finally yielding lock literally quickened Gregor. With a deep breath of relief he said to himself: "So I didn't need the locksmith," and laid his head on the handle to open the door wide.

Since he had to pull the door towards him, he was still invisible when it was really wide open. He had to edge himself slowly round the near half of the double door, and to do it very carefully if he was not to fall plump upon his back just on the threshold. He was still carrying out this difficult manoeuvre, with no time to observe anything else, when he heard the chief clerk utter a loud "Oh!" — it sounded like a gust of wind — and now he could see the man, standing as he was nearest to the door, clapping one hand before his open mouth and slowly backing away as if driven by some invisible steady pressure. His mother — in spite of the chief clerk's being there her hair was still undone and sticking up in all directions — first clasped her hands and looked at his father, then took two steps towards Gregor and fell on the floor among her outspread skirts, her face quite hidden on her breast. His father knotted his fist with a fierce expression on his face as if he meant to knock Gregor back into his room, then looked uncertainly round the living room, covered his eyes with his hands and wept till his great chest heaved.

Gregor did not go now into the living room, but leaned against the inside of the firmly shut wing of the door, so that only half his body was visible and his head above it bending sideways to look at the others. The light had meanwhile strengthened; on the other side of the street one could see clearly a section of the endlessly long, dark gray building opposite — it was a hospital — abruptly punctuated by its row of regular windows; the rain was still falling, but only in large singly discernible and literally singly splashing drops. The breakfast dishes were set out on the table lavishly, for breakfast was the most important meal of the day to Gregor's father, who lingered it out for hours over various newspapers. Right opposite Gregor on the wall hung a photograph of himself on military service, as a lieutenant, hand on sword, a carefree smile on his face, inviting one to respect his uniform and military bearing. The door leading to the hall was open, and one could see that the front door stood open too, showing the landing beyond and the beginning of the stairs going down.

"Well," said Gregor, knowing perfectly that he was the only one who had retained any composure, "I'll put my clothes on at once, pack up my samples and start off. Will you only let me go? You see, sir, I'm not obstinate, and I'm willing to work; traveling is a hard life, but I couldn't live without it. Where are you going, sir? To the office? Yes? Will you give a true account of all this? One can be temporarily incapacitated, but that's just the moment for remembering former services and bearing in mind that later on, when the incapacity has been got over, one will certainly work with all the more industry and concentration. I'm loyally bound to serve the chief, you know that very well. Besides, I have to provide for my parents and my sister. I'm in great difficulties, but I'll get out of them again. Don't make things any worse for me than they are. Stand up for me in the firm. Travelers are not popular there, I know. People think they earn sacks of money and just have a good time. A prejudice there's no particular reason for revising. But you, sir, have a more comprehensive view of affairs than the rest of the staff, yes, let me tell you in confidence, a more comprehensive view than the chief himself, who, being the owner, lets his judgment easily be swayed against one of his employees. And you know very well that the traveler, who is never seen in the office almost the whole year round, can so easily fall a victim to gossip and ill luck and unfounded complaints, which he mostly knows nothing about, except when he comes back exhausted from his rounds, and only then suffers in person from their evil consequences, which he can no longer trace back to the original causes. Sir, sir, don't go away without a word to me to show that you think me in the right at least to some extent!"

But at Gregor's very first words the chief clerk had already backed away and only stared at him with parted lips over one twitching shoulder. And while Gregor was speaking he did not stand still one moment but stole away towards the door, without taking his eyes off Gregor, yet only an inch at a time, as if obeying some secret injunction to leave the room. He was already at the hall, and the suddenness with which he took his last step out of the living room would have made one believe he had burned the sole of his foot. Once in the hall he stretched his right arm before him towards the staircase, as if some supernatural power were waiting there to deliver him.

Gregor perceived that the chief clerk must on no account be allowed to go away in this frame of mind if his position in the firm were not to be endangered to the utmost. His parents did not understand this so well; they had convinced themselves in the course of years that Gregor was settled for life in this firm, and besides they were so occupied with their immediate troubles that all foresight had forsaken them. Yet Gregor had this foresight. The chief clerk must be detained, soothed, persuaded and finally won over; the whole future of Gregor and his family depended on it! If only his sister had been there! She was intelligent; she had begun to cry while Gregor was still lying quietly on his back. And no doubt the chief clerk, so partial to ladies, would have been guided by her; she would have shut the door of the flat and in the hall talked him out of his horror. But she was not there, and Gregor would have to handle the situation himself. And without remembering that he was still unaware what powers of movement he possessed, without even remembering that his words in all possibility, indeed in all likelihood, would again be unintelligible, he let go the wing of the door, pushed himself through the opening, started to walk towards the chief clerk, who was already ridiculously clinging with both hands to the railing on the landing; but immediately, as he was feeling for a support, he fell down with a little cry upon all his numerous legs. Hardly was he down when he experienced for the first time this morning a sense of physical comfort; his legs had firm ground under them; they were completely obedient, as he noted with joy; they even strove to carry him forward in whatever direction he chose; and he was inclined to believe that a final relief from all his sufferings was at hand. But in the same moment as he found himself on the floor, rocking with suppressed eagerness to move, not far from his mother, indeed just in front of her, she, who had seemed so completely crushed, sprang all at once to her feet, her arms and fingers outspread, cried: "Help, for God's sake, help!" bent her head down as if to see Gregor better, yet on the contrary kept backing senselessly away; had quite forgotten that the laden table stood behind her; sat upon it hastily, as if in absence of mind, when she bumped into it; and seemed altogether unaware that the big coffee pot beside her was upset and pouring coffee in a flood over the carpet.

"Mother, Mother," said Gregor in a low voice, and looked up at her. The chief clerk, for the moment, had quite slipped from his mind; instead, he could not resist snapping his jaws together at the sight of the streaming coffee. That made his mother scream again, she fled from the table and fell into the arms of his father, who hastened to catch her. But Gregor had now no time to spare for his parents; the chief clerk was already on the stairs; with his chin on the banisters he was taking one last backward look. Gregor made a spring, to be as sure as possible of overtaking him; the chief clerk must have divined his intention, for he leaped down several steps and vanished; he was still yelling "Ugh!" and it echoed through the whole staircase.

Unfortunately, the flight of the chief clerk seemed completely to upset Gregor's father, who had remained relatively calm until now, for instead of running after the man himself, or at least not hindering Gregor in his pursuit, he seized in his right hand the walking stick which the chief clerk had left behind on a chair, together with a hat and greatcoat, snatched in his left hand a large newspaper from the table and began stamping his feet and flourishing the stick and the newspaper to drive Gregor back into his room. No entreaty of Gregor's availed, indeed no entreaty was even understood, however humbly he bent his head his father only stamped on the floor the more loudly. Behind his father his mother had torn open a window, despite the cold weather, and was leaning far out of it with her face in her hands. A strong draught set in from the street to the staircase, the window curtains blew in, the newspaper on the table fluttered, stray pages whisked over the floor. Pitilessly Gregor's father drove him back, hissing and crying "Shoo!" like a savage. But Gregor was quite unpracticed in walking backwards, it really was a slow business. If he only had a chance to turn round he could get back to his room at once, but he was afraid of exasperating his father by the slowness of such a rotation and at any moment the stick in his father's hand might hit him a fatal blow on the back or on the head. In the end, however, nothing else was left for him to do since to his horror he observed that in moving backwards he could not even control the direction he took; and so, keeping an anxious eye on his father all the time over his shoulder, he began to turn round as quickly as he could, which was in reality very slowly. Perhaps his father noted his good intentions, for he did not interfere except every now and then to help him in the manoeuvre from a distance with the point of the stick. If only he would have stopped making that unbearable hissing noise! It made Gregor quite lose his head. He had turned almost completely round when the hissing noise so distracted him that he even turned a little the wrong way again. But when at last his head was fortunately right in front of the doorway, it appeared that his body was too broad simply to get through the opening. His father, of course, in his present mood was far from thinking of such a thing as opening the other half of the door, to let Gregor have enough space. He had merely the fixed idea of driving Gregor back into his room as quickly as possible. He would never have suffered Gregor to make the circumstantial preparations for standing up on end and perhaps slipping his way through the door. Maybe he was now making more noise than ever to urge Gregor forward, as if no obstacle impeded him; to Gregor, anyhow, the noise in his rear sounded no longer like the voice of one single father; this was really no joke, and Gregor thrust himself — come what might — into the doorway. One side of his body rose up, he was tilted at an angle in the doorway, his flank was quite bruised, horrid blotches stained the white door, soon he was stuck fast and, left to himself, could not have moved at all, his legs on one side fluttered trembling to the air, those on the other were crushed painfully to the floor — when from behind his father gave him a strong push which was literally a deliverance and he flew far into the room, bleeding freely. The door was slammed behind him with the stick, and then at last there was silence.

II

Not until it was twilight did Gregor awake out of a deep sleep, more like a swoon than a sleep. He would certainly have waked up of his own accord not much later, for he felt himself sufficiently rested and well-slept, but it seemed to him as if a fleeting step and a cautious shutting of the door leading into the hall had aroused him. The electric lights in the street cast a pale sheen here and there on the ceiling and the upper surfaces of the furniture, but down below, where he lay, it was dark. Slowly, awkwardly trying out his feelers, which he now first learned to appreciate, he pushed his way to the door to see what had been happening there. His left side felt like one single long, unpleasantly tense scar, and he had actually to limp on his two rows of legs. One little leg, moreover, had been severely damaged in the course of that morning's events — it was almost a miracle that only one had been damaged — and trailed uselessly behind him.

He had reached the door before he discovered what had really drawn him to it: the smell of food. For there stood a basin filled with fresh milk in which floated little sops of white bread. He could almost have laughed with joy, since he was now still hungrier than in the morning, and he dipped his head almost over the eyes straight into the milk. But soon in disappointment he withdrew it again; not only did he find it difficult to feed because of his tender left side — and he could only feed with the palpitating collaboration of his whole body — he did not like the milk either, although milk had been his favorite drink and that was certainly why his sister had set it there for him, indeed it was almost with repulsion that he turned away from the basin and crawled back to the middle of the room.

He could see through the crack of the door that the gas was turned on in the living room, but while usually at this time his father made a habit of reading the afternoon newspaper in a loud voice to his mother and occasionally to his sister as well, not a sound was now to be heard. Well, perhaps his father had recently given up this habit of reading aloud, which his sister had mentioned so often in conversation and in her letters. But there was the same silence all around, although the flat was certainly not empty of occupants. "What a quiet life our family has been leading," said Gregor to himself, and as he sat there motionless staring into the darkness he felt great pride in the fact that he had been able to provide such a life for his parents and sister in such a fine flat. But what if all the quiet, the comfort, the contentment were now to end in horror? To keep himself from being lost in such thoughts Gregor took refuge in movement and crawled up and down the room.

Once during the long evening one of the side doors was opened a little and quickly shut again, later the other side door too; someone had apparently wanted to come in and then thought better of it. Gregor now stationed himself immediately before the living room door, determined to persuade any hesitating visitor to come in or at least to discover who it might be; but the door was not opened again and he waited in vain. In the early morning, when the doors were locked, they had all wanted to come in, now that he had opened one door and the other had apparently been opened during the day, no one came in and even the keys were on the other side of the doors.

It was late at night before the gas went out in the living room, and Gregor could easily tell that his parents and his sister had all stayed awake until then, for he could clearly hear the three of them stealing away on tiptoe. No one was likely to visit him, not until the morning, that was certain; so he had plenty of time to meditate at his leisure on how he was to arrange his life afresh. But the lofty, empty room in which he had to lie flat on the floor filled him with an apprehension he could not account for, since it had been his very own room for the past five years — and with a half-unconscious action, not without a slight feeling of shame, he scuttled under the sofa, where he felt comfortable at once, although his back was a little cramped and he could not lift his head up, and his only regret was that his body was too broad to get the whole of it under the sofa.

He stayed there all night, spending the time partly in a light slumber, from which his hunger kept waking him up with a start, and partly in worrying and sketching vague hopes, which all led to the same conclusion, that he must lie low for the present and, by exercising patience and the utmost consideration, help the family to bear the inconvenience he was bound to cause them in his present condition.

Very early in the morning, it was still almost night, Gregor had the chance to test the strength of his new resolutions, for his sister, nearly fully dressed, opened the door from the hall and peered in. She did not see him at once, yet when she caught sight of him under the sofa — well, he had to be somewhere, he couldn't have flown away, could he? — she was so startled that without being able to help it she slammed the door shut again. But as if regretting her behavior she opened the door again immediately and came in on tiptoe, as if she were visiting an invalid or even a stranger. Gregor had pushed his head forward to the very edge of the sofa and watched her. Would she notice that he had left the milk standing, and not for lack of hunger, and would she bring in some other kind of food more to his taste? If she did not do it of her own accord, he would rather starve than draw her attention to the fact, although he felt a wild impulse to dart out from under the sofa, throw himself at her feet and beg her for something to eat. But his sister at once noticed, with surprise, that the basin was still full, except for a little milk that had been spilt all around it, she lifted it immediately, not with her bare hands, true, but with a cloth and carried it away. Gregor was wildly curious to know what she would bring instead, and made various speculations about it. Yet what she actually did next, in the goodness of her heart, he could never have guessed at. To find out what he liked she brought him a whole selection of food, all set out on an old newspaper. There were old, half-decayed vegetables, bones from last night's supper covered with a white sauce that had thickened; some raisins and almonds; a piece of cheese that Gregor would have called uneatable two days ago; a dry roll of bread, a buttered roll, and a roll both buttered and salted. Besides all that, she set down again the same basin, into which she had poured some water, and which was apparently to be reserved for his exclusive use. And with fine tact, knowing that Gregor would not eat in her presence, she withdrew quickly and even turned the key, to let him understand that he could take his ease as much as he liked. Gregor's legs all whizzed towards the food. His wounds must have healed completely, moreover, for he felt no disability, which amazed him and made him reflect how more than a month ago he had cut one finger a little with a knife and had still suffered pain from the wound only the day before yesterday. Am I less sensitive now? he thought, and sucked greedily at the cheese, which above all the other edibles attracted him at once and strongly. One after another and with tears of satisfaction in his eyes he quickly devoured the cheese, the vegetables and the sauce; the fresh food, on the other hand, had no charms for him, he could not even stand the smell of it and actually dragged away to some little distance the things he could eat. He had long finished his meal and was only lying lazily on the same spot when his sister turned the key slowly as a sign for him to retreat. That roused him at once, although he was nearly asleep, and he hurried under the sofa again. But it took considerable self-control for him to stay under the sofa, even for the short time his sister was in the room, since the large meal had swollen his body somewhat and he was so cramped he could hardly breathe. Slight attacks of breathlessness afflicted him and his eyes were starting a little out of his head as he watched his unsuspecting sister sweeping together with a broom not only the remains of what he had eaten but even the things he had not touched, as if these were now of no use to anyone, and hastily shoveling it all into a bucket, which she covered with a wooden lid and carried away. Hardly had she turned her back when Gregor came from under the sofa and stretched and puffed himself out.

In this manner Gregor was fed, once in the early morning while his parents and the servant girl were still asleep, and a second time after they had all had their midday dinner, for then his parents took a short nap and the servant girl could be sent out on some errand or other by his sister. Not that they would have wanted him to starve, of course, but perhaps they could not have borne to know more about his feeding than from hearsay, perhaps too his sister wanted to spare them such little anxieties wherever possible, since they had quite enough to bear as it was.

Under what pretext the doctor and the locksmith had been got rid of on that first morning Gregor could not discover, for since what he said was not understood by the others it never struck any of them, not even his sister, that he could understand what they said, and so whenever his sister came into his room he had to content himself with hearing her utter only a sigh now and then and an occasional appeal to the saints. Later on, when she had got a little used to the situation — of course she could never get completely used to it — she sometimes threw out a remark which was kindly meant or could be so interpreted. "Well, he liked his dinner today," she would say when Gregor had made a good clearance of his food; and when he had not eaten, which gradually happened more and more often, she would say almost sadly: "Everything's been left standing again."

But although Gregor could get no news directly, he overheard a lot from the neighboring rooms, and as soon as voices were audible, he would run to the door of the room concerned and press his whole body against it. In the first few days especially there was no conversation that did not refer to him somehow, even if only indirectly. For two whole days there were family consultations at every mealtime about what should be done; but also between meals the same subject was discussed, for there were always at least two members of the family at home, since no one wanted to be alone in the flat and to leave it quite empty was unthinkable. And on the very first of these days the household cook — it was not quite clear what and how much she knew of the situation — went down on her knees to his mother and begged leave to go, and when she departed, a quarter of an hour later, gave thanks for her dismissal with tears in her eyes as if for the greatest benefit that could have been conferred on her, and without any prompting swore a solemn oath that she would never say a single word to anyone about what had happened.

Now Gregor's sister had to cook too, helping her mother; true, the cooking did not amount to much, for they ate scarcely anything. Gregor was always hearing one of the family vainly urging another to eat and getting no answer but: "Thanks, I've had all I want," or something similar. Perhaps they drank nothing either. Time and again his sister kept asking his father if he wouldn't like some beer and offered kindly to go and fetch it herself, and when he made no answer suggested that she could ask the concierge to fetch it, so that he need feel no sense of obligation, but then a round "No" came from his father and no more was said about it.

In the course of that very first day Gregor's father explained the family's financial position and prospects to both his mother and his sister. Now and then he rose from the table to get some voucher or memorandum out of the small safe he had rescued from the collapse of his business five years earlier. One could hear him opening the complicated lock and rustling papers out and shutting it again. This statement made by his father was the first cheerful information Gregor had heard since his imprisonment. He had been of the opinion that nothing at all was left over from his father's business, at least his father had never said anything to the contrary, and of course he had not asked him directly. At that time Gregor's sole desire was to do his utmost to help the family to forget as soon as possible the catastrophe which had overwhelmed the business and thrown them all into a state of complete despair. And so he had set to work with unusual ardor and almost overnight had become a commercial traveler instead of a little clerk, with of course much greater chances of earning money, and his success was immediately translated into good round coin which he could lay on the table for his amazed and happy family. These had been fine times, and they had never recurred, at least not with the same sense of glory, although later on Gregor had earned so much money that he was able to meet the expenses of the whole household and did so. They had simply got used to it, both the family and Gregor; the money was gratefully accepted and gladly given, but there was no special uprush of warm feeling. With his sister alone had he remained intimate, and it was a secret plan of his that she, who loved music, unlike himself, and could play movingly on the violin, should be sent next year to study at the Conservatorium, despite the great expense that would entail, which must be made up in some other way. During his brief visits home the Conservatorium was often mentioned in the talks he had with his sister, but always merely as a beautiful dream which could never come true, and his parents discouraged even these innocent references to it; yet Gregor had made up his mind firmly about it and meant to announce the fact with due solemnity on Christmas Day.

Such were the thoughts, completely futile in his present condition, that went through his head as he stood clinging upright to the door and listening. Sometimes out of sheer weariness he had to give up listening and let his head fall negligently against the door, but he always had to pull himself together again at once, for even the slight sound his head made was audible next door and brought all conversation to a stop. "What can he be doing now?" his father would say after a while, obviously turning towards the door, and only then would the interrupted conversation gradually be set going again.

Gregor was now informed as amply as he could wish — for his father tended to repeat himself in his explanations, partly because it was a long time since he had handled such matters and partly because his mother could not always grasp things at once — that a certain amount of investments, a very small amount it was true, had survived the wreck of their fortunes and had even increased a little because the dividends had not been touched meanwhile. And besides that, the money Gregor brought home every month — he had kept only a few dollars for himself — had never been quite used up and now amounted to a small capital sum. Behind the door Gregor nodded his head eagerly, rejoiced at this evidence of unexpected thrift and foresight. True, he could really have paid off some more of his father's debts to the chief with his extra money, and so brought much nearer the day on which he could quit his job, but doubtless it was better the way his father had arranged it.

Yet this capital was by no means sufficient to let the family live on the interest of it; for one year, perhaps, or at the most two, they could live on the principal, that was all. It was simply a sum that ought not to be touched and should be kept for a rainy day; money for living expenses would have to be earned. Now his father was still hale enough but an old man, and he had done no work for the past five years and could not be expected to do much; during these five years, the first years of leisure in his laborious though unsuccessful life, he had grown rather fat and become sluggish. And Gregor's old mother, how was she to earn a living with her asthma, which troubled her even when she walked through the flat and kept her lying on a sofa every other day panting for breath beside an open window? And was his sister to earn her bread, she who was still a child of seventeen and whose life hitherto had been so pleasant, consisting as it did in dressing herself nicely, sleeping long, helping in the housekeeping, going out to a few modest entertainments and above all playing the violin? At first whenever the need for earning money was mentioned Gregor let go his hold on the door and threw himself down on the cool leather sofa beside it, he felt so hot with shame and grief.

Often he just lay there the long nights through without sleeping at all, scrabbling for hours on the leather. Or he nerved himself to the great effort of pushing an armchair to the window, then crawled up over the window sill and, braced against the chair, leaned against the window panes, obviously in some recollection of the sense of freedom that looking out of a window always used to give him. For in reality day by day things that were even a little way off were growing dimmer to his sight; the hospital across the street, which he used to execrate for being all too often before his eyes, was now quite beyond his range of vision, and if he had not known that he lived in Charlotte Street, a quiet street but still a city street, he might have believed that his window gave on a desert waste where gray sky and gray land blended indistinguishably into each other. His quick-witted sister only needed to observe twice that the armchair stood by the window; after that whenever she had tidied the room she always pushed the chair back to the same place at the window and even left the inner casements open.

If he could have spoken to her and thanked her for all she had to do for him, he could have borne her ministrations better, as it was, they oppressed him. She certainly tried to make as light as possible of whatever was disagreeable in her task, and as time went on she succeeded, of course, more and more, but time brought more enlightenment to Gregor too. The very way she came in distressed him. Hardly was she in the room when she rushed to the window, without even taking time to shut the door, careful as she was usually to shield the sight of Gregor's room from the others, and as if she were almost suffocating tore the casements open with hasty fingers, standing then in the open draught for a while even in the bitterest cold and drawing deep breaths. This noisy scurry of hers upset Gregor twice a day; he would crouch trembling under the sofa all the time, knowing quite well that she would certainly have spared him such a disturbance had she found it at all possible to stay in his presence without opening a window.

On one occasion, about a month after Gregor's metamorphosis, when there was surely no reason for her to be still startled at his appearance, she came a little earlier than usual and found him gazing out of the window, quite motionless, and thus well placed to look like a bogey. Gregor would not have been surprised had she not come in at all, for she could not immediately open the window while he was there, but not only did she retreat, she jumped back as if in alarm and banged the door shut; a stranger might well have thought that he had been lying in wait for her there meaning to bite her. Of course he hid himself under the sofa at once, but he had to wait until midday before she came again, and she seemed more ill at ease than usual. This made him realize how repulsive the sight of him still was to her, and that it was bound to go on being repulsive, and what an effort it must cost her not to run away even from the sight of the small portion of his body that stuck out from under the sofa. In order to spare her that, therefore, one day he carried a sheet on his back to the sofa — it cost him four hours' labor — and arranged it there in such a way as to hide him completely, so that even if she were to bend down she could not see him. Had she considered the sheet unnecessary, she would certainly have stripped it off the sofa again, for it was clear enough that this curtaining and confining of himself was not likely to conduce Gregor's comfort, but she left it where it was, and Gregor even fancied that he caught a thankful glance from her eye when he lifted the sheet carefully a very little with his head to see how she was taking the new arrangement.

For the first fortnight his parents could not bring themselves to the point of entering his room, and he often heard them expressing their appreciation of his sister's activities, whereas formerly they had frequently scolded her for being as they thought a somewhat useless daughter. But now, both of them often waited outside the door, his father and his mother, while his sister tidied his room, and as soon as she came out she had to tell them exactly how things were in the room, what Gregor had eaten, how he had conducted himself this time and whether there was not perhaps some slight improvement in his condition. His mother, moreover, began relatively soon to want to visit him, but his father and sister dissuaded her at first with arguments which Gregor listened to very attentively and altogether approved. Later, however, she had to be held back by main force, and when she cried out: "Do let me in to Gregor, he is my unfortunate son! Can't you understand that I must go to him?" Gregor thought that it might be well to have her come in, not every day, of course, but perhaps once a week; she understood things, after all, much better than his sister, who was only a child despite the efforts she was making and had perhaps taken on so difficult a task merely out of childish thoughtlessness.

Gregor's desire to see his mother was soon fulfilled. During the daytime he did not want to show himself at the window, out of consideration for his parents, but he could not crawl very far around the few square yards of floor space he had, nor could he bear lying quietly at rest all during the night, while he was fast losing any interest he had ever taken in food, so that for mere recreation he had formed the habit of crawling crisscross over the walls and ceiling. He especially enjoyed hanging suspended from the ceiling; it was much better than lying on the floor; one could breathe more freely; one's body swung and rocked lightly; and in the almost blissful absorption induced by this suspension it could happen to his own surprise that he let go and fell plump on the floor. Yet he now had his body much better under control than formerly, and even such a big fall did him no harm. His sister at once remarked the new distraction Gregor had found for himself — he left traces behind him of the sticky stuff on his soles wherever he crawled — and she got the idea in her head of giving him as wide a field as possible to crawl in and of removing the pieces of furniture that hindered him, above all the chest of drawers and the writing desk. But that was more than she could manage all by herself; she did not dare ask her father to help her; and as for the servant girl, a young creature of sixteen who had had the courage to stay on after the cook's departure, she could not be asked to help, for she had begged as an especial favor that she might keep the kitchen door locked and open it only on a definite summons; so there was nothing left but to apply to her mother at an hour when her father was out. And the old lady did come, with exclamations of joyful eagerness, which, however, died away at the door of Gregor's room. Gregor's sister, of course, went in first, to see that everything was in order before letting his mother enter. In great haste Gregor pulled the sheet lower and rucked it more in folds so that it really looked as if it had been thrown accidentally over the sofa. And this time he did not peer out from under it; he renounced the pleasure of seeing his mother on this occasion and was only glad that she had come at all. "Come in, he's out of sight," said his sister, obviously leading her mother in by the hand. Gregor could now hear the two women struggling to shift the heavy old chest from its place, and his sister claiming the greater part of the labor for herself, without listening to the admonitions of her mother who feared she might overstrain herself. It took a long time. After at least a quarter of an hour's tugging his mother objected that the chest had better be left where it was, for in the first place it was too heavy and could never be got out before his father came home, and standing in the middle of the room like that it would only hamper Gregor's movements, while in the second place it was not at all certain that removing the furniture would be doing a service to Gregor. She was inclined to think to the contrary; the sight of the naked walls made her own heart heavy, and why shouldn't Gregor have the same feeling, considering that he had been used to his furniture for so long and might feel forlorn without it. "And doesn't it look," she concluded in a low voice — in fact she had been almost whispering all the time as if to avoid letting Gregor, whose exact whereabouts she did not know, hear even the tones of her voice, for she was convinced that he could not understand her words — "doesn't it look as if we were showing him, by taking away his furniture, that we have given up hope of his ever getting better and are just leaving him coldly to himself? I think it would be best to keep his room exactly as it has always been, so that when he comes back to us he will find everything unchanged and be able all the more easily to forget what has happened in between."

On hearing these words from his mother Gregor realized that the lack of all direct human speech for the past two months together with the monotony of family life must have confused his mind, otherwise he could not account for the fact that he had quite earnestly looked forward to having his room emptied of furnishing. Did he really want his warm room, so comfortably fitted with old family furniture, to be turned into a naked den in which he would certainly be able to crawl unhampered in all directions but at the price of shedding simultaneously all recollection of his human background? He had indeed been so near the brink of forgetfulness that only the voice of his mother, which he had not heard for so long, had drawn him back from it. Nothing should be taken out of his room; everything must stay as it was; he could not dispense with the good influence of the furniture on his state of mind; and even if the furniture did hamper him in his senseless crawling round and round, that was no drawback but a great advantage.

Unfortunately his sister was of the contrary opinion; she had grown accustomed, and not without reason, to consider herself an expert in Gregor's affairs as against her parents, and so her mother's advice was now enough to make her determined on the removal not only of the chest and the writing desk, which had been her first intention, but of all the furniture except the indispensable sofa. This determination was not, of course, merely the outcome of childish recalcitrance and of the self-confidence she had recently developed so unexpectedly and at such cost; she had in fact perceived that Gregor needed a lot of space to crawl about in, while on the other hand he never used the furniture at all, so far as could be seen. Another factor might have been also the enthusiastic temperament of an adolescent girl, which seeks to indulge itself on every opportunity and which now tempted Grete to exaggerate the horror of her brother's circumstances in order that she might do all the more for him. In a room where Gregor lorded it all alone over empty walls no one save herself was likely ever to set foot.

And so she was not to be moved from her resolve by her mother who seemed moreover to be ill at ease in Gregor's room and therefore unsure of herself, was soon reduced to silence and helped her daughter as best she could to push the chest outside. Now, Gregor could do without the chest, if need be, but the writing desk he must retain. As soon as the two women had got the chest out of his room, groaning as they pushed it, Gregor stuck his head out from under the sofa to see how he might intervene as kindly and cautiously as possible. But as bad luck would have it, his mother was the first to return, leaving Grete clasping the chest in the room next door where she was trying to shift it all by herself, without of course moving it from the spot. His mother however was not accustomed to the sight of him, it might sicken her and so in alarm Gregor backed quickly to the other end of the sofa, yet could not prevent the sheet from swaying a little in front. That was enough to put her on the alert. She paused, stood still for a moment and then went back to Grete.

Although Gregor kept reassuring himself that nothing out of the way was happening, but only a few bits of furniture were being changed round, he soon had to admit that all this trotting to and fro of the two women, their little ejaculations and the scraping of furniture along the floor affected him like a vast disturbance coming from all sides at once, and however much he tucked in his head and legs and cowered to the very floor he was bound to confess that he would not be able to stand it for long. They were clearing his room out; taking away everything he loved; the chest in which he kept his fret saw and other tools was already dragged off; they were now loosening the writing desk which had almost sunk into the floor, the desk at which he had done all his homework when he was at the commercial academy, at the grammar school before that, and, yes, even at the primary school — he had no more time to waste in weighing the good intentions of the two women, whose existence he had by now almost forgotten, for they were so exhausted that they were laboring in silence and nothing could be heard but the heavy scuffling of their feet.

And so he rushed out — the women were just leaning against the writing desk in the next room to give themselves a breather — and four times changed his direction, since he really did not know what to rescue first, then on the wall opposite, which was already otherwise cleared, he was struck by the picture of the lady muffled in so much fur and quickly crawled up to it and pressed himself to the glass, which was a good surface to hold on to and comforted his hot belly. This picture at least, which was entirely hidden beneath him, was going to be removed by nobody. He turned his head towards the door of the living room so as to observe the women when they came back.

They had not allowed themselves much of a rest and were already coming; Grete had twined her arm round her mother and was almost supporting her. "Well, what shall we take now?" said Grete, looking round. Her eyes met Gregor's from the wall. She kept her composure, presumably because of her mother, bent her head down to her mother, to keep her from looking up, and said, although in a fluttering, unpremeditated voice: "Come, hadn't we better go back to the living room for a moment?" Her intentions were clear enough to Gregor, she wanted to bestow her mother in safety and then chase him down from the wall. Well, just let her try it! He clung to his picture and would not give it up. He would rather fly in Grete's face.

But Grete's words had succeeded in disquieting her mother, who took a step to one side, caught sight of the huge brown mass on the flowered wallpaper, and before she was really conscious that what she saw was Gregor screamed in a loud, hoarse voice: "Oh God, oh God!" fell with outspread arms over the sofa as if giving up and did not move. "Gregor!" cried his sister, shaking her fist and glaring at him. This was the first time she had directly addressed him since his metamorphosis. She ran into the next room for some aromatic essence with which to rouse her mother from her fainting fit. Gregor wanted to help too — there was still time to rescue the picture — but he was stuck fast to the glass and had to tear himself loose: he then ran after his sister into the next room as if he could advise her, as he used to do; but then had to stand helplessly behind her; she meanwhile searched among various small bottles and when she turned round started in alarm at the sight of him; one bottle fell on the floor and broke; a splinter of glass cut Gregor's face and some kind of corrosive medicine splashed him; without pausing a moment longer Grete gathered up all the bottles she could carry and ran to her mother with them; she banged the door shut with her foot. Gregor was now cut off from his mother, who was perhaps nearly dying because of him; he dared not open the door for fear of frightening away his sister, who had to stay with her mother; there was nothing he could do but wait; and harassed by self-reproach and worry he began now to crawl to and fro, over everything, walls, furniture and ceiling, and finally in his despair, when the whole room seemed to be reeling round him, fell down on to the middle of the big table.

A little while elapsed, Gregor was still lying there feebly and all around was quiet, perhaps that was a good omen. Then the doorbell rang. The servant girl was of course locked in her kitchen, and Grete would have to open the door. It was his father. "What's been happening?" were his first words; Grete's face must have told him everything. Grete answered in a muffled voice, apparently hiding her head on his breast: "Mother has been fainting, but she's better now. Gregor's broken loose." "Just what I expected," said his father, "just what I've been telling you, but you women would never listen." It was clear to Gregor that his father had taken the worst interpretation of Grete's all too brief statement and was assuming that Gregor had been guilty of some violent act. Therefore Gregor must now try to propitiate his father, since he had neither time nor means for an explanation. And so he fled to the door of his own room and crouched against it, to let his father see as soon as he came in from the hall that his son had the good intention of getting back into his room immediately and that it was not necessary to drive him there, but that if only the door were opened he would disappear at once.

Yet his father was not in the mood to perceive such fine distinctions. "Ah!" he cried as soon as he appeared, in a tone which sounded at once angry and exultant. Gregor drew his head back from the door and lifted it to look at his father. Truly, this was not the father he had imagined to himself; admittedly he had been too absorbed of late in his new recreation of crawling over the ceiling to take the same interest as before in what was happening elsewhere in the flat, and he ought really to be prepared for some changes. And yet, and yet, could that be his father? The man who used to lie wearily sunk in bed whenever Gregor set out on a business journey; who welcomed him back of an evening lying in a long chair in a dressing gown; who could not really rise to his feet but only lifted his arms in greeting, and on the rare occasions when he did go out with his family, on one or two Sundays a year and on high holidays, walked between Gregor and his mother, who were slow walkers anyhow, even more slowly than they did, muffled in his old greatcoat, shuffling laboriously forward with the help of his crook-handled stick which he set down most cautiously at every step and, whenever he wanted to say anything, nearly always came to a full stop and gathered his escort around him? Now he was standing there in fine shape; dressed in a smart blue uniform with gold buttons, such as bank messengers wear; his strong double chin bulged over the stiff high collar of his jacket; from under his bushy eyebrows his black eyes darted fresh and penetrating glances; his onetime tangled white hair had been combed flat on either side of a shining and carefully exact parting. He pitched his cap, which bore a gold monogram, probably the badge of some bank, in a wide sweep across the whole room on to a sofa and with the tail-ends of his jacket thrown back, his hands in his trouser pockets, advanced with a grim visage towards Gregor. Likely enough he did not himself know what he meant to do; at any rate he lifted his feet uncommonly high, and Gregor was dumbfounded at the enormous size of his shoe soles. But Gregor could not risk standing up to him, aware as he had been from the very first day of his new life that his father believed only the severest measures suitable for dealing with him. And so he ran before his father, stopping when he stopped and scuttling forward again when his father made any kind of move. In this way they circled the room several times without anything decisive happening; indeed the whole operation did not even look like a pursuit because it was carried out so slowly. And so Gregor did not leave the floor, for he feared that his father might take as a piece of peculiar wickedness any excursion of his over the walls or the ceiling. All the same, he could not stay this course much longer, for while his father took one step he had to carry out a whole series of movements. He was already beginning to feel breathless, just as in his former life his lungs had not been very dependable. As he was staggering along, trying to concentrate his energy on running, hardly keeping his eyes open; in his dazed state never even thinking of any other escape than simply going forward; and having almost forgotten that the walls were free to him, which in this room were well provided with finely carved pieces of furniture full of knobs and crevices — suddenly something lightly flung landed close behind him and rolled before him. It was an apple; a second apple followed immediately; Gregor came to a stop in alarm; there was no point in running on, for his father was determined to bombard him. He had filled his pockets with fruit from the dish on the sideboard and was now shying apple after apple, without taking particularly good aim for the moment. The small red apples rolled about the floor as if magnetized and cannoned into each other. An apple thrown without much force grazed

Gregor's back and glanced off harmlessly. But another following immediately landed right on his back and sank in; Gregor wanted to drag himself forward, as if this startling, incredible pain could be left behind him: but he felt as if nailed to the spot and flattened himself out in a complete derangement of all his senses. With his last conscious look he saw the door of his room being torn open and his mother rushing out ahead of his screaming sister, in her underbodice, for her daughter had loosened her clothing to let her breathe more freely and recover from her swoon, he saw his mother rushing towards his father, leaving one after another behind her on the floor her loosened petticoats, stumbling over her petticoats straight to his father and embracing him, in complete union with him — but here Gregor's sight began to fail — with her hands clasped round his father's neck as she begged for her son's life.

III

The serious injury done to Gregor, which disabled him for more than a month — the apple went on sticking in his body as a visible reminder, since no one ventured to remove it — seemed to have made even his father recollect that Gregor was a member of the family, despite his present unfortunate and repulsive shape, and ought not to be treated as an enemy, that, on the contrary, family duty required the suppression of disgust and the exercise of patience, nothing but patience.

And although his injury had impaired, probably for ever, his power of movement, and for the time being it took him long, long minutes to creep across his room like an old invalid — there was no question now of crawling up the wall — yet in his own opinion he was sufficiently compensated for this worsening of his condition by the fact that towards evening the living-room door, which he used to watch intently for an hour or two beforehand, was always thrown open, so that lying in the darkness of his room, invisible to the family, he could see them all at the lamp-lit table and listen to their talk, by general consent as it were, very different from his earlier eavesdropping.

True, their intercourse lacked the lively character of former times, which he had always called to mind with a certain wistfulness in the small hotel bedrooms where he had been wont to throw himself down, tired out, on damp bedding. They were now mostly very silent. Soon after supper his father would fall asleep in his armchair; his mother and sister would admonish each other to be silent; his mother, bending low over the lamp, stitched at fine sewing for an underwear firm; his sister, who had taken a job as a salesgirl, was learning shorthand and French in the evenings on the chance of bettering herself. Sometimes his father woke up, and as if quite unaware that he had been sleeping said to his mother: "What a lot of sewing you're doing today!" and at once fell asleep again, while the two women exchanged a tired smile.

With a kind of mulishness his father persisted in keeping his uniform on even in the house; his dressing gown hung uselessly on its peg and he slept fully dressed where he sat, as if he were ready for service at any moment and even here only at the beck and call of his superior. As a result, his uniform, which was not brand-new to start with, began to look dirty, despite all the loving care of the mother and sister to keep it clean, and Gregor often spent whole evenings gazing at the many greasy spots on the garment, gleaming with gold buttons always in a high state of polish, in which the old man sat sleeping in extreme discomfort and yet quite peacefully.

As soon as the clock struck ten his mother tried to rouse his father with gentle words and to persuade him after that to get into bed, for sitting there he could not have a proper sleep and that was what he needed most, since he had to go to duty at six. But with the mulishness that had obsessed him since he became a bank messenger he always insisted on staying longer at the table, although he regularly fell asleep again and in the end only with the greatest trouble could be got out of his armchair and into his bed. However insistently Gregor's mother and sister kept urging him with gentle reminders, he would go on slowly shaking his head for a quarter of an hour, keeping his eyes shut, and refuse to get to his feet. The mother plucked at his sleeve, whispering endearments in his ear, the sister left her lessons to come to her mother's help, but Gregor's father was not to be caught. He would only sink down deeper in his chair. Not until the two women hoisted him up by the armpits did he open his eyes and look at them both, one after the other, usually with the remark: "This is a life. This is the peace and quiet of my old age." And leaning on the two of them he would heave himself up, with difficulty, as if he were a great burden to himself, suffer them to lead him as far as the door and then wave them off and go on alone, while the mother abandoned her needlework and the sister her pen in order to run after him and help him farther.

Who could find time, in this overworked and tired-out family, to bother about Gregor more than was absolutely needful? The household was reduced more and more; the servant girl was turned off; a gigantic bony charwoman with white hair flying round her head came in morning and evening to do the rough work; everything else was done by Gregor's mother, as well as great piles of sewing. Even various family ornaments, which his mother and sister used to wear with pride at parties and celebrations, had to be sold, as Gregor discovered of an evening from hearing them all discuss the prices obtained. But what they lamented most was the fact that they could not leave the flat which was much too big for their present circumstances, because they could not think of any way to shift Gregor. Yet Gregor saw well enough that consideration for him was not the main difficulty preventing the removal, for they could have easily shifted him in some suitable box with a few air holes in it; what really kept them from moving into another flat was rather their own complete hopelessness and the belief that they had been singled out for a misfortune such as had never happened to any of their relations or acquaintances. They fulfilled to the uttermost all that the world demands of poor people, the father fetched breakfast for the small clerks in the bank, the mother devoted her energy to making underwear for strangers, the sister trotted to and fro behind the counter at the behest of customers, but more than this they had not the strength to do. And the wound in Gregor's back began to nag at him afresh when his mother and sister, after getting his father into bed, came back again, left their work lying, drew close to each other and sat cheek by cheek; when his mother, pointing towards his room, said: "Shut that door now, Grete," and he was left again in darkness, while next door the women mingled their tears or perhaps sat dry-eyed staring at the table.

Gregor hardly slept at all by night or by day. He was often haunted by the idea that next time the door opened he would take the family's affairs in hand again just as he used to do; once more, after this long interval, there appeared in his thoughts the figures of the chief and the chief clerk, the commercial travelers and the apprentices, the porter who was so dull-witted, two or three friends in other firms, a chambermaid in one of the rural hotels, a sweet and fleeting memory, a cashier in a milliner's shop, whom he had wooed earnestly but too slowly — they all appeared, together with strangers or people he had quite forgotten, but instead of helping him and his family they were one and all unapproachable and he was glad when they vanished. At other times he would not be in the mood to bother about his family, he was only filled with rage at the way they were neglecting him, and although he had no clear idea of what he might care to eat he would make plans for getting into the larder to take the food that was after all his due, even if he were not hungry. His sister no longer took thought to bring him what might especially please him, but in the morning and at noon before she went to business hurriedly pushed into his room with her foot any food that was available, and in the evening cleared it out again with one sweep of the broom, heedless of whether it had been merely tasted, or — as most frequently happened — left untouched. The cleaning of his room, which she now did always in the evenings, could not have been more hastily done. Streaks of dirt stretched along the walls, here and there lay balls of dust and filth. At first Gregor used to station himself in some particularly filthy corner when his sister arrived, in order to reproach her with it, so to speak. But he could have sat there for weeks without getting her to make any improvements; she could see the dirt as well as he did, but she had simply made up her mind to leave it alone. And yet, with a touchiness that was new to her, which seemed anyhow to have infected the whole family, she jealously guarded her claim to be the sole caretaker of Gregor's room. His mother once subjected his room to a thorough cleaning, which was achieved only by means of several buckets of water — all this dampness of course upset Gregor too and he lay widespread, sulky and motionless on the sofa — but she was well punished for it. Hardly had his sister noticed the changed aspect of his room that evening than she rushed in high dudgeon into the living room and, despite the imploringly raised hands of her mother, burst into a storm of weeping, while her parents — her father had of course been startled out of his chair — looked on at first in helpless amazement; then they too began to go into action; the father reproached the mother on his right for not having left the cleaning of Gregor's room to his sister; shrieked at the sister on his left that never again was she to be allowed to clean Gregor's room; while the mother tried to pull the father into his bedroom, since he was beyond himself with agitation; the sister, shaken with sobs, then beat upon the table with her small fists; and Gregor hissed loudly with rage because not one of them thought of shutting the door to spare him such a spectacle and so much noise.

Still, even if the sister, exhausted by her daily work, had grown tired of looking after Gregor as she did formerly, there was no need for his mother's intervention or for Gregor's being neglected at all. The charwoman was there. This old widow, whose strong bony frame had enabled her to survive the worst of a long life could offer, by no means recoiled from Gregor. Without being in the least curious she had once by chance opened the door of his room and at the sight of Gregor, who, taken by surprise, began to rush to and fro although no one was chasing him, merely stood there with her arms folded. From that time she never failed to open his door a little for a moment, morning and evening, to have a look at him. At first she even used to call him to her, with words which apparently she took to be friendly, such as: "Come along, then, you old dung beetle!" or "Look at the old dung beetle, then!" To such allocutions Gregor made no answer, but stayed motionless where he was, as if the door had never been opened. Instead of being allowed to disturb him so senselessly whenever the whim took her, she should rather have been ordered to clean out his room daily, that charwoman! Once, early in the morning — heavy rain was lashing on the windowpanes, perhaps a sign that spring was on the way — Gregor was so exasperated when she began addressing him again that he ran at her, as if to attack her, although slowly and feebly enough. But the charwoman instead of showing fright merely lifted high a chair that happened to be beside the door, and as she stood there with her mouth wide open it was clear that she meant to shut it only when she brought the chair down on Gregor's back. "So you're not coming any nearer?" she asked, as Gregor turned away again, and quietly put the chair back into the corner.

Gregor was now eating hardly anything. Only when he happened to pass the food laid out for him did he take a bit of something in his mouth as a pastime, kept it there for an hour at a time and usually spat it out again. At first he thought it was chagrin over the state of his room that prevented him from eating, yet he soon got used to the various changes in his room. It had become a habit in the family to push into his room things there was no room for elsewhere, and there were plenty of these now, since one of the rooms had been let to three lodgers. These serious gentlemen — all three of them with full beards, as Gregor once observed through a crack in the door — had a passion for order, not only in their own room but, since they were now members of the household, in all its arrangements, especially in the kitchen. Superfluous, not to say dirty, objects they could not bear. Besides, they had brought with them most of the furnishings they needed. For this reason many things could be dispensed with that it was no use trying to sell but that should not be thrown away either. All of them found their way into Gregor's room. The ash can likewise and the kitchen garbage can. Anything that was not needed for the moment was simply flung into Gregor's room by the charwoman, who did everything in a hurry; fortunately Gregor usually saw only the object, whatever it was, and the hand that held it. Perhaps she intended to take the things away again as time and opportunity offered, or to collect them until she could throw them all out in a heap, but in fact they just lay wherever she happened to throw them, except when Gregor pushed his way through the junk heap and shifted it somewhat, at first out of necessity, because he had not room enough to crawl, but later with increasing enjoyment, although after such excursions, being sad and weary to death, he would lie motionless for hours. And since the lodgers often ate their supper at home in the common living room, the living-room door stayed shut many an evening, yet Gregor reconciled himself quite easily to the shutting of the door, for often enough on evenings when it was opened he had disregarded it entirely and lain in the darkest corner of his room, quite unnoticed by the family. But on one occasion the charwoman left the door open a little and it stayed ajar even when the lodgers came in for supper and the lamp was lit. They set themselves at the top end of the table where formerly Gregor and his father and mother had eaten their meals, unfolded their napkins and took knife and fork in hand. At once his mother appeared in the other doorway with a dish of meat and close behind her his sister with a dish of potatoes piled high. The food steamed with a thick vapor. The lodgers bent over the food set before them as if to scrutinize it before eating, in fact the man in the middle, who seemed to pass for an authority with the other two, cut a piece of meat as it lay on the dish, obviously to discover if it were tender or should be sent back to the kitchen. He showed satisfaction, and Gregor's mother and sister, who had been watching anxiously, breathed freely and began to smile.

The family itself took its meals in the kitchen. Nonetheless, Gregor's father came into the living room before going into the kitchen and with one prolonged bow, cap in hand, made a round of the table. The lodgers all stood up and murmured something in their beards. When they were alone again they ate their food in almost complete silence. It seemed remarkable to Gregor that among the various noises coming from the table he could always distinguish the sound of their masticating teeth, as if this were a sign to Gregor that one needed teeth in order to eat, and that with toothless jaws even of the finest make one could do nothing. "I'm hungry enough," said Gregor sadly to himself, "But not for that kind of food. How these lodgers are stuffing themselves, and here am I dying of starvation!"

On that very evening — during the whole of his time there Gregor could not remember ever having heard the violin — the sound of violin-playing came from the kitchen. The lodgers had already finished their supper, the one in the middle had brought out a newspaper and given the other two a page apiece, and now they were leaning back at ease reading and smoking. When the violin began to play they pricked up their ears, got to their feet, and went on tiptoe to the hall door where they stood huddled together. Their movements must have been heard in the kitchen, for Gregor's father called out: "Is the violin-playing disturbing you, gentlemen? It can be stopped at once." "On the contrary," said the middle lodger, "could not Fräulein Samsa come and play in this room, beside us, where it is much more convenient and comfortable?" "Oh certainly," cried Gregor's father, as if he were the violin-player. The lodgers came back into the living room and waited. Presently Gregor's father arrived with the music stand, his mother carrying the music and his sister with the violin. His sister quietly made everything ready to start playing; his parents, who had never let rooms before and so had an exaggerated idea of the courtesy due to lodgers, did not venture to sit down on their own chairs; his father leaned against the door, the right hand thrust between two buttons of his livery coat, which was formally buttoned up; but his mother was offered a chair by one of the lodgers and, since she left the chair just where he had happened to put it, sat down in a corner to one side.

Gregor's sister began to play; the father and mother, from either side, intently watched the movements of her hands. Gregor, attracted by the playing, ventured to move forward a little until his head was actually inside the living room. He felt hardly any surprise at his growing lack of consideration for the others; there had been a time when he prided himself on being considerate. And yet just on this occasion he had more reason than ever to hide himself, since owing to the amount of dust which lay thick in his room and rose into the air at the slightest movement, he too was covered with dust; fluff and hair and remnants of food trailed with him, caught on his back and along his sides; his indifference to everything was much too great for him to turn on his back and scrape himself clean on the carpet, as once he had done several times a day. And in spite of his condition, no shame deterred him from advancing a little over the spotless floor of the living room.

To be sure, no one was aware of him. The family was entirely absorbed in the violin-playing; the lodgers, however, who first of all had stationed themselves, hands in pockets, much too close behind the music stand so that they could all have read the music, which must have bothered his sister, had soon retreated to the window, half-whispering with downbent heads, and stayed there while his father turned an anxious eye on them. Indeed, they were making it more than obvious that they had been disappointed in their expectation of hearing good or enjoyable violin-playing, that they had had more than enough of the performance and only out of courtesy suffered a continued disturbance of their peace. From the way they all kept blowing the smoke of their cigars high in the air through nose and mouth one could divine their irritation. And yet Gregor's sister was playing so beautifully. Her face leaned sideways, intently and sadly her eyes followed the notes of music. Gregor crawled a little farther forward and lowered his head to the ground so that it might be possible for his eyes to meet hers. Was he an animal, that music had such an effect upon him? He felt as if the way were opening before him to the unknown nourishment he craved. He was determined to push forward till he reached his sister, to pull at her skirt and so let her know that she was to come into his room with her violin, for no one here appreciated her playing as he would appreciate it. He would never let her out of his room, at least, not so long as he lived; his frightful appearance would become, for the first time, useful to him; he would watch all the doors of his room at once and spit at intruders; but his sister should need no constraint, she should stay with him of her own free will; she should sit beside him on the sofa, bend down her ear to him and hear him confide that he had had the firm intention of sending her to the Conservatorium, and that, but for his mishap, last Christmas — surely Christmas was long past? — he would have announced it to everybody without allowing a single objection. After this confession his sister would be so touched that she would burst into tears, and Gregor would then raise himself to her shoulder and kiss her on the neck, which, now that she went to business, she kept free of any ribbon or collar.

"Mr. Samsa!" cried the middle lodger, to Gregor's father, and pointed, without wasting any more words, at Gregor, now working himself slowly forwards. The violin fell silent, the middle lodger first smiled to his friends with a shake of the head and then looked at Gregor again. Instead of driving Gregor out, his father seemed to think it more needful to begin by soothing down the lodgers, although they were not at all agitated and apparently found Gregor more entertaining than the violin-playing. He hurried toward them and, spreading out his arms, tried to urge them back into their own room and at the same time to block their view of Gregor. They now began to be really a little angry, one could not tell whether because of the old man's behavior or because it had just dawned on them that all unwittingly they had such a neighbor as Gregor next door. They demanded explanations of his father, they waved their arms like him, tugged uneasily at their beards, and only with reluctance backed towards their room. Meanwhile Gregor's sister, who stood there as if lost when her playing was so abruptly broken off, came to life again, pulled herself together all at once after standing for a while holding violin and bow in nervelessly hanging hands and staring at her music, pushed her violin into the lap of her mother, who was still sitting in her chair fighting asthmatically for breath, and ran into the lodgers' room to which they were now being shepherded by her father rather more quickly than before. One could see the pillows and blankets on the beds flying under her accustomed fingers and being laid in order. Before the lodgers had actually reached their room she had finished making the beds and slipped out.

The old man seemed once more to be so possessed by his mulish self-assertiveness that he was forgetting all the respect he should show to his lodgers. He kept driving them on and driving them on until in the very door of the bedroom the middle lodger stamped his foot loudly on the floor and so brought him to a halt. "I beg to announce," said the lodger, lifting one hand and looking also at Gregor's mother and sister, "that because of the disgusting conditions prevailing in this household and family" — here he spat on the floor with emphatic brevity — "I give you notice on the spot.

Naturally I won't pay you a penny for the days I have lived here, on the contrary I shall consider bringing an action for damages against you, based on claims — believe me — that will be easily susceptible of proof." He ceased and stared straight in front of him, as if he expected something. In fact his two friends at once rushed into the breach with these words: "And we too give notice on the spot." On that he seized the door-handle and shut the door with a slam.

Gregor's father, groping with his hands, staggered forward and fell into his chair; it looked as if he were stretching himself there for his ordinary evening nap, but the marked jerkings of his head, which was as if uncontrollable, showed that he was far from asleep. Gregor had simply stayed quietly all the time on the spot where the lodgers had espied him. Disappointment at the failure of his plan, perhaps also the weakness arising from extreme hunger, made it impossible for him to move. He feared, with a fair degree of certainty, that at any moment the general tension would discharge itself in a combined attack upon him, and he lay waiting. He did not react even to the noise made by the violin as it fell off his mother's lap from under her trembling fingers and gave out a resonant note.

"My dear parents," said his sister, slapping her hand on the table by way of introduction, "things can't go on like this. Perhaps you don't realize that, but I do. I won't utter my brother's name in the presence of this creature, and so all I say is: we must try to get rid of it. We've tried to look after it and to put up with it as far as is humanly possible, and I don't think anyone could reproach us in the slightest."

"She is more than right," said Gregor's father to himself. His mother, who was still choking for lack of breath, began to cough hollowly into her hand with a wild look in her eyes.

His sister rushed over to her and held her forehead. His father's thoughts seemed to have lost their vagueness at Grete's words, he sat more upright, fingering his service cap that lay among the plates still lying on the table from the lodgers' supper, and from time to time looked at the still form of Gregor.

"We must try to get rid of it," his sister now said explicitly to her father, since her mother was coughing too much to hear a word, "it will be the death of both of you, I can see that coming. When one has to work as hard as we do, all of us, one can't stand this continual torment at home on top of it. At least I can't stand it any longer." And she burst into such a passion of sobbing that her tears dropped on her mother's face, where she wiped them off mechanically.

"My dear," said the old man sympathetically, and with evident understanding, "but what can we do?"

Gregor's sister merely shrugged her shoulders to indicate the feeling of helplessness that had now overmastered her during her weeping fit, in contrast to her former confidence.

"If he could understand us," said her father, half questioningly; Grete, still sobbing, vehemently waved a hand to show how unthinkable that was.

"If he could understand us," repeated the old man, shutting his eyes to consider his daughter's conviction that understanding was impossible, "then perhaps we might come to some agreement with him. But as it is — "

"He must go," cried Gregor's sister, "That's the only solution, Father. You must just try to get rid of the idea that this is Gregor. The fact that we've believed it for so long is the root of all our trouble. But how can it be Gregor? If this were Gregor, he would have realized long ago that human beings can't live with such a creature, and he'd have gone away on his own accord. Then we wouldn't have any brother, but we'd be able to go on living and keep his memory in honor. As it is, this creature persecutes us, drives away our lodgers, obviously wants the whole apartment to himself and would have us all sleep in the gutter. Just look, Father," she shrieked all at once, "he's at it again!" And in an access of panic that was quite incomprehensible to Gregor she even quitted her mother, literally thrusting the chair from her as if she would rather sacrifice her mother than stay so near to Gregor, and rushed behind her father, who also rose up, being simply upset by her agitation, and half-spread his arms out as if to protect her.

Yet Gregor had not the slightest intention of frightening anyone, far less his sister. He had only begun to turn round in order to crawl back to his room, but it was certainly a startling operation to watch, since because of his disabled condition he could not execute the difficult turning movements except by lifting his head and then bracing it against the floor over and over again. He paused and looked round. His good intentions seemed to have been recognized; the alarm had only been momentary. Now they were all watching him in melancholy silence. His mother lay in her chair, her legs stiffly outstretched and pressed together, her eyes almost closing for sheer weariness; his father and his sister were sitting beside each other, his sister's arm around the old man's neck.

Perhaps I can go on turning round now, thought Gregor, and began his labors again. He could not stop himself from panting with the effort, and had to pause now and then to take breath. Nor did anyone harass him, he was left entirely to himself. When he had completed the turn-round he began at once to crawl straight back. He was amazed at the distance separating him from his room and could not understand how in his weak state he had managed to accomplish the same journey so recently, almost without remarking it. Intent on crawling as fast as possible, he barely noticed that not a single word, not an ejaculation from his family, interfered with his progress. Only when he was already in the doorway did he turn his head round, not completely, for his neck muscles were getting stiff, but enough to see that nothing had changed behind him except that his sister had risen to her feet. His last glance fell on his mother, who was not quite overcome by sleep.

Hardly was he well inside his room when the door was hastily pushed shut, bolted and locked. The sudden noise in his rear startled him so much that his little legs gave beneath him. It was his sister who had shown such haste. She had been standing ready waiting and had made a light spring forward, Gregor had not even heard her coming, and she cried "At last!" to her parents as she turned the key in the lock.

"And what now?" said Gregor to himself, looking round in the darkness. Soon he made the discovery that he was now unable to stir a limb. This did not surprise him, rather it seemed unnatural that he should ever actually have been able to move on these feeble little legs. Otherwise he felt relatively comfortable. True, his whole body was aching, but it seemed that the pain was gradually growing less and would finally pass away. The rotting apple in his back and the inflamed area around it, all covered with soft dust, already hardly troubled him. He thought of his family with tenderness and love. The decision that he must disappear was one that he held to even more strongly than his sister, if that were possible. In this state of vacant and peaceful meditation he remained until the tower clock struck three in the morning. The first broadening of light in the world outside the window entered his consciousness once more. Then his head sank to the floor of its own accord and from his nostrils came the last faint flicker of his breath.

When the charwoman arrived early in the morning — what between her strength and her impatience she slammed all the doors so loudly, never mind how often she had been begged not to do so, that no one in the whole apartment could enjoy any quiet sleep after her arrival — she noticed nothing unusual as she took her customary peep into Gregor's room. She thought he was lying motionless on purpose, pretending to be in the sulks; she credited him with every kind of intelligence. Since she happened to have the long-handed broom in her hand she tried to tickle him up with it from the doorway. When that too produced no reaction she felt provoked and poked at him a little harder, and only when she had pushed him along the floor without meeting any resistance was her attention aroused. It did not take her long to establish the truth of the matter, and her eyes widened, she let out a whistle, yet did not waste much time over it but tore open the door of the Samsas' bedroom and yelled into the darkness at the top of her voice: "Just look at this, it's dead; it's lying here dead and done for!"

Mr. and Mrs. Samsa started up in their double bed and before they realized the nature of the charwoman's announcement had some difficulty in overcoming the shock of it. But then they got out of bed quickly, one on either side, Mr. Samsa throwing a blanket over his shoulders, Mrs. Samsa in nothing but her nightgown; in this array they entered Gregor's room. Meanwhile the door of the living room opened, too, where Grete had been sleeping since the advent of the lodgers; she was completely dressed as if she had not been to bed, which seemed to be confirmed also by the paleness of her face. "Dead?" said Mrs. Samsa, looking questioningly at the charwoman, although she could have investigated for herself, and the fact was obvious enough without investigation. "I should say so," said the charwoman, proving her words by pushing Gregor's corpse a long way to one side with her broomstick. Mrs. Samsa made a movement as if to stop her, but checked it. "Well," said Mr. Samsa, "now thanks be to God." He crossed himself, and the three women followed his example. Grete, whose eyes never left the corpse, said: "Just see how thin he was. It's such a long time since he's eaten anything. The food came out again just as it went in." Indeed, Gregor's body was completely flat and dry, as could only now be seen when it was no longer supported by the legs and nothing prevented one from looking closely at it.

"Come in beside us, Grete, for a little while," said Mrs. Samsa with a tremulous smile, and Grete, not without looking back at the corpse, followed her parents into their bedroom. The charwoman shut the door and opened the window wide. Although it was so early in the morning a certain softness was perceptible in the fresh air. After all, it was already the end of March.

The three lodgers emerged from their room and were surprised to see no breakfast; they had been forgotten. "Where's our breakfast?" said the middle lodger peevishly to the charwoman. But she put her finger to her lips and hastily, without a word, indicated by gestures that they should go into Gregor's room. They did so and stood, their hands in the pockets of their somewhat shabby coats, around Gregor's corpse in the room where it was now fully light.

At that the door of the Samsas' bedroom opened and Mr. Samsa appeared in his uniform, his wife on one arm, his daughter on the other. They all looked a little as if they had been crying; from time to time Grete hid her face on her father's arm.

"Leave my house at once!" said Mr. Samsa, and pointed to the door without disengaging himself from the women. "What do you mean by that?" said the middle lodger, taken somewhat aback, with a feeble smile. The two others put their hands behind them and kept rubbing them together, as if in gleeful expectation of a fine set-to in which they were bound to come off the winners. "I mean just what I say," answered Mr. Samsa, and advanced in a straight line with his two companions towards the lodger. He stood his ground at first quietly, looking at the floor as if his thoughts were taking a new pattern in his head. "Then let us go, by all means," he said, and looked up at Mr. Samsa as if in a sudden access of humility he were expecting some renewed sanction for this decision. Mr. Samsa merely nodded briefly once or twice with meaning eyes. Upon that the lodger really did go with long strides into the hall, his two friends had been listening and had quite stopped rubbing their hands for some moments and now went scuttling after him as if afraid that Mr. Samsa might get into the hall before them and cut them off from their leader. In the hall they all three took their hats from the rack, their sticks from the umbrella stand, bowed in silence and quitted the apartment. With a suspiciousness which proved quite unfounded Mr. Samsa and the two women followed them out to the landing; leaning over the banister they watched the three figures slowly but surely going down the long stairs, vanishing from sight at a certain turn of the staircase on every floor and coming into view again after a moment or so; the more they dwindled, the more the Samsa family's interest in them dwindled, and when a butcher's boy met them and passed them on the stairs coming up proudly with a tray on his head, Mr. Samsa and the two women soon left the landing and as if a burden had been lifted from them went back into their apartment.

They decided to spend this day in resting and going for a stroll; they had not only deserved such a respite from work, but absolutely needed it. And so they sat down at the table and wrote three notes of excuse, Mr. Samsa to his board of management, Mrs. Samsa to her employer and Grete to the head of her firm. While they were writing, the charwoman came in to say that she was going now, since her morning's work was finished. At first they only nodded without looking up, but as she kept hovering there they eyed her irritably. "Well?" said Mr. Samsa. The charwoman stood grinning in the doorway as if she had good news to impart to the family but meant not to say a word unless properly questioned. The small ostrich feather standing upright on her hat, which had annoyed Mr. Samsa ever since she was engaged, was waving gaily in all directions. "Well, what is it then?" asked Mr. Samsa, who obtained more respect from the charwoman than the others. "Oh," said the charwoman, giggling so amiably that she could not at once continue, "just this, you don't need to bother about how to get rid of the thing next door. It's been seen to already." Mrs. Samsa and Grete bent over their letters again, as if preoccupied; Mr. Samsa, who perceived that she was eager to begin describing it all in detail, stopped her with a decisive hand. But since she was not allowed to tell her story, she remembered the great hurry she was in, being obviously deeply huffed: "Bye, everybody," she said, whirling off violently, and departed with a frightful slamming of doors.

"She'll be given notice tonight," said Mr. Samsa, but neither from his wife nor his daughter did he get any answer, for the charwoman seemed to have shattered again the composure they had barely achieved. They rose, went to the window and stayed there, clasping each other tight. Mr. Samsa turned to his chair to look at them and quietly observed them for a little. Then he called out: "Come along, now, do. Let bygones be bygones. And you might have some consideration for me." The two of them complied at once, hastened to him, caressed him and quickly finished their letters.

Then they all three left the apartment together, which was more than they had done for months, and went by tram into the open country outside the town. The tram, in which they were the only passengers, was filled with warm sunshine. Leaning comfortably back in their seats they canvassed their prospects for the future, and it appeared on closer inspection that these were not at all bad, for the jobs they had got, which so far they had never really discussed with each other, were all three admirable and likely to lead to better things later on. The greatest immediate improvement in their condition would of course arise from moving to another house; they wanted to take a smaller and cheaper but also better situated and more easily run apartment than the one they had, which Gregor had selected. While they were thus conversing, it struck both Mr. and Mrs. Samsa, almost at the same moment, as they became aware of their daughter's increasing vivacity, that in spite of all the sorrow of recent times, which had made her cheeks pale, she had bloomed into a pretty girl with a good figure. They grew quieter and half unconsciously exchanged glances of complete agreement, having come to the conclusion that it would soon be time to find a good husband for her. And it was like a confirmation of their new dreams and excellent intentions that at the end of their journey their daughter sprang to her feet first and stretched her young body.

HERMAN MELVILLE

Billy Budd, Foretopman

WHAT BEFELL HIM IN THE YEAR OF THE GREAT MUTINY ETC.

Dedicated to Jack Chase, Englishman

Wherever that great heart may now be
here on Earth or harbored in Paradise
Captain of the main-top in the year 1843
in the U.S. Frigate "United States."

PREFACE

The year 1797, the year of this narrative, belongs to a period which as every thinker now feels, involved a crisis for Christendom not exceeded in its undetermined momentousness at the time by any other era whereof there is record. The opening proposition made by the Spirit of that Age, involved the rectification of the Old World's hereditary wrongs. In France to some extent this was bloodily effected. But what then? Straightway the Revolution itself became a wrongdoer, one more oppressive than the kings. Under Napoleon it enthroned upstart kings, and initiated that prolonged agony of continual war whose final throe was Waterloo. During those years not the wisest could have foreseen that the outcome of all would be what to some thinkers apparently it has since turned out to be, a political advance along nearly the whole line for Europeans.

Now, as elsewhere hinted, it was something caught from the Revolutionary Spirit that at Spithead emboldened the man-of-war's men to rise against real abuses, longstanding ones, and afterwards at the Nore to make inordinate and aggressive demands, successful resistance to which was confirmed only when the ringleaders were hung for an admonitory spectacle to the anchored fleet. Yet in a way analogous to the operation of the Revolution at large the Great Mutiny, though by Englishmen naturally deemed monstrous at the time, doubtless gave the first latent prompting to most important reforms in the British Navy.

I
BILLY BUDD, FORETOPMAN
(AN INSIDE NARRATIVE.)

In the time before steamships, or then more frequently than now, a stroller along the docks of any considerable seaport would occasionally have his attention arrested by a group of bronzed mariners, man-of-war's men or merchant-sailors in holiday attire ashore on liberty. In certain instances they would flank, or, like a body-guard quite surround some superior figure of their own class, moving along with them like Aldebaran among the lesser lights of his constellation. That signal object was the "Handsome Sailor" of the less prosaic time alike of the military and merchant navies. With no perceptible trace of the vainglorious about him, rather with the off-hand unaffectedness of natural regality, he seemed to accept the spontaneous homage of his shipmates. A somewhat remarkable instance recurs to me. In Liverpool, now half a century ago I saw under the shadow of the great dingy street-wall of Prince's Dock (an obstruction long since removed) a common sailor, so intensely black that he must needs have been a native African of the unadulterate blood of Ham. A symmetric figure much above the average height. The two ends of a gay silk handkerchief thrown loose about the neck danced upon the displayed ebony of his chest; in his ears were big hoops of gold, and a Scotch Highland bonnet with a tartan band set off his shapely head.

It was a hot noon in July; and his face, lustrous with perspiration, beamed with barbaric good humor. In jovial sallies right and left his white teeth flashing into view, he rollicked along, the center of a company of his shipmates. These were made up of such an assortment of tribes and complexions as would have well fitted them to be marched up by Anacharsis Cloots before the bar of the first French Assembly as Representatives of the Human Race. At each spontaneous tribute rendered by the wayfarers to this black pagod of a fellow — the tribute of a pause and stare, and less frequent an exclamation, — the motley retinue showed that they took that sort of pride in the evoker of it which the Assyrian priests doubtless showed from their grand sculptured Bull when the faithful prostrated themselves.

To return.

If in some cases a bit of a nautical Murat in setting forth his person ashore, the handsome sailor of the period in question evinced nothing of the dandified Billy-be-Damn, an amusing character all but extinct now, but occasionally to be encountered, and in a form yet more amusing than the original, at the tiller of the boats on the tempestuous Erie Canal or, more likely, vaporing in the groggeries along the tow-path. Invariably a proficient in his perilous calling, he was also more or less of a mighty boxer or wrestler. It was strength and beauty. Tales of his prowess were recited. Ashore he was the champion; afloat the spokesman; on every suitable occasion always foremost. Close-reefing top-sails in a gale, there he was, astride the weather yard-arm-end, foot in the Flemish horse as "stirrup," both hands tugging at the "ear-ring" as at a bridle, in very much the attitude of young Alexander curbing the fiery Bucephalus. A superb figure, tossed up as by the horns of Taurus against the thunderous sky, cheerily hallooing to the strenuous file along the spar.

The moral nature was seldom out of keeping with the physical make. Indeed, except as toned by the former, the comeliness and power, always attractive in masculine conjunction, hardly could have drawn the sort of honest homage the Handsome Sailor in some examples received from his less gifted associates.

Such a cynosure, at least in aspect, and something such too in nature, though with important variations made apparent as the story proceeds, was welkin-eyed Billy Budd, or Baby Budd as more familiarly under circumstances hereafter to be given he at last came to be called aged twenty-one, a foretopman of the British fleet toward the close of the last decade of the eighteenth century. It was not very long prior to the time of the narration that follows that he had entered the King's Service, having been impressed on the Narrow Seas from a homeward-bound English merchantman into a seventy-four outward-bound, *H.M.S. Indomitable*; which ship, as was not unusual in those hurried days having been obliged to put to sea short of her proper complement of men. Plump upon Billy at first sight in the gangway the boarding officer Lieutenant Ratcliffe pounced, even before the merchantman's crew was formally mustered on the quarter-deck for his deliberate inspection. And him only he elected. For whether it was because the other men when ranged before him showed to ill advantage after Billy, or whether he had some scruples in view of the merchantman being rather short-handed, however it might be, the officer contented himself with his first spontaneous choice. To the surprise of the ship's company, though much to the Lieutenant's satisfaction Billy made no demur. But, indeed, any demur would have been as idle as the protest of a goldfinch popped into a cage.

Noting this uncomplaining acquiescence, all but cheerful one might say, the shipmates turned a surprised glance of silent reproach at the sailor. The shipmaster was one of those worthy mortals found in every vocation even the humbler ones — the sort of person whom everybody agrees in calling "a respectable man." And — nor so strange to report as it may appear to be — though a ploughman of the troubled waters, life-long contending with the intractable elements, there was nothing this honest soul at heart loved better than simple peace and quiet. For the rest, he was fifty or thereabouts, a little inclined to corpulence, a prepossessing face, unwhiskered, and of an agreeable color — a rather full face, humanely intelligent in expression. On a fair day with a fair wind and all going well, a certain musical chime in his voice seemed to be the veritable unobstructed outcome of the innermost man. He had much prudence, much conscientiousness, and there were occasions when these virtues were the cause of overmuch disquietude in him. On a passage, so long as his craft was in any proximity to land, no sleep for Captain Graveling. He took to heart those serious responsibilities not so heavily borne by some shipmasters.

Now while Billy Budd was down in the forecastle getting his kit together, the *Indomitable's* lieutenant, burly and bluff, nowise disconcerted by Captain Graveling's omitting to proffer the customary hospitalities on an occasion so unwelcome to him, an omission simply caused by preoccupation of thought, unceremoniously invited himself into the cabin, and also to a flask from the spirit-locker, a receptacle which his experienced eye instantly discovered. In fact he was one of those sea-dogs in whom all the hardship and peril of naval life in the great prolonged wars of his time never impaired the natural instinct for sensuous enjoyment. His duty he always faithfully did; but duty is sometimes a dry obligation, and he was for irrigating its aridity whensoever possible with a fertilizing decoction of strong waters. For the cabin's proprietor there was nothing left but to play the part of the enforced host with whatever grace and alacrity were practicable. As necessary adjuncts to the flask, he silently placed tumbler and water-jug before the irrepressible guest. But excusing himself from partaking just then, he dismally watched the unembarrassed officer deliberately diluting his grog a little, then tossing it off in three swallows, pushing the empty tumbler away, yet not so far as to be beyond easy reach, at the same time settling himself in his seat and smacking his lips with high satisfaction, looking straight at the host.

These proceedings over, the Master broke the silence; and there lurked a rueful reproach in the tone of his voice; "Lieutenant, you are going to take my best man from me, the jewel of 'em."

"Yes, I know" rejoined the other, immediately

drawing back the tumbler preliminary to a replenishing; "Yes I know. Sorry."

"Beg pardon, but you don't understand, Lieutenant. See here now. Before I shipped that young fellow, my forecastle was a rat-pit of quarrels. It was black times. I tell you, aboard the *'Rights'* here. I was worried to that degree my pipe had no comfort for me. But Billy came; and it was like a Catholic priest striking peace in an Irish shindy. Not that he preached to them or said or did anything in particular; but a virtue went out of him, sugaring the sour ones. They took to him like hornets to treacle; all but the buffer of the gang, the big shaggy chap with the fire-red whiskers. He indeed out of envy, perhaps, of the newcomer, and thinking such a 'sweet and pleasant fellow,' as he mockingly designated him to the others, could hardly have the spirit of a game-cock, must needs bestir himself in trying to get up an ugly row with him. Billy forebore with him and reasoned with him in a pleasant way — he is something like myself, lieutenant, to whom aught like a quarrel is hateful — but nothing served. So, in the second dog-watch one day the Red Whiskers in presence of the others, under pretence of showing Billy just whence a sirloin steak was cut — for the fellow had once been a butcher — insultingly gave him a dig under the ribs. Quick as lightning Billy let fly his arm. I dare say he never meant to do quite as much as he did, but anyhow he gave the burly fool a terrible drubbing. It took about half a minute, I should think. And, Lord bless you, the lubber was astonished at the celerity. And will you believe it, Lieutenant, the Red Whiskers now really loves Billy — loves him, or is the biggest hypocrite that ever I heard of. But they all love him. Some of 'em do his washing, darn his old trousers for him; the carpenter is at odd times making a pretty little chest of drawers for him. Anybody will do anything for Billy Budd; and it's the happy family here. But now Lieutenant, if that young fellow goes — I know how it will be aboard the *'Rights.'* Not again very soon shall I, coming up from dinner, lean over the capstan smoking a quiet pipe — no, not very soon again, I think. Ay, Lieutenant, you are going to take away the jewel of 'em; you are going to take away my peacemaker!" And with that the good soul had really some ado in checking a rising sob.

"Well," said the officer who had listened with amused interest to all this, and now waxing merry with his tipple; "Well, blessed are the peacemakers especially the fighting peacemakers! And such are the seventy-four beauties some of which you see poking their noses out of the port-holes of yonder warship lying-to for me" pointing through the cabin window at the *Indomitable*. "But courage! don't look so downhearted, man. Why, I pledge you in advance the royal approbation. Rest assured that His Majesty will be delighted to know that in a time when his hardtack is not sought for by sailors with such avidity as should be; a time also when some shipmasters privily resent the borrowing from them a tar or two for the service; His Majesty, I say, will be delighted to learn that *one* shipmaster at least cheerfully surrenders to the King, the flower of his flock, a sailor who with equal loyalty makes no dissent. — But where's my beauty? Ah," looking through the cabin's open door "Here he comes; and, by Jove — lugging along his chest — Apollo with his portmanteau! — My man," stepping out to him, "you can't take that big box aboard a warship. The boxes there are mostly shot-boxes. Put your duds in a bag, lad. Boot and saddle for the cavalryman, bag and hammock for the man-of-war's man."

The transfer from chest to bag was made. And, after seeing his man into the cutter and then following him down, the lieutenant pushed off from the *Rights-of-Man*. That was the merchant ship's name; though by her master and crew abbreviated in sailor fashion into *The Rights*. The hard-headed Dundee owner was a staunch admirer of Thomas Paine whose book in rejoinder to Burke's arraignment of the French Revolution had then been published for some time and had gone everywhere. In christening his vessel after the title of Paine's volume the man of Dundee was something like his contemporary shipowner, Stephen Girard of Philadelphia, whose sympathies, alike with his native land and its liberal philosophers, he evinced by naming his ships after Voltaire, Diderot, and so forth.

But now, when the boat swept under the merchantman's stern, and officer and oarsmen were noting — some bitterly and others with a grin, — the name emblazoned there; just then it was that the new recruit jumped up from the bow where the coxswain had directed him to sit, and waving his hat to his silent shipmates sorrowfully looking over at him from the taffrail, bade the lads a genial good-bye. Then making a salutation as to the ship herself, "And good-bye to you too, old *Rights of Man*!"

"Down, Sir!" roared the lieutenant, instantly assuming all the rigor of his rank, though with difficulty repressing a smile.

To be sure, Billy's action was a terrible breach of naval decorum. But in that decorum he had never been instructed; in consideration of which the lieutenant would hardly have been so energetic in reproof but for the concluding farewell to the ship. This he rather took as meant to convey a covert sally on the new recruit's part, a sly slur at impressment in general, and that of himself in especial. And yet, more likely, if satire it was in effect, it was hardly so by intention, for Billy, though happily endowed with the gaiety of high health, youth and a free heart, was yet by no means of a satirical turn. The will to it and the sinister dexterity were alike wanting. To deal in double meaning and insinuations of any sort was quite foreign to his nature.

As to his enforced enlistment, that he seemed

to take pretty much as he was wont to take any vicissitude of weather. Like the animals, though no philosopher, he was, without knowing it, practically a fatalist. And, it may be, that he rather liked this adventurous turn in his affairs, which promised an opening into novel scenes and martial excitements.

Aboard the *Indomitable* our merchant-sailor was forthwith rated as an able-seaman and assigned to the starboard watch of the foretop. He was soon at home in the service, not at all disliked for his unpretentious good looks and a sort of genial happy-go-lucky air. No merrier man in his mess: in marked contrast to certain other individuals included like himself among the impressed portion of the ship's company; for these when not actively employed were sometimes, and more particularly in the last dog-watch when the drawing near of twilight induced revery, apt to fall into a saddish mood which in some partook of sullenness. But they were not so young as our foretopman, and no few of them must have known a hearth of some sort, others may have had wives and children left, too probably, in uncertain circumstances, and hardly any but must have had acknowledged kith and kin, while for Billy, as will shortly be seen, his entire family was practically invested in himself.

II

Though our new-made foretopman was well received in the top and on the gun-decks, hardly here was he that cynosure he had previously been among those minor ship's companies of the merchant marine, with which companies only had he hitherto consorted.

He was young; and despite his all but fully developed frame in aspect looked even younger than he really was, owing to a lingering adolescent expression in the as yet smooth face all but feminine in purity in natural complexion but where, thanks to his seagoing, the lily was quite suppressed and the rose had some ado visibly to flush through the tan.

To one essentially such a novice in the complexities of factious life, the abrupt transition from his former and simpler sphere to the ampler and more knowing world of a great warship; this might well have abashed him had there been any conceit or vanity in his composition. Among her miscellaneous multitude, the *Indomitable* mustered several individuals who however inferior in grade were of no common natural stamp, sailors more signally susceptive of that air which continuous martial discipline and repeated presence in battle can in some degree impart even to the average man. As the *handsome sailor* Billy Budd's position aboard the seventy-four was something analogous to that of a rustic beauty transplanted from the provinces and brought into competition with the high-born dames of the court. But this change of circumstances he scarce noted. As little did he observe that something about him provoked an ambiguous smile in one or two harder faces among the blue-jackets. Nor less unaware was he of the peculiar favorable effect his person and demeanor had upon the more intelligent gentlemen of the quarter-deck. Nor could this well have been otherwise. Cast in a mould peculiar to the finest physical examples of those Englishmen in whom the Saxon strain would seem not at all to partake of any Norman or other admixture, he showed in face that humane look of reposeful good nature which the Greek sculptor in some instances gave to his heroic strong man, Hercules. But this again was subtly modified by another and pervasive quality. The ear, small and shapely, the arch of the foot, the curve in mouth and nostril, even the indurated hand dyed to the orange-tawny of the toucan's bill, a hand telling alike of the halyards and tar-bucket; but, above all, something in the mobile expression, and every chance attitude and movement, something suggestive of a mother eminently favored by Love and the Graces; all this strangely indicated a lineage in direct contradiction to his lot. The mysteriousness here, became less mysterious through a matter-of-fact elicited when Billy at the capstan was being formally mustered into the service. Asked by the officer, a small brisk little gentleman as it chanced among other questions, his place of birth, he replied, "Please, Sir, I don't know."

"Don't know where you were born? — Who was your father?"

"God knows, Sir."

Struck by the straightforward simplicity of these replies, the officer next asked "Do you know anything about your beginning?"

"No, Sir. But I have heard that I was found in a pretty silk-lined basket hanging one morning from the knocker of a good man's door in Bristol."

"*Found* say you? Well," throwing back his head and looking up and down the new recruit; "Well it turns out to have been a pretty good find. Hope they'll find some more like you, my man; the fleet sadly needs them."

Yes, Billy Budd was a foundling, a presumable bye-blow, and, evidently, no ignoble one. Noble descent was as evident in him as in a blood horse.

For the rest, with little or no sharpness of faculty or any trace of the wisdom of the serpent, nor yet quite a dove, he possessed that kind and degree of intelligence going along with the unconventional rectitude of a sound human creature, one to whom not yet has been proffered the questionable apple of knowledge. He was illiterate; he could not read, but he could sing, and like the illiterate nightingale was sometimes the composer of his own song.

Of self-consciousness he seemed to have little or none, or about as much as we may reasonably impute to a dog of St. Bernard's breed.

Habitually living with the elements and knowing little more of the land than as a beach, or, rather, that portion of the terraqueous globe providentially set apart for dancehouses doxies and tapsters, in short what sailors call a "fiddlers' green," his simple nature remained unsophisticated by those moral obliquities which are not in every case incompatible with that manufacturable thing known as respectability. But are sailors, frequenters of "fiddlers' greens," without vices? No; but less often than with landsmen do their vices, so called, partake of crookedness of heart, seeming less to proceed from viciousness than exuberance of vitality after long constraint; frank manifestations in accordance with natural law. By his original constitution aided by the coöperating influences of his lot, Billy in many respects, was little more than a sort of upright barbarian, much such perhaps as Adam presumably might have been ere the urbane Serpent wriggled himself into his company.

And here be it submitted that apparently going to corroborate the doctrine of man's fall, a doctrine now popularly ignored, it is observable that where certain virtues pristine and unadulterate peculiarly characterize anybody in the external uniform of civilization, they will upon scrutiny seem not to be derived from custom or convention but rather to be out of keeping with these, as if indeed exceptionally transmitted from a period prior to Cain's city and citified man. The character marked by such qualities has to an unvitiated taste an untampered-with flavor like that of berries while the man thoroughly civilized even in a fair specimen of the breed has to the same moral palate a questionable smack as of a compounded wine. To any stray inheritor of these primitive qualities found, like Caspar Hauser, wandering dazed in any Christian capital of our time the good-natured poet's famous invocation, near two thousand years ago, of the good rustic out of his latitude in the Rome of the Caesars, still appropriately holds: —

"Honest and poor, faithful in word and thought,
What has thee, Fabian, to the city brought."

Though our Handsome Sailor had as much of masculine beauty as one can expect anywhere to see; nevertheless, like the beautiful woman in one of Hawthorne's minor tales, there was just one thing amiss in him. No visible blemish, indeed, as with the lady; no, but an occasional liability to a vocal defect. Though in the hour of elemental uproar or peril, he was everything that a sailor should be, yet under sudden provocation of strong heart-feeling his voice otherwise singularly musical, as if expressive of the harmony within, was apt to develop an organic hesitancy, in fact more or less of a stutter or even worse. In this particular Billy was a striking instance that the arch interferer, the envious marplot of Eden still has more or less to do with every human consignment to this planet of earth. In every case, one way or another he is sure to slip in his little card, as much as to remind us — I too have a hand here.

The avowal of such an imperfection in the Handsome Sailor should be evidence not alone that he is not presented as a conventional hero, but also that the story in which he is the main figure is no romance.

III

At the time of Billy Budd's arbitrary enlistment into the *Indomitable* that ship was on her way to join the Mediterranean fleet. No long time elapsed before the junction was effected. As one of that fleet the seventy-four participated in its movements, though at times on account of her superior sailing qualities, in the absence of frigates, despatched on separate duty as a scout and at times on less temporary service. But with all this the story has little concernment, restricted as it is to the inner life of one particular ship and the career of an individual sailor.

It was the summer of 1797. In the April of that year had occurred the commotion at Spithead followed in May by a second and yet more serious outbreak in the fleet at the Nore. The latter is known, and without exaggeration in the epithet, as the Great Mutiny. It was indeed a demonstration more menacing to England than the contemporary manifestoes and conquering and proselyting armies of the French Directory.

To the British Empire the Nore Mutiny was what a strike in the fire-brigade would be to London threatened by general arson. In a crisis when the Kingdom might well have anticipated the famous signal that some years later published along the naval line of battle what it was that upon occasion England expected of Englishmen; *that* was the time when at the mast-heads of the three-deckers and seventy-fours moored in her own roadstead — a fleet, the right arm of a Power then all but the sole free conservative one of the Old World, the blue-jackets, to be numbered by thousands, ran up with huzzas the British colors with the union and cross wiped out; by that cancellation transmuting the flag of founded law and freedom defined, into the enemy's red meteor of unbridled and unbounded revolt. Reasonable discontent growing out of practical grievances in the fleet had been ignited into irrational combustion as by live cinders blown across the Channel from France in flames.

The event converted into irony for a time those spirited strains of Dibdin — as a song-writer no mean auxiliary to the English Government at the European conjuncture — strains celebrating, among other things, the patriotic devotion of the British tar:

"And as for my life, 'tis the King's!"

Such an episode in the Island's grand naval story her naval historians naturally abridge; one of them (G. P. R. James) candidly acknowledging that fain would he pass it over did not "impartiality forbid fastidiousness." And yet his mention is less a narration than a reference, having to do hardly at all with details. Nor are these readily to be found in the libraries. Like some other events in every age befalling states everywhere including America the Great Mutiny was of such character that national pride along with views of policy would fain shade it off into the historical background. Such events cannot be ignored, but there is a considerate way of historically treating them. If a well-constituted individual refrains from blazoning aught amiss or calamitous in his family; a nation in the like circumstance may without reproach be equally discreet.

Though after parleyings between Government and the ring-leaders, and concessions by the former as to some glaring abuses, the first uprising — that of Spithead — with difficulty was put down, or matters for a time pacified; yet at the Nore the unforeseen renewal of insurrection on a yet larger scale, and emphasized in the conferences that ensued by demands deemed by the authorities not only inadmissible but aggressively insolent, indicated — if the red flag did not sufficiently do so, what was the spirit animating the men. Final suppression, however, there was; but only made possible perhaps by the unswerving loyalty of the marine corps a voluntary resumption of loyalty among influential sections of the crews.

To some extent the Nore Mutiny may be regarded as analogous to the distempering irruption of contagious fever in a frame constitutionally sound, and which anon throws it off.

At all events, of these thousands of mutineers were some of the tars who not so very long afterwards — whether wholly prompted thereto by patriotism, or pugnacious instinct, or by both, — helped to win a coronet for Nelson at the Nile, and the naval crown of crowns for him at Trafalgar. To the mutineers those battles and especially Trafalgar were a plenary absolution; and a grand one; for all that goes to make up scenic naval display and heroic magnificence in arms, those battles especially Trafalgar stand unmatched in human annals.

IV
CONCERNING "THE GREATEST SAILOR SINCE THE WORLD BEGAN" — TENNYSON?

In this matter of writing, resolve as one may to keep to the main road, some by-paths have an enticement not readily to be withstood. I am going to err into such a by-path. If the reader will keep me company I shall be glad. At the least we can promise ourselves that pleasure which is wickedly said to be in sinning, for a literary sin the divergence will be.

Very likely it is no new remark that the inventions of our time have at last brought about a change in sea-warfare in degree corresponding to the revolution in all warfare effected by the original introduction from China into Europe of gunpowder. The first European fire-arm, a clumsy contrivance, was, as is well known, scouted by no few of the knights as a base implement good enough peradventure for weavers too craven to stand up crossing steel with steel in frank fight. But as ashore knightly valor though shorn of its blazonry did not cease with the knights, neither on the seas though nowadays in encounters there a certain kind of displayed gallantry be fallen out of date as hardly applicable under changed circumstances, did the nobler qualities of such naval magnates as Don John of Austria, Doria, Van Tromp, Jean Bart, the long line of British admirals and the American Decaturs of 1812 become obsolete with their wooden walls.

Nevertheless, to anybody who can hold the Present at its worth without being inappreciative of the Past, it may be forgiven, if to such an one the solitary old hulk at Portsmouth, Nelson's *Victory*, seems to float there, not alone as the decaying monument of a fame incorruptible, but also as a poetic reproach, softened by its picturesqueness, to the *Monitors* and yet mightier hulls of the European ironclads. And this not altogether because such craft are unsightly, unavoidably lacking the symmetry and grand lines of the old battleships, but equally for other reasons.

There are some, perhaps, who while not altogether inaccessible to that poetic reproach just alluded to, may yet on behalf of the new order, be disposed to parry it; and this to the extent of iconoclasm, if need be. For example, prompted by the sight of the star inserted in the *Victory's* quarter-deck designating the spot where the Great Sailor fell, these martial utilitarians may suggest considerations implying that Nelson's ornate publication of his person in battle was not only unnecessary, but not military, nay, savored of foolhardiness and vanity. They may add, too, that at Trafalgar it was in effect nothing less than a challenge to death; and death came; and that but for his bravado the victorious admiral might possibly have survived the battle, and so, instead of having his sagacious dying injunctions overruled by his immediate successor in command he himself when the contest was decided might have brought his shattered fleet to anchor, a proceeding which might have averted the deplorable loss of life by shipwreck in the elemental tempest that followed the martial one.

Well, should we set aside the more disputable

point whether for various reasons it was possible to anchor the fleet, then plausibly enough the Benthamites of war may urge the above.

But the *might-have-been* is but boggy ground to build on. And certainly in foresight as to the larger issue of an encounter, and anxious preparations for it — buoying the deadly way and mapping it out, as at Copenhagen — few commanders have been so painstakingly circumspect as this same reckless declarer of his person in fight.

Personal prudence even when dictated by quite other than selfish considerations surely is no special virtue in a military man; while an excessive love of glory, impassioning a less burning impulse the honest sense of duty, is the first. If the name *Wellington* is not so much of a trumpet to the blood as the simpler name *Nelson*, the reason for this may perhaps be inferred from the above. Alfred in his funeral ode on the victor of Waterloo ventures not to call him the greatest soldier of all time, though in the same ode he invokes Nelson as "the greatest sailor since the world began."

At Trafalgar Nelson on the brink of opening the fight sat down and wrote his last brief will and testament. If under the presentiment of the most magnificent of all victories to be crowned by his own glorious death, a sort of priestly motive led him to dress his person in the jewelled vouchers of his own shining deeds; if thus to have adorned himself for the altar and the sacrifice were indeed vain-glory, then affectation and fustian is each more heroic line in the great epics and dramas, since in such lines the poet but embodies in verse those exaltations of sentiment that a nature like Nelson, the opportunity being given, vitalizes into acts.

V

Yes, the outbreak at the Nore was put down. But not every grievance was redressed. If the contractors, for example, were no longer permitted to ply some practices peculiar to their tribe everywhere, such as providing shoddy cloth, rations not sound, or false in the measure; not the less impressment, for one thing, went on. By custom sanctioned for centuries, and judicially maintained by a Lord Chancellor as late as Mansfield, that mode of manning the fleet, a mode now fallen into a sort of abeyance but never formally renounced, it was not practicable to give up in those years. Its abrogation would have crippled the indispensable fleet, one wholly under canvas, no steam-power, its innumerable sails and thousands of cannon, everything in short, worked by muscle alone; a fleet the more insatiate in demand for men, because then multiplying its ships of all grades against contingencies present and to come of the convulsed Continent.

Discontent foreran the Two Mutinies, and more or less it lurkingly survived them. Hence it was not unreasonable to apprehend some return of trouble sporadic or general. One instance of such apprehensions: In the same year with this story, Nelson, then Vice-Admiral Sir Horatio, being with the fleet off the Spanish coast, was directed by the Admiral in command to shift his pennant from the *Captain* to the *Theseus*; and for this reason: that the latter ship having newly arrived on the station from home where it had taken part in the Great Mutiny, danger was apprehended from the temper of the men; and it was thought that an officer like Nelson was the one, not indeed to terrorize the crew into base subjection, but to win them, by force of his mere presence back to an allegiance if not as enthusiastic as his own, yet as true. So it was that for a time on more than one quarter-deck anxiety did exist. At sea precautionary vigilance was strained against relapse. At short notice an engagement might come on. When it did, the lieutenants assigned to batteries felt it incumbent on them, in some instances to stand with drawn swords behind the men working the guns.

VI

But on board the seventy-four in which Billy now swung his hammock, very little in the manner of the men and nothing obvious in the demeanor of the officers would have suggested to an ordinary observer that the Great Mutiny was a recent event. In their general bearing and conduct the commissioned officers of a warship naturally take their tone from the commander, that is if he have that ascendancy of character that ought to be his.

Captain the Honorable Edward Fairfax Vere, to give his full title, was a bachelor of forty or thereabouts, a sailor of distinction even in a time prolific of renowned seamen. Though allied to the higher nobility his advancement had not been altogether owing to influences connected with that circumstance. He had seen much service, been in various engagements, always acquitting himself as an officer mindful of the welfare of his men, but never tolerating an infraction of discipline; thoroughly versed in the science of his profession, and intrepid to the verge of temerity, though never injudiciously so. For his gallantry in the West Indian waters as flag-lieutenant under Rodney in that Admiral's crowning victory over De Grasse, he was made a post-captain.

Ashore in the garb of a civilian scarce any one would have taken him for a sailor, more especially that he never garnished unprofessional talk with nautical terms, and grave in his bearing, evinced little appreciation of mere humor. It was not out of keeping with these traits that on a passage when nothing demanded his paramount action, he was the most undemonstrative of men. Any landsman observing this gentleman not conspicuous by his stature and wearing no pronounced insignia, emerging from his cabin to the open deck and noting the silent deference of the officers retiring to leeward, might have taken him for the King's guest, a civilian aboard the King's ship, some highly honorable discreet envoy on his way to an important post. But in fact this unobtrusiveness of demeanor may have proceeded from a certain unaffected modesty of manhood sometimes accompanying a resolute nature, a modesty evinced at all times not calling for pronounced action, and which shown in any rank of life suggests a virtue aristocratic in kind.

As with some others engaged in various departments of the world's more heroic activities, Captain Vere though practical enough upon occasion would at times betray a certain dreaminess of mood. Standing alone on the weather-side of the quarter-deck, one hand holding by the rigging he would absently gaze off at the blank sea. At the presentation to him then of some minor matter interrupting the current of his thoughts he would show more or less irascibility; but instantly he would control it.

In the navy he was popularly known by the appellation — Starry Vere. How such a designation happened to fall upon one who whatever his sturdy qualities was without any brilliant ones was in this wise: A favorite kinsman, Lord Denton, a free-hearted fellow, had been the first to meet and congratulate him upon his return to England from his West Indian cruise; and but the day previous turning over a copy of Andrew Marvell's poems had lighted, not for the first time however, upon the lines entitled *Appleton House*, the name of one of the seats of their common ancestor, a hero in the German wars of the seventeenth century, in which poem occur the lines,

"This 'tis to have been from the first
In a domestic heaven nursed,
Under the discipline severe
Of Fairfax and the starry Vere."

And so, upon embracing his cousin fresh from Rodney's victory wherein he had played so gallant a part, brimming over with just family pride in the sailor of their house, he exuberantly exclaimed, "Give ye joy, Ed; give ye joy, my starry Vere!" This got currency, and the novel prefix serving in familiar parlance readily to distinguish the *Indomitable's* Captain from another Vere his senior, a distant relative an officer of like rank in the navy, it remained permanently attached to the surname.

VII

In view of the part that the Commander of the *Indomitable* plays in scenes shortly to follow, it may be well to fill out that sketch of him outlined in the previous chapter. Aside from his qualities as a sea-officer Captain Vere was an exceptional character. Unlike no few of England's renowned sailors, long and arduous service with signal devotion to it, had not resulted in absorbing and *salting* the entire man. He had a marked leaning toward everything intellectual. He loved books, never going to sea without a newly replenished library, compact but of the best. The isolated leisure, in some cases so wearisome, falling at intervals to commanders even during a war-cruise, never was tedious to Captain Vere. With nothing of that literary taste which less heeds the thing conveyed than the vehicle, his bias was toward those books to which every serious mind of superior order occupying any active post of authority in the world, naturally inclines; books treating of actual men and events no matter of what era — history, biography and unconventional writers, who, free from cant and convention, like Montaigne, honestly, and in the spirit of common sense philosophize upon realities.

In this love of reading he found confirmation of his own more reserved thoughts — confirmation which he had vainly sought in social converse, so that as touching most fundamental topics, there had got to be established in him some positive convictions which he forefelt would abide in him essentially unmodified so long as his intelligent part remained unimpaired. In view of the troubled period in which his lot was cast this was well for him. His settled convictions were as a dyke against those invading waters of novel opinion social political and otherwise, which carried away as in a torrent no few minds in those days, minds by nature not inferior to his own. While other members of that aristocracy to which by birth he belonged were incensed at the innovators mainly because their theories were inimical to the privileged classes, not alone Captain Vere disinterestedly opposed them because they seemed to him incapable of embodiment in lasting institutions, but at war with the peace of the world and the true welfare of mankind.

With minds less stored than his and less earnest, some officers of his rank, with whom at times he would necessarily consort, found him lacking in the companionable quality, a dry and bookish gentleman as they deemed. Upon any chance withdrawal from their company one would be apt to say to another something like this: "Vere is a noble fellow, Starry Vere. 'Spite the gazettes, Sir Horatio" meaning him with the Lord title "is at bottom scarce a better seaman or fighter. But between you and me now don't you think there is a queer streak of the pedantic running through him? Yes, like the King's yarn in a coil of navy-rope?"

Some apparent ground there was for this sort of confidential criticism; since not only did the

Captain's discourse never fall into the jocosely familiar, but in illustrating of any point touching the stirring personages and events of the time he would be as apt to cite some historic character or incident of antiquity as that he would cite from the moderns. He seemed unmindful of the circumstance that to his bluff company such remote allusions however pertinent they might really be were altogether alien to men whose reading was mainly confined to the journals. But considerateness in such matters is not easy to natures constituted like Captain Vere's. Their honesty prescribes to them directness, sometimes far-reaching like that of a migratory fowl that in its flight never heeds when it crosses a frontier.

VIII

The lieutenants and other commissioned gentlemen forming Captain Vere's staff it is not necessary here to particularize nor needs it to make any mention of any of the warrant-officers. But among the petty officers was one who having much to do with the story, may as well be forthwith introduced. This portrait I essay, but shall never hit it. This was John Claggart, the Master-at-arms. But that sea-title may to landsmen seem somewhat equivocal. Originally doubtless that petty-officer's function was the instruction of the men in the use of arms, sword or cutlass. But very long ago, owing to the advance in gunnery making hand-to-hand encounters less frequent and giving to nitre and sulphur the pre-eminence over steel, that function ceased; the master-at-arms of a great warship becoming a sort of Chief of Police charged among other matters with the duty of preserving order on the populous lower gun-decks.

Claggart was a man of about five-and-thirty, somewhat spare and tall, yet of no ill figure upon the whole. His hand was too small and shapely to have been accustomed to hard toil. The face was a notable one; the features all except the chin cleanly cut as those on a Greek medallion; yet the chin, beardless as Tecumseh's, had something of strange protuberant heaviness in its make that recalled the prints of the Rev. Dr. Titus Oates, the historic deponent with the clerical drawl in the time of Charles II and the fraud of the alleged Popish Plot. It served Claggart in his office that his eye could cast a tutoring glance. His brow was of the sort phrenologically associated with more than average intellect; silken jet curls partly clustering over it, making a foil to the pallor below, a pallor tinged with a faint shade of amber akin to the hue of time-tinted marbles of old. This complexion, singularly contrasting with the red or deeply bronzed visages of the sailors, and in part the result of his official seclusion from the sunlight, though it was not exactly displeasing, nevertheless seemed to hint of something defective or abnormal in the constitution and blood. But his general aspect and manner were so suggestive of an education and career incongruous with his naval function that when not actively engaged in it he looked like a man of high quality, social and moral, who for reasons of his own was keeping incog. Nothing was known of his former life. It might be that he was an Englishman; and yet there lurked a bit of accent in his speech suggesting that possibly he was not such by birth, but through naturalization in early childhood. Among certain grizzled sea-gossips of the gun-decks and forecastle went a rumor perdue that the master-at-arms was a *chevalier* who had volunteered into the King's navy by way of compounding for some mysterious swindle whereof he had been arraigned at the King's Bench. The fact that nobody could substantiate this report was, of course, nothing against its secret currency. Such a rumor once started on the gun-decks in reference to almost anyone below the rank of a commissioned officer would, during the period assigned to this narrative, have seemed not altogether wanting in credibility to the tarry old wiseacres of a man-of-war crew. And indeed a man of Claggart's accomplishments, without prior nautical experience entering the navy at mature life, as he did, and necessarily allotted at the start to the lowest grade in it; a man too who never made allusion to his previous life ashore; these were circumstances which in the dearth of exact knowledge as to his true antecedents opened to the invidious a vague field for unfavorable surmise.

But the sailors' dog-watch gossip concerning him derived a vague plausibility from the fact that now for some period the British Navy could so little afford to be squeamish in the matter of keeping up the muster-rolls, that not only were press-gangs notoriously abroad both afloat and ashore, but there was little or no secret about another matter, namely that the London police were at liberty to capture any able-bodied suspect, any questionable fellow at large and summarily ship him to the dock-yard or fleet. Furthermore, even among voluntary enlistments there were instances where the motive thereto partook neither of patriotic impulse nor yet of a random desire to experience a bit of sea-life and martial adventure. Insolvent debtors of minor grade, together with the promiscuous lame ducks of morality found in the navy a convenient and secure refuge. Secure, because once enlisted aboard a King's-Ship, they were as much in sanctuary, as the transgressor of the middle ages harboring himself under the shadow of the altar. Such sanctioned irregularities which for obvious reasons the Government would hardly think to parade at the time and which consequently, and as affecting the least influential class of mankind, have all but dropped into oblivion lend color to something for the truth whereof I do not vouch, and hence have some scruple in stating; something I remember having seen in print, though the book I cannot recall; but the same thing was personally communicated to me now more than forty years ago by an old pensioner in a cocked hat with whom I had a most interesting talk on the terrace at Greenwich, a Baltimore negro, a Trafalgar man. It was to this effect: In the case of a warship short of hands whose speedy sailing was imperative, the deficient quota in lack of any other way of making it good, would be eked out by drafts culled direct from the jails. For reasons previously suggested it would not perhaps be easy at the present day directly to prove or disprove the allegation. But allowed as a verity, how significant would it be of England's straits at the time confronted by those wars which like a flight of harpies rose shrieking from the din and dust of the fallen Bastille. That era appears measurably clear to us who look back at it, and but read of it. But to the grandfathers of us graybeards, the more thoughtful of them, the genius of it presented an aspect like that of Camoëns' Spirit of the Cape, an eclipsing menace mysterious and prodigious. Not America was exempt from apprehension. At the height of Napoleon's unexampled conquests, there were Americans who had fought at Bunker Hill who looked forward to the possibility that the Atlantic might prove no barrier against the ultimate schemes of this French portentous upstart from the revolutionary chaos who seemed in act of fulfilling judgment prefigured in the Apocalypse.

But the less credence was to be given to the gun-deck talk touching Claggart, seeing that no man holding his office in a man-of-war can ever hope to be popular with the crew. Besides, in derogatory comments upon anyone against whom they have a grudge, or for any reason or no reason mislike, sailors are much like landsmen, they are apt to exaggerate or romance it.

About as much was really known to the *Indomitable's* tars of the master-at-arms' career before entering the service as an astronomer knows about a comet's travels prior to its first observable appearance in the sky. The verdict of the sea quidnunc's has been cited only by way of showing what sort of moral impression the man made upon rude uncultivated natures whose conceptions of human wickedness were necessarily of the narrowest, limited to ideas of vulgar rascality, — a thief among the swinging hammocks during a night-watch, or the man-brokers and land-sharks of the sea-ports.

It was no gossip, however, but fact, that though, as before hinted, Claggart upon his entrance into the navy was, as a novice, assigned to the least honorable section of a man-of-war's crew, embracing the drudgery, he did not long remain there.

The superior capacity he immediately evinced, his constitutional sobriety, ingratiating deference to superiors, together with a peculiar ferreting genius manifested on a singular occasion, all this capped by a certain austere patriotism abruptly advanced him to the position of master-at-arms.

Of this maritime Chief of Police the ship's corporals, so called, were the immediate subordinates, and compliant ones; and this, as is to be noted in some business departments ashore, almost to a degree inconsistent with entire moral volition. His place put various converging wires of underground influence under the Chief's control, capable when astutely worked through his understrappers of operating to the mysterious discomfort if nothing worse, of any of the sea-commonalty.

IX

Life in the foretop well agreed with Billy Budd. There, when not actually engaged on the yards yet higher aloft, the topmen, who as such had been picked out for youth and activity, constituted an aerial club lounging at ease against the smaller stunsails rolled up into cushions, spinning yarns like the lazy gods, and frequently amused with what was going on in the busy world of the decks below. No wonder then that a young fellow of Billy's disposition was well content in such society. Giving no cause of offense to anybody, he was always alert at a call. So in the merchant service it had been with him. But now such a punctiliousness in duty was shown that his topmates would sometimes good-naturedly laugh at him for it. This heightened alacrity had its cause, namely, the impression made upon him by the first formal gangway-punishment he had ever witnessed, which befell the day following his impressment. It had been incurred by a little fellow, young, a novice an after-guardsman absent from his assigned post when the ship was being put about; a dereliction resulting in a rather serious hitch to that maneuver, one demanding instantaneous promptitude in letting go and making fast. When Billy saw the culprit's naked back under the scourge gridironed with red welts, and worse; when he marked the dire expression on the liberated man's face as with his woolen shirt flung over him by the executioner he rushed forward from the spot to bury himself in the crowd, Billy was horrified. He resolved that never through remissness would he make himself liable to such a visitation or do or omit aught that might merit even verbal reproof. What then was his surprise and concern when ultimately he found himself getting into petty trouble occasionally about such matters as the stowage of his bag or something amiss in his hammock, matters under the police oversight of the ship's corporals of the lower decks, and which brought down on him a vague threat from one of them.

So heedful in all things as he was, how could this be? He could not understand it, and it more than vexed him. When he spoke to his young topmates about it they were either lightly incredulous, or found something comical in his unconcealed anxiety. "Is it your bag, Billy?" said one "well, sew yourself up in it, bully boy, and then you'll be sure to know if anybody meddles with it."

Now there was a veteran aboard who because his years began to disqualify him for more active work had been recently assigned duty as mainmast-man in his watch, looking to the gear belayed at the rail roundabout that great spar near the deck. At off-times the foretopman had picked up some acquaintance with him, and now in his trouble it occurred to him that he might be the sort of person to go to for wise counsel. He was an old Dansker long anglicized in the service, of few words, many wrinkles and some honorable scars. His wizened face, time-tinted and weather-stained to the complexion of an antique parchment, was here and there peppered blue by the chance explosion of a gun-cartridge in action. He was an *Agamemnon*-man; some two years prior to the time of this story having served under Nelson, when but Sir Horatio, in that ship immortal in naval memory, and which dismantled and in part broken up to her bare ribs is seen a grand skeleton in Haydon's etching. As one of a boarding-party from the *Agamemnon* he had received a cut slantwise along one temple and cheek, leaving a long pale scar like a streak of dawn's light falling athwart the dark visage. It was on account of that scar and the affair in which it was known that he had received it, as well as from his blue-peppered complexion that the Dansker went among the *Indomitable's* crew by the name of "Boarder-in-the-smoke."

Now the first time that his small weazel-eyes happened to light on Billy Budd, a certain grim internal merriment set all his ancient wrinkles into antic play. Was it that his eccentric unsentimental old sapience primitive in its kind saw or thought it saw something which in contrast with the warship's environment looked oddly incongruous in the handsome sailor? But after slyly studying him at intervals, the old Merlin's equivocal merriment was modified; for now when the twain would meet, it would start in his face a quizzing sort of look, but it would be but momentary and sometimes replaced by an expression of speculative query as to what might eventually befall a nature like that, dropped into a world not without some man-traps and against whose subtleties simple courage lacking experience and address and without any touch of defensive ugliness, is of little avail; and where such innocence as man is capable of does yet in a moral emergency not always sharpen the faculties or enlighten the will.

However it was the Dansker in his ascetic way rather took to Billy. Nor was this only because of a certain philosophic interest in such a character. There was another cause. While the old man's eccentricities, sometimes bordering on the ursine, repelled the juniors, Billy, undeterred thereby, revering him as a salt hero would make advances, never passing the old Agamemnon-man without a salutation marked by that respect which is seldom lost on the aged however crabbed at times or whatever their station in life. There was a vein of dry humor, or what not, in the mast-man; and, whether in freak of patriarchal irony touching Billy's youth and athletic frame, or for some other and more recondite reason, from the first in addressing him he always substituted Baby for Billy. The Dansker in fact being the originator of the name by which the foretopman eventually became known aboard ship.

Well then, in his mysterious little difficulty going in quest of the wrinkled one, Billy found him off duty in a dog-watch ruminating by himself seated on a shot-box of the upper gun-deck now and then surveying with a somewhat cynical regard certain of the more swaggering promenaders there. Billy recounted his trouble, again wondering how it all happened. The salt seer attentively listened, accompanying the foretopman's recital with queer twitchings of his wrinkles and problematical little sparkles of his small ferret eyes. Making an end of his story, the foretopman asked, "And now, Dansker, do tell me what you think of it."

The old man, shoving up the front of his tarpaulin and deliberately rubbing the long slant scar at the point where it entered the thin hair, laconically said, "Baby Budd, *Jemmy Legs*" (meaning the master-at-arms) "is down on you."

"*Jemmy Legs!*" ejaculated Billy his welkin eyes expanding; "what for? Why he calls me *the sweet and pleasant young fellow,* they tell me."

"Does he so?" grinned the grizzled one; then said "Ay Baby Lad a sweet voice has *Jemmy Legs*."

"No, not always. But to me he has. I seldom pass him but there comes a pleasant word."

"And that's because he's down upon you, Baby Budd."

Such reiteration along with the manner of it, incomprehensible to a novice, disturbed Billy almost as much as the mystery for which he had sought explanation. Something less unpleasingly oracular he tried to extract; but the old sea-Chiron thinking perhaps that for the nonce he had sufficiently instructed his young Achilles, pursed his lips, gathered his wrinkles together and would commit himself to nothing further.

Years, and those experiences which befall certain shrewder men subordinated life-long to the will of superiors, all this had developed in the Dansker the pithy guarded cynicism that was his leading characteristic.

X

The next day an incident served to confirm Billy Budd in his incredulity as to the Dansker's strange summing up of the case submitted.

The ship at noon going large before the wind was rolling on her course, and he below at dinner and engaged in some sportful talk with the members of his mess, chanced in a sudden lurch to spill the entire contents of his soup-pan upon the new scrubbed deck. Claggart, the Master-at-arms, official rattan in hand, happened to be passing along the battery in a bay of which the mess was lodged, and the greasy liquid streamed just across his path. Stepping over it, he was proceeding on his way without comment, since the matter was nothing to take notice of under the circumstances, when he happened to observe who it was that had done the spilling. His countenance changed. Pausing, he was about to ejaculate something hasty at the sailor, but checked himself, and pointing down to the streaming soup, playfully tapped him from behind with his rattan, saying in a low musical voice peculiar to him at times "Handsomely done, my lad! And handsome is as handsome did it too!" And with that passed on. Not noted by Billy as not coming within his view was the involuntary smile, or rather grimace, that accompanied Claggart's equivocal words. Aridly it drew down the thin corners of his shapely mouth. But everybody taking his remark as meant for humorous, and at which therefore as coming from a superior they were bound to laugh "with counterfeited glee," acted accordingly; and Billy tickled, it may be, by the allusion to his being the handsome sailor, merrily joined in; then addressing his messmates exclaimed "There now, who says that *Jemmy Legs* is down on me!"

"And who said he was, Beauty?" demanded one Donald with some surprise. Whereat the foretopman looked a little foolish recalling that it was only one person, Board-her-in-the-smoke who had suggested what to him was the smoky idea that this master-at-arms was in any peculiar way hostile to him. Meantime that functionary resuming his path must have momentarily worn some expression less guarded than that of the bitter smile and, usurping the face from the heart, some distorting expression perhaps, for a drummer-boy, heedlessly frolicking along from the opposite direction, and chancing to come into light collision with his person was strangely disconcerted by his aspect. Nor was the impression lessened when the official, impulsively giving him a sharp cut with the rattan, vehemently exclaimed "Look where you go!"

XI

What was the matter with the master-at-arms? And, be the matter what it might, how could it have direct relation to Billy Budd with whom prior to the affair of the spilled soup he had never come into any special contact official or otherwise? What indeed could the trouble have to do with one so little inclined to give offense as the merchant-ship's *peacemaker*, even him who in Claggart's own phrase was "the sweet and pleasant young fellow"? Yes, why should *Jemmy Legs*, to borrow the Dansker's expression, be *down* on the Handsome Sailor?

But at heart and not for nothing, as the late chance encounter may indicate to the discerning, down on him, secretly down on him, he assuredly was.

Now to invent something touching the more private career of Claggart, something involving Billy Budd, of which something the latter should be wholly ignorant, some romantic incident implying that Claggart's knowledge of the young bluejacket began at some period anterior to catching sight of him on board the seventy-four — all this, not so difficult to do, might avail in a way more or less interesting to account for whatever enigma may appear to lurk in the case. But in fact there was nothing of the sort. And yet the cause, necessarily to be assumed as the sole one assignable, is in its very realism as much charged with that prime element of Radcliffian romance, the *mysterious,* as any that the ingenuity of the author of the *Mysteries of Udolpho* could devise. For what can more partake of the mysterious than an antipathy spontaneous and profound such as is evoked in certain exceptional mortals by the mere aspect of some other mortal, however harmless he may be? if not called forth by this very harmlessness itself.

Now there can exist no irritating juxtaposition of dissimilar personalities comparable to that which is possible aboard a great warship fully manned and at sea. There, every day among all ranks almost every man comes into more or less of contact with almost every other man. Wholly there to avoid even the sight of an aggravating object one must needs give it Jonah's toss or jump overboard himself. Imagine how all this might eventually operate on some peculiar human creature the direct reverse of a saint?

But before the adequate comprehending of Claggart by a normal nature these hints are insufficient. To pass from a normal nature to him one must cross "the deadly space between." And this is best done by indirection.

Long ago an honest scholar my senior, said to me in reference to one who like himself is now no more, a man so unimpeachably respectable that against him nothing was ever openly said though among the few something was whispered, "Yes, X — — is a nut not to be cracked by the tap of a lady's fan. You are aware that I am the adherent of no organized religion much less of any philosophy built into a system. Well, for all that, I think that to try and get into X ——, enter his labyrinth and get out again, without a clue derived from some source other than what is known as *knowledge of the world* — that were hardly possible, at least for me."

"Why," said I, "X —— however singular a study

to some, is yet human, and knowledge of the world assuredly implies the knowledge of human nature, and in most of its varieties."

"Yes, but a superficial knowledge of it, serving ordinary purposes. But for anything deeper, I am not certain whether to know the world and to know human nature be not two distinct branches of knowledge, which while they may coexist in the same heart, yet either may exist with little or nothing of the other. Nay, in an average man of the world, his constant rubbing with its blunts that fine spiritual insight indispensable to the understanding of the essential in certain exceptional characters, whether evil ones or good. In a matter of some importance I have seen a girl wind an old lawyer about her little finger. Nor was it the dotage of senile love. Nothing of the sort. But he knew law better than he knew the girl's heart. Coke and Blackstone hardly shed so much light into obscure spiritual places as the Hebrew prophets. And who were they? Mostly recluses."

At the time my inexperience was such that I did not quite see the drift of all this. It may be that I see it now. And, indeed, if that lexicon which is based on Holy Writ were any longer popular, one might with less difficulty define and denominate certain phenomenal men. As it is, one must turn to some authority not liable to the charge of being tinctured with the Biblical element.

In a list of definitions included in the authentic translation of Plato, a list attributed to him, occurs this: "Natural Depravity: a depravity according to nature." A definition which though savoring of Calvinism, by no means involves Calvin's dogma as to total mankind. Evidently its intent makes it applicable but to individuals. Not many are the examples of this depravity which the gallows and jail supply. At any rate for notable instances, since these have no vulgar alloy of the brute in them, but invariably are dominated by intellectuality, one must go elsewhere. Civilization, especially if of the austerer sort, is auspicious to it. It folds itself in the mantle of respectability. It has its certain negative virtues serving as silent auxiliaries. It never allows wine to get within its guard. It is not going too far to say that it is without vices or small sins. There is a phenomenal pride in it that excludes them from anything mercenary or avaricious. In short the depravity here meant partakes nothing of the sordid or sensual. It is serious, but free from acerbity. Though no flatterer of mankind it never speaks ill of it.

But the thing which in eminent instances signalizes so exceptional a nature is this: though the man's even temper and discreet bearing would seem to intimate a mind peculiarly subject to the law of reason, not the less in his heart he would seem to riot in complete exemption from that law having apparently little to do with reason further than to employ it as an ambidexter implement for effecting the irrational. That is to say: toward the accomplishment of an aim which in wantonness of malignity would seem to partake of the insane, he will direct a cool judgment sagacious and sound.

These men are true madmen, and of the most dangerous sort, for their lunacy is not continuous but occasional evoked by some special object; it is probably secretive which is as much to say it is self-contained, so that when moreover, most active it is to the average mind not distinguishable from sanity, and for the reason above suggested that whatever its aims may be, and the aim is never declared — the method and the outward proceeding is always perfectly rational.

Now something such an one was Claggart, in whom was the mania of an evil nature, not engendered by vicious training or corrupting books or licentious living, but born with him and innate, in short "a depravity according to nature."

XII
LAWYERS, EXPERTS, CLERGY
AN EPISODE

By the way, can it be the phenomenon, disowned or at least concealed, that in some criminal cases puzzles the courts? For this cause have our juries at times not only to endure the prolonged contentions of lawyers with their fees, but also the yet more perplexing strife of the medical experts with theirs? But why leave it to them? Why not subpoena (?) as well the clerical proficients? Their vocation bringing them into peculiar contact with so many human beings, and sometimes in their least guarded hour, in interviews very much more confidential than those of phyician and patient; this would seem to qualify them to know something about those intricacies involved in the question of moral responsibility; whether in a given case, say, the crime proceeded from mania in the brain or rabies of the heart. As to any differences among themselves these clerical proficients might develop on the stand, these could hardly be greater than the direct contradictions exchanged between the remunerated medical experts.

Dark sayings are these, some will say. But why? Is it because they somewhat savor of Holy Writ in its phrase "mysteries of iniquity"? If they do, such savor was far from being intended for little will it commend these pages to many a reader of today.

The point of the present story turning on the hidden nature of the master-at-arms has necessitated this chapter. With an added hint or two in connection with the incident at the mess, the resumed narrative must be left to vindicate as it may, its own credibility.

XIII
PALE IRE, ENVY AND DESPAIR

That Claggart's figure was not amiss, and his face, save the chin, well moulded, has already been said. Of these favorable points he seemed not insensible, for he was not only neat but careful in his dress. But the form of Billy Budd was heroic; and if his face was without the intellectual look of the pallid Claggart's, not the less was it lit, like his, from within, though from a different source. The bonfire in his heart made luminous the rose-tan in his cheek.

In view of the marked contrast between the persons of the twain, it is more than probable that when the master-at-arms in the scene last given applied to the sailor the proverb *Handsome is as handsome does*; he there let escape an ironic inkling, not caught by the young sailors who heard it, as to what it was that had first moved him against Billy, namely, his significant personal beauty.

Now envy and antipathy passions irreconcilable in reason, nevertheless in fact may spring conjoined like Chang and Eng in one birth. Is Envy then such a monster? Well, though many an arraigned mortal has in hopes of mitigated penalty pleaded guilty to horrible actions, did ever anybody seriously confess to envy? Something there is in it universally felt to be more shameful than even felonious crime. And not only does everybody disown it but the better sort are inclined to incredulity when it is in earnest imputed to an intelligent man. But since its lodgment is in the heart not the brain, no degree of intellect supplies a guarantee against it. But Claggart's was no vulgar form of the passion. Nor, as directed toward Billy Budd, did it partake of that streak of apprehensive jealousy that marred Saul's visage perturbedly brooding on the comely young David. Claggart's envy struck deeper. If askance he eyed the good looks, cheery health and frank enjoyment of young life in Billy Budd, it was because these went along with a nature that as Claggart magnetically felt, had in its simplicity never willed malice or experienced the reactionary bite of that serpent. To him, the spirit lodged within Billy, and looking out from his welkin eyes as from windows, that ineffability it was which made the dimple in his dyed cheek, suppled his joints, and dancing in his yellow curls made him preeminently the Handsome Sailor. One person excepted the master-at-arms was perhaps the only man in the ship intellectually capable of adequately appreciating the moral phenomenon presented in Billy Budd. And the insight but intensified his passion, which assuming various secret forms within him, at times assumed that of cynic disdain — disdain of innocence — To be nothing more than innocent! Yet in an aesthetic way he saw the charm of it, the courageous free-and-easy temper of it, and fain would have shared it, but he despaired of it.

With no power to annul the elemental evil in him, though readily enough he could hide it; apprehending the good, but powerless to be it; a nature like Claggart's surcharged with energy as such natures almost invariably are, what recourse is left to it but to recoil upon itself and like the scorpion for which the Creator alone is responsible, act out to the end the part allotted it.

XIV

Passion, and passion in its profoundest, is not a thing demanding a palatial stage whereon to play its part. Down among the groundlings, among the beggars and rakers of the garbage, profound passion is enacted. And the circumstances that provoke it, however trivial or mean, are no measure of its power. In the present instance the stage is a scrubbed gun-deck, and one of the external provocations a man-of-war's man's spilled soup.

Now when the Master-at-arms noticed whence came that greasy fluid streaming before his feet, he must have taken it — to some extent wilfully, — perhaps not for the mere accident it assuredly was, but for the sly escape of a spontaneous feeling on Billy's part more or less answering to the antipathy on his own. In effect a foolish demonstration he must have thought, and very harmless, like the futile kick of a heifer, which yet were the heifer a shod stallion, would not be so harmless. Even so was it that into the gall of Claggart's envy he infused the vitriol of his contempt. But the incident confirmed to him certain tell-tale reports purveyed to his ear by *Squeak*, one of his more cunning corporals, a grizzled little man, so nicknamed by the sailors on account of his squeaky voice, and sharp visage ferreting about the dark corners of the lower decks after interlopers, satirically suggesting to them the idea of a rat in a cellar.

From his Chief's employing him as an implicit tool in laying little traps for the worriment of the Foretopman — for it was from the Master-at-arms that the petty persecutions heretofore adverted to had proceeded — the corporal having naturally enough concluded that his master could have no love for the sailor, made it his business, faithful understrapper that he was, to foment the ill blood by perverting to his Chief certain innocent frolics of the good natured Foretopman, besides inventing for his mouth sundry contumelious epithets he claimed to have overheard him let fall. The Master-at-arms never suspected the veracity of these reports, more especially as to the epithets, for he well knew how secretly unpopular may become a master-at-arms at least a master-at-arms of those days zealous in his function, and how the blue-jackets shoot at him in private their raillery and wit; the nickname by which he goes among them *(Jemmy Legs)* implying under the form of merriment their cherished disrespect and dislike.

But in view of the greediness of hate for patrolmen it hardly needed a purveyor to feed Claggart's passion. An uncommon prudence is habitual with the subtler depravity, for it has everything to hide. And in case of an injury but suspected its secretiveness voluntarily cuts it off from enlightenment or disillusion; and, not unreluctantly, action is taken upon surmise as upon certainty. And the retaliation is apt to be in monstrous disproportion to the supposed offense; for when in anybody was revenge in its exactions aught else but an inordinate usurer? But how with Claggart's conscience? For though consciences are unlike as foreheads, every intelligence, not excluding the Scriptural devils who "believe and tremble," has one. But Claggart's conscience being but the lawyer to his will, made ogres of trifles, probably arguing that the motive imputed to Billy in spilling the soup just when he did, together with the epithets alleged, these, if nothing more, made a strong case against him; nay, justified animosity into a sort of retributive righteousness. The Pharisee is the Guy Fawkes prowling in the hid chambers underlying the Claggarts. And they can really form no conception of an unreciprocated malice. Probably, the master-at-arms' clandestine persecutions of Billy were started to try the temper of the man; but it had not developed any quality in him that enmity could make official use of or even pervert into even plausible self-justification; so that the occurrence at the mess, petty if it were, was a welcome one to that peculiar conscience assigned to be the private mentor of Claggart; and for the rest, not improbably it put him upon new experiments.

XV

Not many days after the last incident narrated something befell Billy Budd that more gravelled him than aught that had previously occurred.

It was a warm night for the latitude; and the Foretopman, whose watch at the time was properly below, was dozing on the uppermost deck whither he had ascended from his hot hammock one of hundreds suspended so closely wedged together over a lower gun-deck that there was little or no swing to them. He lay as in the shadow of a hill-side stretched under the lee of the *booms*, a piled ridge of spare spars amidships between foremast and mainmast and among which the ship's largest boat, the launch, was stowed. Alongside of three other slumberers from below, he lay near that end of the booms which approaches from the foremast; his station aloft on duty as a foretopman being just over the deck-station of the forecastlemen, entitling him according to usage to make himself more or less at home in that neighborhood.

Presently he was stirred into semi-consciousness by somebody, who must have previously sounded the sleep of the others, touching his shoulder, and then as the Foretopman raised his head, breathing into his ear in a quick whisper, "Slip into the lee forechains, Billy; there is something in the wind. Don't speak. Quick. I will meet you there;" and disappeared.

Now Billy like sundry other essentially good-natured ones had some of the weaknesses inseparable from essential good-nature; and among these was a reluctance, almost an incapacity of plumply saying *no* to an abrupt proposition not obviously absurd, on the face of it, nor obviously unfriendly, nor iniquitous. And being of warm blood he had not the phlegm tacitly to negative any proposition by an unresponsive inaction. Like his sense of fear, his apprehension as to aught outside of the honest and natural was seldom very quick. Besides, upon the present occasion, the drowse from his sleep still hung upon him.

However it was, he mechanically rose, and sleepily wondering what could be in the wind, betook himself to the designated place, a narrow platform, one of six, outside of the high bulwarks and screened by the great dead-eyes and multiple columned lanyards of the shrouds and backstays; and, in a great warship of that time, of dimensions commensurate to the hull's magnitude; a tarry balcony in short overhanging the sea, and so secluded that one mariner of the *Indomitable*, a nonconformist old tar of a serious turn, made it even in daytime his private oratory.

In this retired nook the stranger soon joined Billy Budd. There was no moon as yet; a haze obscured the star-light. He could not distinctly see the stranger's face. Yet from something in the outline and carriage, Billy took him to be, and correctly, one of the afterguard.

"Hist! Billy," said the man; in the same quick cautionary whisper as before, "You were impressed, weren't you? Well, so was I;" and he paused as to mark the effect. But Billy not knowing exactly what to make of this said nothing. Then the other: "We are not the only impressed ones, Billy. There's a gang of us. — Couldn't you — help — at a pinch?"

"What do you mean?" demanded Billy here thoroughly shaking off his drowse.

"Hist, hist!" the hurried whisper now growing husky, "see here;" and the man held up two small objects faintly twinkling in the night light; "see, they are yours, Billy if you'll only — "

But Billy broke in, and in his resentful eagerness to deliver himself his vocal infirmity somewhat intruded; "D-D-Damme, I don't know what you are d-d-driving at, or what you mean, but you had better g-g-go where you belong!" For the moment the fellow, as confounded, did not stir; and Billy, springing to his feet, said "If you d-don't start I'll t-t-toss you back over the r-rail!" There was no mistaking this and the mysterious emissary decamped, disappearing in the direction of the mainmast in the shadow of the booms.

"Hallo, what's the matter?" here came growling from a forecastleman awakened from his deckdoze by Billy's raised voice. And as the foretopman reappeared and was recognized by him;

"Ah, *Beauty*, is it you? Well, something must have been the matter for you st-st-stuttered."

"Oh," rejoined Billy, now mastering the impediment; "I found an afterguardsman in our part of the ship here and I bid him be off where he belongs."

"And is that all you did about it, foretopman?" gruffly demanded another, an irascible old fellow of brick-colored visage and hair, and who was known to his associate forecastlemen as *Red Pepper*; "Such sneaks I should like to marry to the gunner's daughter!" by that expression meaning that he would like to subject them to disciplinary castigation over a gun.

However, Billy's rendering of the matter satisfactorily accounted to these inquirers for the brief commotion, since of all the sections of a ship's company the forecastlemen, veterans for the most part and bigoted in their sea-prejudices, are the most jealous in resenting territorial encroachments, especially on the part of any of the afterguard, of whom they have but a sorry opinion, chiefly landsmen, never going aloft except to reef or furl the main-sail, and in no wise competent to handle a marlinspike or turn in a *dead-eye*, say.

XVI

This incident sorely puzzled Billy Budd. It was an entirely new experience; the first time in his life that he had ever been personally approached in underhand intriguing fashion. Prior to this encounter he had known nothing of the afterguardsman, the two men being stationed wide apart, one forward and aloft during his watch, the other on deck and aft.

What could it mean? And could they really be guineas, those two glittering objects the interloper had held up to his (Billy's) eyes? Where could the fellow get guineas? Why even buttons spare buttons are not so plentiful at sea. The more he turned the matter over, the more he was nonplussed, and made uneasy and discomforted. In his disgustful recoil from an overture which though he but ill comprehended he instinctively knew must involve evil of some sort, Billy Budd was like a young horse fresh from the pasture suddenly inhaling a vile whiff from some chemical factory and by repeated snortings tries to get it out of his nostrils and lungs. This frame of mind barred all desire of holding further parley with the fellow, even were it but for the purpose of gaining some enlightenment as to his design in approaching him. And yet he was not without natural curiosity to see how such a visitor in the dark would look in broad day.

He espied him the following afternoon in his first dog-watch below one of the smokers on that forward part of the upper gun-deck allotted to the pipe. He recognized him by his general cut and build, more than by his round freckled face and glassy eyes of pale blue, veiled with lashes all but white.

And yet Billy was a bit uncertain whether indeed it were he — yonder chap about his own age, chatting and laughing in free-hearted way, leaning against a gun; a genial young fellow enough to look at, and something of a rattle-brain, to all appearance. Rather chubby too for a sailor even an afterguardsman. In short the last man in the world, one would think, to be overburdened with thoughts, especially those perilous thoughts that must needs belong to a conspirator in any serious project, or even to the underling of such a conspirator.

Although Billy was not aware of it, the fellow, with a sidelong watchful glance had perceived Billy first, and then noting that Billy was looking at him, thereupon nodded a familiar sort of friendly recognition as to an old acquaintance, without interrupting the talk he was engaged in with the group of smokers. A day or two afterwards chancing in the evening promenade on a gun-deck, to pass Billy, he offered a flying word of good-fellowship as it were, which by its unexpectedness, and equivocalness under the circumstances so embarrassed Billy that he knew not how to respond to it, and let it go unnoticed.

Billy was now left more at a loss than before. The ineffectual speculations into which he was led were so disturbingly alien to him that he did his best to smother them. It never entered his mind that here was a matter which from its extreme questionableness, it was his duty as a loyal bluejacket to report in the proper quarter. And, probably, had such a step been suggested to him, he would have been deterred from taking it by the thought, one of novice-magnanimity, that it would savor overmuch of the dirty work of a tell-tale. He kept the thing to himself. Yet upon one occasion, he could not forbear a little disburthening himself to the old Dansker, tempted thereto perhaps by the influence of a balmy night when the ship lay becalmed; the twain, silent for the most part, sitting together on deck, their heads propped against the bulwarks. But it was only a partial and anonymous account that Billy gave, the unfounded scruples above referred to preventing full disclosure to anybody. Upon hearing Billy's version, the sage Dansker seemed to divine more than he was told; and after a little meditation during which his wrinkles were pursed as into a point, quite effacing for the time that quizzing expression his face sometimes wore, — "Didn't I say so, Baby Budd?"

"Say what?" demanded Billy.

"Why, *Jemmy Legs* is *down* on you."

"And what" rejoined Billy in amazement, "has *Jemmy Legs* to do with that cracked afterguardsman?"

"Ho, it was an afterguardsman, then. A cat's-paw, a cat's-paw!" And with that exclamation, which, whether it had reference to a light puff of air just then coming over the calm sea, or subtler relation to the afterguardsman, there is no telling, the old Merlin gave a twisting wrench with his black teeth at his plug of tobacco, vouchsafing no reply to Billy's impetuous question, though now repeated, for it was his wont to relapse into grim silence when interrogated in skeptical sort as to any of his sententious oracles, not always very clear ones, rather partaking of that obscurity which invests most Delphic deliverances from any quarter. Long experience had very likely brought this old man to that bitter prudence which never interferes in aught and never gives advice.

XVII

Yes, despite the Dansker's pithy insistence as to the Master-at-arms being at the bottom of these strange experiences of Billy on board the *Indomitable*, the young sailor was ready to ascribe them to almost anybody but the man who, to use Billy's own expression, "always had a pleasant word for him." This is to be wondered at. Yet not so much to be wondered at. In certain matters, some sailors even in mature life remain unsophisticated enough. But a young seafarer of the disposition of our athletic Foretopman is much of a child-man. And yet a child's utter innocence is but its blank ignorance, and the innocence more or less wanes as intelligence waxes. But in Billy Budd intelligence such as it was, had advanced, while yet his simple-mindedness remained for the most part unaffected. Experience is a teacher indeed; yet did Billy's years make his experience small. Besides, he had none of that intuitive knowledge of the bad which in natures not good or incompletely so foreruns experience, and therefore may pertain, as in some instances it too clearly does pertain, even to youth.

And what could Billy know of man except of man as a mere sailor? And the old-fashioned sailor, the veritable man-before-the-mast, the sailor from boyhood up, he, though indeed of the same species as a landsman is in some respects singularly distinct from him. The sailor is frankness, the landsman is finesse. Life is not a game with the sailor, demanding the long head; no intricate game of chess where few moves are made in straightforwardness, and ends are attained by indirection; an oblique, tedious, barren game hardly worth that poor candle burnt out in playing it.

Yes, as a class, sailors are in character a juvenile race. Even their deviations are marked by juvenility. And this more especially holding true with the sailors of Billy's time. Then, too, certain things which apply to all sailors, do more pointedly operate here and there, upon the junior one. Every sailor, too is accustomed to obey orders without debating them; his life afloat is externally ruled for him; he is not brought into that promiscuous commerce with mankind where unobstructed free agency on equal terms — equal superficially, at least — soon teaches one that unless upon occasion he exercises a distrust keen in proportion to the fairness of the appearance, some foul turn may be served him. A ruled undemonstrative distrustfulness is so habitual, not with business-men so much, as with men who know their kind in less shallow relations than business, namely certain men-of-the-world, that they come at last to employ it all but unconsciously; and some of them would very likely feel real surprise at being charged with it as one of their general characteristics.

XVIII

But after the little matter at the mess Billy Budd no more found himself in strange trouble at times about his hammock or his clothes-bag or what not. While, as to that smile that occasionally sunned him, and the pleasant passing word, these were if not more frequent, yet if anything more pronounced than before.

But for all that, there were certain other demonstrations now. When Claggart's unobserved glance happened to light on belted Billy rolling along the upper gun-deck in the leisure of the second dog-watch exchanging passing broadsides of fun with other young promenaders in the crowd; that glance would follow the cheerful sea-Hyperion with a settled meditative and melancholy expression, his eyes strangely suffused with incipient feverish tears. Then would Claggart look like the man of sorrows. Yes, and sometimes the melancholy expression would have in it a touch of soft yearning, as if Claggart could even have loved Billy but for fate and ban. But this was an evanescence, and quickly repented of, as it were, by an immitigable look, pinching and shrivelling the visage into the momentary semblance of a wrinkled walnut. But sometimes catching sight in advance of the foretopman coming in his direction, he would, upon their nearing, step aside a little to let him pass, dwelling upon Billy for the moment with the glittering dental satire of a Guise. But upon any abrupt unforeseen encounter a red light would flash forth from his eye like a spark from an anvil in a dusk smithy. That quick fierce light was a strange one, darted from orbs which in repose were of a color nearest approaching a deeper violet, the softest of shades.

Though some of these caprices of the pit could not but he observed by their object, yet were they beyond the construing of such a nature. And the *thews* of Billy were hardly compatible with that sort of sensitive spiritual organization which in some cases instinctively conveys to ignorant innocence an admonition of the proximity of the malign. He thought the Master-at-arms acted in a manner rather queer at times. That was all. But the occasional frank air and pleasant word went for what they purported to be, the young sailor never having heard as yet of the "too fair-spoken man."

Had the foretopman been conscious of having done or said anything to provoke the ill will of the official, it would have been different with him, and his sight might have been purged if not sharpened. As it was innocence was his blinder.

So was it with him in yet another matter. Two minor officers — the Armorer, and Captain of the Hold, with whom he had never exchanged a word, his position on the ship not bringing him into contact with them; these men now for the first began to cast upon Billy when they chanced to encounter him, that peculiar glance which evidences that the man from whom it comes has been some way tampered with and to the prejudice of him upon whom the glance lights. Never did it occur to Billy as a thing to be noted or a thing suspicious, though he well knew the fact, that the Armorer and Captain of the Hold, with the ship's yeoman, apothecary and others of that grade, were by naval usage, messmates of the master-at-arms men with ears convenient to his confidential tongue.

But the general popularity that our Handsome Sailor's manly forwardness upon occasion, and irresistible good nature indicating no mental superiority tending to excite an invidious feeling; this good will on the part of most of his shipmates made him the less to concern himself about such mute aspects toward him as those whereto allusion has just been made as far as he could not so fathom as to infer their whole import.

As to the afterguardsman, though Billy for reasons already given necessarily saw little of him, yet when the two did happen to meet, invariably came the fellow's offhand cheerful recognition, sometimes accompanied by a passing pleasant word or two. Whatever that equivocal young person's original design may really have been, or the design of which he might have been the deputy, certain it was from his manner upon these occasions, that he had wholly dropped it.

It was as if his precocity of crookedness (and every vulgar villain is precocious) had for once deceived him, and the man he had sought to entrap as a simpleton had, through his very simplicity ignorantly baffled him.

But shrewd ones may opine that it was hardly possible for Billy to refrain from going up to the afterguardsman and bluntly demanding to know his purpose in the initial interview, so abruptly closed in the fore-chains. Shrewd ones may also think it but natural in Billy to set about sounding some of the other impressed men of the ship in order to discover what basis, if any, there was for the emissary's obscure suggestions as to plotting disaffection aboard. Yes, the shrewd may so think. But something more, or rather, something else than mere shrewdness is perhaps needful for the due understanding of such a character as Billy Budd's.

As to Claggart, the monomania in the man — if that indeed it were — as involuntarily disclosed by starts in the manifestations detailed, yet in general covered over by his self-contained and rational demeanor; this, like a subterranean fire was eating its way deeper and deeper in him. Something decisive must come of it.

XIX

After the mysterious interview in the fore-chains, the one so abruptly ended there by Billy, nothing especially german to the story occurred until the events now about to be narrated.

Elsewhere it has been said that in the lack of frigates (of course better sailers than line-of-battle ships) in the English squadron up the Straits at that period, the *Indomitable* was occasionally employed not only as an available substitute for a scout, but at times on detached service of more important kind. This was not alone because of her sailing qualities, not common in a ship of her rate, but quite as much, probably, that the character of her commander, it was thought, specially adapted him for any duty where under unforeseen difficulties a prompt initiative might have to be taken in some matter demanding knowledge and ability in addition to those qualities implied in good seamanship. It was on an expedition of the latter sort, a somewhat distant one, and when the *Indomitable* was almost at her furthest remove from the fleet that in the latter part of an afternoon-watch she unexpectedly came in sight of a ship of the enemy. It proved to be frigate. The latter, perceiving through the glass that the weight of men and metal would be heavily against her, invoking her light heels crowded sail to get away. After a chase urged almost against hope and lasting until about the middle of the first dog-watch, she signally succeeded in effecting her escape.

Not long after the pursuit had been given up, and ere the excitement incident thereto had altogether waned away, the master-at-arms ascending from his cavernous sphere made his appearance cap in hand by the mainmast respectfully awaiting the notice of Captain Vere then solitary walking the weather-side of the quarter-deck doubtless somewhat chafed at the failure of the pursuit. The spot where Claggart stood was the place allotted to men of lesser grades seeking some more particular interview either with the officer-of-the-deck or the Captain himself. But from the latter it was not often that a sailor or petty-officer of those days would seek a hearing; only some exceptional cause, would, according to established custom, have warranted that.

Presently, just as the Commander absorbed in his reflections was on the point of turning aft in his promenade, he became sensible of Claggart's presence, and saw the doffed cap held in deferential expectancy. Here be it said that Captain Vere's personal knowledge of this petty-officer had only begun at the time of the ship's last sailing from home, Claggart then for the first, in transfer from a ship detained for repairs, supplying on board the *Indomitable* the place of a previous master-at-arms disabled and ashore.

No sooner did the Commander observe who it was that now so deferentially stood awaiting his notice, than a peculiar expression came over him. It was not unlike that which uncontrollably will flit across the countenance of one at unawares encountering a person who though known to him indeed has hardly been long enough known for thorough knowledge, but something in whose aspect nevertheless now for the first provokes a vaguely repellent distaste. But coming to a stand and resuming much of his wonted official manner, save that a sort of impatience lurked in the intonation of the opening word, he said, "Well? what is it, master-at-arms?"

With the air of a subordinate grieved at the necessity of being a messenger of ill tidings, and while conscientiously determined to be frank, yet equally resolved upon shunning overstatement, Claggart at this invitation or rather summons to disburthen, spoke up. What he said, conveyed in the language of no uneducated man, was to the effect following if not altogether in these words, namely, that during the chase and preparations for the possible encounter he had seen enough to convince him that at least one sailor aboard was a dangerous character in a ship mustering some who not only had taken a guilty part in the late serious troubles, but others also who, like the man in question, had entered His Majesty's service under another form than enlistment.

At this point Captain Vere with some impatience, interrupted him:

"Be direct, man; say impressed men."

Claggart made a gesture of subservience, and proceeded.

Quite lately whereof he (Claggart) had begun to suspect that on the gun-decks some sort of movement prompted by the sailor in question was covertly going on, but he had not thought himself warranted in reporting the suspicion so long as it remained indistinct. But from what he had that afternoon observed in the man referred to, the suspicion of somewhat clandestine going on had advanced to a point less removed from certainty. He deeply felt, he added, the serious responsibility assumed in making a report involving such possible consequences to the individual mainly concerned, besides tending to augment those natural anxieties which every naval commander must feel in view of extraordinary outbreaks so recent as those which, he sorrowfully said it, it needed not to name.

Now at the first broaching of the matter Captain Vere taken by surprise could not wholly dissemble his disquietude. But as Claggart went on, the former's aspect changed into restiveness under something in the witness's manner in giving his testimony. However, he refrained from interrupting him. And Claggart, continuing, concluded with this:

"God forbid, your honor, that the *Indomitable's* should be the experience of the — "

"Never mind that!" here peremptorily broke in the superior, his face altering with anger, instinctively divining the ship that the other was about to name, one in which the Nore Mutiny had assumed a singularly tragical character that for a time jeopardized the life of its commander. Under the circumstances he was indignant at the purposed allusion. When the commissioned officers themselves were on all occasions very heedful how they referred to the recent events, for a petty-officer unnecessarily to allude to them in the presence of his Captain, this struck him as a most immodest presumption. Besides, to his quick sense of self-respect, it even looked under the circumstances something like an attempt to alarm him. Nor at first was he without some surprise that one who so far as he had hitherto come under his notice had shown considerable tact in his function should in this particular evince such lack of it.

But these thoughts and kindred dubious ones flitting across his mind were suddenly replaced by an intuitional surmise which though as yet obscure in form served practically to affect his reception of the ill tidings. Certain it is, that long versed in everything pertaining to the complicated gun-deck life, which like every other form of life has its secret mines and dubious side the side popularly disclaimed, Captain Vere did not permit himself to be unduly disturbed by the general tenor of his subordinate's report. Furthermore, if in view of recent events prompt action should be taken at the first palpable sign of recurring insubordination, for all that, not judicious would it be, he thought, to keep the idea of lingering disaffection alive by undue forwardness in crediting an informer even if his own subordinate and charged among other things with police surveillance of the crew. This feeling would not perhaps have so prevailed with him were it not that upon a prior occasion the patriotic zeal officially evinced by Claggart had somewhat irritated him as appearing rather super-sensible and strained. Furthermore something even in the official's self-possessed and somewhat ostentatious manner in making his specifications strangely reminded him of a bandsman, a perjurous witness in a capital case before a court-martial ashore of which when a lieutenant he Captain Vere had been a member.

Now the peremptory check given to Claggart in

the matter of the arrested allusion was quickly followed up by this: "You say that there is at least one dangerous man aboard. Name him."

"William Budd. A foretopman, your honor — "

"William Budd" repeated Captain Vere with unfeigned astonishment; "and mean you the man that Lieutenant Ratcliffe took from the merchantman not very long ago — the young fellow who seems to be so popular with the men — Billy, the Handsome Sailor, as they call him?"

"The same, your honor; but for all his youth and good looks, a deep one. Not for nothing does he insinuate himself into the good will of his shipmates, since at the least all hands will at a pinch say a good word for him at all hazards. Did Lieutenant Ratcliffe happen to tell your honor of that adroit fling of Budd's jumping up in the cutter's bow under the merchantman's stern when he was being taken off? It is even masqued by that sort of good humored air that at heart he resents his impressment. You have but noted his fair cheek. A man-trap may be under his ruddy-tipped daisies."

Now the *Handsome Sailor* as a signal figure among the crew, had naturally enough attracted the Captain's attention from the first. Though in general not very demonstrative to his officers, he had congratulated Lieutenant Ratcliffe upon his good fortune in lighting on such a fine specimen of the genus homo, who in the nude might have posed for a statue of young Adam before the Fall.

As to Billy's adieu to the ship *Rights-of-Man*, which the boarding lieutenant had indeed reported to him, Captain Vere, but in a deferential way more as a good story than aught else, though mistakenly understanding it as a satiric sally, had but thought so much the better of the impressed man for it; as a military sailor, admiring the spirit that could take an arbitrary enlistment so merrily and sensibly. The foretopman's conduct, too, so far as it had fallen under the Captain's notice had confirmed the first happy augury, while the new recruit's qualities as a *sailor-man* seemed to be such that he had thought of recommending him to the executive officer for promotion to a place that would more frequently bring him under his own observation, namely, the captaincy of the mizzentop, replacing there in the starboard watch a man not so young whom partly for that reason he deemed less fitted for the post. Be it parenthesized here that since the mizzen-top-men having not to handle such breadths of heavy canvas as the lower sails on the main-mast and fore-mast, a young man if of the right stuff not only seems best adapted to duty there, but in fact is generally selected for the captaincy of that top, and the company under him are light hands and often but striplings. In sum, Captain Vere had from the beginning deemed Billy Budd to be what in the naval parlance of the time was called a *"King's bargain,"* that is to say, for His Britannic Majesty's navy a capital investment at small outlay or none at all.

After a brief pause during which the reminiscences above mentioned passed vividly through his mind and he weighed the import of Claggart's last suggestion, conveyed in the phrase, "pitfall under the clover," and the more he weighed it the less reliance he felt in the informer's good faith. Suddenly he turned upon him and in a low voice: "Do you come to me, master-at-arms, with so foggy a tale? As to Budd, cite me an act or spoken word of his confirmatory of what you in general charge against him. Stay," drawing nearer to him "heed what you speak. Just now and in a case like this, there is a yard-arm-end for the falsewitness."

"Ah, your honor!" sighed Claggart mildly shaking his shapely head as in sad deprecation of such unmerited severity of tone. Then, bridling — erecting himself as in virtuous self-assertion, he circumstantially alleged certain words and acts, which collectively, if credited, led to presumptions mortally inculpating Budd. And for some of these averments, he added, substantiating proof was not far.

With gray eyes impatient and distrustful essaying to fathom to the bottom Claggart's calm violet ones, Captain Vere again heard him out; then for the moment stood ruminating. The mood he evinced, Claggart — himself for the time liberated from the other's scrutiny — steadily regarded with a look difficult to render, — a look curious of the operation of his tactics, a look such as might have been that of the spokesman of the envious children of Jacob deceptively imposing upon the troubled patriarch the blood-dyed coat of young Joseph.

Though something exceptional in the moral quality of Captain Vere made him, in earnest encounter with a fellow-man, a veritable touch-stone of that man's essential nature, yet now as to Claggart and what was really going on in him his feeling partook less of intuitional conviction than of strong suspicion clogged by strange dubieties. The perplexity he evinced proceeded less from aught touching the man informed against — as Claggart doubtless opined — than from considerations how best to act in regard to the informer. At first indeed he was naturally for summoning that substantiation of his allegations which Claggart said was at hand. But such a proceeding would result in the matter at once getting abroad, which in the present stage of it, he thought, might undesirably affect the ship's company. If Claggart was a false witness, — that closed the affair. And therefore before trying the accusation, he would first practically test the accuser; and he thought this could be done in a quiet undemonstrative way.

The measure he determined upon involved a shifting of the scene, a transfer to a place less exposed to observation than the broad quarter-deck. For although the few gun-room officers there at the time had, in due observance of naval etiquette, withdrawn to leeward the moment Captain Vere had begun his promenade on the deck's weatherside; and though during the colloquy with Claggart they of course ventured not to diminish the distance; and though throughout the interview Captain Vere's voice was far from high, and Claggart's silvery and low; and the wind in the cordage and the wash of the sea helped the more to put them beyond ear-shot; nevertheless, the interview's continuance already had attracted observation from some topmen aloft and other sailors in the waist or further forward.

Having determined upon his measures, Captain Vere forthwith took action. Abruptly turning to Claggart he asked "Master-at-arms, is it now Budd's watch aloft?"

"No, your honor." Whereupon, "Mr. Wilkes!" summoning the nearest midshipman, "tell Albert to come to me." Albert was the Captain's hammock-boy, a sort of sea-valet in whose discretion and fidelity his master had much confidence. The lad appeared. "You know Budd the foretopman?"

"I do, Sir."

"Go find him. It is his watch off. Manage to tell him out of ear-shot that he is wanted aft. Contrive it that he speaks to nobody. Keep him in talk yourself. And not till you get well aft here, not till then let him know that the place where he is wanted is my cabin. You understand. Go. — Master-at-arms, show yourself on the decks below, and when you think it time for Albert to be coming with his man, stand by quietly to follow the sailor in."

XX

Now when the foretopman found himself closeted there, as it were, in the cabin with the Captain and Claggart, he was surprised enough. But it was a surprise unaccompanied by apprehension or distrust. To an immature nature essentially honest and humane, forewarning intimations of subtler danger from one's kind come tardily if at all. The only thing that took shape in the young sailor's mind was this: Yes, the Captain, I have always thought, looks kindly upon me. Wonder if he's going to make me his coxswain. I should like that. And maybe now he is going to ask the master-at-arms about me.

"Shut the door there, sentry," said the commander; "stand without, and let nobody come in. — Now, master-at-arms, tell this man to his face what you told of him to me;" and stood prepared to scrutinize the mutually confronting visages.

With the measured step and calm collected air of an asylum-physician approaching in the public hall some patient beginning to show indications of a coming paroxysm, Claggart deliberately advanced within short range of Billy, and mesmerically looking him in the eye, briefly recapitulated the accusation.

Not at first did Billy take it in. When he did the rose-tan of his cheek looked struck as by white leprosy. He stood like one impaled and gagged. Meanwhile the accuser's eyes removing not as yet from the blue dilated ones, underwent a phenomenal change, their wonted rich violet color blurring into a muddy purple. Those lights of human intelligence losing human expression, gelidly protruding like the alien eyes of certain uncatalogued creatures of the deep. The first mesmeric glance was one of serpent fascination; the last was as the hungry lurch of the torpedo-fish.

"Speak, man!" said Captain Vere to the transfixed one struck by his aspect even more than by Claggart's, "Speak! defend yourself." Which appeal caused but a strange dumb gesturing and gurgling in Billy; amazement at such an accusation so suddenly sprung on inexperienced nonage; this, and, it may be, horror of the accuser, serving to bring out his lurking defect and in this instance for the time intensifying it into a convulsed tongue-tie; while the intent head and entire form straining forward in an agony of ineffectual eagerness to obey the injunction to speak and defend himself, gave an expression to the face like that of a condemned Vestal priestess in the moment of being buried alive, and in the first struggle against suffocation.

Though at the time Captain Vere was quite ignorant of Billy's liability to vocal impediment, he now immediately divined it, since vividly Billy's aspect recalled to him that of a bright young schoolmate of his whom he had once seen struck by much the same startling impotence in the act of eagerly rising in the class to be foremost in response to a testing question put to it by the master. Going close up to the young sailor, and laying a soothing hand on his shoulder, he said: "There is no hurry, my boy. Take your time, take your time." Contrary to the effect intended, these words so fatherly in tone, doubtless touching Billy's heart to the quick, prompted yet more violent efforts at utterance — efforts soon ending for the time in confirming the paralysis, and bringing to his face an expression which was as a crucifixion to behold. The next instant, quick as the flame from a discharged cannon at night, his right arm shot out, and Claggart dropped to the deck. Whether intentionally or but owing to the young athlete's superior height, the blow had taken effect full upon the forehead, so shapely and intellectual-looking a feature in the master-at-arms; so that the body fell over lengthwise, like a heavy plank tilted from erectness. A gasp or two, and he lay motionless.

"Fated boy," breathed Captain Vere in tone so low as to be almost a whisper, "what have you done! But here, help me."

The twain raised the felled one from the loins up into a sitting position. The spare form flexibly acquiesced, but inertly. It was like handling a dead snake. They lowered it back. Regaining erectness Captain Vere with one hand covering his face stood to all appearance as impassive as the object at his feet. Was he absorbed in taking in all the bearings of the event and what was best not only now at once to be done, but also in the sequel? Slowly he uncovered his face; and the effect was as if the moon emerging from eclipse should reappear with quite another aspect than that which had gone into hiding. The father in him, manifested towards Billy thus far in the scene, was replaced by the military disciplinarian. In his official tone he bade the foretopman retire to a state-room aft (pointing it out) and there remain till thence summoned. This order Billy in silence mechanically obeyed. Then going to the cabin-door where it opened on the quarter-deck, Captain Vere said to the sentry without, "Tell somebody to send Albert here." When the lad appeared his master so contrived it that he should not catch sight of the prone one. "Albert," he said to him, "tell the Surgeon I wish to see him. You need not come back till called."

When the Surgeon entered — a self-poised character of that grave sense and experience that hardly anything could take him aback, — Captain Vere advanced to meet him, thus unconsciously intercepting his view of Claggart and interrupting the other's wonted ceremonious salutation, said, "Nay, tell me how it is with yonder man," directing his attention to the prostrate one.

The Surgeon looked, and for all his self-command, somewhat started at the abrupt revelation. On Claggart's always pallid complexion, thick black blood was now oozing from nostril and ear. To the gazer's professional eye it was unmistakably no living man that he saw.

"Is it so then?" said Captain Vere intently watching him. "I thought it. But verify it." Whereupon the customary tests confirmed the Surgeon's first glance, who now looking up in unfeigned concern, cast a look of intense inquisitiveness upon his superior. But Captain Vere, with one hand to his brow was standing motionless. Suddenly, catching the Surgeon's arm convulsively, he exclaimed pointing down to the body — "It is the divine judgment on Ananias! Look!"

Disturbed by the excited manner he had never before observed in the *Indomitable's* Captain, and as yet wholly ignorant of the affair, the prudent Surgeon nevertheless held his peace, only again looking an earnest interrogation as to what it was that had resulted in such a tragedy.

But Captain Vere was now again motionless standing absorbed in thought. But again starting, he vehemently exclaimed — "Struck dead by an angel of God. Yet the angel must hang!"

At these passionate interjections, mere incoherences to the listener as yet unapprised of the antecedent events, the Surgeon was profoundly discomposed. But now as recollecting himself, Captain Vere in less harsh tone briefly related the circumstances leading up to the event.

"But come; we must despatch" he added. "Help me to remove him (meaning the body) to yonder compartment," designating one opposite that where the foretopman remained immured. Anew disturbed by a request that as implying a desire for secrecy, seemed unaccountably strange to him, there was nothing for the subordinate to do but comply.

"Go now" said Captain Vere with something of his wonted manner, "Go now. I shall presently call a drumhead court. Tell the lieutenants what has happened, and tell Mr. Mordant," meaning the captain of marines, "and charge them to keep the matter to themselves."

XXI

Full of disquietude and misgiving the Surgeon left the cabin. Was Captain Vere suddenly affected in his mind, or was it but a transient excitement, brought about by so strange and extraordinary happening? As to the drumhead court, it struck the Surgeon as impolitic, if nothing more. The thing to do, he thought, was to place Billy Budd in confinement, and in a way dictated by usage, and postpone further action in so extraordinary a case to such time as they should rejoin the squadron, and then refer it to the Admiral. He recalled the unwonted agitation of Captain Vere and his excited exclamations so at variance with his normal manner. Was he unhinged? But assuming that he is, it is not so susceptible of proof. What then could he do? No more trying situation is conceivable than that of an officer subordinate under a Captain whom he suspects to be, not mad indeed, but yet not quite unaffected in his intellect. To argue his order to him would be insolence. To resist him would be mutiny. In obedience to Captain Vere he communicated what had happened to the lieutenants and captain of marines; saying nothing as to the Captain's state. They fully shared his own surprise and concern. Like him they seemed to think that such a matter should be referred to the Admiral.

XXII

Who in the rainbow can draw the line where the violet tint ends and the orange tint begins? Distinctly we see the difference of the colors, but where exactly does the one first blendingly enter into the other? So with sanity and insanity. In pronounced cases there is no question about them.

But in some supposed cases, in various degrees supposedly less pronounced, to draw the exact line of demarkation few will undertake though for a fee some professional experts will. There is nothing namable but that some men will undertake to do it for pay.

Whether Captain Vere, as the Surgeon professionally and primarily surmised, was really the sudden victim of any degree of aberration, one must determine for himself by such light as this narrative may afford.

That the unhappy event which has been narrated could not have happened at a worse juncture was but too true. For it was close on the heel of the suppressed insurrections, an after-time very critical to naval authority, demanding from every English sea-commander two qualities not readily interfusable — prudence and rigor. Moreover there was something crucial in the case.

In the jugglery of circumstances preceding and attending the event on board the *Indomitable* and in the light of that martial code whereby it was formally to be judged, innocence and guilt personified in Claggart and Budd — in effect changed places.

In a legal view the apparent victim of the tragedy was he who had sought to victimize a man blameless; and the indisputable deed of the latter, navally regarded, constituted the most heinous of military crimes. Yet more. The essential right and wrong involved in the matter, the clearer that might be, so much the worse for the responsibility of a loyal sea-commander inasmuch as he was not authorized to determine the matter on that primitive basis.

Small wonder then that the *Indomitable's* Captain though in general a man of rapid decision, felt that circumspectness not less than promptitude was necessary. Until he could decide upon his course, and in each detail; and not only so, but until the concluding measure was upon the point of being enacted, he deemed it advisable, in view of all the circumstances to guard as much as possible against publicity. Here he may or may not have erred. Certain it is however that subsequently in the confidential talk of more than one or two gun-rooms and cabins he was not a little criticized by some officers, a fact imputed by his friends, and vehemently by his cousin Jack Denton, to professional jealousy of *Starry Vere*. Some imaginative ground for invidious comment there was. The maintenance of secrecy in the matter, the confining all knowledge of it for a time to the place where the homicide occurred, the quarter-deck cabin; in these particulars lurked some resemblance to the policy adopted in those tragedies of the palace which have occurred more than once in the capital founded by Peter the Barbarian.

The case indeed was such that fain would the *Indomitable's* Captain have deferred taking any action whatever respecting it further than to keep the foretopman a close prisoner till the ship rejoined the squadron and then submitting the matter to the judgment of his Admiral.

But a true military officer is in one particular like a true monk. Not with more of self-abnegation will the latter keep his vows of monastic obedience than the former his vows of allegiance to martial duty.

Feeling that unless quick action were taken on it, the deed of the foretopman, so soon as it should be known on the gun-decks would tend to awaken any slumbering embers of the Nore among the crew, a sense of the urgency of the case overruled in Captain Vere every other consideration. But though a conscientious disciplinarian he was no lover of authority for mere authority's sake. Very far was he from embracing opportunities for monopolizing to himself the perils of moral responsibility none at least that could properly be referred to an official superior or shared with him by his official equals or even subordinates. So thinking he was glad it would not be at variance with usage to turn the matter over to a summary court of his own officers, reserving to himself as the one on whom the ultimate accountability would rest, the right of maintaining a supervision of it, or formally or informally interposing at need. Accordingly a drumhead court was summarily convened, he electing the individuals composing it, the First Lieutenant, the Captain of marines, and the Sailing Master.

In associating an officer of marines with the sea-lieutenants in a case having to do with a sailor the Commander perhaps deviated from general custom. He was prompted thereto by the circumstance that he took that soldier to be a judicious person, thoughtful, and not altogether incapable of grappling with a difficult case unprecedented in his prior experience. Yet even as to him he was not without some latent misgiving, for withal he was an extremely good-natured man, an enjoyer of his dinner, a sound sleeper, and inclined to obesity. A man who though he would always maintain his manhood in battle might not prove altogether reliable in a moral dilemma involving aught of the tragic. As to the First Lieutenant and the Sailing Master Captain Vere could not but be aware that though honest natures, of approved gallantry upon occasion their intelligence was mostly confined to the matter of active seamanship and the fighting demands of their profession. The court was held in the same cabin where the unfortunate affair had taken place. This cabin, the Commander's, embraced the entire area under the poop-deck. Aft, and on either side was a small state-room the one room temporarily a jail and the other a dead-house and a yet smaller compartment leaving a space between, expanding forward into a goodly oblong of length coinciding with the ship's beam. A sky-light of moderate dimension was overhead and at each end of the oblong space were two sashed port-hole windows easily convertible back into embrasures for short carronades.

All being quickly in readiness, Billy Budd was arraigned, Captain Vere necessarily appearing as the sole witness in the case, and as such temporarily sinking his rank, though singularly maintaining it in a matter apparently trivial, namely, that he testified from the ship's weather-side with that object having caused the court to sit on the lee-side. Concisely he narrated all that had led up to the catastrophe, omitting nothing in Claggart's accusation and deposing as to the manner in which the prisoner had received it. At this testimony the three officers glanced with no little surprise at Billy Budd, the last man they would have suspected either of the mutinous design alleged by Claggart or the undeniable deed he himself had done. The First Lieutenant, taking judicial primacy and turning toward the prisoner, said, "Captain Vere has spoken. Is it or is it not as Captain Vere says?" In response came syllables not so much impeded in the utterance as might have been anticipated. They were these: "Captain Vere tells the truth. It is just as Captain Vere says, but it is not as the Master-at-Arms said. I have eaten the King's bread and I am true to the King."

"I believe you, my man," said the witness his voice indicating a suppressed emotion not otherwise betrayed.

"God will bless you for that, Your Honor!" not without stammering said Billy, and all but broke down. But immediately was recalled to self-control by another question, to which with the same emotional difficulty of utterance he said "No, there was no malice between us. I never bore malice against the Master-at-arms. I am sorry that he is dead. I did not mean to kill him. Could I have used my tongue I would not have struck him. But he foully lied to my face and in presence of my Captain, and I had to say something, and I could only say it with a blow, God help me!"

In the impulsive above-board manner of the frank one the court saw confirmed all that was implied in words that just previously had perplexed them coming as they did from the testifier to the tragedy and promptly following Billy's impassioned disclaimer of mutinous intent — Captain Vere's words, "I believe you, my man."

Next it was asked of him whether he knew of or suspected aught savoring of incipient trouble (meaning mutiny, though the explicit term was avoided) going on in any section of the ship's company.

The reply lingered. This was naturally imputed by the court to the same vocal embarrassment which had retarded or obstructed previous answers. But in main it was otherwise here; the question immediately recalling to Billy's mind the interview with the afterguardsman in the fore-chains. But an innate repugnance to playing a part at all approaching that of an informer against one's own shipmates — the same erring sense of uninstructed honor which had stood in the way of his reporting the matter at the time though as a loyal man-of-war-man it was incumbent on him and failure so to do if charged against him and proven, would have subjected him to the heaviest of penalties; this, with the blind feeling now his, that nothing really was being hatched, prevailed with him. When the answer came it was a negative.

"One question more," said the officer of marines now first speaking and with a troubled earnestness, "You tell us that what the Master-at-arms said against you was a lie. Now why should he was non-plussed, evincing a confusion indeed clare there was no malice between you?"

At that question unintentionally touching on a spiritual sphere wholly obscure to Billy's thoughts, he was nonplussed, evincing a confusion indeed that some observers, such as can readily be imagined, would have constructed into involuntary evidence of hidden guilt. Nevertheless he strove some way to answer, but all at once relinquished the vain endeavor, at the same time turning an appealing glance towards Captain Vere as deeming him his best helper and friend. Captain Vere who had been seated for a time, rose to his feet, addressing the interrogator. "The question you put to him comes naturally enough. But how can he rightly answer it? or anybody else? unless indeed it be he who lies within there" designating the compartment where lay the corpse. "But the prone one there will not rise to our summons. In effect though, as it seems to me, the point you make is hardly material. Quite aside from any conceivable motive actuating the Master-at-arms, and irrespective of the provocation to the blow, a martial court must needs in the present case confine its attention to the blow's consequence, which consequence justly is to be deemed not otherwise than as the striker's deed."

This utterance the full significance of which it was not at all likely that Billy took in, nevertheless caused him to turn a wistful interrogative look toward the speaker, a look in its dumb expressiveness not unlike that which a dog of generous breed might turn upon his master seeking in his face some elucidation of a previous gesture ambiguous to the canine intelligence. Nor was the same utterance without marked effect upon the three officers, more especially the soldier. Couched in it seemed to them a meaning unanticipated, involving a prejudgment on the speaker's part. It served to augment a mental disturbance previously evident enough.

The soldier once more spoke; in a tone of suggestive dubiety addressing at once his associates and Captain Vere: "Nobody is present — none of the ship's company, I mean, who might shed lateral light, if any is to be had, upon what remains mysterious in this matter."

"That is thoughtfully put" said Captain Vere; "I see your drift. Ay, there is a mystery; but to use a Scriptural phrase, it is 'a mystery of iniquity,' a matter for psychologic theologians to discuss. But what has a military court to do with it? Not to add that for us any possible investigation of it is cut off by the lasting tongue-tie of — him — in yonder," again designating the mortuary state-room. "The prisoner's deed, — with that alone we have to do."

To this, and particularly the closing reiteration, the marine soldier knowing not how aptly to reply, sadly abstained from saying aught. The First Lieutenant who at the outset had not unnaturally assumed primacy in the court, now overrulingly instructed by a glance from Captain Vere, a glance more effective than words, resumed that primacy. Turning to the prisoner, "Budd," he said, and scarce in equable tones, "Budd, if you have aught further to say for yourself, say it now."

Upon this the young sailor turned another quick glance toward Captain Vere; then, as taking a hint from that aspect, a hint confirming his own instinct that silence was now best, replied to the Lieutenant, "I have said all, Sir."

The marine — the same who had been the sentinel without the cabin-door at the time that the foretopman followed by the master-at-arms, entered it — he, standing by the sailor throughout these judicial proceedings, was now directed to take him back to the after compartment originally assigned to the prisoner and his custodian. As the twain disappeared from view, the three officers as partially liberated from some inward constraint associated with Billy's mere presence, simultaneously stirred in their seats. They exchanged looks of troubled indecision, yet feeling that decide they must and without long delay. For Captain Vere was for the time standing unconsciously with his back toward them, apparently in one of his absent fits, gazing out from a sashed port-hole to windward upon the monotonous blank of the twilight sea. But the court's silence continuing, broken only at moments by brief consultations in low earnest tones, this seemed to assure him and encourage him. Turning, he to-and-fro paced the cabin athwart; in the returning ascent to windward, climbing the slant deck in the ship's lee roll; without knowing it symbolizing thus in his action a mind resolute to surmount difficulties even if against primitive instincts strong as the wind and the sea. Presently he came to a stand before the three. After scanning their faces he stood less as mustering his thoughts for expression, than as one inly deliberating how best to put them to well-meaning men not intellectually mature, men with whom it was necessary to demonstrate certain principles that were axioms to himself. Similar impatience as to talking is perhaps one reason that deters some minds from addressing any popular assemblies.

When speak he did, something both in the substance of what he said and his manner of saying it, showed the influence of unshared studies modifying and tempering the practical training of an active career. This, along with his phraseology now and then was suggestive of the grounds whereon rested that imputation of a certain pedantry socially alleged against him by certain naval men of wholly practical cast, captains who nevertheless would frankly concede that His Majesty's navy mustered no more efficient officer of their grade than *'Starry Vere.'*

What he said was to this effect: "Hitherto I have been but the witness, little more; and I should hardly think now to take another tone, that of your coadjutor, for the time, did I not perceive in you — at the crisis too — a troubled hesitancy, proceeding, I doubt not from the clash of military duty with moral scruple — scruple vitalized by compassion. For the compassion how can I otherwise than share it. But, mindful of paramount obligations I strive against scruples that may tend to enervate decision. Not, gentlemen, that I hide from myself that the case is an exceptional one. Speculatively regarded, it well might be referred to a jury of casuists. But for us here acting not as casuists or moralists, it is a case practical, and under martial law practically to be dealt with.

"But your scruples: do they move as in a dusk? Challenge them. Make them advance and declare themselves. Come now: do they import something like this: If, mindless of palliating circumstances we are bound to regard the death of the Master-at-arms as the prisoner's deed, then does that deed constitute a capital crime whereof the penalty is a mortal one. But in natural justice is nothing but the prisoner's overt act to be considered? How can we adjudge to summary and shameful death a fellow-creature innocent before God, and whom we feel to be so? — Does that state it aright? You sign sad assent. Well, I too feel that, the full force of that. It is Nature. But do these buttons that we wear attest that our allegiance is to Nature? No, to the King. Though the ocean, which is inviolate Nature primeval, though this be the element where we move and have our being as sailors, yet as the King's officers lies our duty in a sphere correspondingly natural? So little is that true, that in receiving our commissions we in the most important regards ceased to be natural free-agents. When war is declared, are we the commissioned fighters previously consulted? We fight at command. If our judgments approve the war, that is but coincidence. So in other particulars. So now. For suppose condemnation to follow these present proceedings. Would it be so much we ourselves that would condemn as it would be martial law operating through us? For that law and the rigor of it, we are not responsible. Our vowed responsibility is in this: That however pitilessly that law may operate, we nevertheless adhere to it and administer it.

"But the exceptional in the matter moves the hearts within you. Even so too is mine moved. But let not warm hearts betray heads that should be cool. Ashore in a criminal case will an upright judge allow himself off the bench to be waylaid by some tender kinswoman of the accused seeking to touch him with her tearful plea? Well the heart sometimes the feminine in man, here is as that piteous woman. And hard though it be, she must here be ruled out."

He paused, earnestly studying them for a moment, then resumed.

"But something in your aspect seems to urge that it is not solely the heart that moves in you, but also the conscience, the private conscience. But tell me whether or not, occupying the position we do, private conscience should not yield to that imperial one formulated in the code under which alone we officially proceed?"

Here the three men moved in their seats, less convinced than agitated by the course of an argument troubling but the more the spontaneous conflict within.

Perceiving which, the speaker paused for a moment; then abruptly changing his tone, went on.

"To steady us a bit, let us recur to the facts. — In war-time at sea a man-of-war's-man strikes his superior in grade, and the blow kills. Apart from its effect the blow itself is, according to the Articles of War, a capital crime. Furthermore — "

"Ay, Sir," emotionally broke in the officer of marines, "in one sense it was. But surely Budd purposed neither mutiny nor homicide."

"Surely not, my good man. And before a court less arbitrary and more merciful than a martial one that plea would largely extenuate. At the Last Assizes it shall acquit. But how here? We proceed under the law of the Mutiny Act. In feature no child can resemble his father more than that Act resembles in spirit the thing from which it derives — War. In His Majesty's service — in this ship indeed — there are Englishmen forced to fight for the King against their will. Against their conscience, for aught we know. Though as their fellow-creatures some of us may appreciate their position, yet as Navy Officers, what reck we of it? Still less recks the enemy. Our impressed men he would fain cut down in the same swath with our volunteers. As regards the enemy's naval conscripts, some of whom may even share our own abhorrence of the regicidal French Directory, it is the same on our side. War looks but to the frontage, the appearance. And the Mutiny Act, War's child, takes after the father. Budd's intent or non-intent is nothing to the purpose.

"But while, put to it by those anxieties in you which I can not but respect, I only repeat myself — while thus strangely we prolong proceedings that should be summary — the enemy may be sighted and an engagement result. We must do; and one of two things must we do — condemn or let go."

"Can we not convict and yet mitigate the penalty?" asked the junior Lieutenant here speaking, and falteringly, for the first.

"Lieutenant, were that clearly lawful for us under the circumstances consider the consequence of such clemency. The people" (meaning the ship's company) "have native sense; most of them are familiar with our naval usage and tradition; and how would they take it? Even could you explain to them — which our official position forbids — they, long moulded by arbitrary discipline have not that kind of intelligent responsiveness that might qualify them to comprehend and discriminate. No, to the people the foretopman's deed however it be worded in the announcement will be plain homicide committed in a flagrant act of mutiny. What penalty for that should follow, they know. But it does not follow. *Why?* They will ruminate. You know what sailors are. Will they not revert to the recent outbreak at the Nore? Ay. They know the well-founded alarm — the panic it struck through England. Your clement sentence they would account pusillanimous. They would think that we flinch, that we are afraid of them — afraid of practicing a lawful rigor singularly demanded at this juncture lest it should provoke new troubles. What shame to us such a conjecture on their part, and how deadly to discipline. You see then, whither prompted by duty and the law I steadfastly drive. But I beseech you, my friends, do not take me amiss. I feel as you do for this unfortunate boy. But did he know our hearts, I take him to be of that generous nature that he would feel even for us on whom in this military necessity so heavy a compulsion is laid."

With that, crossing the deck he resumed his place by the sashed port-hole, tacitly leaving the three to come to a decision. On the cabin's opposite side the troubled court sat silent. Loyal lieges, plain and practical, though at bottom they dissented from some points Captain Vere had put to them, they were without the faculty, hardly had the inclination to gainsay one whom they felt to be an earnest man, one too not less their superior in mind than in naval rank. But it is not improbable that even such of his words as were not without influence over them, less came home to them than his closing appeal to their instinct as sea-officers in the forethought he threw out as to the practical consequences to discipline, considering the unconfirmed tone of the fleet at the time, should a man-of-war's-man's violent killing at sea of a superior in grade be allowed to pass for aught else than a capital crime demanding prompt infliction of the penalty.

Not unlikely they were brought to something more or less akin to that harassed frame of mind which in the year 1842 actuated the commander of the U.S. brig-of-war *Somers* to resolve, under the so-called Articles of War, Articles modelled upon the English Mutiny Act, to resolve upon the execution at sea of a midshipman and two petty-officers as mutineers designing the seizure of the brig. Which resolution was carried out though in a time of peace and within not many days sail of home. An act vindicated by a naval court of inquiry subsequently convened ashore. History, and here cited without comment. True, the circumstances on board the *Somers* were different from those on board the *Indomitable*. But the urgency felt, well-warranted or otherwise, was much the same.

Says a writer whom few know, "Forty years after a battle it is easy for a non-combatant to reason about how it ought to have been fought. It is another thing personally and under fire to direct the fighting while involved in the obscuring smoke of it. Much so with respect to other emergencies involving considerations both practical and moral, and when it is imperative promptly to act. The greater the fog the more it imperils the steamer, and speed is put on though at the hazard of running somebody down. Little ween the snug card-players in the cabin of the responsibilities of the sleepless man on the bridge."

In brief, Billy Budd was formally convicted and sentenced to be hung at the yard-arm in the early morning watch, it being now night. Otherwise, as is customary in such cases, the sentence would forthwith have been carried out. In war-time on the field or in the fleet, a mortal punishment decreed by a drumhead court — on the field sometimes decreed by but a nod from the General — follows without delay on the heel of conviction without appeal.

XXIII

It was Captain Vere himself who of his own motion communicated the finding of the court to the prisoner; for that purpose going to the compartment where he was in custody and bidding the marine there to withdraw for the time.

Beyond the communication of the sentence what took place at this interview was never known. But in view of the character of the twain briefly closeted in that state-room, each radically sharing in the rarer qualities of our nature — so rare indeed as to be all but incredible to average minds however much cultivated — some conjectures may be ventured.

It would have been in consonance with the spirit of Captain Vere should he on this occasion have concealed nothing from the condemned one — should he indeed have frankly disclosed to him the part he himself had played in bringing about the decision, at the same time revealing his actuating motives. On Billy's side it is not improbable that such a confession would have been received in much the same spirit that prompted it. Not without a sort of joy indeed he might have appreciated the brave opinion of him implied in his Captain making such a confidant of him. Nor, as to the sentence itself could he have been insensible that it was imparted to him as to one not afraid to die. Even more may have been. Captain Vere in the end may have developed the passion sometimes latent under an exterior stoical or indifferent. He was old enough to have been Billy's father. The austere devotee of military duty letting himself melt back into what remains primeval in our formalized humanity may in the end have caught Billy to his heart even as Abraham may have caught young Isaac on the brink of resolutely offering him up in obedience to the exacting behest. But there is no telling the sacrament, seldom if in any case revealed to the gadding world wherever under circumstances at all akin to those here attempted to be set forth two of great Nature's nobler order embrace. There is privacy at the time, inviolable to the survivor, and holy oblivion the sequel to each diviner magnanimity, providentially covers all at last.

The first to encounter Captain Vere in act of leaving the compartment was the senior Lieutenant. The face he beheld, for the moment one expressive of the agony of the strong, was to that officer, though a man of fifty, a startling revelation. That the condemned one suffered less than he who mainly had effected the condemnation was apparently indicated by the former's exclamation in the scene soon perforce to be touched upon.

XXIV

Of a series of incidents within a brief term rapidly following each other, the adequate narration may take up a term less brief, especially if explanation or comment here and there seem requisite to the better understanding of such incidents. Between the entrance into the cabin of him who never left it alive, and him who when he did leave it left it as one condemned to die; between this and the closeted interview just given less than an hour and a half had elapsed. It was an interval long enough however to awaken speculations among no few of the ship's company as to what it was that could be detaining in the cabin the master-at-arms and the sailor; for a rumor that both of them had been seen to enter it and neither of them had been seen to emerge, this rumor had got abroad upon the gun-decks and in the tops; the people of a great warship being in one respect like villagers, taking microscopic note of every outward movement or non-movement going on. When therefore in weather not at all tempestuous all hands were called in the second dog-watch, a summons under such circumstances not usual in those hours, the crew were not wholly unprepared for some announcement extraordinary, one having connection too with the continued absence of the two men from their wonted haunts.

There was a moderate sea at the time; and the moon, newly risen and near to being at its full, silvered the white spar-deck wherever not blotted by the clear-cut shadows horizontally thrown of fixtures and moving men. On either side the quarter-deck the marine guard under arms was drawn up; and Captain Vere standing in his place surrounded by all the ward-room officers, addressed his men. In so doing his manner showed neither more nor less than that properly pertaining to his supreme position aboard his own ship. In clear terms and concise he told them what had taken place in the cabin; that the master-at-arms was dead; that he who had killed him had been already tried by a summary court and condemned to death; and that the execution would take place in the early morning watch. The word *mutiny* was not named in what he said. He refrained too from making the occasion an opportunity for any preachment as to the maintenance of discipline, thinking perhaps that under existing circumstances in the navy the consequence of violating discipline should be made to speak for itself.

Their Captain's announcement was listened to by the throng of standing sailors in a dumbness like that of a seated congregation of believers in hell listening to the clergyman's announcement in his Calvinistic text.

At the close, however, a confused murmur went up. It began to wax. All but instantly, then, at a sign, it was pierced and suppressed by shrill whistles of the Boatswain and his mates piping down one watch.

To be prepared for burial Claggart's body was delivered to certain petty-officers of his mess. And here, not to clog the sequel with lateral matters, it may be added that at a suitable hour, the Master-at-arms was committed to the sea with every funeral honor properly belonging to his naval grade.

In this proceeding as in every public one growing out of the tragedy strict adherence to usage was observed. Nor in any point could it have been at all deviated from either with respect to Claggart or Billy Budd without begetting undesirable speculations in the ship's company, sailors, and more particularly men-of-war's men, being of all men the greatest sticklers for usage.

For similar cause all communication between Captain Vere and the condemned one ended with the closeted interview already given, the latter being now surrendered to the ordinary routine preliminary to the end. This transfer under guard from the Captain's quarters was effected without unusual precautions — at least no visible ones.

If possible not to let the men so much as surmise that their officers anticipate aught amiss from them is the tacit rule in a military ship. And the more that some sort of trouble should really be apprehended the more do the officers keep that apprehension to themselves; though not the less unostentatious vigilance may be augmented.

In the present instance the sentry placed over the prisoner had strict orders to let no one have communication with him but the Chaplain. And certain unobtrusive measures were taken absolutely to insure this point.

XXV

In a seventy-four of the old order the deck known as the upper gun-deck was the one covered over by the spar-deck which last though not without its armament was for the most part exposed to the weather. In general it was at all hours free from hammocks; those of the crew swinging on the lower gun-deck, and berth-deck, the latter being not only a dormitory but also the place for the stowing of the sailors' bags, and on both sides lined with the large chests or movable pantries of the many messes of the men.

On the starboard side of the *Indomitable's* upper gundeck, behold Billy Budd under sentry lying prone in irons in one of the bays formed by the regular spacing of the guns comprising the batteries on either side. All these pieces were of the heavier caliber of that period. Mounted on lumbering wooden carriages they were hampered with cumbersome harness of breeching and strong side-tackles for running them out. Guns and carriages, together with the long rammers and shorter lintstocks lodged in loops overhead — all these, as customary, were painted black; and the heavy hempen breechings tarred to the same tint, wore the like livery of the undertakers. In contrast with the funereal tone of these surroundings the prone sailor's exterior apparel, white *jumper* and white duck trousers, each more or less soiled, dimly glimmered in the obscure light of the bay like a patch of discolored snow in early April lingering at some upland cave's black mouth. In effect he is already in his shroud or the garments that shall serve him in lieu of one. Over him but scarce illuminating him, two battle-lanterns swing from two massive beams of the deck above. Fed with the oil supplied by the war-contractors (whose gains, honest or otherwise, are in every land an anticipated portion of the harvest of death) with flickering splashes of dirty yellow light they pollute the pale moonshine all but ineffectually struggling in obstructed flecks through the open ports from which the tompioned cannon protrude. Other lanterns at intervals serve but to bring out somewhat the obscurer bays which like small confessionals or side-chapels in a cathedral branch from the long dim-vistaed broad aisle between the two batteries of that covered tier.

Such was the deck where now lay the Handsome Sailor. Through the rose-tan of his complexion, no pallor could have shown. It would have taken days of sequestration from the winds and the sun to have brought about the effacement of that. But the skeleton in the cheek-bone at the point of its angle was just beginning delicately to be defined under the warm-tinted skin. In fervid hearts self-contained some brief experiences devour our human tissue as secret fire in a ship's hold consumes cotton in the bale.

But now lying between the two guns, as nipped in the vice of fate, Billy's agony, mainly proceeding from a generous young heart's virgin experience of the diabolical incarnate and effective in some men — the tension of that agony was over now. It survived not the something healing in the closeted interview with Captain Vere. Without movement, he lay as in a trance. That adolescent expression previously noted as his, taking on somewhat akin to the look of a slumbering child in the cradle when the warm hearth-glow of the still chamber at night plays on the dimples that at whiles mysteriously form in the cheek, silently coming and going there. For now and then in the gyved one's trance a serene happy light born of some wandering reminiscence or dream would diffuse itself over his face, and then wane away only anew to return.

The Chaplain coming to see him and finding him thus, and perceiving no sign that he was conscious of his presence, attentively regarded him for a space, then slipping aside, withdrew for the time, peradventure feeling that even he the minister of Christ though receiving his stipend from Mars had no consolation to proffer which could result in a peace transcending that which he beheld. But in the small hours he came again. And the prisoner now awake to his surroundings noticed his approach and civilly, all but cheerfully, welcomed him. But it was to little purpose that in the interview following the good man sought to bring Billy Budd to some Godly understanding that he must die, and at dawn. True, Billy himself freely referred to his death as a thing close at hand; but it was something in the way that children will refer to death in general, who yet among their other sports will play a funeral with hearse and mourners.

Not that like children Billy was incapable of conceiving what death really is. No, but he was wholly without irrational fear of it, a fear more prevalent in highly civilized communities than those so-called barbarous ones which in all respects stand nearer to unadulterate Nature. And, as elsewhere said, a barbarian Billy radically was; as much so, for all the costume, as his countrymen the British captives, living trophies, made to march in the Roman triumph of Germanicus. Quite as much so as those later barbarians, young men probably, and picked specimens among the earlier British converts to Christianity, at least nominally such and taken to Rome (as today converts from lesser isles of the sea may be taken to London) of whom the Pope of that time, admiring the strangeness of their personal beauty so unlike the Italian stamp, their clear ruddy complexion and curled flaxen locks, exclaimed, "Angles" (meaning *English* the modern derivative) "Angles do you call them? And is it because they look so like angels?" Had it been later in time one would think that the Pope had in mind Fra Angelico's seraphs some of whom, plucking apples in gardens of the Hesperides have the faint rosebud complexion of the more beautiful English girls.

If in vain the good Chaplain sought to impress the young barbarian with ideas of death akin to those conveyed in the skull, dial and cross-bones on old tombstones; equally futile to all appearance were his efforts to bring home to him the thought of salvation and a Saviour. Billy listened, but less out of awe or reverence perhaps than from a certain natural politeness; doubtless at bottom regarding all that in much the same way that most mariners of his class take any discourse abstract or out of the common tone of the work-a-day world. And this sailor way of taking clerical discourse is not wholly unlike the way in which the pioneer of Christianity full of transcendent miracles was received long ago on tropic isles by any superior *savage* so called — a Tahitian say of Captain Cook's time or shortly after that time. Out of natural courtesy he received but did not appropriate. It was like a gift placed in the palm of an outstretched hand upon which the fingers do not close.

But the *Indomitable's* Chaplain was a discreet man possessing the good sense of a good heart. So he insisted not in his vocation here. At the instance of Captain Vere, a lieutenant had apprised him of pretty much everything as to Billy; and since he felt that innocence was even a better thing than religion wherewith to go to Judgement, he reluctantly withdrew; but in his emotion not without first performing an act strange enough in an Englishman, and under the circumstances yet more so in any regular priest. Stooping over, he kissed on the fair cheek his fellow-man, a felon in martial law, one who though on the confines of death he felt he could never convert to a dogma; nor for all that did he fear for his future.

Marvel not that having been made acquainted with the young sailor's essential innocence (an irruption of heretic thought hard to suppress) the worthy man lifted not a finger to avert the doom of such a martyr to martial discipline. So to do would not only have been as idle as invoking the desert, but would also have been an audacious transgression of the bounds of his function, one as exactly prescribed to him by military law as that of the boatswain or any other naval officer. Bluntly put, a chaplain is the minister of the Prince of Peace serving in the host of the God of War — Mars. As such, he is as incongruous as that musket of Blücher etc. at Christmas. Why then is he there? Because he indirectly subserves the purpose attested by the cannon; because too he lends the sanction of the religion of the meek to that which practically is the abrogation of everything but brute Force.

XXVI

The night so luminous on the spar-deck but otherwise on the cavernous ones below, levels so like the tiered galleries in a coal-mine — the luminous night passed away. But, like the prophet in the chariot disappearing in heaven and dropping his mantle to Elisha, the withdrawing night transferred its pale robe to the breaking day. A meek shy light appeared in the East, where stretched a diaphanous fleece of white furrowed vapor. That light slowly waxed. Suddenly *eight bells* was struck aft, responded to by one louder metallic stroke from forward. It was four o'clock in the morning. Instantly the silver whistles were heard summoning all hands to witness punishment. Up through the great hatchways rimmed with racks of heavy shot, the watch below came pouring overspreading with the watch already on deck the space between the mainmast and foremast including that occupied by the capacious *launch* and the black booms tiered on either side of it, boat and booms making a summit of observation for the powder-boys and younger tars. A different group comprising one watch of topmen leaned over the rail of that sea-balcony, no small one in a seventy-four, looking down on the crowd below. Man or boy none spake but in whisper, and few spake at all. Captain Vere — as before, the central figure among the assembled commissioned officers — stood nigh the break of the poop-deck facing forward. Just below him on the quarter-deck the marines in full equipment were drawn up much as at the scene of the promulgated sentence.

At sea in the old time, the execution by halter of a military sailor was generally from the fore-yard. In the present instance for special reasons the main-yard was assigned. Under an arm of that weather or lee(?) yard the prisoner was presently brought up, the Chaplain attending him. It was noted at the time and remarked upon afterwards, that in this final scene the good man evinced little or nothing of the perfunctory. Brief speech indeed he had with the condemned one, but the genuine Gospel was less on his tongue than in his aspect and manner towards him. The final preparations personal to the latter being speedily brought to an end by two boatswain's-mates, the consummation impended. Billy stood facing aft. At the penultimate moment, his words, his only ones, words wholly unobstructed in the utterance were these — "God bless Captain Vere!" Syllables so unanticipated coming from one with the ignominious hemp about his neck — a conventional felon's benediction directed aft towards the quarters of honor; syllables too delivered in the clear melody of a singing-bird on the point of launching from the twig, had a phenomenal effect, not unenhanced by the rare personal beauty of the young sailor spiritualized now through late experiences so poignantly profound.

Without volition as it were, as if indeed the ship's populace were but the vehicles of some vocal current electric, with one voice from alow and aloft, came a resonant sympathetic echo — "God bless Captain Vere!" And yet at that instant Billy alone must have been in their hearts, even as he was in their eyes.

At the pronounced words and the spontaneous echo that voluminously rebounded them, Captain Vere, either through stoic self-control or a sort of momentary paralysis induced by emotional shock, stood erectly rigid as a musket in the ship-armorer's rack.

The hull deliberately recovering from the periodic roll to leeward was just regaining an even keel, when the last signal a preconcerted dumb one was given. At the same moment it chanced that the vapory fleece hanging low in the East, was shot through with a soft glory as of the fleece of the Lamb of God seen in mystical vision and simultaneously therewith, watched by the wedged mass of upturned faces, Billy ascended; and, ascending, took the full rose of the dawn.

In the pinioned figure, arrived at the yard-end, to the wonder of all no motion was apparent save that created by the ship's motion, in moderate weather so majestic in a great ship ponderously cannoned.

End of Chapter

XXVII
A DIGRESSION

When some days afterwards in reference to the singularity just mentioned, the Purser a rather ruddy rotund person more accurate as an accountant than profound as a philosopher said at mess to the Surgeon, "What testimony to the force lodged in will-power" the latter — saturnine spare and tall, one in whom a discreet causticity went along with a manner less genial than polite, replied, "Your pardon, Mr. Purser. In a hanging scientifically conducted — and under special orders I myself directed how Budd's was to be effected — any movement following the completed suspension and originating in the body suspended, such movement indicates mechanical spasm in the muscular system. Hence the absence of that is no more attributable to will-power as you call it than to horsepower — begging your pardon."

"But this muscular spasm you speak of, is not that in a degree more or less invariable in these cases?"

"Assuredly so, Mr. Purser."

"How then, my good Sir, do you account for its absence in this instance?"

"Mr. Purser, it is clear that your sense of the singularity in this matter equals not mine. You account for it by what you call will-power a term not yet included in the lexicon of science. For me I do not, with my present knowledge pretend to account for it at all. Even should one assume the hypothesis that at the first touch of the halyards the action of Budd's heart, intensified by extraordinary emotion at its climax, abruptly stopped — much like a watch when in carelessly winding it up you strain at the finish, thus snapping the chain — even under that hypothesis how account for the phenomenon that followed?"

"You admit then that the absence of spasmodic movement was phenomenal."

"It was phenomenal, Mr. Purser, in the sense that it was an appearance the cause of which is not immediately to be assigned."

"But tell me, my dear Sir," pertinaciously continued the other, "was the man's death effected by the halter, or was it a species of euthanasia?"

"*Euthanasia*, Mr. Purser, is something like your *will-power*; I doubt its authenticity as a scientific term — begging your pardon again. It is at once imaginative and metaphysical, — in short, Greek. But" abruptly changing his tone, "there is a case in the sick-bay that I do not care to leave to my assistants. Beg your pardon, but excuse me." And rising from the mess he formally withdrew.

XXVIII

The silence at the moment of execution and for a moment or two continuing thereafter, a silence but emphasized by the regular wash of the sea against the hull or the flutter of a sail caused by the helmsman's eyes being tempted astray, this emphasized silence was gradually disturbed by a sound not easily to be verbally rendered. Whoever has heard the freshet-wave of a torrent suddenly swelled by pouring showers in tropical mountains, showers not shared by the plain; whoever has heard the first muffled murmur of its sloping advance through precipitous woods, may form some conception of the sound now heard. The seeming remoteness of its source was because of its murmurous indistinctness since it came from close by, even from the men massed on the ship's open deck. Being inarticulate, it was dubious in significance further than it seemed to indicate some capricious revulsion of thought or feeling such as mobs ashore are liable to, in the present instance possibly implying a sullen revocation on the men's part of their involuntary echoing of Billy's benediction. But ere the murmur had time to wax into clamor it was met by a strategic command, the more telling that it came with abrupt unexpectedness.

"Pipe down the starboard watch Boatswain, and see that they go."

Shrill as the shriek of the sea-hawk the whistles of the Boatswain and his Mates pierced that ominous low sound, dissipating it; and yielding to the mechanism of discipline the throng was thinned by one half. For the remainder most of them were set to temporary employments connected with trimming the yards and so forth, business readily to be got up to serve occasion by any officer-of-the-deck.

Now each proceeding that follows a mortal sentence pronounced at sea by a drum-head court is characterized by promptitude not perceptibly merging into hurry, though bordering that. The hammock, the one which had been Billy's bed when alive, having already been ballasted with shot and otherwise prepared to serve for his canvas coffin, the last office of the sea-undertakers, the Sail-Maker's Mates, were now speedily completed. When everything was in readiness a second call for all hands made necessary by the strategic movement before mentioned was sounded and now to witness burial.

The details of this closing formality it needs not to give. But when the tilted plank let slide its freight into the sea, a second strange human murmur was heard, blended now with another inarticulate sound proceeding from certain larger sea-fowl whose attention having been attracted by the peculiar commotion in the water resulting from the heavy sloped dive of the shotted hammock into the sea flew screaming to the spot. So near the hull did they come, that the stridor or bony creak of their gaunt double-jointed pinions was audible. As the ship under light airs passed on, leaving the burial spot astern, they still kept circling it low down with the moving shadow of their outstretched wings and the croaked requiem of their cries.

Upon sailors as superstitious as those of the age preceding ours, men-of-war's men too who had just beheld the prodigy of repose in the form suspended in air and now foundering in the deeps; to such mariners the action of the sea-fowl though dictated by mere animal greed for prey, was big with no prosaic significance. An uncertain movement began among them, in which some encroachment was made. It was tolerated but for a moment. For suddenly the drum beat to quarters, which familiar sound happening at least twice every day, had upon the present occasion some signal peremptoriness in it. True martial discipline long continued superinduces in average man a sort of impulse of docility whose operation at the official sound of command much resembles in its promptitude the effect of an instinct.

The drum-beat dissolved the multitude, distributing most of them along the batteries of the two covered gun-decks. There, as wont, the guns' crews stood by their respective cannon erect and silent. In due course the First Officer, sword under arm and standing in his place on the quarter-deck formally received the successive reports of the sworded Lieutenants commanding the sections of batteries below; the last of which reports being made the summed report he delivered with the customary salute to the Commander. All this occupied time, which, in the present case, was the object of beating to quarters at an hour prior to the customary one. That such variance from usage was authorized by an officer like Captain Vere, a martinet as some deemed him, was evidence of the necessity for unusual action implied in what he deemed to be temporarily the mood of his men. "With mankind" he would say "forms, measured forms are everything; and that is the import couched in the story of Orpheus with his lyre spell-binding the wild denizens of the wood." And this he once applied to the disruption of forms going on across the Channel and the consequences thereof.

At this unwonted muster at quarters, all proceeded as at the regular hour. The band on the quarter-deck played a sacred air. After which the Chaplain went through with the customary morning service. That done, the drum beat the retreat, and toned by music and religious rites subserving the discipline and purpose of war, the men in their wonted orderly manner dispersed to the places allotted them when not at the guns.

And now it was full day. The fleece of low-hanging vapor had vanished, licked up by the sun that late had so glorified it. And the circumambient air in the clearness of its serenity was like smooth white marble in the polished block not yet removed from the marble-dealer's yard.

XXIX

The symmetry of form attainable in pure fiction can not so readily be achieved in a narration essentially having less to do with fable than with fact. Truth uncompromisingly told will always have its ragged edges; hence the conclusion of such a narration is apt to be less finished than an architectural finial.

How it fared with the Handsome Sailor during the year of the great mutiny has been faithfully given. But though properly the story ends with his life something in way of sequel will not be amiss. Three brief chapters will suffice.

In the general re-christening under the Directory of the craft originally forming the navy of the French Monarchy, the *St. Louis* line-of-battle ship was named the *Athéiste*. Such a name, like some other substituted ones in the Revolutionary fleet while proclaiming the infidel audacity of the ruling power was yet, though not so intended to be, the aptest name, if one consider it, ever given to a warship; far more so indeed that the *Devastation*, the *Erebus* (the *Hell*) and similar names bestowed upon fighting-ships.

On the return-passage to the English fleet from the detached cruise during which occurred the events already recorded, the *Indomitable* fell in with the *Athéiste*. An engagement ensued; during which Captain Vere in the act of putting his ship alongside the enemy with a view of throwing his boarders across her bulwarks, was hit by a musket-ball from a port-hole of the enemy's main cabin. More than disabled he dropped to the deck and was carried below to the same cock-pit where some of his men already lay. The senior Lieutenant took command. Under him the enemy was finally captured and though much crippled was by rare good fortune successfully taken into Gibraltar, an English port not very distant from the scene of the fight. There, Captain Vere with the rest of the wounded was put ashore. He lingered for some days, but the end came. Unhappily he was cut off too early for the Nile and Trafalgar. The spirit that spite its philosophic austerity may yet have indulged in the most secret of all passions, ambition, never attained to the fullness of fame.

Not long before death while lying under the influence of that magical drug which soothing the physical frame mysteriously operates on the subtler element in man, he was heard to murmur words inexplicable to his attendant — "Billy Budd, Billy Budd." That these were not the accents of remorse, would seem clear from what the attendant said to the *Indomitable's* senior officer of marines who as the most reluctant to condemn of the members of the drumhead court, too, well knew though here he kept the knowledge to himself, who Billy Budd was.

XXX

Some few weeks after the execution, among other matters under the head of *News from the Mediterranean*, there appeared in a naval chronicle of the time, an authorized weekly publication, an account of the affair. It was doubtless for the most part written in good faith, though the medium, partly rumor, through which the facts must have reached the writer, served to deflect and in part falsify them. The account was as follows: —

"On the tenth of the last month a deplorable occurrence took place on board *H.M.S. Indomitable.* John Claggart, the ship's master-at-arms, discovering that some sort of plot was incipient among an inferior section of the ship's company, and that the ring-leader was one William Budd; he, Claggart in the act of arraigning the man before the Captain was vindictively stabbed to the heart by the suddenly drawn sheath-knife of Budd.

"The deed and the implement employed, sufficiently suggest that though mustered into the service under an English name, the assassin was no Englishman, but one of those aliens adopting English cognomens whom the present extraordinary necessities of the Service have caused to be admitted into it in considerable numbers.

"The enormity of the crime and the extreme depravity of the criminal, appear the greater in view of the character of the victim, a middle-aged man respectable and discreet, belonging to that minor official grade, the petty-officers, upon whom, as none know better than the commissioned gentlemen, the efficiency of His Majesty's navy so largely depends. His function was a responsible one; at once onerous and thankless and his fidelity in it the greater because of his strong patriotic impulse. In this instance as in so many other instances in these days, the character of this unfortunate man signally refutes, if refutation were needed, that peevish saying attributed to the late Dr. Johnson, that patriotism is the last refuge of a scoundrel.

"The criminal paid the penalty of his crime. The promptitude of the punishment has proved salutary. Nothing amiss is now apprehended aboard *H.M.S. Indomitable*."

The above appearing in a publication now long ago superannuated and forgotten is all that hitherto has stood in human record to attest what manner of men respectively were John Claggart and Billy Budd.

XXXI

Everything is for a term remarkable in navies. Any tangible object associated with some striking incident of the service is converted into a monument. The spar from which the Foretopman was suspended, was for some few years kept trace of by the blue-jackets. Then knowledge followed it from ship to dock-yard and again from dock-yard to ship, still pursuing it even when at last reduced to a mere dock-yard boom. To them a chip of it was as a piece of the Cross. Ignorant though they were of the secret facts of the tragedy, and not thinking but that the penalty was somehow unavoidably inflicted from the naval point of view, for all that they instinctively felt that Billy was a sort of man as incapable of mutiny as of wilful murder. They recalled the fresh young image of the Handsome Sailor, that face never deformed by a sneer or subtler vile freak of the heart within. This impression of him was doubtless deepened by the fact that he was gone, and in a measure mysteriously gone. On the gun-decks of the *Indomitable* the general estimate of his nature and its unconscious simplicity eventually found rude utterance from another foretopman, one of his own watch, gifted as some sailors are with an artless poetic temperament. The tarry hands made some lines which after circulating among the shipboard crew for a while, finally got rudely printed at Portsmouth as a ballad. The title given to it was the sailor's.

BILLY IN THE DARBIES

Good of the Chaplain to enter Lone Bay
And down on his marrow-bones here and pray
For the likes just o' me, Billy Budd. — But look:
Through the port comes the moon-shine astray!
It tips the guard's cutlass and silvers this nook;
But 'twill die in the dawning of Billy's last day.
A jewel-block they'll make of me tomorrow,
Pendant pearl from the yard-arm-end
Like the ear-drop I gave to Bristol Molly —
O, 'tis me, not the sentence they'll suspend.
Ay, Ay, all is up; and I must up too
Early in the morning, aloft from alow.
On an empty stomach, now, never it would do.
They'll give me a nibble — bit o' biscuit ere I go.
Sure, a messmate will reach me the last parting cup;
But, turning heads away from the hoist and the belay,
Heaven knows who will have the running of me up!
No pipe to those halyards — but aren't it all sham?
A blur's in my eyes; it is dreaming that I am.
A hatchet to my painter? all adrift to go?
The drum roll to grog, and Billy never know?
But Donald he has promised to stand by the plank;
So I'll shake a friendly hand ere I sink.
But — no! It is dead then I'll be, come to think. —
I remember Taff the Welshman when he sank.
And his cheek it was like the budding pink.
But me they'll lash me in hammock, drop me deep.
Fathoms down, fathoms down, how I'll dream fast asleep.
I feel it stealing now. Sentry, are you there?
Just ease these darbies at the wrist,
And roll me over fair.
I am sleepy, and the oozy weeds about me twist.

End of Book

April 19th, 1891

JOHN METCALF

Girl in Gingham

Following his divorce, frequent dinners with the Norths had become habit for Peter Thornton. Nancy fussed over him and stitched on lost buttons; Alan plied him with beer and had distracted him in the early months with ferocious games of chess. Now, two and a half years later, his family relationship was declared by their daughter, Amanda, to be that of Uncle the Best.

"I'm ready!" she yelled from upstairs.

"No, don't go up yet, Peter. Have some more coffee," said Nancy. "She still hasn't brushed her teeth."

"TEETH!" bellowed Alan.

"She's getting so bitchy and *cunning*," said Nancy. "She runs the tap, eats some toothpaste, smears it round the basin, but *now* the little swine's learned to wet the brush."

"They *all* seem to hate it, don't they?" said Peter. "Same thing with Jeremy."

"By the way," said Alan, "nothing new with the woman situation, is there?"

"No. Not particularly. Why?"

"Well don't be too long up there. Might have something to interest you."

"What?"

"This wine," said Alan, emptying the bottle into his glass, "confirms one's prejudices against Hungarians."

"What might interest me?"

Alan shook his head and wagged a solemn finger.

"What are you being so mysterious for?" said Peter. "Oh, *no!* You haven't got someone coming over?"

He glanced at Nancy who shrugged.

"Our wife," said Alan, "privy though she is to our councils and most trusted to our ear . . ."

"READY!"

"Before you get *completely* pissed, dear husband," said Nancy, "you can help me with these dishes."

"Your merest whim, my petal," cried Alan, "is my command."

"Oh, Christ!" said Nancy.

As Peter went upstairs, Alan in the kitchen was demanding his apron with the rabbits on it; Nancy's voice; and then he heard the sounds of laughter.

'The woman situation.'

Whom, he wondered, had Alan in mind for him?

The woman situation had started again for him some eight months or so after his wife had left him. The woman situation had started at the same time he'd stopped seeing Dr. Trevore, when he'd realized that he was boring himself; when he'd realized that his erstwhile wife, his son, and he, had been reduced to characters in a soap opera which was broadcast every two weeks from Trevore's sound-proofed studio.

And which character was he?

He was the man whom ladies helped in laundromats. He was the man who dined on frozen pies. Whose sink was full of dishes. He was the man in the raincoat who wept in late-night bars.

That office, and he in it, that psychiatrist's office with its scuffed medical magazines and pieces of varnished driftwood on the waiting room's occasional tables was the stuff of comic novels, skits, the weekly fodder of stand-up comedians.

In the centre of Trevore's desk sat a large, misshapen thing. The rim was squashed in four places indicating that it was probably an ashtray. On its side, Trevore's name was spelled out in spastic white slip. Peter had imagined it a grateful gift from the therapy ward of a loony bin.

It presided over their conversations.

How about exercise? Are you exercising?

No, not much.

How about squash?

I don't know how to play.

I play myself. Squash. I play on Mondays, Wednesdays, and Fridays. In the evenings.

Following one such session he had gone home, opened the bathroom cabinet, regarded the pill bottles which had accumulated over the months. He had taken them all out and stood them on the tank above the toilet. He arranged them into four rows. In the first row he placed the Valium. In the second, the Stelazine. In the third, the Tofranil. In the fourth, the Mareline.

Uncapping the bottles, he tipped the tablets rank by rank into the toilet bowl. Red fell upon yellow, blue fell on red, tranquillizing, antidepressant psychotherapeutic agents fell, swirled and sifted onto agents for the relief of anxiety, emotional disorders, and nausea.

The results had suggested to him the droppings of a Walt Disney rabbit.

Following this, he had twice attempted suicide.

In spite of Montreal's entrenched and burgeoning underworld, the only weapon he had been able to procure, and that in a junk shop, was an ancient .45. Bullets had proved impossible to obtain without a permit.

He shrank from the *mechanics* of a shotgun — bare feet and the cold, oily taste of gun metal filling his mouth and the absurd fear that in the second of death the kick of the barrels would smash his teeth.

His second attempt was with prescription sleeping pills, blue gelatine capsules. He had written to his mother and father, swallowed twenty-five, and lain wakefully on his bed clutching the plastic bracelet which had been secured round Jeremy's wrist at birth. His stomach felt distended and after belching repeatedly the taste of the gelatine had made him vomit.

Subsequently, with a large weariness and a settled habit of sadness, he had become active in the world of those whose world was broken. First it was the single women of his married friends' acquaintance, awkward dinners where he had learned the meaning of 'intelligent,' 'interesting,' 'creative,' and 'kind.' Later, he had encountered childless women, women married but embittered, divorced women with single maladjusted children who demanded to know if he was to be their new uncle. He had even met a twenty-eight-year-old virgin who one night confessed that she hated men because when they became excited their things came out of their bodies, red like dogs.

He had acquired an almost encyclopedic knowledge of Montreal's restaurants.

He had become an authority on films.

He had learned to avoid women who took pottery courses and had come to recognize as danger signs: indoor plants, Alice in Wonderland posters, health food, stuffed toys, parents, menstrual cramps, and more than one cat.

Amanda was trying to whistle.

He whistled a few notes of the tune she was hissing.

"Come *on*," she called.

Her bed was littered with books; she had chosen *Paddington Bear* and *The Sleeping Beauty*. The Bear book was one he had recently given her. When he bought books for his son who now lived in distant Vancouver, he always bought Mandy duplicates. He mailed off a book and a letter weekly into the void from which few answers returned. Mandy snuggled against him as he read.

... *mounted the Prince's white charger* ...

"What's a charger?"

"A big white horse."

... *mounted the Prince's white charger and rode away to his kingdom in a far country.*

"Look at all the flowers in the picture," she said.

"The end," said Peter, getting up and kissing her goodnight.

"Peter? How many flowers are there in the world?"

"THE END."

"More than people? More than cars? Not more than ANTS?"

"I don't know. Go to sleep."

"Will Nanny die?"

"Good night."

As he went along the landing, he heard her half-singing, "Nanny'll die and Grampy, Mummy and Daddy, Uncle Drew *and* the mailman and Mary and the Volkswagen *and* Nanny *and* Grampy ..."

He stood silently in the bathroom for a few moments resting his hands on the edges of the washbasin, staring down. He saw, unbidden, like a succession of frozen movie frames, that other bathroom in a silent apartment where dirt and empty beer cans had accumulated until the lease expired.

In the cabinet, the daily reminder of the blue plastic diaper pin, the sticky bottle of Extract of Wild Strawberries, Gravol, the smiling tin of Johnson's Baby Powder.

The room that had been his son's he had not been able to enter. The frieze of animals sagging from its thumbtacks, a deflated elephant on the dusty carpet, scattered blocks.

He washed his face and then remembered to flush the toilet.

"No trouble?" said Nancy as he came into the livingroom.

"She'll be off in a few minutes."

"A suggestion of cognac?" said Alan. "You'll have to use a tumbler because I broke the last snifter."

Peter sank into his usual armchair.

Nancy was lying on the couch staring into the fire.

Alan rolled the glass in his palms.

"Well?" said Peter.

"Well what? Oh! Oh, yes."

Alan produced from the inner pocket of his jacket an envelope. He straightened a bent corner. He leaned forward and passed the envelope to Peter. He sat back. Peter opened the envelope and glanced at the contents.

"Funny," he said. "Witty. Exquisitely comical."

"I thought you'd react that way."

Peter tossed the letter over to Nancy.

"Oh, Alan!" she said. "That's not very funny."

"It wasn't intended to be," he said.

"'A Scientific Date with CompuMate,'" read Nancy.

"An unfortunate name, agreed," said Alan.

"Sounds like 'copulate,'" said Nancy.

"'Consummate,'" said Peter.

"Shut up!" said Alan. "Listen, I'm being serious. Okay? We've listened to you talking about the situation for hours on end so you can just sit there and hear me out. Now, I want to look at this rationally. The first fact is that you claim you want to get married again. God knows why, but that's *your* funeral. So what's stopping you? It isn't that you're not attractive to women because over the last couple of years there's been a veritable *parade* of the creatures ..."

Peter sipped the cognac, martinis before dinner, wine with, conscious of becoming floatingly, pleasantly, drunk, watching the play of expression on Alan's face rather than paying attention to his words, feeling a great affection for him. It was soothing to be with friends in this room with a fire in the fireplace, in this room which was part of a house, part of a household; soothing to be, however briefly, in some sort of context.

"... so it's not lack of opportunity. Montreal's *bulging* with women ..."

A log in the fire slipped and sparks sailed up. When the fire had burned down and the talk had finished, he would have to go out into the snow. He thought of his apartment. In a closet in his apartment there still sat a carton not unpacked — a 'barrel' the moving men had called it. For two years he had reached over it to take out his coat. He did not know what it contained.

"... and just think of the bunch of ... of Dulcineas you've brought round here," Alan was saying, "eating us out of house and home. And I expect they were the pick of the crop. Now what I'm getting at ..."

Nancy's hand patted the carpet for the packet of cigarettes. Watching the oily curves of the cognac on the glass the word 'meniscus' came into his mind but he knew it wasn't the right word. Bulky as the still-packed carton, sadness sat inside him.

"Well *I* think the whole idea's *silly*," said Nancy. "Any woman who'd sign up for that'd be crazy."

"Why don't you *listen*!" exclaimed Alan with a drunken earnestness. "*Of course!* That's just what I've been saying. The women he's found on his *own* were mostly crazy. Right? What about that blonde one? Eh? You know."

"Marion," said Nancy.

"Right. All *that* nonsense. And that other woman with the adhesive tape over it. If you didn't know Peter, you wouldn't believe they were walking around, would you? *Of course* ninety per cent of these'd be mad as hatters, but what if there was *one* woman just like him. The same reasons, I mean. Why not? What's he got to lose?"

"Peter wouldn't like a woman who'd sign up for that sort of thing."

"How do you know?"

"Because I know Peter."

"And what do you mean 'that sort of thing'?"

"You know very well what I mean."

"Peter!" said Alan. "What do you think?"

"The other day," said Peter, sitting up, "I went into Dominion to get some apples and I was wandering around sort of glazed with the music and everything and I'd come to a halt in front of a shelf and I found myself staring at a box of toothpicks."

"Fascinating," said Alan.

"And do you know what it said on the box? It said: 'Stim-U-Dent: Inter-Dental Stimulators.' "

"Do you want to give it a try or not?"

"I had a hamburger last week," said Peter, "that was served on a paper plate embossed with the word 'Chi-Net.' And I've sipped my milk through straws manufactured by the 'Golden Age Scientific Company.' "

"Stop babbling," said Alan. "It's only fifteen dollars for a month's trial."

Peter laughed.

"Okay?" said Alan. "Or not?"

Peter shrugged.

"Good!" said Alan. "So we can fill in the form. I *love* forms. I'll just get something to rest it on."

He took a large book that was on the side table near the couch.

"What the fuck's this!"

"It's that book club," said Nancy. "I keep forgetting to send the don't-want cards back."

"*Fish Cookery of South-East Asia.*"

"They bury them until they rot," said Nancy.

"What?"

"Fish."

"Who?"

"South-East Asians."

Alan stared at her.

"And you," he said, turning to Peter, "want to get married again."

Spreading out the form, he started to read.

Many of us have come to realize that we need the love and companionship of a compatible Mate with whom we can share our deepest beliefs, our gravest sorrows, our wildest joys. CompuMate promotes harmonious relationships between mature individuals and encourages personal growth through deep and meaningful long-term, male-female interaction. Any single or legally unattached person who is serious-minded and of sound character and who meets the computer's acceptance standards is eligible to become a CompuMember.

"Just who does that computer think it is?" said Nancy.

"Haughtyputer," said Peter.

"Now the first thing, then ..." said Alan.

"Wait," said Peter. "How's all this nonsense supposed to *work*?"

"You answer all these questions and then it matches you with someone who's given the same kind of answers. And then you end up with a Computer Compatible."

"A 'Computer Compatible'?"

"Now don't start being awkward. Are you ready? Okay?"

Mark the Character Traits which are YOU: Popular, Well-to-do, Artistic, Puritan, Sexually Experienced, Bohemian, Diplomatic, Free Spirit, Romantic, Shy, Well-Groomed, Sensual, Sporty, Sensitive, Smoker (non, moderate, heavy), Drinker (non, social, heavy).

"So?" said Alan. "What would you like to be?"

"Artistic," said Nancy.

"Romantic, do you think?" said Alan.

"Of course," said Nancy. "And Sensitive. And Shy."

"Can't I be Sexually Experienced?"

"No," said Alan, "it might put her off."

He marked crosses in the appropriate boxes.

"And for smoking and drinking," he said, "I'm putting 'moderate' and 'social.' Or we won't get any Compatibles at all."

Can Premarital Sex be Justified?

"What choice do I have?"

Never. After Engagement. If in Love. Between Mature Individuals. Always.

"Do people still *get* engaged?" said Nancy.

"*I* was engaged," said Peter.

"Yes, but you're as old as we are."

"Not only was I officially engaged, I purchased an engagement ring complete with diamond."

"You're an antique," said Nancy. "Just like us."

Alan cleared his throat.

Which of the following interests would you like to share with your CompuMatch: Dancing, Athletics, Skiing, Water Sports, Spectator Sports ...

"Hate *all* of them," said Peter.

... Politics, Photography, Music, Animals ...

"Animals?"

... Animals, Fine Arts, Natural Sciences, Parties, Psychology and Sociology.

"I don't like any of them."

"Well you've got to."

"What do you mean, *animals*?"

"How the fuck should I know?" said Alan. "Take her to the zoo."

"It's not open in the winter."

"Oh, stop being difficult!" said Alan. "I'm putting you down for Music, Animals, and Fine Arts."

"And what's more," Peter said to Nancy, "the engagement was announced in the paper with, believe it or not, a photograph of the charming young couple. So how about that?"

"What are your age requirements?" said Alan.

"What?"

"How young and old are you prepared to go? There's a note here that says the wider the range the more choice the computer can provide."

"Remember her father, Nancy?" said Peter. "I even asked him for her hand in marriage."

"*Peter!* Come on! You're not paying attention."

"Sorry, sorry. What was it? How young, you said?"

There flashed through his mind a vision of an evening he had spent some eighteen months earlier. He had met her at a party. She was young and beautiful, her eyes dark and entrancing. At three-thirty in the morning he had escorted her back to her apartment on Sherbrooke West. Her apartment was furnished with plants, posters, and a pinball machine.

It was summer; she gave him a large glass of Kool-Aid. She went into her bedroom.

One of the posters was electric blue.

In the centre was a red circle.

Under the circle was the word NOW.

She reappeared in a long, white nightgown. Her bare feet were brown. Across the road from her apartment was the Montreal Association For the Blind. Yellow floodlights lit the front of the buildings. She insisted they go out into the night because she wanted to share with him something rare, something mysterious.

She flitted across to the island in the middle of the road, her legs dark through the white gown against the lights of the approaching cars. She smiled and beckoned to him. On the lawn in front of the building she urged him to take off his shoes and socks to walk in the dew. His feet looked pale and silly in the dark grass. She took him by the hand and led him to one of the floodlights. Her hand was cool on his. She made him kneel and gaze into the glare of one of the yellow bars of light while she counted aloud to a hundred.

"See!" she cried, when they stood up. "Everything looks purple."

Peter drained the last drops of cognac.

"I'll put the maximum as your age," said Alan, "so how about twenty-five as a minimum? That's ten years."

"Make it thirty."

"Why thirty?"

"The heart," said Peter, "has its reasons."

Alan crossed something out and turned the form over.

"How about race?" he said. "Of your CompuMatch, that is."

"Peter?" said Nancy.

"Umm?"

White. Coloured. Oriental. Any.

"Apart from all *this*," she said, "do you know what sort of girl you *really* want? You know, if you could ... Or is the whole idea just silly?"

"What *sort* of girl?" said Peter.

Protestant. Catholic. Jewish. Unaffiliated. Other.

He held up the empty glass looking through it at the fire.

"Yes," he said. "I know *just* the sort."

He tilted the glass creating changing shapes.

"I want a girl in gingham."

II

Peter sipped the coffee, watching the waitress, watching other diners, half-listening to scraps of conversation near him, extending as long as was decent the minutes until he would have to pay the bill. He ate at Chez Jean-Guy two or three times a week. It was not exactly cheap but he liked the linen, wine, flowers on the table. The food was respectable. As he was a regular, they rarely hurried him and he often sat over coffee, sometimes cognac, glancing through trade journals and the catalogues.

Above the background sound of voices, cutlery, crockery, he heard a sharp click and *Jesus Christ!* from a man at the next table. He hadn't looked at the two men when they'd come in as he'd been watching his waitress stretching to clear off a vacated table. Both men were in their forties and wearing expensively tailored versions of teenage clothing. One wore a necklace and medallion. On the near man a heavy gold braclet.

"What a jeezely-looking thing!"

"Couldn't tell, eh?" said the necklace man. "Swear it was a Parker pen. I came through three international airports with that in my suit pocket."

Peter couldn't see what it was because of the flowers on their table.

"Where in hell did you *find* a thing like that?"

"This one?" said the necklace man. "Tokyo, this one. Never," he said, "never underestimate your Japanese."

"A very ingenious people," said the bracelet man.

"The Jews of the East," said the necklace man.

"Let bygones be bygones," said the bracelet man.

"Of course," said the necklace man, "in the travel business you're always on the move. Locating. Different countries all the time. The personal touch. And it's become — well, I suppose you'd have to call it a hobby of mine."

"Well," said the bracelet man, "it sure is different!"

There was another click.

"Refill all round?" said the bracelet man.

Beckoning to Peter's waitress, the necklace man said to the bracelet man, "Two more vodkatinis, are we?"

Peter felt a surge of irritation. They were ten years older than he was. Why couldn't they accept with dignity what faced them in the morning mirror? Slackening. Caries. The intimation of jowls.

He wondered what they thought about when locked alone in the burnished steel and strip-lighting of a jet plane's toilet.

"Yes," continued the necklace man, "every different place I go, I buy their kind of switchblade. As I say, I suppose you'd call it a hobby."

The waitresses wore blue tunics with white blouses. Peter watched the changing blue planes across her thighs as she placed the martinis in front of them.

"But it's in the south," continued the necklace man, "the southern countries where I've found what I'd call my best pieces. The time before last in Mexico, for example, I bought a crucifix. Crown of thorns. Loincloth. Little nailheads in the hands and feet. Enamelled. Brown beard. But press his navel and you've got yourself five and a half inches."

The waitress smiled at Peter from her buffet and raised the coffee pot. Nodding, he smiled back.

He always tried to get a table at her station. The other girls were French-Canadian but she, he had discovered, was German. It was not the length of leg nor the strange severity of her haircut which attracted him but rather the way she spoke. There was something about her speech; it was nothing as definite as, say, a lisp; if it was an impediment at all it was so slight, so elusive, as to be indefinable. But he was not comfortable with the idea of 'impediment'; it did not quite capture what he seemed to hear. That something, he had almost decided, must be the suggestion of a long-ago-lost accent. He found it charming.

He did not know her name.

Sometimes it was Eva. Sometimes Ilse.

She wore no rings.

The austere tunics reminded him of girls' gym-slips, stirred idle thoughts of Victorian pornography, the backs of hairbrushes, correction, discipline.

Miss Flaybum's Academy. Sexual pleasures he'd never been able to even vaguely understand.

Necklace and Bracelet had exhausted compact cars and the prime lending rate and were now fairly launched into the virtues of aluminum siding.

He watched her deft movements, her smile, the formal inclination of her head as she jotted down each order. The elusive something about her speech, was, he decided, like a faint presence of perfume in an empty room.

He found himself wishing that he wasn't wishing that she wasn't German.

He embroidered upon the possible permutations of Alsace-Lorraine.

Recalled a poster he'd seen outside The Beaver for a movie called *Hitler's Hellcats*. A Nordic beauty aiming a sten-gun, her blouse severely strained. He had come to consider most psychological solemnities such as the gun-penis thing as dubious as Dr. Trevore and his lumpy ashtray. Yet the poster had stayed in his mind for months. And then, too, he remembered the security guard at Man and his World.

Last year with Jeremy. The mechanical delights of La Ronde, ice-creams, orange-crush. The rights of summer. And while Jeremy had been riding out his minutes on the merry-go-round, the paunchy guard *stroking* the revolver butt.

Peter cradled the globe of cognac.

Snapshots of Jeremy.

Half-frightened laughter into the sky as the chains of the swing groaned in the park. Magic markers. Counting his popsicle stick collection. Fear of spider webs. Tiny feet swinging under the kitchen table, the flannelette pyjamas, the pyjamas with elephants. Snapshots already fading, fading like the yellowed snapshots found in albums gathering dust in a thousand junk shops, the last unwanted effects of auctioned families.

Clinging to his refrigerator door were Jeremy's

magnetic letters. He had saved them from that other apartment.

Reliques.

He used them to hold notes to himself, shopping lists, bills. Sometimes late at night, taking out another beer, he used the letters to compose messages.

Four of them presently held a sheet of paper from CompuMate which bore five names. The evening at Alan's had ended like so many evenings, vague memories the next day of snow, a taxi, swallowing down four aspirins with milk from the carton against the morning. He had been surprised and irritated with Alan when the list arrived.

He had ignored it for several days. The very idea was ludicrous. He knew himself to be incapable of phoning strange women.

Marjorie Kirkland
Stella Bluth
Nadja Chayefski
Elspeth McCleod
Anna Stevens

As the days had gone by he found the names wandering his mind. He wondered if Marjorie was once Margery; what nationality Bluth might be; if Nadja's hair was of raven lustre; if Elspeth were elfin and wandered lonely as a cloud, mist, rock, and heather.

But even more vividly he had imagined the conversations, the receiver glistening with sweat, silences, fingers clenched, armpits wet. That, most likely that, or fevered Woody Allen performances, fumbling blather ending with his accidentally garrotting himself with the telephone cord.

How, he had wondered, did one open? And, possibly worse, how did one close? And what could conceivably come between?

Marjorie Kirkland.

Marjorie Kirkland had been quite understanding. Marjorie it turned out, had been married for two years. She had reserved her asperity for CompuMate which, despite several registered letters, had not removed her name from the active list.

Stella Bluth.

Six generous cognacs followed by three Molson Export to prevent dehydration had phoned Stella Bluth. After he had diffidently presented his credentials Stella Bluth had assumed command. It was best, she always found, for each to describe each other to the other and then, if they liked the sound of each other, he could call her again.

It's a good thing you can't see over the phone.

Why?

Because.

Because what?

Just because.

Silence.

Well, if you must *know, my hair's all wet and I'm not completely dressed.*

Stella Bluth was sobering; it took Peter only a few moments to form the impression that she was possibly unhinged. He would have liked to close the conversation at its start but was incapable of replacing the receiver.

She frankly held out little hope; she was a Cancer and he was an Aries and she was sure he knew what *that* meant.

Upon command, he described himself. He was thirty-five and six feet tall. He was divorced. He was of medium build. His hair was brownish. He worked as an appraiser for a firm of auctioneers. Appraiser meant he had to estimate the value of antiques and *objets d'art*. No, it wasn't a French company. He was interested in music and animals.

Are you sure *you're not coloured?*

Quite.

You sound *like you're coloured. Because I'm Catholic.*

Stella was twenty-seven years old. Why lie about it? It was nothing to be ashamed of. She wasn't married and she hadn't been. She wasn't fat and she wasn't thin. They said she had a good figure. Her hair was brunette. She was at Alcan and did seventy-three a minute. She wasn't in the pool; she usually worked personally for Mr. Edwards. Who was quite nice though she didn't want him to get the wrong impression and sometimes he took her to the Golden Hinde in the Queen Elizabeth where they gave you triple martinis. Did he know the Golden Hinde? But she was only a social drinker. That and if she went to a party. She liked hockey and animals.

In the silence, Peter had heard the magnified sound of his breathing.

And she was interested in the environment.

The advent of the two middle-aged ladies caused an eddy in the flow of restaurant movement as they were seated, the table pulled out, lifted back, chairs settled. They spoke loudly in American voices; one asked Ilse in English if she spoke English. They were a parody of affluent American middle-aged womanhood; white and rinsed hair tended, fingers bedizoned with diamond rings. They were explaining to Ilse that they were on a Winter Tour; that the other girls were eating in the hotel; but they had read about Chez Jean-Guy in *Gourmet* magazine. And what did the menu mean?

Rejecting with increasing amazement kidney, cod, sausage blood and sausage garlic, quail and rabbit, they settled on poached salmon.

Peter signalled for his bill.

Three or four people were standing near the door waiting for a table.

Two full weeks had passed before curiosity and imaginings had nudged him into calling Nadja Chayefski. She had seemed abrupt and said she couldn't talk to him but had asked for his address.

A few days later in the mail he received an envelope from Sun Life.

It contained a poem on Sun Life letterhead.

Hey You!

I love you — please, it's not "dirty"!
I love trees and grass and plants and anything that lives.
Do you believe me?

It's not an intended, on purpose thing,
it's just here, in me,
and I want you to know it.

Please, it's not "dirty".

Quite likely you won't need it
or want it.

But that's O.K.

I just wanted you to know.

"The flavour's very different from canned," said one of the American ladies.

Peter smiled as he scanned his bill.

One of the ladies clattered her fork on the plate.

"Your joints swell up," she said, looking at the back of her hand.

They were silent.

"One of the girls was taken sick last night," said the other, the one who had spoken first, the one who was wearing tinted spectacles.

Peter regarded her.

"Carrie told me. The Director had a doctor come," she went on.

She paused.

"It was in the middle of the night."

They were silent again.

The other said suddenly, "It's all different since Herb's gone."

III

Peter had fortified himself for the encounter by drinking a severe vodka during his bath and another while dressing. He had then recleaned his teeth with Close-up: Super-Whitening Toothpaste and Mouthwash in One. Elspeth McCleod lived in a recent apartment building called The Michelangelo which boasted a commissionaire and live foliage in the foyer. On the fence surrounding the hole next door a large sign proclaimed the imminent construction of the El Greco.

The yellow light tacked its way up the indicator panel above which was a plaque that said Otis Elevator. He imagined Otis as the given name of the company's owner, a fat, cigar-smoking, mid-western American; rotund Oris; Rotarian; orotund.

He realized that he was not entirely sober.

"Peter Thornton!" she said, opening wide the door.

His impression was of colour. Her hair was blonde, her dress white, but her face was tanned a stark and startling bronze. She ushered him into a white, Danish living-room, angles, glass tables, teak wall unit, striped grey couch.

"First things first," she said. "What can I get you to drink?"

"Well, whatever ..."

"I've made some martinis if you'd ..."

She went away. In the brighter light of the living-room the tan was even more unlikely. It looked as if she'd been enthusiastically made-up for some theatricals; the Chief's Daughter who falls in love with the Captured White Scout. Obviously, she'd been a little naughty on her Compu-Sheet. She was, he guessed, about forty. A year or two older possibly. Attractive in a carefully arranged kind of way. On the glass table in front of the couch lay a gigantic soapstone seal with a bulbous Eskimo trying to do something to it. He stared. Kitchen sounds, glasses, the slam of the fridge door. He wondered what he was doing there.

"Well," she said, raising her glass, "what's the new word that they're trying to make the Canadian word for 'Cheers!'?"

"Ookpic?" said Peter.

"Or 'Inuit' or something?" she said. "Is that how you say it?"

"Well," said Peter, "cheers!"

The martini stopped his breath and hit his empty stomach like a well-aimed brick.

"So," she said, nodding her head and smiling, "*you're* Peter Thornton."

He smiled.

With her every movement the massive silver charm-bracelet jingled.

"Your tan ..."

"Florida. I've just come back. Three glorious weeks in the sun."

"So you missed the big storm," he said. "An eleven-inch fall, I think they said."

They made faces.

"Are you starving?"

"No, no, not at all."

"Because if you don't mind I'll start dinner now and it'll be ready in about an hour, if you'll excuse me."

The skirt was one of those skirts with lots of pleats in it. Fine legs. Her shoes were white too. He wondered if her legs under the brownness of the stockings were as intensely brown as her face and wrists.

He wandered over and looked at the things in the compartments of the wall unit. A stereo set. A photograph of a girl. A photograph of a boy. A few recent best sellers held upright by the polished halves of a geode — Yoga, Possession, Diet, Herbal Secrets, Yogurt. Some miniature bottles of liquor and a clustering of tiny animals in pink glass. The bowl caught his professional eye. Flower decoration, vigorous in the Kakiemon style. Opaque glaze. It felt right. He checked the hunting-horn mark.

The Chantilly factory before 1750. He wondered what it was doing there, where it had come from, if she knew what it was. It contained a squashy peach.

He followed the sounds to the kitchen.

"Can I do anything to help?"

"Would you like another?" she said, setting down her glass. "This one's cook's privilege."

The kitchen gleamed. Appliances. The table was littered with chrome bar-implements; salt and pepper were contained in two large wooden blocks, each four inches square. He hefted one.

"Teak," she said, as she filled his glass.

"There's really nothing to do," she continued. "I bought a gorgeous cut of salmon."

As Peter watched, she enclosed the fish in two layers of aluminum foil, pinching and securing the seams. She then opened the dishwasher, placed the foil package on the upper rack, slammed and locked the door, and switched on.

Peter stared.

She looked up and caught something of his expression.

"I calculate by weight, you see," she said.

"By weight," repeated Peter.

"That'll need two full cycles," she said.

Peter nodded.

"Anything heavier," she said, "and I'd add two Rinse Holds."

"Ah," said Peter.

He carried the pitcher of martinis and a chrome icebucket thing and she brought the glasses, closing the kitchen door behind them to muffle the throb of the dishwasher. She put on some kind of Latin-Americany music and joined him on the grey striped couch.

"Well," she said, "you must tell me all about appraising. What does an antique appraiser *do*?"

"Well," said Peter, "furniture's the bread-and-butter side of . . ."

"That's a dip I make myself," she said, lifting a white limp leather handbag from the floor by the end of the couch and rummaging.

"But porcelain and silver," said Peter, "are my . . ."

"And I'm sorry about the chips — I was rushed and picked up those awful ones that taste of vinegar by mistake — but the dip's very good. It's very easy in a blender — sour cream and Danish Blue, chives, and a teaspoon of lemon juice."

She found cigarettes at the bottom of the bag.

"Delicious," said Peter. "Absolutely delicious."

And listened to himself crunching.

"Tell me," she said, snapping and snapping the mechanism of the slim gold lighter, "we didn't seem to talk about this, did we? Or did we? I was rather flustered — well, *you* know, and my memory's awful but did you say you *weren't* married? My memory! Sometimes I can't even seem . . ."

"No," said Peter, leaning across and lighting her cigarette with a match. "No, I'm not."

"You're lucky," she said.

He smiled and then sipped.

"Peter," she said, "you listen to me. You pay attention. You're a very lucky man."

"I don't know if I'd agree with that," he said with a smile.

She turned towards him.

"And just how," she said, "did an attractive man like you escape so long?"

"I'm divorced," he said.

"Aha!" she said.

"What about you?"

"I will be soon," she said. "Divorced. It's on the rolls for March."

He nodded.

"And it can't be soon enough," she said. "Let me tell you."

"It's a strange business," he said.

She filled her glass, holding the pitcher with both hands.

"Peter," she said. "Do you know what I'm going to do? I'm going to phone my friend."

"Your friend?"

"We girls have to stick together," she said. "Right? So I'll tell her *not* to come at nine. Because you're not *ughy* and you know what they say?"

"What?"

"Three's a crowd."

She got up and smoothed her dress, straightening pleats with her fingertips, running her fingertips down the pleats at her thigh.

"And I don't think you're likely to molest me," she said. She smiled down at him. "Are you?"

She started from the room.

"You have some more dip," she called back.

He was beginning to feel satisfactorily sloshed. He leaned back on the uncomfortable Danish couch and looked at his watch. He felt relaxed and the pitcher of martinis was still half-full. He sucked his olive. He then initiated some exploratory dental work with the cocktail stick thing.

He had phoned Elspeth McCleod a week earlier on his return from dinner at Chez Jean-Guy. When he had entered his apartment, he had taken off his rubbers and put them on the sheet of newspaper inside the front door. The paper was scratchy with grit and sand; he had been meaning to change it for weeks.

He had tried to read but the conversation of the American ladies had echoed in his mind. Doors slammed. The TV in the next apartment was switched off. In the deepening silence, the refrigerator started and stopped.

Magnetic letters on the fridge door still held his Compu-Sheet. As he had stood over the toilet, he had seen into the empty room he maintained for Jeremy. Light from the bathroom glinted on the rims and spokes of the two-wheeler propped against the bedroom wall, last summer's birthday present. The bicycle had come in a large cardboard carton and he had skinned his knuckles working with an unaccustomed wrench to attach handlebars and pedals. Jeremy had been frightened of the bicycle and had hysterically resisted Peter's efforts, but had loved the carton, playing with it every day until it was forgotten overnight on the balcony and the rain rendered it limp and soggy.

Peter struggled to sit upright on the sloping couch. He dropped the olive into the crystal ashtray.

The toilet flushed and he heard water running.

The bicycle and the carton seemed as if they ought to be symbolic of something but of what, exactly, he was unable to grasp.

"Hello, again!" she said.

"I've been admiring your bowl," he said.

"Bowl? Oh. That belonged to my Drex. Well, he isn't but he *will* be. I've got a red ring around it."

"Pardon?"

"Oh, don't mind me," she said, "it's just my way, the way I am. It's what my girlfriend calls *hers*. She's a riot. My Drex did this, my Drex did that, she says. It stands for Dreadful Ex."

"What," said Peter, "have you got a red ring around?"

"March 17th," she said. "I was looking at it when I was on the phone. On the calendar," she added, in answer to his puzzled look. "Of course, I should have done it years ago. Everyone says so. So in a way I blame myself."

She fumbled at the lighter again.

She gestured encompassing the living-room.

"We used to live in the Town of Mount Royal. Do you know the Town? We lived in a very big house in the most expensive part, the most exclusive part. And we had three cars."

She eased off her shoes and let them fall on the carpet.

"Good old TMR!" she said.

She raised her glass.

"And what else," she said, "what else did we have?"

She started to tally.

"A large garden. And an Italian gardener who came twice a week. And a swimming pool. Fieldstone fireplaces. A woman came four times a week to clean and . . ."

"Sounds very pleasant," said Peter.

"Oh, yes. Very pleasant. Very, very pleasant. I can assure you it was certainly very pleasant."

She laughed.

"Boog hates him so much he won't even visit there. Boog," she said, "will not set foot in that house. I've just come back from Florida visiting him. Did I mention that?"

"Boog?"

"My son. He's working there now. In a hotel until he finds himself."

Peter looked at the white shoes, one of them standing, one lying on its side. He'd always felt absurdly moved by women's shoes. Such frail shells. Compared with men's shoes, like toys. Glass slippers. He'd never been quite sure, though, what he felt, sexually, about feet.

"Boog'll be up for the trial," she said. "It's physical and mental cruelty."

"Trial?"

"Thing."

"I thought physical was supposed to be the hardest to prove?"

"Oh, I've got grounds," she said. "He's admitted it. I've got grounds all right. You just don't know."

"I hope it goes . . ."

"You just don't know," she said. "I could tell you all sorts of things."

Peter knew she would.

He recognized and remembered the condition. He remembered the need to tell friends and acquaintances, the compulsion to inform even strangers of his anguish. He remembered the long drunken nights in patient apartments, words said, actions described, the paralysing replay of words. He said. She said. Words becoming meaningless sounds which were the echo of the pain that would not go away.

He remembered standing in Dominion, the muzak and bright light enveloping, standing in front of the freezer section, glass, chrome, gazing with unseeing eyes at the carcases of butterball turkeys, tears running unheeded.

"He used to lock me in the bedroom," she said.

"Oh, yes!" she said in answer to Peter's raised eyebrow.

"He didn't even like me to leave the house. Always wanted to know where I was. There's nothing wrong with bridge, is there? Just a group of girls. It wasn't as if it was men. Because that isn't true. I mean, you understand these things. You've been married. I know he works very hard. You have to give him that. But he wouldn't for night after night and then sometimes when he did he couldn't, you know, couldn't manage. And then he used to shout at me and say it was my fault and beat me up. He used to hit me with a shoe-tree."

"Good God!" said Peter.

"And if I even spoke to another man at a party he'd beat me up when we got home. That's why Boog left. Boog hates him."

"Boog?"

"My son."

"Yes, I know. You said. But I mean *Boog*."

"In Florida," she said.

Peter stared down into the diminished ice cubes in his glass.

"There isn't any harm in discotheques, is there? I've always been a good girl. Nineteen years. Nineteen years and I've always been a good girl. But that's not what *he's* saying. And after I told him I was leaving, well, he wanted to do things."

She nodded.

"You mean . . .?"

"*You* know," she said. "After I told him, after I'd seen the lawyer, he changed, couldn't get enough of me. Pestered me all the time wanting to do things in chairs and from behind and in the afternoon. I was a good wife to him. I bore him two children. I was always a good girl. He used to listen on the extension phone."

Peter shook his head.

"I shouldn't be telling you these things," she said.

Peter nibbled around the olive.

"He stopped going to the bathroom," she said.

"What?"

"Four or five months," she said, "he stopped going to the bathroom. Before, I mean. Before I left. That isn't normal, is it? You can't tell me that's the action of a normal person."

"What do you mean, 'He stopped going to the bathroom'?"

"Last Christmas," she said, "I bought him a wine-making kit — that was just part of his present — not *last*, Christmas *before* last — and there was a shiny thing in it like sodawater things, you know, the things that make soda-water, the bubbles, but it was for putting corks in bottles. He had a funnel from the office in the upstairs bathroom and another in the powder room — I did mention he was a doctor, didn't I? — the office's in the house, you see, and he did it in bottles and then he used the thing to put corks in."

"When I was a little boy," said Peter, "my mother used to make jam and she stuck on little labels with the name of what it was on it. They were white with a blue border. I remember that. Sticky on the back."

"Rows and rows and rows of bottles," she said. "It isn't very nice, is it? He kept them in the den."

"Perhaps," said Peter, "he was an oenophile."

"You're quite right," she said. "It's filthy. Nobody could call that normal."

She sighed and patted his arm.

"But the past's the past," she said. "Aren't I right?"

"Right," said Peter.

"So let's drink," she said, "to the future! To our futures!"

They drank.

He followed directions to the bathroom.

The dishwasher seemed to be mounting to some sort of climax.

It was nice in the bathroom. There were big mirrors and on the floor a furry carpet. And net curtains looped back on either side of the bath. And a coloured plastic box to put a box of Kleenex in. And a cut-glass jar of bath salts with a pink ribbon round the neck. He weighed himself. Trying not to make a noise, he eased back the mirrored cabinet doors and examined the pills, salves, tubes, pots, and potions. Here there were *two* jars of vaseline; all women had jars of vaseline; it was puzzling. He could think of only two bathroom uses for the stuff — to smear on infants or to facilitate the commission of unnatural acts. Neither seemed likely here, he hoped. Vaseline, he decided, was one of the mysteries of the female life.

He weighed himself again but it was difficult to see the wavering arrow. The toilet seat had a furry cover too and he suddenly wanted to know what it would feel like. He lowered his trousers and sat. It was nice.

He thought of the fallen white shoes, one standing, one lying on its side.

Sad he; sad she.

Children's feet, though, were a different matter. Children's feet were pink, diminutive, not deformed by shoes, veins, callouses, not hardened at the heels by yellowing skin.

Poor sad Peter Thornton he whispered to the furry floor *what are you doing in this sad lady's house?*

He would have liked to have stayed in the bathroom, read, gone to sleep on the carpet. Leaning forward was making him dizzy. He consulted his watch. Sitting on the furry seat was like what sitting on a St. Bernard would be like. Which would rescue him and take him home and give him aspirins and milk. He stared at the tiled wall. Home, he thought, for no good reason, is the sailor home from sea, and the hunter home from the hill.

As he passed the kitchen door he saw Elspeth McCleod standing to one side of the open dishwasher throwing handfuls of green stuff into the billowing steam. The steam was making her hair wilt.

"What are you doing?" he said.

A strand of hair hung across her puzzled face.

"Parsley," she said.

"Parsley?"

"Forgot the garnish," she said.

She locked the dishwasher and started the cycle again.

"Did you know," said Peter, "there's a kind of wine called *Pisse Dru*?"

"You always forget something," she said.

She linked her arm with his and they went back into the living-room.

"I shouldn't really have told you the things I told you," she said, "but some faces you can tell about. I can see from your face that you've been through a lot of suffering. There are two kinds of people in this world — there are faces that have suffered and there are faces that haven't suffered."

She drew away from him and touched his brow, traced the corners of his mouth. Nodding, she snuggled closer again, drawing her legs up onto the couch. Her skirt was rucked. Peter looked at her thigh.

"Your face is nice," she said. "Very strong but very gentle. It's a masculine face."

He regretted the advent of panty-hose. A nasty garment; peculiarly asexual. Before, when he was younger, there had been brownness, sheen, then, shockingly, the stark contrast of white thigh. Always an incredibly intimate whiteness.

"You're a very cautious person, aren't you, Peter?"

"Am I?" he said.

He stared at the Eskimo carving. The larger they got the less artistic they became; great nasty lumpy thing.

"You don't have to be cautious with me," she said.

There was a silence.

The silence extended.

"Well," she said, "I've been telling you all about me. What about you?"

"There isn't much to tell. It all happened three years or more ago."

"But what happened?"

"She seemed to feel there was more in life or something. Or ought to be. And she met another man and ... well, she just left."

"Does she love him?"

"She seems to, yes."

"And you were unhappy?"

He nodded.

"Yes."

He lighted another cigarette.

But she had said *what happened?*

It was a question he couldn't answer. Even after three long years he did not know what had happened. With the passage of time, it had all become, if anything, even more senseless. One day, it seemed to him now, he had been a father who brought home flowers and did the shopping on Saturdays, the next, the occupant of a dismantled apartment.

Of course it could not have happened in quite that way. There had been talk, a lot of talk. Words. 'Growth,' 'Fulfillment,' 'Freedom,' 'human something-or-other.' He suspected now that for all the mornings he had awoken crying, he was merely victim of the clichés of *Cosmopolitan* and *Ms.*

And Jeremy?

What he felt, he did not know. He did not know.

"You're very quiet," she said. "Did I say something?"

"No, no. Sorry. Just thinking."

She sighed and squeezed his arm.

He stared at the Eskimo thing.

"How about another drink?" she said. "Do you think we should?"

They drank. She sighed again.

"You don't find me unattractive, do you? I'm not unattractive, am I?"

"You're *very* attractive."

"I'm not ugly or anything," she said. "I bore him two children."

"Certainly not," said Peter.

"I've got Hester," she said. "He needn't think he can kick me out without a penny."

"Certainly not," said Peter.

"There are some things," she said, "that people shouldn't say to other people. There are some things you just don't say."

"I think I'd agree with that," said Peter.

"My lawyer says it constitutes mental cruelty."

"What does?"

"When he'd done it — you know — *when* he did it, which wasn't very often *I* can tell you and it's not as if I'm unattractive, he'd stand up on the bed and shout at me — would you believe that? And I worried he'd wake the children because it isn't the sort of thing ..."

"Shouting about what? What do you mean shouting?"

"Well that's the point. That's the mental cruelty."

"What is?"

"Because do you know what *I* had to say?"

"No."

"I had to say, 'You are, Robert.' Standing on the bed," she said, "shouting."

"You are what?"

"Not a thought for the children."

"You are what?" said Peter.

"What do you mean?" she said.

"What did he shout when you had to say you are?"

"You mean, what did he shout?" she said.

Drawing away from him, she straightened her back, turned.

"WHO'S YOUR MASTER?"

"Shsss!"

"WHO'S YOUR MASTER?"

"Shss! They'll hear next door."

"Was I speaking loudly?"

"Just a bit."

"I'm sorry."

"It's just ..."

"If I was speaking loudly," she said, "I'm sorry."

"That's terrible."

"I apologize," she said.

She peered into the empty cigarette packet and then dropped it on the glass table. She groped for the white handbag and rummaged again.

"Oh!" she said. "Look what I've found! I knew they were somewhere."

She opened a fat paper wallet of colour snaps.

"These were all taken in Florida," she said. "Did I mention that?"

Leaning heavily against him, giving his thigh a quick squeeze, she started to pass him the photographs one by one. Dutifully, one after another, he stared at beaches, palm trees, hotel facades, swimming pools, swim-suited groups, reclining people in reclining chairs.

That's me.

And with dismissive gestures, *You don't know these other people.*

That's the ocean.

He stared at two lounging young men who were grinning at him. They held tall drinks. They were tanned and muscled. One wore red trunks, the other white. There was a palm tree. The pool was blue. To the side of the picture stood a waiter in a white jacket.

"There's not an ounce of fat on their bodies," she said.

She tapped the photo with a beringed finger.

"They're famous," she said. "There's one — here it is — of me with them in a group. Here. You don't know these other people."

He stared at the captured smiles.

"They're very famous junior league hockey players," she said.

IV

Sitting in The Happy Wanderer finishing his dinner and gazing at the travel posters of ruined castles, bare-knee bands, and Rhinemaids with steins, Peter realized that he had arrived at a decision.

Three weeks or more had passed since Elspeth McCleod. He had not been out much — a movie with Alan and Nancy North, a farewell evening with one of the young assistants who was going to London for a course at the V and A, bridge with Hugh and Noreen. He had allowed the coming March sale to take up most of his time; afternoons and evenings spent in the houses of widows, widowers, the old with their managing children. Afternoons and evenings spent examining the furniture and bric-a-brac of lives, suggesting reserve prices, met always with incredulity that cherished objects would fetch but a fraction of what had been paid for them, bread-and-butter work usually left to the younger men.

Peter realized that the decision which had been growing in him during these days and weeks was probably an inevitable one. It was, he told himself, a decision towards which the course of his life had inevitably and inexorably brought him. He examined the decision, tried out forms of words in his head, declarations. Declarations which began: *The die is cast ... From now on ... From this time forth ...*

His quest, he had decided, was ludicrous. What had he to do with Stella Bluth, Elspeth McCleod, and stretching fore and after, all that sad sisterhood? His life was in need of rationalization and restructuring. All, he told himself, was not lost. He was not exactly young — middle age approached — but neither was he old; not handsome but not unattractive. He had friends, a comfortable income, wide interests. He would embrace the single life, honourably discharge his duties as a parent so far as that was possible, live to himself.

As a sign of this decision, he would make his apartment habitable, invest in it time and care. He would, after two years of camping in it, *move into* his apartment. With growing excitement, he saw that he would paint, polish, scour, and burnish, re-arrange the lighting, buy new furniture. He would cook. He would buy supplies, utensils, Copco enamel pots.

He finished his coffee.

His waitress was the large woman. He watched her making out the bill. He was pleased he'd got her and not the small, Heidi-like one. He pocketed his cigarettes and matches. The large woman's handsome face had reminded him of some other face and the likeness had troubled him for months until he'd recognized it as the impassive gaze of the woman in Giorgione's *Tempesta*. The resemblance was striking. She frowned as she figured the tax from the table on the back of her pad. He imagined her as in the painting, naked, babe at breast. He left a large tip. Past the smelly, damp overcoats and striding towards his local A and P, he saw himself the painting's other character, that enigmatic youth against the violent sky.

In the foyer of the apartment building he checked his mailbox; it contained yet another letter from the Victorian Order of Nurses addressed to Mary Chan.

In his living-room, he took his purchases from the shopping bag and stood them one by one on the coffee table. Cling-Fast Dust Remover, Mr. Clean, J-Cloths, lemon-scented liquid furniture polish, Ajax, Windex.

He wondered where to start. He moved a sticky brandy snifter and picked up a sweater. He opened the closet to throw the sweater in and saw the carton still secured by glossy tape, the barrel. He hesitated and then with sudden resolution reached in to grasp its far corners. To unpack the carton was a kind of declaration, he decided, a laying of ghosts, a line ruled beneath the column. He wrestled the box out into the living-room and then sat on the couch to look at it. Someone had scrawled on the side 'Bedroom.'

He remembered the two moving men, white patches on the walls, echoes, the rooms becoming hollow. At nine in the morning they had been drinking beer. One, he remembered, called the other, 'Kangaroo.'

He hunted for a clean knife in the kitchen and slit the glossy tape. Inside the carton:

three blankets
newspaper-wrapped things
a wooden train (Jeremy's)
bundles of catalogues from Sotheby's and Parke Bernet (his)
an electric appliance which made yogurt (hers)
a scarlet winter coat and her fur hat

He smoothed the fur and spoke her name in the silence. 'Patricia.' And immediately wondered why he had. He had never called her Patricia, always either Pat or a private name he would not now say.

Snowflakes drifting from the darkness into the light of the street lamp, glistening, settling, melting on the fur that framed her face. He tried to see her face within that frame but all he could recall was her face as it was in the few photographs he had kept.

The blankets, too. He touched the topmost blanket; it often must have covered them. He tried to remember her body, tried to remember making love, but she, his wife, Pat, dissolved, faded, assumed the postures of models in *Penthouse* and *Cavalier*.

He wondered why he felt so sad, her real face gone, her real body. The moving men remained more vivid, past drama more acute than present feelings. He wondered if perhaps he was deliberately inducing a sense of desolation. He tried the word 'desolation' in his mind to see if he felt 'desolated' but all the word conjured was the memory of a photograph of Ypres.

He felt, he decided, as if he'd suffered amputation. He was no longer whole. And the pain he felt, the sadness, was part real and perhaps part pain in a phantom limb. This formulation struck him as penetrating and clever and he sat on the couch to think about it but the more he thought about it, about the relation of 'pain' to 'phantom limb,' the more he realized it didn't mean anything at all.

He sat on the couch staring at the carton. The carton was just a cardboard box full of things he once had used and now did not. He sat on the couch feeling sad and holding the wooden train.

The telephone in the bedroom shrilled. Rushing to answer it, he stumbled over a chair in the kitchen. The voice wanted George. The number was right? Then how come no George? Did George *use* to live there?

Peter sat on the edge of his bed and switched on the light which stood on the chest of drawers. The cat woman was on the next door balcony calling kitty — kitty. He could grow herbs in the summer on the balcony in a box — basil and oregano to flavour salads and egg dishes he would cook for friends. He could hang up strings of onions in the kitchen.

Kitty — kitty called the cat woman. *Kitty — kitty.*

He sat on the edge of the bed staring at the chest of drawers. In the chest of drawers, under his shirts, was the list from CompuMate. There remained Anna Stevens. Anna Stevens held for him no interest; the die was cast. But the sheet of paper was a presence. Taking out a daily shirt, he was aware that the list was there, grit and oyster, irritating. To throw the list away was to leave loose ends; to throw the list away was to leave unread, as it were, the final chapter. To throw the list away was, it might be argued, a refusal to test his position. To not phone her could be seen even as a weakness. To phone her was, in a way, part of cleaning up, unpacking, settling in.

He thought of a piece of Battersea enamel that had been through his hands the previous week, a seventeen-eightyish patch-box. The plaque had read:

Happy the Man who Void of Care and Strife
In ease and Friendship lives the Social Life

Exactly so.

Who loves you the most in the world? called the cat woman.

He opened the drawer and took out the paper. It was rather late to phone but on the other hand he didn't much care what her reaction was. He wished to deal with the matter in a summary way. He felt about it, he decided, as he did when he stayed up late to finish a detective story. The action and the minor characters intrigued him but towards the end of the book exhaustion dragged him down and all that remained was the tedium of the explanation — a scene always contrived, the villain revealing all before pulling the trigger, the cast assembled in the library. Tedious, often silly, but essential before he could brush his teeth and go to bed.

He listened to the ringing, twice . . . three times . . . four.

"Oh . . . Miss Stevens, please."

"Speaking."

"I hope I'm not disturbing you calling at this hour?"

In the background Bach or Vivaldi.

"No."

"My name is Thornton. Peter Thornton. I was given your name by CompuMate."

"Oh, God!" she said.

He listened to the breathing silence for a few seconds.

"Hello?"

"I'm sorry," she said. "I didn't mean . . ."

"Is there something wrong?" he said.

"Look!" she said. "This is all a mistake. One of the men I work with filled out a form in my name and he's caused me a great deal of — "

"But that's exactly what happened to me!" said Peter. "A friend thought — "

"Then you know how distasteful — "

"But what a strange coincidence!" said Peter.

"Yes," she said. "It is."

"What do you mean? Don't you believe me?"

"Why shouldn't I?" she said.

"I'm sorry — just your tone."

There was silence.

"Mr. . . . Thornton, did you say? Let's agree that it *is* a strange coincidence and leave it at that. I really don't want to seem rude but it *is* late — "

"I wonder . . ." said Peter.

"What?"

"No. I'm sorry. I'm sorry to have troubled you."

He replaced the receiver. His hand was sweaty.

Later, lying in bed, drifting towards sleep, his thoughts wandered around the conversation. It was not the sort of ending he'd imagined. In the morning, first thing, he'd throw the list away. He had said, 'I wonder . . .' and she had said, 'What?' and then he'd said, 'No.' Had said, 'No. I'm sorry.' Vivaldi in the background. It was not what he'd imagined; not an ending he'd foreseen.

He wondered if somewhere in the city she too was lying in bed awake, wondering what he might have said when he said, 'I wonder . . .', curious, less determined than she'd sounded, provoked perhaps by a coincidence so strange.

But mainly he thought about her voice. Ever since his adolescence he'd been oddly excited by women with a certain kind of voice and she had it. 'Husky' did not describe it; that was the property of torchsingers and the like. 'Deep' or 'low' did not do it justice. For some reason he had come to associate the timbre with coolness, the coolness of moss, of ancient masonry, and over the years had imagined a scene which was somehow the equivalent of the voice.

At a cocktail party, he was introduced to a beautiful woman. They talked. He was holding her glass while she searched her purse for matches. Before taking the glass back, she placed her forefinger across the inside of his wrist for a second. Her finger was slim and cool. The touch was almost solemn yet shockingly erotic because proprietorial. A cool finger across the heat of his pulse, a sophisticated 'yes.'

And that was the sound of the voice.

During the next two days, Peter frequently caught himself thinking of the voice, the telephone conversation, that music, the strange coincidence of their situation. The coincidence was so strange that it might even be considered a sign or portent. While not at all superstitious or neurotic, Peter often made minor decisions, this restaurant or that, to go out, to stay in, by whether ten cars or more had passed while he counted fifty, by whether a bird flew across the portion of sky visible from his bedroom, by whether in ten dealt cards he drew an ace. On days when he forgot his nailclippers on the night-table he felt oddly uncomfortable. This business of Anna Stevens deserved thought. He kept remembering something that Alan had said when he filled in the form — something about the possibility of there being one, the same sort of reasons, one like him.

Her existence in no way altered his earlier decision, of course, but he was forced to admit that he was intrigued. Although he entirely agreed with and approved of her attitude on the phone, her cool rejection had irritated him. An admittedly irrational part of him even felt hurt. On the other hand, had she not taken that position, had she accepted or welcomed his approach, he would probably have let her talk and, whatever might have been said, would have tended to consider the matter closed, brushed teeth and so to bed. Just like who was it — Groucho Marx? — who ever said that any club which would accept him as a member was not the sort of club to which he wished to belong.

Silly.

He acknowledged his perversity.

She, of course, probably *did* consider the matter closed.

That was a problem.

The coincidence so tantalizing, the effect of her voice, her obvious intelligence and self-possession — she had deprived him of anything he could consider a fitting conclusion to this dismal adventure. This was not the way that stories ended. Before embracing his decision, he wanted to feel that his past — he sought an image — burning of boats, clearing a campsite before shouldering a pack and moving on, yes, that was it precisely. Litter buried, fireplace stones dispersed, the fire kicked out.

To phone her again was impossible; he was not a man who importuned strange women. The most sensible course of action was to write. This would obviate any embarrassment on either side and allow them both their dignity. He would include in the letter sufficient information about himself for her to make a reasoned response. If she chose not to reply, then he would accept that refusal as a considered refusal — the circumstances being completely different from an unexpected phone call. If she chose not to reply, he could accept that refusal as a fitting conclusion to what had been a silly business from the start.

If she *did* reply, if she did reply, then, simply, he would see what happened.

On his return from work on the third day, he sat down at the desk in his bedroom to construct the letter. He had determined on a light and civilized approach. The letter's stated intention was to apologize for his gauche intrusion upon her privacy. He presented himself as a victim of Alan's misplaced sense of humour who — but why had he co-operated, why phoned these dreadful women in the first place? *Pitfall.* Light-heartedly? Presumably he'd have phoned *them* in the same spirit he'd phoned *her. Pitfall.* He used up endless sheets of his office scratch-pad.

He wove all necessary information about himself into the fabric of his chronicle of misadventure. All references to his past, marital status, occupation, income, and interests were oblique and present only to make clear word and action. He did not request a meeting or any further contact — the fact of writing implied enough.

He wrote and rewrote, shading an emphasis here, burnishing a highlight, lengthening there, excising. Humour with a dash of pathos dealt with Stella Bluth and Nadia Chayefski. Elspeth McCleod he played as comedy degenerating into farce. He himself emerged as a slightly bruised idealist, rueful, the Philip Marlowe of the antique trade, a man unafraid to admit to loneliness, a man, who, in these untender times, was not ashamed to admit to the possibility of love.

Love, which, strip away our sterile sophistication, our bright brittleness, was perhaps . . . *etc. etc.*

Difficult, this part. Such rhetoric clashed with the letter's general tone. He struggled to bring it under control.

The letter was five pages long. Looking at his watch, he saw with surprise that he'd been working on it for more than three hours. He realized suddenly that he was hungry and exhausted. He felt light-headed, oddly disconnected from his bedroom with its familiar furniture, as if he'd been living for those hours in a different world where a part of him still lingered. He poured himself a large scotch and read the letter through, smiling still at certain turns of phrase. The letter pleased him; it was a fine blend of humour, self-deprecation, and manly emotion. In a quiet way, it was moving.

He decided that he must eat before writing out a fair copy. He investigated the kitchen. He had bought supplies, tins, meat in the fridge, the *Penguin Book of French Provincial Cookery*. The haricot beans he had been soaking with the intention of using in a simplified version of cassoulet seemed to have gone funny. There was a grey scum on the water and they smelled. As he had further work to do on the letter and felt tired, he decided to eat, for the sake of convenience, at Chez Jean-Guy.

He took the scotch and the letter into the living-room and sat down to read it again. It *was* moving. He sipped the scotch. And what was more, he realized, it was *true*.

He mailed the letter the next morning and immediately began to brood about the anarchy of the Montreal postal situation. It was not unheard of for letters to take eight days to cross the city. Letters were sorted ten times, redirected, trundled to Ottawa and back, burned even by union goon squads. Burned, dropped down drains, stabbed through and through by separatist postmen.

His mail was usually delivered at about ten AM and on the third possible day for a reply he drove home at lunchtime to check his mailbox. It contained advertising matter from Simpsons and a Hydro bill.

The weekend intervened.

On Monday, however, the whiteness inside the mail-slot was an envelope addressed in an unfamiliar hand.

The letter read:

Dear Mr. Thornton,

Thank you for your charming and humourous letter. There was no need to apologize. If apologies are needed, then I should apologize for being so abrupt. How were you to know that I'd been made the object of someone's spite? Strange as it may seem, passions in libraries *do* exist — it must be something to do with being so enclosed — I was about to say *cloistered!*

Please don't feel guilty and excuse my curtness — I'm sure with *your* experiences, you'll understand it.

Yours sincerely,
Anna Stevens

Peter studied the letter.

The most important point, of course, was that she had written it at all. Any kind of reply was a clear indication of interest. That she had gone further and unnecessarily revealed the nature of her occupation... He wondered about the words 'cloistered' and 'passions' — words possibly full of obscure promise.

He imagined her voice saying those words.

On the phone she had said, 'one of the men I work with' and the plural was interesting. In most public libraries, the staff was mainly women — one man, perhaps. But 'men'? Possible in the main branch of a large city but Montreal had no large public English-language library. And the private or semi-private libraries — Fraser Hickson, Atwater, Westmount — were definitely female preserves. Could it be that, better and better, she worked in a university? And he wondered about 'one of the men' — why he'd done that, filled in the form. A discontented underling? A rejected suitor, perhaps, spurred by bitterness.

The letter was written in ink not ballpoint — much in her favour. The paper was a heavy bond, pleasant to handle, the handwriting graceful and firm. The emphasis of 'do' and 'cloistered,' and 'your' and the excessive exclamation mark were possibly a little feminine but the letter was not hideous with green or purple ink and circles instead of dots over the i's — characteristics with which he had become familiar over the last three years, infallible indicators of mental or emotional unbalance.

What should be his response? To phone, even now, would be injudicious. Another letter was required, a letter simple and to the point. A letter which explained how he was haunted by how strangely they were yoked by coincidence, which proposed they meet entirely outside the sordid context of CompuMate, perhaps for dinner. Solitary dining uncheering and bad for the digestion. Something along those lines. He would gamble everything on one throw of the dice.

It was as he was labouring over the composition of this letter that the phone rang. He reached over from his desk.

"So what's new?" said Alan.

"Nothing much. You?"

"Just been invited to give a paper in England at a Shakespeare orgy. Expenses paid."

"Will Nancy let you go?"

"I'll have to try being nice to her for a bit," said Alan.

"I'll tell you what *did* happen," said Peter. "I've just met a most interesting new lady."

"What sort of lady?"

"A librarian lady. Very bright. Very good-looking. It all looks very promising."

"Large personalities, has she?" said Alan.

"Really North!" said Peter. "Must you sully everything you touch?"

"Sully my ass," said Alan. "I'd rather have a pair of first-rate knockers than all those old Chinese pots and pans you moon over."

"You have a point, I suppose," said Peter.

"So have they," said Alan. "But listen. Enough of this Pat and Mike stuff. You want to come to dinner? Nancy's doing something disgusting from a new cook book and I want you to eat some before I try it. Half an hour or so? Dress informal."

"I'll pick up some wine," said Peter.

"If you want," said Alan, "bring this librarian creature."

The next morning, after the alarm had gone off, dozing, Peter dreamed a most vivid dream which was part dream and part memory. It was the last day of his summer holiday at his uncle's farm. He was saying goodbye to the girl who lived at the next farm. He was thirteen and loved her achingly. Marjorie was twelve.

He was standing in the lane looking up at her where she sat on her pony. Their conversation was stilted. Suddenly he blurted out:

"Can I kiss you goodbye?"

A deep blush suffused her and she bent to pat the horse's neck.

After a silence she said:

"I'd like to but I can't."

They seemed held there then in the still sunshine, the shade of the hazel trees almost black, the buzz of insects in the roadside flowers. He stared at a place in the rein where the leather was cracked and blackened.

And then she said:

"You can have this to keep."

And she thrust at him her handkerchief, a large, man's handkerchief, white with a green and brown border. And later in the bedroom with the black oak beams where he always slept, he moved aside the basin and ewer and smoothed and folded the handkerchief on the washstand and put it in the brown plastic wallet his Auntie Anne had given him for a going-away present.

On his way to work, to his pots and pans as Alan called them, he drove down to the main post office and mailed the letter. He had thought of driving to a post office in Outremont where she lived and posting the letter there but realized that all mail probably went first to the main branch for sorting.

He did not doubt that she would reply.

He was working now on the catalogue, his desk covered with numbered file cards bearing descriptions of each item — dates, hallmarks, troy weights, factory marks, furniture labels, repairs noted, flaws and defects noted, provenance.

Pots and pans.

Thoughts of Anna Stevens possessed his mind.

A bedroom in Madrid full of sunlight, a red tile floor. Breakfast late, and then, in the afternoon, beer and *tapas* at a sidewalk café, she in a blue and white cotton frock, sun-brown legs. And at five in the afternoon, the black bulls in the bull ring, the yellow and magenta capes. And then through the warm and quickening streets strolling towards dinner at eleven.

He would take her to his favourite places, the farmlands of his childhood, Madrid, Angoulème, to the rows of dealers in Amsterdam in their ancient, leaning buildings, to the Hebrides, to his student rooms in the rue de Vaugirard.

Yes.

They would walk in the Jardin du Luxembourg eating lemon water-ice.

He thought again of Paco Camino, slim in a silver suit of lights, and counted the years in shock. He had seen the boy take his *alternativa*, followed him in those sun-filled student days through San Sebastian, Bilbao, Huesca, Pamplona, down through the orange groves to Seville, watched him work the bulls with mad and terrifying grace.

So many years ago like yesterday. What had become of that nobility? Dead now, perhaps, or fat, or fighting bulls with shaved horns like the rest.

Was he too old, Peter wondered, too old to start again?

File cards. Pots and pans.

The day bore on.

On the way home from work he bought the Montreal *Star*. His mailbox contained a mangled *New Yorker* and a letter from an insurance company informing him that he had been chosen from thousands to receive a prize. He poured himself a drink and sat in his living-room. He got up and put on a record he'd bought in a Greek store on Park Avenue, bazouki music and a man singing, very sad-sounding and Eastern, but after a couple of minutes he took the record off.

The apartment, cleaned and now quite neat, was somehow oppressive. He stroked the intricate surface of the cloisonné vase that stood on the bookcase. Pots and pans. He stood at the window looking out and feeling restless. He wanted to be a part of the life out there but if he went out he had nowhere he wanted to go. The glass of the window was cold. He went into his bedroom and called Alan but there was no answer. Ray, too, was not back from work.

He sat looking through his address book. So many names crossed out, friends of Pat's, acquaintances fallen by the wayside since his divorce. He stared at her familiar handwriting, numbers from their old locality — grocers, beer, laundry, drycleaners, diaper-service.

He thought of Jeremy last summer and the summer before, of those desert hours in the sandbox in the park, the suspicious stares of the suburban mothers and their huddled conversations, the sun crawling towards the hot tears of bedtime.

He saw himself in the living-room at night stupefied with exhaustion listening to the child's breathing, waiting for a sigh or cry, drinking scotch too fast, too tired to eat.

He was unable to concentrate on the news in the *Star* and he found himself doing something that he never did, working his way through the classified section, through the columns of houses for sale. Outremont, lower Westmount, Montreal West.

He pictured them together, a family again, Anna and Jeremy, on picnics, at the seaside, in fields full of flowers.

After the third day of waiting, Anna's reply arrived. He had known that it would be there, had dawdled deliberately on the way home doing some unnecessary shopping. He did not open the letter in the elevator. In his apartment, he hung up his coat. He took a beer from the fridge and poured it into a pewter tankard he rarely used. He took the beer into the living-room and set it down on the table by his chair. He hunted for the brass letter-opener which he never used, a gift from someone once, its handle the three monkeys. He slit open the envelope and drew out the letter.

He read the note quickly, then read it through again. He could feel the smile stretching his face. He raised the tankard and said aloud, "Your health sir! Your very good health."

He felt so happy it was as if he'd breathed in as much as possible, then a bit more — he felt *full*. He blew a kiss to the drawing which hung near the door — gorgeous grainy charcoal, a backview of a nude brushing her hair.

"An army," he said sternly to her back, "marches on its stomach."

He took the dog-eared copy of *Where to Dine in Montreal* from the bookcase and started to thumb through it. He felt he could compile a better guide himself, one which named names, which exposed corruption in high places, which advised of the venerable patisserie, the Bisto sauces, the crêpes manufactured from Aunt Jemima at $6.50. It was mildly depressing to think of the procession of women he had squired to most of Montreal's many restaurants. He wished he could think of some other socially acceptable way of meeting her, of meeting Anna, something less *used*.

He needed a meal that would be lengthy with no pressure from waiters seeking to seat the starving hordes. He considered the St. Amable — tables too close together. Chez Bardet? Too oppressive, too much conscious good taste, everyone on his or her best behaviour. His own favourite going-out place was the Symposium but it was not a restaurant for intimate occasions — at nine o'clock it filled with rattletrap drummers, amplified bazoukis, and men who danced intensely and alone.

He needed, then, an unhurried restaurant with a relaxed atmosphere, but not *too* festive, with tables decently separated, and, as he was dealing with unknown tastes, a cuisine not aggressively ethnic. The idea came to him of the Port and Starboard; if she didn't like seafood, the meat dishes were more than passable, salads good, wine list reasonable, the whole place nautically silly with portholes and pleasant and comfortable.

He felt that, even now, it would be safer to write again with day, place, and time but he knew that he could not stand more writing, more waiting, more hours, days, mailmen and letterboxes.

The conversation was brief, the most convenient arrangement made, and even the part he'd been dreading was carried off with the minimum of awkwardness.

"This is rather ridiculous," he said, "like spy stories — but how will I recognize you?"

"I'll be the one," she said, "carrying a copy of *Pravda* and a saxophone and wearing a red coat."

He laughed deliberately and gratefully.

"Red coat it is," he said. "Until tomorrow, then."

Peter sat the next night, half an hour before the appointed time, in the Crow's Nest drinking a nasty drink called a Capstan. The Crow's Nest was a small bar just outside the main dining room of the Port and Starboard which gave a view of the staircase, the cashdesk, and the cloakroom. The tables in the Crow's Nest were made of barrels and the seats were fashioned from kegs. Special low prices were being offered on drinks called The Capstan, Bluenose, and Blow The Man Down.

Since his last visit, to his horror, the restaurant had fallen prey to a prodigal decorator. The overall effect was of an end-of-lease sale at the premises of an unsuccessful chandler. Every nook, recess, and area of wall had been jammed, plastered, and festooned with nets, buoys, bollards, binnacles, belaying-pins, barnacle-encrusted brass bells, anchors, cutlasses, hawsers, harpoons, lanterns, strings of bunting and lengths of rusted chain.

Peter imagined the whole restaurant as a bad stage set for a musical. At the entrance to the Crow's Nest, facing the wide staircase, stood a ship's figurehead in the form of a mermaid. The sequence formed before his eyes — a muscular matelot in striped jersey and canvas bell-bottom pants dancing down the staircase, leaning forward from the waist, arms akimbo, to plant a chaste kiss upon the mermaid's carmine lips, and then whirling away into the restaurant proper to dance on tables for Annabelle, the Admiral's lovely daughter.

Peter felt nervous and looked frequently at his watch.

His drink was becoming nastier and *thicker* as he neared the maraschino cherry.

He felt constrained in his newly pressed suit and the white shirt he had bought that morning, dressed up, costumed. He fiddled with the knot of his tie. He fiddled with his silver cigarette lighter.

And then, on the stairs, a flash of red movement, legs, red coat, a girl standing on the bottom step looking about her.

He got up from the table and moved towards her. She was tall and had long black hair tied at the nape with a red wool ribbon like the ones that Nancy bought for Amanda. Her eyes were large and dark. She was beautiful.

She turned again and saw him coming towards her.

He raised his eyebrows.

She smiled.

"Anna?"

"Sorry I'm late," she said. "There's a blizzard starting out there — cars abandoned all over the road."

"I have a table through here," he said. "Thought you might like a drink while we're waiting."

"Lovely," she said.

"Shall I check your coat."

"No, thanks. I'm still freezing."

As she manoeuvred round the barrel and kegs to sit down, the hood of her coat caught on the fluke of an anchor and he had to disentangle her.

"I'm sorry," he said, gesturing at the walls. "It wasn't like this the last time I was here."

"I *like* silly places once in a while," she said. "What's *that*?"

"I've been wondering," said Peter. "I think it's a donkey-engine."

She undid the wooden pegs of her coat, slipped her arms out of it, and then settled it back over her shoulders. In the bar's half-gloom, pretending not to be watching, Peter saw that she was wearing a black turtle-neck sweater with some kind of large silver pendant over her breasts.

"Drinks!" said Peter. "What would you like? I'll wade through the lobster traps to the bar."

"Sherry, please. A *fino. Tio Pepe*, if they have it."

"This," said Peter, "is a Capstan, as advertised, and it is unbelievably vile and I'm going to get a scotch to take the taste away."

When he came back from the bar, he raised his glass and said,

"Well, Yo-ho-ho!"

"It does all crowd in on you a bit, doesn't it?" she said.

"I hope the food's still as good," said Peter. "If the decor's anything to go by we might be eating hardtack and tapping out the weevils."

"With lashings of putrid salt pork," she said.

"And dumplings sewn up in canvas," said Peter.

She sipped the sherry and smiled at him.

"I like dry sherry," she said, "but I don't like it as much as martinis but if I drink *them* before I eat I get tiddly and can't taste the food."

"Half-seas over, as it were," said Peter.

"Three sheets to the wind," she said.

"In irons on a lee shore," said Peter.

"You made that up," she said.

"I swear," said Peter, "by all that's nautical. I got it from a Hornblower book."

"What does it mean, then?"

"I don't know," he said, making a severe face, "but it's *not good*."

She giggled.

"You're silly," she said.

"Far from it," said Peter. "You behold one who is Captain of his Fate."

"Men who play," she said, "are more to be trusted than men who do not play."

"Is that one of your Laws?"

"The Third," she said. "And I don't feel so nervous now. Can I have a cigarette?"

"Me neither," said Peter.

They occupied themselves with cigarettes and his lighter and the ashtray.

"Can I ask you something I shouldn't?" said Peter.

"What?"

"Why did you come tonight?"

She shrugged.

"I don't know," she said. "It was against my better judgement but — well, I wasn't doing anything else. And your letter, I liked your letter. Curiosity. Who knows?"

"Meeting people is sort of sordid, isn't it?" said Peter. "I'm sorry."

She laughed.

"I didn't mean to be funny."

"I know you didn't," she said. "You just are."

They looked at each other smiling.

"When that wretched little man in the library sent in my name to that *thing* ..."

"Why did he do that?"

"I think he thought it was funny," she said. "Men who work in libraries tend to be strange — not all of them, of course — but quite a few are eccentric or homosexual or just childish — I suppose like men who choose to teach elementary school or become nurses. The way things are, it's a strange occupation to choose. Shouldn't be, but it is. But you wouldn't *believe* some of the things I went through. Breathers and panters and abuse and men asking me how much I charged — "

"Good God!" said Peter.

"Someone kept sending religious tracts and one man kept sending me postcards — always the same one. On the writing side it always said I MEAN TO HAVE YOU and the picture-side was always a reproduction of a sort of scroll that had a chant or a prayer by Aleister Crowley on it."

She looked enquiry at him and he nodded.

"Always the same thing," she went on, "one of those 'Do What You Want Shall Be All Of The Law' Crowley things — gibberish, horrible — murder being good if you feel like doing it, you know? I was getting really frightened."

"I've always thought it was funny," said Peter,

"that the Great Beast was cremated at Brighton. He should at least have disappeared in a clap of thunder and forked lightning."

"I didn't think *any* of this was very funny," she said.

"True," said Peter. "I was just thinking about Brighton."

"One man," she said, "even sent me a sheet of paper — foolscap — with some obscene doggerel at the bottom and with a drawing of his — his apparatus on the rest."

Peter laughed out loud.

"Really," she said. "And there was an asterisk by the, well, the *tip* of it and beside the asterisk it said 'Actual size'."

She joined in his laughter.

"Did he *need* foolscap?" said Peter.

"But what was funnier than *that*," she said, "if you stop to think about it, I mean, and sad too, it was a Gestetner stencil."

The maître d' appeared at the doorway of the Crow's Nest, menus cradled in his arm, and inclined his head in stately summons. They followed his measured pace and majestic bulk towards the dining-room. In the more brightly lighted foyer and corridor, Peter was violently aware of the swing of Anna's skirt, the trimness and tension of her body beside him.

The dining-room itself was less ravaged; the prints of Ships of the Line remained and the decorator had confined himself to blocks and tackle and a few flurries of swords. They quickly settled the details of the meal; Anna decided on crêpes stuffed with shrimp, clams, mussel and oyster and baked in cream and cheese; Peter on a dish of herring and roe. Anna traded in an hors d'oeuvre for a dry martini and Peter ordered another scotch. Much ado was made with a wine cooler, napery, and the solemnities of label-inspection.

"I was meaning to ask you," said Peter. "Which library do you work in?"

"McGill," she said. "In the rare book and special collections."

"Aha!" said Peter. "I've had dealings with them. We once took some medieval manuscripts there we'd had in an estate sale — sort of contracts or leases — bits of parchment with wavy edges?"

He made scissors with his fingers.

"They're called foot of fine," she said, nodding.

"We wanted them dated," he said, "and not a soul in that place had even a clue."

"You aren't surprising me," she said.

"What's more than one of them? *Feet* of fine? Foot of *fines*?"

"Lovely," she said, putting her hand over his for a second. "You don't know how lovely it is to be talking to someone whom you *know* won't say, 'What's the point of first editions when you can buy it in paperback?' Or, 'Is it fair to students to buy things they can't read?' "

"*They*," said Peter, "are always with us."

"I try," she said, "but I don't like *they*."

"Isn't it *nice*," he said, raising his scotch in salute, "you with your squiggly old manuscripts and me with my old pots and pans, isn't it nice to have two *us's* together instead of an *us* and a *them*?"

"Yes," she said, "it really is nice."

A bus boy arrived with wine glasses, a water pitcher, bread basket and butter dish and they drew apart as he busied himself.

"So tell me," said Peter, "what *are* the Special Collections?"

She laughed.

"The two main ones," she said, "are Winston Churchill and books and pamphlets relating to the Boy Scout movement."

"How depressingly Canadian," he said.

"And of course," she said, "even those were a bequest."

The cork was pulled, wine tasted, glasses filled.

Salads arrived.

"So it's not entirely fascinating?" said Peter.

"I often wish I'd stayed in London," she said.

"What were you doing?"

"Well, after university and library school here, I went there to King's College — I was taking the diploma course in palaeography."

"And then?"

"I *did* stay for a year but then I fled the country and here I am back with Winston Churchill and the Boy Scouts."

"Fled?"

She laughed.

"Yes, I really did flee — all very dramatic and intense. Possessions abandoned and dishes left on the table. It all seems very *young* and silly now."

"Don't be tantalizing."

"Oh, well, I was living with a very agonized Englishman who was trying to decide if he was or wasn't homosexual and one day I knew I just couldn't take it any more. I didn't know what to do. So I ran away. He was a Marxist, too, and that's a bad combination because they *talk* a lot."

She traced the rim of the wine glass with her fingertip.

"Perhaps it was the talking," she said, "more than anything else."

Peter nodded.

"Bad talk," he said, "is not good."

"That's a profound remark," she said. "*You're* not a Marxist, are you?"

"No," said Peter, "nor homosexual."

"That's a relief," she said. "Most nice men are."

The waitress arrived. Dinner was served from casserole and platter onto plates, wine glasses were replenished. When the waitress had withdrawn, Peter said,

"Okay. If we're asking intimate questions, let me ask you one."

She looked up.

"Have *you* got a cat?"

"A cat?"

"A cat."

"Can I take the Fifth?"

"Not allowed."

"Well," she said, "no. I hate them."

He nodded slowly, as if weighing her reply.

She made a mocking little-girl face at him.

"Did I pass?"

"We're not allowed to say," he said, preparing to dissect a herring.

She gestured at the seafood crêpes with her fork.

"*Delicious,* Peter. Like to try some?"

He shook his head.

"All that heaving brown cheese — it looks like a thing a friend of mine makes — he calls it 'Disgusting Potatoes.' You'll like Alan."

As they ate, they chatted of other foods and restaurants, other cities, until the talk turned, inevitably, to the drama of families. Anna's mother was a martyr whose sufferings were inflicted on the entire cast. She ironed underwear and saved paper bags. She rearranged Anna's books in Anna's apartment according to colour. Anna's father was a mining engineer who, unable to stand the provocation of ironed underwear and paper bags, now lived in Edmonton. This desertion was a matter of profound satisfaction to his estranged wife. The script demanded from Anna guilt that she lived in her own apartment.

Peter related the saga of how his much-loved grandfather in an inebriated state had introduced a horse into his grandmother's teetotal kitchen. This event with its conflicting values was, he explained, the archetype of all relationships in his family. It explained, he said, why his mother had a brooding fear of firearms, why his father had built a second bathroom, and why his brother had gone to Australia.

Anna was smiling and stemming with Kleenex after Kleenex the explosive sneezes and sniffles which had overtaken her.

Plates were pushed away and cigarettes lighted.

Talk turned to Peter's job, the shop he had opened and which had folded, the general duplicity of the antique trade. Anna was fascinated by the fakes, the frauds, the piracy of buying and selling. He explained to her that contrary to appearances, provenance, or apparent age, *all* antiques were made in the closing years of the nineteenth century.

She kept making faces of apology for her fits of coughing and urged him to go on, to pay no attention.

He told her of the workshops and factories which turned out Luristan Bronze Age artifacts, Solingen sword blades, Delftware, and eighteenth-century English silver with genuine eighteenth-century hallmarks; of the intricacies of the aging process in the faking of early Quebec pine, how pieces were usually buried first for six to eight weeks in a manure pile; of the vast Chinese industry and the Chinese copies of European copies of Chinese originals.

Her coughing seemed to be getting more rasping and uncontrollable. He suggested ice cream in the hope it would soothe her throat. Her face was startlingly red and she kept mopping at her eyes. He suggested that they leave, that the night air might make her feel better, but she made a pantomime of refusal, of swallowing something followed by immense relief.

They sat waiting for the ice cream to arrive. It had become impossible to talk. She was restlessly plucking at the neck of her sweater, pulling it away from her throat. The coughing tore at her and between bouts her breathing was audible, harsh and wheezing.

"I've got an idea," said Peter. "I'll go and get some of those after-dinner mints from the bowl at the desk. The sweetness might do something for it."

He had to wait behind a noisy crowd of people arguing about whose privilege it was to pay the bill and then for an old man doddering over the choice of a cigar and then the bowl was found to be nearly empty and the girl insisted on refilling it from an enormous bag she had to fetch from a cupboard in the cloakroom. She then searched through drawers and cupboards for an envelope to put the mints in.

As he made his way back to the table, he saw standing there a waitress and the maître d'. They were looking down at Anna. As he came up to them, the maître d' said,

"It is too much to drink."

"She was doing that," said the waitress.

Anna was making movements with her hands as if unaware of what she was doing, rubbing the bunched sweater under and between her breasts. The red ribbon had come undone and her hair hung about her face. The chain of her pendant had snapped and it lay snaked on the table in front of her. There was something disturbing, almost frightening, about the movement of her hands; it was a movement that reminded him of the violence of a sleeping baby.

"Anna?"

Peter knelt beside her chair and lifted back her hair, smoothing it away from her face. Her eyes seemed not to see him. Her skin looked coarse and grainy and sweat glistened under her eyes.

"Can you tell me what's wrong? Anna?"

He prised her fingers loose from the sweater and pulled it down to cover her. Her body was slippery with sweat.

"She would like to go to the ladies' room," said the maître d'.

Peter put his arm around her and prepared to lift her up but her head lolled.

"I don't think she can move," he said to the maître d'.

"She didn't say anything when I brought that order of ice cream," said the waitress. "She was just doing that."

They looked at her. Her breathing scraped at their silence.

"Well," said Peter, straightening up and turning to the maître d', "I don't think she can walk."

"It is wine," said the maître d'.

There was a crash of broken glass and cutlery falling as she collapsed across the table. Her shoulders were working and she was making noises. Vomit spread out around her face.

Her eyes were closed. Heads were turned; some people were standing up. Peter gathered her hair and lifted it from the path of the vomit. The hair was heavy and alive in his hands. Water dripped onto the floor. The maître d' started to pile shards of glass at the corner of the table.

"Anna?" said Peter. "Can you sit up? If I help you?"

"Excuse me," said a voice behind them. "Thought I'd better pop over and take a look."

The dapper middle-aged man bent over her. His tie trailed in the spilled water.

"Are you a doctor?" said Peter.

"She has fainted," said the maître d'.

"Sneezing, coughing, and so forth," said the doctor. "How long's it been going on?"

"About half an hour," said Peter. "Maybe more. What is it? What's wrong?"

"Do you have oxygen?" said the doctor to the maître d'. "Cannister sort of affair with a mask? Well, you should have."

"What's wrong with her?" said Peter.

"Shock," said the doctor. "Anaphylaxis."

"When I brought that ice cream ..." said the waitress.

"I need a room," said the doctor, "and blankets."

"By the side of the cloakroom," said the maître d', "is the wine cellar."

"That sounds just the job," said the doctor. "And now phone for an ambulance — as fast as you like. You," he said to Peter, "take her other arm. Right? Better this way in case she vomits again."

As they lifted her, there was the sudden stench of diarrhea. Urine trickling down her leg.

"Never mind that," said the doctor. "They usually let it all go. Thank God for panty-hose, eh?"

In the long narrow room which served as a wine cellar they lowered her to the carpet. It was cold there and silent with the door closed. Her breath laboured on, harsh, rasping in the quietness. The sour smell of vomit and the sweeter stench of excrement hung on the chilly air. The doctor turned her head to one side. She was unconscious.

The doctor was breathing heavily from his exertion.

"Not getting any younger," he said.

"But what *is* this anaphylactic shock?"

"It's the devil of a thing," said the doctor, looking at his watch. "Like an extreme allergy reaction. Food can do it, insect bites."

There was a knock at the door and a waiter came in.

"The lady's shoe, sir."

"But I don't understand," said Peter. "She was all right. I was only away a few minutes ..."

"Can be as short as two minutes," said the doctor.

"Is it ... serious?"

"Well," said the doctor, scratching at his moustache with his thumbnail, "yes, I'm afraid it is."

"But I don't understand," said Peter.

"Results in a massive fluid imbalance, you see. The, ah, serum in the body engorges the tissue — can't breathe as a result of that. Throat closes. Lungs fill with liquid. That's what all the coughing and sputtering was in aid of. The whole thing — well, it's rather like drowning, you might say, but drowning from the inside."

There was another knock and the maître d' came in with two blankets.

"Any sign of that ambulance?"

The maître d' shrugged and shook his head.

"Phone again. Immediately. We haven't much time. And send us two brandies — none of your wretched bar stuff. You don't want two poisonings in one night. I don't like that fellow," said the doctor to the closing door. "He seated me in a draught."

He covered her with the blankets and knelt taking her pulse.

"No sense of humour these Italians," he said. "They hadn't got one in the war and they haven't developed one since."

Peter stared at her face.

"But what happens?" he said.

"Happens? Oh. Well, the heart beat becomes more rapid and eventually so fast that the heart isn't circulating at all. No crossover of blood between the, ah, whatnames. Everything demanding oxygen, you see, and the heart doing its best to push round what there is — works harder and harder with less and less — a losing game, you might say. And death results from cardiac arrest."

"Death?"

"No, *no*," said the doctor. "Clap on an oxygen mask — takes care of the breathing. And an injection of what you'd call adrenalin or cortisone steadies the heart — right as rain in no time."

He glanced at his watch and then felt the pulse in her neck.

"Boccaccio was a good chap," he said thoughtfully, "but I haven't a lot of time for them since."

The waiter entered with two snifters of brandy on a tray. He stared at Anna as they took the glasses. The doctor swirled the brandy, inhaled, swallowed. Peter drank from his gratefully. The smell of the room was beginning to make him feel queasy.

"Forbes," said the doctor.

"Pardon?"

"Forbes," he said. "I'm Forbes."

"Oh, I'm sorry. Peter Thornton."

"Wife?" said Forbes gesturing with his glass.

"No. I've just met her."

Anna was stirring under the blankets.

"You just hang on, old girl," said Forbes.

"Do they have oxygen and adrenalin and things in the ambulance?"

"Standard equipment, old chap," said Forbes. "Not to worry. We can set her to rights down here."

Forbes checked her pulse again. Peter stared at Forbes' forefinger as it lay across the inside of Anna's wrist. The finger was bright yellow with nicotine. He tried to read the expression on the man's face. The face told him nothing.

They sat waiting. Peter began to count the wine bottles in the racks. The rasp of Anna's breath filled the silence. He counted all the bottles up to the first partition. There were one hundred and sixty-one bottles.

"They put me in one of their silly prisons, you know," said Forbes.

"Pardon?"

"The Italians. And a damned inefficient place it was."

They were silent.

"Come *on*," said Forbes suddenly.

"Is she still all right?"

Forbes knelt by Anna's side again taking her pulse. He considered his watch.

"Is she?"

"Look!" said Forbes. "Scurry up there above-decks, would you, and investigate that bloody ambulance."

Peter hurried out past the mermaid with the carmine lips and up the wide staircase. He pushed open the heavy padded door and stared out into the blizzard. It was difficult to see much further than the width of the road. Sidewalk and curb were obliterated, cars were white mounds. The wind nearly wrenched the heavy door from his grasp. From St. Catherine Street came the muffled sound of horns.

He stood shivering there trying to peer through the flying snow, straining for the sound of a siren.

As he opened the door to the wine cellar, he saw Forbes kneeling over Anna, the blankets thrown back, her sweater pulled up.

"Nothing?" said Forbes.

"You can't even see," said Peter. "Everywhere's blocked."

"Heart's moving into fibrillation," said Forbes, taking off his jacket. "We're going to have to get some oxygen in there."

"But there isn't any."

Forbes held out his wrists.

"Can you manage these damn cuff-links? Wife usually does it."

"What do you mean — oxygen?"

"Tracheotomy, old chap. Bit of a long shot, but ..."

He pulled the blanket off again.

"Sweater?" he said.

They worked her limp arms out of it and pulled it over her head.

From his trouser pocket, Forbes produced a fat red knife.

"Swiss Army job," he said. "Ingenious thing. Use it in the garden. It's got a pair of scissors and a saw."

"But won't she bleed? I mean ..."

"Can't make an omelet, old chap," said Forbes, rolling up his sleeves. "Simple enough. Not to worry."

Peter stared down at her. A small blue and white cotton tab stuck out from the edge of the left cup of her bra. It said: *St. Michael. Registered Trade Mark.*

"Get all that hair out of the way," said Forbes.

Then,

"*Bloody* HELL."

"What? What is it?"

Forbes crouched across her.

He remained like that for long moments.

Then, slowly, he raised himself up, sat back on his heels.

Then Peter, too, became aware of the difference, the change in the room. The room was silent. The sound had stopped.

Forbes took the tip of the blade between forefinger and thumb and eased the blade inwards to the half-closed position. He then pushed the back of the blade with the flat of his hand and the knife closed with a loud click.

Peter stared at her body. Just above her navel and to one side there was a faint brown birthmark. He stared across her at Forbes.

"But she was all right," said Peter. "I only went to the desk. I was only away a few minutes."

"I'm sorry," said Forbes. "Without oxygen, without drugs ..."

He stood up and started to roll down his sleeves.

"It doesn't make sense," said Peter.

"It's all right," said Forbes. "Not your fault."

"But she was all right," said Peter.

"Look, old chap ..."

"We were talking. She was all right."

"You need a drink," said Forbes. "Do you a world of good. I'll take care of details here. Phone and suchlike — have a word with Chummy out there. Then I'll join you. Right?"

Forbes led him to the door.

"Get yourself a drink. Doctor's orders."

Peter went out into the restaurant. It was noisy and warm. Her red coat was still draped over the back of her chair. The table had been cleaned and reset. The carpet was dark where the water had spilled. Someone had sprayed the area with a lemon-scented air-freshener. He sat down. He picked up a fork and sat staring at the flash of light on the tines.

A voice said something.

"Pardon?"

A waitress stood there with an order pad.

"Are you the party that was at this table before?"

He nodded.

"The other girl she's finished her shift. She's gone off now."

He stared at her.

She was middle-aged with frizzy, yellowed hair and glasses. She looked tired. Like the other waitresses, she was wearing baggy red pirate trousers and a blouse with puffed sleeves fastened at the breast with black thongs. Round her waist was a wide leather belt with a brass buckle. Stuck in the belt was a plastic flintlock pistol. She was wearing the sort of boots that are illustrated in children's stories, *Dick Whittington, The Brave Little Tailor, Puss-in-Boots.*

"Anything else?" he repeated.

"Yes," she said. "Something nice for dessert?"

Montreal 1975/Gifford's Cottages, Delta 1976

LEO TOLSTOY

The Death of Ivan Ilych

Translated by Aylmer Maude

I

During an interval in the Melvinski trial in the large building of the Law Courts, the members and public prosecutor met in Ivan Egorovich Shebek's private room, where the conversation turned on the celebrated Krasovski case. Fëdor Vasilievich warmly maintained that it was not subject to their jurisdiction, Ivan Egorovich maintained the contrary, while Peter Ivanovich, not having entered into the discussion at the start, took no part in it but looked through the *Gazette* which had just been handed in.

"Gentlemen," he said, "Ivan Ilych has died!"

"You don't say so!"

"Here, read it yourself," replied Peter Ivanovich, handing Fëdor Vasilievich the paper still damp from the press. Surrounded by a black border were the words: "Praskovya Fëdorovna Golovina, with profound sorrow, informs relatives and friends of the demise of her beloved husband Ivan Ilych Golovin, Member of the Court of Justice, which occurred on February the 4th of this year 1882. The funeral will take place on Friday at one o'clock in the afternoon."

Ivan Ilych had been a colleague of the gentlemen present and was liked by them all. He had been ill for some weeks with an illness said to be incurable. His post had been kept open for him, but there had been conjectures that in case of his death Alexeev might receive his appointment, and that either Vinnikov or Shtabel would succeed Alexeev. So on receiving the news of Ivan Ilych's death the first thought of each of the gentlemen in that private room was of the changes and promotions it might occasion among themselves or their acquaintances.

"I shall be sure to get Shtabel's place or Vinnikov's," thought Fëdor Vasilievich. "I was promised that long ago, and the promotion means an extra eight hundred rubles a year for me besides the allowance."

"Now I must apply for my brother-in-law's transfer from Kaluga," thought Peter Ivanovich. "My wife will be very glad, and then she won't be able to say that I never do anything for her relations."

"I thought he would never leave his bed again," said Peter Ivanovich aloud. "It's very sad."

"But what really was the matter with him?"

"The doctors couldn't say — at least they could, but each of them said something different. When last I saw him I thought he was getting better."

"And I haven't been to see him since the holidays. I always meant to go."

"Had he any property?"

"I think his wife had a little — but something quite trifling."

"We shall have to go to see her, but they live so terribly far away."

"Far away from you, you mean. Everything's far away from your place."

"You see, he never can forgive my living on the other side of the river," said Peter Ivanovich, smiling at Shebek. Then, still talking of the distances between different parts of the city, they returned to the Court.

Besides considerations as to the possible transfers and promotions likely to result from Ivan Ilych's death, the mere fact of the death of a near acquaintance aroused, as usual, in all who heard of it the complacent feeling that, "it is he who is dead and not I."

Each one thought or felt, "Well, he's dead but I'm alive!" But the more intimate of Ivan Ilych's acquaintances, his so-called friends, could not help thinking also that they would now have to fulfil the very tiresome demands of propriety by attending the funeral service and paying a visit of condolence to the widow.

Fëdor Vasilievich and Peter Ivanovich had been his nearest acquaintances. Peter Ivanovich had studied law with Ivan Ilych and had considered himself to be under obligations to him.

Having told his wife at dinner-time of Ivan Ilych's death and of his conjecture that it might be possible to get her brother transferred to their circuit, Peter Ivanovich sacrificed his usual nap, put on his evening clothes, and drove to Ivan Ilych's house.

At the entrance stood a carriage and two cabs. Leaning against the wall in the hall downstairs near the cloak-stand was a coffin-lid covered with cloth of gold, ornamented with gold cord and tassels, that had been polished up with metal powder. Two ladies in black were taking off their fur cloaks. Peter Ivanovich recognized one of them as Ivan Ilych's sister, but the other was a stranger to him. His colleague Schwartz was just coming downstairs, but on seeing Peter Ivanovich enter he stopped and winked at him, as if to say: "Ivan Ilych has made a mess of things — not like you and me."

Schwartz's face with his Piccadilly whiskers and his slim figure in evening dress, had as usual an air of elegant solemnity which contrasted with the playfulness of his character and had a special piquancy here, or so it seemed to Peter Ivanovich.

Peter Ivanovich allowed the ladies to precede him and slowly followed them upstairs. Schwartz did not come down but remained where he was, and Peter Ivanovich understood that he wanted to arrange where they should play bridge that evening. The ladies went upstairs to the widow's room, and Schwartz with seriously compressed lips but a playful look in his eyes, indicated by a twist of his eyebrows the room to the right where the body lay.

Peter Ivanovich, like everyone else on such occasions, entered feeling uncertain what he would have to do. All he knew was that at such times it is always safe to cross oneself. But he was not quite sure whether one should make obeisances while doing so. He therefore adopted a middle course. On entering the room he began crossing himself and made a slight movement resembling a bow. At the same time, as far as the motion of his head and arm allowed, he surveyed the room. Two young men — apparently nephews, one of whom was a high-school pupil — were leaving the room, crossing themselves as they did so. An old woman was standing motionless, and a lady with strangely arched eyebrows was saying something to her in a whisper. A vigorous, resolute Church Reader, in a frock-coat, was reading something in a loud voice with an expression that precluded any contradiction. The butler's assistant, Gerasim, stepping lightly in front of Peter Ivanovich, was strewing something on the floor. Noticing this, Peter Ivanovich was immediately aware of a faint odour of a decomposing body.

The last time he had called on Ivan Ilych, Peter Ivanovich had seen Gerasim in the study. Ivan Ilych had been particularly fond of him and he was performing the duty of a sick nurse.

Peter Ivanovich continued to make the sign of the cross slightly inclining his head in an intermediate direction between the coffin, the Reader, and the icons on the table in a corner of the room. Afterwards, when it seemed to him that this movement of his arm in crossing himself had gone on too long, he stopped and began to look at the corpse.

The dead man lay, as dead men always lie, in a specially heavy way, his rigid limbs sunk in the soft cushions of the coffin, with the head forever bowed on the pillow. His yellow waxen brow with bald patches over his sunken temples was thrust up in the way peculiar to the dead, the protruding nose seeming to press on the upper lip. He was much changed and had grown even thinner since Peter Ivanovich had last seen him, but, as is always the case with the dead, his face was handsomer and above all more dignified than when he was alive. The expression on the face said that what was necessary had been accomplished, and accomplished rightly. Besides this there was in that expression a reproach and a warning to the living. This warning seemed to Peter Ivanovich out of place, or at least not applicable to him. He felt a certain discomfort and so he hurriedly crossed himself once more and turned and went out of the door — too hurriedly and too regardless of propriety, as he himself was aware.

Schwartz was waiting for him in the adjoining room with legs spread wide apart and both hands toying with his top-hat behind his back. The mere sight of that playful, well-groomed, and elegant figure refreshed Peter Ivanovich. He felt that Schwartz was above all these happenings and would not surrender to any depressing influences. His very look said that this incident of a church service for Ivan Ilych could not be a sufficient reason for infringing the order of the session — in other words, that it would certainly not prevent his unwrapping a new pack of cards and shuffling them that evening while a footman placed four fresh candles on the table: in fact, that there was no reason for supposing that this incident would hinder their spending the evening agreeably. Indeed he said this in a whisper as Peter Ivanovich passed him, proposing that they should meet for a game at Fëdor Vasilievich's. But apparently Peter Ivanovich was not destined to play bridge that evening. Praskovya Fëdorovna (a short, fat woman who despite all efforts to the contrary had continued to broaden steadily from her shoulders downwards and who had the same extraordinarily arched eyebrows as the lady who had been standing by the coffin), dressed all in black, her head covered with lace, came out of her own room with some other ladies, conducted them to the room where the dead body lay, and said: "The service will begin immediately. Please go in."

Schwartz, making an indefinite bow, stood still, evidently neither accepting nor declining this invitation. Praskovya Fëdorovna, recognizing Peter Ivanovich, sighed, went close up to him, took his hand, and said: "I know you were a true friend to Ivan Ilych . . ." and looked at him awaiting some suitable response. And Peter Ivanovich knew that, just as it had been the right thing to cross himself in that room, so what he had to do here was to press her hand, sigh, and say, "Believe me. . . ." So he did all this and as he did it felt that the desired result had been achieved: that both he and she were touched.

"Come with me. I want to speak to you before it begins," said the widow. "Give me your arm."

Peter Ivanovich gave her his arm and they went to the inner rooms, passing Schwartz, who winked at Peter Ivanovich compassionately.

"That does for our bridge! Don't object if we find another player. Perhaps you can cut in when you do escape," said his playful look.

Peter Ivanovich sighed still more deeply and despondently, and Praskovya Fëdorovna pressed his arm gratefully. When they reached the drawing-room, upholstered in pink cretonne and lighted by a dim lamp, they sat down at the table — she on a sofa and Peter Ivanovich on a low pouffe, the springs of which yielded spasmodically under his weight. Praskovya Fëdorovna had been on the point of warning him to take another seat, but felt that such a warning was out of keeping with her present condition and so changed her mind. As he sat down on the pouffe Peter Ivanovich recalled how Ivan Ilych had arranged this room and had consulted him regarding this pink cretonne with green leaves. The whole room was full of furniture and knick-knacks, and on her way to the sofa the lace of the widow's black shawl caught on the carved edge of the table. Peter Ivanovich rose to detach it, and the springs of the pouffe, relieved of his weight, rose also and gave him a push. The widow began detaching her shawl herself, and Peter Ivanovich again sat down, suppressing the rebellious springs of the pouffe under him. But the widow had not quite freed herself and Peter Ivanovich got up again, and again the pouffe rebelled and even creaked. When this was all over she took out a clean cambric handkerchief and began to weep. The episode with the shawl and the struggle with the pouffe had cooled Peter Ivanovich's emotions and he sat there with a sullen look on his face. This awkward situation was interrupted by Sokolov, Ivan Ilych's butler, who came to report that the plot in the cemetery that Praskovya Fëdorovna had chosen would cost two hundred rubles. She stopped weeping and, looking at Peter Ivanovich with the air of a victim, remarked in French that it was very hard for her. Peter Ivanovich made a silent gesture signifying his full conviction that it must indeed be so.

"Please smoke," she said in a magnanimous yet crushed voice, and turned to discuss with Sokolov the price of the plot for the grave.

Peter Ivanovich while lighting his cigarette heard her inquiring very circumstantially into the prices of different plots in the cemetery and finally decide which she would take. When that was done she gave instructions about engaging the choir. Sokolov then left the room.

"I look after everything myself," she told Peter Ivanovich, shifting the albums that lay on the table; and noticing that the table was endangered by his cigarette-ash, she immediately passed him an ash-tray, saying as she did so: "I consider it an affectation to say that my grief prevents my attending to practical affairs. On the contrary, if anything can — I won't say console me, but — distract me, it is seeing to everything concerning him." She again took out her handkerchief as if preparing to cry, but suddenly, as if mastering her feeling, she shook herself and began to speak calmly. "But there is something I want to talk to you about."

Peter Ivanovich bowed, keeping control of the springs of the pouffe, which immediately began quivering under him.

"He suffered terribly the last few days."

"Did he?" said Peter Ivanovich.

"Oh, terribly! He screamed unceasingly, not for minutes but for hours. For the last three days he screamed incessantly. It was unendurable. I cannot understand how I bore it; you could hear him three rooms off. Oh, what I have suffered!"

"Is it possible that he was conscious all that time?" asked Peter Ivanovich.

"Yes," she whispered. "To the last moment. He took leave of us a quarter of an hour before he died, and asked us to take Volodya away."

The thought of the sufferings of this man he had known so intimately, first as a merry little boy, then as a school-mate, and later as a grown-up colleague, suddenly struck Peter Ivanovich with horror, despite an unpleasant consciousness of his own and this woman's dissimulation. He again saw that brow, and that nose pressing down on the lip, and felt afraid for himself.

"Three days of frightful suffering and then death! Why, that might suddenly, at any time, happen to me," he thought, and for a moment felt terrified. But — he did not himself know how — the customary reflection at once occurred to him that this had happened to Ivan Ilych and not to him, and that it should not and could not happen to him, and that to think that it could would be yielding to depression which he ought not to do, as Schwartz's expression plainly showed. After which reflection Peter Ivanovich felt reassured, and began to ask with interest about the details of Ivan Ilych's death, as though death was an accident natural to Ivan Ilych but certainly not to himself.

After many details of the really dreadful physical sufferings Ivan Ilych had endured (which details he learnt only from the effect those sufferings had produced on Praskovya Fëdorovna's nerves) the widow apparently found it necessary to get to business.

"Oh, Peter Ivanovich, how hard it is! How terribly, terribly hard!" and she again began to weep.

Peter Ivanovich sighed and waited for her to finish blowing her nose. When she had done so he said, "Believe me . . ." and she again began talking and brought out what was evidently her chief concern with him — namely, to question him as to how she could obtain a grant of money from the government on the occasion of her husband's death. She made it appear that she was asking Peter Ivanovich's advice about her pension, but he soon saw that she already knew about that to the minutest detail, more even than he did himself. She knew how much could be got out of the government in consequence of her husband's death, but wanted to find out whether she could not possibly extract something more. Peter Ivanovich tried to think of some means of doing so, but after reflecting for a while and, out of propriety, condemning the government for its niggardliness, he said he thought that nothing more could be got. Then she sighed and evidently began to devise means of getting rid of her visitor. Noticing this, he put out his cigarette, rose, pressed her hand, and went out into the anteroom.

In the dining-room where the clock stood that Ivan Ilych had liked so much and had bought at an antique shop, Peter Ivanovich met a priest and a few acquaintances who had come to attend the service, and he recognized Ivan Ilych's daughter, a handsome young woman. She was in black and her slim figure appeared slimmer than ever. She had a gloomy, determined, almost angry expression, and bowed to Peter Ivanovich as though he were in some way to blame. Behind her, with the same offended look, stood a wealthy young man, an examining magistrate, whom Peter Ivanovich also knew and who was her fiancé, as he had heard. He bowed mournfully to them and was about to pass into the death-chamber, when from under the stairs appeared the figure of Ivan Ilych's schoolboy son, who was extremely like his father. He seemed a little Ivan Ilych, such as Peter Ivanovich remembered when they studied law together. His tear-stained eyes had in them the look that is seen in the eyes of boys of thirteen or fourteen who are not pure-minded. When he saw Peter Ivanovich he scowled morosely and shamefacedly. Peter Ivanovich nodded to him and entered the death-chamber. The service began: candles, groans, incense, tears, and sobs. Peter Ivanovich stood looking gloomily down at his feet. He did not look once at the dead man, did not yield to any depressing influence, and was one of the first to leave the room. There was no one in the anteroom, but Gerasim darted out of the dead man's room, rummaged with his strong hands among the fur coats to find Peter Ivanovich's and helped him on with it.

"Well, friend Gerasim," said Peter Ivanovich, so as to say something. "It's a sad affair, isn't it?"

"It's God's will. We shall all come to it some day," said Gerasim, displaying his teeth — the even, white teeth of a healthy peasant — and, like a man in the thick of urgent work, he briskly opened the front door, called the coachman, helped Peter Ivanovich into the sledge, and sprang back to the porch as if in readiness for what he had to do next.

Peter Ivanovich found the fresh air particularly pleasant after the smell of incense, the dead body, and carbolic acid.

"Where to, sir?" asked the coachman.

"It's not too late even now.... I'll call round on Fëdor Vasilievich."

He accordingly drove there and found them just finishing the first rubber, so that it was quite convenient for him to cut in.

II

Ivan Ilych's life had been most simple and most ordinary and therefore most terrible.

He had been a member of the Court of Justice, and died at the age of forty-five. His father had been an official who after serving in various ministries and departments in Petersburg had made the sort of career which brings men to positions from which by reason of their long service they cannot be dismissed, though they are obviously unfit to hold any responsible position, and for whom therefore posts are specially created, which though fictitious carry salaries of from six to ten thousand rubles that are not fictitious, and in receipt of which they live on to a great age.

Such was the Privy Councillor and superfluous member of various superfluous institutions, Ilya Epimovich Golovin.

He had three sons, of whom Ivan Ilych was the second. The eldest son was following in his father's footsteps only in another department, and was already approaching that stage in the service at which a similar sinecure would be reached. The third son was a failure. He had ruined his prospects in a number of positions and was now serving in the railway department. His father and brothers, and still more their wives, not merely disliked meeting him, but avoided remembering his existence unless compelled to do so. His sister had married Baron Greff, a Petersburg official of her father's type. Ivan Ilych was *le phénix de la famille* as people said. He was neither as cold and formal as his elder brother nor as wild as the younger, but was a happy mean between them — an intelligent, polished, lively and agreeable man. He had studied with his younger brother at the School of Law, but the latter had failed to complete the course and was expelled when he was in the fifth class. Ivan Ilych finished the course well. Even when he was at the School of Law he was just what he remained for the rest of his life: a capable, cheerful, good-natured, and sociable man, though strict in the fulfilment of what he considered to be his duty: and he considered his duty to be what was so considered by those in authority. Neither as a boy nor as a man was he a toady, but from early youth was by nature attracted to people of high station as a fly is drawn to the light, assimilating their ways and views of life and establishing friendly relations with them. All the enthusiasms of childhood and youth passed without leaving much trace on him; he succumbed to sensuality, to vanity, and latterly among the highest classes to liberalism, but always within limits which his instinct unfailingly indicated to him as correct.

At school he had done things which had formerly seemed to him very horrid and made him feel disgusted with himself when he did them; but when later on he saw that such actions were done by people of good position and that they did not regard them as wrong, he was able not exactly to regard them as right, but to forget about them entirely or not be at all troubled at remembering them.

Having graduated from the School of Law and qualified for the tenth rank of the civil service, and having received money from his father for his equipment, Ivan Ilych ordered himself clothes at Scharmer's, the fashionable tailor, hung a medallion inscribed *respice finem* on his watch-chain, took leave of his professor and the prince who was patron of the school, had a farewell dinner with his comrades at Donon's first-class restaurant, and with his new and fashionable portmanteau, linen, clothes, shaving and other toilet appliances, and a travelling rug, all purchased at the best shops, he set off for one of the provinces where, through his father's influence, he had been attached to the Governor as an official for special service.

In the province Ivan Ilych soon arranged as easy and agreeable a position for himself as he had had at the School of Law. He performed his official tasks, made his career, and at the same time amused himself pleasantly and decorously. Occasionally he paid official visits to country districts, where he behaved with dignity both to his superiors and inferiors, and performed the duties entrusted to him, which related chiefly to the sectarians, with an exactness and incorruptible honesty of which he could not but feel proud.

In official matters, despite his youth and taste for frivolous gaiety, he was exceedingly reserved, punctilious, and even severe; but in society he was often amusing and witty, and always good-natured, correct in his manner, and *bon enfant*, as the governor and his wife — with whom he was like one of the family — used to say of him.

In the province he had an affair with a lady who made advances to the elegant young lawyer, and there was also a milliner; and there were carousals with aides-de-camp who visited the district, and after-supper visits to a certain outlying street of doubtful reputation; and there was too some obsequiousness to his chief and even to his chief's wife, but all this was done with such a tone of good breeding that no hard names could be applied to it. It all came under the heading of the French saying: *"Il faut que jeunesse se passe."* It was all done with clean hands, in clean linen, with French phrases, and above all among people of the best society and consequently with the approval of people of rank.

So Ivan Ilych served for five years and then came a change in his official life. The new and reformed judicial institutions were introduced, and new men were needed. Ivan Ilych became such a new man. He was offered the post of examining magistrate, and he accepted it though the post was in another province and obliged him to give up the connexions he had formed and to make new ones. His friends met to give him a send-off; they had a group-photograph taken and presented him with a silver cigarette-case, and he set off to his new post.

As examining magistrate Ivan Ilych was just as *comme il faut* and decorous a man, inspiring general respect and capable of separating his official duties from his private life, as he had been when acting as an official on special service. His duties now as examining magistrate were far more interesting and attractive than before. In his former position it had been pleasant to wear an undress uniform made by Scharmer, and to pass through the crowd of petitioners and officials who were timorously awaiting an audience with the governor, and who envied him as with free and easy gait he went straight into his chief's private room to have a cup of tea and a cigarette with him. But not many people had then been directly dependent on him — only police officials and the sectarians when he went on special missions — and he liked to treat them politely, almost as comrades, as if he were letting them feel that he who had the power to crush them was treating them in this simple, friendly way. There were then but few such people. But now, as an examining magistrate, Ivan Ilych felt that everyone without exception, even the most important and self-satisfied, was in his power, and that he need only write a few words on a sheet of paper with a certain heading, and this or that important, self-satisfied person would be brought before him in the role of an accused person or a witness, and if he did not choose to allow him to sit down, would have to stand before him and answer his questions. Ivan Ilych never abused his power; he tried on the contrary to soften its expression, but the consciousness of it and of the possibility of softening its effect, supplied the chief interest and attraction of his office. In his work itself, especially in his examinations, he very soon acquired a method of eliminating all considerations irrelevant to the legal aspect of the case, and reducing even the most complicated case to a form in which it would be presented on paper only in its externals, completely excluding his personal opinion of the matter, while above all observing every prescribed formality. The work was new and Ivan Ilych was one of the first men to apply the new Code of 1864.

On taking up the post of examining magistrate in a new town, he made new acquaintances and connexions, placed himself on a new footing, and assumed a somewhat different tone. He took up an attitude of rather dignified aloofness towards the provincial authorities, but picked out the best circle of legal gentlemen and wealthy gentry living in the town and assumed a tone of slight dissatisfaction with the government, of moderate liberalism, and of enlightened citizenship. At the same time, without at all altering the elegance of his toilet, he ceased shaving his chin and allowed his beard to grow as it pleased.

Ivan Ilych settled down very pleasantly in this new town. The society there, which inclined towards opposition to the Governor, was friendly, his salary was larger, and he began to play *vint* [a form of bridge], which he found added not a little to the pleasure of life, for he had a capacity for cards, played good-humouredly, and calculated rapidly and astutely, so that he usually won.

After living there for two years he met his future wife, Praskovya Fëdorovna Mikhel, who was the most attractive, clever, and brilliant girl of the set in which he moved, and among other amusements and relaxations from his labours as examining magistrate, Ivan Ilych established light and playful relations with her.

While he had been an official on special service he had been accustomed to dance, but now as an examining magistrate it was exceptional for him to do so. If he danced now, he did it as if to show that though he served under the reformed order of things, and had reached the fifth official rank, yet when it came to dancing he could do it better than most people. So at the end of an evening he sometimes danced with Praskovya Fëdorovna, and it was chiefly during these dances that he captivated her. She fell in love with him. Ivan Ilych had at first no definite intention of marrying, but when the girl fell in love with him he said to himself: "Really, why shouldn't I marry?"

Praskovya Fëdorovna came of a good family, was not bad looking, and had some little property. Ivan Ilych might have aspired to a more brilliant match, but even this was good. He had his salary, and she, he hoped, would have an equal income. She was well connected, and was a sweet, pretty, and thoroughly correct young woman. To say that Ivan Ilych married because he fell in love with Praskovya Fëdorovna and found that she sympathized with his views of life would be as incorrect as to say that he married because his social circle approved of the match. He was swayed by both these considerations: the marriage gave him personal satisfaction, and at the same time it was considered the right thing by the most highly placed of his associates.

So Ivan Ilych got married.

The preparations for marriage and the beginning of married life, with its conjugal caresses, the new furniture, new crockery, and new linen, were very pleasant until his wife became pregnant — so that Ivan Ilych had begun to think that marriage would not impair the easy, agreeable, gay and always decorous character of his life, approved of by society and regarded by himself as natural, but would even improve it. But from the first months of his wife's pregnancy, something new, unpleasant, depressing, and unseemly, and from which there was no way of escape, unexpectedly showed itself.

His wife, without any reason — *de gaieté de coeur* as Ivan Ilych expressed it to himself — began to disturb the pleasure and propriety of their life. She began to be jealous without any cause, expected him to devote his whole attention to her, found fault with everything, and made coarse and ill-mannered scenes.

At first Ivan Ilych hoped to escape from the unpleasantness of this state of affairs by the same easy and decorous relation to life that had served him heretofore; he tried to ignore his wife's disagreeable moods, continued to live in his usual easy and pleasant way, invited friends to his house for a game of cards, and also tried going out to his club or spending his evenings with friends. But one day his wife began upbraiding him so vigorously, using such coarse words, and continued to abuse him every time he did not fulfil her demands, so resolutely and with such evident determination not to give way till he submitted — that is, till he stayed at home and was bored just as she was — that he became alarmed. He now realized that matrimony — at any rate with Praskovya Fëdorovna — was not always conducive to the pleasures and amenities of life, but on the contrary often infringed both comfort and propriety, and that he must therefore entrench himself against such infringement. And Ivan Ilych began to seek for means of doing so. His official duties were the one thing that imposed upon Praskovya Fëdorovna, and by means of his official work and the duties attached to it he began struggling with his wife to secure his own independence.

With the birth of their child, the attempts to feed it and the various failures in doing so, and with the real and imaginary illnesses of mother and child, in which Ivan Ilych's sympathy was demanded but about which he understood nothing, the need of securing for himself an existence outside his family life became still more imperative.

As his wife grew more irritable and exacting and Ivan Ilych transferred the centre of gravity of his life more and more to his official work, so did he grow to like his work better and became more ambitious than before.

Very soon, within a year of his wedding, Ivan Ilych had realized that marriage, though it may add some comforts to life, is in fact a very intricate and difficult affair towards which in order to perform one's duty, that is, to lead a decorous life approved of by society, one must adopt a definite attitude just as towards one's official duties.

And Ivan Ilych evolved such an attitude towards married life. He only required of it those conveniences — dinner at home, housewife, and bed — which it could give him, and above all that propriety of external forms required by public opinion. For the rest he looked for light-hearted pleasure and propriety, and was very thankful when he found them, but if he met with antagonism and querulousness he at once retired into his separate fenced-off world of official duties, where he found satisfaction.

Ivan Ilych was esteemed a good official, and after three years was made Assistant Public Prosecutor. His new duties, their importance, the possibility of indicting and imprisoning anyone he chose, the publicity his speeches received, and the success he had in all these things, made his work still more attractive.

More children came. His wife became more and more querulous and ill-tempered, but the attitude Ivan Ilych had adopted towards his home life rendered him almost impervious to her grumbling.

After seven years' service in that town he was transferred to another province as Public Prosecutor. They moved, but were short of money and his wife did not like the place they moved to. Though the salary was higher the cost of living was greater, besides which two of their children died and family life became still more unpleasant for him.

Praskovya Fëdorovna blamed her husband for every inconvenience they encountered in their new home. Most of the conversations between husband and wife, especially as to the children's education, led to topics which recalled former disputes, and those disputes were apt to flare up again at any moment. There remained only those rare periods of amorousness which still came to them at times but did not last long. These were islets at which they anchored for a while and then again set out upon that ocean of veiled hostility which showed itself in their aloofness from one another. This aloofness might have grieved Ivan Ilych had he considered that it ought not to exist, but he now regarded the position as normal, and even made it the goal at which he aimed in family life. His aim was to free himself more and more from those unpleasantnesses and to give them a semblance of harmlessness and propriety. He attained this by spending less and less time with his family, and when obliged to be at home he tried to safeguard his position by the presence of outsiders. The chief thing however was that he had his official duties. The whole interest of his life now centred in the official world and that interest absorbed him. The consciousness of his power, being able to ruin anybody he wished to ruin, the importance, even the external dignity of his entry into court, or meetings with his subordinates, his success with superiors and inferiors, and above all his masterly handling of cases, of which he was conscious — all this gave him pleasure and filled his life, together with chats with his colleagues, dinners, and bridge. So that on the whole Ivan Ilych's life continued to flow as he considered it should do — pleasantly and properly.

So things continued for another seven years. His eldest daughter was already sixteen, another child had died, and only one son was left, a schoolboy and a subject of dissension. Ivan Ilych wanted to put him in the School of Law, but to spite him Praskovya Fëdorovna entered him at the High School. The daughter had been educated at home and had turned out well: the boy did not learn badly either.

III

So Ivan Ilych lived for seventeen years after his marriage. He was already a Public Prosecutor of long standing, and had declined several proposed transfers while awaiting a more desirable post, when an unanticipated and unpleasant occurrence quite upset the peaceful course of his life. He was expecting to be offered the post of presiding judge in a University town, but Happe somehow came to the front and obtained the appointment instead. Ivan Ilych became irritable, reproached Happe, and quarrelled both with him and with his immediate superiors — who became colder to him and again passed him over when other appointments were made.

This was in 1880, the hardest year of Ivan Ilych's life. It was then that it became evident on the one hand that his salary was insufficient for them to live on, and on the other that he had been forgotten, and not only this, but that what was for him the greatest and most cruel injustice appeared to others a quite ordinary occurrence. Even his father did not consider it his duty to help him. Ivan Ilych felt himself abandoned by everyone, and that they regarded his position with a salary of 3,500 rubles as quite normal and even fortunate. He alone knew that with the consciousness of the injustices done him, with his wife's incessant nagging, and with the debts he had contracted by living beyond his means, his position was far from normal.

In order to save money that summer he obtained leave of absence and went with his wife to live in the country at her brother's place.

In the country, without his work, he experienced *ennui* for the first time in his life, and not only *ennui* but intolerable depression, and he decided that it was impossible to go on living like that, and that it was necessary to take energetic measures.

Having passed a sleepless night pacing up and down the veranda, he decided to go to Petersburg and bestir himself, in order to punish those who had failed to appreciate him and to get transferred to another ministry.

Next day, despite many protests from his wife and her brother, he started for Petersburg with the sole object of obtaining a post with a salary of five thousand rubles a year. He was no longer bent on any particular department, or tendency, or kind of activity. All he now wanted was an appointment to another post with a salary of five thousand rubles, either in the administration, in the banks, with the railways, in one of the Empress Marya's Institutions, or even in the customs — but it had to carry with it a salary of five thousand rubles and be in a ministry other than that in which they had failed to appreciate him.

And this quest of Ivan Ilych's was crowned with remarkable and unexpected success. At Kursk an acquaintance of his, F. I. Ilyin, got into the first-class carriage, sat down beside Ivan Ilych, and told him of a telegram just received by the Governor of Kursk announcing that a change was about to take place in the ministry: Peter Ivanovich was to be superseded by Ivan Semënovich.

The proposed change, apart from its significance for Russia, had a special significance for Ivan Ilych, because by bringing forward a new man, Peter Petrovich, and consequently his friend Zachar Ivanovich, it was highly favourable for Ivan Ilych, since Zachar Ivanovich was a friend and colleague of his.

In Moscow this news was confirmed, and on reaching Petersburg Ivan Ilych found Zachar Ivanovich and received a definite promise of an appointment in his former department of Justice.

A week later he telegraphed to his wife: "Zachar in Miller's place. I shall receive appointment on presentation of report."

Thanks to this change of personnel, Ivan Ilych had unexpectedly obtained an appointment in his former ministry which placed him two stages above his former colleagues besides giving him five thousand rubles salary and three thousand five hundred rubles for expenses connected with his removal. All his ill humour towards his former enemies and the whole department vanished, and Ivan Ilych was completely happy.

He returned to the country more cheerful and contented than he had been for a long time. Praskovya Fëdorovna also cheered up and a truce was arranged between them. Ivan Ilych told of how he had been fêted by everybody in Petersburg, how all those who had been his enemies were put to shame and now fawned on him, how envious they were of his appointment, and how much everybody in Petersburg had liked him.

Praskovya Fëdorovna listened to all this and appeared to believe it. She did not contradict anything, but only made plans for their life in the town to which they were going. Ivan Ilych saw with delight that these plans were his plans, that he and his wife agreed, and that, after a stumble, his life was regaining its due and natural character of pleasant lightheartedness and decorum.

Ivan Ilych had come back for a short time only, for he had to take up his new duties on the 10th of September. Moreover, he needed time to settle into the new place, to move all his belongings from the province, and to buy and order many additional things: in a word, to make such arrangements as he had resolved on, which were almost exactly what Praskovya Fëdorovna too had decided on.

Now that everything had happened so fortunately, and that he and his wife were at one in their aims and moreover saw so little of one another, they got on together better than they had done since the first years of marriage. Ivan Ilych had thought of taking his family away with him at once, but the insistence of his wife's brother and her sister-in-law, who had suddenly become particularly amiable and friendly to him and his family, induced him to depart alone.

So he departed, and the cheerful state of mind induced by his success and by the harmony between his wife and himself, the one intensifying the other, did not leave him. He found a delightful house, just the thing both he and his wife had dreamt of. Spacious, lofty reception rooms in the old style, a convenient and dignified study, rooms for his wife and daughter, a study for his son — it might have been specially built for them. Ivan Ilych himself superintended the arrangements, chose the wallpapers, supplemented the furniture (preferably with antiques which he considered particularly *comme il faut*), and supervised the upholstering. Everything progressed and progressed and approached the ideal he had set himself: even when things were only half completed they exceeded his expectations. He saw what a refined and elegant character, free from vulgarity, it would all have when it was ready. On falling asleep he pictured to himself how the reception-room would look. Looking at the yet unfinished drawing-room he could see the fireplace, the screen, the what-not, the little chairs dotted here and there, the dishes and plates on the walls, and the bronzes, as they would be when everything was in place. He was pleased by the thought of how his wife and daughter, who shared his taste in this matter, would be impressed by it. They were certainly not expecting as much. He had been particularly successful in finding, and buying cheaply, antiques which gave a particularly aristocratic character to the whole place. But in his letters he intentionally understated everything in order to be able to surprise them. All this so absorbed him that his new duties — though he liked his official work — interested him less than he had expected. Sometimes he even had moments of absent-mindedness during the Court Sessions, and would consider whether he should have straight or curved cornices for his curtains. He was so interested in it all that he often did things himself, rearranging the furniture, or rehanging the curtains. Once when mounting a step-ladder to show the upholsterer, who did not understand, how he wanted the hangings draped, he made a false step and slipped, but being a strong and agile man he clung on and only knocked his side against the knob of the window frame. The bruised place was painful but the pain soon passed, and he felt particularly bright and well just then. He wrote: "I feel fifteen years younger." He thought he would have everything ready by September, but it dragged on till mid-October. But the result was charming not only in his eyes but to everyone who saw it.

In reality it was just what is usually seen in the houses of people of moderate means who want to appear rich, and therefore succeed only in resembling others like themselves: there were damasks, dark wood, plants, rugs, and dull and polished bronzes — all the things people of a certain class have in order to resemble other people of that class. His house was so like the others that it would never have been noticed, but to him it all seemed to be quite exceptional. He was very happy when he met his family at the station and brought them to the newly furnished house all lit up, where a footman in a white tie opened the door into the hall decorated with plants, and when they went on into the drawing-room, and the study uttering exclamations of delight. He conducted them everywhere, drank in their praises eagerly, and beamed with pleasure. At tea that evening, when Praskovya Fëdorovna among other things asked him about his fall, he laughed and showed them how he had gone flying and had frightened the upholsterer.

"It's a good thing I'm a bit of an athlete. Another man might have been killed, but I merely knocked myself, just here; it hurts when it's touched, but it's passing off already — it's only a bruise."

So they began living in their new home — in which, as always happens, when they got thoroughly settled in they found they were just one room short — and with the increased income, which as always was just a little (some five hundred rubles) too little, but it was all very nice.

Things went particularly well at first, before everything was finally arranged and while something had still to be done: this thing bought, that thing ordered, another thing moved, and something else adjusted. Though there were some disputes between husband and wife, they were both so well satisfied and had so much to do that it all passed off without any serious quarrels. When nothing was left to arrange it became rather dull and something seemed to be lacking, but they were then making acquaintances, forming habits, and life was growing fuller.

Ivan Ilych spent his mornings at the law court and came home to dinner, and at first he was generally in a good humour, though he occasionally became irritable just on account of his house. (Every spot on the tablecloth or the upholstery, and every broken window-blind string, irritated him. He had devoted so much trouble to arranging it all that every disturbance of it distressed him.) But on the whole his life ran its course as he believed life should do: easily, pleasantly, and decorously.

He got up at nine, drank his coffee, read the paper, and then put on his undress uniform and went to the law courts. There the harness in which he worked had already been stretched to fit him and he donned it without a hitch: petitioners, inquiries at the chancery, the chancery itself, and the sittings public and administrative. In all this the thing was to exclude everything fresh and vital, which always disturbs the regular course of official business, and to admit only official relations with people, and then only on official grounds. A man would come, for instance, wanting some information. Ivan Ilych, as one in whose sphere the matter did not lie, would have nothing to do with him: but if the man had some business with him in his official capacity, something that could be expressed on officially stamped paper, he would do everything, positively everything he could within the limits of such relations, and in doing so would maintain the semblance of friendly human relations, that is, would observe the courtesies of life. As soon as the official relations ended, so did everything else. Ivan Ilych possessed this capacity to separate his real life from the official side of affairs and not mix the two, in the highest degree, and by long practice and natural aptitude had brought it to such a pitch that sometimes, in the manner of a virtuoso, he would even allow himself to let the human and official relations mingle. He let himself do this just because he felt that he could at any time he chose resume the strictly official attitude again and drop the human relation. And he did it all easily, pleasantly, correctly, and even artistically. In the intervals between the sessions he smoked, drank tea, chatted a little about politics, a little about general topics, a little about cards, but most of all about official appointments. Tired, but with the feelings of a virtuoso — one of the first violins who has played his part in an orchestra with precision — he would return home to find that his wife and daughter had been out paying calls, or had a visitor, and that his son had been to school, had done his homework with his tutor, and was duly learning what is taught at High Schools. Everything was as it should be. After dinner, if they had no visitors, Ivan Ilych sometimes read a book that was being much discussed at the time, and in the evening settled down to work, that is, read official papers, compared the depositions of witnesses, and noted paragraphs of the Code applying to them. This was neither dull nor amusing. It was dull when he might have been playing bridge, but if no bridge was available it was at any rate better than doing nothing or sitting with his wife. Ivan Ilych's chief pleasure was giving little dinners to which he invited men and women of good social position, and just as his drawing-room resembled all other drawing-rooms so did his enjoyable little parties resemble all other such parties.

Once they even gave a dance. Ivan Ilych enjoyed it and everything went off well, except that it led to a violent quarrel with his wife about the cakes and sweets. Praskovya Fëdorovna had made her own plans, but Ivan Ilych insisted on getting everything from an expensive confectioner and ordered too many cakes, and the quarrel occurred because some of those cakes were left over and the confectioner's bill came to forty-five rubles. It was a great and disagreeable quarrel. Praskovya Fëdorovna called him "a fool and an imbecile," and he clutched at his head and made angry allusions to divorce.

But the dance itself had been enjoyable. The best people were there, and Ivan Ilych had danced with Princess Trufonova, a sister of the distinguished founder of the Society "Bear my Burden."

The pleasures connected with his work were pleasures of ambition; his social pleasures were those of vanity; but Ivan Ilych's greatest pleasure was playing bridge. He acknowledged that whatever disagreeable incident happened in his life, the pleasure that beamed like a ray of light above everything else was to sit down to bridge with good players, not noisy partners, and of course to four-handed bridge (with five players it was annoying to have to stand out, though one pretended not to mind), to play a clever and serious game (when the cards allowed it) and then to have supper and drink a glass of wine. After a game of bridge, especially if he had won a little (to win a large sum was unpleasant), Ivan Ilych went to bed in specially good humour.

So they lived. They formed a circle of acquaintances among the best people and were visited by people of importance and by young folk. In their views as to their acquaintances, husband, wife and daughter were entirely agreed, and tacitly and unanimously kept at arm's length and shook off the various shabby friends and relations who, with much show of affection, gushed into the drawing-room with its Japanese plates on the walls. Soon these shabby friends ceased to obtrude themselves and only the best people remained in the Golovins' set.

Young men made up to Lisa, and Petrishchev, an examining magistrate and Dmitri Ivanovich Petrishchev's son and sole heir, began to be so attentive to her that Ivan Ilych had already spoken to Praskovya Fëdorovna about it, and considered whether they should not arrange a party for them, or get up some private theatricals.

So they lived, and all went well, without change, and life flowed pleasantly.

IV

They were all in good health. It could not be called ill health if Ivan Ilych sometimes said that he had a queer taste in his mouth and felt some discomfort in his left side.

But this discomfort increased and, though not exactly painful, grew into a sense of pressure in his side accompanied by ill humour. And his irritability became worse and worse and began to mar the agreeable, easy, and correct life that had established itself in the Golovin family. Quarrels between husband and wife became more and more frequent, and soon the ease and amenity disappeared and even the decorum was barely maintained. Scenes again became frequent, and very few of those islets remained on which husband and wife could meet without an explosion. Praskovya Fëdorovna now had good reason to say that her husband's temper was trying. With characteristic exaggeration she said he had always had a dreadful temper, and that it had needed all her good nature to put up with it for twenty years. It was true that now the quarrels were started by him. His bursts of temper always came just before dinner, often just as he began to eat his soup. Sometimes he noticed that a plate or dish was chipped, or the food was not right, or his son put his elbow on the table, or his daughter's hair was not done as he liked it, and for all this he blamed Praskovya Fëdorovna. At first she retorted and said disagreeable things to him, but once or twice he fell into such a rage at the beginning of dinner that she realized it was due to some physical derangement brought on by taking food, and so she restrained herself and did not answer, but only hurried to get the dinner over. She regarded this self-restraint as highly praiseworthy. Having come to the conclusion that her husband had a dreadful temper and made her life miserable, she began to feel sorry for herself, and the more she pitied herself the more she hated her husband. She began to wish he would die; yet she did not want him to die because then his salary would cease. And this irritated her against him still more. She considered herself dreadfully unhappy just because not even his death could save her, and though she concealed her exasperation, that hidden exasperation of hers increased his irritation also.

After one scene in which Ivan Ilych had been particularly unfair and after which he had said in explanation that he certainly was irritable but that it was due to his not being well, she said that if he was ill it should be attended to, and insisted on his going to see a celebrated doctor.

He went. Everything took place as he had expected and as it always does. There was the usual waiting and the important air assumed by the doctor, with which he was so familiar (resembling that which he himself assumed in court), and the sounding and listening, and the questions which called for answers that were foregone conclusions and were evidently unnecessary, and the look of importance which implied that "if only you put yourself in our hands we will arrange everything — we know indubitably how it has to be done, always in the same way for everybody alike." It was all just as it was in the law courts. The doctor put on just the same air towards him as he himself put on towards an accused person.

The doctor said that so-and-so indicated that there was so-and-so inside the patient, but if the investigation of so-and-so did not confirm this, then he must assume that and that. If he assumed that and that, then ... and so on. To Ivan Ilych only one question was important: was his case serious or not? But the doctor ignored that inappropriate question. From his point of view it was not the one under consideration, the real question was to decide between a floating kidney, chronic catarrh, or appendicitis. It was not a question of Ivan Ilych's life or death, but one between a floating kidney and appendicitis. And that question the doctor solved brilliantly, as it seemed to Ivan Ilych, in favour of the appendix, with the reservation that should an examination of the urine give fresh indications the matter would be reconsidered. All this was just what Ivan Ilych had himself brilliantly accomplished a thousand times in dealing with men on trial. The doctor summed up just as brilliantly, looking over his spectacles triumphantly and even gaily at the accused. From the doctor's summing up Ivan Ilych concluded that things were bad, but that for the doctor, and perhaps for everybody else, it was a matter of indifference, though for him it was bad. And this conclusion struck him painfully, arousing in him a great feeling of pity for himself and of bitterness towards the doctor's indifference to a matter of such importance.

He said nothing of this, but rose, placed the doctor's fee on the table, and remarked with a sigh: "We sick people probably often put inappropriate questions. But tell me, in general, is this complaint dangerous, or not? ..."

The doctor looked at him sternly over his spectacles with one eye, as if to say: "Prisoner, if you will not keep to the questions put to you, I shall be obliged to have you removed from the court."

"I have already told you what I consider necessary and proper. The analysis may show something more." And the doctor bowed.

Ivan Ilych went out slowly, seated himself disconsolately in his sledge, and drove home. All the way home he was going over what the doctor had said, trying to translate those complicated, obscure, scientific phrases into plain language and find in them an answer to the question: "Is my condition bad? Is it very bad? Or is there as yet nothing much wrong?" And it seemed to him that the meaning of what the doctor had said was that it was very bad. Everything in the streets seemed depressing. The cabmen, the houses, the passers-by, and the shops, were dismal. His ache, this dull gnawing ache that never ceased for a moment, seemed to have acquired a new and more serious significance from the doctor's dubious remarks. Ivan Ilych now watched it with a new and oppressive feeling.

He reached home and began to tell his wife about it. She listened, but in the middle of his account his daughter came in with her hat on, ready to go out with her mother. She sat down reluctantly to listen to this tedious story, but could not stand it long, and her mother too did not hear him to the end.

"Well, I am very glad," she said. "Mind now to take your medicine regularly. Give me the prescription and I'll send Gerasim to the chemist's." And she went to get ready to go out.

While she was in the room Ivan Ilych had hardly taken time to breathe, but he sighed deeply when she left it.

"Well," he thought, "perhaps it isn't so bad after all."

He began taking his medicine and following the doctor's directions, which had been altered after the examination of the urine. But then it happened that there was a contradiction between the indications drawn from the examination of the urine and the symptoms that showed themselves. It turned out that what was happening differed from what the doctor had told him, and that he had either forgotten, or blundered, or hidden something from him. He could not, however, be blamed for that, and Ivan Ilych still obeyed his orders implicitly and at first derived some comfort from doing so.

From the time of his visit to the doctor, Ivan Ilych's chief occupation was the exact fulfilment of the doctor's instructions regarding hygiene and the taking of medicine, and the observation of his pain and his excretions. His chief interests came to be people's ailments and people's health. When sickness, deaths, or recoveries were mentioned in his presence, especially when the illness resembled his own, he listened with agitation which he tried to hide, asked questions, and applied what he heard to his own case.

The pain did not grow less, but Ivan Ilych made efforts to force himself to think that he was better. And he could do this so long as nothing agitated him. But as soon as he had any unpleasantness with his wife, any lack of success in his official work, or held bad cards at bridge, he was at once acutely sensible of his disease. He had formerly borne such mischances, hoping soon to adjust what was wrong, to master it and attain success, or make a grand slam. But now every mischance upset him and plunged him into despair. He would say to himself: "There now, just as I was beginning to get better and the medicine had begun to take effect, comes this accursed misfortune, or unpleasantness. ..." And he was furious with the mishap, or with the people who were causing the unpleasantness and killing him, for he felt that this fury was killing him but could not restrain it. One would have thought that it should have been clear to him that this exasperation with circumstances and people aggravated his illness, and that he ought therefore to ignore unpleasant occurrences. But he drew the very opposite conclusion: he said that he needed peace, and he watched for everything that might disturb it and became irritable at the slightest infringement of it. His condition was rendered worse by the fact that he read medical books and consulted doctors. The progress of his disease was so gradual that he could deceive himself when comparing one day with another — the difference was so slight. But when he consulted the doctors it seemed to him that he was getting worse, and even very rapidly. Yet despite this he was continually consulting them.

That month he went to see another celebrity, who told him almost the same as the first had done but put his questions rather differently, and the interview with this celebrity only increased Ivan Ilych's doubts and fears. A friend of a friend of his, a very good doctor, diagnosed his illness again quite differently from the others, and though he predicted recovery, his questions and suppositions bewildered Ivan Ilych still more and increased his doubts. A homoeopathist diagnosed the disease in yet another way, and prescribed medicine which Ivan Ilych took secretly for a week. But after a week, not feeling any improvement and having lost confidence both in the former doctor's treatment and in this one's, he became still more despondent. One day a lady acquaintance mentioned a cure effected by a wonder-working icon. Ivan Ilych caught himself listening attentively and beginning to believe that it had occurred. This incident alarmed him. "Has my mind really weakened to such an extent?" he asked himself. "Nonsense! It's all rubbish. I mustn't give way to nervous fears but having chosen a doctor must keep strictly to his treatment. That is what I will do. Now it's all settled. I won't think about it, but will follow the treatment seriously till summer, and then we shall see. From now there must be no more of this wavering!" This was easy to say but impossible to carry out. The pain in his side oppressed him and seemed to grow worse and more incessant, while the taste in his mouth grew stranger and stranger. It seemed to him that his breath had a disgusting smell, and he was conscious of a loss of appetite and strength. There was no deceiving himself: something terrible, new, and more important than anything before in his life, was taking place within him of which he alone was aware. Those about him did not understand or would not understand it, but thought everything in the world was going on as usual. That tormented Ivan Ilych more than anything. He saw that his household, especially his wife and daughter who were in a perfect whirl of visiting, did not understand anything of it and were annoyed that he was so depressed and so exacting, as if he were to blame for it. Though they tried to disguise it he saw that he was an obstacle in their path, and that his wife had adopted a definite line in regard to his illness and kept to it regardless of anything he said or did. Her attitude was this: "You know," she would say to her friends, "Ivan Ilych can't do as other people do, and keep to the treatment prescribed for him. One day he'll take his drops and keep strictly to his diet and go to bed in good time, but the next day unless I watch him he'll suddenly forget his medicine, eat sturgeon — which is forbidden — and sit up playing cards till one o'clock in the morning."

"Oh, come, when was that?" Ivan Ilych would ask in vexation. "Only once at Peter Ivanovich's."

"And yesterday with Shebek."

"Well, even if I hadn't stayed up, this pain would have kept me awake."

"Be that as it may you'll never get well like that, but will always make us wretched."

Praskovya Fëdorovna's attitude to Ivan Ilych's illness, as she expressed it both to others and to him, was that it was his own fault and was another of the annoyances he caused her. Ivan Ilych felt that this opinion escaped her involuntarily — but that did not make it easier for him.

At the law courts too, Ivan Ilych noticed, or thought he noticed, a strange attitude towards himself. It sometimes seemed to him that people were watching him inquisitively as a man whose place might soon be vacant. Then again, his friends would suddenly begin to chaff him in a friendly way about his low spirits, as if the awful, horrible, and unheard-of thing that was going on within him, incessantly gnawing at him and irresistibly drawing him away, was a very agreeable subject for jests. Schwartz in particular irritated him by his jocularity, vivacity, and *savoir-faire*, which reminded him of what he himself had been ten years ago.

Friends came to make up a set and they sat down to cards. They dealt, bending the new cards to soften them, and he sorted the diamonds in his hand and found he had seven. His partner said "No trumps" and supported him with two diamonds. What more could be wished for? It ought to be jolly and lively. They would make a grand slam. But suddenly Ivan Ilych was conscious of that gnawing pain, that taste in his mouth, and it seemed ridiculous that in such circumstances he should be pleased to make a grand slam.

He looked at his partner Mikhail Mikhaylovich, who rapped the table with his strong hand and instead of snatching up the tricks pushed the cards courteously and indulgently towards Ivan Ilych that he might have the pleasure of gathering them up without the trouble of stretching out his hand for them. "Does he think I am too weak to stretch out my arm?" thought Ivan Ilych, and forgetting what he was doing he over-trumped his partner, missing the grand slam by three tricks. And what was most awful of all was that he saw how upset Mikhail Mikhaylovich was about it but did not himself care. And it was dreadful to realize why he did not care.

They all saw that he was suffering, and said: "We can stop if you are tired. Take a rest." Lie down? No, he was not at all tired, and he finished the rubber. All were gloomy and silent. Ivan Ilych felt that he had diffused this gloom over them and could not dispel it. They had supper and went away, and Ivan Ilych was left alone with the consciousness that his life was poisoned and was poisoning the lives of others, and that this poison did not weaken but penetrated more and more deeply into his whole being.

With this consciousness, and with physical pain besides the terror, he must go to bed, often to lie awake the greater part of the night. Next morning he had to get up again, dress, go to the law courts, speak, and write; or if he did not go out, spend at home those twenty-four hours a day each of which was a torture. And he had to live thus all alone on the brink of an abyss, with no one who understood or pitied him.

V

So one month passed and then another. Just before the New Year his brother-in-law came to town and stayed at their house. Ivan Ilych was at the law courts and Praskovya Fëdorovna had gone shopping. When Ivan Ilych came home and entered his study he found his brother-in-law there — a healthy, florid man — unpacking his portmanteau himself. He raised his head on hearing Ivan Ilych's footsteps and looked up at him for a moment without a word. That stare told Ivan Ilych everything. His brother-in-law opened his mouth to utter an exclamation of surprise but checked himself, and that action confirmed it all.

"I have changed, eh?"

"Yes, there is a change."

And after that, try as he would to get his brother-in-law to return to the subject of his looks, the latter would say nothing about it. Praskovya Fëdorovna came home and her brother went out to her. Ivan Ilych locked the door and began to examine himself in the glass, first full face, then in profile. He took up a portrait of himself taken with his wife, and compared it with what he saw in the glass. The change in him was immense. Then he bared his arms to the elbow, looked at them, drew the sleeves down again, sat down on an ottoman, and grew blacker than night.

"No, no, this won't do!" he said to himself, and jumped up, went to the table, took up some law papers and began to read them, but could not continue. He unlocked the door and went into the reception-room. The door leading to the drawing-room was shut. He approached it on tiptoe and listened.

"No, you are exaggerating!" Praskovya Fëdorovna was saying.

"Exaggerating! Don't you see it? Why, he's a dead man! Look at his eyes — there's no light in them. But what is it that is wrong with him?"

"No one knows. Nikolaevich [that was another doctor] said something, but I don't know what. And Leshchetitsky [this was the celebrated specialist] said quite the contrary ..."

Ivan Ilych walked away, went to his own room, lay down, and began musing: "The kidney, a floating kidney." He recalled all the doctors had told him of how it detached itself and swayed about. And by an effort of imagination he tried to catch that kidney and arrest it and support it. So little was needed for this, it seemed to him. "No, I'll go to see Peter Ivanovich again." [That was the friend whose friend was a doctor.] He rang, ordered the carriage, and got ready to go.

"Where are you going, Jean?" asked his wife, with a specially sad and exceptionally kind look.

This exceptionally kind look irritated him. He looked morosely at her.

"I must go to see Peter Ivanovich."

He went to see Peter Ivanovich, and together they went to see his friend, the doctor. He was in, and Ivan Ilych had a long talk with him.

Reviewing the anatomical and physiological details of what in the doctor's opinion was going on inside him, he understood it all.

There was something, a small thing, in the vermiform appendix. It might all come right. Only stimulate the energy of one organ and check the activity of another, then absorption would take place and everything would come right. He got home rather late for dinner, ate his dinner, and conversed cheerfully, but could not for a long time bring himself to go back to work in his room. At last, however, he went to his study and did what was necessary, but the consciousness that he had put something aside — an important, intimate matter which he would revert to when his work was done — never left him. When he had finished his work he remembered that this intimate matter was the thought of his vermiform appendix. But he did not give himself up to it, and went to the drawing-room for tea. There were callers there, including the examining magistrate who was a desirable match for his daughter, and they were conversing, playing the piano, and singing. Ivan Ilych, as Praskovya Fëdorovna remarked, spent that evening more cheerfully than usual, but he never for a moment forgot that he had postponed the important matter of the appendix. At eleven o'clock he said good-night and went to his bedroom. Since his illness he had slept alone in a small room next to his study. He undressed and took up a novel by Zola, but instead of reading it he fell into thought, and in his imagination that desired improvement in the vermiform appendix occurred. There was the absorption and evacuation and the re-establishment of normal activity. "Yes, that's it!" he said to himself. "One need only assist nature, that's all." He remembered his medicine, rose, took it, and lay down on his back watching for the beneficent action of the medicine and for it to lessen the pain. "I need only take it regularly and avoid all injurious influences. I am already feeling better, much better." He began touching his side: it was not painful to the touch. "There, I really don't feel it. It's much better already." He put out the light and turned on his side. . . . "The appendix is getting better, absorption is occurring." Suddenly he felt the old, familiar, dull, gnawing pain, stubborn and serious. There was the same familiar loathsome taste in his mouth. His heart sank and he felt dazed. "My God! My God!" he muttered. "Again, again! and it will never cease." And suddenly the matter presented itself in a quite different aspect. "Vermiform appendix! Kidney!" he said to himself. "It's not a question of appendix or kidney, but of life and . . . death. Yes, life was there and now it is going, going and I cannot stop it. Yes. Why deceive myself? Isn't it obvious to everyone but me that I'm dying, and that it's only a question of weeks, days . . . it may happen this moment. There was light and now there is darkness. I was here and now I'm going there! Where?" A chill came over him, his breathing ceased, and he felt only the throbbing of his heart.

"When I am not, what will there be? There will be nothing. Then where shall I be when I am no more? Can this be dying? No, I don't want to!" He jumped up and tried to light the candle, felt for it with trembling hands, dropped candle and candlestick on the floor, and fell back on his pillow.

"What's the use? It makes no difference," he said to himself, staring with wide-open eyes into the darkness. "Death. Yes, death. And none of them know or wish to know it, and they have no pity for me. Now they are playing." (He heard through the door the distant sound of a song and its accompaniment.) "It's all the same to them, but they will die too! Fools! I first, and they later, but it will be the same for them. And now they are merry . . . the beasts!"

Anger choked him and he was agonizingly, unbearably miserable. "It is impossible that all men have been doomed to suffer this awful horror!" He raised himself.

"Something must be wrong. I must calm myself — must think it all over from the beginning." And he again began thinking. "Yes, the beginning of my illness: I knocked my side, but I was still quite well that day and the next. It hurt a little, then rather more. I saw the doctors, then followed despondency and anguish, more doctors, and I drew nearer to the abyss. My strength grew less and I kept coming nearer and nearer, and now I have wasted away and there is no light in my eyes. I think of the appendix — but this is death! I think of mending the appendix, and all the while here is death! Can it really be death?" Again terror seized him and he gasped for breath. He leant down and began feeling for the matches, pressing with his elbow on the stand beside the bed. It was in his way and hurt him, he grew furious with it, pressed on it still harder, and upset it. Breathless and in despair he fell on his back, expecting death to come immediately.

Meanwhile the visitors were leaving. Praskovya Fëdorovna was seeing them off. She heard something fall and came in.

"What has happened?"

"Nothing. I knocked it over accidentally."

She went out and returned with a candle. He lay there panting heavily, like a man who has run a thousand yards, and stared upwards at her with a fixed look.

"What is it, Jean?"

"No . . . o . . . thing. I upset it." ("Why speak of it? She won't understand," he thought.)

And in truth she did not understand. She picked up the stand, lit his candle, and hurried away to see another visitor off. When she came back he still lay on his back, looking upwards.

"What is it? Do you feel worse?"

"Yes."

She shook her head and sat down.

"Do you know, Jean, I think we must ask Leshchetitsky to come and see you here."

This meant calling in the famous specialist, regardless of expense. He smiled malignantly and said "No." She remained a little longer and then went up to him and kissed his forehead.

While she was kissing him he hated her from the bottom of his soul and with difficulty refrained from pushing her away.

"Good-night. Please God you'll sleep."

"Yes."

VI

Ivan Ilych saw that he was dying, and he was in continual despair.

In the depth of his heart he knew he was dying, but not only was he not accustomed to the thought, he simply did not and could not grasp it.

The syllogism he had learnt from Kiezewetter's Logic: "Caius is a man, men are mortal, therefore Caius is mortal," had always seemed to him correct as applied to Caius, but certainly not as applied to himself. That Caius — man in the abstract — was mortal, was perfectly correct, but he was not Caius, not an abstract man, but a creature quite, quite separate from all others. He had been little Vanya, with a mamma and a papa, with Mitya and Volodya, with the toys, a coachman and a nurse, afterwards with Katenka and with all the joys, griefs, and delights of childhood, boyhood, and youth. What did Caius know of the smell of that striped leather ball Vanya had been so fond of? Had Caius kissed his mother's hand like that, and did the silk of her dress rustle so for Caius?

Had he rioted like that at school when the pastry was bad? Had Caius been in love like that? Could Caius preside at a session as he did? "Caius really was mortal, and it was right for him to die; but for me, little Vanya, Ivan Ilych, with all my thoughts and emotions, it's altogether a different matter. It cannot be that I ought to die. That would be too terrible."

Such was his feeling.

"If I had to die like Caius I should have known it was so. An inner voice would have told me so, but there was nothing of the sort in me and I and all my friends felt that our case was quite different from that of Caius. And now here it is!" he said to himself. "It can't be. It's impossible! But here it is. How is this? How is one to understand it?"

He could not understand it, and tried to drive this false, incorrect, morbid thought away and to replace it by other proper and healthy thoughts. But that thought, and not the thought only but the reality itself, seemed to come and confront him.

And to replace that thought he called up a succession of others, hoping to find in them some support. He tried to get back into the former current of thoughts that had once screened the thought of death from him. But strange to say, all that had formerly shut off, hidden, and destroyed, his consciousness of death, no longer had that effect. Ivan Ilych now spent most of his time in attempting to re-establish that old current. He would say to himself: "I will take up my duties again — after all I used to live by them." And banishing all doubts he would go to the law courts, enter into conversation with his colleagues, and sit carelessly as was his wont, scanning the crowd with a thoughtful look and leaning both his emaciated arms on the arms of his oak chair; bending over as usual to a colleague and drawing his papers nearer he would interchange whispers with him, and then suddenly raising his eyes and sitting erect would pronounce certain words and open the proceedings. But suddenly in the midst of those proceedings the pain in his side, regardless of the stage the proceedings had reached, would begin its own gnawing work. Ivan Ilych would turn his attention to it and try to drive the thought of it away, but without success. *It* would come and stand before him and look at him, and he would be petrified and the light would die out of his eyes, and he would again begin asking himself whether *It* alone was true. And his colleagues and subordinates would see with surprise and distress that he, the brilliant and subtle judge, was becoming confused and making mistakes. He would shake himself, try to pull himself together, manage somehow to bring the sitting to a close, and return home with the sorrowful consciousness that his judicial labours could not as formerly hide from him what he wanted them to hide, and could not deliver him from *It*. And what was worst of all was that *It* drew his attention to itself not in order to make him take some action but only that he should look at *It*, look it straight in the face: look at it and without doing anything, suffer inexpressibly.

And to save himself from this condition Ivan Ilych looked for consolations — new screens — and new screens were found and for a while seemed to save him, but then they immediately fell to pieces or rather became transparent, as if *It* penetrated them and nothing could veil *It*.

In these latter days he would go into the drawing-room he had arranged — that drawing-room where he had fallen and for the sake of which (how bitterly ridiculous it seemed) he had sacrificed his life — for he knew that his illness originated with that knock. He would enter and see that something had scratched the polished table. He would look for the cause of this and find that it was the bronze ornamentation of an album, that had got bent. He would take up the expensive album which he had lovingly arranged, and feel vexed with his daughter and her friends for their untidiness — for the album was torn here and there and some of the photographs turned upside down. He would put it carefully in order and bend the ornamentation back into position. Then it would occur to him to place all those things in another corner of the room, near the plants. He could call the footman, but his daughter or wife would come to help him. They would not agree, and his wife would contradict him, and he would dispute and grow angry. But that was all right, for then he did not think about *It*. *It* was invisible.

But then, when he was moving something himself, his wife would say: "Let the servants do it. You will hurt yourself again." And suddenly *It* would flash through the screen and he would see it. It was just a flash, and he hoped it would disappear, but he would involuntarily pay attention to his side. "It sits there as before, gnawing just the same!" And he could no longer forget *It*, but could distinctly see it looking at him from behind the flowers. "What is it all for?"

"It really is so! I lost my life over that curtain as I might have done when storming a fort. Is that possible? How terrible and how stupid. It can't be true! It can't, but it is."

He would go to his study, lie down, and again be alone with *It*: face to face with *It*. And nothing could be done with *It* except to look at it and shudder.

VII

How it happened it is impossible to say because it came about step by step, unnoticed, but in the third month of Ivan Ilych's illness, his wife, his daughter, his son, his acquaintances, the doctors, the servants, and above all he himself, were aware that the whole interest he had for other people was whether he would soon vacate his place, and at last release the living from the discomfort caused by his presence and be himself released from his sufferings.

He slept less and less. He was given opium and hypodermic injections of morphine, but this did not relieve him. The dull depression he experienced in a somnolent condition at first gave him a little relief, but only as something new, afterwards it became as distressing as the pain itself or even more so.

Special foods were prepared for him by the doctors' orders, but all those foods became increasingly distasteful and disgusting to him.

For his excretions also special arrangements had to be made, and this was a torment to him every time — a torment from the uncleanliness, the unseemliness, and the smell, and from knowing that another person had to take part in it.

But just through this most unpleasant matter, Ivan Ilych obtained comfort. Gerasim, the butler's young assistant, always came in to carry the things out. Gerasim was a clean, fresh peasant lad, grown stout on town food and always cheerful and bright. At first the sight of him, in his clean Russian peasant costume, engaged in that disgusting task embarrassed Ivan Ilych.

Once when he got up from the commode too weak to draw up his trousers, he dropped into a soft armchair and looked with horror at his bare, enfeebled thighs with the muscles so sharply marked on them.

Gerasim with a firm light tread, his heavy boots emitting a pleasant smell of tar and fresh winter air, came in wearing a clean Hessian apron, the sleeves of his print shirt tucked up over his strong bare young arms; and refraining from looking at his sick master out of consideration for his feelings, and restraining the joy of life that beamed from his face, he went up to the commode.

"Gerasim!" said Ivan Ilych in a weak voice.

Gerasim started, evidently afraid he might have committed some blunder, and with a rapid movement turned his fresh, kind, simple young face which just showed the first downy signs of a beard.

"Yes, sir?"

"That must be very unpleasant for you. You must forgive me. I am helpless."

"Oh, why, sir," and Gerasim's eyes beamed and he showed his glistening white teeth, "what's a little trouble? It's a case of illness with you, sir."

And his deft strong hands did their accustomed task, and he went out of the room stepping lightly. Five minutes later he as lightly returned.

Ivan Ilych was still sitting in the same position in the armchair.

"Gerasim," he said when the latter had replaced the freshly-washed utensil. "Please come here and help me." Gerasim went up to him. "Lift me up. It is hard for me to get up, and I have sent Dmitri away."

Gerasim went up to him, grasped his master with his strong arms deftly but gently, in the same way that he stepped — lifted him, supported him with one hand, and with the other drew up his trousers and would have set him down again, but Ivan Ilych asked to be led to the sofa. Gerasim, without an effort and without apparent pressure, led him, almost lifting him, to the sofa and placed him on it.

"Thank you. How easily and well you do it all!"

Gerasim smiled again and turned to leave the room. But Ivan Ilych felt his presence such a comfort that he did not want to let him go.

"One thing more, please move up that chair. No, the other one — under my feet. It is easier for me when my feet are raised."

Gerasim brought the chair, set it down gently in place, and raised Ivan Ilych's legs on to it. It seemed to Ivan Ilych that he felt better while Gerasim was holding up his legs.

"It's better when my legs are higher," he said. "Place that cushion under them."

Gerasim did so. He again lifted the legs and placed them, and again Ivan Ilych felt better while Gerasim held his legs. When he set them down Ivan Ilych fancied he felt worse.

"Gerasim," he said. "Are you busy now?"

"Not at all, sir," said Gerasim, who had learnt from the townsfolk how to speak to gentlefolk.

"What have you still to do?"

"What have I to do? I've done everything except chopping the logs for tomorrow."

"Then hold my legs up a bit higher, can you?"

"Of course I can. Why not?" And Gerasim raised his master's legs higher and Ivan Ilych thought that in that position he did not feel any pain at all.

"And how about the logs?"

"Don't trouble about that, sir. There's plenty of time."

Ivan Ilych told Gerasim to sit down and hold his legs, and began to talk to him. And strange to say it seemed to him that he felt better while Gerasim held his legs up.

After that Ivan Ilych would sometimes call Gerasim and get him to hold his legs on his shoulders, and he liked talking to him. Gerasim did it all easily, willingly, simply, and with a good nature that touched Ivan Ilych. Health, strength, and vitality in other people were offensive to him, but Gerasim's strength and vitality did not mortify but soothed him.

What tormented Ivan Ilych most was the deception, the lie, which for some reason they all accepted, that he was not dying but was simply ill, and that he only need keep quiet and undergo a treatment and then something very good would result. He however knew that do what they would nothing would come of it, only still more agonizing suffering and death. This deception tortured him — their not wishing to admit what they all knew and what he knew, but wanting to lie to him concerning his terrible condition, and wishing and forcing him to participate in that lie. Those lies — lies enacted over him on the eve of his death and destined to degrade this awful, solemn act to the level of their visitings, their curtains, their sturgeon for dinner — were a terrible agony for Ivan Ilych. And strangely enough, many times when they were going through their antics over him he had been within a hairbreadth of calling out to them: "Stop lying! You know and I know that I am dying. Then at least stop lying about it!" But he had never had the spirit to do it. The awful, terrible act of his dying was, he could see, reduced by those about him to the level of a casual, unpleasant, and almost indecorous incident (as if someone entered a drawing-room diffusing an unpleasant odour) and this was done by that very decorum which he had served all his life long. He saw that no one felt for him, because no one even wished to grasp his position. Only Gerasim recognized it and pitied him. And so Ivan Ilych felt at ease only with him. He felt comforted when Gerasim supported his legs (sometimes all night long) and refused to go to bed, saying: "Don't you worry, Ivan Ilych. I'll get sleep enough later on," or when he suddenly became familiar and exclaimed: "If you weren't sick it would be another matter, but as it is, why should I grudge a little trouble?" Gerasim alone did not lie; everything showed that he alone understood the facts of the case and did not consider it necessary to disguise them, but simply felt sorry for his emaciated and enfeebled master. Once when Ivan Ilych was sending him away he even said straight out: "We shall all of us die, so why should I grudge a little trouble?" — expressing the fact that he did not think his work burdensome, because he was doing it for a dying man and hoped someone would do the same for him when his time came.

Apart from this lying, or because of it, what most tormented Ivan Ilych was that no one pitied him as he wished to be pitied. At certain moments after prolonged suffering he wished most of all (though he would have been ashamed to confess it) for someone to pity him as a sick child is pitied. He longed to be petted and comforted. He knew he was an important functionary, that he had a beard turning grey, and that therefore what he longed for was impossible, but still he longed for it. And in Gerasim's attitude towards him there was something akin to what he wished for, and so that attitude comforted him. Ivan Ilych wanted to weep, wanted to be petted and cried over, and then his colleague Shebek would come, and instead of weeping and being petted, Ivan Ilych would assume a serious, severe, and profound air, and by force of habit would express his opinion on a decision of the Court of Cassation and would stubbornly insist on that view. This falsity around him and within him did more than anything else to poison his last days.

VIII

It was morning. He knew it was morning because Gerasim had gone, and Peter the footman had come and put out the candles, drawn back one of the curtains, and begun quietly to tidy up. Whether it was morning or evening, Friday or Sunday, made no difference, it was all just the same: the gnawing, unmitigated, agonizing pain, never ceasing for an instant, the consciousness of life inexorably waning but not yet extinguished, the approach of that ever dreaded and hateful Death which was the only reality, and always the same falsity. What were days, weeks, hours, in such a case?

"Will you have some tea, sir?"

"He wants things to be regular, and wishes the gentlefolk to drink tea in the morning," thought Ivan Ilych, and only said "No."

"Wouldn't you like to move onto the sofa, sir?"

"He wants to tidy up the room, and I'm in the way. I am uncleanliness and disorder," he thought, and said only:

"No, leave me alone."

The man went on bustling about. Ivan Ilych stretched out his hand. Peter came up, ready to help.

"What is it, sir?"

"My watch."

Peter took the watch which was close at hand and gave it to his master.

"Half-past eight. Are they up?"

"No, sir, except Vladimir Ivanich" (the son) "who has gone to school. Praskovya Fëdorovna ordered me to wake her if you asked for her. Shall I do so?"

"No, there's no need to." "Perhaps I'd better have some tea," he thought, and added aloud: "Yes, bring me some tea."

Peter went to the door, but Ivan Ilych dreaded being left alone. "How can I keep him here? Oh yes, my medicine." "Peter, give me my medicine." "Why not? Perhaps it may still do me some good." He took a spoonful and swallowed it. "No, it won't help. It's all tomfoolery, all deception," he decided as soon as he became aware of the familiar, sickly, hopeless taste. "No, I can't believe in it any longer. But the pain, why this pain? If it would only cease just for a moment!" And he moaned. Peter turned towards him. "It's all right. Go and fetch me some tea."

Peter went out. Left alone Ivan Ilych groaned not so much with pain, terrible though that was, as from mental anguish. Always and for ever the same, always these endless days and nights. If only it would come quicker! If only *what* would come quicker? Death, darkness? ... No, no! Anything rather than death!

When Peter returned with the tea on a tray, Ivan Ilych stared at him for a time in perplexity, not realizing who and what he was. Peter was disconcerted by that look and his embarrassment brought Ivan Ilych to himself.

"Oh, tea! All right, put it down. Only help me to wash and put on a clean shirt."

And Ivan Ilych began to wash. With pauses for rest, he washed his hands and then his face, cleaned his teeth, brushed his hair, and looked in the glass. He was terrified by what he saw, especially by the limp way in which his hair clung to his pallid forehead.

While his shirt was being changed he knew that he would be still more frightened at the sight of his body, so he avoided looking at it. Finally he was ready. He drew on a dressing-gown, wrapped himself in a plaid, and sat down in the armchair to take his tea. For a moment he felt refreshed, but as soon as he began to drink the tea he was again aware of the same taste, and the pain also returned. He finished it with an effort, and then lay down stretching out his legs, and dismissed Peter.

Always the same. Now a spark of hope flashes up, then a sea of despair rages, and always pain; always pain, always despair, and always the same. When alone he had a dreadful and distressing desire to call someone, but he knew beforehand that with others present it would be still worse. "Another dose of morphine — to lose consciousness. I will tell him, the doctor, that he must think of something else. It's impossible, impossible, to go on like this."

An hour and another pass like that. But now there is a ring at the door bell. Perhaps it's the doctor? It is. He comes in fresh, hearty, plump, and cheerful, with that look on his face that seems to say: "There now, you're in a panic about something, but we'll arrange it all for you directly!" The doctor knows this expression is out of place here, but he has put it on once for all and can't take it off — like a man who has put on a frock-coat in the morning to pay a round of calls.

The doctor rubs his hands vigorously and reassuringly.

"Brr! How cold it is! There's such a sharp frost; just let me warm myself!" he says, as if it were only a matter of waiting till he was warm, and then he would put everything right.

"Well now, how are you?"

Ivan Ilych feels that the doctor would like to say: "Well, how are our affairs?" but that even he feels that this would not do, and says instead: "What sort of a night have you had?"

Ivan Ilych looks at him as much as to say: "Are you really never ashamed of lying?" But the doctor does not wish to understand this question, and Ivan Ilych says: "Just as terrible as ever. The pain never leaves me and never subsides. If only something ..."

"Yes, you sick people are always like that. ... There, now I think I am warm enough. Even Praskovya Fëdorovna, who is so particular, could find no fault with my temperature. Well, now I can say good-morning," and the doctor presses his patient's hand.

Then, dropping his former playfulness, he begins with a most serious face to examine the patient, feeling his pulse and taking his temperature, and then begins the sounding and auscultation.

Ivan Ilych knows quite well and definitely that all this is nonsense and pure deception, but when the doctor, getting down on his knee, leans over him, putting his ear first higher then lower, and performs various gymnastic movements over him with a significant expression on his face, Ivan Ilych submits to it all as he used to submit to the speeches of the lawyers, though he knew very well that they were all lying and why they were lying.

The doctor, kneeling on the sofa, is still sounding him when Praskovya Fëdorovna's silk dress rustles at the door and she is heard scolding Peter for not having let her know of the doctor's arrival.

She comes in, kisses her husband, and at once proceeds to prove that she has been up a long time already, and only owing to a misunderstanding failed to be there when the doctor arrived.

Ivan Ilych looks at her, scans her all over, sets against her the whiteness and plumpness and cleanness of her hands and neck, the gloss of her hair, and the sparkle of her vivacious eyes. He hates her with his whole soul. And the thrill of hatred he feels for her makes him suffer from her touch.

Her attitude towards him and his disease is still the same. Just as the doctor had adopted a certain relation to his patient which he could not abandon, so had she formed one towards him — that he was not doing something he ought to do and was himself to blame, and that she reproached him lovingly for this — and she could not now change that attitude.

"You see he doesn't listen to me and doesn't take his medicine at the proper time. And above all he lies in a position that is no doubt bad for him — with his legs up."

She described how he made Gerasim hold his legs up.

The doctor smiled with a contemptuous affability that said: "What's to be done? These sick people do have foolish fancies of that kind, but we must forgive them."

When the examination was over the doctor looked at his watch, and then Praskovya Fëdorovna announced to Ivan Ilych that it was of course as he pleased, but she had sent today for a celebrated specialist who would examine him and have a consultation with Michael Danilovich (their regular doctor).

"Please don't raise any objections. I am doing this for my own sake," she said ironically, letting it be felt that she was doing it all for his sake and only said this to leave him no right to refuse. He remained silent, knitting his brows. He felt that he was so surrounded and involved in a mesh of falsity that it was hard to unravel anything.

Everything she did for him was entirely for her own sake, and she told him she was doing for herself what she actually was doing for herself, as if that was so incredible that he must understand the opposite.

At half-past eleven the celebrated specialist arrived. Again the sounding began and the significant conversations in his presence and in another room, about the kidneys and the appendix, and the questions and answers, with such an air of importance that again, instead of the real question of life and death which now alone confronted him, the question arose of the kidney and appendix which were not behaving as they ought to and would now be attacked by Michael Danilovich and the specialist and forced to amend their ways.

The celebrated specialist took leave of him with a serious though not hopeless look, and in reply to the timid question Ivan Ilych, with eyes glistening with fear and hope, put to him as to whether there was a chance of recovery, said that he could not vouch for it but there was a possibility. The look of hope with which Ivan Ilych watched the doctor out was so pathetic that Praskovya Fëdorovna, seeing it, even wept as she left the room to hand the doctor his fee.

The gleam of hope kindled by the doctor's encouragement did not last long. The same room, the same pictures, curtains, wall-paper, medicine bottles, were all there, and the same aching suffering body, and Ivan Ilych began to moan. They gave him a subcutaneous injection and he sank into oblivion.

It was twilight when he came to. They brought him his dinner and he swallowed some beef tea with difficulty, and then everything was the same again and night was coming on.

After dinner, at seven o'clock, Praskovya Fëdorovna came into the room in evening dress, her full bosom pushed up by her corset, and with traces of powder on her face. She had reminded him in the morning that they were going to the theatre. Sarah Bernhardt was visiting the town and they had a box, which he had insisted on their taking. Now he had forgotten about it and her toilet offended him, but he concealed his vexation when he remembered that he had himself insisted on their securing a box and going because it would be an instructive and aesthetic pleasure for the children.

Praskovya Fëdorovna came in, self-satisfied but yet with a rather guilty air. She sat down and asked how he was, but, as he saw, only for the sake of asking and not in order to learn about it, knowing that there was nothing to learn — and then went on to what she really wanted to say: that she would not on any account have gone but that the box had been taken and Helen and their daughter were going, as well as Petrishchev (the examining magistrate, their daughter's fiancé) and that it was out of the question to let them go alone; but that she would have much preferred to sit with him for a while; and he must be sure to follow the doctor's orders while she was away.

"Oh, and Fëdor Petrovich" (the fiancé) "would like to come in. May he? And Lisa?"

"All right."

Their daughter came in in full evening dress, her fresh young flesh exposed (making a show of that very flesh which in his own case caused so much suffering), strong, healthy, evidently in love, and impatient with illness, suffering, and death, because they interfered with her happiness.

Fëdor Petrovich came in too, in evening dress, his hair curled *à la Capoul*, a tight stiff collar round his long sinewy neck, an enormous white shirt-front and narrow black trousers tightly stretched over his strong thighs. He had one white glove tightly drawn on, and was holding his opera hat in his hand.

Following him the schoolboy crept in unnoticed, in a new uniform, poor little fellow, and wearing gloves. Terribly dark shadows showed under his eyes, the meaning of which Ivan Ilych knew well.

His son had always seemed pathetic to him, and now it was dreadful to see the boy's frightened look of pity. It seemed to Ivan Ilych that Vasya was the only one besides Gerasim who understood and pitied him.

They all sat down and again asked how he was. A silence followed. Lisa asked her mother about the opera-glasses, and there was an altercation between mother and daughter as to who had taken them and where they had been put. This occasioned some unpleasantness.

Fëdor Petrovich inquired of Ivan Ilych whether he had ever seen Sarah Bernhardt. Ivan Ilych did not at first catch the question, but then replied: "No, have you seen her before?"

"Yes, in *Adrienne Lecouvreur*."

Praskovya Fëdorovna mentioned some rôles in which Sarah Bernhardt was particularly good. Her daughter disagreed. Conversation sprang up as to the elegance and realism of her acting — the sort of conversation that is always repeated and is always the same.

In the midst of the conversation Fëdor Petrovich glanced at Ivan Ilych and became silent. The others also looked at him and grew silent. Ivan Ilych was staring with glittering eyes straight before him, evidently indignant with them. This had to be rectified, but it was impossible to do so. The silence had to be broken, but for a time no one dared to break it and they all became afraid that the conventional deception would suddenly become obvious and the truth become plain to all. Lisa was the first to pluck up courage and break that silence, but by trying to hide what everybody was feeling, she betrayed it.

"Well, if we are going it's time to start," she said, looking at her watch, a present from her father, and with a faint and significant smile at Fëdor Petrovich relating to something known only to them. She got up with a rustle of her dress.

They all rose, said good-night, and went away.

When they had gone it seemed to Ivan Ilych that he felt better; the falsity had gone with them. But the pain remained — that same pain and that same fear that made everything monotonously alike, nothing harder and nothing easier. Everything was worse.

Again minute followed minute and hour followed hour. Everything remained the same and there was no cessation. And the inevitable end of it all became more and more terrible.

"Yes, send Gerasim here," he replied to a question Peter asked.

IX

His wife returned late at night. She came in on tiptoe, but he heard her, opened his eyes, and made haste to close them again. She wished to send Gerasim away and to sit with him herself, but he opened his eyes and said: "No, go away."

"Are you in great pain?"

"Always the same."

"Take some opium."

He agreed and took some. She went away.

Till about three in the morning he was in a state of stupefied misery. It seemed to him that he and his pain were being thrust into a narrow, deep black sack, but though they were pushed further and further in they could not be pushed to the bottom. And this, terrible enough in itself, was accompanied by suffering. He was frightened yet wanted to fall through the sack, he struggled but yet co-operated. And suddenly he broke through, fell, and regained consciousness. Gerasim was sitting at the foot of the bed dozing quietly and patiently, while he himself lay with his emaciated stockinged legs resting on Gerasim's shoulders; the same shaded candle was there and the same unceasing pain.

"Go away, Gerasim," he whispered.

"It's all right, sir. I'll stay a while."

"No. Go away."

He removed his legs from Gerasim's shoulders, turned sideways onto his arm, and felt sorry for himself. He only waited till Gerasim had gone into the next room and then restrained himself no longer but wept like a child. He wept on account of his helplessness, his terrible loneliness, the cruelty of man, the cruelty of God, and the absence of God.

"Why hast Thou done all this? Why hast Thou brought me here? Why, why dost Thou torment me so terribly?"

He did not expect an answer and yet wept because there was no answer and could be none. The pain again grew more acute, but he did not stir and did not call. He said to himself: "Go on! Strike me! But what is it for? What have I done to Thee? What is it for?"

Then he grew quiet and not only ceased weeping but even held his breath and became all attention. It was as though he were listening not to an audible voice but to the voice of his soul, to the current of thoughts arising within him.

"What is it you want?" was the first clear conception capable of expression in words, that he heard.

"What do you want? What do you want?" he repeated to himself.

"What do I want? To live and not to suffer," he answered.

And again he listened with such concentrated attention that even his pain did not distract him.

"To live? How?" asked his inner voice.

"Why, to live as I used to — well and pleasantly."

"As you lived before, well and pleasantly?" the voice repeated.

And in imagination he began to recall the best moments of his pleasant life. But strange to say none of those best moments of his pleasant life now seemed at all what they had then seemed — none of them except the first recollections of childhood. There, in childhood, there had been something really pleasant with which it would be possible to live if it could return. But the child who had experienced that happiness existed no longer, it was like a reminiscence of somebody else.

As soon as the period began which had produced the present Ivan Ilych, all that had then seemed joys now melted before his sight and turned into something trivial and often nasty.

And the further he departed from childhood and the nearer he came to the present the more worthless and doubtful were the joys. This began with the School of Law. A little that was really good was still found there — there was lightheartedness, friendship, and hope. But in the upper classes there had already been fewer of such good moments. Then during the first years of his official career, when he was in the service of the Governor, some pleasant moments again occurred: they were the memories of love for a woman. Then all became confused and there was still less of what was good; later on again there was still less that was good, and the further he went the less there was. His marriage, a mere accident, then the disenchantment that followed it, his wife's bad breath and the sensuality and hypocrisy: then that deadly official life and those preoccupations about money, a year of it, and two, and ten, and twenty, and always the same thing. And the longer it lasted the more deadly it became. "It is as if I had been going downhill while I imagined I was going up. And that is really what it was. I was going up in public opinion, but to the same extent life was ebbing away from me. And now it is all done and there is only death."

"Then what does it mean? Why? It can't be that life is so senseless and horrible. But if it really has been so horrible and senseless, why must I die and die in agony? There is something wrong!"

"Maybe I did not live as I ought to have done," it suddenly occurred to him. "But how could that be, when I did everything properly?" he replied, and immediately dismissed from his mind this, the sole solution of all the riddles of life and death, as something quite impossible.

"Then what do you want now? To live? Live how? Live as you lived in the law courts when the usher proclaimed 'The Judge is coming!' The judge is coming, the judge!" he repeated to himself. "Here he is, the judge. But I am not guilty!" he exclaimed angrily. "What is it for?" And he ceased crying, but turning his face to the wall continued to ponder on the same question: Why, and for what purpose, is there all this horror? But however much he pondered he found no answer. And whenever the thought occurred to him, as it often did, that it all resulted from his not having lived as he ought to have done, he at once recalled the correctness of his whole life and dismissed so strange an idea.

X

Another fortnight passed. Ivan Ilych now no longer left his sofa. He would not lie in bed but lay on the sofa, facing the wall nearly all the time. He suffered ever the same unceasing agonies and in his loneliness pondered always on the same insoluble question: "What is this? Can it be that it is Death?" And the inner voice answered: "Yes, it is Death."

"Why these sufferings?" And the voice answered, "For no reason — they just are so." Beyond and besides this there was nothing.

From the very beginning of his illness, ever since he had first been to see the doctor, Ivan Ilych's life had been divided between two contrary and alternating moods: now it was despair and the expectation of this uncomprehended and terrible death, and now hope and an intently interested observation of the functioning of his organs. Now before his eyes there was only a kidney or an intestine that temporarily evaded its duty, and now only that incomprehensible and dreadful death from which it was impossible to escape.

These two states of mind had alternated from the very beginning of his illness, but the further it progressed the more doubtful and fantastic became the conception of the kidney, and the more real the sense of impending death.

He had but to call to mind what he had been three months before and what he was now, to call to mind with what regularity he had been going downhill, for every possibility of hope to be shattered.

Latterly during that loneliness in which he found himself as he lay facing the back of the sofa, a loneliness in the midst of a populous town and surrounded by numerous acquaintances and relations but that yet could not have been more complete anywhere — either at the bottom of the sea or under the earth — during that terrible loneliness Ivan Ilych had lived only in memories of the past. Pictures of his past rose before him one after another. They always began with what was nearest in time and then went back to what was most remote — to his childhood — and rested there. If he thought of the stewed prunes that had been offered him that day, his mind went back to the raw shrivelled French plums of his childhood, their peculiar flavour and the flow of saliva when he sucked their stones, and along with the memory of that taste came a whole series of memories of those days: his nurse, his brother, and their toys. "No, I mustn't think of that.... It is too painful," Ivan Ilych said to himself, and brought himself back to the present — to the button on the back of the sofa and the creases in its morocco. "Morocco is expensive, but it does not wear well: there had been a quarrel about it. It was a different kind of quarrel and a different kind of morocco that time when we tore father's portfolio and were punished, and mamma brought us some tarts...." And again his thoughts dwelt on his childhood, and again it was painful and he tried to banish them and fix his mind on something else.

Then again together with that chain of memories another series passed through his mind — of how his illness had progressed and grown worse. There also the further back he looked the more life there had been. There had been more of what was good in life and more of life itself. The two merged together. "Just as the pain went on getting worse and worse, so my life grew worse and worse," he thought. "There is one bright spot there at the back, at the beginning of life, and afterwards all becomes blacker and blacker and proceeds more and more rapidly — in inverse ratio to the square of the distance from death," thought Ivan Ilych. And the example of a stone falling downwards with increasing velocity entered his mind. Life, a series of increasing sufferings, flies further and further towards its end — the most terrible suffering. "I am flying...." He shuddered, shifted himself, and tried to resist, but was already aware that resistance was impossible, and again with eyes weary of gazing but unable to cease seeing what was before them, he stared at the back of the sofa and waited — awaiting that dreadful fall and shock and destruction.

"Resistance is impossible!" he said to himself. "If I could only understand what it is all for! But that too is impossible. An explanation would be possible if it could be said that I have not lived as I ought to. But it is impossible to say that," and he remembered all the legality, correctitude, and propriety of his life. "That at any rate can certainly not be admitted," he thought, and his lips smiled ironically as if someone could see that smile and be taken in by it. "There is no explanation! Agony, death ... What for?"

XI

Another two weeks went by in this way and during that fortnight an event occurred that Ivan Ilych and his wife had desired. Petrishchev formally proposed. It happened in the evening. The next day Praskovya Fëdorovna came into her husband's room considering how best to inform him of it, but that very night there had been a fresh change for the worse in his condition. She found him still lying on the sofa but in a different position. He lay on his back, groaning and staring fixedly straight in front of him.

She began to remind him of his medicines, but he turned his eyes towards her with such a look that she did not finish what she was saying; so great an animosity, to her in particular, did that look express.

"For Christ's sake let me die in peace!" he said.

She would have gone away, but just then their daughter came in and went up to say good morning. He looked at her as he had done at his wife, and in reply to her inquiry about his health said dryly that he would soon free them all of himself. They were both silent and after sitting with him for a while went away.

"Is it our fault?" Lisa said to her mother. "It's as if we were to blame! I am sorry for papa, but why should we be tortured?"

The doctor came at his usual time. Ivan Ilych answered "Yes" and "No," never taking his angry eyes from him, and at last said: "You know you can do nothing for me, so leave me alone."

"We can ease your sufferings."

"You can't even do that. Let me be."

The doctor went into the drawing-room and told Praskovya Fëdorovna that the case was very serious and that the only recourse left was opium to allay her husband's sufferings, which must be terrible.

It was true, as the doctor said, that Ivan Ilych's physical sufferings were terrible, but worse than the physical sufferings were his mental sufferings, which were his chief torture.

His mental sufferings were due to the fact that that night, as he looked at Gerasim's sleepy, good-natured face with its prominent cheek-bones, the question suddenly occurred to him: "What if my whole life has really been wrong?"

It occurred to him that what had appeared perfectly impossible before, namely that he had not spent his life as he should have done, might after all be true. It occurred to him that his scarcely perceptible attempts to struggle against what was considered good by the most highly placed people, those scarcely noticeable impulses which he had immediately suppressed, might have been the real thing, and all the rest false. And his professional duties and the whole arrangement of his life and of his family, and all his social and official interests, might all have been false. He tried to defend all those things to himself and suddenly felt the weakness of what he was defending. There was nothing to defend.

"But if that is so," he said to himself, "and I am leaving this life with the consciousness that I have lost all that was given me and it is impossible to rectify it — what then?"

He lay on his back and began to pass his life in review in quite a new way. In the morning when he saw first his footman, then his wife, then his daughter, and then the doctor, their every word and movement confirmed to him the awful truth that had been revealed to him during the night. In them he saw himself — all that for which he had lived — and saw clearly that it was not real at all, but a terrible and huge deception which had hidden both life and death. This consciousness intensified his physical suffering tenfold. He groaned and tossed about, and pulled at his clothing which choked and stifled him. And he hated them on that account.

He was given a large dose of opium and became unconscious, but at noon his sufferings began again. He drove everybody away and tossed from side to side.

His wife came to him and said:

"Jean, my dear, do this for me. It can't do any harm and often helps. Healthy people often do it."

He opened his eyes wide.

"What? Take communion? Why? It's unnecessary! However ..."

She began to cry.

"Yes, do, my dear. I'll send for our priest. He is such a nice man."

"All right. Very well," he muttered.

When the priest came and heard his confession, Ivan Ilych was softened and seemed to feel a relief from his doubts and consequently from his sufferings, and for a moment there came a ray of hope. He again began to think of the vermiform appendix and the possibility of correcting it. He received the sacrament with tears in his eyes.

When they laid him down again afterwards he felt a moment's ease, and the hope that he might live awoke in him again. He began to think of the operation that had been suggested to him. "To live! I want to live!" he said to himself.

His wife came in to congratulate him after his communion, and when uttering the usual conventional words she added:

"You feel better, don't you?"

Without looking at her he said "Yes."

Her dress, her figure, the expression of her face, the tone of her voice, all revealed the same thing. "This is wrong, it is not as it should be. All you have lived for and still live for is falsehood and deception, hiding life and death from you." And as soon as he admitted that thought, his hatred and his agonizing physical suffering again sprang up, and with that suffering a consciousness of the unavoidable, approaching end. And to this was added a new sensation of grinding shooting pain and a feeling of suffocation.

The expression of his face when he uttered that "yes" was dreadful. Having uttered it, he looked her straight in the eyes, turned on his face with a rapidity extraordinary in his weak state and shouted:

"Go away! Go away and leave me alone!"

XII

From that moment the screaming began that continued for three days, and was so terrible that one could not hear it through two closed doors without horror. At the moment he answered his wife he realized that he was lost, that there was no return, that the end had come, the very end, and his doubts were still unsolved and remained doubts.

"Oh! Oh! Oh!" he cried in various intonations. He had begun by screaming "I won't!" and continued screaming on the letter *O*.

For three whole days, during which time did not exist for him, he struggled in that black sack into which he was being thrust by an invisible, resistless force. He struggled as a man condemned to death struggles in the hands of the executioner, knowing that he cannot save himself. And every moment he felt that despite all his efforts he was drawing nearer and nearer to what terrified him. He felt that his agony was due to his being thrust into that black hole and still more to his not being able to get right into it. He was hindered from getting into it by his conviction that his life had been a good one. That very justification of his life held him fast and prevented his moving forward, and it caused him most torment of all.

Suddenly some force struck him in the chest and side, making it still harder to breathe, and he fell through the hole and there at the bottom was a light. What had happened to him was like the sensation one sometimes experiences in a railway carriage when one thinks one is going backwards while one is really going forwards and suddenly becomes aware of the real direction.

"Yes, it was all not the right thing," he said to himself, but that's no matter. It can be done. But what *is* the right thing?" he asked himself, and suddenly grew quiet.

This occurred at the end of the third day, two hours before his death. Just then his schoolboy son had crept softly in and gone up to the bedside. The dying man was still screaming desperately and waving his arms. His hand fell on the boy's head, and the boy caught it, pressed it to his lips, and began to cry.

At that very moment Ivan Ilych fell through and caught sight of the light, and it was revealed to him that though his life had not been what it should have been, this could still be rectified. He asked himself, "What *is* the right thing?" and grew still, listening. Then he felt that someone was kissing his hand. He opened his eyes, looked at his son, and felt sorry for him. His wife came up to him and he glanced at her. She was gazing at him open-mouthed, with undried tears on her nose and cheek and a despairing look on her face. He felt sorry for her too.

"Yes, I am making them wretched," he thought. "They are sorry, but it will be better for them when I die." He wished to say this but had not the strength to utter it. "Besides, why speak? I must act," he thought. With a look at his wife he indicated his son and said: "Take him away ... sorry for him ... sorry for you too. ..." He tried to add, "forgive me," but said "forgo" and waved his hand, knowing that He whose understanding mattered would understand.

And suddenly it grew clear to him that what had been oppressing him and would not leave him was all dropping away at once from two sides, from ten sides, and from all sides. He was sorry for them, he must act so as not to hurt them: release them and free himself from these sufferings. "How good and how simple!" he thought. "And the pain?" he asked himself. "What has become of it? Where are you, pain?"

He turned his attention to it.

"Yes, here it is. Well, what of it? Let the pain be."

"And death ... where is it?"

He sought his former accustomed fear of death and did not find it. "Where is it? What death?" There was no fear because there was no death.

In place of death there was light.

"So that's what it is!" he suddenly exclaimed aloud. "What joy!"

To him all this happened in a single instant, and the meaning of that instant did not change. For those present his agony continued for another two hours. Something rattled in his throat, his emaciated body twitched, then the gasping and rattle became less and less frequent.

"It is finished!" said someone near him.

He heard these words and repeated them in his soul.

"Death is finished," he said to himself. "It is no more!"

He drew in a breath, stopped in the midst of a sigh, stretched out, and died.

Acknowledgements

Chinua Achebe "The Voter" from *Girls at War and Other Stories* by Chinua Achebe. Copyright © 1972, 1973 by Chinua Achebe. Reprinted by permission of Doubleday & Company, Inc.

Sherwood Anderson "I Want to Know Why" from *Smart Set*. Copyright © 1921 by B. W. Huebsch, Inc. Renewed 1948 by Eleanor Copenhaver Anderson. Reprinted by permission of Harold Ober Associates Inc.

Margaret Atwood "The Resplendent Quetzal" from *Dancing Girls*. Reprinted by permission of The Canadian Publishers, McClelland and Stewart Limited, Toronto.

James Baldwin "Sonny's Blues" from *Sonny's Blues* by James Baldwin. Reprinted by permission of The Dial Press.

John Barth "Lost in the Funhouse" from *Lost in the Funhouse*. Copyright © 1967 by Atlantic Monthly Company. Reprinted by permission of Doubleday & Company, Inc.

Donald Barthelme "The Balloon" from *The Balloon*. Reprinted by permission of Farrar, Straus & Giroux, Inc.

Saul Bellow "Looking for Mr. Green" from *Looking for Mr. Green*. Reprinted by permission of Viking/Penguin Publishers, Inc.

Clark Blaise "Grids and Doglegs" From *Tribal Justice* by Clark Blaise. Copyright © 1974 by Clark Blaise. Reprinted by permission of Doubleday & Company, Inc.

Heinrich Böll "The Adventure" from *The Adventure*. Reprinted by permission of McGraw-Hill Ryerson, Limited.

Jorge Louis Borges "The Garden of the Forking Paths" from *The Garden of Forking Paths*. Reprinted by permission of Grove Press, Inc.

George Bowering "The Elevator" from *The Elevator*. Reprinted by permission of Oberon Press.

Richard Brautigan "Sea, Sea Rider" from *Trout Fishing in America* by Richard Brautigan. Copyright © 1967 by Richard Brautigan. Reprinted by permission of Delacorte Press/Seymour Lawrence.

Erskine Caldwell "Where the Girls Were Different" from *American Earth*. Copyright © 1931 by Erskine Caldwell. Renewed effective 1959 by Erskine Caldwell. Reprinted by permission of McIntosh and Otis, Inc.

Morley Callaghan "Last Spring They Came Over" from *Morley Callaghan's Stories* by Morley Callaghan. Reprinted by permission of Macmillan of Canada, A Division of Gage Publishing Limited.

Italo Calvino "The Count of Monte Cristo" from *T-Zero* by Italo Calvino. Reprinted by permission of the Roslyn Targ Literary Agency, Inc.

Albert Camus "The Guest" from *Exile and the Kingdom*. Reprinted by permission of Random House, Inc.

Roch Carrier "The Hockey Sweater" from *The Hockey Sweater*. Reprinted by permission of Anansi Press Ltd.

John Cheever "The Country Husband" from *The Stories of John Cheever*. Reprinted by permission of Random House, Inc.

Arthur C. Clarke "The Star" from *The Other Side of the Sky* by Arthur Clarke. Reprinted by permission of Harcourt Brace Jovanovich, Inc.

V. S. Naipaul "A Christmas Story" from *Selected Stories of V. S. Naipaul.* Reprinted by permission of the author.

Alden Nowlan "Miracle at Indian River" from *Miracle at Indian River* by Alden Nowlan © 1968 by Clarke, Irwin & Company Limited. Reprinted by permission of Clarke, Irwin & Company Limited.

Edna O'Brien "Mary" from *Mrs. Reinhardt and Other Stories* by Edna O'Brien. Reprinted by permission of A. M. Heath & Company Ltd.

Flannery O'Connor "A Good Man Is Hard to Find" from *A Good Man Is Hard to Find and Other Stories* by Flannery O'Connor. Reprinted by permission of Harcourt Brace Jovanovich, Inc.

Tillie Olsen "I Stand Here Ironing" from *I Stand Here Ironing and Other Stories* by Tillie Olsen. Reprinted by permission of Delacorte Press, Inc.

Katherine Anne Porter "The Grave" from *The Leaning Tower and Other Stories* by Katherine Anne Porter. Reprinted by permission of Harcourt Brace Jovanovich, Inc.

Leon Rooke "Standing in for Nita". Reprinted by permission of ECW Press Limited.

Sinclair Ross "The Painted Door" from *Lamp at Noon and Other Stories* by Sinclair Ross. Reprinted by permission of The Canadian Publishers, McClelland and Stewart Limited, Toronto.

Philip Roth "Defender of the Faith". Reprinted by permission of Houghton Mifflin, Inc.

Gabrielle Roy "My Aunt Thérésina Veilleux" from *Street of Riches* by Gabrielle Roy. Reprinted by permission of The Canadian Publishers, McClelland and Stewart Limited, Toronto.

William Saroyan "Love, Here Is My Hat" from *Selected Stories of William Saroyan.* Reprinted by permission of the author.

Sam Selvon "When Greek Meets Greek". Reprinted by permission of the author.

Irwin Shaw "The Girls In Their Summer Dresses". Reprinted by permission of Delacorte Press, Inc.

Isaac Bashevis Singer "Gimpel the Fool". Reprinted by permission of Farrar, Straus & Giroux, Inc.

John Steinbeck "The Chrysanthemums" from *Selected Stories of John Steinbeck*. Reprinted by permission of Viking/Penguin Publishers, Inc.

James Thurber "The Catbird Seat" from *Stories of James Thurber*. Reprinted by permission of Mrs. James Thurber.

John Updike "A & P" from *Pigeon Feathers and Other Stories* by John Updike. Reprinted by permission of Alfred A. Knopf, Inc.

W. D. Valgardson "Red Dust" from *Selected Stories of W. D. Valgardson.* Reprinted by permission of Oberon Press.

Kurt Vonnegut, Jr. "Report on the Barnhouse Effect" from *Report on the Barnhouse Effect and Other Stories* by Kurt Vonnegut, Jr. Reprinted by permission of Delacorte Press, Inc.

Eudora Welty "Powerhouse" from *A Curtain of Green and Other Stories* by Eudora Welty. Reprinted by permission of Harcourt Brace Jovanovich, Inc.

Rudy Wiebe "Where Is the Voice Coming From?" from *Selected Stories of Rudy Wiebe.* Reprinted by permission of the author.

Virginia Woolf "The New Dress" from *A Haunted House and Other Stories* by Virginia Woolf. Reprinted by permission of The Hogarth Press, Ltd.

